GUSTAVE FLAUBERT

LIBRARY OF ESSENTIAL WRITERS

GUSTAVE FLAUBERT

◆

FIVE NOVELS

◆

COMPLETE AND UNABRIDGED

Madame Bovary ◆ Salammbô ◆
Sentimental Education ◆ The Temptation of
Saint Anthony ◆ Bouvard and Pécuchet

BARNES & NOBLE

NEW YORK

2007 Barnes & Noble, Inc.

ISBN-13: 978-0-7607-9345-9
ISBN-10: 0-7607-9345-X

Printed and bound in China

1   3   5   7   9   10   8   6   4   2

Contents

INTRODUCTION

─────────────

I AM NOTHING BUT A LITERARY LIZARD," GUSTAVE FLAUBERT WROTE TO HIS MIStress, Louise Colet, in 1846, "warming myself all day in the bright sun of Beauty. That is all." He had, by that time, been writing incessantly for more than ten years without publishing anything. He had completed his first novel, *Sentimental Education*, but had set it aside because it was not satisfactory.

Flaubert, at twenty-five, did indeed seem to many of those who knew and loved him to be a mere idler, incapable of real achievement. Born on December 12, 1821, he had grown up in comfortable middle-class surroundings in Rouen. Bookish and dedicated to writing historical dramas and philosophical tales during his years at boarding school, he showed great interest in the arts but little ambition to succeed in a traditional career. Gustave had been a disappointment to his father, a prominent doctor who had died in 1845. As if it were not bad enough that he had shown little interest in science and medicine, which his father considered the highest achievements of civilization, Gustave had been expelled from school and had then spent two years idling at home before failing to complete the studies in law for which he was sent to Paris. Although he had not followed the dissolute example set by many provincial students let loose in the capital, he had not devoted himself to his chosen profession either. He had the excuse of perennial poor health, but his deployment of that excuse was always treated with some suspicion.

Although Flaubert's mother loyally provided financial support and routinely accommodated him at her home in Croisset while he followed his literary vocation, she always lamented his steadfast refusal to seek proper employment and make a living of his own. Even to Louise Colet—herself a published writer—he seemed the epitome of the amateur dabbler, a *poseur* rather than a productive artist. Both women knew that he was perfectly serious in his intentions, and infinitely painstaking in his methods, but they must have despaired of his ability actually to make a mark on the literary world.

In September 1849 Flaubert completed the first version of *The Temptation of Saint Anthony*, which he rated more highly than the first version of *Sentimental Education*, but when he read it to his friends Louis Bouilhet and Maxime Du Camp they urged him to burn it, lest it scandalize its audience. He did not burn it, but agreed, reluctantly, to shelve it. He immediately wrote to Louis Colet, informing her that he had to see her because he had "something important to tell her." Louise, convinced that he was about to discard her, waited for him with a dagger concealed in the folds of her dress, intending to stab him in revenge—and then had to dispose of the weapon surreptitiously when she realized that he only wanted to inform her of his decision to postpone his literary debut yet again.

For Flaubert, a decision relating to his work was infinitely more momentous than any mere matter of personal passion. His literary procedure contrasted starkly with the methods of the most celebrated French prose writers who came before him, many of whom had written voluminously at great pace. Voltaire, at his peak, had scribbled away with goose quills for fourteen hours a day. Victor Hugo had written his first novel in a week merely to demonstrate that he could do it. Honoré de Balzac locked himself away to pour out entire novels in what was effectively a single sitting. Alexandre Dumas dictated his novels in torrential haste, employing collaborators to do his historical research and relying on his secretaries to supply the punctuation. Flaubert carefully cultivated a lifestyle that accommodated long hours of creative solitude, but instead of pouring out prose like a faucet he spent those hours in a desperate struggle to find *"le mot juste"*: the perfect form of expression for what he wanted to accomplish.

In the event, it was not until 1857 that Flaubert was sufficiently satisfied with a novel actually to publish it. That was *Madame Bovary,* which was promptly prosecuted for "offending public morals." Shortly after its publication Théophile Gautier put Flaubert in touch with another author who was to suffer the same fate in the same year with his own long-delayed first book: Charles Baudelaire, author of *Les Fleurs du Mal.* The two exchanged letters of commiseration, and Baudelaire published a strident defense of *Madame Bovary.* Flaubert's novel escaped the cuts demanded by the censor, and the full text of *Les Fleurs du Mal* was soon restored; the two books went on to become the pillars of modern French literature.

So much of what Flaubert did in *Madame Bovary* has now become the routine practice of novelistic composition that it is very difficult for the modern reader to appreciate the genius of its originality. Because Flaubert worried so intensely about what he was trying to do, and clarified his thoughts in the letters he wrote incessantly to his mother and his mistress—both of whom tolerated his outpourings patiently—we now know as much about his intentions and improvisations as the creative processes of any other author. We can therefore understand exactly how the naturalism of *Madame Bovary* came about.

Flaubert believed that the principal problem of storytelling was the tendency of the teller to get between the reader and the subject matter, thus obscuring the truth. He was primarily concerned with the way in which a narrative voice tended to provide a moral commentary, dictating the reader's approval and disapproval of various characters and events. He believed that the teller ought to be an objective reporter, not a censorious judge, who ought to let readers decide for themselves what to think about the events he reported. It was not what Madame Bovary actually did that "offended public morals" but the fact that the narrative voice of the novel refrained from condemning it.

In order to neutralize the moral stance of his narrative voice, Flaubert found himself compelled to minimize its presence in other ways, too. Sometimes he did this by adopting a camera-like viewpoint which reported what could be seen with the blatant accuracy of one of the photographs that Louis Daguerre had recently invented. His principal trick, however, was to transplant the intrusive aspects of storytelling—filling in background, expressing opinions, and formulating explanations—from the narrative voice to the thought and speech of the characters. This allowed the narrative voice to fade into the background while the characters became much more distinct—making it easier for readers to "identify" with the characters, stepping temporarily into their shoes in order to see a situation as they saw it and respond to it as they responded.

All of this is now the standard method of the novel and the everyday craft of prose fiction—but in the early nineteenth century it all had to be invented. No writer contributed more to its development than Flaubert, and no single work accomplished more by way of demonstration than *Madame Bovary*. Flaubert was elated by the success of his own identification with his instruments. "It is a delicious thing to write," he observed, "to be no longer yourself but to move in an entire universe of your own creating." He got so far under the skin of his self-deceiving heroine that he was able to make her fundamental foolishness self-evident, in a manner that no previous writer, trapped by the necessity of pointing out accidental hypocrisy, had ever contrived.

Flaubert might have gone on to write another contemporary novel in a vein similar to *Madame Bovary*, but, by the time it was published, he had become fascinated by the ancient city of Carthage, the rival of Rome, which had paid the price of its rivalry in being obliterated from the map at the conclusion of the Punic Wars. Other writers had attempted to recapture pharaonic Egypt and long-lost Pompeii in literary representations, but they had done so in a vague and impressionistic manner. Flaubert expressed his desire "to perpetuate a mirage by applying to antiquity the methods of the modern novel": to restore Carthage with as much quasi-photographic clarity as a literary image could contain.

In *Salammbô*, published in 1862, Flaubert elected to represent Carthage at the height of its grandeur, as it trembled on the brink of its long decline towards oblivion. The great Carthaginian hero of the first Punic War (265–242 B.C.),

Hamilcar Barca, became one of the key figures in the plot. While Hamilcar's daughter, Salammbô, provides a prospect of the city from within, the dissatisfied mercenary Mathô provides a view from without—contrasted images which become confused as the characters react to one another, with tragic effect.

Having published *Salammbô*, Flaubert turned his attention back to the manuscripts on his shelf. He had already made one unsatisfactory attempt to rewrite *The Temptation of Saint Anthony*, so he focused his attention on producing a conscientiously updated version of *Sentimental Education*, which was published in 1869. Flaubert's purpose in writing the first version of the novel in 1843–1845 had been to record the "moral history" of his era, without any overt moralizing of his own. He had selected key characters who embodied what he considered to be the relevant range of social and moral opinions, and—after intensive research—had set them to interact. In rewriting the novel he had to take full account of the fact that "moral history" had advanced very considerably in the interim, thanks to the revolution of 1848 and Louis-Napoleon's *coup d'état* of 1851. The latter event had established the Second Empire and, incidentally, mutilated the face of French literary culture by sending Victor Hugo, Alexandre Dumas, and Eugène Sue into exile.

Flaubert was disappointed by the critical reception of *Sentimental Education*; many readers thought its hero's responses to historical events too passive, and his personal erotic entanglements too confused. The author was justified in his disappointment—as a man whose own attitude to current affairs was conscientiously distanced and whose management of his own love life was conspicuously slapdash, he was undoubtedly better able to identify with his hero's vacillations than most of his readers. The real problem, however, was that the contemporary audience was not yet ready to embrace principles he had established in *Madame Bovary* wholeheartedly. The last refuge of judgmental story-telling, even in literary novels that strive with all their might to abandon the conventional platitudes of popular fiction, was the explicit celebration of the rewarding and redeeming aspects of sexual love. Flaubert's clinical treatment of that theme—the core curriculum of sentimental education—was bound to seem discomfitingly cerebral and inconclusive even to many readers who considered themselves gifted with fine artistic sensibilities.

The hesitant response to *Sentimental Education* reinforced Flaubert's determination to make no compromises in rewriting *The Temptation of Saint Anthony*. He was afflicted in the early 1870s by a chain of personal catastrophes—including the death of his mother—which exacerbated his health problems. Even so, he produced a final version of the text for publication in 1874. He retained a dramatic mode of presentation rather than reverting to conventional narrative because it seemed more suited to subject matter that was essentially artificial and melodramatic.

Although the *Temptation* is an extended Voltairean *conte philosphique* rather than a naturalistic novel, Flaubert took his narrative neutrality to its furthest extreme in attempting a distanced and balanced view of the eternal conflict between God and the Devil. In the vast majority of cases it requires very little temptation to lure people from the path of righteousness, but Saint Anthony is established by legend as a man of indomitable virtue, against whom Satan had been forced to loose every weapon in his armory. That phantasmagorical assault had been a popular image in Baroque art, and Flaubert had been prompted to produce is own version by Pieter Brueghel's famous painting, which he had seen in Genoa in 1845.

In the first version of the novel, Flaubert's Anthony had withstood the barrage of temptations but had been left alone and exhausted in the aftermath of the climax, with the Devil's mocking laughter ringing in his ears—an ending largely responsible for Bouilhet and Du Camp's alarm. In the final version, Anthony's victory is more clear-cut, and markedly less likely to offend the pious; as in *Sentimental Education*, though, Flaubert had taken account of the fact that the world had moved on in the meantime, and Satan's ideological artillery is considerably reinforced by the produce of modern science, especially evolutionary science. The high value that Flaubert had been brought up to place on scientific research and progress had as powerful an effect on his philosophical outlook as it had on his literary method; unlike Baudelaire, however—who had included a hymn to Satan in *Les Fleurs du Mal* in spite of refusing to relinquish his fervent Catholicism—Flaubert was no cynic. He was extraordinarily scrupulous in attempting to recognize and describe the force of virtue as something more than stubborn faith in defiance of reason; it is because Satan has such a powerful case to make that Anthony's avoidance of despair is an authentic triumph, and because Satan's armory has so much truth in it that Anthony is enable to turn elements of the vision to the advantage of his own righteousness.

Given his fundamental objective, it is entirely natural that Flaubert, having finally published the *Temptation*, should have set about planning the ultimate naturalistic novel: a novel that would set aside the problems of sentimental education in order to foreground the problems of intellectual education. He elected to describe the philosophical odyssey of two humble clerks intent on using their retirement profitably in the cause of self-enlightenment.

Bouvard and Pécuchet, published in 1881, is usually considered an amiable satirical comedy, whose account of the accidents that befall the two clerks is intended merely to poke fun at them. Indeed, that is what the novel actually amounts to in its incomplete state—but the ever-meticulous Flaubert left behind enough notes at his death in 1880 for the reader to understand that it would have undergone a profound, if temporary, transformation when the central characters reached their intellectual crossroads. At that point, they were to set out opposed accounts of the existential situation and potential future of humankind, Pécuchet taking a pessimistic view while Bouvard became the voice of optimism.

As the first great "modern" writer in France, François Rabelais, had abundantly demonstrated, there are matters so painful in their seriousness that they can best be represented frankly within a framework of broad comedy. Flaubert had dealt in ironic representation before—the *Temptation* has a jesting quality throughout and *Madame Bovary* is a funnier book than some earnest critics will concede—but *Bouvard and Pécuchet* would have taken this principle to its extreme, embedding the culmination of the philosophical debate for which the *Temptation* had laid the preliminary groundwork within the everyday travails of two quintessentially ordinary people—which is, after all, where it truly belongs. The loss of that debate, owing to Flaubert's sudden death from a stroke in 1880, is a tragedy; the fact that he left us its outline only serves to underline the misfortune.

Although Flaubert only published four novels and three short stories in his lifetime, he left behind a greater prose legacy than any other French writer of the nineteenth century. A lizard sunning himself in the radiance of Beauty he may have been, at least for a while, but he absorbed enough heat in his bathing to animate himself marvelously. When he moved, he did so with great effect and accuracy, benefiting tremendously from all his careful preparation. His lifestyle inspired a host of feebler imitators who elected to disguise genuine idleness as desperate artistic questing, but his works provided a sequence of outstanding exemplars for the writers who continued the progress of the modern novel; it is a testament to his meticulousness, as well as a great convenience to his readers, that his novels can be contained in a single volume.

BRIAN STABLEFORD

Brian Stableford teaches fiction writing at the University of Reading, where he also served as a lecturer in philosophy of social science and the sociology of literature and the mass media. He is the author of more than seventy-five books, including fifty novels and short fiction collections and the definitive critical studies *Glorious Perversity: The Decline and Fall of Literary Decadence*, *Scientific Romance in Britain: 1890-1950*, and *The Sociology of Science Fiction*.

MADAME BOVARY

TO

MARIE-ANTOINE-JULES SENARD,

MEMBER OF THE PARIS BAR,

EX-PRESIDENT OF THE NATIONAL ASSEMBLY, AND FORMER

MINISTER OF THE INTERIOR

DEAR AND ILLUSTRIOUS FRIEND—

PERMIT me to inscribe your name at the head of this book, and above its dedication; for it is to you, before all, that I owe its publication. Reading over your magnificent defence, my work has acquired for myself, as it were, an unexpected authority. Accept, then, here, the homage of my gratitude, which, how great soever it is, will never attain the height of your eloquence and your devotion.

GUSTAVE FLAUBERT

CONTENTS

PART I

Chapter I

WE WERE IN CLASS WHEN THE HEAD-MASTER CAME IN, FOLLOWED BY A "new fellow," not wearing the school uniform, and a school servant carrying a large desk. Those who had been asleep woke up, and every one rose as if just surprised at his work.

The head-master made a sign to us to sit down. Then, turning to the class-master, he said to him in a low voice—

"Monsieur Roger, here is a pupil whom I recommend to your care; he'll be in the second. If his work and conduct are satisfactory, he will go into one of the upper classes, as becomes his age."

The "new fellow," standing in the corner behind the door so that he could hardly be seen, was a country lad of about fifteen, and taller than any of us. His hair was cut square on his forehead like a village chorister's; he looked reliable, but very ill at ease. Although he was not broad-shouldered, his short school jacket of green cloth with black buttons must have been tight about the armholes, and showed at the opening of the cuffs red wrists accustomed to being bare. His legs, in blue stockings, looked out from beneath yellow trousers, drawn tight by braces. He wore stout, ill-cleaned, hobnailed boots.

We began repeating the lesson. He listened with all his ears, as attentive as if at a sermon, not daring even to cross his legs or lean on his elbow; and when at two o'clock the bell rang, the master was obliged to tell him to fall into line with the rest of us.

When we came back to work, we were in the habit of throwing our caps on the ground so as to have our hands more free; we used from the door to toss them under the form, so that they hit against the wall and made a lot of dust: it was "the thing."

But, whether he had not noticed the trick, or did not dare to attempt it, the "new fellow" was still holding his cap on his knees even after prayers were over. It was one of those head-gears of composite order, in which we can find traces of the bearskin, shako, billycock hat, sealskin cap, and cotton nightcap; one of those poor things, in fine, whose dumb ugliness has depths of expression, like an imbecile's face. Oval, stiffened with whalebone, it began with three round knobs; then came in succession lozenges of velvet and rabbit-skin separated by a red band; after that a sort of bag that ended in a cardboard polygon covered with complicated braiding, from which hung, at the end of a long thin cord, small twisted gold threads in the manner of a tassel. The cap was new; its peak shone.

"Rise," said the master.

He stood up; his cap fell. The whole class began to laugh. He stooped to pick it up. A neighbour knocked it down again with his elbow; he picked it up once more.

"Get rid of your helmet," said the master, who was a bit of a wag.

There was a burst of laughter from the boys, which so thoroughly put the poor lad out of countenance that he did not know whether to keep his cap in his hand, leave it on the ground, or put it on his head. He sat down again and placed it on his knee.

"Rise," repeated the master, "and tell me your name."

The new boy articulated in a stammering voice an unintelligible name.

"Again!"

The same sputtering of syllables was heard, drowned by the tittering of the class.

"Louder!" cried the master; "louder!"

The "new fellow" then took a supreme resolution, opened an inordinately large mouth, and shouted at the top of his voice as if calling some one the word "Charbovari."

A hubbub broke out, rose in *crescendo* with bursts of shrill voices (they yelled, barked, stamped, repeated "Charbovari! Charbovari!"), then died away into single notes, growing quieter only with great difficulty, and now and again suddenly recommencing along the line of a form whence rose here and there, like a damp cracker going off, a stifled laugh.

However, amid a rain of impositions, order was gradually re-established in the class; and the master having succeeded in catching the name of "Charles Bovary," having had it dictated to him, spelt out, and re-read, at once ordered the poor devil to go and sit down on the punishment form at the foot of the master's desk. He got up, but before going hesitated.

"What are you looking for?" asked the master.

"My c-a-p," timidly said the "new fellow," casting troubled looks round him.

"Five hundred verses for all the class!" shouted in a furious voice, stopped, like the *Quos ego*, a fresh outburst. "Silence!" continued the master indignantly, wiping his brow with his handkerchief, which he had just taken from his cap. "As to you, 'new boy,' you will conjugate '*ridiculus sum*' twenty times." Then, in a gentler tone, "Come, you'll find your cap again; it hasn't been stolen."

Quiet was restored. Heads bent over desks, and the "new fellow" remained for two hours in an exemplary attitude, although from time to time some paper pellet flipped from the tip of a pen came bang in his face. But he wiped his face with one hand and continued motionless, his eyes lowered.

In the evening, at preparation, he pulled out his pens from his desk, arranged his small belongings, and carefully ruled his paper. We saw him working conscientiously, looking out every word in the dictionary, and taking the greatest pains. Thanks, no doubt, to the willingness he showed, he had not to go down to the class below. But though he knew his rules passably, he had little finish in composition. It was the curé of his village who had taught him his first Latin; his parents, from motives of economy, having sent him to school as late as possible.

His father, Monsieur Charles Denis Bartolomé Bovary, retired assistant-surgeon-major, compromised about 1812 in certain conscription scandals, and forced at this time to leave the service, had taken advantage of his fine figure to get hold of a dowry of sixty thousand francs that offered in the person of a hosier's daughter who had fallen in love with his good looks. A fine man, a great talker, making his spurs ring as he walked, wearing whiskers that ran into his moustache, his fingers always garnished with rings and dressed in loud colours, he had the dash of a military man with the easy go of a commercial traveller. Once married, he lived for three or four years on his wife's fortune, dining well, rising late, smoking long porcelain pipes, not coming in at night till after the theatre, and haunting cafés. The father-in-law died, leaving little; he was indignant at this, "went in for the business," lost some money in it, then retired to the country, where he thought he would make money. But, as he knew no more about farming than calico, as he rode his horses instead of sending them to plough, drank his cider in bottle instead of selling it in cask, ate the finest poultry in his farmyard, and greased his hunting-boots with the fat of his pigs, he was not long in finding out that he would do better to give up all speculation.

For two hundred francs a year he managed to live on the border of the provinces of Caux and Picardy, in a kind of place half farm, half private house; and here, soured, eaten up with regrets, cursing his luck, jealous of every one, he shut himself up at the age of forty-five, sick of men, he said, and determined to live in peace.

His wife had adored him once on a time; she had bored him with a thousand servilities that had only estranged him the more. Lively once, expansive and affectionate, in growing older she had become (after the fashion of wine that, exposed to air, turns to vinegar) ill-tempered, grumbling, irritable. She had suffered so much without complaint at first, when she had seen him going after all the village drabs, and when a score of bad houses sent him back to her at night, weary, stinking drunk. Then her pride revolted. After that she was silent, burying her anger in a dumb stoicism that she maintained till her death. She was constantly going about looking after business matters. She called on the lawyers, the president, remembered when bills fell due, got them renewed, and at home ironed, sewed, washed, looked after the workmen, paid the accounts, while he, troubling himself about nothing, eternally besotted in sleepy sulkiness, whence he only roused himself to say disagreeable things to her, sat smoking by the fire and spitting into the cinders.

When she had a child, it had to be sent out to nurse. When he came home, the lad was spoilt as if he were a prince. His mother stuffed him with jam; his father let him run about barefoot, and, playing the philosopher, even said he might as well go about quite naked like the young of animals. As opposed to the maternal ideas, he had a certain virile idea of childhood on which he sought to mould his son, wishing him to be brought up hardily, like a Spartan, to give him a strong constitution. He sent him to bed without any fire, taught him to drink off large draughts of rum and to jeer at religious processions. But, peaceable by nature, the lad answered only poorly to his notions. His mother always kept him near her; she cut out cardboard for him, told him tales, entertained him with endless monologues full of melancholy gaiety and charming nonsense. In her life's isolation she centered on the child's head all her shattered, broken little vanities. She dreamed of high station; she already saw him, tall, handsome, clever, settled as an engineer or in the law. She taught him to read, and even on an old piano she had taught him two or three little songs. But to all this Monsieur Bovary, caring little for letters, said "It was not worth while. Would they ever have the means to send him to a public school, to buy him a practice, or start him in business? Besides, with cheek a man always gets on in the world." Madame Bovary bit her lips, and the child knocked about the village.

He went after the labourers, drove away with clods of earth the ravens that were flying about. He ate blackberries along the hedges, minded the geese with a long switch, went haymaking during harvest, ran about in the woods, played hopscotch under the church porch on rainy days, and at great fêtes begged the beadle to let him toll the bells, that he might hang all his weight on the long rope and feel himself borne upward by it in its swing. Meanwhile he grew like an oak; he was strong of hand, fresh of colour.

When he was twelve years old his mother had her own way; he began his lessons. The curé took him in hand; but the lessons were so short and irregular that they could not be of much use. They were given at spare moments in the sacristy, standing up, hurriedly, between a baptism and a burial; or else the curé, if he had not to go out, sent for his pupil after the *Angelus*. They went up to his room and settled down; the flies and moths fluttered round the candle. It was close, the child fell asleep, and the good man, beginning to doze with his hands on his stomach, was soon snoring with his mouth wide open. On other occasions, when Monsieur le Curé, on his way back after administering the viaticum to some sick person in the neighbourhood, caught sight of Charles playing about the fields, he called him, lectured him for a quarter of an hour, and took advantage of the occasion to make him conjugate his verb at the foot of a tree. The rain interrupted them or an acquaintance passed. All the same he was always pleased with him, and even said the "young man" had a very good memory.

Charles could not go on like this. Madame Bovary took strong steps. Ashamed, or rather tired out, Monsieur Bovary gave in without a struggle, and they waited one year longer, so that the lad should take his first communion.

Six months more passed, and the year after Charles was finally sent to school at Rouen, whither his father took him towards the end of October, at the time of the St. Romain fair.

It would now be impossible for any of us to remember anything about him. He was a youth of even temperament, who played in playtime, worked in schoolhours, was attentive in class, slept well in the dormitory, and ate well in the refectory. He had *in loco parentis* a wholesale ironmonger in the Rue Ganterie, who took him out once a month on Sundays after his shop was shut, sent him for a walk on the quay to look at the boats, and then brought him back to college at seven o'clock before supper. Every Thursday evening he wrote a long letter to his mother with red ink and three wafers; then he went over his history note-books, or read an old volume of Anarchasis that was knocking about the study. When he went for walks he talked to the servant, who, like himself, came from the country.

By dint of hard work he kept always about the middle of the class; once even he got a certificate in natural history. But at the end of his third year his parents withdrew him from the school to make him study medicine, convinced that he could even take his degree by himself.

His mother chose a room for him on the fourth floor of a dyer's she knew, overlooking the Eau-de-Robec. She made arrangements for his board, got him furniture, table and two chairs, sent home for an old cherry-tree bedstead, and bought besides a small cast-iron stove with the supply of wood that was to warm the poor child. Then at the end of a week she departed, after a thousand injunctions to be good now that he was going to be left to himself.

The syllabus that he read on the notice-board stunned him: lectures on anatomy, lectures on pathology, lectures on physiology, lectures on pharmacy, lectures on botany and clinical medicine, and therapeutics, without counting hygiene and materia medica—all names of whose etymologies he was ignorant, and that were to him as so many doors to sanctuaries filled with magnificent darkness.

He understood nothing of it all; it was all very well to listen—he did not follow. Still he worked; he had bound note-books, he attended all the courses, never missed a single lecture. He did his little daily task like a mill-horse, who goes round and round with his eyes bandaged, not knowing what work he is doing.

To spare him expense his mother sent him every week by the carrier a piece of veal baked in the oven, with which he lunched when he came back from the hospital, while he sat kicking his feet against the wall. After this he had to run off to lectures, to the operation-room, to the hospital, and return to his home at the other end of the town. In the evening, after the poor dinner of his landlord, he went back to his room and set to work again in his wet clothes, that smoked as he sat in front of the hot stove.

On the fine summer evenings, at the time when the close streets are empty, when the servants are playing shuttle-cock at the doors, he opened his window and leaned out. The river, that makes of this quarter of Rouen a wretched little Venice, flowed beneath him, between the bridges and the railings, yellow, violet, or blue. Working men, kneeling on the banks, washed their bare arms in the water. On poles projecting from the attics, skeins of cotton were drying in the air. Opposite, beyond the roofs, spread the pure heaven with the red sun setting. How pleasant it must be at home! How fresh under the beech-tree! And he expanded his nostrils to breathe in the sweet odours of the country which did not reach him.

He grew thin, his figure became taller, his face took a saddened look that made it nearly interesting. Naturally, through indifference, he abandoned all the resolutions he had made. Once he missed a lecture; the next day all the lectures; and, enjoying his idleness, little by little he gave up work altogether. He got into the habit of going to the public-house, and had a passion for dominoes. To shut himself up every evening in the dirty public room, to push about on marble tables the small sheep-bones with black dots, seemed to him a fine proof of his freedom, which raised him in his own esteem. It was beginning to see life, the sweetness of stolen pleasures; and when he entered, he put his hand on the door-handle with a joy almost sensual. Then many things hidden within him came out; he learnt couplets by heart and sang them to his boon companions, became enthusiastic about Béranger, learnt how to make punch, and, finally, how to make love.

Thanks to these preparatory labours, he failed completely in his examination for an ordinary degree. He was expected home the same night to celebrate his success. He started on foot, stopped at the beginning of the village, sent for his mother, and told her all. She excused him, threw the blame of his failure on the injustice of the examiners, encouraged him a little, and took upon herself to set matters straight. It was only five years later that Monsieur Bovary knew the truth; it was old then, and he accepted it. Moreover, he could not believe that a man born of him could be a fool.

So Charles set to work again and crammed for his examination, ceaselessly learning all the old questions by heart. He passed pretty well. What a happy day for his mother! They gave a grand dinner.

Where should he go to practise? To Tostes, where there was only one old doctor. For a long time Madame Bovary had been on the look-out for his death, and the old fellow had barely been packed off when Charles was installed, opposite his place, as his successor.

But it was not everything to have brought up a son, to have had him taught medicine, and discovered Tostes, where he could practise it; he must have a wife. She found him one—the widow of a bailiff at Dieppe, who was forty-five and had an income of twelve hundred francs. Though she was ugly, as dry as a bone, her face with as many pimples as the spring has buds, Madame Dubuc had no lack of suitors. To attain her ends Madame Bovary had to oust them all, and she even succeeded in very cleverly baffling the intrigues of a pork-butcher backed up by the priests.

Charles had seen in marriage the advent of an easier life, thinking he would be more free to do as he liked with himself and his money. But his wife was master; he had to say this and not say that in company, to fast every Friday, dress as she liked, harass at her bidding those patients who did not pay. She opened his letters, watched his comings and goings, and listened at the partition-wall when women came to consult him in his surgery.

She must have her chocolate every morning, attentions without end. She constantly complained of her nerves, her chest, her liver. The noise of footsteps made her ill; when people left her, solitude became odious to her; if they came back, it was doubtless to see her die. When Charles returned in the evening, she stretched forth two long thin arms from beneath the sheets, put them round his neck, and having made him sit down on the edge of the bed, began to talk to him of her troubles: he was neglecting her, he loved another. She had been warned she would be unhappy; and she ended by asking him for a dose of medicine and a little more love.

Chapter II

ONE NIGHT TOWARDS ELEVEN O'CLOCK THEY WERE AWAKENED BY THE noise of a horse pulling up outside their door. The servant opened the garret-window and parleyed for some time with a man in the street below. He came for the doctor, had a letter for him. Nastasie came downstairs shivering and undid the bars and bolts one after the other. The man left his horse, and, following the servant, suddenly came in behind her. He pulled out from his wool cap with grey top-knots a letter wrapped up in a rag and presented it gingerly to Charles, who rested on his elbow on the pillow to read it. Nastasie, standing near the bed, held the light. Madame in modesty had turned to the wall and showed only her back.

This letter, sealed with a small seal in blue wax, begged Monsieur Bovary to come immediately to the farm of the Bertaux to set a broken leg. Now from Tostes to the Bertaux was a good eighteen miles across country by way of Longueville and Saint-Victor. It was a dark night; Madame Bovary junior was afraid of accidents for her husband. So it was decided the stable-boy should go on first; Charles would start three hours later when the moon rose. A boy was to be sent to meet him, and show him the way to the farm, and open the gates for him.

Towards four o'clock in the morning, Charles, well wrapped up in his cloak, set out for the Bertaux. Still sleepy from the warmth of his bed, he let himself be lulled by the quiet trot of his horse. When it stopped of its own accord in front of those holes surrounded with thorns that are dug on the margin of furrows, Charles awoke with a start, suddenly remembered the broken leg, and tried to call to mind all the fractures he knew. The rain had stopped, day was breaking, and on the branches of the leafless trees birds roosted motionless, their little feathers bristling in the cold morning wind. The flat country stretched as far as eye could see, and the tufts of trees round the farms at long intervals seemed like dark violet stains on the vast grey surface, that on the horizon faded into the gloom of the sky. Charles from time to time opened his eyes, his mind grew weary, and sleep coming upon him, he soon fell into a doze wherein his recent sensations blending with memories, he became conscious of a double self, at once student and married man, lying in his bed as but now, and crossing the operation theatre as of old. The warm smell of poultices mingled in his brain with the fresh odour of dew; he heard the iron rings rattling along the curtain-rods of the bed and saw his wife sleeping. As he passed Vassonville he came upon a boy sitting on the grass at the edge of a ditch.

"Are you the doctor?" asked the child.

And on Charles's answer he took his wooden shoes in his hands and ran on in front of him.

The general practitioner, riding along, gathered from his guide's talk that Monsieur Rouault must be one of the well-to-do farmers. He had broken his leg the evening before on his way home from a Twelfth-night feast at a neighbour's. His wife had been dead for two years. There was only his daughter, who helped him to keep house, with him.

The ruts were becoming deeper; they were approaching the Bertaux. The little lad, slipping through a hole in the hedge, disappeared; then he came back to the end of a courtyard to open the gate. The horse slipped on the wet grass; Charles had to stoop to pass under the branches. The watchdogs in their kennels barked, dragging at their chains. As he entered the Bertaux the horse took fright and stumbled.

It was a substantial-looking farm. In the stables, over the top of the open doors, one could see great cart-horses quietly feeding from new racks. Right along the outbuildings extended a large dunghill, from which manure liquid oozed, while amidst fowls and turkeys five or six peacocks, a luxury in Chauchois farmyards, were foraging on the top of it. The sheepfold was long, the barn high, with walls smooth as your hand. Under the cartshed were two large carts and four ploughs, with their whips, shafts and harnesses complete, whose fleeces of blue wool were getting soiled by the fine dust that fell from the granaries. The courtyard sloped upwards, planted with trees set out symmetrically, and the chattering noise of a flock of geese was heard near the pond.

A young woman in a blue merino dress with three flounces came to the threshold of the door to receive Monsieur Bovary, whom she led to the kitchen, where a large fire was blazing. The servants' breakfast was boiling beside it in small pots of all sizes. Some damp clothes were drying inside the chimney-corner. The shovel, tongs, and the nozzle of the bellows, all of colossal size, shone like polished steel, while along the walls hung many pots and pans in which the clear flame of the hearth, mingling with the first rays of the sun coming in through the window, was mirrored fitfully.

Charles went up to the first floor to see the patient. He found him in his bed, sweating under his bed-clothes, having thrown his cotton nightcap right away from him. He was a fat little man of fifty, with white skin and blue eyes, the fore part of his head bald, and he wore ear-rings. By his side on a chair stood a large decanter of brandy, whence he poured himself out a little from time to time to keep up his spirits; but as soon as he caught sight of the doctor his elation subsided, and instead of swearing, as he had been doing for the last twelve hours, began to groan feebly.

The fracture was a simple one, without any kind of complication. Charles could not have hoped for an easier case. Then calling to mind the devices of his masters at the bedside of patients, he comforted the sufferer with all sorts of kindly remarks, those caresses of the surgeon that are like the oil they put on bistouries. In order to make some splints a bundle of laths was brought up from the carthouse. Charles selected one, cut it into two pieces and planed it with a fragment of window-pane, while the servant tore up sheets to make bandages, and Mademoiselle Emma tried to sew some pads. As she was a long time before she found her workcase, her father grew impatient; she did not answer, but as she sewed she pricked her fingers, which she then put to her mouth to suck them. Charles was surprised at the whiteness of her nails. They were shiny, delicate at the tips, more polished than the ivory of Dieppe, and almond-shaped. Yet her hand was not beautiful, perhaps not white enough, and a little hard at the knuckles; besides, it was too long, with no soft inflections in the outlines. Her real beauty was in her eyes. Although brown, they seemed black because of the lashes, and her look came at you frankly, with a candid boldness.

The bandaging over, the doctor was invited by Monsieur Rouault himself to "pick a bit" before he left.

Charles went down into the room on the ground-floor. Knives and forks and silver goblets were laid for two on a little table at the foot of a huge bed that had a canopy of printed cotton with figures representing Turks. There was an odour of iris-root and damp sheets that escaped from a large oak chest opposite the window. On the floor in corners were sacks of flour stuck upright in rows. These were the overflow from the neighbouring granary, to which three stone steps led. By way of decoration for the apartment, hanging to a nail in the middle of the wall, whose green paint scaled off from the effects of the saltpetre, was a crayon head of Minerva in a gold frame, underneath which was written in Gothic letters "To dear Papa."

First they spoke of the patient, then of the weather, of the great cold, of the wolves that infested the fields at night. Mademoiselle Rouault did not at all like the country, especially now that she had to look after the farm almost alone. As the room was chilly, she shivered as she ate. This showed something of her full lips, that she had a habit of biting when silent.

Her neck stood out from a white turned-down collar. Her hair, whose two black folds seemed each of a single piece, so smooth were they, was parted in the middle by a delicate line that curved slightly with the curve of the head; and, just showing the tip of the ear, it was joined behind in a thick chignon, with a wavy movement at the temples that the country doctor saw now for the first time in his life. The upper part of her cheek was rose-coloured. She had, like a man, thrust in between two buttons of her bodice a tortoise-shell eyeglass.

When Charles, after bidding farewell to old Rouault, returned to the room before leaving, he found her standing, her forehead against the window, looking into the garden, where the bean props had been knocked down by the wind. She turned round. "Are you looking for anything?" she asked.

"My whip, if you please," he answered.

He began rummaging on the bed, behind the doors, under the chairs. It had fallen to the ground, between the sacks and the wall. Mademoiselle Emma saw it, and bent over the flour sacks. Charles out of politeness made a dash also, and as he stretched out his arm, at the same moment felt his breast brush against the back of the young girl bending beneath him. She drew herself up, scarlet, and looked at him over her shoulder as she handed him his whip.

Instead of returning to the Bertaux in three days as he had promised, he went back the very next day, then regularly twice a week, without counting the visits he paid now and then as if by accident.

Everything, moreover, went well; the patient progressed favourably; and when, at the end of forty-six days, old Rouault was seen trying to walk alone in his "den," Monsieur Bovary began to be looked upon as a man of great capacity. Old Rouault said that he could not have been cured better by the first doctor of Yvetot, or even of Rouen.

As to Charles, he did not stay to ask himself why it was a pleasure to him to go to the Bertaux. Had he done so, he would, no doubt have attributed his zeal to the importance of the case, or perhaps to the money he hoped to make by it. Was it for this, however, that his visits to the farm formed a delightful exception to the meagre occupations of his life? On these days he rose early, set off at a gallop, urging on his horse, then got down to wipe his boots in the grass and put on black gloves before entering. He liked going into the courtyard, and noticing the gate turn against his shoulder, the cock crow on the wall, the lads run to meet him. He liked the granary and the stables; he liked old Rouault, who pressed his hand and called him his saviour; he liked the small wooden shoes of Mademoiselle Emma on the scoured flags of the kitchen—her high heels made her a little taller; and when she walked in front of him, the wooden soles springing up quickly struck with a sharp sound against the leather of her boots.

She always reconducted him to the first step of the stairs. When his horse had not yet been brought round she stayed there. They had said "Good-bye"; there was no more talking. The open air wrapped her round, playing with the soft down on the back of her neck, or blew to and fro on her hips her apron-strings, that fluttered like streamers. Once, during a thaw, the bark of the trees in the yard was oozing, the snow on the roofs of the out-buildings was melting; she stood on the threshold, and went to fetch her sunshade and opened it. The sunshade, of silk of the colour of pigeons' breasts, through which the sun shone, lighted up with shifting hues the white skin of her face. She smiled under the tender warmth, and drops of water could be heard falling one by one on the stretched silk.

During the first period of Charles's visits to the Bertaux, Madame Bovary, junior, never failed to inquire after the invalid, and she had even chosen in the book that she kept on a system of double entry a clean blank page for Monsieur Rouault. But when she heard he had a daughter, she began to make inquiries, and she learnt that Mademoiselle Rouault, brought up at the Ursuline Convent, had received what is called "a good education"; and so knew dancing, geography, drawing, how to embroider and play the piano. That was the last straw.

"So it is for this," she said to herself, "that his face beams when he goes to see her, and that he puts on his new waistcoat at the risk of spoiling it with the rain. Ah! that woman! that woman!"

And she detested her instinctively. At first she solaced herself by allusions that Charles did not understand, then by casual observations that he let pass for fear of a storm, finally by open apostrophes to which he knew not what to answer. "Why did he go back to the Bertaux now that Monsieur Rouault was cured and that these folks hadn't paid yet? Ah! it was because a young lady was there, someone who knew how to talk, to embroider, to be witty. That was what he cared about; he wanted town misses." And she went on:

"The daughter of old Rouault a town miss! Get out! Their grandfather was a shepherd, and they have a cousin who was almost had up at the assizes for a nasty blow in a quarrel. It is not worth while making such a fuss, or showing herself at church on Sundays in a silk gown like a countess. Besides, the poor old chap, if it hadn't been for the colza last year, would have had much ado to pay up his arrears."

For very weariness Charles left off going to the Bertaux. Héloïse made him swear, his hand on the prayer-book, that he would go there no more, after much sobbing and many kisses, in a great outburst of love. He obeyed then, but the strength of his desire protested against the servility of his conduct; and he thought, with a kind of naïve hypocrisy, that this interdict to see her gave him a sort of right to love her. And then the widow was thin; she had long teeth; wore in all weathers a little black shawl, the edge of which hung down between her shoulder-blades; her bony figure was sheathed in her clothes as if they were a scabbard; they were too short, and displayed her ankles with the laces of her large boots crossed over grey stockings.

Charles's mother came to see them from time to time, but after a few days the daughter-in-law seemed to put her own edge on her, and then, like two knives, they scarified him with their reflections and observations. It was wrong of him to eat so much. Why did he always offer a glass of something to every one who came? What obstinacy not to wear flannels!

In the spring it came about that a notary at Ingouville, the holder of the widow Dubuc's property, one fine day went off, taking with him all the money in his office. Héloïse, it is true, still possessed, besides a share in a boat valued at six thousand francs, her house in the Rue St. François; and yet, with all this fortune that had been so trumpeted abroad, nothing, excepting perhaps a little furniture and a few clothes, had appeared in the household. The matter had to be gone into. The house at Dieppe was found to be eaten up with mortgages to its foundations; what she had placed with the notary God only knew, and her share in the boat did not exceed one thousand crowns. She had lied, the good lady! In his exasperation, Monsieur Bovary the elder, smashing a chair on the flags, accused his wife of having caused the misfortune of their son by harnessing him to such a harridan, whose harness wasn't worth her hide. They came to Tostes. Explanations followed. There were scenes. Héloïse in tears, throwing her arms about her husband, conjured him to defend her from his parents. Charles tried to speak up for her. They grew angry and left the house.

But "the blow had struck home." A week after, as she was hanging up some washing in her yard, she was seized with a spitting of blood, and the next day, while Charles had his back turned to her drawing the window-curtain, she said, "O God!" gave a sigh and fainted. She was dead! What a surprise!

When all was over at the cemetery Charles went home. He found no one downstairs; he went up to the first floor to their room; saw her dress still hanging at the foot of the alcove; then, leaning against the writing-table, he stayed until the evening, buried in a sorrowful reverie. She had loved him after all!

Chapter III

O NE MORNING OLD ROUAULT BROUGHT CHARLES THE MONEY FOR SETTING his leg—seventy-five francs in forty-sou pieces, and a turkey. He had heard of his loss, and consoled him as well as he could.

"I know what it is," said he, clapping him on the shoulder; "I've been through it. When I lost my dear departed, I went into the fields to be quite alone. I fell at the foot of a tree; I cried; I called on God; I talked nonsense to Him. I wanted to be like the moles that I saw on the branches, their insides swarming with worms, dead, and an end of it. And when I thought that there were others at that very moment with their nice little wives holding them in their embrace, I struck great blows on the earth with my stick. I was pretty well mad with not eating; the very idea of going to a café disgusted me—you wouldn't believe it. Well, quite softly, one day following another, a spring on a winter, and an autumn after a summer, this wore away, piece by piece, crumb by crumb; it passed away, it is gone, I should say it has sunk; for something always remains at the bottom, as one would say—a weight here, at one's heart. But since it is the lot of all of us, one must not give way altogether, and, because others have died, want to die too. You must pull yourself together, Monsieur Bovary. It will pass away. Come to see us; my daughter thinks of you now and again, d'ye know, and she says you are forgetting her. Spring will soon be here. We'll have some rabbit-shooting in the warrens to amuse you a bit."

Charles followed his advice. He went back to the Bertaux. He found all as he had left it, that is to say, as it was five months ago. The pear-trees were already in blossom, and Farmer Rouault, on his legs again, came and went, making the farm more full of life.

Thinking it his duty to heap the greatest attention upon the doctor because of his sad position, he begged him not to take his hat off, spoke to him in an under-tone as if he had been ill, and even pretended to be angry because nothing rather lighter had been prepared for him than for the others, such as a little clotted cream or stewed pears. He told stories. Charles found himself laughing, but the remembrance of his wife suddenly coming back to him depressed him. Coffee was brought in; he thought no more about her.

He thought less of her as he grew accustomed to living alone. The new delight of independence soon made his loneliness bearable. He could now change his meal-times, go in or out without explanation, and when he was very tired stretch himself at full length on his bed. So he nursed and coddled himself and accepted the consolations that were offered him. On the other hand, the death of his wife had not served him ill in his business, since for a month people had been saying, "The poor young man! what a loss!" His name had been talked about, his practice had increased; and, moreover, he could go to the Bertaux just as he liked. He had an aimless hope, and was vaguely happy; he thought himself better looking as he brushed his whiskers before the looking-glass.

One day he got there about three o'clock. Everybody was in the fields. He went into the kitchen, but did not at once catch sight of Emma; the outside shutters were closed. Through the chinks of the wood the sun sent across the flooring long fine rays that were broken at the corners of the furniture and trembled along the ceiling. Some flies on the table were crawling up the glasses that had been used, and buzzing as they drowned themselves in the dregs of the cider. The daylight that came in by the chimney made velvet of the soot at the back of the fireplace, and touched with blue the cold cinders. Between the window and the hearth Emma was sewing; she wore no fichu; he could see small drops of perspiration on her bare shoulders.

After the fashion of country folks she asked him to have something to drink. He said no; she insisted, and at last laughingly offered to have a glass of liqueur with him. So she went to fetch a bottle of curaçao from the cupboard, reached down two small glasses, filled one to the brim, poured scarcely anything into the other, and, after having clinked glasses, carried hers to her mouth. As it was almost empty she bent back to drink, her head thrown back, her lips pouting, her neck on the strain. She laughed at getting none of it, while with the tip of her tongue passing between her small teeth she licked drop by drop the bottom of her glass.

She sat down again and took up her work, a white cotton stocking she was darning. She worked with her head bent down; she did not speak, nor did Charles. The air coming in under the door blew a little dust over the flags; he watched it drift along, and heard nothing but the throbbing in his head and the faint clucking of a hen that had laid an egg in the yard. Emma from time to time cooled her cheeks with the palms of her hands, and cooled these again on the knobs of the huge fire-dogs.

She complained of suffering since the beginning of the season from giddiness; she asked if sea-baths would do her any good; she began talking of her convent, Charles of his school; words came to them. They went up into her bed-room. She showed him her old music-books, the little prizes she had won, and the oak-leaf crowns, left at the bottom of a cupboard. She spoke to him, too, of her mother, of the country, and even showed him the bed in the garden where, on the first Friday of every month, she gathered flowers to put on her mother's tomb. But the gardener they had understood nothing about it; servants were so careless. She would have dearly liked, if only for the winter, to live in town, although the length of the fine days made the country perhaps even more wearisome in the summer. And, according to what she was saying, her voice was clear, sharp, or, on a sudden all languor, lingered out in modulations that ended almost in murmurs as she spoke to herself, now joyous, opening big naïve eyes, then with her eyelids half closed, her look full of boredom, her thoughts wandering.

Going home at night, Charles went over her words one by one, trying to recall them, to fill out their sense, that he might piece out the life she had lived before he knew her. But he never saw her in his thoughts other than he had seen her the first time, or as he had just left her. Then he asked himself what would become of her—if she would be married, and to whom? Alas! old Rouault was rich, and she!—so beautiful! But Emma's face always rose before his eyes, and a monotone, like the humming of a top, sounded in his ears, "If you should marry after all! if you should marry!" At night he could not sleep; his throat was parched; he was athirst. He got up to drink from the water-bottle and opened the window. The night was covered with stars, a warm wind blowing in the distance; the dogs were barking. He turned his head towards the Bertaux.

Thinking that, after all, he should lose nothing, Charles promised himself to ask her in marriage as soon as occasion offered, but each time such occasion did offer the fear of not finding the right words sealed his lips.

Old Rouault would not have been sorry to be rid of his daughter, who was of no use to him in the house. In his heart he excused her, thinking her too clever for farming, a calling under the ban of Heaven, since one never saw a millionaire in it. Far from having made a fortune by it, the good man was losing every year; for if he was good in bargaining, in which he enjoyed the dodges of the trade, on the other hand, agriculture properly so called, and the internal management of the farm, suited him less than most people. He did not willingly take his hands out of his pockets, and did not spare expense in all that concerned himself, liking to eat well, to have good fires, and to sleep well. He liked old cider, underdone legs of mutton, *glorias* well beaten up. He took his meals in the kitchen alone, opposite the fire, on a little table brought to him all ready laid as on the stage.

When, therefore, he perceived that Charles's cheeks grew red if near his daughter, which meant that he would propose for her one of these days, he chewed the cud of the matter beforehand. He certainly thought him a little meagre, and not quite the son-in-law he would have liked, but he was said to be well-conducted, economical, very learned, and no doubt would not make too many difficulties about the dowry. Now, as old Rouault would soon be forced to sell twenty-two acres of "his property," as he owed a good deal to the mason, to the harness-maker, and as the shaft of the cider-press wanted renewing, "If he asks for her," he said to himself, "I'll give her to him."

At Michaelmas Charles went to spend three days at the Bertaux. The last had passed like the others in procrastinating from hour to hour. Old Rouault was seeing him off; they were walking along the road full of ruts; they were about to part. This was the time. Charles gave himself as far as to the corner of the hedge, and at last, when past it—

"Monsieur Rouault," he murmured, "I should like to say something to you."

They stopped. Charles was silent.

"Well, tell me your story. Don't I know all about it?" said old Rouault, laughing softly.

"Monsieur Rouault—Monsieur Rouault," stammered Charles.

"I ask nothing better," the farmer went on. "Although, no doubt, the little one is of my mind, still we must ask her opinion. So you get off—I'll go back home. If it is 'yes,' you needn't return because of all the people about, and besides it would upset her too much. But so that you mayn't be eating your heart, I'll open wide the outer shutter of the window against the wall; you can see it from the back by leaning over the hedge."

And he went off.

Charles fastened his horse to a tree; he ran into the road and waited. Half-an-hour passed, then he counted nineteen minutes by his watch. Suddenly a noise was heard against the wall; the shutter had been thrown back; the hook was still swinging.

The next day by nine o'clock he was at the farm. Emma blushed as he entered, and she gave a little forced laugh to keep herself in countenance. Old Rouault embraced his future son-in-law. The discussion of money matters was put off; moreover, there was plenty of time before them, as the marriage could not decently take place till Charles was out of mourning, that is to say, about the spring of the next year.

The winter passed waiting for this. Mademoiselle Rouault was busy with her trousseau. Part of it was ordered at Rouen, and she made herself chemises and nightcaps after fashion-plates that she borrowed. When Charles visited the farmer, the preparations for the wedding were talked over; they wondered in what room they should have dinner; they dreamed of the number of dishes that would be wanted, and what should be the entrées.

Emma would, on the contrary, have preferred to have a midnight wedding with torches, but old Rouault could not understand such an idea. So there was a wedding at which forty-three persons were present, at which they remained sixteen hours at table, began again the next day, and to some extent on the days following.

Chapter IV

THE GUESTS ARRIVED EARLY IN CARRIAGES, IN ONE-HORSE CHAISES, TWO-wheeled cars, old open gigs, waggonettes with leather hoods, and the young people from the nearer villages in carts, in which they stood up in rows, holding on to the sides so as not to fall, going at a trot and well shaken up. Some came from a distance of thirty miles, from Goderville, from Normanville, and from Cany. All the relatives of both families had been invited, quarrels between friends arranged, acquaintances long since lost sight of written to.

From time to time one heard the crack of a whip behind the hedge; then the gates opened, a chaise entered. Galloping up to the foot of the steps, it stopped short and emptied its load. They got down from all sides, rubbing knees and stretching arms. The ladies, wearing bonnets, had on dresses in the town fashion, gold watch chains, pelerines with the ends tucked into belts, or little coloured fichus fastened down behind with a pin, and that left the back of the neck bare. The lads, dressed like their papas, seemed uncomfortable in their new clothes (many that day handselled their first pair of boots), and by their sides, speaking never a word, wearing the white dress of their first communion lengthened for the occasion, were some big girls of fourteen or sixteen, cousins or elder sisters no doubt, rubicund, bewildered, their hair greasy with rose-pomade, and very much afraid of dirtying their gloves. As there were not enough stable-boys to unharness all the carriages, the gentlemen turned up their sleeves and set about it themselves. According to their different social positions they wore tail-coats, overcoats, shooting-jackets, cutaway-coats: fine tail-coats, redolent of family respectability, that only came out of the wardrobe on state occasions; overcoats with long tails flapping in the wind and round capes and pockets like sacks; shooting-jackets of coarse cloth, generally worn with a cap with a brass-bound peak; very short cutaway-coats with two small buttons in the back, close together like a pair of eyes, and the tails of which seemed cut out of one piece by a carpenter's hatchet. Some, too (but these, you may be sure, would sit at the bottom of the table), wore their best blouses—that is to say, with collars turned down to the shoulders, the back gathered into small plaits and the waist fastened very low down with a worked belt.

And the shirts stood out from the chests like cuirasses! Everyone had just had his hair cut; ears stood out from the heads; they had been close-shaved; a few, even, who had had to get up before daybreak, and not been able to see to shave, had diagonal gashes under their noses or cuts the size of a three-franc piece along the jaws, which the fresh air *en route* had enflamed, so that the great white beaming faces were mottled here and there with red dabs.

The mairie was a mile and a half from the farm, and they went thither on foot, returning in the same way after the ceremony in the church. The procession, first united like one long coloured scarf that undulated across the fields, along the narrow path winding amid the green corn, soon lengthened out, and broke up into different groups that loitered to talk. The fiddler walked in front with his violin, gay with ribbons at its pegs. Then came the married pair, the relations, the friends, all following pell-mell; the children stayed behind amusing themselves plucking the bell-flowers from oat-ears, or playing amongst themselves unseen. Emma's dress, too long, trailed a little on the ground; from time to time she stopped to pull it up, and then delicately, with her gloved hands, she picked off the coarse grass and the thistledowns, while Charles, empty handed, waited till she had finished. Old Rouault, with a new silk hat and the cuffs of his black coat covering his hands up to the nails, gave his arm to Madame Bovary senior. As to Monsieur Bovary senior, who, heartily despising all these folk, had come simply in a frock-coat of military cut with one row of buttons—he was passing compliments of the bar to a fair young peasant. She bowed, blushed, and did not know what to say. The other wedding guests talked of their business or played tricks behind each other's backs, egging one another on in advance to be jolly. Those who listened could always catch the squeaking of the fiddler, who went on playing across the fields. When he saw that the rest were far behind he stopped to take breath, slowly rosined his bow, so that the strings should sound more shrilly, then set off again, by turns lowering and raising his neck, the better to mark time for himself. The noise of the instrument drove away the little birds from afar.

The table was laid under the cart-shed. On it were four sirloins, six chicken fricassées, stewed veal, three legs of mutton, and in the middle a fine roast suckling-pig, flanked by four chitterlings with sorrel. At the corners were decanters of brandy. Sweet bottled-cider frothed round the corks, and all the glasses had been filled to the brim with wine beforehand. Large dishes of yellow cream, that trembled with the least shake of the table, had designed on their smooth surface the initials of the newly wedded pair in nonpareil arabesques. A confectioner of Yvetot had been intrusted with the tarts and sweets. As he had only just set up in the place, he had taken a lot of trouble, and at dessert he himself brought in a set dish that evoked loud cries of wonderment. To begin with, at its base there was a square of blue cardboard, representing a temple with porticoes, colonnades, and stucco statuettes all round, and in the niches constellations of gilt paper stars; then on the second stage was a dungeon of Savoy cake, surrounded by many fortifications in candied angelica, almonds, raisins, and quarters of oranges; and finally, on the upper platform a green field with rocks set in lakes of jam, nutshell boats, and a small Cupid balancing himself in a chocolate swing whose two up-rights ended in real roses for balls at the top.

Until night they ate. When any of them were too tired of sitting, they went out for a stroll in the yard, or for a game with corks in the granary, and then returned to table. Some towards the finish went to sleep and snored. But with the coffee every one woke up. Then they began songs, showed off tricks, raised heavy weights, performed feats with their fingers, then tried lifting carts on their shoulders, made broad jokes, kissed the women. At night when they left, the horses, stuffed up to the nostrils with oats, could hardly be got into the shafts; they kicked, reared, the harness broke, their masters laughed or swore; and all night in the light of the moon along country roads there were runaway carts at full gallop plunging into the ditches, jumping over yard after yard of stones, clambering up the hills, with women leaning out from the tilt to catch hold of the reins.

Those who stayed at the Bertaux spent the night drinking in the kitchen. The children had fallen asleep under the seats.

The bride had begged her father to be spared the usual marriage pleasantries. However, a fishmonger, one of their cousins (who had even brought a pair of soles for his wedding present), began to squirt water from his mouth through the key-hole, when old Rouault came up just in time to stop him, and explain to him that the distinguished position of his son-in-law would not allow of such liberties. The cousin all the same did not give in to these reasons readily. In his heart he accused old Rouault of being proud, and he joined four or five other guests in a corner, who having, through mere chance, been several times running served with the worst helps of meat, also were of opinion they had been badly used, and were whispering about their host, and with covered hints hoping he would ruin himself.

Madame Bovary, senior, had not opened her mouth all day. She had been consulted neither as to the dress of her daughter-in-law nor as to the arrangement of the feast; she went to bed early. Her husband, instead of following her, sent to Saint-Victor for some cigars, and smoked till daybreak, drinking kirsch-punch, a mixture unknown to the company. This added greatly to the consideration in which he was held.

Charles, who was not of a facetious turn, did not shine at the wedding. He answered feebly to the puns, *doubles entendres*, compliments, and chaff that it was felt a duty to let off at him as soon as the soup appeared.

The next day, on the other hand, he seemed another man. It was he who might rather have been taken for the virgin of the evening before, whilst the bride gave no sign that revealed anything. The shrewdest did not know what to make of it, and they looked at her when she passed near them with an unbounded concentration of mind. But Charles concealed nothing. He called her "my wife," *tutoyéd* her, asked for her of everyone, looked for her everywhere, and often he dragged her into the yards, where he could be seen from far between the trees, putting his arm round her waist, and walking half-bending over her, ruffling the chemisette of her bodice with his head.

Two days after the wedding the married pair left. Charles, on account of his patients, could not be away longer. Old Rouault had them driven back in his cart, and himself accompanied them as far as Vassonville. Here he embraced his daughter for the last time, got down, and went his way. When he had gone about a hundred paces he stopped, and as he saw the cart disappearing, its wheels turning in the dust, he gave a deep sigh. Then he remembered his wedding, the old times, the first pregnancy of his wife; he, too, had been very happy the day when he had taken her from her father to his home, and had carried her off on a pillion, trotting through the snow, for it was near Christmas-time, and the country was all white. She held him by one arm, her basket hanging from the other; the wind blew the long lace of her Cauchois head-dress so that it sometimes flapped across his mouth, and when he turned his head he saw near him, on his shoulder, her little rosy face, smiling silently under the gold bands of her cap. To warm her hands she put them from time to time in his breast. How long ago it all was! Their son would have been thirty by now. Then he looked back and saw nothing on the road. He felt dreary as an empty house; and tender memories mingling with the sad thoughts in his brain, addled by the fumes of the feast, he felt inclined for a moment to take a turn towards the church. As he was afraid, however, that this sight would make him yet more sad, he went right away home.

Monsieur and Madame Charles arrived at Tostes about six o'clock. The neighbours came to the windows to see their doctor's new wife.

The old servant presented herself, curtsied to her, apologised for not having dinner ready, and suggested that madame, in the meantime, should look over her house.

Chapter V

THE BRICK FRONT WAS JUST IN A LINE WITH THE STREET, OR RATHER THE road. Behind the door hung a cloak with a small collar, a bridle, and a black leather cap, and on the floor, in a corner, were a pair of leggings, still covered with dry mud. On the right was the one apartment, that was both dining and sitting room. A canary-yellow paper, relieved at the top by a garland of pale flowers, was puckered everywhere over the badly-stretched canvas; white calico curtains with a red border hung crossways the length of the window; and on the narrow mantelpiece a clock with a head of Hippocrates shone resplendent between two plate candlesticks under oval shades. On the other side of the passage was Charles's consulting-room, a little room about six paces wide, with a table, three chairs, and an office-chair. Volumes of the *Dictionary of Medical Science*, uncut, but the binding rather the worse for the successive sales through which they had gone, occupied almost alone the six shelves of a deal bookcase. The smell of melted butter penetrated through the walls when he saw patients, just as in the kitchen one could hear the people coughing in the consulting-room and recounting their whole histories. Then, opening on the yard, where the stable was, came a large dilapidated room with a stove, now used as a wood-house, cellar, and pantry, full of old rubbish, of empty casks, agricultural implements past service, and a mass of dusty things whose use it was impossible to guess.

The garden, longer than wide, ran between two mud walls with espaliered apricots, to a hawthorn hedge that separated it from the field. In the middle was a slate sundial on a brick pedestal; four flower-beds with eglantines surrounded symmetrically the more useful kitchen-garden bed. Right at the bottom, under the spruce bushes, was a curé in plaster reading his breviary.

Emma went upstairs. The first room was not furnished, but in the second, which was their bedroom, was a mahogany bedstead in an alcove with red drapery. A shell-box adorned the chest of drawers, and on the secretary near the window a bouquet of orange blossoms tied with white satin ribbons stood in a bottle. It was a bride's bouquet; it was the other one's. She looked at it. Charles noticed it; he took it and carried it up to the attic, while Emma seated in an armchair (they were putting her things down around her) thought of her bridal flowers packed up in a bandbox, and wondered, dreaming, what would be done with them if she were to die.

During the first days she occupied herself in thinking about changes in the house. She took the shades off the candlesticks, had new wall-paper put up, the staircase repainted, and seats made in the garden round the sundial; she even in-quired how she could get a basin with a jet fountain and fishes. Finally her hus-band, knowing that she liked to drive out, picked up a second-hand dogcart, which, with new lamps and a splashboard in striped leather, looked almost like a tilbury.

He was happy then, and without a care in the world. A meal together, a walk in the evening on the highroad, a gesture of her hands over her hair, the sight of her straw hat hanging from the window-fastener, and many another thing in which Charles had never dreamed of pleasure, now made up the endless round of his happiness. In bed, in the morning, by her side, on the pillow, he watched the sun-light sinking into the down on her fair cheek, half hidden by the lappets of her nightcap. Seen thus closely, her eyes looked to him enlarged, especially when, on waking up, she opened and shut them rapidly many times. Black in the shade, dark blue in broad daylight, they had, as it were, depths of different colours, that, darker in the centre, grew paler towards the surface of the eye. His own eyes lost them-selves in these depths; he saw himself in miniature down to the shoulders, with his handkerchief round his head and the top of his shirt open. He rose. She came to the window to see him off, and stayed leaning on the sill between two pots of gera-nium, clad in her dressing-gown hanging loosely about her. Charles, in the street, buckled his spurs, his foot on the mounting stone, while she talked to him from above, picking with her mouth some scrap of flower or leaf that she blew out at him. Then this, eddying, floating, described semicircles in the air like a bird, and was caught before it reached the ground in the ill-groomed mane of the old white mare standing motionless at the door. Charles from horseback threw her a kiss; she answered with a nod; she shut the window, and he set off. And then along the high-road, spreading out its long ribbon of dust, along the deep lanes that the trees bent over as in arbours, along paths where the corn reached to the knees, with the sun on his back and the morning air in his nostrils, his heart full of the joys of the past night, his mind at rest, his flesh at ease, be went on, re-chewing his happiness, like those who after dinner taste again the truffles which they are digesting.

Until now what good had he had of his life? His time at school, when he re-mained shut up within the high walls, alone, in the midst of companions richer than he or cleverer at their work, who laughed at his accent, who jeered at his clothes, and whose mothers came to the school with cakes in their muffs? Later on, when he studied medicine, and never had his purse full enough to treat some little work-girl who would have become his mistress? Afterwards, he had lived fourteen months with the widow, whose feet in bed were cold as icicles. But now he had for life this beautiful woman whom he adored. For him the universe did not extend be-yond the circumference of her petticoat, and he reproached himself with not lov-ing her. He wanted to see her again; he turned back quickly, ran up the stairs with a beating heart. Emma, in her room, was dressing; he came up on tiptoe, kissed her back; she gave a cry.

He could not keep from constantly touching her comb, her rings, her fichu; sometimes he gave her great sounding kisses with all his mouth on her cheeks, or else little kisses in a row all along her bare arm from the tip of her fingers up to her shoulder, and she put him away half-smiling, half-vexed, as you do a child who hangs about you.

Before marriage she thought herself in love; but the happiness that should have followed this love not having come, she must, she thought, have been mistaken. And Emma tried to find out what one meant exactly in life by the words *felicity*, *passion*, *rapture*, that had seemed to her so beautiful in books.

Chapter VI

SHE HAD READ *PAUL AND VIRGINIA,* AND SHE HAD DREAMED OF THE LITTLE bamboo-house, the nigger Domingo, the dog Fidèle, but above all of the sweet friendship of some dear little brother, who seeks red fruit for you on trees taller than steeples, or who runs barefoot over the sand, bringing you a bird's nest.

When she was thirteen, her father himself took her to town to place her in the convent. They stopped at an inn in the St. Gervais quarter, where, at their supper, they used painted plates that set forth the story of Mademoiselle de la Vallière. The explanatory legends, chipped here and there by the scratching of knives, all glorified religion, the tendernesses of the heart, and the pomps of court.

Far from being bored at first at the convent, she took pleasure in the society of the good sisters, who, to amuse her, took her to the chapel, which one entered from the refectory by a long corridor. She played very little during recreation hours, knew her catechism well, and it was she who always answered Monsieur le Vicaire's difficult questions. Living thus, without ever leaving the warm atmosphere of the class-rooms, and amid these pale-faced women wearing rosaries with brass crosses, she was softly lulled by the mystic languor exhaled in the perfumes of the altar, the freshness of the holy water, and the lights of the tapers. Instead of attending to mass, she looked at the pious vignettes with their azure borders in her book, and she loved the sick lamb, the sacred heart pierced with sharp arrows, or the poor Jesus sinking beneath the cross he carries. She tried, by way of mortification, to eat nothing a whole day. She puzzled her head to find some vow to fulfil.

When she went to confession, she invented little sins in order that she might stay there longer, kneeling in the shadow, her hands joined, her face against the grating beneath the whispering of the priest. The comparisons of betrothed, husband, celestial lover, and eternal marriage, that recur in sermons, stirred within her soul depths of unexpected sweetness.

In the evening, before prayers, there was some religious reading in the study. On week-nights it was some abstract of sacred history or the Lectures of the Abbé Frayssinous, and on Sundays passages from the *Génie du Christianisme,* as a recreation. How she listened at first to the sonorous lamentations of its romantic melancholies re-echoing through the world and eternity! If her childhood had been spent in the shop-parlour of some business quarter, she might perhaps have opened her heart to those lyrical invasions of Nature, which usually come to us only through translation in books. But she knew the country too well; she knew the lowing of cattle, the milking, the ploughs. Accustomed to calm aspects of life, she turned, on the contrary, to those of excitement. She loved the sea only for the sake of its storms, and the green fields only when broken up by ruins. She wanted to get some personal profit out of things, and she rejected as useless all that did not contribute to the immediate desires of her heart, being of a temperament more sentimental than artistic, looking for emotions, not landscapes.

At the convent there was an old maid who came for a week each month to mend the linen. Patronised by the clergy, because she belonged to an ancient family of noblemen ruined by the Revolution, she dined in the refectory at the table of the good sisters, and after the meal had a bit of chat with them before going back to her work. The girls often slipped out from the study to go and see her. She knew by heart the love-songs of the last century, and sang them in a low voice as she stitched away. She told stories, gave them news, went errands in the town, and on the sly lent the big girls some novel, that she always carried in the pockets of her apron, and of which the good lady herself swallowed long chapters in the intervals of her work. They were all love, lovers, sweethearts, persecuted ladies fainting in lonely pavilions, postillions killed at every stage, horses ridden to death on every page, sombre forests, heart-aches, vows, sobs, tears and kisses, little skiffs by moonlight, nightingales in shady groves, "gentlemen" brave as lions, gentle as lambs, virtuous as no one ever was, always well dressed, and weeping like fountains. For six months, then, Emma, at fifteen years of age, made her hands dirty with books from old lending libraries. With Walter Scott, later on, she fell in love with historical events, dreamed of old chests, guardrooms and minstrels. She would have liked to live in some old manor-house, like those long-waisted chatelaines who, in the shade of pointed arches, spent their days leaning on the stone, chin in hand, watching a cavalier with white plume galloping on his black horse from the distant fields. At this time she had a cult for Mary Stuart and enthusiastic veneration for illustrious or unhappy women. Joan of Arc, Héloïse, Agnès Sorel, the beautiful Ferronière, and Clémence Isaure stood out to her like comets in the dark immensity of heaven, where also were seen, lost in shadow, and all unconnected, St. Louis with his oak, the dying Bayard, some cruelties of Louis XI, a little of St. Bartholomew's, the plume of the Béarnais, and always the remembrance of the plates painted in honour of Louis XIV.

In the music-class, in the ballads she sang, there was nothing but little angels with golden wings, madonnas, lagunes, gondoliers;—mild compositions that allowed her to catch a glimpse athwart the obscurity of style and the weakness of the music of the attractive phantasmagoria of sentimental realities. Some of her companions brought "keepsakes" given them as new year's gifts to the convent. These had to be hidden; it was quite an undertaking; they were read in the dormitory.

Delicately handling the beautiful satin bindings, Emma looked with dazzled eyes at the names of the unknown authors, who had signed their verses for the most part as counts or viscounts.

She trembled as she blew back the tissue paper over the engraving and saw it folded in two and fall gently against the page. Here behind the balustrade of a balcony was a young man in a short cloak, holding in his arms a young girl in a white dress wearing an alms-bag at her belt; or there were nameless portraits of English ladies with fair curls, who looked at you from under their round straw hats with their large clear eyes. Some there were lounging in their carriages, gliding through parks, a greyhound bounding along in front of the equipage, driven at a trot by two small postilions in white breeches. Others, dreaming on sofas with an open letter, gazed at the moon through a slightly open window half draped by a black curtain. The naïve ones, a tear on their cheeks, were kissing doves through the bars of a Gothic cage, or, smiling, their heads on one side, were plucking the leaves of a marguerite with their taper fingers, that curved at the tips like peaked shoes. And you, too, were there, Sultans with long pipes reclining beneath arbours in the arms of Bayadères; Djiaours, Turkish sabres, Greek caps; and you especially, pale landscapes of dithyrambic lands, that often show us at once palm-trees and firs, tigers on the right, a lion to the left, Tartar minarets on the horizon; the whole framed by a very neat virgin forest, and with a great perpendicular sunbeam trembling in the water, where, standing out in relief like white excoriations on a steel-grey ground, swans are swimming about.

And the shade of the argand lamp fastened to the wall above Emma's head lighted up all these pictures of the world, that passed before her one by one in the silence of the dormitory, and to the distant noise of some belated carriage rolling over the Boulevards.

When her mother died she cried much the first few days. She had a funeral picture made with the hair of the deceased, and, in a letter sent to the Bertaux full of sad reflections on life, she asked to be buried later on in the same grave. The goodman thought she must be ill, and came to see her. Emma was secretly pleased that she had reached at a first attempt the rare ideal of pale lives, never attained by mediocre hearts. She let herself glide along with Lamartine meanderings, listened to harps on lakes, to all the songs of dying swans, to the falling of the leaves, the pure virgins ascending to heaven, and the voice of the Eternal discoursing down the valleys. She wearied of it, would not confess it, continued from habit, and at last was surprised to feel herself soothed, and with no more sadness at heart than wrinkles on her brow.

The good nuns, who had been so sure of her vocation, perceived with great astonishment that Mademoiselle Rouault seemed to be slipping from them. They had indeed been so lavish to her of prayers, retreats, novenas, and sermons, they had so often preached the respect due to saints and martyrs, and given so much good advice as to the modesty of the body and the salvation of her soul, that she did as tightly reigned horses: she pulled up short and the bit slipped from her teeth. This nature, positive in the midst of its enthusiasms, that had loved the church for the sake of the flowers, and music for the words of the songs, and literature for its passional stimulus, rebelled against the mysteries of faith as it grew irritated by discipline, a thing antipathetic to her constitution. When her father took her from school, no one was sorry to see her go. The Lady Superior even thought that she had latterly been somewhat irreverent to the community.

Emma at home once more, first took pleasure in looking after the servants, then grew disgusted with the country and missed her convent. When Charles came to the Bertaux for the first time, she thought herself quite disillusioned, with nothing more to learn, and nothing more to feel.

But the uneasiness of her new position, or perhaps the disturbance caused by the presence of this man, had sufficed to make her believe that she at last felt that wondrous passion which, till then, like a great bird with rose-coloured wings, hung in the splendour of the skies of poesy; and now she could not think that the calm in which she lived was the happiness she had dreamed.

Chapter VII

S HE THOUGHT, SOMETIMES, THAT, AFTER ALL, THIS WAS THE HAPPIEST TIME OF her life—the honeymoon, as people called it. To taste the full sweetness of it, it would have been necessary doubtless to fly to those lands with sonorous names where the days after marriage are full of laziness most suave. In post-chaises behind blue silken curtains to ride slowly up steep roads, listening to the song of the postilion re-echoed by the mountains, along with the bells of goats and the muffled sound of a waterfall; at sunset on the shores of gulfs to breathe in the perfume of lemon-trees; then in the evening on the villa-terraces above, hand in hand to look at the stars, making plans for the future. It seemed to her that certain places on earth must bring happiness, as a plant peculiar to the soil, and that cannot thrive elsewhere. Why could not she lean over balconies in Swiss châlets, or enshrine her melancholy in a Scotch cottage, with a husband dressed in a black velvet coat with long tails, and thin shoes, a pointed hat and frills?

Perhaps she would have liked to confide all these things to someone. But how tell an undefinable uneasiness, variable as the clouds, unstable as the winds? Words failed her—the opportunity, the courage.

If Charles had but wished it, if he had guessed it, if his look had but once met her thought, it seemed to her that a sudden plenty would have gone out from her heart, as the fruit falls from a tree when shaken by a hand. But as the intimacy of their life became deeper, the greater became the gulf that separated her from him.

Charles's conversation was commonplace as a street pavement, and everyone's ideas trooped through it in their everyday garb, without exciting emotion, laughter, or thought. He had never had the curiosity, he said, while he lived at Rouen, to go to the theatre to see the actors from Paris. He could neither swim, nor fence, nor shoot, and one day he could not explain some term of horsemanship to her that she had come across in a novel.

A man, on the contrary, should he not know everything, excel in manifold activities, initiate you into the energies of passion, the refinements of life, all mysteries? But this one taught nothing, knew nothing, wished nothing. He thought her happy; and she resented this easy calm, this serene heaviness, the very happiness she gave him.

Sometimes she would draw; and it was great amusement to Charles to stand there bolt upright and watch her bend over her cardboard, with eyes half-closed the better to see her work, or rolling, between her fingers, little bread-pellets. As to the piano, the more quickly her fingers glided over it the more he wondered. She struck the notes with aplomb, and ran from top to bottom of the keyboard without a break. Thus shaken up, the old instrument, whose strings buzzed, could be heard at the other end of the village when the window was open, and often the bailiff's clerk, passing along the highroad bare-headed and in list slippers, stopped to listen, his sheet of paper in his hand.

Emma, on the other hand, knew how to look after her house. She sent the patients' accounts in well-phrased letters that had no suggestion of a bill. When they had a neighbour to dinner on Sundays, she managed to have some tasty dish—piled up pyramids of green-gages on vine leaves, served up preserves turned out into plates—and even spoke of buying finger-glasses for dessert. From all this much consideration was extended to Bovary.

Charles finished by rising in his own esteem for possessing such a wife. He showed with pride in the sitting-room two small pencil sketches by her that he had had framed in very large frames, and hung up against the wall-paper by long green cords. People returning from mass saw him at his door in his wool-work slippers.

He came home late—at ten o'clock, at midnight sometimes. Then he asked for something to eat, and as the servant had gone to bed, Emma waited on him. He took off his coat to dine more at his ease. He told her, one after the other, the people he had met, the villages where he had been, the prescriptions he had written, and, well pleased with himself, he finished the remainder of the boiled beef and onions, picked pieces off the cheese, munched an apple, emptied his water-bottle, and then went to bed, and lay on his back and snored.

As he had been for a time accustomed to wear nightcaps, his handkerchief would not keep down over his ears, so that his hair in the morning was all tumbled pell-mell about his face and whitened with the feathers of the pillow, whose strings came untied during the night. He always wore thick boots that had two long creases over the instep running obliquely towards the ankle, while the rest of the upper continued in a straight line as if stretched on a wooden foot. He said that "was quite good enough for the country."

His mother approved of his economy, for she came to see him as formerly when there had been some violent row at her place; and yet Madame Bovary senior seemed prejudiced against her daughter-in-law. She thought "her ways too fine for their position"; the wood, the sugar, and the candles disappeared as "at a grand establishment," and the amount of firing in the kitchen would have been enough for twenty-five courses. She put her linen in order for her in the presses, and taught her to keep an eye on the butcher when he brought the meat. Emma put up with these lessons. Madame Bovary was lavish of them; and the words "daughter" and "mother" were exchanged all day long, accompanied by little quiverings of the lips, each one uttering gentle words in a voice trembling with anger.

In Madame Dubuc's time the old woman felt that she was still the favourite; but now the love of Charles for Emma seemed to her a desertion from her tenderness, an encroachment upon what was hers, and she watched her son's happiness in sad silence, as a ruined man looks through the windows at people dining in his old house. She recalled to him as remembrances her troubles and her sacrifices, and, comparing these with Emma's negligence, came to the conclusion that it was not reasonable to adore her so exclusively.

Charles knew not what to answer: he respected his mother, and he loved his wife infinitely; he considered the judgment of the one infallible, and yet he thought the conduct of the other irreproachable. When Madame Bovary had gone, he tried timidly and in the same terms to hazard one or two of the more anodyne observations he had heard from his mamma. Emma proved to him with a word that he was mistaken, and sent him off to his patients.

And yet, in accord with theories she believed right, she wanted to make herself in love with him. By moonlight in the garden she recited all the passionate rhymes she knew by heart, and, sighing, sang to him many melancholy adagios; but she found herself as calm after this as before, and Charles seemed no more amorous and no more moved.

When she had thus for a while struck the flint on her heart without getting a spark, incapable, moreover, of understanding what she did not experience as of believing anything that did not present itself in conventional forms, she persuaded herself without difficulty that Charles's passion was nothing very exorbitant. His outbursts became regular; he embraced her at certain fixed times. It was one habit among other habits, and, like a dessert, looked forward to after the monotony of dinner.

A gamekeeper, cured by the doctor of inflammation of the lungs, had given madame a little Italian greyhound; she took her out walking, for she went out sometimes in order to be alone for a moment, and not to see before her eyes the eternal garden and the dusty road. She went as far as the beeches of Banneville, near the deserted pavilion which forms an angle of the wall on the side of the country. Amidst the vegetation of the ditch there are long reeds with leaves that cut you.

She began by looking round her to see if nothing had changed since last she had been there. She found again in the same places the foxgloves and wallflowers, the beds of nettles growing round the big stones, and the patches of lichen along the three windows, whose shutters, always closed, were rotting away on their rusty iron bars. Her thoughts, aimless at first, wandered at random, like her greyhound, who ran round and round in the fields, yelping after the yellow butterflies, chasing the shrew-mice, or nibbling the poppies on the edge of a cornfield. Then gradually her ideas took definite shape, and, sitting on the grass that she dug up with little prods of her sunshade, Emma repeated to herself, "Good heavens! why did I marry?"

She asked herself if by some other chance combination it would not have been possible to meet another man; and she tried to imagine what would have been these unrealised events, this different life, this unknown husband. All, surely, could not be like this one. He might have been handsome, witty distinguished, attractive, such as, no doubt, her old companions of the convent had married. What were they doing now? In town, with the noise of the streets, the buzz of the theatres, and the lights of the ball-room, they were living lives where the heart expands, the senses bourgeon out. But she—her life was cold as a garret whose dormer-window looks on the north, and ennui, the silent spider, was weaving its web in the darkness in every corner of her heart. She recalled the prize-days, when she mounted the platform to receive her little crowns, with her hair in long plaits. In her white frock and open prunella shoes she had a pretty way, and when she went back to her seat, the gentlemen bent over her to congratulate her; the courtyard was full of carriages; farewells were called to her through their windows; the music-master with his violin-case bowed in passing by. How far off all this! How far away!

She called Djali, took her between her knees, and smoothed the long, delicate head, saying, "Come, kiss mistress; you have no troubles."

Then noting the melancholy face of the graceful animal, who yawned slowly, she softened, and comparing her to herself, spoke to her aloud as to somebody in trouble whom one is consoling.

Occasionally there came gusts of wind, breezes from the sea rolling in one sweep over the whole plateau of the Caux country, which brought even to these fields a salt freshness. The rushes, close to the ground, whistled; the branches trembled in a swift rustling, while their summits, ceaselessly swaying, kept up a deep murmur. Emma drew her shawl round her shoulders and rose.

In the avenue a green light dimmed by the leaves lit up the short moss that crackled softly beneath her feet. The sun was setting; the sky showed red between the branches, and the trunks of the trees, uniform, and planted in a straight line, seemed a brown colonnade standing out against a background of gold. A fear took hold of her; she called Djali, and hurriedly returned to Tostes by the highroad, threw herself into an arm-chair, and for the rest of the evening did not speak.

But towards the end of September something extraordinary fell upon her life; she was invited by the Marquis d'Andervilliers to Vaubyessard.

Secretary of State under the Restoration, the Marquis, anxious to re-enter political life, set about preparing for his candidature to the Chamber of Deputies long beforehand. In the winter he distributed a great deal of wood, and in the Conseil Général always enthusiastically demanded new roads for his arrondissement. During the dog-days he had suffered from an abscess, which Charles had cured as if by miracle by giving a timely little touch with the lancet. The steward sent to Tostes to pay for the operation reported in the evening that he had seen some superb cherries in the doctor's little garden. Now cherry-trees did not thrive at Vaubyessard; the Marquis asked Bovary for some slips; made it his business to thank him personally; saw Emma; thought she had a pretty figure, and that she did not bow like a peasant; so that he did not think he was going beyond the bounds of condescension, nor, on the other hand, making a mistake, in inviting the young couple.

One Wednesday at three o'clock, Monsieur and Madame Bovary, seated in their dog-cart, set out for Vaubyessard, with a great trunk strapped on behind and a bonnet-box in front on the apron. Besides these Charles held a bandbox between his knees.

They arrived at nightfall, just as the lamps in the park were being lit to show the way for the carriages.

Chapter VIII

THE CHÂTEAU, A MODERN BUILDING IN ITALIAN STYLE, WITH TWO PROJECTing wings and three flights of steps, lay at the foot of an immense greensward, on which some cows were grazing among groups of large trees set out at regular intervals, while large beds of arbutus, rhododendron, syringas, and guelder roses bulged out their irregular clusters of green along the curve of the gravel path. A river flowed under a bridge; through the mist one could distinguish buildings with thatched roofs scattered over the field bordered by two gentlysloping well-timbered hillocks, and in the background amid the trees rose in two parallel lines the coach-houses and stables, all that was left of the ruined old château.

Charles's dog-cart pulled up before the middle flight of steps; servants appeared; the Marquis came forward, and offering his arm to the doctor's wife, conducted her to the vestibule.

It was paved with marble slabs, was very lofty, and the sound of footsteps and that of voices re-echoed through it as in a church. Opposite rose a straight staircase, and on the left a gallery overlooking the garden led to the billiard-room, through whose door one could hear the click of the ivory balls. As she crossed it to go to the drawing-room, Emma saw standing round the table men with grave faces, their chins resting on high cravats. They all wore orders, and smiled silently as they made their strokes. On the dark wainscoting of the walls large gold frames bore at the bottom names written in black letters. She read: "Jean-Antoine d'Andervilliers d'Yverbonville, Count de la Vaubyessard and Baron de la Fresnaye, killed at the battle of Coutras on the 20th of October 1587." And on another: "Jean-Antoine-Henry-Guy d'Andervilliers de la Vaubyessard, Admiral of France and Chevalier of the Order of St. Michael, wounded at the battle of the HougueSaint-Vaast on the 29th of May 1692; died at Vaubyessard on the 23rd of January 1693." One could hardly make out those that followed, for the light of the lamps lowered over the green cloth threw a dim shadow round the room. Burnishing the horizontal pictures, it broke up against these in delicate lines where there were cracks in the varnish, and from all these great black squares framed in with gold stood out here and there some lighter portion of the painting—a pale brow, two eyes that looked at you, perukes flowing over and powdering red-coated shoulders, or the buckle of a garter above a well-rounded calf.

The Marquis opened the drawing-room door; one of the ladies (the Marchioness herself) came to meet Emma. She made her sit down by her on an ottoman, and began talking to her as amicably as if she had known her a long time. She was a woman of about forty, with fine shoulders, a hook nose, a drawling voice, and on this evening she wore over her brown hair a simple *guipure fichu* that fell in a point at the back. A fair young woman was by a side in a high-backed chair, and gentlemen with flowers in their button-holes were talking to ladies round the fire.

At seven dinner was served. The men, who were in the majority, sat down at the first table in the vestibule; the ladies at the second in the dining-room with the Marquis and Marchioness.

Emma, on entering, felt herself wrapped round by the warm air, a blending of the perfume of flowers and of the fine linen, of the fumes of the viands, and the odour of the truffles. The silver dish-covers reflected the lighted wax candles in the candelabra, the cut crystal covered with light steam reflected from one to the other pale rays; bouquets were placed in a row the whole length of the table; and in the large-bordered plates each napkin, arranged after the fashion of a bishop's mitre, held between its two gaping folds a small oval-shaped roll. The red claws of lobsters hung over the dishes; rich fruit in open baskets was piled up on moss; there were quails in their plumage; smoke was rising; and in silk stockings, knee-breeches, white cravat, and frilled shirt, the steward, grave as a judge, offering ready-carved dishes between the shoulders of the guests, with a touch of the spoon gave you the piece chosen. On the large stove of porcelain inlaid with copper baguettes the statue of a woman, draped to the chin, gazed motionless on the room full of life.

Madame Bovary noticed that many ladies had not put their gloves in their glasses.

But at the upper end of the table, along amongst all these women, bent over his full plate, and his napkin tied round his neck like a child, an old man sat eating, letting drops of gravy drip from his mouth. His eyes were bloodshot, and he wore a little queue tied with a black ribbon. He was the Marquis's father-in-law, the old Duke de Laverdière, once on a time favourite of the Count d'Artois, in the days of the Vaudreuil hunting-parties at the Marquis de Conflans's, and had been, it was said, the lover of Queen Marie Antoinette, between Monsieur de Coigny and Monsieur de Lauzun. He had lived a life of noisy debauch, full of duels, bets, elopements; he had squandered his fortune and frightened all his family. A servant behind his chair named aloud to him in his ear the dishes that he pointed to stammering, and constantly Emma's eyes turned involuntarily to this old man with hanging lips, as to something extraordinary. He had lived at court and slept in the bed of queens!

Iced champagne was poured out. Emma shivered all over as she felt it cold in her mouth. She had never seen pomegranates nor tasted pine-apples. The pow-dered sugar even seemed to her whiter and finer than elsewhere.

The ladies afterwards went to their rooms to prepare for the ball.

Emma made her toilet with the fastidious care of an actress on her début. She did her hair according to the directions of the hairdresser, and put on the barege dress spread out upon the bed. Charles's trousers were tight across the belly.

"My trouser-straps will be rather awkward for dancing," he said.

"Dancing?" repeated Emma.

"Yes!"

"Why, you must be mad! They would make fun of you; keep your place. Be-sides, it is more becoming for a doctor," she added.

Charles was silent. He walked up and down waiting for Emma to finish dressing.

He saw her from behind in the glass between two lights. Her black eyes seemed blacker than ever. Her hair, undulating towards the ears, shone with a blue lustre; a rose in her chignon trembled on its mobile stalk, with artificial dew-drops on the tip of the leaves. She wore a gown of pale saffron trimmed with three bouquets of pompon roses mixed with green.

Charles came and kissed her on her shoulder.

"Let me alone!" she said; "you are tumbling me."

One could hear the flourish of the violin and the notes of a horn. She went downstairs restraining herself from running.

Dancing had begun. Guests were arriving. There was some crushing. She sat down on a form near the door.

The quadrille over, the floor was occupied by groups of men standing up and talking and servants in livery bearing large trays. Along the line of seated women painted fans were fluttering, bouquets half-hid smiling faces, and gold-stoppered scent-bottles were turned in partly-closed hands, whose white gloves outlined the nails and tightened on the flesh at the wrists. Lace trimmings, diamond brooches, medallion bracelets trembled on bodices, gleamed on breasts, clinked on bare arms. The hair, well smoothed over the temples and knotted at the nape, bore crowns, or bunches, or sprays of myosotis, jasmine, pomegranate blossoms, ears of corn, and corn-flowers. Calmly seated in their places, mothers with forbidding countenances were wearing red turbans.

Emma's heart beat rather faster when, her partner holding her by the tips of the fingers, she took her place in a line with the dancers, and waited for the first note to start. But her emotion soon vanished, and, swaying to the rhythm of the or-chestra, she glided forward with slight movements of the neck. A smile rose to her lips at certain delicate phrases of the violin, that sometimes played alone while the other instruments were silent; one could hear the clear clink of the louis d'or that were being thrown down upon the card-tables in the next room; then all struck in again, the cornet-a-piston uttered its sonorous note, feet marked time, skirts swelled and rustled, hands touched and parted; the same eyes falling before you met yours again.

A few men (some fifteen or so), of twenty-five to forty, scattered here and there among the dancers or talking at the doorways, distinguished themselves from the crowd by a certain air of breeding, whatever their differences in age, dress, or face.

Their clothes, better made, seemed of finer cloth, and their hair, brought forward in curls towards the temples, glossy with more delicate pomades. They had the complexion of wealth—that clear complexion that is heightened by the pallor of porcelain, the shimmer of satin, the veneer of old furniture, and that an ordered regimen of exquisite nurture maintains at its best. Their necks moved easily in their low cravats, their long whiskers fell over their turned-down collars, they wiped their lips upon handkerchiefs with embroidered initials that gave forth a subtle perfume. Those who were beginning to grow old had an air of youth, while there was something mature in the faces of the young. In their unconcerned looks was the calm of passions daily satiated, and through all their gentleness of manner pierced that peculiar brutality, the result of a command of half-easy things, in which force is exercised and vanity amused—the management of thoroughbred horses and the society of loose women.

A few steps from Emma a gentleman in a blue coat was talking of Italy with a pale young woman wearing a parure of pearls.

They were praising the breadth of the columns of St. Peter's, Tivoli, Vesuvius, Castellamare, and Cassines, the roses of Genoa, the Coliseum by moonlight. With her other ear Emma was listening to a conversation full of words she did not understand. A circle gathered round a very young man who the week before had beaten "Miss Arabella" and "Romolus," and won two thousand louis jumping a ditch in England. One complained that his racehorses were growing fat; another of the printers' errors that had disfigured the name of his horse.

The atmosphere of the ball was heavy; the lamps were growing dim. Guests were flocking to the billiard-room. A servant got upon a chair and broke the window-panes. At the crash of the glass Madame Bovary turned her head and saw in the garden the faces of peasants pressed against the window looking in at them. Then the memory of the Bertaux came back to her. She saw the farm again, the muddy pond, her father in a blouse under the apple-trees, and she saw herself again as formerly, skimming with her finger the cream off the milk-pans in the dairy. But in the refulgence of the present hour her past life, so distinct until then, faded away completely, and she almost doubted having lived it. She was there; beyond the ball was only shadow overspreading all the rest. She was just eating a maraschino ice that she held with her left hand in a silver-gilt cup, her eyes half-closed, and the spoon between her teeth.

A lady near her dropped her fan. A gentleman was passing.

"Would you be so good," said the lady, "as to pick up my fan that has fallen behind the sofa?"

The gentleman bowed, and as he moved to stretch out his arm, Emma saw the hand of the young woman throw something white, folded in a triangle, into his hat. The gentleman picking up the fan, offered it to the lady respectfully; she thanked him with an inclination of the head, and began smelling her bouquet.

After supper, where were plenty of Spanish and Rhine wines, soups *à la bisque* and *au lait d'amandes,* puddings *à la Trafalgar,* and all sorts of cold meats with jellies that trembled in the dishes, the carriages one after the other began to drive off. Raising the corners of the muslin curtain, one could see the light of their lanterns glimmering through the darkness. The seats began to empty, some card-players were still left; the musicians were cooling the tips of their fingers on their tongues. Charles was half asleep, his back propped against a door.

At three o'clock the cotillion began. Emma did not know how to waltz. Everyone was waltzing, Mademoiselle d'Andervilliers herself and the Marquis; only the guests staying at the castle were still there, about a dozen persons.

One of the waltzers, however, who was familiarly called Viscount, and whose low cut waistcoat seemed moulded to his chest, came a second time to ask Madame Bovary to dance, assuring her that he would guide her, and that she would get through it very well.

They began slowly, then went more rapidly. They turned; all around them was turning—the lamps, the furniture, the wainscoting, the floor, like a disc on a pivot. On passing near the doors the bottom of Emma's dress caught against his trousers. Their legs commingled; he looked down at her; she raised her eyes to his. A torpor seized her; she stopped. They started again, and with a more rapid movement; the Viscount, dragging her along, disappeared with her to the end of the gallery, where, panting, she almost fell, and for a moment rested her head upon his breast. And then, still turning, but more slowly, he guided her back to her seat. She leaned back against the wall and covered her eyes with her hands.

When she opened them again, in the middle of the drawing-room three waltzers were kneeling before a lady sitting on a stool. She chose the Viscount, and the violin struck up once more.

Everyone looked at them. They passed and repassed, she with rigid body, her chin bent down, and he always in the same pose, his figure curved, his elbow rounded, his chin thrown forward. That woman knew how to waltz! They kept up a long time, and tired out all the others.

Then they talked a few moments longer, and after the good-nights, or rather good-mornings, the guests of the château retired to bed.

Charles dragged himself up by the balusters. His "knees were going up into his body." He had spent five consecutive hours standing bolt upright at the card-tables, watching them play whist, without understanding anything about it, and it was with a deep sigh of relief that he pulled off his boots.

Emma threw a shawl over her shoulders, opened the window, and leant out.

The night was dark; some drops of rain were falling. She breathed in the damp wind that refreshed her eyelids. The music of the ball was still murmuring in her ears, and she tried to keep herself awake in order to prolong the illusion of this luxurious life that she would soon have to give up.

Day began to break. She looked long at the windows of the château, trying to guess which were the rooms of all those she had noticed the evening before. She would fain have known their lives, have penetrated, blended with them. But she was shivering with cold. She undressed, and cowered down between the sheets against Charles, who was asleep.

There were a great many people to luncheon. The repast lasted ten minutes; no liqueurs were served, which astonished the doctor. Next, Mademoiselle d'Andervilliers collected some pieces of roll in a small basket to take them to the swans on the ornamental waters, and they went to walk in the hot-houses, where strange plants, bristling with hairs, rose in pyramids under hanging vases, whence, as from overfilled nests of serpents, fell long green cords interlacing. The orangery, which was at the other end, led by a covered way to the outhouses of the château. The Marquis, to amuse the young woman, took her to see the stables. Above the basket-shaped racks porcelain slabs bore the names of the horses in black letters. Each animal in its stall whisked its tail when anyone went near and said "Tchk! tchk!" The boards of the harness-room shone like the flooring of a drawing-room. The carriage harness was piled up in the middle against two twisted columns, and the bits, the whips, the spurs, the curbs, were ranged in a line all along the wall.

Charles, meanwhile, went to ask a groom to put his horse to. The dog-cart was brought to the foot of the steps, and all the parcels being crammed in, the Bovarys paid their respects to the Marquis and Marchioness and set out again for Tostes.

Emma watched the turning wheels in silence. Charles, on the extreme edge of the seat, held the reins with his two arms wide apart, and the little horse ambled along in the shafts that were too big for him. The loose reins hanging over his crupper were wet with foam, and the box fastened on behind the chaise gave great regular bumps against it.

They were on the heights of Thibourville when suddenly some horsemen with cigars between their lips passed laughing. Emma thought she recognised the Viscount, turned back, and caught on the horizon only the movement of the heads rising or falling with the unequal cadence of the trot or gallop.

A mile farther on they had to stop to mend with some string the traces that had broken.

But Charles, giving a last look to the harness, saw something on the ground between his horse's legs, and he picked up a cigar-case with a green silk border and beblazoned in the centre like the door of a carriage.

"There are even two cigars in it," said he; "they'll do for this evening after dinner."

"Why, do you smoke?" she asked.

"Sometimes, when I get a chance."

He put his find in his pocket and whipped up the nag.

When they reached home the dinner was not ready. Madame lost her temper. Nastasie answered rudely.

"Leave the room!" said Emma. "You are forgetting yourself. I give you warning."

For dinner there was onion soup and a piece of veal with sorrel. Charles, seated opposite Emma, rubbed his hands gleefully.

"How good it is to be at home again!"

Nastasie could be heard crying. He was rather fond of the poor girl. She had formerly, during the wearisome time of his widowhood, kept him company many an evening. She had been his first patient, his oldest acquaintance in the place.

"Have you given her warning for good?" he asked at last.

"Yes. Who is to prevent me?" she replied.

Then they warmed themselves in the kitchen while their room was being made ready. Charles began to smoke. He smoked with lips protruded, spitting every moment, recoiling at every puff.

"You'll make yourself ill," she said scornfully.

He put down his cigar and ran to swallow a glass of cold water at the pump. Emma seizing hold of the cigar-case threw it quickly to the back of the cupboard.

The next day was a long one. She walked about her little garden, up and down the same walks, stopping before the beds, before the espalier, before the plaster curate, looking with amazement at all these things of once-on-a-time that she knew so well. How far off the ball seemed already! What was it that thus set so far asunder the morning of the day before yesterday and the evening of to-day? Her journey to Vaubyessard had made a hole in her life, like one of those great crevasses that a storm will sometimes make in one night in mountains. Still she was resigned.

She devoutly put away in her drawers her beautiful dress, down to the satin shoes whose soles were yellowed with the slippery wax of the dancing floor. Her heart was like these. In its friction against wealth something had come over it that could not be effaced.

The memory of this ball, then, became an occupation for Emma. Whenever the Wednesday came round she said to herself as she awoke, "Ah! I was there a week—a fortnight—three weeks ago." And little by little the faces grew confused in her remembrance. She forgot the tune of the quadrilles; she no longer saw the liveries and appointments so distinctly; some details escaped her, but the regret remained with her.

Chapter IX

OFTEN WHEN CHARLES WAS OUT SHE TOOK FROM THE CUPBOARD, BETWEEN the folds of the linen where she had left it, the green silk cigar-case. She looked at it, opened it, and even smelt the odour of the lining—a mixture of verbena and tobacco. Whose was it? The Viscount's? Perhaps it was a present from his mistress. It had been embroidered on some rosewood frame, a pretty little thing, hidden from all eyes, that had occupied many hours, and over which had fallen the soft curls of the pensive worker. A breath of love had passed over the stitches on the canvas; each prick of the needle had fixed there a hope or a memory, and all those interwoven threads of silk were but the continuity of the same silent passion. And then one morning the Viscount had taken it away with him. Of what had they spoken when it lay upon the wide-mantelled chimneys between flower-vases and Pompadour clocks? She was at Tostes; he was at Paris now, far away! What was this Paris like? What a vague name! She repeated it in a low voice, for the mere pleasure of it; it rang in her ears like a great cathedral bell; it shone before her eyes, even on the labels of her pomade-pots.

At night, when the carriers passed under her windows in their carts singing the "Marjolaine," she awoke, and listened to the noise of the iron-bound wheels, which, as they gained the country road, was soon deadened by the soil. "They will be there to-morrow!" she said to herself.

And she followed them in thought up and down the hills, traversing villages, gliding along the highroads by the light of the stars. At the end of some indefinite distance there was always a confused spot, into which her dream died.

She bought a plan of Paris, and with the tip of her finger on the map she walked about the capital. She went up the boulevards, stopping at every turning, between the lines of the streets, in front of the white squares that represented the houses. At last she would close the lids of her weary eyes, and see in the darkness the gas jets flaring in the wind and the steps of carriages lowered with much noise before the peristyles of theatres.

She took in *La Corbeille*, a lady's journal, and the *Sylphe des Salons*. She devoured, without skipping a word, all the accounts of first nights, races, and soirées, took an interest in the début of a singer, in the opening of a new shop. She knew the latest fashions, the addresses of the best tailors, the days of the Bois and the Opera. In Eugène Sue she studied descriptions of furniture; she read Balzac and George Sand, seeking in them imaginary satisfaction for her own desires. Even at table she had her book by her, and turned over the pages while Charles ate and talked to her. The memory of the Viscount always returned as she read. Between him and the imaginary personages she made comparisons. But the circle of which he was the centre gradually widened round him, and the aureole that he bore, fading from his form, broadened out beyond, lighting up her other dreams.

Paris, more vague than the ocean, glimmered before Emma's eyes in an atmosphere of vermilion. The many lives that stirred amid this tumult were, however, divided into parts, classed as distinct pictures. Emma perceived only two or three that hid from her all the rest, and in themselves represented all humanity. The world of ambassadors moved over polished floors in drawing-rooms lined with mirrors, round oval tables covered with velvet and gold-fringed cloths. There were dresses with trains, deep mysteries, anguish hidden beneath smiles. Then came the society of the duchesses; all were pale; all got up at four o'clock; the women, poor angels, wore English point on their petticoats; and the men, unappreciated geniuses under a frivolous outward seeming, rode horses to death at pleasure parties, spent the summer season at Baden, and towards the forties married heiresses. In the private rooms of restaurants, where one sups after midnight by the light of wax candles, laughed the motley crowd of men of letters and actresses. They were prodigal as kings, full of ideal, ambitious, fantastic frenzy. This was an existence outside that of all others, between heaven and earth, in the midst of storms, having something of the sublime. For the rest of the world it was lost, with no particular place, and as if non-existent. The nearer things were, moreover, the more her thoughts turned away from them. All her immediate surroundings, the wearisome country, the middle-class imbeciles, the mediocrity of existence, seemed to her exceptional, a peculiar chance that had caught hold of her, while beyond stretched as far as eye could see an immense land of joys and passions. She confused in her desire the sensualities of luxury with the delights of the heart, elegance of manners with delicacy of sentiment. Did not love, like Indian plants, need a special soil, a particular temperature? Sighs by moonlight, long embraces, tears flowing over yielded hands, all the fevers of the flesh and the languors of tenderness could not be separated from the balconies of great castles full of indolence, from boudoirs with silken curtains and thick carpets, well-filled flower-stands, a bed on a raised daïs, nor from the flashing of precious stones and the shoulder-knots of liveries.

The lad from the posting-house who came to groom the mare every morning passed through the passage with his heavy wooden shoes; there were holes in his blouse; his feet were bare in list slippers. And this was the groom in knee-breeches with whom she had to be content! His work done, he did not come back again all day, for Charles on his return put up his horse himself, unsaddled him and put on the halter, while the servant-girl brought a bundle of straw and threw it as best she could into the manger.

To replace Nastasie (who left Tostes shedding torrents of tears) Emma took into her service a young girl of fourteen, an orphan with a sweet face. She forbade her wearing cotton caps, taught her to address her in the third person, to bring a glass of water on a plate, to knock before coming into a room, to iron, starch, and to dress her—wanted to make a lady's-maid of her. The new servant obeyed without a murmur, so as not to be sent away; and as madame usually left the key in the sideboard, Félicité every evening took a small supply of sugar that she ate alone in her bed after she had said her prayers.

Sometimes in the afternoon she went to chat with the postilions. Madame was in her room upstairs. She wore an open dressing-gown, that showed between the shawl facings of her bodice a pleated chemisette with three gold buttons. Her belt was a corded girdle with great tassels, and her small garnet-coloured slippers had a large knot of ribbon that fell over her instep. She had bought herself a blotting-book, writing-case, pen-holder, and envelopes, although she had no one to write to; she dusted her what-not, looked at herself in the glass, picked up a book, and then, dreaming between the lines, let it drop on her knees. She longed to travel or to go back to her convent. She wished at the same time to die and to live in Paris.

Charles in snow and rain trotted across country. He ate omelettes on farm-house tables, poked his arm into damp beds, received the tepid spurt of blood-lettings in his face, listened to death-rattles, examined basins, turned over a good deal of dirty linen; but every evening he found a blazing fire, his dinner ready, easy-chairs, and a well-dressed woman, charming with an odour of freshness, though no one could say whence the perfume came, or if it were not her skin that made odorous her chemise.

She charmed him by numerous attentions; now it was some new way of ar-ranging paper sconces for the candles, a flounce that she altered on her gown, or an extraordinary name for some very simple dish that the servant had spoilt, but that Charles swallowed with pleasure to the last mouthful. At Rouen she saw some ladies who wore a bunch of charms on their watch-chains; she bought some charms. She wanted for her mantelpiece two large blue glass vases, and some time after an ivory nécessaire with a silver-gilt thimble. The less Charles understood these refinements the more they seduced him. They added something to the pleas-ure of the senses and to the comfort of his fireside. It was like a golden dust sand-ing all along the narrow path of his life.

He was well, looked well; his reputation was firmly established. The country-folk loved him because he was not proud. He petted the children, never went to the public-house, and, moreover, his morals inspired confidence. He was specially suc-cessful with catarrhs and chest complaints. Being much afraid of killing his pa-tients, Charles, in fact, only prescribed sedatives, from time to time an emetic, a footbath, or leeches. It was not that he was afraid of surgery; he bled people copiously like horses, and for the taking out of teeth he had the "devil's own wrist."

Finally, to keep up with the times, he took in *La Ruche Médicale,* a new journal whose prospectus had been sent him. He read it a little after dinner, but in about five minutes, the warmth of the room added to the effect of his dinner sent him to sleep; and he sat there, his chin on his two hands and his hair spreading like a mane to the foot of the lamp. Emma looked at him and shrugged her shoulders. Why, at least, was not her husband one of those men of taciturn passions who work at their books all night, and at last, when about sixty, the age of rheumatism sets in, wear a string of orders on their ill-fitting black coat? She could have wished this name of Bovary, which was hers, had been illustrious, to see it displayed at the booksellers', repeated in the newspapers, known to all France. But Charles had no ambition. An Yvetot doctor whom he had lately met in consultation had somewhat humiliated him at the very bedside of the patient, before the assembled relatives. When, in the evening, Charles told her this anecdote, Emma inveighed loudly against his colleague. Charles was much touched. He kissed her forehead with a tear in his eyes. But she was angered with shame; she felt a wild desire to strike him; she went to open the window in the passage and breathed in the fresh air to calm herself.

"What a man! what a man!" she said in a low voice, biting her lips.

Besides, she was becoming more irritated with him. As he grew older his manner grew heavier; at dessert he cut the corks of the empty bottles, after eating he cleaned his teeth with his tongue; in taking soup he made a gurgling noise with every spoonful; and, as he was getting fatter, the puffed-out cheeks seemed to push the eyes, always small, up to the temples.

Sometimes Emma tucked the red borders of his undervest into his waistcoat, rearranged his cravat, and threw away the dirty gloves he was going to put on; and this was not, as he fancied, for himself; it was for herself, by a diffusion of egotism, of nervous irritation. Sometimes, too, she told him of what she had read, such as a passage in a novel, of a new play, or an anecdote of the "upper ten" that she had seen in a feuilleton; for, after all, Charles was something, an ever-open ear, an ever-ready approbation. She confided many a thing to her greyhound. She would have done so to the logs in the fireplace or to the pendulum of the clock.

At bottom of her heart, however, she was waiting for something to happen. Like shipwrecked sailors, she turned despairing eyes upon the solitude of her life, seeking afar off some white sail in the mists of the horizon. She did not know what this chance would be, what wind would bring it her, towards what shore it would drive her, if it would be a shallop or a three-decker, laden with anguish or full of bliss to the portholes. But each morning, as she awoke, she hoped it would come that day; she listened to every sound, sprang up with a start, wondered that it did not come; then at sunset, always more saddened, she longed for the morrow.

Spring came round. With the first warm weather, when the pear-trees began to blossom, she suffered from dyspnoea.

From the beginning of July she counted how many weeks there were to October, thinking that perhaps the Marquis d'Andervilliers would give another ball at Vaubyessard. But all September passed without letters or visits.

After the ennui of this disappointment her heart once more remained empty, and then the same series of days recommenced. So now they would thus follow one another, always the same, immovable, and bringing nothing. Other lives, however flat, had at least the chance of some event. One adventure sometimes brought with it infinite consequences and the scene changed. But nothing happened to her; God had willed it so! The future was a dark corridor, with its door at the end shut fast.

She gave up music. What was the good of playing? Who would hear her? Since she could never, in a velvet gown with short sleeves, striking with her light fingers the ivory keys of an Erard at a concert, feel the murmur of ecstasy envelop her like a breeze, it was not worth while boring herself with practising. Her drawing cardboard and her embroidery she left in the cupboard. What was the good? What was the good? Sewing irritated her. "I have read everything," she said to herself. And she sat there making the tongs red-hot, or looked at the rain falling.

How sad she was on Sundays when vespers sounded! She listened with dull attention to each stroke of the cracked bell. A cat slowly walking over some roof put up his back in the pale rays of the sun. The wind on the highroad blew up clouds of dust. Afar off a dog sometimes howled; and the bell, keeping time, continued its monotonous ringing that died away over the fields.

But the people came out from church. The women in waxed clogs, the peasants in new blouses, the little bareheaded children skipping along in front of them, all were going home. And till nightfall, five or six men, always the same, stayed playing at corks in front of the large door of the inn.

The winter was severe. The windows every morning were covered with rime, and the light shining through them, dim as through ground-glass, sometimes did not change the whole day long. At four o'clock the lamp had to be lighted.

On fine days she went down into the garden. The dew had left on the cabbages a silver lace with long transparent threads spreading from one to the other. No birds were to be heard; everything seemed asleep, the espalier covered with straw, and the vine, like a great sick serpent under the coping of the wall, along which, on drawing near, one saw the many-footed woodlice crawling. Under the spruce by the hedgerow, the curé in the three-cornered hat reading his breviary had lost his right foot, and the very plaster, scaling off with the frost, had left white scabs on his face.

Then she went up again, shut her door, put on coals, and fainting with the heat of the hearth, felt her boredom weigh more heavily than ever. She would have liked to go down and talk to the servant, but a sense of shame restrained her.

Every day at the same time the schoolmaster in a black skull-cap opened the shutters of his house, and the rural policeman, wearing his sabre over his blouse, passed by. Night and morning the post-horses, three by three, crossed the street to water at the pond. From time to time the bell of a public-house door rang, and when it was windy one could hear the little brass basins that served as signs for the hairdresser's shop creaking on their two rods. This shop had as decoration an old engraving of a fashion-plate stuck against a window-pane and the wax bust of a woman with yellow hair. He, too, the hairdresser, lamented his wasted calling, his hopeless future, and dreaming of some shop in a big town—at Rouen, for example, overlooking the harbour, near the theatre—he walked up and down all day from the mairie to the church, sombre and waiting for customers. When Madame Bovary looked up, she always saw him there, like a sentinel on duty, with his skull-cap over his ears and his vest of lasting.

Sometimes in the afternoon outside the window of her room, the head of a man appeared, a swarthy head with black whiskers, smiling slowly, with a broad, gentle smile that showed his white teeth. A waltz immediately began, and on the organ, in a little drawing-room, dancers the size of a finger, women in pink turbans, Tyrolians in jackets, monkeys in frock-coats, gentlemen in knee-breeches, turned and turned between the sofas, the consoles, multiplied in the bits of looking-glass held together at their corners by a piece of gold paper. The man turned his handle, looking to the right and left, and up at the windows. Now and again, while he shot out a long squirt of brown saliva against the milestone, with his knee he raised his instrument, whose hard straps tired his shoulder; and now, doleful and drawling, or gay and hurried, the music escaped from the box, droning through a curtain of pink taffeta under a brass claw in arabesque. They were airs played in other places at the theatres, sung in drawing-rooms, danced to at night under lighted lustres, echoes of the world that reached even to Emma. Endless sarabands ran through her head, and, like an Indian dancing-girl on the flowers of a carpet, her thoughts leapt with the notes, swung from dream to dream, from sadness to sadness. When the man had caught some coppers in his cap, he drew down an old cover of blue cloth, hitched his organ on to his back, and went off with a heavy tread. She watched him going.

But it was above all the meal-times that were unbearable to her, in this small room on the ground-floor, with its smoking stove, its creaking door, the walls that sweated, the damp flags; all the bitterness in life seemed served up on her plate, and with the smoke of the boiled beef there rose from her secret soul whiffs of sickliness. Charles was a slow eater; she played with a few nuts, or, leaning on her elbow, amused herself with drawing lines along the oil-cloth table-cover with the point of her knife.

She now let everything in her household take care of itself, and Madame Bovary senior, when she came to spend part of Lent at Tostes, was much surprised at the change. She who was formerly so careful, so dainty, now passed whole days without dressing, wore grey cotton stockings, and burnt tallow candles. She kept saying they must be economical since they were not rich, adding that she was very contented, very happy, that Tostes pleased her very much, with other speeches that closed the mouth of her mother-in-law. Besides, Emma no longer seemed inclined to follow her advice; once even, Madame Bovary having thought fit to maintain that mistresses ought to keep an eye on the religion of their servants, she had answered with so angry a look and so cold a smile that the good woman did not try it on again.

Emma was growing difficile, capricious. She ordered dishes for herself, then she did not touch them; one day drank only pure milk, and the next cups of tea by the dozen. Often she persisted in not going out, then, stifling, threw open the windows and put on light dresses. After she had well scolded her servant she gave her presents or sent her out to see neighbours, just as she sometimes threw beggars all the silver in her purse, although she was by no means tender-hearted or easily accessible to the feelings of others, like most country-bred people, who always retain in their souls something of the horny hardness of the paternal hands.

Towards the end of February old Rouault, in memory of his cure, himself brought his son-in-law a superb turkey, and stayed three days at Tostes. Charles being with his patients, Emma kept him company. He smoked in the room, spat on the fire-dogs, talked farming, calves, cows, poultry, and municipal council, so that when he left she closed the door on him with a feeling of satisfaction that surprised even herself. Moreover she no longer concealed her contempt for anything or anybody, and at times she set herself to express singular opinions, finding fault with that which others approved, and approving things perverse and immoral, all of which made her husband open his eyes widely.

Would this misery last forever? Would she never issue from it? Yet she was as good as all the women who were living happily. She had seen duchesses at Vaubyessard with clumsier waists and commoner ways, and she execrated the injustice of God. She leant her head against the walls to weep; she envied lives of stir; longed for masked balls, for violent pleasures, with all the wildness, that she did not know, but that these must surely yield.

She grew pale and suffered from palpitations of the heart. Charles prescribed valerian and camphor baths. Everything that was tried only seemed to irritate her the more.

On certain days she chattered with feverish rapidity, and this over-excitement was suddenly followed by a state of torpor, in which she remained without speaking, without moving. What then revived her was pouring a bottle of eau-de-cologne over her arms.

As she was constantly complaining about Tostes, Charles fancied that her illness was no doubt due to some local cause, and fixing on this idea, began to think seriously of setting up elsewhere.

From that moment she drank vinegar, contracted a sharp little cough, and completely lost her appetite.

It cost Charles much to give up Tostes after living there four years and "when he was beginning to get on there." Yet if it must be! He took her to Rouen to see his old master. It was a nervous complaint: change of air was needed.

After looking about him on this side and on that, Charles learnt that in the Neufchâtel arrondissement there was a considerable market-town called Yonville-l'Abbaye, whose doctor, a Polish refugee, had decamped a week before. Then he wrote to the chemist of the place to ask the number of the population, the distance from the nearest doctor, what his predecessor had made a year, and so forth; and the answer being satisfactory, he made up his mind to move towards the spring, if Emma's health did not improve.

One day when, in view of her departure, she was tidying a drawer, something pricked her finger. It was a wire of her wedding-bouquet. The orange blossoms were yellow with dust and the silver-bordered satin ribbons frayed at the edges. She threw it into the fire. It flared up more quickly than dry straw. Then it was like a red bush in the cinders, slowly devoured. She watched it burn. The little pasteboard berries burst, the wire twisted, the gold lace melted; and the shrivelled paper corollas, fluttering like black butterflies at the back of the stove, at last flew up the chimney.

When they left Tostes in the month of March, Madame Bovary was pregnant.

PART II

Chapter I

YONVILLE-L'ABBAYE (SO CALLED FROM AN OLD CAPUCHIN ABBEY OF WHICH not even the ruins remain), is a market-town twenty-four miles from Rouen, between the Abbeville and Beauvais roads, at the foot of a valley watered by the Rieule, a little river that runs into the Andelle after turning three water-mills near its mouth, where there are a few trout that the lads amuse themselves by fishing for on Sundays.

We leave the highroad at La Boissière and keep straight on to the top of the Leux hill, whence the valley is seen. The river that runs through it makes of it, as it were, two regions with distinct physiognomies—all on the left is pasture land, all on the right arable. The meadow stretches under a bulge of low hills to join at the back with the pasture land of the Bray country, while on the eastern side, the plain, gently rising, broadens out, showing as far as eye can follow its blond cornfields. The water, flowing by the grass, divides with a white line the colour of the roads and of the plains, and the country is like a great unfolded mantle with a green velvet cape bordered with a fringe of silver.

Before us, on the verge of the horizon, lie the oaks of the forest of Argueil, with the steeps of the Saint-Jean hills scarred from top to bottom with red irregular lines; they are rain-tracks, and these brick-tones standing out in narrow streaks against the grey colour of the mountain are due to the quantity of iron springs that flow beyond in the neighbouring country.

Here we are on the confines of Normandy, Picardy, and the Ile-de-France, a bastard land, whose language is without accent as its landscape is without character. It is there that they make the worst Neufchâtel cheeses of all the arrondissement; and, on the other hand, farming is costly because so much manure is needed to enrich this friable soil full of sand and flints.

Up to 1835 there was no practicable road for getting to Yonville, but about this time a cross-road was made which joins that of Abbeville to that of Amiens, and is occasionally used by the Rouen waggoners on their way to Flanders. Yonville-l'Abbaye has remained stationary in spite of its "new outlet." Instead of improving the soil, they persist in keeping up the pasture lands, however depreciated they may be in value, and the lazy borough, growing away from the plain, has naturally spread riverwards. It is seen from afar sprawling along the banks like a cowherd taking a siesta by the water-side.

At the foot of the hill beyond the bridge begins a roadway, planted with young aspens that leads in a straight line to the first houses in the place. These, fenced in by hedges, are in the middle of courtyards full of straggling buildings, wine-presses, cart-sheds, and distilleries scattered under thick trees, with ladders, poles, or scythes hung on to the branches. The thatched roofs, like fur caps drawn over eyes, reach down over about a third of the low windows, whose course convex glasses have knots in the middle like the bottoms of bottles. Against the plaster wall diagonally crossed by black joists, a meagre pear-tree sometimes leans, and the ground-floors have at their door a small swing-gate, to keep out the chicks that come pilfering crumbs of bread steeped in cider on the threshold. But the court-yards grow narrower, the houses closer together, and the fences disappear; a bun-dle of ferns swings under a window from the end of a broomstick; there is a blacksmith's forge and then a wheelwright's, with two or three new carts outside that partly block up the way. Then across an open space appears a white house be-yond a grass mound ornamented by a Cupid, his finger on his lips; two brass vases are at each end of a flight of steps; scutcheons blaze upon the door. It is the no-tary's house, and the finest in the place.

The church is on the other side of the street, twenty paces farther down, at the entrance of the square. The little cemetery that surrounds it, closed in by a wall breast-high, is so full of graves that the old stones, level with the ground, form a continuous pavement, on which the grass of itself has marked out regular green squares. The church was rebuilt during the last years of the reign of Charles X. The wooden roof is beginning to rot from the top, and here and there has black hollows in its blue colour. Over the door, where the organ should be, is a loft for the men, with a spiral staircase that reverberates under their wooden shoes.

The daylight coming through the plain glass windows falls obliquely upon the pews ranged along the walls, which are adorned here and there with a straw mat bearing beneath it the words in large letters, "Mr. So-and-so's pew." Farther on, at a spot where the building narrows, the confessional forms a pendant to a statuette of the Virgin, clothed in a satin robe, coifed with a tulle veil sprinkled with silver stars, and with red cheeks, like an idol of the Sandwich Islands; and, finally, a copy of the "Holy Family, presented by the Minister of the Interior," overlooking the high altar, between four candlesticks, closes in the perspective. The choir stalls, of deal wood, have been left unpainted.

The market, that is to say, a tiled roof supported by some twenty posts, occu-pies of itself about half the public square of Yonville. The town hall, constructed "from the designs of a Paris architect," is a sort of Greek temple that forms the corner next to the chemist's shop. On the ground-floor are three Ionic columns and on the first floor a semicircular gallery, while the dome that crowns it is occupied by a Gallic cock, resting one foot upon the "Charte" and holding in the other the scales of Justice.

But that which most attracts the eye is opposite the Lion d'Or inn the chemist's shop of Monsieur Homais. In the evening especially its argand lamp is lit up and the red and green jars that embellish his shop-front throw far across the street their two streams of colour; then across them as if in Bengal lights is seen the shadow of the chemist leaning over his desk. His house from top to bottom is placarded with inscriptions written in large hand, round hand, printed hand: "Vichy, Seltzer, Barège waters, blood purifiers, Raspail patent medicine, Arabian racahout, Darcet lozenges, Regnault paste, trusses, baths, hygienic chocolate," etc. And the sign-board, which takes up all the breadth of the shop, bears in gold letters, "Homais, Chemist." Then at the back of the shop, behind the great scales fixed to the counter, the word "Laboratory" appears on a scroll above a glass door, which about half-way up once more repeats "Homais" in gold letters on a black ground.

Beyond this there is nothing to see at Yonville. The street (the only one) a gun-shot in length and flanked by a few shops on either side stops short at the turn of the highroad. If it is left on the right hand and the foot of the Saint-Jean hills fol-lowed the cemetery is soon reached.

At the time of the cholera, in order to enlarge this, a piece of wall was pulled down, and three acres of land by its side purchased; but all the new portion is al-most tenantless; the tombs, as heretofore, continue to crowd together towards the gate. The keeper, who is at once gravedigger and church beadle (thus making a double profit out of the parish corpses), has taken advantage of the unused plot of ground to plant potatoes there. From year to year, however, his small field grows smaller, and when there is an epidemic, he does not know whether to rejoice at the deaths or regret the burials.

"You live on the dead, Lestiboudois!" the curé at last said to him one day. This grim remark made him reflect; it checked him for some time; but to this day he car-ries on the cultivation of his little tubers, and even maintains stoutly that they grow naturally.

Since the events about to be narrated, nothing in fact has changed at Yonville. The tin tricolour flag still swings at the top of the church-steeple; the two chintz streamers still flutter in the wind from the linendraper's; the chemist's foetuses, like lumps of white amadou, rot more and more in their turbid alcohol, and above the big door of the inn the old golden lion, faded by rain, still shows passers-by its poo-dle mane.

On the evening when the Bovarys were to arrive at Yonville, Widow Lefrançois, the landlady of this inn, was so very busy that she sweated great drops as she moved her saucepans. To-morrow was market-day. The meat had to be cut beforehand, the fowls drawn, the soup and coffee made. Moreover, she had the boarders' meal to see to, and that of the doctor, his wife, and their servant; the

billiard-room was echoing with bursts of laughter; three millers in the small parlour were calling for brandy; the wood was blazing, the brazen pan was hissing, and
on the long kitchen-table, amid the quarters of raw mutton, rose piles of plates that
rattled with the shaking of the block on which spinach was being chopped. From
the poultry-yard was heard the screaming of the fowls whom the servant was chasing in order to wring their necks.

A man slightly marked with small-pox, in green leather slippers, and wearing
a velvet cap with a gold tassel, was warming his back at the chimney. His face expressed nothing but self-satisfaction, and he appeared to take life as calmly as the
goldfinch suspended over his head in its wicker cage: this was the chemist.

"Artémise!" shouted the landlady, "chop some wood, fill the water bottles,
bring some brandy, look sharp! If only I knew what dessert to offer the guests you
are expecting! Good heavens! Those furniture-movers are beginning their racket
in the billiard-room again; and their van has been left before the front door! The
Hirondelle might run into it when it draws up. Call Polyte and tell him to put it up.
Only to think, Monsieur Homais, that since morning they have had about fifteen
games, and drunk eight jars of cider! Why, they'll tear my cloth for me," she went
on, looking at them from a distance, her strainer in her hand.

"That wouldn't be much of a loss," replied Monsieur Homais. "You would
buy another."

"Another billiard-table!" exclaimed the widow.

"Since that one is coming to pieces, Madame Lefrançois. I tell you again you
are doing yourself harm, much harm! And besides, players now want narrow
pockets and heavy cues. Hazards aren't played now; everything is changed! One
must keep pace with the times! Just look at Tellier!"

The hostess reddened with vexation. The chemist went on—

"You may say what you like; his table is better than yours; and if one were to
think, for example, of getting up a patriotic pool for Poland or the sufferers from
the Lyons floods"—

"It isn't beggars like him that'll frighten us," interrupted the landlady, shrugging her fat shoulders. "Come, come, Monsieur Homais; as long as the Lion d'Or
exists people will come to it. We've feathered our nest; while one of these days
you'll find the Café Français closed with a big placard on the shutters. Change my
billiard-table!" she went on, speaking to herself, "the table that comes in so handy
for folding the washing, and on which, in the hunting season, I have slept six visitors! But that dawdler, Hivert, doesn't come!"

"Are you waiting for him for your gentlemen's dinner?"

"Wait for him! And what about Monsieur Binet? As the clock strikes six you'll
see him come in, for he hasn't his equal under the sun for punctuality. He must al-

ways have his seat in the small parlour. He'd rather die than dine anywhere else. And so squeamish as he is, and so particular about the cider! Not like Monsieur Léon; he sometimes comes at seven, or even half-past, and he doesn't so much as look at what he eats. Such a nice young man! Never speaks a rough word!"

"Well, you see, there's a great difference between an educated man and an old carabineer who is now a tax-collector."

Six o'clock struck. Binet came in.

He wore a blue frock-coat falling in a straight line round his thin body, and his leather cap, with its lappets knotted over the top of his head with string, showed under the turned-up peak a bald forehead, flattened by the constant wearing of a helmet. He wore a black cloth waistcoat, a hair collar, grey trousers, and, all the year round, well-blacked boots, that had two parallel swellings due to the sticking out of his big-toes. Not a hair stood out from the regular line of fair whiskers, which, encircling his jaws, framed, after the fashion of a garden border, his long, wan face, whose eyes were small and the nose hooked. Clever at all games of cards, a good hunter, and writing a fine hand, he had at home a lathe, and amused himself by turning napkin-rings, with which he filled up his house, with the jealousy of an artist and the egotism of a bourgeois.

He went to the small parlour, but the three millers had to be got out first, and during the whole time necessary for laying the cloth, Binet remained silent in his place near the stove. Then he shut the door and took off his cap in his usual way.

"It isn't with saying civil things that he'll wear out his tongue," said the chemist, as soon as he was alone with the landlady.

"He never talks more," she replied. "Last week two travellers in the cloth line were here—such clever chaps, who told such jokes in the evening, that I fairly cried with laughing; and he stood there like a dab fish and never said a word."

"Yes," observed the chemist; "no imagination, no sallies, nothing that makes the society-man."

"Yet they say he has parts," objected the landlady.

"Parts!" replied Monsieur Homais; "he parts! In his own line it is possible," he added in a calmer tone. And he went on—

"Ah! that a merchant, who has large connections, a juris-consult, a doctor, a chemist, should be thus absent-minded, that they should become whimsical or even peevish, I can understand; such cases are cited in history. But at least it is because they are thinking of something. Myself, for example, how often has it happened to me to look on the bureau of my pen to write a label, and to find, after all, that I had put it behind my ear?"

Madame Lefrançois just then went to the door to see if the Hirondelle were not coming. She started. A man dressed in black suddenly came into the kitchen. By the last gleam of the twilight one could see that his face was rubicund and his form athletic.

"What can I do for you, Monsieur le Curé?" asked the landlady, as she reached down from the chimney one of the copper candlesticks placed with their candles in a row. "Will you take something? A thimbleful of cassis? A glass of wine?"

The priest declined very politely. He had come for his umbrella, that he had forgotten the other day at the Ernemont convent, and after asking Madame Lefrançois to have it sent to him at the presbytery in the evening, he left for the church, from which the Angelus was ringing.

When the chemist no longer heard the noise of his boots along the square, he thought the priest's behaviour just now very unbecoming. This refusal to take any refreshment seemed to him the most odious hypocrisy; all priests tippled on the sly, and were trying to bring back the days of the tithe.

The landlady took up the defence of her curé.

"Besides, he could double up four men like you over his knee. Last year he helped our people to bring in the straw; he carried as many as six trusses at once, he is so strong."

"Bravo!" said the chemist. "Now just send your daughters to confess to fellows with such a temperament! I, if I were the Government, I'd have the priests bled once a month. Yes, Madame Lefrançois, every month—a good phlebotomy, in the interests of the police and morals."

"Be quiet, Monsieur Homais. You are an infidel; you've no religion."

The chemist answered: "I have a religion, my religion, and I even have more than all these others with their mummeries and their juggling. I adore God, on the contrary. I believe in the Supreme Being, in a Creator, whatever he may be. I care little who has placed us here below to fulfil our duties as citizens and fathers of families; but I don't need to go to church to kiss silver plates, and fatten, out of my pocket, a lot of good-for-nothings who live better than we do. For one can know him as well in a wood, in a field, or even contemplating the eternal vault like the ancients. My God! mine is the God of Socrates, of Franklin, of Voltaire, and of Béranger! I am for the profession of faith of the 'Savoyard Vicar,' and the immortal principles of '89! And I can't admit of an old boy of a God who takes walks in his garden with a cane in his hand, who lodges his friends in the belly of whales, dies uttering a cry, and rises again at the end of three days; things absurd in themselves, and completely opposed, moreover, to all physical laws, which proves to us, by the way, that priests have always wallowed in turpid ignorance, in which they would fain engulf the people with them."

He ceased looking round for an audience, for in his bubbling over the chemist had for a moment fancied himself in the midst of the town council. But the landlady no longer heeded him; she was listening to a distant rolling. One could distinguish the noise of a carriage mingled with the clattering of loose horseshoes that beat against the ground, and at last the Hirondelle stopped at the door.

It was a yellow box on two large wheels, that, reaching to the tilt, prevented travellers from seeing the road and dirtied their shoulders. The small panes of the narrow windows rattled in their sashes when the coach was closed, and retained here and there patches of mud amid the old layers of dust, that not even storms of rain had altogether washed away. It was drawn by three horses, the first a leader, and when it came down-hill its bottom jolted against the ground.

Some of the inhabitants of Yonville came out into the square; they all spoke at once, asking for news, for explanations, for hampers. Hivert did not know whom to answer. It was he who did the errands of the place in town. He went to the shops and brought back rolls of leather for the shoemaker, old iron for the farrier, a barrel of herrings for his mistress, caps from the milliner's, locks from the hairdresser's, and all along the road on his return journey he distributed his parcels, which he threw, standing upright on his seat and shouting at the top of his voice, over the enclosures of the yards.

An accident had delayed him. Madame Bovary's greyhound had run across the field. They had whistled for him a quarter of an hour; Hivert had even gone back a mile and a half expecting every moment to catch sight of her; but it had been necessary to go on. Emma had wept, grown angry; she had accused Charles of this misfortune. Monsieur Lheureux, a draper, who happened to be in the coach with her, had tried to console her by a number of examples of lost dogs recognising their masters at the end of long years. One, he said, had been told of, who had come back to Paris from Constantinople. Another had gone one hundred and fifty miles in a straight line, and swum four rivers; and his own father had possessed a poodle, which, after twelve years of absence, had all of a sudden jumped on his back in the street as he was going to dine in town.

Chapter II

EMMA GOT OUT FIRST, THEN FÉLICITÉ, MONSIEUR LHEUREUX, AND A NURSE, and they had to wake up Charles in his corner, where he had slept soundly since night set in.

Homais introduced himself; he offered his homages to madame and his respects to monsieur; said he was charmed to have been able to render them some slight service, and added with a cordial air that he had ventured to invite himself, his wife being away.

When Madame Bovary was in the kitchen she went up to the chimney. With the tips of her fingers she caught her dress at the knee, and having thus pulled it up to her ankle, held out her foot in its black boot to the fire above the revolving leg of mutton. The flame lit up the whole of her, penetrating with a crude light the woof of her gowns, the fine pores of her fair skin, and even her eyelids, which she blinked now and again. A great red glow passed over her with the blowing of the wind through the half-open door. On the other side of the chimney a young man with fair hair watched her silently.

As he was a good deal bored at Yonville, where he was a clerk at the notary's, Monsieur Guillaumin, Monsieur Léon Dupuis (it was he who was the second habitué of the Lion d'Or) frequently put back his dinner-hour in the hope that some traveller might come to the inn, with whom he could chat in the evening. On the days when his work was done early, he had, for want of something else to do, to come punctually, and endure from soup to cheese a *tête-à-tête* with Binet. It was therefore with delight that he accepted the landlady's suggestion that he should dine in company with the newcomers, and they passed into the large parlour where Madame Lefrançois, for the purpose of showing off, had had the table laid for four.

Homais asked to be allowed to keep on his skull-cap, for fear of coryza; then, turning to his neighbour—

"Madame is no doubt a little fatigued; one gets jolted so abominably in our Hirondelle."

"That is true," replied Emma; "but moving about always amuses me. I like change of place."

"It is so tedious," sighed the clerk, "to be always riveted to the same places."

"If you were like me," said Charles, "constantly obliged to be in the saddle"—

"But," Léon went on, addressing himself to Madame Bovary, "nothing, it seems to me, is more pleasant—when one can," he added.

"Moreover," said the druggist, "the practice of medicine is not very hard work in our part of the world, for the state of our roads allows us the use of gigs, and generally, as the farmers are well off, they pay pretty well. We have, medically speaking, besides the ordinary cases of enteritis, bronchitis, bilious affections, etc., now and then a few intermittent fevers at harvest-time; but on the whole, little of a serious nature, nothing special to note, unless it be a great deal of scrofula, due, no doubt, to the deplorable hygienic conditions of our peasant dwellings. Ah! you will find many prejudices to combat, Monsieur Bovary, much obstinacy of routine, with which all the efforts of your science will daily come into collision; for people still have recourse to novenas, to relics, to the priest, rather than come straight to the doctor or the chemist. The climate, however, is not, truth to tell, bad, and we even have a few nonogenarians in our parish. The thermometer (I have made some observations) falls in winter to 4 degrees, and in the hottest season rises to 25 or 30 degrees Centigrade at the outside, which gives us 24 degrees Réaumur as the maximum, or otherwise 54 degrees Fahrenheit (English scale), not more. And, as a matter of fact, we are sheltered from the north winds by the forest of Argueil on the one side, from the west winds by the St. Jean range on the other; and this heat, moreover, which, on account of the aqueous vapours given off by the river and the considerable number of cattle in the fields, which, as you know, exhale much ammonia, that is to say, nitrogen, hydrogen, and oxygen (no, nitrogen and hydrogen alone), and which sucking up into itself the humus from the ground, mixing together all those different emanations, unites them into a stack, so to say, and combining with the electricity diffused through the atmosphere, when there is any, might in the long-run, as in tropical countries, engender insalubrious miasmata— this heat, I say, finds itself perfectly tempered on the side whence it comes, or rather whence it should come—that is to say, the southern side—by the southeastern winds, which, having cooled themselves passing over the Seine, reach us sometimes all at once like breezes from Russia."

"At any rate, you have some walks in the neighbourhood?" continued Madame Bovary, speaking to the young man.

"Oh, very few," he answered. "There is a place they call La Pâture, on the top of the hill, on the edge of the forest. Sometimes, on Sundays, I go and stay there with a book, watching the sunset."

"I think there is nothing so admirable as sunsets," she resumed; "but especially by the side of the sea."

"Oh, I adore the sea!" said Monsieur Léon.

"And then, does it not seem to you," continued Madame Bovary, "that the mind travels more freely on this limitless expanse, the contemplation of which elevates the soul, gives ideas of the infinite, the ideal?"

"It is the same with mountainous landscapes," continued Léon. "A cousin of mine who travelled in Switzerland last year told me that one could not picture to oneself the poetry of the lakes, the charm of the waterfalls, the gigantic effect of the glaciers. One sees pines of incredible size across torrents, cottages suspended over precipices, and, a thousand feet below one, whole valleys when the clouds open. Such spectacles must stir to enthusiasm, incline to prayer, to ecstasy; and I no longer marvel at that celebrated musician who, the better to inspire his imagination, was in the habit of playing the piano before some imposing site."

"You play?" she asked.

"No, but I am very fond of music," he replied.

"Ah! don't you listen to him, Madame Bovary," interrupted Homais, bending over his plate. "That's sheer modesty. Why, my dear fellow, the other day in your room you were singing 'L'Ange Gardien' ravishingly. I heard you from the laboratory. You gave it like an actor."

Léon, in fact, lodged at the chemist's, where he had a small room on the second floor, overlooking the Place. He blushed at the compliment of his landlord, who had already turned to the doctor, and was enumerating to him, one after the other, all the principal inhabitants of Yonville. He was telling anecdotes, giving information; the fortune of the notary was not known exactly, and "there was the Tuvache household," who made a good deal of show.

Emma continued, "And what music do you prefer?"

"Oh, German music; that which makes you dream."

"Have you been to the opera?"

"Not yet; but I shall go next year, when I am living at Paris to finish reading for the bar."

"As I had the honour of putting it to your husband," said the chemist, "with regard to this poor Yanoda who has run away, you will find yourself, thanks to his extravagance, in the possession of one of the most comfortable houses of Yonville. Its greatest convenience for a doctor is a door giving on the Walk, where one can go in and out unseen. Moreover, it contains everything that is agreeable in a household—a laundry, kitchen with offices, sitting-room, fruit-room, etc. He was a gay dog, who didn't care what he spent. At the end of the garden, by the side of the water, he had an arbour built just for the purpose of drinking beer in summer; and if madame is fond of gardening she will be able—"

"My wife doesn't care about it," said Charles; "although she has been advised to take exercise, she prefers always sitting in her room reading."

"Like me," replied Léon. "And indeed, what is better than to sit by one's fireside in the evening with a book, while the wind beats against the window and the lamp is burning?"

"What, indeed?" she said, fixing her large black eyes wide open upon him.

"One thinks of nothing," he continued; "the hours slip by. Motionless we traverse countries we fancy we see, and your thought, blending with the fiction, playing with the details, follows the outline of the adventures. It mingles with the characters, and it seems as if it were yourself palpitating beneath their costumes."

"That is true! that is true!" she said.

"Has it ever happened to you," Léon went on, "to come across some vague idea of one's own in a book, some dim image that comes back to you from afar, and as the completest expression of your own slightest sentiment?"

"I have experienced it," she replied.

"That is why," he said, "I especially love the poets. I think verse more tender than prose, and that it moves far more easily to tears."

"Still in the long-run it is tiring," continued Emma. "Now I, on the contrary, adore stories that rush breathlessly along, that frighten one. I detest commonplace heroes and moderate sentiments, such as there are in nature."

"In fact," observed the clerk, "these works, not touching the heart, miss, it seems to me, the true end of art. It is so sweet, amid all the disenchantments of life, to be able to dwell in thought upon noble characters, pure affections, and pictures of happiness. For myself, living here far from the world, this is my one distraction; but Yonville affords so few resources."

"Like Tostes, no doubt," replied Emma; "and so I always subscribed to a lending library."

"If madame will do me the honour of making use of it," said the chemist, who had just caught the last words, "I have at her disposal a library composed of the best authors, Voltaire, Rousseau, Delille, Walter Scott, the *Echo des Feuilletons*; and in addition I receive various periodicals, among them the *Fanal de Rouen* daily, having the advantage to be its correspondent for the districts of Buchy, Forges, Neufchâtel, Yonville, and vicinity."

For two hours and a half they had been at table; for the servant Artémis, carelessly dragging her old list slippers over the flags, brought one plate after the other, forgot everything, and constantly left the door of the billiard-room half open, so that it beat against the wall with its hooks.

Unconsciously, Léon, while talking, had placed his foot on one of the bars of the chair on which Madame Bovary was sitting. She wore a small blue silk necktie, that kept up like a ruff a gauffered cambric collar, and with the movements of her head the lower part of her face gently sunk into the linen or came out from it. Thus side by side, while Charles and the chemist chatted, they entered into one of those vague conversations where the hazard of all that is said brings you back to the fixed centre of a common sympathy. The Paris theatres, titles of novels, new quadrilles, and the world they did not know; Tostes, where she had lived, and

Yonville, where they were; they examined all, talked of everything till to the end of dinner.

When coffee was served Félicité went away to get ready the room in the new house, and the guests soon raised the siege. Madame Lefrançois was asleep near the cinders, while the stable-boy, lantern in hand, was waiting to show Monsieur and Madame Bovary the way home. Bits of straw stuck in his red hair, and he limped with his left leg. When he had taken in his other hand the curé's umbrella, they started.

The town was asleep; the pillars of the market threw great shadows; the earth was all grey as on a summer's night. But as the doctor's house was only some fifty paces from the inn, they had to say good-night almost immediately, and the company dispersed.

As soon as she entered the passage, Emma felt the cold of the plaster fall about her shoulders like damp linen. The walls were new and the wooden stairs creaked. In their bedroom, on the first floor, a whitish light passed through the curtain-less windows. She could catch glimpses of tree-tops, and beyond, the fields, half-drowned in the fog that lay reeking in the moonlight along the course of the river. In the middle of the room, pell-mell, were scattered drawers, bottles, curtain-rods, gilt poles, with mattresses on the chairs and basins on the ground—the two men who had brought the furniture had left everything about carelessly.

This was the fourth time that she had slept in a strange place. The first was the day of her going to the convent; the second, of her arrival at Tostes; the third, at Vaubyessard; and this was the fourth. And each one had marked, as it were, the inauguration of a new phase in her life. She did not believe that things could present themselves in the same way in different places, and since the portion of her life lived had been bad, no doubt that which remained to be lived would be better.

Chapter III

THE NEXT DAY, AS SHE WAS GETTING UP, SHE SAW THE CLERK ON THE PLACE. She had on a dressing-gown. He looked up and bowed. She nodded quickly and reclosed the window.

Léon waited all day for six o'clock in the evening to come, but on going to the inn, he found no one but Monsieur Binet, already at table. The dinner of the evening before had been a considerable event for him; he had never till then talked for two hours consecutively to a "lady." How then had he been able to explain, and in such language, the number of things that he could not have said so well before? He was usually shy, and maintained that reserve which partakes at once of modesty and dissimulation. At Yonville he was considered "well-bred." He listened to the arguments of the older people, and did not seem hot about politics—a remarkable thing for a young man. Then he had some accomplishments; he painted in water-colours, could read the key of *G,* and readily talked literature after dinner when he did not play cards. Monsieur Homais respected him for his education; Madame Homais liked him for his good-nature, for he often took the little Homais into the garden—little brats who were always dirty, very much spoilt, and somewhat lymphatic, like their mother. Besides the servant to look after them, they had Justin, the chemist's apprentice, a second cousin of Monsieur Homais, who had been taken into the house from charity, and who was useful at the same time as a servant.

The druggist proved the best of neighbours. He gave Madame Bovary information as to the tradespeople, sent expressly for his own cider merchant, tasted the drink himself, and saw that the casks were properly placed in the cellar; he explained how to set about getting in a supply of butter cheap, and made an arrangement with Lestiboudois, the sacristan, who, besides his sacerdotal and funereal functions, looked after the principal gardens at Yonville by the hour or the year, according to the taste of the customers.

The need of looking after others was not the only thing that urged the chemist to such obsequious cordiality; there was a plan underneath it all.

He had infringed the law of the 19th Ventôse, year xi, article I, which forbade all persons not having a diploma to practise medicine; so that, after certain anonymous denunciations, Homais had been summoned to Rouen to see the procurer of the king in his own private room; the magistrate receiving him standing up, ermine on shoulder and cap on head. It was in the morning, before the court opened. In the corridors one heard the heavy boots of the gendarmes walking past, and like a far-off noise great locks that were shut. The druggist's ears tingled as if he were about to have an apoplectic stroke; he saw the depths of dungeons, his family in tears, his shop sold, all the jars dispersed; and he was obliged to enter a café and take a glass of rum and seltzer to recover his spirits.

Little by little the memory of this reprimand grew fainter, and he continued, as heretofore, to give anodyne consultations in his back-parlour. But the mayor resented it, his colleagues were jealous, everything was to be feared; gaining over Monsieur Bovary by his attentions was to earn his gratitude, and prevent his speaking out later on, should he notice anything. So every morning Homais brought him "the paper," and often in the afternoon left his shop for a few moments to have a chat with the Doctor.

Charles was dull: patients did not come. He remained seated for hours without speaking, went into his consulting-room to sleep, or watched his wife sewing. Then for diversion he employed himself at home as a workman; he even tried to do up the attic with some paint which had been left behind by the painters. But money matters worried him. He had spent so much for repairs at Tostes, for madame's toilette, and for the moving, that the whole dowry, over three thousand crowns, had slipped away in two years. Then how many things had been spoilt or lost during their carriage from Tostes to Yonville, without counting the plaster curé, who, falling out of the coach at an over-severe jolt, had been dashed into a thousand fragments on the pavement of Quincampoix!

A pleasanter trouble came to distract him, namely, the pregnancy of his wife. As the time of her confinement approached he cherished her the more. It was another bond of the flesh establishing itself, and, as it were, a continued sentiment of a more complex union. When from afar he saw her languid walk, and her figure without stays turning softly on her hips; when opposite one another he looked at her at his ease, while she took tired poses in her armchair, then his happiness knew no bounds; he got up, embraced her, passed his hands over her face, called her little mamma, wanted to make her dance, and, half-laughing, half-crying, uttered all kinds of caressing pleasantries that came into his head. The idea of having begotten a child delighted him. Now he wanted nothing. He knew human life from end to end, and he sat down to it with serenity.

Emma at first felt a great astonishment; then was anxious to be delivered that she might know what it was to be a mother. But not being able to spend as much as she would have liked, to have a swing-bassinette with rose silk curtains, and embroidered caps, in a fit of bitterness she gave up looking after the trousseau, and ordered the whole of it from a village needlewoman, without choosing or discussing anything. Thus she did not amuse herself with those preparations that stimulate the tenderness of mothers, and so her affection was from the very outset, perhaps, to some extent attenuated.

As Charles, however, spoke of the boy at every meal, she soon began to think of him more consecutively.

She hoped for a son; he would be strong and dark; she would call him George; and this idea of having a male child was like an expected revenge for all her impotence in the past. A man, at least, is free; he may travel over passions and over countries, overcome obstacles, taste of the most far-away pleasures. But a woman is always hampered. At once inert and flexible, she has against her the weakness of the flesh and legal dependence. Her will, like the veil of her bonnet, held by a string, flutters in every wind; there is always some desire that draws her, some conventionality that restrains.

She was confined on a Sunday at about six o'clock, as the sun was rising.

"It is a girl!" said Charles.

She turned her head away and fainted.

Madame Homais, as well as Madame Lefrançois of the Lion d'Or, almost immediately came running in to embrace her. The chemist, as a man of discretion, only offered a few provisional felicitations through the half-opened door. He wished to see the child, and thought it well made.

Whilst she was getting well she occupied herself much in seeking a name for her daughter. First she went over all those that have Italian endings, such as Clara, Louisa, Amanda, Atala; she liked Galsuinde pretty well, and Yseult or Léocadie still better. Charles wanted the child to be called after her mother; Emma opposed this. They ran over the calendar from end to end, and then consulted outsiders.

"Monsieur Léon," said the chemist, "with whom I was talking about it the other day, wonders you do not choose Madeleine. It is very much in fashion just now."

But Madame Bovary, senior, cried out loudly against this name of a sinner. As to Monsieur Homais, he had a preference for all those that recalled some great man, an illustrious fact, or a generous idea, and it was on this system that he had baptised his four children. Thus Napoleon represented glory and Franklin liberty; Irma was perhaps a concession to romanticism, but Athalie was an homage to the greatest masterpiece of the French stage. For his philosophical convictions did not interfere with his artistic tastes; in him the thinker did not stifle the man of sentiment; he could make distinctions, make allowances for imagination and fanaticism. In this tragedy, for example, he found fault with the ideas, but admired the style; he detested the conception, but applauded all the details, and loathed the characters while he grew enthusiastic over their dialogue. When he read the fine passages he was transported, but when he thought that mummers would get something out of them for their show, he was disconsolate; and in this confusion of sentiments in which he was involved he would have liked at once to crown Racine with both his hands and discuss with him for a good quarter of an hour.

At last Emma remembered that at the château of Vaubyessard she had heard the Marchioness call a young lady Berthe; from that moment this name was chosen; and as old Rouault could not come, Monsieur Homais was requested to stand godfather. His gifts were all products from his establishment, to wit: six boxes of jujubes, a whole jar of racahout, three cakes of marsh-mallow paste, and six sticks of sugar-candy into the bargain that he had come across in a cupboard. On the evening of the ceremony there was a grand dinner; the curé was present; there was much excitement. Monsieur Homais towards liqueur-time began singing "Le Dieu des bonnes gens." Monsieur Léon sang a barcarolle, and Madame Bovary, senior, who was godmother, a romance of the time of the Empire; finally, M. Bovary, senior, insisted on having the child brought down, and began baptising it with a glass of champagne that he poured over its head. This mockery of the first of the sacraments made the Abbé Bournisien angry; old Bovary replied by a quotation from *La Guerre des Dieux*; the curé wanted to leave; the ladies implored, Homais interfered; and they succeeded in making the priest sit down again, and he quietly went on with the half-finished coffee in his saucer.

Monsieur Bovary, senior, stayed at Yonville a month, dazzling the natives by a superb policeman's cap with silver tassels that he wore in the morning when he smoked his pipe in the square. Being also in the habit of drinking a good deal of brandy, he often sent the servant to the Lion d'Or to buy him a bottle, which was put down to his son's account, and to perfume his handkerchiefs he used up his daughter-in-law's whole supply of eau-de-cologne.

The latter did not at all dislike his company. He had knocked about the world, he talked about Berlin, Vienna, and Strasbourg, of his soldier times, of the mistresses he had had, the grand luncheons of which he had partaken; then he was amiable, and sometimes even, either on the stairs or in the garden, would seize hold of her waist, crying, "Charles, look out for yourself."

Then Madame Bovary, senior, became alarmed for her son's happiness, and fearing that her husband might in the long-run have an immoral influence upon the ideas of the young woman, took care to hurry their departure. Perhaps she had more serious reasons for uneasiness. Monsieur Bovary was not the man to respect anything.

One day Emma was suddenly seized with the desire to see her little girl, who had been put to nurse with the carpenter's wife, and, without looking at the almanack to see whether the six weeks of the Virgin were yet passed, she set out for the Rollets's house, situated at the extreme end of the village, between the highroad and the fields.

It was mid-day, the shutters of the houses were closed, and the slate roofs that glittered beneath the fierce light of the blue sky seemed to strike sparks from the crest of their gables. A heavy wind was blowing; Emma felt weak as she walked; the stones of the pavement hurt her; she was doubtful whether she would not go home again, or go in somewhere to rest.

At this moment Monsieur Léon came out from a neighbouring door with a bundle of papers under his arm. He came to greet her, and stood in the shade in front of Lheureux's shop under the projecting grey awning.

Madame Bovary said she was going to see her baby, but that she was beginning to grow tired.

"If—" said Léon, not daring to go on.

"Have you any business to attend to?" she asked.

And on the clerk's answer, she begged him to accompany her. That same evening this was known in Yonville, and Madame Tuvache, the mayor's wife, declared in the presence of her servant that "Madame Bovary was compromising herself."

To get to the nurse's it was necessary to turn to the left on leaving the street, as if making for the cemetery, and to follow between little houses and yards a small path bordered with privet hedges. They were in bloom, and so were the speedwells, eglantines, thistles, and the sweetbriar that sprang up from the thickets. Through openings in the hedges one could see into the huts, some pig on a dung-heap, or tethered cows rubbing their horns against the trunk of trees. The two side by side, walked slowly, she leaning upon him, and he restraining his pace, which he regulated by hers; in front of them a swarm of midges fluttered, buzzing in the warm air.

They recognised the house by an old walnut-tree which shaded it. Low and covered with brown tiles, there hung outside it, beneath the dormer-window of the garret, a string of onions. Faggots upright against a thorn fence surrounded a bed of lettuces, a few square feet of lavender, and sweet peas strung on sticks. Dirty water was running here and there on the grass, and all round were several indefinite rags, knitted stockings, a red calico jacket, and a large sheet of coarse linen spread over the hedge. At the noise of the gate the nurse appeared with a baby she was suckling on one arm. With her other hand she was pulling along a poor puny little fellow, his face covered with scrofula, the son of a Rouen hosier, whom his parents, too taken up with their business, left in the country.

"Go in," she said; "your little one is there asleep."

The room on the ground-floor, the only one in the dwelling, had at its farther end, against the wall, a large bed without curtains, while a kneading-trough took up the side by the window, one pane of which was mended with a piece of blue paper. In the corner behind the door, shining hob-nailed shoes stood in a row under the slab of the washstand, near a bottle of oil with a feather stuck in its mouth; a *Matthieu Laensberg* lay on the dusty mantelpiece amid gunflints, candle-ends, and bits of amadou. Finally, the last luxury in the apartment was a "Fame" blowing her trumpets, a picture cut out, no doubt, from some perfumer's prospectus and nailed to the wall with six wooden shoe-pegs.

Emma's child was asleep in a wicker-cradle. She took it up in the wrapping that enveloped it and began singing softly as she rocked herself to and fro.

Léon walked up and down the room; it seemed strange to him to see this beautiful woman in her nankeen dress in the midst of all this poverty. Madame Bovary reddened; he turned away, thinking perhaps there had been an impertinent look in his eyes. Then she put back the little girl, who had just been sick over her collar. The nurse at once came to dry her, protesting that it wouldn't show.

"She gives me other doses," she said: "I am always a-washing of her. If you would have the goodness to order Camus, the grocer, to let me have a little soap; it would really be more convenient for you, as I needn't trouble you then."

"Very well! very well!" said Emma. "Good morning, Madame Rollet," and she went out, wiping her shoes at the door.

The good woman accompanied her to the end of the garden, talking all the time of the trouble she had getting up of nights.

"I'm that worn out sometimes as I drop asleep on my chair. I'm sure you might at least give me just a pound of ground coffee; that'd last me a month, and I'd take it of a morning with some milk."

After having submitted to her thanks, Madame Bovary left. She had gone a little way down the path when, at the sound of wooden shoes, she turned round. It was the nurse.

"What is it?"

Then the peasant woman, taking her aside behind an elm tree, began talking to her of her husband, who with his trade and six francs a year that the captain—

"Oh, be quick!" said Emma.

"Well," the nurse went on, heaving sighs between each word, "I'm afraid he'll be put out seeing me have coffee alone, you know men—"

"But you are to have some," Emma repeated; "I will give you some. You bother me!"

"Oh, dear! my poor, dear lady! you see, in consequence of his wounds he has terrible cramps in the chest. He even says that cider weakens him."

"Do make haste, Mère Rollet!"

"Well," the latter continued, making a curtsey, "if it weren't asking too much," and she curtsied once more, "if you would"—and her eyes begged—"a jar of brandy," she said at last, "and I'd rub your little one's feet with it; they're as tender as one's tongue."

Once rid of the nurse, Emma again took Monsieur Léon's arm. She walked fast for some time, then more slowly, and looking straight in front of her, her eyes rested on the shoulder of the young man, whose frock-coat had a black-velvet collar. His brown hair fell over it, straight and carefully arranged. She noticed his nails, which were longer than one wore them at Yonville. It was one of the clerk's chief occupations to trim them, and for this purpose he kept a special knife in his writing-desk.

They returned to Yonville by the water-side. In the warm season the bank, wider than at other times, showed to their foot the garden wells whence a few steps led to the river. It flowed noiselessly, swift, and cold to the eye; long, thin grasses huddled together in it as the current drove them, and spread themselves upon the limpid water like streaming hair; sometimes at the top of the reeds or on the leaf of a water-lily an insect with fine legs crawled or rested. The sun pierced with a ray the small blue bubbles of the waves that, breaking, followed each other; branchless old willows mirrored their grey backs in the water; beyond, all around, the meadows seemed empty. It was the dinner-hour at the farms, and the young woman and her companion heard nothing as they walked but the fall of their steps on the earth of the path, the words they spoke, and the sound of Emma's dress rustling round her.

The walls of the gardens with pieces of bottle on their coping were hot as the glass windows of a conservatory. Wallflowers had sprung up between the bricks, and with the tip of her open sunshade Madame Bovary, as she passed, made some of their faded flowers crumble into a yellow dust, or a spray of overhanging honeysuckle and clematis caught in its fringe and dangled for a moment over the silk.

They were talking of a troupe of Spanish dancers who were expected shortly at the Rouen theatre.

"Are you going?" she asked.

"If I can," he answered.

Had they nothing else to say to one another? Yet their eyes were full of more serious speech, and while they forced themselves to find trivial phrases, they felt the same languor stealing over them both. It was the whisper of the soul, deep, continuous, dominating that of their voices. Surprised with wonder at this strange sweetness, they did not think of speaking of the sensation or of seeking its cause. Coming joys, like tropical shores, throw over the immensity before them their inborn softness, an odorous wind, and we are lulled by this intoxication without a thought of the horizon that we do not even know.

In one place the ground had been trodden down by the cattle; they had to step on large green stones put here and there in the mud. She often stopped a moment to look where to place her foot, and tottering on the stone that shook, her arms outspread, her form bent forward with a look of indecision, she would laugh, afraid of falling into the puddles of water.

When they arrived in front of her garden, Madame Bovary opened the little gate, ran up the steps and disappeared.

Léon returned to his office. His chief was away; he just glanced at the briefs, then cut himself a pen, and at last took up his hat and went out.

He went to La Pâture at the top of the Argueil hills at the beginning of the forest; he threw himself upon the ground under the pines and watched the sky through his fingers.

"How bored I am!" he said to himself, "how bored I am!"

He thought he was to be pitied for living in this village, with Homais for a friend and Monsieur Guillaumin for master. The latter, entirely absorbed by his business, wearing gold-rimmed spectacles and red whiskers over a white cravat, understood nothing of mental refinements, although he affected a stiff English manner, which in the beginning had impressed the clerk.

As to the chemist's spouse, she was the best wife in Normandy, gentle as a sheep, loving her children, her father, her mother, her cousins, weeping for others' woes, letting everything go in her household, and detesting corsets; but so slow of movement, such a bore to listen to, so common in appearance, and of such restricted conversation, that although she was thirty, he only twenty, although they slept in rooms next each other and he spoke to her daily, he never thought that she might be a woman for another, or that she possessed anything else of her sex than the gown.

And what else was there? Binet, a few shopkeepers, two or three publicans, the curé, and, finally, Monsieur Tuvache, the mayor, with his two sons, rich, crabbed, obtuse persons, who farmed their own lands and had feasts among themselves, bigoted to boot, and quite unbearable companions.

But from the general background of all these human faces Emma's stood out isolated and yet farthest off; for between her and him he seemed to see a vague abyss.

In the beginning he had called on her several times along with the druggist. Charles had not appeared particularly anxious to see him again, and Léon did not know what to do between his fear of being indiscreet and the desire for an intimacy that seemed almost impossible.

Chapter IV

WHEN THE FIRST COLD DAYS SET IN EMMA LEFT HER BEDROOM FOR THE sitting-room, a long apartment with a low ceiling, in which there was on the mantel-piece a large bunch of coral spread out against the looking-glass. Seated in her arm-chair near the window, she could see the villagers pass along the pavement.

Twice a day Léon went from his office to the Lion d'Or. Emma could hear him coming from afar; she leant forward listening, and the young man glided past the curtain, always dressed in the same way, and without turning his head. But in the twilight, when, her chin resting on her left hand, she let the embroidery she had begun fall on her knees, she often shuddered at the apparition of this shadow suddenly gliding past. She would get up and order the table to be laid.

Monsieur Homais called at dinner-time. Skull-cap in hand, he came in on tip-toe, in order to disturb no one, always repeating the same phrase, "Good evening, everybody." Then, when he had taken his seat at table between the pair, he asked the doctor about his patients, and the latter consulted him as to the probability of their payment. Next they talked of "what was in the paper." Homais by this hour knew it almost by heart, and he repeated it from end to end, with the reflections of the penny-a-liners, and all the stories of individual catastrophes that had occurred in France or abroad. But the subject becoming exhausted, he was not slow in throwing out some remarks on the dishes before him. Sometimes even, half-rising, he delicately pointed out to madame the tenderest morsel, or turning to the servant, gave her some advice on the manipulation of stews and the hygiene of seasoning. He talked aroma, osmazome, juices, and gelatine in a bewildering manner, Moreover, Homais, with his head fuller of recipes than his shop of jars, excelled in making all kinds of preserves, vinegars, and sweet liqueurs; he knew also all the latest inventions in economic stoves, together with the art of preserving cheeses and of curing sick wines.

At eight o'clock Justin came to fetch him to shut up the shop. Then Monsieur Homais gave him a sly look, especially if Félicité was there, for he had noticed that his apprentice was fond of the doctor's house.

"The young dog," he said, "is beginning to have ideas, and the devil take me if I don't believe he's in love with your servant!"

But a more serious fault with which he reproached Justin was his constantly listening to conversation. On Sunday, for example, one could not get him out of the drawing-room, whither Madame Homais had called him to fetch the children, who were falling asleep in the arm-chairs, and dragging down with their backs calico chair-covers that were too large.

Not many people came to these soirées at the chemist's, his scandal-mongering and political opinions having successfully alienated various respectable persons from him. The clerk never failed to be there. As soon as he heard the bell he ran to meet Madame Bovary, took her shawl, and put away under the shop-counter the thick list shoes that she wore over her boots when there was snow.

First they played some hands at trente-et-un; next Monsieur Homais played écarté with Emma; Léon behind her gave her advice. Standing up with his hands on the back of her chair, he saw the teeth of her comb that bit into her chignon. With every movement that she made to throw her cards the right side of her dress was drawn up. From her turned-up hair a dark colour fell over her back, and growing gradually paler, lost itself little by little in the shade. Then her dress fell on both sides of her chair, puffing out full of folds, and reached the ground. When Léon occasionally felt the sole of his boot resting on it, he drew back as if he had trodden upon some one.

When the game of cards was over, the druggist and the Doctor played dominoes, and Emma, changing her place, leant her elbow on the table, turning over the leaves of *L'Illustration*. She had brought her ladies' journal with her. Léon sat down near her; they looked at the engravings together, and waited for one another at the bottom of the pages. She often begged him to read her the verses; Léon declaimed them in a languid voice, to which he carefully gave a dying fall in the love passages. But the noise of the dominoes annoyed him. Monsieur Homais was strong at the game; he could beat Charles and give him a double-six. Then the three hundred finished, they both stretched themselves out in front of the fire, and were soon asleep. The fire was dying out in the cinders; the teapot was empty, Léon was still reading. Emma listened to him, mechanically turning round the lampshade, on the gauze of which were painted clowns in carriages, and tight-rope dancers with their balancing-poles. Léon stopped, pointing with a gesture to his sleeping audience; then they talked in low tones, and their conversation seemed the more sweet to them because it was unheard.

Thus a kind of bond was established between them, a constant commerce of books and of romances. Monsieur Bovary, little given to jealousy, did not trouble himself about it.

On his birthday he received a beautiful phrenological head, all marked with figures to the thorax and painted blue. This was an attention of the clerk's. He showed him many others, even to doing errands for him at Rouen; and the book of a novelist having made the mania for cactuses fashionable, Léon bought some for Madame Bovary, bringing them back on his knees in the Hirondelle, pricking his fingers with their hard hairs.

She had a board with a balustrade fixed against her window to hold the pots. The clerk, too, had his small hanging garden; they saw each other tending their flowers at their windows.

Of the windows of the village there was one yet more often occupied; for on Sundays from morning to night, and every morning when the weather was bright, one could see at the dormer-window of a garret the profile of Monsieur Binet bending over his lathe, whose monotonous humming could be heard at the Lion d'Or.

One evening on coming home Léon found in his room a rug in velvet and wool with leaves on a pale ground. He called Madame Homais, Monsieur Homais, Justin, the children, the cook; he spoke of it to his chief; every one wanted to see this rug. Why did the doctor's wife give the clerk presents? It looked queer. They decided that she must be his lover.

He made this seem likely, so ceaselessly did he talk of her charms and of her wit; so much so, that Binet once roughly answered him—

"What does it matter to me since I'm not in her set?"

He tortured himself to find out how he could make his declaration to her, and always halting between the fear of displeasing her and the shame of being such a coward, he wept with discouragement and desire. Then he took energetic resolutions, wrote letters that he tore up, put it off to times that he again deferred. Often he set out with the determination to dare all; but this resolution soon deserted him in Emma's presence, and when Charles, dropping in, invited him to jump into his chaise to go with him to see some patient in the neighbourhood, he at once accepted, bowed to madame, and went out. Her husband, was he not something belonging to her?

As to Emma, she did not ask herself whether she loved. Love, she thought, must come suddenly, with great outbursts and lightnings—a hurricane of the skies, which falls upon life, revolutionises it, roots up the will like a leaf, and sweeps the whole heart into the abyss. She did not know that on the terrace of houses it makes lakes when the pipes are choked, and she would thus have remained in her security when she suddenly discovered a rent in the wall of it.

Chapter V

It WAS A SUNDAY IN FEBRUARY, AN AFTERNOON WHEN THE SNOW WAS FALLING. They had all, Monsieur and Madame Bovary, Homais, and Monsieur Léon, gone to see a yarn-mill that was being built in the valley a mile and a half from Yonville. The druggist had taken Napoleon and Athalie to give them some exercise, and Justin accompanied them, carrying the umbrellas on his shoulder.

Nothing, however, could be less curious than this curiosity. A great piece of waste ground, on which pell-mell, amid a mass of sand and stones, were a few brake-wheels, already rusty, surrounded by a quadrangular building pierced by a number of little windows. The building was unfinished; the sky could be seen through the joists of the roofing. Attached to the stop-plank of the gable a bunch of straw mixed with corn-ears fluttered its tricoloured ribbons in the wind.

Homais was talking. He explained to the company the future importance of this establishment, computed the strength of the floorings, the thickness of the walls, and regretted extremely not having a yard-stick such as Monsieur Binet possessed for his own special use.

Emma, who had taken his arm, bent lightly against his shoulder, and she looked at the sun's disc shedding afar through the mist his pale splendour. She turned. Charles was there. His cap was drawn down over his eyebrows, and his two thick lips were trembling, which added a look of stupidity to his face; his very back, his calm back, was irritating to behold, and she saw written upon his coat all the platitude of the bearer.

While she was considering him thus, tasting in her irritation a sort of depraved pleasure, Léon made a step forward. The cold that made him pale seemed to add a more gentle languor to his face; between his cravat and his neck the somewhat loose collar of his shirt showed the skin; the lobe of his ear looked out from beneath a lock of hair, and his large blue eyes, raised to the clouds, seemed to Emma more limpid and more beautiful than those mountain-lakes where the heavens are mirrored.

"Wretched boy!" suddenly cried the chemist.

And he ran to his son, who had just precipitated himself into a heap of lime in order to whiten his boots. At the reproaches with which he was being overwhelmed Napoleon began to roar, while Justin dried his shoes with a wisp of straw. But a knife was wanted; Charles offered his.

"Ah!" she said to herself, "he carries a knife in his pocket like a peasant."

The hoar-frost was falling, and they turned back to Yonville.

In the evening Madame Bovary did not go to her neighbour's, and when Charles had left and she felt herself alone, the comparison re-began with the clearness of a sensation almost actual, and with that lengthening of perspective which memory gives to things. Looking from her bed at the clean fire that was burning, she still saw, as she had down there, Léon standing up with one hand bending his cane, and with the other holding Athalie, who was quietly sucking a piece of ice. She thought him charming; she could not tear herself away from him; she recalled his other attitudes on other days, the words he had spoken, the sound of his voice, his whole person; and she repeated, pouting out her lips as if for a kiss—

"Yes, charming! charming! Is he not in love?" she asked herself; "but with whom? With me?"

All the proofs arose before her at once; her heart leapt. The flame of the fire threw a joyous light upon the ceiling; she turned on her back, stretching out her arms.

Then began the eternal lamentation: "Oh, if Heaven had but willed it! And why not? What prevented it?"

When Charles came home at midnight, she seemed to have just awakened, and as he made a noise undressing, she complained of a headache, then asked carelessly what had happened that evening.

"Monsieur Léon," he said, "went to his room early."

She could not help smiling, and she fell asleep, her soul filled with a new delight.

The next day, at dusk, she received a visit from Monsieur Lheureux, the draper. He was a man of ability, was this shopkeeper. Born a Gascon but bred a Norman, he grafted upon his southern volubility the cunning of the Cauchois. His fat, flabby, beardless face seemed dyed by a decoction of liquorice, and his white hair made even more vivid the keen brilliance of his small black eyes. No one knew what he had been formerly; a pedlar said some, a banker at Routot according to others. What was certain was, that he made complex calculations in his head that would have frightened Binet himself. Polite to obsequiousness, he always held himself with his back bent in the position of one who bows or who invites.

After leaving at the door his hat surrounded with crape, he put down a green bandbox on the table, and began by complaining to madame, with many civilities, that he should have remained till that day without gaining her confidence. A poor shop like his was not made to attract a "fashionable lady"; he emphasised the words; yet she had only to command, and he would undertake to provide her with anything she might wish, either in haberdashery or linen, millinery or fancy goods, for he went to town regularly four times a month. He was connected with the best houses. You could speak of him at the Trois Frères, at the Barbe d'Or, or at the Grand Sauvage; all these gentlemen knew him as well as the insides of their pockets. To-day, then, he had come to show madame, in passing, various articles he happened to have, thanks to the most rare opportunity. And he pulled out half-a-dozen embroidered collars from the box.

Madame Bovary examined them. "I do not require anything," she said.

Then Monsieur Lheureux delicately exhibited three Algerian scarves, several packets of English needles, a pair of straw slippers, and, finally, four eggcups in cocoa-nut wood, carved in open work by convicts. Then, with both hands on the table, his neck stretched out, his figure bent forward, open-mouthed, he watched Emma's look, who was walking up and down undecided amid these goods. From time to time, as if to remove some dust, he filliped with his nail the silk of the scarves spread out at full length, and they rustled with a little noise, making in the green twilight the gold spangles of their tissue scintillate like little stars.

"How much are they?"

"A mere nothing," he replied, "a mere nothing. But there's no hurry; whenever it's convenient. We are not Jews."

She reflected for a few moments, and ended by again declining Monsieur Lheureux's offer. He replied quite unconcernedly—

"Very well. We shall understand one another by and by. I have always got on with ladies—if I didn't with my own!"

Emma smiled.

"I wanted to tell you," he went on good-naturedly, after his joke, "that it isn't the money I should trouble about. Why, I could give you some, if need be."

She made a gesture of surprise.

"Ah!" said he quickly and in a low voice, "I shouldn't have to go far to find you some, rely on that."

And he began asking after Père Tellier, the proprietor of the Café Français, whom Monsieur Bovary was then attending.

"What's the matter with Père Tellier? He coughs so that he shakes his whole house, and I'm afraid he'll soon want a deal covering rather than a flannel vest. He was such a rake as a young man! Those sort of people, madame, have not the least regularity; he's burnt up with brandy. Still it's sad, all the same, to see an acquaintance go off."

And while he fastened up his box he discoursed about the doctor's patients.

"It's the weather, no doubt," he said, looking frowningly at the floor, "that causes these illnesses. I, too, don't feel the thing. One of these days I shall even have to consult the doctor for a pain I have in my back. Well, good-bye, Madame Bovary. At your service; your very humble servant." And he closed the door gently.

Emma had her dinner served in her bedroom on a tray by the fireside; she was a long time over it; everything was well with her.

"How good I was!" she said to herself, thinking of the scarves.

She heard some steps on the stairs. It was Léon. She got up and took from the chest of drawers the first pile of dusters to be hemmed. When he came in she seemed very busy.

The conversation languished; Madame Bovary gave it up every few minutes, whilst he himself seemed quite embarrassed. Seated on a low chair near the fire, he turned round in his fingers the ivory thimble-case. She stitched on, or from time to time turned down the hem of the cloth with her nail. She did not speak; he was silent, captivated by her silence, as he would have been by her speech.

"Poor fellow!" she thought.

"How have I displeased her?" he asked himself.

At last, however, Léon said that he should have, one of these days, to go to Rouen on some office business.

"Your music subscription is out; am I to renew it?"

"No," she replied.

"Why?"

"Because—"

And pursing her lips she slowly drew a long stitch of grey thread.

This work irritated Léon. It seemed to roughen the ends of her fingers. A gallant phrase came into his head, but he did not risk it.

"Then you are giving it up?" he went on.

"What?" she asked hurriedly. "Music? Ah! yes! Have I not my house to look after, my husband to attend to, a thousand things, in fact, many duties that must be considered first?"

She looked at the clock. Charles was late. Then she affected anxiety. Two or three times she even repeated, "He is so good!"

The clerk was fond of Monsieur Bovary. But this tenderness on his behalf astonished him unpleasantly; nevertheless he took up his praises, which he said every one was singing, especially the chemist.

"Ah! he is a good fellow," continued Emma.

"Certainly," replied the clerk.

And he began talking of Madame Homais, whose very untidy appearance generally made them laugh.

"What does it matter?" interrupted Emma. "A good housewife does not trouble about her appearance."

Then she relapsed into silence.

It was the same on the following days; her talks, her manners, everything changed. She took interest in the housework, went to church regularly, and looked after her servant with more severity.

She took Berthe from nurse. When visitors called, Félicité brought her in, and Madame Bovary undressed her to show off her limbs. She declared she adored children; this was her consolation, her joy, her passion, and she accompanied her caresses with lyrical outbursts which would have reminded anyone but the Yonville people of Sachette in *Notre Dame de Paris*.

When Charles came home he found his slippers put to warm near the fire. His waistcoat now never wanted lining, nor his shirt buttons, and it was quite a pleasure to see in the cupboard the night-caps arranged in piles of the same height. She no longer grumbled as formerly at taking a turn in the garden; what he proposed was always done, although she did not understand the wishes to which she submitted without a murmur; and when Léon saw him by his fireside after dinner, his two hands on his stomach, his two feet on the fender, his cheeks red with feeding, his eyes moist with happiness, the child crawling along the carpet, and this woman with the slender waist who came behind his arm-chair to kiss his forehead:

"What madness!" he said to himself. "And how to reach her!"

And thus she seemed so virtuous and inaccessible to him that he lost all hope, even the faintest. But by this renunciation he placed her on an extraordinary pinnacle. To him she stood outside those fleshly attributes from which he had nothing to obtain, and in his heart she rose ever, and became farther removed from him after the magnificent manner of an apotheosis that is taking wing. It was one of those pure feelings that do not interfere with life, that are cultivated because they are rare, and whose loss would afflict more than their passion rejoices.

Emma grew thinner, her cheeks paler, her face longer. With her black hair, her large eyes, her aquiline nose, her birdlike walk, and always silent now, did she not seem to be passing through life scarcely touching it, and to bear on her brow the vague impress of some divine destiny? She was so sad and so calm, at once so gentle and so reserved, that near her one felt oneself seized by an icy charm, as we shudder in churches at the perfume of the flowers mingling with the cold of the marble. The others even did not escape from this seduction. The chemist said—

"She is a woman of great parts, who wouldn't be misplaced in a sub-prefecture."

The housewives admired her economy, the patients her politeness, the poor her charity.

But she was eaten up with desires, with rage, with hate. That dress with the narrow folds hid a distracted heart, of whose torment those chaste lips said nothing. She was in love with Léon, and sought solitude that she might with the more ease delight in his image. The sight of his form troubled the voluptuousness of this meditation. Emma thrilled at the sound of his step; then in his presence the emotion subsided, and afterwards there remained to her only an immense astonishment that ended in sorrow.

Léon did not know that when he left her in despair she rose after he had gone to see him in the street. She concerned herself about his comings and goings; she watched his face; she invented quite a history to find an excuse for going to his room. The chemist's wife seemed happy to her to sleep under the same roof, and her thoughts constantly centred upon this house, like the Lion d'Or pigeons, who came there to dip their red feet and white wings in its gutters. But the more Emma recognised her love, the more she crushed it down, that it might not be evident, that she might make it less. She would have liked Léon to guess it, and she imagined chances, catastrophes that should facilitate this. What restrained her was, no doubt, idleness and fear, and a sense of shame also. She thought she had repulsed him too much, that the time was past, that all was lost. Then, pride, the joy of being able to say to herself, "I am virtuous," and to look at herself in the glass taking resigned poses, consoled her a little for the sacrifice she believed she was making.

Then the lusts of the flesh, the longing for money, and the melancholy of passion all blended themselves into one suffering, and instead of turning her thoughts from it, she clave to it the more, urging herself to pain, and seeking everywhere occasion for it. She was irritated by an ill-served dish or by a half-open door; bewailed the velvets she had not, the happiness she had missed, her too exalted dreams, her narrow home.

What exasperated her was that Charles did not seem to notice her anguish. His conviction that he was making her happy seemed to her an imbecile insult, and his sureness on this point ingratitude. For whose sake, then, was she virtuous? Was it not for him, the obstacle to all felicity, the cause of all misery, and, as it were, the sharp clasp of that complex strap that buckled her in on all sides?

On him alone, then, she concentrated all the various hatreds that resulted from her boredom, and every effort to diminish only augmented it; for this useless trouble was added to the other reasons for despair, and contributed still more to the separation between them. Her own gentleness to herself made her rebel against him. Domestic mediocrity drove her to lewd fancies, marriage tenderness to adulterous desires. She would have liked Charles to beat her, that she might have a better right to hate him, to revenge herself upon him. She was surprised sometimes at the atrocious conjectures that came into her thoughts, and she had to go on smiling, to hear repeated to her at all hours that she was happy, to pretend to be happy, to let it be believed.

Yet she had loathing of this hypocrisy. She was seized with the temptation to flee somewhere with Léon to try a new life; but at once a vague chasm full of darkness opened within her soul.

"Besides, he no longer loves me," she thought. "What is to become of me? What help is to be hoped for, what consolation, what solace?"

She was left broken, breathless, inert, sobbing in a low voice, with flowing tears.

"Why don't you tell master?" the servant asked her when she came in during these crises.

"It is the nerves," said Emma. "Do not speak to him of it; it would worry him."

"Ah! yes," Félicité went on, "you are just like La Guérine, Père Guerin's daughter, the fisherman at Pollet, that I used to know at Dieppe before I came to you. She was so sad, so sad, to see her standing upright on the threshold of her house, she seemed to you like a winding-sheet spread out before the door. Her illness, it appears, was a kind of fog that she had in her head, and the doctors could not do anything, nor the priest either. When she was taken too bad she went off quite alone to the sea-shore, so that the customs officer, going his rounds, often found her lying flat on her face, crying on the shingle. Then, after her marriage, it went off, they say."

"But with me," replied Emma, "it was after marriage that it began."

Chapter VI

ONE EVENING WHEN THE WINDOW WAS OPEN, AND SHE, SITTING BY IT, HAD been watching Lestiboudois, the beadle, trimming the box, she suddenly heard the Angelus ringing.

It was the beginning of April, when the primroses are in bloom, and a warm wind blows over the flower-beds newly turned, and the gardens, like women, seem to be getting ready for the summer fêtes. Through the bars of the arbour and away beyond, the river could be seen in the fields, meandering through the grass in wandering curves. The evening vapours rose between the leafless poplars, touching their outlines with a violet tint, paler and more transparent than a subtle gauze caught athwart their branches. In the distance cattle moved about; neither their steps nor their lowing could be heard; and the bell, still ringing through the air, kept up its peaceful lamentation.

With this repeated tinkling the thoughts of the young woman lost themselves in old memories of her youth and school-days. She remembered the great candlesticks that rose above the vases full of flowers on the altar, and the tabernacle with its small columns. She would have liked to be once more lost in the long line of white veils, marked off here and there by the stiff black hoods of the good sisters bending over their prie-Dieu. At mass on Sundays, when she looked up, she saw the gentle face of the Virgin amid the blue smoke of the rising incense. Then she was moved; she felt herself weak and quite deserted, like the down of a bird whirled by the tempest, and it was unconsciously that she went towards the church, inclined to no matter what devotions, so that her soul was absorbed and all existence lost in it.

On the Place she met Lestiboudois on his way back, for, in order not to shorten his day's labour, he preferred interrupting his work, then beginning it again, so that he rang the Angelus to suit his own convenience. Besides, the ringing over a little earlier warned the lads of catechism hour.

Already a few who had arrived were playing marbles on the stones of the cemetery. Others, astride the wall, swung their legs, kicking with their clogs the large nettles growing between the little enclosure and the newest graves. This was the only green spot. All the rest was but stones, always covered with a fine powder, despite the vestry-broom.

The children in list shoes ran about there as if it were an enclosure made for them. The shouts of their voices could be heard through the humming of the bell. This grew less and less with the swinging of the great rope that, hanging from the

top of the belfry, dragged its end on the ground. Swallows flitted to and fro uttering little cries, cut the air with the edge of their wings, and swiftly returned to their
yellow nests under the tiles of the coping. At the end of the church a lamp was
burning, the wick of a night-light in a glass hung up. Its light from a distance
looked like a white stain trembling in the oil. A long ray of the sun fell across the
nave and seemed to darken the lower sides and the corners.

"Where is the curé?" asked Madame Bovary of one of the lads, who was amusing himself by shaking a swivel in a hole too large for it.

"He is just coming," he answered.

And in fact the door of the presbytery grated; Abbé Bournisien appeared; the
children, pell-mell, fled into the church.

"These young scamps!" murmured the priest, "always the same!" Then, picking up a catechism all in rags that he had struck with his foot, "They respect nothing!" But as soon as he caught sight of Madame Bovary, "Excuse me," he said; "I
did not recognise you."

He thrust the catechism into his pocket, and stopped short, balancing the heavy
vestry key between his two fingers.

The light of the setting sun that fell full upon his face paled the lasting of his
cassock, shiny at the elbows, unravelled at the hem. Grease and tobacco stains followed along his broad chest the lines of the buttons, and grew more numerous the
farther they were from his neckcloth, in which the massive folds of his red chin
rested; this was dotted with yellow spots, that disappeared beneath the coarse hair
of his greyish beard. He had just dined, and was breathing noisily.

"How are you?" he added.

"Not well," replied Emma; "I am ill."

"Well, and so am I," answered the priest. "These first warm days weaken one
most remarkably, don't they? But, after all, we are born to suffer, as St. Paul says.
But what does Monsieur Bovary think of it?"

"He!" she said with a gesture of contempt.

"What!" replied the good fellow, quite astonished, "doesn't he prescribe something for you?"

"Ah!" said Emma, "it is no earthly remedy I need."

But the curé from time to time looked into the church, where the kneeling boys
were shouldering one another, and tumbling over like packs of cards.

"I should like to know——" she went on.

"You look out, Riboudet," cried the priest in an angry voice; "I'll warm your
ears, you imp!" Then turning to Emma. "He's Boudet the carpenter's son; his parents are well off, and let him do just as he pleases. Yet he could learn quickly if he
would, for he is very sharp. And so sometimes for a joke I call him *Ri*boudet (like

the road one takes to go to Maromme), and I even say 'Mon Riboudet.' Ha! ha! 'Mont Riboudet.' The other day I repeated that jest to Monsignor, and he laughed at it; he condescended to laugh at it. And how is Monsieur Bovary?"

She seemed not to hear him. And he went on—

"Always very busy, no doubt; for he and I are certainly the busiest people in the parish. But he is doctor of the body," he added with a thick laugh, "and I of the soul."

She fixed her pleading eyes upon the priest. "Yes," she said, "you solace all sorrows."

"Ah! don't talk to me of it, Madame Bovary. This morning I had to go to Bas-Diauville for a cow that was ill; they thought it was under a spell. All their cows, I don't know how it is—But pardon me! Longuemarre and Boudet! Bless me! will you leave off?"

And with a bound he ran into the church.

The boys were just then clustering round the large desk, climbing over the precentor's footstool, opening the missal; and others on tiptoe were just about to venture into the confessional. But the priest suddenly distributed a shower of cuffs among them. Seizing them by the collars of their coats, he lifted them from the ground, and deposited them on their knees on the stones of the choir, firmly, as if he meant planting them there.

"Yes," said he, when he returned to Emma, unfolding his large cotton handkerchief, one corner of which he put between his teeth, "farmers are much to be pitied."

"Others, too," she replied.

"Assuredly. Town-labourers, for example."

"It is not they—"

"Pardon! I've there known poor mothers of families, virtuous women, I assure you, real saints, who wanted even bread."

"But those," replied Emma, and the corners of her mouth twitched as she spoke, "those, Monsieur le Curé, who have bread and have no—"

"Fire in the winter," said the priest.

"Oh, what does that matter?"

"What! What does it matter? It seems to me that when one has firing and food—for, after all—"

"My God! my God!" she sighed.

"Do you feel unwell?" he asked, approaching her anxiously. "It is indigestion, no doubt? You must get home, Madame Bovary; drink a little tea, that will strengthen you, or else a glass of fresh water with a little moist sugar."

"Why?" And she looked like one awaking from a dream.

"Well, you see, you were putting your hand to your forehead. I thought you felt faint." Then, bethinking himself, "But you were asking me something? What was it? I really don't remember."

"I? Nothing! nothing!" repeated Emma.

And the glance she cast round her slowly fell upon the old man in the cassock. They looked at one another face to face without speaking.

"Then, Madame Bovary," he said at last, "excuse me, but duty first, you know; I must look after my good-for-nothings. The first communion will soon be upon us, and I fear we shall be behind after all. So after Ascension Day I keep them *recta* an extra hour every Wednesday. Poor children! One cannot lead them too soon into the path of the Lord, as, moreover, he has himself recommended us to do by the mouth of his Divine Son. Good health to you, madame; my respects to your husband."

And he went into the church making a genuflexion as soon as he reached the door.

Emma saw him disappear between the double row of forms, walking with heavy tread, his head a little bent over his shoulder, and with his two hands half-open behind him.

Then she turned on her heel all of one piece, like a statue on a pivot, and went homewards. But the loud voice of the priest, the clear voices of the boys still reached her ears, and went on behind her.

"Are you a Christian?"

"Yes, I am a Christian."

"What is a Christian?"

"He who, being baptised—baptised—baptised—"

She went up the steps of the staircase holding on to the banisters, and when she was in her room threw herself into an arm-chair.

The whitish light of the window-panes fell with soft undulations. The furniture in its place seemed to have become more immobile, and to lose itself in the shadow as in an ocean of darkness. The fire was out, the clock went on ticking, and Emma vaguely marvelled at this calm of all things while within herself was such tumult. But little Berthe was there, between the window and the work-table, tottering on her knitted shoes, and trying to come to her mother to catch hold of the ends of her apron-strings.

"Leave me alone," said the latter, putting her from her with her hand.

The little girl soon came up closer against her knees, and leaning on them with her arms, she looked up with her large blue eyes, while a small thread of pure saliva dribbled from her lips on to the silk apron.

"Leave me alone," repeated the young woman quite irritably.

Her face frightened the child, who began to scream.

"Will you leave me alone?" she said, pushing her with her elbow.

Berthe fell at the foot of the drawers against the brass handle, cutting her cheek, which began to bleed, against it. Madame Bovary sprang to lift her up, broke the bell-rope, called for the servant with all her might, and she was just going to curse herself when Charles appeared. It was the dinner-hour; he had come home.

"Look, dear!" said Emma, in a calm voice, "the little one fell down while she was playing, and has hurt herself."

Charles reassured her; the case was not a serious one, and he went for some sticking plaster.

Madame Bovary did not go downstairs to the dining-room; she wished to remain alone to look after the child. Then watching her sleep, the little anxiety she felt gradually wore off, and she seemed very stupid to herself, and very good to have been so worried just now at so little. Berthe, in fact, no longer sobbed. Her breathing now imperceptibly raised the cotton covering. Big tears lay in the corner of the half-closed eyelids, through whose lashes one could see two pale sunken pupils; the plaster stuck on her cheek drew the skin obliquely.

"It is very strange," thought Emma, "how ugly this child is!"

When at eleven o'clock Charles came back from the chemist's shop, whither he had gone after dinner to return the remainder of the sticking-plaster, he found his wife standing by the cradle.

"I assure you it's nothing," he said, kissing her on the forehead. "Don't worry, my poor darling; you will make yourself ill."

He had stayed a long time at the chemist's. Although he had not seemed much moved, Homais, nevertheless, had exerted himself to buoy him up, to "keep up his spirits." Then they had talked of the various dangers that threaten childhood, of the carelessness of servants. Madame Homais knew something of it, having still upon her chest the marks left by a basin full of soup that a cook had formerly dropped on her pinafore, and her good parents took no end of trouble for her. The knives were not sharpened, nor the floors waxed; there were iron gratings to the windows and strong bars across the fireplace; the little Homais, in spite of their spirit, could not stir without someone watching them; at the slightest cold their father stuffed them with pectorals; and until they were turned four they all, without pity, had to wear wadded head-protectors. This, it is true, was a fancy of Madame Homais's; her husband was inwardly afflicted at it. Fearing the possible consequences of such compression to the intellectual organs, he even went so far as to say to her, "Do you want to make Caribs or Botocudos of them?"

Charles, however, had several times tried to interrupt the conversation. "I should like to speak to you," he had whispered in the clerk's ear, who went upstairs in front of him.

"Can he suspect anything?" Léon asked himself. His heart beat, and he racked his brain with surmises.

At last, Charles, having shut the door, asked him to see himself what would be the price at Rouen of a fine daguerreotype. It was a sentimental surprise he intended for his wife, a delicate attention—his portrait in a frock-coat. But he wanted first to know "how much it would be." The inquiries would not put Monsieur Léon out, since he went to town almost every week.

Why? Monsieur Homais suspected some "young man's affair" at the bottom of it, an intrigue. But he was mistaken. Léon was after no love-making. He was sadder than ever, as Madame Lefrançois saw from the amount of food he left on his plate. To find out more about it she questioned the tax-collector. Binet answered roughly that he "wasn't paid by the police."

All the same, his companion seemed very strange to him, for Léon often threw himself back in his chair, and stretching out his arms, complained vaguely of life.

"It's because you don't take enough recreation," said the collector.

"What recreation?"

"If I were you I'd have a lathe."

"But I don't know how to turn," answered the clerk.

"Ah! that's true," said the other, rubbing his chin with an air of mingled contempt and satisfaction.

Léon was weary of loving without any result; moreover, he was beginning to feel that depression caused by the repetition of the same kind of life, when no interest inspires and no hope sustains it. He was so bored with Yonville and the Yonvillers, that the sight of certain persons, of certain houses, irritated him beyond endurance; and the chemist, good fellow though he was, was becoming absolutely unbearable to him. Yet the prospect of a new condition of life frightened as much as it seduced him.

This apprehension soon changed into impatience, and then Paris from afar sounded its fanfare of masked balls with the laugh of grisettes. As he was to finish reading there, why not set out at once? What prevented him? And he began making home-preparations; he arranged his occupations beforehand. He furnished in his head an apartment. He would lead an artist's life there! He would take lessons on the guitar! He would have a dressing-gown, a Basque cap, blue velvet slippers! He even already was admiring two crossed foils over his chimney-piece, with a death's-head on the guitar above them.

The difficulty was the consent of his mother; nothing, however, seemed more reasonable. Even his employer advised him to go to some other chambers where he could advance more rapidly. Taking a middle course, then, Léon looked for some place as second clerk at Rouen; found none, and at last wrote his mother a long letter full of details, in which he set forth the reasons for going to live at Paris immediately. She consented.

He did not hurry. Every day for a month Hivert carried boxes, valises, parcels for him from Yonville to Rouen and from Rouen to Yonville; and when Léon had packed up his wardrobe, had his three arm-chairs restuffed, bought a stock of neckties, in a word, had made more preparations than for a voyage round the world, he put it off from week to week, until he received a second letter from his mother urging him to leave, since he wanted to pass his examination before the vacation.

When the moment for the farewells had come, Madame Homais wept, Justin sobbed; Homais, as a man of nerve, concealed his emotion; he wished to carry his friend's overcoat himself as far as the gate of the notary, who was taking Léon to Rouen in his carriage. The latter had just time to bid farewell to Monsieur Bovary.

When he reached the head of the stairs he stopped, he was so out of breath. On his coming in, Madame Bovary rose hurriedly.

"It is I again!" said Léon.

"I was sure of it!"

She bit her lips, and a rush of blood flowing under her skin made her red from the roots of her hair to the top of her collar. She remained standing, leaning with her shoulder against the wainscot.

"The doctor is not here?" he went on.

"He is out." She repeated, "He is out."

Then there was silence. They looked one at the other, and their thoughts, confounded in the same agony, clung close together like two throbbing breasts.

"I should like to kiss Berthe," said Léon.

Emma went down a few steps and called Félicité.

He threw one long look around him that took in the walls, the brackets, the fireplace, as if to penetrate everything, carry away everything. But she returned, and the servant brought Berthe, who was swinging a windmill roof downwards at the end of a string. Léon kissed her several times on the neck.

"Good-bye, poor child! good-bye, dear little one! good-bye!"

And he gave her back to her mother.

"Take her away," she said.

They remained alone—Madame Bovary, her back turned, her face pressed against a window-pane; Léon held his cap in his hand, knocking it softly against his thigh.

"It is going to rain," said Emma.

"I have a cloak," he answered.

"Ah!"

She turned round, her chin lowered, her forehead bent forward. The light fell on it as on a piece of marble to the curve of the eyebrows, without one's being able to guess what Emma was seeing in the horizon or what she was thinking within herself.

"Well, good-bye," he sighed.

She raised her head with a quick movement.

"Yes, good-bye—go!"

They advanced towards each other; he held out his hand; she hesitated.

"In the English fashion, then," she said, giving her own hand wholly to him, and forcing a laugh.

Léon felt it between his fingers, and the very essence of all his being seemed to pass down into that moist palm. Then he opened his hand; their eyes met again, and he disappeared.

When he reached the market-place, he stopped and hid behind a pillar to look for the last time at this white house with the four green blinds. He thought he saw a shadow behind the window in the room; but the curtain, sliding along the pole as though no one were touching it, slowly opened its long oblique folds, that spread out with a single movement, and thus hung straight and motionless as a plaster wall. Léon set off running.

From afar he saw his employer's gig in the road, and by it a man in a coarse apron holding the horse. Homais and Monsieur Guillaumin were talking. They were waiting for him.

"Embrace me," said the druggist with tears in his eyes. "Here is your coat, my good friend. Mind the cold; take care of yourself; look after yourself."

"Come, Léon, jump in," said the notary.

Homais bent over the splash-board, and in a voice broken by sobs uttered these three sad words—

"A pleasant journey!"

"Good-night," said Monsieur Guillaumin. "Give him his head."

They set out, and Homais went back.

Madame Bovary had opened her window overlooking the garden and watched the clouds. They were gathering round the sunset on the side of Rouen, and swiftly rolled back their black columns, behind which the great rays of the sun looked out like the golden arrows of a suspended trophy, while the rest of the empty heavens was white as porcelain. But a gust of wind bowed the poplars, and suddenly the rain fell; it pattered against the green leaves. Then the sun reappeared, the hens clucked, sparrows shook their wings in the damp thickets, and the pools of water on the gravel as they flowed away carried off the pink flowers of an acacia.

"Ah! how far off he must be already!" she thought.

Monsieur Homais, as usual, came at half-past six during dinner.

"Well," said he, "so we've sent off our young friend!"

"So it seems," replied the doctor. Then turning on his chair, "Any news at home?"

"Nothing much. Only my wife was a little moved this afternoon. You know women—a nothing upsets them, especially my wife. And we should be wrong to object to that, since their nervous organisation is much more malleable than ours."

"Poor Léon!" said Charles. "How will he live at Paris? Will he get used to it?"

Madame Bovary sighed.

"Get along!" said the chemist, smacking his lips. "The outings at restaurants, the masked balls, the champagne—all that'll be jolly enough, I assure you."

"I don't think he'll go wrong," objected Bovary.

"Nor do I," said Monsieur Homais quickly; "although he'll have to do like the rest for fear of passing for a Jesuit. And you don't know what a life those dogs lead in the Latin quarter with actresses. Besides, students are thought a great deal of at Paris. Provided they have a few accomplishments, they are received in the best society; there are even ladies of the Faubourg Saint-Germain who fall in love with them, which subsequently furnishes them opportunities for making very good matches."

"But," said the doctor, "I fear for him that down there—"

"You are right," interrupted the chemist; "that is the reverse of the medal. And one is constantly obliged to keep one's hand in one's pocket there. Thus, we will suppose you are in a public garden. An individual presents himself, well dressed, even wearing an order, and whom one would take for a diplomatist. He approaches you, he insinuates himself; offers you a pinch of snuff, or picks up your hat. Then you become more intimate; he takes you to a café, invites you to his country-house, introduces you, between two drinks, to all sorts of people; and three-fourths of the time it's only to plunder your watch or lead you into some pernicious step."

"That is true," said Charles; "but I was thinking especially of illnesses—of typhoid fever, for example, that attacks students from the provinces."

Emma shuddered.

"Because of the change of regimen," continued the chemist, "and of the perturbation that results therefrom in the whole system. And then the water at Paris, don't you know! The dishes at restaurants, all the spiced food, end by heating the blood, and are not worth, whatever people may say of them, a good soup. For my own part, I have always preferred plain living; it is more healthy. So when I was studying pharmacy at Rouen, I boarded in a boarding-house; I dined with the professors."

And thus he went on, expounding his opinions generally and his personal likings, until Justin came to fetch him for a mulled egg that was wanted.

"Not a moment's peace!" he cried; "always at it! I can't go out for a minute! Like a plough-horse, I have always to be moiling and toiling. What drudgery!" Then, when he was at the door, "By the way, do you know the news?"

"What news?"

"That it is very likely," Homais went on, raising his eyebrows and assuming one of his most serious expressions, "that the agricultural meeting of the Seine-Inférieure will be held this year at Yonville-l'Abbaye. The rumour, at all events, is going the round. This morning the paper alluded to it. It would be of the utmost importance for our district. But we'll talk it over later on. I can see, thank you; Justin has the lantern."

Chapter VII

THE NEXT DAY WAS A DREARY ONE FOR EMMA. EVERYTHING SEEMED TO HER enveloped in a black atmosphere floating confusedly over the exterior of things, and sorrow was engulfed within her soul with soft shrieks such as the winter wind makes in ruined castles. It was that reverie which we give to things that will not return, the lassitude that seizes you after everything was done; that pain, in fine, that the interruption of every wonted movement, the sudden cessation of any prolonged vibration, brings on.

As on the return from Vaubyessard, when the quadrilles were running in her head, she was full of a gloomy melancholy, of a numb despair. Léon reappeared, taller, handsomer, more charming, more vague. Though separated from her, he had not left her; he was there, and the walls of the house seemed to hold his shadow. She could not detach her eyes from the carpet where he had walked, from those empty chairs where he had sat. The river still flowed on, and slowly drove its ripples along the slippery banks. They had often walked there to the murmur of the waves over the moss-covered pebbles. How bright the sun had been! What happy afternoons they had seen alone in the shade at the end of the garden! He read aloud, bareheaded, sitting on a footstool of dry sticks; the fresh wind of the meadow set trembling the leaves of the book and the nasturtiums of the arbour. Ah! he was gone, the only charm of her life, the only possible hope of joy. Why had she not seized this happiness when it came to her? Why not have kept hold of it with both hands, with both knees, when it was about to flee from her? And she cursed herself for not having loved Léon. She thirsted for his lips. The wish took possession of her to run after and rejoin him, throw herself into his arms and say to him, "It is I; I am yours." But Emma recoiled beforehand at the difficulties of the enterprise, and her desires, increased by regret, became only the more acute.

Henceforth the memory of Léon was the centre of her boredom; it burnt there more brightly than the fire travellers have left on the snow of a Russian steppe. She sprang towards him, she pressed against him, she stirred carefully the dying embers, sought all around her anything that could revive it; and the most distant reminiscences, like the most immediate occasions, what she experienced as well as what she imagined, her voluptuous desires that were unsatisfied, her projects of happiness that crackled in the wind like dead boughs, her sterile virtue, her lost hopes, the domestic *tête-à-tête*—she gathered it all up, took everything, and made it all serve as fuel for her melancholy.

The flames, however, subsided, either because the supply had exhausted itself, or because it had been piled up too much. Love, little by little, was quelled by absence; regret stifled beneath habit; and this incendiary light that had empurpled her pale sky was overspread and faded by degrees. In the supineness of her conscience she even took her repugnance towards her husband for aspirations towards her lover, the burning of hate for the warmth of tenderness; but as the tempest still raged, and as passion burnt itself down to the very cinders, and no help came, no sun rose, there was night on all sides, and she was lost in the terrible cold that pierced her.

Then the evil days of Tostes began again. She thought herself now far more unhappy; for she had the experience of grief, with the certainty that it would not end.

A woman who had laid on herself such sacrifices could well allow herself certain whims. She bought a gothic prie-Dieu, and in a month spent fourteen francs on lemons for polishing her nails; she wrote to Rouen for a blue cashmere gown; she chose one of Lheureux's finest scarves, and wore it knotted round her waist over her dressing-gown; and, with closed blinds and a book in her hand, she lay stretched out on a couch in this garb.

She often changed her coiffure; she did her hair *à la Chinoise*, in flowing curls, in plaited coils; she parted it on one side and rolled it under like a man's.

She wanted to learn Italian; she bought dictionaries, a grammar, and a supply of white paper. She tried serious reading, history, and philosophy. Sometimes in the night Charles woke up with a start, thinking he was being called to a patient. "I'm coming," he stammered; and it was the noise of a match Emma had struck to relight the lamp. But her reading fared like her pieces of embroidery, all of which, only just begun, filled her cupboard; she took it up, left it, passed on to other books.

She had attacks in which she could easily have been driven to commit any folly. She maintained one day, in opposition to her husband, that she could drink off a large glass of brandy, and, as Charles was stupid enough to dare her to, she swallowed the brandy to the last drop.

In spite of her vapourish airs (as the housewives of Yonville called them), Emma, all the same, never seemed gay, and usually she had at the corners of her mouth that immobile contraction that puckers the faces of old maids, and those of men whose ambition has failed. She was pale all over, white as a sheet; the skin of her nose was drawn at the nostrils, her eyes looked at you vaguely. After discovering three grey hairs on her temples, she talked much of her old age.

She often fainted. One day she even spat blood, and, as Charles fussed round her showing his anxiety—

"Bah!" she answered, "what does it matter?"

Charles fled to his study and wept there, both his elbows on the table, sitting in an arm-chair at his bureau under the phrenological head.

Then he wrote to his mother to beg her to come, and they had many long consultations together on the subject of Emma.

What should they decide? What was to be done since she rejected all medical treatment?

"Do you know what your wife wants?" replied Madame Bovary senior. "She wants to be forced to occupy herself with some manual work. If she were obliged, like so many others, to earn her living, she wouldn't have these vapours, that come to her from a lot of ideas she stuffs into her head, and from the idleness in which she lives."

"Yet she is always busy," said Charles.

"Ah! always busy at what? Reading novels, bad books, works against religion, and in which they mock at priests in speeches taken from Voltaire. But all that leads you far astray, my poor child. Anyone who has no religion always ends by turning out badly."

So it was decided to stop Emma reading novels. The enterprise did not seem easy. The good lady undertook it. She was, when she passed through Rouen, to go herself to the lending-library and represent that Emma had discontinued her subscription. Would they not have a right to apply to the police if the librarian persisted all the same in his poisonous trade?

The farewells of mother and daughter-in-law were cold. During the three weeks that they had been together they had not exchanged half-a-dozen words apart from the inquiries and phrases when they met at table and in the evening before going to bed.

Madame Bovary left on a Wednesday, the market-day at Yonville.

The Place since morning had been blocked by a row of carts, which, on end and their shafts in the air, spread all along the line of houses from the church to the inn. On the other side there were canvas booths, where cotton checks, blankets, and woolen stockings were sold, together with harness for horses, and packets of blue ribbon, whose ends fluttered in the wind. The coarse hardware was spread out on the ground between pyramids of eggs and hampers of cheeses, from which sticky straw stuck out. Near the corn-machines clucking hens passed their necks through the bars of flat cages. The people, crowding in the same place and unwilling to move thence, sometimes threatened to smash the shop-front of the chemist. On Wednesdays his shop was never empty, and the people pushed in less to buy drugs than for consultations, so great was Homais's reputation in the neighbouring villages. His robust aplomb had fascinated the rustics. They considered him a greater doctor than all the doctors.

Emma was leaning out at the window; she was often there. The window in the provinces replaces the theatre and the promenade, and she amused herself with watching the crowd of boors, when she saw a gentleman in a green velvet coat. He had on yellow gloves, although he wore heavy gaiters; he was coming towards the doctor's house, followed by a peasant walking with bent head and quite a thoughtful air.

"Can I see the doctor?" he asked Justin, who was talking on the doorsteps with Félicité, and, taking him for a servant of the house. "Tell him that Monsieur Rodolphe Boulanger of La Huchette is here."

It was not from territorial vanity that the new arrival added "of La Huchette" to his name, but to make himself the better known. La Huchette, in fact, was an estate near Yonville, where he had just bought the château and two farms that he cultivated himself, without, however, troubling very much about them. He lived as a bachelor, and was supposed to have "at least fifteen thousand francs a year."

Charles came into the room. Monsieur Boulanger introduced his man, who wanted to be bled because he felt "a tingling all over."

"That'll purge me," he urged as an objection to all reasoning.

So Bovary ordered a bandage and a basin, and asked Justin to hold it. Then addressing the countryman, already pale—

"Don't be afraid, my lad."

"No, no, sir," said the other; "get on."

And with an air of bravado he held out his great arm. At the prick of the lancet the blood spurted out, splashing against the looking-glass.

"Hold the basin nearer," exclaimed Charles.

"Lor!" said the peasant, "one would swear it was a little fountain flowing. How red my blood is! That's a good sign, isn't it?"

"Sometimes," answered the doctor, "one feels nothing at first, and then syncope sets in, and more especially with people of strong constitution like this man."

At these words the rustic let go the lancet-case he was twisting between his fingers. A shudder of his shoulders made the chair-back creak. His hat fell off.

"I thought as much," said Bovary, pressing his finger on the vein.

The basin was beginning to tremble in Justin's hands; his knees shook, he turned pale.

"Emma! Emma!" called Charles.

With one bound she came down the staircase.

"Some vinegar," he cried. "O dear! two at once!"

And in his emotion he could hardly put on the compress.

"It is nothing," said Monsieur Boulanger quietly, taking Justin in his arms. He seated him on the table with his back resting against the wall.

Madame Bovary began taking off his cravat. The strings of his shirt had got into a knot, and she was for some minutes moving her light fingers about the young fellow's neck. Then she poured some vinegar on her cambric handkerchief; she moistened his temples with little dabs, and then blew upon them softly. The ploughman revived, but Justin's syncope still lasted, and his eyeballs disappeared in their pale sclerotic like blue flowers in milk.

"We must hide this from him," said Charles.

Madame Bovary took the basin to put it under the table. With the movement she made in bending down, her dress (it was a summer dress with four flounces, yellow, long in the waist and wide in the skirt) spread out around her on the flags of the room; and as Emma, stooping, staggered a little as she stretched out her arms, the stuff here and there gave with the inflections of her bust. Then she went to fetch a bottle of water, and she was melting some pieces of sugar when the chemist arrived. The servant had been to fetch him in the tumult. Seeing his pupil with his eyes open he drew a long breath; then going round him he looked at him from head to foot.

"Fool!" he said, "really a little fool! A fool in four letters! A phlebotomy's a big affair, isn't it! And a fellow who isn't afraid of anything; a kind of squirrel, just as he is who climbs to vertiginous heights to shake down nuts. Oh, yes! you just talk to me, boast about myself! Here's a fine fitness for practising pharmacy later on; for under serious circumstances you may be called before the tribunals in order to enlighten the minds of the magistrates, and you would have to keep your head then, to reason, show yourself a man, or else pass for an imbecile."

Justin did not answer. The chemist went on—

"Who asked you to come? You are always pestering the doctor and madame. On Wednesday, moreover, your presence is indispensable to me. There are now twenty people in the shop. I left everything because of the interest I take in you. Come, get along! Sharp! Wait for me, and keep an eye on the jars."

When Justin, who was rearranging his dress, had gone, they talked for a little while about fainting-fits. Madame Bovary had never fainted.

"That is extraordinary for a lady," said Monsieur Boulanger; "but some people are very susceptible. Thus in a duel, I have seen a second lose consciousness at the mere sound of the loading of pistols."

"For my part," said the chemist, "the sight of other people's blood doesn't affect me at all, but the mere thought of my own flowing would make me faint if I reflected upon it too much."

Monsieur Boulanger, however, dismissed his servant, advising him to calm himself, since his fancy was over.

"It procured me the advantage of making your acquaintance," he added, and he looked at Emma as she said this. Then he put three francs on the corner of the table, bowed negligently, and went out.

He was soon on the other side of the river (this was his way back to La Huchette), and Emma saw him in the meadow, walking under the poplars, slackening his pace now and then as one who reflects.

"She is very pretty," he said to himself; "she is very pretty, this doctor's wife. Fine teeth, black eyes, a dainty foot, a figure like a Parisienne's. Where the devil does she come from? Wherever did this fat fellow pick her up?"

Monsieur Rodolphe Boulanger was thirty-four; he was of brutal temperament and intelligent perspicacity, having, moreover, had much to do with women, and knowing them well. This one had seemed pretty to him; so he was thinking about her and her husband.

"I think he is very stupid. She is tired of him, no doubt. He has dirty nails, and hasn't shaved for three days. While he is trotting after his patients, she sits there botching socks. And she gets bored! She would like to live in town and dance polkas every evening. Poor little woman! She is gaping after love like a carp after water on a kitchen-table. With three words of gallantry she'd adore one, I'm sure of it. She'd be tender, charming. Yes; but how get rid of her afterwards?"

Then the difficulties of love-making seen in the distance made him by contrast think of his mistress. She was an actress at Rouen, whom he kept; and when he had pondered over this image, with which, even in remembrance, he was satiated—

"Ah! Madame Bovary," he thought, "is much prettier, especially fresher. Virginie is decidedly beginning to grow fat. She is so finikin with her pleasures; and, besides, she has a mania for prawns."

The fields were empty, and around him Rodolphe only heard the regular beating of the grass striking against his boots, with the cry of the grasshopper hidden at a distance among the oats. He again saw Emma in her room, dressed as he had seen her, and he undressed her.

"Oh, I will have her," he cried, striking a blow with his stick at a clod in front of him. And he at once began to consider the political part of the enterprise. He asked himself—

"Where shall we meet? By what means? We shall always be having the brat on our hands, and the servant, the neighbours, the husband, all sorts of worries. Pshaw! one would lose too much time over it."

Then he resumed, "She really has eyes that pierce one's heart like a gimlet. And that pale complexion! I adore pale women!"

When he reached the top of the Argueil hills he had made up his mind. "It's only finding the opportunities. Well, I will call in now and then. I'll send them venison, poultry; I'll have myself bled, if need be. We shall become friends; I'll invite them to my place. By Jove!" added he, "there's the agricultural show coming on. She'll be there. I shall see her. We'll begin boldly, for that's the surest way."

Chapter VIII

AT LAST IT CAME, THE FAMOUS AGRICULTURAL SHOW. ON THE MORNING OF the solemnity all the inhabitants at their doors were chatting over the preparations. The pediment of the townhall had been hung with garlands of ivy: a tent had been erected in a meadow for the banquet; and in the middle of the Place, in front of the church, a kind of bombarde was to announce the arrival of the prefect and the names of the successful farmers who had obtained prizes. The National Guard of Buchy (there was none at Yonville) had come to join the corps of firemen, of whom Binet was captain. On that day he wore a collar even higher than usual; and, tightly buttoned in his tunic, his figure was so stiff and motionless that the whole vital portion of his person seemed to have descended into his legs, which rose in a cadence of set steps with a single movement. As there was some rivalry between the tax-collector and the colonel, both, to show off their talents, drilled their men separately. One saw the red epaulettes and the black breast-plates pass and repass alternately; there was no end to it, and it constantly began again. There had never been such a display of pomp. Several citizens had washed down their houses the evening before; tricoloured flags hung from half-open windows; all the public houses were full; and in the lovely weather the starched caps, the golden crosses, and the coloured neckerchiefs seemed whiter than snow, shone in the sun, and relieved with their motley colours the sombre monotony of the frock-coats and blue smocks. The neighbouring farmers' wives, when they got off their horses, pulled out a long pin that fastened round them their dresses, turned up for fear of mud; and the husbands, on the contrary, in order to save their hats, kept their handkerchiefs round them, holding one corner between their teeth.

The crowd came into the main street from both ends of the village. People poured in from the lanes, the alleys, the houses; and from time to time one heard knockers banging against doors closing behind women with their gloves, who were going out to see the fête. What was most admired were two long lamp-stands covered with lanterns, that flanked a platform on which the authorities were to sit. Besides this there were against the four columns of the townhall four kinds of poles, each bearing a small standard of greenish cloth, embellished with inscriptions in gold letters. On one was written, "To Commerce"; on the other, "To Agriculture"; on the third, "To Industry"; and on the fourth, "To the Fine Arts."

But the jubilation that brightened all faces seemed to darken that of Madame Lefrançois, the innkeeper. Standing on her kitchen-steps she muttered to herself, "What rubbish! what rubbish! With their canvas booth! Do they think the prefect will be glad to dine down there under a tent like a gipsy? They call all this fussing doing good to the place! Then it wasn't worth while sending to Neufchâtel for the keeper of a cookshop! And for whom? For cowherds! tatterdemalions!"

The druggist was passing. He had on a frock-coat, nankeen trousers, beaver shoes, and, for a wonder, a hat with a low crown.

"Your servant! Excuse me, I am in a hurry." And as the fat widow asked where he was going—

"It seems odd to you, doesn't it, I who am always more cooped up in my laboratory than the man's rat in his cheese."

"What cheese?" asked the landlady.

"Oh, nothing! nothing!" Homais continued. "I merely wished to convey to you, Madame Lefrançois, that I usually live at home like a recluse. To-day, however, considering the circumstances, it is necessary—"

"Oh, you're going down there!" she said contemptuously.

"Yes, I am going," replied the druggist, astonished. "Am I not a member of the consulting commission?"

Mère Lefrançois looked at him for a few moments, and ended by saying with a smile—

"That's another pair of shoes! But what does agriculture matter to you? Do you understand anything about it?"

"Certainly I understand it, since I am a druggist—that is to say, a chemist. And the object of chemistry, Madame Lefrançois, being the knowledge of the reciprocal and molecular action of all natural bodies, it follows that agriculture is comprised within its domain. And, in fact, the composition of the manure, the fermentation of liquids, the analyses of gases, and the influence of miasmata, what, I ask you, is all this, if it isn't chemistry, pure and simple?"

The landlady did not answer. Homais went on—

"Do you think that to be an agriculturist it is necessary to have tilled the earth or fattened fowls oneself? It is necessary rather to know the composition of the substances in question—the geological strata, the atmospheric actions, the quality of the soil, the minerals, the waters, the density of the different bodies, their capillarity, and what not. And one must be master of all the principles of hygiene in order to direct, criticise the construction of buildings, the feeding of animals, the diet of domestics. And, moreover, Madame Lefrançois, one must know botany, be able to distinguish between plants, you understand, which are the wholesome and those that are deleterious, which are unproductive and which nutritive, if it is well to pull them up here and re-sow them there, to propagate some, destroy others; in brief, one must keep pace with science by means of pamphlets and public papers, be always on the alert to find out improvements."

The landlady never took her eyes off the Café Français and the chemist went on—

"Would to God our agriculturists were chemists, or that at least they would pay more attention to the counsels of science. Thus lately I myself wrote a considerable tract, a memoir of over seventy-two pages, entitled, 'Cider, its Manufacture and its Effects, together with some New Reflections on this Subject,' that I sent to the Agricultural Society of Rouen, and which even procured me the honour of being received among its members—Section, Agriculture; Class, Pomological. Well, if my work had been given to the public—" But the druggist stopped, Madame Lefrançois seemed so preoccupied.

"Just look at them!' she said. "It's past comprehension! Such a cookshop as that!" And with a shrug of the shoulders that stretched out over her breast the stitches of her knitted bodice, she pointed with both hands at her rival's inn, whence songs were heard issuing. "Well, it won't last long," she added, "It'll be over before a week."

Homais drew back with stupefaction. She came down three steps and whispered in his ear—

"What! you didn't know it? There'll be an execution in next week. It's Lheureux who is selling him up; he has killed him with bills."

"What a terrible catastrophe!" cried the druggist, who always found expressions in harmony with all imaginable circumstances.

Then the landlady began telling him this story, that she had heard from Theodore, Monsieur Guillaumin's servant, and although she detested Tellier, she blamed Lheureux. He was "a wheedler, a sneak."

"There!" she said. "Look at him! he is in the market; he is bowing to Madame Bovary, who's got on a green bonnet. Why, she's taking Monsieur Boulanger's arm."

"Madame Bovary!" exclaimed Homais. "I must go at once and pay her my respects. Perhaps she'll be very glad to have a seat in the enclosure under the peristyle." And, without heeding Madame Lefrançois, who was calling him back to tell him more about it, the druggist walked off rapidly with a smile on his lips, with straight knees, bowing copiously to right and left, and taking up much room with the large tails of his frock-coat that fluttered behind him in the wind.

Rodolphe having caught sight of him from afar, hurried on, but Madame Bovary lost her breath; so he walked more slowly, and, smiling at her, said in a rough tone—

"It's only to get away from that fat fellow, you know, the druggist." She pressed his elbow.

"What's the meaning of that?" he asked himself. And he looked at her out of the corner of his eyes.

Her profile was so calm that one could guess nothing from it. It stood out in the light from the oval of her bonnet, with pale ribbons on it like the leaves of weeds. Her eyes with their long curved lashes looked straight before her, and though wide open, they seemed slightly puckered by the cheek-bones, because of the blood pulsing gently under the delicate skin. A pink line ran along the partition between her nostrils. Her head was bent upon her shoulder, and the pearl tips of her white teeth were seen between her lips.

"Is she making fun of me?" thought Rodolphe.

Emma's gesture, however, had only been meant for a warning; for Monsieur Lheureux was accompanying them, and spoke now and again as if to enter into the conversation.

"What a superb day! Everybody is out! The wind is east!"

And neither Madame Bovary nor Rodolphe answered him, whilst at the slightest movement made by them he drew near, saying, "I beg your pardon!" and raised his hat.

When they reached the farrier's house, instead of following the road up to the fence, Rodolphe suddenly turned down a path, drawing with him Madame Bovary. He called out—

"Good evening, Monsieur Lheureux! See you again presently."

"How you got rid of him!" she said, laughing.

"Why," he went on, "allow oneself to be intruded upon by others? And as to-day I have the happiness of being with you—"

Emma blushed. He did not finish his sentence. Then he talked of the fine weather and of the pleasure of walking on the grass. A few daisies had sprung up again.

"Here are some pretty Easter daisies," he said, "and enough of them to furnish oracles to all the amorous maids in the place." He added, "Shall I pick some? What do you think?"

"Are you in love?" she asked, coughing a little.

"H'm, h'm! who knows?" answered Rodolphe.

The meadow began to fill, and the housewives hustled you with their great umbrellas, their baskets, and their babies. One had often to get out of the way of a long file of country folk, servant-maids with blue stockings, flat shoes, silver rings, and who smelt of milk when one passed close to them. They walked along holding one another by the hand, and thus they spread over the whole field from the row of open trees to the banquet tent. But this was the examination time, and the farmers one after the other entered a kind of enclosure formed by a long cord supported on sticks.

The beasts were there, their noses towards the cord, and making a confused line with their unequal rumps. Drowsy pigs were burrowing in the earth with their snouts, calves were bleating, lambs baaing; the cows, on knees folded in, were stretching their bellies on the grass, slowly chewing the cud, and blinking their heavy eyelids at the gnats that buzzed round them. Ploughmen with bare arms were holding by the halter prancing stallions that neighed with dilated nostrils looking towards the mares. These stood quietly, stretching out their heads and flowing manes, while their foals rested in their shadow, or now and then came and sucked them. And above the long undulation of these crowded animals one saw some white mane rising in the wind like a wave, or some sharp horns sticking out, and the heads of men running about. Apart, outside the enclosure, a hundred paces off, was a large black bull, muzzled, with an iron ring in its nostrils, and who moved no more than if he had been in bronze. A child in rags was holding him by a rope.

Between the two lines the committee-men were walking with heavy steps, examining each animal, then consulting one another in a low voice. One who seemed of more importance now and then took notes in a book as he walked along. This was the president of the jury, Monsieur Derozerays de la Panville. As soon as he recognised Rodolphe he came forward quickly, and smiling amiably, said—

"What! Monsieur Boulanger, you are deserting us?"

Rodolphe protested that he was just coming. But when the president had disappeared—

"*Ma foi!*" said he, "I shall not go. Your company is better than his."

And while poking fun at the show, Rodolphe, to move about more easily, showed the gendarme his blue card, and even stopped now and then in front of some fine beast, which Madame Bovary did not at all admire. He noticed this, and began jeering at the Yonville ladies and their dresses; then he apologised for the negligence of his own. He had that incongruity of common and elegant in which the habitually vulgar think they see the revelation of an eccentric existence, of the perturbations of sentiment, the tyrannies of art, and always a certain contempt for social conventions, that seduces or exasperates them. Thus his cambric shirt with plaited cuffs was blown out by the wind in the opening of his waistcoat of grey ticking, and his broad-striped trousers disclosed at the ankle nankeen boots with patent leather gaiters. These were so polished that they reflected the grass. He trampled on horse's dung with them, one hand in the pocket of his jacket and his straw hat on one side.

"Besides," added he, "when one lives in the country—"

"It's waste of time," said Emma.

"That is true," replied Rodolphe. "To think that not one of these people is capable of understanding even the cut of a coat!"

Then they talked about provincial mediocrity, of the lives it crushed, the illusions lost there.

"And I too," said Rodolphe, "am drifting into depression."

"You!" she said in astonishment; "I thought you very light-hearted."

"Ah! yes. I seem so, because in the midst of the world I know how to wear the mask of a scoffer upon my face; and yet, how many a time at the sight of a cemetery by moonlight have I not asked myself whether it were not better to join those sleeping there!"

"Oh! and your friends?" she said. "You do not think of them."

"My friends! What friends? Have I any? Who cares for me?" And he accompanied the last words with a kind of whistling of the lips.

But they were obliged to separate from each other because of a great pile of chairs that a man was carrying behind them. He was so overladen with them that one could only see the tips of his wooden shoes and the ends of his two outstretched arms. It was Lestiboudois, the gravedigger, who was carrying the church chairs about amongst the people. Alive to all that concerned his interests, he had hit upon this means of turning the show to account; and his idea was succeeding, for he no longer knew which way to turn. In fact, the villagers, who were hot, quarrelled for these seats, whose straw smelt of incense, and they leant against the thick backs, stained with the wax of candles, with a certain veneration.

Madame Bovary again took Rodolphe's arm; he went on as if speaking to himself—

"Yes, I have missed so many things. Always alone! Ah! if I had some aim in life, if I had met some love, if I had found someone! Oh, how I would have spent all the energy of which I am capable, surmounted everything, overcome everything!"

"Yet it seems to me," said Emma, "that you are not to be pitied."

"Ah! you think so?" said Rodolphe.

"For, after all," she went on, "you are free—" she hesitated, "rich—"

"Do not mock me," he replied.

And she protested that she was not mocking him, when the report of a cannon resounded. Immediately all began hustling one another pell-mell towards the village.

It was a false alarm. The prefect seemed not to be coming, and the members of the jury felt much embarrassed, not knowing if they ought to begin the meeting or still wait.

At last at the end of the Place a large hired landau appeared, drawn by two thin horses, whom a coachman in a white hat was whipping lustily. Binet had only just

time to shout, "Present arms!" and the colonel to imitate him. All ran towards the
enclosure; everyone pushed forward. A few even forgot their collars; but the
equipage of the prefect seemed to anticipate the crowd, and the two yoked jades,
trapesing in their harness, came up at a little trot in front of the peristyle of the
townhall at the very moment when the National Guard and firemen deployed,
beating drums and marking time.

"Present!" shouted Binet.

"Halt!" shouted the colonel. "Left about, march."

And after presenting arms, during which the clang of the band, letting loose,
rang out like a brass kettle rolling downstairs, all the guns were lowered. Then was
seen stepping down from the carriage a gentleman in a short coat with silver braiding, with bald brow, and wearing a tuft of hair at the back of his head, of a sallow
complexion and the most benign appearance. His eyes, very large and covered by
heavy fids, were half-closed to look at the crowd, while at the same time he raised
his sharp nose, and forced a smile upon his sunken mouth. He recognised the
mayor by his scarf, and explained to him that the prefect was not able to come. He
himself was a councillor at the prefecture; then he added a few apologies. Monsieur
Tuvache answered them with compliments; the other confessed himself nervous;
and they remained thus, face to face, their foreheads almost touching, with the
members of the jury all round, the municipal council, the notable personages, the
National Guard and the crowd. The councillor pressing his little cocked hat to his
breast repeated his bows, while Tuvache, bent like a bow, also smiled, stammered,
tried to say something, protested his devotion to the monarchy and the honour that
was being done to Yonville.

Hippolyte, the groom from the inn, took the head of the horses from the
coachman, and, limping along with his clubfoot, led them to the door of the Lion
d'Or where a number of peasants collected to look at the carriage. The drum beat,
the howitzer thundered, and the gentlemen one by one mounted the platform,
where they sat down in red utrecht velvet arm-chairs that had been lent by Madame
Tuvache.

All these people looked alike. Their fair flabby faces, somewhat tanned by the
sun, were the colour of sweet cider, and their puffy whiskers emerged from stiff
collars, kept up by white cravats with broad bows. All the waistcoats were of velvet, double-breasted; all the watches had, at the end of a long ribbon, an oval cor-
nelian seal; everyone rested his two hands on his thighs, carefully stretching the
stride of their trousers, whose unspunged glossy cloth shone more brilliantly than
the leather of his heavy boots.

The ladies of the company stood at the back under the vestibule between the
pillars, while the common herd was opposite, standing up or sitting on chairs. As a

matter of fact, Lestiboudois had brought thither all those that he had moved from the field, and he even kept running back every minute to fetch others from the church. He caused such confusion with this piece of business that one had great difficulty in getting to the small steps of the platform.

"I think," said Monsieur Lheureux to the chemist, who was passing to his place, "that they ought to have put up two Venetian masts with something rather severe and rich for ornaments; it would have been a very pretty effect."

"To be sure," replied Homais; "but what can you expect? The mayor took everything on his own shoulders. He hasn't much taste. Poor Tuvache! and he is even completely destitute of what is called the genius of art."

Rodolphe, meanwhile, with Madame Bovary, had gone up to the first floor of the townhall, to the "council-room," and, as it was empty, he declared that they could enjoy the sight there more comfortably. He fetched three stools from the round table under the bust of the monarch, and having carried them to one of the windows, they sat down by each other.

There was commotion on the platform, long whisperings, much parleying. At last the councillor got up. They knew now that his name was Lieuvain, and in the crowd the name was passed from one to the other. After he had collated a few pages, and bent over them to see better, he began—

"Gentlemen! May I be permitted first of all (before addressing you on the object of our meeting to-day, and this sentiment will, I am sure, be shared by you all), may I be permitted, I say, to pay a tribute to the higher administration, to the government, to the monarch, gentlemen, our sovereign, to that beloved king, to whom no branch of public or private prosperity is a matter of indifference, and who directs with a hand at once so firm and wise the chariot of the state amid the incessant perils of a stormy sea, knowing, moreover, how to make peace respected as well as war, industry, commerce, agriculture, and the fine arts."

"I ought," said Rodolphe, "to get back a little further."

"Why?" said Emma.

But at this moment the voice of the councillor rose to an extraordinary pitch. He declaimed—

"This is no longer the time, gentlemen, when civil discord ensanguined our public places, when the landlord, the businessman, the working-man himself, falling asleep at night, lying down to peaceful sleep, trembled lest he should be awakened suddenly by the noise of incendiary tocsins, when the most subversive doctrines audaciously sapped foundations."

"Well, someone down there might see me," Rodolphe resumed, "then I should have to invent excuses for a fortnight; and with my bad reputation—"

"Oh, you are slandering yourself," said Emma.

"No! It is dreadful, I assure you."

"But, gentlemen," continued the councillor, "if, banishing from my memory the remembrance of these sad pictures, I carry my eyes back to the actual situation of our dear country, what do I see there? Everywhere commerce and the arts are flourishing; everywhere new means of communication, like so many new arteries in the body of the state, establish within it new relations. Our great industrial centres have recovered all their activity; religion, more consolidated, smiles in all hearts; our ports are full, confidence is born again, and France breathes once more!"

"Besides," added Rodolphe, "perhaps from the world's point of view they are right."

"How so?" she asked.

"What!" said he. "Do you not know that there are souls constantly tormented? They need by turns to dream and to act, the purest passions and the most turbulent joys, and thus they fling themselves into all sorts of fantasies, of follies."

Then she looked at him as one looks at a traveller who has voyaged over strange lands, and went on—

"We have not even this distraction, we poor women!"

"A sad distraction, for happiness isn't found in it."

"But is it ever found?' she asked.

"Yes; one day it comes," he answered.

"And this is what you have understood," said the councillor. "You, farmers, agricultural labourers! you pacific pioneers of a work that belongs wholly to civilisation! you, men of progress and morality, you have understood, I say, that political storms are even more redoubtable than atmospheric disturbances!"

"It comes one day," repeated Rodolphe, "one day suddenly, and when one is despairing of it. Then the horizon expands; it is as if a voice cried, 'It is here!' You feel the need of confiding the whole of your life, of giving everything, sacrificing everything to this being. There is no need for explanations; they understand one another. They have seen each other in dreams!" (And he looked at her.) "In fine, here it is, this treasure so sought after, here before you. It glitters, it flashes; yet one still doubts, one does not believe it; one remains dazzled, as if one went out from darkness into light."

And as he ended Rodolphe suited the action to the word. He passed his hand

over his face, like a man seized with giddiness. Then he let it fall on Emma's. She
took hers away.

"And who would be surprised at it, gentlemen? He only who was so blind, so
plunged (I do not fear to say it), so plunged in the prejudices of another age as still
to misunderstand the spirit of agricultural populations. Where, indeed, is to be
found more patriotism than in the country, greater devotion to the public welfare,
more intelligence, in a word? And, gentlemen, I do not mean that superficial intelligence, vain ornament of idle minds, but rather that profound and balanced intelligence that applies itself above all else to useful objects, thus contributing to the
good of all, to the common amelioration and to the support of the state, born of
respect for law and the practice of duty——"

"Ah! again!" said Rodolphe. "Always 'duty.' I am sick of the word. They are a lot
of old blockheads in flannel vests and of old women with foot-warmers and
rosaries who constantly drone into our ears 'Duty, duty!' Ah! by Jove! one's duty
is to feel what is great, cherish the beautiful, and not accent all the conventions of
society with the ignominy that it imposes upon us."

"Yet—yet—" objected Madame Bovary.

"No, no! Why cry out against the passions? Are they not the one beautiful
thing on the earth, the source of heroism, of enthusiasm, of poetry, music, the arts,
of everything, in a word?"

"But one must," said Emma, "to some extent bow to the opinion of the world
and accept its moral code."

"Ah! but there are two," he replied. "The small, the conventional, that of men,
that which constantly changes, that brays out so loudly, that makes such a commotion here below, of the earth earthy, like the mass of imbeciles you see down there.
But the other, the eternal, that is about us and above, like the landscape that surrounds us, and the blue heavens that give us light."

Monsieur Lieuvain had just wiped his mouth with a pocket-handkerchief. He
continued—

"And what should I do here, gentlemen, pointing out to you the uses of agriculture? Who supplies our wants? Who provides our means of subsistence? Is it not
the agriculturist? The agriculturist, gentlemen, who, sowing with laborious hand
the fertile furrows of the country, brings forth the corn, which, being ground, is
made into a powder by means of ingenious machinery, comes out thence under the
name of flour, and from there, transported to our cities, is soon delivered at the
baker's, who makes it into food for poor and rich alike. Again, is it not the agricul-

turist who fattens, for our clothes, his abundant flocks in the pastures? For how should we clothe ourselves, how nourish ourselves, without the agriculturist? And, gentlemen, is it even necessary to go so far for examples? Who has not frequently reflected on all the momentous things that we get out of that modest animal, the ornament of poultry-yards, that provides us at once with a soft pillow for our bed, with succulent flesh for our tables, and eggs? But I should never end if I were to enumerate one after the other all the different products which the earth, well cultivated, like a generous mother, lavishes upon her children. Here it is the vine, elsewhere the apple tree for cider, there colza, farther on cheeses and flax. Gentlemen, let us not forget flax, which has made such great strides of late years, and to which I will more particularly call your attention."

He had no need to call it, for all the mouths of the multitude were wide open, as if to drink in his words. Tuvache by his side listened to him with staring eyes. Monsieur Derozerays from time to time softly closed his eyelids, and farther on the chemist, with his son Napoleon between his knees, put his hand behind his ear in order not to lose a syllable. The chins of the other members of the jury went slowly up and down in their waistcoats in sign of approval. The firemen at the foot of the platform rested on their bayonets; and Binet, motionless, stood with outturned elbows, the point of his sabre in the air. Perhaps he could hear, but certainly he could see nothing, because of the visor of his helmet, that fell down on his nose. His lieutenant, the youngest son of Monsieur Tuvache, had a bigger one, for his was enormous, and shook on his head, and from it an end of his cotton scarf peeped out. He smiled beneath it with a perfectly infantine sweetness, and his pale little face, whence drops were running, wore an expression of enjoyment and sleepiness.

The square as far as the houses was crowded with people. One saw folk leaning on their elbows at all the windows, others standing at doors, and Justin, in front of the chemist's shop, seemed quite transfixed by the sight of what he was looking at. In spite of the silence Monsieur Lieuvain's voice was lost in the air. It reached you in fragments of phrases, and interrupted here and there by the creaking of chairs in the crowd; then you suddenly heard the long bellowing of an ox, or else the bleating of the lambs, who answered one another at street corners. In fact, the cowherds and shepherds had driven their beasts thus far, and these lowed from time to time, while with their tongues they tore down some scrap of foliage that hung above their mouths.

Rodolphe had drawn nearer to Emma, and said to her in a low voice, speaking rapidly—

"Does not this conspiracy of the world revolt you? Is there a single sentiment it does not condemn? The noblest instincts, the purest sympathies are persecuted, slandered; and if at length two poor souls do meet, all is so organised that they cannot blend together. Yet they will make the attempt; they will flutter their wings; they will call upon each other. Oh! no matter. Sooner or later, in six months, ten years, they will come together, will love; for fate has decreed it, and they are born one for the other."

His arms were folded across his knees, and thus lifting his face towards Emma, close by her, he looked fixedly at her. She noticed in his eyes small golden lines radiating from black pupils; she even smelt the perfume of the pomade that made his hair glossy. Then a faintness came over her; she recalled the Viscount who had waltzed with her at Vaubyessard, and his beard exhaled like this air an odour of vanilla and citron, and mechanically she half-closed her eyes the better to breathe it in. But in making this movement, as she leant back in her chair, she saw in the distance, right on the line of the horizon, the old diligence the Hirondelle, that was slowly descending the hill of Leux, dragging after it a long trail of dust. It was in this yellow carriage that Léon had so often come back to her, and by this route down there that he had gone forever. She fancied she saw him opposite at his window; then all grew confused; clouds gathered; it seemed to her that she was again turning in the waltz under the light of the lustres on the arm of the Viscount, and that Léon was not far away, that he was coming; and yet all the time she was conscious of the scent of Rodolphe's head by her side. This sweetness of sensation pierced through her old desires, and these, like grains of sand under a gust of wind, eddied to and fro in the subtle breath of the perfume which suffused her soul. She opened wide her nostrils several times to drink in the freshness of the ivy round the capitals. She took off her gloves, she wiped her hands, then fanned her face with her handkerchief, while athwart the throbbing of her temples she heard the murmur of the crowd and the voice of the councillor intoning his phrases. He said—

"Continue, persevere; listen neither to the suggestions of routine, nor to the over-hasty councils of a rash empiricism. Apply yourselves, above all, to the amelioration of the soil, to good manures, to the development of the equine, bovine, ovine, and porcine races. Let these shows be to you pacific arenas, where the victor in leaving it will hold forth a hand to the vanquished, and will fraternise with him in the hope of better success. And you, aged servants, humble domestics, whose hard labour no Government up to this day has taken into consideration, come hither to receive the reward of your silent virtues, and be assured that the state henceforward has its eye upon you; that it encourages you, protects you; that it will accede to your just demands, and alleviate as much as in it lies the burden of your painful sacrifices."

Monsieur Lieuvain then sat down; Monsieur Derozerays got up, beginning another speech. His was not perhaps so florid as that of the councillor, but it recommended itself by a more direct style, that is to say, by more special knowledge and more elevated considerations. Thus the praise of the Government took up less space in it; religion and agriculture more. He showed in it the relations of these two, and how they had always contributed to civilisation. Rodolphe with Madame Bovary was talking dreams, presentiments, magnetism. Going back to the cradle of society, the orator painted those fierce times when men lived on acorns in the heart of woods. Then they had left off the skins of beasts, had put on cloth, tilled the soil, planted the vine. Was this a good, and in this discovery was there not more of injury than of gain? Monsieur Derozerays set himself this problem. From magnetism little by little Rodolphe had come to affinities, and while the president was citing Cincinnatus and his plough, Diocletian planting his cabbages, and the Emperors of China inaugurating the year by the sowing of seed, the young man was explaining to the young woman that these irresistible attractions find their cause in some previous state of existence.

"Thus we," he said, "why did we come to know one another? What chance willed it? It was because across the infinite, like two streams that flow but to unite, our special bents of mind had driven us towards each other."

And he seized her hand; she did not withdraw it.

"For good farming generally!" cried the president.

"Just now, for example, when I went to your house."

"To Monsieur Bizat of Quincampoix."

"Did I know I should accompany you?"

"Seventy francs."

"A hundred times I wished to go; and I followed you—I remained."

"Manures!"

"And I shall remain to-night, to-morrow, all other days, all my life!"

"To Monsieur Caron of Argueil, a gold medal!"

"For I have never in the society of any other person found so complete a charm."

"To Monsieur Bain of Givry-Saint-Martin."

"And I shall carry away with me the remembrance of you."

"For a merino ram!"

"But you will forget me; I shall pass away like a shadow."

"To Monsieur Belot of Notre-Dame."

"Oh, no! I shall be something in your thought, in your life, shall I not?"

"Porcine race; prizes—equal, to Messrs. Lehérissé and Cullembourg, sixty francs!"

Rodolphe was pressing her hand, and he felt it all warm and quivering like a captive dove that wants to fly away; but, whether she was trying to take it away or whether she was answering his pressure, she made a movement with her fingers. He exclaimed—

"Oh, I thank you! You do not repulse me! You are good! You understand that I am yours! Let me look at you; let me contemplate you!"

A gust of wind that blew in at the window ruffled the cloth on the table, and in the square below all the great caps of the peasant women were uplifted by it like the wings of white butterflies fluttering.

"Use of oil-cakes," continued the president. He was hurrying on: "Flemish manure—flax-growing—drainage—long leases—domestic service."

Rodolphe was no longer speaking. They looked at one another. A supreme desire made their dry lips tremble, and wearily, without an effort, their fingers intertwined.

"Catherine Nicaise Elizabeth Leroux, of Sassetot-la-Guerrière, for fifty-four years of service at the same farm, a silver medal—value, twenty-five francs!"

"Where is Catherine Leroux?" repeated the councillor.

She did not present herself, and one could hear voices whispering—

"Go up!"

"Don't be afraid!"

"Oh, how stupid she is!"

"Well, is she there?" cried Tuvache.

"Yes; here she is."

"Then let her come up!"

Then there came forward on the platform a little old woman with timid bearing, who seemed to shrink within her poor clothes. On her feet she wore heavy wooden clogs, and from her hips hung a large blue apron. Her pale face framed in a borderless cap was more wrinkled than a withered russet apple. And from the sleeves of her red jacket looked out two large hands with knotty joints, the dust of barns, the potash of washing the grease of wools had so encrusted, roughened, hardened these that they seemed dirty, although they had been rinsed in clear water; and by dint of long service they remained half open, as if to bear humble witness for themselves of so much suffering endured. Something of monastic rigidity dignified her face. Nothing of sadness or of emotion weakened that pale look. In her constant living with animals she had caught their dumbness and their calm. It was the first time that she found herself in the midst of so large a company, and inwardly scared by the flags, the drums, the gentlemen in frock-coats, and the order of the councillor, she stood motionless, not knowing whether to advance or run away, nor why the crowd was pushing her and the jury were smiling at her. Thus stood before these radiant bourgeois this half-century of servitude.

"Approach, venerable Catherine Nicaise Elizabeth Leroux!" said the councillor, who had taken the list of prize-winners from the president; and, looking at the piece of paper and the old woman by turns, he repeated in a fatherly tone—

"Approach! approach!"

"Are you deaf?" said Tuvache, fidgeting in his arm-chair; and he began shouting in her ear, "Fifty-four years of service. A silver medal! Twenty-five francs! For you!"

Then, when she had her medal, she looked at it, and a smile of beatitude spread over her face; and as she walked away they could hear her muttering—

"I'll give it to our curé up home, to say some masses for me!"

"What fanaticism!' exclaimed the chemist, leaning across to the notary.

The meeting was over, the crowd dispersed, and now that the speeches had been read, each one fell back into his place again, and everything into the old grooves; the masters bullied the servants, and these struck the animals, indolent victors, going back to the stalls, a green crown on their horns.

The National Guards, however, had gone up to the first-floor of the townhall with buns spitted on their bayonets, and the drummer of the battalion carried a basket with bottles. Madame Bovary took Rodolphe's arm; he saw her home; they separated at her door; then he walked about alone in the meadow while he waited for the time of the banquet.

The feast was long, noisy, ill served; the guests were so crowded that they could hardly move their elbows; and the narrow planks used for forms almost broke down under their weight. They ate hugely. Each one stuffed himself on his own account. Sweat stood on every brow, and a whitish steam, like the vapour of a stream on an autumn morning, floated above the table between the hanging lamps. Rodolphe, leaning against the calico of the tent, was thinking so earnestly of Emma that he heard nothing. Behind him on the grass the servants were piling up the dirty plates, his neighbours were talking; he did not answer them; they filled his glass, and there was silence in his thoughts in spite of the growing noise. He was dreaming of what she had said, of the line of her lips; her face, as in a magic mirror, shone on the plates of the shakos, the folds of her gown fell along the walls, and days of love unrolled to all infinity before him in the vistas of the future.

He saw her again in the evening during the fireworks, but she was with her husband, Madame Homais, and the druggist, who was worrying about the danger of stray rockets, and every moment he left the company to go and give some advice to Binet.

The pyrotechnic pieces sent to Monsieur Tuvache had, through an excess of caution, been shut up in his cellar, and so the damp powder would not light, and the principal set piece, that was to represent a dragon biting his tail, failed completely.

Now and then a meagre Roman-candle went off; then the gaping crowd sent up a shout that mingled with the cry of the women, whose waists were being squeezed in the darkness. Emma silently nestled gently against Charles's shoulder; then, raising her chin, she watched the luminous rays of the rockets against the dark sky. Rodolphe gazed at her in the light of the burning lanterns.

They went out one by one. The stars shone out. A few drops of rain began to fall. She knotted her fichu round her bare head.

At this moment the councillor's carriage came out from the inn. His coachman, who was drunk, suddenly dozed off, and one could see from the distance, above the hood, between the two lanterns, the mass of his body, that swayed from right to left with the giving of the traces.

"Truly," said the druggist, "one ought to proceed most rigorously against drunkenness! I should like to see written up weekly at the door of the townhall on a board *ad hoc* the names of all those who during the week got intoxicated on alcohol. Besides, with regard to statistics, one would thus have, as it were, public records that one could refer to in case of need. But excuse me!"

And he once more ran off to the captain. The latter was going back to see his lathe again.

"Perhaps you would not do ill," Homais said to him, "to send one of your men, or to go yourself—"

"Leave me alone!" answered the tax-collector. "It's all right!"

"Do not be uneasy," said the druggist, when he returned to his friends. "Monsieur Binet has assured me that all precautions have been taken. No sparks have fallen; the pumps are full. Let us go to rest."

"*Ma foi!* I want it," said Madame Homais, yawning at large. "But never mind; we've had a beautiful day for our fête."

Rodolphe repeated in a low voice, and with a tender look, "Oh, yes! very beautiful!"

And having bowed to one another, they separated.

Two days later, in the Fanal de Rouen, there was a long article on the show. Homais had composed it with verve the very next morning.

"Why these festoons, these flowers, these garlands? Whither hurries this crowd like the waves of a furious sea under the torrents of a tropical sun pouring its heat upon our heads?"

Then he spoke of the condition of the peasants. Certainly the Government was doing much, but not enough. "Courage!" he cried to it; "a thousand reforms are indispensable; let us accomplish them!" Then touching on the entry of the councillor, he did not forget "the martial air of our militia," nor "our most merry village maidens," nor the "bald-headed old men like patriarchs who were there, and of whom some, the remnants of our phalanxes, still felt their hearts beat at the manly sound of the drums." He cited himself among the first of the members of the jury, and he even called attention in a note to the fact that Monsieur Homais, chemist, had sent a memoir on cider to the agricultural society. When he came to the distribution of the prizes, he painted the joy of the prize-winners in dithyrambic strophes. "The father embraced the son, the brother the brother, the husband his consort. More than one showed his humble medal with pride; and no doubt when he got home to his good housewife, he hung it up weeping on the modest walls of his cot.

"About six o'clock a banquet prepared in the meadow of Monsieur Leigeard brought together the principal personages of the fête. The greatest cordiality reigned here. Divers toasts were proposed: Monsieur Lieuvain, the King; Monsieur Tuvache, the Prefect; Monsieur Derozerays, Agriculture; Monsieur Homais, Industry and the Fine Arts, those twin sisters; Monsieur Leplichey, Progress. In the evening some brilliant fireworks on a sudden illumined the air. One would have called it a veritable kaleidoscope, a real operatic scene; and for a moment our little locality might have thought itself transported into the midst of a dream of the *Thousand and One Nights.*

"Let us state that no untoward event disturbed this family meeting." And he added: "Only the absence of the clergy was remarked. No doubt the priests understand progress in another fashion. Just as you please, messieurs the followers of Loyola!"

Chapter IX

SIX WEEKS PASSED. RODOLPHE DID NOT COME AGAIN. AT LAST ONE EVENING HE appeared.

The day after the show he had said to himself—

"We mustn't go back too soon; that would be a mistake."

And at the end of a week he had gone off hunting. After the hunting he had thought it was too late, and then he reasoned thus—

"If from the first day she loved me, she must from impatience to see me again love me more. Let's go on with it!"

And he knew that his calculation had been right when, on entering the room, he saw Emma turn pale.

She was alone. The day was drawing in. The small muslin curtain along the windows deepened the twilight, and the gilding of the barometer, on which the rays of the sun fell, shone in the looking-glass between the meshes of the coral.

Rodolphe remained standing, and Emma hardly answered his first conventional phrases.

"I," he said, "have been busy. I have been ill."

"Seriously?" she cried.

"Well," said Rodolphe, sitting down at her side on a footstool, "no; it was because I did not want to come back."

"Why?"

"Can you not guess?"

He looked at her again, but so hard that she lowered her head, blushing. He went on—

"Emma!"

"Sir," she said, drawing back a little.

"Ah! you see," replied he in a melancholy voice, "that I was right not to come back; for this name, this name that fills my whole soul, and that escaped me, you forbid me to use! Madame Bovary! why all the world calls you thus! Besides, it is not your name; it is the name of another!" he repeated, "of another!" And he hid his face in his hands. "Yes, I think of you constantly. The memory of you drives me to despair. Ah! forgive me! I will leave you! Farewell! I will go far away, so far that you will never hear of me again; and yet—to-day—I know not what force impelled me towards you. For one does not struggle against Heaven; one cannot resist the smile of angels; one is carried away by that which is beautiful, charming, adorable."

It was the first time that Emma had heard such words spoken to herself, and her pride, like one who reposes bathed in warmth, expanded softly and fully at this glowing language.

"But if I did not come," he continued, "if I could not see you, at least I have gazed long on all that surrounds you. At night—every night—I arose; I came hither; I watched your house, its glimmering in the moon, the trees in the garden swaying before your window, and the little lamp, a gleam shining through the window-panes in the darkness. Ah! you never knew that there, so near you, so far from you, was a poor wretch!"

She turned towards him with a sob.

"Oh, you are good!" she said.

"No, I love you, that is all! You do not doubt that! Tell me—one word—only one word!"

And Rodolphe imperceptibly glided from the footstool to the ground; but a sound of wooden shoes was heard in the kitchen, and he noticed the door of the room was not closed.

"How kind it would be of you," he went on, rising, "if you would humour a whim of mine." It was to go over her house; he wanted to know it; and Madame Bovary seeing no objection to this, they both rose, when Charles came in.

"Good morning, doctor," Rodolphe said to him.

The doctor, flattered at this unexpected title, launched out into obsequious phrases. Of this the other took advantage to pull himself together a little.

"Madame was speaking to me," he then said, "about her health."

Charles interrupted him; he had indeed a thousand anxieties; his wife's palpitations of the heart were beginning again. Then Rodolphe asked if riding would not be good.

"Certainly! excellent! just the thing! There's an idea! You ought to follow it up."

And as she objected that she had no horse, Monsieur Rodolphe offered one. She refused his offer; he did not insist. Then to explain his visit he said that his ploughman, the man of the blood-letting, still suffered from giddiness.

"I'll call round," said Bovary.

"No, no! I'll send him to you; we'll come; that will be more convenient for you."

"Ah! very good! I thank you."

And as soon as they were alone, "Why don't you accept Monsieur Boulanger's kind offer?"

She assumed a sulky air, invented a thousand excuses, and finally declared that perhaps it would look odd.

"Well, what the deuce do I care for that?" said Charles, making a pirouette. "Health before everything! You are wrong."

"And how do you think I can ride when I haven't got a habit?"

"You must order one." he answered.

The riding-habit decided her.

When the habit was ready, Charles wrote to Monsieur Boulanger that his wife was at his command, and that they counted on his good-nature.

The next day at noon Rodolphe appeared at Charles's door with two saddle-horses. One had pink rosettes at his ears and a deerskin side-saddle.

Rodolphe had put on high soft boots, saying to himself that no doubt she had never seen anything like them. In fact, Emma was charmed with his appearance as he stood on the landing in his great velvet coat and white corduroy breeches. She was ready; she was waiting for him.

Justin escaped from the chemist's to see her start, and the chemist also came out. He was giving Monsieur Boulanger a little good advice.

"An accident happens so easily. Be careful! Your horses perhaps are mettlesome.

She heard a noise above her; it was Félicité drumming on the window-panes to amuse little Berthe. The child blew her a kiss; her mother answered with a wave of her whip.

"A pleasant ride!" cried Monsieur Homais. "Prudence! above all, prudence!' And he flourished his newspaper as he saw them disappear.

As soon as he felt the ground, Emma's horse set off at a gallop. Rodolphe galloped by her side. Now and then they exchanged a word. Her figure slightly bent, her hand well up, and her right arm stretched out, she gave herself up to the cadence of the movement that rocked her in her saddle. At the bottom of the hill Rodolphe gave his horse its head; they started together at a bound, then at the top suddenly the horses stopped, and her large blue veil fell about her.

It was early in October. There was fog over the land. Hazy clouds hovered on the horizon between the outlines of the hills; others, rent asunder, floated up and disappeared. Sometimes through a rift in the clouds, beneath a ray of sunshine, gleamed from afar the roofs of Yonville, with the gardens at the water's edge, the yards, the walls and the church steeple. Emma half closed her eyes to pick out her house, and never had this poor village where she lived appeared so small. From the height on which they were the whole valley seemed an immense pale lake sending off its vapour into the air. Clumps of trees here and there stood out like black rocks, and the tall lines of the poplars that rose above the mist were like a beach stirred by the wind.

By the side, on the turf between the pines, a brown light shimmered in the warm atmosphere. The earth, ruddy like the powder of tobacco, deadened the noise of their steps, and with the edge of their shoes the horses as they walked kicked the fallen fir cones in front of them.

Rodolphe and Emma thus went along the skirt of the wood. She turned away from time to time to avoid his look, and then she saw only the pine trunks in lines, whose monotonous succession made her a little giddy. The horses were panting; the leather of the saddles creaked.

Just as they were entering the forest the sun shone out.

"God protects us!" said Rodolphe.

"Do you think so?" she said.

"Forward! forward!" he continued.

He "tchk'd" with his tongue. The two beasts set off at a trot. Long ferns by the roadside caught in Emma's stirrup. Rodolphe leant forward and removed them as they rode along. At other times, to turn aside the branches, he passed close to her, and Emma felt his knee brushing against her leg. The sky was now blue, the leaves no longer stirred. There were spaces full of heather in flower, and plots of violets alternated with the confused patches of the trees that were grey, fawn, or golden coloured, according to the nature of their leaves. Often in the thicket was heard the fluttering of wings, or else the hoarse, soft cry of the ravens flying off amidst the oaks.

They dismounted. Rodolphe fastened up the horses. She walked on in front on the moss between the paths. But her long habit got in her way, although she held it up by the skirt; and Rodolphe, walking behind her, saw between the black cloth and the black shoe the fineness of her white stocking, that seemed to him as if it were a part of her nakedness.

She stopped. "I am tired," she said.

"Come, try again," he went on. "Courage!"

Then some hundred paces farther on she again stopped, and through her veil, that fell sideways from her man's hat over her hips, her face appeared in a bluish transparency as if she were floating under azure waves.

"But where are we going?"

He did not answer. She was breathing irregularly. Rodolphe looked round him biting his moustache. They came to a larger space where the coppice had been cut. They sat down on the trunk of a fallen tree, and Rodolphe began speaking to her of his love. He did not begin by frightening her with compliments. He was calm, serious, melancholy.

Emma listened to him with bowed head, and stirred the bits of wood on the ground with the tip of her foot.

But at the words, "Are not our destinies now one?—"

"Oh, no!" she replied. "You know that well. It is impossible!"

She rose to go. He seized her by the wrist. She stopped. Then, having gazed at him for a few moments with an amorous and humid look, she said hurriedly—

"Ah! do not speak of it again! Where are the horses? Let us go back."

He made a gesture of anger and annoyance. She repeated—

"Where are the horses? Where are the horses?"

Then smiling a strange smile, his pupil fixed, his teeth set, he advanced with outstretched arms. She recoiled trembling. She stammered—

"Oh, you frighten me! You hurt me! Let me go!"

"If it must be," he went on, his face changing; and he again became respectful, caressing, timid. She gave him her arm. They went back. He said—

"What was the matter with you? Why? I do not understand. You were mistaken, no doubt. In my soul you are as a Madonna on a pedestal, in a place lofty, secure, immaculate. But I want you for my life. I must have your eyes, your voice, your thought! Be my friend, my sister, my angel!"

And he put out his arm round her waist. She feebly tried to disengage herself. He supported her thus as they walked along.

But they heard the two horses browsing on the leaves.

"Oh! one moment!" said Rodolphe. "Do not let us go! Stay!"

He drew her farther on to a small pool where duckweeds made a greenness on the water. Faded waterlilies lay motionless between the reeds. At the noise of their steps in the grass, frogs jumped away to hide themselves.

"I am wrong! I am wrong!" she said. "I am mad to listen to you!"

"Why? Emma! Emma!"

"Oh, Rodolphe!" said the young woman slowly, leaning on his shoulder.

The cloth of her habit caught against the velvet of his coat. She threw back her white neck, swelling with a sigh, and faltering, in tears, with a long shudder and hiding her face, she gave herself up to him.

The shades of night were falling; the horizontal sun passing between the branches dazzled the eyes. Here and there around her, in the leaves or on the ground, trembled luminous patches, as if humming-birds flying about had scattered their feathers. Silence was everywhere; something sweet seemed to come forth from the trees; she felt her heart, whose beating had begun again, and the blood coursing through her flesh like a stream of milk. Then far away, beyond the wood, on the other hills, she heard a vague prolonged cry, a voice which lingered, and in silence she heard it mingling like music with the last pulsations of her throbbing nerves. Rodolphe, a cigar between his lips, was mending with his penknife one of the two broken bridles.

They returned to Yonville by the same road. On the mud they saw again the traces of their horses side by side, the same thickets, the same stones in the grass;

nothing around them seemed changed; and yet for her something had happened more stupendous than if the mountains had moved in their places. Rodolphe now and again bent forward and took her hand to kiss it.

She was charming on horseback—upright, with her slender waist, her knee bent on the mane of her horse, her face somewhat flushed by the fresh air in the red of the evening.

On entering Yonville she made her horse prance in the road. People looked at her from the windows.

At dinner her husband thought she looked well, but she pretended not to hear him when he inquired about her ride, and she remained sitting there with her elbow at the side of her plate between the two lighted candles.

"Emma!" he said.

"What?"

"Well, I spent the afternoon at Monsieur Alexandre's. He has an old cob, still very fine, only a little broken-kneed, and that could be bought, I am sure, for a hundred crowns." He added, "And thinking it might please you, I have bespoken it—bought it. Have I done right? Do tell me!"

She nodded her head in assent; then a quarter of an hour later—

"Are you going out to-night?" she asked.

"Yes. Why?"

"Oh, nothing, nothing, my dear!"

And as soon as she had got rid of Charles she went and shut herself up in her room.

At first she felt stunned; she saw the trees, the paths, the ditches, Rodolphe, and she again felt the pressure of his arm, while the leaves rustled and the reeds whistled.

But when she saw herself in the glass she wondered at her face. Never had her eyes been so large, so black, of so profound a depth. Something subtle about her being transfigured her. She repeated, "I have a lover! a lover!" delighting at the idea as if a second puberty had come to her. So at last she was to know those joys of love, that fever of happiness of which she had despaired! She was entering upon marvels where all would be passion, ecstasy, delirium. An azure infinity encompassed her, the heights of sentiment sparkled under her thought, and ordinary existence appeared only afar off, down below in the shade, through the interspaces of these heights.

Then she recalled the heroines of the books that she had read, and the lyric legion of these adulterous women began to sing in her memory with the voice of sisters that charmed her. She became herself, as it were, an actual part of these imaginings, and realised the love-dream of her youth as she saw herself in this type of amorous women whom she had so envied. Besides, Emma felt a satisfaction of revenge. Had she not suffered enough? But now she triumphed, and the love so long pent up burst forth in full joyous bubblings. She tasted it without remorse, without anxiety, without trouble.

The day following passed with a new sweetness. They made vows to one another. She told him of her sorrows. Rodolphe interrupted her with kisses; and she, looking at him through half-closed eyes, asked him to call her again by her name—to say that he loved her. They were in the forest, as yesterday, in the shed of some wooden-shoe maker. The walls were of straw, and the roof so low they had to stoop. They were seated side by side on a bed of dry leaves.

From that day forth they wrote to one another regularly every evening. Emma placed her letter at the end of the garden, by the river, in a fissure of the wall. Rodolphe came to fetch it, and put another there, that she always found fault with as too short.

One morning, when Charles had gone out before daybreak, she was seized with the fancy to see Rodolphe at once. She would go quickly to La Huchette, stay there an hour, and be back again at Yonville while everyone was still asleep. This idea made her pant with desire, and she soon found herself in the middle of the field, walking with rapid steps, without looking behind her.

Day was just breaking. Emma from afar recognised her lover's house. Its two dove-tailed weathercocks stood out black against the pale dawn.

Beyond the farmyard there was a detached building that she thought must be the château. She entered it as if the doors at her approach had opened wide of their own accord. A large straight staircase led up to the corridor. Emma raised the latch of a door, and suddenly at the end of the room she saw a man sleeping. It was Rodolphe. She uttered a cry.

"You here? You here?" he repeated. "How did you manage to come? Ah! your dress is damp."

This first piece of daring successful, now every time Charles went out early Emma dressed quickly and slipped on tiptoe down the steps that led to the waterside.

But when the plank for the cows was taken up, she had to go by the walls alongside of the river; the bank was slippery; in order not to fall she caught hold of the tufts of faded wallflowers. Then she went across ploughed fields, in which she sank, stumbling, and clogging her thin shoes. Her scarf, knotted round her head, fluttered to the wind in the meadows. She was afraid of the oxen; she began to run; she arrived out of breath, with rosy cheeks, and breathing out from her whole person a fresh perfume of sap, of verdure, of the open air. At this hour Rodolphe still slept. It was like a spring morning coming into his room.

The yellow curtains along the windows let a heavy, whitish light enter softly. Emma felt about, opening and closing her eyes, while the drops of dew hanging from her hair formed, as it were, a topaz aureole around her face. Rodolphe, laughing, drew her to him and pressed her to his breast.

Then she examined the apartment, opened the drawers of the tables, combed her hair with his comb, and looked at herself in his shaving-glass. Often she even put between her teeth the big pipe that lay on the table by the bed, amongst lemons and pieces of sugar near a bottle of water.

It took them a good quarter of an hour to say good-bye. Then Emma cried. She would have wished never to leave Rodolphe. Something stronger than herself forced her to him; so much so, that one day, seeing her come unexpectedly, he frowned as one put out.

"What is the matter with you?" she said. "Are you ill? Tell me!"

At last he declared with a serious air that her visits were becoming imprudent—that she was compromising herself.

Chapter X

GRADUALLY RODOLPHE'S FEARS TOOK POSSESSION OF HER. AT FIRST, LOVE had intoxicated her, and she had thought of nothing beyond. But now that he was indispensable to her life, she feared to lose anything of this, or even that it should be disturbed. When she came back from his house, she looked all about her, anxiously watching every form that passed in the horizon, and every village window from which she could be seen. She listened for steps, cries, the noise of the ploughs, and she stopped short, white, and trembling more than the aspen leaves swaying overhead.

One morning as she was thus returning, she suddenly thought she saw the long barrel of a carbine that seemed to be aimed at her. It stuck outsideways from the end of a small tub half-buried in the grass on the edge of a ditch. Emma, half-fainting with terror, nevertheless walked on, and a man stepped out of the tub like a Jack-in-the-box. He had gaiters buckled up to the knees, his cap pulled down over his eyes, trembling lips, and a red nose. It was Captain Binet lying in ambush for wild ducks.

"You ought to have called out long ago!" he exclaimed. "When one sees a gun, one should always give warning."

The tax-collector was thus trying to hide the fright he had had, for a prefectorial order having prohibited duck-hunting except in boats, Monsieur Binet, despite his respect for the laws, was infringing them, and so he every moment expected to see the rural guard turn up. But this anxiety whetted his pleasure, and, all alone in his tub, he congratulated himself on his luck and on his 'cuteness.

At sight of Emma he seemed relieved from a great weight, and at once entered upon a conversation.

"It isn't warm; it's nipping."

Emma answered nothing. He went on—

"And you're out so early?"

"Yes," she said stammering; "I am just coming from the nurse where my child is."

"Ah! very good! very good! For myself, I am here, just as you see me, since break of day; but the weather is so muggy, that unless one had the bird at the mouth of the gun—"

"Good evening, Monsieur Binet," she interrupted him, turning on her heel.

"Your servant, madame," he replied drily; and he went back into his tub.

Emma regretted having left the tax-collector so abruptly. No doubt he would form unfavourable conjectures. The story about the nurse was the worst possible excuse, everyone at Yonville knowing that the little Bovary had been at home with her parents for a year. Besides, no one was living in this direction; this path led only to La Huchette. Binet, then, would guess whence she came, and he would not keep silence; he would talk, that was certain. She remained until evening racking her brain with every conceivable lying project, and had constantly before her eyes that imbecile with the game-bag.

Charles after dinner, seeing her gloomy, proposed, by way of distraction, to take her to the chemist's, and the first person she caught sight of in the shop was the tax-collector again. He was standing in front of the counter, lit up by the gleams of the red bottle, and was saying—

"Please give me half an ounce of vitriol."

"Justin," cried the druggist, "bring us the sulphuric acid." Then to Emma, who was going up to Madame Homais's room, "No, stay here; it isn't worth while going up; she is just coming down. Warm yourself at the stove in the meantime. Excuse me. Good-day, doctor" (for the chemist much enjoyed pronouncing the word "doctor," as if addressing another by it reflected on himself some of the grandeur that he found in it). "Now, take care not to upset the mortars! You'd better fetch some chairs from the little room; you know very well that the arm-chairs are not to be taken out of the drawing-room."

And to put his arm-chair back in its place he was darting away from the counter, when Binet asked him for half an ounce of sugar acid.

"Sugar acid!" said the chemist contemptuously, "don't know it; I'm ignorant of it! But perhaps you want oxalic acid. It is oxalic acid, isn't it?"

Binet explained that he wanted a corrosive to make himself some copper-water with which to remove rust from his hunting things.

Emma shuddered. The chemist began saying—

"Indeed the weather is not propitious on account of the damp."

"Nevertheless," replied the tax-collector, with a sly look, "there are people who like it."

She was stifling.

"And give me—"

"Will he never go?" thought she.

"Half an ounce of resin and turpentine, four ounces of yellow wax, and three half ounces of animal charcoal, if you please, to clean the varnished leather of my togs."

The druggist was beginning to cut the wax when Madame Homais appeared, Irma in her arms, Napoleon by her side, and Athalie following. She sat down on the velvet seat by the window, and the lad squatted down on a footstool, while his eldest sister hovered round the jujube box near her papa. The latter was filling funnels and corking phials, sticking on labels, making up parcels. Around him all were silent; only from time to time were heard the weights jingling in the balance, and a few low words from the chemist giving directions to his pupil.

"And how's the little woman?" suddenly asked Madame Homais.

"Silence!" exclaimed her husband, who was writing down some figures in his waste-book.

"Why didn't you bring her?" she went on in a low voice.

"Hush! hush!" said Emma, pointing with her finger to the druggist.

But Binet, quite absorbed in looking over his bill, had probably heard nothing. At last he went out. Then Emma, relieved, uttered a deep sigh.

"How hard you are breathing!" said Madame Homais.

"Well, you see, it's rather warm," she replied.

So the next day they talked over how to arrange their rendezvous. Emma wanted to bribe her servant with a present, but it would be better to find some safe house at Yonville. Rodolphe promised to look for one.

All through the winter, three or four times a week, in the dead of night he came to the garden. Emma had on purpose taken away the key of the gate, which Charles thought lost.

To call her, Rodolphe threw a sprinkle of sand at the shutters. She jumped up with a start; but sometimes he had to wait, for Charles had a mania for chatting by the fireside, and he would not stop. She was wild with impatience; if her eyes could have done it, she would have hurled him out at the window. At last she would begin to undress, then take up a book, and go on reading very quietly as if the book amused her. But Charles, who was in bed, called to her to come too.

"Come, now, Emma," he said, "it is time."

"Yes, I am coming," she answered.

Then, as the candles dazzled him, he turned to the wall and fell asleep. She escaped, smiling, palpitating, undressed.

Rodolphe had a large cloak; he wrapped her in it, and putting his arm round her waist, he drew her without a word to the end of the garden.

It was in the arbour, on the same seat of old sticks where formerly Léon had looked at her so amorously on the summer evenings. She never thought of him now.

The stars shone through the leafless jasmine branches. Behind them they heard the river flowing, and now and again on the bank the rustling of the dry reeds. Masses of shadow here and there loomed out in the darkness, and sometimes, vibrating with one movement, they rose up and swayed like immense black waves pressing forward to engulf them. The cold of the nights made them clasp closer;

the sighs of their lips seemed to them deeper; their eyes, that they could hardly see, larger; and in the midst of the silence low words were spoken that fell on their souls sonorous, crystalline, and that reverberated in multiplied vibrations.

When the night was rainy, they took refuge in the consulting-room between the cart-shed and the stable. She lighted one of the kitchen candles that she had hidden behind the books. Rodolphe settled down there as if at home. The sight of the library, of the bureau, of the whole apartment, in fine, excited his merriment, and he could not refrain from making jokes about Charles, which rather embarrassed Emma. She would have liked to see him more serious, and even on occasions more dramatic; as, for example, when she thought she heard a noise of approaching steps in the alley.

"Someone is coming!" she said.

He blew out the light.

"Have you your pistols?"

"Why?"

"Why, to defend yourself," replied Emma.

"From your husband? Oh, poor devil!" And Rodolphe finished his sentence with a gesture that said, "I could crush him with a flip of my finger."

She was wonder-stricken at his bravery, although she felt in it a sort of indecency and a naïve coarseness that scandalised her.

Rodolphe reflected a good deal on the affair of the pistols. If she had spoken seriously, it was very ridiculous, he thought, even odious; for he had no reason to hate the good Charles, not being what is called devoured by jealousy; and on this subject Emma had taken a great vow that he did not think in the best of taste.

Besides, she was growing very sentimental. She had insisted on exchanging miniatures; they had cut off handfuls of hair, and now she was asking for a ring— a real wedding-ring, in sign of an eternal union. She often spoke to him of the evening chimes, of the voices of nature. Then she talked to him of her mother— hers! and of his mother—his! Rodolphe had lost his twenty years ago. Emma none the less consoled him with caressing words as one would have done a lost child, and she sometimes even said to him, gazing at the moon—

"I am sure that above there together they approve of our love."

But she was so pretty. He had possessed so few women of such ingenuousness. This love without debauchery was a new experience for him, and, drawing him out of his lazy habits, caressed at once his pride and his sensuality. Emma's enthusiasm, which his bourgeois good sense disdained, seemed to him in his heart of hearts charming, since it was lavished on him. Then, sure of being loved, he no longer kept up appearances, and insensibly his ways changed.

He had no longer, as formerly, words so gentle that they made her cry, nor passionate caresses that made her mad, so that their great love, which engrossed her life, seemed to lessen beneath her like the water of a stream absorbed into its channel, and she could see the bed of it. She would not believe it; she redoubled in tenderness, and Rodolphe concealed his indifference less and less.

She did not know if she regretted having yielded to him, or whether she did not wish, on the contrary, to enjoy him the more. The humiliation of feeling herself weak was turning to rancour, tempered by their voluptuous pleasures. It was not affection; it was like a continual seduction. He subjugated her; she almost feared him.

Appearances, nevertheless, were calmer than ever, Rodolphe having succeeded in carrying out the adultery after his own fancy; and at the end of six months, when the spring-time came, they were to one another like a married couple, tranquilly keeping up a domestic flame.

It was the time of year when old Rouault sent his turkey in remembrance of the setting of his leg. The present always arrived with a letter. Emma cut the string that tied it to the basket, and read the following lines:—

MY DEAR CHILDREN—I hope this will find you in good health, and that it will be as good as the others, for it seems to me a little more tender, if I may venture to say so, and heavier. But next time, for a change, I'll give you a turkey-cock, unless you have a preference for some dabs; and send me back the hamper, if you please, with the two old ones. I have had an accident with my cart-sheds, whose covering flew off one windy night among the trees. The harvest has not been over-good either. Finally, I don't know when I shall come to see you. It is so difficult now to leave the house since I am alone, my poor Emma.

Here there was a break in the lines, as if the old fellow had dropped his pen to dream a little while.

For myself, I am very well, except for a cold I caught the other day at the fair at Yvetot, where I had gone to hire a shepherd, having turned away mine because he was too dainty. How we are to be pitied with such a lot of thieves! Besides, he was also rude. I heard from a pedlar, who, travelling through your part of the country this winter, had a tooth drawn, that Bovary was as usual working hard. That doesn't surprise me; and he showed me his tooth; we had some coffee together. I asked him if he had seen you, and he said not, but that he had seen two horses in the stables, from which I conclude that business is looking up. So much the better, my dear children, and may God send you every imaginable happiness! It grieves me not yet to have seen my dear little granddaughter, Berthe Bovary. I have planted an Orleans plum-tree for her in the garden under your room, and I won't have it touched unless it is to have jam made for her by and bye, that I will keep in the cupboard for her when she comes.

Good-bye, my dear children. I kiss you, my girl, you too, my son-in-law, and the little one on both cheeks. I am, with best compliments, your loving father,

THEODORE ROUAULT

She held the coarse paper in her fingers for some minutes. The spelling mistakes were interwoven one with the other, and Emma followed the kindly thought that cackled right through it like a hen half hidden in a hedge of thorns. The writing had been dried with ashes from the hearth, for a little grey powder slipped from the letter on to her dress, and she almost thought she saw her father bending over the hearth to take up the tongs. How long since she had been with him, sitting on the footstool in the chimney-corner, where she used to burn the end of a bit of wood in the great flame of the sea-sedges! She remembered the summer evenings all full of sunshine. The colts neighed when anyone passed by, and galloped, galloped. Under her window there was a beehive, and sometimes the bees wheeling round in the light struck against her window like rebounding balls of gold. What happiness there had been at that time, what freedom, what hope! What an abundance of illusions! Nothing was left of them now. She had got rid of them all in her soul's life, in all her successive conditions of life— maidenhood, her marriage, and her love—thus constantly losing them all her life through, like a traveller who leaves something of his wealth at every inn along his road.

But what then made her so unhappy? What was the extraordinary catastrophe that had transformed her? And she raised her head, looking round as if to seek the cause of that which made her suffer.

An April ray was dancing on the china of the whatnot; the fire burned; beneath her slippers she felt the softness of the carpet; the day was bright, the air warm, and she heard her child shouting with laughter.

In fact, the little girl was just then rolling on the lawn in the midst of the grass that was being turned. She was lying flat on her stomach at the top of a rick. The servant was holding her by her skirt. Lestiboudois was raking by her side, and every time he came near she lent forward, beating the air with both her arms.

"Bring her to me," said her mother, rushing to embrace her. "How I love you, my poor child! How I love you!"

Then noticing that the tips of her ears were rather dirty, she rang at once for warm water, and washed her, changed her linen, her stockings, her shoes, asked a thousand questions about her health, as if on the return from a long journey, and finally, kissing her again and crying a little, she gave her back to the servant, who stood quite thunderstricken at this excess of tenderness.

That evening Rodolphe found her more serious than usual.

"That will pass over," he concluded; "it's a whim."

And he missed three rendezvous running. When he did come, she showed herself cold and almost contemptuous.

"Ah! you're losing your time, my lady!"

And he pretended not to notice her melancholy sighs, nor the handkerchief she took out.

Then Emma repented. She even asked herself why she detested Charles; if it had not been better to have been able to love him? But he gave her no opportunities for such a revival of sentiment, so that she was much embarrassed by her desire for sacrifice, when the druggist came just in time to provide her with an opportunity.

Chapter XI

H E HAD RECENTLY READ A EULOGY ON A NEW METHOD FOR CURING CLUB-foot, and as he was a partisan of progress, he conceived the patriotic idea that Yonville, in order to keep to the fore, ought to have some operations for strephopody or club-foot.

"For," said he to Emma, "what risk is there? See" (and he enumerated on his fingers the advantages of the attempt), "success, almost certain relief and beautifying of the patient, celebrity acquired by the operator. Why, for example, should not your husband relieve poor Hippolyte of the Lion d'Or? Note that he would not fail to tell about his cure to all the travellers, and then" (Homais lowered his voice and looked round him) "who is to prevent me from sending a short paragraph on the subject to the paper? Eh! goodness me! an article gets about; it is talked of; it ends by making a snowball! And who knows? who knows?"

In fact, Bovary might succeed. Nothing proved to Emma that he was not clever; and what a satisfaction for her to have urged him to a step by which his reputation and fortune would be increased! She only wished to lean on something more solid than love.

Charles, urged by the druggist and by her, allowed himself to be persuaded. He sent to Rouen for Dr. Duval's volume, and every evening, holding his head between both hands, plunged into the reading of it.

While he was studying equinus, varus, and valgus, that is to say, *katastrephopody, endostrephopody,* and *exostrephopody* (or better, the various turnings of the foot downwards, inwards, and outwards, with the *hypostrephopody* and *anastrephopody*), otherwise torsion downwards and upwards, Monsieur Homais, with all sorts of arguments, was exhorting the lad at the inn to submit to the operation.

"You will scarcely feel, probably, a slight pain; it is a simple prick, like a little blood-letting, less than the extraction of certain corns."

Hippolyte, reflecting, rolled his stupid eyes.

"However," continued the chemist, "it doesn't concern me. It's for your sake, for pure humanity! I should like to see you, my friend, rid of your hideous caudication, together with that waddling of the lumbar regions which, whatever you say, must considerably interfere with you in the exercise of your calling."

Then Homais represented to him how much jollier and brisker he would feel afterwards, and even gave him to understand that he would be more likely to please the women; and the stable-boy began to smile heavily. Then he attacked him through his vanity—

"Aren't you a man? Hang it! what would you have done if you had had to go into the army, to go and fight beneath the standard? Ah! Hippolyte!"

And Homais retired, declaring that he could not understand this obstinacy, this blindness in refusing the benefactions of science.

The poor fellow gave way, for it was like a conspiracy. Binet, who never interfered with other people's business, Madame Lefrançois, Antémise, the neighbours, even the mayor, Monsieur Tuvache—everyone persuaded him, lectured him, shamed him; but what finally decided him was that it would cost him nothing. Bovary even undertook to provide the machine for the operation. This generosity was an idea of Emma's, and Charles consented to it, thinking in his heart of hearts that his wife was an angel.

So by the advice of the chemist, and after three fresh starts, he had a kind of box made by the carpenter, with the aid of the locksmith, that weighed about eight pounds, and in which iron, wood, sheet-iron, leather, screws, and nuts had not been spared.

But to know which of Hippolyte's tendons to cut, it was necessary first of all to find out what kind of club-foot he had.

He had a foot forming almost a straight line with the leg, which, however, did not prevent it from being turned in, so that it was an equinus together with something of a varus, or else a slight varus with a strong tendency to equinus. But with this equinus, wide in foot like a horse's hoof, with rugose skin, dry tendons, and large toes, on which the black nails looked as if made of iron, the club-foot ran about like a deer from morn till night. He was constantly to be seen on the Place, jumping round the carts, thrusting his limping foot forwards. He seemed even stronger on that leg than the other. By dint of hard service it had acquired, as it were, moral qualities of patience and energy; and when he was given some heavy work, he stood on it in preference to its fellow.

Now, as it was an equinus, it was necessary to cut the tendo Achillis, and, if need were, the anterior tibial muscle could be seen to afterwards for getting rid of the varus; for the doctor did not dare to risk both operations at once; he was even trembling already for fear of injuring some important region that he did not know.

Neither Ambrose Paré, applying for the first time since Celsus, after an interval of fifteen centuries, a ligature to an artery, nor Dupuytren, about to open an abcess in the brain, nor Gensoul when he first took away the superior maxilla, had hearts that trembled, hands that shook, minds so strained as Monsieur Bovary when he approached Hippolyte, his tenotome between his fingers. And as at hospitals, nearby on a table lay a heap of lint, with waxed thread, many bandages—a pyramid of bandages—every bandage to be found at the druggist's. It was Monsieur Homais who since morning had been organising all these preparations, as much to dazzle the multitude as to keep up his illusions. Charles pierced the skin; a dry crackling was heard. The tendon was cut, the operation over. Hippolyte could not get over his surprise, but bent over Bovary's hands to cover them with kisses.

"Come, be calm," said the druggist; "later on you will show your gratitude to your benefactor."

And he went down to tell the result to five or six inquirers who were waiting in the yard, and who fancied that Hippolyte would reappear walking properly. Then Charles, having buckled his patient into the machine, went home, where Emma, all anxiety, awaited him at the door. She threw herself on his neck; they sat down to table; he ate much, and at dessert he even wanted to take a cup of coffee, a luxury he only permitted himself on Sundays when there was company.

The evening was charming, full of prattle, of dreams together. They talked about their future fortune, of the improvements to be made in their house; he saw people's estimation of him growing, his comforts increasing, his wife always loving him; and she was happy to refresh herself with a new sentiment, healthier, better, to feel at last some tenderness for this poor fellow who adored her. The thought of Rodolphe for one moment passed through her mind, but her eyes turned again to Charles; she even noticed with surprise that he had not bad teeth.

They were in bed when Monsieur Homais, in spite of the servant, suddenly entered the room, holding in his hand a sheet of paper just written. It was the paragraph he intended for the *Fanal de Rouen*. He brought it them to read.

"Read it yourself," said Bovary.

He read—

" 'Despite the prejudices that still invest a part of the face of Europe like a net, the light nevertheless begins to penetrate our country places. Thus on Tuesday our little town of Yonville found itself the scene of a surgical operation which is at the same time an act of loftiest philanthropy. Monsieur Bovary, one of our most distinguished practitioners—' "

"Oh, that is too much! too much!" said Charles, choking with emotion.

"No, no! not at all! What next!"

" '—Performed an operation on a club-footed man.' I have not used the scientific term, because you know in a newspaper everyone would not perhaps understand. The masses must—"

"No doubt," said Bovary; "go on!"

"I proceed," said the chemist. " 'Monsieur Bovary, one of our most distinguished practitioners, performed an operation on a club-footed man called Hippolyte Tautain, stable-man for the last twenty-five years at the hotel of the Lion d'Or, kept by Widow Lefrançois, at the Place d'Armes. The novelty of the attempt, and the interest incident to the subject, had attracted such a concourse of persons that there was a veritable obstruction on the threshold of the establishment. The operation, moreover, was performed as if by magic, and barely a few drops of blood appeared on the skin, as though to say that the rebellious tendon had at last given way beneath the efforts of art. The patient, strangely enough— we affirm it as an eye-witness—complained of no pain. His condition up to the present time leaves nothing to be desired. Everything tends to show that his convalescence will be brief; and who knows even if at our next village festivity we shall not see our good Hippolyte figuring in the bacchic dance in the midst of a chorus of joyous boon-companions, and thus proving to all eyes by his verve and his capers his complete cure? Honour, then, to the generous savants! Honour to those indefatigable spirits who consecrate their vigils to the amelioration or to the alleviation of their kind! Honour, thrice honour! Is it not time to cry that the blind shall see, the deaf hear, the lame walk? But that which fanaticism formerly promised to its elect, science now accomplishes for all men. We shall keep our readers informed as to the successive phases of this remarkable cure.' "

This did not prevent Mère Lefrançois from coming five days after, scared, and crying out—

"Help! he is dying! I am going crazy!"

Charles rushed to the Lion d'Or, and the chemist, who caught sight of him passing along the Place hatless, abandoned his shop. He appeared himself breathless, red, anxious, and asking everyone who was going up the stairs—

"Why, what's the matter with our interesting strephopode?"

The strephopode was writhing in hideous convulsions, so that the machine in which his leg was enclosed was knocked against the wall enough to break it.

With many precautions, in order not to disturb the position of the limb, the box was removed, and an awful sight presented itself. The outlines of the foot disappeared in such a swelling that the entire skin seemed about to burst, and it was covered with ecchymosis, caused by the famous machine. Hippolyte had already complained of suffering from it. No attention had been paid to him; they had to acknowledge that he had not been altogether wrong, and he was freed for a few hours. But hardly had the edema gone down to some extent, than the two savants thought fit to put back the limb in the apparatus, strapping it tighter to hasten matters. At last, three days after, Hippolyte being unable to endure it any longer, they once more removed the machine, and were much surprised at the result they saw. The livid tumefaction spread over the leg, with blisters here and there, whence there oozed a black liquid. Matters were taking a serious turn. Hippolyte began to worry himself, and Mère Lefrançois had him installed in the little room near the kitchen, so that he might at least have some distraction.

But the tax-collector, who dined there every day, complained bitterly of such companionship. Then Hippolyte was removed to the billiard-room. He lay there moaning under his heavy coverings, pale, with long beard, sunken eyes, and from time to time turning his perspiring head on the dirty pillow, where the flies alighted. Madame Bovary went to see him. She brought him linen for his poultices; she comforted, and encouraged him. Besides, he did not want for company, especially on market-days, when the peasants were knocking about the billiard-balls round him, fenced with the cues, smoked, drank, sang, and brawled.

"How are you?" they said, clapping him on the shoulder. "Ah! you're not up to much, it seems, but it's your own fault. You should do this! do that!" And then they told him stories of people who had all been cured by other remedies than his. Then by way of consolation they added—

"You give way too much! Get up! You coddle yourself like a king! All the same, old chap, you don't smell nice!"

Gangrene, in fact, was spreading more and more. Bovary himself turned sick at it. He came every hour, every moment. Hippolyte looked at him with eyes full of terror, sobbing—

"When shall I get well? Oh, save me! How unfortunate I am! How unfortunate I am!"

And the doctor left, always recommending him to diet himself.

"Don't listen to him, my lad," said Mère Lefrançois. "Haven't they tortured you enough already? You'll grow still weaker. Here! swallow this."

And she gave him some good beef-tea, a slice of mutton, a piece of bacon, and sometimes small glasses of brandy, that he had not the strength to put to his lips.

Abbé Bournisien, hearing that he was growing worse, asked to see him. He began by pitying his sufferings, declaring at the same time that he ought to rejoice at them since it was the will of the Lord, and take advantage of the occasion to reconcile himself to Heaven.

"For," said the ecclesiastic in a paternal tone, "you rather neglected your duties; you were rarely seen at divine worship. How many years is it since you approached the holy table? I understand that your work, that the whirl of the world may have kept you from care for your salvation. But now is the time to reflect. Yet don't despair. I have known great sinners, who, about to appear before God (you are not yet at this point I know), had implored His mercy, and who certainly died in the best frame of mind. Let us hope that, like them, you will set us a good example. Thus, as a precaution, what is to prevent you from saying morning and evening a 'Hail Mary, full of grace,' and 'Our Father which art in heaven'? Yes, do that, for my sake, to oblige me. That won't cost you anything. Will you promise me?"

The poor devil promised. The curé came back day after day. He chatted with the landlady, and even told anecdotes interspersed with jokes and puns that Hippolyte did not understand. Then, as soon as he could, he fell back upon matters of religion, putting on an appropriate expression of face.

His zeal seemed successful, for the club-foot soon manifested a desire to go on a pilgrimage to Bon-Secours if he were cured; to which Monsieur Bournisien replied that he saw no objection; two precautions were better than one; it was no risk anyhow.

The druggist was indignant at what he called the manouevres of the priest; they were prejudicial, he said, to Hippolyte's convalescence, and he kept repeating to Madame Lefrançois, "Leave him alone! leave him alone! You perturb his morals with your mysticism."

But the good woman would no longer listen to him; he was the cause of it all. From a spirit of contradiction she hung up near the bedside of the patient a basin filled with holy-water and a branch of box.

Religion, however, seemed no more able to succour him than surgery, and the invincible gangrene still spread from the extremities towards the stomach. It was all very well to vary the potions and change the poultices; the muscles each day rotted more and more; and at last Charles replied by an affirmative nod of the head when Mère Lefrançois asked him if she could not, as a forlorn hope, send for Monsieur Canivet of Neufchâtel, who was a celebrity.

A doctor of medicine, fifty years of age, enjoying a good position and self-possessed, Charles's colleague did not refrain from laughing disdainfully when he had uncovered the leg, mortified to the knee. Then having flatly declared that it must be amputated, he went off to the chemist's to rail at the asses who could have reduced a poor man to such a state. Shaking Monsieur Homais by the button of his coat, he shouted out in the shop—

"These are the inventions of Paris! These are the ideas of those gentry of the capital! It is like strabismus, chloroform, lithotrity, a heap of monstrosities that the Government ought to prohibit. But they want to do the clever, and they cram you with remedies without troubling about the consequences. We are not so clever, not we! We are not savants, coxcombs, fops! We are practitioners; we cure people, and we should not dream of operating on anyone who is in perfect health. Straighten club-feet! As if one could straighten club-feet! It is as if one wished, for example, to make a hunchback straight!"

Homais suffered as he listened to this discourse, and he concealed his discomfort beneath a courtier's smile; for he needed to humour Monsieur Canivet, whose prescriptions sometimes came as far as Yonville. So he did not take up the defence of Bovary; he did not even make a single remark, and, renouncing his principles, he sacrificed his dignity to the more serious interests of his business.

This amputation of the thigh by Doctor Canivet was a great event in the village. On that day all the inhabitants got up earlier, and the Grande Rue, although full of people, had something lugubrious about it, as if an execution had been expected. At the grocers they discussed Hippolyte's illness; the shops did no business, and Madame Tuvache, the mayor's wife, did not stir from her window, such was her impatience to see the operator arrive.

He came in his gig, which he drove himself. But the springs of the right side having at length given way beneath the weight of his corpulence, it happened that the carriage as it rolled along leaned over a little, and on the other cushion near him could be seen a large box covered in red sheep-leather, whose three brass clasps shone grandly.

After he had entered like a whirlwind the porch of the Lion d'Or, the doctor, shouting very loud, ordered them to unharness his horse. Then he went into the stable to see that he was eating his oats all right; for on arriving at a patient's he first of all looked after his mare and his gig. People even said about this—

"Ah! Monsieur Canivet's a character!"

And he was the more esteemed for this imperturbable coolness. The universe to the last man might have died, and he would not have missed the smallest of his habits.

Homais presented himself.

"I count on you," said the doctor. "Are we ready? Come along!"

But the druggist, turning red, confessed that he was too sensitive to assist at such an operation.

"When one is a simple spectator," he said, "the imagination, you know, is impressed. And then I have such a nervous system!"

"Pshaw!' interrupted Canivet; "on the contrary, you seem to me inclined to apoplexy. Besides, that doesn't astonish me, for you chemist fellows are always poking about your kitchens, which must end by spoiling your constitutions. Now just look at me. I get up every day at four o'clock; I shave with cold water (and am never cold). I don't wear flannels, and I never catch cold; my carcass is good enough! I live now in one way, now in another, like a philosopher, taking pot-luck; that is why I am not squeamish like you, and it is as indifferent to me to carve a Christian as the first fowl that turns up. Then, perhaps, you will say, habit! habit!"

Then, without any consideration for Hippolyte, who was sweating with agony between his sheets, these gentlemen entered into a conversation, in which the druggist compared the coolness of a surgeon to that of a general; and this comparison was pleasing to Canivet, who launched out on the exigencies of his art. He looked upon it as a sacred office, although the ordinary practitioners dishonoured it. At last, coming back to the patient, he examined the bandages brought by Homais, the same that had appeared for the club-foot, and asked for someone to hold the limb for him. Lestiboudois was sent for, and Monsieur Canivet having turned up his sleeves, passed into the billiard-room, while the druggist stayed with Artémise and the landlady, both whiter than their aprons, and with ears strained towards the door.

Bovary during this time did not dare to stir from his house.

He kept downstairs in the sitting-room by the side of the fireless chimney, his chin on his breast, his hands clasped, his eyes staring. "What a mishap!" he thought, "what a mishap!" Perhaps, after all, he had made some slip. He thought it over, but could hit upon nothing. But the most famous surgeons also made mistakes; and that is what no one would ever believe! People, on the contrary, would laugh, jeer! It would spread as far as Forges, as Neufchâtel, as Rouen, everywhere! Who could say if his colleagues would not write against him. Polemics would ensue; he would have to answer in the papers. Hippolyte might even prosecute him. He saw himself dishonoured, ruined, lost; and his imagination, assailed by a world of hypotheses, tossed amongst them like an empty cask borne by the sea and floating upon the waves.

Emma, opposite, watched him; she did not share his humiliation; she felt another—that of having supposed such a man was worth anything. As if twenty times already she had not sufficiently perceived his mediocrity.

Charles was walking up and down the room; his boots creaked on the floor.

"Sit down," she said; "you fidget me."

He sat down again.

How was it that she—she, who was so intelligent—could have allowed herself to be deceived again? and through what deplorable madness had she thus ruined her life by continual sacrifices? She recalled all her instincts of luxury, all the privations of her soul, the sordidness of marriage, of the household, her dream sinking into the mire like wounded swallows; all that she had longed for, all that she had denied herself, all that she might have had! And for what? for what?

In the midst of the silence that hung over the village a heartrending cry rose on the air. Bovary turned white to fainting. She knit her brows with a nervous gesture, then went on. And it was for him, for this creature, for this man, who understood nothing, who felt nothing! For he was there quite quiet, not even suspecting that the ridicule of his name would henceforth sully hers as well as his. She had made efforts to love him, and she had repented with tears for having yielded to another!

"But it was perhaps a valgus!" suddenly exclaimed Bovary, who was meditating.

At the unexpected shock of this phrase falling on her thought like a leaden bullet on a silver plate, Emma, shuddering, raised her head in order to find out what he meant to say; and they looked at the other in silence, almost amazed to see each other, so far sundered were they by their inner thoughts. Charles gazed at her with the dull look of a drunken man, while he listened motionless to the last cries of the sufferer, that followed each other in long-drawn modulations, broken by sharp spasms like the far-off howling of some beast being slaughtered. Emma bit her wan lips, and rolling between her fingers a piece of coral that she had broken, fixed on Charles the burning glance of her eyes like two arrows of fire about to dart forth. Everything in him irritated her now; his face, his dress, what he did not say, his whole person, his existence, in fine. She repented of her past virtue as of a crime, and what still remained of it crumbled away beneath the furious blows of her pride. She revelled in all the evil ironies of triumphant adultery. The memory of her lover came back to her with dazzling attractions; she threw her whole soul into it, borne away towards this image with a fresh enthusiasm; and Charles seemed to her as much removed from her life, as absent forever, as impossible and annihilated, as if he had been about to die and were passing under her eyes.

There was a sound of steps on the pavement. Charles looked up, and through the lowered blinds he saw at the corner of the market in the broad sunshine Dr. Canivet, who was wiping his brow with his handkerchief. Homais, behind him, was carrying a large red box in his hand, and both were going towards the chemist's.

Then with a feeling of sudden tenderness and discouragement Charles turned to his wife saying to her—

"Oh, kiss me, my own!"

"Leave me!" she said, red with anger.

"What is the matter?" he asked, stupefied. "Be calm; compose yourself. You know well enough that I love you. Come!"

"Enough!" she cried with a terrible look.

And escaping from the room, Emma closed the door so violently that the barometer fell from the wall and smashed on the floor.

Charles sank back into his arm-chair overwhelmed, trying to discover what could be wrong with her, fancying some nervous illness, weeping, and vaguely feeling something fatal and incomprehensible whirling round him.

When Rodolphe came to the garden that evening, he found his mistress waiting for him at the foot of the steps on the lowest stair. They threw their arms round one another, and all their rancour melted like snow beneath the warmth of that kiss.

Chapter XII

THEY BEGAN TO LOVE ONE ANOTHER AGAIN. OFTEN, EVEN IN THE MIDDLE of the day, Emma suddenly wrote to him, then from the window made a sign to Justin, who, taking his apron off, quickly ran to La Huchette. Rodolphe would come; she had sent for him to tell him that she was bored, that her husband was odious, her life frightful.

"But what can I do?" he cried one day impatiently.

"Ah! if you would—"

She was sitting on the floor between his knees, her hair loose, her look lost.

"Why, what?" said Rodolphe.

She sighed.

"We would go and live elsewhere—somewhere!"

"You are really mad!" he said laughing. "How could that be possible?"

She returned to the subject; he pretended not to understand, and turned the conversation.

What he did not understand was all this worry about so simple an affair as love. She had a motive, a reason, and, as it were, a pendant to her affection.

Her tenderness, in fact, grew each day with her repulsion to her husband. The more she gave up herself to the one, the more she loathed the other. Never had Charles seemed to her so disagreeable, to have such stodgy fingers, such vulgar ways, to be so dull as when they found themselves together after her meeting with Rodolphe. Then, while playing the spouse and virtue, she was burning at the thought of that head whose black hair fell in a curl over the sunburnt brow, of that form at once so strong and elegant, of that man, in a word, who had such experience in his reasoning, such passion in his desires. It was for him that she filed her nails with the care of a chaser, and that there was never enough cold-cream for her skin, nor of patchouli for her handkerchiefs. She loaded herself with bracelets, rings, and necklaces. When he was coming she filled the two large blue glass vases with roses, and prepared her room and her person like a courtesan expecting a prince. The servant had to be constantly washing linen, and all day Félicité did not stir from the kitchen, where little Justin, who often kept her company, watched her at work.

With his elbows on the long board on which she was ironing, he greedily watched all these women's clothes spread out about him, the dimity petticoats, the fichus, the collars, and the drawers with running strings, wide at the hips and growing narrower below.

"What is that for?" asked the young fellow, passing his hand over the crinoline or the hooks and eyes.

"Why, haven't you ever seen anything?" Félicité answered laughing. "As if your mistress, Madame Homais, didn't wear the same."

"Oh, I daresay! Madame Homais!" And he added with a meditative air, "As if she were a lady like madame!"

But Félicité grew impatient of seeing him hanging round her. She was six years older than he, and Theodore, Monsieur Guillaumin's servant, was beginning to pay court to her.

"Let me alone," she said, moving her pot of starch. "You'd better be off and pound almonds; you are always dangling about women. Before you meddle with such things, bad boy, wait till you've got a beard to your chin."

"Oh, don't be cross! I'll go and clean her boots."

And he at once took down from the shelf Emma's boots, all coated with mud, the mud of the rendezvous, that crumbled into powder beneath his fingers, and that he watched as it gently rose in a ray of sunlight.

"How afraid you are of spoiling them!" said the servant, who wasn't so particular when she cleaned them herself, because as soon as the stuff of the boots was no longer fresh madame handed them over to her.

Emma had a number in her cupboard that she squandered one after the other, without Charles allowing himself the slightest observation. So also he disbursed three hundred francs for a wooden leg that she thought proper to make a present of to Hippolyte. Its top was covered with cork, and it had spring joints, a complicated mechanism, covered over by black trousers ending in a patent-leather boot. But Hippolyte, not daring to use such a handsome leg every day, begged Madame Bovary to get him another more convenient one. The doctor, of course, had again to defray the expense of this purchase.

So little by little the stable-man took up his work again. One saw him running about the village as before, and when Charles heard from afar the sharp noise of the wooden leg, he at once went in another direction.

It was Monsieur Lheureux, the shopkeeper, who had undertaken the order; this provided him with an excuse for visiting Emma. He chatted with her about the new goods from Paris, about a thousand feminine trifles, made himself very obliging, and never asked for his money. Emma yielded to this lazy mode of satisfying all her caprices. Thus she wanted to have a very handsome riding-whip that was at an umbrella-maker's at Rouen to give to Rodolphe. The week after Monsieur Lheureux placed it on her table.

But the next day he called on her with a bill for two hundred and seventy francs, not counting the centimes. Emma was much embarrassed; all the drawers of the writing-table were empty; they owed over a fortnight's wages to Lestiboudois, two quarters to the servant, for any quantity of other things, and Bovary was impatiently expecting Monsieur Derozeray's account, which he was in the habit of paying every year about Midsummer.

She succeeded at first in putting off Lheureux. At last he lost patience; he was being sued; his capital was out, and unless he got some in he should be forced to take back all the goods she had received.

"Oh, very well, take them!" said Emma.

"I was only joking," he replied; "the only thing I regret is the whip. My word! I'll ask monsieur to return it to me."

"No, no!" she said.

"Ah! I've got you!" thought Lheureux.

And, certain of his discovery, he went out repeating to himself in an undertone, and with his usual low whistle—

"Good! we shall see! we shall see!"

She was thinking how to get out of this when the servant coming in put on the mantelpiece a small roll of blue paper "from Monsieur Derozeray's." Emma pounced upon and opened it. It contained fifteen napoleons; it was the account. She heard Charles on the stairs; threw the gold to the back of her drawer, and took out the key.

Three days after Lheureux reappeared.

"I have an arrangement to suggest to you," he said. "If, instead of the sum agreed on, you would take—"

"Here it is," she said placing fourteen napoleons in his hand.

The tradesman was dumbfounded. Then, to conceal his disappointment, he was profuse in apologies and proffers of service, all of which Emma declined; then she remained a few moments fingering in the pocket of her apron the two five-franc pieces that he had given her in change. She promised herself she would economise in order to pay back later on. "Pshaw!" she thought, "he won't think about it again."

Besides the riding-whip with its silver-gilt handle, Rodolphe had received a seal with the motto *Amor nel cor;* furthermore, a scarf for a muffler, and, finally, a cigar-case exactly like the Viscount's, that Charles had formerly picked up in the road, and that Emma had kept. These presents, however, humiliated him; he refused several; she insisted, and he ended by obeying, thinking her tyrannical and over-exacting.

Then she had strange ideas.

"When midnight strikes," she said, "you must think of me."

And if he confessed that he had not thought of her, there were floods of re-proaches that always ended with the eternal question—

"Do you love me?"

"Why, of course I love you," he answered.

"A great deal?"

"Certainly!"

"You haven't loved any others?"

"Did you think you'd got a virgin?" he exclaimed laughing.

Emma cried, and he tried to console her, adorning his protestations with puns.

"Oh," she went on, "I love you! I love you so that I could not live without you, do you see? There are times when I long to see you again, when I am torn by all the anger of love. I ask myself, Where is he? Perhaps he is talking to other women. They smile upon him; he approaches. Oh no; no one else pleases you. There are some more beautiful, but I love you best. I know how to love best. I am your ser-vant, your concubine! You are my king, my idol! You are good, you are beautiful, you are clever, you are strong!"

He had so often heard these things said that they did not strike him as origi-nal. Emma was like all his mistresses; and the charm of novelty, gradually falling away like a garment, laid bare the eternal monotony of passion, that has always the same forms and the same language. He did not distinguish, this man of so much experience, the difference of sentiment beneath the saneness of expression. Because lips libertine and venal had murmured such words to him, he believed but little in the candour of hers; exaggerated speeches hiding mediocre affections must be discounted; as if the fulness of the soul did not sometimes overflow in the emptiest metaphors, since no one can ever give the exact measure of his needs, nor of his conceptions, nor of his sorrows; and since human speech is like a cracked tin kettle, on which we hammer out tunes to make bears dance when we long to move the stars.

But with that superior critical judgment that belongs to him who, in no matter what circumstance, holds back, Rodolphe saw other delights to be got out of this love. He thought all modesty in the way. He treated her quite *sans façon*. He made of her something supple and corrupt. Hers was an idiotic sort of attachment, full of admiration for him, of voluptuousness for her, a beatitude that benumbed her; her soul sank into this drunkenness, shrivelled up, drowned in it, like Clarence in his butt of Malmsey.

By the mere effect of her love Madame Bovary's manners changed. Her looks grew bolder, her speech more free; she even committed the impropriety of walk-ing out with Monsieur Rodolphe, a cigarette in her mouth, "as if to defy the peo-ple." At last, those who still doubted doubted no longer when one day they saw her getting out of the Hirondelle, her waist squeezed into a waistcoat like a man; and Madame Bovary senior, who, after a fearful scene with her husband, had taken refuge at her son's, who was not the least scandalised of the women-folk. Many other things displeased her. First, Charles had not attended to her advice about the forbidding of novels; then the "ways of the house" annoyed her; she allowed herself to make some remarks, and there were quarrels, especially one on account of Félicité.

Madam Bovary senior, the evening before, passing along the passage, had surprised her in company of a man—a man with a brown collar, about forty years old, who, at the sound of her step, had quickly escaped through the kitchen. Then Emma began to laugh, but the good lady grew angry, declaring that unless morals were to be laughed at one ought to look after those of one's servants.

"Where were you brought up?" asked the daughter-in-law, with so impertinent a look that Madame Bovary asked her if she were not perhaps defending her own case.

"Leave the room!" said the young woman, springing up with a bound.

"Emma! Mamma!" cried Charles, trying to reconcile them.

But both had fled in their exasperation. Emma was stamping her feet as she repeated—

"Oh! what manners! What a peasant!"

He ran to his mother; she was beside herself. She stammered—

"She is an insolent, giddy-headed thing, or perhaps worse!"

And she was for leaving at once if the other did not apologise.

So Charles went aback again to his wife and implored her to give way; he knelt to her; she ended by saying—

"Very well! I'll go to her."

And in fact she held out her hand to her mother-in-law with the dignity of a marchioness as she said—

"Excuse me, madame."

Then, having gone up again to her room, she threw herself flat on her bed and cried there like a child, her face buried in the pillow.

She and Rodolphe had agreed that in the event of anything extraordinary occurring, she should fasten a small piece of white paper to the blind, so that if by chance he happened to be in Yonville, he could hurry to the lane behind the house. Emma made the signal; she had been waiting three-quarters of an hour when she suddenly caught sight of Rodolphe at the corner of the market. She felt tempted to open the window and call him, but he had already disappeared. She fell back in despair.

Soon, however, it seemed to her that someone was walking on the pavement.

It was he, no doubt. She went downstairs, crossed the yard. He was there outside. She threw herself into his arms.

"Do take care!" he said.

"Ah! if you knew!" she replied.

And she began telling him everything, hurriedly, disjointedly, exaggerating the facts, inventing many, and so prodigal of parentheses that he understood nothing of it.

"Come, my poor angel, courage! Be comforted! be patient!"

"But I have been patient; I have suffered for four years. A love like ours ought to show itself in the face of heaven. They torture me! I can bear it no longer! Save me!"

She clung to Rodolphe. Her eyes, full of tears, flashed like flames beneath a wave; her breast heaved; he had never loved her so much, so that he lost his head and said—

"What is it? What do you wish?"

"Take me away," she cried, "carry me off! Oh, I pray you!"

And she threw herself upon his mouth, as if to seize there the unexpected consent if breathed forth in a kiss.

"But—" Rodolphe resumed.

"What?"

"Your little girl!"

She reflected a few moments, then replied—

"We will take her! It can't be helped!"

"What a woman!" he said to himself, watching her as she went. For she had run into the garden. Someone was calling her.

On the following days Madame Bovary senior was much surprised at the change in her daughter-in-law. Emma, in fact, was showing herself more docile, and even carried her deference so far as to ask for a recipe for pickling gherkins.

Was it the better to deceive them both? Or did she wish by a sort of voluptuous stoicism to feel the more profoundly the bitterness of the things she was about to leave?

But she paid no heed to them; on the contrary, she lived as lost in the anticipated delight of her coming happiness. It was an eternal subject for conversation with Rodolphe. She leant on his shoulder murmuring—

"Ah! when we are in the mail-coach! Do you think about it? Can it be? It seems to me that the moment I feel the carriage start, it will be as if we were rising in a balloon, as if we were setting out for the clouds. Do you know that I count the hours. And you?"

Never had Madame Bovary been so beautiful as at this period; she had that indefinable beauty that results from joy, from enthusiasm, from success, and that is only the harmony of temperament with circumstances. Her desires, her sorrows, the experience of pleasure, and her ever-young illusions, that had, as soil and rain and winds and the sun make flowers grow, gradually developed her, and she at length blossomed forth in all the plenitude of her nature. Her eyelids seemed chiselled expressly for her long amorous looks in which the pupil disappeared, while a strong inspiration expanded her delicate nostrils and raised the fleshy corner of her lips, shaded in the light by a little black down. One would have thought that an artist apt in conception had arranged the curls of hair upon her neck; they fell in a thick mass, negligently, and with the changing chances of their adultery, that unbound them every day. Her voice now took more mellow inflections, her figure also; something subtle and penetrating escaped even from the folds of her gown and from the line of her foot. Charles, as when they were first married, thought her delicious and quite irresistible.

When he came home in the middle of the night, he did not dare to wake her. The porcelain night-light threw a round trembling gleam upon the ceiling, and the drawn curtains of the little cot formed as it were a white hut standing out in the shade, and by the bedside Charles looked at them. He seemed to hear the light breathing of his child. She would grow big now; every season would bring rapid progress. He already saw her coming from school as the day drew in, laughing, with ink-stains on her jacket, and carrying her basket on her arm. Then she would have to be sent to a boarding-school; that would cost much; how was it to be done? Then he reflected. He thought of hiring a small farm in the neighbourhood, that he would superintend every morning on his way to his patients. He would save up what he brought in; he would put it in the savings-bank. Then he would buy shares somewhere, no matter where; besides, his practice would increase; he counted upon that, for he wanted Berthe to be well-educated, to be accomplished, to learn to play the piano. Ah! how pretty she would be later on when she was fifteen, when, resembling her mother, she would, like her, wear large straw hats in the summer-time; from a distance they would be taken for two sisters. He pictured her to himself working in the evening by their side beneath the light of the lamp; she would embroider him slippers; she would look after the house; she would fill all the home with her charm and her gaiety. At last, they would think of her marriage; they would find her some good young fellow with a steady business; he would make her happy; this would last forever.

Emma was not asleep; she pretended to be; and while he dozed off by her side she awakened to other dreams.

To the gallop of four horses she was carried away for a week towards a new land, whence they would return no more. They went on and on, their arms entwined, without a word. Often from the top of a mountain there suddenly glimpsed some splendid city with domes, and bridges, and ships, forests of citron trees, and cathedrals of white marble, on whose pointed steeples were storks' nests. They went at a walking-pace because of the great flag-stones, and on the ground there were bouquets of flowers, offered you by women dressed in red bodices. They heard the chiming of bells, the neighing of mules, together with the murmur of guitars and the noise of fountains, whose rising spray refreshed heaps of fruit arranged like a pyramid at the foot of pale statues that smiled beneath playing waters. And then, one night they came to a fishing village, where brown nets were drying in the wind along the cliffs and in front of the huts. It was there that they would stay; they would live in a low, flat-roofed house, shaded by a palm-tree, in the heart of a gulf, by the sea. They would row in gondolas, swing in hammocks, and their existence would be easy and large as their silk gowns, warm and star-spangled as the nights they would contemplate. However, in the immensity of this future that she conjured up, nothing special stood forth; the days, all magnificent, resembled each other like waves; and it swayed in the horizon, infinite, har-monised, azure, and bathed in sunshine. But the child began to cough in her cot or Bovary snored more loudly, and Emma did not fall asleep till morning, when the dawn whitened the windows, and when little Justin was already in the square tak-ing down the shutters of the chemist's shop.

She had sent for Monsieur Lheureux, and had said to him—

"I want a cloak—a large lined cloak with a deep collar."

"You are going on a journey?" he asked.

"No; but—never mind. I may count on you, may I not, and quickly?"

He bowed.

"Besides, I shall want," she went on, "a trunk—not too heavy—handy."

"Yes, yes, I understand. About three feet by a foot and a half, as they are being made just now."

"And a travelling bag."

"Decidedly," thought Lheureux, "there's a row on here."

"And," said Madame Bovary, taking her watch from her belt, "take this; you can pay yourself out of it."

But the tradesman cried out that she was wrong; they knew one another; did he doubt her? What childishness!

She insisted, however, on his taking at least the chain, and Lheureux had al-ready put it in his pocket and was going, when she called him back.

"You will leave everything at your place. As to the cloak"—she seemed to be reflecting—"do not bring it either; you can give me the maker's address, and tell him to have it ready for me."

It was the next month that they were to run away. She was to leave Yonville as if she was going on some business to Rouen. Rodolphe would have booked the seats, procured the passports, and even have written to Paris in order to have the whole mail-coach reserved for them as far as Marseilles, where they would buy a carriage, and go on thence without stopping to Genoa. She would take care to send her luggage to Lheureux's, whence it would be taken direct to the Hirondelle, so that no one would have any suspicion. And in all this there never was any allusion to the child. Rodolphe avoided speaking of her; perhaps he no longer thought about it.

He wished to have two more weeks before him to arrange some affairs; then at the end of a week he wanted two more; then he said he was ill; next he went on a journey. The month of August passed, and, after all these delays, they decided that it was to be irrevocably fixed for the 4th September—a Monday.

At length the Saturday before arrived.

Rodolphe came in the evening earlier than usual.

"Everything is ready?" she asked him.

"Yes."

Then they walked round a garden-bed, and went to sit down near the terrace on the kerb-stone of the wall.

"You are sad," said Emma.

"No; why?"

And yet he looked at her strangely in a tender fashion.

"Is it because you are going away?" she went on; "because you are leaving what is dear to you—your life? Ah! I understand. I have nothing in the world! You are all to me; so shall I be to you. I will be your people, your country; I will tend, I will love you!"

"How sweet you are!" he said, seizing her in his arms.

"Really!" she said with a voluptuous laugh. "Do you love me? Swear it then!"

"Do I love you—love you? I adore you, my love!'

The moon, full and purple-coloured, was rising right out of the earth at the end of the meadow. She rose quickly between the branches of the poplars, that hid her here and there like a black curtain pierced with holes. Then she appeared dazzling with whiteness in the empty heavens that she lit up, and now sailing more slowly along, let fall upon the river a great stain that broke up into an infinity of stars; and the silver sheen seemed to writhe through the very depths like a headless serpent covered with luminous scales; it also resembled some monster candelabra all along which sparkled drops of diamonds running together. The soft night was about them; masses of shadow filled the branches. Emma, her eyes half closed, breathed in with deep sighs the fresh wind that was blowing. They did not speak, lost as they were in the rush of their reverie. The tenderness of the old days came back to their hearts, full and silent as the flowing river, with the softness of the perfume of the syringas, and threw across their memories shadows more immense and more sombre than those of the still willows that lengthened out over the grass. Often some night-animal, hedgehog or weasel, setting out on the hunt, disturbed the lovers, or sometimes they heard a ripe peach falling all alone from the espalier.

"Ah! what a lovely night!" said Rodolphe.

"We shall have others," replied Emma; and, as if speaking to herself. "Yet, it will be good to travel. And yet, why should my heart be so heavy? Is it dread of the unknown? The effect of habits left? Or rather——? No; it is the excess of happiness. How weak I am, am I not? Forgive me!"

"There is still time!" he cried. "Reflect! perhaps you may repent!"

"Never!" she cried impetuously. And coming closer to him: "What ill could come to me? There is no desert, no precipice, no ocean I would not traverse with you. The longer we live together the more it will be like an embrace, every day closer, more heart to heart. There will be nothing to trouble us, no cares, no obstacle. We shall be alone, all to ourselves eternally. Oh, speak! Answer me!"

At regular intervals he answered, "Yes—Yes——" She had passed her hands through his hair, and she repeated in a childlike voice, despite the big tears which were falling, "Rodolphe! Rodolphe! Ah! Rodolphe! dear little Rodolphe!"

Midnight struck.

"Midnight!" said she. "Come, it is to-morrow. One day more!"

He rose to go; and as if the movement he made had been the signal for their flight, Emma said, suddenly assuming a gay air—

"You have the passports?"

"Yes."

"You are forgetting nothing?"

"No."

"Are you sure?"

"Certainly."

"It is at the Hotel de Provence, is it not, that you will wait for me at mid-day?"

He nodded.

"Till to-morrow then!" said Emma in a last caress; and she watched him go.

He did not turn round. She ran after him, and, leaning over the water's edge between the bulrushes—

"To-morrow!" she cried.

He was already on the other side of the river and walking fast across the meadow.

After a few moments Rodolphe stopped; and when he saw her with her white gown gradually fade away in the shade like a ghost, he was seized with such a beating of the heart that he leant against a tree lest he should fall.

"What an imbecile I am!" he said with a fearful oath. "No matter! She was a pretty mistress!"

And immediately Emma's beauty, with all the pleasures of their love, came back to him. For a moment he softened; then he rebelled against her.

"For, after all," he exclaimed, gesticulating, "I can't exile myself—have a child on my hands."

He was saying these things to give himself firmness.

"And besides, the worry, the expense! Ah! no, no, no, no! a thousand times no! It would have been too stupid."

Chapter XIII

NO SOONER WAS RODOLPHE AT HOME THAN HE SAT DOWN QUICKLY AT HIS bureau under the stag's head that hung as a trophy on the wall. But when he had the pen between his fingers, he could think of nothing, so that, resting on his elbows, he began to reflect. Emma seemed to him to have receded into a far-off past, as if the resolution he had taken had suddenly placed a distance between them.

To get back something of her, he fetched from the cupboard at the bedside an old Rheims biscuit-box, in which he usually kept his letters from women, and from it came an odour of dry dust and withered roses. First he saw a handkerchief with pale little spots. It was a handkerchief of hers. Once when they were walking her nose had bled; he had forgotten it. Near it, chipped at all the corners, was a miniature given him by Emma: her toilette seemed to him pretentious, and her languishing look in the worst possible taste. Then, from looking at this image and recalling the memory of its original, Emma's features little by little grew confused in his remembrance, as if the living and the painted face, rubbing one against the other, had effaced each other. Finally, he read some of her letters; they were full of explanations relating to their journey, short, technical, and urgent, like business notes. He wanted to see the long ones again, those of old times. In order to find them at the bottom of the box, Rodolphe disturbed all the others, and mechanically began rummaging amidst this mass of papers and things, finding pell-mell bouquets, garters, a black mask, pins, and hair—hair! dark and fair, some even, catching in the hinges of the box, broke when it was opened.

Thus dallying with his souvenirs, he examined the writing and the style of the letters, as varied as their orthography. They were tender or jovial, facetious, melancholy; there were some that asked for love, others that asked for money. A word recalled faces to him, certain gestures, the sound of a voice; sometimes, however, he remembered nothing at all.

In fact, these women, rushing at once into his thoughts, cramped each other and lessened, as reduced to a uniform level of love that equalised them all. So taking handfuls of the mixed-up letters, he amused himself for some moments with letting them fall in cascades from his right into his left hand. At last, bored and weary, Rodolphe took back the box to the cupboard, saying to himself, "What a lot of rubbish!" Which summed up his opinion; for pleasures, like schoolboys in a school courtyard, had so trampled upon his heart that no green thing grew there, and that which passed through it, more heedless than children, did not even, like them, leave a name carved upon the wall.

"Come," said he, "let's begin."

He wrote—

"Courage, Emma! courage! I would not bring misery into your life."

"After all, that's true," thought Rodolphe. "I am acting in her interest; I am honest."

"Have you carefully weighed your resolution? Do you know to what an abyss I was dragging you, poor angel? No, you do not, do you? You were coming confident and fearless, believing in happiness in the future. Ah! unhappy that we are—insensate!'

Rodolphe stopped here to think of some good excuse.

"If I told her all my fortune is lost? No! Besides, that would stop nothing. It would all have to be begun over again later on. As if one could make women like that listen to reason!" He reflected, then went on—

"I shall not forget you, oh! believe it; and I shall ever have a profound devotion for you; but some day, sooner or later, this ardour (such is the fate of human things) would have grown less, no doubt. Lassitude would have come to us, and who knows if I should not even have had the atrocious pain of witnessing your remorse, of sharing it myself, since I should have been its cause? The mere idea of the grief that would come to you tortures me, Emma. Forget me! Why did I ever know you? Why were you so beautiful? Is it my fault? O my God! No, no! Accuse only fate."

"That's a word that always tells," he said to himself.

"Ah, if you had been one of those frivolous women one sees, certainly I might, through egotism, have tried an experiment, in that case without danger for you. But that delicious exaltation, at once your charm and your torment, has prevented you from understanding, adorable woman that you are, the falseness of our future position. Nor had I reflected upon this at first, and I rested in the shade of that ideal happiness as beneath that of the manchineel-tree, without foreseeing the consequences."

"Perhaps she'll think I'm giving it up from avarice. Ah, well! so much the worse; it must be stopped!"

"The world is cruel, Emma. Wherever we might have gone, it would have perse-cuted us. You would have had to put up with indiscreet questions, calumny, contempt, in-sult perhaps. Insult to you! Oh! And I, who would place you on a throne! I who bear with me your memory as a talisman! For I am going to punish myself by exile for all the ill I have done you. I am going away. Whither I know not. I am mad. Adieu! Be good al-ways. Preserve the memory of the unfortunate who has lost you. Teach my name to your child; let her repeat it in her prayers."

The wicks of the candles flickered. Rodolphe got up to shut the window, and when he had sat down again—

"I think it's all right. Ah! and this for fear she should come and hunt me up."

"I shall be far away when you read these sad lines, for I have wished to flee as quickly as possible to shun the temptation of seeing you again. No weakness! I shall re-turn, and perhaps later on we shall talk together very coldly of our old love. Adieu!"

And there was a last "adieu" divided into two words! "A Dieu!" which he thought in very excellent taste.

"Now how am I to sign?" he said to himself. *"'Yours devotedly?' No! 'Your friend?' Yes, that's it."*

                   "Your friend."

He re-read his letter. He considered it very good.

"Poor little woman!" he thought with emotion. "She'll think me harder than a rock. There ought to have been some tears on this; but I can't cry; it isn't my fault." Then, having emptied some water into a glass, Rodolphe dipped his finger into it, and let a big drop fall on the paper, that made a pale stain on the ink. Then look-ing for a seal, he came upon the one *"Amor nel cor."*

"That doesn't at all fit in with the circumstances. Pshaw! never mind!"

After which he smoked three pipes and went to bed.

The next day when he was up (at about two o'clock—he had slept late), Rodolphe had a basket of apricots picked. He put his letter at the bottom under some vine leaves, and at once ordered Girard, his ploughman, to take it with care to Madame Bovary. He made use of this means for corresponding with her, send-ing according to the season fruits or game.

"If she asks after me," he said, "you will tell her that I have gone on a journey. You must give the basket to her herself, into her own hands. Get along and take care!"

Girard put on his new blouse, knotted his handkerchief round the apricots, and, walking with great heavy steps in his thick iron-bound goloshes, made his way to Yonville.

Madame Bovary, when he got to her house, was arranging a bundle of linen on the kitchen-table with Félicité.

"Here," said the ploughboy, "is something for you from master."

She was seized with apprehension, and as she sought in her pocket for some coppers, she looked at the peasant with haggard eyes, while he himself looked at her with amazement, not understanding how such a present could so move anyone. At last he went out. Félicité remained. She could bear it no longer; she ran into the sitting room as if to take the apricots there, overturned the basket, tore away the leaves, found the letter, opened it, and, as if some fearful fire were behind her, Emma flew to her room terrified.

Charles was there; she saw him; he spoke to her; she heard nothing, and she went on quickly up the stairs, breathless, distraught, dumb, and ever holding this horrible piece of paper, that crackled between her fingers like a plate of sheet-iron. On the second floor she stopped before the attic-door, that was closed.

Then she tried to calm herself; she recalled the letter; she must finish it; she did not dare to. And where? How? She would be seen! "Ah, no! here," she thought, "I shall be all right."

Emma pushed open the door and went in.

The slates threw straight down a heavy heat that gripped her temples, stifled her; she dragged herself to the closed garret-window. She drew back the bolt, and the dazzling light burst in with a leap.

Opposite, beyond the roofs, stretched the open country till it was lost to sight. Down below, underneath her, the village square was empty; the stones of the pavement glittered, the weathercocks on the houses were motionless. At the corner of the street, from a lower storey, rose a kind of humming with strident modulations. It was Binet turning.

She leant against the embrasure of the window, and re-read the letter with angry sneers. But the more she fixed her attention upon it, the more confused were her ideas. She saw him again, heard him, encircled him with her arms, and the throbs of her heart, that beat against her breast like blows of a sledge-hammer, grew faster and faster, with uneven intervals. She looked about her with the wish that the earth might crumble into pieces. Why not end it all? What restrained her? She was free. She advanced, looked at the paving-stones, saying to herself, "Come! come!"

The luminous ray that came straight up from below drew the weight of her body towards the abyss. It seemed to her that the ground of the oscillating square went up the walls, and that the floor dipped on end like a tossing boat. She was right at the edge, almost hanging, surrounded by vast space. The blue of the heavens suffused her, the air was whirling in her hollow head; she had but to yield, to let herself be taken; and the humming of the lathe never ceased, like an angry voice calling her.

"Emma! Emma!" cried Charles.

She stopped.

"Wherever are you? Come!"

The thought that she had just escaped from death almost made her faint with terror. She closed her eyes; then she shivered at the touch of a hand on her sleeve; it was Félicité.

"Master is waiting for you, madame; the soup is on the table."

And she had to go down to sit at table.

She tried to eat. The food choked her. Then she unfolded her napkin as if to examine the darns, and she really thought of applying herself to this work, counting the threads in the linen. Suddenly the remembrance of the letter returned to her. How had she lost it? Where could she find it? But she felt such weariness of spirit that she could not even invent a pretext for leaving the table. Then she became a coward; she was afraid of Charles; he knew all, that was certain! Indeed he pronounced these words in a strange manner:

"We are not likely to see Monsieur Rodolphe soon again, it seems."

"Who told you?" she said, shuddering.

"Who told me!" he replied, rather astonished at her abrupt tone. "Why, Girard, whom I met just now at the door of the Café Français. He has gone on a journey, or is to go."

She gave a sob.

"What surprises you in that? He absents himself like that from time to time for a change, and, *ma foi*, I think he's right, when one has a fortune and is a bachelor. Besides, he has jolly times, has our friend. He's a bit of a rake. Monsieur Langlois told me—"

He stopped for propriety's sake because the servant came in. She put back into the basket the apricots scattered on the sideboard. Charles, without noticing his wife's colour, had them brought to him, took one, and bit into it.

"Ah! perfect!' said he; "just taste!"

And he handed her the basket, which she put away from her gently.

"Do just smell! What an odour!" he remarked, passing it under her nose several times.

"I am choking," she cried, leaping up. But by an effort of will the spasm passed; then—

"It is nothing," she said, "it is nothing! It is nervousness. Sit down and go on eating." For she dreaded lest he should begin questioning her, attending to her, that she should not be left alone.

Charles, to obey her, sat down again, and he spat the stones of the apricots into his hands, afterwards putting them on his plate.

Suddenly a blue tilbury passed across the square at a rapid trot. Emma uttered a cry and fell back rigid to the ground.

In fact, Rodolphe, after many reflections, had decided to set out for Rouen. Now, as from La Huchette to Buchy there is no other way than by Yonville, he had to go through the village, and Emma had recognised him by the rays of the lanterns, which like lightning flashed through the twilight.

The chemist, at the tumult which broke out in the house, ran thither. The table with all the plates was upset; sauce, meat, knives, the salt, and cruet-stand were strewn over the room; Charles was calling for help; Berthe, scared, was crying; and Félicité, whose hands trembled, was unlacing her mistress, whose whole body shivered convulsively.

"I'll run to my laboratory for some aromatic vinegar," said the druggist.

Then as she opened her eyes on smelling the bottle—

"I was sure of it," he remarked; "that would wake any dead person for you!"

"Speak to us," said Charles; "collect yourself; it is I—your Charles, who loves you. Do you know me? See! here is your little girl! Oh, kiss her!"

The child stretched out her arms to her mother to cling to her neck. But turning away her head, Emma said in a broken voice—

"No, no! no one!"

She fainted again. They carried her to her bed. She lay there stretched at full length, her lips apart, her eyelids closed, her hands open, motionless, and white as a waxen image. Two streams of tears flowed from her eyes and fell slowly upon the pillow.

Charles, standing up, was at the back of the alcove, and the chemist, near him, maintained that meditative silence that is becoming on the serious occasions of life.

"Do not be uneasy," he said, touching his elbow; "I think the paroxysm is past."

"Yes, she is resting a little now," answered Charles, watching her sleep. "Poor girl! poor girl! She has gone off now!"

Then Homais asked how the accident had come about. Charles answered that she had been taken ill suddenly while she was eating some apricots.

"Extraordinary!" continued the chemist. "But it might be that the apricots had brought on the syncope. Some natures are so sensitive to certain smells; and it would even be a very fine question to study both in its pathological and physiological relation. The priests know the importance of it, they who have introduced aromatics into all their ceremonies. It is to stupefy the senses and to bring on ecstasies—a thing, moreover, very easy in persons of the weaker sex, who are more delicate than the other. Some are cited who faint at the smell of burnt hartshorn, of new bread—"

"Take care; you'll wake her!" said Bovary in a low voice.

"And not only," the druggist went on, "are human beings subject to such anomalies, but animals also. Thus you are not ignorant of the singularly aphrodisiac effect produced by the *Nepeta cataria*, vulgarly called cat-mint, on the feline race; and, on the other hand, to quote an example whose authenticity I can answer for, Bridaux (one of my old comrades, at present established in the Rue Malpalu) possesses a dog that falls into convulsions as soon as you hold out a snuff-box to him. He often even makes the experiment before his friends at his summer-house at Guillaume Wood. Would anyone believe that a simple sternutation could produce such ravages on a quadrupedal organism? It is extremely curious, is it not?"

"Yes," said Charles, who was not listening to him.

"This shows us," went on the other, smiling with benign self-sufficiency, "the innumerable irregularities of the nervous system. With regard to madame, she has always seemed to me, I confess, very susceptible. And so I should by no means recommend to you, my dear friend, any of those so-called remedies that, under the pretence of attacking the symptoms, attack the constitution. No; no useless physicking! Diet, that is all; sedatives, emollients, dulcification. Then, don't you think that perhaps her imagination should be worked upon?"

"In what way? How?" said Bovary.

"Ah! that is it. Such is indeed the question. 'That is the question,' as I lately read in a newspaper."

But Emma, awaking, cried out—

"The letter! the letter!"

They thought she was delirious; and she was by midnight. Brain-fever had set in.

For forty-three days Charles did not leave her. He gave up all his patients; he no longer went to bed; he was constantly feeling her pulse, putting on sinapisms and cold-water compresses. He sent Justin as far as Neufchâtel for ice; the ice melted on the way; he sent him back again. He called Monsieur Canivet into consultation; he sent for Dr. Larivière, his old master, from Rouen; he was in despair. What alarmed him most was Emma's prostration, for she did not speak, did not listen, did not even seem to suffer, as if her body and soul were both resting together after all their troubles.

About the middle of October she could sit up in bed supported by pillows. Charles wept when he saw her eat her first bread-and-jelly. Her strength returned to her; she got up for a few hours of an afternoon, and one day, when she felt better, he tried to take her, leaning on his arm, for a walk round the garden. The sand of the paths was disappearing beneath the dead leaves; she walked slowly, dragging along her slippers, and leaning against Charles's shoulder. She smiled all the time.

They went thus to the bottom of the garden near the terrace. She drew herself up slowly, shading her eyes with her hand to look. She looked far off, as far as she could, but on the horizon were only great bonfires of grass smoking on the hills.

"You will tire yourself, my darling!" said Bovary. And, pushing her gently to make her go into the arbour, "Sit down on this seat; you'll be comfortable."

"Oh! no; not there!" she said in a faltering voice.

She was seized with giddiness, and from that evening her illness recommenced, with a more uncertain character, it is true, and more complex symptoms. Now she suffered in her heart, then in the chest, the head, the limbs; she had vomitings, in which Charles thought he saw the first signs of cancer.

And besides this, the poor fellow was worried about money matters.

Chapter XIV

TO BEGIN WITH, HE DID NOT KNOW HOW HE COULD PAY MONSIEUR HOMAIS for all the physic supplied by him, and though, as a medical man, he was not obliged to pay for it, he nevertheless blushed a little at such an obligation. Then the expenses of the household, now that the servant was mistress, became terrible. Bills rained in upon the house; the tradesmen grumbled; Monsieur Lheureux especially harassed him. In fact, at the height of Emma's illness, the latter, taking advantage of the circumstances to make his bill larger, had hurriedly brought the cloak, the travelling-bag, two trunks instead of one, and a number of other things. It was very well for Charles to say he did not want them. The tradesman answered arrogantly that these articles had been ordered, and that he would not take them back; besides, it would vex madame in her convalescence; the doctor had better think it over; in short, he was resolved to sue him rather than give up his rights and take back his goods. Charles subsequently ordered them to be sent back to the shop. Félicité forgot; he had other things to attend to; then thought no more about them. Monsieur Lheureux returned to the charge, and, by turns threatening and whining, so managed that Bovary ended by signing a bill at six months. But hardly had he signed this bill than a bold idea occurred to him: it was to borrow a thousand francs from Lheureux. So, with an embarrassed air, he asked if it were possible to get them, adding that it would be for a year, at any interest he wished. Lheureux ran off to his shop, brought back the money, and dictated another bill, by which Bovary undertook to pay to his order on the 1st of September next the sum of one thousand and seventy francs, which, with the hundred and eighty already agreed to, made just twelve hundred and fifty, thus lending at six per cent in addition to one-fourth for commission; and the things bringing him in a good third at the least, this ought in twelve months to give him a profit of a hundred and thirty francs. He hoped that the business would not stop there; that the bills would not be paid; that they would be renewed; and that his poor little money, having thriven at the doctor's as at a hospital, would come back to him one day considerably more plump, and fat enough to burst his bag.

Everything, moreover, succeeded with him. He was adjudicator for a supply of cider to the hospital at Neufchâtel; Monsieur Guillaumin promised him some shares in the turf-pits of Gaumesnil, and he dreamt of establishing a new diligence service between Argueil and Rouen, which no doubt would not be long in ruining the ramshackle van of the Lion d'Or, and that, travelling faster, at a cheaper rate, and carrying more luggage, would thus put into his hands the whole commerce of Yonville.

Charles several times asked himself by what means he should next year be able to pay back so much money. He reflected, imagined expedients, such as applying to his father or selling something. But his father would be deaf, and he—he had nothing to sell. Then he foresaw such worries that he quickly dismissed so disagreeable a subject of meditation from his mind. He reproached himself with forgetting Emma, as if, all his thoughts belonging to this woman, it was robbing her of something not to be constantly thinking of her.

The winter was severe, Madame Bovary's convalescence slow. When it was fine they wheeled her arm-chair to the window that overlooked the square, for she now had an antipathy to the garden, and the blinds on that side were always down. She wished the horse to be sold; what she formerly liked now displeased her. All her ideas seemed to be limited to the care of herself. She stayed in bed taking little meals, rang for the servant to inquire about her gruel or to chat with her. The snow on the market-roof threw a white, still light into the room; then the rain began to fall; and Emma waited daily with a mind full of eagerness for the inevitable return of some trifling events which nevertheless had no relation to her. The most important was the arrival of the Hirondelle in the evening. Then the landlady shouted out, and other voices answered, while Hippolyte's lantern, as he fetched the boxes from the boot, was like a star in the darkness. At mid-day Charles came in; then he went out again; next she took some beef-tea, and towards five o'clock, as the day drew in, the children coming back from school, dragging their wooden shoes along the pavement, knocked the clapper of the shutters with their rulers one after the other.

It was at this hour that Monsieur Bournisien came to see her. He inquired after her health, gave her news, exhorted her to religion in a coaxing little gossip that was not without its charm. The mere thought of his cassock comforted her.

One day, when at the height of her illness, she had thought herself dying, and had asked for the communion; and, while they were making the preparations in her room for the sacrament, while they were turning the night table covered with syrups into an altar, and while Félicité was strewing dahlia flowers on the floor, Emma felt some power passing over her that freed her from her pains, from all perception, from all feeling. Her body, relieved, no longer thought; another life was beginning; it seemed to her that her being, mounting toward God, would be annihilated in that love like a burning incense that melts into vapour. The bed-clothes were sprinkled with holy water, the priest drew from the holy pyx the white wafer; and it was fainting with a celestial joy that she put out her lips to accept the body of the Saviour presented to her. The curtains of the alcove floated gently round her like clouds, and the rays of the two tapers burning on the night-table seemed to shine like dazzling halos. Then she let her head fall back, fancying she heard in space the music of seraphic harps, and perceived in an azure sky, on a golden throne in the midst of saints holding green palms, God the Father, resplendent with majesty, who with a sign sent to earth angels with wings of fire to carry her away in their arms.

This splendid vision dwelt in her memory as the most beautiful thing that it was possible to dream, so that now she strove to recall her sensation, that still lasted, however, but in a less exclusive fashion and with a deeper sweetness. Her soul, tortured by pride, at length found rest in Christian humility, and, tasting the joy of weakness, she saw within herself the destruction of her will, that must have left a wide entrance for the inroads of heavenly grace. There existed, then, in the place of happiness, still greater joys—another love beyond all loves, without pause and without end, one that would grow eternally! She saw amid the illusions of her hope a state of purity floating above the earth mingling with heaven, to which she aspired. She wanted to become a saint. She bought chaplets and wore amulets; she wished to have in her room, by the side of her bed, a reliquary set in emeralds that she might kiss it every evening.

The curé marvelled at this humour, although Emma's religion, he thought, might, from its fervour, end by touching on heresy, extravagance. But not being much versed in these matters, as soon as they went beyond a certain limit he wrote to Monsieur Boulard, bookseller to Monsignor, to send him "something good for a lady who was very clever." The bookseller, with as much indifference as if he had been sending off hardware to niggers, packed up, pell-mell, everything that was then the fashion in the pious book trade. There were little manuals in questions and answers, pamphlets of aggressive tone after the manner of Monsieur de Maistre, and certain novels in rose-coloured bindings and with a honied style, manufactured by troubadour seminarists or penitent blue-stockings. There were the "Think of it; the Man of the World at Mary's Feet, by Monsieur de ———, décoré with many Orders"; "The Errors of Voltaire, for the Use of the Young," etc.

Madame Bovary's mind was not yet sufficiently clear to apply herself seriously to anything; moreover, she began this reading in too much hurry. She grew provoked at the doctrines of religion; the arrogance of the polemic writings displeased her by their inveteracy in attacking people she did not know; and the secular stories, relieved with religion, seemed to her written in such ignorance of the world, that they insensibly estranged her from the truths for whose proof she was looking. Nevertheless, she persevered; and when the volume slipped from her hands, she fancied herself seized with the finest Catholic melancholy that an ethereal soul could conceive.

As for the memory of Rodolphe, she had thrust it back to the bottom of her heart, and it remained there more solemn and more motionless than a king's mummy in a catacomb. An exhalation escaped from this embalmed love, that, penetrating through everything, perfumed with tenderness the immaculate atmosphere in which she longed to live. When she knelt on her Gothic prie-Dieu, she addressed to the Lord the same suave words that she had murmured formerly to her lover in the outpourings of adultery. It was to make faith come; but no delights descended from the heavens, and she arose with tired limbs and with a vague feeling of a gigantic dupery.

This searching after faith, she thought, was only one merit the more, and in the pride of her devoutness Emma compared herself to those grand ladies of long ago whose glory she had dreamed of over a portrait of La Vallière, and who, trailing with so much majesty the lace-trimmed trains of their long gowns, retired into solitudes to shed at the feet of Christ all the tears of hearts that life had wounded.

Then she gave herself up to excessive charity. She sewed clothes for the poor, she sent wood to women in childbed; and Charles one day, on coming home, found three good-for-nothings in the kitchen seated at the table eating soup. She had her little girl, whom during her illness her husband had sent back to the nurse, brought home. She wanted to teach her to read; even when Berthe cried, she was not vexed. She had made up her mind to resignation, to universal indulgence. Her language about everything was full of ideal expressions. She said to her child, "Is your stomach-ache better, my angel?"

Madame Bovary senior found nothing to censure except perhaps this mania of knitting jackets for orphans instead of mending her own house-linen; but, harassed with domestic quarrels, the good woman took pleasure in this quiet house, and she even stayed there till after Easter, to escape the sarcasms of old Bovary, who never failed on Good Friday to order chitterlings.

Besides the companionship of her mother-in-law, who strengthened her a little by the rectitude of her judgment and her grave ways, Emma almost every day had other visitors. These were Madame Langlois, Madame Caron, Madame Dubreuil, Madame Tuvache, and regularly from two to five o'clock the excellent Madame Homais, who, for her part, had never believed any of the tittle-tattle about her neighbour. The little Homais also came to see her; Justin accompanied them. He went up with them to her bedroom, and remained standing near the door, motionless and mute. Often even Madame Bovary, taking no heed of him, began her toilette. She began by taking out her comb, shaking her head with a quick movement, and when he for the first time saw all this mass of hair that fell to her knees unrolling in black ringlets, it was to him, poor child! like a sudden entrance into something new and strange, whose splendour terrified him.

Emma, no doubt, did not notice his silent attentions or his timidity. She had no suspicion that the love vanished from her life was there, palpitating by her side, beneath that coarse holland shirt, in that youthful heart open to the emanations of her beauty. Besides, she now enveloped all things with such indifference, she had words so affectionate with looks so haughty, such contradictory ways, that one could no longer distinguish egotism from charity, or corruption from virtue. One evening, for example, she was angry with the servant, who had asked to go out, and stammered as she tried to find some pretext. Then suddenly—

"So you love him?" she said.

And without waiting for any answer from Félicité, who was blushing, she added, "There! run along; enjoy yourself!"

In the beginning of spring she had the garden turned up from end to end, despite Bovary's remonstrances. However, he was glad to see her at last manifest a wish of any kind. As she grew stronger she displayed more wilfulness. First, she found occasion to expel Mère Rollet, the nurse, who during her convalescence had contracted the habit of coming too often to the kitchen with her two nurslings and her boarder, better off for teeth than a cannibal. Then she got rid of the Homais family, successively dismissed all the other visitors, and even frequented church less assiduously, to the great approval of the druggist, who said to her in a friendly way—

"You were going in a bit for the cassock!"

As formerly, Monsieur Bournisien dropped in every day when he came out after catechism class. He preferred staying out of doors to taking the air "in the grove," as he called the arbour. This was the time when Charles came home. They were hot; some sweet cider was brought out, and they drank together to madame's complete restoration.

Binet was there; that is to say, a little lower down against the terrace wall, fishing for crayfish. Bovary invited him to have a drink, and he thoroughly understood the uncorking of the stone bottles.

"You must," he said, throwing a satisfied glance all round him, even to the very extremity of the landscape, "hold the bottle perpendicularly on the table, and after the strings are cut, press up the cork with little thrusts, gently, gently, as indeed they do seltzer-water at restaurants."

But during his demonstration the cider often spurted right into their faces, and then the ecclesiastic, with a thick laugh, never missed this joke—

"Its goodness strikes the eye!"

He was in fact, a good fellow and one day he was not even scandalised at the chemist, who advised Charles to give madame some distraction by taking her to the theatre at Rouen to hear the illustrious tenor, Lagardy. Homais, surprised at this silence, wanted to know his opinion, and the priest declared that he considered music less dangerous for morals than literature.

But the chemist took up the defence of letters. The theatre, he contended, served for railing at prejudices, and, beneath a mask of pleasure, taught virtue.

"*Castigat ridendo mores,* Monsieur Bournisien! Thus consider the greater part of Voltaire's tragedies; they are cleverly strewn with philosophical reflections, that make them a very school of morals and diplomacy for the people."

"I," said Binet, "once saw a piece called the *Gamin de Paris,* in which there was the character of an old general that is really hit off to a T. He sets down a young swell who had seduced a working girl, who at the ending—"

"Certainly," continued Homais, "there is bad literature as there is bad pharmacy, but to condemn in a lump the most important of the fine arts seems to me a stupidity, a Gothic idea, worthy of the abominable times that imprisoned Galileo."

"I know very well," objected the curé, "that there are good works, good authors. However, if it were only those persons of different sexes united in a bewitching apartment, decorated rouge, those lights, those effeminate voices, all this must, in the long-run, engender a certain mental libertinage, give rise to immodest thoughts and impure temptations. Such, at any rate, is the opinion of all the Father. Finally," he added, suddenly assuming a mystic tone of voice while he rolled a pinch of snuff between his fingers, "if the Church has condemned the theatre, she must be right; we must submit to her decrees."

"Why," asked the druggist, "should she excommunicate actors? For formerly they openly took part in religious ceremonies. Yes, in the middle of the chancel they acted; they performed a kind of farce called *Mysteries,* which often offended against the laws of decency."

The ecclesiastic contented himself with uttering a groan, and the chemist went on—

"It's like it is in the Bible; there there are, you know, more than one piquant detail, matters really libidinous!"

And on a gesture of irritation from Monsieur Bournisien—

"Ah! you'll admit that it is not a book to place in the hands of a young girl, and I should be sorry if Athalie—"

"But it is the Protestants, and not we," cried the other impatiently, "Who recommend the Bible."

"No matter," said Homais. "I am surprised that in our days, in this century of enlightenment, anyone should still persist in proscribing an intellectual relaxation that is inoffensive, moralising, and sometimes even hygienic; is it not, doctor?"

"No doubt," replied the doctor carelessly, either because, sharing the same ideas, he wished to offend no one, or else because he had not any ideas.

The conversation seemed at an end when the chemist thought fit to shoot a Parthian arrow.

"I've known priests who put on ordinary clothes to go and see dancers kicking about."

"Come, come!" said the curé.

"Ah! I've known some!" And separating the words of his sentence, Homais repeated, "I—have—known—some!"

"Well, they were wrong," said Bournisien, resigned to anything.

"By Jove! they go in far more than that," exclaimed the druggist.

"Sir!" replied the ecclesiastic, with such angry eyes that the druggist was intimidated by them.

"I only mean to say," he replied in less brutal a tone, "that toleration is the surest way to draw people to religion."

"That is true! that is true!" agreed the good fellow, sitting down again on his chair. But he stayed only a few moments.

Then, as soon as he had gone, Monsieur Homais said to the doctor—

"That's what I call a cock-fight. I beat him, did you see, in a way!—Now take my advice. Take madame to the theatre, if it were only for once in your life, to enrage one of these ravens, hang it! If anyone could take my place, I would accompany you myself. Be quick about it. Lagardy is only going to give one performance; he's engaged to go to England at a high salary. From what I hear, he's a regular dog; he's rolling in money; he's taking three mistresses and a cook along with him. All these great artists burn the candle at both ends; they require a dissolute life, that stirs the imagination to some extent. But they die at the hospital, because they haven't the sense when young to lay by. Well, a pleasant dinner! Good-bye till to-morrow."

The idea of the theatre quickly germinated in Bovary's head, for he at once communicated it to his wife, who at first refused, alleging the fatigue, the worry, the expense; but, for a wonder, Charles did not give in, so sure was he that this recreation would be good for her. He saw nothing to prevent it: his mother had sent them three hundred francs which he had no longer expected; the current debts were not very large, and the falling in of Lheureux's bills was still so far off that there was no need to think about them. Besides, imagining that she was refusing from delicacy, he insisted the more; so that by dint of worrying her she at last made up her mind, and the next day at eight o'clock they set out in the Hirondelle.

The druggist, whom nothing whatever kept at Yonville, but who thought himself bound not to budge from it, sighed as he saw them go.

"Well, a pleasant journey!" he said to them; "happy mortals that you are!"

Then addressing himself to Emma, who was wearing a blue silk gown with four flounces—

"You are as lovely as a Venus. You'll cut a figure at Rouen."

The diligence stopped at the Croix-Rouge in the Place Beauvoisine. It was the inn that is in every provincial faubourg, with large stables and small bedrooms, where one sees in the middle of the court chickens pilfering the oats under the muddy gigs of the commercial travellers;—a good old house, with worm-eaten balconies that creak in the wind on winter nights, always full of people, noise, and feeding, whose black tables are sticky with coffee and brandy, the thick windows made yellow by the flies, the damp napkins stained with cheap wine, and that always smells of the village, like ploughboys dressed in Sunday-clothes, has a café on the street, and towards the countryside a kitchen-garden. Charles at once set out. He muddled up the stage-boxes with the gallery, the pit with the boxes; asked for explanations, did not understand them; was sent from the box-office to the acting-manager; came back to the inn, returned to the theatre, and thus several times traversed the whole length of the town from the theatre to the boulevard.

Madame Bovary bought a bonnet, gloves, and a bouquet. The doctor was much afraid of missing the beginning, and, without having had time to swallow a plate of soup, they presented themselves at the doors of the theatre, which were still closed.

Chapter XV

THE CROWD WAS WAITING AGAINST THE WALL, SYMMETRICALLY ENCLOSED between the balustrades. At the corner of the neighbouring streets huge bills repeated in quaint letters "Lucie de Lammermoor—Lagardy—Opera—etc." The weather was fine, the people were hot, perspiration trickled amid the curls, and handkerchiefs taken from pockets were mopping red foreheads; and now and then a warm wind that blew from the river gently stirred the border of the tick awnings hanging from the doors of the public-houses. A little lower down, however, one was refreshed by a current of icy air that smelt of tallow, leather, and oil. This was an exhalation from the Rue des Charrettes, full of large black warehouses where they make casks.

For fear of seeming ridiculous, Emma before going in wished to have a little stroll in the harbour, and Bovary prudently kept his tickets in his hand, in the pocket of his trousers, which he pressed against his stomach.

Her heart began to beat as soon as she reached the vestibule. She involuntarily smiled with vanity on seeing the crowd rushing to the right by the other corridor while she went up the staircase to the reserved seats. She was as pleased as a child to push with her finger the large tapestried door. She breathed in with all her might the dusty smell of the lobbies, and when she was seated in her box she bent forward with the air of a duchess.

The theatre was beginning to fill; opera-glasses were taken from their cases, and the subscribers, catching sight of one another, were bowing. They came to seek relaxation in the fine arts after the anxieties of business; but "business" was not forgotten; they still talked cottons, spirits of wine, or indigo. The heads of old men were to be seen, inexpressive and peaceful, with their hair and complexions looking like silver medals tarnished by steam of lead. The young beaux were strutting about in the pit, showing in the opening of their waistcoats their pink or apple-green cravats, and Madame Bovary from above admired them leaning on their canes with golden knobs in the open palm of their yellow gloves.

Now the lights of the orchestra were lit, the lustre, let down from the ceiling, throwing by the glimmering of its facets a sudden gaiety over the theatre; then the musicians came in one after the other; and first there was the protracted hubbub of the basses grumbling, violins squeaking, cornets trumpeting, flutes and flageolets fifing. But three knocks were heard on the stage, a rolling of drums began, the brass instruments played some chords, and the curtain rising, discovered a country-scene.

It was the cross-roads of a wood, with a fountain shaded by an oak to the left. Peasants and lords with plaids on their shoulders were singing a hunting-song together; then a captain suddenly came on, who evoked the spirit of evil by lifting both his arms to heaven. Another appeared; they went away, and the hunters started afresh.

She felt herself transported to the reading of her youth, into the midst of Walter Scott. She seemed to hear through the mist the sound of the Scotch bagpipes re-echoing over the heather. Then her remembrance of the novel helping her to understand the libretto, she followed the story phrase by phrase, while vague thoughts that came back to her dispersed at once again with the bursts of music. She gave herself up to the lullaby of the melodies, and felt all her being vibrate as if the violin bows were drawn over her nerves. She had not eyes enough to look at the costumes, the scenery, the actors, the painted trees that shook when anyone walked, and the velvet caps, cloaks, swords—all those imaginary things that floated amid the harmony as in the atmosphere of another world. But a young woman stepped forward, throwing a purse to a squire in green. She was left alone, and the flute was heard like the murmur of a fountain or the warbling of birds. Lucie attacked her cavatina in G major bravely. She plained of love; she longed for wings. Emma, too, fleeing from life, would have liked to fly away in an embrace. Suddenly Edgar-Lagardy appeared.

He had that splendid palor that gives something of the majesty of marble to the ardent races of the South. His vigourous form was tightly clad in a brown-coloured doublet; a small chiselled poniard hung against his left thigh, and he cast round laughing looks showing his white teeth. They said that a Polish princess having heard him sing one night on the beach at Biarritz, where he mended boats, had fallen in love with him. She had ruined herself for him. He had deserted her for other women, and this sentimental celebrity did not fail to enhance his artistic reputation. The diplomatic mummer took care always to slip into his advertisements some poetic phrase on the fascination of his person and the susceptibility of his soul. A fine organ, imperturbable coolness, more temperament than intelligence, more power of emphasis than of real singing, made up the charm of this admirable charlatan nature, in which there was something of the hairdresser and the toréador.

From the first scene he evoked enthusiasm. He pressed Lucy in his arms, he left her, he came back, he seemed desperate; he had outbursts of rage, then elegiac gurglings of infinite sweetness, and the notes escaped from his bare neck full of sobs and kisses. Emma lent forward to see him, clutching the velvet of the box with her nails. She was filling her heart with these melodious lamentations that were drawn out to the accompaniment of the double-basses, like the cries of the drowning in the tumult of a tempest. She recognised all the intoxication and the anguish that had almost killed her. The voice of the prima donna seemed to her to be but echoes of her conscience, and this illusion that charmed her as some very thing of her own life. But no one on earth had loved her with such love. He had not wept like Edgar that last moonlit night when they said, "To-morrow! to-morrow!" The theatre rang with cheers; they recommenced the entire movement; the lovers spoke of the flowers on their tomb, of vows, exile, fate, hopes; and when they uttered the final adieu, Emma gave a sharp cry that mingled with the vibrations of the last chords.

"But why," asked Bovary, "does that gentleman persecute her?"

"No, no!" she answered; "he is her lover!"

"Yet he vows vengeance on her family, while the other one who came on before said, 'I love Lucie and she loves me!' Besides, he went off with her father arm in arm. For he certainly is her father, isn't he—the ugly little man with a cock's feather in his hat?"

Despite Emma's explanations, as soon as the recitative duet began in which Gilbert lays bare his abominable machinations to his master Ashton, Charles, seeing the false troth-ring that is to deceive Lucie, thought it was a love-gift sent by Edgar. He confessed, moreover, that he did not understand the story because of the music, which interfered very much with the words.

"What does it matter?" said Emma. "Do be quiet!"

"Yes, but you know," he went on, leaning against her shoulder, "I like to understand things."

"Be quiet! be quiet!" she cried impatiently.

Lucie advanced, half supported by her women, a wreath of orange blossoms in her hair, and paler than the white satin of her gown. Emma dreamed of her marriage day; she saw herself at home again amid the corn in the little path as they walked to the church. Oh, why had not she, like this woman, resisted, implored? She, on the contrary, had been joyous, without seeing the abyss into which she was throwing herself. Ah! if in the freshness of her beauty, before the soiling of marriage and the disillusions of adultery, she could have anchored her life upon some great, strong heart, then virtue, tenderness, voluptuousness, and duty blending, she would never have fallen from so high a happiness. But that happiness, no doubt, was a lie inverted for the despair of all desire. She now knew the smallness of the passions that art exaggerated. So, striving to divert her thoughts, Emma determined now to see in this reproduction of her sorrows only a plastic fantasy, well enough to please the eye, and she even smiled internally with disdainful pity when at the back of the stage under the velvet hangings a man appeared in a black cloak.

His large Spanish hat fell at a gesture he made, and immediately the instruments and the singers began the sextet. Edgar, flashing with fury, dominated all the others with his clearer voice; Ashton hurled homicidal provocations at him in deep notes; Lucie uttered her shrill plaint, Arthur at one side, his modulated tones in the middle register, and the bass of the minister pealed forth like an organ, while the voices of the women repeating his words took them up in chorus delightfully. They were all in a row gesticulating, and anger, vengeance, jealousy, terror, and stupefaction breathed forth at once from their half-opened mouths. The outraged lover brandished his naked sword; his guipure ruffle rose with jerks to the movements of his chest, and he walked from right to left with long strides, clanking against the boards the silver-gilt spurs of his soft boots, widening out at the ankles. He, she thought, must have an inexhaustible love to lavish it upon the crowd with such effusion. All her small fault-findings faded before the poetry of the part that absorbed her; and, drawn towards this man by the illusion of the character, she tried to imagine to herself his life—that life resonant, extraordinary, splendid, and that might have been hers if fate had willed it. They would have known one another, loved one another. With him, through all the kingdoms of Europe she would have travelled from capital to capital, sharing his fatigues and his pride, picking up the flowers thrown to him, herself embroidering his costumes. Then each evening, at the back of a box, behind the golden trellis-work, she would have drunk in eagerly the expansions of this soul that would have sung for her alone; from the stage, even as he acted, he would have looked at her. But the mad idea seized her that he was looking at her; it was certain. She longed to run to his arms, to take refuge in his strength, as in the incarnation of love itself, and to say to him, to cry out, "Take me away! carry me with you! let us go! Thine, thine! all my ardour and all my dreams!"

The curtain fell.

The smell of the gas mingled with that of the breaths, the waving of the fans, made the air more suffocating. Emma wanted to go out; the crowd filled the corridors, and she fell back in her arm-chair with palpitations that choked her. Charles, fearing that she would faint, ran to the refreshment-room to get a glass of barleywater.

He had great difficulty in getting back to his seat, for his elbows were jerked at every step because of the glass he held in his hands, and he even spilt three-fourths on the shoulders of a Rouen lady in short sleeves, who feeling the cold liquid running down to her loins, uttered cries like a peacock, as if she were being assassinated. Her husband, who was a mill-owner, railed at the clumsy fellow, and while she was with her handkerchief wiping up the stains from her handsome cherry-coloured taffeta gown, he angrily muttered about indemnity, costs, reimbursement. At last Charles reached his wife, saying to her, quite out of breath—

"*Ma foi!* I thought I should have had to stay there. There is such a crowd—*such* a crowd!"

He added—

"Just guess whom I met up there! Monsieur Léon!"

"Léon?"

"Himself! He's coming along to pay his respects." And as he finished these words the ex-clerk of Yonville entered the box.

He held out his hand with the ease of a gentleman; and Madame Bovary extended hers, without doubt obeying the attraction of a stronger will. She had not felt it since that spring evening when the rain fell upon the green leaves, and they had said good-bye standing at the window. But soon recalling herself to the necessities of the situation, with an effort she shook off the torpor of her memories, and began stammering a few hurried words.

"Ah, good-day! What! you here?"

"Silence!" cried a voice from the pit, for the third act was beginning.

"So you are at Rouen?"

"Yes."

"And since when?"

"Turn them out! turn them out!" People were looking at them. They were silent.

But from that moment she listened no more; and the chorus of the guests, the scene between Ashton and his servant, the grand duet in D major, all were for her as far off as if the instruments had grown less sonorous and the characters more remote. She remembered the games at cards at the druggist's, and the walk to the nurse's, the reading in the arbour, the *tête-à-tête* by the fireside—all that poor love, so calm and so protracted, so discreet, so tender, and that she had nevertheless forgotten. And why had he come back? What combination of circumstances had brought him back into her life. He was standing behind her, leaning with his shoulder against the wall of the box; now and again she felt herself shuddering beneath the hot breath from his nostrils falling upon her hair.

"Does this amuse you?" he said, bending over her so closely that the end of his moustache brushed her cheek. She replied carelessly—

"Oh, dear me, no, not much."

Then he proposed that they should leave the theatre and go and take an ice somewhere.

"Oh, not yet; let us stay," said Bovary. "Her hair's undone; this is going to be tragic."

But the mad scene did not at all interest Emma, and the acting of the singer seemed to her exaggerated.

"She screams too loud," said she, turning to Charles, who was listening.

"Yes—perhaps—a little," he replied, undecided between the frankness of his pleasure and his respect for his wife's opinion.

Then with a sigh Léon said—

"The heat is—"

"Unbearable! Yes!"

"Do you feel unwell?" asked Bovary.

"Yes, I am stifling; let us go."

Monsieur Léon put her long lace shawl carefully about her shoulders, and all three went off to sit down in the harbour, in the open air, outside the windows of a café.

First they spoke of her illness, although Emma interrupted Charles from time to time, for fear, she said, of boring Monsieur Léon; and the latter told them that he had come to spend two years at Rouen in a large office, in order to get practice in his profession, which was different in Normandy and Paris. Then he inquired after Berthe, the Homais, Mère Lefrançois, and as they had, in the husband's presence, nothing more to say to one another, the conversation soon came to an end.

People coming out of the theatre passed along the pavement, humming or shouting at the top of their voices, *"O bel ange, ma Lucie!"* Then Léon, playing the dilettante, began to talk music. He had seen Tamburini, Rubini, Persiani, Grisi, and, compared with them, Lagardy, despite his grand outbursts, was nowhere.

"Yet," interrupted Charles, who was slowly sipping his rum-sherbet, "they say that he is quite admirable in the last act. I regret leaving before the end, because it was beginning to amuse me."

"Why," said the clerk, "he will soon give another performance."

But Charles replied that they were going back next day. "Unless," he added, turning to his wife, "you would like to stay alone, pussy?"

And changing his tactics at this unexpected opportunity that presented itself to his hopes, the young man sang the praises of Lagardy in the last number. It was really superb, sublime. Then Charles insisted—

"You would get back on Sunday. Come, make up your mind. You are wrong if you feel that this is doing you the least good."

The tables round them, however, were emptying; a waiter came and stood discreetly near them. Charles, who understood, took out his purse; the clerk held back his arm, and did not forget to leave two more pieces of silver that he made chink on the marble.

"I am really sorry," said Bovary, "about the money which you are—"

The other made a careless gesture full of cordiality, and taking his hat said—

"It is settled, isn't it? To-morrow at six o'clock?"

Charles explained once more that he could not absent himself longer, but that nothing prevented Emma—

"But," she stammered, with a strange smile, "I am not sure—"

"Well, you must think it over. We'll see. Night brings counsel." Then to Léon, who was walking along with them, "Now that you are in our part of the world, I hope you'll come and ask us for some dinner now and then."

The clerk declared he would not fail to do so, being obliged, moreover, to go to Yonville on some business for his office. And they parted before the Saint-Herbland Passage just as the cathedral struck half-past eleven.

PART III

Chapter I

MONSIEUR LÉON, WHILE STUDYING LAW, HAD GONE PRETTY OFTEN TO THE dancing-rooms, where he was even a great success amongst the grisettes, who thought he had a distinguished air. He was the best-mannered of the students; he wore his hair neither too long nor too short, didn't spend all his quarter's money on the first day of the month, and kept on good terms with his professors. As for excesses, he had always abstained from them, as much from cowardice as from refinement.

Often when he stayed in his room to read, or else when sitting of an evening under the lime-trees of the Luxembourg, he let his *Code* fall to the ground, and the memory of Emma came back to him. But gradually this feeling grew weaker, and other desires gathered over it, although it still persisted through them all. For Léon did not lose all hope; there was for him, as it were, a vague promise floating in the future, like a golden fruit suspended from some fantastic tree.

Then, seeing her again after three years of absence, his passion reawakened. He must, he thought, at last make up his mind to possess her. Moreover, his timidity had worn off by contact with his gay companions, and he returned to the provinces despising everyone who had not with varnished shoes trodden the asphalt of the boulevards. By the side of a Parisienne in her laces, in the drawing-room of some illustrious physician, a person driving his carriage and wearing many orders, the poor clerk would no doubt have trembled like a child; but here, at Rouen, on the harbour, with the wife of this small doctor he felt at his ease, sure beforehand he would shine. Self-possession depends on its environment. We don't speak on the first floor as on the fourth; and the wealthy woman seems to have, about her, to guard her virtue, all her bank-notes, like a cuirass, in the lining of her corset.

On leaving the Bovarys the night before, Léon had followed them through the streets at a distance; then having seen them stop at the Croix-Rouge, he turned on his heel, and spent the night meditating a plan.

So the next day about five o'clock he walked into the kitchen of the inn, with a choking sensation in his throat, pale cheeks, and that resolution of cowards that stops at nothing.

"The gentleman isn't in," answered a servant.

This seemed to him a good omen. He went upstairs.

She was not disturbed at his approach; on the contrary, she apologised for having neglected to tell him where they were staying.

"Oh, I divined it!" said Léon.

He pretended he had been guided towards her by chance, by instinct. She began to smile; and at once, to repair his folly, Léon told her that he had spent his morning in looking for her in all the hotels in the town, one after the other.

"So you have made up your mind to stay?" he added.

"Yes," she said, "and I am wrong. One ought not to accustom oneself to impossible pleasures when there are a thousand demands upon one."

"Oh, I can imagine!"

"Ah! no; for you, you are a man!"

But men too had their trials, and the conversation went off into certain philosophical reflections. Emma expatiated much on the misery of earthly affections, and the eternal isolation in which the heart remains entombed.

To show off, or from a naïve imitation of this melancholy which called forth his, the young man declared that he had been awfully bored during the whole course of his studies. The law irritated him, other vocations attracted him, and his mother never ceased worrying him in every one of her letters. As they talked they explained more and more fully the motives of their sadness, working themselves up in their progressive confidence. But they sometimes stopped short of the complete exposition of their thought, and then sought to invent a phrase that might express it all the same. She did not confess her passion for another; he did not say that he had forgotten her.

Perhaps he no longer remembered his suppers with girls after masked balls; and no doubt she did not recollect the rendezvous of old when she ran across the fields in the morning to her lover's house. The noises of the town hardly reached them, and the room seemed small, as if on purpose to hem in their solitude more closely. Emma, in a dimity dressing-gown, leant her head against the back of the old arm-chair; the yellow wall-paper formed, as it were, a golden back-ground behind her, and her bare head was mirrored in the glass with the white parting in the middle, and the tip of her ears peeping out from the folds of her hair.

"But pardon me!" she said. "It is wrong of me. I weary you with my eternal complaints."

"No, never, never!"

"If you knew," she went on, raising to the ceiling her beautiful eyes, in which a tear was trembling, "all that I had dreamed!"

"And I! Oh, I too have suffered! Often I went out; I went away. I dragged myself along the quays, seeking distraction amid the din of the crowd without being able to banish the heaviness that weighed upon me. In an engraver's shop on the boulevard there is an Italian print of one of the Muses. She is draped in a tunic, and she is looking at the moon, with forget-me-nots in her flowing hair. Something drove me there continually; I stayed there hours together." Then in a trembling voice, "She resembled you a little."

Madame Bovary turned away her head that he might not see the irrepressible smile she felt rising to her lips.

"Often," he went on, "I wrote you letters that I tore up."

She did not answer. He continued—

"I sometimes fancied that some chance would bring you. I thought I recognised you at street-corners, and I ran after all the carriages through whose windows I saw a shawl fluttering, a veil like yours."

She seemed resolved to let him go on speaking without interruption. Crossing her arms and bending down her face, she looked at the rosettes on her slippers, and at intervals made little movements inside the satin of them with her toes.

At last she sighed.

"But the most wretched thing, is it not—is to drag out, as I do, a useless existence. If our pains were only of some use to someone, we should find consolation in the thought of the sacrifice."

He started off in praise of virtue, duty, and silent immolation, having himself an incredible longing for self-sacrifice that he could not satisfy.

"I should much like," she said, "to be a nurse at a hospital."

"Alas! men have none of these holy missions, and I see nowhere any calling— unless perhaps that of a doctor."

With a slight shrug of her shoulders, Emma interrupted him to speak of her illness, which had almost killed her. What a pity! She should not be suffering now! Léon at once envied the calm of the tomb, and one evening he had even made his will, asking to be buried in that beautiful rug with velvet stripes he had received from her. For this was how they would have wished to be, each setting up an ideal to which they were now adapting their past life. Besides, speech is a rolling-mill that always thins out the sentiment.

But at this invention of the rug she asked, "But why?"

"Why?" He hesitated. "Because I loved you so!" And congratulating himself at having surmounted the difficulty, Léon watched her face out of the corner of his eyes.

It was like the sky when a gust of wind drives the clouds across. The mass of sad thoughts that darkened them seemed to be lifted from her blue eyes; her whole face shone. He waited. At last she replied—

"I always suspected it."

Then they went over all the trifling events of that far-off existence, whose joys and sorrows they had just summed up in one word. They recalled the arbour with clematis, the dresses she had worn, the furniture of her room, the whole of her house.

"And our poor cactuses, where are they?"

"The cold killed them this winter."

"Ah! how I have thought of them, do you know? I often saw them again as of yore, when on the summer mornings the sun beat down upon your blinds, and I saw your two bare arms passing out amongst the flowers."

"Poor friend!" she said, holding out her hand to him.

Léon swiftly pressed his lips to it. Then, when he had taken a deep breath—

"At that time you were to me I know not what incomprehensible force that took captive my life. Once, for instance, I went to see you; but you, no doubt, do not remember it."

"I do," she said; "go on."

"You were downstairs in the ante-room, ready to go out, standing on the last stair; you were wearing a bonnet with small blue flowers; and without any invitation from you, in spite of myself, I went with you. Every moment, however, I grew more and more conscious of my folly, and I went on walking by you, not daring to follow you completely, and unwilling to leave you. When you went into a shop, I waited in the street, and I watched you through the window taking off your gloves and counting the change on the counter. Then you rang at Madame Tuvache's; you were let in, and I stood like an idiot in front of the great heavy door that had closed after you."

Madame Bovary, as she listened to him, wondered that she was so old. All these things reappearing before her seemed to widen out her life; it was like some sentimental immensity to which she returned; and from time to time she said in a low voice, her eyes half closed—

"Yes, it is true—true—true!"

They heard eight strike on the different clocks of the Beauvoisine quarter, that is full of schools, churches, and large empty hotels. They no longer spoke, but they felt as they looked upon each other a buzzing in their heads, as if something sonorous had escaped from the fixed eyes of each of them. They were hand in hand now, and the past, the future, reminiscences and dreams, all were confounded in the sweetness of this ecstasy. Night was darkening over the walls, on which still shone, half hidden in the shade, the coarse colours of four bills representing four scenes from the *Tour de Nesle*, with a motto in Spanish and French at the bottom. Through the sash-window a patch of dark sky was seen between the pointed roofs.

She rose to light two wax-candles on the drawers, then she sat down again.

"Well!" said Léon.

"Well!" she replied.

He was thinking how to resume the interrupted conversation, when she said to him—

"How is it that no one until now has ever expressed such sentiments to me?"

The clerk said that ideal natures were difficult to understand. He from the first moment had loved her, and he despaired when he thought of the happiness that would have been theirs, if thanks to fortune, meeting her earlier, they had been indissolubly bound to one another.

"I have sometimes thought of it," she went on.

"What a dream!" murmured Léon. And fingering gently the blue binding of her long white sash, he added, "And who prevents us from beginning now?"

"No, my friend," she replied; "I am too old; you are too young. Forget me! Others will love you; you will love them."

"Not as you!" he cried.

"What a child you are! Come, let us be sensible. I wish it."

She showed him the impossibility of their love, and that they must remain, as formerly, on the simple terms of a fraternal friendship.

Was she speaking thus seriously? No doubt Emma did not herself know, quite absorbed as she was by the charm of the seduction, and the necessity of defending herself from it; and contemplating the young man with a moved look, she gently repulsed the timid caresses that his trembling hands attempted.

"Ah! forgive me!" he cried, drawing back.

Emma was seized with a vague fear at this shyness, more dangerous to her than the boldness of Rodolphe when he advanced to her open-armed. No man had ever seemed to her so beautiful. An exquisite candour emanated from his being. He lowered his long fine eyelashes, that curled upwards. His cheek, with the soft skin reddened, she thought, with desire of her person, and Emma felt an invincible longing to press her lips to it. Then, leaning towards the clock as if to see the time—

"Ah! how late it is!" she said; "how we do chatter!"

He understood the hint and took up his hat.

"It has even made me forget the theatre. And poor Bovary has left me here especially for that. Monsieur Lormeaux, of the Rue Grand-Pont, was to take me and his wife."

And the opportunity was lost, as she was to leave the next day.

"Really!" said Léon.

"Yes."

"But I must see you again," he went on. "I wanted to tell you—"

"What?"

"Something—important—serious. Oh, no! Besides, you will not go; it is impossible. If you should—listen to me. Then you have not understood me; you have not guessed—"

"Yet you speak plainly," said Emma.

"Ah! you can jest. Enough! enough! Oh, for pity's sake, let me see you once—only once!"

"Well—" She stopped; then, as if thinking better of it, "Oh, not here!"

"Where you will."

"Will you—" She seemed to reflect; then abruptly, "To-morrow at eleven o'clock in the cathedral."

"I shall be there," he cried, seizing her hands, which she disengaged.

And as they were both standing up, he behind her, and Emma with her head bent, he stooped over her and pressed long kisses on her neck.

"You are mad! Ah! you are mad!" she said, with sounding little laughs, while the kisses multiplied.

Then bending his head over her shoulder, he seemed to beg the consent of her eyes. They fell upon him full of an icy dignity.

Léon stepped back to go out. He stopped on the threshold; then he whispered with a trembling voice, "To-morrow!"

She answered with a nod, and disappeared like a bird into the next room.

In the evening Emma wrote the clerk an interminable letter, in which she cancelled the rendezvous; all was over; they must not, for the sake of their happiness, meet again. But when the letter was finished, as she did not know Léon's address, she was puzzled.

"I'll give it to him myself," she said; "he will come."

The next morning, at the open window, and humming on his balcony, Léon himself varnished his pumps with several coatings. He put on white trousers, fine socks, a green coat, emptied all the scent he had into his handkerchief, then having had his hair curled, he uncurled it again, in order to give it a more natural elegance.

"It is still too early," he thought, looking at the hairdresser's cuckoo-clock, that pointed to the hour of nine. He read an old fashion journal, went out, smoked a cigar, walked up three streets, thought it was time, and went slowly towards the porch of Notre Dame.

It was a beautiful summer morning. Silver plate sparkled in the jeweller's windows, and the light falling obliquely on the cathedral made mirrors of the corners of the grey stones; a flock of birds fluttered in the grey sky round the trefoil bell-turrets; the square, resounding with cries, was fragrant with the flowers that bordered its pavement, roses, jasmines, pinks, narcissi, and tuberoses, unevenly spaced out between moist grasses, cat-mint, and chickweed for the birds; the fountains gurgled in the centre, and under large umbrellas, amidst melons piled up in heaps, flower-women, bare-headed, were twisting paper round bunches of violets.

The young man took one. It was the first time that he had bought flowers for a woman, and his breast, as he smelt them, swelled with pride, as if this homage that he meant for another had recoiled upon himself.

But he was afraid of being seen; he resolutely entered the church. The beadle, who was just then standing on the threshold in the middle of the left doorway, under the "Dancing Marianne," with feather cap, and rapier dangling against his calves, came in, more majestic than a cardinal, and as shining as a saint on a holy pyx.

He came towards Léon, and, with that smile of wheedling benignity assumed by ecclesiastics when they question children—

"The gentleman, no doubt, does not belong to these parts? The gentleman would like to see the curiosities of the church?"

"No!" said the other.

And he first went round the lower aisles. Then he went out to look at the Place. Emma was not coming yet. He went up again to the choir.

The nave was reflected in the full fonts with the beginning of the arches and some portions of the glass windows. But the reflections of the paintings, broken by the marble rim, were continued farther on upon the flag-stones, like a many-coloured carpet. The broad daylight from without streamed into the church in three enormous rays from the three opened portals. From time to time at the upper end a sacristan passed, making the oblique genuflexion of devout persons in a hurry. The crystal lustres hung motionless. In the choir a silver lamp was burning, and from the side chapels and dark places of the church sometimes rose sounds like sighs, with the clang of a closing grating, its echo reverberating under the lofty vault.

Léon with solemn steps walked along by the walls. Life had never seemed so good to him. She would come directly, charming, agitated, looking back at the glances that followed her, and with her flounced dress, her gold eyeglass, her thin shoes, with all sorts of elegant trifles that he had never enjoyed, and with the ineffable seduction of yielding virtue. The church like a huge boudoir spread around her; the arches bent down to gather in the shade the confession of her love; the windows shone resplendent to illumine her face, and the censers would burn that she might appear like an angel amid the fumes of the sweet-smelling odours.

But she did not come. He sat down on a chair, and his eyes fell upon a blue stained window representing boatmen carrying baskets. He looked at it long, attentively, and he counted the scales of the fishes and the button-holes of the doublets, while his thoughts wandered off towards Emma.

The beadle, standing aloof, was inwardly angry at this individual who took the liberty of admiring the cathedral by himself. He seemed to him to be conducting himself in a monstrous fashion, to be robbing him in a sort, and almost committing sacrilege.

But a rustle of silk on the flags, the tip of a bonnet, a lined cloak—it was she! Léon rose and ran to meet her.

Emma was pale. She walked fast.

"Read!" she said, holding out a paper to him. "Oh, no!"

And she abruptly withdrew her hand to enter the chapel of the Virgin, where, kneeling on a chair, she began to pray.

The young man was irritated at this bigot fancy; then he nevertheless experienced a certain charm in seeing her, in the middle of a rendezvous, thus lost in her devotions, like an Andalusian marchioness; then he grew bored, for she seemed never coming to an end.

Emma prayed, or rather strove to pray, hoping that some sudden resolution might descend to her from heaven; and to draw down divine aid she filled full her eyes with the splendours of the tabernacle. She breathed in the perfumes of the full-blown flowers in the large vases, and listened to the stillness of the church, that only heightened the tumult of her heart.

She rose, and they were about to leave, when the beadle came forward, hurriedly saying—

"Madame, no doubt, does not belong to these parts? Madame would like to see the curiosities of the church?"

"Oh, no!" cried the clerk.

"Why not?" said she. For she clung with her expiring virtue to the Virgin, the sculptures, the tombs—anything.

Then, in order to proceed "by rule," the beadle conducted them right to the entrance near the square, where, pointing out with his cane a large circle of block-stones without inscription or carving—

"This," he said majestically, "is the circumference of the beautiful bell of Ambroise. It weighed forty thousand pounds. There was not its equal in all Europe. The workman who cast it died of the joy—"

"Let us go on," said Léon.

The old fellow started off again; then, having got back to the chapel of the Virgin, he stretched forth his arm with an all-embracing gesture of demonstration, and, prouder than a country squire showing you his espaliers, went on—

"This simple stone covers Pierre de Brézé, lord of Varenne and of Brissac, grand marshal of Poitou, and governor of Normandy, who died at the battle of Montlhéry on the 16th of July, 1465."

Léon bit his lips, fuming.

"And on the right, this gentleman all encased in iron, on the prancing horse, is his grandson, Louise de Brézé, lord of Breval and of Montchauvet, Count de Maulevrier, Baron de Mauny, chamberlain to the king, Knight of the Order, and also governor of Normandy; died on the 23rd of July, 1531—a Sunday, as the inscription specifies; and below, this figure, about to descend into the tomb, portrays the same person. It is not possible, is it, to see a more perfect representation of annihilation?"

Madame Bovary put up her eyeglasses. Léon, motionless, looked at her, no longer even attempting to speak a single word, to make a gesture, so discouraged was he at this twofold obstinacy of gossip and indifference.

The everlasting guide went on—

"Near him, this kneeling woman who weeps is his spouse, Diane de Poitiers, Countess de Brézé, Duchess de Valentinois, born in 1499, died in 1566, and to the left, the one with the child is the Holy Virgin. Now turn to this side; here are the tombs of the Ambroise. They were both cardinals and archbishops of Rouen. That one was minister under Louis XII. He did a great deal for the cathedral. In his will he left thirty thousand gold crowns for the poor."

And without stopping, still talking, he pushed them into a chapel full of balustrades, some put away, and disclosed a kind of block that certainly might once have been an ill-made statue.

"Truly," he said with a groan, "it adorned the tomb of Richard Cœur de Lion, King of England and Duke of Normandy. It was the Calvinists, sir, who reduced it to this condition. They had buried it for spite in the earth, under the episcopal seat of Monsignor. See! this is the door by which Monsignor passes to his house. Let us pass on quickly to see the gargoyle windows."

But Léon hastily took some silver from his pocket and seized Emma's arm. The beadle stood dumbfounded, not able to understand this untimely munificence when there were still so many things for the stranger to see. So calling him back, he cried—

"Sir! sir! The steeple! the steeple!"

"No, thank you!" said Léon.

"You are wrong, sir! It is four hundred and forty feet high, nine less than the great pyramid of Egypt. It is all cast; it—"

Léon was fleeing, for it seemed to him that his love, that for nearly two hours now had become petrified in the church like the stones, would vanish like a vapour through that sort of truncated funnel, of oblong cage, of open chimney that rises so grotesquely from the cathedral like the extravagant attempt of some fantastic brazier.

"But where are we going?" she said.

Making no answer, he walked on with a rapid step; and Madame Bovary was already dipping her finger in the holy water when behind them they heard a panting breath interrupted by the regular sound of a cane. Léon turned back.

"Sir!"

"What is it?"

And he recognised the beadle, holding under his arms and balancing against his stomach some twenty large sewn volumes. They were works "which treated of the cathedral."

"Idiot!" growled Léon, rushing out of the church.

A lad was playing about the close.

"Go and get me a cab!"

The child bounded off like a ball by the Rue Quatre-Vents; then they were alone a few minutes, face to face, and a little embarrassed.

"Ah! Léon! Really—I don't know—if I ought," she whispered. Then with a more serious air, "Do you know, it is very improper?"

"How so?" replied the clerk. "It is done at Paris."

And that, as an irresistible argument, decided her.

Still the cab did not come. Léon was afraid she might go back into the church. At last the cab appeared.

"At all events, go out by the north porch," cried the beadle, who was left alone on the threshold, "so as to see the Resurrection, the Last Judgment, Paradise, King David, and the Condemned in Hell-flames."

"Where to, sir?" asked the coachman.

"Where you like," said Léon, forcing Emma into the cab.

And the lumbering machine set out. It went down the Rue Grand-Pont, crossed the Place des Arts, the Quai Napoleon, the Pont Neuf, and stopped short before the statue of Pierre Corneille.

"Go on," cried a voice that came from within.

The cab went on again, and as soon as it reached the Carrefour Lafayette, set off down-hill, and entered the station at a gallop.

"No, straight on!" cried the same voice.

The cab came out by the gate, and soon having reached the Cours, trotted quietly beneath the elm-trees. The coachman wiped his brow, put his leather hat between his knees, and drove his carriage beyond the side alley by the meadow to the margin of the waters.

It went along by the river, along the towing-path paved with sharp pebbles, and for a long while in the direction of Oyssel, beyond the isles.

But suddenly it turned with a dash across Quatremares, Sotteville, La Grande-Chaussée, the Rue d'Elbeuf, and made its third halt in front of the Jardin des Plantes.

"Get on, will you?" cried the voice more furiously.

And at once resuming its course, it passed by Saint-Sever, by the Quai des Curandiers, the Quai aux Meules, once more over the bridge, by the Place du Champ de Mars, and behind the hospital gardens, where old men in black coats were walking in the sun along the terrace all green with ivy. It went up the Boulevard Bouvreuil, along the Boulevard Cauchoise, then the whole of Mont-Riboudet to the Deville hills.

It came back; and then, without any fixed plan or direction, wandered about at hazard. The cab was seen at Saint-Pol, at Lescure, at Mont Gargan, at La Rougue-Marc and Place du Gaillardbois; in the Rue Maladrerie, Rue Dinanderie, before Saint-Romain, Saint-Vivien, Saint-Maclou, Saint-Nicaise—in front of the Customs, at the "Vieille Tour," the "Trois Pipes," and the Monumental Cemetery. From time to time the coachman on his box cast despairing eyes at the public-houses. He could not understand what furious desire for locomotion urged these individuals never to wish to stop. He tried to now and then, and at once exclamations of anger burst forth behind him. Then he lashed his perspiring jades afresh, but indifferent to their jolting, running up against things here and there, not caring if he did, demoralised, and almost weeping with thirst, fatigue, and depression.

And on the harbour, in the midst of the drays and casks, and in the streets, at the corners, the good folk opened large wonder-stricken eyes at this sight, so extraordinary in the provinces, a cab with blinds drawn, and which appeared thus constantly shut more closely than a tomb, and tossing about like a vessel.

Once in the middle of the day, in the open country, just as the sun beat most fiercely against the old plated lanterns, a bared hand passed beneath the small blinds of yellow canvas, and threw out some scraps of paper that scattered in the wind, and farther off alighted like white butterflies on a field of red clover all in bloom.

At about six o'clock the carriage stopped in a back street of the Beauvoisine Quarter, and a woman got out, who walked with her veil down, and without turning her head.

Chapter II

O N REACHING THE INN, MADAME BOVARY WAS SURPRISED NOT TO SEE THE
diligence. Hivert, who had waited for her fifty-three minutes, had at last
started.

Yet nothing forced her to go; but she had given her word that she would return
that same evening. Moreover, Charles expected her, and in her heart she felt already that cowardly docility that is for some women at once the chastisement and
atonement of adultery.

She packed her box quickly, paid her bill, took a cab in the yard, hurrying on
the driver, urging him on, every moment inquiring about the time and the miles
traversed. He succeeded in catching up the Hirondelle as it neared the first houses
of Quincampoix.

Hardly was she seated in her corner than she closed her eyes, and opened them
at the foot of the hill, when from afar she recognised Félicité, who was on the lookout in front of the farrier's shop. Hivert pulled in his horses, and the servant, climbing up to the window, said mysteriously—

"Madame, you must go at once to Monsieur Homais. It's for something important."

The village was silent as usual. At the corner of the streets were small pink
heaps that smoked in the air, for this was the time for jam-making, and everyone at
Yonville prepared his supply on the same day. But in front of the chemist's shop
one might admire a far larger heap, and that surpassed the others with the superiority that a laboratory must have over ordinary stores, a general need over individual fancy.

She went in. The large arm-chair was upset, and even the *Fanal de Rouen* lay on
the ground, outspread between two pestles. She pushed open the lobby door, and in the
middle of the kitchen, amid brown jars full of picked currants, of powdered sugar and
lump sugar, of the scales on the table, and of the pans on the fire, she saw all the
Homais, small and large, with aprons reaching to their chins, and with forks in their
hands. Justin was standing up with bowed head, and the chemist was screaming—

"Who told you to go and fetch it in the capharnaüm."

"What is it? What is the matter?"

"What is it?" replied the druggist. "We are making preserves; they are simmering; but they were about to boil over, because there is too much juice, and I ordered another pan. Then he, from indolence, from laziness, went and took,
hanging on its nail in my laboratory, the key of the capharnaüm."

It was thus the druggist called a small room under the leads, full of the utensils and the goods of his trade. He often spent long hours there alone, labelling, decanting, and doing up again; and he looked upon it not as a simple store, but as a veritable sanctuary, whence there afterwards issued, elaborated by his hands, all sorts of pills, boluses, infusions, lotions, and potions, that would bear far and wide his celebrity. No one in the world set foot there, and he respected it so, that he swept it himself. Finally, if the pharmacy, open to all comers, was the spot where he displayed his pride, the capharnaüm was the refuge where, egoistically concentrating himself, Homais delighted in the exercise of his predilections, so that Justin's thoughtlessness seemed to him a monstrous piece of irreverence, and, redder than the currants, he repeated—

"Yes, from the capharnaüm! The key that locks up the acids and caustic alkalies! To go and get a spare pan! a pan with a lid! and that I shall perhaps never use! Everything is of importance in the delicate operations of our art! But, devil take it! one must make distinctions, and not employ for almost domestic purposes that which is meant for pharmaceutical! It is as if one were to carve a fowl with a scalpel; as if a magistrate—"

"Now be calm," said Madame Homais.

And Athalie, pulling at his coat, cried "Papa! papa!"

"No, let me alone," went on the druggist, "let me alone, hang it! My word! One might as well set up for a grocer. That's it! go it! respect nothing! break, smash, let loose the leeches, burn the mallow-paste, pickle the gherkins in the window jars, tear up the bandages!"

"I thought you had—" said Emma.

"Presently! Do you know to what you exposed yourself? Didn't you see anything in the corner, on the left, on the third shelf? Speak, answer, articulate something."

"I—don't—know," stammered the young fellow.

"Ah! you don't know! Well, then, I do know! You saw a bottle of blue glass, sealed with yellow wax, that contains a white powder, on which I have even written 'Dangerous!' And do you know what is in it? Arsenic! And you go and touch it! You take a pan that was next to it!"

"Next to it!" cried Madame Homais, clasping her hands. "Arsenic! You might have poisoned us all."

And the children began howling as if they already had frightful pains in their entrails.

"Or poison a patient!" continued the druggist. "Do you want to see me in the prisoner's dock with criminals, in a court of justice? To see me dragged to the scaffold? Don't you know what care I take in managing things, although I am so thoroughly used to it? Often I am horrified myself when I think of my responsibility; for the Government persecutes us, and the absurd legislation that rules us is a veritable Damocles's sword over our heads."

Emma no longer dreamed of asking what they wanted her for, and the druggist went on in breathless phrases—

"That is your return for all the kindnesses we have shown you! That is how you recompense me for the really paternal care that I lavish on you! For without me where would you be? What would you be doing? Who provides you with food, education, clothes, and all the means of figuring one day with honour in the ranks of society? But you must pull hard at the oar if you're to do that, and get, as, people say, callosities upon your hands. *Fabricando fit faber, age quod agis.*"

He was so exasperated he quoted Latin. He would have quoted Chinese or Greenlandish had he known those two languages, for he was in one of those crises in which the whole soul shows indistinctly what it contains, like the ocean, which, in the storm, opens itself from the seaweeds on its shores down to the sands of its abysses.

And he went on—

"I am beginning to repent terribly of having taken you up! I should certainly have done better to have left you to rot in your poverty and the dirt in which you were born. Oh, you'll never be fit for anything but to herd animals with horns! You have no aptitude for science! You hardly know how to stick on a label! And there you are, dwelling with me snug as a parson, living in clover, taking your ease!"

But Emma, turning to Madame Homais, "I was told to come here—"

"Oh, dear me!" interrupted the good woman with a sad air, "how am I to tell you? It is a misfortune!"

She could not finish, the druggist was thundering—"Empty it! Clean it! Take it back! Be quick!"

And seizing Justin by the collar of his blouse, he shook a book out of his pocket. The lad stooped, but Homais was the quicker, and, having picked up the volume, contemplated it with staring eyes and open mouth.

"*Conjugal—love!*" he said, slowly separating the two words. "Ah! very good! very good! very pretty! And illustrations! Oh, this is too much!"

Madame Homais came forward.

"No, do not touch it!"

The children wanted to look at the pictures.

"Leave the room," he said imperiously; and they went out.

First he walked up and down with the open volume in his hand, rolling his eyes, choking, tumid, apoplectic. Then he came straight to his pupil, and, planting himself in front of him with crossed arms—

"Have you every vice, then, little wretch? Take care! you are on a downward path. Did not you reflect that this infamous book might fall into the hands of my children, kindle a spark in their minds, tarnish the purity of Athalie, corrupt Napoleon. He is already formed like a man. Are you quite sure, anyhow, that they have not read it? Can you certify to me—"

"But really, sir," said Emma, "you wished to tell me—"

"Ah, yes! madame. Your father-in-law is dead."

In fact, Monsieur Bovary senior had expired the evening before suddenly from an attack of apoplexy as he got up from table, and by way of greater precaution, on account of Emma's sensibility, Charles had begged Homais to break the horrible news to her gradually. Homais had thought over his speech; he had rounded, polished it, made it rhythmical; it was a masterpiece of prudence and transitions, of subtle turns and delicacy; but anger had got the better of rhetoric.

Emma, giving up all chance of hearing any details, left the pharmacy; for Monsieur Homais had taken up the thread of his vituperations. However, he was growing calmer, and was now grumbling in a paternal tone whilst he fanned himself with his skull-cap.

"It is not that I entirely disapprove of the work. Its author was a doctor! There are certain scientific points in it that it is not ill a man should know, and I would even venture to say that a man must know. But later—later! At any rate, not till you are man yourself and your temperament is formed."

When Emma knocked at the door, Charles, who was waiting for her, came forward with open arms and said to her with tears in his voice—

"Ah! my dear!"

And he bent over her gently to kiss her. But at the contact of his lips the memory of the other seized her, and she passed her hand over her face shuddering.

But she made answer, "Yes, I know, I know!"

He showed her the letter in which his mother told the event without any sentimental hypocrisy. She only regretted her husband had not received the consolations of religion, as he had died at Daudeville, in the street, at the door of a café after a patriotic dinner with some ex-officers.

Emma gave him back the letter; then at dinner, for appearance's sake, she affected a certain repugnance. But as he urged her to try, she resolutely began eating, while Charles opposite her sat motionless in a dejected attitude.

Now and then he raised his head and gave her a long look full of distress. Once he sighed, "I should have liked to see him again!"

She was silent. At last, understanding that she must say something, "How old was your father?" she asked.

"Fifty-eight."

"Ah!"

And that was all.

A quarter of an hour after he added, "My poor mother! what will become of her now?"

She made a gesture that signified she did not know. Seeing her so taciturn, Charles imagined her much affected, and forced himself to say nothing, not to reawaken this sorrow which moved him. And, shaking off his own—

"Did you enjoy yourself yesterday?" he asked.

"Yes."

When the cloth was removed, Bovary did not rise, nor did Emma; and as she looked at him, the monotony of the spectacle drove little by little all pity from her heart. He seemed to her paltry, weak, a cipher—in a word, a poor thing in every way. How to get rid of him? What an interminable evening! Something stupefying like the fumes of opium seized her.

They heard in the passage the sharp noise of a wooden leg on the boards. It was Hippolyte bringing back Emma's luggage. In order to put it down he described painfully a quarter of a circle with his stump.

"He doesn't even remember any more about it," she thought, looking at the poor devil, whose coarse red hair was wet with perspiration.

Bovary was searching at the bottom of his purse for a centime, and without appearing to understand all there was of humiliation for him in the mere presence of this man, who stood there like a personified reproach to his incurable incapacity.

"Hallo! you've a pretty bouquet," he said, noticing Léon's violets on the chimney.

"Yes," she replied indifferently; "it's a bouquet I bought just now from a beggar."

Charles picked up the flowers, and freshening his eyes, red with tears, against them, smelt them delicately.

She took them quickly from his hand and put them in a glass of water.

The next day Madame Bovary senior arrived. She and her son wept much. Emma, on the pretext of giving orders, disappeared. The following day they had a talk over the mourning. They went and sat down with their workboxes by the waterside under the arbour.

Charles was thinking of his father, and was surprised to feel so much affection for this man, whom till then he had thought he cared little about. Madame Bovary senior was thinking of her husband. The worst days of the past seemed enviable to her. All was forgotten beneath the instinctive regret of such a long habit, and from time to time whilst she sewed, a big tear rolled along her nose and hung suspended there a moment. Emma was thinking that it was scarcely forty-eight hours since they had been together, far from the world, all in a frenzy of joy, and not having eyes enough to gaze upon each other. She tried to recall the slightest details of that past day. But the presence of her husband and mother-in-law worried her. She would have liked to hear nothing, to see nothing, so as not to disturb the meditation on her love, that, do what she would, became lost in external sensations.

She was unpicking the lining of a dress, and the strips were scattered around her. Madame Bovary senior was plying her scissors without looking up, and Charles, in his list slippers and his old brown surtout that he used as a dressing-gown, sat with both hands in his pockets, and did not speak either; near them Berthe, in a little white pinafore, was raking the sand in the walks with her spade.

Suddenly she saw Monsieur Lheureux, the linen-draper, come in through the gate.

He came to offer his services "under the sad circumstances." Emma answered that she thought she could do without. The shopkeeper was not to be beaten.

"I beg your pardon," he said, "but I should like to have a private talk with you." Then in a low voice, "It's about that affair—you know."

Charles crimsoned to his ears. "Oh, yes! certainly." And in his confusion, turning to his wife, "Couldn't you, my darling?"

She seemed to understand him, for she rose; and Charles said to his mother, "It is nothing particular. No doubt, some household trifle." He did not want her to know the story of the bill, fearing her reproaches.

As soon as they were alone, Monsieur Lheureux in sufficiently clear terms began to congratulate Emma on the inheritance, then to talk of indifferent matters, of the espaliers, of the harvest, and of his own health, which was always so-so, always having ups and downs. In fact, he had to work devilish hard, although he didn't make enough, in spite of all people said, to find butter for his bread.

Emma let him talk on. She had bored herself so prodigiously the last two days.

"And so you're quite well again?" he went on. "*Ma foi!* I saw your husband in a sad state. He's a good fellow, though we did have a little misunderstanding."

She asked what misunderstanding, for Charles had said nothing of the dispute about the goods supplied to her.

"Why, you know well enough," cried Lheureux. "It was about your little fancies—the travelling trunks."

He had drawn his hat over his eyes, and, with his hands behind his back, smiling and whistling, he looked straight at her in an unbearable manner. Did he suspect anything? She was lost in all kinds of apprehensions. At last, however, he went on—

"We made it up, all the same, and I've come again to propose another arrangement."

This was to renew the bill Bovary had signed. The doctor, of course, would do as he pleased; he was not to trouble himself, especially just now, when he would have a lot of worry. "And he would do better to give it over to someone else—to you, for example. With a power of attorney it could be easily managed, and then we (you and I) would have our little business transactions together."

She did not understand. He was silent. Then, passing to his trade, Lheureux declared that madame must require something. He would send her a black barège, twelve yards, just enough to make a gown.

"The one you've on is good enough for the house, but you want another for calls. I saw that the very moment that I came in. I've the eye of an American!"

He did not send the stuff; he brought it. Then he came again to measure it; he came again on other pretexts, always trying to make himself agreeable, useful, "en-feoffing himself," as Homais would have said, and always dropping some hint to Emma about the power of attorney. He never mentioned the bill; she did not think of it. Charles, at the beginning of her convalescence, had certainly said something about it to her, but so many emotions had passed through her head that she no longer remembered it. Besides, she took care not to talk of any money questions. Madame Bovary seemed surprised at this, and attributed the change in her ways to the religious sentiments she had contracted during her illness.

But as soon as she was gone, Emma greatly astounded Bovary by her practical good sense. It would be necessary to make inquiries, to look into mortgages, and see if there were any occasion for a sale by auction or a liquidation. She quoted technical terms casually, pronounced the grand words of order, the future, fore-sight, and constantly exaggerated the difficulties of settling his father's affairs so much, that at last one day she showed him the rough draft of a power of attorney to manage and administer his business, arrange all loans, sign and endorse all bills, pay all sums, etc. She had profited by Lheureux's lessons.

Charles naïvely asked her where this paper came from.

"Monsieur Guillaumin"; and with the utmost coolness she added, "I don't trust him overmuch. Notaries have such a bad reputation. Perhaps we ought to consult— we only know—no one."

"Unless Léon—" replied Charles, who was reflecting.

But it was difficult to explain matters by letter. Then she offered to make the journey, but he thanked her. She insisted. It was quite a contest of mutual consid-eration. At last she cried with affected waywardness—

"No, I will go!"

"How good you are!" he said, kissing her forehead.

The next morning she set out in the Hirondelle to go to Rouen to consult Mon-sieur Léon, and she stayed there three days.

Chapter III

THEY WERE THREE FULL, EXQUISITE DAYS—A TRUE HONEYMOON.
They were at the Hotel-de-Boulogne, on the harbour; and they lived there, with drawn blinds and closed doors, with flowers on the floor, and iced syrups that were brought them early in the morning.

Towards evening they took a covered boat and went to dine on one of the islands. It was the time when one hears by the side of the dockyard the caulking-mallets sounding against the hull of vessels. The smoke of the tar rose up between the trees; there were large fatty drops on the water, undulating in the purple colour of the sun, like floating plaques of Florentine bronze.

They rowed down in the midst of moored boats, whose long oblique cables grazed lightly against the bottom of the boat. The din of the town gradually grew distant; the rolling of carriages, the tumult of voices, the yelping of dogs on the decks of vessels. She took off her bonnet, and they landed on their island.

They sat down in the low-ceilinged room of a tavern, at whose door hung black nets. They ate fried smelts, cream and cherries. They lay down upon the grass; they kissed behind the poplars; and they would fain, like two Robinsons, have lived forever in this little place, which seemed to them in their beatitude the most magnificent on earth. It was not the first time that they had seen trees, a blue sky, meadows; that they had heard the water flowing and the wind blowing in the leaves; but, no doubt, they had never admired all this, as if Nature had not existed before, or had only begun to be beautiful since the gratification of their desires.

At night they returned. The boat glided along the shores of the islands. They sat at the bottom, both hidden by the shade, in silence. The square oars rang in the iron thwarts, and, in the stillness, seemed to mark time, like the beating of a metronome, while at the stern the rudder that trailed behind never ceased its gentle splash against the water.

Once the moon rose; then they did not fail to make fine phrases, finding the orb melancholy and full of poetry. She even began to sing—

"One night, do you remember, we were sailing," etc.

Her musical but weak voice died away along the waves, and the winds carried off the trills that Léon heard pass like the flapping of wings about him.

She was opposite him, leaning against the partition of the shallop, through one of whose raised blinds the moon streamed in. Her black dress, whose drapery spread out like a fan, made her seem more slender, taller. Her head was raised, her hands clasped, her eyes turned towards heaven. At times the shadow of the willows hid her completely; then she reappeared suddenly, like a vision in the moonlight.

Léon, on the floor by her side, found under his hand a ribbon of scarlet silk. The boatman looked at it, and at last said—

"Perhaps it belongs to the party I took out the other day. A lot of jolly folk, gentlemen and ladies, with cakes, champagne, cornets—everything in style! There was one especially, a tall handsome man with small moustaches, who was that funny! And they all kept saying, 'Now tell us something, Adolphe—Dolpe,' I think."

She shivered.

"You are in pain?" asked Léon, coming closer to her.

"Oh, it's nothing! No doubt, it is only the night air."

"And who doesn't want for women, either," softly added the sailor, thinking he was paying the stranger a compliment.

Then, spitting on his hands, he took the oars again.

Yet they had to part. The adieux were sad. He was to send his letters to Mère Rollet, and she gave him such precise instructions about a double envelope that he admired greatly her amorous astuteness.

"So you can assure me it is all right?" she said with her last kiss.

"Yes, certainly."

"But why," he thought afterwards as he came back through the streets alone, "is she so very anxious to get this power of attorney?"

Chapter IV

LEON SOON PUT ON AN AIR OF SUPERIORITY BEFORE HIS COMRADES, AVOIDED their company, and completely neglected his work.

He waited for her letters; he re-read them; he wrote to her. He called her to mind with all the strength of his desires and of his memories. Instead of lessening with absence, this longing to see her again grew, so that at last on Saturday morning he escaped from his office.

When, from the summit of the hill, he saw in the valley below the church-spire with its tin flag swinging in the wind, he felt that delight mingled with triumphant vanity and egoistic tenderness that millionaires must experience when they come back to their native village.

He went rambling round her house. A light was burning in the kitchen. He watched for her shadow behind the curtains, but nothing appeared.

Mère Lefrançois, when she saw him, uttered many exclamations. She thought he "had grown and was thinner," while Artémise, on the contrary, thought him stouter and darker.

He dined in the little room as of yore, but alone, without the tax-gatherer; for Binet, tired of waiting for the Hirondelle, had definitely put forward his meal one hour, and now he dined punctually at five, and yet he declared usually the rickety old concern "was late."

Léon, however, made up his mind, and knocked at the doctor's door. Madame was in her room, and did not come down for a quarter of an hour. The doctor seemed delighted to see him, but he never stirred out that evening, nor all the next day.

He saw her alone in the evening, very late, behind the garden in the lane;—in the lane, as she had the other one! It was a stormy night, and they talked under an umbrella by lightning flashes.

Their separation was becoming intolerable. "I would rather die!" said Emma. She was writhing in his arms, weeping. "Adieu! adieu! When shall I see you again?"

They came back again to embrace once more, and it was then that she promised him to find soon, by no matter what means, a regular opportunity for seeing one another in freedom at least once a week. Emma never doubted she should be able to do this. Besides, she was full of hope. Some money was coming to her.

On the strength of it she bought a pair of yellow curtains with large stripes for her room, whose cheapness Monsieur Lheureux had commended; she dreamed of getting a carpet, and Lheureux, declaring that it wasn't "drinking the sea," politely undertook to supply her with one. She could no longer do without his services. Twenty times a day she sent for him, and he at once put by his business without a murmur. People could not understand either why Mère Rollet breakfasted with her every day, and even paid her private visits.

It was about this time, that is to say, the beginning of winter, that she seemed seized with great musical fervour.

One evening when Charles was listening to her, she began the same piece four times over, each time with much vexation, while he, not noticing any difference, cried—

"Bravo! very good! You are wrong to stop. Go on!"

"Oh, no; it is execrable! My fingers are quite rusty."

The next day he begged her to play him something again.

"Very well; to please you!"

And Charles confessed she had gone off a little. She played wrong notes and blundered; then, stopping short—

"Ah! it is no use. I ought to take some lessons; but—" She bit her lips and added, "Twenty francs a lesson, that's too dear!"

"Yes, so it is—rather," said Charles, giggling stupidly. "But it seems to me that one might be able to do it for less; for there are artists of no reputation, and who are often better than the celebrities."

"Find them!" said Emma.

The next day when he came home he looked at her shyly, and at last could no longer keep back the words.

"How obstinate you are sometimes! I went to Barfuchères to-day. Well, Madame Liégard assured me that her three young ladies who are at La Miséricorde have lessons at fifty sous apiece, and that from an excellent mistress!"

She shrugged her shoulders and did not open her piano again. But when she passed by it (if Bovary were there), she sighed—

"Ah! my poor piano!"

And when anyone came to see her, she did not fail to inform them that she had given up music, and could not begin again now for important reasons. Then people commiserated her—

"What a pity! she had so much talent!"

They even spoke to Bovary about it. They put him to shame, and especially the chemist.

"You are wrong. One should never let any of the faculties of nature lie fallow. Besides, just think, my good friend, that by inducing madame to study, you are economising on the subsequent musical education of your child. For my own part, I think that mothers ought themselves to instruct their children. That is an idea of

Rousseau's, still rather new perhaps, but that will end by triumphing, I am certain of it, like mothers nursing their own children and vaccination."

So Charles returned once more to this question of the piano. Emma replied bitterly that it would be better to sell it. This poor piano, that had given her vanity so much satisfaction—to see it go was to Bovary like the indefinable suicide of a part of herself.

"If you liked," he said, "a lesson from time to time, that wouldn't after all be very ruinous."

"But lessons," she replied, "are only of use when followed up."

And thus it was she set about obtaining her husband's permission to go to town once a week to see her lover. At the end of a month she was even considered to have made considerable progress.

Chapter V

SHE WENT ON THURSDAYS. SHE GOT UP AND DRESSED SILENTLY, IN ORDER NOT to awaken Charles, who would have made remarks about her getting ready too early. Next she walked up and down, went to the windows, and looked out at the Place. The early dawn was broadening between the pillars of the market, and the chemist's shop, with the shutters still up, showed in the pale light of the dawn the large letters of his signboard.

When the clock pointed to a quarter past seven, she went off to the Lion d'Or, whose door Artémise opened yawning. The girl then made up the coals covered by the cinders, and Emma remained alone in the kitchen. Now and again she went out. Hivert was leisurely harnessing his horses, listening, moreover, to Mère Lefrançois, who, passing her head and nightcap through a grating, was charging him with commissions and giving him explanations that would have confused anyone else. Emma kept beating the soles of her boots against the pavement of the yard.

At last, when he had eaten his soup, put on his cloak, lighted his pipe, and grasped his whip, he calmly installed himself on his seat.

The Hirondelle started at a slow trot, and for about a mile stopped here and there to pick up passengers who waited for it, standing at the border of the road, in front of their yard gates.

Those who had secured seats the evening before kept it waiting; some even were still in bed in their houses. Hivert called, shouted, swore; then he got down from his seat and went and knocked loudly at the doors. The wind blew through the cracked windows.

The four seats, however, filled up. The carriage rolled off; rows of apple-trees followed one upon another, and the road between its two long ditches, full of yellow water, rose, constantly narrowing towards the horizon.

Emma knew it from end to end; she knew that after a meadow there was a sign-post, next an elm, a barn, or the hut of a lime-kiln tender. Sometimes even, in the hope of getting some surprise, she shut her eyes, but she never lost the clear perception of the distance to be traversed.

At last the brick houses began to follow one another more closely, the earth resounded beneath the wheels, the Hirondelle glided between the gardens, where through an opening one saw statues, a periwinkle plant, clipped yews, and a swing. Then on a sudden the town appeared. Sloping down like an amphitheatre, and drowned in the fog, it widened out beyond the bridges confusedly. Then the open country spread away with a monotonous movement till it touched in the distance the vague line of the pale sky. Seen thus from above, the whole landscape looked immovable as a picture; the anchored ships were massed in one corner, the river curved round the foot of the green hills, and the isles, oblique in shape, lay on the water, like large, motionless, black fishes. The factory chimneys belched forth immense brown fumes that were blown away at the top. One heard the rumbling of the foundries, together with the clear chimes of the churches that stood out in the mist. The leafless trees on the boulevards made violet thickets in the midst of the houses, and the roofs, all shining with the rain, threw back unequal reflections, according to the height of the quarters in which they were. Sometimes a gust of wind drove the clouds towards the Saint Catherine hills, like aerial waves that broke silently against a cliff.

A giddiness seemed to her to detach itself from this mass of existence, and her heart swelled as if the hundred and twenty thousand souls that palpitated there had all at once sent into it the vapour of the passions she fancied theirs. Her love grew in the presence of this vastness, and expanded with tumult to the vague murmurings that rose towards her. She poured it out upon the square, on the walks, on the streets, and the old Norman city outspread before her eyes as an enormous capital, as a Babylon into which she was entering. She leant with both hands against the window, drinking in the breeze; the three horses galloped, the stones grated in the mud, the diligence rocked, and Hivert, from afar, hailed the carts on the road, while the bourgeois who had spent the night at the Guillaume woods came quietly down the hill in their little family carriages.

They stopped at the barrier; Emma undid her overshoes, put on other gloves, rearranged her shawl, and some twenty paces farther she got down from the Hirondelle.

The town was then awakening. Shop-boys in caps were cleaning up the shop-fronts, and women, with baskets against their hips, at intervals uttered sonorous cries at the corners of streets. She walked with downcast eyes, close to the walls, and smiling with pleasure under her lowered black veil.

For fear of being seen, she did not usually take the most direct road. She plunged into dark alleys, and, all perspiring, reached the bottom of the Rue Nationale, near the fountain that stands there. It is the quarter for theatres, public-houses, and whores. Often a cart would pass near her, bearing some shaking scenery. Waiters in aprons were sprinkling sand on the flagstones between green shrubs. It all smelt of absinthe, cigars, and oysters.

She turned down a street; she recognised him by his curling hair that escaped from beneath his hat.

Léon walked along the pavement. She followed him to the hotel. He went up, opened the door, entered— What an embrace!

Then, after the kisses, the words gushed forth. They told each other the sorrows of the week, the presentiments, the anxiety for the letters; but now everything was forgotten; they gazed into each other's faces with voluptuous laughs, and tender names.

The bed was large, of mahogany, in the shape of a boat. The curtains were in red levantine, that hung from the ceiling and bulged out too much towards the bell-shaped bedside; and nothing in the world was so lovely as her brown head and white skin standing out against this purple colour, when, with a movement of shame, she crossed her bare arms, hiding her face in her hands.

The warm room, with its discreet carpet, its gay ornaments, and its calm light, seemed made for the intimacies of passion. The curtain-rods, ending in arrows, their brass pegs, and the great balls of the fire-dogs shone suddenly when the sun came in. On the chimney between the candelabra there were two of those pink shells in which one hears the murmur of the sea if one holds them to the ear.

How they loved that dear room, so full of gaiety, despite its rather faded splendour! They always found the furniture in the same place, and sometimes hairpins, that she had forgotten the Thursday before, under the pedestal of the clock. They lunched by the fireside on a little round table, inlaid with rosewood. Emma carved, put bits on his plate with all sorts of coquettish ways, and she laughed with a sonorous and libertine laugh when the froth of the champagne ran over from the glass to the rings on her fingers. They were so completely lost in the possession of each other that they thought themselves in their own house, and that they would live there till death, like two spouses eternally young. They said "our room," "our carpet," she even said "my slippers," a gift of Léon's, a whim she had had. They were pink satin, bordered with swansdown. When she sat on his knees, her leg, then too short, hung in the air, and the dainty shoe, that had no back to it, was held in only by the toes to her bare foot.

He for the first time enjoyed the inexpressible delicacy of feminine refinements. He had never met this grace of language, this reserve of clothing, these poses of the weary dove. He admired the exaltation of her soul and the lace on her petticoat. Besides, was she not "a lady" and a married woman—a real mistress, in fine?

By the diversity of her humour, in turn mystical or mirthful, talkative, taciturn, passionate, careless, she awakened in him a thousand desires, called up instincts or memories. She was the mistress of all the novels, the heroine of all the dramas, the vague "she" of all the volumes of verse. He found again on her shoulder the amber colouring of the "odalisque bathing"; she had the long waist of feudal châtelaines, and she resembled the "pale woman of Barcelona." But above all she was the Angel!

Often looking at her, it seemed to him that his soul, escaping towards her, spread like a wave about the outline of her head, and descended drawn down into the whiteness of her breast. He knelt on the ground before her, and with both elbows on her knees looked at her with a smile, his face upturned.

She bent over him, and murmured, as if choking with intoxication—

"Oh, do not move! do not speak! look at me! Something so sweet comes from your eyes that helps me so much!"

She called him "child." "Child, do you love me?"

And she did not listen for his answer in the haste of her lips that fastened to his mouth.

On the clock there was a bronze cupid, who smirked as he bent his arm beneath a golden garland. They had laughed at it many a time, but when they had to part everything seemed serious to them.

Motionless in front of each other, they kept repeating, "Till Thursday, till Thursday."

Suddenly she seized his head between her hands, kissed him hurriedly on the forehead, crying, "Adieu!" and rushed down the stairs.

She went to a hairdresser's in the Rue de la Comédie to have her hair arranged. Night fell; the gas was lighted in the shop. She heard the bell at the theatre calling the mummers to the performance, and she saw, passing opposite, men with white faces and women in faded gowns going in at the stage-door.

It was hot in the room, small, and too low, where the stove was hissing in the midst of wigs and pommades. The smell of the tongs, together with the greasy hands that handled her head, soon stunned her, and she dozed a little in her wrapper. Often, as he did her hair, the man offered her tickets for a masked ball.

Then she went away. She went up the streets; reached the Croix-Rouge, put on her overshoes, that she had hidden in the morning under the seat, and sank into her place among the impatient passengers. Some got out at the foot of the hill. She remained alone in the carriage. At every turning all the lights of the town were seen more and more completely, making a great luminous vapour about the dim houses. Emma knelt on the cushions, and her eyes wandered over the dazzling light. She sobbed; called on Léon, sent him tender words and kisses lost in the wind.

On the hillside a poor devil wandered about with his stick in the midst of the diligences. A mass of rags covered his shoulders, and an old staved-in beaver, turned out like a basin, hid his face; but when he took it off he discovered in the place of eyelids empty and bloody orbits. The flesh hung in red shreds, and there flowed from it liquids that congealed into green scales down to the nose, whose black nostrils sniffed convulsively. To speak to you he threw back his head with an idiotic laugh; then his blueish eyeballs, rolling constantly, at the temples beat against the edge of the open wound. He sang a little song as he followed the carriages—

> *"Maids in the warmth of a summer day*
> *Dream of love, and of love alway."*

And all the rest was about birds and sunshine and green leaves.

Sometimes he appeared suddenly behind Emma, bareheaded, and she drew back with a cry. Hivert made fun of him. He would advise him to get a booth at the Saint Romain fair, or else ask him, laughing, how his young woman was.

Often they had started when, with a sudden movement, his hat entered the diligence through the small window, while he clung with his other arm to the footboard, between the wheels splashing mud. His voice, feeble at first and quavering, grew sharp; it resounded in the night like the indistinct moan of a vague distress; and through the ringing of the bells, the murmur of the trees, and the rumbling of the empty vehicle, it had a far-off sound that disturbed Emma. It went to the bottom of her soul, like a whirlwind in an abyss, and carried her away into the distances of a boundless melancholy. But Hivert, noticing a weight behind, gave the blind man sharp cuts with his whip. The thong lashed his wounds, and he fell back into the mud with a yell. Then the passengers in the Hirondelle ended by falling asleep, some with open mouths, others with lowered chins, leaning against their neighbour's shoulder, or with their arm passed through the strap, oscillating regularly with the jolting of the carriage; and the reflection of the lantern swinging without, on the crupper of the wheeler, penetrating into the interior through the chocolate calico curtains, threw sanguineous shadows over all these motionless people. Emma, drunk with grief, shivered in her clothes, feeling her feet grow colder and colder, and death in her soul.

Charles at home was waiting for her; the Hirondelle was always late on Thursdays. Madame arrived at last, and scarcely kissed the child. The dinner was not ready. No matter! She excused the servant. This girl now seemed allowed to do just as she liked.

Often her husband, noting her pallor, asked if she were unwell.

"No," said Emma.

"But," he replied, "you seem so strange this evening."

"Oh, it's nothing! nothing!"

There were even days when she had no sooner come in than she went up to her room; and Justin, happening to be there, moved about noiselessly, quicker at helping her than the best of maids. He put the matches ready, the candlestick, a book, arranged her nightgown, turned back the bedclothes.

"Come!" said she, "that will do. Now you can go."

For he stood there, his hands hanging down and his eyes wide open, as if enmeshed in the innumerable threads of a sudden reverie.

The following day was frightful, and those that came after still more unbearable, because of her impatience to once again seize her happiness; an ardent lust, inflamed by the images of past experience, and that burst forth freely on the seventh day beneath Léon's caresses. His ardours were hidden beneath outbursts of wonder and gratitude. Emma tasted this love in a discreet, absorbed fashion, maintained it by all the artifices of her tenderness, and trembled a little lest it should be lost later on.

She often said to him, with her sweet, melancholy voice—

"Ah! you too, you will leave me! You will marry! You will be like all the others."

He asked, "What others?"

"Why, like all men," she replied. Then added, repulsing him with a languid movement—

"You are all evil!"

One day, as they were talking philosophically of earthly disillusions, to experiment on his jealousy, or yielding, perhaps, to an over-strong need to pour out her heart, she told him that formerly, before him, she had loved someone. "Not like you," she went on quickly, protesting by the head of her child that "nothing had passed between them."

The young man believed her, but none the less questioned her to find out what *he* was.

"He was a ship's captain, my dear."

Was this not preventing any inquiry, and, at the same time, assuming a higher ground through this pretended fascination exercised over a man who must have been of warlike nature and accustomed to receive homage?

The clerk then felt the lowliness of his position; he longed for epaulettes, crosses, titles. All that would please her—he gathered that from her spendthrift habits.

Emma nevertheless concealed many of these extravagant fancies, such as her wish to have a blue tilbury to drive into Rouen, drawn by an English horse and driven by a groom in top-boots. It was Justin who had inspired her with this whim, by begging her to take him into her service as *valet-de-chambre*, and if the privation of it did not lessen the pleasure of her arrival at each rendezvous, it certainly augmented the bitterness of the return.

Often, when they talked together of Paris, she ended by murmuring, "Ah! how happy we should be there!"

"Are we not happy?" gently answered the young man, passing his hands over her hair.

"Yes, that is true," she said. "I am mad. Kiss me!"

To her husband she was more charming than ever. She made him pistachio-creams and played him waltzes after dinner. So he thought himself the most fortunate of men, and Emma was without uneasiness, when, one evening, suddenly he said—

"It is Mademoiselle Lempereur, isn't it, who gives you lessons?"

"Yes."

"Well, I saw her just now," Charles went on, "at Madame Liégeard's. I spoke to her about you, and she doesn't know you."

This was like a thunderclap. However, she replied quite naturally—

"Ah! no doubt she forgot my name."

"But perhaps," said the doctor, "there are several Demoiselles Lempereur at Rouen who are music-mistresses."

"Possibly!" Then quickly—"But I have my receipts here. See!"

And she went to the writing-table, ransacked all the drawers, rummaged the papers, and at last lost her head so completely that Charles earnestly begged her not to take so much trouble about those wretched receipts.

"Oh, I will find them," she said.

And, in fact, on the following Friday, as Charles was putting on one of his boots in the dark cabinet where his clothes were kept, he felt a piece of paper between the leather and his sock. He took it out and read—

"Received, for three months' lessons and several pieces of music, the sum of sixty-three francs.—FELICIE LEMPEREUR, professor of music."

"How the devil did it get into my boots?"

"It must," she replied, "have fallen from the old box of bills that is on the edge of the shelf."

From that moment her existence was but one long tissue of lies, in which she enveloped her love as in veils to hide it. It was a want, a mania, a pleasure carried to such an extent that if she said she had the day before walked on the right side of a road, one might know she had taken the left.

One morning, when she had gone, as usual, rather lightly clothed, it suddenly began to snow, and as Charles was watching the weather from the window, he caught sight of Monsieur Bournisien in the chaise of Monsieur Tuvache, who was driving him to Rouen. Then he went down to give the priest a thick shawl that he was to hand over to Emma as soon as he reached the Croix-Rouge. When he got to the inn, Monsieur Bournisien asked for the wife of the Yonville doctor. The landlady replied that she very rarely came to her establishment. So that evening, when he recognised Madame Bovary in the Hirondelle, the curé told her his dilemma, without, however, appearing to attach much importance to it, for he began praising a preacher who was doing wonders at the Cathedral, and whom all the ladies were rushing to hear.

Still, if he did not ask for any explanation, others, later on, might prove less discreet. So she thought well to get down each time at the Croix-Rouge, so that the good folk of her village who saw her on the stairs should suspect nothing.

One day, however, Monsieur Lheureux met her corning out of the Hotel de Boulogne on Léon's arm; and she was frightened, thinking he would gossip. He was not such a fool. But three days after he came to her room, shut the door, and said, "I must have some money."

She declared she could not give him any. Lheureux burst into lamentations, and reminded her of all the kindnesses he had shown her.

In fact, of the two bills signed by Charles, Emma up to the present had paid only one. As to the second, the shopkeeper, at her request, had consented to replace it by another, which again had been renewed for a long date. Then he drew from his pocket a list of goods not paid for; to wit, the curtains, the carpet, the material for the arm-chairs, several dresses, and divers articles of dress, the bills for which amounted to about two thousand francs.

She bowed her head. He went on—

"But if you haven't any ready money, you have an estate." And he reminded her of a miserable little hovel situated at Barneville, near Aumale, that brought in almost nothing. It had formerly been part of a small farm sold by Monsieur Bovary senior; for Lheureux knew everything, even to the number of acres and the names of the neighbours.

"If I were in your place," he said, "I should clear myself of my debts, and have some money left over."

She pointed out the difficulty of getting a purchaser. He held out the hope of finding one; but she asked him how she should manage to sell it.

"Haven't you your power of attorney?" he replied.

The phrase came to her like a breath of fresh air. "Leave me the bill," said Emma.

"Oh, it isn't worth while," answered Lheureux.

He came back the following week and boasted of having, after much trouble, at last discovered a certain Langlois, who, for a long time, had had an eye on the property, but without mentioning his price.

"Never mind the price!" she cried.

But they would, on the contrary, have to wait, to sound the fellow. The thing was worth a journey, and, as she could not undertake it, he offered to go to the

place to have an interview with Langlois. On his return he announced that the purchaser proposed four thousand francs.

Emma was radiant at this news.

"Frankly," he added, "that's a good price."

She drew half the sum at once, and when she was about to pay her account the
shopkeeper said—

"It really grieves me, on my word! to see you depriving yourself all at once of
such a big sum as that."

Then she looked at the bank-notes, and dreaming of the unlimited number of
rendezvous represented by those two thousand francs, she stammered—

"What! what!"

"Oh!" he went on, laughing good-naturedly, "one puts anything one likes on
receipts. Don't you think I know what household affairs are?" And he looked at
her fixedly, while in his hand he held two long papers that he slid between his nails.
At last, opening his pocket-book, he spread out on the table four bills to order, each
for a thousand francs.

"Sign these," he said, "and keep it all!"

She cried out, scandalised.

"But if I give you the surplus," replied Monsieur Lheureux impudently, "is not
that helping you?"

And taking a pen he wrote at the bottom of the account, "Received of Madame
Bovary four thousand francs."

"Now who can trouble you, since in six months you'll draw the arrears for your
cottage, and I don't make the last bill due till after you've been paid?"

Emma grew rather confused in her calculations, and her ears tingled as if gold
pieces, bursting from their bags, rang all round her on the floor. At last Lheureux
explained that he had a very good friend, Vinçart, a broker at Rouen, who would
discount these four bills. Then he himself would hand over to madame the remainder after the actual debt was paid.

But instead of two thousand francs he brought only eighteen hundred, for the
friend Vinçart (which was *only fair*) had deducted two hundred francs for commission and discount. Then he carelessly asked for a receipt.

"You understand—in business—sometimes. And with the date, if you please,
with the date."

A horizon of realisable whims opened out before Emma. She was prudent
enough to lay by a thousand crowns, with which the first three bills were paid when
they fell due; but the fourth, by chance, came to the house on a Thursday, and
Charles, quite upset, patiently awaited his wife's return for an explanation.

If she had not told him about this bill, it was only to spare him such domestic worries; she sat on his knees, caressed him, cooed to him, gave a long enumeration of all the indispensable things that had been got on credit.

"Really, you must confess, considering the quantity, it isn't too dear."

Charles, at his wit's end, soon had recourse to the eternal Lheureux, who swore he would arrange matters if the doctor would sign him two bills, one of which was for seven hundred francs, payable in three months. In order to arrange for this he wrote his mother a pathetic letter. Instead of sending a reply she came herself; and when Emma wanted to know whether he had got anything out of her, "Yes," he replied; "but she wants to see the account." The next morning at day-break Emma ran to Lheureux to beg him to make out another account for not more than a thousand francs, for to show the one for four thousand it would be necessary to say that she had paid two-thirds, and confess, consequently, the sale of the estate—a negotiation admirably carried out by the shopkeeper, and which, in fact, was only actually known later on.

Despite the low price of each article, Madame Bovary senior of course thought the expenditure extravagant.

"Couldn't you do without a carpet? Why have you re-covered the arm-chairs? In my time there was a single arm-chair in a house, for elderly persons—at any rate it was so at my mother's, who was a good woman, I can tell you. Everybody can't be rich! No fortune can hold out against waste! I should be ashamed to coddle my-self as you do! And yet I am old. I need looking after. And there! there! fitting up gowns! fallals! What! silk for lining at two francs, when you can get jaconet for ten sous, or even for eight, that would do well enough!"

Emma, lying on a lounge, replied as quietly as possible—"Ah! Madame, enough! enough!"

The other went on lecturing her, predicting they would end in the workhouse. But it was Bovary's fault. Luckily he had promised to destroy that power of attorney.

"What?"

"Ah! he swore he would," went on the good woman.

Emma opened the window, called Charles, and the poor fellow was obliged to confess the promise torn from him by his mother.

Emma disappeared, then came back quickly, and majestically handed her a thick piece of paper.

"Thank you," said the old woman. And she threw the power of attorney into the fire.

Emma began to laugh, a strident, piercing, continuous laugh; she had an attack of hysterics.

"Oh, my God!" cried Charles. "Ah! you really are wrong! You come here and make scenes with her!"

His mother, shrugging her shoulders, declared it was "all put on."

But Charles, rebelling for the first time, took his wife's part, so that Madame Bovary senior said she would leave. She went the very next day, and on the threshold, as he was trying to detain her, she replied—

"No, no! You love her better than me, and you are right. It is natural. For the rest, so much the worse! You will see. Good day—for I am not likely to come soon again, as you say, to make scenes."

Charles nevertheless was very crestfallen before Emma, who did not hide the resentment she still felt at his want of confidence, and it needed many prayers before she would consent to have another power of attorney. He even accompanied her to Monsieur Guillaumin to have a second one, just like the other, drawn up.

"I understand," said the notary; "a man of science can't be worried with the practical details of life."

And Charles felt relieved by this comfortable reflection, which gave his weakness the flattering appearance of higher preoccupation.

And what an outburst the next Thursday at the hotel in their room with Léon! She laughed, cried, sang, sent for sherbets, wanted to smoke cigarettes, seemed to him wild and extravagant, but adorable, superb.

He did not know what recreation of her whole being drove her more and more to plunge into the pleasures of life. She was becoming irritable, greedy, voluptuous; and she walked about the streets with him carrying her head high, without fear, so she said, of compromising herself. At times, however, Emma shuddered at the sudden thought of meeting Rodolphe, for it seemed to her that, although they were separated forever, she was not completely free from her subjugation to him.

One night she did not return to Yonville at all. Charles lost his head with anxiety, and little Berthe would not go to bed without her mamma, and sobbed enough to break her heart. Justin had gone out searching the road at random. Monsieur Homais even had left his pharmacy.

At last, at eleven o'clock, able to bear it no longer, Charles harnessed his chaise, jumped in, whipped up his horse, and reached the Croix-Rouge about two o'clock in the morning. No one there! He thought that the clerk had perhaps seen her; but where did he live? Happily, Charles remembered his employer's address, and rushed off there.

Day was breaking, and he could distinguish the escutcheons over the door, and knocked. Someone, without opening the door, shouted out the required information, adding a few insults to those who disturb people in the middle of the night.

The house inhabited by the clerk had neither bell, knocker, nor porter. Charles knocked loudly at the shutters with his hands. A policeman happened to pass by. Then he was frightened, and went away.

"I am mad," he said; "no doubt they kept her to dinner at Monsieur Lormeaux's." But the Lormeaux no longer lived at Rouen.

"She probably stayed to look after Madame Dubreuil. Why, Madame Dubreuil has been dead these ten months! Where can she be?"

An idea occurred to him. At a café he asked for a Directory, and hurriedly looked for the name of Mademoiselle Lempereur, who lived at No. 74 Rue de la Renelle-des-Maroquiniers.

As he was turning into the street, Emma herself appeared at the other end of it. He threw himself upon her rather than embraced her, crying—

"What kept you yesterday?"

"I was not well."

"What was it? Where? How?"

She passed her hand over her forehead and answered, "At Mademoiselle Lempereur's."

"I was sure of it! I was going there."

"Oh, it isn't worth while," said Emma. "She went out just now; but for the future don't worry. I do not feel free, you see, if I know that the least delay upsets you like this."

This was a sort of permission that she gave herself, so as to get perfect freedom in her escapades. And she profited by it freely, fully. When she was seized with the desire to see Léon, she set out upon any pretext; and as he was not expecting her on that day, she went to fetch him at his office.

It was a great delight at first, but soon he no longer concealed the truth, which was, that his master complained very much about these interruptions.

"Pshaw! come along," she said.

And he slipped out.

She wanted him to dress all in black, and grow a pointed beard, to look like the portraits of Louis XIII. She wanted to see his lodgings; thought them poor. He blushed at them, but she did not notice this, then advised him to buy some curtains like hers, and as he objected to the expense—

"Ah! ah! you care for your money," she said laughing.

Each time Léon had to tell her everything that he had done since their last meeting. She asked him for some verses—some verses "for herself," a "love poem" in honour of her. But he never succeeded in getting a rhyme for the second verse; and at last ended by copying a sonnet in a "Keepsake." This was less from vanity than from the one desire of pleasing her. He did not question her ideas; he accepted all her tastes; he was rather becoming her mistress than she his. She had tender words and kisses that thrilled his soul. Where could she have learnt this corruption almost incorporeal in the strength of its profanity and dissimulation?

Chapter VI

DURING THE JOURNEYS HE MADE TO SEE HER, LÉON HAD OFTEN DINED AT the chemist's, and he felt obliged from politeness to invite him in turn.

"With pleasure!" Monsieur Homais replied; "besides, I must invigorate my mind, for I am getting rusty here. We'll go to the theatre, to the restaurant; we'll make a night of it!"

"Oh, my dear!" tenderly murmured Madame Homais, alarmed at the vague perils he was preparing to brave.

"Well, what? Do you think I'm not sufficiently ruining my health living here amid the continual emanations of the pharmacy? But there! that is the way with women! They are jealous of science, and then are opposed to our taking the most legitimate distractions. No matter! Count upon me. One of these days I shall turn up at Rouen, and we'll go the pace together."

The druggist would formerly have taken good care not to use such an expression, but he was cultivating a gay Parisian style, which he thought in the best taste; and, like his neighbour, Madame Bovary, he questioned the clerk curiously about the customs of the capital; he even talked slang to dazzle the bourgeois, saying *bender, crummy, dandy, maccaroni, the cheese, cut my stick* and *"I'll hook it,"* for "I am going."

So one Thursday Emma was surprised to meet Monsieur Homais in the kitchen of the Lion d'Or, wearing a traveller's costume, that is to say, wrapped in an old cloak which no one knew he had, while he carried a valise in one hand and the foot-warmer of his establishment in the other. He had confided his intentions to no one, for fear of causing the public anxiety by his absence.

The idea of seeing again the place where his youth had been spent no doubt excited him, for during the whole journey he never ceased talking, and as soon as he had arrived, he jumped quickly out of the diligence to go in search of Léon. In vain the clerk tried to get rid of him. Monsieur Homais dragged him off to the large Café de la Normandie, which he entered majestically, not raising his hat, thinking it very provincial to uncover in any public place.

Emma waited for Léon three quarters of an hour. At last she ran to his office, and, lost in all sorts of conjectures, accusing him of indifference, and reproaching herself for her weakness, she spent the afternoon, her face pressed against the window-panes.

At two o'clock they were still at table opposite each other. The large room was emptying; the stove-pipe, in the shape of a palm-tree, spread its gilt leaves over the white ceiling, and near them, outside the window, in the bright sunshine, a little fountain gurgled in a white basin, where, in the midst of watercress and asparagus, three torpid lobsters stretched across to some quails that lay heaped up in a pile on their sides.

Homais was enjoying himself. Although he was even more intoxicated with the luxury than the rich fare, the Pomard wine all the same rather excited his faculties; and when the omelette *au rhum* appeared, he began propounding immoral theories about women. What seduced him above all else was *chic*. He admired an elegant toilette in a well-furnished apartment, and as to bodily qualities, he didn't dislike a young girl.

Léon watched the clock in despair. The druggist went on drinking, eating, and talking.

"You must be very lonely," he said suddenly, "here at Rouen. To be sure your lady-love doesn't live far away."

And as the other blushed—

"Come now, be frank. Can you deny that at Yonville—"

The young man stammered something.

"At Madame Bovary's, you're not making love to—"

"To whom?"

"The servant!"

He was not joking; but vanity getting the better of all prudence, Léon, in spite of himself protested. Besides, he only liked dark women.

"I approve of that," said the chemist; "they have more passion."

And whispering into his friend's ear, he pointed out the symptoms by which one could find out if a woman had passion. He even launched into an ethnographic digression: the German was vapourish, the French woman licentious, the Italian passionate.

"And negresses?" asked the clerk.

"They are an artistic taste!" said Homais. "Waiter! two cups of coffee!"

"Are we going?" at last asked Léon impatiently.

"Ja!"

But before leaving he wanted to see the proprietor of the establishment and made him a few compliments. Then the young man, to be alone, alleged he had some business engagement.

"Ah! I will escort you," said Homais.

And all the while he was walking through the streets with him he talked of his wife, his children, of their future, and of his business; told him in what a decayed condition it had formerly been, and to what a degree of perfection he had raised it.

Arrived in front of the Hotel de Boulogne, Léon left him abruptly, ran up the stairs, and found his mistress in great excitement. At mention of the chemist she flew into a passion. He, however, piled up good reasons; it wasn't his fault; didn't she know Homais—did she believe that he would prefer his company? But she turned away; he drew her back, and, sinking on his knees, clasped her waist with his arms in a languorous pose, full of concupiscence and supplication.

She was standing up, her large flashing eyes looked at him seriously, almost terribly. Then tears obscured them, her red eyelids were lowered, she gave him her hands, and Léon was pressing them to his lips when a servant appeared to tell the gentleman that he was wanted.

"You will come back?" she said.

"Yes."

"But when?"

"Immediately."

"It's a trick," said the chemist, when he saw Léon. "I wanted to interrupt this visit, that seemed to me to annoy you. Let's go and have a glass of *garus* at Bridoux'."

Léon vowed that he must get back to his office. Then the druggist joked him about quill-drivers and the law.

"Leave Cujas and Barthole alone a bit. Who the devil prevents you? Be a man! Let's go to Bridoux's. You'll see his dog. It's very interesting."

And as the clerk still insisted—

"I'll go with you. I'll read a paper while I wait for you, or turn over the leaves of a *Code*."

Léon, bewildered by Emma's anger, Monsieur Homais's chatter, and, perhaps, by the heaviness of the luncheon, was undecided, and, as it were, fascinated by the chemist, who kept repeating—

"Let's go to Bridoux's. It's just by here, in the Rue Malpalu."

Then, through cowardice, through stupidity, through that indefinable feeling that drags us into the most distasteful acts, he allowed himself to be led off to Bridoux's, whom they found in his small yard, superintending three workmen, who panted as they turned the large wheel of a machine for making seltzer-water. Homais gave them some good advice. He embraced Bridoux; they took some *garus*. Twenty times Léon tried to escape, but the other seized him by the arm saying—

"Presently! I'm coming! We'll go to the *Fanal de Rouen* to see the fellows there. I'll introduce you to Thomassin."

At last he managed to get rid of him, and rushed straight to the hotel. Emma was no longer there. She had just gone in a fit of anger. She detested him now. This failing to keep their rendezvous seemed to her an insult, and she tried to rake up other reasons to separate herself from him. He was incapable of heroism, weak, banal, more spiritless than a woman, avaricious too, and cowardly.

Then, growing calmer, she at length discovered that she had, no doubt, calumniated him. But the disparaging of those we love always alienates us from them to some extent. We must not touch our idols; the gilt sticks to our fingers.

They gradually came to talking more frequently of matters outside their love, and in the letters that Emma wrote him she spoke of flowers, verses, the moon and the stars, naïve resources of a waning passion striving to keep itself alive by all external aids. She was constantly promising herself a profound felicity on her next journey. Then she confessed to herself that she felt nothing extraordinary. This disappointment quickly gave way to a new hope, and Emma returned to him more inflamed, more eager than ever. She undressed brutally, tearing off the thin laces of her corset that nestled around her hips like a gliding snake. She went on tiptoe, barefooted, to see once more that the door was closed, then, pale, serious, and, without speaking, with one movement, she threw herself upon his breast with a long shudder.

Yet there was upon that brow covered with cold drops, on those quivering lips, in those wild eyes, in the strain of those arms, something vague and dreary that seemed to Léon to glide between them subtly as if to separate them.

He did not dare to question her; but, seeing her so skilled, she must have passed, he thought, through every experience of suffering and of pleasure. What had once charmed now frightened him a little. Besides, he rebelled against his absorption, daily more marked, by her personality. He begrudged Emma this constant victory. He even strove not to love her; then, when he heard the creaking of her boots, he turned coward, like drunkards at the sight of strong drinks.

She did not fail, in truth, to lavish all sorts of attentions upon him, from the delicacies of food to the coquettries of dress and languishing looks. She brought roses in her breast from Yonville, which she threw into his face; was anxious about his health, gave him advice as to his conduct; and, in order the more surely to keep her hold on him, hoping perhaps that heaven would take her part, she tied a medal of the Virgin round his neck. She inquired like a virtuous mother about his companions. She said to him—

"Don't see them; don't go out; think only of ourselves; love me!"

She would have liked to be able to watch over his life, and the idea occurred to her of having him followed in the streets. Near the hotel there was always a kind of loafer who accosted travellers, and who would not refuse. But her pride revolted at this.

"Bah! so much the worse. Let him deceive me! What does it matter to me? As if I cared for him!"

One day, when they had parted early and she was returning alone along the boulevard, she saw the walls of her convent; then she sat down on a form in the shade of the elm-trees. How calm that time had been! How she longed for the in-effable sentiments of love that she had tried to figure to herself out of books! The first month of her marriage, her rides in the wood, the viscount that waltzed, and Lagardy singing, all repassed before her eyes. And Léon suddenly appeared to her as far off as the others.

"Yet I love him," she said to herself.

No matter! She was not happy—she never had been. Whence came this insuf-ficiency in life—this instantaneous turning to decay of everything on which she leant? But if there were somewhere a being strong and beautiful, a valiant nature, full at once of exaltation and refinement, a poet's heart in an angel's form, a lyre with sounding chords ringing out elegaic epithalamia to heaven, why, perchance, should she not find him? Ah! how impossible! Besides, nothing was worth the trou-ble of seeking it; everything was a lie. Every smile hid a yawn of boredom, every joy a curse, all pleasure satiety, and the sweetest kisses left upon your lips only the unattainable desire for a greater delight.

A metallic clang droned through the air, and four strokes were heard from the convent-clock. Four o'clock! And it seemed to her that she had been there on that form an eternity. But an infinity of passions may be contained in a minute, like a crowd in a small space.

Emma lived all absorbed in hers, and troubled no more about money matters than an archduchess.

Once, however, a wretched-looking man, rubicund and bald, came to her house, saying he had been sent by Monsieur Vinçart of Rouen. He took out the pins that held together the side-pockets of his long green overcoat, stuck them into his sleeve, and politely handed her a paper.

It was a bill for seven hundred francs, signed by her, and which Lheureux, in spite of all his professions, had paid away to Vinçart. She sent her servant for him. He could not come. Then the stranger, who had remained standing, casting right and left curious glances, that his thick, fair eyebrows hid, asked with a naïve air—

"What answer am I to take Monsieur Vinçart?"

"Oh," said Emma, "tell him that I haven't it. I will send next week; he must wait; yes, till next week."

And the fellow went without another word.

But the next day at twelve o'clock she received a summons, and the sight of the stamped paper, on which appeared several times in large letters, "Maître Hareng, bailiff at Buchy," so frightened her that she rushed in hot haste to the linen-draper's. She found him in his shop, doing up a parcel.

"Your obedient!" he said; "I am at your service."

But Lheureux, all the same, went on with his work, helped by a young girl of about thirteen, somewhat hunchbacked, who was at once his clerk and his servant.

Then, his clogs clattering on the shop-boards, he went up in front of Madame Bovary to the first door, and introduced her into a narrow closet, where, in a large bureau in sapon-wood, lay some ledgers, protected by a horizontal padlocked iron bar. Against the wall, under some remnants of calico, one glimpsed a safe, but of such dimensions that it must contain something besides bills and money. Monsieur Lheureux, in fact, went in for pawnbroking, and it was there that he had put Madame Bovary's gold chain, together with the earrings of poor old Tellier, who, at last forced to sell out, had bought a meagre store of grocery at Quincampoix, where he was dying of catarrh amongst his candles, that were less yellow than his face.

Lheureux sat down in a large cane arm-chair, saying: "What news?"

"See!"

And she showed him the paper.

"Well, how can I help it?"

Then she grew angry, reminding him of the promise he had given not to pay away her bills. He acknowledged it.

"But I was pressed myself; the knife was at my own throat."

"And what will happen now?" she went on.

"Oh, it's very simple; a judgment and then a distraint—that's about it!"

Emma kept down a desire to strike him, and asked gently if there was no way of quieting Monsieur Vinçart.

"I dare say! Quiet Vinçart! You don't know him; he's more ferocious than an Arab!"

Still Monsieur Lheureux must interfere.

"Well, listen. It seems to me so far I've been very good to you." And opening one of his ledgers, "See," he said. Then running up the page with his finger, "Let's see! let's see! August 3d, two hundred francs; June 17th, a hundred and fifty; March 23d, forty-six. In April—"

He stopped, as if afraid of making some mistake.

"Not to speak of the bills signed by Monsieur Bovary, one for seven hundred francs, and another for three hundred. As to your little instalments, with the interest, why, there's no end to 'em; one gets quite muddled over 'em. I'll have nothing more to do with it."

She wept; she even called him "her good Monsieur Lheureux." But he always fell back upon "that rascal Vinçart." Besides, he hadn't a brass farthing; no one was paying him now-a-days; they were eating his coat off his back; a poor shopkeeper like him couldn't advance money.

Emma was silent, and Monsieur Lheureux, who was biting the feathers of a quill, no doubt became uneasy at her silence, for he went on—

"Unless one of these days I have something coming in, I might—"

"Besides," said she, "as soon as the balance of Barneville—"

"What!"

And on hearing that Langlois had not yet paid he seemed much surprised. Then in a honied voice—

"And we agree, you say?"

"Oh! to anything you like."

On this he closed his eyes to reflect, wrote down a few figures, and declaring it would be very difficult for him, that the affair was shady, and that he was being bled, he wrote out four bills for two hundred and fifty francs each, to fall due month by month.

"Provided that Vinçart will listen to me! However, it's settled. I don't play the fool; I'm straight enough."

Next he carelessly showed her several new goods, not one of which, however, was in his opinion worthy of madame.

"When I think that there's a dress at threepence-half-penny a yard, and warranted fast colours! And yet they actually swallow it! Of course you understand one doesn't tell them what it really is!" He hoped by this confession of dishonesty to others to quite convince her of his probity to her.

Then he called her back to show her three yards of guipure that he had lately picked up "at a sale."

"Isn't it lovely?" said Lheureux. "It is very much used now for the backs of arm-chairs. It's quite the rage."

And, more ready than a juggler, he wrapped up the guipure in some blue paper and put it in Emma's hands.

"But at least let me know—"

"Yes, another time," he replied, turning on his heel.

That same evening she urged Bovary to write to his mother, to ask her to send as quickly as possible the whole of the balance due from the father's estate. The mother-in-law replied that she had nothing more, the winding up was over, and there was due to them besides Barneville an income of six hundred francs, that she would pay them punctually.

Then Madame Bovary sent in accounts to two or three patients, and she made large use of this method, which was very successful. She was always careful to add a postscript: "Do not mention this to my husband; you know how proud he is. Excuse me. Yours obediently." There were some complaints; she intercepted them.

To get money she began selling her old gloves, her old hats, the old odds and ends, and she bargained rapaciously, her peasant blood standing her in good stead. Then on her journey to town she picked up nick-nacks second-hand, that, in default of anyone else, Monsieur Lheureux would certainly take off her hands. She bought ostrich feathers, Chinese porcelain, and trunks; she borrowed from Félicité, from Madame Lefrançois, from the landlady at the Croix-Rouge, from everybody, no matter where. With the money she at last received from Barneville she paid two bills; the other fifteen hundred francs fell due. She renewed the bills, and thus it was continually.

Sometimes, it is true, she tried to make a calculation, but she discovered things so exorbitant that she could not believe them possible. Then she recommenced, soon got confused, gave it all up, and thought no more about it.

The house was very dreary now. Tradesmen were seen leaving it with angry faces. Handkerchiefs were lying about on the stoves, and little Berthe, to the great scandal of Madame Homais, wore stockings with holes in them. If Charles timidly ventured a remark, she answered roughly that it wasn't her fault.

What was the meaning of all these fits of temper? He explained everything through her old nervous illness, and reproaching himself with having taken her infirmities for faults, accused himself of egotism, and longed to go and take her in his arms.

"Ah, no!" he said to himself; "I should worry her."

And he did not stir.

After dinner he walked about alone in the garden; he took little Berthe on his knees, and unfolding his medical journal, tried to teach her to read. But the child, who never had any lessons, soon looked up with large, sad eyes and began to cry. Then he comforted her; went to fetch water in her can to make rivers on the sand path, or broke off branches from the privet hedges to plant trees in the beds. This did not spoil the garden much, all choked now with long weeds. They owed Lestiboudois for so many days. Then the child grew cold and asked for her mother.

"Call the servant," said Charles. "You know, dearie, that mamma does not like to be disturbed."

Autumn was setting in, and the leaves were already falling, as they did two years ago when she was ill. Where would it all end? And he walked up and down, his hands behind his back.

Madame was in her room, which no one entered. She stayed there all day long, torpid, half dressed, and from time to time burning Turkish pastilles which she had bought at Rouen in an Algerian's shop. In order not to have at night this sleeping man stretched at her side, by dint of manoeuvring, she at last succeeded in banishing him to the second floor, while she read till morning extravagant books, full of pictures of orgies and thrilling situations. Often, seized with fear, she cried out, and Charles hurried to her.

"Oh, go away!" she would say.

Or at other times, consumed more ardently than ever by that inner flame to which adultery added fuel, panting, tremulous, all desire, she threw open her window, breathed in the cold air, shook loose in the wind her masses of hair, too heavy, and, gazing upon the stars, longed for some princely love. She thought of him, of Léon. She would then have given anything for a single one of those meetings that surfeited her.

These were her gala days. She wanted them to be sumptuous, and when he alone could not pay the expenses, she made up the deficit liberally, which happened pretty well every time. He tried to make her understand that they would be quite as comfortable somewhere else, in a smaller hotel, but she always found some objection.

One day she drew six small silver-gilt spoons from her bag (they were old Rouault's wedding present), begging him to pawn them at once for her, and Léon obeyed, though the proceeding annoyed him. He was afraid of compromising himself.

Then, on reflection, he began to think his mistress's ways were growing odd, and that they were perhaps not wrong in wishing to separate him from her.

In fact, someone had sent his mother a long anonymous letter to warn her that he was "ruining himself with a married woman," and the good lady at once conjuring up the eternal bugbear of families, the vague pernicious creature, the siren, the monster, who dwells fantastically in depths of love, wrote to Lawyer Dubocage, his employer, who behaved perfectly in the affair. He kept him for three quarters of an hour trying to open his eyes, to warn him of the abyss into which he was falling. Such an intrigue would damage him later on, when he set up for himself. He implored him to break with her, and, if he would not make this sacrifice in his own interest, to do it at least for his, Dubocage's sake.

At last Léon swore he would not see Emma again, and he reproached himself with not having kept his word, considering all the worry and lectures this woman might still draw down upon him, without reckoning the jokes made by his companions as they sat round the stove in the morning. Besides, he was soon to be head-clerk; it was time to settle down. So he gave up his flute, exalted sentiments, and poetry; for every bourgeois in the flush of his youth, were it but for a day, a moment, has believed himself capable of immense passions, of lofty enterprises. The most mediocre libertine has dreamed of sultanas; every notary bears within him the débris of a poet.

He was bored now when Emma suddenly began to sob on his breast, and his heart, like the people who can only stand a certain amount of music, dozed to the sound of a love whose delicacies he no longer noted.

They knew one another too well for any of those surprises of possession that increase its joys a hundred-fold. She was as sick of him as he was weary of her. Emma found again in adultery all the platitudes of marriage.

But how to get rid of him? Then, though she might feel humiliated at the baseness of such enjoyment, she clung to it from habit or from corruption, and each day she hungered after them the more, exhausting all felicity in wishing for too much of it. She accused Léon of her baffled hopes, as if he had betrayed her; and she even longed for some catastrophe that would bring about their separation, since she had not the courage to make up her mind to it herself.

She none the less went on writing him love letters, in virtue of the notion that a woman must write to her lover.

But whilst she wrote it was another man she saw, a phantom fashioned out of her most ardent memories, of her finest reading, her strongest lusts, and at last he became so real, so tangible, that she palpitated wondering, without, however, the power to imagine him clearly, so lost was he, like a god, beneath the abundance of his attributes. He dwelt in that azure land where silk ladders hang from balconies under the breath of flowers, in the light of the moon. She felt him near her; he was coming, and would carry her right away in a kiss.

Then she fell back exhausted, for these transports of vague love wearied her more than great debauchery.

She now felt constant ache all over her. Often she even received summonses, stamped paper that she barely looked at. She would have liked not to be alive, or to be always asleep.

On Mid-Lent she did not return to Yonville, but in the evening went to a masked ball. She wore velvet breeches, red stockings, a club wig, and three-cornered hat cocked on one side. She danced all night to the wild tones of the trombones; people gathered round her, and in the morning she found herself on the steps of the theatre together with five or six masks, *débardeuses* and sailors, Léon's comrades, who were talking about having supper.

The neighbouring cafés were full. They caught sight of one on the harbour, a very indifferent restaurant, whose proprietor showed them to a little room on the fourth floor.

The men were whispering in a corner, no doubt consulting about expenses. There were a clerk, two medical students, and a shopman—what company for her! As to the women, Emma soon perceived from the tone of their voices that they must almost belong to the lowest class. Then she was frightened, pushed back her chair, and cast down her eyes.

The others began to eat; she ate nothing. Her head was on fire, her eyes smarted, and her skin was ice-cold. In her head she seemed to feel the floor of the ball-room rebounding again beneath the rhythmical pulsation of the thousands of dancing feet. And now the smell of the punch, the smoke of the cigars, made her giddy. She fainted, and they carrier her to the window.

Day was breaking, and a great stain of purple colour broadened out in the pale horizon over the St. Catherine hills. The livid river was shivering in the wind; there was no one on the bridges; the street lamps were going out.

She revived, and began thinking of Berthe asleep yonder in the servant's room. Then a cart filled with long strips of iron passed by, and made a deafening metallic vibration against the walls of the houses.

She slipped away suddenly, threw off her costume, told Léon she must get back, and at last was alone at the Hotel de Boulogne. Everything, even herself, was now unbearable to her. She wished that, taking wing like a bird, she could fly somewhere, far away to regions of purity, and there grow young again.

She went out, crossed the Boulevard, the Place Cauchoise, and the Faubourg, as far as an open street that overlooked some gardens. She walked rapidly, the fresh air calming her; and, little by little, the faces of the crowd, the masks, the quadrilles, the lights, the supper, those women, all, disappeared like mists fading away. Then, reaching the Croix-Rouge, she threw herself on the bed in her little room on the second floor, where there were pictures of the *Tour de Nesle*. At four o'clock Hivert awoke her.

When she got home, Félicité showed her behind the clock a grey paper. She read—

"In virtue of the seizure in execution of a judgment."

What judgment? As a matter of fact, the evening before another paper had been brought that she had not yet seen, and she was stunned by these words—

"By order of the king, law, and justice, to Madame Bovary." Then, skipping several lines, she read, "Within twenty-four hours, without fail—" But what? "To pay the sum of eight thousand francs." And there was even at the bottom, "She will be constrained thereto by every form of law, and notably by a writ of distraint on her furniture and effects."

What was to be done? In twenty-four hours—to-morrow. Lheureux, she thought, wanted to frighten her again; for she saw through all his devices, the object of his kindnesses. What reassured her was the very magnitude of the sum.

However, by dint of buying and not paying, of borrowing, signing bills, and renewing these bills, that grew at each new falling-in, she had ended by preparing a capital for Monsieur Lheureux which he was impatiently awaiting for his speculations.

She presented herself at his place with an offhand air.

"You know what has happened to me? No doubt it's a joke!"

"No."

"How so?"

He turned away slowly, and, folding his arms, said to her—

"My good lady, did you think I should go on to all eternity being your purveyor and banker, for the love of God? Now be just. I must get back what I've laid out. Now be just."

She cried out against the debt.

"Ah! so much the worse. The court has admitted it. There's a judgment. It's been notified to you. Besides, it isn't my fault. It's Vinçart's."

"Could you not—?"

"Oh, nothing whatever."

"But still, now talk it over."

And she began beating about the bush; she had known nothing about it; it was a surprise.

"Whose fault is that?" said Lheureux, bowing ironically. "While I'm slaving like a nigger, you go gallivanting about."

"Ah! no lecturing."

"It never does any harm," he replied.

She turned coward; she implored him; she even pressed her pretty white and slender hand against the shopkeeper's knee.

"There, that'll do! Anyone'd think you wanted to seduce me!"

"You are a wretch!" she cried.

"Oh, oh! go it! go it!"

"I will show you up. I shall tell my husband."

"All right! I too, I'll show your husband something."

And Lheureux drew from his strong box the receipt for eighteen hundred francs that she had given him when Vinçart had discounted the bills.

"Do you think," he added, "that he'll not understand your little theft, the poor dear man?"

She collapsed, more overcome than if felled by the blow of a pole-axe. He was walking up and down from the window to the bureau, repeating all the while—

"Ah! I'll show him! I'll show him!" Then he approached her, and in a soft voice said—

"It isn't pleasant, I know; but, after all, no bones are broken, and, since that is the only way that is left for you paying back my money—"

"But where am I to get any?" said Emma, wringing her hands.

"Bah! when one has friends like you!"

And he looked at her in so keen, so terrible a fashion, that she shuddered to her very heart.

"I promise you," she said, "to sign—"

"I've enough of your signatures."

"I will sell something."

"Get along!" he said, shrugging his shoulders; "you've not got anything."

And he called through the peep-hole that looked down into the shop—

"Annette, don't forget the three coupons of No. 14."

The servant appeared. Emma understood, and asked how much money would be wanted to put a stop to the proceedings.

"It is too late."

"But if I brought you several thousand francs—a quarter of the sum—a third—perhaps the whole?"

"No; it's no use!"

And he pushed her gently towards the staircase.

"I implore you Monsieur Lheureux, just a few days more!"

She was sobbing.

"There! tears now!"

"You are driving me to despair!"

"What do I care?' said he, shutting the door.

Chapter VII

SHE WAS STOICAL THE NEXT DAY WHEN MAÎTRE HARENG, THE BAILIFF, WITH two assistants, presented himself at her house to draw up the inventory for the distraint.

They began with Bovary's consulting-room, and did not write down the phrenological head, which was considered an "instrument of his profession"; but in the kitchen they counted the plates, the saucepans, the chairs, the candlesticks, and in the bedroom all the nick-nacks on the whatnot. They examined her dresses, the linen, the dressing-room; and her whole existence, to its most intimate details, was, like a corpse on whom a post-mortem is made, outspread before the eyes of these three men.

Maître Hareng, buttoned up in his thin black coat, wearing a white choker and very tight foot-straps, repeated from time to time—"Allow me, madame. You allow me?" Often he uttered exclamations. "Charming! very pretty." Then he began writing again, dipping his pen into the horn inkstand in his left hand.

When they had done with the rooms they went up to the attic. She kept a desk there in which Rodolphe's letters were locked. It had to be opened.

"Ah! a correspondence," said Maître Hareng, with a discreet smile. "But allow me, for I must make sure the box contains nothing else." And he tipped up the papers lightly, as if to shake out napoleons. Then she grew angered to see this coarse hand, with fingers red and pulpy like slugs, touching these pages against which her heart had beaten.

They went at last. Félicité came back. Emma had sent her out to watch for Bovary in order to keep him off, and they hurriedly installed the man in possession under the roof, where he swore he would remain.

During the evening Charles seemed to her careworn. Emma watched him with a look of anguish, fancying she saw an accusation in every line of his face. Then, when her eyes wandered over the chimney-piece ornamented with Chinese screens, over the large curtains, the arm-chairs, all those things, in a word, that had softened the bitterness of her life, remorse seized her, or rather an immense regret, that, far from crushing, irritated her passion. Charles placidly poked the fire, both his feet on the fire-dogs.

Once the man, no doubt bored in his hiding-place, made a slight noise.

"Is anyone walking upstairs?" said Charles.

"No," she replied; "it is a window that has been left open, and is rattling in the wind."

The next day, Sunday, she went to Rouen to call on all the brokers whose names she knew. They were at their country-places or on journeys. She was not discouraged; and those whom she did manage to see she asked for money, declaring she must have some, and that she would pay it back. Some laughed in her face; all refused.

At two o'clock she hurried to Léon, and knocked at the door. No one answered. At length he appeared.

"What brings you here?"

"Do I disturb you?"

"No; but—" And he admitted that his landlord didn't like his having "women" there.

"I must speak to you," she went on.

Then he took down the key, but she stopped him.

"No, no! Down there, in our home!"

And they went to their room at the Hotel de Boulogne.

On arriving she drank off a large glass of water. She was very pale. She said to him—

"Léon, you will do me a service?"

And, shaking him by both hands that she grasped tightly, she added—

"Listen, I want eight thousand francs."

"But you are mad!"

"Not yet."

And thereupon, telling him the story of the distraint, she explained her distress to him; for Charles knew nothing of it; her mother-in-law detested her; old Rouault could do nothing; but he, Léon, he would set about finding this indispensable sum.

"How on earth can I?"

"What a coward you are!" she cried.

Then he said stupidly, "You are exaggerating the difficulty. Perhaps with a thousand crowns or so the fellow could be stopped."

All the greater reason to try and do something; it was impossible that they could not find three thousand francs. Besides, Léon could be security instead of her.

"Go, try, try! I will love you so!"

He went out, and came back at the end of an hour, saying, with solemn face—

"I have been to three people with no success."

Then they remained sitting face to face at the two chimney corners, motionless, in silence. Emma shrugged her shoulders as she stamped her feet. He heard her murmuring—

"If I were in your place *I* should soon get some."

"But where?"

"At your office." And she looked at him.

An infernal boldness looked out from her burning eyes, and their lids drew close together with a lascivious and encouraging look, so that the young man felt himself growing weak beneath the mute will of this woman who was urging him to a crime. Then he was afraid, and to avoid any explanation he smote his forehead, crying—

"Morel is to come back to-night; he will not refuse me, I hope" (this was one of his friends, the son of a very rich merchant); "and I will bring it you to-morrow," he added.

Emma did not seem to welcome this hope with all the joy he had expected. Did she suspect the lie? He went on, blushing—

"However, if you don't see me by three o'clock, do not wait for me, my darling. I must be off now; forgive me! Good-bye!"

He pressed her hand, but it felt quite lifeless. Emma had no strength left for any sentiment.

Four o'clock struck, and she rose to return to Yonville, mechanically obeying the force of old habits.

The weather was fine. It was one of those March days, clear and sharp, when the sun shines in a perfectly white sky. The Rouen folk, in Sunday-clothes, were walking about with happy looks. She reached the Place du Parvis. People were coming out after vespers; the crowd flowed out through the three doors like a stream through the three arches of a bridge, and in the middle one, more motionless than a rock, stood the beadle.

Then she remembered the day when, all anxious and full of hope, she had entered beneath this large nave, that had opened out before her, less profound than her love; and she walked on weeping beneath her veil, giddy, staggering, almost fainting.

"Take care!" cried a voice issuing from the gate of a courtyard that was thrown open.

She stopped to let pass a black horse, pawing the ground between the shafts of a tilbury, driven by a gentleman in sable furs. Who was it? She knew him. The carriage darted by and disappeared.

Why, it was he—the Viscount. She turned away; the street was empty. She was so overwhelmed, so sad, that she had to lean against a wall to keep herself from falling.

Then she thought she had been mistaken. Anyhow, she did not know. All within her and around her was abandoning her. She felt lost, sinking at random into indefinable abysses, and it was almost with joy that, on reaching the Croix Rouge, she saw the good Homais, who was watching a large box full of pharmaceutical stores being hoisted on to the Hirondelle. In his hand he held tied in a silk handkerchief six *cheminots* for his wife.

Madame Homais was very fond of these small, heavy turban-shaped loaves, that are eaten in Lent with salt butter; a last vestige of Gothic food that goes back, perhaps, to the time of the Crusades, and with which the robust Normans gorged themselves of yore, fancying they saw on the table, in the light of the yellow torches, between tankards of hippocras and huge boars' heads, the heads of Saracens to be devoured. The druggist's wife crunched them up as they had done—heroically, despite her wretched teeth. And so whenever Homais journeyed to town, he never failed to bring her home some that he bought at the great baker's in the Rue Massacre.

"Charmed to see you," he said, offering Emma a hand to help her into the Hirondelle. Then he hung up his *cheminots* to the cords of the netting, and remained bareheaded in an attitude pensive and Napoleonic.

But when the blind man appeared as usual at the foot of the hill he exclaimed—

"I can't understand why the authorities tolerate such culpable industries. Such unfortunates should be locked up and forced to work. Progress, my word! creeps at a snail's pace. We are floundering about in mere barbarism."

The blind man held out his hat, that flapped about at the door, as if it were a bag in the lining that had come unnailed.

"This," said the chemist, "is a scrofulous affection."

And though he knew the poor devil, he pretended to see him for the first time, murmured something about "cornea," "opaque cornea," "sclerotic," "facies," then asked him in a paternal tone—

"My friend, have you long had this terrible infirmity? Instead of getting drunk at the public, you'd do better to die yourself."

He advised him to take good wine, good beer, and good joints. The blind man went on with his song; he seemed, moreover, almost idiotic. At last Monsieur Homais opened his purse—

"Now there's a sou; give me back two liards, and don't forget my advice: you'll be the better for it."

Hivert openly cast some doubt on the efficacy of it. But the druggist said that he would cure himself with an antiphlogistic pommade of his own composition, and he gave his address: "Monsieur Homais, near the market, pretty well known."

"Now," said Hivert, "for all this trouble you'll give us your performance."

The blind man sank down on his haunches, with his head thrown back, whilst he rolled his greenish eyes, lolled out his tongue, and rubbed his stomach with both hands, as he uttered a kind of hollow yell like a famished dog. Emma, filled with disgust, threw him over her shoulder a five-franc piece. It was all her fortune. It seemed to her very fine thus to throw it away.

The coach had gone on again when suddenly Monsieur Homais leant out through the window, crying—

"No farinaceous or milk food, wear wool next the skin, and expose the diseased parts to the smoke of juniper berries."

The sight of the well-known objects that defiled before her eyes gradually diverted Emma from her present trouble. An intolerable fatigue overwhelmed her, and she reached her home stupefied, discouraged, almost asleep.

"Come what may come!" she said to herself. "And then, who knows? Why, at any moment could not some extraordinary event occur? Lheureux even might die!"

At nine o'clock in the morning she was awakened by the sound of voices in the Place. There was a crowd round the market reading a large bill fixed to one of the posts, and she saw Justin, who was climbing on to a stone and tearing down the bill. But at this moment the rural guard seized him by the collar. Monsieur Homais came out of his shop, and Mère Lefrançois, in the midst of the crowd, seemed to be perorating.

"Madame! madame!" cried Félicité, running in, "it's abominable!"

And the poor girl, deeply moved, handed her a yellow paper that she had just torn off the door. Emma read with a glance that all her furniture was for sale.

Then they looked at one another silently. The servant and mistress had no secret one from the other. At last Félicité sighed—

"If I were you, madame, I should go to Monsieur Guillaumin."

"Do you think—"

And this question meant to say—

"You who know the house through the servant, has the master spoken sometimes of me?"

"Yes, you'd do well to go there."

She dressed, put on her black gown, and her hood with jet beads, and that she might not be seen (there was still a crowd on the Place), she took the path by the river, outside the village.

She reached the notary's gate quite breathless. The sky was sombre, and a little snow was falling. At the sound of the bell, Theodore in a red waistcoat appeared on the steps; he came to open the door almost familiarly, as to an acquaintance, and showed her into the dining-room.

A large porcelain stove crackled beneath a cactus that filled up the niche in the wall, and in black wood frames against the oak-stained paper hung Steuben's *Esmeralda* and Schopin's *Potiphar*. The ready-laid table, the two silver chafing-dishes, the crystal door-knobs, the parquet and the furniture, all shone with a scrupulous, English cleanliness; the windows were ornamented at each corner with stained glass.

"Now this," thought Emma, "is the dining-room I ought to have."

The notary came in pressing his palm-leaf dressing-gown to his breast with his left arm, while with the other hand he raised and quickly put on again his brown velvet cap, pretentiously cocked on the right side, whence looked out the ends of three fair curls drawn from the back of the head, following the line of his bald skull.

After he had offered her a seat he sat down to breakfast, apologising profusely for his rudeness.

"I have come," she said, "to beg you, sir——"

"What, madame? I am listening."

And she began explaining her position to him. Monsieur Guillaumin knew it, being secretly associated with the linen-draper, from whom he always got capital for the loans on mortgages that he was asked to make.

So he knew (and better than she herself) the long story of the bills, small at first, bearing different names as endorsers, made out at long dates, and constantly renewed up to the day, when, gathering together all the protested bills, the shop-keeper had bidden his friend Vinçart take in his own name all the necessary proceedings, not wishing to pass for a tiger with his fellow-citizens.

She mingled her story with recriminations against Lheureux, to which the notary replied from time to time with some insignificant word. Eating his cutlet and drinking his tea, he buried his chin in his sky-blue cravat, into which were thrust two diamond pins, held together by a small gold chain; and he smiled a singular smile, in a sugary, ambiguous fashion. But noticing that her feet were damp, he said——

"Do get closer to the stove; put your feet up against the porcelain."

She was afraid of dirtying it. The notary replied in a gallant tone——

"Beautiful things spoil nothing."

Then she tried to move him, and, growing moved herself, she began telling him about the poorness of her home, her worries, her wants. He could understand that; an elegant woman! and, without leaving off eating, he had turned completely round towards her, so that his knee brushed against her boot, whose sole curled round as it smoked against the stove.

But when she asked for a thousand écus, he closed his lips, and declared he was very sorry he had not had the management of her fortune before, for there were hundreds of ways very convenient, even for a lady, of turning her money to account. They might, either in the turf-peats of Grumesnil or building-ground at Havre, almost without risk, have ventured on some excellent speculations; and he let her consume herself with rage at the thought of the fabulous sums that she would certainly have made.

"How was it," he went on, "that you didn't come to me?"

"I hardly know," she said.

"Why, hey? Did I frighten you so much? It is I, on the contrary, who ought to complain. We hardly know one another; yet I am very devoted to you. You do not doubt that, I hope?"

He held out his hand, took hers, covered it with a greedy kiss, then held it on his knee; and he played delicately with her fingers whilst he murmured a thousand blandishments. His insipid voice murmured like a running brook; a light shone in his eyes through the glimmering of his spectacles, and his hand was advancing up Emma's sleeve to press her arm. She felt against her cheek his panting breath. This man oppressed her horribly.

She sprang up and said to him—

"Sir, I am waiting."

"For what?" said the notary, who suddenly became very pale.

"This money."

"But—" Then, wielding to the outburst of too powerful a desire, "Well, yes!"

He dragged himself towards her on his knees, regardless of his dressing-gown.

"For pity's sake, stay! I love you!"

He seized her by her waist. Madame Bovary's face flushed purple. She recoiled with a terrible look, crying—

"You are taking a shameless advantage of my distress, sir! I am to be pitied—not to be sold."

And she went out.

The notary remained quite stupefied, his eyes fixed on his fine embroidered slippers. They were a love gift, and the sight of them at last consoled him. Besides, he reflected that such an adventure might have carried him too far.

"What a wretch! what a scoundrel! what an infamy!" she said to herself, as she fled with nervous steps beneath the aspens of the path. The disappointment of her failure increased the indignation of her outraged modesty; it seemed to her that Providence pursued her implacably, and, strengthening herself in her pride, she had never felt so much esteem for herself nor so much contempt for others. A spirit of warfare transformed her. She would have liked to strike all men, to spit in their faces, to crush them, and she walked rapidly straight on, pale, quivering, maddened, searching the empty horizon with tear-dimmed eyes, and as it were rejoicing in the hate that was choking her.

When she saw her house a numbness came over her. She could not go on; and yet she must. Besides, whither could she flee?

Félicité was waiting for her at the door. "Well?"

"No!" said Emma.

And for a quarter of an hour the two of them went over the various persons in Yonville who might perhaps be inclined to help her. But each time that Félicité named someone Emma replied—

"Impossible! they will not!"

"And the master'll soon be in."

"I know that well enough. Leave me alone."

She had tried everything; there was nothing more to be done now; and when Charles came in she would have to say to him—

"Go away! This carpet on which you are walking is no longer ours. In your own house you do not possess a chair, a pin, a straw, and it is I, poor man, who have ruined you."

Then there would be a great sob; next he would weep abundantly, and at last, the surprise past, he would forgive her.

"Yes," she murmured, grinding her teeth, "he will forgive me, he who would give me a million if I would forgive him for having known me! Never! never!"

This thought of Bovary's superiority to her exasperated her. Then, whether she confessed or did not confess, presently, immediately, to-morrow, he would know the catastrophe all the same; so she must wait for this horrible scene, and bear the weight of his magnanimity. The desire to return to Lheureux's seized her— what would be the use? To write to her father—it was too late; and perhaps she began to repent now that she had not yielded to that other, when she heard the trot of a horse in the alley. It was he; he was opening the gate; he was whiter than the plaster wall. Rushing to the stairs, she ran out quickly to the square; and the wife of the mayor, who was talking to Lestiboudois in front of the church, saw her go in to the tax-collector's.

She hurried off to tell Madame Caron, and the two ladies went up to the attic, and, hidden by some linen spread across props, stationed themselves comfortably for overlooking the whole of Binet's room.

He was alone in his garret, busy imitating in wood one of those indescribable bits of ivory, composed of crescents, of spheres hollowed out one within the other, the whole as straight as an obelisk, and of no use whatever; and he was beginning on the last piece—he was nearing his goal. In the twilight of the workshop the white dust was flying from his tools like a shower of sparks under the hoofs of a galloping horse; the two wheels were turning, droning; Binet smiled, his chin lowered, his nostrils distended, and, in a word, seemed lost in one of those complete happinesses that, no doubt, belong only to commonplace occupations, which amuse the mind with facile difficulties, and satisfy by a realisation of that beyond which such minds have not a dream.

"Ah! there she is!" exclaimed Madame Tuvache.

But it was impossible because of the lathe to hear what she was saying.

At last these ladies thought they made out the word "francs," and Madame Tuvache whispered in a low voice—

"She is begging him to give her time for paying her taxes."

"Apparently!" replied the other.

They saw her walking up and down, examining the napkin-rings, the candlesticks, the banister rails against the walls, while Binet stroked his beard with satisfaction.

"Do you think she wants to order something of him?" said Madame Tuvache.

"Why, he doesn't sell anything," objected her neighbour.

The tax-collector seemed to be listening with wide-open eyes, as if he did not understand. She went on in a tender, suppliant manner. She came nearer to him, her breast heaving; they no longer spoke.

"Is she making him advances?" said Madame Tuvache.

Binet was scarlet to his very ears. She took hold of his hands.

"Oh, it's too much!"

And no doubt she was suggesting something abominable to him; for the tax-collector—yet he was brave, had fought at Bautzen and at Lutzen, had been through the French campaign, and had even been recommended for the cross—suddenly, as at the sight of a serpent, recoiled as far as he could from her, crying—

"Madame! what do you mean?"

"Women like that ought to be whipped," said Madame Tuvache.

"But where is she?" continued Madame Caron, for she had disappeared whilst they spoke; then catching sight of her going up the Grande Rue, and turning to the right as if making for the cemetery, they were lost in conjectures.

"Nurse Rolet," she said on reaching the nurse's, "I am choking; unlace me!" She fell on the bed sobbing. Nurse Rolet covered her with a petticoat and remained standing by her side. Then, as she did not answer, the good woman withdrew, took her wheel and began spinning flax.

"Oh, leave off!" she murmured, fancying she heard Binet's lathe.

"What's bothering her?" said the nurse to herself. "Why has she come here?"

She had rushed thither, impelled by a kind of horror that drove her from her home.

Lying on her back, motionless, and with staring eyes, she saw things but vaguely, although she tried to with idiotic persistence. She looked at the scales on the walls, two brands smoking end to end, and a long spider crawling over her head in a rent in the beam. At last she began to collect her thoughts. She remembered— one day—Léon— Oh! how long ago that was—the sun was shining on the river, and the clematis were perfuming the air. Then, carried away as by a rushing torrent, she soon began to recall the day before.

"What time is it?" she asked.

Mère Rolet went out, raised the fingers of her right hand to that side of the sky that was brightest, and came back slowly, saying—

"Nearly three."

"Ah! thanks, thanks!"

For he would come; he would have found some money. But he would, perhaps, go down yonder, not guessing she was here, and she told the nurse to run to her house to fetch him.

"Be quick!"

"But, my dear lady, I'm going, I'm going!"

She wondered now that she had not thought of him from the first. Yesterday he had given his word; he would not break it. And she already saw herself at Lheureux's spreading out her three bank-notes on his bureau. Then she would have to invent some story to explain matters to Bovary. What should it be?

The nurse, however, was a long while gone. But, as there was no clock in the cot, Emma feared she was perhaps exaggerating the length of time. She began walking round the garden, step by step; she went into the path by the hedge, and returned quickly, hoping that the woman would have come back by another road. At last, weary of waiting, assailed by fears that she thrust from her, no longer conscious whether she had been here a century or a moment, she sat down in a corner, closed her eyes, and stopped her ears. The gate grated; she sprang up. Before she had spoken Mère Rolet said to her—

"There is no one at your house!"

"What?"

"Oh, no one! And the doctor is crying. He is calling for you; they're looking for you."

Emma answered nothing. She gasped as she turned her eyes about her, while the peasant woman, frightened at her face, drew back instinctively, thinking her mad. Suddenly she struck her brow and uttered a cry; for the thought of Rodolphe, like a flash of lightning in a dark night, had passed into her soul. He was so good, so delicate, so generous! And besides, should he hesitate to do her this service, she would know well enough how to constrain him to it by re-waking, in a single moment, their lost love. So she set out towards La Huchette, not seeing that she was hastening to offer herself to that which but a while ago had so angered her, not in the least conscious of her prostitution.

Chapter VIII

S HE ASKED HERSELF AS SHE WALKED ALONG, "WHAT AM I GOING TO SAY? HOW shall I begin?" And as she went on she recognised the thickets, the trees, the sea-rushes on the hill, the château yonder. All the sensations of her first tenderness came back to her, and her poor aching heart opened out amorously. A warm wind blew in her face; the melting snow fell drop by drop from the buds to the grass.

She entered, as she used to, through the small park-gate. Then came to the avenue bordered by a double row of dense lime-trees. They were swaying their long whispering branches to and fro. The dogs in their kennels all barked, and the noise of their voices resounded, but brought out no one.

She went up the large straight staircase with wooden balusters that led to the corridor paved with dusty flags, into which several doors in a row opened, as in a monastery or an inn. His was at the top, right at the end, on the left. When she placed her fingers on the lock her strength suddenly deserted her. She was afraid, almost wished he would not be there, though this was her only hope, her last chance of salvation. She collected her thoughts for one moment, and, strengthening herself by the feeling of present necessity, went in.

He was in front of the fire, both his feet on the mantelpiece, smoking a pipe.

"What! it is you!" he said, getting up hurriedly.

"Yes, it is I, Rodolphe. I should like to ask your advice." And, despite all her efforts, it was impossible for her to open her lips.

"You have not changed; you are charming as ever!"

"Oh," she replied bitterly, "they are poor charms since you disdained them."

Then he began a long explanation of his conduct, excusing himself in vague terms, in default of being able to invent better.

She yielded to his words, still more to his voice and the sight of him, so that she pretended to believe, or perhaps believed, in the pretext he gave for their rupture; this was a secret on which depended the honour, the very life of a third person.

"No matter!" she said, looking at him sadly. "I have suffered much."

He replied philosophically—

"Such is life!"

"Has life," Emma went on, "been good to you at least, since our separation?"

"Oh, neither good nor bad."

"Perhaps it would have been better never to have parted."

"Yes, perhaps."

"You think so?" she said, drawing nearer, and she sighed. "Oh, Rodolphe! if you but knew! I loved you so!"

It was then that she took his hand, and they remained some time, their fingers intertwined, like that first day at the Show. With a gesture of pride he struggled against this emotion. But sinking upon his breast she said to him—

"How did you think I could live without you? One cannot lose the habit of happiness. I was desolate. I thought I should die. I will tell you about all that and you will see. And you—you fled from me!"

For, all the three years, he had carefully avoided her in consequence of that natural cowardice that characterises the stronger sex. Emma went on with dainty little nods, more coaxing than an amorous kitten—

"You love others, confess it! Oh, I understand them, dear! I excuse them. You probably seduced them as you seduced me. You are indeed a man; you have everything to make one love you. But we'll begin again, won't we? We will love one another. See! I am laughing; I am happy! Oh, speak!"

And she was charming to see, with her eyes, in which trembled a tear, like the rain of a storm in a blue corolla.

He had drawn her upon his knees, and with the back of his hand was caressing her smooth hair, where in the twilight was mirrored like a golden arrow one last ray of the sun. She bent down her brow; at last he kissed her on the eyelids quite gently with the tips of his lips.

"Why, you have been crying! What for?"

She burst into tears. Rodolphe thought this was an outburst of her love. As she did not speak, he took this silence for a last remnant of resistance, and then he cried out—

"Oh, forgive me! You are the only one who pleases me. I was imbecile and cruel. I love you. I will love you always. What is it? Tell me!" He was kneeling by her.

"Well, I am ruined, Rodolphe! You must lend me three thousand francs."

"But—but—" said he, getting up slowly, while his face assumed a grave expression.

"You know," she went on quickly, "that my husband had placed his whole fortune at a notary's. He ran away. So we borrowed; the patients don't pay us. Moreover, the settling of the estate is not yet done; we shall have the money later on. But to-day, for want of three thousand francs, we are to be sold up. It is to be at once, this very moment, and, counting upon your friendship, I have come to you."

"Ah!" thought Rodolphe, turning very pale, "that was what she came for." At last he said with a calm air—

"Dear madame, I have not got them."

He did not lie. If he had had them, he would, no doubt, have given them, although it is generally disagreeable to do such fine things: a demand for money being, of all the winds that blow upon love, the coldest and most destructive.

First she looked at him for some moments.

"You have not got them!" she repeated several times. "You have not got them! I ought to have spared myself this last shame. You never loved me. You are no better than the others."

She was betraying, ruining herself.

Rodolphe interrupted her, declaring he was "hard up" himself.

"Ah! I pity you," said Emma. "Yes—very much."

And fixing her eyes upon an embossed carabine that shone against its panoply, "But when one is so poor one doesn't have silver on the butt of one's gun. One doesn't buy a clock inlaid with tortoise-shell," she went on, pointing to a buhl timepiece, "nor silver-gilt whistles for one's whips," and she touched them, "nor charms for one's watch. Oh, he wants for nothing! even to a liqueur-stand in his room! For you love yourself; you live well. You have a château, farms, woods; you go hunting; you travel to Paris. Why, if it were but that," she cried, taking up two studs from the mantlepiece, "but the least of these trifles, one can get money for them. Oh, I do not want them; keep them!"

And she threw the two links away from her, their gold chain breaking as it struck against the wall.

"But I! I would have given you everything. I would have sold all, worked for you with my hands, I would have begged on the highroads for a smile, for a look, to hear you say 'Thanks!' And you sit there quietly in your arm-chair, as if you had not made me suffer enough already! But for you, and you know it, I might have lived happily. What made you do it? Was it a bet? Yet you loved me—you said so. And but a moment since— Ah! it would have been better to have driven me away. My hands are hot with your kisses, and there is the spot on the carpet where at my knees you swore an eternity of love! You made me believe you; for two years you held me in the most magnificent, the sweetest dream! Eh! Our plans for the journey, do you remember? Oh, your letter! your letter! it tore my heart! And then when I come back to him—to him, rich, happy, free—to implore the help the first stranger would give, a suppliant, and bringing back to him all my tenderness, he repulses me because it would cost him three thousand francs!"

"I haven't got them," replied Rodolphe, with that perfect calm with which resigned rage covers itself as with a shield.

She went out. The walls trembled, the ceiling was crushing her, and she passed back through the long alley, stumbling against the heaps of dead leaves scattered by the wind. At last she reached the ha-ha hedge in front of the gate; she broke her nails against the lock in her haste to open it. Then a hundred steps farther on, breathless, almost falling, she stopped. And now turning round, she once more saw the impassive château, with the park, the gardens, the three courts, and all the windows of the façade.

She remained lost in stupor, and having no more consciousness of herself than through the beating of her arteries, that she seemed to hear bursting forth like a deafening music filling all the fields. The earth beneath her feet was more yielding than the sea, and the furrows seemed to her immense brown waves breaking into foam. Everything in her head, of memories, ideas, went off at once like a thousand pieces of fireworks. She saw her father, Lheureux's closet, their room at home, another landscape. Madness was coming upon her; she grew afraid, and managed to recover herself, in a confused way, it is true, for she did not in the least remember the cause of the terrible condition she was in, that is to say, the question of money. She suffered only in her love, and felt her soul passing from her in this memory, as wounded men, dying, feel their life ebb from their bleeding wounds.

Night was falling, crows were flying about.

Suddenly it seemed to her that fiery spheres were exploding in the air like fulminating balls when they strike, and were whirling, whirling, to melt at last upon the snow between the branches of the trees. In the midst of each of them appeared the face of Rodolphe. They multiplied and drew near her, penetrating her. It all disappeared; she recognised the lights of the houses that shone through the fog.

Now her situation, like an abyss, rose up before her. She was panting as if her heart would burst. Then in an ecstasy of heroism, that made her almost joyous, she ran down the hill, crossed the cow-plank, the footpath, the alley, the market, and reached the chemist's shop. She was about to enter, but at the sound of the bell someone might come, and slipping in by the gate, holding her breath, feeling her way along the walls, she went as far as the door of the kitchen, where a candle stuck on the stove was burning. Justin in his shirt-sleeves was carrying out a dish.

"Ah! they are dining; I will wait."

He returned; she tapped at the window. He went out.

"The key! the one for upstairs where he keeps the—"

"What?"

And he looked at her, astonished at the pallor of her face, that stood out white against the black background of the night. She seemed to him extraordinarily beautiful and majestic as a phantom. Without understanding what she wanted, he had the presentiment of something terrible.

But she went on quickly in a low voice, in a sweet, melting voice, "I want it; give it to me."

As the partition wall was thin, they could hear the clatter of the forks on the plates in the dining-room.

She pretended that she wanted to kill the rats that kept her from sleeping.

"I must tell master."

"No, stay!" Then with an indifferent air, "Oh, it's not worth while; I'll tell him presently. Come, light me upstairs."

She entered the corridor into which the laboratory door opened. Against the wall was a key labelled capharnaüm.

"Justin!" called the druggist impatiently.

"Let us go up."

And he followed her. The key turned in the lock, and she went straight to the third shelf, so well did her memory guide her, seized the blue jar, tore out the cork, plunged in her hand, and withdrawing it full of a white powder, she began eating it.

"Stop!" he cried, rushing at her.

"Hush! someone will come."

He was in despair, was calling out.

"Say nothing, or all the blame will fall on your master."

Then she went home, suddenly calmed, and with something of the serenity of one that had performed a duty.

When Charles, distracted by the news of the distraint, returned home, Emma had just gone out. He cried aloud, wept, fainted, but she did not return. Where could she be? He sent Félicité to Homais, to Monsieur Tuvache, to Lheureux, to the Lion d'Or, everywhere, and in the intervals of his agony he saw his reputation destroyed, their fortune lost, Berthe's future ruined. By what?—Not a word! He waited till six in the evening. At last, unable to bear it any longer, and fancying she had gone to Rouen, he set out along the highroad, walked a mile, met no one, again waited, and returned home. She had come back.

"What was the matter? Why? Explain to me."

She sat down at her writing-table and wrote a letter, which she sealed slowly, adding the date and the hour. Then she said in a solemn tone—

"You are to read it to-morrow; till then, I pray you, do not ask me a single question. No, not one!"

"But—"

"Oh, leave me!"

She lay down full length on her bed. A bitter taste that she felt in her mouth awakened her. She saw Charles, and again closed her eyes.

She was studying herself curiously, to see if she were not suffering. But no! nothing as yet. She heard the ticking of the clock, the crackling of the fire, and Charles breathing as he stood upright by her bed.

"Ah! it is but a little thing, death!" she thought. "I shall fall asleep and all will be over."

She drank a mouthful of water and turned to the wall. The frightful taste of ink continued.

"I am thirsty; oh! so thirsty," she sighed.

"What is it?" said Charles, who was handing her a glass.

"It is nothing! Open the window; I am choking."

She was seized with a sickness so sudden that she had hardly time to draw out her handkerchief from under the pillow.

"Take it away," she said quickly; "throw it away."

He spoke to her; she did not answer. She lay motionless, afraid that the slightest movement might make her vomit. But she felt an icy cold creeping from her feet to her heart.

"Ah! it is beginning," she murmured.

"What did you say?"

She turned her head from side to side with a gentle movement full of agony, while constantly opening her mouth as if something very heavy were weighing upon her tongue. At eight o'clock the vomiting began again.

Charles noticed that at the bottom of the basin there was a sort of white sediment sticking to the sides of the porcelain.

"This is extraordinary—very singular," he repeated.

But she said in a firm voice, "No, you are mistaken."

Then gently, and almost as caressing her, he passed his hand over her stomach. She uttered a sharp cry. He fell back terror-stricken.

Then she began to groan, faintly at first. Her shoulders were shaken by a strong shuddering, and she was growing paler than the sheets in which her clenched fingers buried themselves. Her unequal pulse was now almost imperceptible.

Drops of sweat oozed from her bluish face, that seemed as if rigid in the exhalations of a metallic vapour. Her teeth chattered, her dilated eyes looked vaguely about her, and to all questions she replied only with a shake of the head; she even smiled once or twice. Gradually, her moaning grew louder; a hollow shriek burst from her; she pretended she was better and that she would get up presently. But she was seized with convulsions and cried out—

"Ah! my God! It is horrible!"

He threw himself on his knees by her bed.

"Tell me! what have you eaten? Answer, for heaven's sake!"

And he looked at her with a tenderness in his eyes such as she had never seen.

"Well, there—there!" she said in a faint voice. He flew to the writing-table, tore open the seal, and read aloud: "Accuse no one." He stopped, passed his hands across his eyes, and read it over again.

"What! help—help!"

He could only keep repeating the word: "Poisoned! poisoned!" Félicité ran to Homais, who proclaimed it in the market-place; Madame Lefrançois heard it at the Lion d'Or; some got up to go and tell their neighbours, and all night the village was on the alert.

Distraught, faltering, reeling, Charles wandered about the room. He knocked against the furniture, tore his hair, and the chemist had never believed that there could be so terrible a sight.

He went home to write to Monsieur Canivet and to Doctor Larivière. He lost his head, and made more than fifteen rough copies. Hippolyte went to Neufchâtel, and Justin so spurred Bovary's horse that he left it foundered and three parts dead by the hill at Bois-Guillaume.

Charles tried to look up his medical dictionary, but could not read it; the lines were dancing.

"Be calm," said the druggist; "we have only to administer a powerful antidote. What is the poison?"

Charles showed him the letter. It was arsenic.

"Very well," said Homais, "we must make an analysis."

For he knew that in cases of poisoning an analysis must be made; and the other, who did not understand, answered—

"Oh, do anything! save her!"

Then going back to her, he sank upon the carpet, and lay there with his head leaning against the edge of her bed, sobbing.

"Don't cry," she said to him. "Soon I shall not trouble you any more."

"Why was it? Who drove you to it?"

She replied. "It had to be, my dear!"

"Weren't you happy? Is it my fault? I did all I could!"

"Yes, that is true—you are good—you."

And she passed her hand slowly over his hair. The sweetness of this sensation deepened his sadness; he felt his whole being dissolving in despair at the thought that he must lose her, just when she was confessing more love for him than ever. And he could think of nothing; he did not know, he did not dare; the urgent need for some immediate resolution gave the finishing stroke to the turmoil of his mind.

So she had done, she thought, with all the treachery, and meanness, and numberless desires that had tortured her. She hated no one now; a twilight dimness was settling upon her thoughts, and, of all earthly noises, Emma heard none but the intermittent lamentations of this poor heart, sweet and indistinct like the echo of a symphony dying away.

"Bring me the child," she said, raising herself on her elbow.

"You are not worse, are you?" asked Charles.

"No, no!"

The child, serious, and still half-asleep, was carried in on the servant's arm in her long white nightgown, from which her bare feet peeped out. She looked wonderingly at the disordered room, and half-closed her eyes, dazzled by the candles burning on the table. They reminded her, no doubt, of the morning of New Year's day and Mid-Lent, when thus awakened early by candlelight she came to her mother's bed to fetch her presents, for she began saying—

"But where is it, mamma?" And as everybody was silent, "But I can't see my little stocking."

Félicité held her over the bed while she still kept looking towards the mantelpiece.

"Has nurse taken it?" she asked.

And at this name, that carried her back to the memory of her adulteries and her calamities, Madame Bovary turned away her head, as at the loathing of another bitterer poison that rose to her mouth. But Berthe remained perched on the bed.

"Oh, how big your eyes are, mamma! How pale you are! how hot you are!"

Her mother looked at her.

"I am frightened!" cried the child, recoiling.

Emma took her hand to kiss it; the child struggled.

"That will do. Take her away," cried Charles, who was sobbing in the alcove.

Then the symptoms ceased for a moment; she seemed less agitated; and at every insignificant word, at every respiration a little more easy, he regained hope. At last, when Canivet came in, he threw himself into his arms.

"Ah! it is you. Thanks! You are good! But she is better. See! look at her."

His colleague was by no means of this opinion, and, as he said of himself, "never beating about the bush," he prescribed an emetic in order to empty the stomach completely.

She soon began vomiting blood. Her lips became drawn. Her limbs were convulsed, her whole body covered with brown spots, and her pulse slipped beneath the fingers like a stretched thread, like a harp-string nearly breaking.

After this she began to scream horribly. She cursed the poison, railed at it, and implored it to be quick, and thrust away with her stiffened arms everything that Charles, in more agony than herself, tried to make her drink. He stood up, his handkerchief to his lips, with a rattling sound in his throat, weeping, and choked by sobs that shook his whole body. Félicité was running hither and thither in the room. Homais, motionless, uttered great sighs; and Monsieur Canivet, always retaining his self-command, nevertheless began to feel uneasy.

"The devil! yet she has been purged, and from the moment that the cause ceases—"

"The effect must cease," said Homais, "that is evident."

"Oh, save her!" cried Bovary.

And, without listening to the chemist, who was still venturing the hypothesis, "It is perhaps a salutary paroxysm," Canivet was about to administer some theriac, when they heard the cracking of a whip; all the windows rattled, and a post-chaise drawn by three horses abreast, up to their ears in mud, drove at a gallop round the corner of the market. It was Doctor Larivière.

The apparition of a god would not have caused more commotion. Bovary raised his hands; Canivet stopped short; and Homais pulled off his skull-cap long before the doctor had come in.

He belonged to that great school of surgery begotten of Bichat, to that generation, now extinct, of philosophical practitioners, who, loving their art with a fanatical love, exercised it with enthusiasm and wisdom. Everyone in his hospital trembled when he was angry; and his students so revered him that they tried, as soon as they were themselves in practice, to imitate him as much as possible. So that in all the towns about they were found wearing his long wadded merino overcoat and black frock-coat, whose buttoned cuffs slightly covered his brawny hands—very beautiful hands, and that never knew gloves, as though to be more ready to plunge into suffering. Disdainful of honours, of titles, and of academies, like one of the old Knight-Hospitallers, generous, fatherly to the poor, and practising virtue without believing in it, he would almost have passed for a saint if the keenness of his intellect had not caused him to be feared as a demon. His glance, more penetrating than his bistouries, looked straight into your soul, and dissected every lie athwart all assertions and all reticences. And thus he went along, full of that debonair majesty that is given by the consciousness of great talent, of fortune, and of forty years of a labourious and irreproachable life.

He frowned as soon as he had passed the door when he saw the cadaverous face of Emma stretched out on her back with her mouth open. Then, while apparently listening to Canivet, he rubbed his fingers up and down beneath his nostrils, and repeated—

"Good! good!"

But he made a slow gesture with his shoulders. Bovary watched him; they looked at one another; and this man, accustomed as he was to the sight of pain, could not keep back a tear that fell on his shirt-frill.

He tried to take Canivet into the next room. Charles followed him.

"She is very ill, isn't she? If we put on sinapisms? Anything! Oh, think of something, you who have saved so many!"

Charles caught him in both his arms, and gazed at him wildly, imploringly, half-fainting against his breast.

"Come, my poor fellow, courage! There is nothing more to be done."

And Doctor Larivière turned away.

"You are going?"

"I will come back."

He went out only to give an order to the coachman, with Monsieur Canivet, who did not care either to have Emma die under his hands.

The chemist rejoined them on the Place. He could not by temperament keep away from celebrities, so he begged Monsieur Larivière to do him the signal honour of accepting some breakfast.

He sent quickly to the Lion d'Or for some pigeons; to the butcher's for all the cutlets that were to be had; to Tuvache for cream; and to Lestiboudois for eggs; and the druggist himself aided in the preparations, while Madame Homais was saying as she pulled together the strings of her jacket—

"You must excuse us, sir, for in this poor place, when one hasn't been told the night before—"

"Wine glasses!" whispered Homais.

"If only we were in town, we could fall back upon stuffed trotters."

"Be quiet! Sit down, doctor!"

He thought fit, after the first few mouthfuls, to give some details as to the catastrophe.

"We first had a feeling of siccity in the pharynx, then intolerable pains at the epigastrium, super-purgation, coma."

"But how did she poison herself?"

"I don't know, doctor, and I don't even know where she can have procured the arsenious acid."

Justin, who was just bringing in a pile of plates, began to tremble.

"What's the matter?" said the chemist.

At this question the young man dropped the whole lot on the ground with a crash.

"Imbecile!" cried Homais, "awkward lout! blockhead! confounded ass!"

But suddenly controlling himself—

"I wished, doctor, to make an analysis, and *primo* I delicately introduced a tube—"

"You would have done better," said the physician, "to introduce your fingers into her throat."

His colleague was silent, having just before privately received a severe lecture about his emetic, so that this good Canivet, so arrogant and so verbose at the time of the club-foot, was to-day very modest. He smiled without ceasing in an approving manner.

Homais dilated in Amphytrionic pride, and the affecting thought of Bovary vaguely contributed to his pleasure by a kind of egotistic reflex upon himself. Then the presence of the doctor transported him. He displayed his erudition, cited pell-mell cantharides, upas, the manchineel, vipers.

"I have even read that various persons have found themselves under toxicological symptoms, and, as it were, thunderstricken by black-pudding that had been subjected to a too vehement fumigation. At least, this was stated in a very fine report drawn up by one of our pharmaceutical chiefs, one of our masters, the illustrious Cadet de Gassicourt!"

Madame Homais reappeared, carrying one of those shaky machines that are heated with spirits of wine; for Homais liked to make his coffee at table, having, moreover, torrefied it, pulverised it, and mixed it himself.

"*Saccharum,* doctor?" said he, offering the sugar.

Then he had all his children brought down, anxious to have the physician's opinion on their constitutions.

At last Monsieur Larivière was about to leave, when Madame Homais asked for a consultation about her husband. He was making his blood too thick by going to sleep every evening after dinner.

"Oh, it isn't his blood that's too thick," said the physician.

And, smiling a little at his unnoticed joke, the doctor opened the door. But the chemist's shop was full of people; he had the greatest difficulty in getting rid of Monsieur Tuvache, who feared his spouse would get inflammation of the lungs, because she was in the habit of spitting on the ashes; then of Monsieur Binet, who sometimes experienced sudden attacks of great hunger; and of Madame Caron, who suffered from tinglings; of Lheureux, who had vertigo; of Lestiboudois, who had rheumatism; and of Madame Lefrançois, who had heartburn. At last the three horses started; and it was the general opinion that he had not shown himself at all obliging.

Public attention was distracted by the appearance of Monsieur Bournisien, who was going across the market with the holy oil.

Homais, as was due to his principles, compared priests to ravens attracted by the odour of death. The sight of an ecclesiastic was personally disagreeable to him, for the cassock made him think of the shroud, and he detested the one from some fear of the other.

Nevertheless, not shrinking from what he called his mission, he returned to Bovary's in company with Canivet, whom Monsieur Larivière, before leaving, had strongly urged to make this visit; and he would, but for his wife's objections, have taken his two sons with him, in order to accustom them to great occasions; that this might be a lesson, an example, a solemn picture, that should remain in their heads later on.

The room when they went in was full of mournful solemnity. On the work-table, covered over with a white cloth, there were five or six small balls of cotton in a silver dish, near a large crucifix between two lighted candles.

Emma, her chin sunken upon her breast, had her eyes inordinately wide open, and her poor hands wandered over the sheets with that hideous and soft movement of the dying, that seems as if they wanted already to cover themselves with the shroud. Pale as a statue and with eyes red as fire, Charles, not weeping, stood opposite her at the foot of the bed, while the priest, bending one knee, was muttering words in a low voice.

She turned her face slowly, and seemed filled with joy on seeing suddenly the violet stole, no doubt finding again, in the midst of a temporary lull in her pain, the lost voluptuousness of her first mystical transports, with the visions of eternal beatitude that were beginning.

The priest rose to take the crucifix; then she stretched forward her neck as one who is athirst, and glueing her lips to the body of the Man-God, she pressed upon it with all her expiring strength the fullest kiss of love that she had ever given. Then he recited the *Misereatur* and the *Indulgentiam,* dipped his right thumb in the oil, and began to give extreme unction. First, upon the eyes, that had so coveted all worldly pomp; then upon the nostrils, that had been greedy of the warm breeze and amorous odours; then upon the mouth, that had uttered lies, that had curled with pride and cried out in lewdness; then upon the hands that had delighted in sensual touches; and finally upon the soles of the feet, so swift of yore, when she was running to satisfy her desires, and that would now walk no more.

The curé wiped his fingers, threw the bit of cotton dipped in oil into the fire, and came and sat down by the dying woman, to tell her that she must now blend her sufferings with those of Jesus Christ and abandon herself to the divine mercy.

Finishing his exhortations, he tried to place in her hand a blessed candle, symbol of the celestial glory with which she was soon to be surrounded. Emma, too weak, could not close her fingers, and the taper, but for Monsieur Bournisien would have fallen to the ground.

However, she was not quite so pale, and her face had an expression of serenity as if the sacrament had cured her.

The priest did not fail to point this out; he even explained to Bovary that the Lord sometimes prolonged the life of persons when he thought it meet for their salvation; and Charles remembered the day when, so near death, she had received the communion. Perhaps there was no need to despair, he thought.

In fact, she looked around her slowly, as one awakening from a dream; then in a distinct voice she asked for her looking-glass, and remained some time bending over it, until the big tears fell from her eyes. Then she turned away her head with a sigh and fell back upon the pillows.

Her chest soon began panting rapidly; the whole of her tongue protruded from her mouth; her eyes, as they rolled, grew paler, like the two globes of a lamp that is going out, so that one might have thought her already dead but for the fearful labouring of her ribs, shaken by violent breathing, as if the soul were struggling to free itself. Félicité knelt down before the crucifix, and the druggist himself slightly bent his knees, while Monsieur Canivet looked out vaguely at the Place. Bournisien had again begun to pray, his face bowed against the edge of the bed, his long black cassock trailing behind him in the room. Charles was on the other side, on his knees, his arms outstretched towards Emma. He had taken her hands and pressed them, shuddering at every beat of her heart, as at the shaking of a falling ruin. As the death-rattle became stronger the priest prayed faster; his prayers mingled with the stifled sobs of Bovary, and sometimes all seemed lost in the muffled murmur of the Latin syllables that tolled like a passing bell.

Suddenly on the pavement was heard a loud noise of clogs and the clattering of a stick; and a voice rose—a raucous voice—that sang—

> "Maids in the warmth of a summer day
> Dream of love and of love alway."

Emma raised herself like a galvanised corpse, her hair undone, her eyes fixed, staring.

> "Where the sickle blades have been,
> Nannette, gathering ears of corn,
> Passes bending down, my queen,
> To the earth where they were born."

"The blind man!" she cried. And Emma began to laugh, an atrocious, frantic, despairing laugh, thinking she saw the hideous face of the poor wretch that stood out against the eternal night like a menace.

> *"The wind is strong this summer day,*
> *Her petticoat has flown away."*

She fell back upon the mattress in a convulsion. They all drew near. She was dead.

Chapter IX

THERE IS ALWAYS AFTER THE DEATH OF ANYONE A KIND OF STUPEFACTION; so difficult is it to grasp this advent of nothingness and to resign ourselves to believe in it. But still, when he saw that she did not move, Charles threw himself upon her, crying—

"Farewell! farewell!"

Homais and Canivet dragged him from the room.

"Restrain yourself!"

"Yes," said he, struggling, "I'll be quiet. I'll not do anything. But leave me alone. I want to see her. She is my wife!"

And he wept.

"Cry," said the chemist; "let nature take her course; that will solace you."

Weaker than a child, Charles let himself be led downstairs into the sitting-room, and Monsieur Homais soon went home. On the Place he was accosted by the blind man, who, having dragged himself as far as Yonville in the hope of getting the antiphlogistic pommade, was asking every passer-by where the druggist lived.

"There now! as if I hadn't got other fish to fry. Well, so much the worse; you must come later on."

And he entered the shop hurriedly.

He had to write two letters, to prepare a soothing potion for Bovary, to invent some lie that would conceal the poisoning, and work it up into an article for the *Fanal*, without counting the people who were waiting to get the news from him; and when the Yonvillers had all heard his story of the arsenic that she had mistaken for sugar in making a vanilla cream, Homais once more returned to Bovary's.

He found him alone (Monsieur Canivet had left), sitting in an arm-chair near the window, staring with an idiotic look at the flags of the floor.

"Now," said the chemist, "you ought yourself to fix the hour for the ceremony."

"Why? What ceremony?" Then, in a stammering, frightened voice, "Oh, no! not that. No! I want to see her here."

Homais, to keep himself in countenance, took up a water-bottle on the what-not to water the geraniums.

"Ah! thanks," said Charles; "you are good."

But he did not finish, choking beneath the crowd of memories that this action of the druggist recalled to him.

Then to distract him, Homais thought fit to talk a little horticulture: plants wanted humidity. Charles bowed his head in sign of approbation.

"Besides, the fine days will soon be here again."

"Ah!" said Bovary.

The druggist, at his wit's end, began softly to draw aside the small window-curtain.

"Hallo! there's Monsieur Tuvache passing."

Charles repeated like a machine—

"Monsieur Tuvache passing!"

Homais did not dare to speak to him again about the funeral arrangements; it was the priest who succeeded in reconciling him to them.

He shut himself up in his consulting-room, took a pen, and after sobbing for some time, wrote—

"I wish her to be buried in her wedding-dress, with white shoes, and a wreath. Her hair is to be spread out over her shoulders. Three coffins, one of oak, one of mahogany, one of lead. Let no one say anything to me. I shall have strength. Over all there is to be placed a large piece of green velvet. This is my wish; see that it is done."

The two men were much surprised at Bovary's romantic ideas. The chemist at once went to him and said—

"This velvet seems to me a superfetation. Besides, the expense—"

"What's that to you?" cried Charles. "Leave me! You did not love her. Go!"

The priest took him by the arm for a turn in the garden. He discoursed on the vanity of earthly things. God was very great, was very good: one must submit to his decrees without a murmur; nay, must even thank him.

Charles burst out into blasphemies: "I hate your God!"

"The spirit of rebellion is still upon you," sighed the ecclesiastic.

Bovary was far away. He was walking with great strides along by the wall, near the espalier, and he ground his teeth; he raised to heaven looks of malediction, but not so much as a leaf stirred.

A fine rain was falling: Charles, whose chest was bare, at last began to shiver; he went in and sat down in the kitchen.

At six o'clock a noise like a clatter of old iron was heard on the Place; it was the Hirondelle coming in, and he remained with his forehead against the window-pane, watching all the passengers get out, one after the other. Félicité put down a mattress for him in the drawing-room. He threw himself upon it and fell asleep.

Although a philosopher, Monsieur Homais respected the dead. So bearing no grudge to poor Charles, he came back again in the evening to sit up with the body, bringing with him three volumes and a pocket-book for taking notes.

Monsieur Bournisien was there, and two large candles were burning at the head of the bed, that had been taken out of the alcove. The druggist, on whom the silence weighed, was not long before he began formulating some regrets about this "unfortunate young woman," and the priest replied that there was nothing to do now but pray for her.

"Yet," Homais went on, "one of two things; either she died in a state of grace (as the Church has it), and then she has no need of our prayers; or else she departed impertinent (that is, I believe, the ecclesiastical expression), and then—"

Bournisien interrupted him, replying testily that it was none the less necessary to pray.

"But," objected the chemist, "since God knows all our needs, what can be the good of prayer?"

"What!" cried the ecclesiastic, "prayer! Why, aren't you a Christian?"

"Excuse me," said Homais; "I admire Christianity. To begin with, it enfranchised the slaves, introduced into the world a morality—"

"That isn't the question. All the texts—"

"Oh! oh! As to texts, look at history; it is known that all the texts have been falsified by the Jesuits."

Charles came in, and advancing towards the bed, slowly drew the curtains.

Emma's head was turned towards her right shoulder, the corner of her mouth, which was open, seemed like a black hole at the lower part of her face; her two thumbs were bent into the palms of her hands; a kind of white dust besprinkled her lashes, and her eyes were beginning to disappear in that viscous pallor that looks like a thin web, as if spiders had spun it over. The sheet sunk in from her breast to her knees, and then rose at the tips of her toes, and it seemed to Charles that infinite masses, an enormous load, were weighing upon her.

The church clock struck two. They could hear the loud murmur of the river flowing in the darkness at the foot of the terrace. Monsieur Bournisien from time to time blew his nose noisily, and Homais's pen was scratching over the paper.

"Come, my good friend," he said, "withdraw; this spectacle is tearing you to pieces."

Charles once gone, the chemist and the curé recommenced their discussions.

"Read Voltaire," said the one, "read D'Holbach, read the *Encyclopædia!*"

"Read the *Letters of some Portuguese Jews,*" said the other; "read *The Meaning of Christianity,* by Nicolas, formerly a magistrate."

They grew warm, they grew red, they both talked at once without listening to each other. Bournisien was scandalised at such audacity; Homais marvelled at such stupidity; and they were on the point of insulting one another when Charles suddenly reappeared. A fascination drew him. He was continually coming upstairs.

He stood opposite her, the better to see her, and he lost himself in a contemplation so deep that it was no longer painful.

He recalled stories of catalepsy, the marvels of magnetism, and he said to himself that by willing it with all his force he might perhaps succeed in reviving her. Once he even bent towards her, and cried in a low voice, "Emma! Emma!" His strong breathing made the flames of the candles tremble against the wall.

At daybreak Madame Bovary senior arrived. Charles as he embraced her burst into another flood of tears. She tried, as the chemist had done, to make some remarks to him on the expenses of the funeral. He became so angry that she was silent, and he even commissioned her to go to town at once and buy what was necessary.

Charles remained alone the whole afternoon; they had taken Berthe to Madame Homais's; Félicité was in the room upstairs with Madame Lefrançois.

In the evening he had some visitors. He rose, pressed their hands, unable to speak. Then they sat down near one another, and formed a large semicircle in front of the fire. With lowered faces, and swinging one leg crossed over the other knee, they uttered deep sighs at intervals; each one was inordinately bored, and yet none would be the first to go.

Homais, when he returned at nine o'clock (for the last two days only Homais seemed to have been on the Place), was laden with a stock of camphor, of benzine, and aromatic herbs. He also carried a large jar full of chlorine water, to keep off all miasmata. Just then the servant, Madame Lefrançois, and Madame Bovary senior were busy about Emma, finishing dressing her, and they were drawing down the long stiff veil that covered her to her satin shoes.

Félicité was sobbing—"Ah! my poor mistress! my poor mistress!"

"Look at her," said the landlady, sighing; "how pretty she still is! Now, couldn't you swear she was going to get up in a minute?"

Then they bent over her to put on her wreath. They had to raise the head a little, and a rush of black liquid issued, as if she were vomiting, from her mouth.

"Oh, goodness! The dress; take care!" cried Madame Lefrançois. "Now, just come and help," she said to the chemist. "Perhaps you're afraid?"

"I afraid?" replied he, shrugging his shoulders. "I dare say! I've seen all sorts of things at the hospital when I was studying pharmacy. We used to make punch in the dissecting room! Nothingness does not terrify a philosopher; and, as I often say, I even intend to leave my body to the hospitals, in order, later on, to serve science."

The curé on his arrival inquired how Monsieur Bovary was, and, on the reply of the druggist, went on—"The blow, you see, is still too recent."

Then Homais congratulated him on not being exposed, like other people, to the loss of a beloved companion; whence there followed a discussion on the celibacy of priests.

"For," said the chemist, "it is unnatural that a man should do without women! There have been crimes——"

"But, good heaven!" cried the ecclesiastic, "how do you expect an individual who is married to keep the secrets of the confessional, for example?"

Homais fell foul of the confessional. Bournisien defended it; he enlarged on the acts of restitution that it brought about. He cited various anecdotes about thieves who had suddenly become honest. Military men on approaching the tribunal of penitence had felt the scales fall from their eyes. At Fribourg there was a minister——

His companion was asleep. Then he felt somewhat stifled by the over-heavy atmosphere of the room; he opened the window; this awoke the chemist.

"Come, take a pinch of snuff," he said to him. "Take it, it'll relieve you."

A continual barking was heard in the distance. "Do you hear that dog howling?" said the chemist.

"They smell the dead," replied the priest. "It's like bees; they leave their hives on the decease of any person."

Homais made no remark upon these prejudices, for he had again dropped asleep. Monsieur Bournisien, stronger than he, went on moving his lips gently for some time, then insensibly his chin sank down, he let fall his big black boot, and began to snore.

They sat opposite one another, with protruding stomachs, puffed-up faces, and frowning looks, after so much disagreement uniting at last in the same human weakness, and they moved no more than the corpse by their side, that seemed to be sleeping.

Charles coming in did not wake them. It was the last time; he came to bid her farewell.

The aromatic herbs were still smoking, and spirals of bluish vapour blended at the window-sash with the fog that was coming in. There were few stars, and the night was warm. The wax of the candles fell in great drops upon the sheets of the bed. Charles watched them burn, tiring his eyes against the glare of their yellow flame.

The watering on the satin gown shimmered white as moonlight. Emma was lost beneath it; and it seemed to him that, spreading beyond her own self, she blended confusedly with everything around her—the silence, the night, the passing wind, the damp odours rising from the ground.

Then suddenly he saw her in the garden at Tostes, on a bench against the thorn hedge, or else at Rouen in the streets, on the threshold of their house, in the yard at Bertaux. He again heard the laughter of the happy boys beneath the apple-trees: the room was filled with the perfume of her hair; and her dress rustled in his arms with a noise like electricity. The dress was still the same.

For a long while he thus recalled all his lost joys, her attitudes, her movements, the sound of her voice. Upon one fit of despair followed another, and even others, inexhaustible as the waves of an overflowing sea.

A terrible curiosity seized him. Slowly, with the tips of his fingers, palpitating, he lifted her veil. But he uttered a cry of horror that awoke the other two.

They dragged him down into the sitting-room. Then Félicité came up to say that he wanted some of her hair.

"Cut some off," replied the druggist.

And as she did not dare to, he himself stepped forward, scissors in hand. He trembled so that he pierced the skin of the temple in several places. At last, stiffening himself against emotion, Homais gave two or three great cuts at random that left white patches amongst that beautiful black hair.

The chemist and the curé plunged anew into their occupations, not without sleeping from time to time, of which they accused each other reciprocally at each fresh awakening. Then Monsieur Bournisien sprinkled the room with holy water and Homais threw a little chlorine water on the floor.

Félicité had taken care to put on the chest of drawers, for each of them, a bottle of brandy, some cheese, and a large roll; and the druggist, who could not hold out any longer, about four in the morning sighed—

"My word! I should like to take some sustenance."

The priest did not need any persuading; he went out to go and say mass, came back, and then they ate and hob-nobbed, giggling a little without knowing why, stimulated by that vague gaiety that comes upon us after times of sadness, and at the last glass the priest said to the druggist, as he clapped him on the shoulder—

"We shall end by understanding one another."

In the passage downstairs they met the undertaker's men, who were coming in. Then Charles for two hours had to suffer the torture of hearing the hammer resound against the wood. Next day they lowered her into her oak coffin, that was fitted into the other two; but as the bier was too large, they had to fill up the gaps with the wool of a mattress. At last, when the three lids had been planed down, nailed, soldered, it was placed outside in front of the door; the house was thrown open, and the people of Yonville began to flock round.

Old Rouault arrived, and fainted on the Place when he saw the black cloth.

Chapter X

H E HAD ONLY RECEIVED THE CHEMIST'S LETTER THIRTY-SIX HOURS AFTER the event; and, from consideration for his feelings, Homais had so worded it that it was impossible to make out what it was all about.

First, the old fellow had fallen as if struck by apoplexy. Next, he understood that she was not dead, but she might be. At last, he had put on his blouse, taken his hat, fastened his spurs to his boots, and set out at full speed; and the whole of the way old Rouault, panting, was torn by anguish. Once even he was obliged to dismount. He was dizzy; he heard voices round about him; he felt himself going mad.

Day broke. He saw three black hens asleep in a tree. He shuddered, horrified at this omen. Then he promised the Holy Virgin three chasubles for the church, and that he would go barefooted from the cemetery at Bertaux to the chapel of Vassonville.

He entered Maromme shouting for the people of the inn, burst open the door with a thrust of his shoulder, made for a sack of oats, emptied a bottle of sweet cider into the manger, and again mounted his nag, whose feet struck fire as it dashed along.

He said to himself that no doubt they would save her; the doctors would discover some remedy surely. He remembered all the miraculous cures he had been told about. Then she appeared to him dead. She was there, before his eyes, lying on her back in the middle of the road. He reined up, and the hallucination disappeared.

At Quincampoix, to give himself heart, he drank three cups of coffee one after the other. He fancied they had made a mistake in the name in writing. He looked for the letter in his pocket, felt it there, but did not dare to open it.

At last he began to think it was all a joke; someone's spite, the jest of some wag; and besides, if she were dead, one would have known it. But no! There was nothing extraordinary about the country; the sky was blue, the trees swayed; a flock of sheep passed. He saw the village; he was seen coming bending forward upon his horse, belabouring it with great blows, the girths dripping with blood.

When he had recovered consciousness, he fell, weeping, into Bovary's arms: "My girl! Emma! my child! tell me—"

The other replied, sobbing, "I don't know! I don't know! It's a curse!"

The druggist separated them. "These horrible details are useless. I will tell this gentleman all about it. Here are the people coming. Dignity! Come now! Philosophy!"

The poor fellow tried to show himself brave, and repeated several times, "Yes! courage!"

"Oh," cried the old man, "so I will have, by God! I'll go along o' her to the end!"

The bell began tolling. All was ready; they had to start. And seated in a stall of the choir, side by side, they saw pass and repass in front of them continually the three chanting choristers.

The serpent-player was blowing with all his might. Monsieur Bournisien, in full vestments, was singing in a shrill voice. He bowed before the tabernacle, raising his hands, stretched out his arms. Lestiboudois went about the church with his whalebone stick. The bier stood near the lectern, between four rows of candles. Charles felt inclined to get up and put them out.

Yet he tried to stir himself to a feeling of devotion, to throw himself into the hope of a future life in which he should see her again. He imagined to himself she had gone on a long journey, far away, for a long time. But when he thought of her lying there, and that all was over, that they would lay her in the earth, he was seized with a fierce, gloomy, despairful rage. At times he thought he felt nothing more, and he enjoyed this lull in his pain, whilst at the same time he reproached himself for being a wretch.

The sharp noise of an iron-ferruled stick was heard on the stones, striking them at irregular intervals. It came from the end of the church, and stopped short at the lower aisles. A man in a coarse brown jacket knelt down painfully. It was Hippolyte, the stable-boy at the Lion d'Or. He had put on his new leg.

One of the choristers went round the nave making a collection, and the coppers chinked one after the other on the silver plate.

"Oh, make haste! I am in pain!" cried Bovary, angrily throwing him a five-franc piece. The churchman thanked him with a deep bow.

They sang, they knelt, they stood up; it was endless! He remembered that once, in the early times, they had been to mass together, and they had sat down on the other side, on the right, by the wall. The bell began again. There was a great moving of chairs; the bearers slipped their three staves under the coffin, and everyone left the church.

Then Justin appeared at the door of the shop. He suddenly went in again, pale, staggering.

People were at the windows to see the procession pass. Charles at the head walked erect. He affected a brave air, and saluted with a nod those who, coming out from the lanes or from their doors, stood amidst the crowd.

The six men, three on either side, walked slowly, panting a little. The priests, the choristers, and the two choir-boys recited the *De profundis,* and their voices echoed over the fields, rising and falling with their undulations. Sometimes they disappeared in the windings of the path; but the great silver cross rose always between the trees.

The women followed in black cloaks with turned-down hoods; each of them carried in her hands a large lighted candle, and Charles felt himself growing weaker at this continual repetition of prayers and torches, beneath this oppressive odour of wax and of cassocks. A fresh breeze was blowing; the rye and colza were sprouting, little dew-drops trembled at the roadsides and on the hawthorn hedges. All sorts of joyous sounds filled the air; the jolting of a cart rolling afar off in the ruts, the crowing of a cock, repeated again and again, or the gambling of a foal running away under the apple-trees. The pure sky was fretted with rosy clouds; a bluish haze rested upon the cots covered with iris. Charles as he passed recognised each courtyard. He remembered mornings like this, when, after visiting some patient, he came out from one and returned to her.

The black cloth bestrewn with white beads blew up from time to time, laying bare the coffin. The tired bearers walked more slowly, and it advanced with constant jerks, like a boat that pitches with every wave.

They reached the cemetery. The men went right down to a place in the grass where a grave was dug. They ranged themselves all round; and while the priest spoke, the red soil thrown up at the sides kept noiselessly slipping down at the corners.

Then when the four ropes were arranged the coffin was placed upon them. He watched it descend; it seemed descending forever. At last a thud was heard; the ropes creaked as they were drawn up. Then Bournisien took the spade handed to him by Lestiboudois; with his left hand all the time sprinkling water, with the right he vigourously threw in a large spadeful; and the wood of the coffin, struck by the pebbles, gave forth that dread sound that seems to us the reverberation of eternity.

The ecclesiastic passed the holy water sprinkler to his neighbour. This was Homais. He swung it gravely, then handed it to Charles, who sank to his knees in the earth and threw in handfuls of it, crying, "Adieu!" He sent her kisses; he dragged himself towards the grave, to engulf himself with her. They led him away, and he soon grew calmer, feeling perhaps, like the others, a vague satisfaction that it was all over.

Old Rouault on his way back began quietly smoking a pipe, which Homais in his innermost conscience thought not quite the thing. He also noticed that Monsieur Binet had not been present, and that Tuvache had "made off" after mass, and that Theodore, the notary's servant, wore a blue coat, "as if one could not have got a black coat, since that is the custom, by Jove!" And to share his observations with others he went from group to group. They were deploring Emma's death, especially Lheureux, who had not failed to come to the funeral.

"Poor little woman! What a trouble for her husband!"

The druggist continued, "Do you know that but for me he would have committed some fatal attempt upon himself?"

"Such a good woman! To think that I saw her only last Saturday in my shop."

"I haven't had leisure," said Homais, "to prepare a few words that I would have cast upon her tomb."

Charles on getting home undressed, and old Rouault put on his blue blouse. It was a new one, and as he had often during the journey wiped his eyes on the sleeves, the dye had stained his face, and the traces of tears made lines in the layer of dust that covered it.

Madame Bovary senior was with them. All three were silent. At last the old fellow sighed—

"Do you remember, my friend, that I went to Tostes once when you had just lost your first deceased? I consoled you at that time. I thought of something to say then, but now—" Then, with a loud groan that shook his whole chest, "Ah! this is the end for me, do you see! I saw my wife go, then my son, and now to-day it's my daughter."

He wanted to go back at once to Bertaux, saying that he could not sleep in this house. He even refused to see his granddaughter.

"No, no! It would grieve me too much. Only you'll kiss her many times for me. Good-bye! you're a good fellow! And then I shall never forget that," he said, slapping his thigh. "Never fear, you shall always have your turkey."

But when he reached the top of the hill he turned back, as he had turned once before on the road of Saint-Victor when he had parted from her. The windows of the village were all on fire beneath the slanting rays of the sun sinking behind the field. He put his hand over his eyes, and saw in the horizon an enclosure of walls, where trees here and there formed black clusters between white stones; then he went on his way at a gentle trot, for his nag had gone lame.

Despite their fatigue, Charles and his mother stayed very long that evening talking together. They spoke of the days of the past and of the future. She would come to live at Yonville; she would keep house for him; they would never part again. She was ingenious and caressing, rejoicing in her heart at gaining once more an affection that had wandered from her for so many years. Midnight struck. The village as usual was silent, and Charles, awake, thought always of her.

Rodolphe, who, to distract himself, had been rambling about the wood all day, was sleeping quietly in his château, and Léon, down yonder, always slept.

There was another who at that hour was not asleep.

On the grave between the pine-trees a child was on his knees weeping, and his heart, rent by sobs, was beating in the shadow beneath the load of an immense regret, sweeter than the moon and fathomless as the night. The gate suddenly grated. It was Lestiboudois; he came to fetch his spade, that he had forgotten. He recognised Justin climbing over the wall, and at last knew who was the culprit who stole his potatoes.

Chapter XI

THE NEXT DAY CHARLES HAD THE CHILD BROUGHT BACK. SHE ASKED FOR her mamma. They told her she was away; that she would bring her back some playthings. Berthe spoke of her again several times, then at last thought no more of her. The child's gaiety broke Bovary's heart, and he had to bear besides the intolerable consolations of the chemist.

Money troubles soon began again, Monsieur Lheureux urging on anew his friend Vinçart, and Charles pledged himself for exorbitant sums; for he would never consent to let the smallest of the things that had belonged to *her* be sold. His mother was exasperated with him; he grew even more angry than she did. He had altogether changed. She left the house.

Then everyone began "taking advantage" of him. Mademoiselle Lempereur presented a bill for six months' teaching, although Emma had never taken a lesson (despite the receipted bill she had shown Bovary); it was an arrangement between the two women. The man at the circulating library demanded three years' subscriptions; Mère Rolet claimed the postage due for some twenty letters, and when Charles asked for an explanation, she had the delicacy to reply—

"Oh, I don't know. It was for her business affairs."

With every debt he paid Charles thought he had come to the end of them. But, others followed ceaselessly. He sent in accounts for professional attendance. He was shown the letters his wife had written. Then he had to apologise.

Félicité now wore Madame Bovary's gowns; not all, for he had kept some of them, and he went to look at them in her dressing-room, locking himself up there; she was about her height, and often Charles, seeing her from behind, was seized with an illusion, and cried out—

"Oh, stay, stay!"

But at Whitsuntide she ran away from Yonville, carried off by Theodore, stealing all that was left of the wardrobe.

It was about this time that the widow Dupuis had the honour to inform him of the "marriage of Monsieur Léon Dupuis her son, notary at Yvetot, to Mademoiselle Léocadié Lebœuf of Bondeville." Charles, among the other congratulations he sent him, wrote this sentence—

"How glad my poor wife would have been!"

One day when, wandering aimlessly about the house, he had gone up to the attic, he felt a pellet of fine paper under his slipper. He opened it and read: "Courage, Emma, courage. I would not bring misery into your life." It was

Rodolphe's letter, fallen to the ground between the boxes, where it had remained, and that the wind from the dormer window had just blown towards the door. And Charles stood, motionless and staring, in the very same place where, long ago, Emma, in despair, and paler even than he, had thought of dying. At last he discovered a small R at the bottom of the second page. What did this mean? He remembered Rodolphe's attentions, his sudden disappearance, his constrained air when they had met two or three times since. But the respectful tone of the letter deceived him.

"Perhaps they loved one another platonically," he said to himself.

Besides, Charles was not of those who go to the bottom of things; he shrank from the proofs, and his vague jealousy was lost in the immensity of his woe.

Everyone, he thought, must have adored her; all men assuredly must have coveted her. She seemed but the more beautiful to him for this; he was seized with a lasting, furious desire for her, that inflamed his despair, and that was boundless, because it was now unrealisable.

To please her, as if she were still living, he adopted her predilections, her ideas; he bought patent leather boots and took to wearing white cravats. He put cosmetics on his moustache, and, like her, signed notes of hand. She corrupted him from beyond the grave.

He was obliged to sell his silver piece by piece; next he sold the drawing-room furniture. All the rooms were stripped; but the bedroom, her own room, remained as before. After his dinner Charles went up there. He pushed the round table in front of the fire, and drew up *her* arm-chair. He sat down opposite it. A candle burnt in one of the gilt candlesticks. Berthe by his side was painting prints.

He suffered, poor man, at seeing her so badly dressed, with laceless boots, and the arm-holes of her pinafore torn down to the hips; for the charwoman took no care of her. But she was so sweet, so pretty, and her little head bent forward so gracefully, letting the dear fair hair fall over her rosy cheeks, that an infinite joy came upon him, a happiness mingled with bitterness, like those ill-made wines that taste of resin. He mended her toys, made her puppets from cardboard, or sewed up half-torn dolls. Then, if his eyes fell upon the workbox, a ribbon lying about, or even a pin left in a crack of the table, he began to dream, and looked so sad that she became as sad as he.

No one now came to see them, for Justin had run away to Rouen, where he was a grocer's assistant, and the druggist's children saw less and less of the child, Monsieur Homais not caring, seeing the difference of their social position, to continue the intimacy.

The blind man, whom he had not been able to cure with the pommade, had gone back to the hill of Bois-Guillaume, where he told the travellers of the vain attempt of the druggist, to such an extent, that Homais when he went to town hid himself behind the curtains of the Hirondelle to avoid meeting him. He detested him, and wishing, in the interests of his own reputation, to get rid of him at all costs, he directed against him a secret battery, that betrayed the depth of his intellect and the baseness of his vanity. Thus, for six consecutive months, one could read in the *Fanal de Rouen* editorials such as these—

"All who bend their steps towards the fertile plains of Picardy have, no doubt, remarked, by the Bois-Guillaume hill, a wretch suffering from a horrible facial wound. He importunes, persecutes one, and levies a regular tax on all travellers. Are we still living in the monstrous times of the Middle Ages, when vagabonds were permitted to display in our public places leprosy and scrofulas they had brought back from the Crusades?"

Or—

"In spite of the laws against vagabondage, the approaches to our great towns continue to be infected by bands of beggars. Some are seen going about alone, and these are not, perhaps, the least dangerous. What are our ediles about?"

Then Homais invented anecdotes—

"Yesterday, by the Bois-Guillaume hill, a skittish horse—" And then followed the story of an accident caused by the presence of the blind man.

He managed so well that the fellow was locked up. But he was released. He began again, and Homais began again. It was a struggle. Homais won it, for his foe was condemned to life-long confinement in an asylum.

This success emboldened him, and henceforth there was no longer a dog run over, a barn burnt down, a woman beaten in the parish, of which he did not immediately inform the public, guided always by the love of progress and the hate of priests. He instituted comparisons between the elementary and clerical schools to the detriment of the latter; called to mind the massacre of St. Bartholomew *àpropos* of a grant of one hundred francs to the church, and denounced abuses, aired new views. That was his phrase. Homais was digging and delving; he was becoming dangerous.

However, he was stifling in the narrow limits of journalism, and soon a book, a work was necessary to him. Then he composed "General Statistics of the Canton of Yonville, followed by Climatological Remarks." The statistics drove him to philosophy. He busied himself with great questions: the social problem, moralisation of the poorer classes, pisciculture, caoutchouc, railways, etc. He even began to blush at being a bourgeois. He affected the artistic style, he smoked. He bought two *chic* Pompadour statuettes to adorn his drawing-room.

He by no means gave up his shop. On the contrary, he kept well abreast of new discoveries. He followed the great movement of chocolates; he was the first to introduce "cocoa" and "revalenta" into the Seine-Inférieure. He was enthusiastic about the hydro-electric Pulvermacher chains; he wore one himself, and when at night he took off his flannel vest, Madame Homais stood quite dazzled before the golden spiral beneath which he was hidden, and felt her ardour redouble for this man more bandaged than a Scythian, and splendid as one of the Magi.

He had fine ideas about Emma's tomb. First he proposed a broken column with some drapery, next a pyramid, then a Temple of Vesta, a sort of rotunda, or else a "mass of ruins." And in all his plans Homais always stuck to the weeping willow, which he looked upon as the indispensable symbol of sorrow.

Charles and he made a journey to Rouen together to look at some tombs at a funeral furnisher's, accompanied by an artist, one Vaufrylard, a friend of Bridoux's, who made puns all the time. At last, after having examined some hundred designs, having ordered an estimate and made another journey to Rouen, Charles decided in favour of a mausoleum, which on the two principal sides was to have "a spirit bearing an extinguished torch."

As to the inscription, Homais could think of nothing so fine as *Sta viator*, and he got no further; he racked his brain, he constantly repeated *Sta viator*. At last he hit upon *Amabilem conjugem calcas*, which was adopted.

A strange thing was that Bovary, while continually thinking of Emma, was forgetting her. He grew desperate as he felt this image fading from his memory in spite of all efforts to retain it. Yet every night he dreamt of her; it was always the same dream. He drew near her, but when he was about to clasp her she fell into decay in his arms.

For a week he was seen going to church in the evening. Monsieur Bournisien even paid him two or three visits, then gave him up. Moreover, the old fellow was growing intolerant, fanatic, said Homais. He thundered against the spirit of the age, and never failed, every other week, in his sermon, to recount the death agony of Voltaire, who died devouring his excrements, as everyone knows.

In spite of the economy with which Bovary lived, he was far from being able to pay off his old debts. Lheureux refused to renew any more bills. A distraint became imminent. Then he appealed to his mother, who consented to let him take a mortgage on her property, but with a great many recriminations against Emma; and in return for her sacrifice she asked for a shawl that had escaped the depredations of Félicité. Charles refused to give it her; they quarrelled.

She made the first overtures of reconciliation by offering to have the little girl, who could help her in the house, to live with her. Charles consented to this, but when the time for parting came, all his courage failed him. Then there was a final, complete rupture.

As his affections vanished, he clung more closely to the love of his child. She made him anxious, however, for she coughed sometimes, and had red spots on her cheeks.

Opposite his house, flourishing and merry, was the family of the chemist, with whom everything was prospering. Napoléon helped him in the laboratory, Athalie embroidered him a skull-cap, Irma cut out rounds of paper to cover the preserves, and Franklin recited Pythagoras's table in a breath. He was the happiest of fathers, the most fortunate of men.

Not so! A secret ambition devoured him. Homais hankered after the cross of the Legion of Honour. He had plenty of claims to it.

"First, having at the time of the cholera distinguished myself by a boundless devotion; second, by having published, at my expense, various works of public utility, such as" (and he recalled his pamphlet entitled, "Cider, its manufacture and effects," besides observations on the lanigerous plant-louse, sent to the Academy; his volume of statistics, and down to his pharmaceutical thesis); "without counting that I am a member of several learned societies" (he was member of a single one).

"In short!" he cried, making a pirouette, "if it were only for distinguishing myself at fires!"

Then Homais inclined towards the Government. He secretly did the prefect great service during the elections. He sold himself—in a word, prostituted himself. He even addressed a petition to the sovereign in which he implored him to "do him justice"; he called him "our good king," and compared him to Henri IV.

And every morning the druggist rushed for the paper to see if his nomination were in it. It was never there. At last, unable to bear it any longer, he had a grass plot in his garden designed to represent the Star of the Cross of Honour, with two little strips of grass running from the top to imitate the ribband. He walked round it with folded arms, meditating on the folly of the Government and the ingratitude of men.

From respect, or from a sort of sensuality that made him carry on his investigations slowly, Charles had not yet opened the secret drawer of a rosewood desk which Emma had generally used. One day, however, he sat down before it, turned the key, and pressed the spring. All Léon's letters were there. There could be no doubt this time. He devoured them to the very last, ransacked every corner, all the furniture, all the drawers, behind the walls, sobbing, crying aloud, distraught, mad. He found a box and broke it open with a kick. Rodolphe's portrait flew full in his face in the midst of the overturned love-letters.

People wondered at his despondency. He never went out, saw no one, refused even to visit his patients. Then they said "he shut himself up to drink."

Sometimes, however, some curious person climbed on to the garden hedge, and saw with amazement this long-bearded, shabbily clothed, wild man, who wept aloud as he walked up and down.

In the evening in summer he took his little girl with him and led her to the cemetery. They came back at nightfall, when the only light left in the Place was that in Binet's window.

The voluptuousness of his grief was, however, incomplete, for he had no one near him to share it, and he paid visits to Madame Lefrançois to be able to speak of *her*. But the landlady only listened with half an ear, having troubles like himself. For Lheureux had at last established the *Favorites du Commerce*, and Hivert, who enjoyed a great reputation for doing errands, insisted on a rise of wages, and was threatening to go over "to the opposition shop."

One day when he had gone to the market at Argueil to sell his horse—his last resource—he met Rodolphe.

They both turned pale when they caught sight of one another. Rodolphe, who had only sent his card, first stammered some apologies, then grew bolder, and even pushed his assurance (it was in the month of August and very hot) to the length of inviting him to have a bottle of beer at the public-house.

Leaning on the table opposite him, he chewed his cigar as he talked, and Charles was lost in reverie at this face that she had loved. He seemed to see again something of her in it. It was a marvel to him. He would have liked to have been this man.

The other went on talking agriculture, cattle, pasturage, filling out with banal phrases all the gaps where an allusion might slip in. Charles was not listening to him; Rodolphe noticed it, and he followed the succession of memories that crossed his face. This gradually grew redder; the nostrils throbbed fast, the lips quivered. There was at last a moment when Charles, full of a sombre fury, fixed his eyes on Rodolphe, who, in something of fear, stopped talking. But soon the same look of weary lassitude came back to his face.

"I don't blame you," he said.

Rodolphe was dumb. And Charles, his head in his hands, went on in a broken voice, and with the resigned accent of infinite sorrow—

"No, I don't blame you now."

He even added a fine phrase, the only one he ever made—

"It is the fault of fatality!"

Rodolphe, who had managed the fatality, thought the remark very offhand from a man in his position, comic even, and a little mean.

The next day Charles went to sit down on the seat in the arbour. Rays of light were straying through the trellis, the vine leaves threw their shadows on the sand, the jasmines perfumed the air, the heavens were blue, Spanish flies buzzed round the lilies in bloom, and Charles was suffocating like a youth beneath the vague love influences that filled his aching heart.

At seven o'clock little Berthe, who had not seen him all the afternoon, went to fetch him to dinner.

His head was thrown back against the wall, his eyes closed, his mouth open, and in his hand was a long tress of black hair.

"Come along, papa," she said.

And thinking he wanted to play, she pushed him gently. He fell to the ground. He was dead.

Thirty-six hours after, at the druggist's request, Monsieur Canivet came thither. He made a post-mortem and found nothing.

When everything had been sold, twelve francs seventy-five centimes remained, that served to pay for Mademoiselle Bovary's going to her grandmother. The good woman died the same year; old Rouault was paralysed, and it was an aunt who took charge of her. She is poor, and sends her to a cotton-factory to earn a living.

Since Bovary's death three doctors have followed one another at Yonville without any success, so severely did Homais attack them. He has an enormous practice; the authorities treat him with consideration, and public opinion protects him.

He has just received the cross of the Legion of Honour.

THE END

SALAMMBÔ
A ROMANCE OF ANCIENT CARTHAGE

Contents

Chapter I

The Feast

I T WAS AT MEGARA, A SUBURB OF CARTHAGE, IN THE GARDENS OF HAMILCAR. THE soldiers whom he had commanded in Sicily were having a great feast to celebrate the anniversary of the battle of Eryx, and as the master was away, and they were numerous, they ate and drank with perfect freedom.

The captains, who wore bronze cothurni, had placed themselves in the central path, beneath a gold-fringed purple awning, which reached from the wall of the stables to the first terrace of the palace; the common soldiers were scattered beneath the trees, where numerous flat-roofed buildings might be seen, wine-presses, cellars, storehouses, bakeries, and arsenals, with a court for elephants, dens for wild beasts, and a prison for slaves.

Fig-trees surrounded the kitchens; a wood of sycamores stretched away to meet masses of verdure, where the pomegranate shone amid the white tufts of the cotton-plant; vines, grape-laden, grew up into the branches of the pines; a field of roses bloomed beneath the plane-trees; here and there lilies rocked upon the turf; the paths were strewn with black sand mingled with powdered coral, and in the centre the avenue of cypress formed, as it were, a double colonnade of green obelisks from one extremity to the other.

Far in the background stood the palace, built of yellow mottled Numidian marble, broad courses supporting its four terraced stories. With its large, straight, ebony staircase, bearing the prow of a vanquished galley at the corners of every step, its red doors quartered with black crosses, its brass gratings protecting it from scorpions below, and its trellises of gilded rods closing the apertures above, it seemed to the soldiers in its haughty opulence as solemn and impenetrable as the face of Hamilcar.

The Council had appointed his house for the holding of this feast; the convalescents lying in the temple of Eschmoun had set out at daybreak and dragged themselves thither on their crutches. Every minute others were arriving. They poured in ceaselessly by every path like torrents rushing into a lake; through the trees the slaves of the kitchens might be seen running scared and half-naked; the gazelles fled bleating on the lawns; the sun was setting, and the perfume of citron trees rendered the exhalation from the perspiring crowd heavier still.

Men of all nations were there, Ligurians, Lusitanians, Balearians, Negroes, and fugitives from Rome. Beside the heavy Dorian dialect were audible the resonant

Celtic syllables rattling like chariots of war, while Ionian terminations conflicted with consonants of the desert as harsh as the jackal's cry. The Greek might be recognized by his slender figure, the Egyptian by his elevated shoulders, the Cantabriun by his broad calves. There were Carians proudly nodding their helmet plumes, Cappadocian archers displaying large flowers painted on their bodies with the juice of herbs, and a few Lydians in women's robes, dining in slippers and earrings. Others were ostentatiously daubed with vermilion, and resembled coral statues.

They stretched themselves on the cushions, they ate squatting round large trays, or lying face downwards they drew out the pieces of meat and sated themselves, leaning on their elbows in the peaceful posture of lions tearing their prey. The last comers stood leaning against the trees watching the low tables half hidden beneath the scarlet coverings, and awaiting their turn.

Hamilcar's kitchens being insufficient, the Council had sent them slaves, ware, and beds, and in the middle of the garden, as on a battle-field when they burn the dead, large bright fires might be seen, at which oxen were roasting. Anise-sprinkled loaves alternated with great cheeses heavier than discuses, crateras filled with wine, and cantharuses filled with water, together with baskets of gold filigree-work containing flowers. Every eye was dilated with the joy of being able at last to gorge at pleasure, and songs were beginning here and there.

First they were served with birds and green sauce in plates of red clay relieved by drawings in black, then with every kind of shell-fish that is gathered on the Punic coasts, wheaten porridge, beans and barley, and snails dressed with cumin on dishes of yellow amber.

Afterwards the tables were covered with meats: antelopes with their horns, peacocks with their feathers, whole sheep cooked in sweet wine, haunches of she-camels and buffaloes, hedgehogs with garum, fried grasshoppers, and preserved dormice. Large pieces of fat floated in the midst of saffron in bowls of Tamrapanni wood. Everything was running over with wine, truffles, and asafœtida. Pyramids of fruit were crumbling upon honeycombs, and they had not forgotten a few of those plump little dogs with pink silky hair and fattened on olive lees—a Carthaginian dish held in abhorrence among other nations. Surprise at the novel fare excited the greed of the stomach. The Gauls with their long hair drawn up on the crown of the head, snatched at the watermelons and lemons, and crunched them up with the rind. The Negroes, who had never seen a lobster, tore their faces with its red prickles. But the shaven Greeks, whiter than marble, threw the leavings of their plates behind them, while the herdsmen from Brutium, in their wolf-skin garments, devoured in silence with their faces in their portions.

Night fell. The velarium, spread over the cypress avenue, was drawn back, and torches were brought.

The apes, sacred to the moon, were terrified on the cedar tops by the wavering lights of the petroleum as it burned in the porphyry vases. They uttered screams which afforded mirth to the soldiers.

Oblong flames trembled in cuirasses of brass. Every kind of scintillation flashed from the gem-incrusted dishes. The crateras with their borders of convex mirrors multiplied and enlarged the images of things; the soldiers thronged around, looking at their reflections with amazement, and grimacing to make themselves laugh. They tossed the ivory stools and golden spatulas to one another across the tables. They gulped down all the Greek wines in their leathern bottles, the Campanian wines enclosed in amphoras, the Cantabrian wines brought in casks, with the wines of the jujube, cinnamomum and lotus. There were pools of these on the ground that made the foot slip. The smoke of the meats ascended into the foliage with the vapour of the breath. Simultaneously were heard the snapping of jaws, the noise of speech, songs, and cups, the crash of Campanian vases shivering into a thousand pieces, or the limpid sound of a large silver dish.

In proportion as their intoxication increased they more and more recalled the injustice of Carthage. The Republic, in fact, exhausted by the war, had allowed all the returning bands to accumulate in the town. Gisco, their general, had however been prudent enough to send them back severally in order to facilitate the liquidation of their pay, and the Council had believed that they would in the end consent to some reduction. But at present ill-will was caused by the inability to pay them. This debt was confused in the minds of the people with the 3200 Euboic talents exacted by Lutatius, and equally with Rome they were regarded as enemies to Carthage. The Mercenaries understood this, and their indignation found vent in threats and outbreaks. At last they demanded permission to assemble to celebrate one of their victories, and the peace party yielded, at the same time revenging themselves on Hamilcar who had so strongly upheld the war. It had been terminated notwithstanding all his efforts, so that, despairing of Carthage, he had entrusted the government of the Mercenaries to Gisco. To appoint his palace for their reception was to draw upon him something of the hatred that was borne to them. Moreover, the expense must be excessive, and he would incur nearly the whole.

Proud of having brought the Republic to submit, the Mercenaries thought that they were at last about to return to their homes with the payment for their blood in the hoods of their cloaks. But as seen through the mists of intoxication, their fatigues seemed to them prodigious and but ill-rewarded. They showed one another their wounds, they told of their combats, their travels and the hunting in their native lands. They imitated the cries and the leaps of wild beasts. Then came unclean wagers; they buried their heads in the amphoras and drank on without interruption, like thirsty dromedaries. A Lusitanian of gigantic stature ran over the tables, carrying a man in each hand at arm's length, and spitting out fire through his nostrils. Some Lacedæmonians, who had not taken off their cuirasses, were leaping with a heavy step. Some advanced like women, making obscene gestures; others stripped naked to fight amid the cups after the fashion of gladiators, and a company of Greeks danced around a vase whereon nymphs were to be seen, while a negro tapped with an ox-bone on a brazen buckler.

Suddenly they heard a plaintive song, a song loud and soft, rising and falling in the air like the wing-beating of a wounded bird.

It was the voice of the slaves in the ergastulum. Some soldiers rose at a bound to release them and disappeared.

They returned, driving forward through the dust amid shouts, twenty men, distinguished by their greater paleness of face. Small black felt caps of conical shape covered their shaven heads; they all wore wooden shoes, and yet made a noise as of old iron like driving chariots.

They reached the avenue of cypress, where they were lost among the crowd of those questioning them. One of them had remained apart, standing. Through the rents in his tunic his shoulders could be seen striped with long scars. Drooping his chin, he looked round him with distrust, closing his eyelids somewhat against the dazzling light of the torches, but when he saw that none of the armed men were unfriendly to him, a great sigh escaped from his breast; he stammered, he sneered through the bright tears that bathed his face. At last he seized a brimming cantharus by its rings, raised it straight up into the air with his outstretched arms, from which his chains hung down, and then looking to heaven, and still holding the cup he said:

"Hail first to thee, Baal-Eschmoun, the deliverer, whom the people of my country call Æsculapius! and to you, genii of the fountains, light, and woods! and to you, ye gods hidden beneath the mountains and in the caverns of the earth! and to you, strong men in shining armour who have set me free!"

Then he let fall the cup and related his history. He was called Spendius. The Carthaginians had taken him in the battle of Æginusæ, and he thanked the Mercenaries once more in Greek, Ligurian and Punic; he kissed their hands; finally he congratulated them on the banquet, while expressing his surprise at not perceiving the cups of the Sacred Legion. These cups, which bore an emerald vine on each of their six golden faces, belonged to a corps composed exclusively of young patricians of the tallest stature. They were a privilege, almost a sacerdotal distinction, and accordingly nothing among the treasures of the Republic was more coveted by the Mercenaries. They detested the Legion on this account, and some of them had been known to risk their lives for the inconceivable pleasure of drinking out of these cups.

Accordingly they commanded that the cups should be brought. They were in the keeping of the Syssitia, companies of traders, who had a common table. The slaves returned. At that hour all the members of the Syssitia were asleep.

"Let them be awakened!" responded the Mercenaries.

After a second excursion it was explained to them that the cups were shut up in a temple.

"Let it be opened!" they replied.

And when the slaves confessed with trembling that they were in the possession of Gisco, the general, they cried out:

"Let him bring them!"

Gisco soon appeared at the far end of the garden with an escort of the Sacred Legion. His full, black cloak, which was fastened on his head to a golden mitre starred with precious stones, and which hung all about him down to his horse's hoofs, blended in the distance with the colour of the night. His white beard, the radiancy of his head-dress, and his triple necklace of broad blue plates beating against his breast, were alone visible.

When he entered, the soldiers greeted him with loud shouts, all crying:

"The cups! The cups!"

He began by declaring that if reference were had to their courage, they were worthy of them.

The crowd applauded and howled with joy.

He knew it, he who had commanded them over yonder, and had returned with the last cohort in the last galley!

"True! True!" said they.

Nevertheless, Gisco continued, the Republic had respected their national divisions, their customs, and their modes of worship; in Carthage they were free! As to the cups of the Sacred Legion, they were private property. Suddenly a Gaul, who was close to Spendius, sprang over the tables and ran straight up to Gisco, gesticulating and threatening him with two naked swords.

Without interrupting his speech, the General struck him on the head with his heavy ivory staff, and the Barbarian fell. The Gauls howled, and their frenzy, which was spreading to the others, would soon have swept away the legionaries. Gisco shrugged his shoulders as he saw them growing pale. He thought that his courage would be useless against these exasperated brute beasts. It would be better to revenge himself upon them by some artifice later; accordingly, he signed to his soldiers and slowly withdrew. Then, turning in the gateway towards the Mercenaries, he cried to them that they would repent of it.

The feast recommenced. But Gisco might return, and by surrounding the suburb, which was beside the last ramparts, might crush them against the walls. Then they felt themselves alone in spite of their crowd, and the great town sleeping beneath them in the shade suddenly made them afraid, with its piles of staircases, its lofty black houses, and its vague gods fiercer even than its people. In the distance a few ships'-lanterns were gliding across the harbour, and there were lights in the temple of Khamon. They thought of Hamilcar. Where was he? Why had he forsaken them when peace was concluded? His differences with the Council were doubtless but a pretence in order to destroy them. Their unsatisfied hate recoiled upon him, and they cursed him, exasperating one another with their own anger. At this juncture they collected together beneath the plane-trees to see a slave who, with eyeballs fixed, neck contorted, and lips covered with foam, was rolling on the ground, and beating the soil with his limbs. Some one cried out that he was poisoned. All then believed themselves poisoned. They fell upon the slaves, a terrible clamour was raised, and a vertigo of destruction came like a whirlwind upon the drunken army. They struck about them at random, they smashed, they slew; some hurled torches into the foliage; others, leaning over the lions' balustrade, massacred the animals with arrows; the most daring ran to the elephants, desiring to cut down their trunks and eat ivory.

Some Balearic slingers, however, who had gone round the corner of the palace, in order to pillage more conveniently, were checked by a lofty barrier, made of Indian cane. They cut the lock-straps with their daggers, and then found themselves beneath the front that faced Carthage, in another garden full of trimmed vegetation. Lines of white flowers all following one another in regular succession formed long parabolas like star-rockets on the azure-coloured earth. The gloomy bushes exhaled warm and honied odours. There were trunks of trees smeared with cinnabar, which resembled columns covered with blood. In the centre were twelve pedestals, each supporting a great glass ball, and these hollow globes were indistinctly filled with reddish lights, like enormous and still palpitating eyeballs. The soldiers lighted themselves with torches as they stumbled on the slope of the deeply laboured soil.

But they perceived a little lake divided into several basins by walls of blue stones. So limpid was the wave that the flames of the torches quivered in it at the very bottom, on a bed of white pebbles and golden dust. It began to bubble, luminous spangles glided past, and great fish with gems about their mouths, appeared near the surface.

With much laughter the soldiers slipped their fingers into the gills, and brought them to the tables. They were the fish of the Barca family, and were all descended from those primordial lotes which had hatched the mystic egg wherein the goddess was concealed. The idea of committing a sacrilege revived the greediness of the Mercenaries; they speedily placed fire beneath some brazen vases, and amused themselves by watching the beautiful fish struggling in the boiling water.

The surge of soldiers pressed on. They were no longer afraid. They commenced to drink again. Their ragged tunics were wet with the perfumes that flowed in large drops from their foreheads, and resting both fists on the tables, which seemed to them to be rocking like ships, they rolled their great drunken eyes around to devour by sight what they could not take. Others walked amid the dishes on the purple table covers, breaking ivory stools, and phials of Tyrian glass to pieces with their feet. Songs mingled with the death-rattle of the slaves expiring amid the broken cups. They demanded wine, meat, gold. They cried out for women. They raved in a hundred languages. Some thought that they were at the vapour baths on account of the steam which floated around them, or else, catching sight of the foliage, imagined that they were at the chase, and rushed upon their companions as upon wild beasts. The conflagration spread to all the trees, one after another, and the lofty mosses of verdure, emitting long white spirals, looked like volcanoes beginning to smoke. The clamour redoubled; the wounded lions roared in the shade.

In an instant the highest terrace of the palace was illuminated, the central door opened, and a woman, Hamilcar's daughter herself, clothed in black garments, appeared on the threshold. She descended the first staircase, which ran obliquely along the first story, then the second, and the third, and stopped on the last terrace at the head of the galley staircase. Motionless and with head bent, she gazed upon the soldiers.

Behind her, on each side, were two long shadows of pale men, clad in white, red-fringed robes, which fell straight to their feet. They had no beard, no hair, no eyebrows. In their hands, which sparkled with rings, they carried enormous lyres, and with shrill voice they all sang a hymn to the divinity of Carthage. They were the eunuch priests of the temple of Tanith, who were often summoned by Salammbô to her house.

At last she descended the galley staircase. The priests followed her. She advanced into the avenue of cypress, and walked slowly through the tables of the captains, who drew back somewhat as they watched her pass.

Her hair, which was powdered with violet sand, and combined into the form of a tower, after the fashion of the Chanaanite maidens, added to her height. Tresses of pearls were fastened to her temples, and fell to the corners of her mouth, which was as rosy as a half-open pomegranate. On her breast was a collection of luminous stones, their variegation imitating the scales of the murena. Her arms were adorned with diamonds, and issued naked from her sleeveless tunic, which was starred with red flowers on a perfectly black ground. Between her ankles she wore a golden chainlet to regulate her steps, and her large dark purple mantle, cut of an unknown material, trailed behind her, making, as it were, at each step, a broad wave which followed her.

The priests played nearly stifled chords on their lyres from time to time, and in the intervals of the music might be heard the tinkling of the little golden chain, and the regular patter of her papyrus sandals.

No one as yet was acquainted with her. It was only known that she led a retired life, engaged in pious practices. Some soldiers had seen her in the night on the summit of her palace kneeling before the stars amid the eddyings from kindled perfuming-pans. It was the moon that had made her so pale, and there was something from the gods that enveloped her like a subtle vapour. Her eyes seemed to gaze far beyond terrestrial space. She bent her head as she walked, and in her right hand she carried a little ebony lyre.

They heard her murmur:

"Dead! All dead! No more will you come obedient to my voice as when, seated on the edge of the lake, I used to throw seeds of the watermelon into your mouths! The mystery of Tanith ranged in the depths of your eyes that were more limpid than the globules of rivers." And she called them by their names, which were those of the months—"Siv! Sivan! Tammouz, Eloul, Tischri, Schebar! Ah! have pity on me, goddess!"

The soldiers thronged about her without understanding what she said. They wondered at her attire, but she turned a long frightened look upon them all, then sinking her head beneath her shoulders, and waving her arms, she repeated several times:

"What have you done? what have you done?

"Yet you had bread, and meats and oil, and all the malobathrum of the granaries for your enjoyment! I had brought oxen from Hecatompylos; I had sent hunters into the desert!" Her voice swelled; her cheeks purpled. She added, "Where, pray, are you now? In a conquered town, or in the palace of a master? And what master? Hamilcar the Suffet, my father, the servant of the Baals! It was he who withheld from Lutatius those arms of yours, red now with the blood of his slaves! Know you of any in your own lands more skilled in the conduct of battles? Look! our palace steps are encumbered with our victories! Ah! desist not! burn it! I will carry away with me the genius of my house, my black serpent slumbering up yonder on lotus leaves! I will whistle and he will follow me, and if I embark in a galley he will speed in the wake of my ship over the foam of the waves."

Her delicate nostrils were quivering. She crushed her nails against the gems on her bosom. Her eyes drooped, and she resumed:

"Ah! poor Carthage! lamentable city! No longer hast thou for thy protection the strong men of former days who went beyond the oceans to build temples on their shores. All the lands laboured about thee, and the sea-plains, ploughed by thine oars, rocked with thy harvests." Then she began to sing the adventures of Melkarth, the god of the Sidonians, and the father of her family.

She told of the ascent of the mountains of Ersiphonia, the journey to Tartessus, and the war against Masisabal to avenge the queen of the serpents:

"He pursued the female monster, whose tail undulated over the dead leaves like a silver brook, into the forest, and came to a plain where women with dragon-croups were round a great fire, standing erect on the points of their tails. The blood-coloured moon was shining within a pale circle, and their scarlet tongues, cloven like the harpoons of fishermen, reached curling forth to the very edge of the flame."

Then Salammbô, without pausing, related how Melkarth, after vanquishing Masisabal, placed her severed head on the prow of his ship. "At each throb of the waves it sank beneath the foam, but the sun embalmed it; it became harder than gold; nevertheless the eyes ceased not to weep, and the tears fell into the water continually."

She sang all this in an old Chanaanite idiom, which the Barbarians did not understand. They asked one another what she could be saying to them with those frightful gestures which accompanied her speech, and mounted round about her on the tables, beds, and sycamore boughs, they strove with open mouths and craned necks to grasp the vague stories hovering before their imaginations, through the dimness of the theogonies, like phantoms wrapped in cloud.

Only the beardless priests understood Salammbô; their wrinkled hands, which hung over the strings of their lyres, quivered, and from time to time they would draw forth a mournful chord; for, feebler than old women, they trembled at once with mystic emotion, and with the fear inspired by men. The Barbarians heeded them not, but listened continually to the maiden's song.

None gazed at her like a young Numidian chief, who was placed at the captains' tables among soldiers of his own nation. His girdle so bristled with darts that it formed a swelling in his ample cloak, which was fastened on his temples with a leather lace. The cloth parted asunder as it fell upon his shoulders, and enveloped his countenance in shadow, so that only the fires of his two fixed eyes could be seen. It was by chance that he was at the feast, his father having domiciled him with the Barca family, according to the custom by which kings used to send their children into the households of the great in order to pave the way for alliances; but Narr' Havas had lodged there for six months without having hitherto seen Salammbô, and now, seated on his heels, with his head brushing the handles of his javelins, he was watching her with dilated nostrils, like a leopard crouching among the bamboos.

On the other side of the tables was a Libyan of colossal stature, and with short black curly hair. He had retained only his military jacket, the brass plates of which were tearing the purple of the couch. A necklace of silver moons was tangled in his hairy breast. His face was stained with splashes of blood; he was leaning on his left elbow with a smile on his large, open mouth.

Salammbô had abandoned the sacred rhythm. With a woman's subtlety she was simultaneously employing all the dialects of the Barbarians in order to appease their anger. To the Greeks she spoke Greek; then she turned to the Ligurians, the Campanians, the Negroes, and listening to her each one found again in her voice the sweetness of his native land. She now, carried away by the memories of Carthage, sang of the ancient battles against Rome; they applauded. She kindled at the gleaming of the naked swords, and cried aloud with outstretched arms. Her lyre fell, she was silent; and, pressing both hands upon her heart, she remained for some minutes with closed eyelids enjoying the agitation of all these men.

Matho, the Libyan, leaned over towards her. Involuntarily she approached him, and impelled by grateful pride, poured him a long stream of wine into a golden cup in order to conciliate the army.

"Drink!" she said.

He took the cup, and was carrying it to his lips when a Gaul, the same that had been hurt by Giscò, struck him on the shoulder, while in a jovial manner he gave utterance to pleasantries in his native tongue. Spendius was not far off, and he volunteered to interpret them.

"Speak!" said Matho.

"The gods protect you; you are going to become rich. When will the nuptials be?"

"What nuptials?"

"Yours! for with us," said the Gaul, "when a woman gives drink to a soldier, it means that she offers him her couch."

He had not finished when Narr' Havas, with a bound, drew a javelin from his girdle, and, leaning his right foot upon the edge of the table, hurled it against Matho.

The javelin whistled among the cups, and piercing the Libyan's arm, pinned it so firmly to the cloth, that the shaft quivered in the air.

Matho quickly plucked it out; but he was weaponless and naked; at last he lifted the over-laden table with both arms, and flung it against Narr' Havas into the very centre of the crowd that rushed between them. The soldiers and Numidians pressed together so closely that they were unable to draw their swords. Matho advanced dealing great blows with his head. When he raised it, Narr' Havas had disappeared. He sought for him with his eyes. Salammbô also was gone.

Then directing his looks to the palace he perceived the red door with the black cross closing far above, and he darted away.

They saw him run between the prows of the galleys, and then reappear along the three staircases until he reached the red door against which he dashed his whole body. Panting, he leaned against the wall to keep himself from falling.

But a man had followed him, and through the darkness, for the lights of the feast were hidden by the corner of the palace, he recognised Spendius.

"Begone!" said he.

The slave without replying began to tear his tunic with his teeth; then kneeling beside Matho he tenderly took his arm, and felt it in the shadow to discover the wound.

By a ray of the moon which was then gliding between the clouds, Spendius perceived a gaping wound in the middle of the arm. He rolled the piece of stuff all around it, but the other said irritably, "Leave me! leave me!"

"Oh no!" replied the slave. "You released me from the ergastulum. I am yours! you are my master! command me!"

Matho walked round the terrace brushing against the walls. He strained his ears at every step, glancing down into the silent apartments through the spaces between the gilded reeds. At last he slopped with a look of despair.

"Listen!" said the slave to him. "Oh! do not despise me for my feebleness! I have lived in the palace. I can wind like a viper through the walls. Come! in the Ancestors' Chamber there is an ingot of gold beneath every flagstone; an underground path leads to their tombs."

"Well! what matters it?" said Matho.

Spendius was silent.

They were on the terrace. A huge mass of shadow stretched before them, appearing as if it contained vague accumulations, like the gigantic billows of a black and petrified ocean.

But a luminous bar rose towards the East; far below, on the left, the canals of Megara were beginning to stripe the verdure of the gardens with their windings of white. The conical roofs of the heptagonal temples, the staircases, terraces, and ramparts were being carved by degrees upon the paleness of the dawn; and a girdle of white foam rocked around the Carthaginian peninsula, while the emerald sea appeared as if it were curdled in the freshness of the morning. Then as the rosy sky grew larger, the lofty houses, bending over the sloping soil, reared and massed themselves like a herd of black goats coming down from the mountains. The deserted streets lengthened; the palm-trees that topped the walls here and there were motionless; the brimming cisterns seemed like silver bucklers lost in the courts; the beacon on the promontory of Hermæum was beginning to grow pale. The horses of Eschmoun, on the very summit of the Acropolis in the cypress wood, feeling that the light was coming, placed their hoofs on the marble parapet, and neighed towards the sun.

It appeared, and Spendius raised his arms with a cry.

Everything stirred in a diffusion of red, for the god, as if he were rending himself, now poured full-rayed upon Carthage the golden rain of his veins. The beaks of the galleys sparkled, the roof of Khamon appeared to be all in flames, while far within the temples, whose doors were opening, glimmerings of light could be seen. Large chariots, arriving from the country, rolled their wheels over the flagstones in the streets. Dromedaries, baggage-laden, came down the ramps. Money-changers raised the pent-houses of their shops at the cross ways, storks took to flight, white sails fluttered. In the wood of Tanith might be heard the tambourines of the sacred courtesans, and the furnaces for baking the clay coffins were beginning to smoke on the Mappalian point.

Spendius leaned over the terrace; his teeth chattered and he repeated:

"Ah! yes—yes—master! I understand why you scorned the pillage of the house just now."

Matho was as if he had just been awaked by the hissing of his voice, and did not seem to understand. Spendius resumed:

"Ah! what riches! and the men who possess them have not even the steel to defend them!"

Then, pointing with his right arm outstretched to some of the populace who were crawling on the sand outside the mole to look for gold dust:

"See!" he said to him, "the Republic is like these wretches: bending on the brink of the ocean, she buries her greedy arms in every shore, and the noise of the billows so fills her ear that she cannot hear behind her the tread of a master's heel!"

He drew Matho to quite the other end of the terrace, and showed him the garden, wherein the soldiers' swords, hanging on the trees, were like mirrors in the sun:

"But here there are strong men whose hatred is roused! and nothing binds them to Carthage, neither families, oaths nor gods!"

Matho remained leaning against the wall; Spendius came close, and continued in a low voice:

"Do you understand me, soldier? We should walk purple-clad like satraps. We should bathe in perfumes; and I should in turn have slaves! Are you not weary of sleeping on the hard ground, of drinking the vinegar of the camps, and of continually hearing the trumpet? But you will rest later, will you not? When they pull off your cuirass to cast your corpse to the vultures! or perhaps blind, lame, and weak you will go, leaning on a stick, from door to door to tell of your youth to pickle-sellers and little children. Remember all the injustice of your chiefs, the campings in the snow, the marchings in the sun, the tyrannies of discipline, and the everlasting menace of the cross! And after all this misery they have given you a necklace of honour, as they hang a girdle of bells round the breast of an ass to deafen it on its journey, and prevent it from feeling fatigue. A man like you, braver than Pyrrhus! If only you had wished it! Ah! how happy will you be in large cool halls, with the sound of lyres, lying on flowers, with women and buffoons! Do not tell me that the enterprise is impossible. Have not the Mercenaries already possessed Rhegium and other fortified places in Italy? Who is to prevent you? Hamilcar is away; the people execrate the rich; Gisco can do nothing with the cowards who surround him. But you are brave! and they will obey you. Command them! Carthage is ours; let us fall upon it!"

"No!" said Matho, "the curse of Moloch weighs upon me. I felt it in her eyes, and just now I saw a black ram retreating in a temple." Looking around him he added: "But where is she?"

Then Spendius understood that a great disquiet possessed him, and did not venture to speak again.

The trees behind them were still smoking; half-burned carcasses of apes dropped from their blackened boughs from time to time into the midst of the dishes. Drunken soldiers snored open-mouthed by the side of the corpses, and those who were not asleep lowered their heads dazzled by the light of day. The trampled soil was hidden beneath splashes of red. The elephants poised their bleeding trunks between the stakes of their pens. In the open granaries might be seen sacks of spilled wheat, below the gate was a thick line of chariots which had been heaped up by the Barbarians, and the peacocks perched in the cedars were spreading their tails and beginning to utter their cry.

Matho's immobility, however, astonished Spendius; he was even paler than he had recently been, and he was following something on the horizon with fixed eyeballs, and with both fists resting on the edge of the terrace. Spendius couched down, and so at last discovered at what he was gazing. In the distance a golden speck was turning in the dust on the road to Utica; it was the nave of a chariot drawn by two mules; a slave was running at the end of the pole, and holding them by the bridle. Two women were seated in the chariot. The manes of the animals were puffed between their ears after the Persian fashion, beneath a network of blue pearls. Spendius recognised them, and restrained a cry.

A large veil floated behind in the wind.

Chapter II

At Sicca

TWO DAYS AFTERWARDS THE MERCENARIES LEFT CARTHAGE.

They had each received a piece of gold on the condition that they should go into camp at Sicca, and they had been told with all sorts of caresses:

"You are the saviours of Carthage! But you would starve it if you remained there; it would become insolvent. Withdraw! The Republic will be grateful to you later for all this condescension. We are going to levy taxes immediately; your pay shall be in full, and galleys shall be equipped to take you back to your native lands."

They did not know how to reply to all this talk. These men, accustomed as they were to war, were wearied by residence in a town; there was no difficulty in convincing them, and the people mounted the walls to see them go away.

They defiled through the street of Khamon, and the Cirta gate, pell-mell, archers with hoplites, captains with soldiers, Lusitanians with Greeks. They marched with a bold step, rattling their heavy cothurni on the paving stones. Their armour was dinted by the catapult, and their faces blackened by the sunburn of battles. Hoarse cries issued from their thick beards, their tattered coats of mail flapped upon the pommels of their swords, and through the holes in the brass might be seen their naked limbs, as frightful as engines of war. Sarissae, axes, spears, felt caps and bronze helmets, all swung together with a single motion. They filled the street thickly enough to have made the walls crack, and the long mass of armed soldiers overflowed between the lofty bitumen-smeared houses six storys high. Behind their gratings of iron or reed the women, with veiled heads, silently watched the Barbarians pass.

The terraces, fortifications, and walls were hidden beneath the crowd of Carthaginians, who were dressed in garments of black. The sailors' tunics showed like drops of blood among the dark multitude, and nearly naked children, whose skin shone beneath their copper bracelets, gesticulated in the foliage of the columns, or amid the branches of a palm tree. Some of the Ancients were posted on the platform of the towers, and people did not know why a personage with a long beard stood thus in a dreamy attitude here and there. He appeared in the distance against the background of the sky, vague as a phantom and motionless as stone.

All, however, were oppressed with the same anxiety; it was feared that the Barbarians, seeing themselves so strong, might take a fancy to stay. But they were leaving with so much good faith that the Carthaginians grew bold and mingled with the soldiers. They overwhelmed them with protestations and embraces. Some with exaggerated politeness and audacious hypocrisy even sought to induce them not to leave the city. They threw perfumes, flowers, and pieces of silver to them. They gave them amulets to avert sickness; but they had spit upon them three times to attract death, or had enclosed jackal's hair within them to put cowardice into their hearts. Aloud, they invoked Melkarth's favour, and in a whisper, his curse.

Then came the mob of baggage, beasts of burden, and stragglers. The sick groaned on the backs of dromedaries, while others limped along leaning on broken pikes. The drunkards carried leathern bottles, and the greedy quarters of meat, cakes, fruits, butter wrapped in fig leaves, and snow in linen bags. Some were to be seen with parasols in their hands, and parrots on their shoulders. They had mastiffs, gazelles, and panthers following behind them. Women of Libyan race, mounted on asses, inveighed against the Negresses who had forsaken the lupanaria of Malqua for the soldiers; many of them were suckling children suspended on their bosoms by leathern thongs. The mules were goaded on at the point of the sword, their backs bending beneath the load of tents, while there were numbers of serving-men and water-carriers, emaciated, jaundiced with fever, and filthy with vermin, the scum of the Carthaginian populace, who had attached themselves to the Barbarians.

When they had passed, the gates were shut behind them, but the people did not descend from the walls. The army soon spread over the breadth of the isthmus.

It parted into unequal masses. Then the lances appeared like tall blades of grass, and finally all was lost in a train of dust; those of the soldiers who looked back towards Carthage could now only see its long walls with their vacant battlements cut out against the edge of the sky.

Then the Barbarians heard a great shout. They thought that some from among them (for they did not know their own number) had remained in the town, and were amusing themselves by pillaging a temple. They laughed a great deal at the idea of this, and then continued their journey.

They were rejoiced to find themselves, as in former days, marching all together in the open country; and some of the Greeks sang the old song of the Mamertines:

"With my lance and sword I plough and reap; I am master of the house! The disarmed man falls at my feet and calls me Lord and Great King."

They shouted, they leaped, the merriest began to tell stories; the time of their miseries was past. As they arrived at Tunis, some of them remarked that a troop of Balearic slingers was missing. They were doubtless not far off; and no further heed was paid to them.

Some went to lodge in the houses, others camped at the foot of the walls, and the townspeople came out to chat with the soldiers.

During the whole night fires were seen burning on the horizon in the direction of Cartilage; the light stretched like giant torches across the motionless lake. No one in the army could tell what festival was being celebrated.

On the following day the Barbarians passed through a region that was covered with cultivation. The domains of the patricians succeeded one another along the border of the route; channels of water flowed through woods of palm; there were long, green lines of olive-trees; rose-coloured vapours floated in the gorges of the hills, while blue mountains reared themselves behind. A warm wind was blowing. Chameleons were crawling on the broad leaves of the cactus.

The Barbarians slackened their speed.

They marched on in isolated detachments, or lagged behind one another at long intervals. They ate grapes along the margin of the vines. They lay on the grass and gazed with stupefaction upon the large, artificially twisted horns of the oxen, the sheep clothed with skins to protect their wool, the furrows crossing one another so as to form lozenges, and the ploughshares like ships' anchors, with the pomegranate trees that were watered with silphium. Such wealth of the soil and such inventions of wisdom dazzled them.

In the evening they stretched themselves on the tents without unfolding them; and thought with regret of Hamilcar's feast, as they fell asleep with their faces towards the stars.

In the middle of the following day they halted on the bank of a river, amid clumps of rose-bays. Then they quickly threw aside lances, bucklers and belts. They bathed with shouts, and drew water in their helmets, while others drank lying flat on their stomachs, and all in the midst of the beasts of burden whose baggage was slipping from them.

Spendius, who was seated on a dromedary stolen in Hamilcar's parks, perceived Matho at a distance, with his arm hanging against his breast, his head bare, and his face bent down, giving his mule drink, and watching the water flow. Spendius immediately ran through the crowd calling him, "Master! master!"

Matho gave him but scant thanks for his blessings, but Spendius paid no heed to this, and began to march behind him, from time to time turning restless glances in the direction of Carthage.

He was the son of a Greek rhetor and a Campanian prostitute. He had at first grown rich by dealing in women; then, ruined by a shipwreck, he had made war against the Romans with the herdsmen of Samnium. He had been taken and had escaped; he had been retaken, and had worked in the quarries, panted in the vapour-baths, shrieked under torture, passed through the hands of many masters, and experienced every frenzy. At last, one day, in despair, he had flung himself into the sea from the top of a trireme where he was working at the oar. Some of Hamilcar's sailors had picked him up when at the point of death, and had brought him to the ergastulum of Megara, at Carthage. But, as fugitives were to be given back to the Romans, he had taken advantage of the confusion to fly with the soldiers.

During the whole of the march he remained near Matho; he brought him food, assisted him to dismount, and spread a carpet in the evening beneath his head. Matho at last was touched by these attentions, and by degrees unlocked his lips.

He had been born in the gulf of Syrtis. His father had taken him on a pilgrimage to the temple of Ammon. Then he had hunted elephants in the forests of the Garamantes. Afterwards he had entered the service of Carthage. He had been appointed tetrarch at the capture of Drepanum. The Republic owed him four horses, twenty-three medimni of wheat, and a winter's pay. He feared the gods, and wished to die in his native land.

Spendius spoke to him of his travels, and of the peoples and temples that he had visited. He knew many things: he could make sandals, boar-spears and nets; he could tame wild beasts and could cook fish.

Sometimes he would interrupt himself, and utter a hoarse cry from the depths of his throat; Matho's mule would quicken his pace, the others would hasten after them, and then Spendius would begin again though still torn with agony. This subsided at last on the evening of the fourth day.

They were marching side by side to the right of the army on the side of a hill; below them stretched the plain lost in the vapours of the night. The lines of soldiers also were defiling below, making undulations in the shade. From time to time these passed over eminences lit up by the moon; then stars would tremble on the points of the pikes, the helmets would glimmer for an instant, all would disappear, and others would come on continually. Startled flocks bleated in the distance, and a something of infinite sweetness seemed to sink upon the earth.

Spendius, with his head thrown back and his eyes half-closed, inhaled the freshness of the wind with great sighs; he spread out his arms, moving his fingers that he might the better feel the caress that streamed over his body. Hopes of vengeance came back to him and transported him. He pressed his hand upon his mouth to check his sobs, and half-swooning with intoxication, let go the halter of his dromedary, which was proceeding with long, regular steps. Matho had relapsed into his former melancholy; his legs hung down to the ground, and the grass made a continuous rustling as it beat against his cothurni.

The journey, however, spread itself out without ever coming to an end. At the extremity of a plain they would always reach a round-shaped plateau; then they would descend again into a valley, and the mountains which seemed to block up the horizon would, in proportion as they were approached, glide as it were from their positions. From time to time a river would appear amid the verdure of tamarisks to lose itself at the turning of the hills. Sometimes a huge rock would tower aloft like the prow of a vessel or the pedestal of some vanished colossus.

At regular intervals they met with little quadrangular temples, which served as stations for the pilgrims who repaired to Sicca. They were closed like tombs. The Libyans struck great blows upon the doors to have them opened. But no one inside responded.

Then the cultivation become more rare. They suddenly entered upon belts of sand bristling with thorny thickets. Flocks of sheep were browsing among the stones; a woman with a blue fleece about her waist was watching them. She fled screaming when she saw the soldiers' pikes among the rocks.

They were marching through a kind of large passage bordered by two chains of reddish coloured hillocks, when their nostrils were greeted with a nauseous odour, and they thought that they could see something extraordinary on the top of a carob tree: a lion's head reared itself above the leaves.

They ran thither. It was a lion with his four limbs fastened to a cross like a criminal. His huge muzzle fell upon his breast, and his two fore-paws, half-hidden beneath the abundance of his mane, were spread out wide like the wings of a bird. His ribs stood severally out beneath his distended skin; his hind legs, which were nailed against each other, were raised somewhat, and the black blood, flowing through his hair, had collected in stalactites at the end of his tail, which hung down perfectly straight along the cross. The soldiers made merry around; they called him consul, and Roman citizen, and threw pebbles into his eyes to drive away the gnats.

But a hundred paces further on they saw two more, and then there suddenly appeared a long file of crosses bearing lions. Some had been so long dead that nothing was left against the wood but the remains of their skeletons; others which were half eaten away had their jaws twisted into horrible grimaces; there were some enormous ones; the shafts of the crosses bent beneath them, and they swayed in the wind, while bands of crows wheeled ceaselessly in the air above their heads. It was thus that the Carthaginian peasants avenged themselves when they captured a wild beast; they hoped to terrify the others by such an example. The Barbarians ceased their laughter and were long lost in amazement. "What people is this," they thought, "that amuses itself by crucifying lions!"

They were, besides, especially the men of the North, vaguely uneasy, troubled, and already sick. They tore their hands with the darts of the aloes; great mosquitoes buzzed in their ears, and dysentery was breaking out in the army. They were weary at not yet seeing Sicca. They were afraid of losing themselves and of reaching the desert, the country of sands and terrors. Many even were unwilling to advance further. Others started back to Carthage.

At last on the seventh day, after following the base of a mountain for a long time, they turned abruptly to the right, and there then appeared a line of walls resting on white rocks and blending with them. Suddenly the entire city rose; blue, yellow, and white veils moved on the walls in the redness of the evening. These were the priestesses of Tanith, who had hastened thither to receive the men. They stood ranged along the rampart, striking tambourines, playing lyres, and shaking crotala, while the rays of the sun, setting behind them in the mountains of Numidia, shot between the strings of their lyres over which their naked arms were stretched. At intervals their instruments would become suddenly still, and a cry would break forth strident, precipitate, frenzied, continuous, a sort of barking which they made by striking both corners of the mouth with the tongue. Others, more motionless than the Sphynx, rested on their elbows with their chins on their hands, and darted their great black eyes upon the army as it ascended.

Although Sicca was a sacred town it could not hold such a multitude; the temple alone, with its appurtenances, occupied half of it. Accordingly the Barbarians established themselves at their ease on the plain; those who were disciplined in regular troops, and the rest according to nationality or their own fancy.

The Greeks ranged their tents of skin in parallel lines; the Iberians placed their canvas pavilions in a circle; the Gauls made themselves huts of planks; the Libyans cabins of dry stones, while the Negroes with their nails hollowed out trenches in the sand to sleep in. Many, not knowing where to go, wandered about among the baggage, and at nightfall lay down in their ragged mantles on the ground.

The plain, which was wholly bounded by mountains, expanded around them. Here and there a palm tree leaned over a sand hill, and pines and oaks flecked the sides of the precipices: sometimes the rain of a storm would hang from the sky like a long scarf, while the country everywhere was still covered with azure and serenity; then a warm wind would drive before it tornadoes of dust, and a stream would descend in cascades from the heights of Sicca, where, with its roofing of gold on its columns of brass, rose the temple of the Carthaginian Venus, the mistress of the land. She seemed to fill it with her soul. In such convulsions of the soil, such alternations of temperature, and such plays of light would she manifest the extravagance of her might with the beauty of her eternal smile. The mountains at their summits were crescent-shaped; others were like women's bosoms presenting their swelling breasts, and the Barbarians felt a heaviness that was full of delight weighing down their fatigues.

Spendius had bought a slave with the money brought him by his dromedary.

The whole day long he lay asleep stretched before Matho's tent. Often he would awake, thinking in his dreams that he heard the whistling of the thongs; with a smile he would pass his hands over the scars on his legs at the place where the fetters had long been worn, and then he would fall asleep again.

Matho accepted his companionship, and when he went out Spendius would escort him like a lictor with a long sword on his thigh; or perhaps Matho would rest his arm carelessly on the other's shoulder, for Spendius was small.

One evening when they were passing together through the streets in the camp they perceived some men covered with white cloaks; among them was Narr' Havas, the prince of the Numidians. Matho started.

"Your sword!" he cried; "I will kill him!"

"Not yet!" said Spendius, restraining him. Narr' Havas was already advancing towards him.

He kissed both his thumbs in token of alliance, showing nothing of the anger which he had experienced at the drunkenness of the feast; then he spoke at length against Carthage, but did not say what brought him among the Barbarians.

"Was it to betray them, or else the Republic?" Spendius asked himself; and as he expected to profit by every disorder, he felt grateful to Narr' Havas for the future perfidies of which he suspected him.

The chief of the Numidians remained amongst the Mercenaries. He appeared desirous of attaching Matho to himself. He sent him fat goats, gold dust, and ostrich feathers. The Libyan, who was amazed at such caresses, was in doubt whether to respond to them or to become exasperated at them. But Spendius pacified him, and Matho allowed himself to be ruled by the slave, remaining ever irresolute and in an unconquerable torpor, like those who have once taken a draught of which they are to die.

One morning when all three went out lion-hunting, Narr' Havas concealed a dagger in his cloak. Spendius kept continually behind him, and when they returned the dagger had not been drawn.

Another time Narr' Havas took them a long way off, as far as the boundaries of his kingdom. They came to a narrow gorge, and Narr' Havas smiled as he declared that he had forgotten the way. Spendius found it again.

But most frequently Matho would go off at sunrise, as melancholy as an augur, to wander about the country. He would stretch himself on the sand, and remain there motionless until the evening.

He consulted all the soothsayers in the army one after the other—those who watch the trail of serpents, those who read the stars, and those who breathe upon the ashes of the dead. He swallowed galbanum, seseli, and viper's venom which freezes the heart; Negro women, singing barbarous words in the moonlight, pricked the skin of his forehead with golden stylets; he loaded himself with neck-laces and charms; he invoked in turn Baal-Khamon, Moloch, the seven Kabiri, Tanith, and the Venus of the Greeks. He engraved a name upon a copper plate, and buried it in the sand at the threshold of his tent. Spendius used to hear him groan-ing and talking to himself.

One night he went in.

Matho, as naked as a corpse, was lying on a lion's skin flat on his stomach, with his face in both his hands; a hanging lamp lit up his armour, which was hooked on to the tent-pole above his head.

"You are suffering?" said the slave to him. "What is the matter with you? An-swer me?" And he shook him by the shoulder calling him several times, "Master! master!"

At last Matho lifted large troubled eyes towards him.

"Listen!" he said in a low voice, and with a finger on his lips. "It is the wrath of the Gods! Hamilcar's daughter pursues me! I am afraid of her, Spendius!" He pressed himself close against his breast like a child terrified by a phantom. "Speak to me! I am sick! I want to get well! I have tried everything! But you, you perhaps know some stronger gods, or some resistless invocation?"

"For what purpose?" asked Spendius.

Striking his head with both his fists, he replied:

"To rid me of her!"

Then speaking to himself with long pauses he said:

"I am no doubt the victim of some holocaust which she has promised to the gods?—She holds me fast by a chain which people cannot see. If I walk, it is she that is advancing; when I stop, she is resting! Her eyes burn me, I hear her voice. She en-compasses me, she penetrates me. It seems to me that she has become my soul!

"And yet between us there are, as it were, the invisible billows of a boundless ocean! She is far away and quite inaccessible! The splendour of her beauty forms a cloud of light around her, and at times I think that I have never seen her—that she does not exist—and that it is all a dream!"

Matho wept thus in the darkness; the Barbarians were sleeping. Spendius, as he looked at him, recalled the young men who once used to entreat him with golden vases in their hands, when he led his herd of courtesans through the towns; a feel-ing of pity moved him, and he said—

"Be strong, my master! Summon your will, and beseech the gods no more, for they turn not aside at the cries of men! Weeping like a coward! And you are not hu-miliated that a woman can cause you so much suffering?"

"Am I a child?" said Matho. "Do you think that I am moved by their faces and songs? We kept them at Drepanum to sweep out our stables. I have embraced them

amid assaults, beneath falling ceilings, and while the catapult was still vibrating!—
But she, Spendius, she!—"

The slave interrupted him:

"If she were not Hamilcar's daughter—"

"No!" cried Matho. "She has nothing in common with other daughters of men!
Have you seen her great eyes beneath her great eyebrows, like suns beneath triumphal arches? Think: when she appeared all the torches grew pale. Her naked
breast shone here and there through the diamonds of her necklace; behind her you
perceived as it were the odour of a temple, and her whole being emitted something
that was sweeter than wine and more terrible than death. She walked, however, and
then she stopped."

He remained gaping with his head cast down and his eyeballs fixed.

"But I want her! I need her! I am dying for her! I am transported with frenzied
joy at the thought of clasping her in my arms, and yet I hate her, Spendius! I should
like to beat her! What is to be done? I have a mind to sell myself and become her
slave! *You* have been that! You were able to get sight of her; speak to me of her!
Every night she ascends to the terrace of her palace, does she not? Ah! the stones
must quiver beneath her sandals, and the stars bend down to see her!"

He fell back in a perfect frenzy, with a rattling in his throat like a wounded bull.

Then Matho sang: "He pursued into the forest the female monster, whose tail
undulated over the dead leaves like a silver brook." And with lingering tones he
imitated Salammbô's voice, while his outspread hands were held like two light
hands on the strings of a lyre.

To all the consolations offered by Spendius, he repeated the same words; their
nights were spent in these wailings and exhortations.

Matho sought to drown his thoughts in wine. After his fits of drunkenness he
was more melancholy still. He tried to divert himself at huckle-bones, and lost the
gold plates of his necklace one by one. He had himself taken to the servants of the
Goddess; but he came down the hill sobbing, like one returning from a funeral.

Spendius, on the contrary, became more bold and gay. He was to be seen in the
leafy taverns discoursing in the midst of the soldiers. He mended old cuirasses. He
juggled with daggers. He went and gathered herbs in the fields for the sick. He was
facetious, dexterous, full of invention and talk; the Barbarians grew accustomed to
his services, and he came to be loved by them.

However, they were awaiting an ambassador from Carthage to bring them
mules laden with baskets of gold; and ever beginning the same calculation over
again, they would trace figures with their fingers in the sand. Every one was arranging his life beforehand; they would have concubines, slaves, lands; others intended to bury their treasure, or risk it on a vessel. But their tempers were

provoked by want of employment; there were constant disputes between horse-soldiers and foot-soldiers, Barbarians and Greeks, while there was a never-ending din of shrill female voices.

Every day men came flocking in nearly naked, and with grass on their heads to protect them from the sun; they were the debtors of the rich Carthaginians and had been forced to till the lands of the latter, but had escaped. Libyans came pouring in with peasants ruined by the taxes, outlaws, and malefactors. Then the horde of traders, all the dealers in wine and oil, who were furious at not being paid, laid the blame upon the Republic. Spendius declaimed against it. Soon the provisions ran low; and there was talk of advancing in a body upon Carthage, and calling in the Romans.

One evening, at supper-time, dull cracked sounds were heard approaching, and something red appeared in the distance among the undulations of the soil.

It was a large purple litter, adorned with ostrich feathers at the corners. Chains of crystal and garlands of pearls beat against the closed hangings. It was followed by camels sounding the great bells that hung at their breasts, and having around them horsemen clad from shoulder to heel in armour of golden scales.

They halted three hundred paces from the camp to take their round bucklers, broad swords, and Bœotian helmets out of the cases which they carried behind their saddles. Some remained with the camels, while the others resumed their march. At last the ensigns of the Republic appeared, that is to say, staves of blue wood terminating in horses' heads or fir cones. The Barbarians all rose with applause; the women rushed towards the guards of the Legion and kissed their feet.

The litter advanced on the shoulders of twelve Negroes who walked in step with short, rapid strides; they went at random to right or left, being embarrassed by the tent-ropes, the animals that were straying about, or the tripods where food was being cooked. Sometimes a fat hand, laden with rings, would partially open the litter, and a hoarse voice would utter loud reproaches; then the bearers would stop and take a different direction through the camp.

But the purple curtains were raised, and a human head, impassible and bloated, was seen resting on a large pillow; the eyebrows, which were like arches of ebony, met each other at the points; golden dust sparkled in the frizzled hair, and the face was so wan that it looked as if it had been powdered with marble raspings. The rest of the body was concealed beneath the fleeces which filled the litter.

In the man so reclining the soldiers recognised the Suffet Hanno, he whose slackness had assisted to lose the battle of the Ægatian islands; and as to his victory at Hecatompylos over the Libyans, even if he did behave with clemency, thought the Barbarians, it was owing to cupidity, for he had sold all the captives on his own account, although he had reported their deaths to the Republic.

After seeking for some time for a convenient place from which to harangue the soldiers, he made a sign; the litter stopped, and Hanno, supported by two slaves, put his tottering feet to the ground.

He wore boots of black felt strewn with silver moons. His legs were swathed in bands like those wrapped about a mummy, and the flesh crept through the crossings of the linen; his stomach came out beyond the scarlet jacket which covered his thighs; the folds of his neck fell down to his breast like the dewlaps of an ox; his tunic, which was painted with flowers, was bursting at the arm-pits; he wore a scarf, a girdle, and an ample black cloak with laced double sleeves. But the abundance of his garments, his great necklace of blue stones, his golden clasps, and heavy earrings only rendered his deformity still more hideous. He might have been taken for some big idol rough-hewn in a block of stone; for a pale leprosy, which was spread over his whole body, gave him the appearance of an inert thing. His nose, however, which was hooked like a vulture's beak, was violently dilated to breathe in the air, and his little eyes, with their gummed lashes, shone with a hard and metallic lustre. He held a spatula of aloe-wood in his hand wherewith to scratch his skin.

At last two heralds sounded their silver horns; the tumult subsided, and Hanno commenced to speak.

He began with an eulogy of the gods and the Republic; the Barbarians ought to congratulate themselves on having served it. But they must show themselves more reasonable; times were hard, "and if a master has only three olives, is it not right that he should keep two for himself?"

The old Suffet mingled his speech in this way with proverbs and apologues, nodding his head the while to solicit some approval.

He spoke in Punic, and those surrounding him (the most alert, who had hastened thither without their arms), were Campanians, Gauls, and Greeks, so that no one in the crowd understood him. Hanno, perceiving this, stopped and reflected, swaying himself heavily from one leg to the other.

It occurred to him to call the captains together; then his heralds shouted the order in Greek, the language which, from the time of Xanthippus, had been used for commands in the Carthaginian armies.

The guards dispersed the mob of soldiers with strokes of the whip; and the captains of the Spartan phalanxes and the chiefs of the Barbarian cohorts soon arrived with the insignia of their rank, and in the armour of their nation. Night had fallen, a great tumult was spreading through the plain; fires were burning here and there; and the soldiers kept going from one to another asking what the matter was, and why the Suffet did not distribute the money?

He was setting the infinite burdens of the Republic before the captains. Her treasury was empty. The tribute to Rome was crushing her. "We are quite at a loss what to do! She is much to be pitied!"

From time to time he would rub his limbs with his aloe-wood spatula, or perhaps he would break off to drink a ptisan made of the ashes of a weasel and asparagus boiled in vinegar from a silver cup handed to him by a slave; then he would wipe his lips with a scarlet napkin and resume:

"What used to be worth a shekel of silver is now worth three shekels of gold, while the cultivated lands which were abandoned during the war bring in nothing! Our purpura fisheries are nearly gone, and even pearls are becoming exorbitant; we have scarcely unguents enough for the service of the gods! As for the things of the table, I shall say nothing about them; it is a calamity! For want of galleys we are without spices, and it is a matter of great difficulty to procure silphium on account of the rebellions on the Cyrenian frontier. Sicily, where so many slaves used to be had, is now closed to us! Only yesterday I gave more money for a bather and four scullions than I used at one time to give for a pair of elephants!"

He unrolled a long piece of papyrus; and, without omitting a single figure, read all the expenses that the government had incurred; so much for repairing the temples, for paving the streets, for the construction of vessels, for the coral-fisheries, for the enlargement of the Syssitia, and for engines in the mines in the country of the Cantabrians.

But the captains understood Punic as little as the soldiers, although the Mercenaries saluted one another in that language. It was usual to place a few Carthaginian officers in the Barbarian armies to act as interpreters; after the war they had concealed themselves through fear of vengeance, and Hanno had not thought of taking them with him; his hollow voice, too, was lost in the wind.

The Greeks, girthed in their iron waist-belts, strained their ears as they strove to guess at his words, while the mountaineers, covered with furs like bears, looked at him with distrust, or yawned as they leaned on their brass-nailed clubs. The heedless Gauls sneered as they shook their lofty heads of hair, and the men of the desert listened motionless, cowled in their garments of grey wool; others kept coming up behind; the guards, crushed by the mob, staggered on their horses; the Negroes held out burning fir branches at arm's length; and the big Carthaginian, mounted on a grassy hillock, continued his harangue.

The Barbarians, however, were growing impatient; murmuring arose, and every one apostrophized him. Hanno gesticulated with his spatula; and those who wished the others to be quiet shouted still more loudly, thereby adding to the din.

Suddenly a man of mean appearance bounded to Hanno's feet, snatched up a herald's trumpet, blew it, and Spendius (for it was he) announced that he was going to say something of importance. At this declaration, which was rapidly uttered in five different languages, Greek, Latin, Gallic, Libyan and Balearic, the captains, half laughing and half surprised, replied: "Speak! Speak!"

Spendius hesitated; he trembled; at last, addressing the Libyans who were the most numerous, he said to them:

"You have all heard this man's horrible threats!"

Hanno made no exclamation, therefore he did not understand Libyan; and, to carry on the experiment, Spendius repeated the same phrase in the other Barbarian dialects.

They looked at one another in astonishment; then, as by a tacit agreement, and believing perhaps that they had understood, they bent their heads in token of assent.

Then Spendius began in vehement tones:

"He said first that all the Gods of the other nations were but dreams beside the Gods of Carthage! He called you cowards, thieves, liars, dogs, and the sons of dogs! But for you (he said that!) the Republic would not be forced to pay tribute to the Romans; and through your excesses you have drained it of perfumes, aromatics, slaves, and silphium, for you are in league with the nomads on the Cyrenian frontier! But the guilty shall be punished! He read the enumeration of their torments; they shall be made to work at the paving of the streets, at the equipment of the vessels, at the adornment of the Syssitia, while the rest shall be sent to scrape the earth in the mines in the country of the Cantabrians."

Spendius repeated the same statements to the Gauls, Greeks, Campanians and Balearians. The Mercenaries, recognising several of the proper names which had met their ears, were convinced that he was accurately reporting the Suffet's speech. A few cried out to him, "You lie!" but their voices were drowned in the tumult of the rest; Spendius added:

"Have you not seen that he has left a reserve of his horse-soldiers outside the camp? At a given signal they will hasten hither to slay you all."

The Barbarians turned in that direction, and as the crowd was then scattering, there appeared in the midst of them, and advancing with the slowness of a phantom, a human being, bent, lean, entirely naked, and covered down to his flanks with long hair bristling with dried leaves, dust and thorns. About his loins and his knees he had wisps of straw and linen rags; his soft and earthy skin hung on his emaciated limbs like tatters on dried boughs; his hands trembled with a continuous quivering, and as he walked he leaned on a staff of olive-wood.

He reached the Negroes who were bearing the torches. His pale gums were displayed in a sort of idiotic titter; his large, scared eyes gazed upon the crowd of Barbarians around him.

But uttering a cry of terror he threw himself behind them, shielding himself with their bodies. "There they are! There they are!" he stammered out, pointing to the Suffet's guards, who were motionless in their glittering armour. Their horses, dazzled by the light of the torches which crackled in the darkness, were pawing the ground; the human spectre struggled and howled:

"They have killed them!"

At these words, which were screamed in Balearic, some Balearians came up and recognised him; without answering them he repeated:

"Yes, all killed, all! crushed like grapes! The fine young men! the slingers! my companions and yours!"

They gave him wine to drink, and he wept; then he launched forth into speech.

Spendius could scarcely repress his joy, as he explained the horrors related by Zarxas to the Greeks and Libyans; he could not believe them, so appropriately did they come in. The Balearians grew pale as they learned how their companions had perished.

It was a troop of three hundred slingers who had disembarked the evening before, and had on that day slept too late. When they reached the square of Khamon the Barbarians were gone, and they found themselves defenceless, their clay bullets having been put on the camels with the rest of the baggage. They were allowed to advance into the street of Satheb as far as the brass sheathed oaken gate; then the people with a single impulse had sprung upon them.

Indeed, the soldiers remembered a great shout; Spendius, who was flying at the head of the columns, had not heard it.

Then the corpses were placed in the arms of the Patæc gods that fringed the temple of Khamon. They were upbraided with all the crimes of the Mercenaries; their gluttony, their thefts, their impiety, their disdain, and the murder of the fishes in Salammbô's garden. Their bodies were subjected to infamous mutilations; the priests burned their hair in order to torture their souls; they were hung up in pieces in the meat-shops; some even buried their teeth in them, and in the evening funeral-piles were kindled at the cross-ways to finish them.

These were the flames that had gleamed from a distance across the lake. But some houses having taken fire, any dead or dying that remained were speedily thrown over the walls; Zarxas had remained among the reeds on the edge of the lake until the following day; then he had wandered about through the country, seeking for the army by the footprints in the dust. In the morning he hid himself in caves; in the evening he resumed his march with his bleeding wounds, famished, sick, living on roots and carrion; at last one day he perceived lances on the horizon, and he had followed them, for his reason was disturbed through his terrors and miseries.

The indignation of the soldiers, restrained so long as he was speaking, broke forth like a tempest; they were going to massacre the guards together with the Suffet. A few interposed, saying that they ought to hear him and know at least whether they should be paid. Then they all cried: "Our money!" Hanno replied that he had brought it.

They ran to the outposts, and the Suffet's baggage arrived in the midst of the tents, pressed forward by the Barbarians. Without waiting for the slaves, they very quickly unfastened the baskets; in them they found hyacinth robes, sponges, scrapers, brushes, perfumes, and antimony pencils for painting the eyes—all belonging to the guards, who were rich men and accustomed to such refinements. Next they uncovered a large bronze tub on a camel: it belonged to the Suffet who had it for bathing in during his journey; for he had taken all manner of precautions, even going so far as to bring caged weasels from Hecatompylos, which were burnt alive to make his ptisan. But, as his malady gave him a great appetite, there were also many comestibles and many wines, pickle, meats and fishes preserved in honey, with little pots of Commagene, or melted goose-fat covered with snow and chopped straw. There was a considerable supply of it; the more they opened the baskets the more they found, and laughter arose like conflicting waves.

As to the pay of the Mercenaries it nearly filled two esparto-grass baskets; there were even visible in one of them some of the leathern discs which the Republic used to economise its specie; and as the Barbarians appeared greatly surprised, Hanno told them that, their accounts being very difficult, the Ancients had not had leisure to examine them. Meanwhile they sent them this.

Then everything was in disorder and confusion: mules, serving men, litter, provisions, and baggage. The soldiers took the coin in the bags to stone Hanno. With great difficulty he was able to mount an ass; and he fled, clinging to its hair, howling, weeping, shaken, bruised, and calling down the curse of all the gods upon the army. His broad necklace of precious stones rebounded up to his ears. His cloak which was too long, and which trailed behind him, he kept on with his teeth, and from afar the Barbarians shouted at him, "Begone coward! pig! sink of Moloch! sweat your gold and your plague! quicker! quicker!" The routed escort galloped beside him.

But the fury of the Barbarians did not abate. They remembered that several of them who had set out for Carthage had not returned; no doubt they had been killed. So much injustice exasperated them, and they began to pull up the stakes of their tents, to roll up their cloaks, and to bridle their horses; every one took his helmet and sword, and instantly all was ready. Those who had no arms rushed into the woods to cut staves.

Day dawned; the people of Sicca were roused, and stirring in the streets.

"They are going to Carthage," said they, and the rumour of this soon spread through the country.

From every path and every ravine men arose. Shepherds were seen running down from the mountains.

Then, when the Barbarians had set out, Spendius circled the plain, riding on a Punic stallion, and attended by his slave, who led a third horse.

A single tent remained. Spendius entered it.

"Up, master! rise! we are departing!"

"And where are you going?" asked Matho.

"To Carthage!" cried Spendius.

Matho bounded upon the horse which the slave held at the door.

Chapter III

SALAMMBÔ

THE MOON WAS RISING JUST ABOVE THE WAVES, AND ON THE TOWN WHICH was still wrapped in darkness there glittered white and luminous specks:—the pole of a chariot, a dangling rag of linen, the corner of a wall, or a golden necklace on the bosom of a god. The glass balls on the roofs of the temples beamed like great diamonds here and there. But ill-defined ruins, piles of black earth, and gardens formed deeper masses in the gloom, and below Malqua fishermen's nets stretched from one house to another like gigantic bats spreading their wings. The grinding of the hydraulic wheels which conveyed water to the highest storys of the palaces, was no longer heard; and the camels, lying ostrich fashion on their stomachs, rested peacefully in the middle of the terraces. The porters were asleep in the streets on the thresholds of the houses; the shadows of the colossuses stretched across the deserted squares; occasionally in the distance the smoke of a still burning sacrifice would escape through the bronze tiling, and the heavy breeze would waft the odours of aromatics blended with the scent of the sea and the exhalation from the sun-heated walls. The motionless waves shone around Carthage, for the moon was spreading her light at once upon the mountain-circled gulf and upon the lake of Tunis, where flamingoes formed long rose-coloured lines amid the banks of sand, while further on beneath the catacombs the great salt lagoon shimmered like a piece of silver. The blue vault of heaven sank on the horizon in one direction into the dustiness of the plains, and in the other into the mists of the sea, and on the summit of the Acropolis, the pyramidal cypress trees, fringing the temple of Eschmoun, swayed murmuring like the regular waves that beat slowly along the mole beneath the ramparts.

Salammbô ascended to the terrace of her palace, supported by a female slave who carried an iron dish filled with live coals.

In the middle of the terrace there was a small ivory bed covered with lynx skins, and cushions made with the feathers of the parrot, a fatidical animal consecrated to the gods; and at the four corners rose four long perfuming-pans filled with nard, incense, cinnamomum, and myrrh. The slave lit the perfumes. Salammbô looked at the polar star; she slowly saluted the four points of heaven, and knelt down on the ground in the azure dust which was strewn with golden stars in imitation of the firmament. Then with both elbows against her sides, her fore-arms straight and her hands open, she threw back her head beneath the rays of the moon, and said:

"O Rabetna!—Baalet!—Tanith!" and her voice was lengthened in a plaintive fashion as if calling to some one. "Anaïtis! Astarte! Derceto! Astoreth! Mylitta! Athara! Elissa! Tiratha!—By the hidden symbols—by the resounding sistra—by the furrows of the earth—by the eternal silence and by the eternal fruitfulness—mistress of the gloomy sea and of the azure shores, O Queen of the watery world, all hail!"

She swayed her whole body twice or thrice, and then cast herself face downwards in the dust with both arms outstretched.

But the slave nimbly raised her, for according to the rites some one must catch the suppliant at the moment of his prostration; this told him that the gods accepted him, and Salammbô's nurse never failed in this pious duty.

Some merchants from Darytian Gætulia had brought her to Carthage when quite young, and after her enfranchisement she would not forsake her old masters, as was shown by her right ear, which was pierced with a large hole. A petticoat of many-coloured stripes fitted closely on her hips, and fell to her ankles, where two tin rings clashed together. Her somewhat flat face was yellow like her tunic. Silver bodkins of great length formed a sun behind her head. She wore a coral button on the nostril, and she stood beside the bed more erect than a Hermes, and with her eyelids cast down.

Salammbô walked to the edge of the terrace; her eyes swept the horizon for an instant, and then were lowered upon the sleeping town, while the sigh that she heaved swelled her bosom, and gave an undulating movement to the whole length of the long white simar which hung without clasp or girdle about her. Her curved and painted sandals were hidden beneath a heap of emeralds, and a net of purple thread was filled with her disordered hair.

But she raised her head to gaze upon the moon, and murmured, mingling her speech with fragments of hymns:

"How lightly turnest thou, supported by the impalpable ether! It brightens about thee, and 'tis the stir of thine agitation that distributes the winds and fruitful dews. According as thou dost wax and wane the eyes of cats and spots of panthers lengthen or grow short. Wives shriek thy name in the pangs of childbirth! Thou makest the shells to swell, the wine to bubble, and the corpse to putrefy! Thou formest the pearls at the bottom of the sea!

"And every germ, O goddess! ferments in the dark depths of thy moisture.

"When thou appearest, quietness is spread abroad upon the earth; the flowers close, the waves are soothed, wearied man stretches his breast toward thee, and the world with its oceans and mountains looks at itself in thy face as in a mirror. Thou art white, gentle, luminous, immaculate, helping, purifying, serene!"

The crescent of the moon was then over the mountain of the Hot Springs, in the hollow formed by its two summits, on the other side of the gulf. Below it there was a little star, and all around it a pale circle. Salammbô went on:

"But thou art a terrible mistress!—Monsters, terrifying phantoms, and lying dreams come from thee; thine eyes devour the stones of buildings, and the apes are ever ill each time thou growest young again.

"Whither goest thou? Why dost thou change thy forms continually? Now, slender and curved thou glidest through space like a mastless galley; and then, amid the stars, thou art like a shepherd keeping his flock. Shining and round, thou dost graze the mountain-tops like the wheel of a chariot.

"O Tanith! thou dost love me? I have looked so much on thee! But no! thou sailest through thine azure, and I—I remain on the motionless earth.

"Taanach, take your nebal and play softly on the silver string, for my heart is sad!"

The slave lifted a sort of harp of ebony wood, taller than herself, and triangular in shape like a delta; she fixed the point in a crystal globe, and with both hands began to play.

The sounds followed one another hurried and deep, like the buzzing of bees, and with increasing sonorousness floated away into the night with the complaining of the waves, and the rustling of the great trees on the summit of the Acropolis.

"Hush!" cried Salammbô.

"What ails you, mistress? The blowing of the breeze, the passing of a cloud, everything disquiets you just now!"

"I do not know," she said.

"You are wearied with too long prayers!"

"Oh! Taanach, I would fain be dissolved in them like a flower in wine!"

"Perhaps it is the smoke of your perfumes?"

"No!" said Salammbô; "the spirit of the gods dwells in fragrant odours."

Then the slave spoke to her of her father. It was thought that he had gone towards the amber country, behind the pillars of Melkarth. "But if he does not return," she said, "you must nevertheless, since it was his will, choose a husband among the sons of the Ancients, and then your grief will pass away in a man's arms."

"Why?" asked the young girl. All those that she had seen had horrified her with their fallow-deer laughter and their coarse limbs.

"Sometimes, Taanach, from the depths of my being there exhale as it were hot fumes heavier than the vapours from a volcano. Voices call me, a globe of fire rolls and mounts within my bosom, it stifles me, I am at the point of death; and then, something sweet, flowing from my brow to my feet, passes through my flesh—it is a caress enfolding me, and I feel myself crushed as if some god were stretched upon me. Oh! would that I could lose myself in the mists of the night, the waters of the fountains, the sap of the trees, that I could issue from my body, and be but a breath, or a ray, and glide, mount up to thee, O Mother!"

She raised her arms to their full length, arching her form, which in its long garment was as pale and light as the moon. Then she fell back, panting, on the ivory couch; but Taanach passed an amber necklace with dolphin's teeth about her neck to banish terrors, and Salammbô said in an almost stifled voice: "Go and bring me Schahabarim."

Her father had not wished her to enter the college of priestesses, nor even to be made at all acquainted with the popular Tanith. He was reserving her for some alliance that might serve his political ends; so that Salammbô lived alone in the midst of the palace. Her mother was long since dead.

She had grown up with abstinences, fastings and purifications, always surrounded by grave and exquisite things, her body saturated with perfumes, and her soul filled with prayers. She had never tasted wine, nor eaten meat, nor touched an unclean animal, nor set her heels in the house of death.

She knew nothing of obscene images, for as each god was manifested in different forms, the same principle often received the witness of contradictory culls, and Salammbô worshipped the goddess in her sidereal presentation. An influence had descended upon the maiden from the moon; when the planet passed diminishing away, Salammbô grew weak. She languished the whole day long, and revived at evening. During an eclipse she had nearly died.

But Rabetna, in jealousy, revenged herself for the virginity withdrawn from her sacrifices, and she tormented Salammbô with possessions, all the stronger for being vague, which were spread through this belief and excited by it.

Unceasingly was Hamilcar's daughter disquieted about Tanith. She had learned her adventures, her travels, and all her names, which she would repeat without their having any distinct signification for her. In order to penetrate into the depths of her dogma, she wished to become acquainted, in the most secret part of the temple, with the old idol in the magnificent mantle, whereon depended the destinies of Carthage, for the idea of a god did not stand out clearly from his representation, and to hold, or even see the image of one, was to take away part of his virtue, and in a measure to rule him.

But Salammbô turned around. She had recognised the sound of the golden bells which Schahabarim wore at the hem of his garment.

He ascended the staircases; then at the threshold of the terrace he stopped and folded his arms.

His sunken eyes shone like the lamps of a sepulchre; his long thin body floated in its linen robe which was weighted by the bells, the latter alternating with balls of emeralds at his heels. He had feeble limbs, an oblique skull and a pointed chin; his skin seemed cold to the touch, and his yellow face, which was deeply furrowed with wrinkles, was as if it contracted in a longing, in an everlasting grief.

He was the high priest of Tanith, and it was he who had educated Salammbô.

"Speak!" he said. "What will you?"

"I hoped—you had almost promised me—" She stammered and was confused; then suddenly: "Why do you despise me? what have I forgotten in the rites? You are my master, and you told me that no one was so accomplished in the things pertaining to the goddess as I; but there are some of which you will not speak. Is it so, O father?"

Schahabarim remembered Hamilcar's orders, and replied:

"No, I have nothing more to teach you!"

"A genius" she resumed, "impels me to this love. I have climbed the steps of Eschmoun, god of the planets and intelligences; I have slept beneath the golden olive of Melkarth, patron of the Tyrian colonies; I have pushed open the doors of Baal-Khamon, the enlightener and fertiliser; I have sacrificed to the subterranean Kabiri, to the gods of woods, winds, rivers and mountains; but, can you understand? they are all too far away, too high, too insensible, while she—I feel her mingled in my life; she fills my soul, and I quiver with inward startings, as though she were leaping in order to escape. Methinks I am about to hear her voice, and see her face, lightnings dazzle me and then I sink back again into the darkness."

Schahabarim was silent. She entreated him with suppliant looks. At last he made a sign for the dismissal of the slave, who was not of Chanaanitish race. Taanach disappeared, and Schahabarim, raising one arm in the air, began:

"Before the gods darkness alone was, and a breathing stirred dull and indistinct as the conscience of a man in a dream. It contracted, creating Desire and Cloud, and from Desire and Cloud there issued primitive Matter. This was a water, muddy, black, icy and deep. It contained senseless monsters, incoherent portions of the forms to be born, which are painted on the walls of the sanctuaries.

"Then Matter condensed. It became an egg. It burst. One half formed the earth and the other the firmament. Sun, moon, winds and clouds appeared, and at the crash of the thunder intelligent creatures awoke. Then Eschmoun spread himself in the starry sphere; Khamon beamed in the sun; Melkarth thrust him with his arms behind Gades; the Kabiri descended beneath the volcanoes, and Rabetna like a nurse bent over the world pouring out her light like milk, and her night like a mantle."

"And then?" she said.

He had related the secret of the origins to her, to divert her from sublimer prospects; but the maiden's desire kindled again at his last words, and Schahabarim, half yielding resumed:

"She inspires and governs the loves of men."

"The loves of men!" repeated Salammbô dreamily.

"She is the soul of Carthage," continued the priest; "and although she is everywhere diffused, it is here the she dwells, beneath the sacred veil."

"O father!" cried Salammbô, "I shall see her, shall I not? you will bring me to her! I had long been hesitating; I am devoured with curiosity to see her form. Pity! help me! let us go?"

He repulsed her with a vehement gesture that was full of pride.

"Never! Do you not know that it means death? The hermaphrodite Baals are unveiled to us alone who are men in understanding and women in weakness. Your desire is sacrilege; be satisfied with the knowledge that you possess!"

She fell upon her knees placing two fingers against her ears in token of repentance; and crushed by the priest's words, and filled at once with anger against him, with terror and with humiliation, she burst into sobs. Schahabarim remained erect, and more insensible than the stones of the terrace. He looked down upon her quivering at his feet, and felt a kind of joy on seeing her suffer for his divinity whom he himself could not wholly embrace. The birds were already singing, a cold wind was blowing, and little clouds were drifting in the paling sky.

Suddenly he perceived on the horizon, behind Tunis, what looked like slight mists trailing along the ground; then these became a great curtain of dust extending perpendicularly, and, amid the whirlwinds of the thronging mass, dromedaries' heads, lances and shields appeared. It was the army of the Barbarians advancing upon Carthage.

Chapter IV

BENEATH THE WALLS OF CARTHAGE

OME COUNTRY PEOPLE, RIDING ON ASSES OR RUNNING ON FOOT, ARRIVED IN
the town, pale, breathless, and mad with fear. They were flying before the
army. It had accomplished the journey from Sicca in three days, in order to
reach Carthage and wholly exterminate it.

The gates were shut. The Barbarians appeared almost immediately; but they
stopped in the middle of the isthmus, on the edge of the lake.

At first they made no hostile announcement. Several approached with palm
branches in their hands. They were driven back with arrows, so great was the terror.

In the morning and at nightfall prowlers would sometimes wander along the
walls. A little man carefully wrapped in a cloak, and with his face concealed beneath a very low visor, was especially noticed. He would remain whole hours gazing at the aqueduct, and so persistently that he doubtless wished to mislead the
Carthaginians as to his real designs. Another man, a sort of giant who walked bare-
headed, used to accompany him.

But Carthage was defended throughout the whole breadth of the isthmus: first
by a trench, then by a grassy rampart, and lastly by a wall thirty cubits high, built
of freestone, and in two storys. It contained stables for three hundred elephants
with stores for their caparisons, shackles, and food; other stables again for four
thousand horses with supplies of barley and harness, and barracks for twenty thousand soldiers with armour and all materials for war. Towers rose from the second
story, all provided with battlements, and having bronze bucklers hung on cramps
on the outside.

This first line of wall gave immediate shelter to Malqua, the sailors' and dyers'
quarter. Masts might be seen whereon purple sails were drying, and on the highest
terraces clay furnaces for heating the pickle were visible.

Behind, the lofty houses of the city rose in an amphitheatre of cubical form.
They were built of stone, planks, shingle, reeds, shells, and beaten earth. The
woods belonging to the temples were like lakes of verdure in this mountain of
diversely-coloured blocks. It was levelled at unequal distances by the public
squares, and was cut from top to bottom by countless intersecting lanes. The enclosures of the three old quarters which are now lost might be distinguished; they
rose here and there like great reefs, or extended in enormous fronts, blackened,

half-covered with flowers, and broadly striped by the casting of filth, while streets passed through their yawning apertures like rivers beneath bridges.

The hill of the Acropolis, in the centre of Byrsa, was hidden beneath a disordered array of monuments. There were temples with wreathed columns bearing bronze capitals and metal chains, cones of dry stones with bands of azure, copper cupolas, marble architraves, Babylonian buttresses, obelisks poised on their points like inverted torches. Peristyles reached to pediments; volutes were displayed through colonnades; granite walls supported tile partitions; the whole mounting, half-hidden, the one above the other in a marvellous and incomprehensible fashion. In it might be felt, the succession of the ages, and, as it were, the memorials of forgotten fatherlands.

Behind the Acropolis the Mappalian road, which was lined with tombs, extended through red lands in a straight line from the shore to the catacombs; then spacious dwellings occurred at intervals in the gardens, and this third quarter, Megara, which was the new town, reached as far as the edge of the cliff, where rose a giant pharos that blazed forth every night.

In this fashion was Carthage displayed before the soldiers quartered in the plain.

They could recognize the markets and crossways in the distance, and disputed with one another as to the sites of the temples. Khamon's, fronting the Syssitia, had golden tiles; Melkarth, to the left of Eschmoun, had branches of coral on its roofing; beyond, Tanith's copper cupola swelled among the palm trees; the dark Moloch was below the cisterns, in the direction of the pharos. At the angles of the pediments, on the tops of the walls, at the corners of the squares, everywhere, divinities with hideous heads might be seen, colossal or squat, with enormous bellies, or immoderately flattened, opening their jaws, extending their arms, and holding forks, chains or javelins in their hands; while the blue of the sea stretched away behind the streets which were rendered still steeper by the perspective.

They were filled from morning till evening with a tumultuous people; young boys shaking little bells, shouted at the doors of the baths; the shops for hot drinks smoked, the air resounded with the noise of anvils, the white cocks, sacred to the Sun, crowed on the terraces, the oxen that were being slaughtered bellowed in the temples, slaves ran about with baskets on their heads; and in the depths of the porticoes a priest would sometimes appear, draped in a dark cloak, barefooted, and wearing a pointed cap.

The spectacle afforded by Carthage irritated the Barbarians; they admired it and execrated it, and would have liked both to annihilate it and to dwell in it. But what was there in the Military Harbour defended by a triple wall? Then behind the town, at the back of Megara, and higher than the Acropolis, appeared Hamilcar's palace.

Matho's eyes were directed thither every moment. He would ascend the olive trees and lean over with his hand spread out above his eyebrows. The gardens were empty, and the red door with its black cross remained constantly shut.

More than twenty times he walked round the ramparts, seeking some breach by which he might enter. One night he threw himself into the gulf and swam for three hours at a stretch. He reached the foot of the Mappalian quarter and tried to climb up the face of the cliff. He covered his knees with blood, broke his nails, and then fell back into the waves and returned.

His impotence exasperated him. He was jealous of this Carthage which contained Salammbô, as if of some one who had possessed her. His nervelessness left him to be replaced by a mad and continual eagerness for action. With flaming cheek, angry eyes, and hoarse voice, he would walk with rapid strides through the camp; or seated on the shore he would scour his great sword with sand. He shot arrows at the passing vultures. His heart overflowed into frenzied speech.

"Give free course to your wrath like a runaway chariot," said Spendius. "Shout, blaspheme, ravage and slay. Grief is allayed with blood, and since you cannot sate your love, gorge your hate; it will sustain you!"

Matho resumed the command of his soldiers. He drilled them pitilessly. He was respected for his courage and especially for his strength. Moreover he inspired a sort of mystic dread, and it was believed that he conversed at night with phantoms. The other captains were animated by his example. The army soon grew disciplined. From their houses the Carthaginians could hear the bugle-nourishes that regulated their exercises. At last the Barbarians drew near.

To crush them in the isthmus it would have been necessary for two armies to take them simultaneously in the rear, one disembarking at the end of the gulf of Utica, and the second at the mountain of the Hot Springs. But what could be done with the single sacred Legion, mustering at most six thousand men? If the enemy bent towards the east they would join the nomads and intercept the commerce of the desert. If they fell back to the west, Numidia would rise. Finally, lack of provisions would sooner or later lead them to devastate the surrounding country like grasshoppers, and the rich trembled for their fine country-houses, their vineyards and their cultivated lands.

Hanno proposed atrocious and impracticable measures, such as promising a heavy sum for every Barbarian's head, or setting fire to their camp with ships and machines. His colleague Gisco, on the other hand, wished them to be paid. But the Ancients detested him owing to his popularity; for they dreaded the risk of a master, and through terror of monarchy strove to weaken whatever contributed to it or might re-establish it.

Outside the fortifications there were people of another race and of unknown origin, all hunters of the porcupine, and eaters of shell-fish and serpents. They used to go into caves to catch hyenas alive, and amuse themselves by making them run in the evening on the sands of Megara between the stelæ of the tombs. Their huts, which were made of mud and wrack, hung on the cliff like swallows' nests. There they lived, without government and without gods, pell-mell, completely naked, at once feeble and fierce, and execrated by the people of all time on account of their unclean food. One morning the sentries perceived that they were all gone.

At last some members of the Great Council arrived at a decision. They came to the camp without necklaces or girdles, and in open sandals like neighbours. They walked at a quiet pace, waving salutations to the captains, or stopped to speak to the soldiers, saying that all was finished and that justice was about to be done to their claims.

Many of them saw a camp of Mercenaries for the first time. Instead of the confusion which they had pictured to themselves, there prevailed everywhere terrible silence and order. A grassy rampart formed a lofty wall round the army immovable by the shock of catapults. The ground in the streets was sprinkled with fresh water; through the holes in the tents they could perceive tawny eyeballs gleaming in the shade. The piles of pikes and hanging panoplies dazzled them like mirrors. They conversed in low tones. They were afraid of upsetting something with their long robes.

The soldiers requested provisions, undertaking to pay for them out of the money that was due.

Oxen, sheep, guinea fowl, fruit and lupins were sent to them, with smoked scombri, that excellent scombri which Carthage dispatched to every port. But they walked scornfully around the magnificent cattle, and disparaging what they coveted, offered the worth of a pigeon for a ram, or the price of a pomegranate for three goats. The Eaters of Uncleanness came forward as arbitrators, and declared that they were being duped. Then they drew their swords with threats to slay.

Commissaries of the Great Council wrote down the number of years for which pay was due to each soldier. But it was no longer possible to know how many Mercenaries had been engaged, and the Ancients were dismayed at the enormous sum which they would have to pay. The reserve of silphium must be sold, and the trading towns taxed; the Mercenaries would grow impatient; Tunis was already with them; and the rich, stunned by Hanno's ragings and his colleague's reproaches, urged any citizens who might know a Barbarian to go to see him immediately in order to win back his friendship, and to speak him fair. Such a show of confidence would soothe them.

Traders, scribes, workers in the arsenal, and whole families visited the Barbarians.

The soldiers allowed all the Carthaginians to come in, but by a single passage so narrow that four men abreast jostled one another in it. Spendius, standing against the barrier, had them carefully searched; facing him Matho was examining the multitude, trying to recognize some one whom he might have seen at Salammbô's palace.

The camp was like a town, so full of people and of movement was it. The two distinct crowds mingled without blending, one dressed in linen or wool, with felt caps like fir-cones, and the other clad in iron and wearing helmets. Amid serving men and itinerant vendors there moved women of all nations, as brown as ripe dates, as greenish as olives, as yellow as oranges, sold by sailors, picked out of dens, stolen from caravans, taken in the sacking of towns, women that were jaded with love so long as they were young, and plied with blows when they were old, and that died in routs on the roadsides among the baggage and the abandoned beasts of burden. The wives of the nomads had square, tawny robes of dromedary's hair swinging at their heels; musicians from Cyrenaïca, wrapped in violet gauze and with painted eyebrows, sang, squatting on mats; old Negresses with hanging breasts gathered the animals' dung that was drying in the sun to light their fires; the Syracusan women had golden plates in their hair; the Lusitanians had necklaces of shells; the Gauls wore wolf skins upon their white bosoms; and sturdy children, vermin-covered, naked and uncircumcised, butted with their heads against passers-by, or came behind them like young tigers to bite their hands.

The Carthaginians walked through the camp, surprised at the quantities of things with which it was running over. The most miserable were melancholy, and the rest dissembled their anxiety.

The soldiers struck them on the shoulder, and exhorted them to be gay. As soon as they saw any one, they invited him to their amusements. If they were playing at discus, they would manage to crush his feet, or if at boxing to fracture his jaw with the very first blow. The slingers terrified the Carthaginians with their slings, the Psylli with their vipers, and the horsemen with their horses, while their victims, addicted as they were to peaceful occupations, bent their heads and tried to smile at all these outrages. Some, in order to show themselves brave, made signs that they should like to become soldiers. They were set to split wood and to curry mules. They were buckled up in armour, and rolled like casks through the streets of the camp. Then, when they were about to leave, the Mercenaries plucked out their hair with grotesque contortions.

But many, from foolishness or prejudice, innocently believed that all the Carthaginians were very rich, and they walked behind them entreating them to grant them something. They requested everything that they thought fine: a ring, a girdle, sandals, the fringe of a robe, and when the despoiled Carthaginian cried—

"But I have nothing left. What do you want?" they would reply, "Your wife!" Others even said, "Your life!"

The military accounts were handed to the captains, read to the soldiers, and definitively approved. Then they claimed tents; they received them. Next the polemarchs of the Greeks demanded some of the handsome suits of armour that were manufactured at Carthage; the Great Council voted sums of money for their purchase. But it was only fair, so the horsemen pretended, that the Republic should indemnify them for their horses; one had lost three at such a siege, another, five during such a march, another, fourteen in the precipices. Stallions from Hecatompylos were offered to them, but they preferred money.

Next they demanded that they should be paid in money (in pieces of money, and not in leathern coins) for all the corn that was owing to them, and at the highest price that it had fetched during the war; so that they exacted four hundred times as much for a measure of meal as they had given for a sack of wheat. Such injustice was exasperating; but it was necessary, nevertheless, to submit.

Then the delegates from the soldiers and from the Great Council swore renewed friendship by the Genius of Carthage and the gods of the Barbarians. They exchanged excuses and caresses with oriental demonstrativeness and verbosity. Then the soldiers claimed, as a proof of friendship, the punishment of those who had estranged them from the Republic.

Their meaning, it was pretended, was not understood, and they explained themselves more clearly by saying that they must have Hanno's head.

Several times in the day, they left their camp, and walked along the foot of the walls, shouting a demand that the Suffet's head should be thrown to them, and holding out their robes to receive it.

The Great Council would perhaps have given way but for a last exaction, more outrageous than the rest; they demanded maidens, chosen from illustrious families, in marriage for their chiefs. It was an idea which had emanated from Spendius, and which many thought most simple and practicable. But the assumption of their desire to mingle with Punic blood made the people indignant; and they were bluntly told that they were to receive no more. Then they exclaimed that they had been deceived, and that if their pay did not arrive within three days, they would themselves go and take it in Carthage.

The bad faith of the Mercenaries was not so complete as their enemies thought. Hamilcar had made them extravagant promises, vague, it is true, but at the same time solemn and reiterated. They might have believed that when they disembarked at Carthage the town would be abandoned to them, and that they should have treasures divided among them; and when they saw that scarcely their wages would be paid, the disillusion touched their pride no less than their greed.

Had not Dionysius, Pyrrhus, Agathocles, and the generals of Alexander furnished examples of marvellous good fortune? Hercules, whom the Chanaanites confounded with the sun, was the ideal which shone on the horizon of armies. They knew that simple soldiers had worn diadems, and the echoes of crumbling empires would furnish dreams to the Gaul in his oak forest, to the Ethiopian amid his sands. But there was a nation always ready to turn courage to account; and the robber driven from his tribe, the parricide wandering on the roads, the perpetrator of sacrilege pursued by the gods, all who were starving or in despair strove to reach the port where the Carthaginian broker was recruiting soldiers. Usually the Republic kept its promises. This time, however, the eagerness of its avarice had brought it into perilous disgrace. Numidians, Libyans, the whole of Africa was about to fall upon Carthage. Only the sea was open to it, and there it met with the Romans; so that, like a man assailed by murderers, it felt death all around it.

It was quite necessary to have recourse to Gisco, and the Barbarians accepted his intervention. One morning they saw the chains of the harbour lowered, and three flat-bottomed boats passing through the canal of the Tænia entered the lake.

Gisco was visible on the first at the prow. Behind him rose an enormous chest, higher than a catafalque, and furnished with rings like hanging crowns. Then appeared the legion of interpreters, with their hair dressed like sphinxes, and with parrots tattooed on their breasts. Friends and slaves followed, all without arms, and in such numbers that they shouldered one another. The three long, dangerously-loaded barges advanced amid the shouts of the onlooking army.

As soon as Gisco disembarked, the soldiers ran to meet him. He had a sort of tribune erected with knapsacks, and declared that he should not depart before he had paid them all in full.

There was an outburst of applause, and it was a long time before he was able to speak.

Then he censured the wrongs done to the Republic, and to the Barbarians; the fault lay with a few mutineers who had alarmed Carthage by their violence. The best proof of good intention on the part of the latter was that it was he, the eternal adversary of the Suffet Hanno, who was sent to them. They must not credit the people with the folly of desiring to provoke brave men, nor with ingratitude enough not to recognise their services; and Gisco began to pay the soldiers, commencing with the Libyans. As they had declared that the lists were untruthful, he made no use of them.

They defiled before him according to nationality, opening their fingers to show the number of their years of service; they were marked in succession with green paint on the left arm; the scribes dipped into the yawning coffer, while others made holes wills a style on a sheet of lead.

A man passed walking heavily like an ox.

"Come up beside me," said the Suffet, suspecting some fraud; "how many years have you served?"

"Twelve," replied the Libyan.

Gisco slipped his fingers under his chin, for the chin-piece of the helmet used in course of time to occasion two callosities there; these were called carobs, and "to have the carobs" was an expression used to denote a veteran.

"Thief!" exclaimed the Suffet, "your shoulders ought to have what your face lacks!" and tearing off his tunic he laid bare his back which was covered with a bleeding scab; he was a labourer from Hippo-Zarytus. Hootings were raised, and he was decapitated.

As soon as night fell, Spendius went and roused the Libyans, and said to them:

"When the Ligurians, Greeks, Balearians, and men of Italy are paid, they will return. But as for you, you will remain in Africa, scattered through your tribes, and without any means of defence! It will be then that the Republic will take its revenge! Mistrust the journey! Are you going to believe everything that is said? Both the Suffets are agreed, and this one is imposing on you! Remember the Island of Bones, and Xanthippus, whom they sent back to Sparta in a rotten galley!"

"How are we to proceed?" they asked.

"Reflect!" said Spendius.

The two following days were spent in paying the men of Magdala, Leptis, and Hecatompylos; Spendius went about among the Gauls.

"They are paying off the Libyans, and then they will discharge the Greeks, the Balearians, the Asiatics and all the rest! But you, who are few in number, will receive nothing! You will see your native lands no more! You will have no ships, and they will kill you to save your food!"

The Gauls came to the Suffet. Autaritus, he whom he had wounded at Hamilcar's palace, put questions to him, but was repelled by the slaves, and disappeared swearing that he would be revenged.

The demands and complaints multiplied. The most obstinate penetrated at night into the Suffet's tent; they took his hands and sought to move him by making him feel their toothless mouths, their wasted arms, and the scars of their wounds. Those who had not yet been paid were growing angry, those who had received the money demanded more for their horses; and vagabonds and outlaws assumed soldiers' arms and declared that they were being forgotten. Every minute there arrived whirlwinds of men, as it were; the tents strained and fell; the multitude, thick pressed between the ramparts of the camp, swayed with loud shouts from the gates to the centre. When the tumult grew excessively violent Gisco would rest one elbow on his ivory sceptre and stand motionless looking at the sea with his fingers buried in his beard.

Matho frequently went off to speak with Spendius; then he would again place himself in front of the Suffet, and Gisco could feel his eyes continually like two flaming phalaricas darted against him. Several times they hurled reproaches at each other over the heads of the crowd, but without making themselves heard. The distribution, meanwhile, continued, and the Suffet found expedients to remove every obstacle.

The Greeks tried to quibble about differences in currency, but he furnished them with such explanations that they retired without a murmur. The Negroes demanded white shells such as are used for trading in the interior of Africa, but when he offered to send to Carthage for them they accepted money like the rest.

But the Balearians had been promised something better, namely, women. The Suffet replied that a whole caravan of maidens was expected for them, but the journey was long and would require six moons more. When they were fat and well rubbed with benjamin they should be sent in ships to the ports of the Balearians.

Suddenly Zarxas, now handsome and vigorous, leaped like a mountebank upon the shoulders of his friends and cried:

"Have you reserved any of them for the corpses?" at the same time pointing to the gale of Khamon in Carthage.

The brass plates with which it was furnished from top to bottom shone in the sun's latest fires, and the Barbarians believed that they could discern on it a trail of blood. Every time that Gisco wished to speak their shouts began again. At last he descended with measured steps, and shut himself up in his tent.

When he left it at sunrise his interpreters, who used to sleep outside, did not stir; they lay on their backs with their eyes fixed, their tongues between their teeth, and their faces of a bluish colour. White mucus flowed from their nostrils, and their limbs were stiff, as if they had all been frozen by the cold during the night. Each had a little noose of rushes round his neck.

From that time onward the rebellion was unchecked. The murder of the Balearians which had been recalled by Zarxas strengthened the distrust inspired by Spendius. They imagined that the Republic was always trying to deceive them. An end must be put to it! The interpreters should be dispensed with! Zarxas sang war-songs with a sling around his head; Autaritus brandished his great sword; Spendius whispered a word to one or gave a dagger to another. The boldest endeavoured to pay themselves, while those who were less frenzied wished to have the distribution continued. No one now relinquished his arms, and the anger of all combined into a tumultuous hatred of Gisco.

Some got up beside him. So long as they vociferated abuse they were listened to with patience; but if they tried to utter the least word in his behalf they were immediately stoned, or their heads were cut off by a sabre-stroke from behind. The heap of knapsacks was redder than an altar.

They became terrible after their meal and when they had drunk wine! This was an enjoyment forbidden in the Punic armies under pain of death, and they raised their cups in the direction of Carthage in derision of its discipline. Then they returned to the slaves of the exchequer and again began to kill. The word *strike*, though different in each language, was understood by all.

Gisco was well aware that he was being abandoned by his country; but in spite of its ingratitude he would not dishonour it. When they reminded him that they had been promised ships, he swore by Moloch to provide them himself at his own expense, and pulling off his necklace of blue stones he threw it into the crowd as the pledge of his oath.

Then the Africans claimed the corn in accordance with the engagements made by the Great Council. Gisco spread out the accounts of the Syssitia traced in violet pigment on sheep skins; and read out all that had entered Carthage month by month and day by day.

Suddenly he stopped with gaping eyes, as if he had just discovered his sentence of death among the figures.

The Ancients had, in fact, fraudulently reduced them, and the corn sold during the most calamitous period of the war was set down at so low a rate that, blindness apart, it was impossible to believe it.

"Speak!" they shouted. "Louder! Ah! he is trying to lie, the coward! Don't trust him."

For some time he hesitated. At last he resumed his task.

The soldiers, without suspecting that they were being deceived, accepted the accounts of the Syssitia as true. But the abundance that had prevailed at Carthage made them furiously jealous. They broke open the sycamore chest; it was three pails empty. They had seen such sums coming out of it, that they thought it inexhaustible; Gisco must have buried some in his tent. They scaled the knapsacks. Matho led them, and as they shouted "The money! the money!" Gisco at last replied:

"Let your general give it to you!"

He looked them in the face without speaking, with his great yellow eyes, and his long face that was paler than his beard. An arrow, held by its feathers, hung from the large gold ring in his ear, and a stream of blood was trickling from his tiara upon his shoulder.

At a gesture from Matho all advanced. Gisco held out his arms; Spendius tied his wrists with a slip knot; another knocked him down, and he disappeared amid the disorder of the crowd which was stumbling over the knapsacks.

They sacked his tent. Nothing was found in it except things indispensable to life; and, on a closer search, three images of Tanith, and, wrapped up in an ape's skin, a black stone which had fallen from the moon. Many Carthaginians had chosen to accompany him; they were eminent men, and all belonged to the war party.

They were dragged outside the tents and thrown into the pit used for the reception of filth. They were tied with iron chains around the body to solid stakes, and were offered food at the point of the javelin.

Autaritus overwhelmed them with invectives as he inspected them, but being quite ignorant of his language they made no reply; and the Gaul from time to time threw pebbles at their faces to make them cry out.

The next day a sort of languor took possession of the army. Now that their anger was over they were seized with anxiety. Matho was suffering from vague melancholy. It seemed to him that Salammbô had indirectly been insulted. These rich men were a kind of appendage to her person. He sat down in the night on the edge of the pit, and recognised in their groanings something of the voice of which his heart was full.

All, however, upbraided the Libyans, who alone had been paid. But while national antipathies revived, together with personal hatreds, it was felt that it would be perilous to give way to them. Reprisals after such an outrage would be formidable. It was necessary, therefore, to anticipate the vengeance of Carthage. Conventions and harangues never ceased. Every one spoke, no one was listened to; Spendius, usually so loquacious, shook his head at every proposal.

One evening he asked Matho carelessly whether there were not springs in the interior of the town.

"Not one!" replied Matho.

The next day Spendius drew him to the bank of the lake.

"Master!" said the former slave, "If your heart is dauntless, I will bring you into Carthage."

"How?" repeated the other, panting.

"Swear to execute all my commands and to follow me like a shadow!"

Then Matho, raising his arm towards the planet of Chabar, exclaimed:

"By Tanith, I swear!"

Spendius resumed:

"To-morrow after sunset you will wait for me at the foot of the aqueduct between the ninth and tenth arcades. Bring with you an iron pick, a crestless helmet, and leathern sandals."

The aqueduct of which he spoke crossed the entire isthmus obliquely—a considerable work, afterwards enlarged by the Romans. In spite of her disdain of other nations, Carthage had awkwardly borrowed this novel invention from them, just as Rome herself had built Punic galleys; and five rows of superposed arches, of a dumpy kind of architecture, with buttresses at their foot and lions' heads at the top, reached to the western part of the Acropolis, where they sank beneath the town to incline what was nearly a river into the cisterns of Megara.

Spendius met Matho here at the hour agreed upon. He fastened a sort of harpoon to the end of a cord and whirled it rapidly like a sling; the iron instrument caught fast, and they began to climb up the wall, the one after the other.

But when they had ascended to the first story the cramp fell back every time that they threw it, and in order to discover some fissure they had to walk along the edge of the cornice. At every row of arches they found that it became narrower. Then the cord relaxed. Several times it nearly broke.

At last they reached the upper platform. Spendius stooped down from time to time to feel the stones with his hand.

"Here it is," he said; "let us begin!" And leaning on the pick which Matho had brought they succeeded in disengaging one of the flagstones.

In the distance they perceived a troop of horsemen galloping on horses without bridles. Their golden bracelets leaped in the vague drapings of their cloaks. A man could be seen in front crowned with ostrich feathers, and galloping with a lance in each hand.

"Narr' Havas!" exclaimed Matho.

"What matter?" returned Spendius, and he leaped into the hole which they had just made by removing the flagstone,

Matho at his command tried to thrust out one of the blocks. But he could not move his elbows for want of room.

"We shall return," said Spendius; "go on in front." Then they ventured into the channel of water.

It reached to their waists. Soon they staggered, and were obliged to swim. Their limbs knocked against the walls of the narrow duct. The water flowed almost immediately beneath the stones above, and their faces were torn by them. Then the current carried them away. Their breasts were crushed with air heavier than that of a sepulchre, and stretching themselves out as much as possible with their heads between their arms and their knees close together, they passed like arrows into the darkness, choking, gurgling, and almost dead. Suddenly all became black before them, and the speed of the waters redoubled. They fell.

When they came to the surface again, they remained for a few minutes extended on their backs, inhaling the air delightfully. Arcades, one behind another, opened up amid large walls separating the various basins. All were filled, and the water stretched in a single sheet throughout the length of the cisterns. Through the air-holes in the cupolas on the ceiling there fell a pale brightness which spread upon the waves discs, as it were, of light, while the darkness round about thickened towards the walls and threw them back to an indefinite distance. The slightest noise made a great echo.

Spendius and Matho commenced to swim again, and passing through the opening of the arches, traversed several chambers in succession. Two other rows of smaller basins extended in a parallel direction on each side. They lost themselves; they turned, and came back again. At last something offered a resistance to their heels. It was the pavement of the gallery that ran along the cisterns.

Then, advancing with great precautions, they felt along the wall to find an outlet. But their feet slipped, and they fell into the great centre-basins. They had to climb up again, and there they fell again. They experienced terrible fatigue, which made them feel as if all their limbs had been dissolved in the water while swimming. Their eyes closed; they were in the agonies of death.

Spendius struck his hand against the bars of a grating. They shook it, it gave way, and they found themselves on the steps of a staircase. A door of bronze closed it above. With the point of a dagger they moved the bar, which was opened from without, and suddenly the pure open air surrounded them.

The night was filled with silence, and the sky seemed at an extraordinary height. Clusters of trees projected over the long lines of walls. The whole town was asleep. The fires of the outposts shone like lost stars.

Spendius, who had spent three years in the ergastulum, was but imperfectly acquainted with the different quarters. Matho conjectured that to reach Hamilcar's palace they ought to strike to the left and cross the Mappalian district.

"No," said Spendius, "take me to the temple of Tanith."

Matho wished to speak.

"Remember!" said the former slave, and raising his arm he showed him the glittering planet of Chabar.

Then Matho turned in silence towards the Acropolis.

They crept along the nopal hedges which bordered the paths. The water trickled from their limbs upon the dust. Their damp sandals made no noise; Spendius, with eyes that flamed more than torches, searched the bushes at every step—and he walked behind Matho with his hands resting on the two daggers which he carried on his arms, and which hung from below the armpit by a leathern band.

Chapter V

TANITH

AFTER LEAVING THE GARDENS MATHO AND SPENDIUS FOUND THEMSELVES checked by the rampart of Megara. But they discovered a breach in the great wall and passed through.

The ground sloped downwards, forming a kind of very broad valley. It was an exposed place.

"Listen," said Spendius, "and first of all fear nothing! I shall fulfil my promise—"

He stopped abruptly, and seemed to reflect as though searching for his words—"Do you remember that time at sunrise when I showed Carthage to you on Salammbô's terrace? We were strong that day, but you would listen to nothing!" Then in a grave voice: "Master, in the sanctuary of Tanith there is a mysterious veil, which fell from heaven and which covers the goddess."

"I know," said Matho.

Spendius resumed: "It is itself divine, for it forms part of her. The gods reside where their images are. It is because Carthage possesses it that Carthage is powerful." Then leaning over to his ear: "I have brought you with me to carry it off!"

Matho recoiled in horror. "Begone! look for some one else! I will not help you in this execrable crime!"

"But Tanith is your enemy," retorted Spendius; "she is persecuting you and you are dying through her wrath. You will be revenged upon her. She will obey you, and you will become almost immortal and invincible."

Matho bent his head. Spendius continued:

"We should succumb; the army would be annihilated of itself. We have neither flight, not succor, nor pardon to hope for! What chastisement from the gods can you be afraid of since you will have their power in your own hands? Would you rather die on the evening of a defeat, in misery beneath the shelter of a bush, or amid the outrages of the populace and the flames of funeral piles? Master, one day you will enter Carthage among the colleges of the pontiffs, who will kiss your sandals; and if the veil of Tanith weighs upon you still, you will reinstate it in its temple. Follow me! come and take it."

Matho was consumed by a terrible longing. He would have liked to possess the veil while refraining from the sacrilege. He said to himself that perhaps it would not be necessary to take it in order to monopolise its virtue. He did not go to the bottom of his thought but stopped at the boundary, where it terrified him.

"Come on!" he said; and they went off with rapid strides, side by side, and without speaking.

The ground rose again, and the dwellings were near. They turned into the narrow streets amid the darkness. The strips of esparto-grass with which the doors were closed, beat against the walls. Some camels were ruminating in a square before heaps of cut grass. Then they passed beneath a gallery covered with foliage. A pack of dogs were barking. But suddenly the space grew wider and they recognised the western face of the Acropolis. At the foot of Byrsa there stretched a long black mass: it was the temple of Tanith, a whole made up of monuments and galleries, courts and fore-courts, and bounded by a low wall of dry stones. Spendius and Matho leaped over it.

This first barrier enclosed a wood of plane-trees as a precaution against plague and infection in the air. Tents were scattered here and there, in which, during the daytime, depilatory pastes, perfumes, garments, moon-shaped cakes, and images of the goddess with representations of the temple hollowed out in blocks of alabaster, were on sale.

They had nothing to fear, for on nights when the planet did not appear, all rites were suspended; nevertheless Matho slackened his speed, and stopped before the three ebony steps leading to the second enclosure.

"Forward!" said Spendius.

Pomegranates, almond trees, cypresses and myrtles alternated in regular succession; the path, which was paved with blue pebbles, creaked beneath their footsteps, and full-blown roses formed a hanging bower over the whole length of the avenue. They arrived before an oval hole protected by a grating. Then Matho, who was frightened by the silence, said to Spendius:

"It is here that they mix the fresh water and the bitter."

"I have seen all that," returned the former slave, "in Syria, in the town of Maphug;" and they ascended into the third enclosure by a staircase of six silver steps.

A huge cedar occupied the centre. Its lowest branches were hidden beneath scraps of material and necklaces hung upon them by the faithful. They walked a few steps further on, and the front of the temple was displayed before them.

Two long porticoes, with their architraves resting on dumpy pillars, flanked a quadrangular tower, the platform of which was adorned with the crescent of a moon. On the angles of the porticoes and at the four corners of the tower stood vases filled with kindled aromatics. The capitals were laden with pomegranates and coloquintidas. Twining knots, lozenges, and rows of pearls alternated on the walls, and a hedge of silver filigree formed a wide semicircle in front of the brass staircase which led down from the vestibule.

There was a cone of stone at the entrance between a stela of gold and one of emerald, and Matho kissed his right hand as he passed beside it.

The first room was very lofty; its vaulted roof was pierced by numberless apertures, and if the head were raised the stars might be seen. All round the wall rush baskets were heaped up with the firstfruits of adolescence in the shape of beards and curls of hair; and in the centre of the circular apartment the body of a woman issued from a sheath which was covered with breasts. Fat, bearded, and with eyelids downcast, she looked as though she were smiling, while her hands were crossed upon the lower part of her big body, which was polished by the kisses of the crowd.

Then they found themselves again in the open air in a transverse corridor, wherein there was an altar of small dimensions leaning against an ivory door. There was no further passage; the priests alone could open it; for the temple was not a place of meeting for the multitude, but the private abode of a divinity.

"The enterprise is impossible," said Matho. "You had not thought of this! Let us go back!" Spendius was examining the walls.

He wanted the veil, not because he had confidence in its virtue (Spendius believed only in the Oracle), but because he was persuaded that the Carthaginians would be greatly dismayed on seeing themselves deprived of it. They walked all round behind in order to find some outlet.

Aedicules of different shapes were visible beneath clusters of turpentine trees. Here and there rose a stone phallus, and large stags roamed peacefully about, spurning the fallen fir-cones with their cloven hoofs.

But they retraced their steps between two long galleries which ran parallel to each other. There were small open cells along their sides, and tambourines and cymbals hung against their cedar columns from top to bottom. Women were sleeping stretched on mats outside the cells. Their bodies were greasy with unguents, and exhaled an odour of spices and extinguished perfuming-pans; while they were so covered with tattooings, necklaces, rings, vermilion, and antimony that, but for the motion of their breasts, they might have been taken for idols as they lay thus on the ground. There were lotus-trees encircling a fountain in which fish like Salammbô's were swimming; and then in the background, against the wall of the temple, spread a vine, the branches of which were of glass and the grape-bunches of emerald, the rays from the precious stones making a play of light through the painted columns upon the sleeping faces.

Matho felt suffocated in the warm atmosphere pressed down upon him by the cedar partitions. All these symbols of fecundation, these perfumes, radiations, and breathings overwhelmed him. Through all the mystic dazzling he kept thinking of

Salammbô. She became confused with the goddess herself, and his love unfolded itself all the more, like the great lotus-plants blooming upon the depths of the waters.

Spendius was calculating how much money he would have made in former
days by the sale of these women; and with a rapid glance he estimated the weight
of the golden necklaces as he passed by.

The temple was impenetrable on this side as on the other, and they returned
behind the first chamber. While Spendius was searching and ferreting, Matho was
prostrate before the door supplicating Tanith. He besought her not to permit the
sacrilege, and strove to soften her with caressing words, such as are used to an
angry person.

Spendius noticed a narrow aperture above the door.

"Rise!" he said to Matho, and he made him stand erect with his back against the
wall. Placing one foot in his hands, and then the other upon his head, he reached
up to the air-hole, made his way into it and disappeared. Then Matho felt a knotted cord—that one which Spendius had rolled around his body before entering the
cisterns—fall upon his shoulders, and bearing upon it with both hands he soon
found himself by the side of the other in a large hall filled with shadow.

Such an attempt was something extraordinary. The inadequacy of the means
for preventing it was a sufficient proof that it was considered impossible. The sanctuaries were protected by terror more than by their walls. Matho expected to die at
every step.

However a light was flickering far back in the darkness, and they went up to it.
It was a lamp burning in a shell on the pedestal of a statue which wore the cap of
the Kabiri. Its long blue robe was strewn with diamond discs, and its heels were fastened to the ground by chains which sank beneath the pavement. Matho suppressed
a cry. "Ah! there she is! there she is!" he stammered out. Spendius took up the lamp
in order to light himself.

"What an impious man you are!" murmured Matho, following him nevertheless.

The apartment which they entered had nothing in it but a black painting representing another woman. Her legs reached to the top of the wall, and her body
filled the entire ceiling; a huge egg hung by a thread from her navel, and she fell
head downwards upon the other wall, reaching as far as the level of the pavement,
which was touched by her pointed fingers.

They drew a hanging aside, in order to go on further; but the wind blew and
the light went out.

Then they wandered about, lost in the complications of the architecture.
Suddenly they felt something strangely soft beneath their feet. Sparks crackled
and leaped; they were walking in fire. Spendius touched the ground and perceived that it was carefully carpeted with lynx skins; then it seemed to them that

a big cord, wet, cold, and viscous, was gliding between their legs. Through some fissures cut in the wall there fell thin white rays, and they advanced by this uncertain light. At last they distinguished a large black serpent. It darted quickly away and disappeared.

"Let us fly!" exclaimed Matho. "It is she! I feel her; she is coming."

"No, no," replied Spendius, "the temple is empty."

Then a dazzling light made them lower their eyes. Next they perceived all around them an infinite number of beasts, lean, panting, with bristling claws, and mingled together one above another in a mysterious and terrifying confusion. There were serpents with feet, and bulls with wings, fishes with human heads were devouring fruit, flowers were blooming in the jaws of crocodiles, and elephants with uplifted trunks were sailing proudly through the azure like eagles. Their incomplete or multiplied limbs were distended with terrible exertion. As they thrust out their tongues they looked as though they would fain give forth their souls; and every shape was to be found among them as if the germ-receptacle had been suddenly hatched and had burst, emptying itself upon the walls of the hall.

Round the latter were twelve globes of blue crystal, supported by monsters resembling tigers. Their eyeballs were starting out of their heads like those of snails, with their dumpy loins bent they were turning round toward the background where the supreme Rabbet, the Omnifecund, the last invented, shone splendid in a chariot of ivory.

She was covered with scales, leathers, flowers, and birds as high as the waist. For earrings she had silver cymbals, which flapped against her cheeks. Her large fixed eyes gazed upon you, and a luminous stone, set in an obscene symbol on her brow, lighted the whole hall by its reflection in red copper mirrors above the door.

Mantho took a step forward; but a flag stone yielded beneath his heels and immediately the spheres began to revolve and the monsters to roar; music rose melodious and pealing, like the harmony of the planets; the tumultuous soul of Tanith was poured streaming forth. She was about to arise, as lofty as the hall and with open arms. Suddenly the monsters closed their jaws and the crystal globes revolved no longer.

Then a mournful modulation lingered for a time through the air and at last died away.

"And the veil?" said Spendius.

Nowhere could it be seen. Where was it to be found? How could it be discovered? What if the priests had hidden it? Matho experienced anguish of heart and felt as though he had been deceived in his belief.

"This way!" whispered Spendius. An inspiration guided him. He drew Matho behind Tanith's chariot, where a cleft a cubit wide ran down the wall from top to bottom.

Then they penetrated into a small and completely circular room, so lofty that it was like the interior of a pillar. In the centre there was a big black stone, of semi-spherical shape like a tambourine; flames were burning upon it; an ebony cone, bearing a head and two arms, rose behind.

But beyond it seemed as though there were a cloud wherein were twinkling stars; faces appeared in the depths of its folds—Eschmoun with the Kabiri, some of the monsters that had already been seen, the sacred beasts of the Babylonians, and others with which they were not acquainted. It passed beneath the idol's face like a mantle, and spread fully out was drawn up on the wall, to which it was fastened by the corners, appearing at once bluish as the night, yellow as the dawn, purple as the sun, multitudinous, diaphanous, sparkling, light. It was the mantle of the goddess, the holy zaïmph which might not be seen.

Both turned pale.

"Take it!" said Matho at last.

Spendius did not hesitate, and leaning upon the idol he unfastened the veil, which sank to the ground. Matho laid his hand upon it; then he put his head through the opening, then he wrapped it about his body, and he spread out his arms the better to view it.

"Let us go!" said Spendius.

Matho stood panting with his eyes fixed upon the pavement. Suddenly he exclaimed:

"But what if I went to her? I fear her beauty no longer! What could she do against me? I am now more than a man. I could pass through flames or walk upon the sea! I am transported! Salammbô! Salammbô! I am your master!"

His voice was like thunder. He seemed to Spendius to have grown taller and transformed.

A sound of footsteps drew near, a door opened, and a man appeared, a priest with lofty cap and staring eyes. Before he could make a gesture Spendius had rushed upon him, and clasping him in his arms had buried both his daggers in his sides. His head rang upon the pavement.

Then they stood for a while, as motionless as the corpse, listening. Nothing could be heard but the murmuring of the wind through the half-opened door.

The latter led into a narrow passage. Spendius advanced along it, Matho followed him, and they found themselves almost immediately in the third enclosure, between the lateral porticoes, in which were the dwellings of the priests.

Behind the cells there must be a shorter way out. They hastened along.

Spendius squatted down at the edge of the fountain and washed his blood-stained hands. The women slept. The emerald vine shone. They resumed their advance.

But something was running behind them under the trees; and Matho, who bore the veil, several times felt that it was being pulled very gently from below. It was a large cynocephalus, one of those which dwelt at liberty within the enclosure of the goddess. It clung to the mantle as though it had been conscious of the theft. They did not dare to strike it, however, fearing that it might redouble its cries; suddenly its anger subsided, and it trotted close beside them swinging its body with its long hanging arms. Then at the barrier it leaped at a bound into a palm tree.

When they had left the last enclosure they directed their steps towards Hamilcar's palace, Spendius understanding that it would be useless to try to dissuade Matho.

They went by the street of the Tanners, the square of Muthumbal, the green market and the cross-ways of Cynasyn. At the angle of a wall a man drew back frightened by the sparkling thing which pierced the darkness.

"Hide the zaïmph!" said Spendius.

Other people passed them, but without perceiving them.

At last they recognised the houses of Megara.

The pharos, which was built behind them on the summit of the cliff, lit up the heavens with a great red brightness, and the shadow of the palace, with its rising terraces, projected a monstrous pyramid, as it were, upon the gardens. They entered through the hedge of jujube-trees, beating down the branches with blows of the dagger.

The traces of the feast of the Mercenaries were everywhere still manifest. The parks were broken up, the trenches drained, the doors of the ergastulum open. No one was to be seen about the kitchens or cellars. They wondered at the silence, which was occasionally broken by the hoarse breathing of the elephants moving in their shackles, and the crepitation of the pharos, in which a pile of aloes was burning.

Matho, however, kept repeating:

"But where is she? I wish to see her! Lead me!"

"It is a piece of insanity!" Spendius kept saying. "She will call, her slaves will run up, and in spite of your strength you will die!"

They reached thus the galley staircase. Matho raised his head, and thought that he could perceive far above a vague brightness, radiant and soft. Spendius sought to restrain him, but he dashed up the steps.

As he found himself again in places where he had already seen her, the interval of the days that had passed was obliterated from his memory. But now had she been singing among the tables; she had disappeared, and he had since been continually ascending this staircase. The sky above his head was covered with fires; the sea filled the horizon; at each step he was surrounded by a still greater immensity, and he continued to climb upward with that strange facility which we experience in dreams.

The rustling of the veil as it brushed against the stones recalled his new power to him; but in the excess of his hope he could no longer tell what he was to do; this uncertainty alarmed him.

From time to time he would press his face against the quadrangular openings in the closed apartments, and he thought that in several of the latter he could see persons asleep.

The last story, which was narrower, formed a sort of dado on the summit of the terraces. Matho walked round it slowly.

A milky light filled the sheets of talc which closed the little apertures in the wall, and in their symmetrical arrangement they looked in the darkness like rows of delicate pearls. He recognised the red door with the black cross. The throbbing of his heart increased. He would fain have fled. He pushed the door and it opened.

A galley-shaped lamp hung burning in the back part of the room, and three rays, emitted from its silver keel, trembled on the lofty wainscots, which were painted red with black bands. The ceiling was an assemblage of small beams, with amethysts and topazes amid their gilding in the knots of the wood. On both the great sides of the apartment there stretched a very low bed made with white leathern straps; while above, semi-circles like shells, opened in the thickness of the wall, suffered a garment to come out and hang down to the ground.

There was an oval basin with a step of onyx round it; delicate slippers of serpent skin were standing on the edge, together with an alabaster flagon. The trace of a wet footstep might be seen beyond. Exquisite scents were evaporating.

Matho glided over the pavement, which was encrusted with gold, mother-of-pearl, and glass; and, in spite of the polished smoothness of the ground, it seemed to him that his feet sank as though he were walking on sand.

Behind the silver lamp he had perceived a large square of azure held in the air by four cords from above, and he advanced with loins bent and month open.

Flamingoes' wings, fitted on branches of black coral, lay about among purple cushions, tortoiseshell strigils, cedar boxes, and ivory spatulas. There were antelopes' horns with rings and bracelets strung upon them; and clay vases were cooling in the wind in the cleft of the wall on a lattice-work of reeds. Several times he struck his foot, for the ground had various levels of unequal height, which formed a succession of apartments, as it were, in the room. In the background there were silver balustrades surrounding a carpet strewn with painted flowers. At last he came to the hanging bed beside an ebony stool serving to get into it.

But the light ceased at the edge; and the shadow, like a great curtain, revealed only a corner of the red mattress with the extremity of a little naked loot lying upon its ankle. Then Matho look up the lamp very gently.

She was sleeping with her cheek in one hand and with the other arm extended.

Her ringlets were spread about her in such abundance that she appeared to be lying on black feathers, and her ample white tunic wound in soft draperies to her feet following the curves of her person. Her eyes were just visible beneath her half-closed eyelids. The curtains, which stretched perpendicularly, enveloped her in a bluish atmosphere, and the motion of her breathing, communicating itself to the cords, seemed to rock her in the air. A long mosquito was buzzing.

Matho stood motionless holding the silver lamp at arm's length; but on a sudden the mosquito-net caught fire and disappeared, and Salammbô awoke.

The fire had gone out of itself. She did not speak. The lamp caused great luminous moires to flicker on the wainscots.

"What is it?" she said.

He replied:

" 'Tis the veil of the goddess!"

"The veil of the goddess!" cried Salammbô, and supporting herself on both clenched hands she leaned shuddering out. He resumed:

"I have been in the depths of the sanctuary to seek it for you! Look!" The zaïmph shone a mass of rays.

"Do you remember it?" said Matho. "You appeared at night in my dreams, but I did not guess the mute command of your eyes!" She put out one foot upon the ebony stool. "Had I understood I should have hastened hither, I should have forsaken the army, I should not have left Carthage. To obey you I would go down through the caverns of Hadrumetum into the kingdom of the shades!—Forgive me! it was as though mountains were weighing upon my days; and yet something drew me on! I tried to come to you! Should I ever have dared this without the Gods!—Let us go! you must follow me! or, if you do not wish to do so, I will remain. What matters it to me!—Drown my soul in your breath! Let my lips be crushed with kissing your hands!"

"Let me see it!" she said. "Nearer! nearer!"

Day was breaking, and the sheets of talc in the walls were filled with a vinous colour. Salammbô leaned fainting against the cushions of the bed.

"I love you!" cried Matho.

"Give it!" she stammered out, and they drew closer together.

She kept advancing, clothed in her white trailing simar, and with her large eyes fastened on the veil. Matho gazed at her, dazzled by the splendours of her head, and, holding out the zaïmph towards her, was about to enfold her in an embrace. She was stretching out her arms. Suddenly she stopped, and they stood looking at each other, open-mouthed.

Then without understanding the meaning of his solicitation a horror seized upon her. Her delicate eyebrows rose, her lips opened; she trembled. At last she struck one of the brass pateras which hung at the corners of the red mattress, crying:

"To the rescue! to the rescue! Back, sacrilegious man! infamous and accursed! Help, Taanach, Kroum, Ewa, Micipsa, Schaoul!"

And the scared face of Spendius, appearing in the wall between the clay flagons, cried out these words:

"Fly! they are hastening hither!"

A great tumult came upwards shaking the staircases, and a flood of people, women, serving-men, and slaves, rushed into the room with slakes, tomahawks, cutlasses, and daggers. They were nearly paralysed with indignation on perceiving a man; the female servants uttered funeral wailings, and the eunuchs grew pale beneath their black skins.

Matho was standing behind the balustrades. With the zaïmph which was wrapped about him, he looked like a sidereal god surrounded by the firmament. The slaves were going to fall upon him, but she stopped them:

"Touch it not! It is the mantle of the goddess!"

She had drawn back into a corner; but she took a step towards him, and stretched forth her naked arm:

"A curse upon you, you who have plundered Tanith! Hatred, vengeance, massacre, and grief! May Gurzil, god of battles, rend you! may Mastiman, god of the the dead, stifle you! and may the Other—he who may not be named—burn you!"

Matho uttered a cry as though he had received a sword-thrust. She repeated several times: "Begone! begone!"

The crowd of servants spread out, and Matho, with hanging head, passed slowly through the midst of them; but at the door he stopped, for the fringe of the zaïmph had caught on one of the golden stars with which the flagstones were paved. He pulled it off abruptly with a movement of his shoulder and went down the staircases.

Spendius, bounding from terrace to terrace, and leaping over the hedges and trenches, had escaped from the gardens. He reached the foot of the pharos. The wall was discontinued at this spot, so inaccessible was the cliff. He advanced to the edge, lay down on his back, and let himself slide, feet foremost, down the whole length of it to the bottom; then by swimming he reached the Cape of the Tombs, made a wide circuit of the salt lagoon, and re-entered the camp of the Barbarians in the evening.

The sun had risen; and, like a retreating lion, Matho went down the paths, casting terrible glances around him.

A vague clamor reached his ears. It had stalled from the palace, and it was beginning afresh in the distance, towards the Acropolis. Some said that the treasure of the Republic had been seized in the temple of Moloch; others spoke of the assassination of a priest. It was thought, moreover, that the Barbarians had entered the city.

Matho, who did not know how to get out of the enclosures, walked straight before him. He was seen, and an outcry was raised. Everyone understood; and there was consternation, and then immense wrath.

From the bottom of the Mappalian quarter, from the heights of the Acropolis, from the catacombs, from the borders of the lake, the multitude came in haste. The patricians left their palaces, and the traders left their shops; the women forsook their children; swords, hatchets, and sticks were seized; but the obstacle which had stayed Salammbô stayed them. How could the veil be taken back? The mere sight of it was a crime; it was of the nature of the gods, and contact with it was death.

The despairing priests wrung their hands on the peristyles of the temples. The guards of the Legion galloped about at random; the people climbed upon the houses, the terraces, the shoulders of the colossuses, and the masts of the ships. He went on, nevertheless, and the rage, and the terror also, increased at each of his steps; the streets cleared at his approach, and the torrent of flying men streamed on both sides up to the tops of the walls. Everywhere he could perceive only eyes opened widely as if to devour him, chattering teeth and outstretched fists, and Salammbô's imprecations resounded many times renewed.

Suddenly a long arrow whistled past, then another, and stones began to buzz about him; but the missiles, being badly aimed (for there was the dread of hitting the zaïmph), passed over his head. Moreover, he made a shield of the veil, holding it to the right, to the left, before him and behind him; and they could devise no expedient. He quickened his steps more and more, advancing through the open streets. They were barred with cords, chariots, and snares; and all his windings brought him back again. At last he entered the square of Khamon where the Balearians had perished, and stopped, growing pale as one about to die. This time he was surely lost, and the multitude clapped their hands.

He ran up to the great gate, which was closed. It was very high, made throughout of heart of oak, with iron nails and sheathed with brass. Matho flung himself against it. The people stamped their feet with joy as they saw the impotence of his fury; then he took his sandal, spit upon it, and beat the immovable panels with it. The whole city howled. The veil was forgotten now, and they were about to crush him. Matho gazed with wide vacant eyes upon the crowd. His temples were throbbing with violence enough to stun him, and he felt a numbness as of intoxication creeping over him. Suddenly he caught sight of the long chain used in working the swinging of the gate. With a bound he grasped it, stiffening his arms, and making a buttress of his feet, and at last the huge leaves partly opened.

Then when he was outside he took the great zaïmph from his neck, and raised it as high as possible above his head. The material, upborne by the sea breeze, shone in the sunlight with its colours, its gems, and the figures of its gods. Matho bore it thus across the whole plain as far as the soldiers' tents, and the people on the walls watched the fortune of Carthage depart.

Chapter VI

HANNO

"I OUGHT TO HAVE CARRIED HER OFF!" MATHO SAID IN THE EVENING TO Spendius. "I should have seized her, and torn her from her house! No one would have dared to touch me!"

Spendius was not listening to him. Stretched on his back he was taking delicious rest beside a large jar filled with honey-coloured water, into which he would dip his head from time to time in order to drink more copiously.

Matho resumed:

"What is to be done? How can we re-enter Carthage?"

"I do not know," said Spendius.

Such impassibility exasperated Matho and he exclaimed:

"Why! the fault is yours! You carry me away, and then you forsake me, coward that you are! Why, pray, should I obey you? Do you think that you are my master? Ah! you prostituter, you slave, you son of a slave!" He ground his teeth and raised his broad hand above Spendius.

The Greek did not reply. An earthen lamp was burning gently against the tent-pole, where the zaïmph shone amid the hanging panoply. Suddenly Matho put on his cothurni, buckled on his brazen jacket of mail, and took his helmet.

"Where are you going?" asked Spendius.

"I am returning! Let me alone! I will bring her back! And if they show themselves I will crush them like vipers! I will put her to death, Spendius! Yes," he repeated, "I will kill her! You shall see, I will kill her!"

But Spendius, who was listening eagerly, snatched up the zaïmph abruptly and threw it into a corner, heaping up fleeces above it. A murmuring of voices was heard, torches gleamed, and Narr' Havas entered, followed by about twenty men.

They wore white woollen cloaks, long daggers, copper necklaces, wooden earrings, and boots of hyena skin; and standing on the threshold they leaned upon their lances like herdsmen resting themselves. Narr' Havas was the handsomest of all; his slender arms were bound with straps ornamented with pearls. The golden circlet which fastened his ample garment about his head held an ostrich feather which hung down behind upon his shoulder; his teeth were displayed in a continual smile; his eyes seemed sharpened like arrows, and there was something observant and airy about his whole demeanour.

He declared that he had come to join the Mercenaries, for the Republic had long been threatening his kingdom. Accordingly he was interested in assisting the Barbarians, and he might also be of service to them.

"I will provide you with elephants (my forests are full of them), wine, oil, barley, dates, pitch and sulphur for sieges, twenty thousand foot-soldiers and ten thousand horses. If I address myself to you, Matho, it is because the possession of the zaïmph has made you chief man in the army. Moreover," he added, "we are old friends."

Matho, however, was looking at Spendius, who, seated on the sheep-skins, was listening, and giving little nods of assent the while. Narr' Havas continued speaking. He called the gods to witness he cursed Carthage. In his imprecations he broke a javelin. All his men uttered simultaneously a loud howl, and Matho, carried away by so much passion, exclaimed that he accepted the alliance.

A white bull and a black sheep, the symbols of day and night, were then brought, and their throats were cut on the edge of a ditch. When the latter was full of blood they dipped their arms into it. Then Narr' Havas spread out his hand upon Matho's breast, and Matho did the same to Narr' Havas. They repeated the stain upon the canvas of their tents. Afterwards they passed the night in eating, and the remaining portions of the meat were burnt together with the skin, bones, horns, and hoofs.

Matho had been greeted with great shouting when he had come back bearing the veil of the goddess; even those who were not of the Chanaanitish religion were made by their vague enthusiasm to feel the arrival of a genius. As to seizing the zaïmph, no one thought of it, for the mysterious manner in which he had acquired it was sufficient in the minds of the Barbarians to justify its possession; such were the thoughts of the soldiers of the African race. The others, whose hatred was not of such long standing, did not know how to make up their minds. If they had had ships they would immediately have departed.

Spendius, Narr' Havas, and Matho despatched men to all the tribes on Punic soil.

Carthage was sapping the strength of these nations. She wrung exorbitant taxes from them, and arrears or even murmurings were punished with fetters, the axe, or the cross. It was necessary to cultivate whatever suited the Republic, and to furnish what she demanded; no one had the right of possessing a weapon; when villages rebelled the inhabitants were sold; governors were esteemed like wine-presses, according to the quantity which they succeeded in extracting. Then beyond the regions immediately subject to Carthage extended the allies, paying only a moderate tribute, and behind the allies roamed the Nomads, who might be let loose upon them. By this system the crops were always abundant, the studs skilfully managed, and the plantations superb.

The elder Cato, a master in the matters of tillage and slaves, was amazed at it ninety-two years later, and the death-cry which he repeated continually at Rome was but the exclamation of jealous greed.

During the last war the exactions had been increased, so that nearly all the towns of Libya had surrendered to Regulus. To punish them, a thousand talents, twenty thousand oxen, three hundred bags of gold dust, and considerable advances of grain had been exacted from them, and the chiefs of the tribes had been crucified or thrown to the lions.

Tunis especially execrated Carthage! Older than the metropolis, it could not forgive her her greatness, and it fronted her walls crouching in the mire on the water's edge like a venomous beast watching her. Transportations, massacres, and epidemics did not weaken it. It had assisted Archagathas, the son of Agathocles, and the Eaters of Uncleanness found arms there at once.

The couriers had not yet set out when universal rejoicing broke out in the provinces. Without waiting for anything they strangled the comptrollers of the houses and the functionaries of the Republic in the baths; they took the old weapons that had been concealed out of the caves; they forged swords with the iron of the ploughs; the children sharpened javelins at the doors, and the women gave their necklaces, rings, earrings, and everything that could be employed for the destruction of Carthage. Piles of lances were heaped up in the county towns like sheaves of maize. Cattle and money were sent off. Matho speedily paid the Mercenaries their arrears, and owing to this, which was Spendius's idea, he was appointed commander-in-chief—the schalischim of the Barbarians.

Reinforcements of men poured in at the same time. The aborigines appeared first, and were followed by the slaves from the country; caravans of Negroes were seized and armed, and merchants on their way to Carthage, despairing of any more certain profit, mingled with the Barbarians. Numerous bands were continually arriving. From the heights of the Acropolis the growing army might be seen.

But the guards of the Legion were posted as sentries on the platform of the aqueduct, and near them rose at intervals brazen vats, in which floods of asphalt were boiling. Below in the plain the great crowd stirred tumultuously. They were in a state of uncertainty, feeling the embarrassment with which Barbarians are always inspired when they meet with walls.

Utica and Hippo-Zarytus refused their alliance. Phoenician colonies like Carthage, they were self-governing, and always had clauses inserted in the treaties concluded by the Republic to distinguish them from the latter. Nevertheless they respected this stronger sister of theirs who protected them, and they did not think that she could be vanquished by a mass of Barbarians; these would on the contrary be themselves exterminated. They desired to remain neutral and to live at peace.

But their position rendered them indispensable. Utica, at the foot of the gulf, was convenient for bringing assistance into Carthage from without. If Utica alone were taken, Hippo-Zarytus, six hours further distant along the coast, would take its place, and the metropolis, being revictualled in this way, would be impregnable.

Spendius wished the siege to be undertaken immediately. Narr' Havas was opposed to this: an advance should first be made upon the frontier. This was the opinion of the veterans, and of Matho himself, and it was decided that Spendius should go to attack Utica, and Matho Hippo-Zarytus, while in the third place the main body should rest on Tunis and occupy the plain of Carthage, Autaritus being in command. As to Narr' Havas, he was to return to his own kingdom to procure elephants and to scour the roads with his cavalry.

The women cried out loudly against this decision; they coveted the jewels of the Punic ladies. The Libyans also protested. They had been summoned against Carthage, and now they were going away from it! The soldiers departed almost alone. Matho commanded his own companions, together with the Iberians, Lusitanians, and the men of the West, and of the islands; all those who spoke Greek had asked for Spendius on account of his cleverness.

Great was the stupefaction when the army was seen suddenly in motion; it stretched along beneath the mountain of Ariana on the road to Utica beside the sea. A fragment remained before Tunis, the rest disappeared to reappear on the other shore of the gulf on the outskirts of the woods in which they were lost.

They were perhaps eighty thousand men. The two Tyrian cities would offer no resistance, and they would return against Carthage. Already there was a considerable army attacking it from the base of the isthmus, and it would soon perish from famine, for it was impossible to live without the aid of the provinces, the citizens not paying contributions as they did at Rome. Carthage was wanting in political genius. Her eternal anxiety for gain prevented her from having the prudence which results from loftier ambitions. A galley anchored on the Libyan sands, it was with toil that she maintained her position. The nations roared like billows around her, and the slightest storm shook this formidable machine.

The treasury was exhausted by the Roman war and by all that had been squandered and lost in the bargaining with the Barbarians. Nevertheless soldiers must be had, and not a government would trust the Republic! Ptolemæus had lately refused it two thousand talents. Moreover the rape of the veil disheartened them. Spendius had clearly foreseen this.

But the nation, feeling that it was haled, clasped its money and its gods to its heart, and its patriotism was sustained by the very constitution of its government.

First, the power rested with all, without any one being strong enough to engross it. Private debts were considered as public debts, men of Chanaanitish race had a monopoly of commerce, and by multiplying the profits of piracy with those of usury, by hard dealings in lands and slaves and with the poor, fortunes were sometimes made. These alone opened up all the magistracies, and although authority and money were perpetuated in the same families, people tolerated the oligarchy because they hoped ultimately to share in it.

The societies of merchants, in which the laws were elaborated, chose the inspectors of the exchequer, who on leaving office nominated the hundred members of the Council of the Ancients, themselves dependent on the Grand Assembly, or general gathering of all the rich. As to the two Suffets, the relics of the monarchy and the less than consuls, they were taken from distinct families on the same day. All kinds of enmities were contrived between them, so that they might mutually weaken each other. They could not deliberate concerning war, and when they were vanquished the Great Council crucified them.

The power of Carthage emanated, therefore, from the Syssitia, that is to say, from a large court in the centre of Malqua, at the place, it was said, where the first bark of Phœnician sailors had touched, the sea having retired a long way since then. It was a collection of little rooms of archaic architecture, built of palm trunks with corners of stone, and separated from one another so as to accommodate the various societies separately. The rich crowded there all day to discuss their own concerns and those of the government, from the procuring of pepper to the extermination of Rome. Thrice in a moon they would have their beds brought up to the lofty terrace running along the wall of the court, and they might be seen from below at table in the air, without cothurni or cloaks, with their diamond-covered fingers wandering over the dishes, and their large earrings hanging down among the flagons—all fat and lusty, half-naked, smiling and eating beneath the blue sky, like great sharks sporting in the sea.

But just now they were unable to dissemble their anxiety; they were too pale for that. The crowd which waited for them at the gates escorted them to their palaces in order to obtain some news from them. As in times of pestilence, all the houses were shut; the streets would fill and suddenly clear again; people ascended the Acropolis or ran to the harbour, and the Great Council deliberated every night. At last the people were convened in the square of Khamon, and it was decided to leave the management of things to Hanno, the conqueror of Hecatompylos.

He was a true Carthaginian, devout, crafty, and pitiless towards the people of Africa. His revenues equalled those of the Barcas. No one had such experience in administrative affairs.

He decreed the enrolment of all healthy citizens, he placed catapults on the towers, he exacted exorbitant supplies of arms, he even ordered the construction of fourteen galleys which were not required, and he desired everything to be registered and carefully set down in writing. He had himself conveyed to the arsenal, the pharos, and the treasuries of the temples; his great litter was continually to be seen swinging from step to step as it ascended the staircases of the Acropolis. And then in his palace at night, being unable to sleep, he would yell out warlike manoeuvres in terrible tones so as to prepare himself for the fray.

In their extremity of terror all became brave. The rich ranged themselves in line along the Mappalian district at cockcrow, and tucking up their robes practised themselves in handling the pike. But for want of an instructor they had disputes about it. They would sit down breathless upon the tombs and then begin again. Several even dieted themselves. Some imagined that it was necessary to eat a great deal in order to acquire strength, while others who were inconvenienced by their corpulence weakened themselves with fasts in order to become thin.

Utica had already called several times upon Carthage for assistance; but Hanno would not set out until the engines of war had been supplied with the last screw. He lost three moons more in equipping the one hundred and twelve elephants that were lodged in the ramparts. They were the conquerors of Regulus; the people loved them; it was impossible to treat such old friends too well. Hanno had the brass plates which adorned their breasts recast, their tusks gilt, their towers enlarged, and caparisons, edged with very heavy fringes, cut out of the handsomest purple. Finally, as their drivers were called Indians (after the first ones, no doubt, who came from the Indies) he ordered them all to be costumed after the Indian fashion; that is to say, with white pads round their temples, and small drawers of byssus, which with their transverse folds looked like two valves of a shell applied to the hips.

The army under Autaritus still remained before Tunis. It was hidden behind a wall made with mud from the lake, and protected on the top by thorny brushwood. Some Negroes had planted tall sticks here and there bearing frightful faces— human masks made with birds' feathers, and jackals' or serpents' heads—which gaped towards the enemy for the purpose of terrifying him; and the Barbarians, reckoning themselves invincible through these means, danced, wrestled, and juggled, convinced that Carthage would perish before long. Any one but Hanno would easily have crushed such a multitude, hampered as it was with herds and women. Moreover, they knew nothing of drill, and Autaritus was so disheartened that he had ceased to require it.

They stepped aside when he passed by rolling his big blue eyes. Then on reaching the edge of the lake he would draw back his sealskin cloak, unfasten the cord which tied up his long red hair, and soak the latter in the water. He regretted that he had not deserted to the Romans along with the two thousand Gauls of the temple of Eryx.

Often the sun would suddenly lose his rays in the middle of the day. Then the gulf and the open sea would seem as motionless as molten lead. A cloud of brown dust stretching perpendicularly would speed whirling along; the palm trees would bend and the sky disappear, while stones would be heard rebounding on the animals' cruppers; and the Gaul, his lips glued against the holes in his tent, would gasp with exhaustion and melancholy. His thoughts would be of the scent of the pastures on autumn mornings, of snowflakes, or of the bellowing of the urus lost in the fog, and closing his eyelids he would in imagination behold the fires in long, straw-roofed cottages flickering on the marshes in the depths of the woods.

Others regretted their native lands as well as he, even though they might not be so far away. Indeed the Carthaginian captives could distinguish the velaria spread over the courtyards of their houses, beyond the gulf on the slopes of Byrsa. But sentries marched round them continually. They were all fastened to a common chain. Each one wore an iron carcanet, and the crowd was never weary of coming to gaze at them. The women would show their little children the handsome robes hanging in tatters on their wasted limbs.

Whenever Autaritus looked at Gisco he was seized with rage at the recollection of the insult that he had received, and he would have killed him but for the oath which he had taken to Narr' Havas. Then he would go back into his tent and drink a mixture of barley and cumin until he swooned away from intoxication—to awake afterwards in broad day light consumed with horrible thirst.

Matho, meanwhile, was besieging Hippo-Zarytus. But the town was protected by a lake, communicating with the sea. It had three lines of circumvallation, and upon the heights which surrounded it there extended a wall fortified with towers. He had never commanded in such an enterprise before. Moreover, he was beset with thoughts of Salammbô, and he raved in the delight of her beauty as in the sweetness of a vengeance that transported him with pride. He felt an acrid, frenzied, permanent want to see her again. He even thought of presenting himself as the bearer of a flag of truce, in the hope that once within Carthage he might make his way to her. Often he would cause the assault to be sounded and waiting for nothing rush upon the mole which it was sought to construct in the sea. He would snatch up the stones with his hands, overturn, strike, and deal sword-thrusts everywhere. The Barbarians would dash on pell-mell; the ladders would break with a loud crash, and masses of men would tumble into the water, causing it to fly up in red waves against the walls. Finally the tumult would subside, and the soldiers would retire to make a fresh beginning.

Matho would go and seat himself outside the tents, wipe his blood-splashed face with his arm, and gaze at the horizon in the direction of Carthage.

In front of him, among the olives, palms, myrtles and planes, stretched two broad ponds which met another lake, the outlines of which could not be seen. Behind one mountain other mountains reared themselves, and in the middle of the immense lake rose an island perfectly black and pyramidal in form. On the left, at the extremity of the gulf, were sand-heaps like arrested waves, large and pale, while the sea, flat as a pavement of lapis-lazuli, ascended by insensible degrees to the edge of the sky. The verdure of the country was lost in places beneath long sheets of yellow; carobs were shining like knobs of coral; vine branches drooped from the tops of the sycamores; the murmuring of the water could be heard; crested larks were hopping about, and the sun's latest fires gilded the carapaces of the tortoises as they came forth from the reeds to inhale the breeze.

Matho would heave deep sighs. He would lie flat on his face, with his nails buried in the soil, and weep; he felt wretched, paltry, forsaken. Never would he possess her, and he was unable even to take a town.

At night when alone in his tent he would gaze upon the zaïmph. Of what use to him was this thing which belonged to the gods?—and doubts crept into the Barbarian's thoughts. Then, on the contrary, it would seem to him that the vesture of the goddess was depending from Salammbô, and that a portion of her soul hovered in it, subtler than a breath; and he would feel it, breathe it in, bury his face in it, and kiss it with sobs. He would cover his shoulders with it in order to delude himself into believing that lie was beside her.

Sometimes he would suddenly steal away, stride in the starlight over the sleeping soldiers as they lay wrapped in their cloaks, spring upon a horse on reaching the camp gates, and two hours later be at Utica in Spendius's tent.

At first he would speak of the siege, but his coming was only to ease his sorrow by talking about Salammbô. Spendius exhorted him to be prudent.

"Drive away these trifles from your soul, which is degraded by them! Formerly you were used to obey; now you command an army, and if Carthage is not conquered we shall at least be granted provinces. We shall become kings!"

But how was it that the possession of the zaïmph did not give them the victory? According to Spendius they must wait.

Matho fancied that the veil affected people of Chanaanitish race exclusively, and, in his Barbarian-like subtlety, he said to himself: "The zaïmph will accordingly do nothing for me, but since they have lost it, it will do nothing for them."

Afterwards a scruple troubled him. He was afraid of offending Moloch by worshipping Aptouknos, the god of the Libyans, and he timidly asked Spendius to which of the gods it would be advisable to sacrifice a man.

"Keep on sacrificing!" laughed Spendius.

Matho, who could not understand such indifference, suspected the Greek of having a genius of whom he would not speak.

All modes of worship, as well as all races, were to be met with in these armies of Barbarians, and consideration was had to the gods of others, for they too, inspired fear. Many mingled foreign practices with their native religion. It was to no purpose that they did not adore the stars; if a constellation were fatal or helpful, sacrifices were offered to it; an unknown amulet found by chance at a moment of peril became a divinity; or it might be a name and nothing more, which would be repeated without any attempt to understand its meaning. But after pillaging temples, and seeing numbers of nations and slaughters, many ultimately ceased to believe in anything but destiny and death;—and every evening these would fall asleep with the placidity of wild beasts. Spendius had spit upon the images of Jupiter Olympius; nevertheless he dreaded to speak aloud in the dark, nor did he fail every day to put on his right boot first.

He reared a long quadrangular terrace in front of Utica, but in proportion as it ascended the rampart was also heightened, and what was thrown down by the one side was almost immediately raised again by the other. Spendius took care of his men; he dreamed of plans and strove to recall the stratagems which he had heard described in his travels. But why did Narr' Havas not return? There was nothing but anxiety.

Hanno had at last concluded his preparations. One night when there was no moon he transported his elephants and soldiers on rafts across the gulf of Carthage. Then they wheeled round the mountain of the Hot Springs so as to avoid Autaritus, and continued their march so slowly that instead of surprising the Barbarians in the morning, as the Suffet had calculated, they did not reach them until it was broad daylight on the third day.

Utica had on the east a plain which extended to the large lagoon of Carthage; behind it a valley ran at right angles between two low and abruptly terminated mountains; the Barbarians were encamped further to the left in such a way as to blockade the harbour; and they were sleeping in their tents (for on that day both sides were too weary to fight and were resting) when the Carthaginian army appeared at the turning of the hills.

Some camp followers furnished with slings were stationed at intervals on the wings. The first line was formed of the guards of the Legion in golden scale-armour, mounted on their big horses, which were without mane, hair, or ears, and had silver horns in the middle of their foreheads to make them look like rhinoceroses. Between their squadrons were youths wearing small helmets and swinging an ashen javelin in each hand. The long files of the heavy infantry marched behind. All these traders had piled as many weapons upon their bodies as possible. Some might be seen carrying an axe, a lance, a club, and two swords all at once; others bristled with darts like porcupines, and their arms stood out from their cuirasses in sheets of horn or iron plates. At last the scaffoldings of the lofty engines appeared: carrobalistas, onagers, catapults and scorpions, rocking on chariots drawn by mules and quadrigas of oxen; and in proportion as the army drew out, the captains ran panting right and left to deliver commands, close up the files, and preserve the intervals. Such of the Ancients as held commands had come in purple cassocks, the magnificent fringes of which tangled in the white straps of their cothurni. Their faces, which were smeared all over with vermilion, shone beneath enormous helmets surmounted with images of the gods; and, as they had shields with ivory borders covered with precious stones, they might have been taken for suns passing over walls of brass.

But the Carthaginians manoeuvred so clumsily that the soldiers in derision urged them to sit down. They called out that they were just going to empty their big stomachs, to dust the gilding of their skin, and to give them iron to drink.

A strip of green cloth appeared at the top of the pole planted before Spendius's tent: it was the signal. The Carthaginian army replied to it with a great noise of trumpets, cymbals, flutes of asses' bones, and tympanums. The Barbarians had already leaped outside the palisades, and were facing their enemies within a javelin's throw of them.

A Balearic slinger took a step forward, put one of his clay bullets into his thong, and swung round his arm. An ivory shield was shivered, and the two armies mingled together.

The Greeks made the horses rear and fall back upon their masters by pricking their nostrils with the points of their lances. The slaves who were to hurl stones had picked such as were too big, and they accordingly fell close to them. The Punic foot-soldiers exposed the right side in cutting with their long swords. The Barbarians broke their lines; they slaughtered them freely; they stumbled over the dying and dead, quite blinded by the blood that spirted into their faces. The confused heap of pikes, helmets, cuirasses and swords turned round about, widening out and closing in with elastic contractions. The gaps increased more and more in the Carthaginian cohorts, the engines could not be got out of the sand; and finally the Suffet's litter (his grand litter with crystal pendants), which from the beginning might have been seen tossing among the soldiers like a bark on the waves, suddenly foundered. He was no doubt dead. The Barbarians found themselves alone.

The dust around them fell and they were beginning to sing, when Hanno himself appeared on the top of an elephant. He sat bare-headed beneath a parasol of byssus which was carried by a negro behind him. His necklace of blue plates flapped against the flowers on his black tunic; his huge arms were compressed within circles of diamonds, and with open mouth he brandished a pike of inordinate size, which spread out at the end like a lotus, and flashed more than a mirror.

Immediately the earth shook—and the Barbarians saw all the elephants of Carthage, with their gilt tusks and blue-painted ears, hastening up in single line, clothed with bronze and shaking the leathern towers which were placed above their scarlet caparisons, in each one of which were three archers bending large bows.

The soldiers were barely in possession of their arms; they had taken up their positions at random. They were frozen with terror; they stood undecided.

Javelins, arrows, phalaricas, and masses of lead were already being showered down upon them from the towers. Some clung to the fringes of the caparisons in order to climb up, but their hands were struck off with cutlasses and they fell backwards upon the swords' points. The pikes were too weak and broke, and the elephants passed through the phalanxes like wild boars through tufts of grass; they plucked up the stakes of the camp with their trunks, and traversed it from one end to the other, overthrowing the tents with their breasts. All the Barbarians had fled. They were hiding themselves in the hills bordering the valley by which the Carthaginians had come.

The victorious Hanno presented himself before the gates of Utica. He had a trumpet sounded. The three Judges of the town appeared in the opening of the battlements on the summit of a tower.

But the people of Utica would not receive such well-armed guests. Hanno was furious. At last they consented to admit him with a feeble escort.

The streets were too narrow for the elephants. They had to be left outside.

As soon as the Suffet was in the town the principal men came to greet him. He had himself taken to the vapour baths, and called for his cooks.

Three hours afterward he was still immersed in the oil of cinnamomum with which the basin had been filled; and while he bathed he ate flamingoes' tongues with honied poppy-seeds on a spread ox-hide. Beside him was his Greek physician, motionless, in a long yellow robe, directing the reheating of the bath from time to time, and two young boys leaned over the steps of the basin and rubbed his legs. But attention to his body did not check his love for the commonwealth, for he was dictating a letter to be sent to the Great Council, and as some prisoners had just been taken he was asking himself what terrible punishment could be devised.

"Stop!" said he to a slave who stood writing in the hollow of his hand. "Let some of them be brought to me! I wish to see them!"

And from the bottom of the hall, full of a whitish vapour on which the torches cast red spots, three Barbarians were thrust forward: a Samnite, a Spartan, and a Cappadocian.

"Proceed!" said Hanno.

"Rejoice, light of the Baals! your Suffet has exterminated the ravenous hounds!

Blessings on the Republic! Give orders for prayers!" He perceived the captives and burst out laughing: "Ah! ha! my line fellows of Sicca! You are not shouting so loudly to-day! It is I! Do you recognize me? And where are your swords? What really terrible fellows!" and he pretended to be desirous to hide himself as if he were afraid of them. "You demanded horses, women, estates, magistracies, no doubt, and priesthoods! Why not? Well, I will provide you with the estates, and such as you will never come out of! You shall be married to gibbets that are perfectly new! Your pay? it shall be melted into your mouths in leaden ingots! and I will put you into good and very exalted positions among the clouds, so as to bring you close to the eagles!"

The three long-haired and ragged Barbarians looked at him without understanding what he said. Wounded in the knees, they had been seized by having ropes thrown over them, and the ends of the great chains on their hands trailed upon the pavement. Hanno was indignant at their impassibility.

"On your knees! on your knees! jackals! dust! vermin! excrements! And they make no reply! Enough! be silent! Let them be flayed alive! No! presently!"

He was breathing like a hippopotamus and rolling his eyes. The perfumed oil overflowed beneath the mass of his body, and clinging to the scales on his skin, made it look pink in the light of the torches.

He resumed:

"For four days we suffered greatly from the sun. Some mules were lost in crossing the Macaras. In spite of their position, the extraordinary courage—Ah! Demonades! how I suffer! Have the bricks reheated, and let them be red-hot!"

A noise of rakes and furnaces was heard. The incense smoked more strongly in the large perfuming-pans, and the shampooers, who were quite naked and were sweating like sponges, crushed a paste composed of wheat, sulphur, black wine, bitch's milk, myrrh, galbanum and storax upon his joints. He was consumed with incessant thirst, but the yellow-robed man did not yield to this inclination, and held out to him a golden cup in which viper broth was smoking.

"Drink!" said he, "that the strength of sun-born serpents may penetrate into the marrow of your bones, and take courage, O reflection of the gods! You know, moreover, that a priest of Eschmoun watches those cruel stars round the Dog from which your malady is derived. They are growing pale like the spots on your skin, and you are not to die from them."

"Oh! yes, that is so, is it not?" repeated the Suffet, "I am not to die from them!" And his violaceous lips gave forth a breath more nauseous than the exhalation from a corpse. Two coals seemed to burn in the place of his eyes, which had lost their eyebrows; a mass of wrinkled skin hung over his forehead; both his ears stood out from his head and were beginning to increase in size; and the deep lines forming semicircles round his nostrils gave him a strange and terrifying appearance, the look of a wild beast. His unnatural voice was like a roar; he said:

"Perhaps you are right, Demonades. In fact there are many ulcers here which have closed. I feel robust. Here! look how I am eating!"

And less from greediness than from ostentation, and the desire to prove to himself that he was in good health, he cut into the forcemeats of cheese and marjoram, the boned fish, gourds, oysters with eggs, horse-radishes, truffles, and brochettes of small birds. As he looked at the prisoners he revelled in the imagination of their tortures. Nevertheless he remembered Sicca, and the rage caused by all his woes found vent in the abuse of these three men.

"Ah! traitors! ah! wretches! infamous, accursed creatures! And you outraged me!—me! the Suffet! Their services, the price of their blood, say they! Ah! yes! their blood! their blood!" Then speaking to himself—"All shall perish! not one shall be sold! It would be better to bring them to Carthage! I should be seen—but, doubtless, I have not brought chains enough? Write: Send me—How many of them are there? go and ask Muthumbal! Go! no pity! and let all their hands be cut off and brought to me in baskets!"

But strange cries at once hoarse and shrill penetrated into the hall above Hanno's voice and the rattling of the dishes that were being placed around him. They increased, and suddenly the furious trumpeting of the elephants burst forth as if the battle were beginning again. A great tumult was going on around the town.

The Carthaginians had not attempted to pursue the Barbarians. They had taken up their quarters at the foot of the walls with their baggage, mules, serving men, and all their train of satraps; and they made merry in their beautiful pearl-bordered tents, while the camp of the Mercenaries was now nothing but a heap of ruins in the plain. Spendius had recovered his courage. He despatched Zarxas to Matho, scoured the woods, rallied his men (the losses had been inconsiderable)—and they were reforming their lines, enraged at having been conquered without a fight, when they discovered a vat of petroleum which had no doubt been abandoned by the Carthaginians. Then Spendius had some pigs carried off from the farms, smeared them with bitumen, set them on fire, and drove them towards Utica.

The elephants were terrified by the flames and fled. The ground sloped upwards, javelins were thrown at them, and they turned back—and with great blows of ivory and trampling of feet they ripped up the Carthaginians, stifled them, flattened them, the Barbarians descended the hill behind them; the Punic camp, which was without entrenchments was sacked at the first rush, and the Carthaginians were crushed against the gates, which were not opened through fear of the Mercenaries.

Day broke, and Matho's foot-soldiers were seen coming up from the west. At the same time horsemen appeared; they were Narr' Havas with his Numidians.

Leaping ravines and bushes they ran down the fugitives like greyhounds pursuing hares. This change of fortune interrupted the Suffet. He called out to be assisted to leave the vapour bath.

The three captives were still before him. Then a Negro (the same who had carried his parasol in the battle) leaned over to his ear.

"Well?" replied the Suffet slowly. "Ah! kill them!" he added in an abrupt tone.

The Ethiopian drew a long dagger from his girdle and the three heads fell. One of them rebounded among the remains of the feast, and leaped into the basin, where it floated for some time with open mouth and staring eyes. The morning light entered through the chinks in the wall; the three bodies streamed with great bubbles like three fountains, and a sheet of blood flowed over the mosaics with their powdering of blue dust. The Suffet dipped his hand into this hot mire and rubbed his knees with it: it was a cure.

When evening had come he stole away from the town with his escort, and made his way into the mountain to rejoin his army.

He succeeded in finding the remains of it.

Four days afterward he was on the top of a defile at Gorza, when the troops under Spendius appeared below. Twenty stout lances might easily have checked them by attacking the head of their column, but the Carthaginians watched them pass by in a slate of stupefaction. Hanno recognised the king of the Numidians in the rearguard; Narr' Havas bowed to him, at the same time making a sign which he did not understand.

The return to Carthage took place amid all kinds of terrors. They marched only at night, hiding in the olive woods during the day. There were deaths at every halting-place; several times they believed themselves lost. At last they reached Cape Hermæum, where vessels came to receive them.

Hanno was so fatigued, so desperate—the loss of the elephants in particular overwhelmed him—that he demanded poison from Demonades in order to put an end to it all. Moreover he could already feel himself stretched upon the cross.

Carthage had not strength enough to be indignant with him. Its losses had amounted to one hundred thousand nine hundred and seventy-two shekels of silver, fifteen thousand six hundred and twenty-three shekels of gold, eighteen elephants, fourteen members of the Great Council, three hundred of the rich, eight thousand citizens, corn enough for three moons, a considerable quantity of baggage, and all the engines of war! The defection of Narr' Havas was certain, and both sieges were beginning again. The army under Autaritus now extended from Tunis to Rhades. From the top of the Acropolis long columns of smoke might be seen in the country ascending to the sky; they were the mansions of the rich, which were on fire.

One man alone could have saved the Republic. People repented that they had slighted him, and the peace party itself voted holocausts for Hamilcar's return.

The sight of the zaïmph had upset Salammbô. At night she thought that she would awake terrified and shrieking. Every day she sent food to the temples. Taanach was worn out with executing her orders, and Schahabarim never left her.

Chapter VII

Hamilcar Barca

THE ANNOUNCER OF THE MOONS, WHO WATCHED ON THE SUMMIT OF THE temple of Eschmoun every night in order to signal the disturbances of the planet with his trumpet, one morning perceived towards the west something like a bird skimming the surface of the sea with its long wings.

It was a ship with three tiers of oars and with a horse carved on the prow. The sun was rising; the Announcer of the Moons put up his hand before his eyes, and then grasping his clarion with outstretched arms sounded a loud brazen cry over Carthage.

People came out of every house; they would not believe what was said; they disputed with one another; the mole was covered with people. At last they recognised Hamilcar's trireme.

It advanced in fierce and haughty fashion, cleaving the foam around it, the lateen-yard quite square and the sail bulging down the whole length of the mast; its gigantic oars kept time as they beat the water; every now and then the extremity of the keel, which was shaped like a plough-share, would appear, and the ivory-headed horse, rearing both its feet beneath the spur which terminated the prow, would seem to be speeding over the plains of the sea.

As it rounded the promontory the wind ceased, the sail fell, and a man was seen standing bareheaded beside the pilot. It was he, Hamilcar, the Suffet! About his sides he wore gleaming sheets of steel; a red cloak, fastened to his shoulders, left his arms visible; two pearls of great length hung from his ears, and his black, bushy beard rested on his breast.

The galley, however, tossing amid the rocks, was proceeding along the side of the mole, and the crowd followed it on the flag-stones, shouting:

"Greeting! blessing! Eye of Khamon! ah! deliver us! 'Tis the fault of the rich! they want to put you to death! Take care of yourself, Barca!"

He made no reply, as if the loud clamour of oceans and battles had completely deafened him. But when he was below the staircase leading down from the Acropolis, Hamilcar raised his head, and looked with folded arms upon the temple of Eschmoun. His gaze mounted higher still, to the great pure sky; he shouted an order in a harsh voice to his sailors; the trireme leaped forward; it grazed the idol set up at the corner of the mole to stay the storms; and in the merchant harbour, which was full of filth, fragments of wood, and rinds of fruit, it pushed aside and crushed against the other ships moored to stakes and terminating in crocodiles' jaws. The people hastened thither, and some threw themselves into the water to swim to it. It was already at the very end before the gate which bristled with nails. The gate rose, and the trireme disappeared beneath the deep arch.

The Military Harbour was completely separated from the town; when ambassadors arrived, they had to proceed between two walls through a passage which had its outlet on the left in front of the temple of Khamoun. This great expanse of water was as round as a cup, and was bordered with quays on which sheds were built for sheltering the ships. Before each of these rose two pillars bearing the horns of Ammon on their capitals and forming continuous porticoes all round the basin. On an island in the centre stood a house for the marine Suffet.

The water was so limpid that the bottom was visible with its paving of white pebbles. The noise of the streets did not reach so far, and Hamilcar as he passed recognised the triremes which he had formerly commanded.

Not more than twenty perhaps remained, under shelter on the land, leaning over on their sides or standing upright on their keels, with lofty poops and swelling prows, and covered with gildings and mystic symbols. The chimæras had lost their wings, the Pataec Gods their arms, the bulls their silver horns—and half-painted, motionless, and rotten as they were, yet full of associations, and still emitting the scent of voyages, they all seemed to say to him, like mutilated soldiers on seeing their master again, " 'Tis we! 'tis we! and *you* too are vanquished!"

No one excepting the marine Suffet might enter the admiral's house. So long as there was no proof of his death he was considered as still in existence. In this way the Ancients avoided a master the more, and they had not failed to comply with the custom in respect to Hamilcar.

The Suffet proceeded into the deserted apartments. At every step he recognised armour and furniture—familiar objects which nevertheless astonished him, and in a perfuming-pan in the vestibule there even remained the ashes of the perfumes that had been kindled at his departure for the conjuration of Melkarth. It was not thus that he had hoped to return. Everything that he had done, everything that he had seen, unfolded itself in his memory: assaults, conflagrations, legions, tempests, Drepanum, Syracuse, Lilybæum, Mount Etna, the plateau of Eryx, live years of battles—until the fatal day when arms had been laid down and Sicily had been lost. Then he once more saw the woods of citron-trees, and herdsmen with their goats on gray mountains; and his heart leaped at the thought of the establishment of another Carthage down yonder. His projects and his recollections buzzed through his head, which was still dizzy from the pitching of the vessel; he was overwhelmed with anguish, and, becoming suddenly weak, he felt the necessity of drawing near to the gods.

Then he went up to the highest story of his house, and taking a nail-studded staple from a golden shell, which hung on his arm, he opened a small oval chamber.

It was softly lighted by means of delicate black discs let into the wall and as transparent as glass. Between the rows of these equal discs, holes, like those for the urns in columbaria, were hollowed out. Each of them contained a round dark stone, which appeared to be very heavy. Only people of superior understanding honoured these abaddirs, which had fallen from the moon. By their fall they denoted the stars, the sky, and fire; by their colour dark night, and by their density the cohesion of terrestrial things. A stilling atmosphere filled this mystic place. The round stones lying in the niches were whitened somewhat with sea-sand which the wind had no doubt driven through the door. Hamilcar counted them one after the other with the tip of his finger; then he hid his face in a saffron-coloured veil, and, falling on his knees, stretched himself on the ground with both arms extended.

The daylight outside was beginning to strike on the folding shutters of black lattice-work. Arborescences, hillocks, eddies, and ill-defined animals appeared in their diaphanous thickness; and the light came terrifying and yet peaceful as it must be behind the sun in the dull spaces of future creations. He strove to banish from his thoughts all forms, and all symbols and appellations of the gods, that he might the better apprehend the immutable spirit which outward appearances took away. Something of the planetary vitalities penetrated him, and he felt withal a wiser and more intimate scorn of death and of every accident. When he rose he was filled with serene fearlessness and was proof against pity or dread, and as his chest was choking he went to the top of the tower which overlooked Carthage.

The town sank downwards in a long hollow curve, with its cupolas, its temples, its golden roofs, its houses, its clusters of palm trees here and there, and its glass balls with streaming rays, while the ramparts formed, as it were, the gigantic border of this horn of plenty which poured itself out before him. Far below he could see the harbours, the squares, the interiors of the courts, the plan of the streets, and the people, who seemed very small and but little above the level of the pavement. Ah! if Hanno had not arrived too late on the morning of the Aegatian isands! He fastened his eyes on the extreme horizon and stretched forth his quivering arms in the direction of Rome.

The steps of the Acropolis were occupied by the multitude. In the square of Khamon the people were pressing forward to see the Suffet come out, and the terraces were gradually being loaded with people; a few recognised him, and he was saluted; but he retired in order the better to excite the impatience of the people.

Hamilcar found the most important men of his party below in the hall: Istatten, Subeldia, Hictamon, Yeoubas and others. They related to him all that had taken place since the conclusion of the peace: the greed of the Ancients, the departure of the soldiers, their return, their demands, the capture of Gisco, the theft of the za-imph, the relief and subsequent abandonment of Utica; but no one ventured to tell him of the events which concerned himself. At last they separated, to meet again during the night at the assembly of the Ancients in the temple of Moloch.

They had just gone out when a tumult arose outside the door. Some one was trying to enter in spite of the servants; and as the disturbance was increasing Hamilcar ordered the stranger to be shown in.

An old negress made her appearance, broken, wrinkled, trembling, stupid-looking, wrapped to the heels in ample blue veils. She advanced face to lace with the Suffet, and they looked at each other for some time; suddenly Hamilcar started; at a wave of his hand the slaves withdrew. Then, signing to her to walk with precaution, he drew her by the arm into a remote apartment.

The negress threw herself upon the floor to kiss his feet; he raised her brutally.

"Where have you left him, Iddibal?"

"Down there, Master;" and extricating herself from her veils, she rubbed her face with her sleeve; the black colour, the senile trembling, the bent figure disappeared, and there remained a strong old man whose skin seemed tanned by sand, wind, and sea. A tuft of white hair rose on his skull like the crest of a bird; and he indicated his disguise, as it lay on the ground, with an ironic glance.

"You have done well, Iddibal! 'Tis well!" Then piercing him, as it were, with his keen gaze: "No one yet suspects?"

The old man swore to him by the Kabiri that the mystery had been kept. They never left their cottage, which was three days' journey from Hadrumetum, on a shore peopled with turtles, and with palms on the dune. "And in accordance with your command, O Master! I teach him to hurl the javelin and to drive a team."

"He is strong, is he not?"

"Yes, Master, and intrepid as well! He has no fear of serpents, or thunder, or phantoms. He runs barefooted like a herdsman along the brinks of precipices."

"Speak! speak!"

"He invents snares for wild beasts. Would you believe it, that last moon he surprised an eagle; he dragged it away, and the bird's blood and the child's were scattered in the air in large drops like driven roses. The animal in its fury enwrapped him in the beating of its wings; he strained it against his breast, and as it died his laughter increased, piercing and proud like the clashing of swords."

Hamilcar bent his head, dazzled by such presages of greatness.

"But he has been for some time restless and disturbed. He gazes at the sails passing far out at sea; he is melancholy, he rejects bread, he inquires about the gods, and he wishes to become acquainted with Carthage."

"No, no! not yet!" exclaimed the Suffet.

The old slave seemed to understand the peril which alarmed Hamilcar, and he resumed:

"How is he to be restrained? Already I am obliged to make him promises, and I have come to Carthage only to buy him a dagger with a silver handle and pearls all around it." Then he told how, having perceived the Suffet on the terrace, he had passed himself off on the warders of the harbour as one of Salammbô's women, so as to make his way in to him.

Hamilcar remained for a long time apparently lost in deliberation; at last he said:

"To-morrow you will present yourself at sunset behind the purple factories in Megara, and imitate a jackal's cry three times. If you do not see me, you will return to Carthage on the first day of every moon. Forget nothing! Love him! You may speak to him now about Hamilcar."

The slave resumed his costume, and they left the house and the harbour together.

Hamilcar went on his way alone on foot and without an escort, for the meetings of the Ancients were, under extraordinary circumstances, always secret, and were resorted to mysteriously.

At first he went along the western front of the Acropolis, and then passed through the Green Market, the galleries of Kinisdo, and the Perfumers' suburb. The scattered lights were being extinguished, the broader streets grew still, then shadows glided through the darkness. They followed him, others appeared, and like him they all directed their course towards the Mappalian district.

The temple of Moloch was built at the foot of a steep defile in a sinister spot. From below nothing could be seen but lofty walls rising indefinitely like those of a monstrous tomb. The night was gloomy, a greyish fog seemed to weigh upon the sea, which beat against the cliff with a noise as of death-rattles and sobs; and the shadows gradually vanished as if they had passed through the walls.

But as soon as the doorway was crossed one found oneself in a vast quadrangular court bordered by arcades. In the centre rose a mass of architecture with eight equal faces. It was surmounted by cupolas which thronged around a second story supporting a kind of rotunda, from which sprang a cone with a re-entrant curve and terminating in a ball on the summit.

Fires were burning in cylinders of filigree-work fitted upon poles, which men were carrying to and fro. These lights flickered in the gusts of wind and reddened the golden combs which fastened their plaited hair on the nape of the neck. They ran about calling to one another to receive the Ancients.

Here and there on the flag-stones huge lions were couched like sphinxes, living symbols of the devouring Sun. They were slumbering with half-closed eyelids. But roused by the footsteps and voices they rose slowly, came towards the Ancients, whom they recognised by their dress, and rubbed themselves against their thighs, arching their backs with sonorous yawns; the vapour of their breath passed across the light of the torches. The stir increased, doors closed, all the priests fled, and the Ancients disappeared beneath the columns which formed a deep vestibule round the temple.

These columns were arranged in such a way that their circular ranks, which were contained one within another, showed the Saturnian period with its years, the years with their months, and the months with their days, and finally reached to the walls of the sanctuary.

Here it was that the Ancients laid aside their sticks of narwhal's horn—for a law which was always observed inflicted the punishment of death upon any one entering the meeting with any kind of weapon. Several wore a rent repaired with a strip of purple at the bottom of their garment, to show that they had not been economical in their dress when mourning for their relatives, and this testimony to their affliction prevented the slit from growing larger. Others had their beards inclosed in little bags of violet skin, and fastened to their ears by two cords. They all accosted one another by embracing breast to breast. They surrounded Hamilcar with congratulations; they might have been taken for brothers meeting their brother again.

These men were generally thick-set, with curved noses like those of the Assyrian colossi. In a few, however, the more prominent cheek-bone, the taller figure, and the narrower foot, betrayed an African origin and nomad ancestors. Those who lived continually shut up in their counting-houses had pale faces; others showed in theirs the severity of the desert, and strange jewels sparkled on all the fingers of their hands, which were burnt by unknown suns. The navigators might be distinguished by their rolling gait, while the men of agriculture smelt of the wine-press, dried herbs, and the sweat of mules. These old pirates had lands under tillage, these money-grubbers would fit out ships, these proprietors of cultivated lands supported slaves who followed trades. All were skilled in religious discipline, expert in strategy, pitiless and rich. They looked wearied of prolonged cares. Their flaming eyes expressed distrust, and their habits of travelling and lying, trafficking and commanding, gave an appearance of cunning and violence, a sort of discreet and convulsive brutality to their whole demeanour. Further, the influence of the god cast a gloom upon them.

They first passed through a vaulted hall which was shaped like an egg. Seven doors, corresponding to the seven planets, displayed seven squares of different colours against the wall. After traversing a long room they entered another similar hall.

A candelabrum completely covered with chiselled flowers was burning at the far end, and each of its eight golden branches bore a wick of byssus in a diamond chalice. It was placed upon the last of the long steps leading to a great altar, the corners of which terminated in horns of brass. Two lateral staircases led to its flattened summit; the stones of it could not be seen; it was like a mountain of heaped cinders, and something indistinct was slowly smoking on the top of it. Then further back, higher than the candelabrum, and much higher than the altar, rose the Moloch, all of iron, and with gaping apertures in his human breast. His outspread wings were stretched upon the wall, his tapering hands reached down to the ground; three black stones bordered by yellow circles represented three eyeballs on his brow, and his bull's head was raised with a terrible effort as if in order to bellow.

Ebony stools were ranged round the apartment. Behind each of them was a bronze shaft resting on three claws and supporting a torch. All these lights were reflected in the mother-of-pearl lozenges which formed the pavement of the hall. So lofty was the latter that the red colour of the walls grew black as it rose towards the vaulted roof, and the three eyes of the idol appeared far above like stars half lost in the night.

The Ancients sat down on the ebony stools alter putting the trains of their robes over their heads. They remained motionless with their hands crossed inside their broad sleeves, and the mother-of-pearl pavement seemed like a luminous river streaming from the altar to the door and flowing beneath their naked feet.

The four pontiffs had their places in the centre, sitting back to back on four ivory seats which formed a cross, the high-priest of Eschmoun in a hyacinth robe, the high-priest of Tanith in a white linen robe, the high-priest of Khamon in a tawny woollen robe, and the high-priest of Moloch in a purple robe.

Hamilcar advanced towards the candelabrum. He walked all round it, looking at the burning wicks; then he threw a scented powder upon them, and violet flames appeared at the extremities of the branches.

Then a shrill voice rose; another replied to it, and the hundred Ancients, the four pontiffs, and Hamilcar, who remained standing, simultaneously intoned a hymn, and their voices—ever repeating the same syllables and strengthening the sounds—rose, grew loud, became terrible, and then suddenly were still.

There was a pause for some time. At last Hamilcar drew from his breast a little three-headed statuette, as blue as sapphire, and placed it before him. It was the image of Truth, the very genius of his speech. Then he replaced it in his bosom, and all, as if seized with sudden wrath, cried out:

"They are good friends of yours, are the Barbarians! Infamous traitor! You come back to see us perish, do you not? Let him speak!—No! no!"

They were taking their revenge for the constraint to which political ceremonial had just obliged them; and even though they had wished for Hamilcar's return, they were now indignant that he had not anticipated their disasters, or rather that he had not endured them as well as they.

When the tumult had subsided, the pontiff of Moloch rose:

"We ask you why you did not return to Carthage?"

"What is that to you?" replied the Suffet disdainfully.

Their shouts were redoubled.

"Of what do you accuse me? I managed the war badly perhaps! You have seen how I order my battles, you who conveniently allow Barbarians—"

"Enough! enough!"

He went on in a low voice so as to make himself the better listened to:

"Oh! that is true! I am wrong, lights of the Baals; there are intrepid men among you! Gisco, rise!" And surveying the step of the altar with half-closed eyelids, as if he sought for some one, he repeated:

"Rise, Gisco! You can accuse me; they will protect you! But where is he?" Then, as if he remembered himself: "Ah! in his house, no doubt! surrounded by his sons, commanding his slaves, happy, and counting on the wall the necklaces of honour which his country has given to him!"

They moved about raising their shoulders as if they were being scourged with thongs. "You do not even know whether he is living or dead!" And without giving any heed to their clamours he said that in deserting the Suffet they had deserted the Republic. So, too, the peace with Rome, however advantageous it might appear to them, was more fatal than twenty battles. A few—those who were the least rich of the Council and were suspected of perpetual leanings towards the people or towards tyranny—applauded. Their opponents, chiefs of the Syssitia and administrators, triumphed over them in point of numbers; and the more eminent of them had ranged themselves close to Hanno, who was sitting at the other end of the hall before the lofty door, which was closed by a hanging of hyacinth colour.

He had covered the ulcers on his face with paint. But the gold dust on his hair had fallen upon his shoulders, where it formed two brilliant sheets, so that his hair appeared whitish, fine, and frizzled like wool. His hands were enveloped in linen soaked in a greasy perfume, which dripped upon the pavement, and his disease had no doubt considerably increased, for his eyes were hidden beneath the folds of his eyelids. He had thrown back his head in order to see. His partisans urged him to speak. At last in a hoarse and hideous voice he said:

"Less arrogance, Barca! We have all been vanquished! Each one supports his own misfortune! Be resigned!"

"Tell us rather," said Hamilcar, smiling, "how it was that you steered your galleys into the Roman fleet?"

"I was driven by the wind," replied Hanno.

"You are like a rhinoceros trampling on his dung: you are displaying your own folly! be silent!" And they began to indulge in recriminations respecting the battle of the Aegatian islands.

Hanno accused him of not having come to meet him.

"But that would have left Eryx undefended. You ought to have stood out from the coast; what prevented you? Ah! I forgot! all elephants are afraid of the sea!"

Hamilcar's followers thought this jest so good that they burst out into loud laughter. The vault rang with it like the beating of tympanums.

Hanno denounced the unworthiness of such an insult; the disease had come upon him from a cold taken at the siege of Hecatompylos, and tears flowed down his face like winter rain on a ruined wall.

Hamilcar resumed:

"If you had loved me as much as him there would be great joy in Carthage now! How many times did I not call upon you! and you always refused me money!"

"We had need of it," said the chiefs of the Syssitia.

"And when things were desperate with me—we drank mules' urine and ate the straps of our sandals; when I would fain have had the blades of grass soldiers, and made battalions with the rottenness of our dead, you recalled the vessels that I had left!"

"We could not risk everything," replied Baat-Baal, who possessed gold mines in Darytian Gætulia.

"But what did you do here, at Carthage, in your houses, behind your walls? There are Gauls on the Eridanus who ought to have been roused, Chanaanites at Cyrene who would have come, and while the Romans send ambassadors to Ptolemæus—"

"Now he is extolling the Romans to us!" Some one shouted out to him: "How much have they paid you to defend them?"

"Ask that of the plains of Bruttium, of the ruins of Locri, of Metapontum, and of Heraclea! I have burnt all their trees, I have pillaged all their temples, and even to the death of their grandchildren's grandchildren—"

"Why! you declaim like a rhetor!" said Kapouras, a very illustrious merchant. "What is it that you want?"

"I say that we must be more ingenious or more terrible! If the whole of Africa rejects your yoke the reason is, my feeble masters, that you do not know how to fasten it upon her shoulders! Agathocles, Regulus, Cœpio, any bold man has only to land and capture her; and when the Libyans in the east concert with the Numidians in the west, and the Nomads come from the south, and the Romans from the north"—a cry of horror rose—"Oh! you will beat your breasts, and roll in the dust, and tear your cloaks! No matter! you will have to go and turn the mill-stone in the Suburra, and gather grapes on the hills of Latium."

They smote their right thighs to mark their sense of the scandal, and the sleeves of their robes rose like large wings of startled birds. Hamilcar, carried away by a spirit, continued his speech, standing on the highest step of the altar, quivering and terrible; he raised his arms, and the rays from the candelabrum which burned behind him passed between his fingers like javelins of gold.

"You will lose your ships, your country seats, your chariots, your hanging beds, and the slaves who rub your feet! The jackal will couch in your palaces, and the ploughshare will upturn your tombs. Nothing will be left but the eagles' scream and a heap of ruins. Carthage, thou wilt fall!"

The four pontiffs spread out their hands to avert the anathema. All had risen. But the marine Suffet, being a sacerdotal magistrate under the protection of the Sun, was inviolable so long as the assembly of the rich had not judged him. Terror was associated with the altar. They drew back.

Hamilcar had ceased speaking, and was panting with eye fixed, his face as pale as the pearls of his tiara, almost frightened at himself, and his spirit lost in funereal visions. From the height on which he stood, all the torches on the bronze shafts seemed to him like a vast crown of fire laid level with the pavement; black smoke issuing from them mounted up into the darkness of the vault; and for some minutes the silence was so profound that they could hear in the distance the sound of the sea.

Then the Ancients began to question one another. Their interests, their existence, were attacked by the Barbarians. But it was impossible to conquer them without the assistance of the Suffet, and in spite of their pride this consideration made them forget every other. His friends were taken aside. There were interested reconciliations, understandings, and promises. Hamilcar would not take any further part in any government. All conjured him. They besought him; and as the word treason occurred in their speech, he fell into a passion. The sole traitor was the Great Council, for as the enlistment of the soldiers expired with the war, they became free as soon as the war was finished; he even exalted their bravery and all the advantages which might be derived from interesting them in the Republic by donations and privileges.

Then Magdassin, a former provincial governor, said, as he rolled his yellow eyes:

"Truly Barca, with your travelling you have become a Greek, or a Latin, or something! Why speak you of rewards for these men? Rather let ten thousand Barbarians perish than a single one of us!"

The Ancients nodded approval, murmuring: "Yes, is there need for so much trouble? They can always be had!"

"And they can be got rid of conveniently, can they not? They are deserted as they were by you in Sardinia. The enemy is apprised of the road which they are to take, as in the case of those Gauls in Sicily, or perhaps they are disembarked in the middle of the sea. As I was returning I saw the rock quite white with their bones!"

"What a misfortune!" said Kapouras impudently.

"Have they not gone over to the enemy a hundred times?" cried the others.

"Why, then," exclaimed Hamilcar, "did you recall them to Carthage, notwithstanding your laws? And when they are in your town, poor and numerous amid all your riches, it does not occur to you to weaken them by the slightest division! Afterwards you dismiss the whole of them with their women and children, without keeping a single hostage! Did you expect that they would murder themselves to spare you the pain of keeping your oaths? You hate them because they are strong! You hate me still more, who am their master! Oh! I felt it just now when you were kissing my hands and were all putting a constraint upon yourselves not to bite them!"

If the lions that were sleeping in the court had come howling in, the uproar could not have been more frightful. But the pontiff of Eschmoun rose, and, standing perfectly upright, with his knees close together, his elbows pressed to his body, and his hands half open, he said:

"Barca, Carthage has need that you take the general command of the Punic forces against the Mercenaries!"

"I refuse," replied Hamilcar.

"We will give you full authority," cried the chiefs of the Syssitia.

"No!"

"With no control, no partition, all the money that you want, all the captives, all the booty, fifty zereths of land for every enemy's corpse."

"No! no! because it is impossible to conquer with you!"

"He is afraid!"

"Because you are cowardly, greedy, ungrateful, pusillanimous and mad!"

"He is careful of them!"

"In order to put himself at their head," said someone.

"And return against us," said another; and from the bottom of the hall Hanno howled:

"He wants to make himself king!"

Then they bounded up, overturning the scats and the torches: the crowd of them rushed towards the altar; they brandished daggers. But Hamilcar dived into his sleeves and drew from them two broad cutlasses; and half stooping, his left foot advanced, his eyes flaming and his teeth clenched, he defied them as he stood there beneath the golden candelabrum.

Thus they had brought weapons with them as a precaution; it was a crime; they looked with terror at one another. As all were guilty, every one became quickly reassured; and by degrees they turned their backs on the Suffet and came down again maddened with humiliation. For the second time they recoiled before him. They remained standing for some time. Several who had wounded their fingers put them to their mouths or rolled them gently in the hem of their mantles, and they were about to depart when Hamilcar heard these words:

"Why! it is a piece of delicacy to avoid distressing his daughter!"

A louder voice was raised:

"No doubt, since she takes her lovers from among the Mercenaries!"

At first he tottered, then his eyes rapidly sought for Shahabarim. But the priest of Tanith had alone remained in his place; and Hamilcar could see only his lofty cap in the distance. All were sneering in his face. In proportion as his anguish increased their joy redoubled, and those who were behind shouted amid the hootings:

"He was seen coming out of her room!"

"One morning in the month of Tammouz!"

"It was the thief who stole the zaïmph!"

"A very handsome man!"

"Taller than you!"

He snatched off his tiara, the ensign of his rank—his tiara with its eight mystic rows, and with an emerald shell in the centre—and with both hands and with all his strength dashed it to the ground; the golden circles rebounded as they broke, and the pearls rang upon the pavement. Then they saw a long scar upon the whiteness of his brow; it moved like a serpent between his eyebrows; all his limbs trembled. He ascended one of the lateral staircases which led on to the altar, and walked upon the latter! This was to devote himself to the god, to offer himself as a holocaust. The motion of his mantle agitated the lights of the candelabrum, which was lower than his sandals, and the fine dust raised by his footsteps surrounded him like a cloud as high as the waist. He stopped between the legs of the brass colossus. He took up two handfuls of the dust, the mere sight of which made every Carthaginian shudder with horror, and said:

"By the hundred torches of your Intelligences! by the eight fires of the Kabiri! by the stars, the meteors, and the volcanoes! by everything that burns! by the thirst of the desert and the saltness of the ocean! by the cave of Hadrumetum and the empire of Souls! by extermination! by the ashes of your sons and the ashes of the brothers of your ancestors with which I now mingle my own!—you, the Hundred of the Council of Carthage, have lied in your accusation of my daughter! And I, Hamilcar Barca, marine Suffet, chief of the rich and ruler of the people, in the presence of bull-headed Moloch, I swear"—they expected something frightful, but he resumed in a loftier and calmer tone—"that I will not even speak to her about it!"

The sacred servants entered wearing their golden combs, some with purple sponges and others with branches of palm. They raised the hyacinth curtain which was stretched before the door; and through the opening of this angle there was visible behind the other halls the great pink sky which seemed to be a continuation of the vault and to rest at the horizon upon the blue sea. The sun was issuing from the waves and mounting upwards. It suddenly struck upon the breast of the brazen colossus, which was divided into seven compartments closed by gratings. His red-toothed jaws opened in a horrible yawn; his enormous nostrils were dilated, the broad daylight animated him, and gave him a terrible and impatient aspect, as if he would fain have leaped without to mingle with the star, the god, and together traverse the immensities.

The torches, however, which were scattered on the ground, were still burning, while here and there on the mother-of-pearl pavement was stretched from them what looked like spots of blood. The Ancients were reeling from exhaustion; they filled their lungs inhaling the freshness of the air; the sweat flowed down their livid faces; they had shouted so much that they could now scarcely make their voices heard. But their wrath against the Suffet was not at all abated; they hurled menaces at him by way of farewells, and Hamilcar answered them again.

"Until the next night, Barca, in the temple of Eschmoun!"

"I shall be there!"

"We will have you condemned by the rich!"

"And I you by the people!"

"Take care that you do not end on the cross!"

"And you that you are not torn to pieces in the streets!"

As soon as they were on the threshold of the court they again assumed a calm demeanor.

Their runners and coachmen were waiting for them at the door. Most of them departed on white mules. The Suffet leaped into his chariot and took the reins; the two animals, curving their necks, and rhythmically beating the rebounding pebbles, went up the whole of the Mappalian Way at full gallop, and the silver vulture at the extremity of the pole seemed to fly, so quickly did the chariot pass along.

The road crossed a field planted with slabs of stone, which were pointed on the top like pyramids, and had open hands carved out in the centre as if all the dead men lying beneath had stretched them out towards heaven to demand something. Next there came scattered cabins built of earth, branches, and bulrush-hurdles, and all of a conical shape. These dwellings, which became constantly denser as the road ascended towards the Suffet's gardens, were irregularly separated from one another by little pebble walls, trenches of spring water, ropes of esparto-grass, and nopal hedges. But Hamilcar's eyes were fastened on a great tower, the three storys of which formed three monster cylinders—the first being built of stone, the second of brick, and the third all of cedar—supporting a copper cupola upon twenty-four pillars of juniper, from which slender interlacing chains of brass hung down after the manner of garlands. This lofty edifice overlooked the buildings—the emporiums and mercantile houses—which stretched to the right, while the women's palace rose at the end of the cypress trees, which were ranged in line like two walls of bronze.

When the echoing chariot had entered through the narrow gateway it stopped beneath a broad shed in which there were shackled horses eating from heaps of chopped grass.

All the servants hastened up. They formed quite a multitude, those who worked on the country estates having been brought to Carthage through fear of the soldiers. The labourers, who were clad in animals' skins, had chains riveted to their ankles and trailing after them; the workers in the purple factories had arms as red as those of executioners; the sailors wore green caps; the fishermen coral necklaces; the huntsmen carried nets on their shoulders; and the people belonging to Megara wore black or white tunics, leathern drawers, and caps of straw, felt or linen, according to their service or their different occupations.

Behind pressed a tattered populace. They lived without employment remote from the apartments, slept at night in the gardens, ate the refuse from the kitchens—a human mouldiness vegetating in the shadow of the palace. Hamilcar tolerated them from foresight even more than from scorn. They had all put a flower in the ear in token of their joy, and many of them had never seen him.

But men with head-dresses like the Sphinx's, and furnished with great sticks, dashed into the crowd, striking right and left. This was to drive back the slaves, who were curious to see their master, so that he might not be assailed by their numbers or inconvenienced by their smell.

Then they all threw themselves flat on the ground, crying:

"Eye of Baal, may your house flourish!" And through these people as they lay thus on the ground in the avenue of cypress trees, Abdalonim, the Steward of the stewards, waving a white mitre, advanced towards Hamilcar with a censer in his hand.

Salammbô was then coming down the galley staircase. All her slave women followed her; and, at each of her steps, they also descended. The heads of the Negresses formed big black spots on the line of the bands of the golden plates clasping the foreheads of the Roman women. Others had silver arrows, emerald butterflies, or long bodkins set like suns in their hair. Rings, clasps, necklaces, fringes, and bracelets shone amid the confusion of white, yellow, and blue garments; a rustling of light material became audible; the pattering of sandals might be heard together with the dull sound of naked feet as they were set down on the wood; and here and there a tall eunuch, head and shoulders above them, smiled with his face in air. When the shouting of the men had subsided they hid their faces in their sleeves, and together uttered a strange cry like the howling of a she-wolf, and so frenzied and strident was it that it seemed to make the great ebony staircase, with its thronging women, vibrate from top to bottom like a lyre.

The wind lifted their veils, and the slender stems of the papyrus plants rocked gently. It was the month of Schebaz and the depth of winter. The flowering pomegranates swelled against the azure of the sky, and the sea appeared through the branches with an island in the distance half lost in the mist.

Hamilcar stopped on perceiving Salammbô. She had come to him after the death of several male children. Moreover, the birth of daughters was considered a calamity in the religions of the Sun. The gods had afterwards sent him a son; but he still felt something of the betrayal of his hope, and the shock, as it were, of the curse which he had uttered against her. Salammbô, however, continued to advance.

Long bunches of various-coloured pearls fell from her ears to her shoulders, and as far as her elbows. Her hair was crisped so as to simulate a cloud. Round her neck she wore little quadrangular plates of gold, representing a woman between two rampant lions; and her costume was a complete reproduction of the equipment of the goddess. Her broad-sleeved hyacinth robe fitted close to her figure, widening out below. The vermilion on her lips gave additional whiteness to her teeth, and the antimony on her eyelids greater length to her eyes. Her sandals, which were cut out in bird's plumage, had very high heels, and she was extraordinarily pale, doubtless on account of the cold.

At last she came close to Hamilcar, and without looking at him, without raising her head, said to him:

"Greeting, eye of Baalim, eternal glory! triumph! leisure! satisfaction! riches! Long has my heart been sad and the house drooping. But the returning master is like reviving Tammouz; and beneath your gaze, O father, joyfulness and a new existence will everywhere prevail!"

And taking from Taanach's hands a little oblong vase wherein smoked a mixture of meal, butter, cardamom, and wine: "Drink freely," said she, "of the returning cup, which your servant has prepared!"

He replied: "A blessing upon you!" and he mechanically grasped the golden vase which she held out to him.

He scanned her, however, with such harsh attention, that Salammbô was troubled and stammered out:

"They have told you, O Master!"

"Yes! I know!" said Hamilcar in a low voice.

Was this a confession, or was she speaking of the Barbarians? And he added a few vague words upon the public embarrassments which he hoped by his own sole efforts to clear away.

"O father!" exclaimed Salammbô, "you will not obliterate what is irreparable!"

Then he drew back and Salammbô was astonished at his amazement; for she was not thinking of Carthage but of the sacrilege in which she found herself implicated. This man, who made legions tremble and whom she hardly knew, terrified her like a god; he had guessed, he knew all, something awful was about to happen. "Pardon!" she cried.

Hamilcar slowly bowed his head.

Although she wished to accuse herself she dared not open her lips; and yet she felt stifled with the need of complaining and being comforted. Hamilcar was struggling against a longing to break his oath. He kept it out of pride or from the dread of putting an end to his uncertainty; and he looked into her face with all his might so as to lay hold on what she kept concealed at the bottom of her heart.

By degrees the panting Salammbô, crushed by such heavy looks, let her head sink below her shoulders. He was now sure that she had erred in the embrace of a Barbarian; he shuddered and raised both his fists. She uttered a shriek and fell down among her women, who crowded around her.

Hamilcar turned on his heel. All the stewards followed him.

The door of the emporiums was opened, and he entered a vast round hall from which long passages leading to other halls branched off like the spokes from the nave of a wheel. A stone disc stood in the centre with balustrades to support the cushions that were heaped up upon carpets.

The Suffet walked at first with rapid strides; he breathed noisily, he struck the ground with his heel, and drew his hand across his forehead like a man annoyed by flies. But he shook his head, and as he perceived the accumulation of his riches he became calm; his thoughts, which were attracted by the vistas in the passages, wandered to the other halls that were full of still rarer treasures. Bronze plates, silver ingots, and iron bars alternated with pigs of tin brought from the Cassiterides over the Dark Sea; gums from the country of the Blacks were running over their bags of palm bark; and gold dust heaped up in leathern bottles was insensibly creeping out through the worn-out seams. Delicate filaments drawn from marine plants hung amid flax from Egypt, Greece, Taprobane and Judæa; madrepores bristled like large bushes at the foot of the walls; and an indefinable odour—the exhalation from perfumes, leather, spices, and ostrich feathers, the latter tied in great bunches at the very top of the vault—floated through the air. An arch was formed above the door before each passage with elephants' teeth placed upright and meeting together at the points.

At last he ascended the stone disc. All the stewards stood with arms folded and heads bent while Abdalonim reared his pointed mitre with a haughty air.

Hamilcar questioned the Chief of the Ships. He was an old pilot with eyelids chafed by the wind, and white locks fell to his hips as if dashing foam of the tempests had remained on his beard.

He replied that he had sent a fleet by Gades and Thymiamata to try to reach Eziongaber by doubling the Southern Horn and the promontory of Aromata.

Others had advanced continuously towards the west for four moons without meeting with any shore; but the ships' prows became entangled in weeds, the horizon echoed continually with the noise of cataracts, blood-coloured mists darkened the sun, a perfume-laden breeze lulled the crews to sleep; and their memories were so disturbed that they were now unable to tell anything. However, expeditions had ascended the rivers of the Scythians, had made their way into Colchis, and into the countries of the Jugrians and of the Estians, had carried off fifteen hundred maidens in the Archipelago, and sunk all the strange vessels sailing beyond Cape Oestrymon, so that the secret of the routes should not be known. King Ptolemæus was detaining the incense from Schesbar; Syracuse, Elathia, Corsica, and the islands had furnished nothing, and the old pilot lowered his voice to announce that a trireme was taken at Rusicada by the Numidians— "for they are with them, Master."

Hamilcar knit his brows; then he signed to the Chief of the Journeys to speak. This functionary was enveloped in a brown, ungirdled robe, and had his head covered with a long scarf of white stuff which passed along the edge of his lips and fell upon his shoulder behind.

The caravans had set out regularly at the winter equinox. But of fifteen hundred men directing their course towards the extreme boundaries of Ethiopia with excellent camels, new leathern bottles, and supplies of painted cloth, but one had reappeared at Carthage—the rest having died of fatigue or become mad through the terror of the desert—and he said that far beyond the Black Harousch, after passing the Atarantes and the country of the great apes, he had seen immense kingdoms, wherein the pettiest utensils were all of gold, a river of the colour of milk and as broad as the sea, forests of blue trees, hills of aromatics, monsters with human faces vegetating on the rocks with eyeballs which expanded like flowers to look at you; and then crystal mountains supporting the sun behind lakes all covered with dragons. Others had returned from India with peacocks, pepper, and new textures. As to those who go by way of the Syrtes and the temple of Ammon to purchase chalcedony, they had no doubt perished in the sands. The caravans from Gaetulia and Phazzana had furnished their usual supplies; but he, the Chief of the Journeys, did not venture to fit one out just now.

Hamilcar understood; the Mercenaries were in occupation of the country. He leaned upon his other elbow with a hollow groan; and the Chief of the Farms was so afraid to speak that he trembled horribly in spite of his thick shoulders and his big red eyeballs. His face, which was as snub-nosed as a mastiff's, was surmounted by a net woven of threads of bark; he wore a waist-belt of hairy leopard's skin, wherein gleamed two formidable cutlasses.

As soon as Hamilcar turned away he began to cry aloud and invoke all the Baals. It was not his fault! he could not help it! He had watched the temperature, the soil, the stars, had planted at the winter solstice and pruned at the waning of the moon, had inspected the slaves and had been careful of their clothes.

But Hamilcar grew angry at this loquacity. He clacked his tongue, and the man with the cutlasses went on in rapid tones:

"Ah, Master! they have pillaged everything! sacked everything! destroyed everything! Three thousand trees have been cut down at Maschala, and at Ubada the granaries have been looted and the cisterns filled up! At Tedes they have carried off fifteen hundred gomors of meal; at Marrazana they have killed the shepherds, eaten the flocks, burnt your house—your beautiful house with its cedar beams, which you used to visit in the summer! The slaves at Tuburbo who were reaping barley fled to the mountains; and the asses, the mules both great and small, the oxen from Taormina, and the antelopes—not a single one left! all carried away! It is a curse! I shall not survive it!" He went on again in tears: "Ah! if you knew how full the cellars were, and how the ploughshares shone! Ah! the fine rams! ah! the fine bulls!—"

Hamilcar's wrath was choking him. It burst forth:

"Be silent! Am I a pauper, then? No lies! speak the truth! I wish to know all that I have lost to the last shekel, to the last cab! Abdalonim, bring me the accounts of the ships, of the caravans, of the farms, of the house! And if your consciences are not clear, woe be on your heads! Go out!"

All the stewards went out walking backwards, with their fists touching the ground.

Abdalonim went up to a set of pigeon-holes in the wall, and from the midst of them took out knotted cords, strips of linen or papyrus, and sheeps' shoulder-blades inscribed with delicate writing. He laid them at Hamilcar's feet, placed in his hands a wooden frame furnished on the inside with three threads on which balls of gold, silver, and horn were strung, and began:

"One hundred and ninety-two houses in the Mappalian district let to the New Carthaginians at the rate of one bekah a moon."

"No! it is too much! be lenient towards the poor people! and you will try to learn whether they are attached to the Republic, and write down the names of those who appear to you to be the most daring! What next?"

Abdalonim hesitated in surprise at such generosity.

Hamilcar snatched the strips of linen from his hands.

"What is this? three palaces around Khamon at twelve kesitahs a month! Make it twenty! I do not want to be eaten up by the rich."

The Steward of the stewards, after a long salutation, resumed:

"Lent to Tigillas until the end of the season two kikars at three per cent, maritime interest; to Bar-Malkarth fifteen hundred shekels on the security of thirty slaves. But twelve have died in the salt-marshes."

"That is because they were not hardy," said the Suffet, laughing. "No matter! if he is in want of money, satisfy him! We should always lend, and at different rates of interest, according to the wealth of the individual."

Then the servant hastened to read all that had been brought in by the iron-mines of Annaba, the coral fisheries, the purple factories, the farming of the tax on the resident Greeks, the export of silver to Arabia, where it had ten times the value of gold, and the captures of vessels, deduction of a tenth being made for the temple of the goddess. "Each time I declared a quarter less, Master!" Hamilcar was reckoning with the balls; they rang beneath his fingers.

"Enough! What have you paid?"

"To Stratonicles of Corinth, and to three Alexandrian merchants, on these letters here (they have been realised), ten thousand Athenian drachmas, and twelve Syrian talents of gold. The food for the crews, amounting to twenty minae a month for each trireme——"

"I know! How many lost?"

"Here is the account on these sheets of lead," said the Steward. "As to the ships chartered in common, it has often been necessary to throw the cargoes into the seas, and so the unequal losses have been divided among the partners. For the ropes which were borrowed from the arsenals, and which it was impossible to restore, the Syssitia exacted eight hundred kesitahs before the expedition to Utica."

"They again!" said Hamilcar, hanging his head; and he remained for a time as if quite crushed by the weight of all the hatreds that he could feel upon him. "But I do not see the Megara expenses?"

Abdalonim, turning pale, went to another set of pigeon-holes, and took from them some planchettes of sycamore wood strung in packets on leathern strings.

Hamilcar, curious about these domestic details, listened to him and grew calm with the monotony of the tones in which the figures were enumerated. Abdalonim became slower. Suddenly he let the wooden sheets fall to the ground and threw himself flat on his face with his arms stretched out in the position of a condemned criminal. Hamilcar picked up the tablets without any emotion; and his lips parted and his eyes grew larger when he perceived an exorbitant consumption of meat, fish, birds, wines, and aromatics, with broken vases, dead slaves, and spoiled carpets set down as the expense of a single day.

Abdalonim, still prostrate, told him of the feast of the Barbarians. He had not been able to avoid the command of the Ancients. Moreover, Salammbô desired money to be lavished for the better reception of the soldiers.

At his daughter's name Hamilcar leaped to his feet. Then with compressed lips he crouched down upon the cushions, tearing the fringes with his nails, and panting with staring eyes.

"Rise!" said he; and he descended.

Abdalonim followed him; his knees trembled. But seizing an iron bar he began like one distraught to loosen the paving stones. A wooden disc sprang up and soon there appeared throughout the length of the passage several of the large covers employed for stopping up the trenches in which grain was kept.

"You see, Eye of Baal," said the servant, trembling, "they have not taken everything yet! and these are each fifty cubits deep and filled up to the brim! During your voyage I had them dug out in the arsenals, in the gardens, everywhere! your house is full of corn as your heart is of wisdom."

A smile passed over Hamilcar's face. "It is well, Abdalonim!" Then bending over to his ear: "You will have it brought from Etruria, Brutium, whence you will, and no matter at what price! Heap it and keep it! I alone must possess all the corn in Carthage."

Then when they were at the extremity of the passage, Abdalonim, with one of the keys hanging at his girdle, opened a large quadrangular chamber divided in the centre by pillars of cedar. Gold, silver, and brass coins were arranged on tables or packed into niches, and rose as high as the joists of the roof along the four walls. In the corners there were huge baskets of hippopotamus skin supporting whole rows of smaller bags; there were hillocks formed of heaps of bullion on the pavement; and here and there a pile that was too high had given way and looked like a ruined column. The large Carthaginian pieces, representing Tanith with a horse beneath a palm-tree, mingled with those from the colonies, which were marked with a bull, star, globe, or crescent. Then there might be seen pieces of all values, dimensions, and ages arranged in unequal amounts—from the ancient coins of Assyria, slender as the nail, to the ancient ones of Latium, thicker than the hand, with the buttons of Egina, the tablets of Bactriana, and the short bars of Lacedæmon;

many were covered with rust, or had grown greasy, or, having been taken in nets or from among the ruins of captured cities, were green with the water or blackened by fire. The Suffet had very speedily calculated whether the sums present corresponded with the gains and losses which had just been read to him; and he was going away when he perceived three brass jars completely empty. Abdalonim turned away his head to mark his horror, and Hamilcar, resigning himself to it, said nothing.

They crossed other passages and other halls, and at last reached a door where, to ensure its better protection and in accordance with a Roman custom lately introduced into Carthage, a man was fastened by the waist to a long chain let into the wall. His beard and nails had grown to an immoderate length, and he swayed himself from right to left with that continual oscillation which is characteristic of captive animals. As soon as he recognised Hamilcar he darted towards him, crying:

"Pardon, Eye of Baal! pity! kill me! For ten years I have not seen the sun! In your father's name, pardon!"

Hamilcar, without answering him, clapped his hands and three men appeared; and all four simultaneously stiffening their arms, drew back from its rings the enormous bar which closed the door. Hamilcar took a torch and disappeared into the darkness.

This was believed to be the family burying-place; but nothing would have been found in it except a broad well. It was dug out merely to baffle robbers, and it concealed nothing. Hamilcar passed along beside it; then stooping down he made a very heavy millstone turn upon its rollers, and through this aperture entered an apartment which was built in the shape of a cone.

The walls were covered with scales of brass; and in the centre, on a granite pedestal, stood the statue of one of the Kabiri called Aletes, the discoverer of the mines in Celtiberia. On the ground, at its base, and arranged in the form of a cross, were large gold shields and monster close-necked silver vases, of extravagant shape and unfitted for use; for it was customary to cast quantities of metal in this way, so that dilapidation and even removal should be almost impossible.

With his torch he lit a miner's lamp which was fastened to the idol's cap, and green, yellow, blue, violet, wine-coloured, and blood-coloured fires suddenly illuminated the hall. It was filled with gems which were either in gold calabashes fastened like sconces upon sheets of brass, or were ranged in native masses at the foot of the wall. There were callaides shot away from the mountains with slings, carbuncles formed by the urine of the lynx, glossopetræ which had fallen from the moon, tyanos, diamonds, sandastra, beryls, with the three kinds of rubies, the four kinds of sapphires, and the twelve kinds of emeralds. They gleamed like splashes of milk, blue icicles, and silver dust, and shed their light in sheets, rays, and stars.

Ceraunia, engendered by the thunder, sparkled by the side of chalcedonies, which are a cure for poison. There were topazes from Mount Zabarca to avert terrors, opals from Bactriana to prevent abortions, and horns of Ammon, which are placed under the bed to induce dreams.

The fires from the stones and the flames from the lamp were mirrored in the great golden shields. Hamilcar stood smiling with folded arms, and was less delighted by the sight of his riches than by the consciousness of their possession. They were inaccessible, exhaustless, infinite. His ancestors sleeping beneath his feet transmitted something of their eternity to his heart. He felt very near to the subterranean deities. It was as the joy of one of the Kabiri; and the great luminous rays striking upon his face looked like the extremity of an invisible net linking him across the abysses with the centre of the world.

A thought came which made him shudder, and placing himself behind the idol he walked straight up to the wall. Then among the tattooings on his arm he scrutinised a horizontal line with two other perpendicular ones which in Chanaanitish figures expressed the number thirteen. Then he counted as far as the thirteenth of the brass plates and again raised his ample sleeve; and with his right hand stretched out he read other more complicated lines on his arm, at the same time moving his fingers daintily about like one playing on a lyre. At last he struck seven blows with his thumb, and an entire section of the wall turned about in a single block.

It served to conceal a sort of cellar containing mysterious things which had no name and were of incalculable value. Hamilcar went down the three steps, took up a llama's skin which was floating on a black liquid in a silver vat, and then re-ascended.

Abdalonim again began to walk before him. He struck the pavement with his tall cane, the pommel of which was adorned with bells, and before every apartment cried aloud the name of Hamilcar amid eulogies and benedictions.

Along the walls of the circular gallery, from which the passages branched off, were piled little beams of algummim, bags of Lawsonia, cakes of Lemnos-earth, and tortoise carapaces filled with pearls. The Suffet brushed them with his robe as he passed without even looking at some gigantic pieces of amber, an almost divine material formed by the rays of the sun.

A cloud of odourous vapour burst forth.

"Push open the door!"

They went in.

Naked men were kneading pastes, crushing herbs, stirring coals, pouring oil into jars, and opening and shutting the little ovoid cells which were hollowed out all round in the wall, and were so numerous that the apartment was like the interior of a hive. They were brimful of myrobalan, bdellium, saffron, and violets.

Gums, powders, roots, glass phials, branches of filipendula, and rose-petals were scattered about everywhere, and the scents were stifling in spite of the cloud-wreaths from the styrax shrivelling on a brazen tripod in the centre.

The Chief of the Sweet Odours, pale and long as a waxen torch, came up to Hamilcar to crush a roll of metopion in his hands, while two others rubbed his heels with leaves of baccharis. He repelled them; they were Cyreneans of infamous morals, but valued on account of the secrets which they possessed.

To show his vigilance the Chief of the Odours offered the Suffet a little mal-obathrum to taste in an electrum spoon; then he pierced three Indian bezoars with an awl. The master, who knew the artifices employed, took a horn full of balm, and after holding it near the coals inclined it over his robe. A brown spot appeared; it was a fraud. Then he gazed fixedly at the Chief of the Odours, and without say-ing anything flung the gazelle's horn full in his face.

However indignant he might be at adulterations made to his own prejudice, when he perceived some parcels of nard which were being packed up for countries beyond the sea, he ordered antimony to be mixed with it so as to make it heavier.

Then he asked where three boxes of psagdas designed for his own use were to be found.

The Chief of the Odours confessed that he did not know; some soldiers had come howling in with knives and he had opened the boxes for them.

"So you are more afraid of them than of me!" cried the Suffet; and his eyeballs flashed like torches through the smoke upon the tall, pale man who was beginning to understand. "Abdalonim! you will make him run the gauntlet before sunset: tear him!"

This loss, which was less than the others, had exasperated him; for in spite of his efforts to banish them from his thoughts he was continually coming again across the Barbarians. Their excesses were blended with his daughter's shame, and he was angry with the whole household for knowing of the latter and for not speaking of it to him. But something impelled him to bury himself in his misfor-tune; and in an inquisitorial fit he visited the sheds behind the mercantile house to see the supplies of bitumen, wood, anchors and cordage, honey and wax, the cloth warehouse, the stores of food, the marble yard and the silphium barn.

He went to the other side of the gardens to make an inspection in their cot-tages, of the domestic artisans whose productions were sold. There were tailors embroidering cloaks, others making nets, others painting cushions or cutting out sandals, and Egyptian workmen polished papyrus with a shell, while the weavers' shuttles rattled and the armourers' anvils rang.

Hamilcar said to them:

"Beat away at the swords! I shall want them." And he drew the antelope's skin that had been steeped in poisons from his bosom to have it cut into a cuirass more solid than one of brass and unassailable by steel or flame.

As soon as he approached the workmen, Abdalonim, to give his wrath another direction, tried to anger him against them by murmured disparagement of their work. "What a performance! It is a shame! The Master is indeed too good." Hamilcar moved away without listening to him.

He slackened his pace, for the paths were barred by great trees calcined from one end to the other, such as may be met with in woods where shepherds have encamped; and the palings were broken the water in the trenches was disappearing, while fragments of glass and the bones of apes were to be seen amid the miry puddles. A scrap of cloth hung here and there from the bushes, and the rotten flowers formed a yellow muck-heap beneath the citron trees. In fact, the servants had neglected everything, thinking that the master would never return.

At every step he discovered some new disaster, some further proof of the thing which he had forbidden himself to learn. Here he was soiling his purple boots as he crushed the filth under-foot; and he had not all these men before him at the end of a catapult to make them fly into fragments! He felt humiliated at having defended them; it was a delusion and a piece of treachery; and as he could not revenge himself upon the soldiers, or the Ancients, or Salammbô, or anybody, and his wrath required some victim, he condemned all the slaves of the gardens to the mines at a single stroke.

Abdalonim shuddered each time that he saw him approaching the parks. But Hamilcar took the path towards the mill, from which there might be heard issuing a mournful melopœia.

The heavy mill-stones were turning amid the dust. They consisted of two cones of porphyry laid the one upon the other—the upper one of the two, which carried a funnel, being made to revolve upon the second by means of strong bars. Some men were pushing these with their breasts and arms, while others were yoked to them and were pulling them. The friction of the straps had formed purulent scabs round about their armpits such as are seen on asses' withers, and the end of the limp black rag, which scarcely covered their loins, hung down and flapped against their hams like a long tail. Their eyes were red, the irons on their feet clanked, and all their breasts panted rhythmically. On their mouths they had muzzles fastened by two little bronze chains to render it impossible for them to eat the flour, and their hands were enclosed in gauntlets without fingers, so as to prevent them from taking any.

At the master's entrance the wooden bars creaked still more loudly. The grain grated as it was being crushed. Several fell upon their knees; the others, continuing their work, stepped across them.

He asked for Giddenem, the governor of the slaves, and that personage appeared, his rank being displayed in the richness of his dress. His tunic, which was slit up the sides, was of fine purple; his ears were weighted with heavy rings; and the strips of cloth enfolding his legs were joined together with a lacing of gold which extended from his ankles to his hips, like a serpent winding about a tree. In his fingers, which were laden with rings, he held a necklace of jet beads, so as to recognise the men who were subject to the sacred disease.

Hamilcar signed to him to unfasten the muzzles. Then with the cries of famished animals they all rushed upon the flour, burying their faces in the heaps of it and devouring it.

"You are weakening them!" said the Suffet.

Giddenem replied that such treatment was necessary in order to subdue them.

"It was scarcely worth while sending you to the slaves' school at Syracuse. Fetch the others!"

And the cooks, butlers, grooms, runners, and litter-carriers, the men belonging to the vapour-baths, and the women with their children, all ranged themselves in a single line in the garden from the mercantile house to the deer park. They held their breath. An immense silence prevailed in Megara. The sun was lengthening across the lagoon at the foot of the catacombs. The peacocks were screeching. Hamilcar walked along step by step.

"What am I to do with these old creatures?" he said. "Sell them! There are too many Gauls: they are drunkards! and too many Cretans: they are liars! Buy me some Capadocians, Asiatics, and Negroes."

He was astonished that the children were so few. "The house ought to have births every year, Giddenem. You will leave the huts open every night to let them mingle freely."

He then had the thieves, the lazy, and the mutinous shown to him. He distributed punishments, with reproaches to Giddenem; and Giddenem, ox-like, bent his low forehead, with its two broad intersecting eyebrows.

"See, Eye of Baal," he said, pointing out a sturdy Libyan, "here is one who was caught with the rope round his neck."

"Ah! you wish to die?" said the Suffet scornfully.

"Yes!" replied the slave in an intrepid tone.

Then, without heeding the precedent or the pecuniary loss, Hamilcar said to the serving-men:

"Away with him!"

Perhaps in his thoughts he intended a sacrifice. It was a misfortune which he inflicted upon himself in order to avert more terrible ones.

Giddenem had hidden those who were mutilated behind the others. Hamilcar perceived them:

"Who cut off your arm?"

"The soldiers, Eye of Baal."

Then to a Samnite who was staggering like a wounded heron:

"And you, who did that to you?"

It was the governor, who had broken his leg with an iron bar.

This silly atrocity made the Suffet indignant; he snatched the jet necklace out of Giddenem's hands.

"Cursed be the dog that injures the flock! Gracious Tanith, to cripple slaves! Ah! you ruin your master! Let him be smothered in the dunghill. And those that are missing? Where are they? Have you helped the soldiers to murder them?"

His face was so terrible that all the women fled. The slaves drew back and formed a large circle around them; Giddenem was frantically kissing his sandals; Hamilcar stood upright with his arms raised above him.

But with his understanding as clear as in the sternest of his battles, he recalled a thousand odious things, ignominies from which he had turned aside; and in the gleaming of his wrath he could once more see all his disasters simultaneously as in the lightnings of a storm. The governors of the country estates had fled through terror of the soldiers, perhaps through collusion with them; they were all deceiving him; he had restrained himself too long.

"Bring them here!" he cried; "and brand them on the forehead with red-hot irons as cowards!"

Then they brought and spread out in the middle of the garden, fetters, carcanets, knives, chains for those condemned to the mines, cippi for fastening the legs, numellæ for confining the shoulders, and scorpions or whips with triple thongs terminating in brass claws.

All were placed facing the sun, in the direction of Moloch the Devourer, and were stretched on the ground on their stomachs or on their backs, those, however, who were sentenced to be flogged standing upright against the trees with two men beside them, one counting the blows and the other striking.

In striking he used both his arms, and the whistling thongs made the bark of the plane-trees fly. The blood was scattered like rain upon the foliage, and red masses writhed with howls at the foot of the trees. Those who were under the iron tore their faces with their nails. The wooden screws could be heard creaking; dull knockings resounded; sometimes a sharp cry would suddenly pierce the air. In the direction of the kitchens, men were brisking up burning coals with fans amid tattered garments and scattered hair, and a smell of burning flesh was perceptible.

Those who were under the scourge, swooning, but kept in their positions by the bonds on their arms, rolled their heads upon their shoulders and closed their eyes. The others who were watching them began to shriek with terror, and the lions, remembering the feast perhaps, stretched themselves out yawning against the edge of the dens.

Then Salammbô was seen on the platform of her terrace. She ran wildly about it from left to right. Hamilcar perceived her. It seemed to him that she was holding up her arms towards him to ask for pardon; with a gesture of horror he plunged into the elephants' park.

These animals were the pride of the great Punic houses. They had carried their ancestors, had triumphed in the wars, and they were reverenced as being the favourites of the Sun.

Those of Megara were the strongest in Carthage. Before he went away Hamilcar had required Abdalonim to swear that he would watch over them. But they had died from their mutilations; and only three remained, lying in the middle of the court in the dust before the ruins of their manger.

They recognised him and came up to him.

One had its ears horribly slit, another had a large wound in its knee, while the trunk of the third was cut off.

They looked sadly at him, like reasonable creatures; and the one that had lost its trunk tried by stooping its huge head and bending its hams to stroke him softly with the hideous extremity of its stump.

At this caress from the animal two tears started into his eyes. He rushed at Abdalonim.

"Ah! wretch! the cross! the cross!"

Abdalonim fell back swooning upon the ground.

The bark of a jackal rang from behind the purple factories, the blue smoke of which was ascending slowly into the sky; Hamilcar paused.

The thought of his son had suddenly calmed him like the touch of a god. He caught a glimpse of a prolongation of his might, an indefinite continuation of his personality, and the slaves could not understand whence this appeasement had come upon him.

As he bent his steps towards the purple factories he passed before the ergastulum, which was a long house of black stone built in a square pit with a small pathway all round it and four staircases at the corners.

Iddibal was doubtless waiting until the night to finish his signal. "There is no hurry yet," thought Hamilcar; and he went down into the prison. Some cried out to him: "Return;" the boldest followed him.

The open door was flapping in the wind. The twilight entered through the narrow loopholes, and in the interior broken chains could be distinguished hanging from the walls.

This was all that remained of the captives of war!

Then Hamilcar grew extraordinarily pale, and those who were leaning over the pit outside saw him resting one hand against the wall to keep himself from falling.

But the jackal uttered its cry three times in succession. Hamilcar raised his head; he did not speak a word nor make a gesture. Then when the sun had completely set he disappeared behind the nopal hedge, and in the evening he said as he entered the assembly of the rich in the temple of Eschmoun:

"Luminaries of the Baalim, I accept the command of the Punic forces against the army of the Barbarians!"

Chapter VIII

The Battle of the Macaras

O N THE FOLLOWING DAY HE DREW TWO HUNDRED AND TWENTY-THREE THOUsand kikars of gold from the Syssitia, and decreed a tax of fourteen shekels upon the rich. Even the women contributed; payment was made in behalf of the children, and he compelled the colleges of priests to furnish money—a monstrous thing, according to Carthaginian customs.

He demanded all the horses, mules, and arms. A few tried to conceal their wealth, and their property was sold; and, to intimidate the avarice of the rest, he himself gave sixty suits of armour, and fifteen hundred gomers of meal, which was as much as was given by the Ivory Company.

He sent into Liguria to buy soldiers, three thousand mountaineers accustomed to fight with bears; they were paid for six moons in advance at the rate of four minæ a day.

Nevertheless an army was wanted. But he did not, like Hanno, accept all the citizens. First he rejected those engaged in sedentary occupations, and then those who were big-bellied or had a pusillanimous look; and he admitted those of ill-repute, the scum of Malqua, sons of Barbarians, freed men. For reward he promised some of the New Carthaginians complete rights of citizenship.

His first care was to reform the Legion. These handsome young fellows, who regarded themselves as the military majesty of the Republic, governed themselves. He reduced their officers to the ranks; he treated them harshly, made them run, leap, ascend the declivity of the Byrsa at a single burst, hurl javelins, wrestle together, and sleep in the squares at night. Their families used to come to see them and pity them.

He ordered shorter swords and stronger buskins. He fixed the number of serving-men, and reduced the amount of baggage; and as there were three hundred Roman pila kept in the temple of Moloch, he took them in spite of the pontiff's protests.

He organised a phalanx of seventy-two elephants with those which had returned from Utica, and others which were private property, and rendered them formidable. He armed their drivers with mallet and chisel to enable them to split their skulls in the fight if they ran away.

He would not allow his generals to be nominated by the Grand Council. The Ancients tried to urge the laws in objection, but he set them aside; no one ventured to murmur again, and everything yielded to the violence of his genius.

He assumed sole charge of the war, the government, and the finances; and as a precaution against accusations he demanded the Suffet Hanno as examiner of his accounts.

He set to work upon the ramparts, and had the old and now useless inner walls demolished in order to furnish stones. But difference of fortune, replacing the hierarchy of race, still kept the sons of the vanquished and those of the conquerors apart; thus the patricians viewed the destruction of these ruins with an angry eye, while the plebeians, scarcely knowing why, rejoiced.

The troops defiled under arms through the streets from morning till night; every moment the sound of trumpets was heard; chariots passed bearing shields, tents, and pikes; the courts were full of women engaged in tearing up linen; the enthusiasm spread from one to another, and Hamilcar's soul filled the Republic.

He had divided his soldiers into even numbers, being careful to place a strong man and a weak one alternately throughout the length of his files, so that he who was less vigorous or more cowardly might be at once led and pushed forward by two others. But with his three thousand Ligurians, and the best in Carthage, he could form only a simple phalanx of four thousand and ninety-six hoplites, protected by bronze helmets, and handling ashen sarissae fourteen cubits long.

There were two thousand young men, each equipped with a sling, a dagger, and sandals. He reinforced them with eight hundred others armed with round shields and Roman swords.

The heavy cavalry was composed of the nineteen hundred remaining guardsmen of the Legion, covered with plates of vermilion bronze, like the Assyrian Clinabarians. He had further four hundred mounted archers, of those that were called Tarentines, with caps of weasel's skin, two-edged axes, and leathern tunics. Finally there were twelve hundred Negroes from the quarter of the caravans, who were mingled with the Clinabarians, and were to run beside the stallions with one hand resting on the manes. All was ready, and yet Hamilcar did not start.

Often at night he would go out of Carthage alone and make his way beyond the lagoon towards the mouths of the Macaras. Did he intend to join the Mercenaries? The Ligurians encamped in the Mappalian district surrounded his house.

The apprehensions of the rich appeared justified when, one day, three hundred Barbarians were seen approaching the walls. The Suffet opened the gates to them; they were deserters; drawn by fear or by fidelity, they were hastening to their master.

Hamilcar's return had not surprised the Mercenaries; according to their ideas the man could not die. He was returning to fulfil his promise—a hope by no means absurd, so deep was the abyss between Country and Army. Moreover they did not believe themselves culpable; the feast was forgotten.

The spies whom they surprised undeceived them. It was a triumph for the bitter; even the lukewarm grew furious. Then the two sieges overwhelmed them with weariness; no progress was being made; a battle would be better! Thus many men had left the ranks and were scouring the country. But at news of the arming they returned; Matho leaped for joy. "At last! at last!" he cried.

Then the resentment which he cherished against Salammbô was turned against Hamilcar. His hate could now perceive a definite prey; and as his vengeance grew easier of conception he almost believed that he had realised it and he revelled in it already. At the same time he was seized with a loftier tenderness, and consumed by more acrid desire. He saw himself alternately in the midst of the soldiers brandishing the Suffet's head on a pike, and then in the room with the purple bed, clasping the maiden in his arms, covering her face with kisses, passing his hands over her long, black hair; and the imagination of this, which he knew could never be realised, tortured him. He swore to himself that, since his companions had appointed him schalishim, he would conduct the war; the certainty that he would not return from it urged him to render it a pitiless one.

He came to Spendius and said to him:

"You will go and get your men! I will bring mine! Warn Autaritus! We are lost if Hamilcar attacks us! Do you understand me? Rise!"

Spendius was stupefied before such an air of authority. Matho usually allowed himself to be led, and his previous transports had quickly passed away. But just now he appeared at once calmer and more terrible; a superb will gleamed in his eyes like the flame of sacrifice.

The Greek did not listen to his reasons. He was living in one of the Carthaginian pearl-bordered tents, drinking cool beverages from silver cups, playing at the cottubos, letting his hair grow, and conducting the siege with slackness. Moreover, he had entered into communications with some in the town and would not leave, being sure that it would open its gates before many days were over.

Narr' Havas, who wandered about among the three armies, was at that time with him. He supported his opinion, and even blamed the Libyan for wishing in his excess of courage to abandon their enterprise.

"Go, if you are afraid!" exclaimed Matho; "you promised us pitch, sulphur, elephants, loot-soldiers, horses! where are they?"

Narr' Havas reminded him that he had exterminated Hanno's last cohorts; as to the elephants, they were being hunted in the woods, he was arming the foot-soldiers, the horses were on their way; and the Numidian rolled his eyes like a woman and smiled in an irritating manner as he stroked the ostrich feather which fell upon his shoulder. In his presence Matho was at a loss for a reply.

But a man who was a stranger entered, wet with perspiration, scared, and with bleeding feet and loosened girdle; his breathing shook his lean sides enough to have burst them, and speaking in an unintelligible dialect he opened his eyes wide as if he were telling of some battle. The king sprang outside and called his horsemen.

They ranged themselves in the plain before him in the form of a circle. Narr' Havas, who was mounted, bent his head and bit his lips. At last he separated his men into two equal divisions, and told the first to wait; then with an imperious gesture he carried off the others at a gallop and disappeared on the horizon in the direction of the mountains.

"Master!" murmured Spendius, "I do not like these extraordinary chances—the Suffet returning, Narr' Havas going away—"

"Why! what does it matter?" said Matho disdainfully.

It was a reason the more for anticipating Hamilcar by uniting with Autaritus. But if the siege of the towns were raised, the inhabitants would come out and attack them in the rear, while they would have the Carthaginians in front. After much talking the following measures were resolved upon and immediately executed.

Spendius proceeded with fifteen thousand men as far as the bridge built across the Macaras, three miles from Utica; the corners of it were fortified with four huge towers provided with catapults; all the paths and gorges in the mountains were stopped up with trunks of trees, pieces of rock, interlacings of thorn, and stone walls; on the summits heaps of grass were made which might be lighted as signals, and shepherds who were able to see at a distance were posted at intervals.

No doubt Hamilcar would not, like Hanno, advance by the mountain of the Hot Springs. He would think that Autaritus, being master of the interior, would close the route against him. Moreover, a check at the opening of the campaign would ruin him, while if he gained a victory he would soon have to make a fresh beginning, the Mercenaries being further off. Again, he could disembark at Cape Grapes and march thence upon one of the towns. But he would then find himself between the two armies, an indiscretion which he could not commit with his scanty forces. Accordingly he must proceed along the base of Mount Ariana, then turn to the left to avoid the mouths of the Macaras, and come straight to the bridge. It was there that Matho expected him.

At night he used to inspect the pioneers by torchlight. He would hasten to Hippo-Zarytus or to the works on the mountains, would come back again, would never rest. Spendius envied his energy; but in the management of spies, the choice of sentries, the working of the engines and all means of defence, Matho listened docilely to his companion. They spoke no more of Salammbô—one not thinking about her, and the other being prevented by a feeling of shame.

Often he would go towards Carthage, striving to catch sight of Hamilcar's troops. His eyes would dart along the horizon; he would lie flat on the ground, and believe that he could hear an army in the throbbing of his arteries.

He told Spendius that if Hamilcar did not arrive within three days he would go with all his men to meet him and offer him battle. Two further days elapsed. Spendius restrained him; but on the morning of the sixth day he departed.

The Carthaginians were no less impatient for war than the Barbarians. In tents and in houses there was the same longing and the same distress; all were asking one another what was delaying Hamilcar.

From time to time he would mount to the cupola of the temple of Eschmoun beside the Announcer of the Moons and take note of the wind.

One day—it was the third of the month of Tibby—they saw him descending from the Acropolis with hurried steps. A great clamour arose in the Mappalian district. Soon the streets were astir, and the soldiers were everywhere beginning to arm surrounded by weeping women who threw themselves upon their breasts; then they ran quickly to the square of Khamon to take their places in the ranks. No one was allowed to follow them or even to speak to them, or to approach the ramparts; for some minutes the whole town was as silent as a great tomb. The soldiers as they leaned on their lances were thinking, and the others in the houses were sighing.

At sunset the army went out by the western gate; but instead of taking the road to Tunis or making for the mountains in the direction of Utica, they continued their march along the edge of the sea; and they soon reached the Lagoon, where round spaces quite whitened with salt glittered like gigantic silver dishes forgotten on the shore.

Then the pools of water multiplied. The ground gradually became softer, and the feet sank in it. Hamilcar did not turn back. He went on still at their head; and his horse, which was yellow-spotted like a dragon, advanced into the mire flinging froth around him, and with great straining of the loins. Night—a moonless night—fell. A few cried out that they were about to perish; he snatched their arms from them, and gave them to the serving-men. Nevertheless the mud became deeper and deeper. Some had to mount the beasts of burden; others clung to the horses' tails; the sturdy pulled the weak, and the Ligurian corps drove on the infantry with the points of their pikes. The darkness increased. They had lost their way. All stopped.

Then some of the Suffet's slaves went on ahead to look for the buoys which had been placed at intervals by his order. They shouted through the darkness, and the army followed them at a distance.

At last they felt the resistance of the ground. Then a whitish curve became dimly visible, and they found themselves on the bank of the Macaras. In spite of the cold no fires were lighted.

In the middle of the night squalls of wind arose. Hamilcar had the soldiers roused, but not a trumpet was sounded: their captains tapped them softly on the shoulder.

A man of lofty stature went down into the water. It did not come up to his girdle; it was possible to cross.

The Suffet ordered thirty-two of the elephants to be posted in the river a hundred paces further on, while the others, lower down, would check the lines of men that were carried away by the current; and holding their weapons above their heads they all crossed the Macaras as though between two walls. He had noticed that the western wind had driven the sand so as to obstruct the river and form a natural causeway across it.

He was now on the loft bank in front of Utica, and in a vast plain, the latter being advantageous for his elephants, which formed the strength of his army.

This feat of genius filled the soldiers with enthusiasm. They recovered extraordinary confidence. They wished to hasten immediately against the Barbarians; but the Suffet made them rest for two hours. As soon as the sun appeared they moved into the plain in three lines—first came the elephants, and then the light infantry with the cavalry behind it, the phalanx marching next.

The Barbarians encamped at Utica, and the fifteen thousand about the bridge were surprised to see the ground undulating in the distance. The wind, which was blowing very hard, was driving tornadoes of sand before it; they rose as though snatched from the soil, ascended in great light-coloured strips, then parted asunder and began again, hiding the Punic army the while from the Mercenaries. Owing to the horns, which stood up on the edge of the helmets, some thought that they could perceive a herd of oxen; others, deceived by the motion of the cloaks, pretended that they could distinguish wings, and those who had travelled a good deal shrugged their shoulders and explained everything by the illusions of the mirage. Nevertheless something of enormous size continued to advance. Little vapours, as subtle as the breath, ran across the surface of the desert; the sun, which was higher now, shone more strongly: a harsh light, which seemed to vibrate, threw back the depths of the sky, and permeating objects, rendered distance incalculable. The immense plain expanded in every direction beyond the limits of vision; and the almost insensible undulations of the soil extended to the extreme horizon, which was closed by a great blue line which they knew to be the sea. The two armies, having left their tents, stood gazing; the people of Utica were massing on the ramparts to have a better view.

At last they distinguished several transverse bars bristling with level points.

They became thicker, larger; black hillocks swayed to and fro; square thickets suddenly appeared; they were elephants and lances. A single shout went up: "The Carthaginians!" and without signal or command the soldiers at Utica and those at the bridge ran pell-mell to fall in a body upon Hamilcar.

Spendius shuddered at the name. "Hamilcar! Hamilcar!" he repeated, panting, and Matho was not there! What was to be done? No means of flight! The suddenness of the event, his terror of the Suffet, and above all, the urgent need of forming an immediate resolution, distracted him; he could see himself pierced by a thousand swords, decapitated, dead. Meanwhile he was being called for; thirty thousand men would follow him; he was seized with fury against himself; he fell back upon the hope of victory; it was full of bliss, and he believed himself more intrepid than Epaminondas. He smeared his cheeks with vermilion in order to conceal his paleness, then he buckled on his knemids and his cuirass, swallowed a patera of pure wine, and ran after his troops, who were hastening towards those from Utica.

They united so rapidly that the Suffet had not time to draw up his men in battle array. By degrees he slackened his speed. The elephants stopped; they rocked their heavy heads with their chargings of ostrich feathers, striking their shoulders the while with their trunks.

Behind the intervals between them might be seen the cohorts of the velites, and further on the great helmets of the Clinabarians, with steel heads glancing in the sun, cuirasses, plumes, and waving standards. But the Carthaginian army, which amounted to eleven thousand three hundred and ninety-six men, seemed scarcely to contain them, for it formed an oblong, narrow at the sides and pressed back upon itself.

Seeing them so weak, the Barbarians, who were thrice as numerous, were seized with extravagant joy. Hamilcar was not to be seen. Perhaps he had remained down yonder? Moreover what did it matter? The disdain which they felt for these traders strengthened their courage; and before Spendius could command a manoeuvre they had all understood it, and already executed it.

They deployed in a long, straight line, overlapping the wings of the Punic army in order to completely encompass it. But when there was an interval of only three hundred paces between the armies, the elephants turned round instead of advancing; then the Clinabarians were seen to face about and follow them; and the surprise of the Mercenaries increased when they saw the archers running to join them. So the Carthaginians were afraid, they were fleeing! A tremendous hooting broke out from among the Barbarian troops, and Spendius exclaimed from the top of his dromedary: "Ah! I knew it! Forward! forward!"

Then javelins, darts, and sling-bullets burst forth simultaneously. The elephants feeling their croups stung by the arrows began to gallop more quickly; a great dust enveloped them, and they vanished like shadows in a cloud.

But from the distance there came a loud noise of footsteps dominated by the shrill sound of the trumpets, which were being blown furiously. The space which the Barbarians had in front of them, which was full of eddies and tumult, attracted like a whirlpool; some dashed into it. Cohorts of infantry appeared; they closed up; and at the same time all the rest saw the foot-soldiers hastening up with the horsemen at a gallop.

Hamilcar had, in fact, ordered the phalanx to break its sections, and the elephants, light troops, and cavalry to pass through the intervals so as to bring themselves speedily upon the wings, and so well had he calculated the distance from the Barbarians, that at the moment when they reached him, the entire Carthaginian army formed one long straight line.

In the centre bristled the phalanx, formed of syntagmata or full squares having sixteen men on each side. All the leaders of all the files appeared amid long, sharp lanceheads, which jutted out unevenly around them, for the first six ranks crossed their sarissae, holding them in the middle, and the ten lower ranks rested them upon the shoulders of their companions in succession before them. Their faces were all half hidden beneath the visors of their helmets; their right legs were all covered with bronze knemids; broad cylindrical shields reached down to their knees; and the horrible quadrangular mass moved in a single body, and seemed to live like an animal and work like a machine. Two cohorts of elephants flanked it in regular array; quivering, they shook off the splinters of the arrows that clung to their black skins. The Indians, squatting on their withers among the tufts of white feathers, restrained them with their spoon-headed harpoons, while the men in the towers, who were hidden up to their shoulders, moved about iron distaffs furnished with lighted tow on the edges of their large bended bows. Right and left of the elephants hovered the slingers, each with a sling around his loins, a second on his head, and a third in his right hand. Then came the Clinabarians, each flanked by a negro, and pointing their lances between the ears of their horses, which, like themselves, were completely covered with gold. Afterwards, at intervals, came the light-armed soldiers with shields of lynx skin, beyond which projected the points of the javelins which they held in their left hands; while the Tarentines, each having two coupled horses, relieved this wall of soldiers at its two extremities.

The army of the Barbarians, on the contrary, had not been able to preserve its line. Undulations and blanks were to be found through its extravagant length; all were panting and out of breath with their running.

The phalanx moved heavily along with thrusts from all its sarissae; and the too slender line of the Mercenaries soon yielded in the centre beneath the enormous weight.

Then the Carthaginian wings expanded in order to fall upon them, the elephants following. The phalanx, with obliquely pointed lances, cut through the Barbarians; there were two enormous, struggling bodies; and the wings with slings and arrows beat them back upon the phalangites. There was no cavalry to get rid of them, except two hundred Numidians operating against the right squadron of the Clinabarians. All the rest were hemmed in, and unable to extricate themselves from the lines. The peril was imminent, and the need of coming to some resolution urgent.

Spendius ordered attacks, to be made simultaneously on both flanks of the phalanx so as to pass clean through it. But the narrower ranks glided below the longer ones and recovered their position, and the phalanx turned upon the Barbarians as terrible in flank as it had just been in front.

They struck at the staves of the sarissae, but the cavalry in the rear embarrassed their attack; and the phalanx, supported by the elephants, lengthened and contracted, presenting itself in the form of a square, a cone, a rhombus, a trapezium, a pyramid. A twofold internal movement went on continually from its head to its rear; for those who were at the lowest part of the files hastened up to the first ranks, while the latter, from fatigue, or on account of the wounded, fell further back. The Barbarians found themselves thronged upon the phalanx. It was impossible for it to advance; there was, as it were, an ocean wherein leaped red crests and scales of brass, while the bright shields rolled like silver foam. Sometimes broad currents would descend from one extremity to the other, and then go up again, while a heavy mass remained motionless in the centre. The lances dipped and rose alternately. Elsewhere there was so quick a play of naked swords that only the points were visible, while turmae of cavalry formed wide circles which closed again like whirlwinds behind them.

Above the voices of the captains, the ringing of clarions and the grating of lyres, bullets of lead and almonds of clay whistled through the air, dashing the sword from the hand or the brain out of the skull. The wounded, sheltering themselves with one arm beneath their shields, pointed their swords by resting the pommels upon the ground, while others, lying in pools of blood, would turn and bite the heels of those above them. The multitude was so compact, the dust so thick, and the tumult so great that it was impossible to distinguish anything; the cowards who offered to surrender were not even heard. Those whose hands were empty clasped one another close; breasts cracked against cuirasses, and corpses hung with head thrown back between a pair of contracted arms. There was a company of sixty Umbrians who, firm on their hams, their pikes before their eyes, immovable and grinding their teeth, forced two syntagmata to recoil simultaneously. Some Epirote shepherds ran upon the left squadron of the Clinabarians, and whirling their staves, seized the horses by the mane; the animals threw their riders and fled across the plain. The Punic slingers scattered here and there stood gaping. The phalanx began to waver, the captains ran to and fro in distraction, the rearmost in the files were pressing upon the soldiers, and the Barbarians had reformed; they were recovering; the victory was theirs.

But a cry, a terrible cry broke forth, a roar of pain and wrath: it came from the seventy-two elephants which were rushing on in double line, Hamilcar having waited until the Mercenaries were massed together in one spot to let them loose against them; the Indians had goaded them so vigorously that blood was trickling down their broad ears. Their trunks, which were smeared with minium, were stretched straight out in the air like red serpents; their breasts were furnished with spears and their backs with cuirasses; their tusks were lengthened with steel blades curved like sabres—and to make them more ferocious they had been intoxicated with a mixture of pepper, wine, and incense. They shook their necklaces of bells, and shrieked; and the elephantarchs bent their heads beneath the stream of phalaricas which was beginning to fly from the tops of the towers.

In order to resist them the better the Barbarians rushed forward in a compact crowd; the elephants flung themselves impetuously upon the centre of it. The spurs on their breasts, like ships' prows, clove through the cohorts, which flowed surging back. They stifled the men with their trunks, or else snatching them up from the ground delivered them over their heads to the soldiers in the towers; with their tusks they disembowelled them, and hurled them into the air, and long entrails hung from their ivory fangs like bundles of ropes from a mast. The Barbarians strove to blind them, to hamstring them; others would slip beneath their bodies, bury a sword in them up to the hilt, and perish crushed to death; the most intrepid clung to their straps; they would go on sawing the leather amid flames, bullets, and arrows, and the wicker tower would fall like a tower of stone. Fourteen of the animals on the extreme right, irritated by their wounds, turned upon the second rank; the Indians seized mallet and chisel, applied the latter to a joint in the head, and with all their might struck a great blow.

Down sank the huge beasts, falling one above another. It was like a mountain; and upon the heap of dead bodies and armour a monstrous elephant, called "The Fury of Baal," which had been caught by the leg in some chains, stood howling until the evening with an arrow in its eye.

The others, however, like conquerors, delighting in extermination, overthrew, crushed, stamped, and raged against the corpses and the *débris*. To repel the maniples in serried circles around them, they turned about on their hind feet as they advanced, with a continual rotatory motion. The Carthaginians felt their energy increase, and the battle began again.

The Barbarians were growing weak; some Greek hoplites threw away their arms, and terror seized upon the rest. Spendius was seen stooping upon his dromedary, and spurring it on the shoulders with two javelins. Then they all rushed away from the wings and ran towards Utica.

The Clinabarians, whose horses were exhausted, did not try to overtake them. The Ligurians, who were weakened by thirst, cried out for an advance towards the river. But the Carthaginians, who were posted in the centre of the syntagmata, and had suffered less, stamped their feet with longing for the vengeance which was flying from them; and they were already darting forward in pursuit of the Mercenaries when Hamilcar appeared.

He held in his spotted and sweat-covered horse with silver reins. The bands fastened to the horns on his helmet flapped in the wind behind him, and he had placed his oval shield beneath his left thigh. With a motion of his triple-pointed pike he checked the army.

The Tarentines leaped quickly upon their spare horses, and set off right and left towards the river and towards the town.

The phalanx exterminated all the remaining Barbarians at leisure. When the swords appeared they would stretch out their throats and close their eyelids. Others defended themselves to the last, and were knocked down from a distance with flints like mad dogs. Hamilcar had desired the taking of prisoners, but the Carthaginians obeyed him grudgingly, so much pleasure did they derive from plunging their swords into the bodies of the Barbarians. As they were too hot they set about their work with bare arms like mowers; and when they desisted to take breath they would follow with their eyes a horseman galloping across the country after a fleeing soldier. He would succeed in seizing him by the hair, hold him thus for a while, and then fell him with a blow of his axe.

Night fell. Carthaginians and Barbarians had disappeared. The elephants which had taken to flight roamed in the horizon with their fired towers. These burned here and there in the darkness like beacons half lost in the mist; and no movement could be discerned in the plain save the undulation of the river, which was heaped with corpses, and was drifting them away to the sea.

Two hours afterwards Matho arrived. He caught sight in the starlight of long, uneven heaps lying upon the ground.

They were files of Barbarians. He stooped down; all were dead. He called into the distance, but no voice replied.

That very morning he had left Hippo-Zarytus with his soldiers to march upon Carthage. At Utica the army under Spendius had just set out, and the inhabitants were beginning to lire the engines. All had fought desperately. But, the tumult which was going on in the direction of the bridge increasing in an incomprehensible fashion, Matho had struck across the mountain by the shortest road, and as the Barbarians were fleeing over the plain he had encountered nobody.

Facing him were little pyramidal masses rearing themselves in the shade, and on this side of the river and closer to him were motionless lights on the surface of the ground. In fact the Carthaginians had fallen back behind the bridge, and to deceive the Barbarians the Suffet had stationed numerous posts upon the other bank.

Matho, still advancing, thought that he could distinguish Punic ensigns, for horses' heads which did not stir appeared in the air fixed upon the tops of piles of staves which could not be seen; and further off he could hear a great clamour, a noise of songs, and clashing of cups.

Then, not knowing where he was nor how to find Spendius, assailed with anguish, scared, and lost in the darkness, he returned more impetuously by the same road. The dawn was growing grey when from the top of the mountain he perceived the town with the carcasses of the engines blackened by the flames and looking like giant skeletons leaning against the walls.

All was peaceful amid extraordinary silence and heaviness. Among his soldiers on the verge of the tents men were sleeping nearly naked, each upon his back, or with his forehead against his arm which was supported by his cuirass. Some were unwinding bloodstained bandages from their legs. Those who were doomed to die rolled their heads about gently; others dragged themselves along and brought them drink. The sentries walked up and down along the narrow paths in order to warm themselves, or stood in a fierce attitude with their faces turned towards the horizon, and their pikes on their shoulders. Matho found Spendius sheltered beneath a rag of canvas, supported by two sticks set in the ground, his knee in his hands and his head cast down.

They remained for a long time without speaking.

At last Matho murmured: "Conquered!"

Spendius rejoined in a gloomy voice: "Yes, conquered!"

And to all questions he replied by gestures of despair.

Meanwhile sighs and death-rattles reached them. Matho partially opened the canvas. Then the sight of the soldiers reminded him of another disaster on the same spot, and he ground his teeth: "Wretch! once already—"

Spendius interrupted him: "You were not there either."

"It is a curse!" exclaimed Matho. "Nevertheless, in the end I will get at him! I will conquer him! I will slay him! Ah! if I had been there!—" The thought of having missed the battle rendered him even more desperate than the defeat. He snatched up his sword and threw it upon the ground. "But how did the Carthaginians beat you?"

The former slave began to describe the manoeuvres. Matho seemed to see them, and he grew angry. The army from Utica ought to have taken Hamilcar in the rear instead of hastening to the bridge.

"Ah! I know!" said Spendius.

"You ought to have made your ranks twice as deep, avoided exposing the velites against the phalanx, and given free passage to the elephants. Everything might have been recovered at the last moment; there was no necessity to fly."

Spendius replied:

"I saw him pass along in his large red cloak, with uplifted arms and higher than the dust, like an eagle flying upon the flank of the cohorts; and at every nod they closed up or darted forward; the throng carried us towards each other; he looked at me, and I felt the cold steel as it were in my heart."

"He selected the day, perhaps?" whispered Matho to himself.

They questioned eachother, trying to discover what it was that had brought the Suffet just when circumstances were most unfavourable. They went on to talk over the situation, and Spendius, to extenuate his fault, or to revive his courage, asserted that some hope still remained.

"And if there be none, it matters not!" said Matho; "alone, I will carry on the war!"

"And I too!" exclaimed the Greek, leaping up; he strode to and fro, his eyes sparkling, and a strange smile wrinkling his jackal face.

"We will make a fresh start; do not leave me again! I am not made for battles in the sunlight—the flashing of the swords troubles my sight; it is a disease, I lived too long in the ergastulum. But give me walls to scale at night, and I will enter the citadels, and the corpses shall be cold before cock-crow! Show me any one, any-thing, an enemy, a treasure, a woman—a woman," he repeated, "were she a king's daughter, and I will quickly bring your desire to your feet. You reproach me for having lost the battle against Hanno, nevertheless I won it back again. Confess it! my herd of swine did more for us than a phalanx of Spartans." And yielding to the need that he felt of exalting himself and taking his revenge, he enumerated all that he had done for the cause of the Mercenaries. "It was I who urged on the Gaul in the Suffet's gardens! And later, at Sicca, I maddened them all with fear of the Re-public! Gisco was sending them back, but I prevented the interpreters speaking. Ah! how their tongues hung out of their mouths! do you remember? I brought you into Carthage; I stole the zaïmph. I led you to her. I will do more yet: you shall see!" He burst out laughing like a madman.

Matho regarded him with gaping eyes. He felt in a measure uncomfortable in the presence of this man, who was at once so cowardly and so terrible.

The Greek resumed in jovial tones and cracking his fingers:

"Evoe! Sun after rain! I have worked in the quarries, and I have drunk Massic wine beneath a golden awning in a vessel of my own like a Ptolemæus. Calamity should help to make us cleverer. By dint of work we may make fortune bend. She loves politicians. She will yield!"

He returned to Matho and took him by the arm.

"Master, at present the Carthaginians are sure of their victory. You have quite an army which has not fought, and your men obey *you*. Place them in the front; mine will follow to avenge themselves. I have still three thousand Carians, twelve hundred slingers and archers, whole cohorts! A phalanx even might be formed; let us return!"

Matho, who had been stunned by the disaster, had hitherto thought of no means of repairing it. He listened with open mouth, and the bronze plates which circled his sides rose with the leapings of his heart. He picked up his sword, crying:

"Follow me; forward!"

But when the scouts returned, they announced that the Carthaginian dead had been carried off, that the bridge was in ruins, and that Hamilcar had disappeared.

Chapter IX

In the Field

Hamilcar had thought that the mercenaries would await him at Utica, or that they would return against him; and finding his forces insufficient to make or to sustain an attack, he had struck southwards along the right bank of the river, thus protecting himself immediately from a surprise.

He intended first to wink at the revolt of the tribes and to detach them all from the cause of the Barbarians; then when they were quite isolated in the midst of the provinces he would fall upon them and exterminate them.

In fourteen days he pacified the region comprised between Thouccaber and Utica, with the towns of Tignicabah, Tessourah, Vacca, and others further to the west. Zounghar built in the mountains, Assouras celebrated for its temple, Djeraado fertile in junipers, Thapitis, and Hagour sent embassies to him. The country people came with their hands full of provisions, implored his protection, kissed his feet and those of the soldiers, and complained of the Barbarians. Some came to offer him bags containing heads of Mercenaries slain, so they said, by themselves, but which they had cut off corpses; for many had lost themselves in their flight, and were found dead here and there beneath the olive trees and among the vines.

On the morrow of his victory, Hamilcar, to dazzle the people, had sent to Carthage the two thousand captives taken on the battlefield. They arrived in long companies of one hundred men each, all with their arms fastened behind their backs with a bar of bronze which caught them at the nape of the neck, and the wounded, bleeding as they still were, running also along; horsemen followed them, driving them on with blows of the whip.

Then there was a delirium of joy! People repeated that there were six thousand Barbarians killed; the others would not hold out, and the war was finished; they embraced one another in the streets, and rubbed the faces of the Patæc Gods with butter and cinnamomum to thank them. These, with their big eyes, their big bodies, and their arms raised as high as the shoulder, seemed to live beneath their freshened paint, and to participate in the cheerfulness of the people. The rich left their doors open; the city resounded with the noise of the timbrels; the temples were illuminated every night, and the servants of the goddess went down to Malqua and set up stages of sycamore-wood at the corners of the cross-ways, and prostituted themselves there. Lands were voted to the conquerors, holocausts to Melkarth, three hundred gold crowns to the Suffet, and his partisans proposed to decree to him new prerogatives and honours.

He had begged the Ancients to make overtures to Autaritus for exchanging all the Barbarians, if necessary, for the aged Gisco, and the other Carthaginians detained like him. The Libyans and Nomads composing the army under Autaritus knew scarcely anything of these Mercenaries, who were men of Italiote or Greek race; and the offer by the Republic of so many Barbarians for so few Carthaginians, showed that the value of the former was nothing and that of the latter considerable. They dreaded a snare. Autaritus refused.

Then the Ancients decreed the execution of the captives, although the Suffet had written to them not to put them to death. He reckoned upon incorporating the best of them with his own troops and of thus instigating defections. But hatred swept away all circumspection.

The two thousand Barbarians were tied to the stelæ of the tombs in the Mappalian quarter; and traders, scullions, embroiderers, and even women—the widows of the dead with their children—all who would, came to kill them with arrows. They aimed slowly at them, the better to prolong their torture, lowering the weapon and then raising it in turn; and the multitude pressed forward howling. Paralytics had themselves brought thither in hand-barrows; many took the precaution of bringing their food, and remained on the spot until the evening; others passed the night there. Tents had been set up in which drinking went on. Many gained large sums by hiring out bows.

Then all these crucified corpses were left upright, looking like so many red statues on the tombs, and the excitement even spread to the people of Malqua, who were the descendants of the aboriginal families, and were usually indifferent to the affairs of their country. Out of gratitude for the pleasure it had been giving them they now interested themselves in its fortunes, and felt that they were Carthaginians, and the Ancients thought it a clever thing to have thus blended the entire people in a single act of vengeance.

The sanction of the gods was not wanting; for crows alighted from all quarters of the sky. They wheeled in the air as they flew with loud hoarse cries, and formed a huge cloud rolling continually upon itself. It was seen from Clypea, Rhades, and the promontory of Hermæum. Sometimes it would suddenly burst asunder, its black spirals extending far away, as an eagle clove the centre of it, and then departed again; here and there on the terraces the domes, the peaks of the obelisks, and the pediments of the temples there were big birds holding human fragments in their reddened beaks.

Owing to the smell the Carthaginians resigned themselves to unbind the corpses. A few of them were burnt; the rest were thrown into the sea, and the waves, driven by the north wind, deposited them on the shore at the end of the gulf before the camp of Autaritus.

This punishment had no doubt terrified the Barbarians, for from the top of Eschmoun they could be seen striking their tents, collecting their flocks, and hoisting their baggage upon asses, and on the evening of the same day the entire army withdrew.

It was to march to and fro between the mountain of the Hot Springs and Hippo-Zarytus, and so debar the Suffet from approaching the Tyrian towns, and from the possibility of a return to Carthage.

Meanwhile the two other armies were to try to overtake him in the south, Spendius in the east, and Matho in the west, in such a way that all three should unite to surprise and entangle him. Then they received a reinforcement which they had not looked for: Narr' Havas reappeared with three hundred camels laden with bitumen, twenty-five elephants, and six thousand horsemen.

To weaken the Mercenaries the Suffet had judged it prudent to occupy his attention at a distance in his own kingdom. From the heart of Carthage he had to come to an understanding with Masgaba, a Gætulian brigand who was seeking to found an empire. Strengthened by Punic money, the adventurer had raised the Numidian States with promises of freedom. But Narr' Havas, warned by his nurse's son, had dropped into Cirta, poisoned the conquerors with the water of the cisterns, struck off a few heads, set all right again, and had just arrived against the Suffet more furious than the Barbarians.

The chiefs of the four armies concerted the arrangements for the war. It would be a long one, and everything must be foreseen.

It was agreed first to entreat the assistance of the Romans, and this mission was offered to Spendius, but as a fugitive he dared not undertake it. Twelve men from the Greek colonies embarked at Annaba in a sloop belonging to the Numidians. Then the chiefs exacted an oath of complete obedience from all the Barbarians. Everyday the captains inspected clothes and boots; the sentries were even forbidden to use a shield, for they would often lean it against their lance and fall asleep as they stood; those who had any baggage trailing after them were obliged to gel rid of it; everything was to be carried, in Roman fashion, on the back. As a precaution against the elephants Matho instituted a corps of cataphract cavalry, men and horses being hidden beneath cuirasses of hippopotamus skin bristling with nails; and to protect the horses' hoofs boots of plaited esparto-grass were made for them.

It was forbidden to pillage the villages, or to tyrannise over the inhabitants who were not of Punic race. But as the country was becoming exhausted, Matho ordered the provisions to be served out to the soldiers individually, without troubling about the women. At first the men shared with them. Many grew weak for lack of food. It was the occasion of incessant quarrels and invectives, many drawing away the companions of the rest by the bait or even by the promise of their own portion. Matho commanded them all to be driven away pitilessly. They took refuge in the camp of Autaritus; but the Gaulish and Libyan women forced them by their outrageous treatment to depart.

At last they came beneath the walls of Carthage to implore the protection of Ceres and Proserpine, for in Byrsa there was a temple with priests consecrated to these goddesses in expiation of the horrors formerly committed at the siege of Syracuse. The Syssitia, alleging their right to waifs and strays, claimed the youngest in order to sell them; and some fair Lacedæmonian women were taken by New Carthaginians in marriage.

A few persisted in following the armies. They ran on the flank of the syntagmata by the side of the captains. They called to their husbands, pulled them by the cloak, cursed them as they beat their breasts, and held out their little naked and weeping children at arm's length. The sight of them was unmanning the Barbarians; they were an embarrassment and a peril. Several times they were repulsed, but they came back again; Matho made the horsemen belonging to Narr' Havas charge them with the point of the lance; and on some Balearians shouting out to him that they must have women, he replied: "*I* have none!"

Just now he was invaded by the genius of Moloch. In spite of the rebellion of his conscience, he performed terrible deeds, imagining that he was thus obeying the voice of a god. When he could not ravage the fields, Matho would cast stones into them to render them sterile.

He urged Autaritus and Spendius with repeated messages to make haste. But the Suffet's operations were incomprehensible. He encamped at Eidous, Monchar, and Tehent successively; some scouts believed that they saw him in the neighbourhood of Ischiil, near the frontiers of Narr' Havas, and it was reported that he had crossed the river above Tebourba as though to return to Carthage. Scarcely was he in one place when he removed to another. The routes that he followed always remained unknown. The Suffet preserved his advantages without offering battle, and while pursued by the Barbarians seemed to be leading them.

These marches and counter marches were still more fatiguing to the Carthaginians; and Hamilcar's forces, receiving no reinforcements, diminished from day to day. The country people were now more backward in bringing him in provisions. In every direction he encountered taciturn hesitation and hatred; and in spite of his entreaties to the Great Council no succour came from Carthage.

It was said, perhaps it was believed, that he had need of none. It was a trick, or his complaints were unnecessary; and Hanno's partisans, in order to do him an ill turn, exaggerated the importance of his victory. The troops which he commanded he was welcome to; but they were not going to supply all his demands continually in that way. The war was quite burdensome enough! it had cost too much, and from pride the patricians belonging to his faction supported him but slackly.

Then Hamilcar, despairing of the Republic, took by force from the tribes all that he wanted for the war—grain, oil, wood, cattle, and men. But the inhabitants were not long in taking to flight. The villages passed through were empty, and the cabins were ransacked without anything being discerned in them. The Punic army was soon encompassed by a terrible solitude.

The Carthaginians, who were furious, began to sack the provinces; they filled up the cisterns and fired the houses. The sparks, being carried by the wind, were scattered far off, and whole forests were on fire on the mountains; they bordered the valleys with a crown of flames, and it was often necessary to wait in order to pass beyond them. Then the soldiers resumed their march over the warm ashes in the full glare of the sun.

Sometimes they would see what looked like the eyes of a tiger cat gleaming in a bush by the side of the road. This was a Barbarian crouching upon his heels, and smeared with dust, that he might not be distinguished from the colour of the foliage; or perhaps when passing along a ravine those on the wings would suddenly hear the rolling of stones, and raising their eyes would perceive a bare-footed man bounding along through the opening of the gorge.

Meanwhile Utica and Hippo-Zarytus were free since the Mercenaries were no longer besieging them. Hamilcar commanded them to come to his assistance. But not caring to compromise themselves, they answered him with vague words, with compliments and excuses.

He went up again abruptly into the North, determined to open up one of the Tyrian towns, though he were obliged to lay siege to it. He required a station on the coast, so as to be able to draw supplies and men from the islands or from Cyrene, and he coveted the harbour of Utica as being the nearest to Carthage.

The Suffet therefore left Zouitin and turned the lake of Hippo-Zarytus with circumspection. But he was soon obliged to lengthen out his regiments into column in order to climb the mountain which separates the two valleys. They were descending at sunset into its hollow, funnel-shaped summit, when they perceived on the level of the ground before them bronze she-wolves which seemed to be running across the grass.

Suddenly large plumes arose and a terrible song burst forth, accompanied by the rhythm of flutes. It was the army under Spendius; for some Campanians and Greeks, in their execration of Carthage, had assumed the ensigns of Rome. At the same time long pikes, shields of leopard's skin, linen cuirasses, and naked shoulders were seen on the left. These were the Iberians under Matho, the Lusitanians, Balearians, and Gætulians; the horses of Narr' Havas were heard to neigh; they spread around the hill; then came the loose rabble commanded by Autaritus—— Gauls, Libyans, and Nomads; while the Eaters of Uncleanness might be recognised among them by the fish bones which they wore in their hair.

Thus the Barbarians, having contrived their marches with exactness, had come together again. But themselves surprised, they remained motionless for some minutes in consultation.

The Suffet had collected his men into an orbicular mass, in such a way as to offer an equal resistance in every direction. The infantry were surrounded by their tall, pointed shields fixed close to one another in the turf. The Clinabarians were outside and the elephants at intervals further off. The Mercenaries were worn out with fatigue; it was better to wait till next day; and the Barbarians feeling sure of their victory occupied themselves the whole night in eating.

They lighted large bright fires, which, while dazzling themselves, left the Punic army below them in the shade. Hamilcar caused a trench fifteen feet broad and ten cubits deep to be dug in Roman fashion round his camp, and the earth thrown out to be raised on the inside into a parapet, on which sharp interlacing stakes were planted; and at sunrise the Mercenaries were amazed to perceive all the Carthaginians thus entrenched as if in a fortress.

They could recognise Hamilcar in the midst of the tents walking about and giving orders. His person was clad in a brown cuirass cut in little scales; he was followed by his horse, and stopped from time to time to point out something with his right arm outstretched.

Then more than one recalled similar mornings when, amid the din of clarions, he passed slowly before them, and his looks strengthened them like cups of wine. A kind of emotion overcame them. Those, on the contrary, who were not acquainted with Hamilcar, were mad with joy at having caught him.

Nevertheless if all attacked at once they would do one another mutual injury in the insufficiency of space. The Numidians might dash through; but the Clinabarians, who were protected by cuirasses, would crush them. And then how were the palisades to be crossed? As to the elephants, they were not sufficiently well trained.

"You are all cowards!" exclaimed Matho.

And with the best among them he rushed against the entrenchment. They were repulsed by a volley of stones; for the Suffet had taken their abandoned catapults on the bridge.

This want of success produced an abrupt change in the fickle minds of the Barbarians. Their extreme bravery disappeared; they wished to conquer, but with the smallest possible risk. According to Spendius they ought to maintain carefully the position that they held, and starve out the Punic army. But the Carthaginians began to dig wells, and as there were mountains surrounding the hill, they discovered water.

From the summit of their palisade they launched arrows, earth, dung, and pebbles which they gathered from the ground, while the six catapults rolled incessantly throughout the length of the terrace.

But the springs would dry up of themselves; the provisions would be exhausted, and the catapults worn out; the Mercenaries, who were ten times as numerous, would triumph in the end. The Suffet devised negotiations so as to gain time, and one morning the Barbarians found a sheep's skin covered with writing within their lines. He justified himself for his victory: the Ancients had forced him into the war, and to show them that he was keeping his word, he offered them the pillaging of Utica or Hippo-Zarytus at their choice; in conclusion, Hamilcar declared that he did not fear them because he had won over some traitors, and thanks to them would easily manage the rest.

The Barbarians were disturbed: this proposal of immediate booty made them consider; they were apprehensive of treachery, not suspecting a snare in the Suffet's boasting, and they began to look upon one another with mistrust. Words and steps were watched; terrors awaked them in the night. Many forsook their companions and chose their army as fancy dictated, and the Gauls with Autaritus went and joined themselves with the men of Cisalpine Gaul, whose language they understood.

The four chiefs met together every evening in Matho's tent, and squatting round a shield, attentively moved backwards and forwards the little wooden figures invented by Pyrrhus for the representation of manoeuvres. Spendius would demonstrate Hamilcar's resources, and with oaths by all the gods entreat that the opportunity should not be wasted. Matho would walk about angry and gesticulating. The war against Carthage was his own personal affair; he was indignant that the others should interfere in it without being willing to obey him. Autaritus would divine his speech from his countenance and applaud. Narr' Havas would elevate his chin to mark his disdain; there was not a measure that he did not consider fatal; and he had ceased to smile. Sighs would escape him as though he were thrusting back sorrow for an impossible dream, despair for an abortive enterprise.

While the Barbarians deliberated in uncertainty, the Suffet increased his defences: he had a second trench dug within the palisades, a second wall raised, and wooden towers constructed at the corners; and his slaves went as far as the middle of the outposts to drive caltrops into the ground. But the elephants, whose allowances were lessened, struggled in their shackles. To economise the grass he ordered the Clinabarians to kill the least strong among the stallions. A few refused to do so, and he had them decapitated. The horses were eaten. The recollection of this fresh meat was a source of great sadness to them in the days that followed.

From the bottom of the amphitheatre in which they were confined they could see the four bustling camps of the Barbarians all around them on the heights. Women moved about with leathern bottles on their heads, goats strayed bleating beneath the piles of pikes; sentries were being relieved, and eating was going on around tripods. In fact, the tribes furnished them abundantly with provisions, and they did not themselves suspect how much their inaction alarmed the Punic army.

On the second day the Carthaginians had remarked a troop of three hundred men apart from the rest in the camp of the nomads. These were the rich who had been kept prisoners since the beginning of the war. Some Libyans ranged them along the edge of the trench, took their station behind them, and hurled javelins, making themselves a rampart of their bodies. The wretched creatures could scarcely be recognised, so completely were their faces covered with vermin and filth. Their hair had been plucked out in places, leaving bare the ulcers on their heads, and they were so lean and hideous that they were like mummies in tattered shrouds. A few trembled and sobbed with a stupid look; the rest cried out to their friends to fire upon the Barbarians. There was one who remained quite motionless with face cast down, and without speaking; his long white beard fell to his chain-covered hands; and the Carthaginians, feeling as it were the downfall of the Republic in the bottom of their hearts, recognised Gisco. Although the place was a dangerous one they pressed forward to see him. On his head had been placed a grotesque tiara of hippopotamus leather incrusted with pebbles. It was Autaritus's idea; but it was displeasing to Matho.

Hamilcar in exasperation, and resolved to cut his way through in one way or another, had the palisades opened; and the Carthaginians went at a furious rate half way up the hill or three hundred paces. Such a flood of Barbarians descended upon them that they were driven back to their lines. One of the guards of the Legion who had remained outside was stumbling among the stones. Zarxas ran up to him, knocked him down, and plunged a dagger into his throat; he drew it out, threw himself upon the wound—and gluing his lips to it with mutterings of joy, and star-lings which shook him to the heels, pumped up the blood by breastfuls; then he quietly sat down upon the corpse, raised his face with his neck thrown back the better to breathe in the air, like a hind that has just drunk at a mountain stream, and in a shrill voice began to sing a Balearic song, a vague melody full of prolonged modulations, with interruptions and alternations like echoes answering one another in the mountains; he called upon his dead brothers and invited them to a feast; then he let his hands fall between his legs, slowly bent his head, and wept. This atrocious occurrence horrified the Barbarians, especially the Greeks.

From that time forth the Carthaginians did not attempt to make any sally; and they had no thought of surrender, certain as they were that they would perish in tortures.

Nevertheless the provisions, in spite of Hamilcar's carefulness, diminished frightfully. There was not left per man more than ten k'hommers of wheat, three hins of millet, and twelve betzas of dried fruit. No more meat, no more oil, no more salt food, and not a grain of barley for the horses, which might be seen stretching down their wasted necks seeking in the dust for blades of trampled straw. Often the sentries on vedette upon the terrace would see in the moonlight a dog belonging to the Barbarians coming to prowl beneath the entrenchment among the heaps of filth; it would be knocked down with a stone, and then, after a descent had been effected along the palisades by means of the straps of a shield, it would be eaten without a word. Sometimes horrible barkings would be heard and the man would not come up again. Three phalangites, in the fourth dilochia of the twelfth syntagma, killed one another with knives in a dispute about a rat.

All regretted their families, and their houses; the poor their hive-shaped huts, with the shells on the threshold and the hanging net, and the patricians their large halls filled with bluish shadows, where at the most indolent hour of the day they used to rest listening to the vague noise of the streets mingled with the rustling of the leaves as they stirred in their gardens—to go deeper into the thought of this, and to enjoy it more, they would half close their eyelids, only to be roused by the shock of a wound. Every minute there was some engagement, some fresh alarm; the towers were burning, the Eaters of Uncleanness were leaping across the palisades; their hands would be struck off with axes; others would hasten up; an iron hail would fall upon the tents. Galleries of rushen hurdles were raised as a protection against the projectiles. The Carthaginians shut themselves up within them and stirred out no more.

Everyday the sun coming over the hill used, after the early hours, to forsake the bottom of the gorge and leave them in the shade. The grey slopes of the ground, covered with flints spotted with scanty lichen, ascended in front and in the rear, and above their summits stretched the sky in its perpetual purity, smoother and colder to the eye than a metal cupola. Hamilcar was so indignant with Carthage that he felt inclined to throw himself among the Barbarians and lead them against her. Moreover, the porters, sutlers, and slaves were beginning to murmur, while neither people, nor Great Council, nor any one sent as much as a hope. The situation was intolerable, especially owing to the thought that it would become worse.

At the news of the disaster Carthage had leaped, as it were, with anger and hate; the Suffet would have been less execrated if he had allowed himself to be conquered from the first.

But time and money were lacking for the hire of other Mercenaries. As to a levy of soldiers in the town, how were they to be equipped? Hamilcar had taken all the arms! and then who was to command them? The best captains were down yonder with him! Meanwhile, some men despatched by the Suffet arrived in the streets with shouts. The Great Council were roused by them, and contrived to make them disappear.

It was an unnecessary precaution; everyone accused Barca of having behaved with slackness. He ought to have annihilated the Mercenaries after his victory. Why had he ravaged the tribes? The sacrifices already imposed had been heavy enough! and the patricians deplored their contributions of fourteen shekels, and the Syssitia their two hundred and twenty-three thousand gold kikars; those who had given nothing lamented like the rest. The populace was jealous of the New Carthaginians, to whom he had promised full rights of citizenship; and even the Ligurians, who had fought with such intrepidity, were confounded with the Barbarians and cursed like them; their race became a crime, the proof of complicity. The traders on the threshold of their shops, the workmen passing plumb-line in hand, the vendors of pickle rinsing their baskets, the attendants in the vapour baths and the retailers of hot drinks all discussed the operations of the campaign. They would trace battle-plans with their fingers in the dust, and there was not a sorry rascal to be found who could not have corrected Hamilcar's mistakes.

It was a punishment, said the priests, for his long-continued impiety. He had offered no holocausts; he had not purified his troops; he had even refused to take augurs with him; and the scandal of sacrilege strengthened the violence of restrained hate, and the rage of betrayed hopes. People recalled the Sicilian disasters, and all the burden of his pride that they had borne for so long! The colleges of the pontiffs could not forgive him for having seized their treasure, and they demanded a pledge from the Great Council to crucify him should he ever return.

The heats of the month of Eloul, which were excessive in that year, were another calamity. Sickening smells rose from the borders of the Lake, and were wafted through the air together with the fumes of the aromatics that eddied at the corners of the streets. The sounds of hymns were constantly heard. Crowds of people occupied the staircases of the temples; all the walls were covered with black veils; tapers burnt on the brows of the Patæc Gods, and the blood of camels slain for sacrifice ran along the flights of stairs forming red cascades upon the steps. Carthage was agitated with funereal delirium. From the depths of the narrowest lanes, and the blackest dens, there issued pale faces, men with viper-like profiles and grinding their teeth. The houses were filled with the women's piercing shrieks, which, escaping through the gratings, caused those who stood talking in the squares to turn round. Sometimes it was thought that the Barbarians were arriving; they had been seen behind the mountain of the Hot Springs; they were encamped at Tunis; and the voices would multiply and swell, and be blended into one single clamour. Then universal silence would reign, some remaining where they had climbed upon the frontals of the buildings, screening their eyes with their open hand, while the rest lay flat on their faces at the foot of the ramparts straining their ears. When their terror had passed off their anger would begin again. But the conviction of their own impotence would soon sink them into the same sadness as before.

It increased every evening when all ascended the terraces, and bowing down nine times uttered a loud cry in salutation of the sun, as it sank slowly behind the lagoon, and then suddenly disappeared among the mountains in the direction of the Barbarians.

They were waiting for the thrice holy festival when, from the summit of a funeral pile, an eagle flew heavenwards as a symbol of the resurrection of the year, and a message from the people to their Baal; they regarded it as a sort of union, a method of connecting themselves with the might of the Sun. Moreover, filled as they now were with hatred, they turned frankly towards homicidal Moloch, and all forsook Tanith. In fact, Rabbetna, having lost her veil, was as if she had been despoiled of part of her virtue. She denied the beneficence of her waters, she had abandoned Carthage; she was a deserter, an enemy. Some threw stones at her to insult her. But many pitied her while they inveighed against her; she was still beloved, and perhaps more deeply than she had been.

All their misfortunes came, therefore, from the loss of the zaïmph. Salammbô had indirectly participated in it; she was included in the same ill will; she must be punished. A vague idea of immolation spread among the people. To appease the Baalim it was without doubt necessary to offer them something of incalculable worth, a being handsome, young, virgin, of old family, a descendant of the gods, a human star. Everyday the gardens of Megara were invaded by strange men; the slaves, trembling on their own account, dared not resist them. Nevertheless, they did not pass beyond the galley staircase. They remained below with their eyes raised to the highest terrace; they were waiting for Salammbô, and they would cry out for hours against her like dogs baying at the moon.

Chapter X

THE SERPENT

THESE CLAMOURINGS OF THE POPULACE DID NOT ALARM HAMILCAR'S DAUGHter. She was disturbed by loftier anxieties: her great serpent, the black python, was drooping; and in the eyes of the Carthaginians, the serpent was at once a national and a private fetish. It was believed to be the offspring of the dust of the earth, since it emerges from its depths and has no need of feet to traverse it; its mode of progression called to mind the undulations of rivers, its temperature the ancient, viscous, and fecund darkness, and the orbit which it describes when biting its tail the harmony of the planets, and the intelligence of Eschmoun.

Salammbô's serpent had several times already refused the four live sparrows which were offered to it at the full moon and at every new moon. Its handsome skin, covered like the firmament with golden spots upon a perfectly black ground, was now yellow, relaxed, wrinkled, and too large for its body. A cottony mouldiness extended round its head; and in the corners of its eyelids might be seen little red specks which appeared to move. Salammbô would approach its silver-wire basket from time to time, and would draw aside the purple curtains, the lotus leaves, and the bird's down; but it was continually rolled up upon itself, more motionless than a withered bindweed; and from looking at it she at last came to feel a kind of spiral within her heart, another serpent, as it were, mounting up to her throat by degrees and strangling her.

She was in despair at having seen the zaïmph, and yet she felt a sort of joy, an intimate pride at having done so. A mystery shrank within the splendour of its folds; it was the cloud that enveloped the gods, and the secret of the universal existence, and Salammbô, horror-stricken at herself, regretted that she had not raised it.

She was almost always crouching at the back of her apartment, holding her bended left leg in her hands, her mouth half open, her chin sunk, her eye fixed. She recollected her father's face with terror; she wished to go away into the mountains of Rhœnicia, on a pilgrimage to the temple of Aphaka, where Tanith descended in the form of a star; all kinds of imaginings attracted her and terrified her; moreover, a solitude which every day became greater encompassed her. She did not even know what Hamilcar was about.

Wearied at last with her thoughts she would rise, and trailing along her little sandals whose soles clacked upon her heels at every step, she would walk at random through the large silent room. The amethysts and topazes of the ceiling made luminous spots quiver here and there, and Salammbô as she walked would turn her head a little to see them. She would go and take the hanging amphoras by the neck; she would cool her bosom beneath the broad fans, or perhaps amuse herself by burning cinnamomum in hollow pearls. At sunset Taanach would draw back the black felt lozenges that closed the openings in the wall; then her doves, rubbed with musk like the doves of Tanith, suddenly entered, and their pink feet glided over the glass pavement, amid the grains of barley which she threw to them in handfuls like a sower in a field. But on a sudden she would burst into sobs and lie stretched on the large bed of ox-leather straps without moving, repeating a word that was ever the same, with open eyes, pale as one dead, insensible, cold; and yet she could hear the cries of the apes in the tufts of the palm trees, with the continuous grinding of the great wheel which brought a flow of pure water through the stories into the porphyry centre-basin.

Sometimes for several days she would refuse to eat. She could see in a dream troubled stars wandering beneath her feet. She would call Schahabarim, and when he came she had nothing to say to him.

She could not live without the relief of his presence. But she rebelled inwardly against this domination; her feeling towards the priest was one at once of terror, jealously, hatred, and a species of love, in gratitude for the singular voluptuousness which she experienced by his side.

He had recognised the influence of Rabbet, being skilful to discern the gods who sent diseases; and to cure Salammbô he had her apartment watered with lotions of vervain, and maidenhair; she ate mandrakes every morning; she slept with her head on a cushion filled with aromatics blended by the pontiffs; he had even employed baaras, a fiery-coloured root which drives back fatal geniuses into the North; lastly, turning towards the polar star, he murmured thrice the mysterious name of Tanith; but Salammbô still suffered and her anguish deepened.

No one in Carthage was so learned as he. In his youth he had studied at the College of the Mogbeds, at Borsippa, near Babylon; had then visited Samothrace, Pessinus, Ephesus, Thessaly, Judæa, and the temples of the Nabathæ, which are lost in the sands; and had travelled on foot along the banks of the Nile from the cataracts to the sea. Shaking torches with veil-covered face, he had cast a black cock upon a fire of sandarach before the breast of the Sphinx, the Father of Terror. He had descended into the caverns of Proserpine; he had seen the five hundred pillars of the labyrinth of Lemnos revolve, and the candelabrum of Tarentum, which bore as many sconces on its shaft as there are days in the year, shine in its splendour; at times he received Greeks by night in order to question them. The constitution of the world disquieted him no less than the nature of the gods; he had observed the equinoxes with the armils placed in the portico of Alexandria, and accompanied the bematists of Evergetes, who measure the sky by calculating the number of their steps, as far as Cyrene; so that there was now growing in his thoughts a religion of his own, with no distinct formula, and on that very account full of infatuation and fervour. He no longer believed that the earth was formed like a fir-cone; he believed it to be round, and eternally falling through immensity with such prodigious speed that its fall was not perceived.

From the position of the sun above the moon he inferred the predominance of Baal, of whom the planet itself is but the reflection and figure; moreover, all that he saw in terrestrial things compelled him to recognise the male exterminating principle as supreme. And then he secretly charged Rabbet with the misfortune of his life. Was it not for her that the grand-pontiff had once advanced amid the tumult of cymbals, and with a patera of boiling water taken from him his future virility? And he followed with a melancholy gaze the men who were disappearing with the priestesses in the depths of the turpentine trees.

His days were spent in inspecting the censers, the gold vases, the tongs, the rakes for the ashes of the altar, and all the robes of the statues down to the bronze bodkin that served to curl the hair of an old Tanith in the third ædicule near the emerald vine. At the same hours he would raise the great hangings of the same swinging doors; would remain with his arms outspread in the same attitude; or prayed prostrate on the same flag-stones, while around him a people of priests moved barefooted through the passages filled with an eternal twilight.

But Salammbô was in the barrenness of his life like a flower in the cleft of a sepulchre. Nevertheless he was hard upon her, and spared her neither penances nor bitter words. His condition established, as it were, the equality of a common sex between them, and he was less angry with the young girl for his inability to possess her than for finding her so beautiful, and above all so pure. Often he saw that she grew weary in following his thought. Then he would turn away sadder than before; he would feel himself more forsaken, more empty, more alone.

Strange words escaped him sometimes, which passed before Salammbô like broad lightnings illuminating the abysses. This would be at night on the terrace when, both alone, they gazed upon the stars, and Carthage spread below under their feet, with the gulf and the open sea dimly lost in the colour of the darkness.

He would set forth to her the theory of the souls that descend upon the earth, following the same route as the sun through the signs of the zodiac. With outstretched arm he showed the gate of human generation in the Ram, and that of the return to the gods in Capricorn; and Salammbô strove to see them, for she took these conceptions for realities; she accepted pure symbols and even manners of speech as being true in themselves, a distinction not always very clear even to the priest.

"The souls of the dead," said he, "resolve themselves into the moon, as their bodies do into the earth. Their tears compose its humidity; 'tis a dark abode full of mire, and wreck, and tempest."

She asked what would become of her then.

"At first you will languish as light as a vapour hovering upon the waves; and after more lengthened ordeals and agonies, you will pass into the forces of the sun, the very source of Intelligence!"

He did not speak, however, of Rabbet. Salammbô imagined that it was through shame for his vanquished goddess, and calling her by a common name which designated the moon, she launched into blessings upon the soft and fertile planet. At last he exclaimed:

"No! no! she draws all her fecundity from the other! Do you not see her hovering about him like an amorous woman running after a man in a field?" And he exalted the virtue of light unceasingly.

Far from depressing her mystic desires, he sought, on the contrary, to excite them, and he even seemed to take joy in grieving her by the revelation of a pitiless doctrine. In spite of the pains of her love Salammbô threw herself upon it with transport.

But the more that Schahabarim felt himself in doubt about Tanith, the more he wished to believe in her. At the bottom of his soul he was arrested by remorse. He needed some proof, some manifestation from the gods, and in the hope of obtaining it the priest devised an enterprise which might save at once his country and his belief.

Thenceforward he set himself to deplore before Salammbô the sacrilege and the misfortunes which resulted from it even in the regions of the sky. Then he suddenly announced the peril of the Suffet, who was assailed by three armies under the command of Matho—for on account of the veil Matho was, in the eyes of the Carthaginians, the king, as it were, of the Barbarians—and he added that the safety of the Republic and of her father depended upon her alone.

"Upon me!" she exclaimed. "How can I—?"

But the priest, with a smile of disdain said:

"You will never consent!"

She entreated him. At last Schahabarim said to her:

"You must go to the Barbarians and recover the zaïmph!"

She sank down upon the ebony stool, and remained with her arms stretched out between her knees and a shivering in all her limbs, like a victim at the altar's foot awaiting the blow of the club. Her temples were ringing, she could see fiery circles revolving, and in her stupor she had lost the understanding of all things save one, that she was certainly going to die soon.

But if Rabbetna triumphed, if the zaïmph were restored and Carthage delivered, what mattered a woman's life? thought Schahabarim. Moreover, she would perhaps obtain the veil and not perish.

He stayed away for three days; on the evening of the fourth she sent for him.

The better to inflame her heart he reported to her all the invectives howled against Hamilcar in open council; he told her that she had erred, that she owed reparation for her crime, and that Rabbetna commanded the sacrifice.

A great uproar came frequently across the Mappalian district to Megara. Schahabarim and Salammbô went out quickly, and gazed from the top of the galley staircase.

There were people in the square of Khamon shouting for arms. The Ancients would not provide them, esteeming such an effort useless; others who had set out without a general had been massacred. At last they were permitted to depart, and as a sort of homage to Moloch, or from a vague need of destruction, they tore up tall cypress trees in the woods of the temples, and having kindled them at the torches of the Kabiri, were carrying them through the streets singing. These monstrous flames advanced swaying gently; they transmitted fires to the glass balls on the crests of the temples, to the ornaments of the colossuses and the beaks of the ships, passed beyond the terraces and formed suns as it were, which rolled through the town. They descended the Acropolis. The gate of Malqua opened.

"Are you ready?" exclaimed Schahabarim, "or have you asked them to tell your father that you abandoned him?" She hid her face in her veils, and the great lights retired, sinking gradually the while to the edge of the waves.

An indeterminate dread restrained her; she was afraid of Moloch and of Matho. This man, with his giant stature, who was master of the zaïmph, ruled Rabbetna as much as did Baal, and seemed to her to be surrounded by the same figurations; and then the souls of the gods sometimes visited the bodies of men. Did not Schahabarim in speaking of him say that she was to vanquish Moloch? They were mingled with each other; she confused them together; both of them were pursuing her.

She wished to learn the future, and approached the serpent, for auguries were drawn from the attitudes of serpents. But the basket was empty; Salammbô was disturbed.

She found him with his tail rolled round one of the silver balustrades beside the hanging bed, which he was rubbing in order to free himself from his old yellowish skin, while his body stretched forth gleaming and clear like a sword half out of the sheath.

Then on the days following, in proportion as she allowed herself to be convinced, and was more disposed to succour Tanith, the python recovered and grew; he seemed to be reviving.

The certainty that Schahabarim was giving expression to the will of the gods then became established in her conscience. One morning she awoke resolved, and she asked what was necessary to make Matho restore the veil.

"To claim it," said Schahabarim.

"But if he refuses?" she rejoined.

The priest scanned her fixedly with a smile such as she had never seen.

"Yes, what is to be done?" repeated Salammbô.

He rolled between his fingers the extremities of the bands which fell from his tiara upon his shoulders, standing motionless with eyes cast down. At last seeing that she did not understand:

"You will be alone with him."

"Well?" she said.

"Alone in his tent."

"What then?"

Schahabarim bit his lips. He sought for some phrase, some circumlocution.

"If you are to die, that will be later," he said; "later! fear nothing! and whatever he may undertake to do, do not call out! do not be frightened! You will be humble, you understand, and submissive to his desire, which is ordained of heaven!"

"But the veil?"

"The gods will take thought for it," replied Schahabarim.

"Suppose you were to accompany me, O father?" she added.

"No!"

He made her kneel down, and keeping his left hand raised and his right extended, he swore in her behalf to bring back the mantle of Tanith into Carthage. With terrible imprecations she devoted herself to the gods, and each time that Schahabarim pronounced a word she falteringly repeated it.

He indicated to her all the purifications and fastings that she was to observe, and how she was to reach Matho. Moreover, a man acquainted with the routes would accompany her.

She felt as if she had been set free. She thought only of the happiness of seeing the zaïmph again, and she now blessed Schahabarim for his exhortations.

It was the period at which the doves of Carthage migrated to Sicily to the mountain of Eryx and the temple of Venus. For several days before their departure they sought out and called to one another so as to collect together; at last one evening they flew away; the wind blew them along, and the big white cloud glided across the sky high above the sea.

The horizon was filled with the colour of blood. They seemed to descend gradually to the waves; then they disappeared as though swallowed up, and falling of themselves into the jaws of the sun. Salammbô, who watched them retiring, bent her head, and then Taanach, believing that she guessed her sorrow, said gently to her:

"But they will come back, Mistress."

"Yes! I know."

"And you will see them again."

"Perhaps!" she said, sighing.

She had not confided her resolve to any one; in order to carry it out with the greater discretion she sent Taanach to the suburb of Kinisdo to buy all the things that she required instead of requesting them from the stewards: vermilion, aromatics, a linen girdle, and new garments. The old slave was amazed at these preparations, without daring, however, to ask any questions; and the day, which had been fixed by Schahabarim, arrived when Salammbô was to set out.

About the twelfth hour she perceived, in the depths of the sycamore trees, a blind old man with one hand resting on the shoulder of a child who walked before him, while with the other he carried a kind of cithara of black wood against his hip. The eunuchs, slaves, and women had been scrupulously sent away; no one might know the mystery that was preparing.

Taanach kindled four tripods filled with strobus and cardamomum in the corners of the apartment; then she unfolded large Babylonian hangings, and stretched them on cords all around the room, for Salammbô did not wish to be seen even by the walls. The kinnor-player squatted behind the door and the young boy standing upright applied a reed flute to his lips. In the distance the roar of the streets was growing feebler, violet shadows were lengthening before the peristyles of the temples, and on the other side of the gulf the mountain bases, the fields of olive-trees, and the vague yellow lands undulated indefinitely, and were blended together in a bluish haze; not a sound was to be heard, and an unspeakable depression weighed in the air.

Salammbô crouched down upon the onyx step on the edge of the basin; she raised her ample sleeves, fastening them behind her shoulders, and began her ablutions in methodical fashion, according to the sacred rites.

Next Taanach brought her something liquid and coagulated in an alabaster phial; it was the blood of a black dog slaughtered by barren women on a winter's night amid the rubbish of a sepulchre. She rubbed it upon her ears, her heels, and the thumb of her right hand, and even her nail remained somewhat red, as if she had crushed a fruit.

The moon rose; then the cithara and the flute began to play together.

Salammbô unfastened her earrings, her necklace, her bracelets, and her long white simar; she unknotted the band in her hair, shaking the latter for a few minutes softly over her shoulders to cool herself by thus scattering it. The music went on outside; it consisted of three notes ever the same, hurried and frenzied; the strings grated, the flute blew; Taanach kept time by striking her hands; Salammbô, with a swaying of her whole body, chanted prayers, and her garments fell one after another around her.

The heavy tapestry trembled, and the python's head appeared above the cord that supported it. The serpent descended slowly like a drop of water flowing along a wall, crawled among the scattered stuffs, and then, gluing its tail to the ground, rose perfectly erect; and his eyes, more brilliant than carbuncles, darted upon Salammbô.

A horror of cold, or perhaps a feeling of shame, at first made her hesitate. But she recalled Schahabarim's orders and advanced; the python turned downwards, and resting the centre of its body upon the nape of her neck, allowed its head and tail to hang like a broken necklace with both ends trailing to the ground. Salammbô rolled it around her sides, under her arms and between her knees; then taking it by the jaw she brought the little triangular mouth to the edge of her teeth, and half shutting her eyes, threw herself back beneath the rays of the moon. The white light seemed to envelop her in a silver mist, the prints of her humid steps shone upon the flag-stones, stars quivered in the depth of the water; it tightened upon her its black rings that were spotted with scales of gold. Salammbô panted beneath the excessive weight, her loins yielded, she felt herself dying, and with the tip of its tail the serpent gently beat her thigh; then the music becoming still it fell off again.

Taanach came back to her; and after arranging two candelabra, the lights of which burned in crystal balls filled with water, she tinged the inside of her hands with Lawsonia, spread vermilion upon her cheeks, and antimony along the edge of her eyelids, and lengthened her eyebrows with a mixture of gum, musk, ebony, and crushed legs of flies.

Salammbô seated on a chair with ivory uprights, gave herself up to the attentions of the slave. But the touchings, the odour of the aromatics, and the fasts that she had undergone, were enervating her. She became so pale that Taanach stopped.

"Go on!" said Salammbô, and bearing up against herself, she suddenly revived. Then she was seized with impatience; she urged Taanach to make haste, and the old slave grumbled:

"Well! well! Mistress!—Besides, you have no one waiting for you!"

"Yes!" said Salammbô, "some one is waiting for me."

Taanach drew back in surprise, and in order to learn more about it, said:

"What orders do you give me, Mistress? for if you are to remain away—"

But Salammbô was sobbing; the slave exclaimed:

"You are suffering! what is the matter? Do not go away! take me! When you were quite little and used to cry, I took you to my heart and made you laugh with the points of my breasts; you have drained them, Mistress!" She struck herself upon her dried-up bosom. "Now I am old! I can do nothing for you! you no longer love me! you hide your griefs from me, you despise the nurse!" And tears of tenderness and vexation flowed down her cheeks in the gashes of her tattooing.

"No!" said Salammbô, "no, I love you! be comforted!"

With a smile like the grimace of an old ape, Taanach resumed her task. In accordance with Schahabarim's recommendations, Salammbô had ordered the slave to make her magnificent; and she was obeying her mistress with barbaric taste full at once of refinement and ingenuity.

Over a first delicate and vinous-coloured tunic she passed a second embroidered with birds' feathers. Golden scales clung to her hips, and from this broad girdle descended her blue flowing silver-starred trousers. Next Taanach put upon her a long robe made of the cloth of the country of Seres, white and streaked with green lines. On the edge of her shoulder she fastened a square of purple weighted at the hem with grains of sandrastum; and above all these garments she placed a black mantle with a flowing train; then she gazed at her, and proud of her work could not help saying:

"You will not be more beautiful on the day of your bridal!"

"My bridal!" repeated Salammbô; she was musing with her elbow resting upon the ivory chair.

But Taanach set up before her a copper mirror, which was so broad and high that she could see herself completely in it. Then she rose, and with a light touch of her finger raised a lock of her hair which was falling too low.

Her hair was covered with gold dust, was crisped in front, and hung down behind over her back in long twists ending in pearls. The brightness of the candelabra heightened the paint on her cheeks, the gold on her garments, and the whiteness of her skin; around her waist, and on her arms, hands and toes, she had such a wealth of gems that the mirror sent back rays upon her like a sun—and Salammbô, standing by the side of Taanach, who leaned over to see her, smiled amid this dazzling display.

Then she walked to and fro embarrassed by the time that was still left.

Suddenly the crow of a cock resounded. She quickly pinned a long yellow veil upon her hair, passed a scarf around her neck, thrust her feet into blue leather boots, and said to Taanach:

"Go and see whether there is not a man with two horses beneath the myrtles."

Taanach had scarcely re-entered when she was descending the galley staircase. "Mistress!" cried the nurse.

Salammbô turned round with one finger on her mouth as a sign for discretion and immobility.

Taanach stole softly along the prows to the foot of the terrace, and from a distance she could distinguish by the light of the moon a gigantic shadow walking obliquely in the cypress avenue to the left of Salammbô, a sign which presaged death.

Taanach went up again into the chamber. She threw herself upon the ground tearing her face with her nails; she plucked out her hair, and uttered piercing shrieks with all her might.

It occurred to her that they might be heard; then she became silent, sobbing quite softly with her head in her hands and her face on the pavement.

Chapter XI

IN THE TENT

THE MAN WHO GUIDED SALAMMBÔ MADE HER ASCEND AGAIN BEYOND THE pharos in the direction of the Catacombs, and then go down the long suburb of Molouya, which was full of steep lanes. The sky was beginning to grow grey. Sometimes palm-wood beams jutting out from the walls obliged them to bend their heads. The two horses which were at the walk would often slip; and thus they reached the Teveste gate.

Its heavy leaves were half open; they passed through, and it closed behind them.

At first they followed the foot of the ramparts for a time, and at the height of the cisterns they took their way along the Taenia, a narrow strip of yellow earth separating the gulf from the lake and extending as far as Rhades.

No one was to be seen around Carthage, whether on the sea or in the country. The slate-coloured waves chopped softly, and the light wind blowing their foam hither and thither spotted them with white rents. In spite of all her veils, Salammbô shivered in the freshness of the morning; the motion and the open air dazed her. Then the sun rose; it preyed on the back of her head, and she involuntarily dozed a little. The two animals ambled along side by side, their feet sinking into the silent sand.

When they had passed the mountain of the Hot Springs, they went on at a more rapid rate, the ground being firmer.

But although it was the season for sowing and ploughing, the fields were as empty as the desert as far as the eye could reach. Here and there were scattered heaps of corn; at other places the barley was shedding its reddened ears. The villages showed black upon the clear horizon, with shapes incoherently carved.

From time to time a half-calcined piece of wall would be found standing on the edge of the road. The roofs of the cottages were falling in, and in the interiors might be distinguished fragments of pottery, rags of clothing, and all kinds of unrecognisable utensils and broken things. Often a creature clothed in tatters, with earthy face and flaming eyes would emerge from these ruins. But he would very quickly begin to run or would disappear into a hole. Salammbô and her guide did not stop.

Deserted plains succeeded one another. Charcoal dust which was raised by their feet behind them, stretched in unequal trails over large spaces of perfectly white soil. Sometimes they came upon little peaceful spots, where a brook flowed amid the long grass; and as they ascended the other bank Salammbô would pluck damp leaves to cool her hands. At the corner of a wood of rose-bays her horse shied violently at the corpse of a man which lay extended on the ground.

The slave immediately settled her again on the cushions. He was one of the servants of the Temple, a man whom Schahabarim used to employ on perilous missions.

With extreme precaution he now went on foot beside her and between the horses; he would whip the animals with the end of a leathern lace wound round his arm, or would perhaps take balls made of wheat, dates, and yolks of eggs wrapped in lotus leaves from a scrip hanging against his breast, and offer them to Salammbô without speaking, and running all the time.

In the middle of the day three Barbarians clad in animals' skins crossed their path. By degrees others appeared wandering in troops of ten, twelve, or twenty-five men; many were driving goats or a limping cow. Their heavy sticks bristled with brass points; cutlasses gleamed in their clothes, which were savagely dirty, and they opened their eyes with a look of menace and amazement. As they passed some sent them a vulgar benediction; others obscene jests; and Schahabarim's man replied to each in his own idiom. He told them that this was a sick youth going to be cured at a distant temple.

However, the day was closing in. Barkings were heard, and they approached them.

Then in the twilight they perceived an enclosure of dry stones shutting in a rambling edifice. A dog was running along the top of the wall. The slave threw some pebbles at him and they entered a lofty vaulted hall.

A woman was crouching in the centre warming herself at a fire of brushwood, the smoke of which escaped through the holes in the ceiling. She was half hidden by her white hair which fell to her knees; and unwilling to answer, she muttered with idiotic look words of vengeance against the Barbarians and the Carthaginians.

The runner ferreted right and left. Then he returned to her and demanded something to eat. The old woman shook her head, and murmured with her eyes fixed upon the charcoal:

"I was the hand. The ten fingers are cut off. The mouth eats no more."

The slave showed her a handful of gold pieces. She rushed upon them, but soon resumed her immobility.

At last he placed a dagger which he had in his girdle beneath her throat. Then, trembling, she went and raised a large stone, and brought back an amphora of wine with fish from Hippo-Zarytus preserved in honey.

Salammbô turned away from this unclean food, and fell asleep on the horses' caparisons which were spread in a corner of the hall.

He awoke her before daylight.

The dog was howling. The slave went up to it quietly, and struck off its head with a single blow of his dagger. Then he rubbed the horses' nostrils with blood to revive them. The old woman cast a malediction at him from behind. Salammbô perceived this, and pressed the amulet which she wore above her heart.

They resumed their journey.

From time to time she asked whether they would not arrive soon. The road undulated over little hills. Nothing was to be heard but the grating of the grasshoppers. The sun heated the yellowed grass; the ground was all chinked with crevices which in dividing formed, as it were, monstrous paving-stones. Sometimes a viper passed, or eagles flew by; the slave still continued running. Salammbô mused beneath her veils, and in spite of the heat did not lay them aside through fear of soiling her beautiful garments.

At regular distances stood towers built by the Carthaginians for the purpose of keeping watch upon the tribes. They entered these for the sake of the shade, and then set out again.

For prudence sake they had made a wide détour the day before. But they met with no one just now; the region being a sterile one, the Barbarians had not passed that way.

Gradually the devastation began again. Sometimes a piece of mosaic would be displayed in the centre of a field, the sole remnant of a vanished mansion; and the leafless olive trees looked at a distance like large bushes of thorns. They passed through a town in which the houses were burnt to the ground. Human skeletons might be seen along the walls. There were some, too, of dromedaries and mules. Half-gnawed carrion blocked the streets.

Night fell. The sky was lowering and cloudy.

They ascended again for two hours in a westerly direction, when suddenly they perceived a quantity of little flames before them.

These were shining at the bottom of an amphitheatre. Gold plates, as they displaced one another, glanced here and there. These were the cuirasses of the Clinabarians in the Punic camp; then in the neighbourhood they distinguished other and more numerous lights, for the armies of the Mercenaries, now blended together, extended over a great space.

Salammbô made a movement as though to advance. But Schahabarim's man took her further away, and they passed along by the terrace which enclosed the camp of the Barbarians. A breach became visible in it, and the slave disappeared.

A sentry was walking upon the top of the entrenchment with a bow in his hand and a pike on his shoulder.

Salammbô drew still nearer; the Barbarian knelt and a long arrow pierced the hem of her cloak. Then as she stood motionless and shrieking, he asked her what she wanted.

"To speak to Matho," she replied. "I am a fugitive from Carthage."

He gave a whistle, which was repeated at intervals further away.

Salammbô waited; her frightened horse moved round and round, sniffing.

When Matho arrived the moon was rising behind her. But she had a yellow veil with black flowers over her face, and so many draperies about her person, that it was impossible to make any guess about her. From the top of the terrace he gazed upon this vague form standing up like a phantom in the penumbræ of the evening.

At last she said to him:

"Lead me to your tent! I wish it!"

A recollection which he could not define passed through his memory. He felt his heart beating. This air of command intimidated him.

"Follow me!" he said.

The barrier was lowered, and immediately she was in the camp of the Barbarians.

It was filled with a great tumult and a great throng. Bright fires were burning beneath hanging pots; and their purpled reflections illuminating some places left others completely in the dark. There was shouting and calling; shackled horses formed long straight lines amid the tents; the latter were round and square, of leather or of canvas; there were huts of reeds, and holes in the sand such as are made by dogs. Soldiers were carting faggots, resting on their elbows on the ground, or wrapping themselves up in mats and preparing to sleep; and Salammbô's horse sometimes stretched out a leg and jumped in order to pass over them.

She remembered that she had seen them before; but their beards were longer now, their faces still blacker, and their voices hoarser. Matho, who walked before her, waved them off with a gesture of his arm which raised his red mantle. Some kissed his hands; others bending their spines approached him to ask for orders, for he was now veritable and sole chief of the Barbarians; Spendius, Autaritus, and Narr' Havas had become disheartened, and he had displayed so much audacity and obstinacy that all obeyed him.

Salammbô followed him through the entire camp. His tent was at the end, three hundred feet from Hamilcar's entrenchments.

She noticed a wide pit on the right, and it seemed to her that faces were resting against the edge of it on a level with the ground, as decapitated heads might have done. However, their eyes moved, and from these half-opened mouths groanings escaped in the Punic tongue.

Two Negroes holding resin lights stood on both sides of the door. Matho drew the canvas abruptly aside. She followed him.

It was a deep tent with a pole standing up in the centre. It was lighted by a large lamp-holder shaped like a lotus and full of a yellow oil wherein floated handfuls of burning tow, and military things might be distinguished gleaming in the shade. A naked sword leaned against a stool by the side of a shield; whips of hippopotamus leather, cymbals, bells, and necklaces were displayed pell-mell on baskets of esparto-grass; a felt rug lay soiled with crumbs of black bread; some copper money was carelessly heaped upon a round stone in a corner, and through the rents in the canvas the wind brought the dust from without, together with the smell of the elephants, which might be heard eating and shaking their chains.

"Who are you?" said Matho.

She looked slowly around her without replying; then her eyes were arrested in the background, where something bluish and sparkling fell upon a bed of palm-branches.

She advanced quickly. A cry escaped her. Matho stamped his foot behind her.

"Who brings you here? why do you come?"

"To take it!" she replied, pointing to the zaïmph, and with the other hand she tore the veils from her head. He drew back with his elbows behind him, gaping, almost terrified.

She felt as if she were leaning upon the might of the gods; and looking at him face to face she asked him for the zaïmph; she demanded it in words abundant and superb.

Matho did not hear; he was gazing at her, and in his eyes her garments were blended with her body. The clouding of the stuffs, like the splendour of her skin, was something special and belonging to her alone. Her eyes and her diamonds sparkled; the polish of her nails continued the delicacy of the stones which loaded her fingers; the two clasps of her tunic raised her breasts somewhat and brought them closer together, and he in thought lost himself in the narrow interval between them whence there fell a thread holding a plate of emeralds which could be seen lower down beneath the violet gauze. She had as earrings two little sapphire scales, each supporting a hollow pearl filled with liquid scent. A little drop would fall every moment through the holes in the pearl and moisten her naked shoulder. Matho watched it fall.

He was carried away by ungovernable curiosity; and, like a child laying his hand upon a strange fruit, he tremblingly and lightly touched the top of her chest with the tip of his finger: the flesh, which was somewhat cold, yielded with an elastic resistance.

This contact, though scarcely a sensible one, shook Matho to the very depths of his nature. An uprising of his whole being urged him towards her. He would fain have enveloped her, absorbed her, drunk her. His bosom was panting, his teeth were chattering.

Taking her by the wrists he drew her gently to him, and then sat down upon a cuirass beside the palm-tree bed which was covered with a lion's skin. She was standing. He looked up at her, holding her thus between his knees, and repeating:

"How beautiful you are! how beautiful you are!"

His eyes, which were continually fixed upon hers, pained her; and the uncomfortableness, the repugnance increased in so acute a fashion that Salammbô put a constraint upon herself not to cry out. The thought of Schahabarim came back to her, and she resigned herself.

Matho still kept her little hands in his own; and from time to time, in spite of the priest's command, she turned away her face and tried to thrust him off by jerking her arms. He opened his nostrils the better to breathe in the perfume which exhaled from her person. It was a fresh, indefinable emanation, which nevertheless made him dizzy, like the smoke from a perfuming-pan. She smelt of honey, pepper, incense, roses, with another odour still.

But how was she thus with him in his tent, and at his disposal? Someone no doubt had urged her. She had not come for the zaïmph. His arms fell, and he bent his head whelmed in sudden reverie.

To soften him Salammbô said to him in a plaintive voice:

"What have I done to you that you should desire my death?"

"Your death!"

She resumed:

"I saw you one evening by the light of my burning gardens amid fuming cups and my slaughtered slaves, and your anger was so strong that you bounded towards me and I was obliged to fly! Then terror entered into Carthage. There were cries of the devastation of the towns, the burning of the country-seats, the massacre of the soldiery; it was you who had ruined them, it was you who had murdered them! I hate you! Your very name gnaws me like remorse! You are execrated more than the plague, and the Roman war! The provinces shudder at your fury, the furrows are full of corpses! I have followed the traces of your fires as though I were travelling behind Moloch!"

Matho leaped up; his heart was swelling with colossal pride; he was raised to the stature of a god.

With quivering nostrils and clenched teeth she went on:

"As if your sacrilege were not enough, you came to me in my sleep covered with the zaïmph! Your words I did not understand; but I could see that you wished to drag me to some terrible thing at the bottom of an abyss."

Matho, writhing his arms, exclaimed:

"No! no! it was to give it to you! to restore it to you! It seemed to me that the goddess had left her garment for you, and that it belonged to you! In her temple or in your house, what does it matter? are you not all-powerful, immaculate, radiant and beautiful even as Tanith?" And with a look of boundless adoration he added:

"Unless perhaps you are Tanith?"

"I, Tanith!" said Salammbô to herself.

They left off speaking. The thunder rolled in the distance. Some sheep bleated, frightened by the storm.

"Oh! come near!" he went on, "come near! fear nothing!

"Formerly I was only a soldier mingled with the common herd of the Mercenaries, ay, and so meek that I used to carry wood on my back for the others. Do I trouble myself about Carthage! The crowd of its people move as though lost in the dust of your sandals, and all its treasures, with the provinces, fleets, and islands, do not raise my envy like the freshness of your lips and the turn of your shoulders. But I wanted to throw down its walls that I might reach you to possess you! Moreover, I was revenging myself in the meantime! At present I crush men like shells, and I throw myself upon phalanxes; I put aside the sarissae with my hands, I check the stallions by the nostrils; a catapult would not kill me! Oh! if you knew how I think of you in the midst of war! Sometimes the memory of a gesture or of a fold of your garment suddenly seizes me and entwines me like a net! I perceive your eyes in the flames of the phalaricas and on the gilding of the shields! I hear your voice in the sounding of the cymbals. I turn aside, but you are not there! and I plunge again into the battle!"

He raised his arms whereon his veins crossed one another like ivy on the branches of a tree. Sweat flowed down his breast between his square muscles; and his breathing shook his sides with his bronze girdle all garnished with thongs hanging down to his knees, which were firmer than marble. Salammbô, who was accustomed to eunuchs, yielded to amazement at the strength of this man. It was the chastisement of the goddess or the influence of Moloch in motion around her in the five armies. She was overwhelmed with lassitude; and she listened in a state of stupor to the intermittent shouts of the sentinels as they answered one another.

The flames of the lamp flickered in the squalls of hot air. There came at times broad lightning flashes; then the darkness increased; and she could only see Matho's eyeballs like two coals in the night. However, she felt that a fatality was surrounding her, that she had reached a supreme and irrevocable moment, and making an effort she went up again towards the zaïmph and raised her hands to seize it.

"What are you doing?" exclaimed Matho.

"I am going back to Carthage," she placidly replied.

He advanced folding his arms and with so terrible a look that her heels were immediately nailed, as it were, to the spot.

"Going back to Carthage!" He stammered, and, grinding his teeth, repeated:

"Going back to Carthage! Ah! you came to take the zaïmph, to conquer me, and then disappear! No, no! you belong to me! and no one now shall tear you from here! Oh! I have not forgotten the insolence of your large tranquil eyes, and how you crushed me with the haughtiness of your beauty! 'Tis my turn now! You are my captive, my slave, my servant! Call, if you like, on your father and his army, the Ancients, the rich, and your whole accursed people! I am the master of three hundred thousand soldiers! I will go and seek them in Lusitania, in the Gauls, and in the depths of the desert, and I will overthrow your town and burn all its temples; the triremes shall float on the waves of blood! I will not have a house, a stone, or a palm tree remaining! And if men fail me I will draw the bears from the mountains and urge on the lions! Seek not to fly or I kill you!"

Pale and with clenched fists he quivered like a harp whose strings are about to burst. Suddenly sobs stifled him, and he sank down upon his hams.

"Ah! forgive me! I am a scoundrel, and viler than scorpions, than mire and dust! Just now while you were speaking your breath passed across my face, and I rejoiced like a dying man who drinks lying flat on the edge of a stream. Crush me, if only I feel your feet! curse me, if only I hear your voice! Do not go! have pity! I love you! I love you!"

He was on his knees on the ground before her; and he encircled her form with both his arms, his head thrown back, and his hands wandering; the gold discs hanging from his ears gleamed upon his bronzed neck; big tears rolled in his eyes like silver globes; he sighed caressingly, and murmured vague words lighter than a breeze and sweet as a kiss.

Salammbô was invaded by a weakness in which she lost all consciousness of herself. Something at once inward and lofty, a command from the gods, obliged her to yield herself; clouds uplifted her, and she fell back swooning upon the bed amid the lion's hair. The zaïmph fell, and enveloped her; she could see Matho's face bending down above her breast.

"Moloch, thou burnest me!" and the soldier's kisses, more devouring than flames, covered her; she was as though swept away in a hurricane, taken in the might of the sun.

He kissed all her fingers, her arms, her feet, and the long tresses of her hair from one end to the other.

"Carry it off," he said, "what do I care? take me away with it! I abandon the army! I renounce everything! Beyond Gades, twenty days' journey into the sea, you come to an island covered with gold dust, verdure, and birds. On the mountains large flowers filled with smoking perfumes rock like eternal censers; in the citron trees, which are higher than cedars, milk-coloured serpents cause the fruit to fall upon the turf with the diamonds in their jaws; the air is so mild that it keeps you from dying. Oh! I shall find it, you will see. We shall live in crystal grottoes cut out at the foot of the hills. No one dwells in it yet, or I shall become the king of the country."

He brushed the dust off her cothurni; he wanted her to put a quarter of a pomegranate between her lips; he heaped up garments behind her head to make a cushion for her. He sought for means to serve her, and to humble himself, and he even spread the zaïmph over her feet as if it were a mere rug.

"Have you still," he said, "those little gazelle's horns on which your necklaces hang? You will give them to me! I love them!" For he spoke as if the war were finished, and joyful laughs broke from him. The Mercenaries, Hamilcar, every obstacle had now disappeared. The moon was gliding between two clouds. They could see it through an opening in the tent. "Ah, what nights have I spent gazing at her! she seemed to me like a veil that hid your face; you would look at me through her; the memory of you was mingled with her beams; then I could no longer distinguish you!" And with his head between her breasts he wept copiously.

"And this," she thought, "is the formidable man who makes Carthage tremble!"

He fell asleep. Then disengaging herself from his arm she put one foot to the ground, and she perceived that her chainlet was broken.

The maidens of the great families were accustomed to respect these shackles as something that was almost religious, and Salammbô, blushing, rolled the two pieces of the golden chain around her ankles.

Carthage, Megara, her house, her room, and the country that she had passed through, whirled in tumultuous yet distinct images through her memory. But an abyss had yawned and thrown them far back to an infinite distance from her.

The storm was departing; drops of water splashing rarely, one by one, made the tent-roof shake.

Matho slept like a drunken man, stretched on his side, and with one arm over the edge of the couch. His band of pearls was raised somewhat, and uncovered his brow; his teeth were parted in a smile; they shone through his black beard, and there was a silent and almost outrageous gaiety in his half-closed eyelids.

Salammbô looked at him motionless, her head bent and her hands crossed.

A dagger was displayed on a table of cypress-wood at the head of the bed; the sight of the gleaming blade fired her with a sanguinary desire. Mournful voices lingered at a distance in the shade, and like a chorus of geniuses urged her on. She approached it; she seized the steel by the handle. At the rustling of her dress Matho half opened his eyes, putting forth his mouth upon her hands, and the dagger fell.

Shouts arose; a terrible light flashed behind the canvas. Matho raised the latter; they perceived the camp of the Libyans enveloped in great flames.

Their reed huts were burning, and the twisting stems burst in the smoke and flew off like arrows; black shadows ran about distractedly on the red horizon. They could hear the shrieks of those who were in the huts; the elephants, oxen, and horses plunged in the midst of the crowd crushing it together with the stores and baggage that were being rescued from the fire. Trumpets sounded. There were calls of "Matho! Matho!" Some people at the door tried to get in.

"Come along! Hamilcar is burning the camp of Autaritus!"

He made a spring. She found herself quite alone.

Then she examined the zaïmph; and when she had viewed it well she was surprised that she had not the happiness which she had once imagined to herself. She stood with melancholy before her accomplished dream.

But the lower part of the tent was raised, and a monstrous form appeared. Salammbô could at first distinguish only the two eyes and a long white beard which hung down to the ground; for the rest of the body, which was cumbered with the rags of a tawny garment, trailed along the earth; and with every forward movement the hands passed into the beard and then fell again. Crawling in this way it reached her feet, and Salammbô recognised the aged Gisco.

In fact, the Mercenaries had broken the legs of the captive Ancients with a brass bar to prevent them from taking to flight; and they were all rotting pell-mell in a pit in the midst of filth. But the sturdiest of them raised themselves and shouted when they heard the noise of platters, and it was in this way that Gisco had seen Salammbô. He had guessed that she was a Carthaginian woman by the little balls of sandastrum flapping against her cothurni; and having a presentiment of an important mystery he had succeeded, with the assistance of his companions, in getting out of the pit; then with elbows and hands he had dragged himself twenty paces further on as far as Matho's tent. Two voices were speaking within it. He had listened outside and had heard everything.

"It is you!" she said at last, almost terrified.

"Yes, it is I!" he replied, raising himself on his wrists. "They think me dead, do they not?"

She bent her head. He resumed:

"Ah! why have the Baals not granted me this mercy!" He approached so close that he was touching her. "They would have spared me the pain of cursing you!"

Salammbô sprang quickly back, so much afraid was she of this unclean being, who was as hideous as a larva and as terrible as a phantom.

"I am nearly one hundred years old," he said. "I have seen Agathocles; I have seen Regulus and the eagles of the Romans passing over the harvests of the Punic fields! I have seen all the terrors of battles and the sea encumbered with the wrecks of our fleets! Barbarians whom I used to command have chained my four limbs like a slave that has committed murder. My companions are dying around me, one after the other; the odour of their corpses awakes me in the night; I drive away the birds that come to peck out their eyes; and yet not for a single day have I despaired of Carthage! Though I had seen all the armies of the earth against her, and the flames of the siege overtop the height of the temples, I should have still believed in her eternity! But now all is over! all is lost! The gods execrate her! A curse upon you who have quickened her ruin by your disgrace!"

She opened her lips.

"Ah! I was there!" he cried. "I heard you gurgling with love like a prostitute; then he told you of his desire and you allowed him to kiss your hands! But if the frenzy of your unchastity urged you to it, you should at least have done as do the fallow deer, which hide themselves in their copulations, and not have displayed your shame beneath your father's very eyes!"

"What?" she said.

"Ah! you did not know that the two entrenchments are sixty cubits from each other and that your Matho, in the excess of his pride, has posted himself just in front of Hamilcar. Your father is there behind you; and could I climb the path which leads to the platform, I should cry to him: 'Come and see your daughter in the Barbarian's arms! She has put on the garment of the goddess to please him; and in yielding her body to him she surrenders with the glory of your name the majesty of the gods, the vengeance of her country, even the safety of Carthage!" The motion of his toothless mouth moved his beard throughout its length; his eyes were riveted upon her and devoured her; panting in the dust he repeated:

"Ah! sacrilegious one! May you be accursed! accursed! accursed!"

Salammbô had drawn back the canvas; she held it raised at arm's length, and without answering him she looked in the direction of Hamilcar.

"It is this way, is it not?" she said.

"What matters it to you? Turn away! Begone! Rather crush your face against the earth! It is a holy spot which would be polluted by your gaze!"

She threw the zaïmph about her waist, and quickly picked up her veils, mantle, and scarf. "I hasten thither!" she cried; and making her escape Salammbô disappeared.

At first she walked through the darkness without meeting any one, for all were betaking themselves to the fire; the uproar was increasing and great flames purpled the sky behind; a long terrace stopped her.

She turned round to right and left at random, seeking for a ladder, a rope, a stone, something in short to assist her. She was afraid of Gisco, and it seemed to her that shouts and footsteps were pursuing her. Day was beginning to break. She perceived a path in the thickness of the entrenchment. She took the hem of her robe, which impeded her, in her teeth, and in three bounds she was on the platform.

A sonorous shout burst forth beneath her in the shade, the same which she had heard at the foot of the galley staircase, and leaning over she recognised Schahabarim's man with his coupled horses.

He had wandered all night between the two entrenchments; then disquieted by the fire, he had gone back again trying to see what was passing in Matho's camp; and, knowing that this spot was nearest to his tent, he had not stirred from it, in obedience to the priest's command.

He stood up on one of the horses. Salammbô let herself slide down to him; and they fled at full gallop, circling the Punic camp in search of a gate.

Matho had re-entered his tent. The smoky lamp gave but little light, and he also believed that Salammbô was asleep. Then he delicately touched the lion's skin on the palm-tree bed. He called but she did not answer; he quickly tore away a strip of the canvas to let in some light; the zaïmph was gone.

The earth trembled beneath thronging feet. Shouts, neighings, and clashing of armour rose in the air, and clarion flourishes sounded the charge. It was as though a hurricane were whirling around him. Immoderate frenzy made him leap upon his arms, and he dashed outside.

The long files of the Barbarians were descending the mountain at a run, and the Punic squares were advancing against them with a heavy and regular oscillation. The mist, rent by the rays of the sun, formed little rocking clouds which as they rose gradually discovered standards, helmets, and points of pikes. Beneath the rapid evolutions portions of the earth which were still in the shadow seemed to be displaced bodily; in other places it looked as if huge torrents were crossing one another, while thorny masses stood motionless between them. Matho could distinguish the captains, soldiers, heralds, and even the serving-men, who were mounted on asses in the rear. But instead of maintaining his position in order to cover the foot-soldiers, Narr' Havas turned abruptly to the right, as though he wished himself to be crushed by Hamilcar.

His horsemen outstripped the elephants, which were slackening their speed; and all the horses, stretching out their unbridled heads, galloped at so furious a rate that their bellies seemed to graze the earth. Then suddenly Narr' Havas went resolutely up to a sentry. He threw away his sword, lance and javelins, and disappeared among the Carthaginians.

The king of the Numidians reached Hamilcar's tent, and pointing to his men, who were standing still at a distance, he said:

"Barca! I bring them to you. They are yours."

Then he prostrated himself in token of bondage, and to prove his fidelity recalled all his conduct from the beginning of the war.

First, he had prevented the siege of Carthage and the massacre of the captives; then he had taken no advantage of the victory over Hanno after the defeat at Utica. As to the Tyrian towns, they were on the frontiers of his kingdom. Finally he had not taken part in the battle of the Macaras; and he had even expressly absented himself in order to evade the obligation of fighting against the Suffet.

Narr' Havas had in fact wished to aggrandise himself by encroachments upon the Punic provinces, and had alternately assisted and forsaken the Mercenaries according to the chances of victory. But seeing that Hamilcar would ultimately prove the stronger, he had gone over to him; and in his desertion there was perhaps something of a grudge against Matho, whether on account of the command or of his former love.

The Suffet listened without interrupting him. The man who thus presented himself in an army where vengeance was his due was not an auxiliary to be despised; Hamilcar at once divined the utility of such an alliance in his great projects. With the Numidians he would get rid of the Libyans. Then he would draw off the West to the conquest of Iberia; and, without asking Narr' Havas why he had not come sooner, or noticing any of his lies, he kissed him, striking his breast thrice against his own.

It was to bring matters to an end and in despair that he had fired the camp of the Libyans. This army came to him like a relief from the gods; dissembling his joy he replied:

"May the Baals favour you! I do not know what the Republic will do for you, but Hamilcar is not ungrateful."

The tumult increased; some captains entered. He was arming himself as he spoke.

"Come, return! You will use your horsemen to beat down their infantry between your elephants and mine. Courage! exterminate them!"

And Narr' Havas was rushing away when Salammbô appeared.

She leaped down quickly from her horse. She opened her ample cloak and spreading out her arms displayed the zaïmph.

The leathern tent, which was raised at the corners, left visible the entire circuit of the mountain with its thronging soldiers, and as it was in the centre Salammbô could be seen on all sides. An immense shouting burst forth, a long cry of triumph and hope. Those who were marching stopped; the dying leaned on their elbows and turned round to bless her. All the Barbarians knew now that she had recovered the zaïmph; they saw her or believed that they saw her from a distance; and other cries, but those of rage and vengeance, resounded in spite of the plaudits of the Carthaginians. Thus did the five armies in tiers upon the mountain stamp and shriek around Salammbô.

Hamilcar, who was unable to speak, nodded her his thanks. His eyes were directed alternately upon the zaïmph and upon her, and he noticed that her chainlet was broken. Then he shivered, being seized with a terrible suspicion. But soon recovering his impassibility he looked sideways at Narr' Havas without turning his face.

The king of the Numidians held himself apart in a discreet attitude; on his forehead he bore a little of the dust which he had touched when prostrating himself. At last the Suffet advanced towards him with a look full of gravity.

"As a reward for the services which you have rendered me, Narr' Havas, I give you my daughter. Be my son," he added, "and defend your father!"

Narr' Havas gave a great gesture of surprise; then he threw himself upon Hamilcar's hands and covered them with kisses.

Salammbô, calm as a statue, did not seem to understand. She blushed a little as she cast down her eyelids, and her long curved lashes made shadows upon her cheeks.

Hamilcar wished to unite them immediately in indissoluble betrothal. A lance was placed in Salammbô's hands and by her offered to Narr' Havas; their thumbs were tied together with a thong of ox-leather; then corn was poured upon their heads, and the grains that fell around them rang like rebounding hail.

Chapter XII

THE AQUEDUCT

TWELVE HOURS AFTERWARDS ALL THAT REMAINED OF THE MERCENARIES was a heap of wounded, dead, and dying. Hamilcar had suddenly emerged from the bottom of the gorge, and again descended the western slope that looked towards Hippo-Zarytus, and the space being broader at this spot he had taken care to draw the Barbarians into it. Narr' Havas had encompassed them with his horse; the Suffet meanwhile drove them back and crushed them. Then, too, they were conquered beforehand by the loss of the zaïmph; even those who cared nothing about it had experienced anguish and something akin to enfeeblement. Hamilcar, not indulging his pride by holding the field of battle, had retired a little further off on the left to some heights, from which he commanded them.

The shape of the camps could be recognised by their sloping palisades. A long heap of black cinders was smoking on the site of the Libyans; the devastated soil showed undulations like the sea, and the tents with their tattered canvas looked like dim ships half lost in the breakers. Cuirasses, forks, clarions, pieces of wood, iron and brass, corn, straw, and garments were scattered about among the corpses; here and there a phalarica on the point of extinction burned against a heap of baggage; in some places the earth was hidden with shields; horses' carcasses succeeded one another like a series of hillocks; legs, sandals, arms, and coats of mail were to be seen, with heads held in their helmets by the chin-pieces and rolling about like balls; heads of hair were hanging on the thorns; elephants were lying with their towers in pools of blood, with entrails exposed, and gasping. The foot trod on slimy things, and there were swamps of mud although no rain had fallen.

This confusion of dead bodies covered the whole mountain from top to bottom.

Those who survived stirred as little as the dead. Squatting in unequal groups they looked at one another scared and without speaking.

The lake of Hippo-Zarytus shone at the end of a long meadow beneath the setting sun. To the right an agglomeration of white houses extended beyond a girdle of walls; then the sea spread out indefinitely; and the Barbarians, with their chins in their hands, sighed as they thought of their native lands. A cloud of grey dust was falling.

The evening wind blew; then every breast dilated, and as the freshness increased, the vermin might be seen to forsake the dead, who were colder now, and

to run over the hot sand. Crows, looking towards the dying, rested motionless on
the tops of the big stones.

When night had fallen yellow-haired dogs, those unclean beasts which followed the armies, came quite softly into the midst of the Barbarians. At first they
licked the clots of blood on the still tepid stumps; and soon they began to devour
the corpses, biting into the stomachs first of all.

The fugitives reappeared one by one like shadows; the women also ventured to
return, for there were still some of them left, especially among the Libyans, in spite
of the dreadful massacre of them by the Numidians.

Some took ropes' ends and lighted them to use as torches. Others held crossed
pikes. The corpses were placed upon these and were conveyed apart.

They were found lying stretched in long lines, on their backs, with their
mouths open, and their lances beside them; or else they were piled up pell-mell so
that it was often necessary to dig out a whole heap in order to discover those that
were wanting. Then the torch would be passed slowly over their faces. They had
received complicated wounds from hideous weapons. Greenish strips hung from
their foreheads; they were cut in pieces, crushed to the marrow, blue from stran-
gulation, or broadly cleft by the elephants' ivory. Although they had died at almost
the same time there existed differences between their various states of corruption.
The men of the North were puffed up with livid swellings, while the more nervous
Africans looked as though they had been smoked, and were already drying up. The
Mercenaries might be recognised by the tattooing on their hands: the old soldiers
of Antiochus displayed a sparrow-hawk; those who had served in Egypt, the head
of the cynocephalus; those who had served with the princes of Asia, a hatchet, a
pomegranate, or a hammer; those who had served in the Greek republics, the side-
view of a citadel or the name of an archon; and some were to be seen whose arms
were entirely covered with these multiplied symbols, which mingled with their
scars and their recent wounds.

Four great funeral piles were erected for the men of Latin race, the Samnites,
Etruscans, Campanians, and Bruttians.

The Greeks dug pits with the points of their swords. The Spartans removed
their red cloaks and wrapped them round the dead; the Athenians laid them out
with their faces towards the rising sun; the Cantabrians buried them beneath a heap
of pebbles; the Nasamonians bent them double with ox-leather thongs, and the
Garamantians went and interred them on the shore so that they might be perpetually washed by the waves. But the Latins were grieved that they could not collect
the ashes in urns; the Nomads regretted the heat of the sands in which bodies were
mummified, and the Celts, the three rude stones beneath a rainy sky at the end of
an islet-covered gulf.

Vociferations arose, followed by a lengthened silence. This was to oblige the souls to return. Then the shouting was resumed persistently at regular intervals.

They made excuses to the dead for their inability to honour them as the rites prescribed: for, owing to this deprivation, they would pass for infinite periods through all kinds of chances and metamorphoses; they questioned them and asked them what they desired; others loaded them with abuse for having allowed themselves to be conquered.

The bloodless faces lying back here and there on wrecks of armour showed pale in the light of the great funeral-pile; tears provoked tears, the sobs became shriller, the recognitions and embracings more frantic. Women stretched themselves on the corpses, mouth to mouth and brow to brow; it was necessary to beat them in order to make them withdraw when the earth was being thrown in. They blackened their cheeks; they cut off their hair; they drew their own blood and poured it into the pits; they gashed themselves in imitation of the wounds that disfigured the dead. Roarings burst forth through the crashing of the cymbals. Some snatched off their amulets and spat upon them. The dying rolled in the bloody mire biting their mutilated fists in their rage; and forty-three Samnites, quite a "sacred spring," cut one another's throats like gladiators. Soon wood for the funeral-piles failed, the flames were extinguished, every spot was occupied; and weary from shouting, weakened, tottering, they fell asleep close to their dead brethren, those who still clung to life full of anxieties, and the others desiring never to wake again.

In the greyness of the dawn some soldiers appeared on the outskirts of the Barbarians, and filed past with their helmets raised on the points of their pikes; they saluted the Mercenaries and asked them whether they had no messages to send to their native lands.

Others approached, and the Barbarians recognised some of their former companions.

The Suffet had proposed to all the captives that they should serve in his troops. Several had fearlessly refused; and quite resolved neither to support them nor to abandon them to the Great Council, he had sent them away with injunctions to fight no more against Carthage. As to those who had been rendered docile by the fear of tortures, they had been furnished with the weapons taken from the enemy; and they were now presenting themselves to the vanquished, not so much in order to seduce them as out of an impulse of pride and curiosity.

At first they told of the good treatment which they had received from the Suffet; the Barbarians listened to them with jealousy although they despised them. Then at the first words of reproach the cowards fell into a passion; they showed them from a distance their own swords and cuirasses and invited them with abuse to come and take them. The Barbarians picked up flints; all took to flight; and nothing more could be seen on the summit of the mountain except the lance-points projecting above the edge of the palisades.

Then the Barbarians were overwhelmed with a grief that was heavier than the humiliation of the defeat. They thought of the emptiness of their courage, and they stood with their eyes fixed and grinding their teeth.

The same thought came to them all. They rushed tumultuously upon the Carthaginian prisoners. It chanced that the Suffet's soldiers had been unable to discover them, and as he had withdrawn from the field of battle they were still in the deep pit.

They were ranged on the ground on a flattened spot. Sentries formed a circle round them, and the women were allowed to enter thirty or forty at a time. Wishing to profit by the short time that was allowed to them, they ran from one to the other, uncertain and panting; then bending over the poor bodies they struck them with all their might like washerwomen beating linen; shrieking their husband's names they tore them with their nails and put out their eyes with the bodkins of their hair. The men came next and tortured them from their feet, which they cut off at the ankles, to their foreheads, from which they took crowns of skin to put upon their own heads. The Eaters of Uncleanness were atrocious in their devices. They envenomed the wounds by pouring into them dust, vinegar, and fragments of pottery; others waited behind; blood flowed, and they rejoiced like vintagers round fuming vats.

Matho, however, was seated on the ground, at the very place where he had happened to be when the battle ended, his elbows on his knees, and his temples in his hands; he saw nothing, heard nothing, and had ceased to think.

At the shrieks of joy uttered by the crowd he raised his head. Before him a strip of canvas caught on a pole, and trailing on the ground, sheltered in confused fashion baskets, carpets, and a lion's skin. He recognised his tent; and he riveted his eyes upon the ground as though Hamilcar's daughter, when she disappeared, had sunk into the earth.

The torn canvas flapped in the wind; the long rags of it sometimes passed across his mouth, and he perceived a red mark like the print of a hand. It was the hand of Narr' Havas, the token of their alliance. Then Matho rose. He took a firebrand which was still smoking, and threw it disdainfully upon the wrecks of his tent. Then with the toe of his cothurn he pushed the things which fell out back towards the flame so that nothing might be left.

Suddenly, without any one being able to guess from what point he had sprung up, Spendius appeared.

The former slave had fastened two fragments of a lance against his thigh; he limped with a piteous look, breathing forth complaints the while.

"Remove that," said Matho to him. "I know that you are a brave fellow!" For he was so crushed by the injustice of the gods that he had not strength enough to be indignant with men.

Spendius beckoned to him and led him to a hollow of the mountain, where Zarxas and Autaritus were lying concealed.

They had fled like the slave, the one although he was cruel, and the other in spite of his bravery. But who, said they, could have expected the treachery of Narr' Havas, the burning of the camp of the Libyans, the loss of the zaïmph, the sudden attack by Hamilcar, and, above all, his manoeuvres which forced them to return to the bottom of the mountain beneath the instant blows of the Carthaginians? Spendius made no acknowledgment of his terror, and persisted in maintaining that his leg was broken.

At last the three chiefs and the schalischim asked one another what decision should now be adopted.

Hamilcar closed the road to Carthage against them; they were caught between his soldiers and the provinces belonging to Narr' Havas; the Tyrian towns would join the conquerors; the Barbarians would find themselves driven to the edge of the sea, and all these united forces would crush them. This would infallibly happen.

Thus no means presented themselves of avoiding the war. Accordingly they must prosecute it to the bitter end. But how were they to make the necessity of an interminable battle understood by all these disheartened people, who were still bleeding from their wounds.

"I will undertake that!" said Spendius.

Two hours afterwards a man who came from the direction of Hippo-Zarytus climbed the mountain at a run. He waved some tablets at arm's length, and as he shouted very loudly the Barbarians surrounded him.

The tablets had been despatched by the Greek soldiers in Sardinia. They recommended their African comrades to watch over Gisco and the other captives. A Samian trader, one Hipponax, coming from Carthage, had informed them that a plot was being organised to promote their escape, and the Barbarians were urged to take every precaution; the Republic was powerful.

Spendius's stratagem did not succeed at first as he had hoped. This assurance of the new peril, so far from exciting frenzy, raised fears; and remembering Hamilcar's warning, lately thrown into their midst, they expected something unlooked for and terrible. The night was spent in great distress; several even got rid of their weapons, so as to soften the Suffet when he presented himself.

But on the following day, at the third watch, a second runner appeared, still more breathless and blackened with dust. The Greek snatched from his hand a roll of papyrus covered with Phœnician writing. The Mercenaries were entreated not to be disheartened; the brave men of Tunis were coming with large reinforcements.

Spendius first read the letter three times in succession; and held up by two Cappadocians, who bore him seated on their shoulders, he had himself conveyed from place to place and reread it. For seven hours he harangued.

He reminded the Mercenaries of the promises of the Great Council; the Africans of the cruelties of the stewards, and all the Barbarians of the injustice of Carthage. The Suffet's mildness was only a bait to capture them; those who surrendered would be sold as slaves, and the vanquished would perish under torture. As to flight, what routes could they follow? Not a nation would receive them. Whereas by continuing their efforts they would obtain at once freedom, vengeance, and money! And they would not have long to wait, since the people of Tunis, the whole of Libya, was rushing to relieve them. He showed the unrolled papyrus: "Look at it! read! see their promises! I do not lie."

Dogs were straying about with their black muzzles all plastered with red. The men's uncovered heads were growing hot in the burning sun. A nauseous smell exhaled from the badly buried corpses. Some even projected from the earth as far as the waist. Spendius called them to witness what he was saying: then he raised his fists in the direction of Hamilcar.

Matho, moreover, was watching him, and to cover his cowardice he displayed an anger by which he gradually found himself carried away. Devoting himself to the gods he heaped curses upon the Carthaginians. The torture of the captives was child's play. Why spare them, and be ever dragging this useless cattle after one? "No! we must put an end to it! their designs are known! a single one might ruin us! no pity! Those who are worthy will be known by the speed of their legs and the force of their blows."

Then they turned again upon the captives. Several were still in the last throes; they were finished by a thrust of a heel in the mouth or a stab with the point of a javelin.

Then they thought of Gisco. Nowhere could he be seen; they were disturbed with anxiety. They wished at once to convince themselves of his death and to participate in it. At last three Samnite shepherds discovered him at a distance of fifteen paces from the spot where Matho's tent lately stood. They recognized him by his long beard and they called the rest.

Stretched on his back, his arms against his hips, and his knees close together, he looked like a dead man laid out for the tomb. Nevertheless his wasted sides rose and fell, and his eyes, wide-opened in his pallid face, gazed in a continuous and intolerable fashion.

The Barbarians looked at him at first with great astonishment. Since he had been living in the pit he had been almost forgotten; rendered uneasy by old memories they stood at a distance and did not venture to raise their hands against him.

But those who were behind were murmuring and pressing forward when a Garamantian passed through the crowd; he was brandishing a sickle; all understood his thought; their faces purpled, and smitten with shame they shrieked:

"Yes! yes!"

The man with the curved steel approached Gisco. He took his head, and, resting it upon his knee, sawed it off with rapid strokes; it fell; two great jets of blood made a hole in the dust. Zarxas leaped upon it, and lighter than a leopard ran towards the Carthaginians.

Then when he had covered two thirds of the mountain he drew Gisco's head from his breast by the beard, whirled his arm rapidly several times—and the mass, when thrown at last, described a long parabola and disappeared behind the Punic entrenchments.

Soon at the edge of the palisades there rose two crossed standards, the customary sign for claiming a corpse.

Then four heralds, chosen for their width of chest, went out with great clarions, and speaking through the brass tubes declared that henceforth there would be between Carthaginians and Barbarians neither faith, pity, nor gods, that they refused all overtures beforehand, and that envoys would be sent back with their hands cut off.

Immediately afterwards, Spendius was sent to Hippo-Zarytus to procure provisions; the Tyrian city sent them some the same evening. They ate greedily. Then when they were strengthened they speedily collected the remains of their baggage and their broken arms; the women massed themselves in the centre, and heedless of the wounded left weeping behind them, they set out along the edge of the shore like a herd of wolves taking its departure.

They were marching upon Hippo-Zarytus, resolved to take it, for they had need of a town.

Hamilcar, as he perceived them at a distance, had a feeling of despair in spite of the pride which he experienced in seeing them fly before him. He ought to have attacked them immediately with fresh troops. Another similar day and the war was over! If matters were protracted they would return with greater strength; the Tyrian towns would join them; his clemency towards the vanquished had been of no avail. He resolved to be pitiless.

The same evening he sent the Great Council a dromedary laden with bracelets collected from the dead, and with horrible threats ordered another army to be despatched.

All had for a long time believed him lost; so that on learning his victory they felt a stupefaction which was almost terror. The vaguely announced return of the zaïmph completed the wonder. Thus the gods and the might of Carthage seemed now to belong to him.

None of his enemies ventured upon complaint or recrimination. Owing to the enthusiasm of some and the pusillanimity of the rest, an army of five thousand men was ready before the interval prescribed had elapsed.

This army promptly made its way to Utica in order to support the Suffet's rear, while three thousand of the most notable citizens embarked in vessels which were to land them at Hippo-Zarytus, whence they were to drive back the Barbarians.

Hanno had accepted the command; but he intrusted the army to his lieutenant, Magdassin, so as to lead the troops which were to be disembarked himself, for he could no longer endure the shaking of the litter. His disease had eaten away his lips and nostrils, and had hollowed out a large hole in his face; the back of his throat could be seen at a distance of ten paces, and he knew himself to be so hideous that he wore a veil over his head like a woman.

Hippo-Zarytus paid no attention to his summonings nor yet to those of the Barbarians; but every morning the inhabitants lowered provisions to the latter in baskets, and shouting from the tops of the towers pleaded the exigencies of the Republic and conjured them to withdraw. By means of signs they addressed the same protestations to the Carthaginians who were stationed on the sea.

Hanno contented himself with blockading the harbour without risking an attack. However, he persuaded the judges of Hippo-Zarytus to admit three hundred soldiers. Then he departed to the Cape Grapes, and made a long circuit so as to hem in the Barbarians, an inopportune and even dangerous operation. His jealousy prevented him from relieving the Suffet; he arrested his spies, impeded him in all his plans, and compromised the success of the enterprise. At last Hamilcar wrote to the Great Council to rid him of Hanno, and the latter returned to Carthage furious at the baseness of the Ancients and the madness of his colleague. Hence, after so many hopes, the situation was now still more deplorable; but there was an effort not to reflect upon it and even not to talk about it.

As if all this were not sufficient misfortune at one time, news came that the Sardinian Mercenaries had crucified their general, seized the strongholds, and everywhere slaughtered those of Chanaanitish race. The Roman people threatened the Republic with immediate hostilities unless she gave twelve hundred talents with the whole of the island of Sardinia. They had accepted the alliance of the Barbarians, and they despatched to them flat-bottomed boats laden with meal and dried meat. The Carthaginians pursued these, and captured five hundred men; but three days afterwards a fleet coming from Byzacena, and conveying provisions to Carthage, foundered in a storm. The gods were evidently declaring against her.

Upon this the citizens of Hippo-Zarytus, under pretence of an alarm, made Hanno's three hundred men ascend their walls; then coming behind them they took them by the legs, and suddenly threw them over the ramparts. Some who were not killed were pursued, and went and drowned themselves in the sea.

Utica was enduring the presence of soldiers, for Magdassin had acted like Hanno, and in accordance with his orders and deaf to Hamilcar's prayers, was surrounding the town. As for these, they were given wine mixed with mandrake, and were then slaughtered in their sleep. At the same time the Barbarians arrived; Magdassin fled; the gates were opened; and thenceforward the two Tyrian towns displayed an obstinate devotion to their new friends and an inconceivable hatred to their former allies.

This abandonment of the Punic cause was a counsel and a precedent. Hopes of deliverance revived. Populations hitherto uncertain hesitated no longer. Everywhere there was a stir. The Suffet learnt this, and he had no assistance to look for! He was now irrevocably lost.

He immediately dismissed Narr' Havas, who was to guard the borders of his kingdom. As for himself, he resolved to re-enter Carthage in order to obtain soldiers and begin the war again.

The Barbarians posted at Hippo-Zarytus perceived his army as it descended the mountain.

Where could the Carthaginians be going? Hunger, no doubt, was urging them on; and, distracted by their sufferings, they were coming in spite of their weakness to give battle. But they turned to the right: they were fleeing. They might be overtaken and all be crushed. The Barbarians dashed in pursuit of them.

The Carthaginians were checked by the river. It was wide this time and the west wind had not been blowing. Some crossed by swimming, and the rest on their shields. They resumed their march. Night fell. They were out of sight.

The Barbarians did not stop; they went higher to find a narrower place. The people of Tunis hastened thither, bringing those of Utica along with them. Their numbers increased at every bush; and the Carthaginians, as they lay on the ground, could hear the tramping of their feet in the darkness. From time to time Barca had a volley of arrows discharged behind him in order to check them, and several were killed. When day broke they were in the Ariana Mountains, at the spot where the road makes a bend.

Then Matho, who was marching at the head, thought that he could distinguish something green on the horizon on the summit of an eminence. Then the ground sank, and obelisks, domes, and houses appeared! It was Carthage. He leaned against a tree to keep himself from falling, so rapidly did his heart beat.

He thought of all that had come to pass in his existence since the last time that he had passed that way! It was an infinite surprise, it stunned him. Then he was transported with joy at the thought of seeing Salammbô again. The reasons which he had for execrating her returned to his recollection, but he very quickly rejected them. Quivering and with straining eyeballs he gazed at the lofty terrace of a palace above the palm trees beyond Eschmoun; a smile of ecstasy lighted his face as if some great light had reached him; he opened his arms, and sent kisses on the breeze, and murmured: "Come! come!" A sigh swelled his breast, and two long tears like pearls fell upon his beard.

"What stays you?" cried Spendius. "Make haste! Forward! The Suffet is going to escape us! But your knees are tottering, and you are looking at me like a drunken man!"

He stamped with impatience and urged Matho, his eyes twinkling as at the approach of an object long aimed at.

"Ah! we have reached it! We are there! I have them!"

He had so convinced and triumphant an air that Matho was surprised from his torpor, and felt himself carried away by it. These words, coming when his distress was at its height, drove his despair to vengeance, and pointed to food for his wrath. He bounded upon one of the camels that were among the baggage, snatched up its halter, and with the long rope, struck the stragglers with all his might, running right and left alternately, in the rear of the army, like a dog driving a flock.

At his thundering voice the lines of men closed up; even the lame hurried their steps; the intervening space lessened in the middle of the isthmus. The foremost of the Barbarians were marching in the dust raised by the Carthaginians. The two armies were coming close, and were on the point of touching. But the Malqua gate, the Tagaste gate, and the great gate of Khamon threw wide their leaves. The Punic square divided; three columns were swallowed up, and eddied beneath the porches. Soon the mass, being too tightly packed, could advance no further; pikes clashed in the air, and the arrows of the Barbarians were shivering against the walls.

Hamilcar was to be seen on the threshold of Khamon. He turned round and shouted to his men to move aside. He dismounted from his horse; and pricking it on the croup with the sword which he held, sent it against the Barbarians.

It was a black stallion, which was fed on balls of meal, and would bend its knees to allow its master to mount. Why was he sending it away? Was this a sacrifice?

The noble horse galloped into the midst of the lances, knocked down men, and, entangling its feet in its entrails, fell down, then rose again with furious leaps;

and while they were moving aside, trying to stop it, or looking at it in surprise, the Carthaginians had united again; they entered, and the enormous gate shut echoing behind them.

It would not yield. The Barbarians came crushing against it—and for some minutes there was an oscillation throughout the army, which became weaker and weaker, and at last ceased.

The Carthaginians had placed soldiers on the aqueduct, they began to hurl stones, balls, and beams. Spendius represented that it would be best not to persist. The Barbarians went and posted themselves further off, all being quite resolved to lay siege to Carthage.

The rumour of the war, however, had passed beyond the confines of the Punic empire; and from the pillars of Hercules to beyond Cyrene shepherds mused on it as they kept their flocks, and caravans talked about it at night in the light of the stars. This great Carthage, mistress of the seas, splendid as the sun, and terrible as a god, actually found men who were daring enough to attack her! Her fall even had been asserted several times; and all had believed it for all wished it: the subject populations, the tributary villages, the allied provinces, the independent hordes, those who execrated her for her tyranny or were jealous of her power, or coveted her wealth. The bravest had very speedily joined the Mercenaries. The defeat at the Macaras had checked all the rest. At last they had recovered confidence, had gradually advanced and approached; and now the men of the eastern regions were lying on the sandhills of Clypea on the other side of the gulf. As soon as they perceived the Barbarians they showed themselves.

They were not Libyans from the neighbourhood of Carthage, who had long composed the third army, but nomads from the tableland of Barca, bandits from Cape Phiscus and the promontory of Dernah, from Phazzana and Marmarica. They had crossed the desert, drinking at the brackish wells walled in with camels' bones; the Zuaeces, with their covering of ostrich feathers, had come on quadrigæ; the Garamantians, masked with black veils, rode behind on their painted mares; others were mounted on asses, onagers, zebras, and buffaloes; while some dragged after them the roofs of their sloop-shaped huts together with their families and idols. There were Ammonians with limbs wrinkled by the hot water of the springs; Atarantians, who curse the sun; Troglodytes, who bury their dead with laughter beneath brandies of trees; and the hideous Auseans, who eat grasshoppers; the Achyrmachidæ, who eat lice; and the vermilion-painted Gysantians, who eat apes.

All were ranged along the edge of the sea in a great straight line. Afterwards they advanced like tornadoes of sand raised by the wind. In the centre of the isth-

mus the throng stopped, the Mercenaries, who were posted in front of them, close
to the walls, being unwilling to move.

Then from the direction of Ariana appeared the men of the West, the people
of the Numidians. In fact, Narr' Havas governed only the Massylians; and, moreover, as they were permitted by custom to abandon their king when reverses were
sustained, they had assembled on the Zainus, and then had crossed it at Hamilcar's
first movement. First were seen running up all the hunters from Malethut-Baal and
Garaphos, clad in lions' skins, and with the staves of their pikes driving small lean
horses with long manes; then marched the Gætulians in cuirasses of serpents' skin;
then the Pharusians, wearing lofty crowns made of wax and resin; and the Cauni-
ans, Macarians, and Tillabarians, each holding two javelins and a round shield of
hippopotamus leather. They stopped at the foot of the Catacombs among the first
pools of the Lagoon.

But when the Libyans had moved away, the multitude of the Negroes appeared
like a cloud on a level with the ground, in the place which the others had occupied.
They were there from the White Harousch, the Black Harousch, the desert of
Augila, and even from the great country of Agazymba, which is four months' journey south of the Garamantians, and from regions further still! In spite of their red
wooden jewels, the filth of their black skin made them look like mulberries that had
been long rolling in the dust. They had bark-thread drawers, dried-grass tunics,
fallow-deer muzzles on their heads; they shook rods furnished with rings, and
brandished cows' tails at the end of sticks, after the fashion of standards, howling
the while like wolves.

Then behind the Numidians, Marusians, and Gætulians pressed the yellowish
men, who are spread through the cedar forests beyond Taggir. They had cat-skin
quivers flapping against their shoulders, and they led in leashes enormous dogs,
which were as high as asses, and did not bark.

Finally, as though Africa had not been sufficiently emptied, and it had been
necessary to seek further fury in the very dregs of the races, men might be seen behind the rest, with beast-like profiles and grinning with idiotic laughter—wretches
ravaged by hideous diseases, deformed pigmies, mulattoes of doubtful sex, albinos
whose red eyes blinked in the sun; stammering out unintelligible sounds, they put
a finger into their mouths to show that they were hungry.

The confusion of weapons was as great as that of garments and peoples. There
was not a deadly invention that was not present—from wooden daggers, stone
hatchets and ivory tridents, to long sabres toothed like saws, slender, and formed
of a yielding copper blade. They handled cutlasses which were forked into several
branches like antelopes' horns, bills fastened to the ends of ropes, iron triangles,

clubs and bodkins. The Ethiopians from the Bambotus had little poisoned darts hidden in their hair. Many had brought pebbles in bags. Others, empty handed, chattered with their teeth.

This multitude was stirred with a ceaseless swell. Dromedaries, smeared all over with tar-like streaks, knocked down the women, who carried their children on their hips. The provisions in the baskets were pouring out; in walking, pieces of salt, parcels of gum, rotten dates, and gourou nuts were crushed underfoot; and sometimes on vermin-covered bosoms there would hang a slender cord supporting a diamond that the Satraps had sought, an almost fabulous stone, sufficient to purchase an empire. Most of them did not even know what they desired. They were impelled by fascination or curiosity; and nomads who had never seen a town were frightened by the shadows of the walls.

The isthmus was now hidden by men; and this long surface, whereon the tents were like huts amid an inundation, stretched as far as the first lines of the other Barbarians, which were streaming with steel and were posted symmetrically upon both sides of the aqueduct.

The Carthaginians had not recovered from the terror caused by their arrival when they perceived the siege-engines sent by the Tyrian towns coming straight towards them like monsters and like buildings—with their masts, arms, ropes, articulations, capitals and carapaces, sixty carroballistas, eighty onagers, thirty scorpions, fifty tollenos, twelve rams, and three gigantic catapults which hurled pieces of rock of the weight of fifteen talents. Masses of men clinging to their bases pushed them on; at every step a quivering shook them, and in this way they arrived in front of the walls.

But several days were still needed to finish the preparations for the siege. The Mercenaries, taught by their defeats, would not risk themselves in useless engagements; and on both sides there was no haste, for it was well known that a terrible action was about to open, and that the result of it would be complete victory or complete extermination.

Carthage might hold out for a long time; her broad walls presented a series of re-entrant and projecting angles, an advantageous arrangement for repelling assaults.

Nevertheless a portion had fallen down in the direction of the Catacombs, and on dark nights lights could be seen in the dens of Malqua through the disjointed blocks. These in some places overlooked the top of the ramparts. It was here that the Mercenaries' wives, who had been driven away by Matho, were living with their new husbands. On seeing the men again their hearts could stand it no longer. They waved their scarfs at a distance; then they came and chatted in the darkness with the soldiers through the cleft in the wall, and one morning the Great Council learned that they had all fled. Some had passed through between the stones; others with greater intrepidity had let themselves down with ropes.

At last Spendius resolved to accomplish his design.

The war, by keeping him at a distance, had hitherto prevented him; and since the return to before Carthage, it seemed to him that the inhabitants suspected his enterprise. But soon they diminished the sentries on the aqueduct. There were not too many people for the defence of the walls.

The former slave practised himself for some days in shooting arrows at the flamingoes on the lake. Then one moonlight evening he begged Matho to light a great fire of straw in the middle of the night, while all his men were to shout at the same time; and taking Zarxas with him, he went away along the edge of the gulf in the direction of Tunis.

When on a level with the last arches they returned straight towards the aqueduct; the place was unprotected: they crawled to the base of the pillars.

The sentries on the platform were walking quietly up and down.

Towering flames appeared; clarions rang; and the soldiers on vedette, believing that there was an assault, rushed away in the direction of Carthage.

One man had remained. He showed black against the background of the sky. The moon was shining behind him, and his shadow, which was of extravagant size, looked in the distance like an obelisk proceeding across the plain.

They waited until he was in position just before them. Zarxas seized his sling, but whether from prudence or from ferocity Spendius stopped him. "No, the whiz of the bullet would make a noise! Let me!"

Then he bent his bow with all his strength, resting the lower end of it against the great toe of his left foot; he took aim, and the arrow went off.

The man did not fall. He disappeared.

"If he were wounded we should hear him!" said Spendius; and he mounted quickly from story to story as he had done the first time, with the assistance of a rope and a harpoon. Then when he had reached the top and was beside the corpse, he let it fall again. The Balearian fastened a pick and a mallet to it and turned back.

The trumpets sounded no longer. All was now quiet. Spendius had raised one of the flag-stones and, entering the water, had closed it behind him.

Calculating the distance by the number of his steps, he arrived at the exact spot where he had noticed an oblique fissure; and for three hours until morning he worked in continuous and furious fashion, breathing with difficulty through the interstices in the upper flag-stones, assailed with anguish, and twenty times believing that he was going to die. At last a crack was heard, and a huge stone ricocheting on the lower arches rolled to the ground—and suddenly a cataract, an entire river, fell from the skies into the plain. The aqueduct, being cut through in the centre, was emptying itself. It was death to Carthage and victory for the Barbarians.

In an instant the awakened Carthaginians appeared on the walls, the houses, and the temples. The Barbarians pressed forward with shouts. They danced in delirium around the great waterfall, and came up and wet their heads in it in the extravagance of their joy.

A man in a torn, brown tunic was perceived on the summit of the aqueduct. He stood leaning over the very edge with both hands on his hips, and was looking down below him as though astonished at his work.

Then he drew himself up. He surveyed the horizon with a haughty air which seemed to say: "All that is now mine!" The applause of the Barbarians burst forth, while the Carthaginians, comprehending their disaster at last, shrieked with despair. Then he began to run about the platform from one end to the other—and like a chariot-driver triumphant at the Olympic Games, Spendius, distraught with pride, raised his arms aloft.

Chapter XIII

Moloch

THE BARBARIANS HAD NO NEED OF A CIRCUMVALLATION ON THE SIDE OF Africa, for it was theirs. But to facilitate the approach to the walls, the entrenchments bordering the ditch were thrown down. Matho next divided the army into great semicircles so as to encompass Carthage the better. The hoplites of the Mercenaries were placed in the first rank, and behind them the slingers and horsemen; quite at the back were the baggage, chariots, and horses; and the engines bristled in front of this throng at a distance of three hundred paces from the towers.

Amid the infinite variety of their nomenclature (which changed several times in the course of the centuries) these machines might be reduced to two systems: some acted like slings, and the rest like bows.

The first, which were the catapults, was composed of a square frame with two vertical uprights and a horizontal bar. In its anterior portion was a cylinder, furnished with cables, which held back a great beam bearing a spoon for the reception of projectiles; its base was caught in a skein of twisted thread, and when the ropes were let go it sprang up and struck against the bar, which, checking it with a shock, multiplied its power.

The second presented a more complicated mechanism. A cross-bar had its centre fixed on a little pillar, and from this point of junction there branched off at right angles a sort of channel; two caps containing twists of horse-hair stood at the extremities of the cross-bar; two small beams were fastened to them to hold the extremities of a rope which was brought to the bottom of the channel upon a tablet of bronze. This metal plate was released by a spring, and sliding in grooves impelled the arrows.

The catapults were likewise called onagers, after the wild asses which fling up stones with their feet, and the ballistas scorpions, on account of a hook which stood upon the tablet, and being lowered by a blow of the fist, released the spring.

Their construction required learned calculations; the wood selected had to be of the hardest substance, and their gearing all of brass; they were stretched with levers, tackle-blocks, capstans or tympanums; the direction of the shooting was changed by means of strong pivots; they were moved forward on cylinders, and the most considerable of them, which were brought piece by piece, were set up in front of the enemy.

Spendius arranged three great catapults opposite the three principal angles; he placed a ram before every gate, a ballista before every tower, while carroballistas were to move about in the rear. But it was necessary to protect them against the fire thrown by the besieged, and first of all to fill up the trench which separated them from the walls.

They pushed forward galleries formed of hurdles of green reeds, and oaken semicircles like enormous shields gliding on three wheels; the workers were sheltered in little huts covered with raw hides and stuffed with wrack; the catapults and ballistas were protected by rope curtains which had been steeped in vinegar to render them incombustible. The women and children went to procure stones on the strand, and gathered earth with their hands and brought it to the soldiers.

The Carthaginians also made preparations.

Hamilcar had speedily reassured them by declaring that there was enough water left in the cisterns for one hundred and twenty-three days. This assertion, together with his presence, and above all that of the zaïmph among them, gave them good hopes. Carthage recovered from its dejection; those who were not of Chanaanitish origin were carried away by the passion of the rest.

The slaves were armed, the arsenals were emptied, and every citizen had his own post and his own employment. Twelve hundred of the fugitives had survived, and the Suffet made them all captains; and carpenters, armourers, blacksmiths, and goldsmiths were intrusted with the engines. The Carthaginians had kept a few in spite of the conditions of the peace with Rome. These were repaired. They understood such work.

The two northern and eastern sides, being protected by the sea and the gulf, remained inaccessible. On the wall fronting the Barbarians they collected tree-trunks, mill-stones, vases filled with sulphur, and vats filled with oil, and built furnaces. Stones were heaped up on the platforms of the towers, and the houses bordering immediately on the rampart were crammed with sand in order to strengthen it and increase its thickness.

The Barbarians grew angry at the sight of these preparations. They wished to fight at once. The weights which they put into the catapults were so extravagantly heavy that the beams broke, and the attack was delayed.

At last on the thirteenth day of the month of Schabar—at sunrise—a great blow was heard at the gate of Khamon.

Seventy-five soldiers were pulling at ropes arranged at the base of a gigantic beam which was suspended horizontally by chains hanging from a framework, and which terminated in a ram's head of pure brass. It had been swathed in ox-hides; it was bound at intervals with iron bracelets; it was thrice as thick as a man's body, one hundred and twenty cubits long, and under the crowd of naked arms pushing it forward and drawing it back, it moved to and fro with a regular oscillation.

The other rams before the other gates began to be in motion. Men might be seen mounting from step to step in the hollow wheels of the tympanums. The pulleys and caps grated, the rope curtains were lowered, and showers of stones and showers of arrows burst forth simultaneously; all the scattered slingers ran up. Some approached the rampart hiding pots of resin under their shields; then they would hurl these with all their might. This hail of bullets, darts, and flames passed above the first ranks in the form of a curve which fell behind the walls. But long cranes, used for masting vessels, were reared on the summit of the ramparts; and from them there descended some of those enormous pincers which terminated in two semicircles toothed on the inside. They bit the rams. The soldiers clung to the beam and drew it back. The Carthaginians hauled in order to pull it up; and the action was prolonged until the evening.

When the Mercenaries resumed their task on the following day, the tops of the walls were completely carpeted with bales of cotton, sails, and cushions; the battlements were stopped up with mats; and a line of forks and blades, fixed upon sticks, might be distinguished among the cranes on the rampart. A furious resistance immediately began.

Trunks of trees fastened to cables fell and rose alternately and battered the rams; cramps hurled by the ballistas tore away the roofs of the huts; and streams of flints and pebbles poured from the platforms of the towers.

At last the rams broke the gates of Khamon and Tagaste. But the Carthaginians had piled up such an abundance of materials on the inside that the leaves did not open. They remained standing.

Then they drove augers against the walls; these were applied to the joints of the blocks, so as to detach the latter. The engines were better managed, the men serving them were divided into squads, and they were worked from morning till evening without interruption and with the monotonous precision of a weaver's loom.

Spendius attended to them untiringly. It was he who stretched the skeins of the ballistas. In order that the twin tensions might completely correspond, the ropes as they were tightened were struck on the right and left alternately until both sides gave out an equal sound. Spendius would mount upon the timbers. He would strike the ropes softly with the extremity of his foot, and strain his ears like a musician tuning a lyre. Then when the beam of the catapult rose, when the pillar of the ballista trembled with the shock of the spring, when the stones were shooting in rays, and the darts pouring in streams, he would incline his whole body and fling his arms into the air as though to follow them.

The soldiers admired his skill and executed his commands. In the gaiety of their work they gave utterance to jests on the names of the machines. Thus the plyers for seizing the rams were called "wolves," and the galleries were covered with "vines;" they were lambs, or they were going to gather the grapes; and as they loaded their pieces they would say to the onagers: "Come, pick well!" and to the scorpions: "Pierce them to the heart!" These jokes, which were ever the same, kept up their courage.

Nevertheless the machines did not demolish the rampart. It was formed of two walls and was completely filled with earth. The upper portions were beaten down, but each time the besieged raised them again. Matho ordered the construction of wooden towers which should be as high as the towers of stone. They cast turf, stakes, pebbles and chariots with their wheels into the trench so as to fill it up the more quickly; but before this was accomplished the immense throng of Barbarians undulated over the plain with a single movement and came beating against the foot of the walls like an overflowing sea.

They moved forward the rope ladders, straight ladders, and sambucas, the latter consisting of two poles from which a series of bamboos terminating in a movable bridge were lowered by means of tackling. They formed numerous straight lines resting against the wall, and the Mercenaries mounted them in files, holding their weapons in their hands. Not a Carthaginian showed himself; already two thirds of the rampart had been covered. Then the battlements opened, vomiting flames and smoke like dragon jaws; the sand scattered and entered the joints of their armour; the petroleum fastened on their garments; the liquid lead hopped on their helmets and made holes in their flesh; a rain of sparks splashed against their faces, and eyeless orbits seemed to weep tears as big as almonds. There were men all yellow with oil, with their hair in flames. They began to run and set fire to the rest. They were extinguished with mantles steeped in blood, which were thrown from a distance over their faces. Some who had no wounds remained motionless, stiffer than stakes, their mouths open and their arms outspread.

The assault was renewed for several days in succession, the Mercenaries hoping to triumph by extraordinary energy and audacity.

Sometimes a man raised on the shoulders of another would drive a pin between the stones, and then making use of it as a step to reach further, would place a second and a third; and, protected by the edge of the battlements, which stood out from the wall, they would gradually raise themselves in this way; but on reaching a certain height they always fell back again. The great trench was full to overflowing; the wounded were massed pell-mell with the dead and dying beneath the footsteps of the living. Calcined trunks formed black spots amid opened entrails, scattered brains, and pools of blood; and arms and legs projecting half way out of a heap, would stand straight up like props in a burning vineyard.

The ladders proving insufficient the tollenos were brought into requisition—instruments consisting of a long beam set transversely upon another, and bearing at its extremity a quadrangular basket which would hold thirty foot-soldiers with their weapons.

Matho wished to ascend in the first that was ready. Spendius stopped him.

Some men bent over a capstan; the great beam rose, became horizontal, reared itself almost vertically, and being overweighted at the end, bent like a huge reed. The soldiers, who were crowded together, were hidden up to their chins; only their helmet-plumes could be seen. At last when it was twenty cubits high in the air it turned several times to the right and to the left, and then was depressed; and like a giant arm holding a cohort of pigmies in its hand, it laid the basketful of men upon the edge of the wall. They leaped into the crowd and never returned.

All the other tollenos were speedily made ready. But a hundred times as many would have been needed for the capture of the town. They were utilised in a murderous fashion: Ethiopian archers were placed in the baskets; then, the cables having been fastened, they remained suspended and shot poisoned arrows. The fifty tollenos commanding the battlements thus surrounded Carthage like monstrous vultures; and the Negroes laughed to see the guards on the rampart dying in grievous convulsions.

Hamilcar sent hoplites to these posts, and every morning made them drink the juice of certain herbs which protected them against the poison.

One evening when it was dark he embarked the best of his soldiers on lighters and planks, and turning to the right of the harbour, disembarked on the Taenia. Then he advanced to the first lines of the Barbarians, and taking them in flank, made a great slaughter. Men hanging to ropes would descend at night from the top of the wall with torches in their hands, burn the works of the Mercenaries, and then mount up again.

Matho was exasperated; every obstacle strengthened his wrath, which led him into terrible extravagances. He mentally summoned Salammbô to an interview; then he waited. She did not come; this seemed to him a fresh piece of treachery—and henceforth he execrated her. If he had seen her corpse he would perhaps have gone away. He doubled the outposts, he planted forks at the foot of the rampart, he drove caltrops into the ground, and he commanded the Libyans to bring him a whole forest that he might set it on fire and burn Carthage like a den of foxes.

Spendius went on obstinately with the siege. He sought to invent terrible machines such as had never before been constructed.

The other Barbarians, encamped at a distance on the isthmus, were amazed at these delays; they murmured, and they were let loose.

Then they rushed with their cutlasses and javelins, and beat against the gates with them. But the nakedness of their bodies facilitating the infliction of wounds, the Carthaginians massacred them freely; and the Mercenaries rejoiced at it, no doubt through jealousy about the plunder. Hence there resulted quarrels and combats between them. Then, the country having been ravaged, provisions were soon scarce. They grew disheartened. Numerous hordes went away, but the crowd was so great that the loss was not apparent.

The best of them tried to dig mines, but the earth, being badly supported, fell in. They began again in other places, but Hamilcar always guessed the direction that they were taking by holding his ear against a bronze shield. He bored countermines beneath the path along which the wooden towers were to move, and when they were pushed forward they sank into the holes.

At last all recognised that the town was impregnable, unless a long terrace were raised to the same height as the walls, so as to enable them to fight on the same level. The top of it should be paved so that the machines might be rolled along. Then Carthage would find it quite impossible to resist.

The town was beginning to suffer from thirst. The water which was worth two kesitahs the bath at the opening of the siege was now sold for a shekel of silver; the stores of meat and corn were also becoming exhausted; there was a dread of famine, and some even began to speak of useless mouths, which terrified everyone.

From the square of Khamon to the temple of Melkarth the streets were cumbered with corpses; and, as it was the end of the summer, the combatants were annoyed by great black flies. Old men carried off the wounded, and the devout continued the fictitious funerals of their relatives and friends who had died far away during the war. Waxen statues with clothes and hair were displayed across the gates. They melted in the heat of the tapers burning beside them; the paint flowed down upon their shoulders, and tears streamed over the faces of the living, as they chanted mournful songs beside them. The crowd meanwhile ran to and fro; armed bands passed; captains shouted orders, while the shock of the rams beating against the rampart was constantly heard.

The temperature became so heavy that the bodies swelled and would no longer fit into the coffins. They were burned in the centre of the courts. But the fires, being too much confined, kindled the neighbouring walls, and long flames suddenly burst from the houses like blood spirting from an artery. Thus Moloch was in possession of Carthage; he clasped the ramparts, he rolled through the streets, he devoured the very corpses.

Men wearing cloaks made of collected rags in token of despair, stationed themselves at the corners of the cross-ways. They declaimed against the Ancients and against Hamilcar, predicted complete ruin to the people, and invited them to universal destruction and license. The most dangerous were the henbane-drinkers; in their crisis they believed themselves wild beasts, and leaped upon the passers-by to rend them. Mobs formed around them, and the defence of Carthage was forgotten. The Suffet devised the payment of others to support his policy.

In order to retain the genius of the gods within the town their images had been covered with chains. Black veils were placed upon the Patæc gods, and hair-cloths around the altars; and attempts were made to excite the pride and jealousy of the Baals by singing in their ears: "Thou art about to suffer thyself to be vanquished! Are the others perchance more strong? Show thyself! aid us! that the peoples may not say: 'Where are now their gods?' "

The colleges of the pontiffs were agitated by unceasing anxiety. Those of Rabbetna were especially afraid—the restoration of the zaïmph having been of no avail. They kept themselves shut up in the third enclosure which was as impregnable as a fortress. Only one among them, the high priest Schahabarim, ventured to go out.

He used to visit Salammbô. But he would either remain perfectly silent, gazing at her with fixed eyeballs, or else would be lavish of words, and the reproaches that he uttered were harder than ever.

With inconceivable inconsistency he could not forgive the young girl for having followed his commands; Schahabarim had guessed all, and this haunting thought revived the jealousies of his impotence. He accused her of being the cause of the war. Matho, according to him, was besieging Carthage to recover the zaïmph; and he poured out imprecations and sarcasms upon this Barbarian who pretended to the possession of holy things. Yet it was not this that the priest wished to say.

But just now Salammbô felt no terror of him. The anguish which she used formerly to suffer had left her. A strange peacefulness possessed her. Her gaze was less wandering, and shone with limpid fire.

Meanwhile the python had become ill again; and as Salammbô, on the contrary, appeared to be recovering, old Taanach rejoiced in the conviction that by its decline it was taking away the languor of her mistress.

One morning she found it coiled up behind the bed of ox-hides, colder than marble, and with its head hidden by a heap of worms. Her cries brought Salammbô to the spot. She turned it over for a while with the tip of her sandal, and the slave was amazed at her insensibility.

Hamilcar's daughter no longer prolonged her fasts with so much fervour. She passed whole days on the top of her terrace, leaning her elbows against the balustrade, and amusing herself by looking out before her. The summits of the walls at the end of the town cut uneven zigzags upon the sky, and the lances of the sentries formed what was like a border of corn-ears throughout their length. Further away she could see the manoeuvres of the Barbarians between the towers; on days when the siege was interrupted she could even distinguish their occupations. They mended their weapons, greased their hair, and washed their bloodstained arms in the sea; the tents were closed; the beasts of burden were feeding; and in the distance the scythes of the chariots, which were all ranged in a semicircle, looked like a silver scimitar lying at the base of the mountains. Schahabarim's talk recurred to her memory. She was waiting for Narr' Havas, her betrothed. In spite of her hatred she would have liked to see Matho again. Of all the Carthaginians she was perhaps the only one who would have spoken to him without fear.

Her father often came into her room. He would sit down panting on the cushions, and gaze at her with an almost tender look, as if he found some rest from his fatigues in the sight of her. He sometimes questioned her about her journey to the camp of the Mercenaries. He even asked her whether any one had urged her to it; and with a shake of the head she answered, No—so proud was Salammbô of having saved the zaïmph.

But the Suffet always came back to Matho under pretence of making military inquiries. He could not understand how the hours which she had spent in the tent had been employed. Salammbô, in fact, said nothing about Gisco; for as words had an effective power in themselves, curses, if reported to any one, might be turned against him; and she was silent about her wish to assassinate, lest she should be blamed for not having yielded to it. She said that the schalischim appeared furious, that he had shouted a great deal, and that he had then fallen asleep. Salammbô told no more, through shame perhaps, or else because she was led by her extreme ingenuousness to attach but little importance to the soldier's kisses. Moreover, it all floated through her head in a melancholy and misty fashion, like the recollection of a depressing dream; and she would not have known in what way or in what words to express it.

One evening when they were thus face to face with each other, Taanach came in looking quite scared. An old man with a child was yonder in the courts, and wished to see the Suffet.

Hamilcar turned pale, and then quickly replied:

"Let him come up!"

Iddibal entered without prostrating himself. He held a young boy, covered with a goat's-hair cloak, by the hand, and at once raised the hood which screened his face.

"Here he is, Master! Take him!"

The Suffet and the slave went into a corner of the room.

The child remained in the centre standing upright, and with a gaze of attention rather than of astonishment he surveyed the ceiling, the furniture, the pearl neck-laces trailing on the purple draperies, and the majestic maiden who was bending over towards him.

He was perhaps ten years old, and was not taller than a Roman sword. His curly hair shaded his swelling forehead. His eyeballs looked as if they were seek-ing for space. The nostrils of his delicate nose were broad and palpitating, and upon his whole person was displayed the indefinable splendour of those who are destined to great enterprises. When he had cast aside his extremely heavy cloak, he remained clad in a lynx skin, which was fastened about his waist, and he rested his little naked feet, which were all white with dust, resolutely upon the pavement. But he no doubt divined that important matters were under discussion, for he stood motionless, with one hand behind his back, his chin lowered, and a finger in his mouth.

At last Hamilcar attracted Salammbô with a sign and said to her in a low voice:

"You will keep him with you, you understand! No one, even though belonging to the house, must know of his existence!"

Then, behind the door, he again asked Iddibal whether he was quite sure that they had not been noticed.

"No!" said the slave, "the streets were empty."

As the war filled all the provinces he had feared for his master's son. Then, not knowing where to hide him, he had come along the coasts in a sloop, and for three days Iddibal had been tacking about in the gulf and watching the ramparts. At last, that evening, as the environs of Khamon seemed to be deserted, he had passed briskly through the channel and landed near the arsenal, the entrance to the har-bour being free.

But soon the Barbarians posted an immense raft in front of it in order to pre-vent the Carthaginians from coming out. They were again rearing the wooden towers, and the terrace was rising at the same time.

Outside communications were cut off and an intolerable famine set in.

The besieged killed all the dogs, all the mules, all the asses, and then the fifteen elephants which the Suffet had brought back. The lions of the temple of Moloch had become ferocious, and the hierodules no longer durst approach them. They were fed at first with the wounded Barbarians; then they were thrown corpses that were still warm; they refused them, and they all died. People wandered in the twi-light along the old enclosures, and gathered grass and flowers among the stones to boil them in wine, wine being cheaper than water. Others crept as far as the enemy's outposts, and entered the tents to steal food, and the stupefied Barbarians sometimes allowed them to return. At last a day arrived when the Ancients re-solved to slaughter the horses of Eschmoun privately. They were holy animals whose manes were plaited by the pontiffs with gold ribbons, and whose existence denoted the motion of the sun—the idea of fire in its most exalted form. Their flesh was cut into equal portions and buried behind the altar. Then every evening the Ancients, alleging some act of devotion, would go up to the temple and regale themselves in secret, and each would take away a piece beneath his tunic for his children. In the deserted quarters remote from the walls, the inhabitants, whose misery was not so great, had barricaded themselves through fear of the rest.

The stones from the catapults, and the demolitions commanded for purposes of defence, had accumulated heaps of ruins in the middle of the streets. At the quietest times masses of people would suddenly rush along with shouts; and from the top of the Acropolis the conflagrations were like purple rags scattered upon the terraces and twisted by the wind.

The three great catapults did not stop in spite of all these works. Their ravages were extraordinary: thus a man's head rebounded from the pediment of the Syssitia; a woman who was being confined in the street of Kinisdo was crushed by a block of marble, and her child was carried with the bed as far as the crossways of Cinasyn, where the coverlet was found.

The most annoying were the bullets of the slingers. They fell upon the roofs, and in the gardens, and in the middle of the courts, while people were at table before a slender meal with their hearts big with sighs. These cruel projectiles bore engraved letters which stamped themselves upon the flesh—and insults might be read on corpses such as "pig," "jackal," "vermin," and sometimes jests: "Catch it!" or "I have well deserved it!"

The portion of the rampart which extended from the corner of the harbours to the height of the cisterns was broken down. Then the people of Malqua found themselves caught between the old enclosure of Byrsa behind, and the Barbarians in front. But there was enough to be done in thickening the wall and making it as high as possible without troubling about them; they were abandoned; all perished; and although they were generally hated, Hamilcar came to be greatly abhorred.

On the morrow he opened the pits in which he kept stores of corn, and his stewards gave it to the people. For three days they gorged themselves.

Their thirst, however, only became the more intolerable, and they could constantly see before them the long cascade formed by the clear falling water of the aqueduct. A thin vapor, with a rainbow beside it, went up from its base, beneath the rays of the sun, and a little stream curving through the plain fell into the gulf.

Hamilcar did not give way. He was reckoning upon an event, upon something decisive and extraordinary.

His own slaves tore off the silver plates from the temple of Melkarth; four long boats were drawn out of the harbour, they were brought by means of capstans to the foot of the Mappalian quarter, the wall facing the shore was bored, and they set out for the Gauls to buy Mercenaries there at no matter what price. Nevertheless, Hamilcar was distressed at his inability to communicate with the king of the Numidians, for he knew that he was behind the Barbarians, and ready to fall upon them. But Narr' Havas, being too weak, was not going to make any venture alone; and the Suffet had the rampart raised twelve palms higher, all the material in the arsenals piled up in the Acropolis, and the machines repaired once more.

Sinews taken from bulls' necks, or else stags' hamstrings, were commonly employed for the twists of the catapults. However, neither stags nor bulls were in existence in Carthage. Hamilcar asked the Ancients for the hair of their wives; all sacrificed it, but the quantity was not sufficient. In the buildings of the Syssitia there were twelve hundred marriageable slaves destined for prostitution in Greece and Italy, and their hair, having been rendered elastic by the use of unguents, was wonderfully well adapted for engines of war. But the subsequent loss would be too great. Accordingly it was decided that a choice should be made of the finest heads of hair among the wives of the plebeians. Careless of their country's needs, they shrieked in despair when the servants of the Hundred came with scissors to lay hands upon them.

The Barbarians were animated with increased fury. They could be seen in the distance taking fat from the dead to grease their machines, while others pulled out the nails and stitched them end to end to make cuirasses. They devised a plan of putting into the catapults vessels filled with serpents which had been brought by the Negroes; the clay pots broke on the flag-stones, the serpents ran about, seemed to multiply, and, so numerous were they, to issue naturally from the walls. Then the Barbarians, not satisfied with their invention, improved upon it; they hurled all kinds of filth, human excrements, pieces of carrion, corpses. The plague reappeared. The teeth of the Carthaginians fell out of their mouths, and their gums were discoloured like those of camels after too long a journey.

The machines were set up on the terrace, although the latter did not as yet reach everywhere to the height of the rampart. Before the twenty-three towers on the fortifications stood twenty-three others of wood. All the tollenos were mounted again, and in the centre, a little further back, appeared the formidable helepolis of Demetrius Poliorcetes, which Spendius had at last reconstructed. Of pyramidal shape, like the pharos of Alexandria, it was one hundred and thirty cubits high and twenty-three wide, with nine stories, diminishing as they approached the summit, and protected by scales of brass; they were pierced with numerous doors and were filled with soldiers, and on the upper platform there stood a catapult flanked by two ballistas.

Then Hamilcar planted crosses for those who should speak of surrender, and even the women were brigaded. The people lay in the streets and waited full of distress.

Then one morning before sunrise (it was the seventh day of the month of Nyssan) they heard a great shout uttered by all the Barbarians simultaneously; the leaden-tubed trumpets pealed, and the great Paphlagonian horns bellowed like bulls. All rose and ran to the rampart.

A forest of lances, pikes, and swords bristled at its base. It leaped against the walls, the ladders grappled them; and Barbarians' heads appeared in the intervals of the battlements.

Beams supported by long files of men were battering at the gates; and, in order to demolish the wall at places where the terrace was wanting, the Mercenaries came up in serried cohorts, the first line crawling, the second bending their hams, and the others rising in succession to the last who stood upright; while elsewhere, in order to climb up, the tallest advanced in front and the lowest in the rear, and all rested their shields upon their helmets with their left arms, joining them together at the edges so tightly that they might have been taken for an assemblage of large tortoises. The projectiles slid over these oblique masses.

The Carthaginians threw down mill-stones, pestles, vats, casks, beds, everything that could serve as a weight and could knock down. Some watched at the embrasures with fishermen's nets, and when the Barbarian arrived he found himself caught in the meshes, and struggled like a fish. They demolished their own battlements; portions of wall fell down raising a great dust; and as the catapults on the terrace were shooting over against one another, the stones would strike together and shiver into a thousand pieces, making a copious shower upon the combatants.

Soon the two crowds formed but one great chain of human bodies; it overflowed into the intervals in the terrace, and, somewhat looser at the two extremities, swayed perpetually without advancing. They clasped one another, lying flat on the ground like wrestlers. They crushed one another. The women leaned over the battlements and shrieked. They were dragged away by their veils, and the whiteness of their suddenly uncovered sides shone in the arms of the Negroes as the latter buried their daggers in them. Some corpses did not fall, being too much pressed by the crowd, and, supported by the shoulders of their companions, advanced for some minutes quite upright and with staring eyes. Some who had both temples pierced by a javelin swayed their heads about like bears. Mouths, opened to shout, remained gaping; severed hands flew through the air. Mighty blows were dealt, which were long talked of by the survivors.

Meanwhile arrows darted from the towers of wood and stone. The tollenos moved their long yards rapidly; and as the Barbarians had sacked the old cemetery of the aborigines beneath the Catacombs, they hurled the tombstones against the

Carthaginians. Sometimes the cables broke under the weight of too heavy baskets, and masses of men, all with uplifted arms, would fall from the sky.

Up to the middle of the day the veterans had attacked the Taenia fiercely in order to penetrate into the harbour and destroy the fleet. Hamilcar had a fire of damp straw lit upon the roofing of Khamon, and as the smoke blinded them they fell back to the left, and came to swell the horrible rout which was pressing forward in Malqua. Some syntagmata composed of sturdy men, chosen expressly for the purpose, had broken in three gates. They were checked by lofty barriers made of planks studded with nails, but a fourth yielded easily; they dashed over it at a run and rolled into a pit in which there were hidden snares. At the south-west angle Autaritus and his men broke down the rampart, the fissure in which had been stopped up with bricks. The ground behind rose, and they climbed it nimbly. But on the top they found a second wall composed of stones and long beams lying quite flat and alternating like the squares on a chess-board. It was a Gaulish fashion, and had been adapted by the Suffet to the requirements of the situation; the Gauls imagined themselves before a town in their own country. Their attack was weak, and they were repulsed.

All the roundway, from the street of Khamon as far as the Green Market, now belonged to the Barbarians, and the Samnites were finishing off the dying with blows of stakes; or else with one foot on the wall were gazing down at the smoking ruins beneath them, and the battle which was beginning again in the distance.

The slingers, who were distributed through the rear, were still shooting. But the springs of the Acarnanian slings had broken from use, and many were throwing stones with the hand like shepherds; the rest hurled leaden bullets with the handle of a whip. Zarxas, his shoulders covered with his long black hair, went about everywhere, and led on the Barbarians. Two pouches hung at his hips; he thrust his left hand into them continually, while his right arm whirled round like a chariot-wheel.

Matho had at first refrained from fighting, the better to command all the Barbarians at once. He had been seen along the gulf with the Mercenaries, near the lagoon with the Numidians, and on the shores of the lake among the Negroes, and from the back part of the plain he urged forward masses of soldiers who came ceaselessly against the ramparts. By degrees he had drawn near; the smell of blood, the sight of carnage, and the tumult of clarions had at last made his heart leap. Then he had gone back into his tent, and throwing off his cuirass had taken his lion's skin as being more convenient for battle. The snout tilted upon his head, bordering his face with a circle of fangs; the two fore-paws were crossed upon his breast, and the claws of the hinder ones fell beneath his knees.

He had kept on his strong waist-belt, wherein gleamed a two-edged axe, and with his great sword in both hands he had dashed impetuously through the breach. Like a pruner cutting willow-branches and trying to strike off as much as possible so as to make the more money, he marched along mowing down the Carthaginians around him. Those who tried to seize him in flank he knocked down with blows of the pommel; when they attacked him in front he ran them through; if they fled he clove them. Two men leaped together upon his back; he bounded backwards against a gate and crushed them. His sword fell and rose. It shivered on the angle of a wall. Then he took his heavy axe, and front and rear he ripped up the Carthaginians like a flock of sheep. They scattered more and more, and he was quite alone when he reached the second enclosure at the foot of the Acropolis. The materials which had been flung from the summit cumbered the steps and were heaped up higher than the wall. Matho turned back amid the ruins to summons his companions.

He perceived their crests scattered over the multitude; they were sinking and their wearers were about to perish; he dashed towards them; then the vast wreath of red plumes closed in, and they soon rejoined him and surrounded him. But an enormous crowd was discharging from the side streets. He was caught by the hips, lifted up and carried away outside the rampart to a spot where the terrace was high.

Matho shouted a command and all the shields sank upon the helmets; he leaped upon them in order to catch hold somewhere so as to re-enter Carthage; and, flourishing his terrible axe, ran over the shields, which resembled waves of bronze, like a marine god, with brandished trident, over his billows.

However, a man in a white robe was walking along the edge of the rampart, impassible, and indifferent to the death which surrounded him. Sometimes he would spread out his right hand above his eyes in order to find out some one. Matho happened to pass beneath him. Suddenly his eyeballs flamed, his livid face contracted; and raising both his lean arms he shouted out abuse at him.

Matho did not hear it; but he felt so furious and cruel a look entering his heart that he uttered a roar. He hurled his long axe at him; some people threw themselves upon Schahabarim; and Matho seeing him no more fell back exhausted.

A terrible creaking drew near, mingled with the rhythm of hoarse voices singing together.

It was the great helepolis surrounded by a crowd of soldiers. They were dragging it with both hands, hauling it with ropes, and pushing it with their shoulders—for the slope rising from the plain to the terrace, though extremely gentle, was found impracticable for machines of such prodigious weight. However, it had eight wheels banded with iron, and it had been advancing slowly in this way since the morning, like a mountain raised upon another. Then there appeared an immense ram issuing from its base. The doors along the three fronts which faced the town fell down, and cuirassed soldiers appeared in the interior like pillars of iron. Some might be seen climbing and descending the two staircases which crossed the stories. Some were waiting to dart out as soon as the cramps of the doors touched the walls; in the middle of the upper platform the skeins of the ballistas were turning, and the great beam of the catapult was being lowered.

Hamilcar was at that moment standing upright on the roof of Melkarth. He had calculated that it would come directly towards him, against what was the most invulnerable place in the wall, which was for that very reason denuded of sentries. His slaves had for a long time been bringing leathern bottles along the roundway, where they had raised with clay two transverse partitions forming a sort of basin. The water was flowing insensibly along the terrace, and strange to say, it seemed to cause Hamilcar no anxiety.

But when the helepolis was thirty paces off, he commanded planks to be placed over the streets between the houses from the cisterns to the rampart; and a file of people passed from hand to hand helmets and amphoras, which were emptied continually. The Carthaginians, however, grew indignant at this waste of water. The ram was demolishing the wall, when suddenly a fountain sprang forth from the disjointed stones. Then the lofty brazen mass, nine stories high, which contained and engaged more than three thousand soldiers, began to rock gently like a ship. In fact, the water, which had penetrated the terrace, had broken up the path before it; its wheels stuck in the mire; the head of Spendius, with distended cheeks blowing an ivory cornet, appeared between leathern curtains on the first story. The great machine, as though convulsively upheaved, advanced perhaps ten paces; but the ground softened more and more, the mire reached to the axles, and the helepolis stopped, leaning over frightfully to one side. The catapult rolled to the edge of the platform, and carried away by the weight of its beam, fell, shattering the lower stories beneath it. The soldiers who were standing on the doors slipped into the abyss, or else held on to the extremities of the long beams, and by their weight increased the inclination of the helepolis, which was going to pieces with creakings in all its joints.

The other Barbarians rushed up to help them, massing themselves into a compact crowd. The Carthaginians descended from the rampart, and, assailing them in the rear, killed them at leisure. But the chariots furnished with the sickles hastened up, and galloped round the outskirts of the multitude. The latter ascended the wall again; night came on; and the Barbarians gradually retired.

Nothing could now be seen on the plain but a sort of perfectly black, swarming mass, which extended from the bluish gulf to the purely white lagoon; and the lake, which had received streams of blood, stretched further away like a great purple pool.

The terrace was now so laden with corpses that it looked as though it had been constructed of human bodies. In the centre stood the helepolis covered with armour; and from time to time huge fragments broke off from it, like stones from a crumbling pyramid. Broad tracks made by the streams of lead might be distinguished on the walls. A broken-down wooden tower burned here and there, and the houses showed dimly like the stages of a ruined amphitheatre. Heavy fumes of smoke were rising, and rolling with them sparks which were lost in the dark sky.

The Carthaginians, however, who were consumed by thirst, had rushed to the cisterns. They broke open the doors. A miry swamp stretched at the bottom.

What was to be done now? Moreover, the Barbarians were countless, and when their fatigue was over they would begin again.

The people deliberated all night in groups at the corners of the streets. Some said that they ought to send away the women, the sick, and the old men; others proposed to abandon the town, and found a colony far away. But vessels were lacking, and when the sun appeared no decision had been made.

There was no fighting that day, all being too much exhausted. The sleepers looked like corpses.

Then the Carthaginians, reflecting upon the cause of their disasters, remembered that they had not dispatched to Phœnicia the annual offering due to Tyrian Melkarth, and a great terror came upon them. The gods were indignant with the Republic, and were, no doubt, about to prosecute their vengeance.

They were considered as cruel masters, who were appeased with supplications and allowed themselves to be bribed with presents. All were feeble in comparison with Moloch the Devourer. The existence, the very flesh of men, belonged to him; and hence in order to preserve it, the Carthaginians used to offer up a portion of it to him, which calmed his fury. Children were burned on the forehead, or on the nape of the neck, with woollen wicks; and as this mode of satisfying Baal brought in much money to the priests, they failed not to recommend it as being easier and more pleasant.

This time, however, the Republic itself was at stake. But as every profit must be purchased by some loss, and as every transaction was regulated according to the needs of the weaker and the demands of the stronger, there was no pain great enough for the god, since he delighted in such as was of the most horrible description, and all were now at his mercy. He must accordingly be fully gratified. Precedents showed that in this way the scourge would be made to disappear. Moreover, it was believed that an immolation by fire would purify Carthage. The ferocity of the people was predisposed towards it. The choice, too, must fall exclusively upon the families of the great.

The Ancients assembled. The sitting was a long one. Hanno had come to it.

As he was now unable to sit he remained lying down near the door, half hidden among the fringes of the lofty tapestry; and when the pontiff of Moloch asked them whether they would consent to surrender their children, his voice suddenly broke forth from the shadow like the roaring of a genius in the depths of a cavern. He regretted, he said, that he had none of his own blood to give; and he gazed at Hamilcar, who faced him at the other end of the hall. The Suffet was so much disconcerted by this look that it made him lower his eyes. All successively bent their heads in approval; and in accordance with the rites he had to reply to the high priest: "Yes; be it so." Then the Ancients decreed the sacrifice in traditional circumlocution—because there are things more troublesome to say than to perform.

The decision was almost immediately known in Carthage, and lamentations resounded. The cries of women might everywhere be heard; their husbands consoled them, or railed at them with remonstrances.

But three hours afterwards extraordinary tidings were spread abroad: the Suffet had discovered springs at the foot of the cliff. There was a rush to the place. Water might be seen in holes dug in the sand, and some were already lying flat on the ground and drinking.

Hamilcar did not himself know whether it was by the determination of the gods or through the vague recollection of a revelation which his father had once made to him; but on leaving the Ancients he had gone down to the shore and had begun to dig the gravel with his slaves.

He gave clothing, boots, and wine. He gave all the rest of the corn that he was keeping by him. He even let the crowd enter his palace, and he opened kitchens, stores, and all the rooms—Salammbô's alone excepted. He announced that six thousand Gaulish Mercenaries were coming, and that the king of Macedonia was sending soldiers.

But on the second day the springs diminished, and on the evening of the third they were completely dried up. Then the decree of the Ancients passed everywhere from lip to lip, and the priests of Moloch began their task.

Men in black robes presented themselves in the houses. In many instances the owners had deserted them under pretence of some business, or of some dainty that they were going to buy; and the servants of Moloch came and took the children away. Others themselves surrendered them stupidly. Then they were brought to the temple of Tanith, where the priestesses were charged with their amusement and support until the solemn day.

They visit Hamilcar suddenly and found him in his gardens.

"Barca! we come for that that you know of—your son!" They added that some people had met him one evening during the previous moon in the centre of the Mappalian district being led by an old man.

He was as though suffocated at first. But speedily understanding that any denial would be vain, Hamilcar bowed; and he brought them into the commercial house. Some slaves who had run up at a sign kept watch round about it.

He entered Salammbô's room in a state of distraction. He seized Hannibal with one hand, snatched up the cord of a trailing garment with the other, tied his feet and hands with it, thrust the end into his mouth to form a gag, and hid him under the bed of ox-hides by letting an ample drapery fall to the ground.

Afterwards he walked about from right to left, raised his arms, wheeled round, bit his lips. Then he stood still with staring eyeballs, and panted as though he were about to die.

But he clapped his hands three times. Giddenem appeared.

"Listen!" he said, "go and take from among the slaves a male child from eight to nine years of age, with black hair and swelling forehead! Bring him here! make haste!"

Giddenem soon entered again, bringing forward a young boy.

He was a miserable child, at once lean and bloated; his skin looked greyish, like the infected rag hanging to his sides; his head was sunk between his shoulders, and with the back of his hand he was rubbing his eyes, which were filled with flies.

How could he ever be confounded with Hannibal! and there was no time to choose another. Hamilcar looked at Giddenem; he felt inclined to strangle him.

"Begone!" he cried; and the master of the slaves fled.

The misfortune which he had so long dreaded was therefore come, and with extravagant efforts he strove to discover whether there was not some mode, some means to escape it.

Abdalonim suddenly spoke from behind the door. The Suffet was being asked for. The servants of Moloch were growing impatient.

Hamilcar repressed a cry as though a red hot iron had burnt him; and he began anew to pace the room like one distraught. Then he sank down beside the balustrade, and, with his elbows on his knees, pressed his forehead into his shut fists.

The porphyry basin still contained a little clear water for Salammbô's ablutions. In spite of his repugnance and all his pride, the Suffet dipped the child into it, and, like a slave merchant, began to wash him and rub him with strigils and red earth. Then he took two purple squares from the receptacles round the wall, placed one on his breast and the other on his back, and joined them together on the collar bones with two diamond clasps. He poured perfume upon his head, passed an electrum necklace around his neck, and put on him sandals with heels of pearl—sandals belonging to his own daughter! But he stamped with shame and vexation; Salammbô, who busied herself in helping him, was as pale as he. The child, dazzled by such splendour, smiled and, growing bold even, was beginning to clap his hands and jump, when Hamilcar took him away.

He held him firmly by the arm as though he were afraid of losing him, and the child, who was hurt, wept a little as he ran beside him.

When on a level with the ergastulum, under a palm tree, a voice was raised, a mournful and supplicant voice. It murmured: "Master! oh! master!"

Hamilcar turned and beside him perceived a man of abject appearance, one of the wretches who led a haphazard existence in the household.

"What do you want?" said the Suffet.

The slave, who trembled horribly, stammered:

"I am his father!"

Hamilcar walked on; the other followed him with stooping loins, bent hams, and head thrust forward. His face was convulsed with unspeakable anguish, and he was choking with suppressed sobs, so eager was he at once to question him, and to cry: "Mercy!"

At last he ventured to touch him lightly with one finger on the elbow.

"Are you going to—?" He had not strength to finish, and Hamilcar stopped quite amazed at such grief.

He had never thought—so immense was the abyss separating them from each other—that there could be anything in common between them. It even appeared to him a sort of outrage, an encroachment upon his own privileges. He replied with a look colder and heavier than an executioner's axe; the slave swooned and fell in the dust at his feet. Hamilcar strode across him.

The three black-robed men were waiting in the great hall, and standing against the stone disc. Immediately he tore his garments, and rolled upon the pavement uttering piercing cries.

"Ah! poor little Hannibal! Oh! my son! my consolation! my hope! my life! Kill me also! take me away! Woe! Woe!" He ploughed his face with his nails, tore out his hair, and shrieked like the women who lament at funerals. "Take him away then! my suffering is too great! begone! kill me like him!" The servants of Moloch were astonished that the great Hamilcar was so weak-spirited. They were almost moved by it.

A noise of naked feet became audible, with a broken throat-rattling like the breathing of a wild beast speeding along, and a man, pale, terrible, and with outspread arms appeared on the threshold of the third gallery, between the ivory pots; he exclaimed:

"My child!"

Hamilcar threw himself with a bound upon the slave, and covering the man's mouth with his hand exclaimed still more loudly:

"It is the old man who reared him! he calls him 'my child!' it will make him mad! enough! enough!" And hustling away the three priests and their victim he went out with them and with a great kick shut the door behind him.

Hamilcar strained his ears for some minutes in constant fear of seeing them return. He then thought of getting rid of the slave in order to be quite sure that he would see nothing; but the peril had not wholly disappeared, and, if the gods were provoked at the man's death, it might be turned against his son. Then, changing his intention, he sent him by Taanach the best from his kitchens—a quarter of a goat, beans, and preserved pomegranates. The slave, who had eaten nothing for a long time, rushed upon them; his tears fell into the dishes.

Hamilcar at last returned to Salammbô, and unfastened Hannibal's cords. The child in exasperation bit his hand until the blood came. He repelled him with a caress.

To make him remain quiet Salammbô tried to frighten him with Lamia, a Cyrenian ogress.

"But where is she?" he asked.

He was told that brigands were coming to put him into prison. "Let them come," he rejoined, "and I will kill them!"

Then Hamilcar told him the frightful truth. But he fell into a passion with his father, contending that he was quite able to annihilate the whole people, since he was the master of Carthage.

At last, exhausted by his exertions and anger, he fell into a wild sleep. He spoke in his dreams, his back leaning against a scarlet cushion; his head was thrown back somewhat, and his little arm, outstretched from his body, lay quite straight in an attitude of command.

When the night had grown dark Hamilcar lifted him up gently, and, without a torch, went down the galley staircase. As he passed through the mercantile house he took up a basket of grapes and a flagon of pure water; the child awoke before the statue of Aletes in the vault of gems, and he smiled—like the other—on his father's arm at the brilliant lights which surrounded him.

Hamilcar felt quite sure that his son could not be taken from him. It was an impenetrable spot communicating with the beach by a subterranean passage which he alone knew, and casting his eyes around he inhaled a great draught of air. Then he set him down upon a stool beside some golden shields.

No one at present could see him; he had no further need for watching; and he relieved his feelings. Like a mother finding again her first-born that was lost, he threw himself upon his son; he clasped him to his breast, he laughed and wept at the same time, he called him by the fondest names and covered him with kisses; little Hannibal was frightened by this terrible tenderness and was silent now.

Hamilcar returned with silent steps, feeling the walls around him, and came into the great hall where the moonlight entered through one of the apertures in the dome; in the centre the slave lay sleeping after his repast, stretched at full length upon the marble pavement. He looked at him and was moved with a sort of pity. With the tip of his cothurn he pushed forward a carpet beneath his head. Then he raised his eyes and gazed at Tanith, whose slender crescent was shining in the sky, and felt himself stronger than the Baals and full of contempt for them.

The arrangements for the sacrifice were already begun.

Part of a wall in the temple of Moloch was thrown down in order to draw out the brazen god without touching the ashes of the altar. Then as soon as the sun appeared the hierodules pushed it towards the square of Khamon.

It moved backwards sliding upon cylinders; its shoulders overlapped the walls. No sooner did the Carthaginians perceive it in the distance than they speedily took to flight, for the Baal could be looked upon with impunity only when exercising his wrath.

A smell of aromatics spread through the streets. All the temples had just been opened simultaneously, and from them there came forth tabernacles borne upon chariots, or upon litters carried by the pontiffs. Great plumes swayed at the corners of them, and rays were emitted from their slender pinnacles which terminated in balls of crystal, gold, silver or copper.

These were the Chanaanitish Baalim, offshoots of the supreme Baal, who were returning to their first cause to humble themselves before his might and annihilate themselves in his splendour.

Melkarth's pavilion, which was of fine purple, sheltered a petroleum flame; on Khamon's, which was of hyacinth colour, there rose an ivory phallus bordered with a circle of gems; between Eschmoun's curtains, which were blue as the ether, a sleeping python formed a circle with his tail, and the Patæc gods, held in the arms of their priests, looked like great infants in swaddling clothes with their heels touching the ground.

Then came all the inferior forms of the Divinity: Baal-Samin, god of celestial space; Baal-Peor, god of the sacred mountains; Baal-Zeboub, god of corruption, with those of the neighbouring countries and congenerous races: the Iarbal of Libya, the Adrammelech of Chaldæa, Kijun of the Syrians; Derceto, with her virgin's face, crept on her fins, and the corpse of Tammouz was drawn along in the midst of a catafalque among torches and heads of hair. In order to subdue the kings of the firmament to the Sun, and prevent their particular influences from disturbing his, diversely coloured metal stars were brandished at the end of long poles; and all were there, from the dark Nebo, the genius of

Mercury, to the hideous Rahab, which is the constellation of the Crocodile. The Abaddirs, stones which had fallen from the moon, were whirling in slings of silver thread; little loaves, representing the female form, were borne on baskets by the priests of Ceres; others brought their fetishes and amulets; forgotten idols reappeared, while the mystic symbols had been taken from the very ships as though Carthage wished to concentrate herself wholly upon a single thought of death and desolation.

Before each tabernacle a man balanced a large vase of smoking incense on his head. Clouds hovered here and there, and the hangings, pendants, and embroideries of the sacred pavilions might be distinguished amid the thick vapours. These advanced slowly owing to their enormous weight. Sometimes the axles became fast in the streets; then the pious took advantage of the opportunity to touch the Baalim with their garments, which they preserved afterwards as holy things.

The brazen statue continued to advance towards the square of Khamon. The rich, carrying sceptres with emerald balls, set out from the bottom of Megara; the Ancients, with diadems on their heads, had assembled in Kinisdo, and masters of the finances, governors of provinces, sailors, and the numerous horde employed at funerals, all with the insignia of their magistracies or the instruments of their calling, were making their way towards the tabernacles which were descending from the Acropolis between the colleges of the pontiffs.

Out of deference to Moloch they had adorned themselves with the most splendid jewels. Diamonds sparkled on their black garments; but their rings were too large and fell from their wasted hands—nor could there have been anything so mournful as this silent crowd where earrings tapped against pale faces, and gold tiaras clasped brows contracted with stern despair.

At last the Baal arrived exactly in the centre of the square. His pontiffs arranged an enclosure with trellis-work to keep off the multitude, and remained around him at his feet.

The priests of Khamon, in tawny woollen robes, formed a line before their temple beneath the columns of the portico; those of Eschmoun, in linen mantles with necklaces of koukouphas' heads and pointed tiaras, posted themselves on the steps of the Acropolis; the priests of Melkarth, in violet tunics, took the western side; the priests of the Abaddirs, clasped with bands of Phrygian stuffs, placed themselves on the east, while towards the south, with the necromancers all covered with tattooings, and the shriekers in patched cloaks, were ranged the curates of the Patæc gods, and the Yidonim, who put the bone of a dead man into their mouths to learn the future. The priests of Ceres, who were dressed in blue robes, had prudently stopped in the street of Satheb, and in low tones were chanting a thesmophorion in the Megarian dialect.

From time to time files of men arrived, completely naked, their arms out-stretched, and all holding one another by the shoulders. From the depths of their breasts they drew forth a hoarse and cavernous intonation; their eyes, which were fastened upon the colossus, shone through the dust, and they swayed their bodies simultaneously, and at equal distances, as though they were all affected by a single movement. They were so frenzied that to restore order the hierodules compelled them, with blows of the stick, to lie flat upon the ground, with their faces resting against the brass trellis-work.

Then it was that a man in a white robe advanced from the back of the square. He penetrated the crowd slowly, and people recognised a priest of Tanith—the high-priest Schahabarim. Hootings were raised, for the tyranny of the male prin-ciple prevailed that day in all consciences, and the goddess was actually so com-pletely forgotten that the absence of her pontiffs had not been noticed. But the amazement increased when he was seen to open one of the doors in the trellis-work intended for those who entered to offer up victims. It was an outrage to their god, thought the priests of Moloch, that he had just committed, and they sought with eager gestures to repel him. Fed on the meat of the holocausts, clad in purple like kings, and wearing triple-storied crowns, they despised the pale eunuch, weakened with his macerations, and angry laughter shook their black beards, which were dis-played on their breasts in the sun.

Schahabarim walked on, giving no reply, and, traversing the whole enclosure with deliberation, reached the legs of the colossus; then, spreading out both arms, he touched it on both sides, which was a solemn form of adoration. For a long time Rabbet had been torturing him, and in despair, or perhaps for lack of a god that completely satisfied his ideas, he had at last decided for this one.

The crowd, terrified by this act of apostasy, uttered a lengthened murmur. It was felt that the last tie which bound their souls to a merciful divinity was breaking.

But owing to his mutilation Schahabarim could take no part in the cult of the Baal. The men in the red cloaks shut him out from the enclosure; then, when he was outside, he went round all the colleges in succession, and the priest, henceforth without a god, disappeared in the crowd. It scattered at his approach.

Meanwhile a fire of aloes, cedar, and laurel was burning between the legs of the colossus. The tips of its long wings dipped into the flame; the unguents with which it had been rubbed flowed like sweat over its brazen limbs. Around the cir-cular flagstone on which its feet rested, the children, wrapped in black veils, formed a motionless circle; and its extravagantly long arms reached down their palms to them as though to seize the crown that they formed and carry it to the sky.

The rich, the Ancients, the women, the whole multitude, thronged behind the priests and on the terraces of the houses. The large painted stars revolved no longer; the tabernacles were set upon the ground; and the fumes from the censers ascended perpendicularly, spreading their bluish branches through the azure like gigantic trees.

Many fainted; others became inert and petrified in their ecstasy. Infinite anguish weighed upon the breasts of the beholders. The last shouts died out one by one—and the people of Carthage stood breathless, and absorbed in the longing of their terror.

At last the high priest of Moloch passed his left hand beneath the children's veils, plucked a lock of hair from their foreheads, and threw it upon the flames. Then the men in the red cloaks chanted the sacred hymn:

"Homage to thee, Sun! king of the two zones, self-generating Creator, Father and Mother, Father and Son, God and Goddess, Goddess and God!" And their voices were lost in the outburst of instruments sounding simultaneously to drown the cries of the victims. The eight-stringed scheminiths, the kinnors which had ten strings, and the nebals which had twelve, grated, whistled, and thundered. Enormous leathern bags, bristling with pipes, made a shrill clashing noise; the tabourines, beaten with all the players' might, resounded with heavy, rapid blows; and, in spite of the fury of the clarions, the salsalim snapped like grasshoppers' wings.

The hierodules, with a long hook, opened the seven-storied compartments on the body of the Baal. They put meal into the highest, two turtle-doves into the second, an ape into the third, a ram into the fourth, a sheep into the fifth, and as no ox was to be had for the sixth, a tawny hide taken from the sanctuary was thrown into it. The seventh compartment yawned empty still.

Before undertaking anything it was well to make trial of the arms of the god. Slender chainlets stretched from his fingers up to his shoulders and fell behind, where men by pulling them made the two hands rise to a level with the elbows, and come close together against the belly; they were moved several times in succession with little abrupt jerks. Then the instruments were still. The fire roared.

The pontiffs of Moloch walked about on the great flagstone scanning the multitude.

An individual sacrifice was necessary, a perfectly voluntary oblation, which was considered as carrying the others along with it. But no one had appeared up to the present, and the seven passages lending from the barriers to the colossus were completely empty. Then the priests, to encourage the people, drew bodkins from their girdles and gashed their faces. The Devotees, who were stretched on the ground outside, were brought within the enclosure. A bundle of horrible irons was thrown to them, and each chose his own torture. They drove in spits between their breasts; they split their cheeks; they put crowns of thorns upon their heads; then they twined their arms together, and surrounded the children in another large circle which widened and contracted in turns. They reached to the balustrade, they threw themselves back again, and then began once more, attracting the crowd to them by the dizziness of their motion with its accompanying blood and shrieks.

By degrees people came into the end of the passages; they flung into the flames pearls, gold vases, cups, torches, all their wealth; the offerings became constantly more numerous and more splendid. At last a man who tottered, a man pale and hideous with terror, thrust forward a child; then a little black mass was seen between the hands of the colossus, and sank into the dark opening. The priests bent over the edge of the great flagstone—and a new song burst forth celebrating the joys of death and of new birth into eternity.

The children ascended slowly, and as the smoke formed lofty eddies as it escaped, they seemed at a distance to disappear in a cloud. Not one stirred. Their wrists and ankles were tied, and the dark drapery prevented them from seeing anything and from being recognised.

Hamilcar, in a red cloak, like the priests of Moloch was beside the Baal, standing upright in front of the great toe of its right foot. When the fourteenth child was brought every one could see him make a great gesture of horror. But he soon resumed his former attitude, folded his arms, and looked upon the ground. The high pontiff stood on the other side of the statue as motionless as he. His head, laden with an Assyrian mitre, was bent, and he was watching the gold plate on his breast; it was covered with fatidical stones, and the flame mirrored in it formed irisated lights. He grew pale and dismayed. Hamilcar bent his brow; and they were both so near the funeral-pile that the hems of their cloaks brushed it as they rose from time to time.

The brazen arms were working more quickly. They paused no longer. Every time that a child was placed in them the priests of Moloch spread out their hands upon him to burden him with the crimes of the people, vociferating: "They are not men but oxen!" and the multitude round about repeated: "Oxen! oxen!" The devout exclaimed: "Lord! eat!" and the priests of Proserpine, complying through terror with the needs of Carthage, muttered the Eleusinian formula: "Pour out rain! bring forth!"

The victims, when scarcely at the edge of the opening, disappeared like a drop of water on a red-hot plate, and white smoke rose amid the great scarlet colour.

Nevertheless, the appetite of the god was not appeased. He ever wished for more. In order to furnish him with a larger supply, the victims were piled up on his hands with a big chain above them which kept them in their place. Some devout persons had at the beginning wished to count them, to see whether their number corresponded with the days of the solar year; but others were brought, and it was impossible to distinguish them in the giddy motion of the horrible arms. This lasted for a long, indefinite time until the evening. Then the partitions inside assumed a darker glow, and burning flesh might be seen. Some even believed that they could descry hair, limbs, and whole bodies.

Night fell; clouds accumulated above the Baal. The funeral-pile, which was flameless now, formed a pyramid of coals up to his knees; completely red like a giant covered with blood, he looked, with his head thrown back, as though he were staggering beneath the weight of his intoxication.

In proportion as the priests made haste, the frenzy of the people increased; as the number of the victims was diminishing, some cried out to spare them, others that still more were needful. The walls, with their burden of people, seemed to be giving way beneath the howlings of terror and mystic voluptuousness. Then the faithful came into the passages, dragging their children, who clung to them; and they beat them in order to make them let go, and handed them over to the men in red. The instrument-players sometimes stopped through exhaustion; then the cries of the mothers might be heard, and the frizzling of the fat as it fell upon the coals. The henbane-drinkers crawled on all fours around the colossus, roaring like tigers; the Yidonim vaticinated, the Devotees sang with their cloven lips; the trellis-work had been broken through, all wished for a share in the sacrifice; and fathers, whose children had died previously, cast their effigies, their playthings, their preserved bones into the fire. Some who had knives rushed upon the rest. They slaughtered one another. The hierodules took the fallen ashes at the edge of the flagstone in bronze fans, and cast them into the air that the sacrifice might be scattered over the town and even to the region of the stars.

The loud noise and great light had attracted the Barbarians to the foot of the walls; they clung to the wreck of the helepolis to have a better view, and gazed open-mouthed in horror.

Chapter XIV

THE PASS OF THE HATCHET

THE CARTHAGINIANS HAD NOT RE-ENTERED THEIR HOUSES WHEN THE clouds accumulated more thickly; those who raised their heads towards the colossus could feel big drops on their foreheads, and the rain fell.

It fell the whole night plentifully, in floods; the thunder growled; it was the voice of Moloch; he had vanquished Tanith; and she, being now fecundated, opened up her vast bosom in heaven's heights. Sometimes she could be seen in a clear and luminous spot stretched upon cushions of cloud; and then the darkness would close in again as though she were still too weary and wished to sleep again; the Carthaginians, all believing that water is brought forth by the moon, shouted to make her travail easy.

The rain beat upon the terraces and overflowed them, forming lakes in the courts, cascades on the staircases, and eddies at the corners of the streets. It poured in warm heavy masses and urgent streams; big frothy jets leaped from the corners of all the buildings; and it seemed as though whitish cloths hung dimly upon the walls, and the washed temple-roofs shone black in the gleam of the lightning. Torrents descended from the Acropolis by a thousand paths; houses suddenly gave way, and small beams, plaster, rubbish, and furniture passed along in the streams which ran impetuously over the pavement.

Amphoras, flagons, and canvases had been placed out of doors; but the torches were extinguished; brands were taken from the funeral-pile of the Baal, and the Carthaginians bent back their necks and opened their mouths to drink. Others by the side of the miry pools, plunged their arms into them up to the arm-pits, and filled themselves so abundantly with water that they vomited it forth like buffaloes. The freshness gradually spread; they breathed in the damp air with play of limb, and in the happiness of their intoxication boundless hope soon arose. All their miseries were forgotten. Their country was born anew.

They felt the need, as it were, of directing upon others the extravagant fury which they had been unable to employ against themselves. Such a sacrifice could not be vain; although they felt no remorse they found themselves carried away by the frenzy which results from complicity in irreparable crimes.

The Barbarians had encountered the storm in their ill-closed tents; and they were still quite chilled on the morrow as they tramped through the mud in search of their stores and weapons, which were spoiled and lost.

Hamilcar went himself to see Hanno, and, in virtue of his plenary powers, intrusted the command to him. The old Suffet hesitated for a few minutes between his animosity and his appetite for authority, but he accepted nevertheless.

Hamilcar next took out a galley armed with a catapult at each end. He placed it in the gulf in front of the raft; then he embarked his stoutest troops on board such vessels as were available. He was apparently taking to flight; and running northward before the wind he disappeared in the mist.

But three days afterwards, when the attack was about to begin again, some people arrived tumultuously from the Libyan coast. Barca had come among them. He had carried off provisions everywhere, and he was spreading through the country.

Then the Barbarians were indignant as though he were betraying them. Those who were most weary of the siege, and especially the Gauls, did not hesitate to leave the walls in order to try to rejoin him. Spendius wanted to reconstruct the helepolis; Matho had traced an imaginary line from his tent to Megara, and inwardly swore to follow it, and none of their men stirred. But the rest, under the command of Autaritus, went off, abandoning the western part of the rampart, and so profound was the carelessness exhibited that no one even thought of replacing them.

Narr' Havas spied them from afar in the mountains. During the night he led all his men along the sea-shore on the outer side of the Lagoon, and entered Carthage.

He presented himself as a savior with six thousand men all carrying meal under their cloaks, and forty elephants laden with forage and dried meat. The people flocked quickly around them; they gave them names. The sight of these strong animals, sacred to Baal, gave the Carthaginians even more joy than the arrival of such relief; it was a token of the tenderness of the god, a proof that he was at last about to interfere in the war to defend them.

Narr' Havas received the compliments of the Ancients. Then he ascended to Salammbô's palace.

He had not seen her again since the time when in Hamilcar's tent amid the five armies he had felt her little, cold, soft hand fastened to his own; she had left for Carthage after the betrothal. His love, which had been diverted by other ambitions, had come back to him; and now he expected to enjoy his rights, to marry her, and take her.

Salammbô did not understand how the young man could ever become her master! Although she asked Tanith every day for Matho's death, her horror of the Libyan was growing less. She vaguely felt that the hate with which he had persecuted her was something almost religious—and she would fain have seen in Narr' Havas's person a reflection, as it were, of that malice which still dazzled her. She desired to know him better, and yet his presence would have embarrassed her. She sent him word that she could not receive him.

Moreover, Hamilcar had forbidden his people to admit the King of the Numidians to see her; by putting off his reward to the end of the war he hoped to retain his devotion—and, through dread of the Suffet, Narr' Havas withdrew.

But he bore himself haughtily towards the Hundred. He changed their arrangements. He demanded privileges for his men, and placed them on important posts; thus the Barbarians stared when they perceived Numidians on the towers.

The surprise of the Carthaginians was greater still when three hundred of their own people, who had been made prisoners during the Sicilian war, arrived on board an old Punic trireme. Hamilcar, in fact, had secretly sent back to the Quirites the crews of the Latin vessels, taken before the defection of the Tyrian towns; and, to reciprocate the courtesy, Rome was now sending him back her captives. She scorned the overtures of the Mercenaries in Sardinia, and would not even recognise the inhabitants of Utica as subjects.

Hiero, who was ruling at Syracuse, was carried away by this example. For the preservation of his own States it was necessary that an equilibrium should exist between the two peoples; he was interested, therefore, in the safety of the Chanaanites, and he declared himself their friend, and sent them twelve hundred oxen, with fifty-three thousand nebels of pure wheat.

A deeper reason prompted aid to Carthage. It was felt that if the Mercenaries triumphed, every one, from soldier to plate-washer, would rise, and that no government and no house could resist them.

Meanwhile Hamilcar was scouring the eastern districts. He drove back the Gauls, and all the Barbarians found that they were themselves in something like a state of siege.

Then he set himself to harass them. He would arrive and then retire, and by constantly renewing this manoeuvre, he gradually detached them from their encampments. Spendius was obliged to follow them, and in the end Matho yielded in like manner.

He did not pass beyond Tunis. He shut himself up within its walls. This persistence was full of wisdom, for soon Narr' Havas was to be seen issuing from the gate of Khamon with his elephants and soldiers. Hamilcar was recalling him, but the other Barbarians were already wandering about in the provinces in pursuit of the Suffet.

The latter had received three thousand Gauls from Clypea. He had horses brought to him from Cyrenaica, and armour from Brutium, and began the war again.

Never had his genius been so impetuous and fertile. For five moons he dragged his enemies after him. He had an end to which he wished to guide them.

The Barbarians had at first tried to encompass him with small detachments, but he always escaped them. They ceased to separate. Their army amounted to about forty thousand men, and several times they enjoyed the sight of seeing the Carthaginians fall back.

The horsemen of Narr' Havas were what they found most tormenting. Often, at times of the greatest weariness, when they were advancing over the plains, and dozing beneath the weight of their arms, a great line of dust would suddenly rise on the horizon; there would be a galloping up to them, and a rain of darts would pour from the bosom of a cloud filled with flaming eyes. The Numidians in their white cloaks would utter loud shouts, raise their arms, press their rearing stallions with their knees, and, wheeling them round abruptly, would then disappear. They had always supplies of javelins and dromedaries some distance off, and they would return more terrible than before, howl like wolves, and take to flight like vultures. The Barbarians posted at the extremities of the files fell one by one; and this would continue until evening, when an attempt would be made to enter the mountains.

Although they were perilous for elephants, Hamilcar made his way in among them. He followed the long chain which extends from the promontory of Hermæum to the top of Zagouan. This, they believed, was a device for hiding the insufficiency of his troops. But the continual uncertainty in which he kept them exasperated them at last more than any defeat. They did not lose heart, and marched after him.

At last one evening they surprised a body of velites amid some big rocks at the entrance of a pass between the Silver Mountain and the Lead Mountain; the entire army was certainly in front of them, for a noise of footsteps and clarions could be heard; the Carthaginians immediately fled through the gorge. It descended into a plain, and was shaped like an iron hatchet with a surrounding of lofty cliffs. The Barbarians dashed into it in order to overtake the velites; quite at the bottom other Carthaginians were running tumultuously amid galloping oxen. A man in a red cloak was to be seen; it was the Suffet; they shouted this to one another; and they were carried away with increased fury and joy. Several, from laziness or prudence, had remained on the threshold of the pass. But some cavalry, debouching from a wood, beat them down upon the rest with blows of pike and sabre; and soon all the Barbarians were below in the plain.

Then this great human mass, after swaying to and fro for some time, stood still; they could discover no outlet.

Those who were nearest to the pass went back again, but the passage had entirely disappeared. They hailed those in front to make them go on; they were being crushed against the mountain, and from a distance they inveighed against their companions, who were unable to find the route again.

In fact the Barbarians had scarcely descended when men who had been crouching behind the rocks raised the latter with beams and overthrew them, and as the slope was steep the huge blocks had rolled down pell-mell and completely stopped up the narrow opening.

At the other extremity of the plain stretched a long passage, split in gaps here and there, and leading to a ravine which ascended to the upper plateau, where the Punic army was stationed. Ladders had been placed beforehand in this passage against the wall of cliff; and, protected by the windings of the gaps, the velites were able to seize and mount them before being overtaken. Several even made their way to the bottom of the ravine; they were drawn up with cables, for the ground at this spot was of moving sand, and so much inclined that it was impossible to climb it even on the knees. The Barbarians arrived almost immediately. But a portcullis, forty cubits high, and made to fit the intervening space exactly, suddenly sank before them like a rampart fallen from the skies.

The Suffet's combinations had therefore succeeded. None of the Mercenaries knew the mountain, and, marching as they did at the head of their columns, they had drawn on the rest. The rocks, which were somewhat narrow at the base, had been easily cast down; and, while all were running, his army had raised shouts, as of distress, on the horizon. Hamilcar, it is true, might have lost his velites, only half of whom remained, but he would have sacrificed twenty times as many for the success of such an enterprise.

The Barbarians pressed forward until morning, in compact files, from one end of the plain to the other. They felt the mountain with their hands, seeking to discover a passage.

At last day broke; and they perceived all about them a great white wall hewn with the pick. And no means of safety, no hope! The two natural outlets from this blind alley were closed by the portcullis and the heaps of rocks.

Then they all looked at one another without speaking. They sank down in collapse, feeling an icy coldness in their loins, and an overwhelming weight upon their eyelids.

They rose, and bounded against the rocks. But the lowest were weighted by the pressure of the others, and were immovable. They tried to cling to them so as to reach the top, but the bellying shape of the great masses rendered all hold impossible. They sought to cleave the ground on both sides of the gorge, but their instruments broke. They made a large fire with the tent poles, but the fire could not burn the mountain.

They returned to the portcullis; it was garnished with long nails as thick as stakes, as sharp as the spines of a porcupine, and closer than the hairs of a brush. But they were animated by such rage that they dashed themselves against it. The first were pierced to the backbone, those coming next surged over them, and all fell back, leaving human fragments and bloodstained hair on those horrible branches.

When their discouragement was somewhat abated, they made an examination of the provisions. The Mercenaries, whose baggage was lost, possessed scarcely enough for two days; and all the rest found themselves destitute—for they had been awaiting a convoy promised by the villages of the South.

However, some bulls were roaming about, those which the Carthaginians had loosed in the gorge to attract the Barbarians. They killed them with lance thrusts and ate them, and when their stomachs were filled their thoughts were less mournful.

The next day they slaughtered all the mules to the number of about forty; then they scraped the skins, boiled the entrails, pounded the bones, and did not yet despair; the army from Tunis had no doubt been warned, and was coming.

But on the evening of the fifth day their hunger increased; they gnawed their sword-belts, and the little sponges which bordered the bottom of their helmets.

These forty thousand men were massed into the species of hippodrome formed by the mountain about them. Some remained in front of the portcullis, or at the foot of the rocks; the rest covered the plain confusedly. The strong shunned one another, and the timid sought out the brave, who, nevertheless, were unable to save them.

To avoid infection, the corpses of the velites had been speedily buried; and the position of the graves was no longer visible.

All the Barbarians lay drooping on the ground. A veteran would pass between their lines here and there; and they would howl curses against the Carthaginians, against Hamilcar, and against Matho, although he was innocent of their disaster; but it seemed to them that their pains would have been less if he had shared them. Then they groaned, and some wept softly like little children.

They came to the captains and besought them to grant them something that would alleviate their sufferings. The others made no reply; or, seized with fury, would pick up a stone and fling it in their faces.

Several, in fact, carefully kept a reserve of food in a hole in the ground—a few handfuls of dates, or a little meal; and they ate this during the night, with their heads bent beneath their cloaks. Those who had swords kept them naked in their hands, and the most suspicious remained standing with their backs against the mountain.

They accused their chiefs and threatened them. Autaritus was not afraid of showing himself. With the Barbaric obstinacy which nothing could discourage, he would advance twenty times a day to the rocks at the bottom, hoping every time to find them perchance displaced; and swaying his heavy fur-covered shoulders, he reminded his companions of a bear coming forth from its cave in springtime to see whether the snows are melted.

Spendius, surrounded by the Greeks, hid himself in one of the gaps; as he was afraid, he caused a rumour of his death to be spread.

They were now hideously lean; their skin was overlaid with bluish marblings. On the evening of the ninth day three Iberians died.

Their frightened companions left the spot. They were stripped, and the white, naked bodies lay in the sunshine on the sand.

Then the Garamantians began to prowl slowly round about them. They were men accustomed to existence in solitude, and they reverenced no god. At last the oldest of the band made a sign, and bending over the corpses they cut strips from them with their knives, then squatted upon their heels and ate. The rest looked on from a distance; they uttered cries of horror—many, nevertheless, being, at the bottom of their souls, jealous of such courage.

In the middle of the night some of these approached, and, dissembling their eagerness, asked for a small mouthful, merely to try, they said. Bolder ones came up; their number increased; there was soon a crowd. But almost all of them let their hands fall on feeling the cold flesh on the edge of their lips; others, on the contrary, devoured it with delight.

That they might be led away by example, they urged one another on mutually. Such as had at first refused went to see the Garamantians, and returned no more. They cooked the pieces on coals at the point of the sword; they salted them with dust, and contended for the best morsels. When nothing was left of the three corpses, their eyes ranged over the whole plain to find others.

But were they not in possession of Carthaginians—twenty captives taken in the last encounter, whom no one had noticed up to the present? These disappeared; moreover, it was an act of vengeance. Then, as they must live, as the taste for this food had become developed, and as they were dying, they cut the throats of the water-carriers, grooms, and all the serving-men belonging to the Mercenaries. They killed some of them everyday. Some ate much, recovered strength, and were sad no more.

Soon this resource failed. Then the longing was directed to the wounded and sick. Since they could not recover, it was as well to release them from their tortures; and, as soon as a man began to stagger, all exclaimed that he was now lost, and ought to be made use of for the rest. Artifices were employed to accelerate their death; the last remnant of their foul portion was stolen from them; they were trodden on as though by inadvertence; those in the last throes wishing to make believe that they were strong, strove to stretch out their arms, to rise, to laugh. Men who had swooned came to themselves at the touch of a notched blade sawing off a limb—and they still slew, ferociously and needlessly, to sate their fury.

A mist heavy and warm, such as comes in those regions at the end of winter, sank on the fourteenth day upon the army. This change of temperature brought numerous deaths with it, and corruption was developed with frightful rapidity in the warm dampness which was kept in by the sides of the mountain. The drizzle that fell upon the corpses softened them, and soon made the plain one broad tract of rottenness. Whitish vapours floated overhead; they pricked the nostrils, penetrated the skin, and troubled the sight; and the Barbarians thought that through the exhalations of the breath they could see the souls of their companions. They were overwhelmed with immense disgust. They wished for nothing more; they preferred to die.

Two days afterwards the weather became fine again, and hunger seized them once more. It seemed to them that their stomachs were being wrenched from them with tongs. Then they rolled about in convulsions, flung handfuls of dust into their mouths, bit their arms, and burst into frantic laughter.

They were still more tormented by thirst, for they had not a drop of water, the leathern bottles having been completely dried up since the ninth day. To cheat their need they applied their tongues to the metal plates on their waist-belts, their ivory pommels, and the steel of their swords. Some former caravan-leaders tightened their waists with ropes. Others sucked a pebble. They drank urine cooled in their brazen helmets.

And they still expected the army from Tunis! The length of time which it took in coming was, according to their conjectures, an assurance of its early arrival. Besides, Matho, who was a brave fellow, would not desert them. " 'Twill be to-morrow!" they would say to one another; and then to-morrow would pass.

At the beginning they had offered up prayers and vows, and practised all kinds of incantations. Just now their only feeling to their divinities was one of hatred, and they strove to revenge themselves by believing in them no more.

Men of violent disposition perished first; the Africans held out better than the Gauls. Zarxas lay stretched at full length among the Balearians, his hair over his arm, inert. Spendius found a plant with broad leaves filled abundantly with juice, and after declaring that it was poisonous, so as to keep off the rest, he fed himself upon it.

They were too weak to knock down the flying crows with stones. Sometimes when a gypaëtus was perched on a corpse, and had been mangling it for a long time, a man would set himself to crawl towards it with a javelin between his teeth.

He would support himself with one hand, and after taking a good aim, throw his weapon. The white-feathered creature, disturbed by the noise, would desist and look about in a tranquil fashion like a cormorant on a rock, and would then again thrust in its hideous, yellow beak, while the man, in despair, would fall flat on his face in the dust. Some succeeded in discovering chameleons and serpents. But it was the love of life that kept them alive. They directed their souls to this idea exclusively, and clung to existence by an effort of the will that prolonged it.

The most stoical kept close to one another, seated in a circle here and there, among the dead in the middle of the plain; and wrapped in their cloaks they gave themselves up silently to their sadness.

Those who had been born in towns recalled the resounding streets, the taverns, theatres, baths, and the barbers' shops where there are tales to be heard. Others could once more see country districts at sunset, when the yellow corn waves, and the great oxen ascend the hills again with the ploughshares on their necks. Travellers dreamed of cisterns, hunters of their forests, veterans of battles; and in the somnolence that benumbed them their thoughts jostled one another with the precipitancy and clearness of dreams. Hallucinations came suddenly upon them; they sought for a door in the mountain in order to flee, and tried to pass through it. Others thought that they were sailing in a storm and gave orders for the handling of a ship, or else fell back in terror, perceiving Punic battalions in the clouds. There were some who imagined themselves at a feast, and sang.

Many through a strange mania would repeat the same word or continually make the same gesture. Then when they happened to raise their heads and look at one another they were choked with sobs on discovering the horrible ravages made in their faces. Some had ceased to suffer, and to while away the hours told of the perils which they had escaped.

Death was certain and imminent to all. How many times had they not tried to open up a passage! As to implore terms from the conqueror, by what means could they do so? They did not even know where Hamilcar was.

The wind was blowing from the direction of the ravine. It made the sand flow perpetually in cascades over the portcullis; and the cloaks and hair of the Barbarians were being covered with it as though the earth were rising upon them and desirous of burying them. Nothing stirred; the eternal mountain seemed still higher to them every morning.

Sometimes flights of birds darted past beneath the blue sky in the freedom of the air. The men closed their eyes that they might not see them.

At first they felt a buzzing in their ears, their nails grew black, the cold reached to their breasts; they lay upon their sides and expired without a cry.

On the nineteenth day two thousand Asiatics were dead, with fifteen hundred from the Archipelago, eight thousand from Libya, the youngest of the Mercenaries and whole tribes—in all twenty thousand soldiers, or half of the army.

Autaritus, who had only fifty Gauls left, was going to kill himself in order to put an end to this state of things, when he thought he saw a man on the top of the mountain in front of him.

Owing to his elevation this man did not appear taller than a dwarf. However, Autaritus recognised a shield shaped like a trefoil on his left arm. "A Carthaginian!" he exclaimed, and immediately throughout the plain, before the portcullis and beneath the rocks, all rose. The soldier was walking along the edge of the precipice; the Barbarians gazed at him from below.

Spendius picked up the head of an ox; then having formed a diadem with two belts, he fixed it on the horns at the end of a pole in token of pacific intentions. The Carthaginian disappeared. They waited.

At last in the evening a sword-belt suddenly fell from above like a stone loosened from the cliff. It was made of red leather covered with embroidery, with three diamond stars, and stamped in the centre, it bore the mark of the Great Council: a horse beneath a palm-tree. This was Hamilcar's reply, the safe-conduct that he sent them.

They had nothing to fear; any change of fortune brought with it the end of their woes. They were moved with extravagant joy, they embraced one another, they wept. Spendius, Autaritus, and Zarxas, four Italiotes, a Negro and two Spartans offered themselves as envoys. They were immediately accepted. They did not know, however, by what means they should get away.

But a cracking sound in the direction of the rocks; and the most elevated of them, after rocking to and fro, rebounded to the bottom. In fact, if they were immovable on the side of the Barbarians—for it would have been necessary to urge them up an incline plane, and they were, moreover, heaped together owing to the narrowness of the gorge—on the others, on the contrary, it was sufficient to drive against them with violence to make them descend. The Carthaginians pushed them, and at daybreak they projected into the plain like the steps of an immense ruined staircase.

The Barbarians were still unable to climb them. Ladders were held out for their assistance; all rushed upon them. The discharge of a catapult drove the crowd back; only the Ten were taken away.

They walked amid the Clinabarians, leaning their hands on the horses' croups for support.

Now that their first joy was over they began to harbour anxieties. Hamilcar's demands would be cruel. But Spendius reassured them.

"*I* will speak!" And he boasted that he knew excellent things to say for the safety of the army.

Behind all the bushes they met with ambushed sentries, who prostrated themselves before the sword-belt which Spendius had placed over his shoulder.

When they reached the Punic camp the crowd flocked around them, and they thought that they could hear whisperings and laughter. The door of a tent opened.

Hamilcar was at the very back of it seated on a stool beside a table on which there shone a naked sword. He was surrounded by captains, who were standing.

He started back on perceiving these men, and then bent over to examine them.

Their pupils were strangely dilated, and there was a great black circle round their eyes, which extended to the lower parts of their ears; their bluish noses stood out between their hollow cheeks, which were chinked with deep wrinkles; the skin of their bodies was too large for their muscles, and was hidden beneath a slate-coloured dust; their lips were glued to their yellow teeth; they exhaled an infectious odour; they might have been taken for half-opened tombs, for living sepulchres.

In the centre of the tent, on a mat on which the captains were about to sit down, there was a dish of smoking gourds. The Barbarians fastened their eyes upon it with a shivering in all their limbs, and tears came to their eyelids; nevertheless they restrained themselves.

Hamilcar turned away to speak to some one. Then they all flung themselves upon it, flat on the ground. Their faces were soaked in the fat, and the noise of their deglutition was mingled with the sobs of joy which they uttered. Through astonishment, doubtless, rather than pity, they were allowed to finish the mess. Then when they had risen Hamilcar with a sign commanded the man who bore the sword-belt to speak. Spendius was afraid; he stammered.

Hamilcar, while listening to him, kept turning round on his finger a big gold ring, the same which had stamped the seal of Carthage upon the sword-belt. He let it fall to the ground; Spendius immediately picked it up; his servile habits came back to him in the presence of his master. The others quivered with indignation at such baseness.

But the Greek raised his voice and spoke for a long time in a rapid, insidious, and even violent fashion, setting forth the crimes of Hanno, whom he knew to be Barca's enemy, and striving to move Hamilcar's pity by the details of their miseries and the recollection of their devotion; in the end he became forgetful of himself, being carried away by the warmth of his temper.

Hamilcar replied that he accepted their excuses. Peace, then, was about to be concluded, and now it would be a definitive one! But he required that ten Mercenaries, chosen by himself, should be delivered up to him without weapons or tunics.

They had not expected such clemency; Spendius exclaimed: "Ah! twenty if you wish, master!"

"No! ten will suffice," replied Hamilcar quietly.

They were sent out of the tent to deliberate. As soon as they were alone, Autaritus protested against the sacrifice of their companions, and Zarxas said to Spendius:

"Why did you not kill him? his sword was there beside you!"

"Him!" said Spendius. "Him! him!" he repeated several times, as though the thing had been impossible, and Hamilcar were an immortal.

They were so overwhelmed with weariness that they stretched themselves on their backs on the ground, not knowing at what resolution to arrive.

Spendius urged them to yield. At last they consented, and went in again.

Then the Suffet put his hand into the hands of the ten Barbarians in turn, and pressed their thumbs; then he rubbed it on his garment, for their viscous skin gave a rude, soft impression to the touch, a greasy tingling which induced horripilation. Afterwards he said to them:

"You are really all the chiefs of the Barbarians, and you have sworn for them?"

"Yes!" they replied.

"Without constraint, from the bottom of your souls, with the intention of fulfilling your promises?"

They assured him that they were rest in order to fulfil them.

"Well!" rejoined the Suffet, "in accordance with the convention concluded between myself, Barca, and the ambassadors of the Mercenaries, it is you whom I choose and shall keep!"

Spendius fell swooning upon the mat. The Barbarians, as though abandoning him, pressed close together; and there was not a word, not a complaint.

Their companions, who were waiting for them, not seeing them return, believed themselves betrayed. The envoys had no doubt given themselves up to the Suffet.

They waited for two days longer; then on the morning of the third, their resolution was taken. With ropes, picks, and arrows, arranged like rungs between strips of canvas, they succeeded in scaling the rocks; and leaving the weakest, about three thousand in number, behind them, they began their march to rejoin the army at Tunis.

Above the gorge there stretched a meadow thinly sown with shrubs; the Barbarians devoured the buds. Afterwards they found a field of beans; and everything disappeared as though a cloud of grasshoppers had passed that way. Three hours later they reached a second plateau bordered by a belt of green hills.

Among the undulations of these hillocks, silvery sheaves shone at intervals from one another; the Barbarians, who were dazzled by the sun, could perceive confusedly below great black masses supporting them; these rose, as though they were expanding. They were lances in towers on elephants terribly armed.

Besides the spears on their breasts, the bodkin tusks, the brass plates which covered their sides, and the daggers fastened to their knee-caps, they had at the extremity of their trunks a leathern bracelet, in which the handle of a broad cutlass was inserted; they had set out simultaneously from the back part of the plain, and were advancing on both sides in parallel lines.

The Barbarians were frozen with a nameless terror. They did not even try to flee. They already found themselves surrounded.

The elephants entered into this mass of men; and the spurs on their breasts divided it, the lances on their tusks upturned it like ploughshares; they cut, hewed, and hacked with the scythes on their trunks; the towers, which were full of phalaricas, looked like volcanoes on the march; nothing could be distinguished but a large heap, whereon human flesh, pieces of brass and blood made white spots, grey sheets and red fuses. The horrible animals dug out black furrows as they passed through the midst of it all.

The fiercest was driven by a Numidian who was crowned with a diadem of plumes. He hurled javelins with frightful quickness, giving at intervals a long shrill whistle. The great beasts, docile as dogs, kept an eye on him during the carnage.

The circle of them narrowed by degrees; the weakened Barbarians offered no resistance; the elephants were soon in the centre of the plain. They lacked space; they thronged half-rearing together, and their tusks clashed against one another. Suddenly Narr' Havas quieted them, and wheeling round they trotted back to the hills.

Two syntagmata, however, had taken refuge on the right in a bend of the ground, had thrown away their arms, and were all kneeling with their faces towards the Punic tents imploring mercy with uplifted arms.

Their legs and hands were tied; then when they were stretched on the ground beside one another the elephants were brought back.

Their breasts cracked like boxes being forced; two were crushed at every step; the big feet sank into the bodies with a motion of the haunches which made the elephants appear lame. They went on to the very end.

The level surface of the plain again became motionless. Night fell. Hamilcar was delighting himself with the spectacle of his vengeance, but suddenly he started.

He saw, and all saw, some more Barbarians six hundred paces to the left on the summit of a peak! In fact four hundred of the stoutest Mercenaries, Etruscans, Libyans, and Spartans had gained the heights at the beginning, and had remained there in uncertainty until now. After the massacre of their companions they resolved to make their way through the Carthaginians; they were already descending in serried columns, in a marvellous and formidable fashion.

A herald was immediately dispatched to them. The Suffet needed soldiers; he received them unconditionally, so greatly did he admire their bravery. They could even, said the man of Carthage, come a little nearer, to a place, which he pointed out to them, where they would find provisions.

The Barbarians ran thither and spent the night in eating. Then the Carthaginians broke into clamours against the Suffet's partiality for the Mercenaries.

Did he yield to these outbursts of insatiable hatred or was it a refinement of treachery? The next day he came himself, without a sword and bare-headed, with an escort of Clinabarians, and announced to them that having too many to feed he did not intend to keep them. Nevertheless, as he wanted men and he knew of no means of selecting the good ones, they were to fight together to the death; he would then admit the conquerors into his own body-guard. This death was quite as good as another; and then moving his soldiers aside (for the Punic standards hid the horizon from the Mercenaries) he showed them the one hundred and ninety-two elephants under Narr' Havas, forming a single straight line, their trunks brandishing broad steel blades like giant arms holding axes above their heads.

The Barbarians looked at one another silently. It was not death that made them turn pale, but the horrible compulsion to which they found themselves reduced.

The community of their lives had brought about profound friendship among these men. The camp, with most, took the place of their country; living without a family they transferred the needful tenderness to a companion, and they would fall asleep in the starlight side by side under the same cloak. And then in their perpetual wanderings through all sorts of countries, murders, and adventures, they had contracted affections, one for the other, in which the stronger protected the younger in the midst of battles, helped him to cross precipices, sponged the sweat of fevers from his brow, and stole food for him, and the weaker, a child perhaps, who had been picked up on the roadside, and had then become a Mercenary, repaid this devotion by a thousand kindnesses.

They exchanged their necklaces and earrings, presents which they had made to one another in former days, after great peril, or in hours of intoxication. All asked to die, and none would strike. A young fellow might be seen here and there, saying to another whose beard was grey: "No! no! you are more robust! you will avenge us, kill me!" and the man would reply: "I have fewer years to live! Strike to the heart, and think no more about it!" Brothers gazed on one another with clasped hands, and friend bade friend eternal farewells, standing and weeping upon his shoulder.

They drew off their cuirasses that the sword-points might be thrust in the more quickly. Then there appeared the marks of the great blows which they had received for Carthage, and which looked like inscriptions on columns.

They placed themselves in four equal ranks, after the fashion of gladiators, and began with timid engagements. Some had even bandaged their eyes, and their swords waved gently through the air like blind men's sticks. The Carthaginians hooted, and shouted to them that they were cowards. The Barbarians became animated, and soon the combat was general, headlong, and terrible.

Sometimes two men all covered with blood would stop, fall into each other's arms, and die with mutual kisses. None drew back. They rushed upon the extended blades. Their delirium was so frenzied that the Carthaginians in the distance were afraid.

At last they stopped. Their breasts made a great hoarse noise, and their eyeballs could be seen through their long hair, which hung down as though it had come out of a purple bath. Several were turning round rapidly, like panthers wounded in the forehead. Others stood motionless looking at a corpse at their feet; then they would suddenly tear their faces with their nails, take their swords in both hands, and plunge them into their own bodies.

There were still sixty left. They asked for drink. They were told by shouts to throw away their swords, and when they had done so water was brought to them.

While they were drinking, with their faces buried in the vases, sixty Carthaginians leaped upon them and killed them with stilettos in the back.

Hamilcar had done this to gratify the instincts of his army, and, by means of this treachery, to attach it to his own person.

The war, then, was ended; at least he believed that it was; Matho would not resist; in his impatience the Suffet commanded an immediate departure.

His scouts came to tell him that a convoy had been descried, departing towards the Lead Mountain. Hamilcar did not trouble himself about it. The Mercenaries once annihilated, the Nomads would give him no further trouble. The important matter was to take Tunis. He advanced by forced marches upon it.

He had sent Narr' Havas to Carthage with the news of his victory; and the King of the Numidians, proud of his success, visited Salammbô.

She received him in her gardens under a large sycamore tree, amid pillows of yellow leather, and with Taanach beside her. Her face was covered with a white scarf, which, passing over her mouth and forehead, allowed only her eyes to be seen; but her lips shone in the transparency of the tissue like the gems on her fingers, for Salammbô had both her hands wrapped up, and did not make a gesture during the whole conversation.

Narr' Havas announced the defeat of the Barbarians to her. She thanked him with a blessing for the services which he had rendered to her father. Then he began to tell about the whole campaign.

The doves on the palm trees around them cooed softly, and other birds fluttered amid the grass: ring-necked glareolas, Tartessus quails and Punic guineafowl. The garden, long uncultivated, had multiplied its verdure; coloquintidas mounted into the branches of cassias, the asclepias was scattered over fields of roses, all kinds of vegetation formed entwinings and bowers; and here and there, as in the woods, sun-rays, descending obliquely, marked the shadow of a leaf upon the ground. Domestic animals, grown wild again, fled at the slightest noise. Sometimes a gazelle might be seen trailing scattered peacocks' feathers after its little black hoofs. The clamours of the distant town were lost in the murmuring of the waves. The sky was quite blue, and not a sail was visible on the sea.

Narr' Havas had ceased speaking; Salammbô was looking at him without replying. He wore a linen robe with flowers painted on it, and with gold fringes at the hem; two silver arrows fastened his plaited hair at the tips of his ears; his right hand rested on a pike-staff adorned with circles of electrum and tufts of hair.

As she watched him a crowd of dim thoughts absorbed her. This young man, with his gentle voice and feminine figure, captivated her eyes by the grace of his person, and seemed to her like an elder sister sent by the Baals to protect her. The recollection of Matho came upon her, nor did she resist the desire to learn what had become of him.

Narr' Havas replied that the Carthaginians were advancing towards Tunis to take it. In proportion as he set forth their chances of success and Matho's weakness, she seemed to rejoice in extraordinary hope. Her lips trembled, her breast panted. When he finally promised to kill him himself, she exclaimed: "Yes! kill him! It must be so!"

The Numidian replied that he desired this death ardently, since he would be her husband when the war was over.

Salammbô started, and bent her head.

But Narr' Havas, pursuing the subject, compared his longings to flowers languishing for rain, or to lost travellers waiting for the day. He told her, further, that she was more beautiful than the moon, better than the wind of morning or than the face of a guest. He would bring for her from the country of the Blacks things such as there were none in Carthage, and the apartments in their house should be sanded with gold dust.

Evening fell, and odours of balsam were exhaled. For a long time they looked at each other in silence, and Salammbô's eyes, in the depths of her long draperies, resembled two stars in the rift of a cloud. Before the sun set he withdrew.

The Ancients felt themselves relieved of a great anxiety, when he left Carthage. The people had received him with even more enthusiastic acclamations than on the first occasion. If Hamilcar and the King of the Numidians triumphed alone over the Mercenaries it would be impossible to resist them. To weaken Barca they therefore resolved to make the aged Hanno, him whom they loved, a sharer in the deliverance of Carthage.

He proceeded immediately towards the western provinces, to take his vengeance in the very places which had witnessed his shame. But the inhabitants and the Barbarians were dead, hidden, or fled. Then his anger was vented upon the country. He burnt the ruins of the ruins, he did not leave a single tree nor a blade of grass; the children and the infirm, that were met with, were tortured; he gave the women to his soldiers to be violated before they were slaughtered.

Often, on the crests of the hills, black tents were struck as though overturned by the wind, and broad, brilliantly bordered discs, which were recognised as being chariot-wheels, revolved with a plaintive sound as they gradually disappeared in the valleys. The tribes, which had abandoned the siege of Carthage, were wandering in this way through the provinces, waiting for an opportunity, or for some victory to be gained by the Mercenaries, in order to return. But, whether from terror or famine, they all took the roads to their native lands, and disappeared.

Hamilcar was not jealous of Hanno's successes. Nevertheless he was in a hurry to end matters; he commanded him to fall back upon Tunis; and Hanno, who loved his country, was under the walls of the town on the appointed day.

For its protection it had its aboriginal population, twelve thousand Mercenaries, and, in addition, all the Eaters of Uncleanness, for like Matho they were riveted to the horizon of Carthage, and plebs and schalischim gazed at its lofty walls from afar, looking back in thought to boundless enjoyments. With this harmony of hatred, resistance was briskly organised. Leathern bottles were taken to make helmets; all the palm-trees in the gardens were cut down for lances; cisterns were dug; while for provisions they caught on the shores of the lake big white fish, fed on corpses and filth. Their ramparts, kept in ruins now by the jealousy of Carthage, were so weak that they could be thrown down with a push of the shoulder. Matho stopped up the holes in them with the stones of the houses. It was the last struggle; he hoped for nothing, and yet he told himself that fortune was fickle.

As the Carthaginians approached they noticed a man on the rampart who towered over the battlements from his belt upwards. The arrows that flew about him seemed to frighten him no more than a swarm of swallows. Extraordinary to say, none of them touched him.

Hamilcar pitched his camp on the south side; Narr' Havas, to his right, occupied the plain of Rhades, and Hanno the shore of the lake; and the three generals were to maintain their respective positions, so as all to attack the walls simultaneously.

But Hamilcar wished first to show the Mercenaries that he would punish them like slaves. He had the ten ambassadors crucified beside one another on a hillock in front of the town.

At the sight of this the besieged forsook the rampart.

Matho had said to himself that if he could pass between the walls and Narr' Havas's tents with such rapidity that the Numidians had not time to come out, he could fall upon the rear of the Carthaginian infantry, who would be caught between his division and those inside. He dashed out with his veterans.

Narr' Havas perceived him; he crossed the shore of the lake, and came to warn Hanno to dispatch men to Hamilcar's assistance. Did he believe Barca too weak to resist the Mercenaries? Was it a piece of treachery or folly? No one could ever learn.

Hanno, desiring to humiliate his rival, did not hesitate. He shouted orders to sound the trumpets, and his whole army rushed upon the Barbarians. The latter returned, and ran straight against the Carthaginians; they knocked them down, crushed them under their feet, and, driving them back in this way, reached the tent of Hanno, who was then surrounded by thirty Carthaginians, the most illustrious of the Ancients.

He appeared stupefied by their audacity; he called for his captains. Every one thrust his list under his throat, vociferating abuse. The crowd pressed on; and those who had their hands on him could scarce retain their hold. However, he tried to whisper to them: "I will give you whatever you want! I am rich! Save me!" They dragged him along; heavy as he was his feet did not touch the ground. The Ancients had been carried off. His terror increased. "You have beaten me! I am your captive! I will ransom myself! Listen to me, my friends!" and borne along by all those shoulders which were pressed against his sides, he repeated: "What are you going to do? What do you want? You can see that I am not obstinate! I have always been good-natured!"

A gigantic cross stood at the gate. The Barbarians howled: "Here! here!" But he raised his voice still higher; and in the names of their gods he called upon them to lead him to the schalischim, because he wished to confide to him something on which their safety depended.

They paused, some asserting that it was right to summon Matho. He was sent for.

Hanno fell upon the grass; and he saw around him other crosses also, as though the torture by which he was about to perish had been multiplied beforehand; he made efforts to convince himself that he was mistaken, that there was only one, and even to believe that there were none at all. At last he was lifted up.

"Speak!" said Matho.

He offered to give up Hamilcar; then they would enter Carthage and both be kings.

Matho withdrew, signing to the others to make haste. It was a stratagem, he thought, to gain time.

The Barbarian was mistaken; Hanno was in an extremity when consideration is had to nothing, and, moreover, he so execrated Hamilcar that he would have sacrificed him with all his soldiers on the slightest hope of safety.

The Ancients were languishing on the ground at the foot of the crosses; ropes had already been passed beneath their armpits. Then the old Suffet, understanding that he must die, wept.

They tore off the clothes that were still left on him—and the horror of his person appeared. Ulcers covered the nameless mass; the fat on his legs hid the nails on his feet; from his fingers there hung what looked like greenish strips; and the tears streaming through the tubercles on his cheeks gave to his face an expression of frightful sadness, for they seemed to take up more room than on another human face. His royal fillet, which was half unfastened, trailed with his white hair in the dust.

They thought that they had no ropes strong enough to haul him up to the top of the cross, and they nailed him upon it, after the Punic fashion, before it was erected. But his pride awoke in his pain. He began to overwhelm them with abuse. He foamed and twisted like a marine monster being slaughtered on the shore, and predicted that they would all end more horribly still, and that he would be avenged.

He was. On the other side of the town, whence there now escaped jets of flame with columns of smoke, the ambassadors from the Mercenaries were in their last throes.

Some who had swooned at first had just revived in the freshness of the wind; but their chins still rested upon their breasts, and their bodies had fallen somewhat, in spite of the nails in their arms, which were fastened higher than their heads; from their heels and hands blood fell in big, slow drops, as ripe fruit falls from the branches of a tree—and Carthage, gulf, mountains, and plains all appeared to them to be revolving like an immense wheel; sometimes a cloud of dust, rising from the ground, enveloped them in its eddies; they burned with horrible thirst, their tongues curled in their mouths, and they felt an icy sweat flowing over them with their departing souls.

Nevertheless they had glimpses, at an infinite depth, of streets, marching soldiers, and the swinging of swords; and the tumult of battle reached them dimly like the noise of the sea to shipwrecked men dying on the masts of a ship. The Italiotes, who were sturdier than the rest, were still shrieking. The Lacedæmonians were silent, with eyelids closed; Zarxas, once so vigorous, was bending like a broken reed; the Ethiopian beside him had his head thrown back over the arms of the cross; Autaritus was motionless, rolling his eyes; his great head of hair, caught in a cleft in the wood, fell straight upon his forehead, and his death-rattle seemed rather to be a roar of anger. As to Spendius, a strange courage had come to him; he despised life now in the certainty which he possessed of an almost immediate and an eternal emancipation, and he awaited death with impassibility.

Amid their swooning, they sometimes started at the brushing of feathers passing across their lips. Large wings swung shadows around them, croakings sounded in the air; and as Spendius's cross was the highest, it was upon his that the first vulture alighted. Then he turned his face towards Autaritus, and said slowly to him with an unaccountable smile:

"Do you remember the lions on the road to Sicca?"

"They were our brothers!" replied the Gaul, as he expired.

The Suffet, meanwhile, had bored through the walls and reached the citadel. The smoke suddenly disappeared before a gust of wind, discovering the horizon as far as the walls of Carthage; he even thought that he could distinguish people watching on the platform of Eschmoun; then, bringing back his eyes, he perceived thirty crosses of extravagant size on the shore of the Lake, to the left.

In fact, to render them still more frightful, they had been constructed with tent-poles fastened end to end, and the thirty corpses of the Ancients appeared high up in the sky. They had what looked like white butterflies on their breasts; these were the feathers of the arrows which had been shot at them from below.

A broad gold ribbon shone on the summit of the highest; it hung down to the shoulder, there being no arm on that side, and Hamilcar had some difficulty in recognising Hanno. His spongy bones had given way under the iron pins, portions of his limbs had come off, and nothing was left on the cross but shapeless remains, like the fragments of animals that are hung up on huntsmen's doors.

The Suffet could not have known anything about it; the town in front of him masked everything that was beyond and behind; and the captains who had been successively sent to the two generals had not reappeared. Then fugitives arrived with the tale of the rout, and the Punic army halted. This catastrophe, falling upon them as it did in the midst of their victory, stupefied them. Hamilcar's orders were no longer listened to.

Matho took advantage of this to continue his ravages among the Numidians.

Hanno's camp having been overthrown, he had returned against them. The elephants came out; but the Mercenaries advanced through the plain shaking about flaming firebrands, which they had plucked from the walls, and the great beasts, in fright, ran headlong into the gulf, where they killed one another in their struggles, or were drowned beneath the weight of their cuirasses. Narr' Havas had already launched his cavalry; all threw themselves face downwards upon the ground; then, when the horses were within three paces of them, they sprang beneath their bellies, ripped them open with dagger-strokes, and half the Numidians had perished when Barca came up.

The exhausted Mercenaries could not withstand his troops. They retired in good order to the mountain of the Hot Springs. The Suffet was prudent enough not to pursue them. He directed his course to the mouths of the Macaras.

Tunis was his; but it was now nothing but a heap of smoking rubbish. The ruins fell through the breaches in the walls to the centre of the plain; quite in the background, between the shores of the gulf, the corpses of the elephants drifting before the wind conflicted, like an archipelago of black rocks floating on the water.

Narr' Havas had drained his forests of these animals, taking young and old, male and female, to keep up the war, and the military force of his kingdom could not repair the loss. The people who had seen them perishing at a distance were grieved at it; men lamented in the streets, calling them by their names like deceased friends: "Ah! the Invincible! the Victory! the Thunderer! the Swallow!" On the first day, too, there was no talk except of the dead citizens. But on the morrow the tents of the Mercenaries were seen on the mountain of the Hot Springs. Then so deep was the despair that many people, especially women, flung themselves headlong from the top of the Acropolis.

Hamilcar's designs were not known. He lived alone in his tent with none near him but a young boy, and no one ever ate with them, not even excepting Narr' Havas. Nevertheless he showed great deference to the latter after Hanno's defeat; but the king of the Numidians had too great an interest in becoming his son not to distrust him.

This inertness veiled skilful manoeuvres. Hamilcar seduced the heads of the villages by all sorts of artifices; and the Mercenaries were hunted, repulsed, and enclosed like wild beasts. As soon as they entered a wood, the trees caught fire around them; when they drank of a spring it was poisoned; the caves in which they hid in order to sleep were walled up. Their old accomplices, the populations who had hitherto defended them, now pursued them; and they continually recognised Carthaginian armour in these bands.

Many had their faces consumed with red tetters; this, they thought, had come to them through touching Hanno. Others imagined that it was because they had eaten Salammbô's fishes, and far from repenting of it, they dreamed of even more abominable sacrileges, so that the abasement of the Punic Gods might be still greater. They would fain have exterminated them.

In this way they lingered for three months along the eastern coast, and then behind the mountain of Selloum, and as far as the first sands of the desert. They sought for a place of refuge, no matter where. Utica and Hippo-Zarytus alone had not betrayed them; but Hamilcar was encompassing these two towns. Then they went northwards at haphazard without even knowing the various routes. Their many miseries had confused their understandings.

The only feeling left them was one of exasperation, which went on developing; and one day they found themselves again in the gorges of Cobus and once more before Carthage!

Then the actions multiplied. Fortune remained equal; but both sides were so wearied that they would willingly have exchanged these skirmishes for a great battle, provided that it were really the last.

Matho was inclined to carry this proposal himself to the Suffet. One of his Libyans devoted himself for the purpose. All were convinced as they saw him depart that he would not return.

He returned the same evening.

Hamilcar accepted their challenge. The encounter should take place the following day at sunrise, in the plain of Rhades.

The Mercenaries wished to know whether he had said anything more, and the Libyan added:

"As I remained in his presence, he asked me what I was waiting for. 'To be killed!' I replied. Then he rejoined: 'No! begone! that will be to-morrow with the rest.' "

This generosity astonished the Barbarians; some were terrified by it, and Matho regretted that the emissary had not been killed.

He had still remaining three thousand Africans, twelve hundred Greeks, fifteen hundred Campanians, two hundred Iberians, four hundred Etruscans, five hundred Samnites, forty Gauls, and a troop of Naffurs, nomad bandits met with in the date region—in all seven thousand two hundred and nineteen soldiers, but not one complete syntagma. They had stopped up the holes in their cuirasses with the shoulder-blades of quadrupeds, and replaced their brass cothurni with worn sandals. Their garments were weighted with copper or steel plates; their coats of mail hung in tatters about them, and scars appeared like purple threads through the hair on their arms and faces.

The wraiths of their dead companions came back to their souls and increased their energy; they felt, in a confused way, that they were the ministers of a god diffused in the hearts of the oppressed, and were the pontiffs, so to speak, of universal vengeance! Then they were enraged with grief at what was extravagant injustice, and above all by the sight of Carthage on the horizon. They swore an oath to fight for one another until death.

The beasts of burden were killed, and as much as possible was eaten so as to gain strength; afterwards they slept. Some prayed, turning towards different constellations.

The Carthaginians arrived first in the plain. They rubbed the edges of their shields with oil to make the arrows glide off them easily; the foot-soldiers who wore long hair took the precaution of cutting it on the forehead; and Hamilcar ordered all bowls to be inverted from the fifth hour, knowing that it is disadvantageous to fight with the stomach too full. His army amounted to fourteen thousand men, or about double the number of the Barbarians. Nevertheless, he had never felt such anxiety; if he succumbed it would mean the annihilation of the Republic, and he would perish on the cross; if, on the contrary, he triumphed, he would reach Italy by way of the Pyrenees, the Gauls, and the Alps, and the empire of the Barcas would become eternal. Twenty times during the night he rose to inspect everything himself, down to the most trifling details. As to the Carthaginians, they were exasperated by their lengthened terror. Narr' Havas suspected the fidelity of his Numidians. Moreover, the Barbarians might vanquish them. A strange weakness had come upon him; every moment he drank large cups of water.

But a man whom he did not know opened his tent and laid on the ground a crown of rock-salt, adorned with hieratic designs formed with sulphur, and lozenges of mother-of-pearl; a marriage crown was sometimes sent to a betrothed husband; it was a proof of love, a sort of invitation.

Nevertheless Hamilcar's daughter had no tenderness for Narr' Havas.

The recollection of Matho disturbed her in an intolerable manner; it seemed to her that the death of this man would unburden her thoughts, just as people to cure themselves of the bite of a viper crush it upon the wound. The king of the Numidians was depending upon her; he awaited the wedding with impatience, and, as it was to follow the victory, Salammbô made him this present to stimulate his courage. Then his distress vanished, and he thought only of the happiness of possessing so beautiful a woman.

The same vision had assailed Matho; but he cast it from him immediately, and his love, which he thus thrust back, was poured out upon his companions in arms. He cherished them like portions of his own person, of his hatred—and he felt his spirit higher, and his arms stronger; everything that he was to accomplish appeared clearly before him. If sighs sometimes escaped him, it was because he was thinking of Spendius.

He drew up the Barbarians in six equal ranks. He posted the Etruscans in the centre, all being fastened to a bronze chain; the archers were behind, and on the wings he distributed the Naffurs, who were mounted on short-haired camels, covered with ostrich feathers.

The Suffet arranged the Carthaginians in similar order. He placed the Clinabarians outside the infantry next to the velites, and the Numidians beyond; when day appeared, both sides were thus in line face to face. All gazed at eachother from a distance, with round fierce eyes. There was at first some hesitation; at last both armies moved.

The Barbarians advanced slowly so as not to become out of breath, beating the ground with their feet; the centre of the Punic army formed a convex curve. Then came the burst of a terrible shock, like the crash of two fleets in collision. The first rank of the Barbarians had quickly opened up, and the marksmen, hidden behind the others, discharged their bullets, arrows, and javelins. The curve of the Carthaginians, however, flattened by degrees, became quite straight, and then bent inwards; upon this, the two sections of the velites drew together in parallel lines, like the legs of a compass that is being closed. The Barbarians, who were attacking the phalanx with fury, entered the gap; they were being lost; Matho checked them—and while the Carthaginian wings continued to advance, he drew out the three inner ranks of his line; they soon covered his flanks, and his army appeared in triple array.

But the Barbarians placed at the extremities were the weakest, especially those on the left, who had exhausted their quivers, and the troop of velites, which had at last come up against them, was cutting them up greatly.

Matho made them fall back. His right comprised Campanians, who were armed with axes; he hurled them against the Carthaginian left; the centre attacked the enemy, and those at the other extremity, who were out of peril, kept the velites at a distance.

Then Hamilcar divided his horsemen into squadrons, placed hoplites between them, and sent them against the Mercenaries.

These cone-shaped masses presented a front of horses, and their broader sides were filled and bristling with lances. The Barbarians found it impossible to resist; the Greek foot-soldiers alone had brazen armour, all the rest had cutlasses on the end of poles, scythes taken from the farms, or swords manufactured out of the fellies of wheels; the soft blades were twisted by a blow, and while they were engaged in straightening them under their heels, the Carthaginians massacred them right and left at their ease.

But the Etruscans, riveted to their chain, did not stir; those who were dead, being prevented from falling, formed an obstruction with their corpses; and the great bronze line widened and contracted in turn, as supple as a serpent, and as impregnable as a wall. The Barbarians would come to reform behind it, pant for a minute, and then set off again with the fragments of their weapons in their hands.

Many already had none left, and they leaped upon the Carthaginians, biting their faces like dogs. The Gauls in their pride stripped themselves of the sagum; they showed their great white bodies from a distance, and they enlarged their wounds to terrify the enemy. The voice of the crier announcing the orders could no longer be heard in the midst of the Punic syntagmata; their signals were repeated by the standards, which were raised above the dust, and every one was swept away in the swaying of the great mass that surrounded him.

Hamilcar commanded the Numidians to advance. But the Naffurs rushed to meet them.

Clad in vast black robes, with a tuft of hair on the top of the skull, and a shield of rhinoceros leather, they wielded a steel which had no handle, and which they held by a rope; and their camels, which bristled all over with feathers, uttered long, hoarse cluckings. Each blade fell on the precise spot, then rose again with a smart stroke carrying off a limb with it. The fierce beasts galloped through the syntagmata. Some, whose legs were broken, went hopping along like wounded ostriches.

The Punic infantry returned in a body upon the Barbarians, and cut them off. Their maniples wheeled about at intervals from one another. The more brilliant Carthaginian weapons encircled them like golden crowns; there was a swarming movement in the centre, and the sun, striking down upon the points of the swords, made them glitter with white flickering gleams. However, files of Clinabarians lay stretched upon the plain; some Mercenaries snatched away their armour, clothed themselves in it, and then returned to the fray. The deluded Carthaginians were several times entangled in their midst. They would stand stupidly motionless, or else would back, surge again, and triumphant shouts rising in the distance seemed to drive them along like derelicts in a storm. Hamilcar was growing desperate; all was about to perish beneath the genius of Matho and the invincible courage of the Mercenaries.

But a great noise of tabourines burst forth on the horizon. It was a crowd of old men, sick persons, children of fifteen years of age, and even women, who, being unable to withstand their distress any longer, had set out from Carthage, and, for the purpose of placing themselves under the protection of something formidable, had taken from Hamilcar's palace the only elephant that the Republic now possessed—that one, namely, whose trunk had been cut off.

Then it seemed to the Carthaginians that their country, forsaking its walls, was coming to command them to die for her. They were seized with increased fury, and the Numidians carried away all the rest.

The Barbarians had set themselves with their backs to a hillock in the centre of the plain. They had no chance of conquering, or even of surviving; but they were the best, the most intrepid, and the strongest.

The people from Carthage began to throw spits, larding-pins and hammers, over the heads of the Numidians; those whom consuls had feared died beneath sticks hurled by women; the Punic populace was exterminating the Mercenaries.

The latter had taken refuge on the top of the hill. Their circle closed up after every fresh breach; twice it descended to be immediately repulsed with a shock; and the Carthaginians stretched forth their arms pell-mell, thrusting their pikes between the legs of their companions, and raking at random before them. They slipped in the blood; the steep slope of the ground made the corpses roll to the bottom. The elephant, which was trying to climb the hillock, was up to its belly; it seemed to be sprawling over them with delight; and its shortened trunk, which was broad at the extremity, rose from time to time like an enormous leech.

Then all paused. The Carthaginians ground their teeth as they gazed at the hill, where the Barbarians were standing.

At last they dashed at them abruptly, and the fight began again. The Mercenaries would often let them approach, shouting to them that they wished to surrender; then, with frightful sneers, they would kill themselves at a blow, and as the dead fell, the rest would mount upon them to defend themselves. It was a kind of pyramid, which grew larger by degrees.

Soon there were only fifty, then only twenty, only three, and lastly only two— a Samnite armed with an axe, and Matho who still had his sword.

The Samnite with bent hams swept his axe alternately to right and left, at the same time warning Matho of the blows that were being aimed at him. "Master, this way! that way! stoop down!"

Matho had lost his shoulder-pieces, his helmet, his cuirass; he was completely naked, and more livid than the dead, with his hair quite erect, and two patches of foam at the corners of his lips—and his sword whirled so rapidly that it formed an aureola around him. A stone broke it near the guard; the Samnite was killed and the flood of Carthaginians closed in, they touched Matho. Then he raised both his empty hands towards heaven, closed his eyes, and, opening out his arms like a man throwing himself from the summit of a promontory into the sea, hurled himself among the pikes.

They moved away before him. Several times he ran against the Carthaginians. But they always drew back and turned their weapons aside.

His foot struck against a sword. Matho tried to seize it. He felt himself tied by the wrists and knees, and fell.

Narr' Havas had been following him for some time, step by step, with one of the large nets used for capturing wild beasts, and, taking advantage of the moment when he stooped down, had involved him in it.

Then he was fastened on the elephants with his four limbs forming a cross; and all those who were not wounded escorted him, and rushed with great tumult towards Carthage.

The news of the victory had arrived in some inexplicable way at the third hour of the night; the clepsydra of Khamon had just completed the fifth as they reached Malqua; then Matho opened his eyes. There were so many lights in the houses that the town appeared to be all in flames.

An immense clamour reached him dimly; and lying on his back he looked at the stars.

Then a door closed and he was wrapped in darkness.

On the morrow, at the same hour, the last of the men left in the Pass of the Hatchet expired.

On the day that their companions had set out, some Zuaeces who were returning had tumbled the rocks down, and had fed them for some time.

The Barbarians constantly expected to see Matho appear—and from discouragement, from languor, and from the obstinacy of sick men who object to change their situation, they would not leave the mountain; at last the provisions were exhausted and the Zuaeces went away. It was known that they numbered scarcely more than thirteen hundred men, and there was no need to employ soldiers to put an end to them.

Wild beasts, especially lions, had multiplied during the three years that the war had lasted. Narr' Havas had held a great battue, and—after tying goats at intervals—had run upon them and so driven them towards the Pass of the Hatchet;—and they were now all living in it when a man arrived who had been sent by the Ancients to find out what there was left of the Barbarians.

Lions and corpses were lying over the tract of the plain, and the dead were mingled with clothes and armour. Nearly all had the face or an arm wanting; some appeared to be still intact; others were completely dried up, and their helmets were filled with powdery skulls; feet which had lost their flesh stood out straight from the knemides; skeletons still wore their cloaks; and bones, cleaned by the sun, made gleaming spots in the midst of the sand.

The lions were resting with their breasts against the ground and both paws stretched out, winking their eyelids in the bright daylight, which was heightened by the reflection from the white rocks. Others were seated on their hind-quarters and staring before them, or else were sleeping, rolled into a ball and half hidden by their great manes; they all looked well fed, tired, and dull. They were as motionless as the mountain and the dead. Night was falling; the sky was striped with broad red bands in the west.

In one of the heaps, which in an irregular fashion embossed the plain, something rose up vaguer than a spectre. Then one of the lions set himself in motion, his monstrous form cutting a black shadow on the background of the purple sky, and when he was quite close to the man, he knocked him down with a single blow of his paw.

Then, stretching himself flat upon him, he slowly drew out the entrails with the edge of his teeth.

Afterwards he opened his huge jaws, and for some minutes uttered a lengthened roar which was repeated by the echoes in the mountain, and was finally lost in the solitude.

Suddenly some small gravel rolled down from above. The rustling of rapid steps was heard, and in the direction of the portcullis and of the gorge there appeared pointed muzzles and straight ears, with gleaming, tawny eyes. These were the jackals coming to eat what was left.

The Carthaginian, who was leaning over the top of the precipice to look, went back again.

Chapter XV

MATHO

THERE WERE REJOICINGS AT CARTHAGE—REJOICINGS DEEP, UNIVERSAL, EX-travagant, frantic; the holes of the ruins had been stopped up, the statues of the gods had been repainted, the streets were strewn with myrtle branches, incense smoked at the corners of the crossways, and the throng on the terraces looked, in their variegated garments, like heaps of flowers blooming in the air.

The shouts of the water-carriers watering the pavement rose above the continual screaming of voices; slaves belonging to Hamilcar offered in his name roasted barley and pieces of raw meat; people accosted one another, and embraced one another with tears; the Tyrian towns were taken, the nomads dispersed, and all the Barbarians annihilated. The Acropolis was hidden beneath coloured velaria; the beaks of the triremes, drawn up in line outside the mole, shone like a dyke of diamonds; everywhere there was a sense of the restoration of order, the beginning of a new existence, and the diffusion of vast happiness: it was the day of Salammbô's marriage with the King of the Numidians.

On the terrace of the temple of Khamon there were three long tables laden with gigantic plate, at which the priests, Ancients, and the rich were to sit, and there was a fourth and higher one for Hamilcar, Narr' Havas, and Salammbô; for as she had saved her country by the restoration of the zaïmph, the people turned her wedding into a national rejoicing, and were waiting in the square below till she should appear.

But their impatience was excited by another and more acrid longing: Matho's death has been promised for the ceremony.

It had been proposed at first to flay him alive, to pour lead into his entrails, to kill him with hunger; he should be tied to a tree, and an ape behind him should strike him on the head with a stone; he had offended Tanith, and the cynocephaluses of Tanith should avenge her. Others were of opinion that he should be led about on a dromedary after linen wicks, dipped in oil, had been inserted in his body in several places—and they took pleasure in the thought of the large animal wandering through the streets with this man writhing beneath the fires like a candelabrum blown about by the wind.

But what citizens should be charged with his torture, and why disappoint the rest? They would have liked a kind of death in which the whole town might take part, in which every hand, every weapon, everything Carthaginian, to the very paving-stones in the streets and the waves in the gulf, could tend him, and crush him, and annihilate him. Accordingly the Ancients decided that he should go from his prison to the square of Khamon without any escort, and with his arms fastened to his back; it was forbidden to strike him to the heart, in order that he might live the longer; to put out his eyes, so that he might see his torture through; to hurl anything against his person, or to lay more than three fingers upon him at a time.

Although he was not to appear until the end of the day, the people sometimes fancied that he could be seen, and the crowd would rush towards the Acropolis, and empty the streets, to return with lengthened murmurings. Some people had remained standing in the same place since the day before, and they would call on one another from a distance and show their nails which they had allowed to grow, the better to bury them in his flesh. Others walked restlessly up and down; some were as pale as though they were awaiting their own execution.

Suddenly lofty feather fans rose above the heads, behind the Mappalian district. It was Salammbô leaving her palace; a sigh of relief found vent.

But the procession was long in coming; it marched with deliberation.

First there filed past the priests of the Patæc Gods, then those of Eschmoun, of Melkarth, and all the other colleges in succession, with the same insignia, and in the same order as had been observed at the time of the sacrifice. The pontiffs of Moloch passed with heads bent, and the multitude stood aside from them in a kind of remorse. But the priests of Rabbetna advanced with a proud step, and with lyres in their hands; the priestesses followed them in transparent robes of yellow or black, uttering cries like birds and writhing like vipers, or else whirling round to the sound of flutes to imitate the dance of the stars, while their light garments wafted puffs of delicate scents through the streets.

The Kedeschim, with painted eyelids, who symbolised the hermaphrodism of the Divinity, received applause among these women, and, being perfumed and dressed like them, they resembled them in spite of their flat breasts and narrower hips. Moreover, on this day the female principle dominated and confused all things; a mystic voluptuousness moved in the heavy air; the torches were already lighted in the depths of the sacred woods; there was to be a great celebration there during the night; three vessels had brought courtesans from Sicily, and others had come from the desert.

As the colleges arrived they ranged themselves in the courts of the temples, on the outer galleries, and along double staircases which rose against the walls, and drew together at the top. Files of white robes appeared between the colonnades, and the architecture was peopled with human statues, motionless as statues of stone.

Then came the masters of the exchequer, the governors of the provinces, and all the rich. A great tumult prevailed below. Adjacent streets were discharging the crowd, hierodules were driving it back with blows of sticks; and then Salammbô appeared in a litter surmounted by a purple canopy, and surrounded by the Ancients crowned with their golden tiaras.

Thereupon an immense shout arose; the cymbals and crotala sounded more loudly, the tabourines thundered, and the great purple canopy sank between the two pylons.

It appeared again on the first landing. Salammbô was walking slowly beneath it; then she crossed the terrace to take her seat behind on a kind of throne cut out of the carapace of a tortoise. An ivory stool with three steps was pushed beneath her feet; two Negro children knelt on the edge of the first step, and sometimes she would rest both arms, which were laden with rings of excessive weight, upon their heads.

From ankle to hip she was covered with a network of narrow meshes which were in imitation of fish scales, and shone like mother-of-pearl; her waist was clasped by a blue zone, which allowed her breasts to be seen through two crescent-shaped slashings; the nipples were hidden by carbuncle pendants. She had a head-dress made of peacock's feathers studded with gems; an ample cloak, as white as snow, fell behind her—and with her elbows at her sides, her knees pressed together, and circles of diamonds on the upper part of her arms, she remained perfectly upright in a hieratic attitude.

Her father and her husband were on two lower seats, Narr' Havas dressed in a light simar and wearing his crown of rock-salt, from which there strayed two tresses of hair as twisted as the horns of Ammon; and Hamilcar in a violet tunic figured with gold vine branches, and with a battle-sword at his side.

The python of the temple of Eschmoun lay on the ground amid pools of pink oil in the space enclosed by the tables, and, biting its tail, described a large black circle. In the middle of the circle there was a copper pillar bearing a crystal egg; and, as the sun shone upon it, rays were emitted on every side.

Behind Salammbô stretched the priests of Tanith in linen robes; on her right the Ancients, in their tiaras, formed a great gold line, and on the other side the rich with their emerald sceptres a great green line—while quite in the background, where the priests of Moloch were ranged, the cloaks looked like a wall of purple. The other colleges occupied the lower terraces. The multitude obstructed the streets. It reached to the house-tops, and extended in long files to the summit of the Acropolis. Having thus the people at her feet, the firmament above her head, and around her the immensity of the sea, the gulf, the mountains, and the distant provinces, Salammbô in her splendour was blended with Tanith, and seemed the very genius of Carthage, and its embodied soul.

The feast was to last all night, and lamps with several branches were planted like trees on the painted woollen cloths which covered the low tables. Large electrum flagons, blue glass amphoras, tortoise-shell spoons, and small round loaves were crowded between the double row of pearl-bordered plates; bunches of grapes with their leaves had been rolled round ivory vine-stocks after the fashion of the thyrsus; blocks of snow were melting on ebony trays, and lemons, pomegranates, gourds, and watermelons formed hillocks beneath the lofty silver plate; boars with open jaws were wallowing in the dust of spices; hares, covered with their fur, appeared to be bounding amid the flowers; there were shells filled with forcemeat; the pastry had symbolic shapes; when the covers of the dishes were removed doves flew out.

The slaves, meanwhile, with tunics tucked up, were going about on tiptoe; from time to time a hymn sounded on the lyres, or a choir of voices rose. The clamour of the people, continuous as the noise of the sea, floated vaguely around the feast, and seemed to lull it in a broader harmony; some recalled the banquet of the Mercenaries; they gave themselves up to dreams of happiness; the sun was beginning to go down, and the crescent of the moon was already rising in another part of the sky.

But Salammbô turned her head as though some one had called her; the people, who were watching her, followed the direction of her eyes.

The door of the dungeon, hewn in the rock at the foot of the temple, on the summit of the Acropolis, had just opened; and a man was standing on the threshold of this black hole.

He came forth bent double, with the scared look of fallow deer when suddenly enlarged.

The light dazzled him; he stood motionless awhile. All had recognised him, and they held their breath.

In their eyes the body of this victim was something peculiarly theirs, and was adorned with almost religious splendour. They bent forward to see him, especially the women. They burned to gaze upon him who had caused the deaths of their children and husbands; and from the bottom of their souls there sprang up in spite of themselves an infamous curiosity, a desire to know him completely, a wish mingled with remorse which turned to increased execration.

At last he advanced; then the stupefaction of surprise disappeared. Numbers of arms were raised, and he was lost to sight.

The staircase of the Acropolis had sixty steps. He descended them as though he were rolled down in a torrent from the top of a mountain; three times he was seen to leap, and then he alighted below on his feet.

His shoulders were bleeding, his breast was panting with great shocks; and he made such efforts to burst his bonds that his arms, which were crossed on his naked loins, swelled like pieces of a serpent.

Several streets began in front of him, leading from the spot at which he found himself. In each of them a triple row of bronze chains fastened to the navels of the Patæc gods extended in parallel lines from one end to the other; the crowd was massed against the houses, and servants, belonging to the Ancients, walked in the middle brandishing thongs.

One of them drove him forward with a great blow; Matho began to move.

They thrust their arms over the chains shouting out that the road had been left too wide for him; and he passed along, felt, pricked, and slashed by all those fingers; when he reached the end of one street another appeared; several times he flung himself to one side to bite them; they speedily dispersed, the chains held him back, and the crowd burst out laughing.

A child rent his ear; a young girl, hiding the point of a spindle in her sleeve, split his cheek; they tore handfuls of hair from him and strips of flesh; others smeared his face with sponges steeped in filth and fastened upon sticks. A stream of blood started from the right side of his neck, frenzy immediately set in. This last Barbarian was to them a representative of all the Barbarians, and all the army; they were taking vengeance on him for their disasters, their terrors, and their shame. The rage of the mob developed with its gratification; the curving chains were over-strained, and were on the point of breaking; the people did not feel the blows of the slaves who struck at them to drive them back; some clung to the projections of the houses; all the openings in the walls were stopped up with heads; and they howled at him the mischief that they could not inflict upon him.

It was atrocious, filthy abuse mingled with ironical encouragements and imprecations; and, his present tortures not being enough for them, they foretold to him others that should be still more terrible in eternity.

This vast baying filled Carthage with stupid continuity. Frequently a single syllable—a hoarse, deep, and frantic intonation—would be repeated for several minutes by the entire people. The walls would vibrate with it from top to bottom, and both sides of the street would seem to Matho to be coming against him, and carrying him off the ground, like two immense arms stifling him in the air.

Nevertheless he remembered that he had experienced something like it before. The same crowd was on the terraces, there were the same looks and the same wrath; but then he had walked free, all had then dispersed, for a god covered him— and the recollection of this, gaining precision by degrees, brought a crushing sadness upon him. Shadows passed before his eyes; the town whirled round in his head, his blood streamed from a wound in his hip, he felt that he was dying; his hams bent, and he sank quite gently upon the pavement.

Someone went to the peristyle of the temple of Melkarth, took thence the bar of a tripod, heated red hot in the coals, and, slipping it beneath the first chain, pressed it against his wound. The Mesh was seen to smoke; the hootings of the people drowned his voice; he was standing again.

Six paces further on, and he fell a third and again a fourth time; but some new torture always made him rise. They discharged little drops of boiling oil through tubes at him; they strewed pieces of broken glass beneath his feet; still he walked on. At the corner of the street of Satheb he leaned his back against the wall beneath the pent-house of a shop, and advanced no further.

The slaves of the Council struck him with their whips of hippopotamus leather, so furiously and long that the fringes of their tunics were drenched with sweat. Matho appeared insensible; suddenly he started off and began to run at random, making a noise with his lips like one shivering with severe cold. He threaded the street of Boudes, and the street of Sœpo, crossed the Green Market, and reached the square of Khamon.

He now belonged to the priests; the slaves had just dispersed the crowd, and there was more room. Matho gazed round him and his eyes encountered Salammbô.

At the first step that he had taken she had risen; then, as he approached, she had involuntarily advanced by degrees to the edge of the terrace; and soon all external things were blotted out, and she saw only Matho. Silence fell in her soul—one of those abysses wherein the whole world disappears beneath the pressure of a single thought, a memory, a look. This man who was walking towards her attracted her.

Excepting his eyes he had no appearance of humanity left; he was a long, perfectly red shape; his broken bonds hung down his thighs, but they could not be distinguished from the tendons of his wrists, which were laid quite bare; his mouth remained wide open; from his eye-sockets there darted flames which seemed to rise up to his hair—and the wretch still walked on!

He reached the foot of the terrace. Salammbô was leaning over the balustrade; those frightful eyeballs were scanning her, and there rose within her a consciousness of all that he had suffered for her. Although he was in his death agony she could see him once more kneeling in his tent, encircling her waist with his arms, and stammering out gentle words; she thirsted to feel them and hear them again; she did not want him to die! At this moment Matho gave a great start; she was on the point of shrieking aloud. He fell backwards and did not stir again.

Salammbô was borne back, nearly swooning, to her throne by the priests who flocked about her. They congratulated her; it was her work. All clapped their hands and stamped their feet, howling her name.

A man darted upon the corpse. Although he had no beard he had the cloak of a priest of Moloch on his shoulder, and in his belt that species of knife which they employed for cutting up the sacred meat, and which terminated, at the end of the handle, in a golden spatula. He cleft Matho's breast with a single blow, then snatched out the heart and laid it upon the spoon; and Schahabarim, uplifting his arm, offered it to the sun.

The sun sank behind the waves; his rays fell like long arrows upon the red heart. As the beatings diminished the planet sank into the sea; and at the last palpitation it disappeared.

Then from the gulf to the lagoon, and from the isthmus to the pharos, in all the streets, on all the houses, and on all the temples, there was a single shout; sometimes it paused, to be again renewed; the buildings shook with it; Carthage was convulsed, as it were, in the spasm of Titanic joy and boundless hope.

Narr' Havas, drunk with pride, passed his left arm beneath Salammbô's waist in token of possession; and taking a gold patera in his right hand, he drank to the Genius of Carthage.

Salammbô rose like her husband, with a cup in her hand, to drink also. She fell down again with her head lying over the back of the throne—pale, stiff, with parted lips—and her loosened hair hung to the ground.

Thus died Hamilcar's daughter for having touched the mantle of Tanith.

SENTIMENTAL EDUCATION
OR,
THE HISTORY OF A YOUNG MAN

CONTENTS

Chapter I

A Promising Pupil

ON THE 15TH OF SEPTEMBER, 1840, ABOUT SIX O'CLOCK IN THE MORNING, THE *ville de Montereau,* just on the point of starting, was sending forth great whirlwinds of smoke, in front of the Quai St. Bernard.

People came rushing on board in breathless haste. The traffic was obstructed by casks, cables, and baskets of linen. The sailors answered nobody. People jostled one another. Between the two paddle-boxes was piled up a heap of parcels; and the uproar was drowned in the loud hissing of the steam, which, making its way through the plates of sheet-iron, enveloped everything in a white cloud, while the bell at the prow kept ringing continuously.

At last, the vessel set out; and the two banks of the river, stocked with warehouses, timber-yards, and manufactories, opened out like two huge ribbons being unrolled.

A young man of eighteen, with long hair, holding an album under his arm, remained near the helm without moving. Through the haze he surveyed steeples, buildings of which he did not know the names; then, with a parting glance, he took in the the Île St. Louis, the Cité, Nôtre Dame; and presently, as Paris disappeared from his view, he heaved a deep sigh.

Frederick Moreau, having just taken his Bachelor's degree, was returning home to Nogent-sur-Seine, where he would have to lead a languishing existence for two months, before going back to begin his legal studies. His mother had sent him, with enough to cover his expenses, to Havre to see an uncle, from whom she had expectations of his receiving an inheritance. He had returned from that place only yesterday; and he indemnified himself for not having the opportunity of spending a little time in the capital by taking the longest possible route to reach his own part of the country.

The hubbub had subsided. The passengers had all taken their places. Some of them stood warming themselves around the machinery, and the chimney spat forth with a slow, rhythmic rattle its plume of black smoke. Little drops of dew trickled over the copper plates; the deck quivered with the vibration from within; and the two paddle-wheels, rapidly turning round, lashed the water. The edges of the river were covered with sand. The vessel swept past rafts of wood which began to oscillate under the rippling of the waves, or a boat without sails in which a man sat fishing. Then the wandering haze cleared off; the sun appeared; the hill which ran along the course of the Seine to the right subsided by degrees, and another rose nearer on the opposite bank.

It was crowned with trees, which surrounded low-built houses, covered with roofs in the Italian style. They had sloping gardens divided by fresh walls, iron railings, grass-plots, hot-houses, and vases of geraniums, laid out regularly on the terraces where one could lean forward on one's elbow. More than one spectator longed, on beholding those attractive residences which looked so peaceful, to be the owner of one of them, and to dwell there till the end of his days with a good billiard-table, a sailing-boat, and a woman or some other object to dream about. The agreeable novelty of a journey by water made such outbursts natural. Already the wags on board were beginning their jokes. Many began to sing. Gaiety prevailed, and glasses of brandy were poured out.

Frederick was thinking about the apartment which he would occupy over there, on the plan of a drama, on subjects for pictures, on future passions. He found that the happiness merited by the excellence of his soul was slow in arriving. He declaimed some melancholy verses. He walked with rapid step along the deck. He went on till he reached the end at which the bell was; and, in the centre of a group of passengers and sailors, he saw a gentleman talking soft nothings to a country-woman, while fingering the gold cross which she wore over her breast. He was a jovial blade of forty with frizzled hair. His robust form was encased in a jacket of black velvet, two emeralds sparkled in his cambric shirt, and his wide, white trousers fell over odd-looking red boots of Russian leather set off with blue designs.

The presence of Frederick did not discompose him. He turned round and glanced several times at the young man with winks of enquiry. He next offered cigars to all who were standing around him. But getting tired, no doubt, of their society, he moved away from them and took a seat further up. Frederick followed him.

The conversation, at first, turned on the various kinds of tobacco, then quite naturally it glided into a discussion about women. The gentleman in the red boots gave the young man advice; he put forward theories, related anecdotes, referred to himself by way of illustration, and he gave utterance to all these things in a paternal tone, with the ingenuousness of entertaining depravity.

He was republican in his opinions. He had travelled; he was familiar with the inner life of theatres, restaurants, and newspapers, and knew all the theatrical celebrities, whom he called by their Christian names. Frederick told him confidentially about his projects; and the elder man took an encouraging view of them.

But he stopped talking to take a look at the funnel, then he went mumbling rapidly through a long calculation in order to ascertain "how much each stroke of the piston at so many times per minute would come to," etc., and having found the number, he spoke about the scenery, which he admired immensely. Then he gave expression to his delight at having got away from business.

Frederick regarded him with a certain amount of respect, and politely manifested a strong desire to know his name. The stranger, without a moment's hesitation, replied:

"Jacques Arnoux, proprietor of *L'Art Industriel*, Boulevard Montmartre."

A man-servant in a gold-laced cap came up and said:

"Would Monsieur have the kindness to go below? Mademoiselle is crying."

L'Art Industriel was a hybrid establishment, wherein the functions of an art-journal and a picture-shop were combined. Frederick had seen this title several times in the bookseller's window in his native place on big prospectuses, on which the name of Jacques Arnoux displayed itself magisterially.

The sun's rays fell perpendicularly, shedding a glittering light on the iron hoops around the masts, the plates of the barricades, and the surface of the water, which, at the prow, was cut into two furrows that spread out as far as the borders of the meadows. At each winding of the river, a screen of pale poplars presented itself with the utmost uniformity. The surrounding country at this point had an empty look. In the sky there were little white clouds which remained motionless, and the sense of weariness, which vaguely diffused itself over everything, seemed to retard the progress of the steamboat and to add to the insignificant appearance of the passengers. Putting aside a few persons of good position who were travelling first class, they were artisans or shopmen with their wives and children. As it was customary at that time to wear old clothes when travelling, they nearly all had their heads covered with shabby Greek caps or discoloured hats, thin black coats that had become quite threadbare from constant rubbing against writing-desks, or frock-coats with the casings of their buttons loose from continual service in the shop. Here and there some roll-collar waistcoat afforded a glimpse of a calico shirt stained with coffee. Pinchbeck pins were stuck into cravats that were all torn. List shoes were kept up by stitched straps. Two or three roughs who held in their hands bamboo canes with leathern loops, kept looking askance at their fellow-passengers; and fathers of families opened their eyes wide while making enquiries. People chatted either standing up or squatting over their luggage; some went to sleep in various corners of the vessel; several occupied themselves with eating. The deck was soiled with walnut shells, butt-ends of cigars, peelings of pears, and the droppings of pork-butchers' meat, which had been carried wrapped up in paper. Three cabinet-makers in blouses took their stand in front of the bottle case; a harp-player in rags was resting with his elbows on his instrument. At intervals could be heard the sound of falling coals in the furnace, a shout, or a laugh;

and the captain kept walking on the bridge from one paddle-box to the other without stopping for a moment.

Frederick, to get back to his place, pushed forward the grating leading into the part of the vessel reserved for first-class passengers, and in so doing disturbed two sportsmen with their dogs.

What he then saw was like an apparition. She was seated in the middle of a bench all alone, or, at any rate, he could see no one, dazzled as he was by her eyes. At the moment when he was passing, she raised her head; his shoulders bent involuntarily; and, when he had seated himself, some distance away, on the same side, he glanced towards her.

She wore a wide straw hat with red ribbons which fluttered in the wind behind her. Her black tresses, twining around the edges of her large brows, descended very low, and seemed amorously to press the oval of her face. Her robe of light muslin spotted with green spread out in numerous folds. She was in the act of embroidering something; and her straight nose, her chin, her entire person was cut out on the background of the luminous air and the blue sky.

As she remained in the same attitude, he took several turns to the right and to the left to hide from her his change of position; then he placed himself close to her parasol which lay against the bench, and pretended to be looking at a sloop on the river.

Never before had he seen more lustrous dark skin, a more seductive figure, or more delicately shaped fingers than those through which the sunlight gleamed. He stared with amazement at her work-basket, as if it were something extraordinary. What was her name, her place of residence, her life, her past? He longed to become familiar with the furniture of her apartment, all the dresses that she had worn, the people whom she visited; and the desire of physical possession yielded to a deeper yearning, a painful curiosity that knew no bounds.

A negress, wearing a silk handkerchief tied round her head, made her appearance, holding by the hand a little girl already tall for her age. The child, whose eyes were swimming with tears, had just awakened. The lady took the little one on her knees. "Mademoiselle was not good, though she would soon be seven; her mother would not love her any more. She was too often pardoned for being naughty." And Frederick heard those things with delight, as if he had made a discovery, an acquisition.

He assumed that she must be of Andalusian descent, perhaps a creole: had she brought this negress across with her from the West Indian Islands?

Meanwhile his attention was directed to a long shawl with violet stripes thrown behind her back over the copper support of the bench. She must have, many a time, wrapped it around her waist, as the vessel sped through the midst of the waves; drawn it over her feet, gone to sleep in it!

Frederick suddenly noticed that with the sweep of its fringes it was slipping off, and it was on the point of falling into the water when, with a bound, he secured it. She said to him:

"Thanks, Monsieur."

Their eyes met.

"Are you ready, my dear?" cried my lord Arnoux, presenting himself at the hood of the companion-ladder.

Mademoiselle Marthe ran over to him, and, clinging to his neck, she began pulling at his moustache. The strains of a harp were heard—she wanted to see the music played; and presently the performer on the instrument, led forward by the negress, entered the place reserved for saloon passengers. Arnoux recognized in him a man who had formerly been a model, and "thou'd" him, to the astonishment of the bystanders. At length the harpist, flinging back his long hair over his shoulders, stretched out his hands and began playing.

It was an Oriental ballad all about poniards, flowers, and stars. The man in rags sang it in a sharp voice; the twanging of the harp strings broke the harmony of the tune with false notes. He played more vigorously: the chords vibrated, and their metallic sounds seemed to send forth sobs, and, as it were, the plaint of a proud and vanquished love. On both sides of the river, woods extended as far as the edge of the water. A current of fresh air swept past them, and Madame Arnoux gazed vaguely into the distance. When the music stopped, she moved her eyes several times as if she were starting out of a dream.

The harpist approached them with an air of humility. While Arnoux was searching his pockets for money, Frederick stretched out towards the cap his closed hand, and then, opening it in a shamefaced manner, he deposited in it a louis d'or. It was not vanity that had prompted him to bestow this alms in her presence, but the idea of a blessing in which he thought she might share—an almost religious impulse of the heart.

Arnoux, pointing out the way, cordially invited him to go below. Frederick declared that he had just lunched; on the contrary, he was nearly dying of hunger; and he had not a single centime in his purse.

After that, it occurred to him that he had a perfect right, as well as anyone else, to remain in the cabin.

Ladies and gentlemen were seated before round tables, lunching, while an attendant went about serving out coffee. Monsieur and Madame Arnoux were in the far corner to the right. He took a seat on the long bench covered with velvet, having picked up a newspaper which he found there.

They would have to take the diligence at Montereau for Châlons. Their tour in Switzerland would last a month. Madame Arnoux blamed her husband for his weakness in dealing with his child. He whispered in her ear something agreeable, no doubt, for she smiled. Then, he got up to draw down the window curtain at her back. Under the low, white ceiling, a crude light filled the cabin. Frederick, sitting opposite to the place where she sat, could distinguish the shade of her eyelashes. She just moistened her lips with her glass and broke a little piece of crust between her fingers. The lapis-lazuli locket fastened by a little gold chain to her wrist made a ringing sound, every now and then, as it touched her plate. Those present, however, did not appear to notice it.

At intervals one could see, through the small portholes, the side of a boat taking away passengers or putting them on board. Those who sat round the tables stooped towards the openings, and called out the names of the various places they passed along the river.

Arnoux complained of the cooking. He grumbled particularly at the amount of the bill, and got it reduced. Then, he carried off the young man towards the forecastle to drink a glass of grog with him. But Frederick speedily came back again to gaze at Madame Arnoux, who had returned to the awning, beneath which she seated herself. She was reading a thin, grey-covered volume. From time to time, the corners of her mouth curled and a gleam of pleasure lighted up her forehead. He felt jealous of the inventor of those things which appeared to interest her so much. The more he contemplated her, the more he felt that there were yawning abysses between them. He was reflecting that he should very soon lose sight of her irrevocably, without having extracted a few words from her, without leaving her even a souvenir!

On the right, a plain stretched out. On the left, a strip of pasture-land rose gently to meet a hillock where one could see vineyards, groups of walnut-trees, a mill embedded in the grassy slopes, and, beyond that, little zigzag paths over the white mass of rocks that reached up towards the clouds. What bliss it would have been to ascend side by side with her, his arm around her waist, while her gown would sweep the yellow leaves, listening to her voice and gazing up into her glowing eyes! The steamboat might stop, and all they would have to do was to step out of it; and yet this thing, simple as it might be, was not less difficult than it would have been to move the sun.

A little further on, a château appeared with pointed roof and square turrets. A flower garden spread out in the foreground; and avenues ran, like dark archways, under the tall linden trees. He pictured her to himself passing along by this group of trees. At that moment a young lady and a young man showed themselves on the steps in front of the house, between the trunks of the orange trees. Then the entire scene vanished.

The little girl kept skipping playfully around the place where he had stationed himself on the deck. Frederick wished to kiss her. She hid herself behind her nurse. Her mother scolded her for not being nice to the gentleman who had rescued her own shawl. Was this an indirect overture?

"Is she going to speak to me?" he asked himself.

Time was flying. How was he to get an invitation to the Arnoux's house? And he could think of nothing better than to draw her attention to the autumnal hues, adding:

"We are close to winter—the season of balls and dinner-parties."

But Arnoux was entirely occupied with his luggage. They had arrived at the point of the river's bank facing Surville. The two bridges drew nearer. They passed a ropewalk, then a range of low-built houses, inside which there were pots of tar and splinters of wood; and brats went along the sand turning head over heels. Frederick recognised a man with a sleeved waistcoat, and called out to him:

"Make haste!"

They were at the landing-place. He looked around anxiously for Arnoux amongst the crowd of passengers, and the other came and shook hands with him, saying:

"A pleasant time, dear Monsieur!"

When he was on the quay, Frederick turned around. She was standing beside the helm. He cast a look towards her into which he tried to put his whole soul. She remained motionless, as if he had done nothing. Then, without paying the slightest attentions to the obeisances of his man-servant:

"Why didn't you bring the trap down here?"

The man made excuses.

"What a clumsy fellow you are! Give me some money."

And after that he went off to get something to eat at an inn.

A quarter of an hour later, he felt an inclination to turn into the coachyard, as if by chance. Perhaps he would see her again.

"What's the use of it?" said he to himself.

The vehicle carried him off. The two horses did not belong to his mother. She had borrowed one of M. Chambrion, the tax-collector, in order to have it yoked alongside of her own. Isidore, having set forth the day before, had taken a rest at Bray until evening, and had slept at Montereau, so that the animals, with restored vigour, were trotting briskly.

Fields on which the crops had been cut stretched out in apparently endless succession; and by degrees Villeneuve, St. Georges, Ablon, Châtillon, Corbeil, and the other places—his entire journey—came back to his recollection with such vividness that he could now recall to mind fresh details, more intimate particulars . . . . Under the lowest flounce of her gown, her foot showed itself encased in a dainty silk boot of maroon shade. The awning made of ticking formed a wide canopy over her head, and the little red tassels of the edging kept perpetually trembling in the breeze.

She resembled the women of whom he had read in romances. He would have added nothing to the charms of her person, and would have taken nothing from them. The universe had suddenly become enlarged. She was the luminous point towards which all things converged; and, rocked by the movement of the vehicle, with half-closed eyelids, and his face turned towards the clouds, he abandoned himself to a dreamy, infinite joy.

At Bray, he did not wait till the horses had got their oats; he walked on along the road ahead by himself. Arnoux had, when he spoke to her, addressed her as "Marie." He now loudly repeated the name "Marie!" His voice pierced the air and was lost in the distance.

The western sky was one great mass of flaming purple. Huge stacks of wheat, rising up in the midst of the stubble fields, projected giant shadows. A dog began to bark in a farm-house in the distance. He shivered, seized with disquietude for which he could assign no cause.

When Isidore had come up with him, he jumped up into the front seat to drive. His fit of weakness was past. He had thoroughly made up his mind to effect an introduction into the house of the Arnoux, and to become intimate with them. Their house should be amusing; besides, he liked Arnoux; then, who could tell? Thereupon a wave of blood rushed up to his face; his temples throbbed; he cracked his whip, shook the reins, and set the horses going at such a pace that the old coachman repeatedly exclaimed:

"Easy! easy now, or they'll get broken-winded!"

Gradually Frederick calmed down, and he listened to what the man was saying. Monsieur's return was impatiently awaited. Mademoiselle Louise had cried in her anxiety to go in the trap to meet him.

"Who, pray, is Mademoiselle Louise?"

"Monsieur Roque's little girl, you know."

"Ah! I had forgotten," rejoined Frederick, carelessly.

Meanwhile, the two horses could keep up the pace no longer. They were both getting lame; and nine o'clock struck at St. Laurent's when he arrived at the parade in front of his mother's house.

This house of large dimensions, with a garden looking out on the open country, added to the social importance of Madame Moreau, who was the most respected lady in the district.

She came of an old family of nobles, of which the male line was now extinct. Her husband, a plebeian whom her parents forced her to marry, met his death by a sword-thrust, during her pregnancy, leaving her an estate much encumbered. She received visitors three times a week, and from time to time, gave a fashionable dinner. But the number of wax candles was calculated beforehand, and she looked forward with some impatience to the payment of her rents. These pecuniary embarrassments, concealed as if there were some guilt attached to them, imparted a certain gravity to her character. Nevertheless, she displayed no prudery, no sourness, in the practice of her peculiar virtue. Her most trifling charities seemed munificent alms. She was consulted about the selection of servants, the education of young girls, and the art of making preserves, and Monseigneur used to stay at her house on the occasion of his episcopal visitations.

Madame Moreau cherished a lofty ambition for her son. Through a sort of prudence grounded on the expectation of favours, she did not care to hear blame cast on the Government. He would need patronage at the start; then, with its aid, he might become a councillor of State, an ambassador, a minister. His triumphs at the college of Sens warranted this proud anticipation; he had carried off there the prize of honour.

When he entered the drawing-room, all present arose with a great racket; he was embraced; and the chairs, large and small, were drawn up in a big semi-circle around the fireplace. M. Gamblin immediately asked him what was his opinion about Madame Lafarge. This case, the rage of the period, did not fail to lead to a violent discussion. Madame Moreau stopped it, to the regret, however, of M. Gamblin. He deemed it serviceable to the young man in his character of a future lawyer, and, nettled at what had occurred, he left the drawing-room.

Nothing should have caused surprise on the part of a friend of Père Roque! The reference to Père Roque led them to talk of M. Dambreuse, who had just become the owner of the demesne of La Fortelle. But the tax-collector had drawn Frederick aside to know what he thought of M. Guizot's latest work. They were all anxious to get some information about his private affairs, and Madame Benoît went cleverly to work with that end in view by inquiring about his uncle. How was that worthy relative? They no longer heard from him. Had he not a distant cousin in America?

The cook announced that Monsieur's soup was served. The guests discreetly retired. Then, as soon as they were alone in the dining-room, his mother said to him in a low tone:

"Well?"

The old man had received him in a very cordial manner, but without disclosing his intentions.

Madame Moreau sighed.

"Where is she now?" was his thought.

The diligence was rolling along the road, and, wrapped up in the shawl, no doubt, she was leaning against the cloth of the coupé, her beautiful head nodding asleep.

He and his mother were just going up to their apartments when a waiter from the Swan of the Cross brought him a note.

"What is that, pray?"

"It is Deslauriers, who wants me," said he.

"Ha! your chum!" said Madame Moreau, with a contemptuous sneer. "Certainly it is a nice hour to select!"

Frederick hesitated. But friendship was stronger. He got his hat.

"At any rate, don't be long!" said his mother to him.

Chapter II

DAMON AND PYTHIAS

CHARLES DESLAURIERS' FATHER, AN EX-CAPTAIN IN THE LINE, WHO HAD LEFT the service in 1818, had come back to Nogent, where he had married, and with the amount of the dowry bought up the business of a process-server, which brought him barely enough to maintain him. Embittered by a long course of unjust treatment, suffering still from the effects of old wounds, and always regretting the Emperor, he vented on those around him the fits of rage that seemed to choke him. Few children received so many whackings as his son. In spite of blows, however, the brat did not yield. His mother, when she tried to interpose, was also ill-treated. Finally, the captain planted the boy in his office, and all the day long kept him bent over his desk copying documents, with the result that his right shoulder was noticeably higher than his left.

In 1833, on the invitation of the president, the captain sold his office. His wife died of cancer. He then went to live at Dijon. After that he started in business at Troyes, where he was connected with the slave trade; and, having obtained a small scholarship for Charles, placed him at the college of Sens, where Frederick came across him. But one of the pair was twelve years old, while the other was fifteen; besides, a thousand differences of character and origin tended to keep them apart.

Frederick had in his chest of drawers all sorts of useful things—choice articles, such as a dressing-case. He liked to lie late in bed in the morning, to look at the swallows, and to read plays; and, regretting the comforts of home, he thought college life rough. To the process-server's son it seemed a pleasant life. He worked so hard that, at the end of the second year, he had got into the third form. However, owing to his poverty or to his quarrelsome disposition, he was regarded with intense dislike. But when on one occasion, in the courtyard where pupils of the middle grade took exercise, an attendant openly called him a beggar's child, he sprang at the fellow's throat, and would have killed him if three of the ushers had not intervened. Frederick, carried away by admiration, pressed him in his arms. From that day forward they became fast friends. The affection of a *grandee* no doubt flattered the vanity of the youth of meaner rank, and the other accepted as a piece of good fortune this devotion freely offered to him. During the holidays Charles's father allowed him to remain in the college. A translation of Plato which he opened by chance excited his enthusiasm. Then he became smitten with a love of metaphysical studies; and he made rapid progress, for he approached the subject with all the energy of youth and the self-confidence of an emancipated intellect. Jouffroy, Cousin, Laromiguière, Malebranche, and the Scotch metaphysicians—everything that could be found in the library dealing with this branch of knowledge passed through his hands. He found it necessary to steal the key in order to get the books.

Frederick's intellectual distractions were of a less serious description. He made sketches of the genealogy of Christ carved on a post in the Rue des Trois Rois, then of the gateway of a cathedral. After a course of mediæval dramas, he took up memoirs—Froissart, Comines, Pierre de l'Estoile, and Brantôme.

The impressions made on his mind by this kind of reading took such a hold of it that he felt a need within him of reproducing those pictures of bygone days. His ambition was to be, one day, the Walter Scott of France. Deslauriers dreamed of formulating a vast system of philosophy, which might have the most far-reaching applications.

They chatted over all these matters at recreation hours, in the playground, in front of the moral inscription painted under the clock. They kept whispering to each other about them in the chapel, even with St. Louis staring down at them. They dreamed about them in the dormitory, which looked out on a burial-ground. On walking-days they took up a position behind the others, and talked without stopping.

They spoke of what they would do later, when they had left college. First of all, they would set out on a long voyage with the money which Frederick would take out of his own fortune on reaching his majority. Then they would come back to Paris; they would work together, and would never part; and, as a relaxation from their labours, they would have love-affairs with princesses in boudoirs lined with satin, or dazzling orgies with famous courtesans. Their rapturous expectations were followed by doubts. After a crisis of verbose gaiety, they would often lapse into profound silence.

On summer evenings, when they had been walking for a long time over stony paths which bordered on vineyards, or on the high-road in the open country, and when they saw the wheat waving in the sunlight, while the air was filled with the fragrance of angelica, a sort of suffocating sensation took possession of them, and they stretched themselves on their backs, dizzy, intoxicated. Meanwhile the other lads, in their shirt-sleeves, were playing at base or flying kites. Then, as the usher called in the two companions from the playground, they would return, taking the path which led along by the gardens watered by brooklets; then they would pass through the boulevards overshadowed by the old city walls. The deserted streets rang under their tread. The grating flew back; they ascended the stairs; and they felt as sad as if they had had a great debauch.

The proctor maintained that they mutually cried up each other. Nevertheless, if Frederick worked his way up to the higher forms, it was through the exhortations of his friend; and, during the vacation in 1837, he brought Deslauriers to his mother's house.

Madame Moreau disliked the young man. He had a terrible appetite. He was fond of making republican speeches. To crown all, she got it into her head that he had been the means of leading her son into improper places. Their relations towards each other were watched. This only made their friendship grow stronger, and they bade one another adieu with heartfelt pangs when, in the following year, Deslauriers left the college in order to study law in Paris.

Frederick anxiously looked forward to the time when they would meet again. For two years they had not laid eyes on each other; and, when their embraces were over, they walked over the bridges to talk more at their ease.

The captain, who had now set up a billiard-room at Villenauxe, reddened with anger when his son called for an account of the expense of tutelage, and even cut down the cost of victuals to the lowest figure. But, as he intended to become a candidate at a later period for a professor's chair at the school, and as he had no money, Deslauriers accepted the post of principal clerk in an attorney's office at Troyes. By dint of sheer privation he spared four thousand francs; and, by not drawing upon the sum which came to him through his mother, he would always have enough to enable him to work freely for three years while he was waiting for a better position. It was necessary, therefore, to abandon their former project of living together in the capital, at least for the present.

Frederick hung down his head. This was the first of his dreams which had crumbled into dust.

"Be consoled," said the captain's son. "Life is long. We are young. We'll meet again. Think no more about it!"

He shook the other's hand warmly, and, to distract his attention, questioned him about his journey.

Frederick had nothing to tell. But, at the recollection of Madame Arnoux, his vexation disappeared. He did not refer to her, restrained by a feeling of bashfulness. He made up for it by expatiating on Arnoux, recalling his talk, his agreeable manner, his stories; and Deslauriers urged him strongly to cultivate this new acquaintance.

Frederick had of late written nothing. His literary opinions were changed. Passion was now above everything else in his estimation. He was equally enthusiastic about Werther, René, Franck, Lara, Lélia, and other ideal creations of less merit. Sometimes it seemed to him that music alone was capable of giving expression to his internal agitation. Then, he dreamed of symphonies; or else the surface of things seized hold of him, and he longed to paint. He had, however, composed verses. Deslauriers considered them beautiful, but did not ask him to write another poem.

As for himself, he had given up metaphysics. Social economy and the French Revolution absorbed all his attention. Just now he was a tall fellow of twenty-two, thin, with a wide mouth, and a resolute look. On this particular evening, he wore a poor-looking paletot of lasting; and his shoes were white with dust, for he had come all the way from Villenauxe on foot for the express purpose of seeing Frederick.

Isidore arrived while they were talking. Madame begged of Monsieur to return home, and, for fear of his catching cold, she had sent him his cloak.

"Wait a bit!" said Deslauriers. And they continued walking from one end to the other of the two bridges which rest on the narrow islet formed by the canal and the river.

When they were walking on the side towards Nogent, they had, exactly in front of them, a block of houses which projected a little. At the right might be seen the church, behind the mills in the wood, whose sluices had been closed up; and, at the left, the hedges covered with shrubs, along the skirts of the wood, formed a boundary for the gardens, which could scarcely be distinguished. But on the side towards Paris the high road formed a sheer descending line, and the meadows lost themselves in the distance under the vapours of the night. Silence reigned along this road, whose white track clearly showed itself through the surrounding gloom. Odours of damp leaves ascended towards them. The waterfall, where the stream had been diverted from its course a hundred paces further away, kept rumbling with that deep harmonious sound which waves make in the night time.

Deslauriers stopped, and said:

" 'Tis funny to have these worthy folks sleeping so quietly! Patience! A new '89 is in preparation. People are tired of constitutions, charters, subtleties, lies! Ah, if I had a newspaper, or a platform, how I would shake off all these things! But, in order to undertake anything whatever, money is required. What a curse it is to be a tavern-keeper's son, and to waste one's youth in quest of bread!"

He hung down his head, bit his lips, and shivered under his threadbare overcoat.

Frederick flung half his cloak over his friend's shoulder. They both wrapped themselves up in it; and, with their arms around each other's waists, they walked down the road side by side.

"How do you think I can live over there without you?" said Frederick.

The bitter tone of his friend had brought back his own sadness.

"I would have done something with a woman who loved me. What are you laughing at? Love is the feeding-ground, and, as it were, the atmosphere of genius.

Extraordinary emotions produce sublime works. As for seeking after her whom I want, I give that up! Besides, if I should ever find her, she will repel me. I belong to the race of the disinherited, and I shall be extinguished with a treasure that will be of paste or of diamond—I know not which."

Somebody's shadow fell across the road, and at the same time they heard these words:

"Excuse me, gentlemen!"

The person who had uttered them was a little man attired in an ample brown frock-coat, and with a cap on his head which under its peak afforded a glimpse of a sharp nose.

"Monsieur Roque?" said Frederick.

"The very man!" returned the voice.

This resident in the locality explained his presence by stating that he had come back to inspect the wolf-traps in his garden near the water-side.

"And so you are back again in the old spot? Very good! I ascertained the fact through my little girl. Your health is good, I hope? You are not going away again?"

Then he left them, repelled, probably, by Frederick's chilling reception.

Madame Moreau, indeed, was not on visiting terms with him, Père Roque lived in peculiar relations with his servant-girl, and was held in very slight esteem, although he was the vice-president at elections, and M. Dambreuse's manager.

"The banker who resides in the Rue d'Anjou," observed Deslauriers. "Do you know what you ought to do, my fine fellow?"

Isidore once more interrupted. His orders were positive not to go back without Frederick. Madame would be getting uneasy at his absence.

"Well, well, he will go back," said Deslauriers. "He's not going to stay out all night."

And, as soon as the man-servant had disappeared:

"You ought to ask that old chap to introduce you to the Dambreuses. There's nothing so useful as to be a visitor at a rich man's house. Since you have a black coat and white gloves, make use of them. You must mix in that set. You can introduce me into it later. Just think!—a man worth millions! Do all you can to make him like you, and his wife, too. Become her lover!"

Frederick uttered an exclamation by way of protest.

"Why, I can quote classical examples for you on that point, I rather think! Remember Rastignac in the *Comédie Humaine*. You will succeed, I have no doubt."

Frederick had so much confidence in Deslauriers that he felt his firmness giving way, and forgetting Madame Arnoux, or including her in the prediction made with regard to the other, he could not keep from smiling.

The clerk added:

"A last piece of advice: pass your examinations. It is always a good thing to have a handle to your name: and, without more ado, give up your Catholic and Satanic poets, whose philosophy is as old as the twelfth century! Your despair is silly. The very greatest men have had more difficult beginnings, as in the case of Mirabeau. Besides, our separation will not be so long. I will make that pickpocket of a father of mine disgorge. It is time for me to be going back. Farewell! Have you got a hundred sous to pay for my dinner?"

Frederick gave him ten francs, what was left of those he had got that morning from Isidore.

Meanwhile, some forty yards away from the bridges, a light shone from the garret-window of a low-built house.

Deslauriers noticed it. Then he said emphatically, as he took off his hat:

"Your pardon, Venus, Queen of Heaven, but Penury is the mother of wisdom. We have been slandered enough for that—so have mercy."

This allusion to an adventure in which they had both taken part, put them into a jovial mood. They laughed loudly as they passed through the streets.

Then, having settled his bill at the inn, Deslauriers walked back with Frederick as far as the crossway near the Hotel-Dieu, and after a long embrace, the two friends parted.

Chapter III

SENTIMENT AND PASSION

TWO MONTHS LATER, FREDERICK, HAVING DEBARKED ONE MORNING IN THE Rue Coq-Heron, immediately thought of paying his great visit.

Chance came to his aid. Père Roque had brought him a roll of papers and requested him to deliver them up himself to M. Dambreuse; and the worthy man accompanied the package with an open letter of introduction in behalf of his young fellow-countryman.

Madame Moreau appeared surprised at this proceeding. Frederick concealed the delight that it gave him.

M. Dambreuse's real name was the Count d'Ambreuse; but since 1825, gradually abandoning his title of nobility and his party, he had turned his attention to business; and with his ears open in every office, his hand in every enterprise, on the watch for every opportunity, as subtle as a Greek and as laborious as a native of Auvergne, he had amassed a fortune which might be called considerable. Furthermore, he was an officer of the Legion of Honour, a member of the General Council of the Aube, a deputy, and one of these days would be a peer of France. However, affable as he was in other respects, he wearied the Minister by his continual applications for relief, for crosses, and licences for tobacconists' shops; and in his complaints against authority he was inclined to join the Left Centre.

His wife, the pretty Madame Dambreuse, of whom mention was made in the fashion journals, presided at charitable assemblies. By wheedling the duchesses, she appeased the rancours of the aristocratic faubourg, and led the residents to believe that M. Dambreuse might yet repent and render them some services.

The young man was agitated when he called on them.

"I should have done better to take my dress-coat with me. No doubt they will give me an invitation to next week's ball. What will they say to me?"

His self-confidence returned when he reflected that M. Dambreuse was only a person of the middle class, and he sprang out of the cab briskly on the pavement of the Rue d'Anjou.

When he had pushed forward one of the two gateways he crossed the courtyard, mounted the steps in front of the house, and entered a vestibule paved with coloured marble. A straight double staircase, with red carpet, fastened with copper rods, rested against the high walls of shining stucco. At the end of the stairs there was a banana-tree, whose wide leaves fell down over the velvet of the baluster. Two bronze candelabra, with porcelain globes, hung from little chains; the atmosphere was heavy with the fumes exhaled by the vent-holes of the hot-air stoves; and all that could be heard was the ticking of a big clock fixed at the other end of the vestibule, under a suit of armour.

A bell rang; a valet made his appearance, and introduced Frederick into a little apartment, where one could observe two strong boxes, with pigeon-holes filled with pieces of pasteboard. In the centre of it, M. Dambreuse was writing at a roll-top desk.

He ran his eye over Père Roque's letter, tore open the canvas in which the papers had been wrapped, and examined them.

At some distance, he presented the appearance of being still young, owing to his slight figure. But his thin white hair, his feeble limbs, and, above all, the extraordinary pallor of his face, betrayed a shattered constitution. There was an expression of pitiless energy in his sea-green eyes, colder than eyes of glass. His cheek-bones projected, and his finger-joints were knotted.

At length, he arose and addressed to the young man a few questions with regard to persons of their acquaintance at Nogent and also with regard to his studies, and then dismissed him with a bow. Frederick went out through another lobby, and found himself at the lower end of the courtyard near the coach-house.

A blue brougham, to which a black horse was yoked, stood in front of the steps before the house. The carriage door flew open, a lady sprang in, and the vehicle, with a rumbling noise, went rolling along the gravel. Frederick had come up to the courtyard gate from the other side at the same moment. As there was not room enough to allow him to pass, he was compelled to wait. The young lady, with her head thrust forward past the carriage blind, talked to the door-keeper in a very low tone. All he could see was her back, covered with a violet mantle. However, he took a glance into the interior of the carriage, lined with blue rep, with silk lace and fringes. The lady's ample robes filled up the space within. He stole away from this little padded box with its perfume of iris, and, so to speak, its vague odour of feminine elegance. The coachman slackened the reins, the horse brushed abruptly past the starting-point, and all disappeared.

Frederick returned on foot, following the track of the boulevard.

He regretted not having been able to get a proper view of Madame Dambreuse. A little higher than the Rue Montmartre, a regular jumble of vehicles made him turn round his head, and on the opposite side, facing him, he read on a marble plate:

"JACQUES ARNOUX."

How was it that he had not thought about her sooner? It was Deslauriers' fault; and he approached the shop, which, however, he did not enter. He was waiting for *her* to appear.

The high, transparent plate-glass windows presented to one's gaze statuettes, drawings, engravings, catalogues and numbers of *L'Art Industriel,* arranged in a skilful fashion; and the amounts of the subscription were repeated on the door, which was decorated in the centre with the publisher's initials. Against the walls could be seen large pictures whose varnish had a shiny look, two chests laden with porcelain, bronze, alluring curiosities; a little staircase separated them, shut off at the top by a Wilton portière; and a lustre of old Saxe, a green carpet on the floor, with a table of marqueterie, gave to this interior the appearance rather of a drawing-room than of a shop.

Frederick pretended to be examining the drawings. After hesitating for a long time, he went in. A clerk lifted the portière, and in reply to a question, said that Monsieur would not be in the shop before five o'clock. But if the message could be conveyed—

"No! I'll come back again," Frederick answered blandly.

The following days were spent in searching for lodgings; and he fixed upon an apartment in a second story of a furnished mansion in the Rue Hyacinthe.

With a fresh blotting-case under his arm, he set forth to attend the opening lecture of the course. Three hundred young men, bare-headed, filled an amphitheatre, where an old man in a red gown was delivering a discourse in a monotonous voice. Quill pens went scratching over the paper. In this hall he found once more the dusty odour of the school, a reading-desk of similar shape, the same wearisome monotony! For a fortnight he regularly continued his attendance at law lectures. But he left off the study of the Civil Code before getting as far as Article 3, and he gave up the Institutes at the *Summa Divisio Personarum.*

The pleasures that he had promised himself did not come to him; and when he had exhausted a circulating library, gone over the collections in the Louvre, and been at the theatre a great many nights in succession, he sank into the lowest depths of idleness.

His depression was increased by a thousand fresh annoyances. He found it necessary to count his linen and to bear with the door keeper, a bore with the figure of a male hospital nurse who came in the morning to make up his bed, smelling of alcohol and grunting. He did not like his apartment, which was ornamented with an alabaster time-piece. The partitions were thin; he could hear the students making punch, laughing and singing.

Tired of this solitude, he sought out one of his old schoolfellows named Baptiste Martinon; and he discovered this friend of his boyhood in a middle-class boarding-house in the Rue Saint-Jacques, cramming up legal procedure before a coal fire. A woman in a print dress sat opposite him darning his socks.

Martinon was what people call a very fine man—big, chubby, with a regular physiognomy, and blue eyes far up in his face. His father, an extensive landowner, had destined him for the magistracy; and wishing already to present a grave exterior, he wore his beard cut like a collar round his neck.

As there was no rational foundation for Frederick's complaints, and as he could not give evidence of any misfortune, Martinon was unable in any way to understand his lamentations about existence. As for him, he went every morning to the school, after that took a walk in the Luxembourg, in the evening swallowed his half-cup of coffee; and with fifteen hundred francs a year, and the love of this workwoman, he felt perfectly happy.

"What happiness!" was Frederick's internal comment.

At the school he had formed another acquaintance, a youth of aristocratic family, who on account of his dainty manners, suggested a resemblance to a young lady.

M. de Cisy devoted himself to drawing, and loved the Gothic style. They frequently went together to admire the Sainte-Chapelle and Nôtre Dame. But the young patrician's rank and pretensions covered an intellect of the feeblest order. Everything took him by surprise. He laughed immoderately at the most trifling joke, and displayed such utter simplicity that Frederick at first took him for a wag, and finally regarded him as a booby.

The young man found it impossible, therefore, to be effusive with anyone; and he was constantly looking forward to an invitation from the Dambreuses.

On New Year's Day, he sent them visiting-cards, but received none in return.

He made his way back to the office of *L'Art Industriel*.

A third time he returned to it, and at last saw Arnoux carrying on an argument with five or six persons around him. He scarcely responded to the young man's bow; and Frederick was wounded by this reception. None the less he cogitated over the best means of finding his way to her side.

His first idea was to come frequently to the shop on the pretext of getting pictures at low prices. Then he conceived the notion of slipping into the letter-box of the journal a few "very strong" articles, which might lead to friendly relations. Perhaps it would be better to go straight to the mark at once, and declare his love? Acting on this impulse, he wrote a letter covering a dozen pages, full of lyric movements and apostrophes; but he tore it up, and did nothing, attempted nothing— bereft of motive power by his want of success.

Above Arnoux's shop, there were, on the first floor, three windows which were lighted up every evening. Shadows might be seen moving about behind them, especially one; this was hers; and he went very far out of his way in order to gaze at these windows and to contemplate this shadow.

A negress who crossed his path one day in the Tuileries, holding a little girl by the hand, recalled to his mind Madame Arnoux's negress. She was sure to come there, like the others; every time he passed through the Tuileries, his heart began to beat with the anticipation of meeting her. On sunny days he continued his walk as far as the end of the Champs-Élysées.

Women seated with careless ease in open carriages, and with their veils floating in the wind, filed past close to him, their horses advancing at a steady walking pace, and with an unconscious see-saw movement that made the varnished leather of the harness crackle. The vehicles became more numerous, and, slackening their motion after they had passed the circular space where the roads met, they took up the entire track. The horses' manes and the carriage lamps were close to each other. The steel stirrups, the silver curbs and the brass rings, flung, here and there, luminous points in the midst of the short breeches, the white gloves, and the furs, falling over the blazonry of the carriage doors. He felt as if he were lost in some far-off world. His eyes wandered along the rows of female heads, and certain vague resemblances brought back Madame Arnoux to his recollection. He pictured her to himself, in the midst of the others, in one of those little broughams like Madame Dambreuse's brougham.

But the sun was setting, and the cold wind raised whirling clouds of dust. The coachmen let their chins sink into their neckcloths; the wheels began to revolve more quickly; the road-metal grated; and all the equipages descended the long sloping avenue at a quick trot, touching, sweeping past one another, getting out of one another's way; then, at the Place de la Concorde, they went off in different directions. Behind the Tuileries, there was a patch of slate-coloured sky. The trees of the garden formed two enormous masses violet-hued at their summits. The gaslamps were lighted; and the Seine, green all over, was torn into strips of silver moire, near the piers of the bridges.

He went to get a dinner for forty-three sous in a restaurant in the Rue de la Harpe. He glanced disdainfully at the old mahogany counter, the soiled napkins, the dingy silver-plate, and the hats hanging up on the wall.

Those around him were students like himself. They talked about their professors, and about their mistresses. Much he cared about professors! Had he a mistress? To avoid being a witness of their enjoyment, he came as late as possible. The tables were all strewn with remnants of food. The two waiters, worn out with attendance on customers, lay asleep, each in a corner of his own; and an odour of cooking, of an argand lamp, and of tobacco, filled the deserted dining-room. Then he slowly toiled up the streets again. The gas lamps vibrated, casting on the mud long yellowish shafts of flickering light. Shadowy forms surmounted by umbrellas glided along the footpaths. The pavement was slippery: the fog grew thicker, and it seemed to him that the moist gloom, wrapping him around, descended into the depths of his heart.

He was smitten with a vague remorse. He renewed his attendance at lectures. But as he was entirely ignorant of the matters which formed the subject of explanation, things of the simplest description puzzled him. He set about writing a novel entitled *Sylvio, the Fisherman's Son*. The scene of the story was Venice. The hero was himself, and Madame Arnoux was the heroine. She was called Antonia; and, to get possession of her, he assassinated a number of noblemen, and burned a portion of the city; after which achievements he sang a serenade under her balcony, where fluttered in the breeze the red damask curtains of the Boulevard Montmartre.

The reminiscences, far too numerous, on which he dwelt produced a disheartening effect on him; he went no further with the work, and his mental vacuity redoubled.

After this, he begged of Deslauriers to come and share his apartment. They might make arrangements to live together with the aid of his allowance of two thousand francs; anything would be better than this intolerable existence. Deslauriers could not yet leave Troyes. He urged his friend to find some means of distracting his thoughts, and, with that end in view, suggested that he should call on Sénécal.

Sénécal was a mathematical tutor, a hard-headed man with republican convictions, a future Saint-Just, according to the clerk. Frederick ascended the five flights, up which he lived, three times in succession, without getting a visit from him in return. He did not go back to the place.

He now went in for amusing himself. He attended the balls at the Opera House. These exhibitions of riotous gaiety froze him the moment he had passed the door. Besides, he was restrained by the fear of being subjected to insult on the subject of money, his notion being that a supper with a domino, entailing considerable expense, was rather a big adventure.

It seemed to him, however, that he must needs love her. Sometimes he used to wake up with his heart full of hope, dressed himself carefully as if he were going to keep an appointment, and started on interminable excursions all over Paris. Whenever a woman was walking in front of him, or coming in his direction, he would say: "Here she is!" Every time it was only a fresh disappointment. The idea of Madame Arnoux strengthened these desires. Perhaps he might find her on his way; and he conjured up dangerous complications, extraordinary perils from which he would save her, in order to get near her.

So the days slipped by with the same tiresome experiences, and enslavement to contracted habits. He turned over the pages of pamphlets under the arcades of the Odéon, went to read the *Revue des Deux Mondes* at the café, entered the hall of the Collége de France, and for an hour stopped to listen to a lecture on Chinese or political economy. Every week he wrote long letters to Deslauriers, dined from time to time with Martinon, and occasionally saw M. de Cisy. He hired a piano and composed German waltzes.

One evening at the theatre of the Palais-Royal, he perceived, in one of the stage-boxes, Arnoux with a woman by his side. Was it she? The screen of green taffeta, pulled over the side of the box, hid her face. At length, the curtain rose, and the screen was drawn aside. She was a tall woman of about thirty, rather faded, and, when she laughed, her thick lips uncovered a row of shining teeth. She chatted familiarly with Arnoux, giving him, from time to time, taps, with her fan, on the fingers. Then a fair-haired young girl with eyelids a little red, as if she had just been weeping, seated herself between them. Arnoux after that remained stooped over her shoulder, pouring forth a stream of talk to which she listened without replying. Frederick taxed his ingenuity to find out the social position of these women, modestly attired in gowns of sober hue with flat, turned-up collars.

At the close of the play, he made a dash for the passages. The crowd of people going out filled them up. Arnoux, just in front of him, was descending the staircase step by step, with a woman on each arm.

Suddenly a gas-burner shed its light on him. He wore a crape hat-band. She was dead, perhaps? This idea tormented Frederick's mind so much, that he hurried, next day, to the office of *L'Art Industriel,* and paying, without a moment's delay, for one of the engravings exposed in the window for sale, he asked the shop-assistant how was Monsieur Arnoux.

The shop-assistant replied:

"Why, quite well!"

Frederick, growing pale, added:

"And Madame?"

"Madame, also."

Frederick forgot to carry off his engraving.

The winter drew to an end. He was less melancholy in the spring time, and began to prepare for his examination. Having passed it indifferently, he started immediately afterwards for Nogent.

He refrained from going to Troyes to see his friend, in order to escape his mother's comments. Then, on his return to Paris at the end of the vacation, he left his lodgings, and took two rooms on the Quai Napoleon which he furnished. He had given up all hope of getting an invitation from the Dambreuses. His great passion for Madame Arnoux was beginning to die out.

Chapter IV

THE INEXPRESSIBLE SHE!

ONE MORNING, IN THE MONTH OF DECEMBER, WHILE GOING TO ATTEND A law lecture, he thought he could observe more than ordinary animation in the Rue Saint-Jacques. The students were rushing precipitately out of the cafés, where, through the open windows, they were calling one another from one house to the other. The shop keepers in the middle of the footpath were looking about them anxiously; the window-shutters were fastened; and when he reached the Rue Soufflot, he perceived a large assemblage around the Panthéon.

Young men in groups numbering from five to a dozen walked along, arm in arm, and accosted the larger groups, which had stationed themselves here and there. At the lower end of the square, near the railings, men in blouses were holding forth, while policemen, with their three-cornered hats drawn over their ears, and their hands behind their backs, were strolling up and down beside the walls making the flags ring under the tread of their heavy boots. All wore a mysterious, wondering look; they were evidently expecting something to happen. Each held back a question which was on the edge of his lips.

Frederick found himself close to a fair-haired young man with a prepossessing face and a moustache and a tuft of beard on his chin, like a dandy of Louis XIII's time. He asked the stranger what was the cause of the disorder.

"I haven't the least idea," replied the other, "nor have they, for that matter! 'Tis their fashion just now! What a good joke!"

And he burst out laughing. The petitions for Reform, which had been signed at the quarters of the National Guard, together with the property-census of Humann and other events besides, had, for the past six months, led to inexplicable gatherings of riotous crowds in Paris, and so frequently had they broken out anew, that the newspapers had ceased to refer to them.

"This lacks graceful outline and colour," continued Frederick's neighbour. "I am convinced, messire, that we have degenerated. In the good epoch of Louis XI, and even in that of Benjamin Constant, there was more mutinousness amongst the students. I find them as pacific as sheep, as stupid as greenhorns, and only fit to be grocers. Gadzooks! And these are what we call the youth of the schools!"

He held his arms wide apart after the fashion of Frederick Lemaître in *Robert Macaire*.

"Youth of the schools, I give you my blessing!"

After this, addressing a rag picker, who was moving a heap of oyster-shells up against the wall of a wine-merchant's house:

"Do you belong to them—the youth of the schools?"

The old man lifted up a hideous countenance in which one could trace, in the midst of a grey beard, a red nose and two dull eyes, bloodshot from drink.

"No, you appear to me rather one of those men with patibulary faces whom we see, in various groups, liberally scattering gold. Oh, scatter it, my patriarch, scatter it! Corrupt me with the treasures of Albion! Are you English? I do not reject the presents of Artaxerxes! Let us have a little chat about the union of customs!"

Frederick felt a hand laid on his shoulder. It was Martinon, looking exceedingly pale.

"Well!" said he with a big sigh, "another riot!"

He was afraid of being compromised, and uttered complaints. Men in blouses especially made him feel uneasy, suggesting a connection with secret societies.

"You mean to say there are secret societies," said the young man with the moustaches. "That is a worn-out dodge of the Government to frighten the middle-class folk!"

Martinon urged him to speak in a lower tone, for fear of the police.

"You believe still in the police, do you? As a matter of fact, how do you know, Monsieur, that I am not myself a police spy?"

And he looked at him in such a way, that Martinon, much discomposed, was, at first, unable to see the joke. The people pushed them on, and they were all three compelled to stand on the little staircase which led, by one of the passages, to the new amphitheatre.

The crowd soon broke up of its own accord. Many heads could be distinguished. They bowed towards the distinguished Professor Samuel Rondelot, who, wrapped in his big frock-coat, with his silver spectacles held up high in the air, and breathing hard from his asthma, was advancing at an easy pace, on his way to deliver his lecture. This man was one of the judicial glories of the nineteenth century, the rival of the Zachariæs and the Ruhdorffs. His new dignity of peer of France had in no way modified his external demeanour. He was known to be poor, and was treated with profound respect.

Meanwhile, at the lower end of the square, some persons cried out:

"Down with Guizot!"

"Down with Pritchard!"

"Down with the sold ones!"

"Down with Louis Philippe!"

The crowd swayed to and fro, and, pressing against the gate of the courtyard, which was shut, prevented the professor from going further. He stopped in front of the staircase. He was speedily observed on the lowest of three steps. He spoke; the loud murmurs of the throng drowned his voice. Although at another time they might love him, they hated him now, for he was the representative of authority. Every time he tried to make himself understood, the outcries recommenced. He gesticulated with great energy to induce the students to follow him. He was answered by vociferations from all sides. He shrugged his shoulders disdainfully, and plunged into the passage. Martinon profited by his situation to disappear at the same moment.

"What a coward!" said Frederick.

"He was prudent," returned the other.

There was an outburst of applause from the crowd, from whose point of view this retreat, on the part of the professor, appeared in the light of a victory. From every window, faces, lighted with curiosity, looked out. Some of those in the crowd struck up the "Marseillaise;" others proposed to go to Béranger's house.

"To Laffitte's house!"

"To Chateaubriand's house!"

"To Voltaire's house!" yelled the young man with the fair moustaches.

The policemen tried to pass around, saying in the mildest tones they could assume:

"Move on, messieurs! Move on! Take yourselves off!"

Somebody exclaimed:

"Down with the slaughterers!"

This was a form of insult usual since the troubles of the month of September. Everyone echoed it. The guardians of public order were hooted and hissed. They began to grow pale. One of them could endure it no longer, and, seeing a low-sized young man approaching too close, laughing in his teeth, pushed him back so roughly, that he tumbled over on his back some five paces away, in front of a wine-merchant's shop. All made way; but almost immediately afterwards the policeman rolled on the ground himself, felled by a blow from a species of Hercules, whose hair hung down like a bundle of tow under an oilskin cap. Having stopped for a few minutes at the corner of the Rue Saint-Jacques, he had very quickly laid down a large case, which he had been carrying, in order to make a spring at the policeman, and, holding down that functionary, punched his face unmercifully. The other policemen rushed to the rescue of their comrade. The terrible shop-assistant was so powerfully built that it took four of them at least to get the better of him. Two of them shook him, while keeping a grip on his collar; two others dragged his arms; a fifth gave him digs of the knee in the ribs; and all of them called him "brigand," "assassin," "rioter." With his breast bare, and his clothes in rags, he protested that he was innocent; he could not, in cold blood, look at a child receiving a beating.

"My name is Dussardier. I'm employed at Messieurs Valincart Brothers' lace
and fancy warehouse, in the Rue de Cléry. Where's my case? I want my case!"

He kept repeating:

"Dussardier, Rue de Cléry. My case!"

However, he became quiet, and, with a stoical air, allowed himself to be led towards the guard-house in the Rue Descartes. A flood of people came rushing after
him. Frederick and the young man with the moustaches walked immediately behind, full of admiration for the shopman, and indignant at the violence of power.

As they advanced, the crowd became less thick.

The policemen from time to time turned round, with threatening looks; and the
rowdies, no longer having anything to do, and the spectators not having anything to
look at, all drifted away by degrees. The passers-by, who met the procession, as they
came along, stared at Dussardier, and in loud tones, gave vent to abusive remarks
about him. One old woman, at her own door, bawled out that he had stolen a loaf
of bread from her. This unjust accusation increased the wrath of the two friends. At
length, they reached the guard-house. Only about twenty persons were now left in
the attenuated crowd, and the sight of the soldiers was enough to disperse them.

Frederick and his companion boldly asked to have the man who had just been
imprisoned delivered up. The sentinel threatened, if they persisted, to ram them
into jail too. They said they required to see the commander of the guard-house,
and stated their names, and the fact that they were law-students, declaring that the
prisoner was one also.

They were ushered into a room perfectly bare, in which, amid an atmosphere
of smoke, four benches might be seen lining the roughly-plastered walls. At the
lower end there was an open wicket. Then appeared the sturdy face of Dussardier,
who, with his hair all tousled, his honest little eyes, and his broad snout, suggested
to one's mind in a confused sort of way the physiognomy of a good dog.

"Don't you recognise us?" said Hussonnet.

This was the name of the young man with the moustaches.

"Why—" stammered Dussardier.

"Don't play the fool any further," returned the other. "We know that you are,
just like ourselves, a law-student."

In spite of their winks, Dussardier failed to understand. He appeared to be collecting his thoughts; then, suddenly:

"Has my case been found?"

Frederick raised his eyes, feeling much discouraged.

Hussonnet, however, said promptly:

"Ha! your case, in which you keep your notes of lectures? Yes, yes, make your
mind easy about it!"

They made further pantomimic signs with redoubled energy, till Dussardier at last realised that they had come to help him; and he held his tongue, fearing that he might compromise them. Besides, he experienced a kind of shamefacedness at seeing himself raised to the social rank of student, and to an equality with those young men who had such white hands.

"Do you wish to send any message to anyone?" asked Frederick.

"No, thanks, to nobody."

"But your family?"

He lowered his head without replying; the poor fellow was a bastard. The two friends stood quite astonished at his silence.

"Have you anything to smoke?" was Frederick's next question.

He felt about, then drew forth from the depths of one of his pockets the remains of a pipe—a beautiful pipe, made of white talc with a shank of blackwood, a silver cover, and an amber mouthpiece.

For the last three years he had been engaged in completing this masterpiece. He had been careful to keep the bowl of it constantly thrust into a kind of sheath of chamois, to smoke it as slowly as possible, without ever letting it lie on any cold stone substance, and to hang it up every evening over the head of his bed. And now he shook out the fragments of it into his hand, the nails of which were covered with blood, and with his chin sunk on his chest, his pupils fixed and dilated, he contemplated this wreck of the thing that had yielded him such delight with a glance of unutterable sadness.

"Suppose we give him some cigars, eh?" said Hussonnet in a whisper, making a gesture as if he were reaching them out.

Frederick had already laid down a cigar-holder, filled, on the edge of the wicket.

"Pray take this. Good-bye! Cheer up!"

Dussardier flung himself on the two hands that were held out towards him. He pressed them frantically, his voice choked with sobs.

"What? For me!—for me!"

The two friends tore themselves away from the effusive display of gratitude which he made, and went off to lunch together at the Café Tabourey, in front of the Luxembourg.

While cutting up the beefsteak, Hussonnet informed his companion that he did work for the fashion journals, and manufactured catchwords for *L'Art Industriel*.

"At Jacques Arnoux's establishment?" said Frederick.

"Do you know him?"

"Yes!—no!—that is to say, I have seen him—I have met him."

He carelessly asked Hussonnet if he sometimes saw Arnoux's wife.

"From time to time," the Bohemian replied.

Frederick did not venture to follow up his enquiries. This man henceforth would fill up a large space in his life. He paid the lunch-bill without any protest on the other's part.

There was a bond of mutual sympathy between them; they gave one another their respective addresses, and Hussonnet cordially invited Frederick to accompany him to the Rue de Fleurus.

They had reached the middle of the garden, when Arnoux's clerk, holding his breath, twisted his features into a hideous grimace, and began to crow like a cock. Thereupon all the cocks in the vicinity responded with prolonged "cock-a-doodle-doos."

"It is a signal," explained Hussonnet.

They stopped close to the Théâtre Bobino, in front of a house to which they had to find their way through an alley. In the skylight of a garret, between the nasturtiums and the sweet peas, a young woman showed herself, bare-headed, in her stays, her two arms resting on the edge of the roof-gutter.

"Good-morrow, my angel! good-morrow, ducky!" said Hussonnet, sending her kisses.

He made the barrier fly open with a kick, and disappeared.

Frederick waited for him all the week. He did not venture to call at Hussonnet's residence, lest it might look as if he were in a hurry to get a lunch in return for the one he had paid for. But he sought the clerk all over the Latin Quarter. He came across him one evening, and brought him to his apartment on the Quai Napoleon.

They had a long chat, and unbosomed themselves to each other. Hussonnet yearned after the glory and the gains of the theatre. He collaborated in the writing of vaudevilles which were not accepted, "had heaps of plans," could turn a couplet; he sang out for Frederick a few of the verses he had composed. Then, noticing on one of the shelves a volume of Hugo and another of Lamartine, he broke out into sarcastic criticisms of the romantic school. These poets had neither good sense nor correctness, and, above all, were not French! He plumed himself on his knowledge of the language, and analysed the most beautiful phrases with that snarling severity, that academic taste which persons of playful disposition exhibit when they are discussing serious art.

Frederick was wounded in his predilections, and he felt a desire to cut the discussion short. Why not take the risk at once of uttering the word on which his happiness depended? He asked this literary youth whether it would be possible to get an introduction into the Arnoux's house through his agency.

The thing was declared to be quite easy, and they fixed upon the following day.

Hussonnet failed to keep the appointment, and on three subsequent occasions he did not turn up. One Saturday, about four o'clock, he made his appearance. But, taking advantage of the cab into which they had got, he drew up in front of the Théâtre Français to get a box-ticket, got down at a tailor's shop, then at a dressmaker's, and wrote notes in the doorkeeper's lodge. At last they came to the Boulevard Montmartre. Frederick passed through the shop, and went up the staircase. Arnoux recognised him through the glass-partition in front of his desk, and while continuing to write he stretched out his hand and laid it on Frederick's shoulder.

Five or six persons, standing up, filled the narrow apartment, which was lighted by a single window looking out on the yard, a sofa of brown damask wool occupying the interior of an alcove between two door-curtains of similar material. Upon the chimney-piece, covered with old papers, there was a bronze Venus. Two candelabra, garnished with rose-coloured wax-tapers, supported it, one at each side. At the right, near a cardboard chest of drawers, a man, seated in an armchair, was reading the newspaper, with his hat on. The walls were hidden from view beneath the array of prints and pictures, precious engravings or sketches by contemporary masters, adorned with dedications testifying the most sincere affection for Jacques Arnoux.

"You're getting on well all this time?" said he, turning round to Frederick.

And, without waiting for an answer, he asked Hussonnet in a low tone:

"What is your friend's name?" Then, raising his voice:

"Take a cigar out of the box on the cardboard stand."

The office of *L'Art Industriel,* situated in a central position in Paris, was a convenient place of resort, a neutral ground wherein rivalries elbowed each other familiarly. On this day might be seen there Anténor Braive, who painted portraits of kings; Jules Burrieu, who by his sketches was beginning to popularise the wars in Algeria; the caricaturist Sombary, the sculptor Vourdat, and others. And not a single one of them corresponded with the student's preconceived ideas. Their manners were simple, their talk free and easy. The mystic Lovarias told an obscene story; and the inventor of Oriental landscape, the famous Dittmer, wore a knitted shirt under his waistcoat, and went home in the omnibus.

The first topic that came on the carpet was the case of a girl named Apollonie, formerly a model, whom Burrieu alleged that he had seen on the boulevard in a carriage. Hussonnet explained this metamorphosis through the succession of persons who had loved her.

"How well this sly dog knows the girls of Paris!" said Arnoux.

"After you, if there are any of them left, sire," replied the Bohemian, with a military salute, in imitation of the grenadier offering his flask to Napoleon.

Then they talked about some pictures in which Apollonie had sat for the female figures. They criticised their absent brethren, expressing astonishment at the sums paid for their works; and they were all complaining of not having been sufficiently remunerated themselves, when the conversation was interrupted by the entrance of a man of middle stature, who had his coat fastened by a single button, and whose eyes glittered with a rather wild expression.

"What a lot of shopkeepers you are!" said he. "God bless my soul! what does that signify? The old masters did not trouble their heads about the million—Correggio, Murillo—"

"Add Pellerin," said Sombary.

But, without taking the slightest notice of the epigram, he went on talking with such vehemence, that Arnoux was forced to repeat twice to him:

"My wife wants you on Thursday. Don't forget!"

This remark recalled Madame Arnoux to Frederick's thoughts. No doubt, one might be able to reach her through the little room near the sofa. Arnoux had just opened the portière leading into it to get a pocket-handkerchief, and Frédéric had seen a wash-stand at the far end of the apartment.

But at this point a kind of muttering sound came from the corner of the chimney-piece; it was caused by the personage who sat in the armchair reading the newspaper. He was a man of five feet nine inches in height, with rather heavy eyelashes, a head of grey hair, and an imposing appearance; and his name was Regimbart.

"What's the matter now, citizen?" said Arnoux.

"Another fresh piece of rascality on the part of Government!"

The thing that he was referring to was the dismissal of a schoolmaster.

Pellerin again took up his parallel between Michael Angelo and Shakespeare. Dittmer was taking himself off when Arnoux pulled him back in order to put two bank notes into his hand. Thereupon Hussonnet said, considering this an opportune time:

"Couldn't you give me an advance, my dear master—?"

But Arnoux had resumed his seat, and was administering a severe reprimand to an old man of mean aspect, who wore a pair of blue spectacles.

"Ha! a nice fellow you are, Père Isaac! Here are three works cried down, destroyed! Everybody is laughing at me! People know what they are now! What do you want me to do with them? I'll have to send them off to California—or to the devil! Hold your tongue!"

The specialty of this old worthy consisted in attaching the signatures of the great masters at the bottom of these pictures. Arnoux refused to pay him, and dismissed him in a brutal fashion. Then, with an entire change of manner, he bowed to a gentleman of affectedly grave demeanour, who wore whiskers and displayed a white tie round his neck and the cross of the Legion of Honour over his breast.

With his elbow resting on the window-fastening, he kept talking to him for a long time in honeyed tones. At last he burst out:

"Ah! well, I am not bothered with brokers, Count."

The nobleman gave way, and Arnoux paid him down twenty-five louis. As soon as he had gone out:

"What a plague these big lords are!"

"A lot of wretches!" muttered Regimbart.

As it grew later, Arnoux was much more busily occupied. He classified articles, tore open letters, set out accounts in a row; at the sound of hammering in the warehouse he went out to look after the packing; then he went back to his ordinary work; and, while he kept his steel pen running over the paper, he indulged in sharp witticisms. He had an invitation to dine with his lawyer that evening, and was starting next day for Belgium.

The others chatted about the topics of the day—Cherubini's portrait, the hemicycle of the Fine Arts, and the next Exhibition. Pellerin railed at the Institute. Scandalous stories and serious discussions got mixed up together. The apartment with its low ceiling was so much stuffed up that one could scarcely move; and the light of the rose-coloured wax-tapers was obscured in the smoke of their cigars, like the sun's rays in a fog.

The door near the sofa flew open, and a tall, thin woman entered with abrupt movements, which made all the trinkets of her watch rattle under her black taffeta gown.

It was the woman of whom Frederick had caught a glimpse last summer at the Palais-Royal. Some of those present, addressing her by name, shook hands with her. Hussonnet had at last managed to extract from his employer the sum of fifty francs. The clock struck seven.

All rose to go.

Arnoux told Pellerin to remain, and accompanied Mademoiselle Vatnaz into the dressing-room.

Frederick could not hear what they said; they spoke in whispers. However, the woman's voice was raised:

"I have been waiting ever since the job was done, six months ago."

There was a long silence, and then Mademoiselle Vatnaz reappeared. Arnoux had again promised her something.

"Oh! oh! later, we shall see!"

"Good-bye! happy man," said she, as she was going out.

Arnoux quickly re-entered the dressing-room, rubbed some cosmetic over his moustaches, raised his braces, stretched his straps; and, while he was washing his hands:

"I would require two over the door at two hundred and fifty apiece, in Boucher's style. Is that understood?"

"Be it so," said the artist, his face reddening.

"Good! and don't forget my wife!"

Frederick accompanied Pellerin to the top of the Faubourg Poissonnière, and asked his permission to come to see him sometimes, a favour which was graciously accorded.

Pellerin read every work on aesthetics, in order to find out the true theory of the Beautiful, convinced that, when he had discovered it, he would produce masterpieces. He surrounded himself with every imaginable auxiliary—drawings, plaster-casts, models, engravings; and he kept searching about, eating his heart out. He blamed the weather, his nerves, his studio, went out into the street to find inspiration there, quivered with delight at the thought that he had caught it, then abandoned the work in which he was engaged, and dreamed of another which should be finer. Thus, tormented by the desire for glory, and wasting his days in discussions, believing in a thousand fooleries—in systems, in criticisms, in the importance of a regulation or a reform in the domain of Art—he had at fifty as yet turned out nothing save mere sketches. His robust pride prevented him from experiencing any discouragement, but he was always irritated, and in that state of exaltation, at the same time factitious and natural, which is characteristic of comedians.

On entering his studio one's attention was directed towards two large pictures, in which the first tones of colour laid on here and there made on the while canvas spots of brown, red, and blue. A network of lines in chalk stretched overhead, like stitches of thread repeated twenty times; it was impossible to understand what it meant. Pellerin explained the subject of these two compositions by pointing out with his thumb the portions that were lacking. The first was intended to represent "The Madness of Nebuchadnezzar," and the second "The Burning of Rome by Nero." Frederick admired them.

He admired academies of women with dishevelled hair, landscapes in which trunks of trees, twisted by the storm, abounded, and above all freaks of the pen, imitations from memory of Callot, Rembrandt, or Goya, of which he did not know the models. Pellerin no longer set any value on these works of his youth. He was now all in favour of the grand style; he dogmatised eloquently about Phidias and Winckelmann. The objects around him strengthened the force of his language; one saw a death's head on a prie-dieu, yataghans, a monk's habit. Frederick put it on.

When he arrived early, he surprised the artist in his wretched folding-bed, which was hidden from view by a strip of tapestry; for Pellerin went to bed late, being an assiduous frequenter of the theatres. An old woman in tatters attended on him. He dined at a cook-shop, and lived without a mistress. His acquirements, picked up in the most irregular fashion, rendered his paradoxes amusing. His hatred of the vulgar and the "bourgeois" overflowed in sarcasms, marked by a superb lyricism, and he had such religious reverence for the masters that it raised him almost to their level.

But why had he never spoken about Madame Arnoux? As for her son, at one time he called Pellerin a decent fellow, at other times a charlatan. Frederick was waiting for some disclosures on his part.

One day, while turning over one of the portfolios in the studio, he thought he could trace in the portrait of a female Bohemian some resemblance to Mademoiselle Vatnaz; and, as he felt interested in this lady, he desired to know what was her exact social position.

She had been, as far as Pellerin could ascertain, originally a schoolmistress in the provinces. She now gave lessons in Paris, and tried to write for the small journals.

According to Frederick, one would imagine from her manners with Arnoux that she was his mistress.

"Pshaw! he has others!"

Then, turning away his face, which reddened with shame as he realised the baseness of the suggestion, the young man added, with a swaggering air:

"Very likely his wife pays him back for it?"

"Not at all; she is virtuous."

Frederick again experienced a feeling of compunction, and the result was that his attendance at the office of the art journal became more marked than before.

The big letters which formed the name of Arnoux on the marble plate above the shop seemed to him quite peculiar and pregnant with significance, like some sacred writing. The wide footpath, by its descent, facilitated his approach; the door almost turned of its own accord; and the handle, smooth to the touch, gave him the sensation of friendly and, as it were, intelligent fingers clasping his. Unconsciously, he became quite as punctual as Regimbart.

Every day Regimbart seated himself in the chimney corner, in his armchair, got hold of the *National,* and kept possession of it, expressing his thoughts by exclamations or by shrugs of the shoulders. From time to time he would wipe his forehead with his pocket-handkerchief, rolled up in a ball, which he usually stuck in between two buttons of his green frock-coat. He had trousers with wrinkles, bluchers, and a long cravat; and his hat, with its turned-up brim, made him easily recognised, at a distance, in a crowd.

At eight o'clock in the morning he descended the heights of Montmartre, in order to imbibe white wine in the Rue Nôtre Dame des Victoires. A late breakfast, following several games of billiards, brought him on to three o'clock. He then directed his steps towards the Passage des Panoramas, where he had a glass of absinthe. After the sitting in Arnoux's shop, he entered the Bordelais smoking-divan, where he swallowed some bitters; then, in place of returning home to his wife, he preferred to dine alone in a little café in the Rue Gaillon, where he desired them to serve up to him "household dishes, natural things." Finally, he made his way to another billiard-room, and remained there till midnight, in fact, till one o'clock in the morning, up till the last moment, when, the gas being put out and the window-shutters fastened, the master of the establishment, worn out, begged of him to go.

And it was not the love of drinking that attracted Citizen Regimbart to these places, but the inveterate habit of talking politics at such resorts. With advancing age, he had lost his vivacity, and now exhibited only a silent moroseness. One would have said, judging from the gravity of his countenence, that he was turning over in his mind the affairs of the whole world. Nothing, however, came from it; and nobody, even amongst his own friends, knew him to have any occupation, although he gave himself out as being up to his eyes in business.

Arnoux appeared to have a very great esteem for him. One day he said to Frederick:

"He knows a lot, I assure you. He is an able man."

On another occasion Regimbart spread over his desk papers relating to the kaolin mines in Brittany. Arnoux referred to his own experience on the subject.

Frederick showed himself more ceremonious towards Regimbart, going so far as to invite him from time to time to take a glass of absinthe; and, although he considered him a stupid man, he often remained a full hour in his company solely because he was Jacques Arnoux's friend.

After pushing forward some contemporary masters in the early portions of their career, the picture-dealer, a man of progressive ideas, had tried, while clinging to his artistic ways, to extend his pecuniary profits. His object was to emancipate the fine arts, to get the sublime at a cheap rate. Over every industry associated with Parisian luxury he exercised an influence which proved fortunate with respect to little things, but fatal with respect to great things. With his mania for pandering to public opinion, he made clever artists swerve from their true path, corrupted the strong, exhausted the weak, and got distinction for those of mediocre talent; he set them up with the assistance of his connections and of his magazine. Tyros in painting were ambitious of seeing their works in his shop-window, and upholsterers brought specimens of furniture to his house. Frederick regarded him, at the same time, as a millionaire, as a *dilettante*, and as a man of action. However, he found

many things that filled him with astonishment, for my lord Arnoux was rather sly
in his commercial transactions.

He received from the very heart of Germany or of Italy a picture purchased in
Paris for fifteen hundred francs, and, exhibiting an invoice that brought the price
up to four thousand, sold it over again through complaisance for three thousand
live hundred. One of his usual tricks with painters was to exact as a drink-
allowance an abatement in the purchase-money of their pictures, under the pretence that he would bring out an engraving of it. He always, when selling such
pictures, made a profit by the abatement; but the engraving never appeared. To
those who complained that he had taken an advantage of them, he would reply by
a slap on the stomach. Generous in other ways, he squandered money on cigars for
his acquaintances, "thee'd" and "thou'd" persons who were unknown, displayed
enthusiasm about a work or a man; and, after that, sticking to his opinion, and, regardless of consequences, spared no expense in journeys, correspondence, and ad-
vertising. He looked upon himself as very upright, and, yielding to an irresistible
impulse to unbosom himself, ingenuously told his friends about certain indelicate
acts of which he had been guilty. Once, in order to annoy a member of his own
trade who inaugurated another art journal with a big banquet, he asked Frederick
to write, under his own eyes, a little before the hour fixed for the entertainment,
letters to the guests recalling the invitations.

"This impugns nobody's honour, do you understand?"

And the young man did not dare to refuse the service.

Next day, on entering with Hussonnet M. Arnoux's office, Frederick saw
through the door (the one opening on the staircase) the hem of a lady's dress disappearing.

"A thousand pardons!" said Hussonnet. "If I had known that there were
women—"

"Oh! as for that one, she is my own," replied Arnoux. "She just came in to pay
me a visit as she was passing."

"You don't say so!" said Frederick.

"Why, yes; she is going back home again."

The charm of the things around him was suddenly withdrawn. That which had
seemed to him to be diffused vaguely through the place had now vanished—or,
rather, it had never been there. He experienced an infinite amazement, and, as it
were, the painful sensation of having been betrayed.

Arnoux, while rummaging about in his drawer, began to smile. Was he laughing at him? The clerk laid down a bundle of moist papers on the table.

"Ha! the placards," exclaimed the picture-dealer. "I am not ready to dine this
evening."

Regimbart took up his hat.

"What, are you leaving me?"

"Seven o'clock," said Regimbart.

Frederick followed him.

At the corner of the Rue Montmartre, he turned round. He glanced towards the windows of the first floor, and he laughed internally with self-pity as he recalled to mind with what love he had so often contemplated them. Where, then, did she reside? How was he to meet her now? Once more around the object of his desire a solitude opened more immense than ever!

"Are you coming to take it?" asked Regimbart.

"To take what?"

"The absinthe."

And, yielding to his importunities, Frederick allowed himself to be led towards the Bordelais smoking-divan. Whilst his companion, leaning on his elbow, was staring at the decanter, he was turning his eyes to the right and to the left. But he caught a glimpse of Pellerin's profile on the footpath outside; the painter gave a quick tap at the window-pane, and he had scarcely sat down when Regimbart asked him why they no longer saw him at the office of *L'Art Industriel*.

"May I perish before ever I go back there again. The fellow is a brute, a mere tradesman, a wretch, a downright rogue!"

These insulting words harmonised with Frederick's present angry mood. Nevertheless, he was wounded, for it seemed to him that they hit at Madame Arnoux more or less.

"Why, what has he done to you?" said Regimbart.

Pellerin stamped with his foot on the ground, and his only response was an energetic puff.

He had been devoting himself to artistic work of a kind that he did not care to connect his name with, such as portraits for two crayons, or pasticcios from the great masters for amateurs of limited knowledge; and, as he felt humiliated by these inferior productions, he preferred to hold his tongue on the subject as a general rule. But "Arnoux's dirty conduct" exasperated him too much. He had to relieve his feelings.

In accordance with an order, which had been given in Frederick's very presence, he had brought Arnoux two pictures. Thereupon the dealer took the liberty of criticising them. He found fault with the composition, the colouring, and the drawing—above all the drawing; he would not, in short, take them at any price. But, driven to extremities by a bill falling due, Pellerin had to give them to the Jew Isaac; and, a fortnight later, Arnoux himself sold them to a Spaniard for two thousand francs.

"Not a sou less! What rascality! and, faith, he has done many other things just as bad. One of these mornings we'll see him in the dock!"

"How you exaggerate!" said Frederick, in a timid voice.

"Come, now, that's good; I exaggerate!" exclaimed the artist, giving the table a great blow with his fist.

This violence had the effect of completely restoring the young man's self-command. No doubt he might have acted more nicely; still, if Arnoux found these two pictures—

"Bad! say it out! Are you a judge of them? Is this your profession? Now, you know, my youngster, I don't allow this sort of thing on the part of mere amateurs."

"Ah! well, it's not my business," said Frederick.

"Then, what interest have you in defending him?" returned Pellerin, coldly.

The young man faltered:

"But—since I am his friend—"

"Go, and give him a hug for me. Good evening!"

And the painter rushed away in a rage, and, of course, without paying for his drink.

Frederick, whilst defending Arnoux, had convinced himself. In the heat of his eloquence, he was filled with tenderness towards this man, so intelligent and kind, whom his friends calumniated, and who had now to work all alone, abandoned by them. He could not resist a strange impulse to go at once and see him again. Ten minutes afterwards he pushed open the door of the picture-warehouse.

Arnoux was preparing, with the assistance of his clerks, some huge placards for an exhibition of pictures.

"Halloa! what brings you back again?"

This question, simple though it was, embarrassed Frederick, and, at a loss for an answer, he asked whether they had happened to find a notebook of his—a little notebook with a blue leather cover.

"The one that you put your letters to women in?" said Arnoux.

Frederic, blushing like a young girl, protested against such an assumption.

"Your verses, then?" returned the picture-dealer.

He handled the pictorial specimens that were to be exhibited, discovering their form, colouring, and frames; and Frederick felt more and more irritated by his air of abstraction, and particularly by the appearance of his hands—large hands, rather soft, with flat nails. At length, M. Arnoux arose, and saying, "That's disposed of!" he chucked the young man familiarly under the chin. Frederick was offended at this liberty, and recoiled a pace or two; then he made a dash for the shop-door, and passed out through it, as he imagined, for the last time in his life. Madame Arnoux herself had been lowered by the vulgarity of her husband.

During the same week he got a letter from Deslauriers, informing him that the clerk would be in Paris on the following Thursday. Then he flung himself back violently on this affection as one of a more solid and lofty character. A man of this sort was worth all the women in the world. He would no longer have any need of Regimbart, of Pellerin, of Hussonnet, of anyone! In order to provide his friend with as comfortable lodgings as possible, he bought an iron bedstead and a second armchair, and stripped off some of his own bed-covering to garnish this one properly. On Thursday morning he was dressing himself to go to meet Deslauriers when there was a ring at the door.

Arnoux entered.

"Just one word. Yesterday I got a lovely trout from Geneva. We expect you by-and-by—at seven o'clock sharp. The address is the Rue de Choiseul 24 *bis*. Don't forget!"

Frederick was obliged to sit down; his knees were tottering under him. He repeated to himself, "At last! at last!" Then he wrote to his tailor, to his hatter, and to his bootmaker; and he despatched these three notes by three different messengers.

The key turned in the lock, and the door-keeper appeared with a trunk on his shoulder.

Frederick, on seeing Deslauriers, began to tremble like an adulteress under the glance of her husband.

"What has happened to you?" said Deslauriers. "Surely you got my letter?"

Frederick had not enough energy left to lie. He opened his arms, and flung himself on his friend's breast.

Then the clerk told his story. His father thought to avoid giving an account of the expense of tutelage, fancying that the period limited for rendering such accounts was ten years; but, well up in legal procedure, Deslauriers had managed to get the share coming to him from his mother into his clutches—seven thousand francs clear—which he had there with him in an old pocket-book.

" 'Tis a reserve fund, in case of misfortune. I must think over the best way of investing it, and find quarters for myself to-morrow morning. To-day I'm perfectly free, and am entirely at your service, my old friend."

"Oh! don't put yourself about," said Frederick. "If you had anything of importance to do this evening—"

"Come, now! I would be a selfish wretch—"

This epithet, flung out at random, touched Frederick to the quick, like a reproachful hint.

The door-keeper had placed on the table close to the fire some chops, cold meat, a large lobster, some sweets for dessert, and two bottles of Bordeaux.

Deslauriers was touched by these excellent preparations to welcome his arrival.

"Upon my word, you are treating me like a king!"

They talked about their past and about the future; and, from time to time, they grasped each other's hands across the table, gazing at each other tenderly for a moment.

But a messenger came with a new hat. Deslauriers, in a loud tone, remarked that this head-gear was very showy. Next came the tailor himself to fit on the coat, to which he had given a touch with the smoothing-iron.

"One would imagine you were going to be married," said Deslauriers.

An hour later, a third individual appeared on the scene, and drew forth from a big black bag a pair of shining patent leather boots. While Frederick was trying them on, the bootmaker slyly drew attention to the shoes of the young man from the country.

"Does Monsieur require anything?"

"Thanks," replied the clerk, pulling behind his chair his old shoes fastened with strings.

This humiliating incident annoyed Frederick. At length he exclaimed, as if an idea had suddenly taken possession of him:

"Ha! deuce take it! I was forgetting."

"What is it, pray?"

"I have to dine in the city this evening."

"At the Dambreuses'? Why did you never say anything to me about them in your letters?"

"It is not at the Dambreuses', but at the Arnoux's."

"You should have let me know beforehand," said Deslauriers. "I would have come a day later."

"Impossible," returned Frederick, abruptly. "I only got the invitation this morning, a little while ago."

And to redeem his error and distract his friend's mind from the occurrence, he proceeded to unfasten the tangled cords round the trunk, and to arrange all his belongings in the chest of drawers, expressed his willingness to give him his own bed, and offered to sleep himself in the dressing-room bedstead. Then, as soon as it was four o'clock, he began the preparations for his toilet.

"You have plenty of time," said the other.

At last he was dressed and off he went.

"That's the way with the rich," thought Deslauriers.

And he went to dine in the Rue Saint-Jacques, at a little restaurant kept by a man he knew.

Frederick stopped several times while going up the stairs, so violently did his heart beat. One of his gloves, which was too tight, burst, and, while he was fastening back the torn part under his shirt-cuff, Arnoux, who was mounting the stairs behind him, took his arm and led him in.

The anteroom, decorated in the Chinese fashion, had a painted lantern hanging from the ceiling, and bamboos in the corners. As he was passing into the drawing-room, Frederick stumbled against a tiger's skin. The place had not yet been lighted up, but two lamps were burning in the boudoir in the far corner.

Mademoiselle Marthe came to announce that her mamma was dressing. Arnoux raised her as high as his mouth in order to kiss her; then, as he wished to go to the cellar himself to select certain bottles of wine, he left Frederick with the little girl.

She had grown much larger since the trip in the steamboat. Her dark hair descended in long ringlets, which curled over her bare arms. Her dress, more puffed out than the petticoat of a *danseuse,* allowed her rosy calves to be seen, and her pretty childlike form had all the fresh odour of a bunch of flowers. She received the young gentleman's compliments with a coquettish air, fixed on him her large, dreamy eyes, then slipping on the carpet amid the furniture, disappeared like a cat.

After this he no longer felt ill at ease. The globes of the lamps, covered with a paper lace-work, sent forth a white light, softening the colour of the walls, hung with mauve satin. Through the fender-bars, as through the slits in a big fan, the coal could be seen in the fireplace, and close beside the clock there was a little chest with silver clasps. Here and there things lay about which gave the place a look of home—a doll in the middle of the sofa, a fichu against the back of a chair, and on the work-table a knitted woollen vest, from which two ivory needles were hanging with their points downwards. It was altogether a peaceful spot, suggesting the idea of propriety and innocent family life.

Arnoux returned, and Madame Arnoux appeared at the other doorway. As she was enveloped in shadow, the young man could at first distinguish only her head. She wore a black velvet gown, and in her hair she had fastened a long Algerian cap, in a red silk net, which coiling round her comb, fell over her left shoulder.

Arnoux introduced Frederick.

"Oh! I remember Monsieur perfectly well," she responded.

Then the guests arrived, nearly all at the same time—Dittmer, Lovarias, Burrieu, the composer Rosenwald, the poet Théophile Lorris, two art critics, colleagues of Hussonnet, a paper manufacturer, and in the rear the illustrious Pierre Paul Meinsius, the last representative of the grand school of painting, who blithely carried along with his glory his forty-five years and his big paunch.

When they were passing into the dining-room, Madame Arnoux took his arm. A chair had been left vacant for Pellerin. Arnoux, though he took advantage of him, was fond of him. Besides, he was afraid of his terrible tongue, so much so, that, in order to soften him, he had given a portrait of him in *L'Art Industriel,* accompanied by exaggerated eulogies; and Pellerin, more sensitive about distinction than about money, made his appearance about eight o'clock quite out of breath. Frederick fancied that they had been a long time reconciled.

He liked the company, the dishes, everything. The dining-room, which resembled a mediæval parlour, was hung with stamped leather. A Dutch whatnot faced a rack for chibouks, and around the table the Bohemian glasses, variously coloured, had, in the midst of the flowers and fruits, the effect of an illumination in a garden.

He had to make his choice between ten sorts of mustard. He partook of daspachio, of curry, of ginger, of Corsican blackbirds, and a species of Roman macaroni called lasagna; he drank extraordinary wines, lip-fraeli and tokay. Arnoux indeed prided himself on entertaining people in good style. With an eye to the procurement of eatables, he paid court to mail-coach drivers, and was in league with the cooks of great houses, who communicated to him the secrets of rare sauces.

But Frederick was particularly amused by the conversation. His taste for travelling was tickled by Dittmer, who talked about the East; he gratified his curiosity about theatrical matters by listening to Rosenwald's chat about the opera; and the atrocious existence of Bohemia assumed for him a droll aspect when seen through the gaiety of Hussonnet, who related, in a picturesque fashion, how he had spent an entire winter with no food except Dutch cheese. Then, a discussion between Lovarias and Burrieu about the Florentine School gave him new ideas with regard to masterpieces, widened his horizon, and he found difficulty in restraining his enthusiasm when Pellerin exclaimed:

"Don't bother me with your hideous reality! What does it mean—reality? Some see things black, others blue—the multitude sees them brute-fashion. There is nothing less natural than Michael Angelo; there is nothing more powerful! The anxiety about external truth is a mark of contemporary baseness; and art will become, if things go on that way, a sort of poor joke as much below religion as it is below poetry, and as much below politics as it is below business. You will never reach its end—yes, its end!—which is to cause within us an impersonal exaltation, with petty works, in spite of all your finished execution. Look, for instance, at Bassolier's pictures: they are pretty, coquettish, spruce, and by no means dull. You might put them into your pocket, bring them with you when you are travelling. Notaries buy them for twenty thousand francs, while pictures of the ideal type are sold for three sous. But, without ideality, there is no grandeur; without grandeur there is no beauty. Olympus is a mountain. The most swagger monument will always be the Pyramids. Exuberance is better than taste; the desert is better than a street-pavement, and a savage is better than a hairdresser!"

Frederick, as these words fell upon his ear, glanced towards Madame Arnoux.

They sank into his soul like metals falling, into a furnace, added to his passion, and supplied the material of love.

His chair was three seats below hers on the same side. From time to time, she bent forward a little, turning aside her head to address a few words to her little daughter; and as she smiled on these occasions, a dimple took shape in her cheek, giving to her lace an expression of more dainty good-nature.

As soon as the time came for the gentlemen to take their wine, she disappeared. The conversation became more free and easy. M. Arnoux shone in it, and Frederick was astonished at the cynicism of men. However, their preoccupation with woman established between them and him, as it were, an equality, which raised him in his own estimation.

When they had returned to the drawing-room, he took up, to keep himself in countenance, one of the albums which lay about on the table. The great artists of the day had illustrated them with drawings, had written in them snatches of verse or prose, or their signatures simply. In the midst of famous names he found many that he had never heard of before, and original thoughts appeared only underneath a flood of nonsense. All these effusions contained a more or less direct expression of homage towards Madame Arnoux. Frederick would have been afraid to write a line beside them.

She went into her boudoir to look at the little chest with silver clasps which he had noticed on the mantelshelf. It was a present from her husband, a work of the Renaissance. Arnoux's friends complimented him, and his wife thanked him. His tender emotions were aroused, and before all the guests he gave her a kiss.

After this they all chatted in groups here and there. The worthy Meinsius was with Madame Arnoux on an easy chair close beside the fire. She was leaning forward towards his ear; their heads were just touching, and Frederick would have been glad to become deaf, infirm, and ugly if, instead, he had an illustrious name and white hair—in short, if he only happened to possess something which would install him in such intimate association with her. He began once more to eat out his heart, furious at the idea of being so young a man.

But she came into the corner of the drawing-room in which he was sitting, asked him whether he was acquainted with any of the guests, whether he was fond of painting, how long he had been a student in Paris. Every word that came out of her mouth seemed to Frederick something entirely new, an exclusive appendage of her personality. He gazed attentively at the fringes of her head-dress, the ends of which caressed her bare shoulder, and he was unable to take away his eyes; he plunged his soul into the whiteness of that feminine flesh, and yet he did not venture to raise his eyelids to glance at her higher, face to face.

Rosenwald interrupted them, begging of Madame Arnoux to sing something.

He played a prelude, she waited, her lips opened slightly, and a sound, pure, long-continued, silvery, ascended into the air.

Frederick did not understand a single one of the Italian words. The song began with a grave measure, something like church music, then in a more animated strain, with a crescendo movement, it broke into repeated bursts of sound, then suddenly subsided, and the melody came back again in a tender fashion with a wide and easy swing.

She stood beside the keyboard with her arms hanging down and a far-off look on her face. Sometimes, in order to read the music, she advanced her forehead for a moment and her eyelashes moved to and fro. Her contralto voice in the low notes took a mournful intonation which had a chilling effect on the listener, and then her beautiful head, with those great brows of hers, bent over her shoulder; her bosom swelled; her eyes were wide apart; her neck, from which roulades made their escape, fell back as if under aerial kisses. She flung out three sharp notes, came down again, cast forth one higher still, and, after a silence, finished with an organ-point.

Rosenwald did not leave the piano. He continued playing, to amuse himself. From time to time a guest stole away. At eleven o'clock, as the last of them were going off, Arnoux went out along with Pellerin, under the pretext of seeing him home. He was one of those people who say that they are ill when they do not "take a turn" after dinner. Madame Arnoux had made her way towards the anteroom. Dittmer and Hussonnet bowed to her. She stretched out her hand to them. She did the same to Frederick; and he felt, as it were, something penetrating every particle of his skin.

He quitted his friends. He wished to be alone. His heart was overflowing. Why had she offered him her hand? Was it a thoughtless act, or an encouragement? "Come now! I am mad!" Besides, what did it matter, when he could now visit her entirely at his ease, live in the very atmosphere she breathed?

The streets were deserted. Now and then a heavy wagon would roll past, shaking the pavements. The houses came one after another with their grey fronts, their closed windows; and he thought with disdain of all those human beings who lived behind those walls without having seen her, and not one of whom dreamed of her existence. He had no consciousness of his surroundings, of space, of anything, and striking the ground with his heel, rapping with his walking-stick on the shutters of the shops, he kept walking on continually at random, in a state of excitement, carried away by his emotions. Suddenly he felt himself surrounded by a circle of damp air, and found that he was on the edge of the quays.

The gas-lamps shone in two straight lines, which ran on endlessly, and long red flames flickered in the depths of the water. The waves were slate-coloured, while the sky, which was of clearer hue, seemed to be supported by vast masses of shadow that rose on each side of the river. The darkness was intensified by buildings whose outlines the eye could not distinguish. A luminous haze floated above the roofs further on. All the noises of the night had melted into a single monotonous hum.

He stopped in the middle of the Pont Neuf, and, taking off his hat and exposing his chest, he drank in the air. And now he felt as if something that was inexhaustible were rising up from the very depths of his being, an afflux of tenderness that enervated him, like the motion of the waves under his eyes. A church-clock slowly struck one, like a voice calling out to him.

Then, he was seized with one of those shuddering sensations of the soul in which one seems to be transported into a higher world. He felt, as it were, endowed with some extraordinary faculty, the aim of which he could not determine. He seriously asked himself whether he would be a great painter or a great poet; and he decided in favour of painting, for the exigencies of this profession would bring him into contact with Madame Arnoux. So, then, he had found his vocation! The object of his existence was now perfectly clear, and there could be no mistake about the future.

When he had shut his door, he heard some one snoring in the dark closet near his apartment. It was his friend. He no longer bestowed a thought on him.

His own face presented itself to his view in the glass. He thought himself handsome, and for a minute he remained gazing at himself.

Chapter V

"Love Knoweth No Laws"

BEFORE TWELVE O'CLOCK NEXT DAY HE HAD BOUGHT A BOX OF COLOURS, paintbrushes, and an easel. Pellerin consented to give him lessons, and Frederick brought him to his lodgings to see whether anything was wanting among his painting utensils.

Deslauriers had come back, and the second armchair was occupied by a young man. The clerk said, pointing towards him:

" 'Tis he! There he is! Sénécal!" Frederick disliked this young man. His forehead was heightened by the way in which he wore his hair, cut straight like a brush. There was a certain hard, cold look in his grey eyes; and his long black coat, his entire costume, savoured of the pedagogue and the ecclesiastic.

They first discussed topics of the hour, amongst others the *Stabat* of Rossini. Sénécal, in answer to a question, declared that he never went to the theatre.

Pellerin opened the box of colours.

"Are these all for you?" said the clerk.

"Why, certainly!"

"Well, really! What a notion!" And he leaned across the table, at which the mathematical tutor was turning over the leaves of a volume of Louis Blanc. He had brought it with him, and was reading passages from it in low tones, while Pellerin and Frederick were examining together the palette, the knife, and the bladders; then the talk came round to the dinner at Arnoux's.

"The picture-dealer, is it?" asked Sénécal. "A nice gentleman, truly!"

"Why, now?" said Pellerin. Sénécal replied:

"A man who makes money by political turpitude!"

And he went on to talk about a well-known lithograph, in which the Royal Family was all represented as being engaged in edifying occupations: Louis Philippe had a copy of the Code in his hand; the Queen had a Catholic prayer-book; the Princesses were embroidering; the Duc de Nemours was girding on a sword; M. de Joinville was showing a map to his young brothers; and at the end of the apartment could be seen a bed with two divisions. This picture, which was entitled "A Good Family," was a source of delight to commonplace middle-class people, but of grief to patriots.

Pellerin, in a tone of vexation, as if he had been the producer of this work himself, observed by way of answer that every opinion had some value. Sénécal protested: Art should aim exclusively at promoting morality amongst the masses! The only subjects that ought to be reproduced were those which impelled people to virtuous actions; all others were injurious.

"But that depends on the execution," cried Pellerin. "I might produce masterpieces."

"So much the worse for you, then; you have no right——"

"What?"

"No, monsieur, you have no right to excite my interest in matters of which I disapprove. What need have we of laborious trifles, from which it is impossible to derive any benefit—those Venuses, for instance, with all your landscapes? I see there no instruction for the people! Show us rather their miseries! arouse enthusiasm in us for their sacrifices! Ah, my God! there is no lack of subjects—the farm, the workshop——"

Pellerin stammered forth his indignation at this, and, imagining that he had found an argument:

"Molière, do you accept him?"

"Certainly!" said Sénécal. "I admire him as the precursor of the French Revolution."

"Ha! the Revolution! What art! Never was there a more pitiable epoch!"

"None greater, Monsieur!"

Pellerin folded his arms, and looking at him straight in the face:

"You have the appearance of a famous member of the National Guard!"

His opponent, accustomed to discussions, responded:

"I am not, and I detest it just as much as you. But with such principles we corrupt the crowd. This sort of thing, however, is profitable to the Government. It would not be so powerful but for the complicity of a lot of rogues of that sort."

The painter took up the defence of the picture-dealer, for Sénécal's opinions exasperated him. He even went so far as to maintain that Arnoux was really a man with a heart of gold, devoted to his friends, deeply attached to his wife.

"Oho! if you offered him a good sum, he would not refuse to let her serve as a model."

Frederick turned pale.

"So then, he has done you some great injury, Monsieur?"

"Me? no! I saw him once at a café with a friend. That's all."

Sénécal had spoken truly. But he had his teeth daily set on edge by the announcements in *L'Art Industriel*. Arnoux was for him the representative of a world which he considered fatal to democracy. An austere Republican, he suspected that there was something corrupt in every form of elegance, and the more so as he wanted nothing and was inflexible in his integrity.

They found some difficulty in resuming the conversation. The painter soon recalled to mind his appointment, the tutor his pupils; and, when they had gone, after a long silence, Deslauriers asked a number of questions about Arnoux.

"You will introduce me there later, will you not, old fellow?"

"Certainly," said Frederick. Then they thought about settling themselves. Deslauriers had without much trouble obtained the post of second clerk in a solicitor's office; he had also entered his name for the terms at the Law School, and bought the indispensable books; and the life of which they had dreamed now began.

It was delightful, owing to their youth, which made everything assume a beautiful aspect. As Deslauriers had said nothing as to any pecuniary arrangement, Frederick did not refer to the subject. He helped to defray all the expenses, kept the cupboard well stocked, and looked after all the household requirements; but if it happened to be desirable to give the doorkeeper a rating, the clerk took that on his own shoulders, still playing the part, which he had assumed in their college days, of protector and senior.

Separated all day long, they met again in the evening. Each took his place at the fireside and set about his work. But ere long it would be interrupted. Then would follow endless outpourings, unaccountable bursts of merriment, and occasional disputes about the lamp flaring too much or a book being mislaid, momentary ebullitions of anger which subsided in hearty laughter.

While in bed they left open the door of the little room where Deslauriers slept, and kept chattering to each other from a distance.

In the morning they walked in their shirt-sleeves on the terrace. The sun rose; light vapours passed over the river. From the flower-market close beside them the noise of screaming reached their ears; and the smoke from their pipes whirled round in the clear air, which was refreshing to their eyes still puffed from sleep. While they inhaled it, their hearts swelled with great expectations.

When it was not raining on Sunday they went out together, and, arm in arm, they sauntered through the streets. The same reflection nearly always occurred to them at the same time, or else they would go on chatting without noticing anything around them. Deslauriers longed for riches, as a means for gaining power over men. He was anxious to possess an influence over a vast number of people, to make a great noise, to have three secretaries under his command, and to give a big political dinner once a month.

Frederick would have furnished for himself a palace in the Moorish fashion, to spend his life reclining on cashmere divans, to the murmur of a jet of water, attended by negro pages. And these things, of which he had only dreamed, became in the end so definite that they made him feel as dejected as if he had lost them.

"What is the use of talking about all these things," said he, "when we'll never have them?"

"Who knows?" returned Deslauriers.

In spite of his democratic views, he urged Frederick to get an introduction into the Dambreuses' house.

The other, by way of objection, pointed to the failure of his previous attempts.

"Bah! go back there. They'll give you an invitation!"

Towards the close of the month of March, they received amongst other bills of a rather awkward description that of the restaurant-keeper who supplied them with dinners. Frederick, not having the entire amount, borrowed a hundred crowns from Deslauriers. A fortnight afterwards, he renewed the same request, and the clerk administered a lecture to him on the extravagant habits to which he gave himself up in the Arnoux's society.

As a matter of fact, he put no restraint upon himself in this respect. A view of Venice, a view of Naples, and another of Constantinople occupying the centre of three walls respectively, equestrian subjects by Alfred de Dreux here and there, a group by Pradier over the mantelpiece, numbers of *L'Art Industriel* lying on the piano, and works in boards on the floor in the corners, encumbered the apartment which he occupied to such an extent that it was hard to find a place to lay a book on, or to move one's elbows about freely. Frederick maintained that he needed all this for his painting.

He pursued his art-studies under Pellerin. But when he called on the artist, the latter was often out, being accustomed to attend at every funeral and public occurrence of which an account was given in the newspapers, and so it was that Frederick spent entire hours alone in the studio. The quietude of this spacious room, which nothing disturbed save the scampering of the mice, the light falling from the ceiling, or the hissing noise of the stove, made him sink into a kind of intellectual ease. Then his eyes, wandering away from the task at which he was engaged, roamed over the shell-work on the wall, around the objects of virtù on the what-not, along the torsos on which the dust that had collected made, as it were, shreds of velvet; and, like a traveller who has lost his way in the middle of a wood, and whom every path brings back to the same spot, continually, he found underlying every idea in his mind the recollection of Madame Arnoux.

He selected days for calling on her. When he had reached the second floor, he would pause on the threshold, hesitating as to whether he ought to ring or not. Steps drew nigh, the door opened, and the announcement "Madame is gone out," a sense of relief would come upon him, as if a weight had been lifted from his heart. He met her, however. On the first occasion there were three other ladies with her; the next time it was in the afternoon, and Mademoiselle Marthe's writing-master came on the scene. Besides, the men whom Madame Arnoux received were not very punctilious about paying visits. For the sake of prudence he deemed it better not to call again.

But he did not fail to present himself regularly at the office of *L'Art Industriel* every Wednesday in order to get an invitation to the Thursday dinners, and he remained there after all the others, even longer than Regimbart, up to the last moment, pretending to be looking at an engraving or to be running his eye through a newspaper. At last Arnoux would say to him, "Shall you be disengaged to-morrow evening?" and, before the sentence was finished, he would give an affirmative answer. Arnoux appeared to have taken a fancy to him. He showed him how to become a good judge of wines, how to make hot punch, and how to prepare a woodcock ragoût. Frederick followed his advice with docility, feeling an attachment to everything connected with Madame Arnoux—her furniture, her servants, her house, her street.

During these dinners he scarcely uttered a word; he kept gazing at her. She had a little mole close to her temple. Her head-bands were darker than the rest of her hair, and were always a little moist at the edges; from time to time she stroked them with only two fingers. He knew the shape of each of her nails. He took delight in listening to the rustle of her silk skirt as she swept past doors; he stealthily inhaled the perfume that came from her handkerchief; her comb, her gloves, her rings were for him things of special interest, important as works of art, almost endowed with life like individuals; all took possession of his heart and strengthened his passion.

He had not been sufficiently self-contained to conceal it from Deslauriers. When he came home from Madame Arnoux's, he would wake up his friend, as if inadvertently, in order to have an opportunity of talking about her.

Deslauriers, who slept in the little off-room, close to where they had their water-supply, would give a great yawn. Frederick seated himself on the side of the bed. At first, he spoke about the dinner; then he referred to a thousand petty details, in which he saw marks of contempt or of affection. On one occasion, for instance, she had refused his arm, in order to take Dittmer's; and Frederick gave vent to his humiliation:

"Ah! how stupid!"

Or else she had called him her "dear friend."

"Then go after her gaily!"

"But I dare not do that," said Frederick.

"Well, then, think no more about her! Good night!"

Deslauriers thereupon turned on his side, and fell asleep. He felt utterly unable to comprehend this love, which seemed to him the last weakness of adolescence;

and, as his own society was apparently not enough to content Frederick, he conceived the idea of bringing together, once a week, those whom they both recognised as friends.

They came on Saturday about nine o'clock. The three Algerine curtains were carefully drawn. The lamp and four wax-lights were burning. In the middle of the table the tobacco-pot, filled with pipes, displayed itself between the beer-bottles, the tea-pot, a flagon of rum, and some fancy biscuits.

They discussed the immortality of the soul, and drew comparisons between the different professors.

One evening Hussonnet introduced a tall young man, attired in a frock-coat, too short in the wrists, and with a look of embarrassment in his face. It was the young fellow whom they had gone to release from the guard-house the year before.

As he had not been able to restore the box of lace which he had lost in the scuffle, his employer had accused him of theft, and threatened to prosecute him. He was now a clerk in a wagon-office. Hussonnet had come across him that morning at the corner of the street, and brought him along, for Dussardier, in a spirit of gratitude, had expressed a wish to see "the other."

He stretched out towards Frederick the cigar-holder, still full, which he had religiously preserved, in the hope of being able to give it back. The young men invited him to pay them a second visit; and he was not slow in doing so.

They all had sympathies in common. At first, their hatred of the Government reached the height of an unquestionable dogma. Martinon alone attempted to defend Louis Philippe. They overwhelmed him with the commonplaces scattered through the newspapers—the "Bastillization" of Paris, the September laws, Pritchard, Lord Guizot—so that Martinon held his tongue for fear of giving offence to somebody. During his seven years at college he had never incurred the penalty of an imposition, and at the Law School he knew how to make himself agreeable to the professors. He usually wore a big frock-coat of the colour of putty, with india-rubber goloshes; but one evening he presented himself arrayed like a bridegroom, in a velvet roll-collar waistcoat, a white tie, and a gold chain.

The astonishment of the other young men was greatly increased when they learned that he had just come away from M. Dambreuse's house. In fact, the banker Dambreuse had just bought a portion of an extensive wood from Martinon senior; and, when the worthy man introduced his son, the other had invited them both to dinner.

"Was there a good supply of truffles there?" asked Deslauriers. "And did you take his wife by the waist between the two doors, *sicut decet?*"

Hereupon the conversation turned on women. Pellerin would not admit that there were beautiful women (he preferred tigers); besides the human female was an inferior creature in the aesthetic hierarchy.

"What fascinates you is just the very thing that degrades her as an idea; I mean her breasts, her hair——"

"Nevertheless," urged Frederick, "long black hair and large dark eyes——"

"Oh! we know all about that," cried Hussonnet. "Enough of Andalusian beauties on the lawn. Those things are out of date; no thank you! For the fact is, honour bright! a fast woman is more amusing than the Venus of Milo. Let us be Gallic, in Heaven's name, and after the Regency style, if we can!

'*Flow, generous wines; ladies, deign to smile!*'

We must pass from the dark to the fair. Is that your opinion, Father Dussardier?"

Dussardier did not reply. They all pressed him to ascertain what his tastes were.

"Well," said he, colouring, "for my part, I would like to love the same one always!"

This was said in such a way that there was a moment of silence, some of them being surprised at this candour, and others finding in his words, perhaps, the secret yearning of their souls.

Sénécal placed his glass of beer on the mantelpiece, and declared dogmatically that, as prostitution was tyrannical and marriage immoral, it was better to practice abstinence. Deslauriers regarded women as a source of amusement—nothing more. M. de Cisy looked upon them with the utmost dread.

Brought up under the eyes of a grandmother who was a devotee, he found the society of those young fellows as alluring as a place of ill-repute and as instructive as the Sorbonne. They gave him lessons without stint; and so much zeal did he exhibit that he even wanted to smoke in spite of the qualms that upset him every time he made the experiment. Frederick paid him the greatest attention. He admired the shade of this young gentleman's cravat, the fur on his overcoat, and especially his boots, as thin as gloves, and so very neat and fine that they had a look of insolent superiority. His carriage used to wait for him below in the street.

One evening, after his departure, when there was a fall of snow, Sénécal began to complain about his having a coachman. He declaimed against kid-gloved exquisites and against the Jockey Club. He had more respect for a workman than for these fine gentlemen.

"For my part, anyhow, I work for my livelihood! I am a poor man!"

"That's quite evident," said Frederick, at length, losing patience.

The tutor conceived a grudge against him for this remark.

But, as Regimbart said he knew Sénécal pretty well, Frederick, wishing to be civil to a friend of the Arnoux, asked him to come to the Saturday meetings; and the two patriots were glad to be brought together in this way.

However, they took opposite views of things.

Sénécal—who had a skull of the angular type—fixed his attention merely on systems, whereas Regimbart, on the contrary, saw in facts nothing but facts. The thing that chiefly troubled him was the Rhine frontier. He claimed to be an authority on the subject of artillery, and got his clothes made by a tailor of the Polytechnic School.

The first day, when they asked him to take some cakes, he disdainfully shrugged his shoulders, saying that these might suit women; and on the next few occasions his manner was not much more gracious. Whenever speculative ideas had reached a certain elevation, he would mutter: "Oh! no Utopias, no dreams!" On the subject of Art (though he used to visit the studios, where he occasionally out of complaisance gave a lesson in fencing) his opinions were not remarkable for their excellence. He compared the style of M. Marast to that of Voltaire, and Mademoiselle Vatnaz to Madame de Staël, on account of an Ode on Poland in which "there was some spirit." In short, Regimbart bored everyone, and especially Deslauriers, for the Citizen was a friend of the Arnoux family. Now the clerk was most anxious to visit those people in the hope that he might there make the acquaintance of some persons who would be an advantage to him.

"When are you going to take me there with you?" he would say. Arnoux was either overburdened with business, or else starting on a journey. Then it was not worth while, as the dinners were coming to an end.

If he had been called on to risk his life for his friend, Frederick would have done so. But, as he was desirous of making as good a figure as possible, and with this view was most careful about his language and manners, and so attentive to his costume that he always presented himself at the office of *L'Art Industriel* irreproachably gloved, he was afraid that Deslauriers, with his shabby black coat, his attorney-like exterior, and his swaggering kind of talk, might make himself disagreeable to Madame Arnoux, and thus compromise him and lower him in her estimation. The other results would have been bad enough, but the last one would have annoyed him a thousand times more.

The clerk saw that his friend did not wish to keep his promise, and Frederick's silence seemed to him an aggravation of the insult. He would have liked to exercise absolute control over him, to see him developing in accordance with the ideal of their youth; and his inactivity excited the clerk's indignation as a breach of duty and a want of loyalty towards himself. Moreover, Frederick, with his thoughts full of Madame Arnoux, frequently talked about her husband; and Deslauriers now began an intolerable course of boredom by repeating the name a hundred times a day, at the end of each remark, like the parrot-cry of an idiot.

When there was a knock at the door, he would answer, "Come in, Arnoux!" At the restaurant he asked for a Brie cheese "in imitation of Arnoux," and at night, pretending to wake up from a bad dream, he would rouse his comrade by howling out, "Arnoux! Arnoux!" At last Frederick, worn out, said to him one day, in a piteous voice:

"Oh! don't bother me about Arnoux!"

"Never!" replied the clerk:

> *"He always, everywhere, burning or icy cold,*
> *The pictured form of Arnoux——"*

"Hold your tongue, I tell you!" exclaimed Frederick, raising his fist.

Then less angrily he added:

"You know well this is a painful subject to me."

"Oh! forgive me, old fellow," returned Deslauriers with a very low bow. "From this time forth we will be considerate towards Mademoiselle's nerves. Again, I say, forgive me. A thousand pardons!"

And so this little joke came to an end.

But, three weeks later, one evening, Deslauriers said to him:

"Well, I have just seen Madame Arnoux."

"Where, pray?"

"At the Palais, with Balandard, the solicitor. A dark woman, is she not, of the middle height?"

Frederick made a gesture of assent. He waited for Deslauriers to speak. At the least expression of admiration he would have been most effusive, and would have fairly hugged the other. However, Deslauriers remained silent. At last, unable to contain himself any longer, Frederick, with assumed indifference, asked him what he thought of her.

Deslauriers considered that "she was not so bad, but still nothing extraordinary."

"Ha! you think so," said Frederick.

They soon reached the month of August, the time when he was to present himself for his second examination. According to the prevailing opinion, the subjects could be made up in a fortnight. Frederick, having full confidence in his own powers, swallowed up in a trice the first four books of the Code of Procedure, the first three of the Penal Code, many bits of the system of criminal investigation, and a part of the Civil Code, with the annotations of M. Poncelet. The night before, Deslauriers made him run through the whole course, a process which did not finish till morning, and, in order to take advantage of even the last quarter of an hour, continued questioning him while they walked along the footpath together.

As several examinations were taking place at the same time, there were many persons in the precincts, and amongst others Hussonnet and Cisy: young men never failed to come and watch these ordeals when the fortunes of their comrades were at stake.

Frederick put on the traditional black gown; then, followed by the throng, with three other students, he entered a spacious apartment, into which the light penetrated through uncurtained windows, and which was garnished with benches ranged along the walls. In the centre, leather chairs were drawn round a table adorned with a green cover. This separated the candidates from the examiners in their red gowns and ermine shoulder-knots, the head examiners wearing gold-laced flat caps.

Frederick found himself the last but one in the series—an unfortunate place. In answer to the first question, as to the difference between a convention and a contract, he defined the one as if it were the other; and the professor, who was a fair sort of man, said to him, "Don't be agitated, Monsieur! Compose yourself!" Then, having asked two easy questions, which were answered in a doubtful fashion, he passed on at last to the fourth. This wretched beginning made Frederick lose his head. Deslauriers, who was facing him amongst the spectators, made a sign to him to indicate that it was not a hopeless case yet; and at the second batch of questions, dealing with the criminal law, he came out tolerably well. But, after the third, with reference to the "mystic will," the examiner having remained impassive the whole time, his mental distress redoubled; for Hussonnet brought his hands together as if to applaud, whilst Deslauriers liberally indulged in shrugs of the shoulders. Finally, the moment was reached when it was necessary to be examined on Procedure. The professor, displeased at listening to theories opposed to his own, asked him in a churlish tone:

"And so this is your view, monsieur? How do you reconcile the principle of article 1351 of the Civil Code with this application by a third party to set aside a judgment by default?"

Frederick had a great headache from not having slept the night before. A ray of sunlight, penetrating through one of the slits in a Venetian blind, fell on his face. Standing behind the seat, he kept wriggling about and tugging at his moustache.

"I am still awaiting your answer," the man with the gold-edged cap observed.

And as Frederick's movements, no doubt, irritated him:

"You won't find it in that moustache of yours!"

This sarcasm made the spectators laugh. The professor, feeling flattered, adopted a wheedling tone. He put two more questions with reference to adjournment and summary jurisdiction, then nodded his head by way of approval. The examination was over. Frederick retired into the vestibule.

While an usher was taking off his gown, to draw it over some other person immediately afterwards, his friends gathered around him, and succeeded in fairly bothering him with their conflicting opinions as to the result of his examination. Presently the announcement was made in a sonorous voice at the entrance of the hall: "The third was—put off!"

"Sent packing!" said Hussonnet. "Let us go away!"

In front of the doorkeeper's lodge they met Martinon, flushed, excited, with a smile on his face and the halo of victory around his brow. He had just passed his final examination without any impediment. All he had now to do was the thesis. Before a fortnight he would be a licentiate. His family enjoyed the acquaintance of a Minister; "a beautiful career" was opening before him.

"All the same, this puts you into a mess," said Deslauriers.

There is nothing so humiliating as to see blockheads succeed in undertakings in which we fail. Frederick, filled with vexation, replied that he did not care a straw about the matter. He had higher pretensions; and as Hussonnet made a show of leaving, Frederick took him aside, and said to him:

"Not a word about this to them, mind!"

It was easy to keep it secret, since Arnoux was starting the next morning for Germany.

When he came back in the evening the clerk found his friend singularly altered: he danced about and whistled; and the other was astonished at this capricious change of mood. Frederick declared that he did not intend to go home to his mother, as he meant to spend his holidays working.

At the news of Arnoux's departure, a feeling of delight had taken possession of him. He might present himself at the house whenever he liked without any fear of having his visits broken in upon. The consciousness of absolute security would make him self-confident. At last he would not stand aloof, he would not be separated from her! Something more powerful than an iron chain attached him to Paris; a voice from the depths of his heart called out to him to remain.

There were certain obstacles in his path. These he got over by writing to his mother: he first of all admitted that he had failed to pass, owing to alterations made in the course—a mere mischance—an unfair thing; besides, all the great advocates (he referred to them by name) had been rejected at their examinations. But he calculated on presenting himself again in the month of November. Now, having no time to lose, he would not go home this year; and he asked, in addition to the quarterly allowance, for two hundred and fifty francs, to get coached in law by a private tutor, which would be of great assistance to him; and he threw around the entire epistle a garland of regrets, condolences, expressions of endearment, and protestations of filial love.

Madame Moreau, who had been expecting him the following day, was doubly grieved. She threw a veil over her son's misadventure, and in answer told him to "come all the same." Frederick would not give way, and the result was a falling out between them. However, at the end of the week, he received the amount of the quarter's allowance together with the sum required for the payment of the private tutor, which helped to pay for a pair of pearl-grey trousers, a white felt hat, and a gold-headed switch. When he had procured all these things he thought:

"Perhaps this is only a hairdresser's fancy on my part!"

And a feeling of considerable hesitation took possession of him.

In order to make sure as to whether he ought to call on Madame Arnoux, he tossed three coins into the air in succession. On each occasion luck was in his favour. So then Fate must have ordained it. He hailed a cab and drove to the Rue de Choiseul.

He quickly ascended the staircase and drew the bell-pull, but without effect. He felt as if he were about to faint.

Then, with fierce energy, he shook the heavy silk tassel. There was a resounding peal which gradually died away till no further sound was heard. Frederick got rather frightened.

He pasted his ear to the door—not a breath! He looked in through the key-hole, and only saw two reed-points on the wall-paper in the midst of designs of flowers. At last, he was on the point of going away when he changed his mind. This time, he gave a timid little ring. The door flew open, and Arnoux himself appeared on the threshold, with his hair all in disorder, his face crimson, and his features distorted by an expression of sullen embarrassment.

"Hallo! What the deuce brings you here? Come in!"

He led Frederick, not into the boudoir or into the bed-room, but into the dining-room, where on the table could be seen a bottle of champagne and two glasses; and, in an abrupt tone:

"There is something you want to ask me, my dear friend?"

"No! nothing! nothing!" stammered the young man, trying to think of some excuse for his visit. At length, he said to Arnoux that he had called to know whether they had heard from him, as Hussonnet had announced that he had gone to Germany.

"Not at all!" returned Arnoux. "What a feather-headed fellow that is to take everything in the wrong way!"

In order to conceal his agitation, Frederick kept walking from right to left in the dining-room. Happening to come into contact with a chair, he knocked down a parasol which had been laid across it, and the ivory handle got broken.

"Good heavens!" he exclaimed. "How sorry I am for having broken Madame Arnoux's parasol!"

At this remark, the picture-dealer raised his head and smiled in a very peculiar fashion. Frederick, taking advantage of the opportunity thus offered to talk about her, added shyly:

"Could I not see her?"

No. She had gone to the country to see her mother, who was ill.

He did not venture to ask any questions as to the length of time that she would be away. He merely enquired what was Madame Arnoux's native place.

"Chartres. Does this astonish you?"

"Astonish me? Oh, no! Why should it! Not in the least!"

After that, they could find absolutely nothing to talk about. Arnoux, having made a cigarette for himself, kept walking round the table, puffing. Frederick, standing near the stove, stared at the walls, the whatnot, and the floor; and delightful pictures flitted through his memory, or, rather, before his eyes. Then he left the apartment.

A piece of a newspaper, rolled up into a ball, lay on the floor in the anteroom. Arnoux snatched it up, and, raising himself on the tips of his toes, he stuck it into the bell, in order, as he said, that he might be able to go and finish his interrupted siesta. Then, as he grasped Frederick's hand:

"Kindly tell the porter that I am not in."

And he shut the door after him with a bang.

Frederick descended the staircase step by step. The ill-success of this first attempt discouraged him as to the possible results of those that might follow. Then began three months of absolute boredom. As he had nothing to do, his melancholy was aggravated by the want of occupation.

He spent whole hours gazing from the top of his balcony at the river as it flowed between the quays, with their bulwarks of grey stone, blackened here and there by the seams of the sewers, with a pontoon of washerwomen moored close to the bank, where some brats were amusing themselves by making a water-spaniel swim in the slime. His eyes, turning aside from the stone bridge of Nôtre Dame and the three suspension bridges, continually directed their glance towards the Quai-aux-Ormes, resting on a group of old trees, resembling the linden-trees of the Montereau wharf. The Saint-Jacques tower, the Hotel de Ville, Saint-Gervais, Saint-Louis, and Saint-Paul, rose up in front of him amid a confused mass of roofs; and the genius of the July Column glittered at the eastern side like a large gold star, whilst at the other end the dome of the Tuileries showed its outlines against the sky in one great round mass of blue. Madame Arnoux's house must be on this side in the rear!

He went back to his bedchamber; then, throwing himself on the sofa, he abandoned himself to a confused succession of thoughts—plans of work, schemes for the guidance of his conduct, attempts to divine the future. At last, in order to shake off broodings all about himself, he went out into the open air.

He plunged at random into the Latin Quarter, usually so noisy, but deserted at this particular time, for the students had gone back to join their families. The huge walls of the colleges, which the silence seemed to lengthen, wore a still more melancholy aspect. All sorts of peaceful sounds could be heard—the flapping of wings in cages, the noise made by the turning of a lathe, or the strokes of a cobbler's hammer; and the old-clothes men, standing in the middle of the street, looked up at each house fruitlessly. In the interior of a solitary café the barmaid was yawning between her two full decanters. The newspapers were left undisturbed on the tables of reading-rooms. In the ironing establishments linen quivered under the puffs of tepid wind. From time to time he stopped to look at the window of a secondhand book-shop; an omnibus which grazed the footpath as it came rumbling along made him turn round; and, when he found himself before the Luxembourg, he went no further.

Occasionally he was attracted towards the boulevards by the hope of finding there something that might amuse him. After he had passed through dark alleys, from which his nostrils were greeted by fresh moist odours, he reached vast, desolate, open spaces, dazzling with light, in which monuments cast at the side of the pavement notches of black shadow. But once more the wagons and the shops appeared, and the crowd had the effect of stunning him, especially on Sunday, when, from the Bastille to the Madeleine, it kept swaying in one immense flood over the asphalt, in the midst of a cloud of dust, in an incessant clamour. He felt disgusted at the meanness of the faces, the silliness of the talk, and the idiotic self-satisfaction that oozed through these sweating foreheads. However, the consciousness of being superior to these individuals mitigated the weariness which he experienced in gazing at them.

Every day he went to the office of *L'Art Industriel*; and in order to ascertain when Madame Arnoux would be back, he made elaborate enquiries about her mother. Arnoux's answer never varied—"the change for the better was continuing"—his wife, with his little daughter, would be returning the following week. The longer she delayed in coming back, the more uneasiness Frederick exhibited, so that Arnoux, touched by so much affection, brought him five or six times a week to dine at a restaurant.

In the long talks which they had together on these occasions Frederick discovered that the picture-dealer was not a very intellectual type of man. Arnoux might, however, take notice of his chilling manner; and now Frederick deemed it advisable to pay back, in a small measure, his polite attentions.

So, being anxious to do things on a good scale, the young man sold all his new clothes to a secondhand clothes-dealer for the sum of eighty francs, and having increased it with a hundred more francs which he had left, he called at Arnoux's house to bring him out to dine. Regimbart happened to be there, and all three of them set forth for Les Trois Frères Provençaux.

The Citizen began by taking off his surtout, and, knowing that the two others would defer to his gastronomic tastes, drew up the *menu*. But in vain did he make his way to the kitchen to speak himself to the *chef*, go down to the cellar, with every corner of which he was familiar, and send for the master of the establishment, to whom he gave "a blowing up." He was not satisfied with the dishes, the wines, or the attendance. At each new dish, at each fresh bottle, as soon as he had swallowed the first mouthful, the first draught, he threw down his fork or pushed his glass some distance away from him; then, leaning on his elbows on the table-cloth, and stretching out his arms, he declared in a loud tone that he could no longer dine in Paris! Finally, not knowing what to put into his mouth, Regimbart ordered kidney-beans dressed with oil, "quite plain," which, though only a partial success, slightly appeased him. Then he had a talk with the waiter all about the latter's predecessors at the "Provençaux":—"What had become of Antoine? And a fellow named Eugène? And Théodore, the little fellow who always used to attend down stairs? There was much finer fare in those days, and Burgundy vintages the like of which they would never see again."

Then there was a discussion as to the value of ground in the suburbs, Arnoux having speculated in that way, and looked on it as a safe thing. In the meantime, however, he would lie out of the interest on his money. As he did not want to sell out at any price, Regimbart would find out some one to whom he could let the ground; and so these two gentlemen proceeded at the close of the dessert to make calculations with a lead pencil.

They went out to get coffee in the smoking-divan on the ground-floor in the Passage du Saumon. Frederick had to remain on his legs while interminable games of billiards were being played, drenched in innumerable glasses of beer; and he lingered on there till midnight without knowing why, through want of energy, through sheer senselessness, in the vague expectation that something might happen which would give a favourable turn to his love.

When, then, would he next see her? Frederick was in a state of despair about it. But, one evening, towards the close of November, Arnoux said to him:

"My wife, you know, came back yesterday!"

Next day, at five o'clock, he made his way to her house. He began by congratulating her on her mother's recovery from such a serious illness.

"Why, no! Who told you that?"

"Arnoux!"

She gave vent to a slight "Ah!" then added that she had grave fears at first, which, however, had now been dispelled. She was seated close beside the fire in an upholstered easy-chair. He was on the sofa, with his hat between his knees; and the conversation was difficult to carry on, as it was broken off nearly every minute, so he got no chance of giving utterance to his sentiments. But, when he began to complain of having to study legal quibbles, she answered, "Oh! I understand—business!" and she let her face fall, buried suddenly in her own reflections.

He was eager to know what they were, and even did not bestow a thought on anything else. The twilight shadows gathered around them.

She rose, having to go out about some shopping; then she reappeared in a bonnet trimmed with velvet, and a black mantle edged with minever. He plucked up courage and offered to accompany her.

It was now so dark that one could scarcely see anything. The air was cold, and had an unpleasant odour, owing to a heavy fog, which partially blotted out the fronts of the houses. Frederick inhaled it with delight; for he could feel through the wadding of his coat the form of her arm; and her hand, cased in a chamois glove with two buttons, her little hand which he would have liked to cover with kisses, leaned on his sleeve. Owing to the slipperiness of the pavement, they lost their balance a little; it seemed to him as if they were both rocked by the wind in the midst of a cloud.

The glitter of the lamps on the boulevard brought him back to the realities of existence. The opportunity was a good one, there was no time to lose. He gave himself as far as the Rue de Richelieu to declare his love. But almost at that very moment, in front of a china-shop, she stopped abruptly and said to him:

"We are at the place. Thanks. On Thursday—is it not?—as usual."

The dinners were now renewed; and the more visits he paid at Madame Arnoux's, the more his love-sickness increased. The contemplation of this woman had an enervating effect upon him, like the use of a perfume that is too strong. It penetrated into the very depths of his nature, and became almost a kind of habitual sensation, a new mode of existence.

The prostitutes whom he brushed past under the gaslight, the female ballad-singers breaking into bursts of melody, the ladies rising on horseback at full gallop, the shopkeepers' wives on foot, the grisettes at their windows, all women brought her before his mental vision, either from the effect of their resemblance to her or the violent contrast to her which they presented. As he walked along by the shops, he gazed at the cashmeres, the laces, and the jewelled eardrops, imagining how they would look draped around her figure, sewn in her corsage, or lighting up her dark hair. In the flower-girls' baskets the bouquets blossomed for her to choose one as she passed. In the shoemakers' show-windows the little satin slippers with swan's-down edges seemed to be waiting for her foot. Every street led towards her house; the hackney-coaches stood in their places to carry her home the more quickly; Paris was associated with her person, and the great city, with all its noises, roared around her like an immense orchestra.

When he went into the Jardin des Plantes the sight of a palm-tree carried him off into distant countries. They were travelling together on the backs of dromedaries, under the awnings of elephants, in the cabin of a yacht amongst the blue archipelagoes, or side by side on mules with little bells attached to them who went stumbling through the grass against broken columns. Sometimes he stopped in the Louvre before old pictures; and, his love embracing her even in vanished centuries, he substituted her for the personages in the paintings. Wearing a hennin on her head, she was praying on bended knees before a stained-glass window. Lady Paramount of Castile or Flanders, she remained seated in a starched ruff and a body lined with whalebone with big puffs. Then he saw her descending some wide porphyry staircase in the midst of senators under a daï's of ostriches' feathers in a robe of brocade. At another time he dreamed of her in yellow silk trousers on the cushions of a harem—and all that was beautiful, the scintillation of the stars, certain tunes in music, the turn of a phrase, the outlines of a face, led him to think about her in an abrupt, unconscious fashion.

As for trying to make her his mistress, he was sure that any such attempt would be futile.

One evening, Dittmer, on his arrival, kissed her on the forehead; Lovarias did the same, observing:

"You give me leave—don't you?—as it is a friend's privilege?"

Frederick stammered out:

"It seems to me that we are all friends."

"Not all old friends!" she returned.

This was repelling him beforehand indirectly.

Besides, what was he to do? To tell her that he loved her? No doubt, she would decline to listen to him or else she would feel indignant and turn him out of the house. But he preferred to submit to even the most painful ordeal rather than run the horrible risk of seeing her no more. He envied pianists for their talents and soldiers for their scars. He longed for a dangerous attack of sickness, hoping in this way to make her take an interest in him.

One thing caused astonishment to himself, that he felt in no way jealous of Arnoux; and he could not picture her in his imagination undressed, so natural did her modesty appear, and so far did her sex recede into a mysterious background.

Nevertheless, he dreamed of the happiness of living with her, of "theeing" and "thouing" her, of passing his hand lingeringly over her head-bands, or remaining in a kneeling posture on the floor, with both arms clasped round her waist, so as to drink in her soul through his eyes. To accomplish this it would be necessary to conquer Fate; and so, incapable of action, cursing God, and accusing himself of being a coward, he kept moving restlessly within the confines of his passion just as a prisoner keeps moving about in his dungeon. The pangs which he was perpetually enduring were choking him. For hours he would remain quite motionless, or else he would burst into tears; and one day when he had not the strength to restrain his emotion, Deslauriers said to him:

"Why, goodness gracious! what's the matter with you?"

Frederick's nerves were unstrung. Deslauriers did not believe a word of it. At the sight of so much mental anguish, he felt all his old affection reawakening, and he tried to cheer up his friend. A man like him to let himself be depressed, what folly! It was all very well while one was young; but, as one grows older, it is only loss of time.

"You are spoiling my Frederick for me! I want him whom I knew in bygone days. The same boy as ever! I liked him! Come, smoke a pipe, old chap! Shake yourself up a little! You drive me mad!"

"It is true," said Frederick, "I am a fool!"

The clerk replied:

"Ah! old troubadour, I know well what's troubling you! A little affair of the heart? Confess it! Bah! One lost, four found instead! We console ourselves for virtuous women with the other sort. Would you like me to introduce you to some women? You have only to come to the Alhambra."

(This was a place for public balls recently opened at the top of the Champs-Elysées, which had gone down owing to a display of licentiousness somewhat ruder than is usual in establishments of the kind.)

"That's a place where there seems to be good fun. You can take your friends, if you like. I can even pass in Regimbart for you."

Frederick did not think fit to ask the Citizen to go. Deslauriers deprived himself of the pleasure of Sénécal's society. They took only Hussonnet and Cisy along with Dussardier; and the same hackney-coach set the group of five down at the entrance of the Alhambra.

Two Moorish galleries extended on the right and on the left, parallel to one another. The wall of a house opposite occupied the entire backguard; and the fourth side (that in which the restaurant was) represented a Gothic cloister with stained-glass windows. A sort of Chinese roof screened the platform reserved for the musicians. The ground was covered all over with asphalt; the Venetian lanterns fastened to posts formed, at regular intervals, crowns of many-coloured flame above the heads of the dancers. A pedestal here and there supported a stone basin, from which rose a thin streamlet of water. In the midst of the foliage could be seen plaster statues, and Hebes and Cupid, painted in oil, and presenting a very sticky appearance; and the numerous walks, garnished with sand of a deep yellow, carefully raked, made the garden look much larger than it was in reality.

Students were walking their mistresses up and down; drapers' clerks strutted about with canes in their hands; lads fresh from college were smoking their regalias; old men had their dyed beards smoothed out with combs. There were English, Russians, men from South America, and three Orientals in tarbooshes. Lorettes, grisettes, and girls of the town had come there in the hope of finding a protector, a lover, a gold coin, or simply for the pleasure of dancing; and their dresses, with tunics of water-green, cherry-red, or violet, swept along, fluttered between the ebony-trees and the lilacs. Nearly all the men's clothes were of striped material; some of them had white trousers, in spite of the coolness of the evening. The gas was lighted.

Hussonnet was acquainted with a number of the women through his connection with the fashion-journals and the smaller theatres. He sent them kisses with the tips of his fingers, and from time to time he quitted his friends to go and chat with them.

Deslauriers felt jealous of these playful familiarities. He accosted in a cynical manner a tall, fair-haired girl, in a nankeen costume. After looking at him with a certain air of sullenness, she said:

"No! I wouldn't trust you, my good fellow!" and turned on her heel.

His next attack was on a stout brunette, who apparently was a little mad; for she gave a bounce at the very first word he spoke to her, threatening, if he went any further, to call the police. Deslauriers made an effort to laugh; then, coming across a little woman sitting by herself under a gas-lamp, he asked her to be his partner in a quadrille.

The musicians, perched on the platform in the attitude of apes, kept scraping and blowing away with desperate energy. The conductor, standing up, kept beating time automatically. The dancers were much crowded and enjoyed themselves thoroughly. The bonnet-strings, getting loose, rubbed against the cravats; the boots sank under the petticoats; and all this bouncing went on to the accompaniment of the music. Deslauriers hugged the little woman, and, seized with the delirium of the cancan, whirled about, like a big marionnette, in the midst of the dancers. Cisy and Deslauriers were still promenading up and down. The young aristocrat kept ogling the girls, and, in spite of the clerk's exhortations, did not venture to talk to them, having an idea in his head that in the resorts of these women there was always "a man hidden in the cupboard with a pistol who would come out of it and force you to sign a bill of exchange."

They came back and joined Frederick. Deslauriers had stopped dancing; and they were all asking themselves how they were to finish up the evening, when Hussonnet exclaimed:

"Look! Here's the Marquise d'Amaëgui!"

The person referred to was a pale woman with a *retroussé* nose, mittens up to her elbows, and big black earrings hanging down her cheeks, like two dog's ears. Hussonnet said to her:

"We ought to organise a little fête at your house—a sort of Oriental rout. Try to collect some of your friends here for these French cavaliers. Well, what is annoying you? Are you going to wait for your hidalgo?"

The Andalusian hung down her head: being well aware of the by no means lavish habits of her friend, she was afraid of having to pay for any refreshments he ordered. When, at length, she let the word "money" slip from her, Cisy offered five napoleons—all he had in his purse; and so it was settled that the thing should come off.

But Frederick was absent. He fancied that he had recognised the voice of Arnoux, and got a glimpse of a woman's hat; and accordingly he hastened towards an arbour which was not far off.

Mademoiselle Vatnaz was alone there with Arnoux.

"Excuse me! I am in the way?"

"Not in the least!" returned the picture-merchant.

Frederick, from the closing words of their conversation, understood that Arnoux had come to the Alhambra to talk over a pressing matter of business with Mademoiselle Vatnaz; and it was evident that he was not completely reassured, for he said to her, with some uneasiness in his manner:

"You are quite sure?"

"Perfectly certain! You are loved. Ah! what a man you are!"

And she assumed a pouting look, putting out her big lips, so red that they seemed tinged with blood. But she had wonderful eyes, of a tawny hue, with specks of gold in the pupils, full of vivacity, amorousness, and sensuality. They illuminated, like lamps, the rather yellow tint of her thin face. Arnoux seemed to enjoy her exhibition of pique. He stooped over her, saying:

"You are nice—give me a kiss!"

She caught hold of his two ears, and pressed her lips against his forehead.

At that moment the dancing stopped; and in the conductor's place appeared a handsome young man, rather fat, with a waxen complexion. He had long black hair, which he wore in the same fashion as Christ, and a blue velvet waistcoat embroidered with large gold palm-branches. He looked as proud as a peacock, and as stupid as a turkey-cock; and, having bowed to the audience, he began a ditty. A villager was supposed to be giving an account of his journey to the capital. The singer used the dialect of Lower Normandy, and played the part of a drunken man. The refrain—

> *"Ah! I laughed at you there, I laughed at you there,*
> *In that rascally city of Paris!"*

was greeted with enthusiastic stampings of feet. Delmas, "a vocalist who sang with expression," was too shrewd to let the excitement of his listeners cool. A guitar was quickly handed to him and he moaned forth a ballad entitled "The Albanian Girl's Brother."

The words recalled to Frederick those which had been sung by the man in rags between the paddle-boxes of the steamboat. His eyes involuntarily attached themselves to the hem of the dress spread out before him.

After each couplet there was a long pause, and the blowing of the wind through the trees resembled the sound of the waves.

Mademoiselle Vatnaz blushed the moment she saw Dussardier. She soon rose, and stretching out her hand towards him:

"You do not remember me, Monsieur Auguste?"

"How do you know her?" asked Frederick.

"We have been in the same house," he replied.

Cisy pulled him by the sleeve; they went out; and, scarcely had they disappeared, when Madame Vatnaz began to pronounce a eulogy on his character. She even went so far as to add that he possessed "the genius of the heart."

Then they chatted about Delmas, admitting that as a mimic he might be a success on the stage; and a discussion followed in which Shakespeare, the Censorship, Style, the People, the receipts of the Porte Saint-Martin, Alexandre Dumas, Victor Hugo, and Dumersan were all mixed up together.

Arnoux had known many celebrated actresses; the young men bent forward their heads to hear what he had to say about these ladies. But his words were drowned in the noise of the music; and, as soon as the quadrille or the polka was over, they all squatted round the tables, called the waiter, and laughed. Bottles of beer and of effervescent lemonade went off with detonations amid the foliage; women clucked like hens; now and then, two gentlemen tried to fight; and a thief was arrested. The dancers, in the rush of a gallop, encroached on the walks. Panting, with flushed, smiling faces, they filed off in a whirlwind which lifted up the gowns with the coat-tails. The trombones brayed more loudly; the rhythmic movement became more rapid. Behind the mediæval cloister could be heard crackling sounds; squibs went off; artificial suns began turning round; the gleam of the Ben-

gal fires, like emeralds in colour, lighted up for the space of a minute the entire garden; and, with the last rocket, a great sigh escaped from the assembled throng.

It slowly died away. A cloud of gunpowder floated into the air. Frederick and
Deslauriers were walking step by step through the midst of the crowd, when they
happened to see something that made them suddenly stop: Martinon was in the act
of paying some money at the place where umbrellas were left; and he was accompanying a woman of fifty, plain-looking, magnificently dressed, and of problem-
atic social rank.

"That sly dog," said Deslauriers, "is not so simple as we imagine. But where
in the world is Cisy?"

Dussardier pointed out to them the smoking-divan, where they perceived the
knightly youth, with a bowl of punch before him, and a pink hat by his side, to keep
him company. Hussonnet, who had been away for the past few minutes, reappeared
at the same moment.

A young girl was leaning on his arm, and addressing him in a loud voice as
"My little cat."

"Oh! no!" said he to her—"not in public! Call me rather 'Vicomte.' That gives
you a cavalier style—Louis XIII and dainty boots—the sort of thing I like! Yes,
my good friends, one of the old *régime!*—nice, isn't she?"—and he chucked her by
the chin—"Salute these gentlemen! they are all the sons of peers of France. I keep
company with them in order that they may get an appointment for me as an ambassador."

"How insane you are!" sighed Mademoiselle Vatnaz. She asked Dussardier to
see her as far as her own door.

Arnoux watched them going off; then, turning towards Frederick:

"Did you like the Vatnaz? At any rate, you're not quite frank about these affairs. I believe you keep your amours hidden."

Frederick, turning pale, swore that he kept nothing hidden.

"Can it be possible you don't know what it is to have a mistress?" said Arnoux.

Frederick felt a longing to mention a woman's name at random. But the story
might be repealed to her. So he replied that as a matter of fact he had no mistress.

The picture-dealer reproached him for this.

"This evening you had a good opportunity! Why didn't you do like the others,
each of whom went off with a woman?"

"Well, and what about yourself?" said Frederick, provoked by his persistency.

"Oh! myself—that's quite a different matter, my lad! I go home to my own
one!"

Then he called a cab, and disappeared.

The two friends walked towards their own destination. An east wind was blowing. They did not exchange a word. Deslauriers was regretting that he had not succeeded in making a *shine* before a certain newspaper-manager, and Frederick was lost once more in his melancholy broodings. At length, breaking-silence, he said that this public-house ball appeared to him a stupid affair.

"Whose fault is it? If you had not left us, to join that Arnoux of yours—"

"Bah! anything I could have done would have been utterly useless!"

But the clerk had theories of his own. All that was necessary in order to get a thing was to desire it strongly.

"Nevertheless, you yourself, a little while ago—"

"I don't care a straw about that sort of thing!" returned Deslauriers, cutting short Frederick's allusion. "Am I going to get entangled with women?"

And he declaimed against their affectations, their silly ways—in short, he disliked them.

"Don't be acting, then!" said Frederick.

Deslauriers became silent. Then, all at once:

"Will you bet me a hundred francs that I won't *do* the first woman that passes?"

"Yes—it's a bet!"

The first who passed was a hideous-looking beggar-woman, and they were giving up all hope of a chance presenting itself when, in the middle of the Rue de Rivoli, they saw a tall girl with a little bandbox in her hand.

Deslauriers accosted her under the arcades. She turned up abruptly by the Tuileries, and soon diverged into the Place du Carrousel. She glanced to the right and to the left. She ran after a hackney-coach; Deslauriers overtook her. He walked by her side, talking to her with expressive gestures. At length, she accepted his arm, and they went on together along the quays. Then, when they reached the rising ground in front of the Châtelet, they kept tramping up and down for at least twenty minutes, like two sailors keeping watch. But, all of a sudden, they passed over the Pont-au-Change, through the Flower Market, and along the Quai Napoleon. Frederick came up behind them. Deslauriers gave him to understand that he would be in their way, and had only to follow his own example.

"How much have you got still?"

"Two hundred sous pieces."

"That's enough—good night to you!"

Frederick was seized with the astonishment one feels at seeing a piece of foolery coming to a successful issue.

"He has the laugh at me," was his reflection. "Suppose I went back again?"

Perhaps Deslauriers imagined that he was envious of this paltry love! "As if I had not one a hundred times more rare, more noble, more absorbing." He felt a sort of angry feeling impelling him onward. He arrived in front of Madame Arnoux's door.

None of the outer windows belonged to her apartment. Nevertheless, he remained with his eyes pasted on the front of the house—as if he fancied he could, by his contemplation, break open the walls. No doubt, she was now sunk in repose, tranquil as a sleeping flower, with her beautiful black hair resting on the lace of the pillow, her lips slightly parted, and one arm under her head. Then Arnoux's head rose before him, and he rushed away to escape from this vision.

The advice which Deslauriers had given to him came back to his memory. It only filled him with horror. Then he walked about the streets in a vagabond fashion.

When a pedestrian approached, he tried to distinguish the face. From time to time a ray of light passed between his legs, tracing a great quarter of a circle on the pavement; and in the shadow a man appeared with his dosser and his lantern. The wind, at certain points, made the sheet-iron flue of a chimney shake. Distant sounds reached his ears, mingling with the buzzing in his brain; and it seemed to him that he was listening to the indistinct flourish of quadrille music. His movements as he walked on kept up this illusion. He found himself on the Pont de la Concorde.

Then he recalled that evening in the previous winter, when, as he left her house for the first time, he was forced to stand still, so rapidly did his heart beat with the hopes that held it in their clasp. And now they had all withered!

Dark clouds were drifting across the face of the moon. He gazed at it, musing on the vastness of space, the wretchedness of life, the nothingness of everything. The day dawned; his teeth began to chatter, and, half-asleep, wet with the morning mist, and bathed in tears, he asked himself, Why should I not make an end of it? All that was necessary was a single movement. The weight of his forehead dragged him along—he beheld his own dead body floating in the water. Frederick stooped down. The parapet was rather wide, and it was through pure weariness that he did not make the attempt to leap over it.

Then a feeling of dismay swept over him. He reached the boulevards once more, and sank down upon a seat. He was aroused by some police-officers, who were convinced that he had been indulging a little too freely.

He resumed his walk. But, as he was exceedingly hungry, and as all the restaurants were closed, he went to get a "snack" at a tavern by the fish-markets; after which, thinking it too soon to go in yet, he kept sauntering about the Hotel de Ville till a quarter past eight.

Deslauriers had long since got rid of his wench; and he was writing at the table in the middle of his room. About four o'clock, M. de Cisy came in.

Thanks to Dussardier, he had enjoyed the society of a lady the night before; and he had even accompanied her home in the carriage with her husband to the very threshold of their house, where she had given him an assignation. He parted with her without even knowing her name.

"And what do you propose that I should do in that way?" said Frederick.

Thereupon the young gentleman began to cudgel his brains to think of a suitable woman; he mentioned Mademoiselle Vatnaz, the Andalusian, and all the rest. At length, with much circumlocution, he stated the object of his visit. Relying on the discretion of his friend, he came to aid him in taking an important step, after which he might definitely regard himself as a man; and Frederick showed no reluctance. He told the story to Deslauriers without relating the facts with reference to himself personally.

The clerk was of opinion that he was now going on very well. This respect for his advice increased his good humour. He owed to that quality his success, on the very first night he met her, with Mademoiselle Clémence Daviou, embroideress in gold for military outfits, the sweetest creature that ever lived, as slender as a reed, with large blue eyes, perpetually staring with wonder. The clerk had taken advantage of her credulity to such an extent as to make her believe that he had been decorated. At their private conversations he had his frock-coat adorned with a red ribbon, but divested himself of it in public in order, as he put it, not to humiliate his master. However, he kept her at a distance, allowed himself to be fawned upon, like a pasha, and, in a laughing sort of way, called her "daughter of the people." Every time they met, she brought him little bunches of violets. Frederick would not have cared for a love affair of this sort.

Meanwhile, whenever they set forth arm-in-arm to visit Pinson's or Barillot's circulating library, he experienced a feeling of singular depression. Frederick did not realise how much pain he had made Deslauriers endure for the past year, while brushing his nails before going out to dine in the Rue de Choiseul!

One evening, when from the commanding position in which his balcony stood, he had just been watching them as they went out together, he saw Hussonnet, some distance off, on the Pont d'Arcole. The Bohemian began calling him by making signals towards him, and, when Frederick had descended the five flights of stairs:

"Here is the thing—it is next Saturday, the 24th, Madame Arnoux's feast-day."

"How is that, when her name is Marie?"

"And Angèle also—no matter! They will entertain their guests at their country-house at Saint-Cloud. I was told to give you due notice about it. You'll find a vehicle at the magazine-office at three o'clock. So that makes matters all right! Excuse me for having disturbed you! But I have such a number of calls to make!"

Frederick had scarcely turned round when his doorkeeper placed a letter in his hand:

"Monsieur and Madame Dambreuse beg of Monsieur F. Moreau to do them the honour to come and dine with them on Saturday the 24th inst.—R.S.V.P."

"Too late!" he said to himself. Nevertheless, he showed the letter to Deslauriers, who exclaimed:

"Ha! at last! But you don't look as if you were satisfied. Why?"

After some little hesitation, Frederick said that he had another invitation for the same day.

"Be kind enough to let me run across to the Rue de Choiseul. I'm not joking! I'll answer this for you if it puts you about."

And the clerk wrote an acceptance of the invitation in the third person.

Having seen nothing of the world save through the fever of his desires, he pictured it to himself as an artificial creation discharging its functions by virtue of mathematical laws. A dinner in the city, an accidental meeting with a man in office, a smile from a pretty woman, might, by a series of actions deducing themselves from one another, have gigantic results. Certain Parisian drawing-rooms were like those machines which take a material in the rough and render it a hundred times more valuable. He believed in courtesans advising diplomatists, in wealthy marriages brought about by intrigues, in the cleverness of convicts, in the capacity of strong men for getting the better of fortune. In short, he considered it so useful to visit the Dambreuses, and talked about it so plausibly, that Frederick was at a loss to know what was the best course to take.

The least he ought to do, as it was Madame Arnoux's feast-day, was to make her a present. He naturally thought of a parasol, in order to make reparation for his awkwardness. Now he came across a shot-silk parasol with a little carved ivory handle, which had come all the way from China. But the price of it was a hundred and seventy-five francs, and he had not a sou, having in fact to live on the credit of his next quarter's allowance. However, he wished to get it; he was determined to have it; and, in spite of his repugnance to doing so, he had recourse to Deslauriers.

Deslauriers answered Frederick's first question by saying that he had no money.

"I want some," said Frederick—"I want some very badly!"

As the other made the same excuse over again, he flew into a passion.

"You might find it to your advantage some time—"

"What do you mean by that?"

"Oh! nothing."

The clerk understood. He took the sum required out of his reserve-fund, and when he had counted out the money, coin by coin:

"I am not asking you for a receipt, as I see you have a lot of expense!"

Frederick threw himself on his friend's neck with a thousand affectionate protestations. Deslauriers received this display of emotion frigidly. Then, next morning, noticing the parasol on the top of the piano:

"Ah! it was for that!"

"I will send it, perhaps," said Frederick, with an air of carelessness.

Good fortune was on his side, for that evening he got a note with a black border from Madame Dambreuse announcing to him that she had lost an uncle, and excusing herself for having to defer till a later period the pleasure of making his acquaintance. At two o'clock, he reached the office of the art journal. Instead of waiting for him in order to drive him in his carriage, Arnoux had left the city the night before, unable to resist his desire to get some fresh air.

Every year it was his custom, as soon as the leaves were budding forth, to start early in the morning and to remain away several days, making long journeys across the fields, drinking milk at the farmhouses, romping with the village girls, asking questions about the harvest, and carrying back home with him stalks of salad in his pocket-handkerchief. At length, in order to realise a long-cherished dream of his, he had bought a country-house.

While Frederick was talking to the picture-dealer's clerk, Mademoiselle Vatnaz suddenly made her appearance, and was disappointed at not seeing Arnoux. He would, perhaps, be remaining away two days longer. The clerk advised her "to go there"—she could not go there; to write a letter—she was afraid that the letter might get lost. Frederick offered to be the bearer of it himself. She rapidly scribbled off a letter, and implored of him to let nobody see him delivering it.

Forty minutes afterwards, he found himself at Saint-Cloud. The house, which was about a hundred paces farther away than the bridge, stood half-way up the hill. The garden-walls were hidden by two rows of linden-trees, and a wide lawn descended to the bank of the river. The railed entrance before the door was open, and Frederick went in.

Arnoux, stretched on the grass, was playing with a litter of kittens. This amusement appeared to absorb him completely. Mademoiselle Vatnaz's letter drew him out of his sleepy idleness.

"The deuce! the deuce!—this is a bore! She is right, though; I must go."

Then, having stuck the missive into his pocket, he showed the young man through the grounds with manifest delight. He pointed out everything—the stable, the cart-house, the kitchen. The drawing-room was at the right, on the side facing Paris, and looked out on a floored arbour, covered over with clematis. But presently a few harmonious notes burst forth above their heads: Madame Arnoux, fancying that there was nobody near, was singing to amuse herself. She executed quavers, trills, arpeggios. There were long notes which seemed to remain suspended in the air; others fell in a rushing shower like the spray of a waterfall; and her voice passing out through the Venetian blind, cut its way through the deep silence and rose towards the blue sky. She ceased all at once, when M. and Madame Oudry, two neighbours, presented themselves.

Then she appeared herself at the top of the steps in front of the house; and, as she descended, he caught a glimpse of her foot. She wore little open shoes of reddish-brown leather, with three straps crossing each other so as to draw just above her stockings a wirework of gold.

Those who had been invited arrived. With the exception of Maître Lefaucheur, an advocate, they were the same guests who came to the Thursday dinners. Each of them had brought some present—Dittmer a Syrian scarf, Rosenwald a scrap-book of ballads, Burieu a water-colour painting, Sombary one of his own caricatures, and Pellerin a charcoal-drawing, representing a kind of dance of death, a hideous fantasy, the execution of which was rather poor. Hussonnet dispensed with the formality of a present.

Frederick was waiting to offer his, after the others.

She thanked him very much for it. Thereupon, he said:

"Why, 'tis almost a debt. I have been so much annoyed—"

"At what, pray?" she returned. "I don't understand."

"Come! dinner is waiting!" said Arnoux, catching hold of his arm; then in a whisper: "You are not very knowing, certainly!"

Nothing could well be prettier than the dining-room, painted in water-green. At one end, a nymph of stone was dipping her toe in a basin formed like a shell. Through the open windows the entire garden could be seen with the long lawn flanked by an old Scotch fir, three-quarters stripped bare; groups of flowers swelled it out in unequal plots; and at the other side of the river extended in a wide semicircle the Bois de Boulogne, Neuilly, Sèvres, and Meudon. Before the railed gate in front a canoe with sail outspread was tacking about.

They chatted first about the view in front of them, then about scenery in general; and they were beginning to plunge into discussions when Arnoux, at half-past nine o'clock, ordered the horse to be put to the carriage.

"Would you like me to go back with you?" said Madame Arnoux.

"Why, certainly!" and, making her a graceful bow: "You know well, madame, that it is impossible to live without you!"

Everyone congratulated her on having so good a husband.

"Ah! it is because I am not the only one," she replied quietly, pointing towards her little daughter.

Then, the conversation having turned once more on painting, there was some talk about a Ruysdaël, for which Arnoux expected a big sum, and Pellerin asked him if it were true that the celebrated Saul Mathias from London had come over during the past month to make him an offer of twenty-three thousand francs for it.

" 'Tis a positive fact!" and turning towards Frederick: "That was the very same gentleman I brought with me a few days ago to the Alhambra, much against my will, I assure you, for these English are by no means amusing companions."

Frederick, who suspected that Mademoiselle Vatnaz's letter contained some reference to an intrigue, was amazed at the facility with which my lord Arnoux found a way of passing it off as a perfectly honourable transaction; but his new lie, which was quite needless, made the young man open his eyes in speechless astonishment.

The picture-dealer added, with an air of simplicity:

"What's the name, by-the-by, of that young fellow, your friend?"

"Deslauriers," said Frederick quickly.

And, in order to repair the injustice which he felt he had done to his comrade, he praised him as one who possessed remarkable ability.

"Ah! indeed? But he doesn't look such a fine fellow as the other—the clerk in the wagon-office."

Frederick bestowed a mental imprecation on Dussardier. She would now be taking it for granted that he associated with the common herd.

Then they began to talk about the ornamentation of the capital—the new districts of the city—and the worthy Oudry happened to refer to M. Dambreuse as one of the big speculators.

Frederick, taking advantage of the opportunity to make a good figure, said he was acquainted with that gentleman. But Pellerin launched into a harangue against shopkeepers—he saw no difference between them, whether they were sellers of candles or of money. Then Rosenwald and Burieu talked about old china; Arnoux chatted with Madame Oudry about gardening; Sombary, a comical character of the old school, amused himself by chaffing her husband, referring to him sometimes as "Odry," as if he were the actor of that name, and remarking that he must be descended from Oudry, the dog-painter, seeing that the bump of the animals was visible on his forehead. He even wanted to feel M. Oudry's skull; but the latter excused himself on account of his wig; and the dessert ended with loud bursts of laughter.

When they had taken their coffee, while they smoked, under the linden-trees, and strolled about the garden for some time, they went out for a walk along the river.

The party stopped in front of a fishmonger's shop, where a man was washing eels. Mademoiselle Marthe wanted to look at them. He emptied the box in which he had them out on the grass; and the little girl threw herself on her knees in order to catch them, laughed with delight, and then began to scream with terror. They all got spoiled, and Arnoux paid for them.

He next took it into his head to go out for a sail in the cutter.

One side of the horizon was beginning to assume a pale aspect, while on the other side a wide strip of orange colour showed itself in the sky, deepening into purple at the summits of the hills, which were steeped in shadow. Madame Arnoux seated herself on a big stone with this glittering splendour at her back. The other ladies sauntered about here and there. Hussonnet, at the lower end of the river's bank, went making ducks and drakes over the water.

Arnoux presently returned, followed by a weather-beaten long boat, into which, in spite of the most prudent remonstrances, he packed his guests. The boat got upset, and they had to go ashore again.

By this time wax-tapers were burning in the drawing-room, all hung with chintz, and with branched candlesticks of crystal fixed close to the walls. Mère Oudry was sleeping comfortably in an armchair, and the others were listening to M. Lefaucheux expatiating on the glories of the Bar. Madame Arnoux was sitting by herself near the window. Frederick came over to her.

They chatted about the remarks which were being made in their vicinity. She admired oratory; he preferred the renown gained by authors. But, she ventured to suggest, it must give a man greater pleasure to move crowds directly by addressing them in person, face to face, than it does to infuse into their souls by his pen all the sentiments that animate his own. Such triumphs as these did not tempt Frederick much, as he had no ambition.

Then he broached the subject of sentimental adventures. She spoke pityingly of the havoc wrought by passion, but expressed indignation at hypocritical vileness, and this rectitude of spirit harmonised so well with the regular beauty of her face that it seemed indeed as if her physical attractions were the outcome of her moral nature.

She smiled, every now and then, letting her eyes rest on him for a minute. Then he felt her glances penetrating his soul like those great rays of sunlight which descend into the depths of the water. He loved her without mental reservation, without any hope of his love being returned, unconditionally; and in those silent transports, which were like outbursts of gratitude, he would fain have covered her forehead with a rain of kisses. However, an inspiration from within carried him beyond himself—he felt moved by a longing for self-sacrifice, an imperative impulse towards immediate self-devotion, and all the stronger from the fact that he could not gratify it.

He did not leave along with the rest. Neither did Hussonnet. They were to go back in the carriage; and the vehicle was waiting just in front of the steps when Arnoux rushed down and hurried into the garden to gather some flowers there. Then the bouquet having been tied round with a thread, as the stems fell down unevenly, he searched in his pocket, which was full of papers, took out a piece at random, wrapped them up, completed his handiwork with the aid of a strong pin, and then offered it to his wife with a certain amount of tenderness.

"Look here, my darling! Excuse me for having forgotten you!"

But she uttered a little scream: the pin, having been awkwardly fixed, had cut her, and she hastened up to her room. They waited nearly a quarter of an hour for her. At last, she reappeared, carried off Marthe, and threw herself into the carriage.

"And your bouquet?" said Arnoux.

"No! no—it is not worth while!" Frederick was running off to fetch it for her; she called out to him:

"I don't want it!"

But he speedily brought it to her, saying that he had just put it into an envelope again, as he had found the flowers lying on the floor. She thrust them behind the leathern apron of the carriage close to the seat, and off they started.

Frederick, seated by her side, noticed that she was trembling frightfully. Then, when they had passed the bridge, as Arnoux was turning to the left:

"Why, no! you are making a mistake!—that way, to the right!"

She seemed irritated; everything annoyed her. At length, Marthe having closed her eyes, Madame Arnoux drew forth the bouquet, and flung it out through the carriage-door, then caught Frederick's arm, making a sign to him with the other hand to say nothing about it.

After this, she pressed her handkerchief against her lips, and sat quite motionless.

The two others, on the dickey, kept talking about printing and about subscribers. Arnoux, who was driving recklessly, lost his way in the middle of the Bois de Boulogne. Then they plunged into narrow paths. The horse proceeded along at a walking pace; the branches of the trees grazed the hood. Frederick could see nothing of Madame Arnoux save her two eyes in the shade. Marthe lay stretched across her lap while he supported the child's head.

"She is tiring you!" said her mother.

He replied:

"No! Oh, no!"

Whirlwinds of dust rose up slowly. They passed through Auteuil. All the houses were closed up; a gas-lamp here and there lighted up the angle of a wall; then once more they were surrounded by darkness. At one time he noticed that she was shedding tears.

Was this remorse or passion? What in the world was it? This grief, of whose exact nature he was ignorant, interested him like a personal matter. There was now a new bond between them, as if, in a sense, they were accomplices; and he said to her in the most caressing voice he could assume:

"You are ill?"

"Yes, a little," she returned.

The carriage rolled on, and the honeysuckles and the syringas trailed over the garden fences, sending forth puffs of enervating odour into the night air. Her gown fell around her feet in numerous folds. It seemed to him as if he were in communication with her entire person through the medium of this child's body which lay stretched between them. He stooped over the little girl, and spreading out her pretty brown tresses, kissed her softly on the forehead.

"You are good!" said Madame Arnoux.

"Why?"

"Because you are fond of children."

"Not all!"

He said no more, but he let his left hand hang down her side wide open, fancying that she would follow his example perhaps, and that he would find her palm touching his. Then he felt ashamed and withdrew it. They soon reached the paved street. The carnage went on more quickly; the number of gas-lights vastly increased— it was Paris. Hussonnet, in front of the lumber-room, jumped down from his seat. Frederick waited till they were in the courtyard before alighting; then he lay in ambush at the corner of the Rue de Choiseul, and saw Arnoux slowly making his way back to the boulevards.

Next morning he began working as hard as ever he could.

He saw himself in an Assize Court, on a winter's evening, at the close of the advocates' speeches, when the jurymen are looking pale, and when the panting audience make the partitions of the prætorium creak; and after having being four hours speaking, he was recapitulating all his proofs, feeling with every phrase, with every word, with every gesture, the chopper of the guillotine, which was suspended behind him, rising up; then in the tribune of the Chamber, an orator who bears on his lips the safety of an entire people, drowning his opponents under his figures of rhetoric, crushing them under a repartee, with thunders and musical intonations in his voice, ironical, pathetic, fiery, sublime. She would be there somewhere in the midst of the others, hiding beneath her veil her enthusiastic tears. After that they would meet again, and he would be unaffected by discouragements, calumnies, and insults, if she would only say, "Ah, that is beautiful!" while drawing her light hand across his brow.

These images flashed, like beacon-lights, on the horizon of his life. His intellect, thereby excited, became more active and more vigorous. He buried himself in study till the month of August, and was successful at his final examination.

Deslauriers, who had found it so troublesome to coach him once more for the second examination at the close of December, and for the third in February, was astonished at his ardour. Then the great expectations of former days returned. In ten years it was probable that Frederick would be deputy; in fifteen a minister. Why not? With his patrimony, which would soon come into his hands, he might, at first, start a newspaper; this would be the opening step in his career; after that they would see what the future would bring. As for himself, he was still ambitious of obtaining a chair in the Law School; and he sustained his thesis for the degree of Doctor in such a remarkable fashion that it won for him the compliments of the professors.

Three days afterwards, Frederick took his own degree. Before leaving for his holidays, he conceived the idea of getting up a picnic to bring to a close their Saturday reunions.

He displayed the utmost gaiety on the occasion. Madame Arnoux was now with her mother at Chartres. But he would soon come across her again, and would end by being her lover.

Deslauriers, admitted the same day to the young advocates' pleading rehearsals at Orsay, had made a speech which was greatly applauded. Although he was sober, he drank a little more wine than was good for him, and said to Dussardier at dessert:

"You are an honest fellow!—and, when I'm a rich man, I'll make you my manager."

All were in a state of delight. Cisy was not going to finish his law-course. Martinon intended to remain during the period before his admission to the Bar in the provinces, where he would be nominated a deputy-magistrate. Pellerin was devoting himself to the production of a large picture representing "The Genius of the Revolution." Hussonnet was, in the following week, about to read for the Director of Public Amusements the scheme of a play, and had no doubt as to its success:

"As for the framework of the drama, they may leave that to me! As for the passions, I have knocked about enough to understand them thoroughly; and as for witticisms, they're entirely in my line!"

He gave a spring, fell on his two hands, and thus moved for some time around the table with his legs in the air. This performance, worthy of a street-urchin, did not get rid of Sénécal's frowns. He had just been dismissed from the boarding-school, in which he had been a teacher, for having given a whipping to an aristocrat's son. His straitened circumstances had got worse in consequence: he laid the blame of this on the inequalities of society, and cursed the wealthy. He poured out his grievances into the sympathetic ears of Regimbart, who had become every day more and more disillusioned, saddened, and disgusted. The Citizen had now turned his attention towards questions arising out of the Budget, and blamed the Court party for the loss of millions in Algeria.

As he could not sleep without having paid a visit to the, Alexandre smoking-divan, he disappeared at eleven o'clock. The rest went away some time afterwards; and Frederick, as he was parting with Hussonnet, learned that Madame Arnoux was to have come back the night before.

He accordingly went to the coach-office to change his time for starting to the next day; and, at about six o'clock in the evening, presented himself at her house. Her return, the door keeper said, had been put off for a week. Frederick dined alone, and then lounged about the boulevards.

Rosy clouds, scarf-like in form, stretched beyond the roofs; the shop-tents were beginning to be taken away; water-carts were letting a shower of spray fall over the dusty pavement; and an unexpected coolness was mingled with emana-tions from café's, as one got a glimpse through their open doors, between some sil-ver plate and gilt ware, of flowers in sheaves, which were reflected in the large sheets of glass. The crowd moved on at a leisurely pace. Groups of men were chat-ting in the middle of the foot-path; and women passed along with an indolent ex-pression in their eyes and that camelia tint in their complexions which intense heat imparts to feminine flesh. Something immeasurable in its vastness seemed to pour itself out and enclose the houses. Never had Paris looked so beautiful. He saw nothing before him in the future but an interminable series of years all full of love.

He stopped in front of the theatre of the Porte Saint-Martin to look at the bill; and, for want of something to occupy him, paid for a seat and went in.

An old-fashioned dramatic version of a fairy-tale was the piece on the stage. There was a very small audience; and through the skylights of the top gallery the vault of heaven seemed cut up into little blue squares, whilst the stage lamps above the orchestra formed a single line of yellow illuminations. The scene represented a slave-market at Pekin, with hand-bells, tomtoms, sweeping robes, sharp-pointed caps, and clownish jokes. Then, as soon as the curtain fell, he wandered into the foyer all alone and gazed out with admiration at a large green landau which stood on the boulevard outside, before the front steps of the theatre, yoked to two white horses, while a coachman with short breeches held the reins.

He had just got back to his seat when, in the balcony, a lady and a gentleman entered the first in front of the stage. The husband had a pale with a narrow strip of grey beard round it, rosette of a Government official, and that frigid look which is supposed to characterise diplomatists.

His wife, who was at least twenty years younger, and who was neither tall nor under-sized, neither ugly nor pretty, wore her fair hair in corkscrew curls in the English fashion, and displayed a long-bodiced dress and a large black lace fan. To make people so fashionable as these come to the theatre at such a season one would imagine either that there was some accidental cause, or that they had got tired of spending the evening in one another's society. The lady kept nibbling at her fan, while the gentleman yawned. Frederick could not recall to mind where he had seen that face.

In the next interval between the acts, while passing through one of the lobbies, he came face to face with both of them. As he bowed in an undecided manner, M. Dambreuse, at once recognising him, came up and apologised for having treated him with unpardonable neglect. It was an allusion to the numerous visiting-cards he had sent in accordance with the clerk's advice. However, he confused the periods, supposing that Frederick was in the second year of his law-course. Then he said he envied the young man for the opportunity of going into the country. He sadly needed a little rest himself, but business kept him in Paris.

Madame Dambreuse, leaning on his arm, nodded her head slightly, and the agreeable sprightliness of her face contrasted with its gloomy expression a short time before.

"One finds charming diversions in it, nevertheless," she said, after her husband's last remark. "What a stupid play that was—was it not, Monsieur?" And all three of them remained there chatting about theatres and new pieces.

Frederick, accustomed to the grimaces of provincial dames, had not seen in any woman such ease of manner combined with that simplicity which is the essence of refinement, and in which ingenuous souls trace the expression of instantaneous sympathy.

They would expect to see him as soon as he returned. M. Dambreuse told him to give his kind remembrances to Père Roque.

Frederick, when he reached his lodgings, did not fail to inform Deslauriers of their hospitable invitation.

"Grand!" was the clerk's reply; "and don't let your mamma get round you! Come back without delay!"

On the day after his arrival, as soon as they had finished breakfast, Madame Moreau brought her son out into the garden.

She said she was happy to see him in a profession, for they were not as rich as people imagined. The land brought in little; the people who farmed it paid badly. She had even been compelled to sell her carriage. Finally, she placed their situation in its true colours before him.

During the first embarrassments which followed the death of her late husband, M. Roque, a man of great cunning, had made her loans of money which had been renewed, and left long unpaid, in spite of her desire to clear them off. He had suddenly made a demand for immediate payment, and she had gone beyond the strict terms of the agreement by giving up to him, at a contemptible figure, the farm of Presles. Ten years later, her capital disappeared through the failure of a banker at Melun. Through a horror which she had of mortgages, and to keep up appearances, which might be necessary in view of her son's future, she had, when Père Roque presented himself again, listened to him once more. But now she was free from debt. In short, there was left them an income of about ten thousand francs, of which two thousand three hundred belonged to him—his entire patrimony.

"It isn't possible!" exclaimed Frederick.

She nodded her head, as if to declare that it was perfectly possible.

But his uncle would leave him something?

That was by no means certain!

And they took a turn around the garden without exchanging a word. At last she pressed him to her heart, and in a voice choked with rising tears:

"Ah! my poor boy! I have had to give up my dreams!"

He seated himself on a bench in the shadow of the large acacia.

Her advice was that he should become a clerk to M. Prouharam, solicitor, who would assign over his office to him; if he increased its value, he might sell it again and find a good practice.

Frederick was no longer listening to her. He was gazing automatically across the hedge into the other garden opposite.

A little girl of about twelve with red hair happened to be there all alone. She had made earrings for herself with the berries of the service-tree. Her bodice, made of grey linen-cloth, allowed her shoulders, slightly gilded by the sun, to be seen. Her short white petticoat was spotted with the stains made by sweets; and there was, so to speak, the grace of a young wild animal about her entire person, at the same time, nervous and thin. Apparently, the presence of a stranger astonished her, for she had stopped abruptly with her watering-pot in her hand darting glances at him with her large bright eyes, which were of a limpid greenish-blue colour.

"That is M. Roque's daughter," said Madame Moreau. "He has just married his servant and legitimised the child that he had by her."

Chapter VI

BLIGHTED HOPES

RUINED, STRIPPED OF EVERYTHING, UNDERMINED!

He remained seated on the bench, as if stunned by a shock. He cursed Fate; he would have liked to beat somebody; and, to intensify his despair, he felt a kind of outrage, a sense of disgrace, weighing down upon him; for Frederick had been under the impression that the fortune coming to him through his father would mount up one day to an income of fifteen thousand livres, and he had so informed the Arnoux' in an indirect sort of way. So then he would be looked upon as a braggart, a rogue, an obscure blackguard, who had introduced himself to them in the expectation of making some profit out of it! And as for her—Madame Arnoux—how could he ever see her again now?

Moreover, that was completely impossible when he had only a yearly income of three thousand francs. He could not always lodge on the fourth floor, have the door keeper as a servant, and make his appearance with wretched black gloves turning blue at the ends, a greasy hat, and the same frock-coat for a whole year. No, no! never! And yet without her existence was intolerable. Many people were well able to live without any fortune, Deslauriers amongst the rest; and he thought himself a coward to attach so much importance to matters of trifling consequence. Need would perhaps multiply his faculties a hundredfold. He excited himself by thinking on the great men who had worked in garrets. A soul like that of Madame Arnoux ought to be touched at such a spectacle, and she would be moved by it to sympathetic tenderness. So, after all, this catastrophe was a piece of good fortune; like those earthquakes which unveil treasures, it had revealed to him the hidden wealth of his nature. But there was only one place in the world where this could be turned to account—Paris; for to his mind, art, science, and love (those three faces of God, as Pellerin would have said) were associated exclusively with the capital. That evening, he informed his mother of his intention to go back there. Madame Moreau was surprised and indignant. She regarded it as a foolish and absurd course. It would be better to follow her advice, namely, to remain near her in an office. Frederick shrugged his shoulders, "Come now"—looking on this proposal as an insult to himself.

Thereupon, the good lady adopted another plan. In a tender voice broken by sobs she began to dwell on her solitude, her old age, and the sacrifices she had made for him. Now that she was more unhappy than ever, he was abandoning her. Then, alluding to the anticipated close of her life:

"A little patience—good heavens! you will soon be free!"

These lamentations were renewed twenty times a day for three months; and at the same time the luxuries of a home made him effeminate. He found it enjoyable to have a softer bed and napkins that were not torn, so that, weary, enervated, overcome by the terrible force of comfort, Frederick allowed himself to be brought to Maître Prouharam's office.

He displayed there neither knowledge nor aptitude. Up to this time, he had been regarded as a young man of great means who ought to be the shining light of the Department. The public would now come to the conclusion that he had imposed upon them.

At first, he said to himself:

"It is necessary to inform Madame Arnoux about it;" and for a whole week he kept formulating in his own mind dithyrambic letters and short notes in an eloquent and sublime style. The fear of avowing his actual position restrained him. Then he thought that it was far better to write to the husband. Arnoux knew life and could understand the true state of the case. At length, after a fortnight's hesitation:

"Bah! I ought not to see them any more: let them forget me! At any rate, I shall be cherished in her memory without having sunk in her estimation! She will believe that I am dead, and will regret me—perhaps."

As extravagant resolutions cost him little, he swore in his own mind that he would never return to Paris, and that he would not even make any enquiries about Madame Arnoux.

Nevertheless, he regretted the very smell of the gas and the noise of the omnibuses. He mused on the things that she might have said to him, on the tone of her voice, on the light of her eyes—and, regarding himself as a dead man, he no longer did anything at all.

He arose very late, and looked through the window at the passing teams of wagoners. The first six months especially were hateful.

On certain days, however, he was possessed by a feeling of indignation even against her. Then he would go forth and wander through the meadows, half covered in winter time by the inundations of the Seine. They were cut up by rows of poplar-trees. Here and there arose a little bridge. He tramped about till evening, rolling the yellow leaves under his feet, inhaling the fog, and jumping over the ditches. As his arteries began to throb more vigorously, he felt himself carried away by a desire to do something wild; he longed to become a trapper in America, to attend on a pasha in the East, to take ship as a sailor; and he gave vent to his melancholy in long letters to Deslauriers.

The latter was struggling to get on. The slothful conduct of his friend and his eternal jeremiads appeared to him simply stupid. Their correspondence soon became a mere form. Frederick had given up all his furniture to Deslauriers, who stayed on in the same lodgings. From time to time his mother spoke to him. At length he one day told her about the present he had made, and she was giving him a rating for it, when a letter was placed in his hands.

"What is the matter now?" she said, "you are trembling?"

"There is nothing the matter with me," replied Frederick.

Deslauriers informed him that he had taken Sénécal under his protection, and that for the past fortnight they had been living together. So now Sénécal was exhibiting himself in the midst of things that had come from the Arnoux's shop. He might sell them, criticise, make jokes about them. Frederick felt wounded in the depths of his soul. He went up to his own apartment. He felt a yearning for death.

His mother called him to consult him about a plantation in the garden.

This garden was, after the fashion of an English park, cut in the middle by a stick fence; and the half of it belonged to Père Roque, who had another for vegetables on the bank of the river. The two neighbours, having fallen out, abstained from making their appearance there at the same hour. But since Frederick's return, the old gentleman used to walk about there more frequently, and was not stinted in his courtesies towards Madame Moreau's son. He pitied the young man for having to live in a country town. One day he told him that Madame Dambreuse had been anxious to hear from him. On another occasion he expatiated on the custom of Champagne, where the stomach conferred nobility.

"At that time you would have been a lord, since your mother's name was De Fouvens. And 'tis all very well to talk—never mind! there's something in a name. After all," he added, with a sly glance at Frederick, "that depends on the Keeper of the Seals."

This pretension to aristocracy contrasted strangely with his personal appearance. As he was small, his big chestnut-coloured frock-coat exaggerated the length of his bust. When he took off his hat, a face almost like that of a woman with an extremely sharp nose could be seen; his hair, which was of a yellow colour, resembled a wig. He saluted people with a very low bow, brushing against the wall.

Up to his fiftieth year, he had been content with the services of Catherine, a native of Lorraine, of the same age as himself, who was strongly marked with small-pox. But in the year 1834, he brought back with him from Paris a handsome blonde with a sheep-like type of countenance and a "queenly carriage." Ere long, she was observed strutting about with large earrings; and everything was explained by the birth of a daughter who was introduced to the world under the name of Elisabeth Olympe Louise Roque.

Catherine, in her first ebullition of jealousy, expected that she would curse this child. On the contrary, she became fond of the little girl, and treated her with the utmost care, consideration, and tenderness, in order to supplant her mother and render her odious—an easy task, inasmuch as Madame Éléonore entirely neglected the little one, preferring to gossip at the tradesmen's shops. On the day after her marriage, she went to pay a visit at the Sub-prefecture, no longer "thee'd" and "thou'd" the servants, and took it into her head that, as a matter of good form, she ought to exhibit a certain severity towards the child. She was present while the little one was at her lessons. The teacher, an old clerk who had been employed at the Mayor's office, did not know how to go about the work of instructing the girl. The pupil rebelled, got her ears boxed, and rushed away to shed tears on the lap of Catherine, who always took her part. After this the two women wrangled, and M. Roque ordered them to hold their tongues. He had married only out of tender regard for his daughter, and did not wish to be annoyed by them.

She often wore a white dress with ribbons, and pantalettes trimmed with lace; and on great festival-days she would leave the house attired like a princess, in order to mortify a little the matrons of the town, who forbade their brats to associate with her on account of her illegitimate birth.

She passed her life nearly always by herself in the garden, went see-sawing on the swing, chased butterflies, then suddenly stopped to watch the floral beetles swooping down on the rose-trees. It was, no doubt, these habits which imparted to her face an expression at the same time of audacity and dreaminess. She had, moreover, a figure like Marthe, so that Frederick said to her, at their second interview:

"Will you permit me to kiss you, mademoiselle?"

The little girl lifted up her head and replied:

"I will!"

But the stick-hedge separated them from one another.

"We must climb over," said Frederick.

"No, lift me up!"

He stooped over the hedge, and raising her off the ground with his hands, kissed her on both cheeks; then he put her back on her own side by a similar process; and this performance was repeated on the next occasions when they found themselves together.

Without more reserve than a child of four, as soon as she heard her friend coming, she sprang forward to meet him, or else, hiding behind a tree, she began yelping like a dog to frighten him.

One day, when Madame Moreau had gone out, he brought her up to his own room. She opened all the scent-bottles, and pomaded her hair plentifully; then, without the slightest embarrassment, she lay down on the bed, where she remained stretched out at full length, wide awake.

"I fancy myself your wife," she said to him.

Next day he found her all in tears. She confessed that she had been "weeping for her sins;" and, when he wished to know what they were, she hung down her head, and answered:

"Ask me no more!"

The time for first communion was at hand. She had been brought to confession in the morning. The sacrament scarcely made her wiser. Occasionally, she got into a real passion; and Frederick was sent for to appease her.

He often brought her with him in his walks. While he indulged in day-dreams as he walked along, she would gather wild poppies at the edges of the corn-fields; and, when she saw him more melancholy than usual, she tried to console him with her pretty childish prattle. His heart, bereft of love, fell back on this friendship inspired by a little girl. He gave her sketches of old fogies, told her stories, and devoted himself to reading books for her.

He began with the *Annales Romantiques,* a collection of prose and verse celebrated at the period. Then, forgetting her age, so much was he charmed by her intelligence, he read for her in succession, *Atala, Cinq-Mars,* and *Les Feuilles d' Antomne.* But one night (she had that very evening heard *Macbeth* in Letourneur's simple translation) she woke up, exclaiming:

"The spot! the spot!" Her teeth chattered, she shivered, and, fixing terrified glances on her right hand, she kept rubbing it, saying:

"Always a spot!"

At last a doctor was brought, who directed that she should be kept free from violent emotions.

The townsfolk saw in this only an unfavourable prognostic for her morals. It was said that "young Moreau" wished to make an actress of her later.

Soon another event became the subject of discussion—namely, the arrival of uncle Barthélemy. Madame Moreau gave up her sleeping-apartment to him, and was so gracious as to serve up meat to him on fast-days.

The old man was not very agreeable. He was perpetually making comparisons between Havre and Nogent, the air of which he considered heavy, the bread bad, the streets ill-paved, the food indifferent, and the inhabitants very lazy. "How wretched trade is with you in this place!" He blamed his deceased brother for his extravagance, pointing out by way of contrast that he had himself accumulated an income of twenty-seven thousand livres a year. At last, he left at the end of the week, and on the footboard of the carriage gave utterance to these by no means reassuring words:

"I am always very glad to know that you are in a good position."

"You will get nothing," said Madame Moreau as they re-entered the dining-room.

He had come only at her urgent request, and for eight days she had been seeking, on her part, for an opening—only too clearly perhaps. She repented now of having done so, and remained seated in her armchair with her head bent down and her lips tightly pressed together. Frederick sat opposite, staring at her; and they were both silent, as they had been live years before on his return home by the Montereau steamboat. This coincidence, which presented itself even to her mind, recalled Madame Arnoux to his recollection.

At that moment the crack of a whip outside the window reached their ears, while a voice was heard calling out to him.

It was Père Roque, who was alone in his tilted cart. He was going to spend the whole day at La Fortelle with M. Dambreuse, and cordially offered to drive Frederick there.

"You have no need of an invitation as long as you are with me. Don't be afraid!"

Frederick felt inclined to accept this offer. But how would he explain his fixed sojourn at Nogent? He had not a proper summer suit. Finally, what would his mother say? He accordingly decided not to go.

From that time, their neighbour exhibited less friendliness. Louise was growing tall; Madame Éléonore fell dangerously ill; and the intimacy broke off, to the great delight of Madame Moreau, who feared lest her son's prospects of being settled in life might be affected by association with such people.

She was thinking of purchasing for him the registrarship of the Court of Justice. Frederick raised no particular objection to this scheme. He now accompanied her to mass; in the evening he took a hand in a game of "all fours." He became accustomed to provincial habits of life, and allowed himself to slide into them; and even his love had assumed a character of mournful sweetness, a kind of soporific charm. By dint of having poured out his grief in his letters, mixed it up with everything he read, given full vent to it during his walks through the country, he had almost exhausted it, so that Madame Arnoux was for him, as it were, a dead woman whose tomb he wondered that he did not know, so tranquil and resigned had his affection for her now become.

One day, the 12th of December, 1845, about nine o'clock in the morning, the cook brought up a letter to his room. The address, which was in big characters, was written in a hand he was not acquainted with; and Frederick, feeling sleepy, was in no great hurry to break the seal. At length, when he did so, he read:

Justice of the Peace at Havre,
111th Arrondissement.

MONSIEUR—Monsieur Moreau, your uncle, having died intestate—

He had fallen in for the inheritance! As if a conflagration had burst out behind the wall, he jumped out of bed in his shirt, with his feet bare. He passed his hand over his face, doubting the evidence of his own eyes, believing that he was still dreaming, and in order to make his mind more clearly conscious of the reality of the event, he flung the window wide open.

There had been a fall of snow; the roofs were white, and he even recognised in the yard outside a washtub which had caused him to stumble after dark the evening before.

He read the letter over three times in succession. Could there be anything more certain? His uncle's entire fortune! A yearly income of twenty-seven thousand livres! And he was overwhelmed with frantic joy at the idea of seeing Madame Arnoux once more. With the vividness of a hallucination he saw himself beside her, at her house, bringing her some present in silver paper, while at the door stood a tilbury—no, a brougham rather!—a black brougham, with a servant in brown livery. He could hear his horse pawing the ground and the noise of the curb-chain mingling with the rippling sound of their kisses. And every day this was renewed indefinitely. He would receive them in his own house: the dining-room would be furnished in red leather; the boudoir in yellow silk; sofas everywhere! and such a variety of whatnots, china vases, and carpets! These images came in so tumultuous a fashion into his mind that he felt his head turning round. Then he thought of his mother; and he descended the stairs with the letter in his hand.

Madame Moreau made an effort to control her emotion, but could not keep herself from swooning. Frederick caught her in his arms and kissed her on the forehead.

"Dear mother, you can now buy back your carriage—laugh then! shed no more tears! be happy!"

Ten minutes later the news had travelled as far as the faubourgs. Then M. Benoist, M. Gamblin, M. Chambion, and other friends hurried towards the house. Frederick got away for a minute in order to write to Deslauriers. Then other visitors turned up. The afternoon passed in congratulations. They had forgotten all about "Roque's wife," who, however, was declared to be "very low."

When they were alone, the same evening, Madame Moreau said to her son that she would advise him to set up as an advocate at Troyes. As he was better known in his own part of the country than in any other, he might more easily find there a profitable connection.

"Ah, it is too hard!" exclaimed Frederick. He had scarcely grasped his good fortune in his hands when he longed to carry it to Madame Arnoux. He announced his express determination to live in Paris.

"And what are you going to do there?"

"Nothing!"

Madame Moreau, astonished at his manner, asked what he intended to become.

"A minister," was Frederick's reply. And he declared that he was not at all joking, that he meant to plunge at once into diplomacy, and that his studies and his instincts impelled him in that direction. He would first enter the Council of State under M. Dambreuse's patronage.

"So then, you know him?"

"Oh, yes—through M. Roque."

"That is singular," said Madame Moreau. He had awakened in her heart her former dreams of ambition. She internally abandoned herself to them, and said no more about other matters.

If he had yielded to his impatience, Frederick would have started that very instant. Next morning every seat in the diligence had been engaged; and so he kept eating out his heart till seven o'clock in the evening.

They had sat down to dinner when three prolonged tolls of the church-bell fell on their ears; and the housemaid, coming in, informed them that Madame Éléonore had just died.

This death, after all, was not a misfortune for anyone, not even for her child. The young girl would only find it all the better for herself afterwards.

As the two houses were close to one another, a great coming and going and a clatter of tongues could be heard; and the idea of this corpse being so near them threw a certain funereal gloom over their parting. Madame Moreau wiped her eyes two or three times. Frederick felt his heart oppressed.

When the meal was over, Catherine stopped him between two doors. Mademoiselle had peremptorily expressed a wish to see him. She was waiting for him in the garden. He went out there, strode over the hedge, and knocking more or less against the trees, directed his steps towards M. Roque's house. Lights were glittering through a window in the second story then a form appeared in the midst of the darkness, and a voice whispered:

" 'Tis I!"

She seemed to him taller than usual, owing to her black dress, no doubt. Not knowing what to say to her, he contented himself with catching her hands, and sighing forth:

"Ah! my poor Louise!"

She did not reply. She gazed at him for a long time with a look of sad, deep earnestness.

Frederick was afraid of missing the coach; he fancied that he could hear the rolling of wheels some distance away, and, in order to put an end to the interview without any delay:

"Catherine told me that you had something—"

"Yes—'tis true! I wanted to tell you—"

He was astonished to find that she addressed him in the plural; and, as she again relapsed into silence:

"Well, what?"

"I don't know. I forget! Is it true that you're going away?"

"Yes, I'm starting just now."

She repeated: "Ah! just now?—for good?—we'll never see one another again?"

She was choking with sobs.

"Good-bye! good-bye! embrace me then!"

And she threw her arms about him passionately.

Chapter VII

CHANGE OF FORTUNE

THEN HE HAD TAKEN HIS PLACE BEHIND THE OTHER PASSENGERS IN THE front of the diligence, and when the vehicle began to shake as the five horses started into a brisk trot all at the same time, he allowed himself to plunge into an intoxicating dream of the future. Like an architect drawing up the plan of a palace, he mapped out his life beforehand. He filled it with dainties and with splendours; it rose up to the sky; a profuse display of allurements could be seen there; and so deeply was he buried in the contemplation of these things that he lost sight of all external objects.

At the foot of the hill of Sourdun his attention was directed to the stage which they had reached in their journey. They had travelled only about five kilometres at the most. He was annoyed at this tardy rate of travelling. He pulled down the coach-window in order to get a view of the road. He asked the conductor several times at what hour they would reach their destination. However, he eventually regained his composure, and remained seated in his corner of the vehicle with eyes wide open.

The lantern, which hung from the postilion's seat, threw its light on the buttocks of the shaft-horses. In front, only the manes of the other horses could be seen undulating like white billows. Their breathing caused a kind of fog to gather at each side of the team. The little iron chains of the harness rang; the windows shook in their sashes; and the heavy coach went rolling at an even pace over the pavement. Here and there could be distinguished the wall of a barn, or else an inn standing by itself. Sometimes, as they entered a village, a baker's oven threw out gleams of light; and the gigantic silhouettes of the horses kept rushing past the walls of the opposite houses. At every change of horses, when the harness was unfastened, there was a great silence for a minute. Overhead, under the awning, some passenger might be heard tapping with his feet, while a woman sitting at the threshold of the door screened her candle with her hand. Then the conductor would jump on the footboard, and the vehicle would start on its way again.

At Mormans, the striking of the clocks announced that it was a quarter past one.

"So then we are in another day," he thought, "we have been in it for some time!"

But gradually his hopes and his recollections, Nogent, the Rue de Choiseul, Madame Arnoux, and his mother, all got mixed up together.

He was awakened by the dull sound of wheels passing over planks: they were crossing the Pont de Charenton—it was Paris. Then his two travelling companions, the first taking off his cap, and the second his silk handkerchief, put on their hats, and began to chat.

The first, a big, red-faced man in a velvet frock-coat, was a merchant; the second was coming up to the capital to consult a physician; and, fearing that he had disturbed this gentleman during the night, Frederick spontaneously apologised to him, so much had the young man's heart been softened by the feelings of happiness that possessed it. The wharf of the wet dock being flooded, no doubt, they went straight ahead; and once more they could see green fields. In the distance, tall factory-chimneys were sending forth their smoke. Then they turned into Ivry. Then drove up a street: all at once, he saw before him the dome of the Panthéon.

The plain, quite broken up, seemed a waste of ruins. The enclosing wall of the fortifications made a horizontal swelling there; and, on the footpath, on the ground at the side of the road, little branchless trees were protected by laths bristling with nails. Establishments for chemical products and timber-merchants' yards made their appearance alternately. High gates, like those seen in farmhouses, afforded glimpses, through their opening leaves, of wretched yards within, full of filth, with puddles of dirty water in the middle of them. Long wine-shops, of the colour of ox's blood, displayed in the first floor, between the windows, two billiard-cues crossing one another, with a wreath of painted flowers. Here and there might be noticed a half-built plaster hut, which had been allowed to remain unfinished. Then the double row of houses was no longer interrupted; and over their bare fronts enormous tin cigars showed themselves at some distance from each other, indicating tobacconists' shops. Midwives' signboards represented in each case a matron in a cap rocking a doll under a counterpane trimmed with lace. The corners of the walls were covered with placards, which, three-quarters torn, were quivering in the wind like rags. Workmen in blouses, brewers' drays, laundresses' and butchers' carts passed along. A thin rain was falling. It was cold. There was a pale sky; but two eyes, which to him were as precious as the sun, were shining behind the haze.

They had to wait a long time at the barrier, for vendors of poultry, wagoners, and a flock of sheep caused an obstruction there. The sentry, with his great-coat thrown back, walked to and fro in front of his box, to keep himself warm. The clerk who collected the city-dues clambered up to the roof of the diligence, and a cornet-à-piston sent forth a flourish. They went down the boulevard at a quick trot, the whipple-trees clapping and the traces hanging loose. The lash of the whip went cracking through the moist air. The conductor uttered his sonorous shout:

"Look alive! look alive! oho!" and the scavengers drew out of the way, the pedestrians sprang back, the mud gushed against the coach-windows; they crossed

dung-carts, cabs, and omnibuses. At length, the iron gate of the Jardin des Plantes
came into sight.

The Seine, which was of a yellowish colour, almost reached the platforms of
the bridges. A cool breath of air issued from it. Frederick inhaled it with his utmost energy, drinking in this good air of Paris, which seems to contain the efflu-
via of love and the emanations of the intellect. He was touched with emotion at
the first glimpse of a hackney-coach. He gazed with delight on the thresholds of
the wine-merchants' shops garnished with straw, on the shoeblacks with their
boxes, on the lads who sold groceries as they shook their coffee-burners. Women
hurried along at a jog-trot with umbrellas over their heads. He bent forward to try
whether he could distinguish their faces—chance might have led Madame Arnoux
to come out.

The shops displayed their wares. The crowd grew denser; the noise in the
streets grew louder. After passing the Quai Saint-Bernard, the Quai de la Tournelle, and the Quai Montebello, they drove along the Quai Napoleon. He was anxious to see the windows there; but they were too far away from him. Then they
once more crossed the Seine over the Pont-Neuf, and descended in the direction of
the Louvre; and, having traversed the Rues Saint-Honoré, Croix des Petits-
Champs, and Du Bouloi, he reached the Rue Coq-Héron, and entered the courtyard of the hotel.

To make his enjoyment last the longer, Frederick dressed himself as slowly as
possible, and even walked as far as the Boulevard Montmartre. He smiled at the
thought of presently beholding once more the beloved name on the marble plate.
He cast a glance upwards; there was no longer a trace of the display in the windows, the pictures, or anything else.

He hastened to the Rue de Choiseul. M. and Madame Arnoux no longer
resided there, and a woman next door was keeping an eye on the porter's lodge.
Frederick waited to see the porter himself. After sometime he made his appearance—
it was no longer the same man. He did not know their address.

Frederick went into a café, and, while at breakfast, consulted the Commercial
Directory. There were three hundred Arnoux in it, but no Jacques Arnoux. Where,
then, were they living? Pellerin ought to know.

He made his way to the very top of the Faubourg Poissonnière, to the artist's
studio. As the door had neither a bell nor a knocker, he rapped loudly on it with his
knuckles, and then called out—shouted. But the only response was the echo of his
voice from the empty house.

After this he thought of Hussonnet; but where could he discover a man of that
sort? On one occasion he had waited on Hussonnet when the latter was paying a
visit to his mistress's house in the Rue de Fleurus. Frederick had just reached the

Rue de Fleurus when he became conscious of the fact that he did not even know the lady's name.

He had recourse to the Prefecture of Police. He wandered from staircase to staircase, from office to office. He found that the Intelligence Department was closed for the day, and was told to come back again next morning.

Then he called at all the picture-dealers' shops that he could discover, and enquired whether they could give him any information as to Arnoux's whereabouts. The only answer he got was that M. Arnoux was no longer in the trade.

At last, discouraged, weary, sickened, he returned to his hotel, and went to bed. Just as he was stretching himself between the sheets, an idea flashed upon him which made him leap up with delight:

"Regimbart! what an idiot I was not to think of him before!"

Next morning, at seven o'clock, he arrived in the Rue Notre Dame des Victoires, in front of a dram-shop, where Regimbart was in the habit of drinking white wine. It was not yet open. He walked about the neighbourhood, and at the end of about half-an-hour, presented himself at the place once more. Regimbart had left it.

Frederick rushed out into the street. He fancied that he could even notice Regimbart's hat some distance away. A hearse and some mourning coaches intercepted his progress. When they had got out of the way, the vision had disappeared.

Fortunately, he recalled to mind that the Citizen breakfasted every day at eleven o'clock sharp, at a little restaurant in the Place Gaillon. All he had to do was to wait patiently till then; and, after sauntering about from the Bourse to the Madeleine, and from the Madeleine to the Gymnase, so long that it seemed as if it would never come to an end, Frederick, just as the clocks were striking eleven, entered the restaurant in the Rue Gaillon, certain of finding Regimbart there.

"Don't know!" said the restaurant-keeper, in an unceremonious tone.

Frederick persisted: the man replied:

"I have no longer any acquaintance with him, Monsieur"—and, as he spoke, he raised his eyebrows majestically and shook his head in a mysterious fashion.

But, in their last interview, the Citizen had referred to the Alexandre smoking-divan. Frederick swallowed a cake, jumped into a cab, and asked the driver whether there happened to be anywhere on the heights of Sainte-Geneviève a certain Café Alexandre. The cabman drove him to the Rue des Francs Bourgeois Saint-Michel, where there was an establishment of that name, and in answer to his question:

"M. Regimbart, if you please?" the keeper of the café said with an unusually gracious smile:

"We have not seen him as yet, Monsieur," while he directed towards his wife, who sat behind the counter, a look of intelligence. And the next moment, turning towards the clock:

"But he'll be here, I hope, in ten minutes, or at most a quarter of an hour. Celestin, hurry with the newspapers! What would Monsieur like to take?"

Though he did not want to take anything, Frederick swallowed a glass of rum, then a glass of kirsch, then a glass of curaçoa, then several glasses of grog, both cold and hot. He read through that day's *Siècle,* and then read it over again; he examined the caricatures in the *Charivari* down to the very tissue of the paper. When he had finished, he knew the advertisements by heart. From time to time, the tramp of boots on the footpath outside reached his ears—it was he! and some one's form would trace its outlines on the window-panes; but it invariably passed on.

In order to get rid of the sense of weariness he experienced, Frederick shifted his seat. He took up his position at the lower end of the room; then at the right; after that at the left; and he remained in the middle of the bench with his arms stretched out. But a cat, daintily pressing down the velvet at the back of the seat, startled him by giving a sudden spring, in order to lick up the spots of syrup on the tray; and the child of the house, an insufferable brat of four, played noisily with a rattle on the bar steps. His mother, a pale-faced little woman, with decayed teeth, was smiling in a stupid sort of way. What in the world could Regimbart be doing? Frederick waited for him in an exceedingly miserable frame of mind.

The rain clattered like hail on the covering of the cab. Through the opening in the muslin curtain he could see the poor horse in the street more motionless than a horse made of wood. The stream of water, becoming enormous, trickled down between two spokes of the wheels, and the coachman was nodding drowsily with the horsecloth wrapped round him for protection, but fearing lest his fare might give him the slip, he opened the door every now and then, with the rain dripping from him as if falling from a mountain torrent; and, if things could get worn out by looking at them, the clock ought to have by this time been utterly dissolved, so frequently did Frederick rivet his eyes on it. However, it kept going. "Mine host" Alexandre walked up and down repeating, "He'll come! Cheer up! he'll come!" and, in order to divert his thoughts, talked politics, holding forth at some length. He even carried civility so far as to propose a game of dominoes.

At length when it was half-past four, Frederick, who had been there since about twelve, sprang to his feet, and declared that he would not wait any longer.

"I can't understand it at all myself," replied the café-keeper, in a tone of straightforwardness. "This is the first time that M. Ledoux has failed to come!"

"What! Monsieur Ledoux?"

"Why, yes, Monsieur!"

"I said Regimbart," exclaimed Frederick, exasperated.

"Ah! a thousand pardons! You are making a mistake! Madame Alexandre, did not Monsieur say M. Ledoux?"

And, questioning the waiter: "You heard him yourself, just as I did?"

No doubt, to pay his master off for old scores, the waiter contented himself with smiling.

Frederick drove back to the boulevards, indignant at having his time wasted, raging against the Citizen, but craving for his presence as if for that of a god, and firmly resolved to drag him forth, if necessary, from the depths of the most remote cellars. The vehicle in which he was driving only irritated him the more, and he accordingly got rid of it. His ideas were in a state of confusion. Then all the names of the cafés which he had heard pronounced by that idiot burst forth at the same time from his memory like the thousand pieces of an exhibition of fireworks—the Café Gascard, the Café Grimbert, the Café Halbout, the Bordelais smoking-divan, the Havanais, the Havrais, the Bœuf à la Mode, the Brasserie Allemande, and the Mère Morel; and he made his way to all of them in succession. But in one he was told that Regimbart had just gone out; in another, that he might perhaps call at a later hour; in a third, that they had not seen him for six months; and, in another place, that he had the day before ordered a leg of mutton for Saturday. Finally, at Vautier's dining-rooms, Frederick, on opening the door, knocked against the waiter.

"Do you know M. Regimbart?"

"What, monsieur! do I know him? 'Tis I who have the honour of attending on him. He's upstairs—he is just finishing his dinner!"

And, with a napkin under his arm, the master of the establishment himself accosted him:

"You're asking him for M. Regimbart, monsieur? He was here a moment ago."

Frederick gave vent to an oath, but the proprietor of the dining-rooms stated that he would find the gentleman as a matter of certainty at Bouttevilain's.

"I assure you, on my honour, he left a little earlier than usual, for he had a business appointment with some gentlemen. But you'll find him, I tell you again, at Bouttevilain's, in the Rue Saint-Martin, No. 92, the second row of steps at the left, at the end of the courtyard—first floor—door to the right!"

At last, he saw Regimbart, in a cloud of tobacco-smoke, by himself, at the lower end of the refreshment-room, near the billiard-table, with a glass of beer in front of him, and his chin lowered in a thoughtful attitude.

"Ah! I have been a long time searching for you!"

Without rising, Regimbart extended towards him only two fingers, and, as if he had seen Frederick the day before, he gave utterance to a number of commonplace remarks about the opening of the session.

Frederick interrupted him, saying in the most natural tone he could assume:

"Is Arnoux going on well?"

The reply was a long time coming, as Regimbart was gargling the liquor in his throat:

"Yes, not badly."

"Where is he living now?"

"Why, in the Rue Paradis Poissonnière," the Citizen returned with astonishment.

"What number?"

"Thirty-seven—confound it! what a funny fellow you are!"

Frederick rose.

"What! are you going?"

"Yes, yes! I have to make a call—some business matter I had forgotten! Goodbye!"

Frederick went from the smoking-divan to the Arnoux's residence, as if carried along by a tepid wind, with a sensation of extreme ease such as people experience in dreams.

He found himself soon on the second floor in front of a door, at the ringing of whose bell a servant appeared. A second door was flung open. Madame Arnoux was seated near the fire. Arnoux jumped up, and rushed across to embrace Frederick. She had on her lap a little boy not quite three years old. Her daughter, now as tall as herself, was standing up at the opposite side of the mantelpiece.

"Allow me to present this gentleman to you," said Arnoux, taking his son up in his arms. And he amused himself for some minutes in making the child jump up in the air very high, and then catching him with both hands as he came down.

"You'll kill him!—ah! good heavens, have done!" exclaimed Madame Arnoux.

But Arnoux, declaring that there was not the slightest danger, still kept tossing up the child, and even addressed him in words of endearment such as nurses use in the Marseillaise dialect, his natal tongue: "Ah! my fine picheoun! my ducksy of a little nightingale!"

Then, he asked Frederick why he had been so long without writing to them, what he had been doing down in the country, and what brought him back.

"As for me, I am at present, my dear friend, a dealer in faïence. But let us talk about yourself!"

Frederick gave as reasons for his absence a protracted lawsuit and the state of his mother's health. He laid special stress on the latter subject in order to make himself interesting. He ended by saying that this time he was going to settle in Paris for good; and he said nothing about the inheritance, lest it might be prejudicial to his past.

The curtains, like the upholstering of the furniture, were of maroon damask wool. Two pillows were close beside one another on the bolster. On the coal-fire a kettle was boiling; and the shade of the lamp, which stood near the edge of the chest of drawers, darkened the apartment. Madame Arnoux wore a large blue merino dressing-gown. With her face turned towards the fire and one hand on the shoulder of the little boy, she unfastened with the other the child's bodice. The youngster in his shirt began to cry, while scratching his head, like the son of M. Alexandre.

Frederick expected that he would have felt spasms of joy; but the passions grow pale when we find ourselves in an altered situation; and, as he no longer saw Madame Arnoux in the environment wherein he had known her, she seemed to him to have lost some of her fascination; to have degenerated in some way that he could not comprehend—in fact, not to be the same. He was astonished at the serenity of his own heart. He made enquiries about some old friends, about Pellerin, amongst others.

"I don't see him often," said Arnoux. She added:

"We no longer entertain as we used to do formerly!"

Was the object of this to let him know that he would get no invitation from them? But Arnoux, continuing to exhibit the same cordiality, reproached him for not having come to dine with them uninvited; and he explained why he had changed his business.

"What are you to do in an age of decadence like ours? Great painting is gone out of fashion! Besides, we may import art into everything. You know that, for my part, I am a lover of the beautiful. I must bring you one of these days to see my earthenware works."

And he wanted to show Frederick immediately some of his productions in the store which he had between the ground-floor and the first floor.

Dishes, soup-tureens, and washhand-basins encumbered the floor. Against the walls were laid out large squares of pavement for bathrooms and dressing-rooms, with mythological subjects in the Renaissance style; whilst in the centre, a pair of whatnots, rising up to the ceiling, supported ice-urns, flower-pots, candelabra, little flower-stands, and large statuettes of many colours, representing a negro or a shepherdess in the Pompadour fashion. Frederick, who was cold and hungry, was bored with Arnoux's display of his wares. He hurried off to the Café Anglais, where he ordered a sumptuous supper, and while eating, said to himself:

"I was well off enough below there with all my troubles! She scarcely took any notice of me! How like a shopkeeper's wife!"

And in an abrupt expansion of healthfullness, he formed egoistic resolutions. He felt his heart as hard as the table on which his elbows rested. So then he could by this time plunge fearlessly into the vortex of society. The thought of the Dambreuses recurred to his mind. He would make use of them. Then he recalled

Deslauriers to mind. "Ah! faith, so much the worse!" Nevertheless, he sent him a note by a messenger, making an appointment with him for the following day, in order that they might breakfast together.

Fortune had not been so kind to the other.

He had presented himself at the examination for a fellowship with a thesis on the law of wills, in which he maintained that the powers of testators ought to be restricted as much as possible; and, as his adversary provoked him in such a way as to make him say foolish things, he gave utterance to many of these absurdities without in any way inducing the examiners to falter in deciding that he was wrong. Then chance so willed it that he should choose by lot, as a subject for a lecture, Prescription. Thereupon, Deslauriers gave vent to some lamentable theories: the questions in dispute in former times ought to be brought forward as well as those which had recently arisen; why should the proprietor be deprived of his estate because he could furnish his title-deeds only after the lapse of thirty-one years? This was giving the security of the honest man to the inheritor of the enriched thief. Every injustice was consecrated by extending this law, which was a form of tyranny, the abuse of force! He had even exclaimed: "Abolish it; and the Franks will no longer oppress the Gauls, the English oppress the Irish, the Yankee oppress the Redskins, the Turks oppress the Arabs, the whites oppress the blacks, Poland——"

The President interrupted him: "Well! well! Monsieur, we have nothing to do with your political opinions—you will have them represented in your behalf by-and-by!"

Deslauriers did not wish to have his opinions represented; but this unfortunate Title XX of the *Third Book of the Civil Code* had become a sort of mountain over which he stumbled. He was elaborating a great work on "Prescription considered as the Basis of the Civil Law and of the Law of Nature amongst Peoples"; and he got lost in Dunod, Rogerius, Balbus, Merlin, Vazeille, Savigny, Traplong, and other weighty authorities on the subject. In order to have more leisure for the purpose of devoting himself to this task, he had resigned his post of head-clerk. He lived by giving private tuitions and preparing theses; and at the meetings of newly-fledged barristers to rehearse legal arguments he frightened by his display of virulence those who held conservative views, all the young doctrinaires who acknowledged M. Guizot as their master—so that in a certain set he had gained a sort of celebrity, mingled, in a slight degree, with lack of confidence in him as an individual.

He came to keep the appointment in a big paletot, lined with red flannel, like the one Sénécal used to wear in former days.

Human respect on account of the passers-by prevented them from straining one another long in an embrace of friendship; and they made their way to Véfour's arm-in-arm, laughing pleasantly, though with tear-drops lingering in the depths of their eyes. Then, as soon as they were free from observation, Deslauriers exclaimed:

"Ah! damn it! we'll have a jolly time of it now!"

Frederick was not quite pleased to find Deslauriers all at once associating himself in this way with his own newly-acquired inheritance. His friend exhibited too much pleasure on account of them both, and not enough on his account alone.

After this, Deslauriers gave details about the reverse he had met with, and gradually told Frederick all about his occupations and his daily existence, speaking of himself in a stoical fashion, and of others in tones of intense bitterness. He found fault with everything; there was not a man in office who was not an idiot or a rascal. He flew into a passion against the waiter for having a glass badly rinsed, and, when Frederick uttered a reproach with a view to mitigating his wrath: "As if I were going to annoy myself with such numbskulls, who, you must know, can earn as much as six and even eight thousand francs a year, who are electors, perhaps eligible as candidates. Ah! no, no!"

Then, with a sprightly air, "But I've forgotten that I'm talking to a capitalist, to a Mondor, for you are a Mondor now!"

And, coming back to the question of the inheritance, he gave expression to this view—that collateral successorship (a thing unjust in itself, though in the present case he was glad it was possible) would be abolished one of these days at the approaching revolution.

"Do you believe in that?" said Frederick.

"Be sure of it!" he replied. "This sort of thing cannot last. There is too much suffering. When I see into the wretchedness of men like Sénécal—"

"Always Sénécal!" thought Frederick.

"But, at all events, tell me the news? Are you still in love with Madame Arnoux? Is it all over—eh?"

Frederick, not knowing what answer to give him, closed his eyes and hung down his head.

With regard to Arnoux, Deslauriers told him that the journal was now the property of Hussonnet, who had transformed it. It was called "*L'Art,* a literary institution—a company with shares of one hundred francs each; capital of the firm, forty thousand francs," each shareholder having the right to put into it his own contributions; for "the company has for its object to publish the works of beginners, to spare talent, perchance genius, the sad crises which drench," etc.

"You see the dodge!" There was, however, something to be effected by the change—the tone of the journal could be raised; then, without any delay, while retaining the same writers, and promising a continuation of the feuilleton, to supply the subscribers with a political organ: the amount to be advanced would not be very great.

"What do you think of it? Come! would you like to have a hand in it?"

Frederick did not reject the proposal; but he pointed out that it was necessary for him to attend to the regulation of his affairs.

"After that, if you require anything—"

"Thanks, my boy!" said Deslauriers.

Then, they smoked puros, leaning with their elbows on the shelf covered with velvet beside the window. The sun was shining; the air was balmy. Flocks of birds, fluttering about, swooped down into the garden. The statues of bronze and marble, washed by the rain, were glistening. Nursery-maids wearing aprons, were seated on chairs, chatting together; and the laughter of children could be heard mingling with the continuous plash that came from the sheaf-jets of the fountain.

Frederick was troubled by Deslauriers' irritability; but under the influence of the wine which circulated through his veins, half-asleep, in a state of torpor, with the sun shining full on his face, he was no longer conscious of anything save a profound sense of comfort, a kind of voluptuous feeling that stupefied him, as a plant is saturated with heat and moisture. Deslauriers, with half-closed eyelids, was staring vacantly into the distance. His breast swelled, and he broke out in the following strain:

"Ah! those were better days when Camille Desmoulins, standing below there on a table, drove the people on to the Bastille. Men really lived in those times; they could assert themselves, and prove their strength! Simple advocates commanded generals. Kings were beaten by beggars; whilst now—"

He stopped, then added all of a sudden:

"Pooh! the future is big with great things!"

And, drumming a battle-march on the window-panes, he declaimed some verses of Barthélemy, which ran thus:

> " *That dread Assembly shall again appear,*
> *Which, after forty years, fills you with fear,*
> *Marching with giant stride and dauntless soul'*

—I don't know the rest of it! But 'tis late; suppose we go?"

And he went on setting forth his theories in the street.

Frederick, without listening to him, was looking at certain materials and articles of furniture in the shop-windows which would be suitable for his new residence in Paris; and it was, perhaps, the thought of Madame Arnoux that made him stop before a second-hand dealer's window, where three plates made of fine ware were exposed to view. They were decorated with yellow arabesques with metallic reflections, and were worth a hundred crowns apiece. He got them put by.

"For my part, if I were in your place," said Deslauriers, "I would rather buy silver plate," revealing by this love of substantial things the man of mean extraction.

As soon as he was alone, Frederick repaired to the establishment of the celebrated Pomadère, where he ordered three pairs of trousers, two coats, a pelisse trimmed with fur, and five waistcoats. Then he called at a bootmaker's, a shirt-maker's, and a hatter's, giving them directions in each shop to make the greatest possible haste. Three days later, on the evening of his return from Havre, he found his complete wardrobe awaiting him in his Parisian abode; and impatient to make use of it, he resolved to pay an immediate visit to the Dambreuses. But it was too early yet—scarcely eight o'clock.

"Suppose I went to see the others?" said he to himself.

He came upon Arnoux, all alone, in the act of shaving in front of his glass. The latter proposed to drive him to a place where they could amuse themselves, and when M. Dambreuse was referred to, "Ah, that's just lucky! You'll see some of his friends there. Come on, then! It will be good fun!"

Frederick asked to be excused. Madame Arnoux recognised his voice, and wished him good-day, through the partition, for her daughter was indisposed, and she was also rather unwell herself. The noise of a soup-ladle against a glass could be heard from within, and all those quivering sounds made by things being lightly moved about, which are usual in a sickroom. Then Arnoux left his dressing-room to say good-bye to his wife. He brought forward a heap of reasons for going out:

"You know well that it is a serious matter! I must go there; 'tis a case of necessity. They'll be waiting for me!"

"Go, go, my dear! Amuse yourself!"

Arnoux hailed a hackney-coach:

"Palais Royal, No. 7 Montpensier Gallery." And, as he let himself sink back in the cushions:

"Ah! how tired I am, my dear fellow! It will be the death of me! However, I can tell it to you—to you!"

He bent towards Frederick's ear in a mysterious fashion:

"I am trying to discover again the red of Chinese copper!"

And he explained the nature of the glaze and the little fire.

On their arrival at Chevet's shop, a large hamper was brought to him, which he stowed away in the hackney-coach. Then he bought for his "poor wife" pine-apples and various dainties, and directed that they should be sent early next morning.

After this, they called at a costumer's establishment; it was to a ball they were going.

Arnoux selected blue velvet breeches, a vest of the same material, and a red wig; Frederick a domino; and they went down the Rue de Laval towards a house the second floor of which was illuminated by coloured lanterns.

At the foot of the stairs they heard violins playing above.

"Where the deuce are you bringing me to?" said Frederick.

"To see a nice girl! don't be afraid!"

The door was opened for them by a groom; and they entered the anteroom, where paletots, mantles, and shawls were thrown together in a heap on some chairs. A young woman in the costume of a dragoon of Louis XIV's reign was passing at that moment. It was Mademoiselle Rosanette Bron, the mistress of the place.

"Well?" said Arnoux.

" 'Tis done!" she replied.

"Ah! thanks, my angel!"

And he wanted to kiss her.

"Take care, now, you foolish man! You'll spoil the paint on my face!"

Arnoux introduced Frederick.

"Step in there, Monsieur; you are quite welcome!"

She drew aside a door-curtain, and cried out with a certain emphasis:

"Here's my lord Arnoux, girl, and a princely friend of his!"

Frederick was at first dazzled by the lights. He could see nothing save some silk and velvet dresses, naked shoulders, a mass of colours swaying to and fro to the accompaniment of an orchestra hidden behind green foliage, between walls hung with yellow silk, with pastel portraits here and there and crystal chandeliers in the style of Louis XVI's period. High lamps, whose globes of roughened glass resembled snowballs, looked down on baskets of flowers placed on brackets in the corners; and at the opposite side, at the rear of a second room, smaller in size, one could distinguish, in a third, a bed with twisted posts, and at its head a Venetian mirror.

The dancing stopped, and there were bursts of applause, a hubbub of delight, as Arnoux was seen advancing with his hamper on his head; the eatables contained in it made a lump in the centre.

"Make way for the lustre!"

Frederick raised his eyes: it was the lustre of old Saxe that had adorned the shop attached to the office of *L'Art Industriel*. The memory of former days was brought back to his mind. But a foot-soldier of the line in undress, with that silly expression of countenance ascribed by tradition to conscripts, planted himself right in front of him, spreading out his two arms in order to emphasise his astonishment, and, in spite of the hideous black moustaches, unusually pointed, which disfigured his face, Frederick recognised his old friend Hussonnet. In a half-Alsatian, half-negro kind of gibberish, the Bohemian loaded him with congratulations, calling him his colonel. Frederick, put out of countenance by the crowd of personages assembled around him, was at a loss for an answer. At a tap on the desk from a fiddlestick, the partners in the dance fell into their places.

They were about sixty in number, the women being for the most part dressed either as village-girls or marchionesses, and the men, who were nearly all of mature age, being got up as wagoners, 'longshoremen, or sailors.

Frederick having taken up his position close to the wall, stared at those who were going through the quadrille in front of him.

An old beau, dressed like a Venetian Doge in a long gown of purple silk, was dancing with Mademoiselle Rosanette, who wore a green coat, laced breeches, and boots of soft leather with gold spurs. The pair in front of them consisted of an Albanian laden with yataghans and a Swiss girl with blue eyes and skin white as milk, who looked as plump as a quail with her chemise-sleeves and red corset exposed to view. In order to turn to account her hair, which fell down to her hips, a tall blonde, a walking lady in the opera, had assumed the part of a female savage; and over her brown swaddling-cloth she displayed nothing save leathern breeches, glass bracelets, and a tinsel diadem, from which rose a large sheaf of peacock's feathers. In front of her, a gentleman who had intended to represent Pritchard, muffled up in a grotesquely big black coat, was beating time with his elbows on his snuff-box. A little Watteau shepherd in blue-and-silver, like moonlight, dashed his crook against the thyrsus of a Bacchante crowned with grapes, who wore a leopard's skin over her left side, and buskins with gold ribbons, On the other side, a Polish lady, in a spencer of nacarat-coloured velvet, made her gauze petticoat flutter over her pearl-gray stockings, which rose above her fashionable pink boots bordered with white fur. She was smiling on a big-paunched man of forty, disguised as a choir-boy, who was skipping very high, lifting up his surplice with one hand, and with the other his red clerical cap. But the queen, the star, was Mademoiselle Loulou, a celebrated dancer at public halls. As she had now become wealthy, she wore a large lace collar over her vest of smooth black velvet; and her wide trousers of poppy-coloured silk, clinging closely to her figure, and drawn tight round her waist by a cashmere scarf, had all over their seams little natural white camellias. Her pale face, a little puffed, and with the nose somewhat *retroussé*, looked all the more pert from the disordered appearance of her wig, over which she had with a touch of her hand clapped a man's grey felt hat, so that it covered her right ear; and, with every bounce she made, her pumps, adorned with diamond buckles, nearly reached the nose of her neighbour, a big mediæval baron, who was quite entangled in his steel armour. There was also an angel, with a gold sword in her hand, and two swan's wings over her back, who kept rushing up and down, every minute losing her partner who appeared as Louis XIV, displaying an utter ignorance of the figures and confusing the quadrille.

Frederick, as he gazed at these people, experienced a sense of forlornness, a feeling of uneasiness. He was still thinking of Madame Arnoux and it seemed to him as if he were taking part in some plot that was being hatched against her.

When the quadrille was over, Mademoiselle Rosanette accosted him. She was slightly out of breath, and her gorget, polished like a mirror, swelled up softly under her chin.

"And you, Monsieur," said she, "don't you dance?"

Frederick excused himself; he did not know how to dance.

"Really! but with me? Are you quite sure?" And, poising herself on one hip, with her other knee a little drawn back, while she stroked with her left hand the mother-of-pearl pommel of her sword, she kept staring at him for a minute with a half-beseeching, half-teasing air. At last she said "Good night! then," made a pirouette, and disappeared.

Frederick, dissatisfied with himself, and not well knowing what to do, began to wander through the ball-room.

He entered the boudoir padded with pale blue silk, with bouquets of flowers from the fields, whilst on the ceiling, in a circle of gilt wood, Cupids, emerging out of an azure sky, played over the clouds, resembling down in appearance. This display of luxuries, which would to-day be only trifles to persons like Rosanette, dazzled him, and he admired everything—the artificial convolvuli which adorned the surface of the mirror, the curtains on the mantelpiece, the Turkish divan, and a sort of tent in a recess in the wall, with pink silk hangings and a covering of white muslin overhead. Furniture made of dark wood with inlaid work of copper filled the sleeping apartment, where, on a platform covered with swan's-down, stood the large canopied bedstead trimmed with ostrich-feathers. Pins, with heads made of precious stones, stuck into pincushions, rings trailing over trays, lockets with hoops of gold, and little silver chests, could be distinguished in the shade under the light shed by a Bohemian urn suspended from three chainlets. Through a little door, which was slightly ajar, could be seen a hot-house occupying the entire breadth of a terrace, with an aviary at the other end.

Here were surroundings specially calculated to charm him. In a sudden revolt of his youthful blood he swore that he would enjoy such things; he grew bold; then, coming back to the place opening into the drawing-room, where there was now a larger gathering—it kept moving about in a kind of luminous pulverulence—he stood to watch the quadrilles, blinking his eyes to see better, and inhaling the soft perfumes of the women, which floated through the atmosphere like an immense kiss.

But, close to him, on the other side of the door, was Pellerin—Pellerin, in full dress, his left arm over his breast and with his hat and a torn white glove in his right.

"Halloa! 'Tis a long time since we saw you! Where the deuce have you been? Gone to travel in Italy? 'Tis a commonplace country enough—Italy, eh? not so unique as people say it is? No matter! Will you bring me your sketches one of these days?"

And, without giving him time to answer, the artist began talking about himself. He had made considerable progress, having definitely satisfied himself as to the stupidity of the line. We ought not to look so much for beauty and unity in a work as for character and diversity of subject.

"For everything exists in nature; therefore, everything is legitimate; everything is plastic. It is only a question of catching the note, mind you! I have discovered the secret." and giving him a nudge, he repeated several times, "I have discovered the secret, you see! Just look at that little woman with the headdress of a sphinx who is dancing with a Russian postilion—that's neat, dry, fixed, all in flats and in stiff tones—indigo under the eyes, a patch of vermilion on the cheek, and bistre on the temples—pif! paf!" And with his thumb he drew, as it were, pencil-strokes in the air. "Whilst the big one over there," he went on, pointing towards a fishwife in a cherry gown with a gold cross hanging from her neck, and a lawn fichu fastened round her shoulders, "is nothing but curves. The nostrils are spread out just like the borders of her cap; the corners of the mouth are rising up; the chin sinks: all is fleshy, melting, abundant, tranquil, and sunshiny—a true Rubens! Nevertheless, they are both perfect! Where, then, is the type?" He grew warm with the subject. "What is this but a beautiful woman? What is it but the beautiful? Ah! the beautiful—tell me what that is—"

Frederick interrupted him to enquire who was the merry-andrew with the face of a he-goat, who was in the very act of blessing all the dancers in the middle of a pastourelle.

"Oh! he's not much!—a widower, the father of three boys. He leaves them without breeches, spends his whole day at the club, and lives with the servant!"

"And who is that dressed like a bailiff talking in the recess of the window to a Marquise de Pompadour?"

"The Marquise is Mademoiselle Vandael, formerly an actress at the Gymnase, the mistress of the Doge, the Comte de Palazot. They have now been twenty years living together—nobody can tell why. Had she fine eyes at one time, this woman? As for the citizen by her side, his name is Captain d'Herbigny, an old man of the hurdy-gurdy sort that you can play on, with nothing in the world except his Cross of the Legion of Honour and his pension. He passes for the uncle of the grisettes at festival times, arranges duels, and dines in the city."

"A rascal?" said Frederick.

"No! an honest man!"

"Ha!"

The artist was going on to mention the names of many others, when, perceiving a gentleman who, like Molière's physician, wore a big black serge gown opening very wide as it descended in order to display all his trinkets:

"The person who presents himself there before you is Dr. Des Rogis, who, full of rage at not having made a name for himself, has written a book of medical pornography, and willingly blacks people's boots in society, while he is at the same time discreet. These ladies adore him. He and his wife (that lean châtelaine in the grey dress) trip about together at every public place—aye, and at other places too. In spite of domestic embarrassments, they have *a day*—artistic teas, at which verses are recited. Attention!"

In fact, the doctor came up to them at that moment; and soon they formed all three, at the entrance to the drawing-room, a group of talkers, which was presently augmented by Hussonnet, then by the lover of the female savage, a young poet who displayed, under a court cloak of Francis I's reign, the most pitiful of anatomies, and finally a sprightly youth disguised as a Turk of the barrier. But his vest with its yellow galloon had taken so many voyages on the backs of strolling dentists, his wide trousers full of creases, were of so faded a red, his turban, rolled about like an eel in the Tartar fashion, was so poor in appearance—in short, his entire costume was so wretched and made-up, that the women did not attempt to hide their disgust. The doctor consoled him by pronouncing eulogies on his mistress, the lady in the dress of a 'longshorewoman. This Turk was a banker's son.

Between two quadrilles, Rosanette advanced towards the mantelpiece, where an obese little old man, in a maroon coat with gold buttons, had seated himself in an armchair. In spite of his withered cheeks, which fell over his white cravat, his hair, still fair, and curling naturally like that of a poodle, gave him a certain frivolity of aspect.

She was listening to him with her face bent close to his. Presently, she accommodated him with a little glass of syrup; and nothing could be more dainty than her hands under their laced sleeves, which passed over the facings of her green coat. When the old man had swallowed it, he kissed them.

"Why, that's M. Oudry, a neighbor of Arnoux!"

"He has lost her!" said Pellerin, smiling.

A Longjumeau postilion caught her by the waist. A waltz was beginning. Then all the women, seated round the drawing-room on benches, rose up quickly at the same time; and their petticoats, their scarfs, and their head-dresses went whirling round.

They whirled so close to him that Frederick could notice the beads of perspiration on their foreheads; and this gyral movement, more and more lively, regular, provocative of dizzy sensations, communicated to his mind a sort of intoxication, which made other images surge up within it, while every woman passed with the same dazzling effect, and each of them with a special kind of exciting influence, according to her style of beauty.

The Polish lady, surrendering herself in a languorous fashion, inspired him with a longing to clasp her to his heart while they were both spinning forward on a sledge along a plain covered with snow. Horizons of tranquil voluptuousness in a chalet at the side of a lake opened out under the footsteps of the Swiss girl, who waltzed with her bust erect and her eyelashes drooping. Then, suddenly, the Bacchante, bending back her head with its dark locks, made him dream of devouring caresses in a wood of oleanders, in the midst of a storm, to the confused accompaniment of labours. The fishwife, who was panting from the rapidity of the music, which was far too great for her, gave vent to bursts of laughter; and he would have liked, while drinking with her in some tavern in the "Porcherons," to rumple her fichu with both hands, as in the good old times. But the 'longshorewoman, whose light toes barely skimmed the floor, seemed to conceal under the suppleness of her limbs and the seriousness of her face all the refinements of modern love, which possesses the exactitude of a science and the mobility of a bird. Rosanette was whirling with arms akimbo; her wig, in an awkward position, bobbing over her collar, flung iris-powder around her; and, at every turn, she was near catching hold of Frederick with the ends of her gold spurs.

During the closing bar of the waltz, Mademoiselle Vatnaz made her appearance. She had an Algerian handkerchief on her head, a number of piastres on her forehead, antimony at the edges of her eyes, with a kind of paletot made of black cashmere falling over a petticoat of sparkling colour, with stripes of silver; and in her hand she held a tambourine.

Behind her back came a tall fellow in the classical costume of Dante, who happened to be—she now made no concealment any longer about it—the ex-singer of the Alhambra, and who, though his name was Auguste Delamare, had first called himself Anténor Delamarre, then Delmas, then Belmar, and at last Delmar, thus modifying and perfecting his name, as his celebrity increased, for he had forsaken the public-house concert for the theatre, and had even just made his *début* in a noisy fashion at the Ambigu in *Gaspardo le Pêcheur*.

Hussonnet, on seeing him, knitted his brows. Since his play had been rejected, he hated actors. It was impossible to conceive the vanity of individuals of this sort, and above all of this fellow. "What a prig! just look at him!"

After a light bow towards Rosanette, Delmar leaned back against the mantelpiece; and he remained motionless with one hand over his heart, his left foot thrust forward, his eyes raised towards heaven, with his wreath of gilt laurels above his cowl, while he strove to put into the expression of his face a considerable amount of poetry in order to fascinate the ladies. They made, at some distance, a great circle around him.

But the Vatnaz, having given Rosanette a prolonged embrace, came to beg of Hussonnet to revise, with a view to the improvement of the style, an educational work which she intended to publish, under the title of "The Young Ladies' Garland," a collection of literature and moral philosophy.

The man of letters promised to assist her in the preparation of the work. Then she asked him whether he could not in one of the prints to which he had access give her friend a slight puff, and even assign to him, later, some part. Hussonnet had forgotten to take a glass of punch on account of her.

It was Arnoux who had brewed the beverage; and, followed by the Comte's groom carrying an empty tray, he offered it to the ladies with a self-satisfied air.

When he came to pass in front of M. Oudry, Rosanette stopped him.

"Well—and this little business?"

He coloured slightly; finally, addressing the old man:

"Our fair friend tells me that you would have the kindness—"

"What of that, neighbour? I am quite at your service!"

And M. Dambreuse's name was pronounced. As they were talking to one another in low tones, Frederick could only hear indistinctly; and he made his way to the other side of the mantelpiece, where Rosanette and Delmar were chatting together.

The mummer had a vulgar countenance, made, like the scenery of the stage, to be viewed from a distance—coarse hands, big feet, and a heavy jaw; and he disparaged the most distinguished actors, spoke of poets with patronising contempt, made use of the expressions "my organ," "my physique," "my powers," enamelling his conversation with words that were scarcely intelligible even to himself, and for which he had quite an affection, such as *"morbidezza,"* "analogue," and "homogeneity."

Rosanette listened to him with little nods of approbation. One could see her enthusiasm bursting out under the paint on her cheeks, and a touch of moisture passed like a veil over her bright eyes of an indefinable colour. How could such a man as this fascinate her? Frederick internally excited himself to greater contempt for him, in order to banish, perhaps, the species of envy which he felt with regard to him.

Mademoiselle Vatnaz was now with Arnoux, and, while laughing from time to time very loudly, she cast glances towards Rosanette, of whom M. Oudry did not lose sight.

Then Arnoux and the Vatnaz disappeared. The old man began talking in a subdued voice to Rosanette.

"Well, yes, 'tis settled then! Leave me alone!"

And she asked Frederick to go and give a look into the kitchen to see whether Arnoux happened to be there.

A battalion of glasses half-full covered the floor; and the saucepans, the pots, the turbot-kettle, and the frying-stove were all in a state of commotion. Arnoux was giving directions to the servants, whom he "thee'd" and "thou'd," beating up the mustard, tasting the sauces, and larking with the housemaid.

"All right," he said; "tell them 'tis ready! I'm going to have it served up."

The dancing had ceased. The women came and sat down; the men were walking about. In the centre of the drawing-room, one of the curtains stretched over a window was swelling in the wind; and the Sphinx, in spite of the observations of everyone, exposed her sweating arms to the current of air.

Where could Rosanette be? Frederick went on further to find her, even into her boudoir and her bedroom. Some, in order to be alone, or to be in pairs, had retreated into the corners. Whisperings intermingled with the shade. There were little laughs stifled under handkerchiefs, and at the sides of women's corsages one could catch glimpses of fans quivering with slow, gentle movements, like the beating of a wounded bird's wings.

As he entered the hot-house, he saw under the large leaves of a caladium near the jet d'eau, Delmar lying on his face on the sofa covered with linen cloth. Rosanette, seated beside him, had passed her fingers through his hair; and they were gazing into each other's faces. At the same moment, Arnoux came in at the opposite side—that which was near the aviary. Delmar sprang to his feet; then he went out at a rapid pace, without turning round; and even paused close to the door to gather a hibiscus flower, with which he adorned his button-hole. Rosanette hung down her head; Frederick, who caught a sight of her profile, saw that she was in tears.

"I say! What's the matter with you?" exclaimed Arnoux.

She shrugged her shoulders without replying.

"Is it on account of him?" he went on.

She threw her arms round his neck, and kissing him on the forehead, slowly:

"You know well that I will always love you, my big fellow! Think no more about it! Let us go to supper!"

A copper chandelier with forty wax tapers lighted up the dining-room, the walls of which were hidden from view under some fine old earthenware that was hung up there; and this crude light, felling perpendicularly, rendered still whiter, amid the side-dishes and the fruits, a huge turbot which occupied the centre of the tablecloth, with plates all round filled with crayfish soup. With a rustle of garments, the women, having arranged their skirts, their sleeves, and their scarfs, took their seats beside one another; the men, standing up, posted themselves at the corners. Pellerin and M. Oudry were placed near Rosanette, Arnoux was facing her. Palazot and his female companion had just gone out.

"Good-bye to them!" said she. "Now let us begin the attack!"

And the choir-boy, a facetious man with a big sign of the cross, said grace.

The ladies were scandalised, and especially the fishwife, the mother of a young girl of whom she wished to make an honest woman. Neither did Arnoux like "that sort of thing," as he considered that religion ought to be respected.

A German clock with a cock attached to it happening to chime out the hour of two, gave rise to a number of jokes about the cuckoo. All kinds of talk followed— puns, anecdotes, bragging remarks, bets, lies taken for truth, improbable assertions, a tumult of words, which soon became dispersed in the form of chats between particular individuals. The wines went round; the dishes succeeded each other; the doctor carved. An orange or a cork would every now and then be flung from a distance. People would quit their seats to go and talk to some one at another end of the table. Rosanette turned round towards Delmar, who sat motionless behind her; Pellerin kept babbling; M. Oudry smiled. Mademoiselle Vatnaz ate, almost alone, a group of crayfish, and the shells crackled under her long teeth. The angel, poised on the piano-stool—the only place on which her wings permitted her to sit down—was placidly masticating without ever stopping.

"What an appetite!" the choir-boy kept repeating in amazement, "what an appetite!"

And the Sphinx drank brandy, screamed out with her throat full, and wriggled like a demon. Suddenly her jaws swelled, and no longer being able to keep down the blood which rushed to her head and nearly choked her, she pressed her napkin against her lips, and threw herself under the table.

Frederick had seen her falling: " 'Tis nothing!" And at his entreaties to be allowed to go and look after her, she replied slowly:

"Pooh! what's the good? That's just as pleasant as anything else. Life is not so amusing!"

Then, he shivered, a feeling of icy sadness taking possession of him, as if he had caught a glimpse of whole worlds of wretchedness and despair—a chafing-dish of charcoal beside a folding-bed, the corpses of the Morgue in leathern aprons, with the tap of cold water that flows over their heads.

Meanwhile, Hussonnet, squatted at the feet of the female savage, was howling in a hoarse voice in imitation of the actor Grassot:

"Be not cruel, O Celuta! this little family fête is charming! Intoxicate me with delight, my loves! Let us be gay! let us be gay!"

And he began kissing the women on the shoulders. They quivered under the tickling of his moustaches. Then he conceived the idea of breaking a plate against his head by rapping it there with a little energy. Others followed his example. The broken earthenware flew about in bits like slates in a storm; and the ' longshore-woman exclaimed:

"Don't bother yourselves about it; these cost nothing. We get a present of them from the merchant who makes them!"

Every eye was riveted on Arnoux. He replied:

"Ha! about the invoice—allow me!" desiring, no doubt, to pass for not being, or for no longer being, Rosanette's lover.

But two angry voices here made themselves heard:

"Idiot!"

"Rascal!"

"I am at your command!"

"So am I at yours!"

It was the mediæval knight and the Russian postilion who were disputing, the latter having maintained that armour dispensed with bravery, while the other re-garded this view as an insult. He desired to fight; all interposed to prevent him, and in the midst of the uproar the captain tried to make himself heard.

"Listen to me, messieurs! One word! I have some experience, messieurs!"

Rosanette, by tapping with her knife on a glass, succeeded eventually in restor-ing silence, and, addressing the knight, who had kept his helmet on, and then the postilion, whose head was covered with a hairy cap:

"Take off that saucepan of yours! and you, there, your wolfs head! Are you going to obey me, damn you? Pray show respect to my epaulets! I am your com-manding officer!"

They complied, and everyone present applauded, exclaiming, "Long live the Maréchale! long live the Maréchale!" Then she took a bottle of champagne off the stove, and poured out its contents into the cups which they successively stretched forth to her. As the table was very large, the guests, especially the women, came over to her side, and stood erect on tiptoe on the slats of the chairs, so as to form, for the space of a minute, a pyramidal group of headdresses, naked shoulders, ex-tended arms, and stooping bodies; and over all these objects a spray of wine played for some time, for the merry-andrew and Arnoux, at opposite corners of the dining-room, each letting fly the cork of a bottle, splashed the faces of those around them.

The little birds of the aviary, the door of which had been left open, broke into the apartment, quite scared, flying round the chandelier, knocking against the window-panes and against the furniture, and some of them, alighting on the heads of the guests, presented the appearance there of large flowers.

The musicians had gone. The piano had been drawn out of the anteroom. The Vatnaz seated herself before it, and, accompanied by the choir-boy, who thumped his tambourine, she made a wild dash into a quadrille, striking the keys like a horse pawing the ground, and wriggling her waist about, the better to mark the time. The Maréchale dragged out Frederick; Hussonnet took the windmill; the 'longshore-woman put out her joints like a circus-clown; the merry-andrew exhibited the manouevres of an orang-outang; the female savage, with outspread arms, imitated the swaying motion of a boat. At last, unable to go on any further, they all stopped; and a window was flung open.

The broad daylight penetrated the apartment with the cool breath of morning. There was an exclamation of astonishment, and then came silence. The yellow flames flickered, making the sockets, of the candlesticks crack from time to time. The floor was strewn with ribbons, flowers, and pearls. The pier-tables were sticky with the stains of punch and syrup. The hangings were soiled, the dresses rumpled and dusty. The plaits of the women's hair hung loose over their shoulders, and the paint, trickling down with the perspiration, revealed pallid faces and red, blinking eyelids.

The Maréchale, fresh as if she had come out of a bath, had rosy cheeks and sparkling eyes. She flung her wig some distance away, and her hair fell around her like a fleece, allowing none of her uniform to be seen except her breeches, the effect thus produced being at the same time comical and pretty.

The Sphinx, whose teeth chattered as if she had the ague, wanted a shawl.

Rosanette rushed up to her own room to look for one, and, as the other came after her, she quickly shut the door in her face.

The Turk remarked, in a loud tone, that M. Oudry had not been seen going out. Nobody noticed the maliciousness of this observation, so worn out were they all.

Then, while waiting for vehicles, they managed to get on their broad-brimmed hats and cloaks. It struck seven. The angel was still in the dining-room, seated at the table with a plate of sardines and fruit stewed in melted butter in front of her, and close beside her was the fishwife, smoking cigarettes, while giving her advice as to the right way to live.

At last, the cabs having arrived, the guests took their departure. Hussonnet, who had an engagement as correspondent for the provinces, had to read through fifty-three newspapers before his breakfast. The female savage had a rehearsal at the theatre; Pellerin had to see a model; and the choir-boy had three appointments. But the angel, attacked by the preliminary symptoms of indigestion, was unable to rise. The mediæval baron carried her to the cab.

"Take care of her wings!" cried the 'longshore-woman through the window.

At the top of the stairs, Mademoiselle Vatnaz said to Rosanette:

"Good-bye, darling! That was a very nice evening party of yours."

Then, bending close to her ear: "Take care of him!"

"Till better times come," returned the Maréchale, in drawling tones, as she turned her back.

Arnoux and Frederick returned together, just as they had come. The dealer in faience looked so gloomy that his companion wished to know if he were ill.

"I? Not at all!"

He bit his moustache, knitted his brows; and Frederick asked him, was it his business that annoyed him.

"By no means!"

Then all of a sudden:

"You know him—Père Oudry—don't you?"

And, with a spiteful expression on his countenance:

"He's rich, the old scoundrel!"

After this, Arnoux spoke about an important piece of ware-making, which had to be finished that day at his works. He wanted to see it; the train was starting in an hour.

"Meantime, I must go and embrace my wife."

"Ha! his wife!" thought Frederick. Then he made his way home to go to bed, with his head aching terribly; and, to appease his thirst, he swallowed a whole carafe of water.

Another thirst had come to him—the thirst for women, for licentious pleasure, and all that Parisian life permitted him to enjoy. He felt somewhat stunned, like a man coming out of a ship, and in the visions that haunted his first sleep, he saw the shoulders of the fishwife, the loins of the 'longshore-woman, the calves of the Polish lady, and the headdress of the female savage flying past him and coming back again continually. Then, two large black eyes, which had not been at the ball, appeared before him; and, light as butterflies, burning as torches, they came and went, ascended to the cornice and descended to his very mouth.

Frederick made desperate efforts to recognise those eyes, without succeeding in doing so. But already the dream had taken hold of him. It seemed to him that he was yoked beside Arnoux to the pole of a hackney-coach, and that the Maréchale, astride of him, was disembowelling him with her gold spurs.

Chapter VIII

FREDERICK ENTERTAINS

REDERICK FOUND A LITTLE MANSION AT THE CORNER OF THE RUE RUMFORT, and he bought it along with the brougham, the horse, the furniture, and two flower-stands which were taken from the Arnoux's house to be placed on each side of his drawing-room door. In the rear of this apartment were a bedroom and a closet. The idea occurred to his mind to put up Deslauriers there. But how could he receive her—*her*, his future mistress? The presence of a friend would be an obstacle. He knocked down the partition-wall in order to enlarge the drawing-room, and converted the closet into a smoking-room.

He bought the works of the poets whom he loved, books of travel, atlases, and dictionaries, for he had innumerable plans of study. He hurried on the workmen, rushed about to the different shops, and in his impatience to enjoy, carried off everything without even holding out for a bargain beforehand.

From the tradesmen's bills, Frederick ascertained that he would have to expend very soon forty thousand francs, not including the succession duties, which would exceed thirty-seven thousand. As his fortune was in landed property, he wrote to the notary at Havre to sell a portion of it in order to pay off his debts, and to have some money at his disposal. Then, anxious to become acquainted at last with that vague entity, glittering and indefinable, which is known as "society," he sent a note to the Dambreuses to know whether he might be at liberty to call upon them. Madame, in reply, said she would expect a visit from him the following day.

This happened to be their reception-day. Carriages were standing in the court-yard. Two footmen rushed forward under the marquee, and a third at the head of the stairs began walking in front of him.

He was conducted through an anteroom, a second room, and then a drawing-room with high windows and a monumental mantelshelf supporting a timepiece in the form of a sphere, and two enormous porcelain vases, in each of which bristled, like a golden bush, a cluster of sconces. Pictures in the manner of Espagnolet hung on the walls. The heavy tapestry portières fell majestically, and the armchairs, the brackets, the tables, the entire furniture, which was in the style of the Second Empire, had a certain imposing and diplomatic air.

Frederick smiled with pleasure in spite of himself.

At last he reached an oval apartment wainscoted in cypress-wood, stuffed with dainty furniture, and letting in the light through a single sheet of plate-glass, which looked out on a garden. Madame Dambreuse was seated at the fireside, with a dozen persons gathered round her in a circle. With a polite greeting, she made a sign to him to take a seat, without, however, exhibiting any surprise at not having seen him for so long a time.

Just at the moment when he was entering the room, they had been praising the eloquence of the Abbé Cœur. Then they deplored the immorality of servants, a topic suggested by a theft which a *valet-de-chambre* had committed, and they began to indulge in tittle-tattle. Old Madame de Sommery had a cold; Mademoiselle de Turvisot had got married; the Montcharrons would not return before the end of January; neither would the Bretancourts, now that people remained in the country till a late period of the year. And the triviality of the conversation was, so to speak, intensified by the luxuriousness of the surroundings; but what they said was less stupid than their way of talking, which was aimless, disconnected, and utterly devoid of animation. And yet there were present men versed in life—an ex-minister, the curé of a large parish, two or three Government officials of high rank. They adhered to the most hackneyed commonplaces. Some of them resembled weary dowagers; others had the appearance of horse-jockeys; and old men accompanied their wives, of whom they were old enough to be the grandfathers.

Madame Dambreuse received all of them graciously. When it was mentioned that anyone was ill, she knitted her brows with a painful expression on her face, and when balls or evening parties were discussed, assumed a joyous air. She would ere long be compelled to deprive herself of these pleasures, for she was going to take away from a boarding-school a niece of her husband, an orphan. The guests extolled her devotedness: this was behaving like a true mother of a family.

Frederick gazed at her attentively. The dull skin of her face looked as if it had been stretched out, and had a bloom in which there was no brilliancy; like that of preserved fruit. But her hair, which was in corkscrew curls, after the English fashion, was finer than silk; her eyes of a sparkling blue; and all her movements were dainty. Seated at the lower end of the apartment, on a small sofa, she kept brushing off the red flock from a Japanese screen, no doubt in order to let her hands be seen to greater advantage—long narrow hands, a little thin, with fingers tilting up at the points. She wore a grey moiré gown with a high-necked body, like a Puritan lady.

Frederick asked her whether she intended to go to La Fortelle this year. Madame Dambreuse was unable to say. He was sure, however, of one thing, that one would be bored to death in Nogent.

Then the visitors thronged in more quickly. There was an incessant rustling of robes on the carpet. Ladies, seated on the edges of chairs, gave vent to little sneering laughs, articulated two or three words, and at the end of five minutes left along with their young daughters. It soon became impossible to follow the conversation, and Frederick withdrew when Madame Dambreuse said to him:

"Every Wednesday, is it not, Monsieur Moreau?" making up for her previous display of indifference by these simple words.

He was satisfied. Nevertheless, he took a deep breath when he got out into the open air; and, needing a less artificial environment, Frederick recalled to mind that he owed the Maréchale a visit.

The door of the anteroom was open. Two Havanese lapdogs rushed forward. A voice exclaimed:

"Delphine! Delphine! Is that you, Felix?"

He stood there without advancing a step. The two little dogs kept yelping continually. At length Rosanette appeared, wrapped up in a sort of dressing-gown of white muslin trimmed with lace, and with her stockingless feet in Turkish slippers.

"Ah! excuse me, Monsieur! I thought it was the hairdresser. One minute; I am coming back!"

And he was left alone in the dining-room. The Venetian blinds were closed. Frederick, as he cast a glance round, was beginning to recall the hubbub of the other night, when he noticed on the table, in the middle of the room, a man's hat, an old felt hat, bruised, greasy, dirty. To whom did this hat belong? Impudently displaying its torn lining, it seemed to say:

"I have the laugh, after all! I am the master!"

The Maréchale suddenly reappeared on the scene. She took up the hat, opened the conservatory, flung it in there, shut the door again (other doors flew open and closed again at the same moment), and, having brought Frederick through the kitchen, she introduced him into her dressing-room.

It could at once be seen that this was the most frequented room in the house, and, so to speak, its true moral centre. The walls, the armchairs, and a big divan with a spring were adorned with a chintz pattern on which was traced a great deal of foliage. On a white marble table stood two large washhand-basins of fine blue earthenware. Crystal shelves, forming a whatnot overhead, were laden with phials, brushes, combs, sticks of cosmetic, and powder-boxes. The fire was reflected in a high cheval-glass. A sheet was hanging outside a bath, and odours of almond-paste and of benzoin were exhaled.

"You'll excuse the disorder. I'm dining in the city this evening."

And as she turned on her heel, she was near crushing one of the little dogs. Frederick declared that they were charming. She lifted up the pair of them, and raising their black snouts up to her face:

"Come! do a laugh—kiss the gentleman!"

A man dressed in a dirty overcoat with a fur collar here entered abruptly.

"Felix, my worthy fellow," said she, "you'll have that business of yours disposed of next Sunday without fail."

The man proceeded to dress her hair. Frederick told her he had heard news of her friends, Madame de Rochegune, Madame de Saint-Florentin, and Madame Lombard, every woman being noble, as if it were at the mansion of the Dambreuses. Then he talked about the theatres. An extraordinary performance was to be given that evening at the Ambigu.

"Shall you go?"

"Faith, no! I'm staying at home."

Delphine appeared. Her mistress gave her a scolding for having gone out without permission.

The other vowed that she was just "returning from market."

"Well, bring me your book. You have no objection, isn't that so?"

And, reading the pass-book in a low tone, Rosanette made remarks on every item. The different sums were not added up correctly.

"Hand me over four sous!"

Delphine handed the amount over to her, and, when she had sent the maid away:

"Ah! Holy Virgin! could I be more unfortunate than I am with these creatures?"

Frederick was shocked at this complaint about servants. It recalled the others too vividly to his mind, and established between the two houses a kind of vexatious equality.

When Delphine came back again, she drew close to the Maréchale's side in order to whisper something in her ear.

"Ah, no! I don't want her!"

Delphine presented herself once more.

"Madame, she insists."

"Ah, what a plague! Throw her out!"

At the same moment, an old lady, dressed in black, pushed forward the door. Frederick heard nothing, saw nothing. Rosanette rushed into her apartment to meet her.

When she reappeared her cheeks were flushed, and she sat down in one of the armchairs without saying a word. A tear fell down her face; then, turning towards the young man, softly:

"What is your Christian name?"

"Frederick."

"Ha! Federico! It doesn't annoy you when I address you in that way?"

And she gazed at him in a coaxing sort of way that was almost amorous.

All of a sudden she uttered an exclamation of delight at the sight of Mademoiselle Vatnaz.

The lady-artist had no time to lose before presiding at her *table d'hôte* at six o'clock sharp; and she was panting for breath, being completely exhausted. She first took out of her pocket a gold chain in a paper, then various objects that she had bought.

"You should know that there are in the Rue Joubert splendid Suède gloves at thirty-six sous. Your dyer wants eight days more. As for the guipure, I told you that they would dye it again. Bugneaux has got the instalment you paid. That's all, I think. You owe me a hundred and eighty-five francs."

Rosanette went to a drawer to get ten napoleons. Neither of the pair had any money. Frederick offered some.

"I'll pay you back," said the Vatnaz, as she stuffed the fifteen francs into her handbag. "But you are a naughty boy! I don't love you any longer—you didn't get me to dance with you even once the other evening! Ah! my dear, I came across a case of stuffed humming-birds which are perfect loves at a shop in the Quai Voltaire. If I were in your place, I would make myself a present of them. Look here! What do you think of it?"

And she exhibited an old remnant of pink silk which she had purchased at the Temple to make a mediæval doublet for Delmar.

"He came to-day, didn't he?"

"No."

"That's singular."

And, after a minute's silence:

"Where are you going this evening?"

"To Alphonsine's," said Rosanette, this being the third version given by her as to the way in which she was going to pass the evening.

Mademoiselle Vatnaz went on: "And what news about the old man of the mountain?"

But, with an abrupt wink, the Maréchale bade her hold her tongue; and she accompanied Frederick out as far as the anteroom to ascertain from him whether he would soon see Arnoux.

"Pray ask him to come—not before his wife, mind!"

At the top of the stairs an umbrella was placed against the wall near a pair of goloshes.

"Vatnaz's goloshes," said Rosanette. "What a foot, eh? My little friend is rather strongly built!"

And, in a melodramatic tone, making the final letter of the word roll:

"Don't tru-us-st her!"

Frederick, emboldened by a confidence of this sort, tried to kiss her on the neck.

"Oh, do it! It costs nothing!"

He felt rather light-hearted as he left her, having no doubt that ere long the Maréchale would be his mistress. This desire awakened another in him; and, in spite of the species of grudge that he owed her, he felt a longing to see Madame Arnoux.

Besides, he would have to call at her house in order to execute the commission with which he had been entrusted by Rosanette.

"But now," thought he (it had just struck six), "Arnoux is probably at home." So he put off his visit till the following day.

She was seated in the same attitude as on the former day, and was sewing a little boy's shirt.

The child, at her feet, was playing with a wooden toy menagerie. Marthe, a short distance away, was writing.

He began by complimenting her on her children. She replied without any exaggeration of maternal silliness.

The room had a tranquil aspect. A glow of sunshine stole in through the window-panes, lighting up the angles of the different articles of furniture, and, as Madame Arnoux sat close beside the window, a large ray, falling on the curls over the nape of her neck, penetrated with liquid gold her skin, which assumed the colour of amber.

Then he said:

"This young lady here has grown very tall during the past three years! Do you remember, Mademoiselle, when you slept on my knees in the carriage?"

Marthe did not remember.

"One evening, returning from Saint-Cloud?"

There was a look of peculiar sadness in Madame Arnoux's face. Was it in order to prevent any allusion on his part to the memories they possessed in common?

Her beautiful black eyes, whose sclerotics were glistening, moved gently under their somewhat drooping lids, and her pupils revealed in their depths an inexpressible kindness of heart. He was seized with a love stronger than ever, a passion that knew no bounds. It enervated him to contemplate the object of his attachment; however, he shook off this feeling. How was he to make the most of himself? by what means? And, having turned the matter over thoroughly in his mind, Frederick could think of none that seemed more effectual than money.

He began talking about the weather, which was less cold than it had been at Havre.

"You have been there?"

"Yes; about a family matter—an inheritance."

"Ah! I am very glad," she said, with an air of such genuine pleasure that he felt quite touched, just as if she had rendered him a great service.

She asked him what he intended to do, as it was necessary for a man to occupy himself with something.

He recalled to mind his false position, and said that he hoped to reach the Council of State with the help of M. Dambreuse, the secretary.

"You are acquainted with him, perhaps?"

"Merely by name."

Then, in a low tone:

"*He* brought you to the ball the other night, did he not?"

Frederick remained silent.

"That was what I wanted to know; thanks!"

After that she put two or three discreet questions to him about his family and the part of the country in which he lived. It was very kind of him not to have forgotten them after having lived so long away from Paris.

"But could I do so?" he rejoined. "Have you any doubt about it?"

Madame Arnoux arose: "I believe that you entertain towards us a true and solid affection. *Au revoir!*"

And she extended her hand towards him in a sincere and virile fashion.

Was this not an engagement, a promise? Frederick felt a sense of delight at merely living; he had to restrain himself to keep from singing. He wanted to burst out, to do generous deeds, and to give alms. He looked around him to see if there were anyone near whom he could relieve. No wretch happened to be passing by; and his desire for self-devotion evaporated, for he was not a man to go out of his way to find opportunities for benevolence.

Then he remembered his friends. The first of whom he thought was Hussonnet, the second, Pellerin. The lowly position of Dussardier naturally called for consideration. As for Cisy, he was glad to let that young aristocrat get a slight glimpse as to the extent of his fortune. He wrote accordingly to all four to come to a housewarming the following Sunday at eleven o'clock sharp; and he told Deslauriers to bring Sénécal.

The tutor had been dismissed from the third boarding-school in which he had been employed for not having given his consent to the distribution of prizes—a custom which he looked upon as dangerous to equality. He was now with an engine-builder, and for the past six months had been no longer living with Deslauriers. There had been nothing painful about their parting.

Sénécal had been visited by men in blouses—all patriots, all workmen, all honest fellows, but at the same time men whose society seemed distasteful to the advocate. Besides, he disliked certain ideas of his friend, excellent though they might be as weapons of warfare. He held his tongue on the subject through motives of ambition, deeming it prudent to pay deference to him in order to exercise control over him, for he looked forward impatiently to a revolutionary movement, in which he calculated on making an opening for himself and occupying a prominent position.

Sénécal's convictions were more disinterested. Every evening, when his work was finished, he returned to his garret and sought in books for something that might justify his dreams. He had annotated the *Contrat Social*; he had crammed himself with the *Revue Indpéndante*; he was acquainted with Mably, Morelly, Fourier, Saint-Simon, Comte, Cabet, Louis Blanc—the heavy cartload of Socialistic writers—those who claim for humanity the dead level of barracks, those who would like to amuse it in a brothel or to bend it over a counter; and from a medley of all these things he constructed an ideal of virtuous democracy, with the double aspect of a farm in which the landlord was to receive a share of the produce, and a spinning-mill, a sort of American Lacedæmon, in which the individual would only exist for the benefit of society, which was to be more omnipotent, absolute, infallible, and divine than the Grand Lamas and the Nebuchadnezzars. He had no doubt as to the approaching realisation of this ideal; and Sénécal raged against everything that he considered hostile to it with the reasoning of a geometrician and the zeal of an Inquisitor. Titles of nobility, crosses, plumes, liveries above all, and even reputations that were too loud-sounding scandalised him, his studies as well as his sufferings intensifying every day his essential hatred of every kind of distinction and every form of social superiority.

"What do I owe to this gentleman that I should be polite to him? If he wants me, he can come to me."

Deslauriers, however, forced him to go to Frederick's reunion.

They found their friend in his bedroom. Spring-roller blinds and double curtains, Venetian mirrors—nothing was wanting there. Frederick, in a velvet vest, was lying back on an easy-chair, smoking cigarettes of Turkish tobacco.

Sénécal wore the gloomy look of a bigot arriving in the midst of a pleasure-party.

Deslauriers gave him a single comprehensive glance; then, with a very low bow:

"Monseigneur, allow me to pay my respects to you!"

Dussardier leaped on his neck. "So you are a rich man now. Ah! upon my soul, so much the better!"

Cisy made his appearance with crape on his hat. Since the death of his grandmother, he was in the enjoyment of a considerable fortune, and was less bent on amusing himself than on being distinguished from others—not being the same as everyone else—in short, on "having the proper stamp." This was his favourite phrase.

However, it was now midday, and they were all yawning.

Frederick was waiting for some one.

At the mention of Arnoux's name, Pellerin made a wry face. He looked on him as a renegade since he had abandoned the fine arts.

"Suppose we pass over him—what do you say to that?"

They all approved of this suggestion.

The door was opened by a man-servant in long gaiters; and the dining-room could be seen with its lofty oak plinths relieved with gold, and its two sideboards laden with plate.

The bottles of wine were heating on the stove; the blades of new knives were glittering beside oysters. In the milky tint of the enamelled glasses there was a kind of alluring sweetness; and the table disappeared from view under its load of game, fruit, and meats of the rarest quality.

These attentions were lost on Sénécal. He began by asking for household bread (the hardest that could be got), and in connection with this subject, spoke of the murders of Buzançais and the crisis arising from lack of the means of subsistence.

Nothing of this sort could have happened if agriculture had been better protected, if everything had not been given up to competition, to anarchy, and to the deplorable maxim of "Let things alone! let things go their own way!" It was in this way that the feudalism of money was established—the worst form of feudalism. But let them take care! The people in the end will get tired of it, and may make the capitalist pay for their sufferings either by bloody proscriptions or by the plunder of their houses.

Frederick saw, as if by a lightning-flash, a flood of men with bare arms invading Madame Dambreuse's drawing-room, and smashing the mirrors with blows of pikes.

Sénécal went on to say that the workman, owing to the insufficiency of wages, was more unfortunate than the helot, the negro, and the pariah, especially if he has children.

"Ought he to get rid of them by asphyxia, as some English doctor, whose name I don't remember—a disciple of Malthus—advises him?"

And, turning towards Cisy: "Are we to be obliged to follow the advice of the infamous Malthus?"

Cisy, who was ignorant of the infamy and even of the existence of Malthus, said by way of reply, that after all, much human misery was relieved, and that the higher classes—

"Ha! the higher classes!" said the Socialist, with a sneer. "In the first place, there are no higher classes. 'Tis the heart alone that makes anyone higher than another. We want no alms, understand! but equality, the fair division of products."

What he required was that the workman might become a capitalist, just as the soldier might become a colonel. The trade-wardenships, at least, in limiting the number of apprentices, prevented workmen from growing inconveniently numerous, and the sentiment of fraternity was kept up by means of the fêtes and the banners.

Hussonnet, as a poet, regretted the banners; so did Pellerin, too—a predilection which had taken possession of him at the Café Dagneaux, while listening to the Phalansterians talking. He expressed the opinion that Fourier was a great man.

"Come now!" said Deslauriers. "An old fool who sees in the overthrow of governments the effects of Divine vengeance. He is just like my lord Saint-Simon and his church, with his hatred of the French Revolution—a set of buffoons who would fain re-establish Catholicism."

M. de Cisy, no doubt in order to get information or to make a good impression, broke in with this remark, which he uttered in a mild tone:

"These two men of science are not, then, of the same way of thinking as Voltaire?"

"That fellow! I make you a present of him!"

"How is that?" Why, I thought—"

"Oh! no, he did not love the people!"

Then the conversation came down to contemporary events: the Spanish marriages, the dilapidations of Rochefort, the new chapter-house of Saint-Denis, which had led to the taxes being doubled. Nevertheless, according to Sénécal, they were not high enough!

"And why are they paid? My God! to erect the palace for apes at the Museum, to make showy staff-officers parade along our squares, or to maintain a Gothic etiquette amongst the flunkeys of the Château!"

"I have read in the *Mode*," said Cisy, "that at the Tuileries ball on the feast of Saint-Ferdinand, everyone was disguised as a miser."

"How pitiable!" said the Socialist, with a shrug of his shoulders, as if to indicate his disgust.

"And the Museum of Versailles!" exclaimed Pellerin. "Let us talk about it! These idiots have foreshortened a Delacroix and lengthened a Gros! At the Louvre they have so well restored, scratched, and made a jumble of all the canvases, that in ten years probably not one will be left. As for the errors in the catalogue, a German has written a whole volume on the subject. Upon my word, the foreigners are laughing at us."

"Yes, we are the laughing-stock of Europe," said Sénécal.

" 'Tis because Art is conveyed in fee-simple to the Crown."

"As long as you haven't universal suffrage—"

"Allow me!"—for the artist, having been rejected at every *salon* for the last twenty years, was filled with rage against Power.

"Ah! let them not bother us! As for me, I ask for nothing. Only the Chambers ought to pass enactments in the interests of Art. A chair of aesthetics should be established with a professor who, being a practical man as well as a philosopher, would succeed, I hope, in grouping the multitude. You would do well, Hussonnet, to touch on this matter with a word or two in your newspaper?"

"Are the newspapers free? are we ourselves free?" said Deslauriers in an angry tone. "When one reflects that there might be as many as twenty-eight different formalities to set up a boat on the river, it makes me feel a longing to go and live amongst the cannibals! The Government is eating us up. Everything belongs to it—philosophy, law, the arts, the very air of heaven; and France, bereft of all energy, lies under the boot of the gendarme and the cassock of the devil-dodger with the death-rattle in her throat!"

The future Mirabeau thus poured out his bile in abundance. Finally he took his glass in his right hand, raised it, and with his other arm akimbo, and his eyes flashing:

"I drink to the utter destruction of the existing order of things—that is to say, of everything included in the words Privilege, Monopoly, Regulation, Hierarchy, Authority, State!"—and in a louder voice—"which I would like to smash as I do this!" dashing on the table the beautiful wine-glass, which broke into a thousand pieces.

They all applauded, and especially Dussardier.

The spectacle of injustices made his heart leap up with indignation. Everything that wore a beard claimed his sympathy. He was one of those persons who fling themselves under vehicles to relieve the horses who have fallen. His erudition was limited to two works, one entitled *Crimes of Kings*, and the other *Mysteries of the Vatican*. He had listened to the advocate with open-mouthed delight. At length, unable to stand it any longer:

"For my part, the thing I blame Louis Philippe for is abandoning the Poles!"

"One moment!" said Hussonnet. "In the first place, Poland has no existence; 'tis an invention of Lafayette! The Poles, as a general rule, all belong to the Faubourg Saint-Marceau, the real ones having been drowned with Poniatowski." In short, "he no longer gave into it;" he had "got over all that suit of thing; it was just like the sea-serpent, the revocation of the Edict of Nantes, and that antiquated humbug about the Saint-Bartholomew massacre!"

Sénécal, while he did not defend the Poles, extolled the latest remarks made by the men of letters. The Popes had been calumniated, inasmuch as they, at any rate, defended the people, and he called the League "the aurora of Democracy, a great move-ment in the direction of equality as opposed to the individualism of Protestants."

Frederick was a little surprised at these views. They probably bored Cisy, for he changed the conversation to the *tableaux vivants* at the Gymnase, which at that time attracted a great number of people.

Sénécal regarded them with disfavour. Such exhibitions corrupted the daugh-ters of the proletariat. Then, it was noticeable that they went in for a display of shameless luxury. Therefore, he approved of the conduct of the Bavarian students who insulted Lola Montès. In imitation of Rousseau, he showed more esteem for the wife of a coal-porter than for the mistress of a king.

"You don't appreciate dainties," retorted Hussonnet in a majestic tone. And he took up the championship of ladies of this class in order to praise Rosanette. Then, as he happened to make an allusion to the ball at her house and to Arnoux's cos-tume, Pellerin remarked:

"People maintain that he is becoming shaky?"

The picture-dealer had just been engaged in a lawsuit with reference to his grounds at Belleville, and he was actually in a kaolin company in Lower Brittany with other rogues of the same sort.

Dussardier knew more about him, for his own master, M. Moussinot, having made enquiries about Arnoux from the banker, Oscar Lefébvre, the latter had said in reply that he considered him by no means solvent, as he knew about bills of his that had been renewed.

The dessert was over; they passed into the drawing-room, which was hung, like that of the Maréchale, in yellow damask in the style of Louis XVI.

Pellerin found fault with Frederick for not having chosen in preference the Neo-Greek style; Sénécal rubbed matches against the hangings; Deslauriers did not make any remark.

There was a bookcase set up there, which he called "a little girl's library." The principal contemporary writers were to be found there. It was impossible to speak about their works, for Hussonnet immediately began relating anecdotes with ref-erence to their personal characteristics, criticising their faces, their habits, their dress, glorifying fifth-rate intellects and disparaging those of the first; and all the while making it clear that he deplored modern decadence.

He instanced some village ditty as containing in itself alone more poetry than all the lyrics of the nineteenth century. He went on to say that Balzac was over-rated, that Byron was effaced, and that Hugo knew nothing about the stage.

"Why, then," said Sénécal, "have you not got the volumes of the working-men poets?"

And M. de Cisy, who devoted his attention to literature, was astonished at not seeing on Frederick's table some of those new physiological studies—the physiology of the smoker, of the angler, of the man employed at the barrier.

They went on irritating him to such an extent that he felt a longing to shove them out by the shoulders.

"But they are making me quite stupid!" And then he drew Dussardier aside, and wished to know whether he could do him any service.

The honest fellow was moved. He answered that his post of cashier entirely sufficed for his wants.

After that, Frederick led Deslauriers into his own apartment, and, taking out of his escritoire two thousand francs:

"Look here, old boy, put this money in your pocket. 'Tis the balance of my old debts to you."

"But—what about the journal?" said the advocate. "You are, of course, aware that I spoke about it to Hussonnet."

And, when Frederick replied that he was "a little short of cash just now," the other smiled in a sinister fashion.

After the liqueurs they drank beer, and after the beer, grog; and then they lighted their pipes once more. At last they left, at five o'clock in the evening, and they were walking along at each others' side without speaking, when Dussardier broke the silence by saying that Frederick had entertained them in excellent style. They all agreed with him on that point.

Then Hussonnet remarked that his luncheon was too heavy. Sénécal found fault with the trivial character of his household arrangements. Cisy took the same view. It was absolutely devoid of the "proper stamp."

"For my part, I think," said Pellerin, "he might have had the grace to give me an order for a picture."

Deslauriers held his tongue, as he had the banknotes that had been given to him in his breeches' pocket.

Frederick was left by himself. He was thinking about his friends, and it seemed to him as if a huge ditch surrounded with shade separated him from them. He had nevertheless held out his hand to them, and they had not responded to the sincerity of his heart.

He recalled to mind what Pellerin and Dussardier had said about Arnoux. Undoubtedly it must be an invention, a calumny? But why? And he had a vision of Madame Arnoux, ruined, weeping, selling her furniture. This idea tormented him all night long. Next day he presented himself at her house.

At a loss to find any way of communicating to her what he had heard, he asked her, as if in casual conversation, whether Arnoux still held possession of his building grounds at Belleville.

"Yes, he has them still."

"He is now, I believe, a shareholder in a kaolin company in Brittany."

"That's true."

"His earthenware-works are going on very well, are they not?"

"Well—I suppose so—"

And, as he hesitated:

"What is the matter with you? You frighten me!"

He told her the story about the renewals. She hung down her head, and said:

"I thought so!"

In fact, Arnoux, in order to make a good speculation, had refused to sell his grounds, had borrowed money extensively on them, and finding no purchasers, had thought of rehabilitating himself by establishing the earthenware manufactory. The expense of this had exceeded his calculations. She knew nothing more about it. He evaded all her questions, and declared repeatedly that it was going on very well.

Frederick tried to reassure her. These in all probability were mere temporary embarrassments. However, if he got any information, he would impart it to her.

"Oh! yes, will you not?" said she, clasping her two hands with an air of charming supplication.

So then, he had it in his power to be useful to her. He was now entering into her existence—finding a place in her heart.

Arnoux appeared.

"Ha! how nice of you to come to take me out to dine!"

Frederick was silent on hearing these words.

Arnoux spoke about general topics, then informed his wife that he would be returning home very late, as he had an appointment with M. Oudry.

"At his house?"

"Why, certainly, at his house."

As they went down the stairs, he confessed that, as the Maréchale had no engagement at home, they were going on a secret pleasure-party to the Moulin Rouge; and, as he always needed somebody to be the recipient of his outpourings, he got Frederick to drive him to the door.

In place of entering, he walked about on the footpath, looking up at the windows on the second floor. Suddenly the curtains parted.

"Ha! bravo! Père Oudry is no longer there! Good evening!"

Frederick did not know what to think now.

From this day forth, Arnoux was still more cordial than before; he invited the young man to dine with his mistress; and ere long Frederick frequented both houses at the same time.

Rosanette's abode furnished him with amusement. He used to call there of an evening on his way back from the club or the play. He would take a cup of tea there, or play a game of loto. On Sundays they played charades; Rosanette, more noisy than the rest, made herself conspicuous by funny tricks, such as running on all-fours or muffling her head in a cotton cap. In order to watch the passers-by through the window, she had a hat of waxed leather; she smoked chibouks; she sang Tyrolese airs. In the afternoon, to kill time, she cut out flowers in a piece of chintz and pasted them against the window-panes, smeared her two little dogs with varnish, burned pastilles, or drew cards to tell her fortune. Incapable of resisting a desire, she became infatuated about some trinket which she happened to see, and could not sleep till she had gone and bought it, then bartered it for another, sold costly dresses for little or nothing, lost her jewellery, squandered money, and would have sold her chemise for a stage-box at the theatre. Often she asked Frederick to explain to her some word she came across when reading a book, but did not pay any attention to his answer, for she jumped quickly to another idea, while heaping questions on top of each other. After spasms of gaiety came childish outbursts of rage, or else she sat on the ground dreaming before the fire with her head down and her hands clasping her knees, more inert than a torpid adder. Without minding it, she made her toilet in his presence, drew on her silk stockings, then washed her face with great splashes of water, throwing back her figure as if she were a shivering naïad; and her laughing white teeth, her sparkling eyes, her beauty, her gaiety, dazzled Frederick, and made his nerves tingle under the lash of desire.

Nearly always he found Madame Arnoux teaching her little boy how to read, or standing behind Marthe's chair while she played her scales on the piano. When she was doing a piece of sewing, it was a great source of delight to him to pick up her scissors now and then. In all her movements there was a tranquil majesty. Her little hands seemed made to scatter alms and to wipe away tears, and her voice, naturally rather hollow, had caressing intonations and a sort of breezy lightness.

She did not display much enthusiasm about literature; but her intelligence exercised a charm by the use of a few simple and penetrating words. She loved travelling, the sound of the wind in the woods, and a walk with uncovered head under the rain.

Frederick listened to these confidences with rapture, fancying that he saw in them the beginning of a certain self-abandonment on her part.

His association with these two women made, as it were, two different strains of music in his life, the one playful, passionate, diverting, the other grave and almost religious, and vibrating both at the same time, they always increased in volume and gradually blended with one another; for if Madame Arnoux happened merely to touch him with her finger, the image of the other immediately presented itself to him as an object of desire, because from that quarter a better opportunity was thrown in his way, and, when his heart happened to be touched while in Rosanette's company, he was immediately reminded of the woman for whom he felt such a consuming passion.

This confusion was, in some measure, due to a similarity which existed between the interiors of the two houses. One of the trunks which was formerly to be seen in the Boulevard Montmartre now adorned Rosanette's dining-room. The same courses were served up for dinner in both places, and even the same velvet cap was to be found trailing over the easy-chairs; then, a heap of little presents— screens, boxes, fans—went to the mistress's house from the wife's and returned again, for Arnoux, without the slightest embarrassment, often took back from the one what he had given to her in order to make a present of it to the other.

The Maréchale laughed with Frederick at the utter disregard for propriety which his habits exhibited. One Sunday, after dinner, she led him behind the door, and showed him in the pocket of Arnoux's overcoat a bag of cakes which he had just pilfered from the table, in order, no doubt, to regale his little family with it at home. M. Arnoux gave himself up to some rogueries which bordered on vileness. It seemed to him a duty to practise fraud with regard to the city dues; he never paid when he went to the theatre, or if he took a ticket for the second seats always tried to make his way into the first; and he used to relate as an excellent joke that it was a custom of his at the cold baths to put into the waiters' collection-box a breeches' button instead of a ten-sous piece—and this did not prevent the Maréchale from loving him.

One day, however, she said, while talking about him:

"Ah! he's making himself a nuisance to me, at last! I've had enough of him! Faith, so much the better—I'll find another instead!"

Frederick believed that the other had already been found, and that his name was M. Oudry.

"Well," said Rosanette, "what does that signify?"

Then, in a voice choked with rising tears:

"I ask very little from him, however, and he won't give me that.

He had even promised a fourth of his profits in the famous kaolin mines. No profit made its appearance any more than the cashmere with which he had been luring her on for the last six months.

Frederick immediately thought of making her a present. Arnoux might regard it as a lesson for himself, and be annoyed at it.

For all that, he was good-natured, his wife herself said so, but so foolish! Instead of bringing people to dine every day at his house, he now entertained his acquaintances at a restaurant. He bought things that were utterly useless, such as gold chains, timepieces, and household articles. Madame Arnoux even pointed out to Frederick in the lobby an enormous supply of tea-kettles, foot-warmers, and samovars. Finally, she one day confessed that a certain matter caused her much anxiety. Arnoux had made her sign a promissory note payable to M. Dambreuse.

Meanwhile Frederick still cherished his literary projects as if it were a point of honour with himself to do so. He wished to write a history of æsthetics, a result of his conversations with Pellerin; next, to write dramas dealing with different epochs of the French Revolution, and to compose a great comedy, an idea traceable to the indirect influence of Deslauriers and Hussonnet. In the midst of his work her face or that of the other passed before his mental vision. He struggled against the longing to see her, but was not long ere he yielded to it; and he felt sadder as he came back from Madame Arnoux's house.

One morning, while he was brooding over his melancholy thoughts by the fireside, Deslauriers came in. The incendiary speeches of Sénécal had filled his master with uneasiness, and once more he found himself without resources.

"What do you want me to do?" said Frederick.

"Nothing! I know you have no money. But it will not be much trouble for you to get him a post either through M. Dambreuse or else through Arnoux. The latter ought to have need of engineers in his establishment."

Frederick had an inspiration. Sénécal would be able to let him know when the husband was away, carry letters for him and assist him on a thousand occasions when opportunities presented themselves. Services of this sort are always rendered between man and man. Besides, he would find means of employing him without arousing any suspicion on his part. Chance offered him an auxiliary; it was a circumstance that omened well for the future, and he hastened to take advantage of it; and, with an affectation of indifference, he replied that the thing was feasible perhaps, and that he would devote attention to it.

And he did so at once. Arnoux took a great deal of pains with his earthenware works. He was endeavouring to discover the copper-red of the Chinese, but his colours evaporated in the process of baking. In order to avoid cracks in his ware, he mixed lime with his potter's clay; but the articles got broken for the most part; the enamel of his paintings on the raw material boiled away; his large plates became bulged; and, attributing these mischances to the inferior plant of his manufactory, he was anxious to start other grinding-mills and other drying-rooms. Frederick recalled some of these things to mind, and, when he met Arnoux, said that he had discovered a very able man, who would be capable of finding his famous red. Arnoux gave a jump; then, having listened to what the young man had to tell him, replied that he wanted assistance from nobody.

Frederick spoke in a very laudatory style about Sénécal's prodigious attainments, pointing out that he was at the same time an engineer, a chemist, and an accountant, being a mathematician of the first rank.

The earthenware-dealer consented to see him.

But they squabbled over the emoluments. Frederick interposed, and, at the end of a week, succeeded in getting them to come to an agreement.

But as the works were situated at Creil, Sénécal could not assist him in any way. This thought alone was enough to make his courage flag, as if he had met with some misfortune. His notion was that the more Arnoux would be kept apart from his wife the better would be his own chance with her. Then he proceeded to make repeated apologies for Rosanette. He referred to all the wrongs she had sustained at the other's hands, referred to the vague threats which she had uttered a few days before, and even spoke about the cashmere without concealing the fact that she had accused Arnoux of avarice.

Arnoux, nettled at the word (and, furthermore, feeling some uneasiness), brought Rosanette the cashmere, but scolded her for having made any complaint to Frederick. When she told him that she had reminded him a hundred times of his promise, he pretended that, owing to pressure of business, he had forgotten all about it.

The next day Frederick presented himself at her abode, and found the Maréchale still in bed, though it was two o'clock, with Delmar beside her finishing a *pâté de foie gras* at a little round table. Before he had advanced many paces, she broke out into a cry of delight, saying: "I have him! I have him!" Then she seized him by the ears, kissed him on the forehead, thanked him effusively, "thee'd" and "thou'd" him, and even wanted to make him sit down on the bed. Her fine eyes, full of tender emotion, were sparkling with pleasure. There was a smile on her humid mouth. Her two round arms emerged through the sleeveless opening of her night-dress, and, from time to time, he could feel through the cambric the well-rounded outlines of her form.

All this time Delmar kept rolling his eyeballs about.

"But really, my dear, my own pet . . ."

It was the same way on the occasion when he saw her next. As soon as Frederick entered, she sat up on a cushion in order to embrace him with more ease, called him a darling, a "dearie," put a flower in his button-hole, and settled his cravat. These delicate attentions were redoubled when Delmar happened to be there. Were they advances on her part? So it seemed to Frederick.

As for deceiving a friend, Arnoux, in his place, would not have had many scruples on that score, and he had every right not to adhere to rigidly virtuous principles with regard to this man's mistress, seeing that his relations with the wife had been strictly honourable, for so he thought—or rather he would have liked Arnoux to think so, in any event, as a sort of justification of his own prodigious cowardice. Nevertheless he felt somewhat bewildered; and presently he made up his mind to lay siege boldly to the Maréchale.

So, one afternoon, just as she was stooping down in front of her chest of drawers, he came across to her, and repeated his overtures without a pause.

Thereupon, she began to cry, saying that she was very unfortunate, but that people should not despise her on that account.

He only made fresh advances. She now adopted a different plan, namely, to laugh at his attempts without stopping. He thought it a clever thing to answer her sarcasms with repartees in the same strain, in which there was even a touch of exaggeration. But he made too great a display of gaiety to convince her that he was in earnest; and their comradeship was an impediment to any outpouring of serious feeling. At last, when she said one day, in reply to his amorous whispers, that she would not take another woman's leavings, he answered.

"What other woman?"

"Ah! yes, go and meet Madame Arnoux again!"

For Frederick used to talk about her often. Arnoux, on his side, had the same mania. At last she lost patience at always hearing this woman's praises sung, and her insinuation was a kind of revenge.

Frederick resented it. However, Rosanette was beginning to excite his love to an unusual degree. Sometimes, assuming the attitude of a woman of experience, she spoke ill of love with a sceptical smile that made him feel inclined to box her ears. A quarter of an hour afterwards, it was the only thing of any consequence in the world, and, with her arms crossed over her breast, as if she were clasping some one close to her: "Oh, yes, 'tis good! 'tis good!" and her eyelids would quiver in a kind of rapturous swoon. It was impossible to understand her, to know, for instance, whether she loved Arnoux, for she made fun of him, and yet seemed jealous of him. So likewise with the Vatnaz, whom she would sometimes call a wretch, and at other times her best friend. In short, there was about her entire person, even to the very arrangement of her chignon over her head, an inexpressible something, which seemed like a challenge; and he desired her for the satisfaction, above all, of conquering her and being her master.

How was he to accomplish this? for she often sent him away unceremoniously, appearing only for a moment between two doors in order to say in a subdued voice, "I'm engaged—for the evening;" or else he found her surrounded by a dozen persons; and when they were alone, so many impediments presented themselves one after the other, that one would have sworn there was a bet to keep matters from going any further. He invited her to dinner; as a rule, she declined the invitation. On one occasion, she accepted it, but did not come.

A Machiavellian idea arose in his brain.

Having heard from Dussardier about Pellerin's complaints against himself, he thought of giving the artist an order to paint the Maréchale's portrait, a life-sized portrait, which would necessitate a good number of sittings. He would not fail to be present at all of them. The habitual incorrectness of the painter would facilitate their private conversations. So then he would urge Rosanette to get the picture executed in order to make a present of her face to her dear Arnoux. She consented, for she saw herself in the midst of the Grand Salon in the most prominent position with a crowd of people staring at her picture, and the newspapers would all talk about it, which at once would set her afloat.

As for Pellerin, he eagerly snatched at the offer. This portrait ought to place him in the position of a great man; it ought to be a masterpiece. He passed in review in his memory all the portraits by great masters with which he was acquainted, and decided finally in favour of a Titian, which would be set off with ornaments in the style of Veronese. Therefore, he would carry out his design without artificial backgrounds in a bold light, which would illuminate the flesh-tints with a single tone, and which would make the accessories glitter.

"Suppose I were to put on her," he thought, "a pink silk dress with an Oriental bournous? Oh, no! the bournous is only a rascally thing! Or suppose, rather, I were to make her wear blue velvet with a grey background, richly coloured? We might likewise give her a white guipure collar with a black fan and a scarlet curtain behind." And thus, seeking for ideas, he enlarged his conception, and regarded it with admiration.

He felt his heart beating when Rosanette, accompanied by Frederick, called at his house for the first sitting. He placed her standing up on a sort of platform in the midst of the apartment, and, finding fault with the light and expressing regret at the loss of his former studio, he first made her lean on her elbow against a pedestal, then sit down in an armchair, and, drawing away from her and coming near her again by turns in order to adjust with a fillip the folds of her dress, he watched her with eyelids half-closed, and appealed to Frederick's taste with a passing word.

"Well, no," he exclaimed; "I return to my own idea. I will set you up in the Venetian style."

She would have a poppy-coloured velvet gown with a jewelled girdle; and her wide sleeve lined with ermine would afford a glimpse of her bare arm, which was to touch the balustrade of a staircase rising behind her. At her left, a large column would mount as far as the top of the canvas to meet certain structures so as to form an arch. Underneath one would vaguely distinguish groups of orange-trees almost black, through which the blue sky, with its streaks of white cloud, would seem cut into fragments. On the baluster, covered with a carpet, there would be, on a silver

dish, a bouquet of flowers, a chaplet of amber, a poniard, and a little chest of an-
tique ivory, rather yellow with age, which would appear to be disgorging gold se-
quins. Some of them, falling on the ground here and there, would form brilliant
splashes, as it were, in such a way as to direct one's glance towards the tip of her
foot, for she would be standing on the last step but one in a natural position, as if
in the act of moving under the glow of the broad sunlight.

He went to look for a picture-case, which he laid on the platform to represent
the step. Then he arranged as accessories, on a stool by way of balustrade, his pea-
jacket, a buckler, a sardine-box, a bundle of pens, and a knife; and when he had
flung in front of Rosanette a dozen big sous, he made her assume the attitude he
required.

"Just try to imagine that these things are riches, magnificent presents. The
head a little on one side! Perfect! and don't stir! This majestic posture exactly suits
your style of beauty."

She wore a plaid dress and carried a big muff, and only kept from laughing out-
right by an effort of self-control.

"As regards the headdress, we will mingle with it a circle of pearls. It always
produces a striking effect with red hair."

The Maréchale burst out into an exclamation, remarking that she had not red
hair.

"Nonsense! The red of painters is not that of ordinary people."

He began to sketch the position of the masses; and he was so much preoccupied with the great artists of the Renaissance that he kept talking about them persistently. For a whole hour he went on musing aloud on those splendid lives, full of
genius, glory, and sumptuous displays, with triumphal entries into the cities, and
galas by torchlight among half-naked women, beautiful as goddesses.

"You were made to live in those days. A creature of your calibre would have
deserved a monseigneur."

Rosanette thought the compliments he paid her very pretty. The day was fixed
for the next sitting. Frederick took it on himself to bring the accessories.

As the heat of the stove had stupefied her a little, they went home on foot
through the Rue du Bac, and reached the Pont Royal.

It was fine weather, piercingly bright and warm. Some windows of houses in
the city shone in the distance, like plates of gold, whilst behind them at the right
the turrets of Nôtre Dame showed their outlines in black against the blue sky,
softly bathed at the horizon in grey vapours.

The wind began to swell; and Rosanette, having declared that she felt hungry,
they entered the "Patisserie Anglaise."

Young women with their children stood eating in front of the marble buffet, where plates of little cakes had glass covers pressed down on them. Rosanette swallowed two cream-tarts. The powdered sugar formed moustaches at the sides of her mouth. From time to time, in order to wipe it, she drew out her handkerchief from her muff, and her face, under her green silk hood, resembled a full-blown rose in the midst of its leaves.

They resumed their walk. In the Rue de la Paix she stood before a goldsmith's shop to look at a bracelet. Frederick wished to make her a present of it.

"No!" said she; "keep your money!"

He was hurt by these words.

"What's the matter now with the ducky? We are melancholy?"

And, the conversation having been renewed, he began making the same protestations of love to her as usual.

"You know well 'tis impossible!"

"Why?"

"Ah! because—"

They went on side by side, she leaning on his arm, and the flounces of her gown kept flapping against his legs. Then, he recalled to mind one winter twilight when on the same footpath Madame Arnoux walked thus by his side, and he became so much absorbed in this recollection that he no longer saw Rosanette, and did not bestow a thought upon her.

She kept looking straight before her in a careless fashion, lagging a little, like a lazy child. It was the hour when people had just come back from their promenade, and equipages were making their way at a quick trot over the hard pavement.

Pellerin's flatteries having probably recurred to her mind, she heaved a sigh.

"Ah! there are some lucky women in the world. Decidedly, I was made for a rich man!"

He replied, with a certain brutality in his tone:

"You have one, in the meantime!" for M. Oudry was looked upon as a man that could count a million three times over.

She asked for nothing better than to get free from him.

"What prevents you from doing so?" And he gave utterance to bitter jests about this old bewigged citizen, pointing out to her that such an intrigue was unworthy of her, and that she ought to break it off.

"Yes," replied the Maréchale, as if talking to herself. " 'Tis what I shall end by doing, no doubt!"

Frederick was charmed by this disinterestedness. She slackened her pace, and he fancied that she was fatigued. She obstinately refused to let him take a cab, and she parted with him at her door, sending him a kiss with her finger-tips.

"Ah! what a pity! and to think that imbeciles take me for a man of wealth!"

He reached home in a gloomy frame of mind.

Hussonnet and Deslauriers were awaiting him. The Bohemian, seated before the table, made sketches of Turks' heads; and the advocate, in dirty boots, lay asleep on the sofa.

"Ha! at last," he exclaimed. "But how sullen you look! Will you listen to me?"

His vogue as a tutor had fallen off, for he crammed his pupils with theories unfavourable for their examinations. He had appeared in two or three cases in which he had been unsuccessful, and each new disappointment flung him back with greater force on the dream of his earlier days—a journal in which he could show himself off, avenge himself, and spit forth his bile and his opinions. Fortune and reputation, moreover, would follow as a necessary consequence. It was in this hope that he had got round the Bohemian, Hussonnet happening to be the possessor of a press.

At present, he printed it on pink paper. He invented hoaxes, composed rebuses, tried to engage in polemics, and even intended, in spite of the situation of the premises, to get up concerts. A year's subscription was to give a right to a place in the orchestra in one of the principal theatres of Paris. Besides, the board of management took on itself to furnish foreigners with all necessary information, artistic and otherwise. But the printer gave vent to threats; there were three quarters' rent due to the landlord. All sorts of embarrassments arose; and Hussonnet would have allowed *L'Art* to perish, were it not for the exhortations of the advocate, who kept every day exciting his mind. He had brought the other with him, in order to give more weight to the application he was now making.

"We've come about the journal," said he.

"What! are you still thinking about that?" said Frederick, in an absent tone.

"Certainly, I am thinking about it!"

And he explained his plan anew. By means of the Bourse returns, they would get into communication with financiers, and would thus obtain the hundred thousand francs indispensable as security. But, in order that the print might be transformed into a political journal, it was necessary beforehand to have a large *clientèle*, and for that purpose to make up their minds to go to some expense—so much for the cost of paper and printing, and for outlay at the office; in short, a sum of about fifteen thousand francs.

"I have no funds," said Frederick.

"And what are we to do, then?" said Deslauriers, with folded arms.

Frederick, hurt by the attitude which Deslauriers was assuming, replied:

"Is that my fault?"

"Ah! very fine. A man has wood in his fire, truffles on his table, a good bed, a library, a carriage, every kind of comfort. But let another man shiver under the slates, dine at twenty sous, work like a convict, and sprawl through want in the mire—is it the rich man's fault?"

And he repeated, "Is it the rich man's fault?" with a Ciceronian irony which smacked of the law-courts.

Frederick tried to speak.

"However, I understand one has certain wants—aristocratic wants; for, no doubt, some woman—"

"Well, even if that were so? Am I not free—?"

"Oh! quite free!"

And, after a minute's silence:

"Promises are so convenient!"

"Good God! I don't deny that I gave them!" said Frederick.

The advocate went on:

"At college we take oaths; we are going to set up a phalanx; we are going to imitate Balzac's Thirteen. Then, on meeting a friend after a separation: 'Goodnight, old fellow! Go about your business!' For he who might help the other carefully keeps everything for himself alone."

"How is that?"

"Yes, you have not even introduced me to the Dambreuses."

Frederick cast a scrutinising glance at him. With his shabby frock-coat, his spectacles of rough glass, and his sallow face, that advocate seemed to him such a typical specimen of the penniless pedant that he could not prevent his lips from curling with a disdainful smile.

Deslauriers perceived this, and reddened.

He had already taken his hat to leave. Hussonnet, filled with uneasiness, tried to mollify him with appealing looks, and, as Frederick was turning his back on him:

"Look here, my boy, become my Mæcenas! Protect the arts!"

Frederick, with an abrupt movement of resignation, took a sheet of paper, and, having scrawled some lines on it, handed it to him. The Bohemian's face lighted up.

Then, passing across the sheet of paper to Deslauriers:

"Apologise, my fine fellow!"

Their friend begged his notary to send him fifteen thousand francs as quickly as possible.

"Ah! I recognise you in that," said Deslauriers.

"On the faith of a gentleman," added the Bohemian, "you are a noble fellow, you'll be placed in the gallery of useful men!"

The advocate remarked:

"You'll lose nothing by it, 'tis an excellent speculation."

"Faith," exclaimed Hussonnet, "I'd stake my head at the scaffold on its success!"

And he said so many foolish things, and promised so many wonderful things, in which perhaps he believed, that Frederick did not know whether he did this in order to laugh at others or at himself.

The same evening he received a letter from his mother. She expressed astonishment at not seeing him yet a minister, while indulging in a little banter at his expense. Then she spoke of her health, and informed him that M. Roque had now become one of her visitors.

"Since he is a widower, I thought there would be no objection to inviting him to the house. Louise is greatly changed for the better." And in a postscript: "You have told me nothing about your fine acquaintance, M. Dambreuse; if I were you, I would make use of him."

Why not? His intellectual ambitions had left him, and his fortune (he saw it clearly) was insufficient, for when his debts had been paid, and the sum agreed on remitted to the others, his income would be diminished by four thousand at least! Moreover, he felt the need of giving up this sort of life, and attaching himself to some pursuit. So, next day, when dining at Madame Arnoux's, he said that his mother was tormenting him in order to make him take up a profession.

"But I was under the impression," she said, "that M. Dambreuse was going to get you into the Council of State? That would suit you very well."

So, then, she wished him to take this course. He regarded her wish as a command.

The banker, as on the first occasion, was seated at his desk, and, with a gesture, intimated that he desired Frederick to wait a few minutes; for a gentleman who was standing at the door with his back turned had been discussing some serious topic with him.

The subject of their conversation was the proposed amalgamation of the different coal-mining companies.

On each side of the glass hung portraits of General Foy and Louis Philippe. Cardboard shelves rose along the panels up to the ceiling, and there were six straw chairs, M. Dambreuse not requiring a more fashionably-furnished apartment for the transaction of business. It resembled those gloomy kitchens in which great banquets are prepared.

Frederick noticed particularly two chests of prodigious size which stood in the corners. He asked himself how many millions they might contain. The banker unlocked one of them, and as the iron plate revolved, it disclosed to view nothing inside but blue paper books full of entries.

At last, the person who had been talking to M. Dambreuse passed in front of Frederick. It was Père Oudry. The two saluted one another, their faces colouring—

a circumstance which surprised M. Dambreuse. However, he exhibited the utmost affability, observing that nothing would be easier than to recommend the young man to the Keeper of the Seals. They would be too happy to have him, he added, concluding his polite attentions by inviting him to an evening party which he would be giving in a few days.

Frederick was stepping into a brougham on his way to this party when a note from the Maréchale reached him. By the light of the carriage-lamps he read:

"Darling, I have followed your advice: I have just expelled my savage. After to-morrow evening, liberty! Say whether I am not brave!"

Nothing more. But it was clearly an invitation to him to take the vacant place. He uttered an exclamation, squeezed the note into his pocket, and set forth.

Two municipal guards on horseback were stationed in the street. A row of lamps burned on the two front gates, and some servants were calling out in the courtyard to have the carriages brought up to the end of the steps before the house under the marquée.

Then suddenly the noise in the vestibule ceased.

Large trees filled up the space in front of the staircase. The porcelain globes shed a light which waved like white moiré satin on the walls.

Frederick rushed up the steps in a joyous frame of mind. An usher announced his name. M. Dambreuse extended his hand. Almost at the very same moment, Madame Dambreuse appeared. She wore a mauve dress trimmed with lace. The ringlets of her hair were more abundant than usual, and not a single jewel did she display.

She complained of his coming to visit them so rarely, and seized the opportunity to exchange a few confidential words with him.

The guests began to arrive. In their mode of bowing they twisted their bodies on one side or bent in two, or merely lowered their heads a little. Then, a married pair, a family passed in, and all scattered themselves about the drawing-room, which was already filled. Under the chandelier in the centre, an enormous ottoman-seat supported a stand, the flowers of which, bending forward, like plumes of feathers, hung over the heads of the ladies seated all around in a ring, while others occupied the easy-chairs, which formed two straight lines symmetrically interrupted by the large velvet curtains of the windows and the lofty bays of the doors with their gilded lintels.

The crowd of men who remained standing on the floor with their hats in their hands seemed, at some distance, like one black mass, into which the ribbons in the button-holes introduced red points here and there, and rendered all the more dull the monotonous whiteness of their cravats. With the exception of the very young men with the down on their faces, all appeared to be bored. Some dandies, with an expression of sullenness on their countenances, were swinging on their heels. There were numbers of men with grey hair or wigs. Here and there glistened a bald pate; and the visages of many of these men, either purple or exceedingly pale, showed in their worn aspect the traces of immense fatigues: for they were persons who devoted themselves either to political or commercial pursuits. M. Dambreuse had also invited a number of scholars and magistrates, two or three celebrated doctors, and he deprecated with an air of humility the eulogies which they pronounced on his entertainment and the allusions to his wealth.

An immense number of men-servants, with fine gold-laced livery, kept moving about on every side. The large branched candlesticks, like bouquets of flame, threw a glow over the hangings. They were reflected in the mirrors; and at the bottom of the dining-room, which was adorned with a jessamine treillage, the sideboard resembled the high altar of a cathedral or an exhibition of jewellery, there were so many dishes, bells, knives and forks, silver and silver-gilt spoons in the midst of crystal ware glittering with iridescence.

The three other reception-rooms overflowed with artistic objects—landscapes by great masters on the walls, ivory and porcelain at the sides of the tables, and Chinese ornaments on the brackets. Lacquered screens were displayed in front of the windows, clusters of camelias rose above the mantel-shelves, and a light music vibrated in the distance, like the humming of bees.

The quadrilles were not numerous, and the dancers, judged by the indifferent fashion in which they dragged their pumps after them, seemed to be going through the performance of a duty.

Frederick heard some phrases, such as the following:

"Were you at the last charity fête at the Hotel Lambert, Mademoiselle?" "No, Monsieur." "It will soon be intolerably warm here." "Oh! yes, indeed; quite suffocating!" "Whose polka, pray, is this?" "Good heavens, Madame, I don't know!"

And, behind him, three greybeards, who had posted themselves in the recess of a window, were whispering some *risqué* remarks. A sportsman told a hunting story, while a Legitimist carried on an argument with an Orléanist. And, wandering about from one group to another, he reached the card-room, where, in the midst of grave-looking men gathered in a circle, he recognised Martinon, now attached to the Bar of the capital.

His big face, with its waxen complexion, filled up the space encircled by his collar-like beard, which was a marvel with its even surface of black hair; and, observing the golden mean between the elegance which his age might yearn for and the dignity which his profession exacted from him, he kept his thumbs stuck under his armpits, according to the custom of beaux, and then put his hands into his waistcoat pockets after the manner of learned personages. Though his boots were polished to excess, he kept his temples shaved in order to have the forehead of a thinker.

After he had addressed a few chilling words to Frederick, he turned once more towards those who were chatting around him. A land-owner was saying: "This is a class of men that dreams of upsetting society."

"They are calling for the organisation of labour," said another: "Can this be conceived?"

"What could you expect," said a third, "when we see M. de Genoude giving his assistance to the *Siècle?*"

"And even Conservatives style themselves Progressives. To lead us to what? To the Republic! as if such a thing were possible in France!"

Everyone declared that the Republic was impossible in France.

"No matter!" remarked one gentleman in a loud tone. "People take too much interest in the Revolution. A heap of histories, of different kinds of works, are published concerning it!"

"Without taking into account," said Martinon, "that there are probably subjects of far more importance which might be studied."

A gentleman occupying a ministerial office laid the blame on the scandals associated with the stage:

"Thus, for instance, this new drama of *La Reine Margot* really goes beyond the proper limits. What need was there for telling us about the Valois? All this exhibits loyalty in an unfavourable light. 'Tis just like your press! There is no use in talking, the September laws are altogether too mild. For my part, I would like to have court-martials, to gag the journalists! At the slightest display of insolence, drag them before a council of war, and then make an end of the business!"

"Oh, take care, Monsieur! take care!" said a professor. "Don't attack the precious boons we gained in 1830! Respect our liberties!" It would be better, he contended, to adopt a policy of decentralisation, and to distribute the surplus populations of the towns through the country districts.

"But they are gangrened!" exclaimed a Catholic. "Let religion be more firmly established!"

Martinon hastened to observe:

"As a matter of fact, it is a restraining force."

All the evil lay in this modern longing to rise above one's class and to possess luxuries.

"However," urged a manufacturer, "luxury aids commerce. Therefore, I approve of the Duc de Nemours' action in insisting on having short breeches at his evening parties."

"M. Thiers came to one of them in a pair of trousers. You know his joke on the subject?"

"Yes; charming! But he turned round to the demagogues, and his speech on the question of incompatibilities was not without its influence in bringing about the attempt of the twelfth of May."

"Oh, pooh!"

"Ay, ay!"

The circle had to make a little opening to give a passage to a man-servant carrying a tray, who was trying to make his way into the card-room.

Under the green shades of the wax-lights the tables were covered with two rows of cards and gold coins. Frederick stopped beside one corner of the table, lost the fifteen napoleons which he had in his pocket, whirled lightly about, and found himself on the threshold of the boudoir in which Madame Dambreuse happened to be at that moment.

It was filled with women sitting close to one another in little groups on seats without backs. Their long skirts, swelling round them, seemed like waves, from which their waists emerged; and their breasts were clearly outlined by the slope of their corsages. Nearly every one of them had a bouquet of violets in her hand. The dull shade of their gloves showed off the whiteness of their arms, which formed a contrast with its human flesh tints. Over the shoulders of some of them hung fringe or mourning-weeds, and, every now and then, as they quivered with emotion, it seemed as if their bodices were about to fall down.

But the decorum of their countenances tempered the exciting effect of their costumes. Several of them had a placidity almost like that of animals; and this resemblance to the brute creation on the part of half-nude women made him think of the interior of a harem—indeed, a grosser comparison suggested itself to the young man's mind.

Every variety of beauty was to be found there—some English ladies, with the profile familiar in "keepsakes"; an Italian, whose black eyes shot forth lava-like flashes, like a Vesuvius; three sisters, dressed in blue; three Normans, fresh as April apples; a tall red-haired girl, with a set of amethysts. And the bright scintillation of diamonds, which trembled in aigrettes worn over their hair, the luminous spots of precious stones laid over their breasts, and the delightful radiance of pearls which adorned their foreheads mingled with the glitter of gold rings, as well as with the lace, powder, the feathers, the vermilion of dainty mouths, and the mother-of-pearl hue of teeth. The ceiling, rounded like a cupola, gave to the boudoir the form of a flower-basket, and a current of perfumed air circulated under the flapping of their fans.

Frederick, planting himself behind them, put up his eyeglass and scanned their shoulders, not all of which did he consider irreproachable. He thought about the Maréchale, and this dispelled the temptations that beset him or consoled him for not yielding to them.

He gazed, however, at Madame Dambreuse, and he considered her charming, in spite of her mouth being rather large and her nostrils too dilated. But she was remarkably graceful in appearance. There was, as it were, an expression of passionate languor in the ringlets of her hair, and her forehead, which was like agate, seemed to cover a great deal, and indicated a masterful intelligence.

She had placed beside her her husband's niece, a rather plain-looking young person. From time to time she left her seat to receive those who had just come in; and the murmur of feminine voices, made, as it were, a cackling like that of birds.

They were talking about the Tunisian ambassadors and their costumes. One lady had been present at the last reception of the Academy. Another referred to the *Don Juan* of Molière, which had recently been performed at the Théâtre Français.

But with a significant glance towards her niece, Madame Dambreuse laid a finger on her lips, while the smile which escaped from her contradicted this display of austerity.

Suddenly, Martinon appeared at the door directly in front of her. She arose at once. He offered her his arm. Frederick, in order to watch the progress of these gallantries on Martinon's part, walked past the card-table, and came up with them in the large drawing-room. Madame Dambreuse very soon quitted her cavalier, and began chatting with Frederick himself in a very familiar tone.

She understood that he did not play cards, and did not dance.

"Young people have a tendency to be melancholy!" Then, with a single comprehensive glance around:

"Besides, this sort of thing is not amusing—at least for certain natures!"

And she drew up in front of the row of armchairs, uttering a few polite remarks here and there, while some old men with double eyeglasses came to pay court to her. She introduced Frederick to some of them. M. Dambreuse touched him lightly on the elbow, and led him out on the terrace.

He had seen the Minister. The thing was not easy to manage. Before he could be qualified for the post of auditor to the Council of State, he should pass an examination. Frederick, seized with an unaccountable self-confidence, replied that he had a knowledge of the subjects prescribed for it.

The financier was not surprised at this, after all the eulogies M. Roque had pronounced on his abilities.

At the mention of this name, a vision of little Louise, her house and her room, passed through his mind, and he remembered how he had on nights like this stood at her window listening to the wagoners driving past. This recollection of his griefs brought back the thought of Madame Arnoux, and he relapsed into silence as he continued to pace up and down the terrace. The windows shone amid the darkness like slabs of flame. The buzz of the ball gradually grew fainter; the carriages were beginning to leave.

"Why in the world," M. Dambreuse went on, "are you so anxious to be attached to the Council of State?"

And he declared, in the tone of a man of broad views, that the public functions led to nothing—he could speak with some authority on that point—business was much better.

Frederick urged as an objection the difficulty of grappling with all the details of business.

"Pooh! I could post you up well in them in a very short time."

Would he like to be a partner in any of his own undertakings?

The young man saw, as by a lightning-flash, an enormous fortune coming into his hands.

"Let us go in again," said the banker. "You are staying for supper with us, are you not?"

It was three o'clock. They left the terrace.

In the dining-room, a table at which supper was served up awaited the guests. M. Dambreuse perceived Martinon, and, drawing near his wife, in a low tone: "Is it you who invited him?"

She answered dryly.

"Yes, of course."

The niece was not present.

The guests drank a great deal of wine, and laughed very loudly; and risky jokes did not give any offence, all present experiencing that sense of relief which follows a somewhat prolonged period of constraint.

Martinon alone displayed anything like gravity. He refused to drink champagne, as he thought this good form, and, moreover, he assumed an air of tact and politeness, for when M. Dambreuse, who had a contracted chest, complained of an oppression, he made repeated enquiries about that gentleman's health, and then let his blue eyes wander in the direction of Madame Dambreuse.

She questioned Frederick in order to find out which of the young ladies he liked best. He had noticed none of them in particular, and besides, he preferred the women of thirty.

"There, perhaps, you show your sense," she returned.

Then, as they were putting on their pelisses and paletots, M. Dambreuse said to him:

"Come and see me one of these mornings and we'll have a chat."

Martinon, at the foot of the stairs, was lighting a cigar, and, as he puffed it, he presented such a heavy profile that his companion allowed this remark to escape from him:

"Upon my word, you have a fine head!"

"It has turned a few other heads," replied the young magistrate, with an air of mingled self-complacency and annoyance.

As soon as Frederick was in bed, he summed up the main features of the evening party. In the first place, his own toilet (he had looked at himself several times in the mirrors), from the cut of his coat to the knot of his pumps left nothing to find fault with. He had spoken to influential men, and seen wealthy ladies at close quarters. M. Dambreuse had shown himself to be an admirable type of man, and Madame Dambreuse an almost bewitching type of woman. He weighed one by one her slightest words, her looks, a thousand things incapable of being analysed. It would be a right good thing to have such a mistress. And, after all, why should he not? He would have as good a chance with her as any other man. Perhaps she was not so hard to win? Then Martinon came back to his recollection; and, as he fell asleep, he smiled with pity for this worthy fellow.

He woke up with the thought of the Maréhale in his mind. Those words of her note, "After tomorrow evening," were in fact an appointment for the very same day.

He waited until nine o'clock, and then hurried to her house.

Some one who had been going up the stairs before him shut the door. He rang the bell; Delphine came out and told him that "Madame" was not there.

Frederick persisted, begging of her to admit him. He had something of a very serious nature to communicate to her; only a word would suffice. At length, the hundred-sous-piece argument proved successful, and the maid let him into the anteroom.

Rosanette appeared. She was in a negligée, with her hair loose, and, shaking her head, she waved her arms when she was some paces away from him to indicate that she could not receive him now.

Frederick descended the stairs slowly. This caprice was worse than any of the others she had indulged in. He could not understand it at all.

In front of the porter's lodge Mademoiselle Vatnaz stopped him.

"Has she received you?"

"No."

"You've been put out?"

"How do you know that?"

" 'Tis quite plain. But come on; let us go away. I am suffocating!"

She made him accompany her along the street; she panted for breath; he could feel her thin arm trembling on his own. Suddenly, she broke out:

"Ah! the wretch!"

"Who, pray?"

"Why, he—he—Delmar!"

This revelation humiliated Frederick. He next asked:

"Are you quite sure of it?"

"Why, when I tell you I followed him!" exclaimed the Vatnaz. "I saw him going in! Now do you understand? I ought to have expected it for that matter—'twas I, in my stupidity, that introduced him to her. And if you only knew all; my God! Why, I picked him up, supported him, clothed him! And then all the paragraphs I got into the newspapers about him! I loved him like a mother!"

Then, with a sneer:

"Ha! Monsieur wants velvet robes! You may be sure 'tis a speculation on his part. And as for her!—to think that I knew her to earn her living as a seamstress! If it were not for me, she would have fallen into the mire twenty times over! But I will plunge her into it yet! I'll see her dying in a hospital—and everything about her will be known!"

And, like a torrent of dirty water from a vessel full of refuse, her rage poured out in a tumultuous fashion into Frederick's ear the recital of her rival's disgraceful acts.

"She lived with Jumillac, with Flacourt, with little Allard, with Bertinaux, with Saint-Valéry, the pockmarked fellow! No, 'twas the other! They are two brothers—it makes no difference. And when she was in difficulties, I settled everything. She is so avaricious! And then, you will agree with me, 'twas nice and kind of me to go to see her, for we are not persons of the same grade! Am I a fast woman—I? Do I sell myself? Without taking into account that she is as stupid as a head of cabbage. She writes 'category' with a 'th.' After all, they are well met. They make a precious couple, though he styles himself an artist and thinks himself a man of genius. But, my God! if he had only intelligence, he would not have done such an infamous thing! Men don't, as a rule, leave a superior woman for a hussy! What do I care about him after all? He is becoming ugly. I hate him! If I met him, mind you, I'd spit in his face." She spat out as she uttered the words. "Yes, this is what I think about him now. And Arnoux, eh? Isn't it abominable? He has forgiven her so often! You can't conceive the sacrifices he has made for her. She ought to kiss his feet! He is so generous, so good!"

Frederick was delighted at hearing Delmar disparaged. He had taken sides with Arnoux. This perfidy on Rosanette's part seemed to him an abnormal and inexcusable thing; and, infected with this elderly spinster's emotion, he felt a sort of tenderness towards her. Suddenly he found himself in front of Arnoux's door. Mademoiselle Vatnaz, without his attention having been drawn to it, had led him down towards the Rue Poissonnière.

"Here we are!" said she. "As for me, I can't go up; but you, surely there is nothing to prevent you?"

"From doing what?"

"From telling him everything, faith!"

Frederick, as if waking up with a start, saw the baseness towards which she was urging him.

"Well?" she said after a pause.

He raised his eyes towards the second floor. Madame Arnoux's lamp was burning. In fact there was nothing to prevent him from going up.

"I am going to wait for you here. Go on, then!"

This direction had the effect of chilling him, and he said:

"I shall be a long time up there; you would do better to return home. I will call on you to-morrow."

"No, no!" replied the Vatnaz, stamping with her foot. "Take him with you! Bring him there! Let him catch them together!"

"But Delmar will no longer be there."

She hung down her head.

"Yes; that's true, perhaps."

And she remained without speaking in the middle of the street, with vehicles all around her; then, fixing on him her wild-cat's eyes:

"I may rely on you, may I not? There is now a sacred bond between us. Do what you say, then; we'll talk about it to-morrow."

Frederick, in passing through the lobby, heard two voices responding to one another.

Madame Arnoux's voice was saying:

"Don't lie! don't lie, pray!"

He went in. The voices suddenly ceased.

Arnoux was walking from one end of the apartment to the other, and Madame was seated on the little chair near the fire, extremely pale and staring straight before her. Frederick stepped back, and was about to retire, when Arnoux grasped his hand, glad that some one had come to his rescue.

"But I am afraid—" said Frederick.

"Stay here, I beg of you!" he whispered in his ear.

Madame remarked:

"You must make some allowance for this scene, Monsieur Moreau. Such things sometimes unfortunately occur in households."

"They do when we introduce them there ourselves," said Arnoux in a jolly tone. "Women have crotchets, I assure you. This, for instance, is not a bad one—

see! No; quite the contrary. Well, she has been amusing herself for the last hour by teasing me with a heap of idle stories."

"They are true," retorted Madame Arnoux, losing patience; "for, in fact, you bought it yourself."

"I?"

"Yes, you yourself, at the Persian House."

"The cashmere," thought Frederick.

He was filled with a consciousness of guilt, and got quite alarmed.

She quickly added:

"It was on Saturday, the fourteenth."

"The fourteenth," said Arnoux, looking up, as if he were searching in his mind for a date.

"And, furthermore, the clerk who sold it to you was a fair-haired young man."

"How could I remember what sort of man the clerk was?"

"And yet it was at your dictation he wrote the address, 18 Rue de Laval."

"How do you know?" said Arnoux in amazement.

She shrugged her shoulders.

"Oh! 'tis very simple: I went to get my cashmere altered, and the superintendent of the millinery department told me that they had just sent another of the same sort to Madame Arnoux."

"Is it my fault if there is a Madame Arnoux in the same street?"

"Yes; but not Jacques Arnoux," she returned.

Thereupon, he began to talk in an incoherent fashion, protesting that he was innocent. It was some misapprehension, some accident, one of those things that happen in some way that is utterly unaccountable. Men should not be condemned on mere suspicion, vague probabilities; and he referred to the case of the unfortunate Lesurques.

"In short, I say you are mistaken. Do you want me to take my oath on it?"

" 'Tis not worth while."

"Why?"

She looked him straight in the face without saying a word, then stretched out her hand, took down the little silver chest from the mantelpiece, and handed him a bill which was spread open.

Arnoux coloured up to his ears, and his swollen and distorted features betrayed his confusion.

"But," he said in faltering tones, "what does this prove?"

"Ah!" she said, with a peculiar ring in her voice, in which sorrow and irony were blended. "Ah!"

Arnoux held the bill in his hands, and turned it round without removing his eyes from it, as if he were going to find in it the solution of a great problem.

"Ah! yes, yes; I remember," said he at length. " 'Twas a commission. You ought to know about that matter, Frederick." Frederick remained silent. "A commission that Père Oudry entrusted to me."

"And for whom?"

"For his mistress."

"For your own!" exclaimed Madame Arnoux, springing to her feet and standing erect before him.

"I swear to you!"

"Don't begin over again. I know everything."

"Ha! quite right. So you're spying on me!"

She returned coldly:

"Perhaps that wounds your delicacy?"

"Since you are in a passion," said Arnoux, looking for his hat, "and can't be reasoned with—"

Then, with a big sigh:

"Don't marry, my poor friend, don't, if you take my advice!"

And he took himself off, finding it absolutely necessary to get into the open air.

Then there was a deep silence, and it seemed as if everything in the room had become more motionless than before. A luminous circle above the lamp whitened the ceiling, while at the corners stretched out bits of shade resembling pieces of black gauze placed on top of one another. The ticking of the clock and the crackling of the fire were the only sounds that disturbed the stillness.

Madame Arnoux had just seated herself in the armchair at the opposite side of the chimney-piece. She bit her lip and shivered. She drew her hands up to her face; a sob broke from her, and she began to weep.

He sat down on the little couch, and in the soothing tone in which one addresses a sick person:

"You don't suspect me of having anything to do with—?"

She made no reply. But, continuing presently to give utterance to her own thoughts:

"I leave him perfectly free! There was no necessity for lying on his part!"

"That is quite true," said Frederick. "No doubt," he added, "it was the result of Arnoux's habits; he had acted thoughtlessly, but perhaps in matters of a graver character—"

"What do you see, then, that can be graver?"

"Oh, nothing!"

Frederick bent his head with a smile of acquiescence. Nevertheless, he urged, Arnoux possessed certain good qualities; he was fond of his children.

"Ay, and he does all he can to ruin them!"

Frederick urged that this was due to an excessively easy-going disposition, for indeed he was a good fellow.

She exclaimed:

"But what is the meaning of that—a good fellow?"

And he proceeded to defend Arnoux in the vaguest kind of language he could think of, and, while expressing his sympathy with her, he rejoiced, he was delighted, at the bottom of his heart. Through retaliation or need of affection she would fly to him for refuge. His love was intensified by the hope which had now grown immeasurably stronger in his breast.

Never had she appeared to him so captivating, so perfectly beautiful. From time to time a deep breath made her bosom swell. Her two eyes, gazing fixedly into space, seemed dilated by a vision in the depths of her consciousness, and her lips were slightly parted, as if to let her soul escape through them. Sometimes she pressed her handkerchief over them tightly. He would have liked to be this dainty little piece of cambric moistened with her tears. In spite of himself, he cast a look at the bed at the end of the alcove, picturing to himself her head lying on the pillow, and so vividly did this present itself to his imagination that he had to restrain himself to keep from clasping her in his arms. She closed her eyelids, and now she appeared quiescent and languid. Then he drew closer to her, and, bending over her, he eagerly scanned her face. At that moment, he heard the noise of boots in the lobby outside—it was the other. They heard him shutting the door of his own room. Frederick made a sign to Madame Arnoux to ascertain from her whether he ought to go there.

She replied "Yes," in the same voiceless fashion, and this mute exchange of thoughts between them was, as it were, an assent—the preliminary step in adultery.

Arnoux was just taking off his coat to go to bed.

"Well, how is she going on?"

"Oh! better," said Frederick; "this will pass off."

But Arnoux was in an anxious state of mind.

"You don't know her; she has got hysterical now! Idiot of a clerk! This is what comes of being too good. If I had not given that cursed shawl to Rosanette!"

"Don't regret having done so a bit. Nobody could be more grateful to you than she is."

"Do you really think so?"

Frederick had not a doubt of it. The best proof of it was her dismissal of Père Oudry.

"Ah! poor little thing!"

And in the excess of his emotion, Arnoux wanted to rush off to her forthwith.

" 'Tisn't worth while. I am calling to see her. She is unwell."

"All the more reason for my going."

He quickly put on his coat again, and took up his candlestick. Frederick cursed his own stupidity, and pointed out to him that for decency's sake he ought to remain this night with his wife. He could not leave her; it would be very nasty.

"I tell you candidly you would be doing wrong. There is no hurry over there. You will go tomorrow. Come; do this for my sake."

Arnoux put down his candlestick, and, embracing him, said:

"You are a right good fellow!"

Chapter IX

THE FRIEND OF THE FAMILY

THEN BEGAN FOR FREDERICK AN EXISTENCE OF MISERY. HE BECAME THE PARasite of the house.

If anyone were indisposed, he called three times a day to know how the patient was, went to the piano-tuner's, contrived to do a thousand acts of kindness; and he endured with an air of contentment Mademoiselle Marthe's poutings and the caresses of little Eugène, who was always drawing his dirty hands over the young man's face. He was present at dinners at which Monsieur and Madame, facing each other, did not exchange a word, unless it happened that Arnoux provoked his wife with the absurd remarks he made. When the meal was over, he would play about the room with his son, conceal himself behind the furniture, or carry the little boy on his back, walking about on all fours, like the Bearnais. At last, he would go out, and she would at once plunge into the eternal subject of complaint—Arnoux.

It was not his misconduct that excited her indignation, but her pride appeared to be wounded, and she did not hide her repugnance towards this man, who showed an absence of delicacy, dignity, and honour.

"Or rather, he is mad!" she said.

Frederick artfully appealed to her to confide in him. Ere long he knew all the details of her life. Her parents were people in a humble rank in life at Chartres. One day, Arnoux, while sketching on the bank of the river (at this period he believed himself to be a painter), saw her leaving the church, and made her an offer of marriage. On account of his wealth, he was unhesitatingly accepted. Besides, he was desperately in love with her. She added:

"Good heavens! he loves me still, after his fashion!"

They spent the few months immediately after their marriage in travelling through Italy.

Arnoux, in spite of his enthusiasm at the sight of the scenery and the masterpieces, did nothing but groan over the wine, and, to find some kind of amusement, organised picnics along with some English people. The profit which he had made by reselling some pictures tempted him to take up the fine arts as a commercial speculation. Then, he became infatuated about pottery. Just now other branches of commerce attracted him; and, as he had become more and more vulgarised, he contracted coarse and extravagant habits. It was not so much for his vices she had to reproach him as for his entire conduct. No change could be expected in him, and her unhappiness was irreparable.

Frederick declared that his own life in the same way was a failure.

He was still a young man, however. Why should he despair? And she gave him good advice: "Work! and marry!" He answered her with bitter smiles; for in place of giving utterance to the real cause of his grief, he pretended that it was of a different character, a sublime feeling, and he assumed the part of an Antony to some extent, the man accursed by fate—language which did not, however, change very materially the complexion of his thoughts.

For certain men action becomes more difficult as desire becomes stronger. They are embarrassed by self-distrust, and terrified by the fear of making themselves disliked. Besides, deep attachments resemble virtuous women: they are afraid of being discovered, and pass through life with downcast eyes.

Though he was now better acquainted with Madame Arnoux (for that very reason perhaps), he was still more faint-hearted than before. Each morning he swore in his own mind that he would take a bold course. He was prevented from doing so by an unconquerable feeling of bashfulness; and he had no example to guide him, inasmuch as she was different from other women. From the force of his dreams, he had placed her outside the ordinary pale of humanity. At her side he felt himself of less importance in the world than the sprigs of silk that escaped from her scissors.

Then he thought of some monstrous and absurd devices, such as surprises at night, with narcotics and false keys—anything appearing easier to him than to face her disdain.

Besides, the children, the two servant-maids, and the relative position of the rooms caused insurmountable obstacles. So then he made up his mind to possess her himself alone, and to bring her to live with him far away in the depths of some solitude. He even asked himself what lake would be blue enough, what seashore would be delightful enough for her, whether it would be in Spain, Switzerland, or the East; and expressly fixing on days when she seemed more irritated than usual, he told her that it would be necessary for her to leave the house, to find out some ground to justify such a step, and that he saw no way out of it but a separation. However, for the sake of the children whom she loved, she would never resort to such an extreme course. So much virtue served to increase his respect for her.

He spent each afternoon in recalling the visit he had paid the night before, and in longing for the evening to come in order that he might call again. When he did not dine with them, he posted himself about nine o'clock at the corner of the street, and, as soon as Arnoux had slammed the hall-door behind him, Frederick quickly ascended the two flights of stairs, and asked the servant-girl in an ingenuous fashion:

"Is Monsieur in?"

Then he would exhibit surprise at finding that Arnoux was gone out.

The latter frequently came back unexpectedly. Then Frederick had to accompany him to the little café in the Rue Sainte-Anne, which Regimbart now frequented.

The Citizen began by giving vent to some fresh grievance which he had against the Crown. Then they would chat, pouring out friendly abuse on one another, for the earthenware manufacturer took Regimbart for a thinker of a high order, and, vexed at seeing him neglecting so many chances of winning distinction, teased the Citizen about his laziness. It seemed to Regimbart that Arnoux was a man full of heart and imagination, but decidedly of lax morals, and therefore he was quite unceremonious towards a personage he respected so little, refusing even to dine at his house on the ground that "such formality was a bore."

Sometimes, at the moment of parting, Arnoux would be seized with hunger. He found it necessary to order an omelet or some roasted apples; and, as there was never anything to eat in the establishment, he sent out for something. They waited. Regimbart did not leave, and ended by consenting in a grumbling fashion to have something himself. He was nevertheless gloomy, for he remained for hours seated before a half-filled glass. As Providence did not regulate things in harmony with his ideas, he was becoming a hypochondriac, no longer cared even to read the newspapers, and at the mere mention of England's name began to bellow with rage. On one occasion, referring to a waiter who attended on him carelessly, he exclaimed:

"Have we not enough of insults from the foreigner?"

Except at these critical periods he remained taciturn, contemplating "an infallible stroke of business that would burst up the whole shop."

Whilst he was lost in these reflections, Arnoux in a monotonous voice and with a slight look of intoxication, related incredible anecdotes in which he always shone himself, owing to his assurance; and Frederick (this was, no doubt, due to some deep-rooted resemblances) felt more or less attracted towards him. He reproached himself for this weakness, believing that on the contrary he ought to hate this man.

Arnoux, in Frederick's presence, complained of his wife's ill-temper, her obstinacy, her unjust accusations. She had not been like this in former days.

"If I were you," said Frederick, "I would make her an allowance and live alone."

Arnoux made no reply; and the next moment he began to sound her praises. She was good, devoted, intelligent, and virtuous; and, passing to her personal beauty, he made some revelations on the subject with the thoughtlessness of people who display their treasures at taverns.

His equilibrium was disturbed by a catastrophe.

He had been appointed one of the Board of Superintendence in a kaolin company. But placing reliance on everything that he was told, he had signed inaccurate reports and approved, without verification, of the annual inventories fraudulently prepared by the manager. The company had now failed, and Arnoux, being legally responsible, was, along with the others who were liable under the guaranty, condemned to pay damages, which meant a loss to him of thirty thousand francs, not to speak of the costs of the judgment.

Frederick read the report of the case in a newspaper, and at once hurried off to the Rue de Paradis.

He was ushered into Madame's apartment. It was breakfast-time. A round table close to the fire was covered with bowls of *café au lait*. Slippers trailed over the carpet, and clothes over the armchairs. Arnoux was attired in trousers and a knitted vest, with his eyes bloodshot and his hair in disorder. Little Eugène was crying at the pain caused by an attack of mumps, while nibbling at a slice of bread and butter. His sister was eating quietly. Madame Arnoux, a little paler than usual, was attending on all three of them.

"Well," said Arnoux, heaving a deep sigh, "you know all about it?"

And, as Frederick gave him a pitying look: "There, you see, I have been the victim of my own trustfulness!"

Then he relapsed into silence, and so great was his prostration, that he pushed his breakfast away from him. Madame Arnoux raised her eyes with a shrug of the shoulders. He passed his hand across his forehead.

"After all, I am not guilty. I have nothing to reproach myself with. 'Tis a misfortune. It will be got over—ay, and so much the worse, faith!"

He took a bite of a cake, however, in obedience to his wife's entreaties.

That evening, he wished that she should go and dine with him alone in a private room at the Maison d'Or. Madame Arnoux did not at all understand this emotional impulse, taking offence, in fact, at being treated as if she were a light woman. Arnoux, on the contrary, meant it as a proof of affection. Then, as he was beginning to feel dull, he went to pay the Maréchale a visit in order to amuse himself.

Up to the present, he had been pardoned for many things owing to his reputation for good-fellowship. His lawsuit placed him amongst men of bad character. No one visited his house.

Frederick, however, considered that he was bound in honour to go there more frequently than ever. He hired a box at the Italian opera, and brought them there with him every week. Meanwhile, the pair had reached that period in unsuitable unions when an invincible lassitude springs from concessions which people get into the habit of making, and which render existence intolerable. Madame Arnoux restrained her pent-up feelings from breaking out; Arnoux became gloomy; and Frederick grew sad at witnessing the unhappiness of these two ill-fated beings.

She had imposed on him the obligation, since she had given him her confidence, of making enquiries as to the state of her husband's affairs. But shame prevented him from doing so. It was painful to him to reflect that he coveted the wife of this man, at whose dinner-table he constantly sat. Nevertheless, he continued his visits, excusing himself on the ground that he was bound to protect her, and that an occasion might present itself for being of service to her.

Eight days after the ball, he had paid a visit to M. Dambreuse. The financier had offered him twenty shares in a coal-mining speculation; Frederick did not go back there again. Deslauriers had written letters to him, which he left unanswered. Pellerin had invited him to go and see the portrait; he always put it off. He gave way, however, to Cisy's persistent appeals to be introduced to Rosanette.

She received him very nicely, but without springing on his neck as she used to do formerly. His comrade was delighted at being received by a woman of easy virtue, and above all at having a chat with an actor. Delmar was there when he called. A drama in which he appeared as a peasant lecturing Louis XIV and prophesying the events of '89 had made him so conspicuous, that the same part was continually assigned to him; and now his function consisted of attacks on the monarchs of all nations. As an English brewer, he inveighed against Charles I; as a student at Salamanca, he cursed Philip II; or, as a sensitive father, he expressed indignation against the Pompadour—this was the most beautiful bit of acting! The brats of the street used to wait at the door leading to the side-scenes in order to see him; and his biography, sold between the acts, described him as taking care of his aged mother, reading the Bible, assisting the poor, in fact, under the aspect of a Saint Vincent de Paul together with a dash of Brutus and Mirabeau. People spoke of him as "Our Delmar." He had a mission; he became another Christ.

All this had fascinated Rosanette; and she had got rid of Père Oudry, without caring one jot about consequences, as she was not of a covetous disposition.

Arnoux, who knew her, had taken advantage of the state of affairs for some time past to spend very little money on her. M. Roque had appeared on the scene, and all three of them carefully avoided anything like a candid explanation. Then, fancying that she had got rid of the other solely on his account, Arnoux increased her allowance, for she was living at a very expensive rate. She had even sold her cashmere in her anxiety to pay off her old debts, as she said; and he was continually giving her money, while she bewitched him and imposed upon him pitilessly.

Therefore, bills and stamped paper rained all over the house. Frederick felt that a crisis was approaching.

One day he called to see Madame Arnoux. She had gone out. Monsieur was at work below stairs in the shop. In fact, Arnoux, in the midst of his Japanese vases, was trying to take in a newly-married pair who happened to be well-to-do people from the provinces. He talked about wheel-moulding and fine-moulding, about spotted porcelain and glazed porcelain; the others, not wishing to appear utterly ignorant of the subject, listened with nods of approbation, and made purchases.

When the customers had gone out, he told Frederick that he had that very morning been engaged in a little altercation with his wife. In order to obviate any remarks about expense, he had declared that the Maréchale was no longer his mistress. "I even told her that she was yours."

Frederick was annoyed at this; but to utter reproaches might only betray him. He faltered: "Ah! you were in the wrong—greatly in the wrong!"

"What does that signify?" said Arnoux. "Where is the disgrace of passing for her lover? I am really so myself. Would you not be flattered at being in that position?"

Had she spoken? Was this a hint? Frederick hastened to reply:

"No! not at all! on the contrary!"

"Well, what then?"

"Yes, 'tis true; it makes no difference so far as that's concerned."

Arnoux next asked: "And why don't you call there oftener?"

Frederick promised that he would make it his business to go there again.

"Ah! I forgot! you ought, when talking about Rosanette, to let out in some way to my wife that you are her lover. I can't suggest how you can best do it, but you'll find out that. I ask this of you as a special favour—eh?"

The young man's only answer was an equivocal grimace. This calumny had undone him. He even called on her that evening, and swore that Arnoux's accusation was false.

"Is that really so?"

He appeared to be speaking sincerely, and, when she had taken a long breath of relief, she said to him:

"I believe you," with a beautiful smile. Then she hung down her head, and, without looking at him:

"Besides, nobody has any claim on you!"

So then she had divined nothing; and she despised him, seeing that she did not think he could love her well enough to remain faithful to her! Frederick, forgetting his overtures while with the other, looked on the permission accorded to him as an insult to himself.

After this she suggested that he ought now and then to pay Rosanette a visit, to get a little glimpse of what she was like.

Arnoux presently made his appearance, and, five minutes later, wished to carry him off to Rosanette's abode.

The situation was becoming intolerable.

His attention was diverted by a letter from a notary, who was going to send him fifteen thousand francs the following day; and, in order to make up for his neglect of Deslauriers, he went forthwith to tell him this good news.

The advocate was lodging in the Rue des Trois-Maries, on the fifth floor, over a courtyard. His study, a little tiled apartment, chilly, and with a grey paper on the walls, had as its principal decoration a gold medal, the prize awarded him on the occasion of taking out his degree as a Doctor of Laws, which was fixed in an ebony frame near the mirror. A mahogany bookcase enclosed under its glass front a hundred volumes, more or less. The writing-desk, covered with sheep-leather, occupied the centre of the apartment. Four old armchairs upholstered in green velvet were placed in the corners; and a heap of shavings made a blaze in the fireplace, where there was always a bundle of sticks ready to be lighted as soon as he rang the bell. It was his consultation-hour, and the advocate had on a white cravat.

The announcement as to the fifteen thousand francs (he had, no doubt, given up all hope of getting the amount) made him chuckle with delight.

"That's right, old fellow, that's right—that's quite right!"

He threw some wood into the fire, sat down again, and immediately began talking about the journal. The first thing to do was to get rid of Hussonnet.

"I'm quite tired of that idiot! As for officially professing opinions, my own notion is that the most equitable and forcible position is to have no opinions at all."

Frederick appeared astonished.

"Why, the thing is perfectly plain. It is time that politics should be dealt with scientifically. The old men of the eighteenth century began it when Rousseau and the men of letters introduced into the political sphere philanthropy, poetry, and other fudge, to the great delight of the Catholics—a natural alliance, however, since the modern reformers (I can prove it) all believe in Revelation. But, if you sing high masses for Poland, if, in place of the God of the Dominicans, who was an executioner, you take the God of the Romanticists, who is an upholsterer, if, in fact, you have not a wider conception of the Absolute than your ancestors, Monarchy will penetrate underneath your Republican forms, and your red cap will never be more than the headpiece of a priest. The only difference will be that the cell system will take the place of torture, the outrageous treatment of Religion that of sacrilege, and the European Concert that of the Holy Alliance; and in this beautiful order which we admire, composed of the wreckage of the followers of Louis XIV, the last remains of the Voltaireans, with some Imperial whitewash on top, and some fragments of the British Constitution, you will see the municipal councils trying to give annoyance to the Mayor, the general councils to their Prefect, the Chambers to the King, the Press to Power, and the Administration to everybody. But simple-minded people get enraptured about the Civil Code, a work fabricated—let them say what they like—in a mean and tyrannical spirit, for the legislator, in place of doing his duty to the State, which simply means to observe customs in a regular fashion, claims to model society like another Lycurgus. Why does the law impede father's of families with regard to the making of wills? Why does it place shackles on the compulsory sale of real estate? Why does it punish as a misdemeanour vagrancy, which ought not even to be regarded as a technical contravention of the Code. And there are other things! I know all about them! and so I am going to write a little novel, entitled 'The History of the Idea of Justice,' which will be amusing. But I am infernally thirsty! And you?"

He leaned out through the window, and called to the porter to go and fetch them two glasses of grog from the public-house over the way.

"To sum up, I see three parties—no! three groups—in none of which do I take the slightest interest: those who have, those who have nothing, and those who are trying to have. But all agree in their idiotic worship of Authority! For example, Mably recommends that the philosophers should be prevented from publishing their doctrines; M. Wronsky, the geometrician, describes the censorship as the 'critical expression of speculative spontaneity'; Père Enfantin gives his blessing to the Hapsburgs for having passed a hand across the Alps in order to keep Italy down; Pierre Leroux wishes people to be compelled to listen to an orator; and Louis Blanc inclines towards a State religion—so much rage for government have these vassals whom we call the people! Nevertheless, there is not a single legitimate government, in spite of their sempiternal principles. But 'principle' signifies 'origin.' It is always necessary to go back to a revolution, to an act of violence, to a transitory fact. Thus, our principle is the national sovereignty embodied in the Parliamentary form, though the Parliament does not assent to this! But in what way could the sovereignty of the people be more sacred than the Divine Right? They are both fictions. Enough of metaphysics; no more phantoms! There is no need of dogmas in order to get the streets swept! It will be said that I am turning society upside down. Well, after all, where would be the harm of that? It is, indeed, a nice thing—this society of yours."

Frederick could have given many answers. But, seeing that his theories were far less advanced than those of Sénécal, he was full of indulgence towards Deslauriers. He contented himself with arguing that such a system would make them generally hated.

"On the contrary, as we should have given to each party a pledge of hatred against his neighbour, all will reckon on us. You are about to enter into it yourself, and to furnish us with some transcendent criticism!"

It was necessary to attack accepted ideas—the Academy, the Normal School, the Consérvatoire, the Comédie Française, everything that resembled an institution. It was in that way that they would give uniformity to the doctrines taught in their review. Then, as soon as it had been thoroughly well-established, the journal would suddenly be converted into a daily publication. Thereupon they could find fault with individuals.

"And they will respect us, you may be sure!"

Deslauriers touched upon that old dream of his—the position of editor-in-chief, so that he might have the unutterable happiness of directing others, of entirely cutting down their articles, of ordering them to be written or declining them. His eyes twinkled under his goggles; he got into a stale of excitement, and drank a few glasses of brandy, one after the other, in an automatic fashion.

"You'll have to stand me a dinner once a week. That's indispensable, even though you should have to squander half your income on it. People would feel pleasure in going to it; it would be a centre for the others, a lever for yourself; and by manipulating public opinion at its two ends—literature and politics—you will see how, before six months have passed, we shall occupy the first rank in Paris."

Frederick, as he listened to Deslauriers, experienced a sensation of rejuvenescence, like a man who, after having been confined in a room for a long time, is suddenly transported into the open air. The enthusiasm of his friend had a contagious effect upon him.

"Yes, I have been an idler, an imbecile—you are right!"

"All in good time," said Deslauriers. "I have found my Frederick again!"

And, holding up his jaw with closed fingers:

"Ah! you have made me suffer! Never mind, I am fond of you all the same."

They stood there gazing into each other's faces, both deeply affected, and were on the point of embracing each other.

A woman's cap appeared on the threshold of the anteroom.

"What brings you here?" said Deslauriers.

It was Mademoiselle Clémence, his mistress.

She replied that, as she happened to be passing, she could not resist the desire to go in to see him, and in order that they might have a little repast together, she had brought some cakes, which she laid on the table.

"Take care of my papers!" said the advocate, sharply. "Besides, this is the third time that I have forbidden you to come at my consultation-hours."

She wished to embrace him.

"All right! Go away! Cut your stick!"

He repelled her; she heaved a great sigh.

"Ah! you are plaguing me again!"

" 'Tis because I love you!"

"I don't ask you to love me, but to oblige me!"

This harsh remark stopped Clémence's tears. She took up her station before the window, and remained there motionless, with her forehead against the pane.

Her attitude and her silence had an irritating effect on Deslauriers.

"When you have finished, you will order your carriage, will you not?"

She turned round with a start.

"You are sending me away?"

"Exactly."

She fixed on him her large blue eyes, no doubt as a last appeal, then drew the two ends of her tartan across each other, lingered for a minute or two, and went away.

"You ought to call her back," said Frederick.

"Come, now!"

And, as he wished to go out, Deslauriers went into the kitchen, which also served as his dressing-room. On the stone floor, beside a pair of boots, were to be seen the remains of a meagre breakfast, and a mattress with a coverlid was rolled up on the floor in a corner.

"This will show you," said he, "that I receive few marchionesses. 'Tis easy to get enough of them, ay, faith! and some others, too! Those who cost nothing take up your time—'tis money under another form. Now, I'm not rich! And then they are all so silly, so silly! Can you chat with a woman yourself?"

As they parted, at the corner of the Pont Neuf, Deslauriers said: "It's agreed, then; you'll bring the thing to me to-morrow as soon as you have it!"

"Agreed!" said Frederick.

When he awoke next morning, he received through the post a cheque on the bank for fifteen thousand francs.

This scrap of paper represented to him fifteen big bags of money; and he said to himself that, with such a sum he could, first of all, keep his carriage for three years instead of selling it, as he would soon be forced to do, or buy for himself two beautiful damaskeened pieces of armour, which he had seen on the Quai Voltaire, then a quantity of other things, pictures, books and what a quantity of bouquets of flowers, presents for Madame Arnoux! anything, in short, would have been preferable to risking losing everything in that journal! Deslauriers seemed to him presumptuous, his insensibility on the night before having chilled Frederick's affection for him; and the young man was indulging in these feelings of regret, when he was quite surprised by the sudden appearance of Arnoux, who sat down heavily on the side of the bed, like a man overwhelmed with trouble.

"What is the matter now?"

"I am ruined!"

He had to deposit that very day at the office of Maître Beaumont, notary, in the Rue Saint-Anne, eighteen thousand francs lent him by one Vanneroy.

" 'Tis an unaccountable disaster. I have, however, given him a mortgage, which ought to keep him quiet. But he threatens me with a writ if it is not paid this afternoon promptly."

"And what next?"

"Oh! the next step is simple enough; he will take possession of my real estate. Once the thing is publicly announced, it means ruin to me—that's all! Ah! if I could find anyone to advance me this cursed sum, he might take Vanneroy's place, and I should be saved! You don't chance to have it yourself?"

The cheque had remained on the night-table near a book. Frederick took up a volume, and placed it on the cheque, while he replied:

"Good heavens, my dear friend, no!"

But it was painful to him to say "no" to Arnoux.

"What, don't you know anyone who would—?"

"Nobody! and to think that in eight days I should be getting in money! There is owing to me probably fifty thousand francs at the end of the month!"

"Couldn't you ask some of the persons that owe you money to make you an advance?"

"Ah! well, so I did!"

"But have you any bills or promissory notes?"

"Not one!"

"What is to be done?" said Frederick.

"That's what I'm asking myself," said Arnoux. " 'Tisn't for myself, my God! but for my children and my poor wife!"

Then, letting each phrase fall from his lips in a broken fashion:

"In fact—I could rough it—I could pack off all I have—and go and seek my fortune—I don't know where!"

"Impossible!" exclaimed Frederick.

Arnoux replied with an air of calmness:

"How do you think I could live in Paris now?"

There was a long silence. Frederick broke it by saying:

"When could you pay back this money?"

Not that he had it; quite the contrary! But there was nothing to prevent him from seeing some friends, and making an application to them.

And he rang for his servant to get himself dressed.

Arnoux thanked him.

"The amount you want is eighteen thousand francs—isn't it?"

"Oh! I could manage easily with sixteen thousand! For I could make two thousand five hundred out of it, or get three thousand on my silver plate, if Vanneroy meanwhile would give me till to-morrow; and, I repeat to you, you may inform the lender, give him a solemn undertaking, that in eight days, perhaps even in five or six, the money will be reimbursed. Besides, the mortgage will be security for it. So there is no risk, you understand?"

Frederick assured him that he thoroughly understood the state of affairs, and added that he was going out immediately.

He would be sure on his return to bestow hearty maledictions on Deslauriers, for he wished to keep his word, and in the meantime, to oblige Arnoux.

"Suppose I applied to M. Dambreuse? But on what pretext could I ask for money? 'Tis I, on the contrary, that should give him some for the shares I took in his coal-mining company. Ah! let him go hang himself—his shares! I am really not liable for them!"

And Frederick applauded himself for his own independence, as if he had refused to do some service for M. Dambreuse.

"Ah, well," said he to himself afterwards, "since I'm going to meet with a loss in this way—for with fifteen thousand francs I might gain a hundred thousand! such things sometimes happen on the Bourse—well, then, since I am breaking my promise to one of them, am I not free? Besides, when Deslauriers might wait? No, no; that's wrong; let us go there."

He looked at his watch.

"Ah! there's no hurry. The bank does not close till five o'clock."

And, at half-past four, when he had cashed the cheque:

" 'Tis useless now; I should not find him in. I'll go this evening." Thus giving himself the opportunity of changing his mind, for there always remain in the conscience some of those sophistries which we pour into it ourselves. It preserves the after-taste of them, like some unwholesome, liquor.

He walked along the boulevards, and dined alone at the restaurant. Then he listened to one act of a play at the Vaudeville, in order to divert his thoughts. But his bank-notes caused him as much embarrassment as if he had stolen them. He would not have been very sorry if he had lost them.

When he reached home again he found a letter containing these words:

"What news? My wife joins me, dear friend, in the hope, etc.—Yours."

And then there was a flourish after his signature.

"His wife! She appeals to me!"

At the same moment Arnoux appeared, to have an answer as to whether he had been able to obtain the sum so sorely needed.

"Wait a moment; here it is," said Frederick.

And, twenty-four hours later, he gave this reply to Deslauriers:

"I have no money."

The advocate came back three days, one after the other, and urged Frederick to write to the notary. He even offered to take a trip to Havre in connection with the matter.

At the end of the week, Frederick timidly asked the worthy Arnoux for his fifteen thousand francs. Arnoux put it off till the following day, and then till the day after. Frederick ventured out late at night, fearing lest Deslauriers might come on him by surprise.

One evening, somebody knocked against him at the corner of the Madeleine. It was he.

And Deslauriers accompanied Frederick as far as the door of a house in the Faubourg Poissonnière.

"Wait for me!"

He waited. At last, after three quarters of an hour, Frederick came out, accompanied by Arnoux, and made signs to him to have patience a little longer. The earthenware merchant and his companion went up the Rue de Hauteville arm-in-arm, and then turned down the Rue de Chabrol.

The night was dark, with gusts of tepid wind. Arnoux walked on slowly, talking about the Galleries of Commerce—a succession of covered passages which would have led from the Boulevard Saint-Denis to the Châtelet, a marvellous speculation, into which he was very anxious to enter; and he stopped from time to time in order to have a look at the grisettes' faces in front of the shop-windows, and then, raising his head again, resumed the thread of his discourse.

Frederick heard Deslauriers' steps behind him like reproaches, like blows falling on his conscience. But he did not venture to claim his money, through a feeling of bashfulness, and also through a fear that it would be fruitless. The other was drawing nearer. He made up his mind to ask.

Arnoux, in a very flippant tone, said that, as he had not got in his outstanding debts, he was really unable to pay back the fifteen thousand francs.

"You have no need of money, I fancy?"

At that moment Deslauriers came up to Frederick, and, taking him aside:

"Be honest. Have you got the amount? Yes or no?"

"Well, then, no," said Frederick; "I've lost it."

"Ah! and in what way?"

"At play."

Deslauriers, without saying a single word in reply, made a very low bow, and went away. Arnoux had taken advantage of the opportunity to light a cigar in a tobacconist's shop. When he came back, be wanted to know from Frederick "who was that young man?"

"Oh! nobody—a friend."

Then, three minutes later, in front of Rosanette's door:

"Come on up," said Arnoux; "she'll be glad to see you. What a savage you are just now!"

A gas-lamp, which was directly opposite, threw its light on him; and, with his cigar between his white teeth and his air of contentment, there was something intolerable about him.

"Ha! now that I think of it, my notary has been at your place this morning about that mortgage-registry business. 'Tis my wife reminded me about it."

"A wife with brains!" returned Frederick automatically.

"I believe you."

And once more Arnoux began to sing his wife's praises. There was no one like her for spirit, tenderness, and thrift; he added in a low tone, rolling his eyes about: "And a woman with so many charms, too!"

"Good-bye!" said Frederick.

Arnoux made a step closer to him.

"Hold on! Why are you going?" And, with his hand half-stretched out towards Frederick, he stared at the young man, quite abashed by the look of anger in his face.

Frederick repeated in a dry tone, "Good-bye!"

He hurried down the Rue de Bréda like a stone rolling headlong, raging against Arnoux, swearing in his own mind that he would never see the man again, nor her either, so broken-hearted and desolate did he feel. In place of the rupture which he had anticipated, here was the other, on the contrary, exhibiting towards her a most perfect attachment from the ends of her hair to the inmost depths of her soul. Frederick was exasperated by the vulgarity of this man. Everything, then, belonged to him! He would meet Arnoux again at his mistress's door; and the mortification of a rupture would be added to rage at his own powerlessness. Besides, he felt humiliated by the other's display of integrity in offering him guaranties for his money. He would have liked to strangle him, and over the pangs of disappointment floated in his conscience, like a fog, the sense of his baseness towards his friend. Rising tears nearly suffocated him.

Deslauriers descended the Rue des Martyrs, swearing aloud with indignation; for his project, like an obelisk that has fallen, now assumed extraordinary proportions. He considered himself robbed, as if he had suffered a great loss. His friendship for Frederick was dead, and he experienced a feeling of joy at it—it was a sort of compensation to him! A hatred of all rich people took possession of him. He leaned towards Sénécal's opinions, and resolved to make every effort to propagate them.

All this time, Arnoux was comfortably seated in an easy-chair near the fire, sipping his cup of tea, with the Maréchale on his knees.

Frederick did not go back there; and, in order to distract his attention from his disastrous passion, he determined to write a "History of the Renaissance." He piled up confusedly on his table the humanists, the philosophers, and the poets, and he went to inspect some engravings of Mark Antony, and tried to understand Machiavelli. Gradually, the serenity of intellectual work had a soothing effect upon him. While his mind was steeped in the personality of others, he lost sight of his own—which is the only way, perhaps, of getting rid of suffering.

One day, while he was quietly taking notes, the door opened, and the man-servant announced Madame Arnoux.

It was she, indeed! and alone? Why, no! for she was holding little Eugène by the hand, followed by a nurse in a white apron. She sat down, and after a preliminary cough:

"It is a long time since you came to see us."

As Frederick could think of no excuse at the moment, she added:

"It was delicacy on your part!"

He asked in return:

"Delicacy about what?"

"About what you have done for Arnoux!" said she.

Frederick made a significant gesture. "What do I care about him, indeed? It was for your sake I did it!"

She sent off the child to play with his nurse in the drawing-room. Two or three words passed between them as to their state of health; then the conversation hung fire.

She wore a brown silk gown, which had the colour of Spanish wine, with a paletot of black velvet bordered with sable. This fur made him yearn to pass his hand over it; and her headbands, so long and so exquisitely smooth, seemed to draw his lips towards them. But he was agitated by emotion, and, turning his eyes towards the door:

" 'Tis rather warm here!"

Frederick understood what her discreet glance meant.

"Ah! excuse me! the two leaves of the door are merely drawn together."

"Yes, that's true!"

And she smiled, as much as to say:

"I'm not a bit afraid!"

He asked her presently what was the object of her visit.

"My husband," she replied with an effort, "has urged me to call on you, not venturing to take this step himself!"

"And why?"

"You know M. Dambreuse, don't you?"

"Yes, slightly."

"Ah! slightly."

She relapsed into silence.

"No matter! finish what you were going to say."

Thereupon she told him that, two days before. Arnoux had found himself unable to meet four bills of a thousand francs, made payable at the banker's order and with his signature attached to them. She felt sorry for having compromised her children's fortune. But anything was preferable to dishonour; and, if M. Dambreuse stopped the proceedings, they would certainly pay him soon, for she was going to sell a little house which she had at Chartres.

"Poor woman!" murmured Frederick. "I will go. Rely on me!"

"Thanks!"

And she arose to go.

"Oh! there is nothing to hurry you yet."

She remained standing, examining the trophy of Mongolian arrows suspended from the ceiling, the bookcase, the bindings, all the utensils for writing. She lifted up the bronze bowl which held his pens. Her feet rested on different portions of the carpet. She had visited Frederick several times before, but always accompanied by Arnoux. They were now alone together—alone in his own house. It was an extraordinary event—almost a successful issue of his love.

She wished to see his little garden. He offered her his arm to show her his property—thirty feet of ground enclosed by some houses, adorned with shrubs at the corners and flower-borders in the middle. The early days of April had arrived. The leaves of the lilacs were already showing their borders of green. A breath of pure air was diffused around, and the little birds chirped, their song alternating with the distant sound that came from a coachmaker's forge.

Frederick went to look for a fire-shovel; and, while they walked on side by side, the child kept making sand-pies in the walk.

Madame Arnoux did not believe that, as he grew older, he would have a great imagination; but he had a winning disposition. His sister, on the other hand, possessed a caustic humour that sometimes wounded her.

"That will change," said Frederick. "We must never despair."

She returned:

"We must never despair!"

This automatic repetition of the phrase he had used appeared to him a sort of encouragement; he plucked a rose, the only one in the garden.

"Do you remember a certain bouquet of roses one evening, in a carriage?"

She coloured a little; and, with an air of bantering pity:

"Ah, I was very young then!"

"And this one," went on Frederick, in a low tone, "will it be the same way with it?"

She replied, while turning about the stem between her fingers, like the thread of a spindle:

"No, I will preserve it."

She called over the nurse, who took the child in her arms; then, on the threshold of the door in the street, Madame Arnoux inhaled the odour of the flower, leaning her head on her shoulder with a look as sweet as a kiss.

When he had gone up to his study, he gazed at the armchair in which she had sat, and every object which she had touched. Some portion of her was diffused around him. The caress of her presence lingered there still.

"So, then, she came here," said he to himself.

And his soul was bathed in the waves of infinite tenderness.

Next morning, at eleven o'clock, he presented himself at M. Dambreuse's house. He was received in the dining-room. The banker was seated opposite his wife at breakfast. Beside her sat his niece, and at the other side of the table appeared the governess, an English woman, strongly pitted with small-pox.

M. Dambreuse invited his young friend to take his place among them, and when he declined:

"What can I do for you? I am listening to whatever you have to say to me."

Frederick confessed, while affecting indifference, that he had come to make a request in behalf of one Arnoux.

"Ha! ha! the ex-picture-dealer," said the banker, with a noiseless laugh which exposed his gums. "Oudry formerly gave security for him; he has given a lot of trouble."

And he proceeded to read the letters and newspapers which lay close beside him on the table.

Two servants attended without making the least noise on the floor; and the loftiness of the apartment, which had three portières of richest tapestry, and two white marble fountains, the polish of the chafing-dish, the arrangement of the side-dishes, and even the rigid folds of the napkins, all this sumptuous comfort impressed Frederick's mind with the contrast between it and another breakfast at the Arnouxs' house. He did not take the liberty of interrupting M. Dambreuse.

Madame noticed his embarrassment.

"Do you occasionally see our friend Martinon?"

"He will be here this evening," said the young girl in a lively tone.

"Ha! so you know him?" said her aunt, fixing on her a freezing look.

At that moment one of the men-servants, bending forward, whispered in her ear.

"Your dressmaker, Mademoiselle—Miss John!"

And the governess, in obedience to this summons, left the room along with her pupil.

M. Dambreuse, annoyed at the disarrangement of the chairs by this movement, asked what was the matter.

" 'Tis Madame Regimbart."

"Wait a moment! Regimbart! I know that name. I have come across his signature."

Frederick at length broached the question. Arnoux deserved some consideration; he was even going, for the sole purpose of fulfilling his engagements, to sell a house belonging to his wife.

"She is considered very pretty," said Madame Dambreuse.

The banker added, with a display of good-nature:

"Are you on friendly terms with them—on intimate terms?"

Frederick, without giving an explicit reply, said that he would be very much obliged to him if he considered the matter.

"Well, since it pleases you, be it so; we will wait. I have some time to spare yet; suppose we go down to my office. Would you mind?"

They had finished breakfast. Madame Dambreuse bowed slightly towards Frederick, smiling in a singular fashion, with a mixture of politeness and irony. Frederick had no time to reflect about it, for M. Dambreuse, as soon as they were alone:

"You did not come to get your shares?"

And, without permitting him to make any excuses:

"Well! well! 'tis right that you should know a little more about the business."

He offered Frederick a cigarette, and began his statement.

The General Union of French Coal Mines had been constituted. All that they were waiting for was the order for its incorporation. The mere fact of the amalgamation had diminished the cost of superintendence, and of manual labour, and increased the profits. Besides, the company had conceived a new idea, which was to interest the workmen in its undertaking. It would erect houses for them, healthful dwellings; finally, it would constitute itself the purveyor of its *employés*, and would have everything supplied to them at net prices.

"And they will be the gainers by it, Monsieur: there's true progress! that's the way to reply effectively to certain Republican brawlings. We have on our Board"—he showed the prospectus—"a peer of France, a scholar who is a member of the Institute, a retired field-officer of genius. Such elements reassure the timid capitalists, and appeal to intelligent capitalists!"

The company would have in its favour the sanction of the State, then the railways, the steam service, the metallurgical establishments, the gas companies, and ordinary households.

"Thus we heat, we light, we penetrate to the very hearth of the humblest home. But how, you will say to me, can we be sure of selling? By the aid of protective laws, dear Monsieur, and we shall get them!—that is a matter that concerns us! For my part, however, I am a downright prohibitionist! The country before anything!"

He had been appointed a director; but he had no time to occupy himself with certain details, amongst other things with the editing of their publications.

"I find myself rather muddled with my authors. I have forgotten my Greek. I should want some one who could put my ideas into shape."

And suddenly: "Will you be the man to perform those duties, with the title of general secretary?"

Frederick did not know what reply to make.

"Well, what is there to prevent you?"

His functions would be confined to writing a report every year for the shareholders. He would find himself day after day in communication with the most notable men in Paris. Representing the company with the workmen, he would ere long be worshipped by them as a natural consequence, and by this means he would be able, later, to push him into the General Council, and into the position of a deputy.

Frederick's ears tingled. Whence came this goodwill? He got confused in returning thanks. But it was not necessary, the banker said, that he should be dependent on anyone. The best course was to take some shares, "a splendid investment besides, for your capital guarantees your position, as your position does your capital."

"About how much should it amount to?" said Frederick.

"Oh, well! whatever you please—from forty to sixty thousand francs, I suppose."

This sum was so trifling in M. Dambreuse's eyes, and his authority was so great, that the young man resolved immediately to sell a farm.

He accepted the offer. M. Dambreuse was to select one of his disengaged days for an appointment in order to finish their arrangements.

"So I can say to Jacques Arnoux—?"

"Anything you like—the poor chap—anything you like!"

Frederick wrote to the Arnouxs' to make their minds easy, and he despatched the letter by a manservant, who brought back the letter: "All right!" His action in the matter deserved better recognition. He expected a visit, or, at least, a letter. He did not receive a visit, and no letter arrived.

Was it forgetfulness on their part, or was it intentional? Since Madame Arnoux had come once, what was to prevent her from coming again? The species of confidence, of avowal, of which she had made him the recipient on the occasion, was nothing better, then, than a manouevre which she had executed through interested motives.

"Are they playing on me? and is she an accomplice of her husband?" A sort of shame, in spite of his desire, prevented him from returning to their house.

One morning (three weeks after their interview), M. Dambreuse wrote to him, saying that he expected him the same day in an hour's time.

On the way, the thought of Arnoux oppressed him once more, and, not having been able to discover any reason for his conduct, he was seized with a feeling of wretchedness, a melancholy presentiment. In order to shake it off, he hailed a cab, and drove to the Rue de Paradis.

Arnoux was away travelling.

"And Madame?"

"In the country, at the works."

"When is Monsieur coming back?"

"To-morrow, without fail."

He would find her alone; this was the opportune moment. Something imperious seemed to cry out in the depths of his consciousness: "Go, then, and meet her!"

But M. Dambreuse? "Ah! well, so much the worse. I'll say that I was ill."

He rushed to the railway-station, and, as soon as he was in the carriage:

"Perhaps I have done wrong. Pshaw! what does it matter?"

Green plains stretched out to the right and to the left. The train rolled on. The little station-houses glistened like stage-scenery, and the smoke of the locomotive kept constantly sending forth on the same side its big fleecy masses, which danced for a little while on the grass, and were then dispersed.

Frederick, who sat alone in his compartment, gazed at these objects through sheer weariness, lost in that languor which is produced by the very excess of impatience. But cranes and warehouses presently appeared. They had reached Creil.

The town, built on the slopes of two low-lying hills (the first of which was bare, and the second crowned by a wood), with its church-tower, its houses of unequal size, and its stone bridge, seemed to him to present an aspect of mingled gaiety, reserve, and propriety. A long flat barge descended to the edge of the water, which leaped up under the lash of the wind.

Fowl perched on the straw at the foot of the crucifix erected on the spot; a woman passed with some wet linen on her head.

After crossing the bridge, he found himself in an isle, where he beheld on his right the ruins of an abbey. A mill with its wheels revolving barred up the entire width of the second arm of the Oise, over which the manufactory projected. Frederick was greatly surprised by the imposing character of this structure. He felt more respect for Arnoux on account of it. Three paces further on, he turned up an alley, which had a grating at its lower end.

He went in. The doorkeeper called him back, exclaiming:

"Have you a permit?"

"For what purpose?"

"For the purpose of visiting the establishment."

Frederick said in a rather curt tone that he had come to see M. Arnoux.

"Who is M. Arnoux?"

"Why, the chief, the master, the proprietor, in fact!"

"No, monsieur! These are MM. Lebœuf and Milliet's works!"

The good woman was surely joking! Some workmen arrived; he came up and spoke to two or three of them. They gave the same response.

Frederick left the premises, staggering like a drunken man; and he had such a look of perplexity, that on the Pont de la Boucherie an inhabitant of the town, who was smoking his pipe, asked whether he wanted to find out anything. This man knew where Arnoux's manufactory was. It was situated at Montataire.

Frederick asked whether a vehicle was to be got. He was told that the only place where he could find one was at the station. He went back there. A shaky-looking calash, to which was yoked an old horse, with torn harness hanging over the shafts, stood all alone in front of the luggage office. An urchin who was looking on offered to go and find Père Pilon. In ten minutes' time he came back, and announced that Père Pilon was at his breakfast. Frederick, unable to stand this any longer, walked away. But the gates of the thoroughfare across the line were closed. He would have to wait till two trains had passed. At last, he made a dash into the open country.

The monotonous greenery made it look like the cover of an immense billiard-table. The scoriae of iron were ranged on both sides of the track, like heaps of stones. A little further on, some factory chimneys were smoking close beside each other. In front of him, on a round hillock, stood a little turreted château, with the quadrangular belfry of a church. At a lower level, long walls formed irregular lines past the trees; and, further down again, the houses of the village spread out.

They had only a single story, with staircases consisting of three steps made of uncemented blocks. Every now and then the bell in front of a grocery-shop could be heard tinkling. Heavy steps sank into the black mire, and a light shower was falling, which cut the pale sky with a thousand hatchings.

Frederick pursued his way along the middle of the street. Then, he saw on his left, at the opening of a pathway, a large wooden arch, whereon was traced, in letters of gold, the word "Faïences."

It was not without an object that Jacques Arnoux had selected the vicinity of Creil. By placing his works as close as possible to the other works (which had long enjoyed a high reputation), he had created a certain confusion in the public mind, with a favourable result so far as his own interests were concerned.

The main body of the building rested on the same bank of a river which flows through the meadowlands. The master's house, surrounded by a garden, could be distinguished by the steps in front of it, adorned with four vases, in which cactuses were bristling.

Heaps of white clay were drying under sheds. There were others in the open air; and in the midst of the yard stood Sénécal with his everlasting blue paletot lined with red.

The ex-tutor extended towards Frederick his cold hand.

"You've come to see the master? He's not there."

Frederick, nonplussed, replied in a stupefied fashion:

"I knew it." But the next moment, correcting himself:

" 'Tis about a matter that concerns Madame Arnoux. Can she receive me?"

"Ha! I have not seen her for the last three days," said Sénécal.

And he broke into a long string of complaints. When he accepted the post of manager, he understood that he would have been allowed to reside in Paris, and not be forced to bury himself in this country district, far from his friends, deprived of newspapers. No matter! he had overlooked all that. But Arnoux appeared to pay no heed to his merits. He was, moreover, shallow and retrograde—no one could be more ignorant. In place of seeking for artistic improvements, it would have been better to introduce firewood instead of coal and gas. The shop-keeping spirit *thrust itself in*—Sénécal laid stress on the last words. In short, he disliked his present occupation, and he all but appealed to Frederick to say a word in his behalf in order that he might get an increase of salary.

"Make your mind easy," said the other.

He met nobody on the staircase. On the first floor, he pushed his way head-foremost into an empty room. It was the drawing-room. He called out at the top of his voice. There was no reply. No doubt, the cook had gone out, and so had the housemaid. At length, having reached the second floor, he pushed a door open. Madame Arnoux was alone in this room, in front of a press with a mirror attached. The belt of her dressing-gown hung down her hips; one entire half of her hair fell in a dark wave over her right shoulder; and she had raised both arms in order to hold up her chignon with one hand and to put a pin through it with the other. She broke into an exclamation and disappeared.

Then, she came back again properly dressed. Her waist, her eyes, the rustle of her dress, her entire appearance, charmed him. Frederick felt it hard to keep from covering her with kisses.

"I beg your pardon," said she, "but I could not—"

He had the boldness to interrupt her with these words:

"Nevertheless—you looked very nice—just now."

She probably thought this compliment a little coarse, for her cheeks reddened. He was afraid that he might have offended her. She went on:

"What lucky chance has brought you here?"

He did not know what reply to make; and, after a slight chuckle, which gave him time for reflection:

"If I told you, would you believe me?"

"Why not?"

Frederick informed her that he had had a frightful dream a few nights before.

"I dreamt that you were seriously ill—near dying."

"Oh! my husband and I are never ill."

"I have dreamt only of you," said he.

She gazed at him calmly: "Dreams are not always realised."

Frederick stammered, sought to find appropriate words to express himself in, and then plunged into a flowing period about the affinity of souls. There existed a force which could, through the intervening bounds of space, bring two persons into communication with each other, make known to each the other's feelings, and enable them to reunite.

She listened to him with downcast face, while she smiled with that beautiful smile of hers. He watched her out of the corner of his eye with delight, and poured out his love all the more freely through the easy channel of a commonplace remark.

She offered to show him the works; and, as she persisted, he made no objection.

In order to divert his attention with something of an amusing nature, she showed him the species of museum that decorated the staircase. The specimens, hung up against the wall or laid on shelves, bore witness to the efforts and the successive fads of Arnoux. After seeking vainly for the red of Chinese copper, he had wished to manufacture majolicas, faïence, Etruscan and Oriental ware, and had, in fact, attempted all the improvements which were realised at a later period.

So it was that one could observe in the series big vases covered with figures of mandarins, porringers of shot reddish-brown, pots adorned with Arabian inscriptions, drinking-vessels in the style of the Renaissance, and large plates on which two personages were outlined as it were on bloodstone, in a delicate, aerial fashion. He now made letters for signboards and wine-labels; but his intelligence was not high enough to attain to art, nor commonplace enough to look merely to profit, so that, without satisfying anyone, he had ruined himself.

They were both taking a view of these things when Mademoiselle Marthe passed.

"So, then, you did not recognise him?" said her mother to her.

"Yes, indeed," she replied, bowing to him, while her clear and sceptical glance—the glance of a virgin—seemed to say in a whisper: "What are you coming here for?" and she rushed up the steps with her head slightly bent over her shoulder.

Madame Arnoux led Frederick into the yard attached to the works, and then explained to him in a grave tone how different clays were ground, cleaned, and sifted.

"The most important thing is the preparation of pastes."

And she introduced him into a hall filled with vats, in which a vertical axis with horizontal arms kept turning. Frederick felt some regret that he had not flatly declined her offer a little while before.

"These things are merely the slobberings," said she.

He thought the word grotesque, and, in a measure, unbecoming on her lips.

Wide straps ran from one end of the ceiling to the other, so as to roll themselves round the drums, and everything kept moving continuously with a provoking mathematical regularity.

They left the spot, and passed close to a ruined hut, which had formerly been used as a repository for gardening implements.

"It is no longer of any use," said Madame Arnoux.

He replied in a tremulous voice:

"Happiness may have been associated with it!"

The clacking of the fire-pump drowned his words, and they entered the workshop where rough drafts were made.

Some men, seated at a narrow table, placed each in front of himself on a revolving disc a piece of paste. Then each man with his left hand scooped out the insides of his own piece while smoothing its surface with the right; and vases could be seen bursting into shape like blossoming flowers.

Madame Arnoux had the moulds for more difficult works shown to him.

In another portion of the building, the threads, the necks, and the projecting lines were being formed. On the floor above, they removed the seams, and stopped up with plaster the little holes that had been left by the preceding operations.

At every opening in the walls, in corners, in the middle of the corridor, everywhere, earthenware vessels had been placed side by side.

Frederick began to feel bored.

"Perhaps these things are tiresome to you?" said she.

Fearing lest it might be necessary to terminate his visit there and then, he affected, on the contrary, a tone of great enthusiasm. He even expressed regret at not having devoted himself to this branch of industry.

She appeared surprised.

"Certainly! I would have been able to live near you."

And as he tried to catch her eye, Madame Arnoux, in order to avoid him, took off a bracket little balls of paste, which had come from abortive readjustments, flattened them out into a thin cake, and pressed her hand over them.

"Might I carry these away with me?" said Frederick.

"Good heavens! are you so childish?"

He was about to reply when in came Sénécal.

The sub-manager, on the threshold, had noticed a breach of the rules. The workshops should be swept every week. This was Saturday, and, as the workmen had not done what was required, Sénécal announced that they would have to remain an hour longer.

"So much the worse for you!"

They stooped over the work assigned to them unmurmuringly, but their rage could be divined by the hoarse sounds which came from their chests. They were, moreover, very easy to manage, having all been dismissed from the big manufactory. The Republican had shown himself a hard taskmaster to them. A mere theorist, he regarded the people only in the mass, and exhibited an utter absence of pity for individuals.

Frederick, annoyed by his presence, asked Madame Arnoux in a low tone whether they could have an opportunity of seeing the kilns. They descended to the ground-floor; and she was just explaining the use of caskets, when Sénécal, who had followed close behind, placed himself between them.

He continued the explanation of his own motion, expatiated on the various kinds of combustibles, the process of placing in the kiln, the pyroscopes, the cylindrical furnaces; the instruments for rounding, the lustres, and the metals, making a prodigious display of chemical terms, such as "chloride," "sulphuret," "borax," and "carbonate." Frederick did not understand a single one of them, and kept turning round every minute towards Madame Arnoux.

"You are not listening," said she. "M. Sénécal, however, is very clear. He knows all these things much better than I."

The mathematician, flattered by this eulogy, proposed to show the way in which colours were laid on. Frederick gave Madame Arnoux an anxious, questioning look. She remained impassive, not caring to be alone with him, very probably, and yet unwilling to leave him.

He offered her his arm.

"No—many thanks! the staircase is too narrow!"

And, when they had reached the top, Sénécal opened the door of an apartment filled with women.

They were handling brushes, phials, shells, and plates of glass. Along the cornice, close to the wall, extended boards with figures engraved on them; scraps of thin paper floated about, and a melting-stove sent forth fumes that made the temperature oppressive, while there mingled with it the odour of turpentine.

The workwomen had nearly all sordid costumes. It was noticeable, however, that one of them wore a Madras handkerchief, and long earrings. Of slight frame, and, at the same time, plump, she had large black eyes and the fleshy lips of a negress. Her ample bosom projected from under her chemise, which was fastened round her waist by the string of her petticoat; and, with one elbow on the board of the work-table and the other arm hanging down, she gazed vaguely at the open country, a long distance away. Beside her were a bottle of wine and some pork chops.

The regulations prohibited eating in the workshops, a rule intended to secure cleanliness at work and to keep the hands in a healthy condition.

Sénécal, through a sense of duty or a longing to exercise despotic authority, shouted out to her ere he had come near her, while pointing towards a framed placard:

"I say, you girl from Bordeaux over there! read out for me Article 9!"

"Well, what then?"

"What then, mademoiselle? You'll have to pay a fine of three francs."

She looked him straight in the face in an impudent fashion.

"What does that signify to me? The master will take off your fine when he comes back! I laugh at you, my good man!"

Sénécal, who was walking with his hands behind his back, like an usher in the study-room, contented himself with smiling.

"Article 13, insubordination, ten francs!"

The girl from Bordeaux resumed her work. Madame Arnoux, through a sense of propriety, said nothing; but her brows contracted. Frederick murmured:

"Ha! you are very severe for a democrat!"

The other replied in a magisterial tone:

"Democracy is not the unbounded license of individualism. It is the equality of all belonging to the same community before the law, the distribution of work, order."

"You are forgetting humanity!" said Frederick.

Madame Arnoux took his arm. Sénécal, perhaps, offended by this mark of silent approbation, went away.

Frederick experienced an immense relief. Since morning he had been looking out for the opportunity to declare itself; now it had arrived. Besides, Madame Arnoux's spontaneous movements seemed to him to contain promises; and he asked her, as if on the pretext of warming their feet, to come up to her room. But, when he was seated close beside her, he began once more to feel embarrassed. He was at a loss for a starting-point. Sénécal, luckily, suggested an idea to his mind.

"Nothing could be more stupid," said he, "than this punishment!"

Madame Arnoux replied: "There are certain severe measures which are indispensable!"

"What! you who are so good! Oh! I am mistaken, for you sometimes take pleasure in making other people suffer!"

"I don't understand riddles, my friend!"

And her austere look, still more than the words she used, checked him. Frederick was determined to go on. A volume of De Musset chanced to be on the chest of drawers; he turned over some pages, then began to talk about love, about his hopes and his transports.

All this, according to Madame Arnoux, was criminal or factitious. The young man felt wounded by this negative attitude with regard to his passion, and, in order to combat it, he cited, by way of proof, the suicides which they read about every day in the newspapers, extolled the great literary types, Phèdre, Dido, Romeo, Desgrieux. He talked as if he meant to do away with himself.

The fire was no longer burning on the hearth; the rain lashed against the window-panes. Madame Arnoux, without stirring, remained with her hands resting on the sides of her armchair. The flaps of her cap fell like the fillets of a sphinx. Her pure profile traced out its clear-cut outlines in the midst of the shadow.

He was anxious to cast himself at her feet. There was a creaking sound in the lobby, and he did not venture to carry out his intention.

He was, moreover, restrained by a kind of religious awe. That robe, mingling with the surrounding shadows, appeared to him boundless, infinite, incapable of being touched; and for this very reason his desire became intensified. But the fear of doing too much, and, again, of not doing enough, deprived him of all judgment.

"If she dislikes me," he thought, "let her drive me away; if she cares for me, let her encourage me."

He said, with a sigh:

"So, then, you don't admit that a man may love—a woman?"

Madame Arnoux replied:

"Assuming that she is at liberty to marry, he may marry her; when she belongs to another, he should keep away from her."

"So happiness is impossible?"

"No! But it is never to be found in falsehood, mental anxiety, and remorse."

"What does it matter, if one is compensated by the enjoyment of supreme bliss?"

"The experience is too costly."

Then he sought to assail her with irony.

"Would not virtue in that case be merely cowardice?"

"Say rather, clear-sightedness. Even for those women who might forget duty or religion, simple good sense is sufficient. A solid foundation for wisdom may be found in self-love."

"Ah, what shopkeeping maxims these are of yours!"

"But I don't boast of being a fine lady."

At that moment the little boy rushed in.

"Mamma, are you coming to dinner?"

"Yes, in a moment."

Frederick arose. At the same instant, Marthe made her appearance.

He could not make up his mind to go away, and, with a look of entreaty:

"These women you speak of are very unfeeling, then?"

"No, but deaf when it is necessary to be so."

And she remained standing on the threshold of her room with her two children beside her. He bowed without saying a word. She mutely returned his salutation.

What he first experienced was an unspeakable astonishment. He felt crushed by this mode of impressing on him the emptiness of his hopes. It seemed to him as if he were lost, like a man who has fallen to the bottom of an abyss and knows that no help will come to him, and that he must die. He walked on, however, but at random, without looking before him. He knocked against stones; he mistook his way. A clatter of wooden shoes sounded close to his ear; it was caused by some of the working-girls who were leaving the foundry. Then he realised where he was.

The railway lamps traced on the horizon a line of flames. He arrived just as the train was starting, let himself be pushed into a carriage, and fell asleep.

An hour later on the boulevards, the gaiety of Paris by night made his journey all at once recede into an already far-distant past. He resolved to be strong, and relieved his heart by vilifying Madame Arnoux with insulting epithets.

"She is an idiot, a goose, a mere brute; let us not bestow another thought on her!"

When he got home, he found in his study a letter of eight pages on blue glazed paper, with the initial "R. A."

It began with friendly reproaches.

"What has become of you, my dear? I am getting quite bored."

But the handwriting was so abominable, that Frederick was about to fling away the entire bundle of sheets, when he noticed in the postscript the following words:

"I count on you to come to-morrow and drive me to the races."

What was the meaning of this invitation? Was it another trick of the Maréchale? But a woman does not make a fool of the same man twice without some object; and, seized with curiosity, he read the letter over again attentively.

Frederick was able to distinguish "Misunderstanding—to have taken a wrong path—disillusions—poor children that we are!—like two rivers that join each other!" etc.

He kept the sheets for a long time between his fingers. They had the odour of orris; and there was in the form of the characters and the irregular spaces between the lines something suggestive, as it were, of a disorderly toilet, that fired his blood.

"Why should I not go?" said he to himself at length. "But if Madame Arnoux were to know about it? Ah! let her know! So much the better! and let her feel jealous over it! In that way I shall be avenged!"

Chapter X

AT THE RACES

THE MARÉCHALE WAS PREPARED FOR HIS VISIT, AND HAD BEEN AWAITING him. "This is nice of you!" she said, fixing a glance of her fine eyes on his face, with an expression at the same time tender and mirthful. When she had fastened her bonnet-strings, she sat down on the divan, and remained silent.

"Shall we go?" said Frederick. She looked at the clock on the mantelpiece.

"Oh, no! not before half-past one!" as if she had imposed this limit to her indecision.

At last, when the hour had struck:

"Ah! well, *andiamo, caro mio!*" And she gave a final touch to her headbands, and left directions for Delphine.

"Is Madame coming home to dinner?"

"Why should we, indeed? We shall dine together somewhere—at the Café Anglais, wherever you wish."

"Be it so!"

Her little dogs began yelping around her.

"We can bring them with us, can't we?"

Frederick carried them himself to the vehicle. It was a hired berlin with two post-horses and a postilion. He had put his man-servant in the back seat. The Maréchale appeared satisfied with his attentions. Then, as soon as she had seated herself, she asked him whether he had been lately at the Arnouxs'.

"Not for the past month," said Frederick.

"As for me, I met him the day before yesterday. He would have even come to-day, but he has all sorts of troubles—another lawsuit—I don't know what. What a queer man!"

Frederick added with an air of indifference:

"Now that I think of it, do you still see—what's that his name is?—that ex-vocalist—Delmar?"

She replied dryly:

"No; that's all over."

So it was clear that there had been a rupture between them. Frederick derived some hope from this circumstance.

They descended the Quartier Bréda at an easy pace. As it happened to be Sunday, the streets were deserted, and some citizens' faces presented themselves at the windows. The carriage went on more rapidly. The noise of wheels made the passers-by turn round; the leather of the hood, which had slid down, was glittering. The man-servant doubled himself up, and the two Havanese, beside one another, seemed like two ermine muffs laid on the cushions. Frederick let himself jog up and down with the rocking of the carriage-straps. The Maréchale turned her head to the right and to the left with a smile on her face.

Her straw hat of mother-of-pearl colour was trimmed with black lace. The hood of her bournous floated in the wind, and she sheltered herself from the rays of the sun under a parasol of lilac satin pointed at the top like a pagoda.

"What loves of little fingers!" said Frederick, softly taking her other hand, her left being adorned with a gold bracelet in the form of a curb-chain.

"I say! that's pretty! Where did it come from?"

"Oh! I've had it a long time," said the Maréchale.

The young man did not challenge this hypocritical answer in any way. He preferred to profit by the circumstance. And, still keeping hold of the wrist, he pressed his lips on it between the glove and the cuff.

"Stop! People will see us!"

"Pooh! What does it signify?"

After passing by the Place de la Concorde, they drove along the Quai de la Conférence and the Quai de Billy, where might be noticed a cedar in a garden. Rosanette believed that Lebanon was situated in China; she laughed herself at her own ignorance, and asked Frederick to give her lessons in geography. Then, leaving the Trocadéro at the right, they crossed the Pont de Jéna, and drew up at length in the middle of the Champ de Mars, near some other vehicles already drawn up in the Hippodrome.

The grass hillocks were covered with common people. Some spectators might be seen on the balcony of the Military School; and the two pavilions outside the weighing-room, the two galleries contained within its enclosure, and a third in front of that of the king, were filled with a fashionably dressed crowd whose deportment showed their regard for this as yet novel form of amusement.

The public around the course, more select at this period, had a less vulgar aspect. It was the era of trouser-straps, velvet collars, and white gloves. The ladies, attired in showy colours, displayed gowns with long waists; and seated on the tiers of the stands, they formed, so to speak, immense groups of flowers, spotted here and there with black by the men's costumes. But every glance was directed towards the celebrated Algerian Bou-Maza, who sat, impassive, between two staff officers in one of the private galleries. That of the Jockey Club contained none but grave-looking gentlemen.

The more enthusiastic portion of the throng were seated underneath, close to the track, protected by two lines of sticks which supported ropes. In the immense oval described by this passage, cocoanut-sellers were shaking their rattles, others were selling programmes of the races, others were hawking cigars, with loud cries. On every side there was a great murmur. The municipal guards passed to and fro. A bell, hung from a post covered with figures, began ringing, Five horses appeared, and the spectators in the galleries resumed their seats.

Meanwhile, big clouds touched with their winding outlines the tops of the elms opposite. Rosanette was afraid that it was going to rain.

"I have umbrellas," said Frederick, "and everything that we need to afford ourselves diversion," he added, lifting up the chest, in which there was a stock of provisions in a basket.

"Bravo! we understand eachother!"

"And we'll understand eachother still better, shall we not?"

"That may be," she said, colouring.

The jockeys, in silk jackets, were trying to draw up their horses in order, and were holding them back with both hands. Somebody lowered a red flag. Then the entire five bent over the bristling manes, and off they started. At first they remained pressed close to each other in a single mass; this presently stretched out and became cut up. The jockey in the yellow jacket was near falling in the middle of the first round; for a long time it was uncertain whether Filly or Tibi should take the lead; then Tom Pouce appeared in front. But Clubstick, who had been in the rear since the start, came up with the others and outstripped them, so that he was the first to reach the winning-post, beating Sir Charles by two lengths. It was a surprise. There was a shout of applause; the planks shook with the stamping of feet.

"We are amusing ourselves," said the Maréchale. "I love you, darling!"

Frederick no longer doubted that his happiness was secure. Rosanette's last words were a confirmation of it.

A hundred paces away from him, in a four-wheeled cabriolet, a lady could be seen. She stretched her head out of the carriage-door, and then quickly drew it in again. This movement was repeated several times. Frederick could not distinguish her face. He had a strong suspicion, however, that it was Madame Arnoux. And yet this seemed impossible! Why should she have come there?

He stepped out of his own vehicle on the pretence of strolling into the weighing-room.

"You are not very gallant!" said Rosanette.

He paid no heed to her, and went on. The four-wheeled cabriolet, turning back, broke into a trot.

Frederick at the same moment, found himself button-holed by Cisy.

"Good-morrow, my dear boy! how are you going on? Hussonnet is over there! Are you listening to me?"

Frederick tried to shake him off in order to get up with the four-wheeled cabriolet. The Maréchale beckoned to him to come round to her. Cisy perceived her, and obstinately persisted in bidding her good-day.

Since the termination of the regular period of mourning for his grandmother, he had realised his ideal, and succeeded in "getting the proper stamp." A Scotch plaid waistcoat, a short coat, large bows over the pumps, and an entrance-card stuck in the ribbon of his hat; nothing, in fact, was wanting to produce what he described himself as his *chic*—a *chic* characterised by Anglomania and the swagger of the musketeer. He began by finding fault with the Champ de Mars, which he referred to as an "execrable turf," then spoke of the Chantilly races, and the droll things that had occurred there, swore that he could drink a dozen glasses of champagne while the clock was striking the midnight hour, offered to make a bet with the Maréchale, softly caressed her two lapdogs; and, leaning against the carriage-door on one elbow, he kept talking nonsense, with the handle of his walking-stick in his mouth, his legs wide apart, and his back stretched out. Frederick, standing beside him, was smoking, while endeavouring to make out what had become of the cabriolet.

The bell having rung, Cisy took himself off, to the great delight of Rosanette, who said he had been boring her to death.

The second race had nothing special about it; neither had the third, save that a man was thrown over the shaft of a cart while it was taking place. The fourth, in which eight horses contested the City Stakes, was more interesting.

The spectators in the gallery had clambered to the top of their seats. The others, standing up in the vehicles, followed with opera-glasses in their hands the movements of the jockeys. They could be seen starting out like red, yellow, white, or blue spots across the entire space occupied by the crowd that had gathered around the ring of the hippodrome. At a distance, their speed did not appear to be very great; at the opposite side of the Champ de Mars, they seemed even to be slackening their pace, and to be merely slipping along in such a way that the horses' bellies touched the ground without their outstretched legs bending at all. But, coming back at a more rapid stride, they looked bigger; they cut the air in their wild gallop. The sun's rays quivered; pebbles went flying about under their hoofs. The wind, blowing out the jockeys' jackets, made them flutter like veils. Each of them lashed the animal he rode with great blows of his whip in order to reach the winning-post—that was the goal they aimed at. One swept away the figures, another was hoisted off his saddle, and, in the midst of a burst of applause, the victorious horse dragged his feet to the weighing-room, all covered with sweat, his knees stiffened, his neck and shoulders bent down, while his rider, looking as if he were expiring in his saddle, clung to the animal's flanks.

The final start was retarded by a dispute which had arisen. The crowd, getting tired, began to scatter. Groups of men were chatting at the lower end of each gallery. The talk was of a free-and-easy description. Some fashionable ladies left, scandalised by seeing fast women in their immediate vicinity.

There were also some specimens of the ladies who appeared at public balls, some light-comedy actresses of the boulevards, and it was not the best-looking portion of them that got the most appreciation. The elderly Georgine Aubert, she whom a writer of vaudevilles called the Louis XI of her profession, horribly painted, and giving vent every now and then to a laugh resembling a grunt, remained reclining at full length in her big calash, covered with a sable fur-tippet, as if it were midwinter. Madame de Remoussat, who had become fashionable by means of a notorious trial in which she figured, sat enthroned on the seat of a brake in company with some Americans; and Thérèse Bachelu, with her look of a Gothic virgin, filled with her dozen furbelows the interior of a trap which had, in place of an apron, a flower-stand filled with roses. The Maréchale was jealous of these magnificent displays. In order to attract attention, she began to make vehement gestures and to speak in a very loud voice.

Gentlemen recognised her, and bowed to her. She returned their salutations while telling Frederick their names. They were all counts, viscounts, dukes, and marquises, and carried a high head, for in all eyes he could read a certain respect for his good fortune.

Cisy had a no less happy air in the midst of the circle of mature men that surrounded them. Their faces wore cynical smiles above their cravats, as if they were laughing at him. At length he gave a tap in the hand of the oldest of them, and made his way towards the Maréchale.

She was eating, with an affectation of gluttony, a slice of *pâté de foie gras*. Frederick, in order to make himself agreeable to her, followed her example, with a bottle of wine on his knees.

The four-wheeled cabriolet reappeared. It *was* Madame Arnoux! Her face was startlingly pale.

"Give me some champagne," said Rosanette.

And, lifting up her glass, full to the brim, as high as possible, she exclaimed:

"Look over there! Look at my protector's wife, one of the virtuous women!"

There was a great burst of laughter all round her; and the cabriolet disappeared from view. Frederick tugged impatiently at her dress, and was on the point of flying into a passion. But Cisy was there, in the same attitude as before, and, with increased assurance, he invited Rosanette to dine with him that very evening.

"Impossible!" she replied; "we're going together to the Café Anglais."

Frederick, as if he had heard nothing, remained silent; and Cisy quitted the Maréchale with a look of disappointment on his face.

While he had been talking to her at the right-hand door of the carriage, Hussonnet presented himself at the opposite side, and, catching the words "Café Anglais":

"It's a nice establishment; suppose we had a pick there, eh?"

"Just as you like," said Frederick, who, sunk down in the corner of the berlin, was gazing at the horizon as the four-wheeled cabriolet vanished from his sight, feeling that an irreparable thing had happened, and that there was an end of his great love. And the other woman was there beside him, the gay and easy love! But, worn out, full of conflicting desires, and no longer even knowing what he wanted, he was possessed by a feeling of infinite sadness, a longing to die.

A great noise of footsteps and of voices made him raise his head. The little ragamuffins assembled round the track sprang over the ropes and came to stare at the galleries. Thereupon their occupants rose to go. A few drops of rain began to fall. The crush of vehicles increased, and Hussonnet got lost in it.

"Well! so much the better!" said Frederick.

"We like to be alone better—don't we?" said the Maréchale, as she placed her hand in his.

Then there swept past him with a glitter of copper and steel a magnificent landau to which were yoked four horses driven in the Daumont style by two jockeys in velvet vests with gold fringes. Madame Dambreuse was by her husband's side, and Martinon was on the other seat facing them. All three of them gazed at Frederick in astonishment.

"They have recognised me!" said he to himself.

Rosanette wished to stop in order to get a better view of the people driving away from the course. Madame Arnoux might again make her appearance! He called out to the postilion:

"Go on! go on! forward!" And the berlin dashed towards the Champs-Élysées in the midst of the other vehicles—calashes, britzkas, wurths, tandems, tilburies, dog-carts, tilted carts with leather curtains, in which workmen in a jovial mood were singing, or one-horse chaises driven by fathers of families. In victorias crammed with people some young fellows seated on the others' feet let their legs both hang down. Large broughams, which had their seats lined with cloth, carried dowagers fast asleep, or else a splendid machine passed with a seat as simple and coquettish as a dandy's black coat.

The shower grew heavier. Umbrellas, parasols, and mackintoshes were put into requisition. People cried out at some distance away: "Good-day!" "Are you quite well?" "Yes!" "No!" "Bye-bye!"—and the faces succeeded each other with the rapidity of Chinese shadows.

Frederick and Rosanette did not say a word to each other, feeling a sort of dizziness at seeing all these wheels continually revolving close to them.

At times, the rows of carriages, too closely pressed together, stopped all at the same time in several lines. Then they remained side by side, and their occupants scanned one another. Over the sides of panels adorned with coats-of-arms indifferent glances were cast on the crowd. Eyes full of envy gleamed from the interiors of hackney-coaches. Depreciatory smiles responded to the haughty manner in which some people carried their heads. Mouths gaping wide expressed idiotic admiration; and, here and there, some lounger, in the middle of the road, fell back with a bound, in order to avoid a rider who had been galloping through the midst of the vehicles, and had succeeded in getting away from them. Then, everything set itself in motion once more; the coachmen let go the reins, and lowered their long whips; the horses, excited, shook their curb-chains, and flung foam around them; and the cruppers and the harness getting moist, were smoking with the watery evaporation, through which struggled the rays of the sinking sun. Passing under the Arc de Triomphe, there stretched out at the height of a man, a reddish light, which shed a glittering lustre on the naves of the wheels, the handles of the carriage-doors, the ends of the shafts, and the rings of the carriage-beds; and on the two sides of the great avenue—like a river in which manes, garments, and human heads were undulating—the trees, all glittering with rain, rose up like two green walls. The blue of the sky overhead, reappearing in certain places, had the soft hue of satin.

Then, Frederick recalled the days, already far away, when he yearned for the inexpressible happiness of finding himself in one of these carriages by the side of one of these women. He had attained to this bliss, and yet he was not thereby one jot the happier.

The rain had ceased falling. The pedestrians, who had sought shelter between the columns of the Public Storerooms, took their departure. Persons who had been walking along the Rue Royale, went up again towards the boulevard. In front of the residence of the Minister of Foreign Affairs a group of boobies had taken up their posts on the steps.

When it had got up as high as the Chinese Baths, as there were holes in the pavement, the berlin slackened its pace. A man in a hazel-coloured paletot was walking on the edge of the footpath. A splash, spurting out from under the springs, showed itself on his back. The man turned round in a rage. Frederick grew pale; he had recognised Deslauriers.

At the door of the Café Anglais he sent away the carriage. Rosanette had gone in before him while he was paying the postilion.

He found her subsequently on the stairs chatting with a gentleman. Frederick took her arm; but in the lobby a second gentleman stopped her.

"Go on," said she; "I am at your service."

And he entered the private room alone. Through the two open windows people could be seen at the casements of the other houses opposite. Large watery masses were quivering on the pavement as it began to dry, and a magnolia, placed on the side of a balcony, shed a perfume through the apartment. This fragrance and freshness had a relaxing effect on his nerves. He sank down on the red divan underneath the glass.

The Maréchale here entered the room, and, kissing him on the forehead:

"Poor pet! there's something annoying you!"

"Perhaps so," was his reply.

"You are not alone; take heart!"—which was as much as to say: "Let us each forget our own concerns in a bliss which we shall enjoy in common."

Then she placed the petal of a flower between her lips and extended it towards him so that he might peck at it. This movement, full of grace and of almost voluptuous gentleness, had a softening influence on Frederick.

"Why do you give me pain?" said he, thinking of Madame Arnoux.

"I give you pain?"

And, standing before him, she looked at him with her lashes drawn close together and her two hands resting on his shoulders.

All his virtue, all his rancour gave way before the utter weakness of his will.

He continued:

"Because you won't love me," and he took her on his knees.

She gave way to him. He pressed his two hands round her waist. The crackling sound of her silk dress inflamed him.

"Where are they?" said Hussonnet's voice in the lobby outside.

The Maréchale arose abruptly, and went across to the other side of the room, where she sat down with her back to the door.

She ordered oysters, and they seated themselves at table.

Hussonnet was not amusing. By dint of writing every day on all sorts of subjects, reading many newspapers, listening to a great number of discussions, and uttering paradoxes for the purpose of dazzling people, he had in the end lost the exact idea of things, blinding himself with his own feeble fireworks. The embarrassments of a life which had formerly been frivolous, but which was now full of difficulty, kept him in a state of perpetual agitation; and his impotency, which he did not wish to avow, rendered him snappish and sarcastic. Referring to a new ballet entitled *Ozaï*, he gave a thorough blowing-up to the dancing, and then, when the opera was in question, he attacked the Italians, now replaced by a company of

Spanish actors, "as if people had not quite enough of Castilles already!" Frederick was shocked at this, owing to his romantic attachment to Spain, and, with a view to diverting the conversation into a new channel, he enquired about the College of France, where Edgar Quinet and Mickiewicz had attended. But Hussonnet, an admirer of M. de Maistre, declared himself on the side of Authority and Spiritualism. Nevertheless, he had doubts about the most well-established facts, contradicted history, and disputed about things whose certainty could not be questioned; so that at mention of the word "geometry," he exclaimed: "What fudge this geometry is!" All this he intermingled with imitations of actors. Sainville was specially his model.

Frederick was quite bored by these quibbles. In an outburst of impatience he pushed his foot under the table, and pressed it on one of the little dogs.

Thereupon both animals began barking in a horrible fashion.

"You ought to get them sent home!" said he, abruptly.

Rosanette did not know anyone to whom she could intrust them.

Then, he turned round to the Bohemian:

"Look here, Hussonnet; sacrifice yourself!"

"Oh! yes, my boy! That would be a very obliging act!"

Hussonnet set off, without even requiring to have an appeal made to him.

In what way could they repay him for his kindness? Frederick did not bestow a thought on it. He was even beginning to rejoice at finding himself alone with her, when a waiter entered.

"Madame, somebody is asking for you!"

"What! again?"

"However, I must see who it is," said Rosanette.

He was thirsting for her; he wanted her. This disappearance seemed to him an act of prevarication, almost a piece of rudeness. What, then, did she mean? Was it not enough to have insulted Madame Arnoux? So much for the latter, all the same! Now he hated all women; and he felt the tears choking him, for his love had been misunderstood and his desire eluded.

The Maréchale returned, and presented Cisy to him.

"I have invited Monsieur. I have done right, have I not?"

"How is that! Oh! certainly."

Frederick, with the smile of a criminal about to be executed, beckoned to the gentleman to take a seat.

The Maréchale began to run her eye through the bill of fare, stopping at every fantastic name.

"Suppose we eat a turban of rabbits *à la Richeliéu* and a pudding *à la d'Or-léans?*"

"Oh! not Orléans, pray!" exclaimed Cisy, who was a Legitimist, and thought of making a pun.

"Would you prefer a turbot à la Chambord?" she next asked.

Frederick was disgusted with this display of politeness.

The Maréchale made up her mind to order a simple fillet of beef cut up into steaks, some crayfishes, truffles, a pine-apple salad, and vanilla ices.

"We'll see what next. Go on for the present! Ah! I was forgetting! Bring me a sausage!—not with garlic!"

And she called the waiter "young man," struck her glass with her knife, and flung up the crumbs of her bread to the ceiling. She wished to drink some Burgundy immediately.

"It is not taken in the beginning," said Frederick.

This was sometimes done, according to the Vicomte.

"Oh! no. Never!"

"Yes, indeed; I assure you!"

"Ha! you see!"

The look with which she accompanied these words meant: "This is a rich man—pay attention to what he says!"

Meantime, the door was opening every moment; the waiters kept shouting; and on an infernal piano in the adjoining room some one was strumming a waltz. Then the races led to a discussion about horsemanship and the two rival systems. Cisy was upholding Baucher and Frederick the Comte d'Aure when Rosanette shrugged her shoulders:

"Enough—my God!—he is a better judge of these things than you are— come now!"

She kept nibbling at a pomegranate, with her elbow resting on the table. The wax-candles of the candelabrum in front of her were flickering in the wind. This white light penetrated her skin with mother-of-pearl tones, gave a pink hue to her lids, and made her eyeballs glitter. The red colour of the fruit blended with the purple of her lips; her thin nostrils heaved; and there was about her entire person an air of insolence, intoxication, and recklessness that exasperated Frederick, and yet filled his heart with wild desires.

Then, she asked, in a calm voice, who owned that big landau with chestnut-coloured livery.

Cisy replied that it was "the Comtesse Dambreuse."

"They're very rich—aren't they?"

"Oh! very rich! although Madame Dambreuse, who was merely a Mademoiselle Boutron and the daughter of a prefect, had a very modest fortune."

Her husband, on the other hand, must have inherited several estates—Cisy enumerated them: as he visited the Dambreuses, he knew their family history.

Frederick, in order to make himself disagreeable to the other, took a pleasure in contradicting him. He maintained that Madame Dambreuse's maiden name was De Boutron, which proved that she was of a noble family.

"No matter! I'd like to have her equipage!" said the Maréchale, throwing herself back on the armchair.

And the sleeve of her dress, slipping up a little, showed on her left wrist a bracelet adorned with three opals.

Frederick noticed it.

"Look here! why—"

All three looked into one another's faces, and reddened.

The door was cautiously half-opened; the brim of a hat could be seen, and then Hussonnet's profile exhibited itself.

"Pray excuse me if I disturb the lovers!"

But he stopped, astonished at seeing Cisy, and that Cisy had taken his own seat.

Another cover was brought; and, as he was very hungry, he snatched up at random from what remained of the dinner some meat which was in a dish, fruit out of a basket, and drank with one hand while he helped himself with the other, all the time telling them the result of his mission. The two bow-wows had been taken home. Nothing fresh at the house. He had found the cook in the company of a soldier—a fictitious story which he had especially invented for the sake of effect.

The Maréchale took down her cloak from the window-screw. Frederick made a rush towards the bell, calling out to the waiter, who was some distance away:

"A carriage!"

"I have one of my own," said the Vicomte.

"But, Monsieur!"

"Nevertheless, Monsieur!"

And they stared into each other's eyes, both pale and their hands trembling.

At last, the Maréchale took Cisy's arm, and pointing towards the Bohemian seated at the table:

"Pray mind him! He's choking himself. I wouldn't care to let his devotion to my pugs be the cause of his death."

The door closed behind him.

"Well?" said Hussonnet.

"Well, what?"

"I thought—"

"What did you think?"

"Were you not—?"

He completed the sentence with a gesture.

"Oh! no—never in all my life!"

Hussonnet did not press the matter further.

He had an object in inviting himself to dinner. His journal—which was no longer called *L'Art,* but *Le Flambart,* with this epigraph, "Gunners, to your cannons!"—not being at all in a flourishing condition, he had a mind to change it into a weekly review, conducted by himself, without any assistance from Deslauriers. He again referred to the old project and explained his latest plan.

Frederick, probably not understanding what he was talking about, replied with some vague words. Hussonnet snatched up several cigars from the tables, said "Good-bye, old chap," and disappeared.

Frederick called for the bill. It had a long list of items; and the waiter, with his napkin under his arm, was expecting to be paid by Frederick, when another, a sallow-faced individual, who resembled Martinon, came and said to him:

"Beg pardon; they forgot at the bar to add in the charge for the cab."

"What cab?"

"The cab the gentleman took a short time ago for the little dogs."

And the waiter put on a look of gravity, as if he pitied the poor young man. Frederick felt inclined to box the fellow's ears. He gave the waiter the twenty francs' change as a *pour-boire.*

"Thanks, Monseigneur," said the man with the napkin, bowing low.

Chapter XI

A Dinner and a Duel

FREDERICK PASSED THE WHOLE OF THE NEXT DAY IN BROODING OVER HIS anger and humiliation. He reproached himself for not having given a slap in the face to Cisy. As for the Maréchale, he swore not to see her again. Others as good-looking could be easily found; and, as money would be required in order to possess these women, he would speculate on the Bourse with the purchase-money of his farm. He would get rich; he would crush the Maréchale and every-one else with his luxury. When the evening had come, he was surprised at not having thought of Madame Arnoux.

"So much the better. What's the good of it?"

Two days after, at eight o'clock, Pellerin came to pay him a visit. He began by expressing his admiration of the furniture and talking in a wheedling tone. Then, abruptly:

"You were at the races on Sunday?"

"Yes, alas!"

Thereupon the painter decried the anatomy of English horses, and praised the horses of Gericourt and the horses of the Parthenon.

"Rosanette was with you?"

And he artfully proceeded to speak in flattering terms about her.

Frederick's freezing manner put him a little out of countenance.

He did not know how to bring about the question of her portrait. His first idea had been to do a portrait in the style of Titian. But gradually the varied colouring of his model had bewitched him; he had gone on boldly with the work, heaping up paste on paste and light on light. Rosanette, in the beginning, was enchanted. Her appointments with Delmar had interrupted the sittings, and left Pellerin all the time to get bedazzled. Then, as his admiration began to subside, he asked himself whether the picture might not be on a larger scale. He had gone to have another look at the Titians, realised how the great artist had filled in his portraits with such finish, and saw wherein his own shortcomings lay; and then he began to go over the outlines again in the most simple fashion. After that, he sought, by scraping them off, to lose there, to mingle there, all the tones of the head and those of the background; and the face had assumed consistency and the shades vigour—the whole work had a look of greater firmness. At length the Maréchale came back again. She even indulged in some hostile criticisms. The painter naturally persevered in his own course. After getting into a violent passion at her silliness, he said to himself that, after all, perhaps she was right. Then began the era of doubts, twinges of reflection which brought about cramps in the stomach, insomnia, feverishness and disgust with himself. He had the courage to make some retouchings, but without much heart, and with a feeling that his work was bad.

He complained merely of having been refused a place in the Salon; then he reproached Frederick for not having come to see the Maréchale's portrait.

"What do I care about the Maréchale?"

Such an expression of unconcern emboldened the artist.

"Would you believe that this brute has no interest in the thing any longer?"

What he did not mention was that he had asked her for a thousand crowns. Now the Maréchale did not give herself much bother about ascertaining who was going to pay, and, preferring to screw money out of Arnoux for things of a more urgent character, had not even spoken to him on the subject.

"Well, and Arnoux?"

She had thrown it over on him. The ex-picture-dealer wished to have nothing to do with the portrait.

"He maintains that it belongs to Rosanette."

"In fact, it is hers."

"How is that? 'Tis she that sent me to you," was Pellerin's answer.

If he had been thinking of the excellence of his work, he would not have dreamed perhaps of making capital out of it. But a sum—and a big sum—would be an effective reply to the critics, and would strengthen his own position. Finally, to get rid of his importunities, Frederick courteously enquired his terms.

The extravagant figure named by Pellerin quite took away his breath, and he replied:

"Oh! no—no!"

"You, however, are her lover—'tis you gave me the order!"

"Excuse me, I was only an intermediate agent."

"But I can't remain with this on my hands!"

The artist lost his temper.

"Ha! I didn't imagine you were so covetous!"

"Nor I that you were so stingy! I wish you good morning!"

He had just gone out when Sénécal made his appearance.

Frederick was moving about restlessly, in a state of great agitation.

"What's the matter?"

Sénécal told his story.

"On Saturday, at nine o'clock, Madame Arnoux got a letter which summoned her back to Paris. As there happened to be nobody in the place at the time to go to

Creil for a vehicle, she asked me to go there myself. I refused, for this was no part of my duties. She left, and came back on Sunday evening. Yesterday morning, Arnoux came down to the works. The girl from Bordeaux made a complaint to him. I don't know what passed between them; but he took off before everyone the fine I had imposed on her. Some sharp words passed between us. In short, he closed accounts with me, and here I am!"

Then, with a pause between every word:

"Furthermore, I am not sorry. I have done my duty. No matter—you were the cause of it."

"How?" exclaimed Frederick, alarmed lest Sénécal might have guessed his secret.

Sénécal had not, however, guessed anything about it, for he replied:

"That is to say, but for you I might have done better."

Frederick was seized with a kind of remorse.

"In what way can I be of service to you now?"

Sénécal wanted some employment, a situation.

"That is an easy thing for you to manage. You know many people of good position, Monsieur Dambreuse amongst others; at least, so Deslauriers told me."

This allusion to Deslauriers was by no means agreeable to his friend. He scarcely cared to call on the Dambreuses again after his undesirable meeting with them in the Champ de Mars.

"I am not on sufficiently intimate terms with them to recommend anyone."

The democrat endured this refusal stoically, and after a minute's silence:

"All this, I am sure, is due to the girl from Bordeaux, and to your Madame Arnoux."

This "your" had the effect of wiping out of Frederick's heart the slight modicum of regard he entertained for Sénécal. Nevertheless, he stretched out his hand towards the key of his escritoire through delicacy.

Sénécal anticipated him:

"Thanks!"

Then, forgetting his own troubles, he talked about the affairs of the nation, the crosses of the Legion of Honour wasted at the Royal Fête, the question of a change of ministry, the Drouillard case and the Bénier case—scandals of the day—declaimed against the middle class, and predicted a revolution.

His eyes were attracted by a Japanese dagger hanging on the wall. He took hold of it; then he flung it on the sofa with an air of disgust.

"Come, then! good-bye! I must go to Nôtre Dame de Lorette."

"Hold on! Why?"

"The anniversary service for Godefroy Cavaignac is taking place there to-day. He died at work—that man! But all is not over. Who knows?"

And Sénécal, with a show of fortitude, put out his hand:

"Perhaps we shall never see each other again! good-bye!"

This "good-bye," repeated several times, his knitted brows as he gazed at the dagger, his resignation, and the solemnity of his manner, above all, plunged Frederick into a thoughtful mood, but very soon he ceased to think about Sénécal.

During the same week, his notary at Havre sent him the sum realised by the sale of his farm—one hundred and seventy-four thousand francs. He divided it into two portions, invested the first half in the Funds, and brought the second half to a stock-broker to take his chance of making money by it on the Bourse.

He dined at fashionable taverns, went to the theatres, and was trying to amuse himself as best he could, when Hussonnet addressed a letter to him announcing in a gay fashion that the Maréchale had got rid of Cisy the very day after the races. Frederick was delighted at this intelligence, without taking the trouble to ascertain what the Bohemian's motive was in giving him the information.

It so happened that he met Cisy, three days later. That aristocratic young gentleman kept his countenance, and even invited Frederick to dine on the following Wednesday.

On the morning of that day, the latter received a notification from a process-server, in which M. Charles Jean Baptiste Oudry apprised him that by the terms of a legal judgment he had become the purchaser of a property situated at Belleville, belonging to M. Jacques Arnoux, and that he was ready to pay the two hundred and twenty-three thousand for which it had been sold. But, as it appeared by the same decree that the amount of the mortgages with which the estate was encumbered exceeded the purchase-money, Frederick's claim would in consequence be completely forfeited.

The entire mischief arose from not having renewed the registration of the mortgage within the proper time. Arnoux had undertaken to attend to this matter formally himself, and had then forgotten all about it. Frederick got into a rage with him for this, and when the young man's anger had passed off:

"Well, afterwards— what?"

"If this can save him, so much the better. It won't kill me! Let us think no more about it!"

But, while moving about his papers on the table, he came across Hussonnet's letter, and noticed the postscript, which had not at first attracted his attention. The Bohemian wanted just five thousand francs to give the journal a start.

"Ah! this fellow is worrying me to death!"

And he sent a curt answer, unceremoniously refusing the application. After that, he dressed himself to go to the Maison d'Or.

Cisy introduced his guests, beginning with the most respectable of them, a big, white-haired gentleman.

"The Marquis Gilbert des Aulnays, my godfather. Monsieur Anselme de For-chambeaux," he said next—(a thin, fair-haired young man, already bald); then, pointing towards a simple-mannered man of forty: "Joseph Boffreu, my cousin; and here is my old tutor, Monsieur Vezou"—a person who seemed a mixture of a ploughman and a seminarist, with large whiskers and a long frock-coat fastened at the end by a single button, so that it fell over his chest like a shawl.

Cisy was expecting some one else—the Baron de Comaing, who "might per-haps come, but it was not certain." He left the room every minute, and appeared to be in a restless frame of mind. Finally, at eight o'clock, they proceeded towards an apartment splendidly lighted up and much more spacious than the number of guests required. Cisy had selected it for the special purpose of display.

A vermilion épergne laden with flowers and fruit occupied the centre of the table, which was covered with silver dishes, after the old French fashion; glass bowls full of salt meats and spices formed a border all around it. Jars of iced red wine stood at regular distances from each other. Five glasses of different sizes were ranged before each plate, with things of which the use could not be divined—a thousand dinner utensils of an ingenious description. For the first course alone, there was a sturgeon's jowl moistened with champagne, a Yorkshire ham with tokay, thrushes with sauce, roast quail, a béchamel vol-au-vent, a stew of red-legged partridges, and at the two ends of all this, fringes of potatoes which were mingled with truffles. The apartment was illuminated by a lustre and some giran-doles, and it was hung with red damask curtains.

Four men-servants in black coats stood behind the armchairs, which were up-holstered in morocco. At this sight the guests uttered an exclamation—the tutor more emphatically than the rest.

"Upon my word, our host has indulged in a foolishly lavish display of luxury. It is too beautiful!"

"Is that so?" said the Vicomte de Cisy; "Come on, then!"

And, as they were swallowing the first spoonful:

"Well, my dear old friend Aulnays, have you been to the Palais-Royal to see *Père et Portier?*"

"You know well that I have no time to go!" replied the Marquis.

His mornings were taken up with a course of arboriculture, his evenings were spent at the Agricultural Club, and all his afternoons were occupied by a study of the implements of husbandry in manufactories. As he resided at Saintonge for three fourths of the year, he took advantage of his visits to the capital to get fresh information; and his large-brimmed hat, which lay on a side-table, was crammed with pamphlets.

But Cisy, abserving that M. de Forchambeaux refused to take wine:

"Go on, damn it, drink! You're not in good form for your last bachelor's meal!"

At this remark all bowed and congratulated him.

"And the young lady," said the tutor, "is charming, I'm sure?"

"Faith, she is!" exclaimed Cisy. "No matter, he is making a mistake; marriage is such a stupid thing!"

"You talk in a thoughtless fashion, my friend!" returned M. des Aulnays, while tears began to gather in his eyes at the recollection of his own dead wife.

And Forchambeaux repeated several times in succession:

"It will be your own case—it will be your own case!"

Cisy protested. He preferred to enjoy himself— to "live in the free-and-easy style of the Regency days." He wanted to learn the shoe-trick, in order to visit the thieves' taverns of the city, like Rodolphe in the *Mysteries of Paris*; drew out of his pocket a dirty clay pipe, abused the servants, and drank a great quantity; then, in order to create a good impression about himself, he disparaged all the dishes. He even sent away the truffles; and the tutor, who was exceedingly fond of them, said through servility;

"These are not as good as your grandmother's snow-white eggs."

Then he began to chat with the person sitting next to him, the agriculturist, who found many advantages from his sojourn in the country, if it were only to be able to bring up his daughters with simple tastes. The tutor approved of his ideas and toadied to him, supposing that this gentleman possessed influence over his former pupil, whose man of business he was anxious to become.

Frederick had come there filled with hostility to Cisy; but the young aristocrat's idiocy had disarmed him. However, as the other's gestures, face, and entire person brought back to his recollection the dinner at the Café Anglais, he got more and more irritated; and he lent his ears to the complimentary remarks made in a low tone by Joseph, the cousin, a fine young fellow without any money, who was a lover of the chase and a University prizeman. Cisy, for the sake of a laugh, called him a "catcher" several times; then suddenly:

"Ha! here comes the Baron!"

At that moment, there entered a jovial blade of thirty, with somewhat rough-looking features and active limbs, wearing his hat over his ear and displaying a flower in his button-hole. He was the Vicomte's ideal. The young aristocrat was delighted at having him there; and stimulated by his presence, he even attempted a pun; for he said, as they passed a heath-cock:

"There's the best of La Bruyére's characters!"

After that, he put a heap of questions to M. de Comaing about persons unknown to society; then, as if an idea had suddenly seized him:

"Tell me, pray! have you thought about me?"

The other shrugged his shoulders:

"You are not old enough, my little man. It is impossible!"

Cisy had begged of the Baron to get him admitted into his club. But the other having, no doubt, taken pity on his vanity:

"Ha! I was forgetting! A thousand congratulations on having won your bet, my dear fellow!"

"What bet?"

"The bet you made at the races to effect an entrance the same evening into that lady's house."

Frederick felt as if he had got a lash with a whip. He was speedily appeased by the look of utter confusion in Cisy's face.

In fact, the Maréchale, next morning, was filled with regret when Arnoux, her first lover, her good friend, had presented himself that very day. They both gave the Vicomte to understand that he was in the way, and kicked him out without much ceremony.

He pretended not to have heard what was said.

The Baron went on:

"What has become of her, this fine Rose? Is she as pretty as ever?" showing by his manner that he had been on terms of intimacy with her.

Frederick was chagrined by the discovery.

"There's nothing to blush at," said the Baron, pursuing the topic, " 'tis a good thing!"

Cisy smacked his tongue.

"Whew! not so good!"

"Ha!"

"Oh dear, yes! In the first place, I found her nothing extraordinary, and then, you pick up the like of her as often as you please, for, in fact, she is for sale!"

"Not for everyone!" remarked Frederick, with some bitterness.

"He imagines that he is different from the others," was Cisy's comment. "What a good joke!"

And a laugh ran round the table.

Frederick felt as if the palpitations of his heart would suffocate him. He swallowed two glasses of water one after the other.

But the Baron had preserved a lively recollection of Rosanette.

"Is she still interested in a fellow named Arnoux?"

"I haven't the faintest idea," said Cisy, "I don't know that gentleman!"

Nevertheless, he suggested that he believed Arnoux was a sort of swindler.

"A moment!" exclaimed Frederick.

"However, there is no doubt about it! Legal proceedings have been taken against him."

"That is not true!"

Frederick began to defend Arnoux, vouched for his honesty, ended by convincing himself of it, and concocted figures and proofs. The Vicomte, full of spite, and tipsy in addition, persisted in his assertions, so that Frederick said to him gravely:

"Is the object of this to give offence to me, Monsieur?"

And he looked Cisy full in the face, with eyeballs as red as his cigar.

"Oh! not at all. I grant you that he possesses something very nice—his wife."

"Do you know her?"

"Faith, I do! Sophie Arnoux; everyone knows her."

"You mean to tell me that?"

Cisy, who had staggered to his feet, hiccoughed:

"Everyone—knows—her."

"Hold your tongue. It is not with women of her sort you keep company!"

"I—flatter myself—it is."

Frederick flung a plate at his face. It passed like a flash of lightning over the table, knocked down two bottles, demolished a fruit-dish, and breaking into three pieces, by knocking against the épergne, hit the Vicomte in the stomach.

All the other guests arose to hold him back. He struggled and shrieked, possessed by a kind of frenzy.

M. des Aulnays kept repeating:

"Come, be calm, my dear boy!"

"Why, this is frightful!" shouted the tutor.

Forchambeaux, livid as a plum, was trembling. Joseph indulged in repeated outbursts of laughter. The attendants sponged out the traces of the wine, and gathered up the remains of the dinner from the floor; and the Baron went and shut the window, for the uproar, in spite of the noise of carriage-wheels, could be heard on the boulevard.

As all present at the moment the plate had been flung had been talking at the same time, it was impossible to discover the cause of the attack—whether it was on account of Arnoux, Madame Arnoux, Rosanette, or somebody else. One thing only they were certain of, that Frederick had acted with indescribable brutality. On his part, he refused positively to testify the slightest regret for what he had done.

M. des Aulnays tried to soften him. Cousin Joseph, the tutor, and Forchambeaux himself joined in the effort. The Baron, all this time, was cheering up Cisy, who, yielding to nervous weakness, began to shed tears.

Frederick, on the contrary, was getting more and more angry, and they would have remained there till daybreak if the Baron had not said, in order to bring matters to a close:

"The Vicomte, Monsieur, will send his seconds to call on you to-morrow."

"Your hour?"

"Twelve, if it suits you."

"Perfectly. Monsieur."

Frederick, as soon as he was in the open air, drew a deep breath. He had been keeping his feelings too long under restraint; he had satisfied them at last. He felt, so to speak, the pride of virility, a superabundance of energy within him which intoxicated him. He required two seconds. The first person he thought of for the purpose was Regimbart, and he immediately directed his steps towards the Rue Saint-Denis. The shop-front was closed, but some light shone through a pane of glass over the door. It opened and he went in, stooping very low as he passed under the penthouse.

A candle at the side of the bar lighted up the deserted smoking-room. All the stools, with their feet in the air, were piled on the table. The master and mistress, with their waiter, were at supper in a corner near the kitchen; and Regimbart, with his hat on his head, was sharing their meal, and even disturbed the waiter, who was compelled every moment to turn aside a little. Frederick, having briefly explained the matter to him, asked Regimbart to assist him. The Citizen at first made no reply. He rolled his eyes about, looked as if he were plunged in reflection, took several strides around the room, and at last said:

"Yes, by all means!" and a homicidal smile smoothed his brow when he learned that the adversary was a nobleman.

"Make your mind easy; we'll rout him with flying colours! In the first place, with the sword—"

"But perhaps," broke in Frederick, "I have not the right."

"I tell you 'tis necessary to take the sword," the Citizen replied roughly. "Do you know how to make passes?"

"A little."

"Oh! a little. This is the way with all of them; and yet they have a mania for committing assaults. What does the fencing-school teach? Listen to me: keep a good distance off, always confining yourself in circles, and parry—parry as you retire; that is permitted. Tire him out. Then boldly make a lunge on him! and, above all, no malice, no strokes of the La Fougère kind. No! a simple one-two, and some disengagements. Look here! do you see? while you turn your wrist as if opening a lock. Père Vauthier, give me your cane. Ha! that will do."

He grasped the rod which was used for lighting the gas, rounded his left arm, bent his right, and began to make some thrusts against the partition. He stamped with his foot, got animated, and pretended to be encountering difficulties, while he exclaimed: "Are you there? Is that it? Are you there?" and his enormous silhouette projected itself on the wall with his hat apparently touching the ceiling. The owner of the café shouted from time to time: "Bravo! very good!" His wife, though a little unnerved, was likewise filled with admiration; and Theodore, who had been in the army, remained riveted to the spot with amazement, the fact being, however, that he regarded M. Regimbart with a species of hero-worship.

Next morning, at an early hour, Frederick hurried to the establishment in which Dussardier was employed. After having passed through a succession of departments all full of clothing-materials, either adorning shelves or lying on tables, while here and there shawls were fixed on wooden racks shaped like toadstools, he saw the young man, in a sort of railed cage, surrounded by account-books, and standing in front of a desk at which he was writing. The honest fellow left his work.

The seconds arrived before twelve o'clock.

Frederick, as a matter of good taste, thought he ought not to be present at the conference.

The Baron and M. Joseph declared that they would be satisfied with the simplest excuses. But Regimbart's principle being never to yield, and his contention being that Arnoux's honour should be vindicated (Frederick had not spoken to him about anything else), he asked that the Vicomte should apologise. M. de Comaing was indignant at this presumption. The Citizen would not abate an inch. As all conciliation proved impracticable, there was nothing for it but to fight.

Other difficulties arose, for the choice of weapons lay with Cisy, as the person to whom the insult had been offered. But Regimbart maintained that by sending the challenge he had constituted himself the offending party. His seconds loudly protested that a buffet was the most cruel of offences. The Citizen carped at the words, pointing out that a buffet was not a blow. Finally, they decided to refer the matter to a military man; and the four seconds went off to consult the officers in some of the barracks.

They drew up at the barracks on the Quai d'Orsay. M. de Comaing, having accosted two captains, explained to them the question in dispute.

The captains did not understand a word of what he was saying, owing to the confusion caused by the Citizen's incidental remarks. In short, they advised the gentlemen who consulted them to draw up a minute of the proceedings; after which they would give their decision. Thereupon, they repaired to a café; and they even, in order to do things with more circumspection, referred to Cisy as H, and Frederick as K.

Then they returned to the barracks. The officers had gone out. They reappeared, and declared that the choice of arms manifestly belonged to H.

They all returned to Cisy's abode. Regimbart and Dussardier remained on the footpath outside.

The Vicomte, when he was informed of the solution of the case, was seized with such extreme agitation that they had to repeat for him several times the decision of the officers; and, when M. de Comaing came to deal with Regimbart's contention, he murmured "Nevertheless," not being very reluctant himself to yield to it. Then he let himself sink into an armchair, and declared that he would not fight.

"Eh? What?" said the Baron. Then Cisy indulged in a confused flood of mouthings. He wished to fight with firearms—to discharge a single pistol at close quarters.

"Or else we will put arsenic into a glass, and draw lots to see who must drink it. That's sometimes done. I've read of it!"

The Baron, naturally rather impatient, addressed him in a harsh tone:

"These gentlemen are waiting for your answer. This is indecent, to put it shortly. What weapons are you going to take? Come! is it the sword?"

The Vicomte gave an affirmative reply by merely nodding his head; and it was arranged that the meeting should take place next morning at seven o'clock sharp at the Maillot gate.

Dussardier, being compelled to go back to his business, Regimbart went to inform Frederick about the arrangement. He had been left all day without any news, and his impatience was becoming intolerable.

"So much the better!" he exclaimed.

The Citizen was satisfied with his deportment.

"Would you believe it? They wanted an apology from us. It was nothing—a mere word! But I knocked them off their beam-ends nicely. The right thing to do, wasn't it?"

"Undoubtedly," said Frederick, thinking that it would have been better to choose another second.

Then, when he was alone, he repeated several times in a very loud tone:

"I am going to fight! Hold on, I am going to fight! 'Tis funny!"

And, as he walked up and down his room, while passing in front of the mirror, he noticed that he was pale.

"Have I any reason to be afraid?"

He was seized with a feeling of intolerable misery at the prospect of exhibiting fear on the ground.

"And yet, suppose I happen to be killed? My father met his death the same way. Yes, I shall be killed!"

And, suddenly, his mother rose up before him in a black dress; incoherent images floated before his mind. His own cowardice exasperated him. A paroxysm of courage, a thirst for human blood, took possession of him. A battalion could not have made him retreat. When this feverish excitement had cooled down, he was overjoyed to feel that his nerves were perfectly steady. In order to divert his thoughts, he went to the opera, where a ballet was being performed. He listened to the music, looked at the *danseuses* through his opera-glass, and drank a glass of punch between the acts. But when he got home again, the sight of his study, of his furniture, in the midst of which he found himself for the last time, made him feel ready to swoon.

He went down to the garden. The stars were shining; he gazed up at them. The idea of fighting about a woman gave him a greater importance in his own eyes, and surrounded him with a halo of nobility. Then he went to bed in a tranquil frame of mind.

It was not so with Cisy. After the Baron's departure, Joseph had tried to revive his drooping spirits, and, as the Vicomte remained in the same dull mood:

"However, old boy, if you prefer to remain at home, I'll go and say so."

Cisy durst not answer "Certainly;" but he would have liked his cousin to do him this service without speaking about it.

He wished that Frederick would die during the night of an attack of apoplexy, or that a riot would break out so that next morning there would be enough of barricades to shut up all the approaches to the Bois de Boulogne, or that some emergency might prevent one of the seconds from being present; for in the absence of seconds the duel would fall through. He felt a longing to save himself by taking an express train—no matter where. He regretted that he did not understand medicine so as to be able to take something which, without endangering his life, would cause it to be believed that he was dead. He finally wished to be ill in earnest.

In order to get advice and assistance from someone, he sent for M. des Aulnays. That worthy man had gone back to Saintonge on receiving a letter informing him of the illness of one of his daughters. This appeared an ominous circumstance to Cisy. Luckily, M. Vezou, his tutor, came to see him. Then he unbosomed himself.

"What am I to do? my God! what am I do?"

"If I were in your place, Monsieur, I should pay some strapping fellow from the market-place to go and give him a drubbing."

"He would still know who brought it about," replied Cisy.

And from time to time he uttered a groan; then:

"But is a man bound to fight a duel?"

" 'Tis a relic of barbarism! What are you to do?"

Out of complaisance the pedagogue invited himself to dinner. His pupil did not eat anything, but, after the meal, felt the necessity of taking a short walk.

As they were passing a church, he said:

"Suppose we go in for a little while—to look?"

M. Vezou asked nothing better, and even offered him holy water.

It was the month of May. The altar was covered with flowers; voices were chanting; the organ was resounding through the church. But he found it impossible to pray, as the pomps of religion inspired him merely with thoughts of funerals. He fancied that he could hear the murmurs of the *De Profundis*.

"Let us go away. I don't feel well."

They spent the whole night playing cards. The Vicomte made an effort to lose in order to exorcise ill-luck, a thing which M. Vezou turned to his own advantage. At last, at the first streak of dawn, Cisy, who could stand it no longer, sank down on the green cloth, and was soon plunged in sleep, which was disturbed by unpleasant dreams.

If courage, however, consists in wishing to get the better of one's own weakness, the Vicomte was courageous, for in the presence of his seconds, who came to seek him, he stiffened himself up with all the strength he could command, vanity making him realise that to attempt to draw back now would destroy him. M. de Comaing congratulated him on his good appearance.

But, on the way, the jolting of the cab and the heat of the morning sun made him languish. His energy gave way again. He could not even distinguish any longer where they were. The Baron amused himself by increasing his terror, talking about the "corpse," and of the way they meant to get back clandestinely to the city. Joseph gave the rejoinder; both, considering the affair ridiculous, were certain that it would be settled.

Cisy kept his head on his breast; he lifted it up slowly, and drew attention to the fact that they had not taken a doctor with them.

" 'Tis needless," said the Baron.

"Then there's no danger?"

Joseph answered in a grave tone:

"Let us hope so!"

And nobody in the carriage made any further remark.

At ten minutes past seven they arrived in front of the Maillot gate. Frederick and his seconds were there, the entire group being dressed all in black. Regimbart, instead of a cravat, wore a stiff horsehair collar, like a trooper; and he carried a long violin-case adapted for adventures of this kind. They exchanged frigid bows. Then they all plunged into the Bois de Boulogne, taking the Madrid road, in order to find a suitable place.

Regimbart said to Frederick, who was walking between him and Dussardier:

"Well, and this scare—what do we care about it? If you want anything, don't annoy yourself about it; I know what to do. Fear is natural to man!"

Then, in a low tone:

"Don't smoke any more; in this case it has a weakening effect."

Frederick threw away his cigar, which had only a disturbing effect on his brain, and went on with a firm step. The Vicomte advanced behind, leaning on the arms of his two seconds. Occasional wayfarers crossed their path. The sky was blue, and from time to time they heard rabbits skipping about. At the turn of a path, a woman in a Madras neckerchief was chatting with a man in a blouse; and in the large avenue under the chestnut-trees some grooms in vests of linen-cloth were walking horses up and down.

Cisy recalled the happy days when, mounted on his own chestnut horse, and with his glass stuck in his eye, he rode up to carriage-doors. These recollections intensified his wretchedness. An intolerable thirst parched his throat. The buzzing of flies mingled with the throbbing of his arteries. His feet sank into the sand. It seemed to him as if he had been walking during a period which had neither beginning nor end.

The seconds, without stopping, examined with keen glances each side of the path they were traversing. They hesitated as to whether they would go to the Catelan Cross or under the walls of the Bagatelle. At last they took a turn to the right; and they drew up in a kind of quincunx in the midst of the pine-trees.

The spot was chosen in such a way that the level ground was cut equally into two divisions. The two places at which the principals in the duel were to take their stand were marked out. Then Regimbart opened his case. It was lined with red sheep's-leather, and contained four charming swords hollowed in the centre, with handles which were adorned with filigree. A ray of light, passing through the leaves, fell on them, and they appeared to Cisy to glitter like silver vipers on a sea of blood.

The Citizen showed that they were of equal length. He took one himself, in order to separate the combatants in case of necessity. M. de Comaing held a walking-stick. There was an interval of silence. They looked at each other. All the faces had in them something fierce or cruel.

Frederick had taken off his coat and his waistcoat. Joseph aided Cisy to do the same. When his cravat was removed a blessed medal could be seen on his neck. This made Regimbart smile contemptuously.

Then M. de Comaing (in order to allow Frederick another moment for reflection) tried to raise some quibbles. He demanded the right to put on a glove, and to catch hold of his adversary's sword with the left hand. Regimbart, who was in a hurry, made no objection to this. At last the Baron, addressing Frederick:

"Everything depends on you, Monsieur! There is never any dishonour in acknowledging one's faults."

Dussardier made a gesture of approval. The Citizen gave vent to his indignation:

"Do you think we came here as a mere sham, damn it! Be on your guard, each of you!"

The combatants were facing one another, with their seconds by their sides.

He uttered the single word:

"Come!"

Cisy became dreadfully pale. The end of his blade was quivering like a horse-whip. His head fell back, his hands dropped down helplessly, and he sank unconscious on the ground. Joseph raised him up and while holding a scent-bottle to his nose, gave him a good shaking.

The Vicomte reopened his eyes, then suddenly grasped at his sword like a madman. Frederick had held his in readiness, and now awaited him with steady eye and uplifted hand.

"Stop! stop!" cried a voice, which came from the road simultaneously with the sound of a horse at full gallop, and the hood of a cab broke the branches. A man bending out his head waved a handkerchief, still exclaiming:

"Stop! stop!"

M. de Comaing, believing that this meant the intervention of the police, lifted up his walking-stick.

"Make an end of it. The Vicomte is bleeding!"

"I?" said Cisy.

In fact, he had in his fall taken off the skin of his left thumb.

"But this was by falling," observed the Citizen.

The Baron pretended not to understand.

Arnoux had jumped out of the cab.

"I have arrived too late? No! Thanks be to God!"

He threw his arms around Frederick, felt him, and covered his face with kisses.

"I am the cause of it. You wanted to defend your old friend! That's right—that's right! Never shall I forget it! How good you are! Ah! my own dear boy!"

He gazed at Frederick and shed tears, while he chuckled with delight. The Baron turned towards Joseph:

"I believe we are in the way at this little family party. It is over, messieurs, is it not? Vicomte, put your arm into a sling. Hold on! here is my silk handkerchief."

Then, with an imperious gesture: "Come! no spite! This is as it should be!"

The two adversaries shook hands in a very lukewarm fashion. The Vicomte, M. de Comaing, and Joseph disappeared in one direction, and Frederick left with his friends in the opposite direction.

As the Madrid Restaurant was not far off, Arnoux proposed that they should go and drink a glass of beer there.

"We might even have breakfast."

But, as Dussardier had no time to lose, they confined themselves to taking some refreshment in the garden.

They all experienced that sense of satisfaction which follows happy *dénouements*. The Citizen, nevertheless, was annoyed at the duel having been interrupted at the most critical stage.

Arnoux had been apprised of it by a person named Compain, a friend of Regimbart; and with an irrepressible outburst of emotion he had rushed to the spot to prevent it, under the impression, however, that he was the occasion of it. He begged of Frederick to furnish him with some details about it. Frederick, touched by these proofs of affection, felt some scruples at the idea of increasing his misapprehension of the facts.

"For mercy's sake, don't say anymore about it!"

Arnoux thought that this reserve showed great delicacy. Then, with his habitual levity, he passed on to some fresh subject.

"What news, Citizen?"

And they began talking about banking transactions, and the number of bills that were falling due. In order to be more undisturbed, they went to another table, where they exchanged whispered confidences.

Frederick could overhear the following words: "You are going to back me up with your signature." "Yes, but you, mind!" "I have negotiated it at last for three hundred!" "A nice commission, faith!"

In short, it was clear that Arnoux was mixed up in a great many shady transactions with the Citizen.

Frederick thought of reminding him about the fifteen thousand francs. But his last step forbade the utterance of any reproachful words even of the mildest description. Besides, he felt tired himself, and this was not a convenient place for talking about such a thing. He put it off till some future day.

Arnoux, seated in the shade of an evergreen, was smoking, with a look of joviality in his face. He raised his eyes towards the doors of private rooms looking out on the garden, and said he had often paid visits to the house in former days.

"Probably not by yourself?" returned the Citizen.

"Faith, you're right there!"

"What blackguardism you do carry on! you, a married man!"

"Well, and what about yourself?" retorted Arnoux; and, with an indulgent smile: "I am even sure that this rascal here has a room of his own somewhere into which he takes his friends."

The Citizen confessed that this was true by simply shrugging his shoulders. Then these two gentlemen entered into their respective tastes with regard to the sex: Arnoux now preferred youth, work-girls; Regimbart hated affected women, and went in for the genuine article before anything else. The conclusion which the earthenware-dealer laid down at the close of this discussion was that women were not to be taken seriously.

"Nevertheless, he is fond of his own wife," thought Frederick, as he made his way home; and he looked on Arnoux as a coarse-grained man. He had a grudge against him on account of the duel, as if it had been for the sake of this individual that he risked his life a little while before.

But he felt grateful to Dussardier for his devotedness. Ere long the book-keeper came at his invitation to pay him a visit every day.

Frederick lent him books—Thiers, Dulaure, Barante, and Lamartine's *Girondins*.

The honest fellow listened to everything the other said with a thoughtful air, and accepted his opinions as those of a master.

One evening he arrived looking quite scared.

That morning, on the boulevard, a man who was running so quickly that he had got out of breath, had jostled against him, and having recognised in him a friend of Sénécal, had said to him:

"He has just been taken! I am making my escape!"

There was no doubt about it. Dussardier had spent the day making enquiries. Sénécal was in jail charged with an attempted crime of a political nature.

The son of an overseer, he was born at Lyons, and having had as his teacher a former disciple of Chalier, he had, on his arrival in Paris, obtained admission into the "Society of Families." His ways were known, and the police kept a watch on him. He was one of those who fought in the outbreak of May, 1839, and since then he had remained in the shade; but, his self-importance increasing more and more, he became a fanatical follower of Alibaud, mixing up his own grievances against society with those of the people against monarchy, and waking up every morning in the hope of a revolution which in a fortnight or a month would turn the world upside down. At last, disgusted at the inactivity of his brethren, enraged at the obstacles that retarded the realisation of his dreams, and despairing of the country, he entered in his capacity of chemist into the conspiracy for the use of incendiary bombs; and he had been caught carrying gunpowder, of which he was going to make a trial at Montmartre—a supreme effort to establish the Republic.

Dussardier was no less attached to the Republican idea, for, from his point of view, it meant enfranchisement and universal happiness. One day—at the age of fifteen—in the Rue Transnonain, in front of a grocer's shop, he had seen soldiers' bayonets reddened with blood and exhibiting human hairs pasted to the butt-ends of their guns. Since that time, the Government had filled him with feelings of rage as the very incarnation of injustice. He frequently confused the assassins with the gendarmes; and in his eyes a police-spy was just as bad as a parricide. All the evil scattered over the earth he ingenuously attributed to Power; and he hated it with a deep-rooted, undying hatred that held possession of his heart and made his sensibility all the more acute. He had been dazzled by Sénécal's declamations. It was of little consequence whether he happened to be guilty or not, or whether the attempt with which he was charged could be characterised as an odious proceeding! Since he was the victim of Authority, it was only right to help him.

"The Peers will condemn him, certainly! Then he will be conveyed in a prison-van, like a convict, and will be shut up in Mont Saint-Michel, where the Government lets people die! Austen had gone mad! Steuben had killed himself! In order to transfer Barbès into a dungeon, they had dragged him by the legs and by the hair. They trampled on his body, and his head rebounded along the staircase at every step they took. What abominable treatment! The wretches!"

He was choking with angry sobs, and he walked about the apartment in a very excited frame of mind.

"In the meantime, something must be done! Come, for my part, I don't know what to do! Suppose we tried to rescue him, eh? While they are bringing him to the Luxembourg, we could throw ourselves on the escort in the passage! A dozen resolute men—that sometimes is enough to accomplish it!"

There was so much fire in his eyes that Frederick was a little startled by his look. He recalled to mind Sénécal's sufferings and his austere life. Without feeling the same enthusiasm about him as Dussardier, he experienced nevertheless that admiration which is inspired by every man who sacrifices himself for an idea. He said to himself that, if he had helped this man, he would not be in his present position; and the two friends anxiously sought to devise some contrivance whereby they could set him free.

It was impossible for them to get access to him.

Frederick examined the newspapers to try to find out what had become of him, and for three weeks he was a constant visitor at the reading-rooms.

One day several numbers of the *Flambard* fell into his hands. The leading article was invariably devoted to cutting up some distinguished man. After that came some society gossip and some scandals. Then there were some chaffing observations about the Odéon Carpentras, pisciculture, and prisoners under sentence of death, when there happened to be any. The disappearance of a packet-boat furnished materials for a whole year's jokes. In the third column a picture-canvasser, under the form of anecdotes or advice, gave some tailors' announcements, together with accounts of evening parties, advertisements as to auctions, and analysis of artistic productions, writing in the same strain about a volume of verse and a pair of boots. The only serious portion of it was the criticism of the small theatres, in which fierce attacks were made on two or three managers; and the interests of art were invoked on the subjects of the decorations of the Rope-dancers' Gymnasium and of the actress who played the part of the heroine at the Délassements.

Frederick was passing over all these items when his eyes alighted on an article entitled "A Lass between three Lads." It was the story of his duel related in a lively Gallic style. He had no difficulty in recognising himself, for he was indicated by this little joke, which frequently recurred: "A young man from the College of Sens who has no sense." He was even represented as a poor devil from the provinces, an obscure booby trying to rub against persons of high rank. As for the Vicomte, he was made to play a fascinating part, first by having forced his way into the supper-room, then by having carried off the lady, and, finally, by having behaved all through like a perfect gentleman.

Frederick's courage was not denied exactly, but it was pointed out that an intermediary—the *protector* himself—had come on the scene just in the nick of time. The entire article concluded with this phrase, pregnant perhaps with sinister meaning:

"What is the cause of their affection? A problem! and, as Bazile says, who the deuce is it that is deceived here?"

This was, beyond all doubt, Hussonnet's revenge against Frederick for having refused him five thousand francs.

What was he to do? If he demanded an explanation from him, the Bohemian would protest that he was innocent, and nothing would be gained by doing this. The best course was to swallow the affront in silence. Nobody, after all, read the *Flambard*.

As he left the reading-room, he saw some people standing in front of a picture-dealer's shop. They were staring at the portrait of a woman, with this line traced underneath in black letters: "Mademoiselle Rosanette Bron, belonging to M. Frederick Moreau of Nogent."

It was indeed she—or, at least, like her—her full face displayed, her bosom uncovered, with her hair hanging loose, and with a purse of red velvet in her hands, while behind her a peacock leaned his beak over her shoulder, covering the wall with his immense plumage in the shape of a fan.

Pellerin had got up this exhibition in order to compel Frederick to pay, persuaded that he was a celebrity, and that all Paris, roused to take his part, would be interested in this wretched piece of work.

Was this a conspiracy? Had the painter and the journalist prepared their attack on him at the same time?

His duel had not put a stop to anything. He had become an object of ridicule, and everyone had been laughing at him.

Three days afterwards, at the end of June, the Northern shares having had a rise of fifteen francs, as he had bought two thousand of them within the past month, he found that he had made thirty thousand francs by them. This caress of fortune gave him renewed self-confidence. He said to himself that he wanted nobody's help, and that all his embarrassments were the result of his timidity and indecision. He ought to have begun his intrigue with the Maréchale with brutal directness and refused Hussonnet the very first day. He should not have compromised himself with Pellerin. And, in order to show that he was not a bit embarrassed, he presented himself at one of Madame Dambreuse's ordinary evening parties.

In the middle of the anteroom, Martinon, who had arrived at the same time as he had, turned round:

"What! so you are visiting here?" with a look of surprise, and as if displeased at seeing him.

"Why not?"

And, while asking himself what could be the cause of such a display of hostility on Martinon's part, Frederick made his way into the drawing-room.

The light was dim, in spite of the lamps placed in the corners, for the three windows, which were wide open, made three large squares of black shadow stand parallel with each other. Under the pictures, flower-stands occupied, at a man's height, the spaces on the walls, and a silver teapot with a samovar cast their reflections in a mirror on the background. There arose a murmur of hushed voices. Pumps could be heard creaking on the carpet. He could distinguish a number of black coats, then a round table lighted up by a large shaded lamp, seven or eight ladies in summer toilets, and at some little distance Madame Dambreuse in a rocking armchair. Her dress of lilac taffeta had slashed sleeves, from which fell muslin puffs, the charming tint of the material harmonising with the shade of her hair; and she sat slightly thrown back with the tip of her foot on a cushion, with the repose of an exquisitely delicate work of art, a flower of high culture.

M. Dambreuse and an old gentleman with a white head were walking from one end of the drawing-room to the other. Some of the guests chatted here and there, sitting on the edges of little sofas, while the others, standing up, formed a circle in the centre of the apartment.

They were talking about votes, amendments, counter-amendments, M. Grandin's speech, and M. Benoist's reply. The third party had decidedly gone too far. The Left Centre ought to have had a better recollection of its origin. Serious attacks had been made on the ministry. It must be reassuring, however, to see that it had no successor. In short, the situation was completely analogous to that of 1834.

As these things bored Frederick, he drew near the ladies. Martinon was beside them, standing up, with his hat under his arm, showing himself in three-quarter profile, and looking so neat that he resembled a piece of Sèvres porcelain. He took up a copy of the *Revue des Deux Mondes* which was lying on the table between an *Imitation* and an *Almanach de Gotha,* and spoke of a distinguished poet in a contemptuous tone, said he was going to the "conferences of Saint-Francis," complained of his larynx, swallowed from time to time a pellet of gummatum, and in the meantime kept talking about music, and played the part of the elegant trifler. Mademoiselle Cécile, M. Dambreuse's niece, who happened to be embroidering a pair of ruffles, gazed at him with her pale blue eyes; and Miss John, the governess, who had a flat nose, laid aside her tapestry on his account. Both of them appeared to be exclaiming internally:

"How handsome he is!"

Madame Dambreuse turned round towards him.

"Please give me my fan which is on that pier-table over there. You are taking the wrong one! 'tis the other!"

She arose, and when he came across to her, they met in the middle of the drawing-room face to face. She addressed a few sharp words to him, no doubt of a reproachful character, judging by the haughty expression of her face. Martinon tried to smile; then he went to join the circle in which grave men were holding discussions. Madame Dambreuse resumed her seat, and, bending over the arm of her chair, said to Frederick:

"I saw somebody the day before yesterday who was speaking to me about you—Monsieur de Cisy. You know him, don't you?"

"Yes, slightly."

Suddenly Madame Dambreuse uttered an exclamation:

"Oh! Duchesse, what a pleasure to see you!"

And she advanced towards the door to meet a little old lady in a Carmelite taffeta gown and a cap of guipure with long borders. The daughter of a companion in exile of the Comte d'Artois, and the widow of a marshal of the Empire, who had been created a peer of France in 1830, she adhered to the court of a former generation as well as to the new court, and possessed sufficient influence to procure many things. Those who stood talking stepped aside, and then resumed their conversation.

It had now turned on pauperism, of which, according to these gentlemen, all the descriptions that had been given were grossly exaggerated.

"However," urged Martinon, "let us confess that there is such a thing as want! But the remedy depends neither on science nor on power. It is purely an individual question. When the lower classes are willing to get rid of their vices, they will free themselves from their necessities. Let the people be more moral, and they will be less poor!"

According to M. Dambreuse, no good could be attained without a superabundance of capital. Therefore, the only practicable method was to intrust, "as the Saint-Simonians, however, proposed (good heavens! there was some merit in their views—let us be just to everybody)—to intrust, I say, the cause of progress to those who can increase the public wealth." Imperceptibly they began to touch on great industrial undertakings—the railways, the coal-mines. And M. Dambreuse, addressing Frederick, said to him in a low whisper:

"You have not called about that business of ours?"

Frederick pleaded illness; but, feeling that this excuse was too absurd:

"Besides, I need my ready money."

"Is it to buy a carriage?" asked Madame Dambreuse, who was brushing past him with a cup of tea in her hand, and for a minute she watched his face with her head bent slightly over her shoulder.

She believed that he was Rosanette's lover—the allusion was obvious. It seemed even to Frederick that all the ladies were staring at him from a distance and whispering to one another.

In order to get a better idea as to what they were thinking about, he once more approached them. On the opposite side of the table, Martinon, seated near Mademoiselle Cécile, was turning over the leaves of an album. It contained lithographs representing Spanish costumes. He read the descriptive titles aloud: "A Lady of Seville," "A Valencia Gardener," "An Andalusian Picador"; and once, when he had reached the bottom of the page, he continued all in one breath:

"Jacques Arnoux, publisher. One of your friends, eh?"

"That is true," said Frederick, hurt by the tone he had assumed.

Madame Dambreuse again interposed:

"In fact, you came here one morning—about a house, I believe—a house belonging to his wife." (This meant: "She is your mistress.")

He reddened up to his ears; and M. Dambreuse, who joined them at the same moment, made this additional remark:

"You appear even to be deeply interested in them."

These last words had the effect of putting Frederick out of countenance. His confusion, which, he could not help feeling, was evident to them, was on the point of confirming their suspicions, when M. Dambreuse drew close to him, and, in a tone of great seriousness, said:

"I suppose you don't do business together?"

He protested by repeated shakes of the head, without realising the exact meaning of the capitalist, who wished to give him advice.

He felt a desire to leave. The fear of appearing faint-hearted restrained him. A servant carried away the teacups. Madame Dambreuse was talking to a diplomatist in a blue coat. Two young girls, drawing their foreheads close together, showed each other their jewellery. The others, seated in a semicircle on armchairs, kept gently moving their white faces crowned with black or fair hair. Nobody, in fact, minded them. Frederick turned on his heels; and, by a succession of long zigzags, he had almost reached the door, when, passing close to a bracket, he remarked, on the top of it, between a china vase and the wainscoting, a journal folded up in two. He drew it out a little, and read these words—*The Flambard*.

Who had brought it there? Cisy. Manifestly no one else. What did it matter, however? They would believe—already, perhaps, everyone believed—in the article. What was the cause of this rancour? Me wrapped himself up in ironical silence. He felt like one lost in a desert. But suddenly he heard Martinon's voice:

"Talking of Arnoux, I saw in the newspapers, amongst the names of those accused of preparing incendiary bombs, that of one of his *employés*, Sénécal. Is that our Sénécal?"

"The very same!"

Martinon repeated several times in a very loud tone:

"What? our Sénécal! our Sénécal!"

Then questions were asked him about the conspiracy. It was assumed that his connection with the prosecutor's office ought to furnish him with some information on the subject.

He declared that he had none. However, he knew very little about this individual, having seen him only two or three times. He positively regarded him as a very ill-conditioned fellow. Frederick exclaimed indignantly:

"Not at all! he is a very honest fellow."

"All the same, Monsieur," said a landowner, "no conspirator can be an honest man."

Most of the men assembled there had served at least four governments; and they would have sold France or the human race in order to preserve their own incomes, to save themselves from any discomfort or embarrassment, or even through sheer baseness, through worship of force. They all maintained that political crimes were inexcusable. It would be more desirable to pardon those which were provoked by want. And they did not fail to put forward the eternal illustration of the father of a family stealing the eternal loaf of bread from the eternal baker.

A gentleman occupying an administrative office even went so far as to exclaim:

"For my part, Monsieur, if I were told that my brother were a conspirator I would denounce him!"

Frederick invoked the right of resistance, and recalling to mind some phrases that Deslauriers had used in their conversations, he referred to Delosmes, Blackstone, the English Bill of Rights, and Article 2 of the Constitution of '91. It was even by virtue of this law that the fall of Napoleon had been proclaimed. It had been recognised in 1830, and inscribed at the head of the Charter. Besides, when the sovereign fails to fulfil the contract, justice requires that he should be overthrown.

"Why, this is abominable!" exclaimed a prefect's wife.

All the rest remained silent, filled with vague terror, as if they had heard the noise of bullets. Madame Dambreuse rocked herself in her chair, and smiled as she listened to him.

A manufacturer, who had formerly been a member of the Carbonari, tried to show that the Orléans family possessed good qualities. No doubt there were some abuses.

"Well, what then?"

"But we should not talk about them, my dear Monsieur! If you knew how all these clamourings of the Opposition injure business!"

"What do I care about business?" said Frederick.

He was exasperated by the rottenness of these old men; and, carried away by the recklessness which sometimes takes possession of even the most timid, he attacked the financiers, the deputies, the government, the king, took up the defence of the Arabs, and gave vent to a great deal of abusive language. A few of those around him encouraged him in a spirit of irony:

"Go on, pray! continue!" whilst others muttered: "The deuce! what enthusiasm!" At last he thought the right thing to do was to retire; and, as he was going away, M. Dambreuse said to him, alluding to the post of secretary:

"No definite arrangement has been yet arrived at; but make haste!"

And Madame Dambreuse:

"You'll call again soon, will you not?"

Frederick considered their parting salutation a last mockery. He had resolved never to come back to this house, or to visit any of these people again. He imagined that he had offended them, not realising what vast funds of indifference society possesses. These women especially excited his indignation. Not a single one of them had backed him up even with a look of sympathy. He felt angry with them for not having been moved by his words. As for Madame Dambreuse, he found in her something at the same time languid and cold, which prevented him from defining her character by a formula. Had she a lover? and, if so, who was her lover? Was it the diplomatist or some other? Perhaps it was Martinon? Impossible! Nevertheless, he experienced a sort of jealousy against Martinon, and an unaccountable ill-will against her.

Dussardier, having called this evening as usual, was awaiting him. Frederick's heart was swelling with bitterness; he unburdened it, and his grievances, though vague and hard to understand, saddened the honest shop-assistant. He even complained of his isolation. Dussardier, after a little hesitation, suggested that they ought to call on Deslauriers.

Frederick, at the mention of the advocate's name, was seized with a longing to see him once more. He was now living in the midst of profound intellectual solitude, and found Dussardier's company quite insufficient. In reply to the latter's question, Frederick told him to arrange matters any way he liked.

Deslauriers had likewise, since their quarrel, felt a void in his life. He yielded without much reluctance to the cordial advances which were made to him. The pair embraced each other, then began chatting about matters of no consequence.

Frederick's heart was touched by Deslauriers' display of reserve, and in order to make him a sort of reparation, he told the other next day how he had lost the fifteen thousand francs without mentioning that these fifteen thousand francs had been originally intended for him. The advocate, nevertheless, had a shrewd suspicion of the truth; and this misadventure, which justified, in his own mind, his prejudices against Arnoux, entirely disarmed his rancour; and he did not again refer to the promise made by his friend on a former occasion.

Frederick, misled by his silence, thought he had forgotten all about it. A few days afterwards, he asked Deslauriers whether there was any way in which he could get back his money.

They might raise the point that the prior mortgage was fraudulent, and might take proceedings against the wife personally.

"No! no! not against her!" exclaimed Frederick, and, yielding to the ex-law-clerk's questions, he confessed the truth. Deslauriers was convinced that Frederick had not told him the entire truth, no doubt through a feeling of delicacy. He was hurt by this want of confidence.

They were, however, on the same intimate terms as before, and they even found so much pleasure in each other's society that Dussardier's presence was an obstacle to their free intercourse. Under the pretence that they had appointments, they managed gradually to get rid of him.

There are some men whose only mission amongst their fellow-men is to serve as go-betweens; people use them in the same way as if they were bridges, by stepping over them and going on further.

Frederick concealed nothing from his old friend. He told him about the coal-mine speculation and M. Dambreuse's prosposal. The advocate grew thoughtful.

"That's queer! For such a post a man with a good knowledge of law would be required!"

"But you could assist me," returned Frederick.

"Yes!—hold on! faith, yes! certainly."

During the same week Frederick showed Dussardier a letter from his mother.

Madame Moreau accused herself of having misjudged M. Roque, who had given a satisfactory explanation of his conduct. Then she spoke of his means, and of the possibility, later, of a marriage with Louise.

"That would not be a bad match," said Deslauriers.

Frederick said it was entirely out of the question. Besides, Père Roque was an old trickster. That in no way affected the matter, in the advocate's opinion.

At the end of July, an unaccountable diminution in value made the Northern shares fall. Frederick had not sold his. He lost sixty thousand francs in one day. His income was considerably reduced. He would have to curtail his expenditure, or take up some calling, or make a brilliant catch in the matrimonial market.

Then Deslauriers spoke to him about Mademoiselle Roque. There was nothing to prevent him from going to get some idea of things by seeing for himself. Frederick was rather tired of city life. Provincial existence and the maternal roof would be a sort of recreation for him.

The aspect of the streets of Nogent, as he passed through them in the moonlight, brought back old memories to his mind; and he experienced a kind of pang, like persons who have just returned home after a long period of travel.

At his mother's house, all the country visitors had assembled as in former days—MM. Gamblin, Heudras, and Chambrion, the Lebrun family, "those young ladies, the Augers," and, in addition, Père Roque, and, sitting opposite to Madame Moreau at a card-table, Mademoiselle Louise. She was now a woman. She sprang to her feet with a cry of delight. They were all in a flutter of excitement. She remained standing motionless, and the paleness of her face was intensified by the light issuing from four silver candlesticks.

When she resumed play, her hand was trembling. This emotion was exceedingly flattering to Frederick, whose pride had been sorely wounded of late. He said to himself: "You, at any rate, will love me!" and, as if he were thus taking his revenge for the humiliations he had endured in the capital, he began to affect the Parisian lion, retailed all the theatrical gossip, told anecdotes as to the doings of society, which he had borrowed from the columns of the cheap newspapers, and, in short, dazzled his fellow-townspeople.

Next morning, Madame Moreau expatiated on Louise's fine qualities; then she enumerated the woods and farms of which she would be the owner. Père Roque's wealth was considerable.

He had acquired it while making investments for M. Dambreuse; for he had lent money to persons who were able to give good security in the shape of mortgages, whereby he was enabled to demand additional sums or commissions. The capital, owing to his energetic vigilance, was in no danger of being lost. Besides, Père Roque never had any hesitation in making a seizure. Then he bought up the mortgaged property at a low price, and M. Dambreuse, having got back his money, found his affairs in very good order.

But this manipulation of business matters in a way which was not strictly legal compromised him with his agent. He could refuse Père Roque nothing, and it was owing to the latter's solicitations that M. Dambreuse had received Frederick so cordially.

The truth was that in the depths of his soul Père Roque cherished a deep-rooted ambition. He wished his daughter to be a countess; and for the purpose of gaining this object, without imperilling the happiness of his child, he knew no other young man so well adapted as Frederick.

Through the influence of M. Dambreuse, he could obtain the title of his maternal grandfather, Madame Moreau being the daughter of a Comte de Fouvens, and besides being connected with the oldest families in Champagne, the Lavernades and the D'Etrignys. As for the Moreaus, a Gothic inscription near the mills of Villeneuve-l'Archevêque referred to one Jacob Moreau, who had rebuilt them in 1596; and the tomb of his own son, Pierre Moreau, first esquire of the king under Louis XIV, was to be seen in the chapel of Saint-Nicholas.

So much family distinction fascinated M. Roque, the son of an old servant. If the coronet of a count did not come, he would console himself with something else; for Frederick might get a deputyship when M. Dambreuse had been raised to the peerage, and might then be able to assist him in his commercial pursuits, and to obtain for him supplies and grants. He liked the young man personally. In short, he desired to have Frederick for a son-in-law, because for a long time past he had been smitten with this notion, which only grew all the stronger day by day. Now he went to religious services, and he had won Madame Moreau over to his views, especially by holding before her the prospect of a title.

So it was that, eight days later, without any formal engagement, Frederick was regarded as Mademoiselle Roque's "intended," and Père Roque, who was not troubled with many scruples, often left them together.

Chapter XII

LITTLE LOUISE GROWS UP

DESLAURIERS HAD CARRIED AWAY FROM FREDERICK'S HOUSE THE COPY OF the deed of subrogation, with a power of attorney in proper form, giving him full authority to act; but, when he had reascended his own five flights of stairs and found himself alone in the midst of his dismal room, in his armchair upholstered in sheep-leather, the sight of the stamped paper disgusted him.

He was tired of these things, and of restaurants at thirty-two sous, of travelling in omnibuses, of enduring want and making futile efforts. He took up the papers again; there were others near them. They were prospectuses of the coal-mining company, with a list of the mines and the particulars as to their contents, Frederick having left all these matters in his hands in order to have his opinion about them.

An idea occurred to him—that of presenting himself at M. Dambreuse's house and applying for the post of secretary. This post, it was perfectly certain, could not be obtained without purchasing a certain number of shares. He recognised the folly of his project, and said to himself:

"Oh! no, that would be a wrong step."

Then he ransacked his brains to think of the best way in which he could set about recovering the fifteen thousand francs. Such a sum was a mere trifle to Frederick. But, if he had it, what a lever it would be in his hands! And the ex-law-clerk was indignant at the other being so well off.

"He makes a pitiful use of it. He is a selfish fellow. Ah! what do I care for his fifteen thousand francs!"

Why had he lent the money? For the sake of Madame Arnoux's bright eyes. She was his mistress! Deslauriers had no doubt about it. "There was another way in which money was useful!"

And he was assailed by malignant thoughts.

Then he allowed his thoughts to dwell even on Frederick's personal appearance. It had always exercised over him an almost feminine charm; and he soon came to admire it for a success which he realised that he was himself incapable of achieving.

"Nevertheless, was not the will the main element in every enterprise? and, since by its means we may triumph over everything—"

"Ha! that would be funny!"

But he felt ashamed of such treachery, and the next moment:

"Pooh! I am afraid?"

Madame Arnoux—from having heard her spoken about so often—had come to be depicted in his imagination as something extraordinary. The persistency of this passion had irritated him like a problem, Her austerity, which seemed a little theatrical, now annoyed him. Besides, the woman of the world—or, rather, his own conception of her—dazzled the advocate as a symbol and the epitome of a thousand pleasures. Poor though he was, he hankered after luxury in its more glittering form.

"After all, even though he should get angry, so much the worse! He has behaved too badly to me to call for any anxiety about him on my part! I have no assurance that she is his mistress! He has denied it. So then I am free to act as I please!"

He could no longer abandon the desire of taking this step. He wished to make a trial of his own strength, so that one day, all of a sudden, he polished his boots himself, bought white gloves, and set forth on his way, substituting himself for Frederick, and almost imagining that he was the other by a singular intellectual evolution, in which there was, at the same time, vengeance and sympathy, imitation and audacity.

He announced himself as "Doctor Deslauriers."

Madame Arnoux was surprised, as she had not sent for any physician.

"Ha! a thousand apologies!—'tis a doctor of law! I have come in Monsieur Moreau's interest."

This name appeared to produce a disquieting effect on her mind.

"So much the better!" thought the ex-law-clerk.

"Since she has a liking for him, she will like me, too!" buoying up his courage with the accepted idea that it is easier to supplant a lover than a husband.

He referred to the fact that he had the pleasure of meeting her on one occasion at the law-courts; he even mentioned the date. This remarkable power of memory astonished Madame Arnoux. He went on in a tone of mild affectation:

"You have already found your affairs a little embarrassing?"

She made no reply.

"Then it must be true."

He began to chat about one thing or another, about her house, about the works; then, noticing some medallions at the sides of the mirror:

"Ha! family portraits, no doubt?"

He remarked that of an old lady, Madame Arnoux's mother.

"She has the appearance of an excellent woman, a southern type."

And, on being met with the objection that she was from Chartres:

"Chartres! pretty town!"

He praised its cathedral and public buildings, and coming back to the portrait, traced resemblances between it and Madame Arnoux, and cast flatteries at her indirectly. She did not appear to be offended at this. He took confidence, and said that he had known Arnoux a long time.

"He is a fine fellow, but one who compromises himself. Take this mortgage, for example—one can't imagine such a reckless act—"

"Yes, I know," said she, shrugging her shoulders.

This involuntary evidence of contempt induced Deslauriers to continue. "That kaolin business of his was near turning out very badly, a thing you may not be aware of, and even his reputation—"

A contraction of the brows made him pause.

Then, falling back on generalities, he expressed his pity for the "poor women whose husbands frittered away their means."

"But in this case, monsieur, the means belong to him. As for me, I have nothing!"

No matter, one never knows. A woman of experience might be useful. He made offers of devotion, exalted his own merits; and he looked into her face through his shining spectacles.

She was seized with a vague torpor; but suddenly said:

"Let us look into the matter, I beg of you."

He exhibited the bundle of papers.

"This is Frederick's letter of attorney. With such a document in the hands of a process-server, who would make out an order, nothing could be easier; in twenty-four hours—" (She remained impassive; he changed his manouevre.)

"As for me, however, I don't understand what impels him to demand this sum, for, in fact, he doesn't want it."

"How is that? Monsieur Moreau has shown himself so kind."

"Oh! granted!"

And Deslauriers began by eulogising him, then in a mild fashion disparaged him, giving it out that he was a forgetful individual, and over-fond of money.

"I thought he was your friend, monsieur?"

"That does not prevent me from seeing his defects. Thus, he showed very little recognition of— how shall I put it?—the sympathy—"

Madame Arnoux was turning over the leaves of a large manuscript book.

She interrupted him in order to get him to explain a certain word.

He bent over her shoulder, and his face came so close to hers that he grazed her cheek. She blushed. This heightened colour inflamed Deslauriers, he hungrily kissed her head.

"What are you doing, Monsieur?" And, standing up against the wall, she compelled him to remain perfectly quiet under the glance of her large blue eyes glowing with anger.

"Listen to me! I love you!"

She broke into a laugh, a shrill, discouraging laugh. Deslauriers felt himself suffocating with anger. He restrained his feelings, and, with the look of a vanquished person imploring mercy:

"Ha! you are wrong! As for me, I would not go like him."

"Of whom, pray, are you talking?"

"Of Frederick."

"Ah! Monsieur Moreau troubles me little. I told you that!"

"Oh! forgive me! forgive me!" Then, drawling his words, in a sarcastic tone:

"I even imagined that you were sufficiently interested in him personally to learn with pleasure—"

She became quite pale. The ex-law-clerk added:

"He is going to be married."

"He!"

"In a month at latest, to Mademoiselle Roque, the daughter of M. Dambreuse's agent. He has even gone down to Nogent for no other purpose but that."

She placed her hand over her heart, as if at the shock of a great blow; but immediately she rang the bell. Deslauriers did not wait to be ordered to leave. When she turned round he had disappeared.

Madame Arnoux was gasping a little with the strain of her emotions. She drew near the window to get a breath of air.

On the other side of the street, on the foot-path, a packer in his shirt-sleeves was nailing down a trunk. Hackney-coaches passed. She closed the window-blinds and then came and sat down. As the high houses in the vicinity intercepted the sun's rays, the light of day stole coldly into the apartment. Her children had gone out; there was not a stir around her. It seemed as if she were utterly deserted.

"He is going to be married! Is it possible?"

And she was seized with a fit of nervous trembling.

"Why is this? Does it mean that I love him?"

Then all of a sudden:

"Why, yes; I love him—I love him!"

It seemed to her as if she were sinking into endless depths. The clock struck three. She listened to the vibrations of the sounds as they died away. And she remained on the edge of the armchair, with her eyeballs fixed and an unchanging smile on her face.

The same afternoon, at the same moment, Frederick and Mademoiselle Louise were walking in the garden belonging to M. Roque at the end of the island.

Old Catherine was watching them, some distance away. They were walking side by side and Frederick said:

"You remember when I brought you into the country?"

"How good you were to me!" she replied. "You assisted me in making sand-pies, in filling my watering-pot, and in rocking me in the swing!"

"All your dolls, who had the names of queens and marchionesses—what has become of them?"

"Really, I don't know!"

"And your pug Moricaud?"

"He's drowned, poor darling!"

"And the *Don Quixote* of which we coloured the engravings together?"

"I have it still!"

He recalled to her mind the day of her first communion, and how pretty she had been at vespers, with her white veil and her large wax-taper, whilst the girls were all taking their places in a row around the choir, and the bell was tinkling.

These memories, no doubt, had little charm for Mademoiselle Roque. She had not a word to say; and, a minute later:

"Naughty fellow! never to have written a line to me, even once!"

Frederick urged by way of excuse his numerous occupations.

"What, then, are you doing?"

He was embarrassed by the question; then he told her that he was studying politics.

"Ha!"

And without questioning him further:

"That gives you occupation; while as for me—!"

Then she spoke to him about the barrenness of her existence, as there was no-body she could go to see, and nothing to amuse her or distract her thoughts. She wished to go on horseback.

"The vicar maintains that this is improper for a young lady! How stupid these proprieties are! Long ago they allowed me to do whatever I pleased; now, they won't let me do anything!"

"Your father, however, is fond of you!"

"Yes; but—"

She heaved a sigh, which meant: "That is not enough to make me happy."

Then there was silence. They heard only the noise made by their boots in the sand, together with the murmur of falling water; for the Seine, above Nogent, is cut into two arms. That which turns the mills discharges in this place the super-abundance of its waves in order to unite further down with the natural course of the stream; and a person coming from the bridge could see at the right, on the other bank of the river, a grassy slope on which a white house looked down. At the left, in the meadow, a row of poplar-trees extended, and the horizon in front was bounded by a curve of the river. It was flat, like a mirror. Large insects hovered over the noiseless water. Tufts of reeds and rushes bordered it unevenly; all kinds of plants which happened to spring up there bloomed out in buttercups, caused yellow clusters to hang down, raised trees in distaff-shape with amaranth-blossoms, and made green rockets spring up at random. In an inlet of the river white water-lilies displayed themselves; and a row of ancient willows, in which wolf-traps were hidden, formed, on that side of the island, the sole protection of the garden.

In the interior, on this side, four walls with a slate coping enclosed the kitchen-garden, in which the square patches, recently dug up, looked like brown plates. The bell-glasses of the melons shone in a row on the narrow hotbed. The artichokes, the kidney-beans, the spinach, the carrots and the tomatoes succeeded each other till one reached a background where asparagus grew in such a fashion that it resembled a little wood of feathers.

All this piece of land had been under the Directory what is called "a folly." The trees had, since then, grown enormously. Clematis obstructed the hornbeams, the walks were covered with moss, brambles abounded on every side. Fragments of statues let their plaster crumble in the grass. The feet of anyone walking through the place got entangled in iron-wire work. There now remained of the pavilion only two apartments on the ground floor, with some blue paper hanging in shreds. Before the façade extended an arbour in the Italian style, in which a vine-tree was supported on columns of brick by a rail-work of sticks.

Soon they arrived at this spot; and, as the light fell through the irregular gaps on the green herbage, Frederick, turning his head on one side to speak to Louise, noticed the shadow of the leaves on her face.

She had in her red hair, stuck in her chignon, a needle, terminated by a glass bell in imitation of emerald, and, in spite of her mourning, she wore (so artless was her bad taste) straw slippers trimmed with pink satin—a vulgar curiosity probably bought at some fair.

He remarked this, and ironically congratulated her.

"Don't be laughing at me!" she replied.

Then surveying him altogether, from his grey felt hat to his silk stockings:

"What an exquisite you are!"

After this, she asked him to mention some works which she could read. He gave her the names of several; and she said:

"Oh! how learned you are!"

While yet very small, she had been smitten with one of those childish passions which have, at the same time, the purity of a religion and the violence of a natural instinct. He had been her comrade, her brother, her master, had diverted her mind, made her heart beat more quickly, and, without any desire for such a result, had poured out into the very depths of her being a latent and continuous intoxication. Then he had parted with her at the moment of a tragic crisis in her existence, when her mother had only just died, and these two separations had been mingled together. Absence had idealised him in her memory. He had come back with a sort of halo round his head; and she gave herself up ingenuously to the feelings of bliss she experienced at seeing him once more.

For the first time in his life Frederick felt himself beloved; and this new pleasure, which did not transcend the ordinary run of agreeable sensations, made his breast swell with so much emotion that he spread out his two arms while he flung back his head.

A large cloud passed across the sky.

"It is going towards Paris," said Louise. "You'd like to follow it—wouldn't you?"

"I! Why?"

"Who knows?"

And surveying him with a sharp look:

"Perhaps you have there" (she searched her mind for the appropriate phrase) "something to engage your affections."

"Oh! I have nothing to engage my affections there."

"Are you perfectly certain?"

"Why, yes, Mademoiselle, perfectly certain!"

In less than a year there had taken place in the young girl an extraordinary transformation, which astonished Frederick. After a minute's silence he added:

"We ought to 'thee' and 'thou' each other, as we used to do long ago—shall we do so?"

"No."

"Why?"

"Because—"

He persisted. She answered, with downcast face:

"I dare not!"

They had reached the end of the garden, which was close to the shell-bank. Frederick, in a spirit of boyish fun, began to send pebbles skimming over the water. She bade him sit down. He obeyed; then, looking at the waterfall:

" 'Tis like Niagara!" He began talking about distant countries and long voyages. The idea of making some herself exercised a fascination over her mind. She would not have been afraid either of tempests or of lions.

Seated close beside each other, they collected in front of them handfuls of sand, then, while they were chatting, they let it slip through their fingers, and the hot wind, which rose from the plains, carried to them in puffs odours of lavender, together with the smell of tar escaping from a boat behind the lock. The sun's rays fell on the cascade. The greenish blocks of stone in the little wall over which the water slipped looked as if they were covered with a silver gauze that was perpetually rolling itself out. A long strip of foam gushed forth at the foot with a harmonious murmur. Then it bubbled up, forming whirlpools and a thousand opposing currents, which ended by intermingling in a single limpid stream of water.

Louise said in a musing tone that she envied the existence of fishes:

"It must be so delightful to tumble about down there at your ease, and to feel yourself caressed on every side."

She shivered with sensuously enticing movements; but a voice exclaimed:

"Where are you?"

"Your maid is calling you," said Frederick.

"All right! all right!" Louise did not disturb herself.

"She will be angry," he suggested.

"It is all the same to me! and besides—" Mademoiselle Roque gave him to understand by a gesture that the girl was entirely subject to her will.

She arose, however, and then complained of a headache. And, as they were passing in front of a large cart-shed containing some faggots:

"Suppose we sat down there, *under shelter?*"

He pretended not to understand this dialectic expression, and even teased her about her accent. Gradually the corners of her mouth were compressed, she bit her lips; she stepped aside in order to sulk.

Frederick came over to her, swore he did not mean to annoy her, and that he was very fond of her.

"Is that true?" she exclaimed, looking at him with a smile which lighted up her entire face, smeared over a little with patches of bran.

He could not resist the sentiment of gallantry which was aroused in him by her fresh youthfulness, and he replied:

"Why should I tell you a lie? Have you any doubt about it, eh?" and, as he spoke, he passed his left hand round her waist.

A cry, soft as the cooing of a dove, leaped up from her throat. Her head fell back, she was going to faint, when he held her up. And his virtuous scruples were futile. At the sight of this maiden offering herself to him he was seized with fear. He assisted her to take a few steps slowly. He had ceased to address her in soothing words, and no longer caring to talk of anything save the most trifling subjects, he spoke to her about some of the principal figures in the society of Nogent.

Suddenly she repelled him, and in a bitter tone:

"You would not have the courage to run away with me!"

He remained motionless, with a look of utter amazement in his face. She burst into sobs, and hiding her face in his breast:

"Can I live without you?"

He tried to calm her emotion. She laid her two hands on his shoulders in order to get a better view of his face, and fixing her green eyes on his with an almost fierce tearfulness:

"Will you be my husband?"

"But," Frederick began, casting about in his inner consciousness for a reply. "Of course, I ask for nothing better."

At that moment M. Roque's cap appeared behind a lilac-tree.

He brought his young friend on a trip through the district in order to show off his property; and when Frederick returned, after two days' absence, he found three letters awaiting him at his mother's house.

The first was a note from M. Dambreuse, containing an invitation to dinner for the previous Tuesday. What was the occasion of this politeness? So, then, they had forgiven his prank.

The second was from Rosanette. She thanked him for having risked his life on her behalf. Frederick did not at first understand what she meant; finally, after a considerable amount of circumlocution, while appealing to his friendship, relying on his delicacy, as she put it, and going on her knees to him on account of the pressing necessity of the case, as she wanted bread, she asked him for a loan of five hundred francs. He at once made up his mind to supply her with the amount.

The third letter, which was from Deslauriers, spoke of the letter of attorney, and was long and obscure. The advocate had not yet taken any definite action. He urged his friend not to disturb himself: " 'Tis useless for you to come back!" even laying singular stress on this point.

Frederick got lost in conjectures of every sort; and he felt anxious to return to Paris. This assumption of a right to control his conduct excited in him a feeling of revolt.

Moreover, he began to experience that nostalgia of the boulevard; and then, his mother was pressing him so much, M. Roque kept revolving about him so constantly, and Mademoiselle Louise was so much attached to him, that it was no longer possible for him to avoid speedily declaring his intentions.

He wanted to think, and he would be better able to form a right estimate of things at a distance.

In order to assign a motive for his journey, Frederick invented a story; and he left home, telling everyone, and himself believing, that he would soon return.

Chapter XIII

ROSANETTE AS A LOVELY TURK

H IS RETURN TO PARIS GAVE HIM NO PLEASURE. IT WAS AN EVENING AT THE close of August. The boulevards seemed empty. The passers-by succeeded each other with scowling faces. Here and there a boiler of asphalt was smoking; several houses had their blinds entirely drawn. He made his way to his own residence in the city. He found the hangings covered with dust; and, while dining all alone, Frederick was seized with a strange feeling of forlornness; then his thoughts reverted to Mademoiselle Roque. The idea of being married no longer appeared to him preposterous. They might travel; they might go to Italy, to the East. And he saw her standing on a hillock, or gazing at a landscape, or else leaning on his arm in a Florentine gallery while she stood to look at the pictures. What a pleasure it would be to him merely to watch this good little creature expanding under the splendours of Art and Nature! When she had got free from the commonplace atmosphere in which she had lived, she would, in a little while, become a charming companion. M. Roque's wealth, moreover, tempted him. And yet he shrank from taking this step, regarding it as a weakness, a degradation.

But he was firmly resolved (whatever he might do) on changing his mode of life—that is to say, to lose his heart no more in fruitless passions; and he even hesitated about executing the commission with which he had been intrusted by Louise. This was to buy for her at Jacques Arnoux's establishment two large-sized statues of many colours representing negroes, like those which were at the Prefecture at Troyes. She knew the manufacturer's number, and would not have any other. Frederick was afraid that, if he went back to their house, he might once again fall a victim to his old passion.

These reflections occupied his mind during the entire evening; and he was just about to go to bed when a woman presented herself.

" 'Tis I," said Mademoiselle Vatnaz, with a laugh. "I have come in behalf of Rosanette."

So, then, they were reconciled?

"Good heavens, yes! I am not ill-natured, as you are well aware. And besides, the poor girl—it would take too long to tell you all about it."

In short, the Maréchale wanted to see him; she was waiting for an answer, her letter having travelled from Paris to Nogent. Mademoiselle Vatnaz did not know what was in it.

Then Frederick asked her how the Maréchale was going on.

He was informed that she was now *with* a very rich man, a Russian, Prince Tzernoukoff, who had seen her at the races in the Champ de Mars last summer.

"He has three carriages, a saddle-horse, livery servants, a groom got up in the English fashion, a country-house, a box at the Italian opera, and a heap of other things. There you are, my dear friend!"

And the Vatnaz, as if she had profited by this change of fortune, appeared gayer and happier. She took off her gloves and examined the furniture and the objects of virtù in the room. She mentioned their exact prices like a second-hand dealer. He ought to have consulted her in order to get them cheaper. Then she congratulated him on his good taste:

"Ha! this is pretty, exceedingly nice! There's nobody like you for these ideas."

The next moment, as her eyes fell on a door close to the pillar of the alcove:

"That's the way you let your friends out, eh?"

And, in a familiar fashion, she laid her finger on his chin. He trembled at the contact of her long hands, at the same time thin and soft. Round her wrists she wore an edging of lace, and on the body of her green dress lace embroidery, like a hussar. Her bonnet of black tulle, with borders hanging down, concealed her forehead a little. Her eyes shone underneath; an odour of patchouli escaped from her headbands. The carcel-lamp placed on a round table, shining down on her like the footlights of a theatre, made her jaw protrude.

She said to him, in an unctuous tone, while she drew forth from her purse three square slips of paper:

"You will take these from me?"

They were three tickets for Delmar's benefit performance.

"What! for him?"

"Certainly."

Mademoiselle Vatnaz, without giving a further explanation, added that she adored him more than ever. If she were to be believed, the comedian was now definitely classed amongst "the leading celebrities of the age." And it was not such or such a personage that he represented, but the very genius of France, the People. He had "the humanitarian spirit; he understood the priesthood of Art." Frederick, in order to put an end to these eulogies, gave her the money for the three seats.

"You need not say a word about this over the way. How late it is, good heavens! I must leave you. Ah! I was forgetting the address—'tis the Rue Grange-Batelier, number 14."

And, at the door:

"Good-bye, beloved man!"

"Beloved by whom?" asked Frederick. "What a strange woman!"

And he remembered that Dussardier had said to him one day, when talking about her:

"Oh, she's not much!" as if alluding to stories of a by no means edifying character.

Next morning he repaired to the Maréchale's abode. She lived in a new house, the spring-roller blinds of which projected into the street. At the head of each flight of stairs there was a mirror against the wall; before each window there was a flower-stand, and all over the steps extended a carpet of oilcloth; and when one got inside the door, the coolness of the staircase was refreshing.

It was a man-servant who came to open the door, a footman in a red waistcoat. On a bench in the anteroom a woman and two men, tradespeople, no doubt, were waiting as if in a minister's vestibule. At the left, the door of the dining-room, slightly ajar, afforded a glimpse of empty bottles on the sideboards, and napkins on the backs of chairs; and parallel with it ran a corridor in which gold-coloured sticks supported an espalier of roses. In the courtyard below, two boys with bare arms were scrubbing a landau. Their voices rose to Frederick's ears, mingled with the intermittent sounds made by a currycomb knocking against a stone.

The man-servant returned. "Madame will receive Monsieur," and he led Frederick through a second anteroom, and then into a large drawing-room hung with yellow brocatel with twisted fringes at the corners which were joined at the ceiling, and which seemed to be continued by flowerings of lustre resembling cables. No doubt there had been an entertainment there the night before. Some cigar-ashes had been allowed to remain on the pier-tables.

At last he found his way into a kind of boudoir with stained-glass windows, through which the sun shed a dim light. Trefoils of carved wood adorned the upper portions of the doors. Behind a balustrade, three purple mattresses formed a divan; and the stem of a narghileh made of platinum lay on top of it. Instead of a mirror, there was on the mantelpiece a pyramid-shaped whatnot, displaying on its shelves an entire collection of curiosities, old silver trumpets, Bohemian horns, jewelled clasps, jade studs, enamels, grotesque figures in china, and a little Byzantine virgin with a vermilion ape; and all this was mingled in a golden twilight with the bluish shade of the carpet, the mother-of-pearl reflections of the foot-stools, and the tawny hue of the walls covered with maroon leather. In the corners, on little pedestals, there were bronze vases containing clusters of flowers, which made the atmosphere heavy.

Rosanette presented herself, attired in a pink satin vest with white cashmere trousers, a necklace of piasters, and a red cap encircled with a branch of jasmine.

Frederick started back in surprise, then said he had brought the thing she had been speaking about, and he handed her the bank-note. She gazed at him in astonishment; and, as he still kept the note in his hand, without knowing where to put it:

"Pray take it!"

She seized it; then, as she flung it on the divan:

"You are very kind."

She wanted it to meet the rent of a piece of ground at Bellevue, which she paid in this way every year. Her unceremoniousness wounded Frederick's sensibility. However, so much the better! this would avenge him for the past.

"Sit down," said she. "There—closer." And in a grave tone: "In the first place, I have to thank you, my dear friend, for having risked your life."

"Oh! that's nothing!"

"What! Why, 'tis a very noble act!"—and the Maréchale exhibited an embarrassing sense of gratitude; for it must have been impressed upon her mind that the duel was entirely on account of Arnoux, as the latter, who believed it himself, was not likely to have resisted the temptation of telling her so.

"She is laughing at me, perhaps," thought Frederick.

He had nothing further to detain him, and, pleading that he had an appointment, he rose.

"Oh! no, stay!"

He resumed his seat, and presently complimented her on her costume.

She replied, with an air of dejection:

" 'Tis the Prince who likes me to dress in this fashion! And one must smoke such machines as that, too!" Rosanette added, pointing towards the narghileh. "Suppose we try the taste of it? Have you any objection?"

She procured a light, and, finding it hard to set fire to the tobacco, she began to stamp impatiently with her foot. Then a feeling of languor took possession of her; and she remained motionless on the divan, with a cushion under her arm and her body twisted a little on one side, one knee bent and the other leg straight out.

The long serpent of red morocco, which formed rings on the floor, rolled itself over her arm. She rested the amber mouthpiece on her lips, and gazed at Frederick while she blinked her eyes in the midst of the cloud of smoke that enveloped her. A gurgling sound came from her throat as she inhaled the fumes, and from time to time she murmured:

"The poor darling! the poor pet!"

He tried to find something of an agreeable nature to talk about. The thought of Vatnaz recurred to his memory.

He remarked that she appeared to him very ladylike.

"Yes, upon my word," replied the Maréchale. "She is very lucky in having me, that same lady!"—without adding another word, so much reserve was there in their conversation.

Each of them felt a sense of constraint, something that formed a barrier to confidential relations between them. In fact, Rosanette's vanity had been flattered by the duel, of which she believed herself to be the occasion. Then, she was very much astonished that he did not hasten to take advantage of his achievement; and, in order to compel him to return to her, she had invented this story that she wanted five hundred francs. How was it that Frederick did not ask for a little love from her in return? This was a piece of refinement that filled her with amazement, and, with a gush of emotion, she said to him:

"Will you come with us to the sea-baths?"

"What does 'us' mean?"

"Myself and my bird. I'll make you pass for a cousin of mine, as in the old comedies."

"A thousand thanks!"

"Well, then, you will take lodgings near ours."

The idea of hiding himself from a rich man humiliated him.

"No! that is impossible."

"Just as you please!"

Rosanette turned away with tears in her eyes. Frederick noticed this, and in order to testify the interest which he took in her, he said that he was delighted to see her at last in a comfortable position.

She shrugged her shoulders. What, then, was troubling her? Was it, perchance, that she was not loved.

"Oh! as for me, I have always people to love me!"

She added:

"It remains to be seen in what way."

Complaining that she was "suffocating with the heat," the Maréchale unfastened her vest; and, without any other garment round her body, save her silk chemise, she leaned her head on his shoulder so as to awaken his tenderness.

A man of less introspective egoism would not have bestowed a thought at such a moment on the possibility of the Vicomte, M. de Comaing, or anyone else appearing on the scene. But Frederick had been too many times the dupe of these very glances to compromise himself by a fresh humiliation.

She wished to know all about his relationships and his amusements. She even enquired about his financial affairs, and offered to lend him money if he wanted it. Frederick, unable to stand it any longer, took up his hat.

"I'm off, my pet! I hope you'll enjoy yourself thoroughly down there. *Au revoir!*"

She opened her eyes wide; then, in a dry tone:

"*An revoir!*"

He made his way out through the yellow drawing-room, and through the second anteroom. There was on the table, between a vase full of visiting-cards and an inkstand, a chased silver chest. It was Madame Arnoux's. Then he experienced a feeling of tenderness, and, at the same time, as it were, the scandal of a profanation. He felt a longing to raise his hands towards it, and to open it. He was afraid of being seen, and went away.

Frederick was virtuous. He did not go back to the Arnouxs' house. He sent his man-servant to buy the two negroes, having given him all the necessary directions; and the case containing them set forth the same evening for Nogent. Next morning, as he was repairing to Deslauriers' lodgings, at the turn where the Rue Vivienne opened out on the boulevard, Madame Arnoux presented herself before him face to face.

The first movement of each of them was to draw back; then the same smile came to the lips of both, and they advanced to meet each other. For a minute, neither of them uttered a single word.

The sunlight fell round her, and her oval face, her long eyelashes, her black lace shawl, which showed the outline of her shoulders, her gown of shot silk, the bouquet of violets at the corner of her bonnet; all seemed to him to possess extraordinary magnificence. An infinite softness poured itself out of her beautiful eyes; and in a faltering voice, uttering at random the first words that came to his lips:

"How is Arnoux?"

"Well, I thank you!"

"And your children?"

"They are very well!"

"Ah! ah! What fine weather we are getting, are we not?"

"Splendid, indeed!"

"You're going out shopping?"

And, with a slow inclination of the head:

"Good-bye!"

She put out her hand, without having spoken one word of an affectionate description, and did not even invite him to dinner at her house. No matter! He would not have given this interview for the most delightful of adventures; and he pondered over its sweetness as he proceeded on his way.

Deslauriers, surprised at seeing him, dissembled his spite; for he cherished still through obstinacy some hope with regard to Madame Arnoux; and he had written to Frederick to prolong his stay in the country in order to be free in his manouevres.

He informed Frederick, however, that he had presented himself at her house in order to ascertain if their contract stipulated for a community of property between husband and wife: in that case, proceedings might be taken against the wife; "and she put on a queer face when I told her about your marriage."

"Now, then! What an invention!"

"It was necessary in order to show that you wanted your own capital! A person who was indifferent would not have been attacked with the species of fainting fit that she had."

"Really?" exclaimed Frederick.

"Ha! my fine fellow, you are betraying yourself! Come! be honest!"

A feeling of nervous weakness stole over Madame Arnoux's lover.

"Why, no! I assure you! upon my word of honour!"

These feeble denials ended by convincing Deslauriers. He congratulated his friend, and asked him for some details. Frederick gave him none, and even resisted a secret yearning to concoct a few. As for the mortgage, he told the other to do nothing about it, but to wait. Deslauriers thought he was wrong on this point, and remonstrated with him in rather a churlish fashion.

He was, besides, more gloomy, malignant, and irascible than ever. In a year, if fortune did not change, he would embark for America or blow out his brains. Indeed, he appeared to be in such a rage against everything, and so uncompromising in his radicalism, that Frederick could not keep from saying to him:

"Here you are going on in the same way as Sénécal!"

Deslauriers, at this remark, informed him that that individual to whom he alluded had been discharged from Sainte-Pelagie, the magisterial investigation having failed to supply sufficient evidence, no doubt, to justify his being sent for trial.

Dussardier was so much overjoyed at the release of Sénécal, that he wanted to invite his friends to come and take punch with him, and begged of Frederick to be one of the party, giving the latter, at the same time, to understand that he would be found in the company of Hussonnet, who had proved himself a very good friend to Sénécal.

In fact, the *Flambard* had just become associated with a business establishment whose prospectus contained the following references: "Vineyard Agency. Office of Publicity. Debt Recovery and Intelligence Office, etc." But the Bohemian was afraid that his connection with trade might be prejudicial to his literary reputation, and he had accordingly taken the mathematician to keep the accounts. Although the situation was a poor one, Sénécal would but for it have died of starvation. Not wishing to mortify the worthy shopman, Frederick accepted his invitation.

Dussardier, three days beforehand, had himself waxed the red floor of his garret, beaten the armchair, and knocked off the dust from the chimney-piece, on which might be seen under a globe an alabaster timepiece between a stalactite and a cocoa-nut. As his two chandeliers and his chamber candlestick were not sufficient, he had borrowed two more candlesticks from the doorkeeper; and these five lights shone on the top of the chest of drawers, which was covered with three napkins in order that it might be fit to have placed on it in such a way as to look attractive some macaroons, biscuits, a fancy cake, and a dozen bottles of beer. At the opposite side, close to the wall, which was hung with yellow paper, there was a little mahogany bookcase containing the *Fables of Lachambeaudie,* the *Mysteries of Paris,* and Norvins' *Napoleon*—and, in the middle of the alcove, the face of Béranger was smiling in a rosewood frame.

The guests (in addition to Deslauriers and Sénécal) were an apothecary who had just been admitted, but who had not enough capital to start in business for himself, a young man of his own house, a town-traveller in wines, an architect, and a gentleman employed in an insurance office. Regimbart had not been able to come. Regret was expressed at his absence.

They welcomed Frederick with a great display of sympathy, as they all knew through Dussardier what he had said at M. Dambreuse's house. Sénécal contented himself with putting out his hand in a dignified manner.

He remained standing near the chimney-piece. The others seated, with their pipes in their mouths, listened to him, while he held forth on universal suffrage, from which he predicted as a result the triumph of Democracy and the practical application of the principles of the Gospel. However, the hour was at hand. The banquets of the party of reform were becoming more numerous in the provinces. Piedmont, Naples, Tuscany—

" 'Tis true," said Deslauriers, interrupting him abruptly. "This cannot last longer!"

And he began to draw a picture of the situation. We had sacrificed Holland to obtain from England the recognition of Louis Philippe; and this precious English alliance was lost, owing to the Spanish marriages. In Switzerland, M. Guizot, in tow with the Austrian, maintained the treaties of 1815. Prussia, with her Zollverein, was preparing embarrassments for us. The Eastern question was still pending.

"The fact that the Grand Duke Constantine sends presents to M. d'Aumale is no reason for placing confidence in Russia. As for home affairs, never have so many blunders, such stupidity, been witnessed. The Government no longer even keeps up its majority. Everywhere, indeed, according to the well-known expression, it is naught! naught! naught! And in the teeth of such public scandals," continued the advocate, with his arms akimbo, "they declare themselves satisfied!"

The allusion to a notorious vote called forth applause. Dussardier uncorked a bottle of beer; the froth splashed on the curtains. He did not mind it. He filled the pipes, cut the cake, offered each of them a slice of it, and several times went downstairs to see whether the punch was coming up; and ere long they lashed themselves up into a state of excitement, as they all felt equally exasperated against Power. Their rage was of a violent character for no other reason save that they hated injustice, and they mixed up with legitimate grievances the most idiotic complaints.

The apothecary groaned over the pitiable condition of our fleet. The insurance agent could not tolerate Marshal Soult's two sentinels. Deslauriers denounced the Jesuits, who had just installed themselves publicly at Lille. Sénécal execrated M. Cousin much more; for eclecticism, by teaching that certitude can be deduced from reason, developed selfishness and destroyed solidarity. The traveller in wines, knowing very little about these matters, remarked in a very loud tone that he had forgotten many infamies:

"The royal carriage on the Northern line must have cost eighty thousand francs. Who'll pay the amount?"

"Aye, who'll pay the amount?" repeated the clerk, as angrily as if this amount had been drawn out of his own pocket.

Then followed recriminations against the lynxes of the Bourse and the corruption of officials. According to Sénécal they ought to go higher up, and lay the blame, first of all, on the princes who had revived the morals of the Regency period.

"Have you not lately seen the Duc de Montpensier's friends coming back from Vincennes, no doubt in a state of intoxication, and disturbing with their songs the workmen of the Faubourg Saint-Antoine?"

"There was even a cry of 'Down with the thieves!' " said the apothecary. "I was there, and I joined in the cry!"

"So much the better! The people are at last waking up since the Teste-Cubières case."

"For my part, that case caused me some pain," said Dussardier, "because it imputed dishonour to an old soldier!"

"Do you know," Sénécal went on, "what they have discovered at the Duchesse de Praslin's house——?"

But here the door was sent flying open with a kick. Hussonnet entered.

"Hail, messeigneurs," said he, as he seated himself on the bed.

No allusion was made to his article, which he was sorry, however, for having written, as the Maréchale had sharply reprimanded him on account of it.

He had just seen at the Théâtre de Dumas the *Chevalier de Maison-Rouge,* and declared that it seemed to him a stupid play.

Such a criticism surprised the democrats, as this drama, by its tendency, or rather by its scenery, flattered their passions. They protested. Sénécal, in order to bring this discussion to a close, asked whether the play served the cause of Democracy.

"Yes, perhaps; but it is written in a style—"

"Well, then, 'tis a good play. What is style? 'Tis the idea!"

And, without allowing Frederick to say a word:

"Now, I was pointing out that in the Praslin case—"

Hussonnet interrupted him:

"Ha! here's another worn-out trick! I'm disgusted at it!"

"And others as well as you," returned Deslauriers.

"It has only got five papers taken. Listen while I read this paragraph."

And drawing his note-book out of his pocket, he read:

" 'We have, since the establishment of the best of republics, been subjected to twelve hundred and twenty-nine press prosecutions, from which the results to the writers have been imprisonment extending over a period of three thousand one hundred and forty-one years, and the light sum of seven million one hundred and ten thousand five hundred francs by way of fine." That's charming, eh?"

They all sneered bitterly.

Frederick, incensed against the others, broke in:

"*The Democratie Pacifique* has had proceedings taken against it on account of its feuilleton, a novel entitled *The Woman's Share.*"

"Come! that's good," said Hussonnet. "Suppose they prevented us from having our share of the women!"

"But what is it that's not prohibited?" exclaimed Deslauriers. "To smoke in the Luxembourg is prohibited; to sing the Hymn to Pius IX is prohibited!"

"And the typographers' banquet has been interdicted," a voice cried, with a thick articulation.

It was that of an architect, who had sat concealed in the shade of the alcove, and who had remained silent up to that moment. He added that, the week before, a man named Rouget had been convicted of offering insults to the king.

"That gurnet is fried," said Hussonnet.

This joke appeared so improper to Sénécal, that he reproached Hussonnet for defending the Juggler of the Hotel de Ville, the friend of the traitor Dumouriez.

"I? quite the contrary!"

He considered Louis Philippe, commonplace, one of the National Guard types of men, all that savoured most of the provision-shop and the cotton night-cap! And laying his hand on his heart, the Bohemian gave utterance to the rhetorical phrases:

"It is always with a new pleasure. . . . Polish nationality will not perish. . . . Our great works will be pursued. . . . Give me some money for my little family. . . ."

They all laughed hugely, declaring that he was a delightful fellow, full of wit. Their delight was redoubled at the sight of the bowl of punch which was brought in by the keeper of a café.

The flames of the alcohol and those of the wax-candles soon heated the apartment, and the light from the garret, passing across the courtyard, illuminated the side of an opposite roof with the flue of a chimney, whose black outlines could be traced through the darkness of night. They talked in very loud tones all at the same time. They had taken off their coats; they gave blows to the furniture; they touched glasses.

Hussonnet exclaimed:

"Send up some great ladies, in order that this may be more Tour de Nesles, have more local colouring, and be more Rembrandtesque, gadzooks!"

And the apothecary, who kept stirring about the punch indefinitely, began to sing with expanded chest:

> *"I've two big oxen in my stable,*
> *Two big white oxen—"*

Sénécal laid his hand on the apothecary's mouth; he did not like disorderly conduct; and the lodgers pressed their faces against the window-panes, surprised at the unwonted uproar that was taking place in Dussardier's room.

The honest fellow was happy, and said that this recalled to his mind their little parties on the Quai Napoleon in days gone by; however, they missed many who used to be present at these reunions, "Pellerin, for instance."

"We can do without him," observed Frederick.

And Deslauriers enquired about Martinon.

"What has become of that interesting gentleman?"

Frederick, immediately giving vent to the ill-will which he bore to Martinon, attacked his mental capacity, his character, his false elegance, his entire personality. He was a perfect specimen of an upstart peasant! The new aristocracy, the mercantile class, was not as good as the old—the nobility. He maintained this, and the democrats expressed their approval, as if he were a member of the one class, and they were in the habit of visiting the other. They were charmed with him. The apothecary compared him to M. d'Alton Shée, who, though a peer of France, defended the cause of the people.

The time had come for taking their departure. They all separated with great handshakings. Dussardier, in a spirit of affectionate solicitude, saw Frederick and Deslauriers home. As soon as they were in the street, the advocate assumed a thoughtful air, and, after a moment's silence:

"You have a great grudge, then, against Pellerin?"

Frederick did not hide his rancour.

The painter, in the meantime, had withdrawn the notorious picture from the show-window. A person should not let himself be put out by trifles. What was the good of making an enemy for himself?

"He has given way to a burst of ill-temper, excusable in a man who hasn't a sou. You, of course, can't understand that!"

And, when Deslauriers had gone up to his own apartments, the shopman did not part with Frederick. He even urged his friend to buy the portrait. In fact, Pellerin, abandoning the hope of being able to intimidate him, had got round them so that they might use their influence to obtain the thing for him.

Deslauriers spoke about it again, and pressed him on the point, urging that the artist's claims were reasonable.

"I am sure that for a sum of, perhaps, five hundred francs—"

"Oh, give it to him! Wait! here it is!" said Frederick.

The picture was brought the same evening. It appeared to him a still more atrocious daub than when he had seen it first. The half-tints and the shades were darkened under the excessive retouchings, and they seemed obscured when brought into relation with the lights, which, having remained very brilliant here and there, destroyed the harmony of the entire picture.

Frederick revenged himself for having had to pay for it by bitterly disparaging it. Deslauriers believed in Frederick's statement on the point, and expressed approval of his conduct, for he had always been ambitious of constituting a phalanx of which he would be the leader. Certain men take delight in making their friends do things which are disagreeable to them.

Meanwhile, Frederick did not renew his visits to the Dambreuses. He lacked the capital for the investment. He would have to enter into endless explanations on the subject; he hesitated about making up his mind. Perhaps he was in the right. Nothing was certain now, the coal-mining speculation any more than other things. He would have to give up society of that sort. The end of the matter was that Deslauriers was dissuaded from having anything further to do with the undertaking.

From sheer force of hatred he had grown virtuous, and again he preferred Frederick in a position of mediocrity. In this way he remained his friend's equal and in more intimate relationship with him.

Mademoiselle Roque's commission had been very badly executed. Her father wrote to him, supplying him with the most precise directions, and concluded his letter with this piece of foolery: "At the risk of giving you *nigger on the brain!*"

Frederick could not do otherwise than call upon the Arnouxs', once more. He went to the warehouse, where he could see nobody. The firm being in a tottering condition, the clerks imitated the carelessness of their master.

He brushed against the shelves laden with earthenware, which filled up the entire space in the centre of the establishment; then, when he reached the lower end, facing the counter, he walked with a more noisy tread in order to make himself heard.

The portières parted, and Madame Arnoux appeared.

"What! you here! you!"

"Yes." she faltered, with some agitation. "I was looking for——"

He saw her handkerchief near the desk, and guessed that she had come down to her husband's warehouse to have an account given to her as to the business, to clear up some matter that caused her anxiety.

"But perhaps there is something you want?" said she.

"A mere nothing, madame."

"These shop-assistants are intolerable! they are always out of the way."

They ought not to be blamed. On the contrary, he congratulated himself on the circumstance.

She gazed at him in an ironical fashion.

"Well, and this marriage?"

"What marriage?"

"Your own!"

"Mine? I'll never marry as long as I live!"

She made a gesture as if to contradict his words.

"Though, indeed, such things must be, after all? We take refuge in the commonplace, despairing of ever realising the beautiful existence of which we have dreamed."

"All your dreams, however, are not so—candid!"

"What do you mean?"

"When you drive to races with women!"

He cursed the Maréchale. Then something recurred to his memory.

"But it was you begged of me yourself to see her at one time in the interest of Arnoux."

She replied with a shake of her head:

"And you take advantage of it to amuse yourself?"

"Good God! let us forget all these foolish things!"

" 'Tis right, since you are going to be married."

And she stifled a sigh, while she bit her lips.

Then he exclaimed:

"But I tell you again I am not! Can you believe that I, with my intellectual requirements, my habits, am going to bury myself in the provinces in order to play cards, look after masons, and walk about in wooden shoes? What object, pray, could I have for taking such a step? You've been told that she was rich, haven't you? Ah! what do I care about money? Could I, after yearning long for that which is most lovely, tender, enchanting, a sort of Paradise under a human form, and having found this sweet ideal at last, when this vision hides every other from my view—"

And taking her head between his two hands, he began to kiss her on the eyelids, repeating:

"No! no! no! never will I marry! never! never!"

She submitted to these caresses, her mingled amazement and delight having bereft her of the power of motion.

The door of the storeroom above the staircase fell back, and she remained with outstretched arms, as if to bid him keep silence. Steps drew near. Then some one said from behind the door:

"Is Madame there?"

"Come in!"

Madame Arnoux had her elbow on the counter, and was twisting about a pen between her fingers quietly when the book-keeper threw aside the portière.

Frederick started up, as if on the point of leaving.

"Madame, I have the honour to salute you. The set will be ready—will it not? I may count on this?"

She made no reply. But by thus silently becoming his accomplice in the deception, she made his face flush with the crimson glow of adultery.

On the following day he paid her another visit. She received him; and, in order to follow up the advantage he had gained, Frederick immediately, without any preamble, attempted to offer some justification for the accidental meeting in the Champ de Mars. It was the merest chance that led to his being in that woman's company. While admitting that she was pretty—which really was not the case—how could she for even a moment absorb his thoughts, seeing that he loved another woman?

"You know it well—I told you it was so!"

Madame Arnoux hung down her head.

"I am sorry you said such a thing."

"Why?"

"The most ordinary proprieties now demand that I should see you no more!"

He protested that his love was of an innocent character. The past ought to be a guaranty as to his future conduct. He had of his own accord made it a point of honour with himself not to disturb her existence, not to deafen her with his complaints.

"But yesterday my heart overflowed."

"We ought not to let our thoughts dwell on that moment, my friend!"

And yet, where would be the harm in two wretched beings mingling their griefs?

"For, indeed, you are not happy any more than I am! Oh! I know you. You have no one who responds to your craving for affection, for devotion. I will do anything you wish! I will not offend you! I swear to you that I will not!"

And he let himself fall on his knees, in spite of himself, giving way beneath the weight of the feelings that oppressed his heart.

"Rise!" she said; "I desire you to do so!"

And she declared in an imperious tone that if he did not comply with her wish, she would never see him again.

"Ha! I defy you to do it!" returned Frederick. "What is there for me to do in the world? Other men strive for riches, celebrity, power! But I have no profession; you are my exclusive occupation, my whole wealth, the object, the centre of my existence and of my thoughts. I can no more live without you than without the air of heaven! Do you not feel the aspiration of my soul ascending towards yours, and that they must intermingle, and that I am dying on your account?"

Madame Arnoux began to tremble in every limb.

"Oh! leave me, I beg of you?"

The look of utter confusion in her face made him pause. Then he advanced a step. But she drew, back, with her two hands clasped.

"Leave me in the name of Heaven, for mercy's sake!"

And Frederick loved her so much that he went away.

Soon afterwards, he was filled with rage against himself, declared in his own mind that he was an idiot, and, after the lapse of twenty-four hours, returned.

Madame was not there. He remained at the head of the stairs, stupefied with anger and indignation. Arnoux appeared, and informed Frederick that his wife had, that very morning, gone out to take up her residence at a little country-house of which he had become tenant at Auteuil, as he had given up possession of the house at Saint-Cloud.

"This is another of her whims. No matter, as she is settled at last; and myself, too, for that matter, so much the better. Let us dine together this evening, will you?"

Frederick pleaded as an excuse some urgent business; then he hurried away of his own accord to Auteuil.

Madame Arnoux allowed an exclamation of joy to escape her lips. Then all his bitterness vanished.

He did not say one word about his love. In order to inspire her with confidence

in him, he even exaggerated his reserve; and on his asking whether he might call
again, she replied: "Why, of course!" putting out her hand, which she withdrew
the next moment.

From that time forth, Frederick increased his visits. He promised extra fares to
the cabman who drove him. But often he grew impatient at the slow pace of the
horse, and, alighting on the ground, he would make a dash after an omnibus, and
climb to the top of it out of breath. Then with what disdain he surveyed the faces
of those around him, who were not going to see her!

He could distinguish her house at a distance, with an enormous honeysuckle
covering, on one side, the planks of the roof. It was a kind of Swiss châlet, painted
red, with a balcony outside. In the garden there were three old chestnut-trees, and
on a rising ground in the centre might be seen a parasol made of thatch, held up by
the trunk of a tree. Under the slatework lining the walls, a big vine-tree, badly fastened, hung from one place to another after the fashion of a rotten cable. The gate-
bell, which it was rather hard to pull, was slow in ringing, and a long time always
elapsed before it was answered. On each occasion he experienced a pang of sus-
pense, a fear born of irresolution.

Then his ears would be greeted with the pattering of the servant-maid's slippers over the gravel, or else Madame Arnoux herself would make her appearance.
One day he came up behind her just as she was stooping down in the act of gathering violets.

Her daughter's capricious disposition had made it necessary to send the girl to
a convent. Her little son was at school every afternoon. Arnoux was now in the
habit of taking prolonged luncheons at the Palais-Royal with Regimbart and their
friend Compain. They gave themselves no bother about anything that occurred, no
matter how disagreeable it might be.

It was clearly understood between Frederick and her that they should not belong to each other. By this convention they were preserved from danger, and they
found it easier to pour out their hearts to each other.

She told him all about her early life at Chartres, which she spent with her
mother, her devotion when she had reached her twelfth year, then her passion for
music, when she used to sing till nightfall in her little room, from which the ramparts could be seen.

He related to her how melancholy broodings had haunted him at college, and
how a woman's face shone brightly in the cloudland of his imagination, so that,
when he first laid eyes upon her, he felt that her features were quite familiar to him.

These conversations, as a rule, covered only the years during which they had
been acquainted with each other. He recalled to her recollection insignificant
details—the colour of her dress at a certain period, a woman whom they had met

on a certain day, what she had said on another occasion; and she replied, quite
astonished:

"Yes, I remember!"

Their tastes, their judgments, were the same, Often one of them, when listening to the other, exclaimed:

"That's the way with me."

And the other replied:

"And with me, too!"

Then there were endless complaints about Providence:

"Why was it not the will of Heaven? If we had only met—!"

"Ah! if I had been younger!" she sighed.

"No, but if I had been a little older."

And they pictured to themselves a life entirely given up to love, sufficiently
rich to fill up the vastest solitudes, surpassing all other joys, defying all forms of
wretchedness, in which the hours would glide away in a continual outpouring of
their own emotions, and which would be as bright and glorious as the palpitating
splendour of the stars.

They were nearly always standing at the top of the stairs exposed to the free
air of heaven. The tops of trees yellowed by the autumn raised their crests in front
of them at unequal heights up to the edge of the pale sky; or else they walked on
to the end of the avenue into a summer-house whose only furniture was a couch of
grey canvas. Black specks stained the glass; the walls exhaled a mouldy smell; and
they remained there chatting freely about all sorts of topics—anything that happened to arise—in a spirit of hilarity. Sometimes the rays of the sun, passing
through the Venetian blind, extended from the ceiling down to the flagstones like
the strings of a lyre. Particles of dust whirled amid these luminous bars. She
amused herself by dividing them with her hand. Frederick gently caught hold of
her; and he gazed on the twinings of her veins, the grain of her skin, and the form
of her fingers. Each of those fingers of hers was for him more than a thing—
almost a person.

She gave him her gloves, and, the week after, her handkerchief. She called him
"Frederick;" he called her "Marie," adoring this name, which, as he said, was expressly made to be uttered with a sigh of ecstasy, and which seemed to contain
clouds of incense and scattered heaps of roses.

They soon came to an understanding as to the days on which he would call to
see her; and, leaving the house as if by mere chance, she walked along the road to
meet him.

She made no effort whatever to excite his love, lost in that listlessness which is
characteristic of intense happiness. During the whole season she wore a brown silk

dressing-gown with velvet borders of the same colour, a large garment, which united the indolence of her attitudes and her grave physiognomy. Besides, she had just reached the autumnal period of womanhood, in which reflection is combined with tenderness, in which the beginning of maturity colours the face with a more intense flame, when strength of feeling mingles with experience of life, and when, having completely expanded, the entire being overflows with a richness in harmony with its beauty. Never had she possessed more sweetness, more leniency. Secure in the thought that she would not err, she abandoned herself to a sentiment which seemed to her won by her sorrows. And, moreover, it was so innocent and fresh! What an abyss lay between the coarseness of Arnoux and the adoration of Frederick!

He trembled at the thought that by an imprudent word he might lose all that he had gained, saying to himself that an opportunity might be found again, but that a foolish step could never be repaired. He wished that she should give herself rather than that he should take her. The assurance of being loved by her delighted him like a foretaste of possession, and then the charm of her person troubled his heart more than his senses. It was an indefinable feeling of bliss, a sort of intoxication that made him lose sight of the possibility of having his happiness completed. Apart from her, he was consumed with longing.

Ere long the conversations were interrupted by long spells of silence. Sometimes a species of sexual shame made them blush in each other's presence. All the precautions they took to hide their love only unveiled it; the stronger it grew, the more constrained they became in manner. The effect of this dissimulation was to intensify their sensibility. They experienced a sensation of delight at the odour of moist leaves; they could not endure the east wind; they got irritated without any apparent cause, and had melancholy forebodings. The sound of a footstep, the creaking of the wainscoting, filled them with as much terror as if they had been guilty. They felt as if they were being pushed towards the edge of a chasm. They were surrounded by a tempestuous atmosphere; and when complaints escaped Frederick's lips, she made accusations against herself.

"Yes, I am doing wrong. I am acting as if I were a coquette! Don't come any more!"

Then he would repeat the same oaths, to which on each occasion she listened with renewed pleasure.

His return to Paris, and the fuss occasioned by New Year's Day, interrupted their meetings to some extent. When he returned, he had an air of greater self-confidence. Every moment she went out to give orders, and in spite of his entreaties she received every visitor that called during the evening.

After this, they engaged in conversations about Léotade, M. Guizot, the Pope, the insurrection at Palermo, and the banquet of the Twelfth Arrondissement, which had caused some disquietude. Frederick eased his mind by railing against Power, for he longed, like Deslauriers, to turn the whole world upside down, so soured had he now become. Madame Arnoux, on her side, had become sad.

Her husband, indulging in displays of wild folly, was flirting with one of the girls in his pottery works, the one who was known as "the girl from Bordeaux." Madame Arnoux was herself informed about it by Frederick. He wanted to make use of it as an argument, "inasmuch as she was the victim of deception."

"Oh! I'm not much concerned about it," she said.

This admission on her part seemed to him to strengthen the intimacy between them. Would Arnoux be seized with mistrust with regard to them?

"No! not now!"

She told him that, one evening, he had left them talking together, and had afterwards come back again and listened behind the door, and as they both were chatting at the time of matters that were of no consequence, he had lived since then in a state of complete security.

"With good reason, too—is that not so?" said Frederick bitterly.

"Yes, no doubt!"

It would have been better for him not to have given so risky an answer.

One day she was not at home at the hour when he usually called. To him there seemed to be a sort of treason in this.

He was next displeased at seeing the flowers which he used to bring her always placed in a glass of water.

"Where, then, would you like me to put them?"

"Oh! not there! However, they are not so cold there as they would be near your heart!"

Not long afterwards he reproached her for having been at the Italian opera the night before without having given him a previous intimation of her intention to go there. Others had seen, admired, fallen in love with her, perhaps; Frederick was fastening on those suspicions of his merely in order to pick a quarrel with her, to torment her; for he was beginning to hate her, and the very least he might expect was that she should share in his sufferings!

One afternoon, towards the middle of February, he surprised her in a state of great mental excitement. Eugène had been complaining about his sore throat. The doctor had told her, however, that it was a trifling ailment—a bad cold, an attack of influenza. Frederick was astonished at the child's stupefied look. Nevertheless, he reassured the mother, and brought forward the cases of several children of the same age who had been attacked with similar ailments, and had been speedily cured.

"Really?"

"Why, yes, assuredly!"

"Oh! how good you are!"

And she caught his hand. He clasped hers tightly in his.

"Oh! let it go!"

"What does it signify, when it is to one who sympathises with you that you offer it? You place every confidence in me when I speak of these things, but you distrust me when I talk to you about my love!"

"I don't doubt you on that point, my poor friend!"

"Why this distrust, as if I were a wretch capable of abusing—"

"Oh! no!—"

"If I had only a proof!—"

"What proof?"

"The proof that a person might give to the first comer—what you have granted to myself!"

And he recalled to her recollection how, on one occasion, they had gone out together, on a winter's twilight, when there was a fog. This seemed now a long time ago. What, then, was to prevent her from showing herself on his arm before the whole world without any fear on her part, and without any mental reservation on his, not having anyone around them who could importune them?

"Be it so!" she said, with a promptness of decision that at first astonished Frederick.

But he replied, in a lively fashion:

"Would you like me to wait at the corner of the Rue Tronchet and the Rue de la Ferme?"

"Good heavens, my friend!" faltered Madame Arnoux.

Without giving her time to reflect, he added:

"Next Tuesday, I suppose?"

"Tuesday?"

"Yes, between two and three o'clock."

"I will be there!"

And she turned aside her face with a movement of shame. Frederick placed his lips on the nape of her neck.

"Oh! this is not right," she said. "You will make me repent."

He turned away, dreading the fickleness which is customary with women. Then, on the threshold, he murmured softly, as if it were a thing that was thoroughly understood:

"On Tuesday!"

She lowered her beautiful eyes in a cautious and resigned fashion.

Frederick had a plan arranged in his mind.

He hoped that, owing to the rain or the sun, he might get her to stop under some doorway, and that, once there, she would go into some house. The difficulty was to find one that would suit.

He made a search, and about the middle of the Rue Tronchet he read, at a distance on a signboard, "Furnished apartments."

The waiter, divining his object, showed him immediately above the ground-floor a room and a closet with two exits. Frederick took it for a month, and paid in advance. Then he went into three shops to buy the rarest perfumery. He got a piece of imitation guipure, which was to replace the horrible red cotton foot-coverlets; he selected a pair of blue satin slippers, only the fear of appearing coarse checked the amount of his purchases. He came back with them; and with more devotion than those who are erecting processional altars, he altered the position of the furniture, arranged the curtains himself, put heather in the fireplace, and covered the chest of drawers with violets. He would have liked to pave the entire apartment with gold. "To-morrow is the time," said he to himself. "Yes, to-morrow! I am not dreaming!" and he felt his heart throbbing violently under the delirious excitement begotten by his anticipations. Then, when everything was ready, he carried off the key in his pocket, as if the happiness which slept there might have flown away along with it.

A letter from his mother was awaiting him when he reached his abode:

"Why such a long absence? Your conduct is beginning to look ridiculous. I understand your hesitating more or less at first with regard to this union. However, think well upon it."

And she put the matter before him with the utmost clearness: an income of forty-five thousand francs. However, "people were talking about it;" and M. Roque was waiting for a definite answer. As for the young girl, her position was truly most embarrassing.

"She is deeply attached to you."

Frederick threw aside the letter even before he had finished reading it, and opened another epistle which came from Deslauriers.

"Dear Old Boy—The *pear* is ripe. In accordance with your promise, we may count on you. We meet to-morrow at daybreak, in the Place du Panthéon. Drop into the Café Soufflot. It is necessary for me to have a chat with you before the manifestation takes place."

"Oh! I know them, with their manifestations! A thousand thanks! I have a more agreeable appointment."

And on the following morning, at eleven o'clock, Frederick had left the house. He wanted to give one last glance at the preparations. Then, who could tell but that, by some chance or other, she might be at the place of meeting before him? As he emerged from the Rue Tronchet, he heard a great clamour behind the Madeleine. He pressed forward, and saw at the far end of the square, to the left, a number of men in blouses and well-dressed people.

In fact, a manifesto published in the newspapers had summoned to this spot all who had subscribed to the banquet of the Reform Party. The Ministry had, almost without a moment's delay, posted up a proclamation prohibiting the meeting. The Parliamentary Opposition had, on the previous evening, disclaimed any connection with it; but the patriots, who were unaware of this resolution on the part of their leaders, had come to the meeting-place, followed by a great crowd of spectators. A deputation from the schools had made its way, a short time before, to the house of Odillon Barrot. It was now at the residence of the Minister for Foreign Affairs; and nobody could tell whether the banquet would take place, whether the Government would carry out its threat, and whether the National Guards would make their appearance. People were as much enraged against the deputies as against Power. The crowd was growing bigger and bigger, when suddenly the strains of the "Marseillaise" rang through the air.

It was the students' column which had just arrived on the scene. They marched along at an ordinary walking pace, in double file and in good order, with angry faces, bare hands, and all exclaiming at intervals:

"Long live Reform! Down with Guizot!"

Frederick's friends were there, sure enough. They would have noticed him and dragged him along with them. He quickly sought refuge in the Rue de l'Arcade.

When the students had taken two turns round the Madeleine, they went down in the direction of the Place de la Concorde. It was full of people; and, at a distance, the crowd pressed close together, had the appearance of a field of dark ears of corn swaying to and fro.

At the same moment, some soldiers of the line ranged themselves in battle-array at the left-hand side of the church.

The groups remained standing there, however. In order to put an end to this, some police-officers in civilian dress seized the most riotous of them in a brutal fashion, and carried them off to the guardhouse. Frederick, in spite of his indignation, remained silent; he might have been arrested along with the others, and he would have missed Madame Arnoux.

A little while afterwards the helmets of the Municipal Guards appeared. They kept striking about them with the flat side of their sabres. A horse fell down. The people made a rush forward to save him, and as soon as the rider was in the saddle, they all ran away.

Then there was a great silence. The thin rain, which had moistened the asphalt, was no longer falling. Clouds floated past, gently swept on by the west wind.

Frederick began running through the Rue Tronchet, looking before him and behind him.

At length it struck two o'clock.

"Ha! now is the time!" said he to himself. "She is leaving her house; she is approaching," and a minute after, "she would have had time to be here."

Up to three he tried to keep quiet. "No, she is not going to be late—a little patience!"

And for want of something to do he examined the most interesting shops that he passed—a bookseller's, a saddler's and a mourning ware-house. Soon he knew the names of the different books, the various kinds of harness, and every sort of material. The persons who looked after these establishments, from seeing him continually going backwards and forwards, were at first surprised, and then alarmed, and they closed up their shop-fronts.

No doubt she had met with some impediment, and for that reason she must be enduring pain on account of it. But what delight would be afforded in a very short time! For she would come—that was certain. "She has given me her promise!" In the meantime an intolerable feeling of anxiety was gradually seizing hold of him. Impelled by an absurd idea, he returned to his hotel, as if he expected to find her there. At the same moment, she might have reached the street in which their meeting was to take place. He rushed out. Was there no one? And he resumed his tramp up and down the footpath.

He stared at the gaps in the pavement, the mouths of the gutters, the candelabra, and the numbers above the doors. The most trifling objects became for him companions, or rather, ironical spectators, and the regular fronts of the houses seemed to him to have a pitiless aspect. He was suffering from cold feet. He felt as if he were about to succumb to the dejection which was crushing him. The reverberation of his footsteps vibrated through his brain.

When he saw by his watch that it was four o'clock, he experienced, as it were, a sense of vertigo, a feeling of dismay. He tried to repeat some verses to himself, to enter on a calculation, no matter of what sort, to invent some kind of story. Impossible! He was beset by the image of Madame Arnoux; he felt a longing to run in order to meet her. But what road ought he to take so that they might not pass each other?

He went up to a messenger, put five francs into his hand, and ordered him to go to the Rue de Paradis to Jacques Arnoux's residence to enquire "if Madame were at home." Then he took up his post at the corner of the Rue de la Ferme and of the Rue Tronchet, so as to be able to look down both of them at the same time. On the boulevard, in the background of the scene in front of him, confused masses of people were gliding past. He could distinguish, every now and then, the aigrette of a dragoon or a woman's hat; and he strained his eyes in the effort to recognise the wearer. A child in rags, exhibiting a jack-in-the-box, asked him, with a smile, for alms.

The man with the velvet vest reappeared. "The porter had not seen her going out." What had kept her in? If she were ill he would have been told about it. Was it a visitor? Nothing was easier than to say that she was not at home. He struck his forehead.

"Ah! I am stupid! Of course, 'tis this political outbreak that prevented her from coming!"

He was relieved by this apparently natural explanation. Then, suddenly: "But her quarter of the city is quiet." And a horrible doubt seized hold of his mind: "Suppose she was not coming at all, and merely gave me a promise in order to get rid of me? No, no!" What had prevented her from coming was, no doubt, some extraordinary mischance, one of those occurrences that baffled all one's anticipations. In that case she would have written to him.

And he sent the hotel errand-boy to his residence in the Rue Rumfort to find out whether there happened to be a letter waiting for him there.

No letter had been brought. This absence of news reassured him.

He drew omens from the number of coins which he took up in his hand out of his pocket by chance, from the physiognomies of the passers-by, and from the colour of different horses; and when the augury was unfavourable, he forced himself to disbelieve in it. In his sudden outbursts of rage against Madame Arnoux, he abused her in muttering tones. Then came fits of weakness that nearly made him swoon, followed, all of a sudden, by fresh rebounds of hopefulness. She would make her appearance presently! She was there, behind his back! He turned round—there was nobody there! Once he perceived, about thirty paces away, a woman of the same height, with a dress of the same kind. He came up to her—it was not she. It struck five—half-past five—six. The gas-lamps were lighted. Madame Arnoux had not come.

The night before, she had dreamed that she had been, for some time, on the footpath in the Rue Tronchet. She was waiting there for something the nature of which she was not quite clear about, but which, nevertheless, was of great importance; and, without knowing why, she was afraid of being seen. But a pestiferous little dog kept barking at her furiously and biting at the hem of her dress. Every time she shook him off he returned stubbornly to the attack, always barking more violently than before. Madame Arnoux woke up. The dog's barking continued. She strained her ears to listen. It came from her son's room. She rushed to the spot in her bare feet. It was the child himself who was coughing. His hands were burning, his face flushed, and his voice singularly hoarse. Every minute he found it more difficult to breathe freely. She waited there till daybreak, bent over the coverlet watching him.

At eight o'clock the drum of the National Guard gave warning to M. Arnoux that his comrades were expecting his arrival. He dressed himself quickly and went away, promising that he would immediately be passing the house of their doctor, M. Colot.

At ten o'clock, when M. Colot did not make his appearance, Madame Arnoux despatched her chambermaid for him. The doctor was away in the country; and the young man who was taking his place had gone out on some business.

Eugène kept his head on one side on the bolster with contracted eyebrows and dilated nostrils. His pale little face had become whiter than the sheets; and there escaped from his larynx a wheezing caused by his oppressed breathing, which became gradually shorter, dryer, and more metallic. His cough resembled the noise made by those barbarous mechanical inventions by which toy-dogs are enabled to bark.

Madame Arnoux was seized with terror. She rang the bell violently, calling out for help, and exclaiming:

"A doctor! a doctor!"

Ten minutes later came an elderly gentleman in a white tie, and with grey whiskers well trimmed. He put several questions as to the habits, the age, and the constitution of the young patient, and studied the case with his head thrown back. He next wrote out a prescription.

The calm manner of this old man was intolerable. He smelt of aromatics. She would have liked to beat him. He said he would come back in the evening.

The horrible coughing soon began again. Some times the child arose suddenly. Convulsive movements shook the muscles of his breast; and in his efforts to breathe his stomach shrank in as if he were suffocating after running too hard. Then he sank down, with his head thrown back and his mouth wide open. With infinite pains, Madame Arnoux tried to make him swallow the contents of the phials, hippo wine, and a potion containing trisulphate of antimony. But he pushed away the spoon, groaning in a feeble voice. He seemed to be blowing out his words.

From time to time she re-read the prescription. The observations of the formulary frightened her. Perhaps the apothecary had made some mistake. Her powerlessness filled her with despair. M. Colot's pupil arrived.

He was a young man of modest demeanour, new to medical work, and he made no attempt to disguise his opinion about the case. He was at first undecided as to what he should do, for fear of compromising himself, and finally he ordered pieces of ice to be applied to the sick child. It took a long time to get ice. The bladder containing the ice burst. It was necessary to change the little boy's shirt. This disturbance brought on an attack of even a more dreadful character than any of the previous ones.

The child began tearing off the linen round his neck, as if he wanted to remove the obstacle that was choking him; and he scratched the walls and seized the curtains of his bedstead, trying to get a point of support to assist him in breathing.

His face was now of a bluish hue, and his entire body, steeped in a cold perspiration, appeared to be growing lean. His haggard eyes were fixed with terror on his mother. He threw his arms round her neck, and hung there in a desperate fashion; and, repressing her rising sobs, she gave utterance in a broken voice to loving words:

"Yes, my pet, my angel, my treasure!"

Then came intervals of calm.

She went to look for playthings—a punchinello, a collection of images, and spread them out on the bed in order to amuse him. She even made an attempt to sing.

She began to sing a little ballad which she used to sing years before, when she was nursing him wrapped up in swaddling-clothes in this same little upholstered chair. But a shiver ran all over his frame, just as when a wave is agitated by the wind. The balls of his eyes protruded. She thought he was going to die, and turned away her eyes to avoid seeing him.

The next moment she felt strength enough in her to look at him. He was still living. The hours succeeded each other—dull, mournful, interminable, hopeless, and she no longer counted the minutes, save by the progress of this mental anguish. The shakings of his chest threw him forward as if to shatter his body. Finally, he vomited something strange, which was like a parchment tube. What was this? She fancied that he had evacuated one end of his entrails. But he now began to breathe freely and regularly. This appearance of well-being frightened her more than anything else that had happened. She was sitting like one petrified, her arms hanging by her sides, her eyes fixed, when M. Colot suddenly made his appearance. The child, in his opinion, was saved.

She did not realise what he meant at first, and made him repeat the words. Was not this one of those consoling phrases which were customary with medical men? The doctor went away with an air of tranquillity. Then it seemed as if the cords that pressed round her heart were loosened.

"Saved! Is this possible?"

Suddenly the thought of Frederick presented itself to her mind in a clear and inexorable fashion. It was a warning sent to her by Providence. But the Lord in His mercy had not wished to complete her chastisement. What expiation could she offer hereafter if she were to persevere in this love-affair? No doubt insults would be flung at her son's head on her account; and Madame Arnoux saw him a young man, wounded in a combat, carried off on a litter, dying. At one spring she threw herself on the little chair, and, letting her soul escape towards the heights of heaven, she vowed to God that she would sacrifice, as a holocaust, her first real passion, her only weakness as a woman.

Frederick had returned home. He remained in his armchair, without even possessing enough of energy to curse her. A sort of slumber fell upon him, and, in the midst of his nightmare, he could hear the rain falling, still under the impression that he was there outside on the footpath.

Next morning, yielding to an incapacity to resist the temptation which clung to him, he again sent a messenger to Madame Arnoux's house.

Whether the true explanation happened to be that the fellow did not deliver his message, or that she had too many things to say to explain herself in a word or two, the same answer was brought back. This insolence was too great! A feeling of angry pride took possession of him. He swore in his own mind that he would never again cherish even a desire; and, like a group of leaves carried away by a hurricane, his love disappeared. He experienced a sense of relief, a feeling of stoical joy, then a need of violent action; and he walked on at random through the streets.

Men from the faubourgs were marching past armed with guns and old swords, some of them wearing red caps, and all singing the "Marseillaise" or the "Girondins." Here and there a National Guard was hurrying to join his mayoral department. Drums could be heard rolling in the distance. A conflict was going on at Porte Saint-Martin. There was something lively and warlike in the air. Frederick kept walking on without stopping. The excitement of the great city made him gay.

On the Frascati hill he got a glimpse of the Maréchale's windows: a wild idea occurred to him, a reaction of youthfulness. He crossed the boulevard.

The yard-gate was just being closed; and Delphine, who was in the act of writing on it with a piece of charcoal, "Arms given," said to him in an eager tone:

"Ah! Madame is in a nice state! She dismissed a groom who insulted her this morning. She thinks there's going to be pillage everywhere. She is frightened to death! and the more so as Monsieur has gone!"

"What Monsieur?"

"The Prince!"

Frederick entered the boudoir. The Maréchale appeared in her petticoat, and her hair hanging down her back in disorder.

"Ah! thanks! You are going to save me! 'tis the second time! You are one of those who never count the cost!"

"A thousand pardons!" said Frederick, catching her round the waist with both hands.

"How now? What are you doing?" stammered the Maréchale, at the same time, surprised and cheered up by his manner.

He replied:

"I am the fashion! I'm reformed!"

She let herself fall back on the divan, and continued laughing under his kisses.

They spent the afternoon looking out through the window at the people in the street. Then he brought her to dine at the Trois Frères Provençaux. The meal was a long and dainty one. They came back on foot for want of a vehicle.

At the announcement of a change of Ministry, Paris had changed. Everyone was in a state of delight. People kept promenading about the streets, and every floor was illuminated with lamps, so that it seemed as if it were broad daylight. The soldiers made their way back to their barracks, worn out and looking quite depressed. The people saluted them with exclamations of "Long live the Line!"

They went on without making any response. Among the National Guard, on the contrary, the officers, flushed with enthusiasm, brandished their sabres, vociferating:

"Long live Reform!"

And every time the two lovers heard this word they laughed.

Frederick told droll stories, and was quite gay.

Making their way through the Rue Duphot, they reached the boulevards. Venetian lanterns hanging from the houses formed wreaths of flame. Underneath, a confused swarm of people kept in constant motion. In the midst of those moving shadows could be seen, here and there, the steely glitter of bayonets. There was a great uproar. The crowd was too compact, and it was impossible to make one's way back in a straight line. They were entering the Rue Caumartin, when suddenly there burst forth behind them a noise like the crackling made by an immense piece of silk in the act of being torn across. It was the discharge of musketry on the Boulevard des Capucines.

"Ha! a few of the citizens are getting a crack," said Frederick calmly; for there are situations in which a man of the least cruel disposition is so much detached from his fellow-men that he would see the entire human race perishing without a single throb of the heart.

The Maréchale was clinging to his arm with her teeth chattering. She declared that she would not be able to walk twenty steps further. Then, by a refinement of hatred, in order the better to offer an outrage in his own soul to Madame Arnoux, he led Rosanette to the hotel in the Rue Tronchet, and brought her up to the room which he had got ready for the other.

The flowers were not withered. The guipure was spread out on the bed. He drew forth from the cupboard the little slippers. Rosanette considered this forethought on his part a great proof of his delicacy of sentiment. About one o'clock she was awakened by distant rolling sounds, and she saw that he was sobbing with his head buried in the pillow.

"What's the matter with you now, my own darling?"

" 'Tis the excess of happiness," said Frederick. "I have been too long yearning after you!"

Chapter XIV

The Barricade

H E WAS ABRUPTLY ROUSED FROM SLEEP BY THE NOISE OF A DISCHARGE OF musketry; and, in spite of Rosanette's entreaties, Frederick was fully determined to go and see what was happening. He hurried down to the Champs-Elysées, from which shots were being fired. At the corner of the Rue Saint-Honoré some men in blouses ran past him, exclaiming:

"No! not that way! to the Palais-Royal!"

Frederick followed them. The grating of the Convent of the Assumption had been torn away. A little further on he noticed three paving-stones in the middle of the street, the beginning of a barricade, no doubt; then fragments of bottles and bundles of iron-wire, to obstruct the cavalry; and, at the same moment, there rushed suddenly out of a lane a tall young man of pale complexion, with his black hair flowing over his shoulders, and with a sort of pea-coloured swaddling-cloth thrown round him. In his hand he held a long military musket, and he dashed along on the tips of his slippers with the air of a somnambulist and with the nimbleness of a tiger. At intervals a detonation could be heard.

On the evening of the day before, the spectacle of the wagon containing five corpses picked up from amongst those that were lying on the Boulevard des Capucines had charged the disposition of the people; and, while at the Tuileries the aides-de-camp succeeded each other, and M. Molé, having set about the composition of a new Cabinet, did not come back, and M. Thiers was making efforts to constitute another, and while the King was cavilling and hesitating, and finally assigned the post of commander-in-chief to Bugeaud in order to prevent him from making use of it, the insurrection was organising itself in a formidable manner, as if it were directed by a single arm.

Men endowed with a kind of frantic eloquence were engaged in haranguing the populace at the street-corners, others were in the churches ringing the tocsin as loudly as ever they could. Lead was cast for bullets, cartridges were rolled about. The trees on the boulevards, the urinals, the benches, the gratings, the gas-burners, everything was torn off and thrown down. Paris, that morning, was covered with barricades. The resistance which was offered was of short duration, so that at eight o'clock the people, by voluntary surrender or by force, had got possession of five barracks, nearly all the municipal buildings, the most favourable strategic points. Of its own accord, without any effort, the Monarchy was melting away in rapid dissolution, and now an attack was made on the guard-house of the Château d'Eau, in order to liberate fifty prisoners, who were not there.

Frederick was forced to stop at the entrance to the square. It was filled with groups of armed men. The Rue Saint-Thomas and the Rue Fromanteau were occupied by companies of the Line. The Rue de Valois was choked up by an enormous barricade. The smoke which fluttered about at the top of it partly opened. Men kept running overhead, making violent gestures; they vanished from sight; then the firing was again renewed. It was answered from the guard-house without anyone being seen inside. Its windows, protected by oaken window-shutters, were pierced with loop-holes; and the monument with its two storys, its two wings, its fountain on the first floor and its little door in the centre, was beginning to be speckled with white spots under the shock of the bullets. The three steps in front of it remained unoccupied.

At Frederick's side a man in a Greek cap, with a cartridge-box over his knitted vest, was holding a dispute with a woman with a Madras neckerchief round her shoulders. She said to him:

"Come back now! Come back!"

"Leave me alone!" replied the husband. "You can easily mind the porter's lodge by yourself. I ask, citizen, is this fair? I have on every occasion done my duty—in 1830, in '32, in '34, and in '39! To-day they're fighting again. I must fight! Go away!"

And the porter's wife ended by yielding to his remonstrances and to those of a National Guard near them—a man of forty, whose simple face was adorned with a circle of white beard. He loaded his gun and fired while talking to Frederick, as cool in the midst of the outbreak as a horticulturist in his garden. A young lad with a packing-cloth thrown over him was trying to coax this man to give him a few caps, so that he might make use of a gun he had, a fine fowling-piece which a "gentleman" had made him a present of.

"Catch on behind my back," said the good man, "and keep yourself from being seen, or you'll get yourself killed!"

The drums beat for the charge. Sharp cries, hurrahs of triumph burst forth. A continual ebbing to and fro made the multitude sway backward and forward. Frederick, caught between two thick masses of people, did not move an inch, all the time fascinated and exceedingly amused by the scene around him. The wounded who sank to the ground, the dead lying at his feet, did not seem like persons really wounded or really dead. The impression left on his mind was that he was looking on at a show.

In the midst of the surging throng, above the sea of heads, could be seen an old man in a black coat, mounted on a white horse with a velvet saddle. He held in one hand a green bough, in the other a paper, and he kept shaking them persistently; but at length, giving up all hope of obtaining a hearing, he withdrew from the scene.

The soldiers of the Line had gone, and only the municipal troops remained to defend the guard-house. A wave of dauntless spirits dashed up the steps; they were flung down; others came on to replace them, and the gate resounded under blows from iron bars. The municipal guards did not give way. But a wagon, stuffed full of hay, and burning like a gigantic torch, was dragged against the walls. Faggots were speedily brought, then straw, and a barrel of spirits of wine. The fire mounted up to the stones along the wall; the building began to send forth smoke on all sides like the crater of a volcano; and at its summit, between the balustrades of the terrace, huge flames escaped with a harsh noise. The first story of the Palais-Royal was occupied by National Guards. Shots were fired through every window in the square; the bullets whizzed, the water of the fountain, which had burst, was mingled with the blood, forming little pools on the ground. People slipped in the mud over clothes, shakos, and weapons. Frederick felt something soft under his foot. It was the hand of a sergeant in a grey great-coat, lying on his face in the stream that ran along the street. Fresh bands of people were continually coming up, pushing on the combatants at the guard-house. The firing became quicker. The wine-shops were open; people went into them from time to time to smoke a pipe and drink a glass of beer, and then came back again to fight. A lost dog began to howl. This made the people laugh.

Frederick was shaken by the impact of a man falling on his shoulder with a bullet through his back and the death-rattle in his throat. At this shot, perhaps directed against himself, he felt himself stirred up to rage; and he was plunging forward when a National Guard stopped him.

" 'Tis useless! the King has just gone! Ah! if you don't believe me, go and see for yourself!"

This assurance calmed Frederick. The Place du Carrousel had a tranquil aspect. The Hotel de Nantes stood there as fixed as ever; and the houses in the rear; the dome of the Louvre in front, the long gallery of wood at the right, and the waste plot of ground that ran unevenly as far as the sheds of the stall-keepers were, so to speak, steeped in the grey hues of the atmosphere, where indistinct murmurs seemed to mingle with the fog; while, at the opposite side of the square, a stiff light, falling through the parting of the clouds on the façade of the Tuileries, cut out all its windows into white patches. Near the Arc de Triomphe a dead horse lay on the ground. Behind the gratings groups consisting of five or six persons were chatting. The doors leading into the chateau were open, and the servants at the thresholds allowed the people to enter.

Below stairs, in a kind of little parlour, bowls of *café au lait* were handed round. A few of those present sat down to the table and made merry; others remained standing, and amongst the latter was a hackney-coachman. He snatched up with both hands a glass vessel full of powdered sugar, cast a restless glance right and left, and then began to eat voraciously, with his nose stuck into the mouth of the vessel.

At the bottom of the great staircase a man was writing his name in a register. Frederick was able to recognise him by his back.

"Hallo, Hussonnet!"

"Yes, 'tis I," replied the Bohemian. "I am introducing myself at court. This is a nice joke, isn't it?"

"Suppose we go upstairs?"

And they reached presently the Salle des Maréchaux. The portraits of those illustrious generals, save that of Bugeaud, which had been pierced through the stomach, were all intact. They were represented leaning on their sabres with a gun-carriage behind each of them, and in formidable attitudes in contrast with the occasion. A large timepiece proclaimed it was twenty minutes past one.

Suddenly the "Marseillaise" resounded. Hussonnet and Frederick bent over the balusters. It was the people. They rushed up the stairs, shaking with a dizzying, wave-like motion bare heads, or helmets, or red caps, or else bayonets or human shoulders with such impetuosity that some people disappeared every now and then in this swarming mass, which was mounting up without a moment's pause, like a river compressed by an equinoctial tide, with a continuous roar under an irresistible impulse. When they got to the top of the stairs, they were scattered, and their chant died away. Nothing could any longer be heard but the tramp of all the shoes intermingled with the chopping sound of many voices. The crowd not being in a mischievous mood, contented themselves with looking about them. But, from time to time, an elbow, by pressing too hard, broke through a pane of glass, or else a vase or a statue rolled from a bracket down on the floor. The wainscotings cracked under the pressure of people against them. Every face was flushed; the perspiration was rolling down their features in large beads. Hussonnet made this remark:

"Heroes have not a good smell."

"Ah! you are provoking," returned Frederick.

And, pushed forward in spite of themselves, they entered an apartment in which a daïs of red velvet rose as far as the ceiling. On the throne below sat a representative of the proletariat in effigy with a black beard, his shirt gaping open, a jolly air, and the stupid look of a baboon. Others climbed up the platform to sit in his place.

"What a myth!" said Hussonnet. "There you see the sovereign people!"

The armchair was lifted up on the hands of a number of persons and passed across the hall, swaying from one side to the other.

"By Jove, 'tis like a boat! The Ship of State is tossing about in a stormy sea! Let it dance the cancan! Let it dance the cancan!"

They had drawn it towards a window, and in the midst of hisses, they launched it out.

"Poor old chap!" said Hussonnet, as he saw the effigy falling into the garden, where it was speedily picked up in order to be afterwards carried to the Bastille and burned.

Then a frantic joy burst forth, as if, instead of the throne, a future of boundless happiness had appeared; and the people, less through a spirit of vindictiveness than to assert their right of possession, broke or tore the glasses, the curtains, the lustres, the tapers, the tables, the chairs, the stools, the entire furniture, including the very albums and engravings, and the corbels of the tapestry. Since they had triumphed, they must needs amuse themselves! The common herd ironically wrapped themselves up in laces and cashmeres. Gold fringes were rolled round the sleeves of blouses. Hats with ostriches' feathers adorned blacksmiths' heads, and ribbons of the Legion of Honour supplied waistbands for prostitutes. Each person satisfied his or her caprice; some danced, others drank. In the queen's apartment a woman gave a gloss to her hair with pomatum. Behind a folding-screen two lovers were playing cards. Hussonnet pointed out to Frederick an individual who was smoking a dirty pipe with his elbows resting on a balcony; and the popular frenzy redoubled with a continuous crash of broken porcelain and pieces of crystal, which, as they rebounded, made sounds resembling those produced by the plates of musical glasses.

Then their fury was overshadowed. A nauseous curiosity made them rummage all the dressing-rooms, all the recesses. Returned convicts thrust their arms into the beds in which princesses had slept, and rolled themselves on the top of them, to console themselves for not being able to embrace their owners. Others, with sinister faces, roamed about silently, looking for something to steal, but too great a multitude was there. Through the bays of the doors could be seen in the suite of apartments only the dark mass of people between the gilding of the walls under a cloud of dust. Every breast was panting. The heat became more and more suffocating; and the two friends, afraid of being stifled, seized the opportunity of making their way out.

In the antechamber, standing on a heap of garments, appeared a girl of the town as a statue of Liberty, motionless, her grey eyes wide open—a fearful sight.

They had taken three steps outside the château when a company of the National Guards, in greatcoats, advanced towards them, and, taking off their foraging-caps, and, at the same time, uncovering their skulls, which were slightly bald, bowed very low to the people. At this testimony of respect, the ragged victors bridled up. Hussonnet and Frederick were not without experiencing a certain pleasure from it as well as the rest.

They were filled with ardour. They went back to the Palais-Royal. In front of the Rue Fromanteau, soldiers' corpses were heaped up on the straw. They passed close to the dead without a single quiver of emotion, feeling a certain pride in being able to keep their countenance.

The Palais overflowed with people. In the inner courtyard seven piles of wood were flaming. Pianos, chests of drawers, and clocks were hurled out through the windows. Fire-engines sent streams of water up to the roofs. Some vagabonds tried to cut the hose with their sabres. Frederick urged a pupil of the Polytechnic School to interfere. The latter did not understand him, and, moreover, appeared to be an idiot. All around, in the two galleries, the populace, having got possession of the cellars, gave themselves up to a horrible carouse. Wine flowed in streams and wetted people's feet; the mudlarks drank out of the tail-ends of the bottles, and shouted as they staggered along.

"Come away out of this," said Hussonnet; "I am disgusted with the people."

All over the Orléans Gallery the wounded lay on mattresses on the ground, with purple curtains folded round them as coverlets; and the small shopkeepers' wives and daughters from the quarter brought them broth and linen.

"No matter!" said Frederick; "for my part, I consider the people sublime."

The great vestibule was filled with a whirlwind of furious individuals. Men tried to ascend to the upper storys in order to put the finishing touches to the work of wholesale destruction. National Guards, on the steps, strove to keep them back. The most intrepid was a chasseur, who had his head bare, his hair bristling, and his straps in pieces. His shirt caused a swelling between his trousers and his coat, and he struggled desperately in the midst of the others. Hussonnet, who had sharp sight, recognised Arnoux from a distance.

Then they went into the Tuileries garden, so as to be able to breathe more freely. They sat down on a bench; and they remained for some minutes with their eyes closed, so much stunned that they had not the energy to say a word. The people who were passing came up to them and informed them that the Duchesse d'Orléans had been appointed Regent, and that it was all over. They were experiencing that species of comfort which follows rapid *dénouements*, when at the windows of the attics in the château appeared men-servants tearing their liveries to pieces. They flung their torn clothes into the garden, as a mark of renunciation. The people hooted at them, and then they retired.

The attention of Frederick and Hussonnet was distracted by a tall fellow who was walking quickly between the trees with a musket on his shoulder. A cartridge-box was pressed against his pea-jacket; a handkerchief was wound round his forehead under his cap. He turned his head to one side. It was Dussardier; and casting himself into their arms:

"Ah! what good fortune, my poor old friends!" without being able to say another word, so much out of breath was he with fatigue.

He had been on his legs for the last twenty-four hours. He had been engaged at the barricades of the Latin Quarter, had fought in the Rue Rabuteau, had saved three dragoons' lives, had entered the Tuileries with Colonel Dunoyer, and, after that, had repaired to the Chamber, and then to the Hotel de Ville.

"I have come from it! all goes well! the people are victorious! the workmen and the employers are embracing one another. Ha! if you knew what I have seen! what brave fellows! what a fine sight it was!"

And without noticing that they had no arms:

"I was quite certain of finding you there! This has been a bit rough—no matter!"

A drop of blood ran down his cheek, and in answer to the questions put to him by the two others:

"Oh! 'tis nothing! a slight scratch from a bayonet!"

"However, you really ought to take care of yourself."

"Pooh! I am substantial! What does this signify? The Republic is proclaimed! We'll be happy henceforth! Some journalists, who were talking just now in front of me, said they were going to liberate Poland and Italy! No more kings! You understand? The entire land free! the entire land free!"

And with one comprehensive glance at the horizon, he spread out his arms in a triumphant attitude. But a long file of men rushed over the terrace on the water's edge.

"Ah, deuce take it! I was forgetting. I must be off. Good-bye!"

He turned round to cry out to them while brandishing his musket:

"Long live the Republic!"

From the chimneys of the château escaped enormous whirlwinds of black smoke which bore sparks along with them. The ringing of the bells sent out over the city a wild and startling alarm. Right and left, in every direction, the conquerors discharged their weapons.

Frederick, though he was not a warrior, felt the Gallic blood leaping in his veins. The magnetism of the public enthusiasm had seized hold of him. He inhaled with a voluptuous delight the stormy atmosphere filled with the odour of gunpowder; and, in the meantime, he quivered under the effluvium of an immense love, a supreme and universal tenderness, as if the heart of all humanity were throbbing in his breast.

Hussonnet said with a yawn:

"It would be time, perhaps, to go and instruct the populace."

Frederick followed him to his correspondence-office in the Place de la Bourse; and he began to compose for the Troyes newspaper an account of recent events in a lyric style—a veritable tit-bit—to which he attached his signature. Then they dined together at a tavern. Hussonnet was pensive; the eccentricities of the Revolution exceeded his own.

After leaving the café, when they repaired to the Hotel de Ville to learn the news, the boyish impulses which were natural to him had got the upper hand once more. He scaled the barricades like a chamois, and answered the sentinels with broad jokes of a patriotic flavour.

They heard the Provisional Government proclaimed by torchlight. At last, Frederick got back to his house at midnight, overcome with fatigue.

"Well," said he to his man-servant, while the latter was undressing him, "are you satisfied?"

"Yes, no doubt, Monsieur; but I don't like to see the people dancing to music."

Next morning, when he awoke, Frederick thought of Deslauriers. He hastened to his friend's lodgings. He ascertained that the advocate had just left Paris, having been appointed a provincial commissioner. At the *soirée* given the night before, he had got into contact with Ledru-Rollin, and laying siege to him in the name of the Law Schools, had snatched from him a post, a mission. However, the doorkeeper explained, he was going to write and give his address in the following week.

After this, Frederick went to see the Maréchale. She gave him a chilling reception. She resented his desertion of her. Her bitterness disappeared when he had given her repeated assurances that peace was restored.

All was quiet now. There was no reason to be afraid. He kissed her, and she declared herself in favour of the Republic, as his lordship the Archbishop of Paris had already done, and as the magistracy, the Council of State, the Institute, the marshals of France, Changarnier, M. de Falloux, all the Bonapartists, all the Legitimists, and a considerable number of Orléanists were about to do with a swiftness indicative of marvellous zeal.

The fall of the Monarchy had been so rapid that, as soon as the first stupefaction that succeeded it had passed away, there was amongst the middle class a feeling of astonishment at the fact that they were still alive. The summary execution of some thieves, who were shot without a trial, was regarded as an act of signal justice. For a month Lamartine's phrase was repeated with reference to the red flag, "which had only gone the round of the Champ de Mars, while the tricoloured flag," etc.; and all ranged themselves under its shade, each party seeing amongst the three colours only its own, and firmly determined, as soon as it would be the most powerful, to tear away the two others.

As business was suspended, anxiety and love of gaping drove everyone into the open air. The careless style of costume generally adopted attenuated differences of social position. Hatred masked itself; expectations were openly indulged in; the multitude seemed full of good-nature. The pride of having gained their rights shone in the people's faces. They displayed the gaiety of a carnival, the manners of a bivouac. Nothing could be more amusing than the aspect of Paris during the first days that followed the Revolution.

Frederick gave the Maréchale his arm, and they strolled along through the streets together. She was highly diverted by the display of rosettes in every buttonhole, by the banners hung from every window, and the bills of every colour that were posted upon the walls, and threw some money here and there into the collection-boxes for the wounded, which were placed on chairs in the middle of the pathway. Then she stopped before some caricatures representing Louis Philippe as a pastry-cook, as a mountebank, as a dog, or as a leech. But she was a little frightened at the sight of Caussidière's men with their sabres and scarfs. At other times it was a tree of Liberty that was being planted. The clergy vied with each other in blessing the Republic, escorted by servants in gold lace; and the populace thought this very fine. The most frequent spectacle was that of deputations from no matter what, going to demand something at the Hotel de Ville, for every trade, every industry, was looking to the Government to put a complete end to its wretchedness. Some of them, it is true, went to offer it advice or to congratulate it, or merely to pay it a little visit, and to see the machine performing its functions. One day, about the middle of the month of March, as they were passing the Pont d'Arcole, having to do some commission for Rosanette in the Latin Quarter, Frederick saw approaching a column of individuals with oddly-shaped hats and long beards. At its head, beating a drum, walked a negro who had formerly been an artist's model; and the man who bore the banner, on which this inscription floated in the wind, "Artist-Painters," was no other than Pellerin.

He made a sign to Frederick to wait for him, and then reappeared five minutes afterwards, having some time before him; for the Government was, at that moment, receiving a deputation from the stone-cutters. He was going with his colleagues to ask for the creation of a Forum of Art, a kind of Exchange where the interests of Æsthetics would be discussed. Sublime masterpieces would be produced, inasmuch as the workers would amalgamate their talents. Ere long Paris would be covered with gigantic monuments. He would decorate them. He had even begun a figure of the Republic. One of his comrades had come to take it, for they were closely pursued by the deputation from the poulterers.

"What stupidity!" growled a voice in the crowd. "Always some humbug, nothing strong!"

It was Regimbart. He did not salute Frederick, but took advantage of the occasion to give vent to his own bitterness.

The Citizen spent his days wandering about the streets, pulling his moustache, rolling his eyes about, accepting and propagating any dismal news that was communicated to him; and he had only two phrases: "Take care! we're going to be run over!" or else, "Why, confound it! they're juggling with the Republic!" He was discontented with everything, and especially with the fact that we had not taken back our natural frontiers.

The very name of Lamartine made him shrug his shoulders. He did not consider Ledru-Rollin "sufficient for the problem," referred to Dupont (of the Eure) as an old numbskull, Albert as an idiot, Louis Blanc as an Utopist, and Blanqui as an exceedingly dangerous man; and when Frederick asked him what would be the best thing to do, he replied, pressing his arm till he nearly bruised it:

"To take the Rhine, I tell you! to take the Rhine, damn it!"

Then he blamed the Reactionaries. They were taking off the mask. The sack of the château of Neuilly and Suresne, the fire at Batignolles, the troubles at Lyons, all the excesses and all the grievances, were just now being exaggerated by having super-added to them Ledru-Rollin's circular, the forced currency of bank-notes, the fall of the funds to sixty francs, and, to crown all, as the supreme iniquity, a final blow, a culminating horror, the duty of forty-five centimes! And over and above all these things, there was again Socialism! Although these theories, as new as the game of goose, had been discussed sufficiently for forty years to fill a number of libraries, they terrified the wealthier citizens, as if they had been a hailstorm of aërolites; and they expressed indignation at them by virtue of that hatred which the advent of every idea provokes, simply because it is an idea—an odium from which it derives subsequently its glory, and which causes its enemies to be always beneath it, however lowly it may be.

Then Property rose in their regard to the level of Religion, and was confounded with God. The attacks made on it appeared to them a sacrilege; almost a species of cannibalism. In spite of the most humane legislation that ever existed, the spectre of '93 reappeared, and the chopper of the guillotine vibrated in every syllable of the word "Republic," which did not prevent them from despising it for its weakness. France, no longer feeling herself mistress of the situation, was beginning to shriek with terror, like a blind man without his stick or an infant that had lost its nurse.

Of all Frenchmen, M. Dambreuse was the most alarmed. The new condition of things threatened his fortune, but, more than anything else, it deceived his experience. A system so good! a king so wise! was it possible? The ground was giving way beneath their feet! Next morning he dismissed three of his servants, sold his horses, bought a soft hat to go out into the streets, thought even of letting his beard grow; and he remained at home, prostrated, reading over and over again newspapers most hostile to his own ideas, and plunged into such a gloomy mood that even the jokes about the pipe of Flocon had not the power to make him smile.

As a supporter of the last reign, he was dreading the vengeance of the people so far as concerned his estates in Champagne when Frederick's lucubration fell into his hands. Then it occurred to his mind that his young friend was a very useful personage, and that he might be able, if not to serve him, at least to protect him, so that, one morning, M. Dambreuse presented himself at Frederick's residence, accompanied by Martinon.

This visit, he said, had no object save that of seeing him for a little while, and having a chat with him. In short, he rejoiced at the events that had happened, and with his whole heart adopted "our sublime motto, *Liberty, Equality, and Fraternity*," having always been at bottom a Republican. If he voted under the other *régime* with the Ministry, it was simply in order to accelerate an inevitable downfall. He even inveighed against M. Guizot, "who has got us into a nice hobble, we must admit!" By way of retaliation, he spoke in an enthusiastic fashion about Lamartine, who had shown himself "magnificent, upon my word of honour, when, with reference to the red flag—"

"Yes, I know," said Frederick. After which he declared that his sympathies were on the side of the working-men.

"For, in fact, more or less, we are all working-men!" And he carried his impartiality so far as to acknowledge that Proudhon had a certain amount of logic in his views. "Oh, a great deal of logic, deuce take it!"

Then, with the disinterestedness of a superior mind, he chatted about the exhibition of pictures, at which he had seen Pellerin's work. He considered it original and well-painted.

Martinon backed up all he said with expressions of approval; and likewise was of his opinion that it was necessary to rally boldly to the side of the Republic. And he talked about the husbandman, his father, and assumed the part of the peasant, the man of the people. They soon came to the question of the elections for the National Assembly, and the candidates in the arrondissement of La Fortelle. The Opposition candidate had no chance.

"You should take his place!" said M. Dambreuse.

Frederick protested.

"But why not?" For he would obtain the suffrages of the Extremists owing to his personal opinions, and that of the Conservatives on account of his family; "And perhaps also," added the banker, with a smile, "thanks to my influence, in some measure."

Frederick urged as an obstacle that he did not know how to set about it.

There was nothing easier if he only got himself recommended to the patriots of the Aube by one of the clubs of the capital. All he had to do was to read out, not a profession of faith such as might he seen every day, but a serious statement of principles.

"Bring it to me; I know what goes down in the locality; and you can, I say again, render great services to the country—to us all—to myself."

In such times people ought to aid each other, and, if Frederick had need of anything, he or his friends—

"Oh, a thousand thanks, my dear Monsieur!"

"You'll do as much for me in return, mind!"

Decidedly, the banker was a decent man.

Frederick could not refrain from pondering over his advice; and soon he was dazzled by a kind of dizziness.

The great figures of the Convention passed before his mental vision. It seemed to him that a splendid dawn was about to rise. Rome, Vienna and Berlin were in a state of insurrection, and the Austrians had been driven out of Venice. All Europe was agitated. Now was the time to make a plunge into the movement, and perhaps to accelerate it; and then he was fascinated by the costume which it was said the deputies would wear. Already he saw himself in a waistcoat with lapels and a tri-coloured sash; and this itching, this hallucination, became so violent that he opened his mind to Dambreuse.

The honest fellow's enthusiasm had not abated.

"Certainly—sure enough! Offer yourself!"

Frederick, nevertheless, consulted Deslauriers.

The idiotic opposition which trammelled the commissioner in his province had augmented his Liberalism. He at once replied, exhorting Frederick with the utmost vehemence to come forward as a candidate. However, as the latter was desirous of having the approval of a great number of persons, he confided the thing to Rosanette one day, when Mademoiselle Vatnaz happened to be present.

She was one of those Parisian spinsters who, every evening when they have given their lessons or tried to sell little sketches, or to dispose of poor manuscripts, return to their own homes with mud on their petticoats, make their own dinner, which they eat by themselves, and then, with their soles resting on a foot-warmer, by the light of a filthy lamp, dream of a love, a family, a hearth, wealth—all that they lack. So it was that, like many others, she had hailed in the Revolution the advent of vengeance, and she delivered herself up to a Socialistic propaganda of the most unbridled description.

The enfranchisement of the proletariat, according to the Vatnaz, was only possible by the enfranchisement of woman. She wished to have her own sex admitted to every kind of employment, to have an enquiry made into the paternity of children, a different code, the abolition, or at least a more intelligent regulation, of marriage. In that case every Frenchwoman would be bound to marry a Frenchman, or to adopt an old man. Nurses and midwives should be officials receiving salaries from the State.

There should be a jury to examine the works of women, special editors for women, a polytechnic school for women, a National Guard for women, everything for women! And, since the Government ignored their rights, they ought to overcome force by force. Ten thousand citizenesses with good guns ought to make the Hotel de Ville quake!

Frederick's candidature appeared to her favourable for carrying out her ideas. She encouraged him, pointing out the glory that shone an the horizon. Rosanette was delighted at the notion of having a man who would make speeches at the Chamber.

"And then, perhaps, they'll give you a good place?"

Frederick, a man prone to every kind of weakness, was infected by the universal mania. He wrote an address and went to show it to M. Dambreuse.

At the sound made by the great door falling back, a curtain gaped open a little behind a casement, and a woman appeared at it. He had not time to find out who she was; but, in the anteroom, a picture arrested his attention—Pellerin's picture—which lay on a chair, no doubt provisionally.

It represented the Republic, or Progress, or Civilisation, under the form of Jesus Christ driving a locomotive, which was passing through a virgin forest. Frederick, after a minute's contemplation, exclaimed:

"What a vile thing!"

"Is it not—eh?" said M. Dambreuse, coming in unexpectedly just at the moment when the other was giving utterance to this opinion, and fancying that it had reference, not so much to the picture as to the doctrine glorified by the work. Martinon presented himself at the same time. They made their way into the study, and Frederick was drawing a paper out of his pocket, when Mademoiselle Cécile, entering suddenly, said, articulating her words in an ingenuous fashion:

"Is my aunt here?"

"You know well she is not," replied the banker. "No matter! act as if you were at home, Mademoiselle."

"Oh! thanks! I am going away!"

Scarcely had she left when Martinon seemed to be searching for his handkerchief.

"I forgot to take it out of my greatcoat—excuse me!"

"All right!" said M. Dambreuse.

Evidently he was not deceived by this manouevre, and even seemed to regard it with favour. Why? But Martinon soon reappeared, and Frederick began reading his address.

At the second page, which pointed towards the preponderance of the financial interests as a disgraceful fact, the banker made a grimace. Then, touching on reforms, Frederick demanded free trade.

"What? Allow me, now!"

The other paid no attention, and went on. He called for a tax on yearly incomes, a progressive tax, a European federation, and the education of the people, the encouragement of the fine arts on the liberal scale.

"When the country could provide men like Delacroix or Hugo with incomes of a hundred thousand francs, where would be the harm?"

At the close of the address advice was given to the upper classes.

"Spare nothing, ye rich; but give! give!"

He stopped, and remained standing. The two who had been listening to him did not utter a word. Martinon opened his eyes wide; M. Dambreuse was quite pale. At last, concealing his emotion under a bitter smile:

"That address of yours is simply perfect!" And he praised the style exceedingly in order to avoid giving his opinion as to the matter of the address.

This virulence on the part of an inoffensive young man frightened him, especially as a sign of the times.

Martinon tried to reassure him. The Conservative party, in a little while, would certainly be able to take its revenge. In several cities the commissioners of the provisional government had been driven away; the elections were not to occur till the twenty-third of April; there was plenty of time. In short, it was necessary for M. Dambreuse to present himself personally in the Aube; and from that time forth, Martinon no longer left his side, became his secretary, and was as attentive to him as any son could be.

Frederick arrived at Rosanette's house in a very self-complacent mood. Delmar happened to be there, and told him of his intention to stand as a candidate at the Seine elections. In a placard addressed to the people, in which he addressed them in the familiar manner which one adopts towards an individual, the actor boasted of being able to understand them, and of having, in order to save them, got himself "crucified for the sake of art," so that he was the incarnation, the ideal of the popular spirit, believing that he had, in fact, such enormous power over the masses that he proposed by-and-by, when he occupied a ministerial office, to quell any outbreak by himself alone; and, with regard to the means he would employ, he gave this answer: "Never fear! I'll show them my head!"

Frederick, in order to mortify him, gave him to understand that he was himself a candidate. The mummer, from the moment that his future colleague aspired to represent the province, declared himself his servant, and offered to be his guide to the various clubs.

They visited them, or nearly all, the red and the blue, the furious and the tranquil, the puritanical and the licentious, the mystical and the intemperate, those that had voted for the death of kings, and those in which the frauds in the grocery trade had been denounced; and everywhere the tenants cursed the landlords; the blouse was full of spite against broadcloth; and the rich conspired against the poor. Many wanted indemnities on the ground that they had formerly been martyrs of the police; others appealed for money in order to carry out certain inventions, or else there were plans of phalansteria, projects for cantonal bazaars, systems of public felicity; then, here and there a flash of genius amid these clouds of folly, sudden as splashes, the law formulated by an oath, and flowers of eloquence on the lips of some soldier-boy, with a shoulder-belt strapped over his bare, shirtless chest. Sometimes, too, a gentleman made his appearance—an aristocrat of humble demeanour, talking in a plebeian strain, and with his hands unwashed, so as to make them look hard. A patriot recognised him; the most virtuous mobbed him; and he went off with rage in his soul. On the pretext of good sense, it was desirable to be always disparaging the advocates, and to make use as often as possible of these expressions: "To carry his stone to the building," "social problem," "workshop."

Delmar did not miss the opportunities afforded him for getting in a word; and when he no longer found anything to say, his device was to plant himself in some conspicuous position with one of his arms akimbo and the other in his waistcoat, turning himself round abruptly in profile, so as to give a good view of his head. Then there were outbursts of applause, which came from Mademoiselle Vatnaz at the lower end of the hall.

Frederick, in spite of the weakness of orators, did not dare to try the experiment of speaking. All those people seemed to him too unpolished or too hostile.

But Dussardier made enquiries, and informed him that there existed in the Rue Saint-Jacques a club which bore the name of the "Club of Intellect." Such a name gave good reason for hope. Besides, he would bring some friends there.

He brought those whom he had invited to take punch with him—the bookkeeper, the traveller in wines, and the architect; even Pellerin had offered to come, and Hussonnet would probably form one of the party, and on the footpath before the door stood Regimbart, with two individuals, the first of whom was his faithful Compain, a rather thick-set man marked with small-pox and with bloodshot eyes; and the second, an ape-like negro, exceedingly hairy, and whom he knew only in the character of "a patriot from Barcelona."

They passed though a passage, and were then introduced into a large room, no doubt used by a joiner, and with walls still fresh and smelling of plaster. Four argand lamps were hanging parallel to each other, and shed an unpleasant light. On a platform, at the end of the room, there was a desk with a bell; underneath it a table, representing the rostrum, and on each side two others, somewhat lower, for the secretaries. The audience that adorned the benches consisted of old painters of daubs, ushers, and literary men who could not get their works published.

In the midst of those lines of paletots with greasy collars could be seen here and there a woman's cap or a workman's linen smock. The bottom of the apartment was even full of workmen, who had in all likelihood come there to pass away an idle hour, and who had been introduced by some speakers in order that they might applaud.

Frederick took care to place himself between Dussardier and Regimbart, who was scarcely seated when he leaned both hands on his walking-stick and his chin on his hands and shut his eyes, whilst at the other end of the room Delmar stood looking down at the assembly. Sénécal appeared at the president's desk.

The worthy bookkeeper thought Frederick would be pleased at this unexpected discovery. It only annoyed him.

The meeting exhibited great respect for the president. He was one who, on the twenty-fifth of February, had desired an immediate organisation of labour. On the following day, at the Prado, he had declared himself in favour attacking the Hotel de Ville; and, as every person at that period took some model for imitation, one copied Saint-Just, another Danton, another Marat; as for him, he tried to be like Blanqui, who imitated Robespierre. His black gloves, and his hair brushed back, gave him a rigid aspect exceedingly becoming.

He opened the proceedings with the declaration of the Rights of Man and of the Citizen—a customary act of faith. Then, a vigorous voice struck up Béranger's "Souvenirs du Peuple."

Other voices were raised:

"No! no! not that!"

" 'La Casquette!' " the patriots at the bottom of the apartment began to howl.

And they sang in chorus the favourite lines of the period:

"Doff your hat before my cap—
Kneel before the working-man!"

At a word from the president the audience became silent.

One of the secretaries proceeded to inspect the letters.

Some young men announced that they burned a number of the *Assemblée Nationale* every evening in front of the Panthéon, and they urged on all patriots to follow their example.

"Bravo! adopted!" responded the audience.

The Citizen Jean Jacques Langreneux, a printer in the Rue Dauphin, would like to have a monument raised to the memory of the martyrs of Thermidor.

Michel Evariste Népomucène, ex-professor, gave expression to the wish that the European democracy should adopt unity of language. A dead language might be used for that purpose—as, for example, improved Latin.

"No; no Latin!" exclaimed the architect.

"Why?" said the college-usher.

And these two gentlemen engaged in a discussion, in which the others also took part, each putting in a word of his own for effect; and the conversation on this topic soon became so tedious that many went away. But a little old man, who wore at the top of his prodigiously high forehead a pair of green spectacles, asked permission to speak in order to make an important communication.

It was a memorandum on the assessment of taxes. The figures flowed on in a continuous stream, as if they were never going to end. The impatience of the audience found vent at first in murmurs, in whispered talk. He allowed nothing to put him out. Then they began hissing; they catcalled him. Sénécal called the persons who were interrupting to order. The orator went on like a machine. It was necessary to catch him by the shoulder in order to stop him. The old fellow looked as if he were waking out of a dream, and, placidly lifting his spectacles, said:

"Pardon me, citizens! pardon me! I am going—a thousand excuses!"

Frederick was disconcerted with the failure of the old man's attempts to read this written statement. He had his own address in his pocket, but an extemporaneous speech would have been preferable.

Finally the president announced that they were about to pass on to the important matter, the electoral question. They would not discuss the big Republican lists. However, the "Club of Intellect" had every right, like every other, to form one, "with all respect for the pachas of the Hotel de Ville, and the citizens who solicited the popular mandate might set forth their claims.

"Go on, now!" said Dussardier.

A man in a cassock, with woolly hair and a petulant expression on his face, had already raised his hand. He said, with a stutter, that his name was Ducretot, priest and agriculturist, and that he was the author of a work entitled "Manures." He was told to send it to a horticultural club.

Then a patriot in a blouse climbed up into the rostrum. He was a plebeian, with broad shoulders, a big face, very mild-looking, with long black hair. He cast on the assembly an almost voluptuous glance, flung back his head, and, finally, spreading out his arms:

"You have repelled Ducretot, O my brothers! and you have done right; but it was not through irreligion, for we are all religious."

Many of those present listened open-mouthed, with the air of catechumens and in ecstatic attitudes.

"It is not either because he is a priest, for we, too, are priests! The workman is a priest, just as the founder of Socialism was—the Master of us all, Jesus Christ!"

The time had arrived to inaugurate the Kingdom of God. The Gospel led directly to '89. After the abolition of slavery, the abolition of the proletariat. They had had the age of hate—the age of love was about to begin.

"Christianity is the keystone and the foundation of the new edifice—"

"You are making game of us?" exclaimed the traveller in wines. "Who has given me such a priest's cap?"

This interruption gave great offence. Nearly all the audience got on benches, and, shaking their fists, shouted: "Atheist! aristocrat! low rascal!" whilst the president's bell kept ringing continuously, and the cries of "Order! order!" redoubled. But, aimless, and, moreover, fortified by three cups of coffee which he had swallowed before coming to the meeting, he struggled in the midst of the others:

"What? I an aristocrat? Come, now!"

When, at length, he was permitted to give an explanation, he declared that he would never be at peace with the priests; and, since something had just been said about economical measures, it would be a splendid one to put an end to the churches, the sacred pyxes, and finally all creeds.

Somebody raised the objection that he was going very far.

"Yes! I am going very far! But, when a vessel is caught suddenly in a storm—"

Without waiting for the conclusion of this simile, another made a reply to his observation:

"Granted! But this is to demolish at a single stroke, like a mason devoid of judgment—"

"You are insulting the masons!" yelled a citizen covered with plaster. And persisting in the belief that provocation had been offered to him, he vomited forth insults, and wished to fight, clinging tightly to the bench whereon he sat. It took no less than three men to put him out.

Meanwhile the workman still remained on the rostrum. The two secretaries gave him an intimation that he should come down. He protested against the injustice done to him.

"You shall not prevent me from crying out, 'Eternal love to our dear France! eternal love all to the Republic!' "

"Citizens!" said Compain, after this—"Citizens!"

And, by dint of repeating "Citizens," having obtained a little silence, he leaned on the rostrum with his two red hands, which looked like stumps, bent forward his body, and blinking his eyes:

"I believe that it would be necessary to give a larger extension to the calf's head."

All who heard him kept silent, fancying that they had misunderstood his words.

"Yes! the calf's head!"

Three hundred laughs burst forth at the same time. The ceiling shook.

At the sight of all these faces convulsed with mirth, Compain shrank back. He continued in an angry tone:

"What! you don't know what the calf's head is!"

It was a paroxysm, a delirium. They held their sides. Some of them even tumbled off the benches to the ground with convulsions of laughter. Compain, not being able to stand it any longer, took refuge beside Regimbart, and wanted to drag him away.

"No! I am remaining till 'tis all over!" said the Citizen.

This reply caused Frederick to make up his mind; and, as he looked about to the right and the left to see whether his friends were prepared to support him, he saw Pellerin on the rostrum in front of him.

The artist assumed a haughty tone in addressing the meeting.

"I would like to get some notion as to who is the candidate amongst all these that represents art. For my part, I have painted a picture."

"We have nothing to do with painting pictures!" was the churlish remark of a thin man with red spots on his cheek-bones.

Pellerin protested against this interruption.

But the other, in a tragic tone:

"Ought not the Government to make an ordinance abolishing prostitution and want?"

And this phrase having at once won to his side the popular favour, he thundered against the corruption of great cities.

"Shame and infamy! We ought to catch hold of wealthy citizens on their way out of the Maison d'Or and spit in their faces—unless it be that the Government countenances debauchery! But the collectors of the city dues exhibit towards our daughters and our sisters an amount of indecency—"

A voice exclaimed, some distance away:

"This is blackguard language! Turn him out!"

"They extract taxes from us to pay for licentiousness! Thus, the high salaries paid to actors—"

"Help!" cried Pellerin.

He leaped from the rostrum, pushed everybody aside, and declaring that he regarded such stupid accusations with disgust, expatiated on the civilising mission of the player. Inasmuch as the theatre was the focus of national education, he would record his vote for the reform of the theatre; and to begin with, no more managements, no more privileges!

"Yes; of any sort!"

The actor's performance excited the audience, and people moved backwards and forwards knocking each other down.

"No more academies! No more institutes!"

"No missions!"

"No more bachelorships! Down with University degrees!"

"Let us preserve them," said Sénécal; "but let them be conferred by universal suffrage, by the people, the only true judge!"

Besides, these things were not the most useful. It was necessary to take a level which would be above the heads of the wealthy. And he represented them as gorging themselves with crimes under their gilded ceilings; while the poor, writhing in their garrets with famine, cultivated every virtue. The applause became so vehement that he interrupted his discourse. For several minutes he remained with his eyes closed, his head thrown back, and, as it were, lulling himself to sleep over the fury which he had aroused.

Then he began to talk in a dogmatic fashion, in phrases as imperious as laws. The State should take possession of the banks and of the insurance offices. Inheritances should be abolished. A social fund should be established for the workers. Many other measures were desirable in the future. For the time being, these would suffice, and, returning to the question of the elections: "We want pure citizens, men entirely fresh. Let some one offer himself."

Frederick arose. There was a buzz of approval made by his friends. But Sénécal, assuming the attitude of a Fouquier-Tinville, began to ask questions as to his Christian name and surname, his antecedents, life, and morals.

Frederick answered succinctly, and bit his lips. Sénécal asked whether anyone saw any impediment to this candidature.

"No! no!"

But, for his part, he saw some. All around him bent forward and strained their ears to listen. The citizen who was seeking for their support had not delivered a certain sum promised by him for the foundation of a democratic journal. Moreover, on the twenty-second of February, though he had had sufficient notice on the subject, he had failed to be at the meeting-place in the Place de Panthéon.

"I swear that he was at the Tuileries!" exclaimed Dussardier.

"Can you swear to having seen him at the Panthéon?"

Dussardier hung down his head. Frederick was silent. His friends, scandalised, regarded him with disquietude.

"In any case," Sénécal went on, "do you know a patriot who will answer to us for your principles?"

"I will!" said Dussardier.

"Oh! this is not enough; another!"

Frederick turned round to Pellerin. The artist replied to him with a great number of gestures, which meant:

"Ah! my dear boy, they have rejected myself! The deuce! What would you have?"

Thereupon Frederick gave Regimbart a nudge.

"Yes, that's true; 'tis time! I'm going."

And Regimbart stepped upon the platform; then, pointing towards the Spaniard, who had followed him:

"Allow me, citizens, to present to you a patriot from Barcelona!"

The patriot made a low bow, rolled his gleaming eyes about, and with his hand on his heart:

"Ciudadanos! mucho aprecio el honor that you have bestowed on me! however great may be vuestra bondad, mayor vuestra atención!"

"I claim the right to speak!" cried Frederick.

"Desde que se proclamo la constitución de Cadiz, ese pacto fundamental de las libertades Españolas, hasta la ultima revolución, nuestra patria cuenta numerosos y heroicos mártires."

Frederick once more made an effort to obtain a hearing:

"But, citizens!—"

The Spaniard went on: "El martes proximo tendra lugar en la iglesia de la Magdelena un servicio fúnebre."

"In fact, this is ridiculous! Nobody understands him!"

This observation exasperated the audience.

"Turn him out! Turn him out!"

"Who? I?" asked Frederick.

"Yourself!" said Sénécal, majestically. "Out with you!"

He rose to leave, and the voice of the Iberian pursued him:

"Y todos los Españoles descarien ver alli reunidas las disputaciónes de los clubs y de la milicia nacional. An oración fúnebre en honour of the libertad Española y del mundo entero will be prononciado por un miembro del clero of Paris en la sala Bonne Nouvelle. Honour al pueblo frances que Ilamaria yo el primero pueblo del mundo, sino fuese ciudadano de otra nación!"

"Aristo!" screamed one blackguard, shaking his fist at Frederick, as the latter, boiling with indignation, rushed out into the yard adjoining the place where the meeting was held.

He reproached himself for his devotedness, without reflecting that, after all, the accusations brought against him were just.

What fatal idea was this candidature! But what asses! what idiots! He drew comparisons between himself and these men, and soothed his wounded pride with the thought of their stupidity.

Then he felt the need of seeing Rosanette. After such an exhibition of ugly traits, and so much magniloquence, her dainty person would be a source of relaxation. She was aware that he had intended to present himself at a club that evening. However, she did not even ask him a single question when he came in. She was sitting near the fire, ripping open the lining of a dress. He was surprised to find her thus occupied.

"Hallo! what are you doing?"

"You can see for yourself," said she, dryly. "I am mending my clothes! So much for this Republic of yours!"

"Why do you call it mine?"

"Perhaps you want to make out that it's mine!"

And she began to upbraid him for everything that had happened in France for the last two months, accusing him of having brought about the Revolution and with having ruined her prospects by making everybody that had money leave Paris, and that she would by-and-by be dying in a hospital.

"It is easy for you to talk lightly about it, with your yearly income! However, at the rate at which things are going on, you won't have your yearly income long."

"That may be," said Frederick. "The most devoted are always misunderstood, and if one were not sustained by one's conscience, the brutes that you mix yourself up with would make you feel disgusted with your own self-denial!"

Rosanette gazed at him with knitted brows.

"Eh? What? What self-denial? Monsieur has not succeeded, it would seem? So much the better! It will teach you to make patriotic donations. Oh, don't lie! I know you have given them three hundred francs, for this Republic of yours has to be kept. Well, amuse yourself with it, my good man!"

Under this avalanche of abuse, Frederick passed from his former disappointment to a more painful disillusion.

He withdrew to the lower end of the apartment. She came up to him.

"Look here! Think it out a bit! In a country as in a house, there must be a master, otherwise, everyone pockets something out of the money spent. At first, everybody knows that Ledru-Rollin is head over ears in debt. As for Lamartine, how can you expect a poet to understand politics? Ah! 'tis all very well for you to shake your head and to presume that you have more brains than others; all the same, what I say is true! But you are always cavilling; a person can't get in a word with you! For instance, there's Fournier-Fontaine, who had stores at Saint-Roch! do you know how much he failed for? Eight hundred thousand francs! And Gomer, the packer opposite to him—another Republican, that one—he smashed the tongs on his wife's head, and he drank so much absinthe that he is going to be put into a private asylum. That's the way with the whole of them—the Republicans! A Republic at twenty-five percent. Ah! yes! plume yourself upon it!"

Frederick took himself off. He was disgusted at the foolishness of this girl, which revealed itself all at once in the language of the populace. He felt himself even becoming a little patriotic once more.

The ill-temper of Rosanette only increased. Mademoiselle Vatnaz irritated him with her enthusiasm. Believing that she had a mission, she felt a furious desire to make speeches, to carry on disputes, and—sharper than Rosanette in matters of this sort—overwhelmed her with arguments.

One day she made her appearance burning with indignation against Hussonnet, who had just indulged in some blackguard remarks at the Woman's Club. Rosanette approved of this conduct, declaring even that she would take men's clothes to go and "give them a bit of her mind, the entire lot of them, and to whip them."

Frederick entered at the same moment.

"You'll accompany me—won't you?"

And, in spite of his presence, a bickering match took place between them, one of them playing the part of a citizen's wife and the other of a female philosopher.

According to Rosanette, women were born exclusively for love, or in order to bring up children, to be housekeepers.

According to Mademoiselle Vatnaz, women ought to have a position in the Government. In former times, the Gaulish women, and also the Anglo-Saxon women, took part in the legislation; the squaws of the Hurons formed a portion of the Council. The work of civilisation was common to both. It was necessary that all should contribute towards it, and that fraternity should be substituted for egoism, association for individualism, and cultivation on a large scale for minute subdivision of land.

"Come, that is good! you know a great deal about culture just now!"

"Why not? Besides, it is a question of humanity, of its future!"

"Mind your own business!"

"This is my business!"

They got into a passion. Frederick interposed. The Vatnaz became very heated, and went so far as to uphold Communism.

"What nonsense!" said Rosanette. "How could such a thing ever come to pass?"

The other brought forward in support of her theory the examples of the Essenes, the Moravian Brethren, the Jesuits of Paraguay, the family of the Pingons near Thiers in Auvergne; and, as she gesticulated a great deal, her gold chain got entangled in her bundle of trinkets, to which was attached a gold ornament in the form of a sheep.

Suddenly, Rosanette turned exceedingly pale.

Mademoiselle Vatnaz continued extricating her trinkets.

"Don't give yourself so much trouble," said Rosanette. "Now, I know your political opinions."

"What?" replied the Vatnaz, with a blush on her face like that of a virgin.

"Oh! oh! you understand me."

Frederick did not understand. There had evidently been something taking place between them of a more important and intimate character than Socialism.

"And even though it should be so," said the Vatnaz in reply, rising up unflinchingly. " 'Tis a loan, my dear—set off one debt against the other."

"Faith, I don't deny my own debts. I owe some thousands of francs—a nice sum. I borrow, at least; I don't rob anyone."

Mademoiselle Vatnaz made an effort to laugh.

"Oh! I would put my hand in the fire for him."

"Take care! it is dry enough to burn."

The spinster held out her right hand to her, and keeping it raised in front of her:

"But there are friends of yours who find it convenient for them."

"Andalusians, I suppose? as castanets?"

"You beggar!"

The Maréchale made her a low bow.

"There's nobody so charming!"

Mademoiselle Vatnaz made no reply. Beads of perspiration appeared on her temples. Her eyes fixed themselves on the carpet. She panted for breath. At last she reached the door, and slamming it vigorously: "Good night! You'll hear from me!"

"Much I care!" said Rosanette. The effort of self-suppression had shattered her nerves. She sank down on the divan, shaking all over, stammering forth words of abuse, shedding tears. Was it this threat on the part of the Vatnaz that had caused so much agitation in her mind? Oh, no! what did she care, indeed, about that one?

It was the golden sheep, a present, and in the midst of her tears the name of Delmar escaped her lips. So, then, she was in love with the mummer?

"In that case, why did she take on with me?" Frederick asked himself. "How is it that he has come back again? Who compels her to keep me? Where is the sense of this sort of thing?"

Rosanette was still sobbing. She remained all the time stretched at the edge of the divan, with her right cheek resting on her two hands, and she seemed a being so dainty, so free from self-consciousness, and so sorely troubled, that he drew closer to her and softly kissed her on the forehead.

Thereupon she gave him assurances of her affection for him; the Prince had just left her, they would be free. But she was for the time being short of money. "You saw yourself that this was so, the other day, when I was trying to turn my old linings to use." No more equipages now! And this was not all; the upholsterer was threatening to resume possession of the bedroom and the large drawing-room furniture. She did not know what to do.

Frederick had a mind to answer:

"Don't annoy yourself about it. I will pay."

But the lady knew how to lie. Experience had enlightened her. He confined himself to mere expressions of sympathy.

Rosanette's fears were not vain. It was necessary to give up the furniture and to quit the handsome apartment in the Rue Drouot. She took another on the Boulevard Poissonnière, on the fourth floor.

The curiosities of her old boudoir were quite sufficient to give to the three rooms a coquettish air. There were Chinese blinds, a tent on the terrace, and in the drawing-room a second-hand carpet still perfectly new, with ottomans covered with pink silk. Frederick had contributed largely to these purchases. He had felt the joy of a newly-married man who possesses at last a house of his own, a wife of his own—and, being much pleased with the place, he used to sleep there nearly every evening.

One morning, as he was passing out through the ante-room, he saw, on the third floor, on the staircase, the shako of a National Guard who was ascending it. Where in the world was he going?

Frederick waited. The man continued his progress up the stairs, with his head slightly bent down. He raised his eyes. It was my lord Arnoux!

The situation was clear. They both reddened simultaneously, overcome by a feeling of embarrassment common to both.

Arnoux was the first to find a way out of the difficulty.

"She is better—isn't that so?" as if Rosanette were ill, and he had come to learn how she was.

Frederick took advantage of this opening.

"Yes, certainly! at least, so I was told by her maid," wishing to convey that he had not been allowed to see her.

Then they stood facing each other, both undecided as to what they would do next, and eyeing one another intently. The question now was, which of the two was going to remain. Arnoux once more solved the problem.

"Pshaw! I'll come back by-and-by. Where are you going? I go with you!"

And, when they were in the street, he chatted as naturally as usual. Unquestionably he was not a man of jealous disposition, or else he was too good-natured to get angry. Besides, his time was devoted to serving his country. He never left off his uniform now. On the twenty-ninth of March he had defended the offices of the *Presse*. When the Chamber was invaded, he distinguished himself by his courage, and he was at the banquet given to the National Guard at Amiens.

Hussonnet, who was still on duty with him, availed himself of his flask and his cigars; but, irreverent by nature, he delighted in contradicting him, disparaging the somewhat inaccurate style of the decrees; and decrying the conferences at the Luxembourg, the women known as the "Vésuviennes," the political section bearing the name of "Tyroliens"; everything, in fact, down to the Car of Agriculture, drawn by horses to the ox-market, and escorted by ill-favoured young girls. Arnoux, on the other hand, was the upholder of authority, and dreamed of uniting the different parties. However, his own affairs had taken an unfavourable turn, and he was more or less anxious about them.

He was not much troubled about Frederick's relations with the Maréchale; for this discovery made him feel justified (in his conscience) in withdrawing the allowance which he had renewed since the Prince had left her. He pleaded by way of excuse for this step the embarrassed condition in which he found himself, uttered many lamentations—and Rosanette was generous. The result was that M. Arnoux regarded himself as the lover who appealed entirely to the heart, an idea that raised him in his own estimation and made him feel young again. Having no doubt that Frederick was paying the Maréchale, he fancied that he was "playing a nice trick" on the young man, even called at the house in such a stealthy fashion as to keep the other in ignorance of the fact, and when they happened to meet, left the coast clear for him.

Frederick was not pleased with this partnership, and his rival's politeness seemed only an elaborate piece of sarcasm. But by taking offence at it, he would have removed from his path every opportunity of ever finding his way back to Madame Arnoux; and then, this was the only means whereby he could hear about her movements. The earthenware-dealer, in accordance with his usual practice, or perhaps with some cunning design, recalled her readily in the course of conversation, and asked him why he no longer came to see her.

Frederick, having exhausted every excuse he could frame, assured him that he had called several times to see Madame Arnoux, but without success. Arnoux was convinced that this was so, for he had often referred in an eager tone at home to the absence of their friend, and she had invariably replied that she was out when he called, so that these two lies, in place of contradicting, corroborated each other.

The young man's gentle ways and the pleasure of finding a dupe in him made Arnoux like him all the better. He carried familiarity to its extreme limits, not through disdain, but through assurance. One day he wrote saying that very urgent business compelled him to be away in the country for twenty-four hours. He begged of the young man to mount guard in his stead. Frederick dared not refuse, so he repaired to the guard-house in the Place du Carrousel.

He had to submit to the society of the National Guards, and, with the exception of a sugar-refiner, a witty fellow who drank to an inordinate extent, they all appeared to him more stupid than their cartridge-boxes. The principal subject of conversation amongst them was the substitution of sashes for belts. Others declaimed against the national workshops.

One man said:

"Where are we going?"

The man to whom the words had been addressed opened his eyes as if he were standing on the verge of an abyss.

"Where are we going?"

Then, one who was more daring than the rest exclaimed:

"It cannot last! It must come to an end!"

And as the same kind of talk went on till night, Frederick was bored to death.

Great was his surprise when, at eleven o'clock, he suddenly beheld Arnoux, who immediately explained that he had hurried back to set him at liberty, having disposed of his own business.

The fact was that he had no business to transact. The whole thing was an invention to enable him to spend twenty-four hours alone with Rosanette. But the worthy Arnoux had placed too much confidence in his own powers, so that, now in the state of lassitude which was the result, he was seized with remorse. He had come to thank Frederick, and to invite him to have some supper.

"A thousand thanks! I'm not hungry. All I want is to go to bed."

"A reason the more for having a snack together. How flabby you are! One does not go home at such an hour as this. It is too late! It would be dangerous!"

Frederick once more yielded. Arnoux was quite a favorite with his brethren-in-arms, who had not expected to see him—and he was a particular crony of the refiner. They were all fond of him, and he was such a good fellow that he was sorry Hussonnet was not there. But he wanted to shut his eyes for one minute, no longer.

"Sit down beside me!" said he to Frederick, stretching himself on the camp-bed without taking off his belt and straps. Through fear of an alarm, in spite of the regulation, he even kept his gun in his hand, then stammered out some words:

"My darling! my little angel!" and ere long was fast asleep.

Those who had been talking to each other became silent; and gradually there was a deep silence in the guard-house. Frederick tormented by the fleas, kept staring about him. The wall, painted yellow, had, half-way up, a long shelf, on which the knapsacks formed a succession of little humps, while underneath, the muskets, which had the colour of lead, rose up side by side; and there could be heard a succession of snores, produced by the National Guards, whose stomachs were outlined through the darkness in a confused fashion. On the top of the stove stood an empty bottle and some plates. Three straw chairs were drawn around the table, on which a pack of cards was displayed. A drum, in the middle of the bench, let its strap hang down.

A warm breath of air making its way through the door caused the lamp to smoke. Arnoux slept with his two arms wide apart; and, as his gun was placed in a slightly crooked position, with the butt-end downward, the mouth of the barrel came up right under his arm. Frederick noticed this, and was alarmed.

"But, no, I'm wrong, there's nothing to be afraid of! And yet, suppose he met his death!"

And immediately pictures unrolled themselves before his mind in endless succession.

He saw himself with her at night in a post-chaise, then on a river's bank on a summer's evening, and under the reflection of a lamp at home in their own house. He even fixed his attention on household expenses and domestic arrangements, contemplating, feeling already his happiness between his hands; and in order to realise it, all that was needed was that the cock of the gun should rise. The end of it could be pushed with one's toe, the gun would go off—it would be a mere accident—nothing more!

Frederick brooded over this idea like a playwright in the agonies of composition. Suddenly it seemed to him that it was not far from being carried into practical operation, and that he was going to contribute to that result—that, in fact, he was yearning for it; and then a feeling of absolute terror took possession of him. In the midst of this mental distress he experienced a sense of pleasure, and he allowed himself to sink deeper and deeper into it, with a dreadful consciousness all the time that his scruples were vanishing. In the wildness of his reverie the rest of the world became effaced, and he could only realise that he was still alive from the intolerable oppression on his chest.

"Let us take a drop of white wine!" said the refiner, as he awoke.

Arnoux sprang to his feet, and, as soon as the white wine was swallowed, he wanted to relieve Frederick of his sentry duty.

Then he brought him to have breakfast in the Rue de Chartres, at Parly's, and as he required to recuperate his energies; he ordered two dishes of meat, a lobster, an omelet with rum, a salad, etc., and finished this off with a brand of Sauterne of 1819 and one of '42 Romanée, not to speak of the champagne at dessert and the liqueurs.

Frederick did not in any way gainsay him. He was disturbed in mind as if by the thought that the other might somehow trace on his countenance the idea that had lately flitted before his imagination. With both elbows on the table and his head bent forward, so that he annoyed Frederick by his fixed stare, he confided some of his hobbies to the young man.

He wanted to take for farming purposes all the embankments on the Northern line, in order to plant potatoes there, or else to organise on the boulevards a monster cavalcade in which the celebrities of the period would figure. He would let all the windows, which would, at the rate of three francs for each person, produce a handsome profit. In short, he dreamed of a great stroke of fortune by means of a monoply. He assumed a moral tone, nevertheless, found fault with excesses and all sorts of misconduct, spoke about his "poor father," and every evening, as he said, made an examination of his conscience offering his soul to God.

"A little curaçao, eh?"

"Just as you please."

As for the Republic, things would right themselves; in fact, he looked on himself as the happiest man on earth; and forgetting himself, he exalted Rosanette's attractive qualities, and even compared her with his wife. It was quite a different thing. You could not imagine a lovelier person!

"Your health!"

Frederick touched glasses with him. He had, out of complaisance, drunk a little too much. Besides, the strong sunlight dazzled him; and when they went up the Rue Vivienne together again, their shoulders touched each other in a fraternal fashion.

When he got home, Frederick slept till seven o'clock. After that he called on the Maréchale. She had gone out with somebody—with Arnoux, perhaps! Not knowing what to do with himself, he continued his promenade along the boulevard, but could not get past the Porte Saint-Martin, owing to the great crowd that blocked the way.

Want had abandoned to their own resources a considerable number of workmen, and they used to come there every evening, no doubt for the purpose of holding a review and awaiting a signal.

In spite of the law against riotous assemblies, these clubs of despair increased to a frightful extent, and many citizens repaired every day to the spot through bravado, and because it was the fashion.

All of a sudden Frederick caught a glimpse, three paces away, of M. Dambreuse along with Martinon. He turned his head away, for M. Dambreuse having got himself nominated as a representative of the people, he cherished a secret spite against him. But the capitalist stopped him.

"One word, my dear monsieur! I have some explanations to make to you."

"I am not asking you for any."

"Pray listen to me!"

It was not his fault in any way. Appeals had been made to him; pressure had, to a certain extent, been placed on him. Martinon immediately endorsed all that he had said. Some of the electors of Nogent had presented themselves in a deputation at his house.

"Besides, I expected to be free as soon as—"

A crush of people on the footpath forced M. Dambreuse to get out of the way. A minute after he reappeared, saying to Martinon:

"This is a genuine service, really, and you won't have any reason to regret—"

All three stood with their backs resting against a shop in order to be able to chat more at their ease.

From time to time there was a cry of, "Long live Napoleon! Long live Barbès! Down with Marie!"

The countless throng kept talking in very loud tones; and all these voices, echoing through the houses, made, so to speak, the continuous ripple of waves in a harbour. At intervals they ceased; and then could be heard voices singing the "Marseillaise."

Under the court-gates, men of mysterious aspect offered sword-sticks to those who passed. Sometimes two individuals, one of whom preceded the other, would wink, and then quickly hurry away. The footpaths were filled with groups of staring idlers. A dense crowd swayed to and fro on the pavement. Entire bands of police-officers, emerging from the alleys, had scarcely made their way into the midst of the multitude when they were swallowed up in the mass of people. Little red flags here and there looked like flames. Coachmen, from the place where they sat high up, gesticulated energetically, and then turned to go back. It was a case of perpetual movement—one of the strangest sights that could be conceived.

"How all this," said Martinon, "would have amused Mademoiselle Cécile!"

"My wife, as you are aware, does not like my niece to come with us," returned M. Dambreuse with a smile.

One could scarcely recognise in him the same man. For the past three months he had been crying, "Long live the Republic!" and he had even voted in favour of the banishment of Orleans. But there should be an end of concessions. He exhibited his rage so far as to carry a tomahawk in his pocket.

Martinon had one, too. The magistracy not being any longer irremovable, he had withdrawn from Parquet, so that he surpassed M. Dambreuse in his display of violence.

The banker had a special antipathy to Lamartine (for having supported Ledru-Rollin) and, at the same time, to Pierre Leroux, Proudhon, Considérant, Lamennais, and all the cranks, all the Socialists.

"For, in fact, what is it they want? The duty on meat and arrest for debt have been abolished. Now the project of a bank for mortgages is under consideration; the other day it was a national bank; and here are five millions in the Budget for the working-men! But luckily, it is over, thanks to Monsieur de Falloux! Good-bye to them! let them go!"

In fact, not knowing how to maintain the three hundred thousand men in the national workshops, the Minister of Public Works had that very day signed an order inviting all citizens between the ages of eighteen and twenty to take service as soldiers, or else to start for the provinces to cultivate the ground there.

They were indignant at the alternative thus put before them, convinced that the object was to destroy the Republic. They were aggrieved by the thought of having to live at a distance from the capital, as if it were a kind of exile. They saw themselves dying of fevers in desolate parts of the country. To many of them, moreover, who had been accustomed to work of a refined description, agriculture seemed a degradation; it was, in short, a mockery, a decisive breach of all the promises which had been made to them. If they offered any resistance, force would be employed against them. They had no doubt of it, and made preparations to anticipate it.

About nine o'clock the riotous assemblies which had formed at the Bastille and at the Châtelet ebbed back towards the boulevard. From the Porte Saint-Denis to the Porte Saint-Martin nothing could be seen save an enormous swarm of people, a single mass of a dark blue shade, nearly black. The men of whom one caught a glimpse all had glowing eyes, pale complexions, faces emaciated with hunger and excited with a sense of wrong.

Meanwhile, some clouds had gathered. The tempestuous sky roused the electricity that was in the people, and they kept whirling about of their own accord with the great swaying movements of a swelling sea, and one felt that there was an incalculable force in the depths of this excited throng, and as it were, the energy of an element. Then they all began exclaiming: "Lamps! lamps!" Many windows had no illumination, and stones were flung at the panes. M. Dambreuse deemed it prudent to withdraw from the scene. The two young men accompanied him home. He predicted great disasters. The people might once more invade the Chamber, and on this point he told them how he should have been killed on the fifteenth of May had it not been for the devotion of a National Guard.

"But I had forgotten! he is a friend of yours—your friend the earthenware manufacturer—Jacques Arnoux!" The rioters had been actually throttling him, when that brave citizen caught him in his arms and put him safely out of their reach.

So it was that, since then, there had been a kind of intimacy between them.

"It would be necessary, one of these days, to dine together, and, since you often see him, give him the assurance that I like him very much. He is an excellent man, and has, in my opinion, been slandered; and he has his wits about him in the morning. My compliments once more! A very good evening!"

Frederick, after he had quitted M. Dambreuse, went back to the Maréchale, and, in a very gloomy fashion, said that she should choose between him and Arnoux. She replied that she did not understand "dumps of this sort," that she did not care about Arnoux, and had no desire to cling to him. Frederick was thirsting to fly from Paris. She did not offer any opposition to this whim; and next morning they set out for Fontainebleau.

The hotel at which they stayed could be distinguished from others by a fountain that rippled in the middle of the courtyard attached to it. The doors of the various apartments opened out on a corridor, as in monasteries. The room assigned to them was large, well-furnished, hung with print, and noiseless, owing to the scarcity of tourists. Alongside the houses, people who had nothing to do kept passing up and down; then, under their windows, when the day was declining, children in the street would engage in a game of base; and this tranquillity, following so soon the tumult they had witnessed in Paris, filled them with astonishment and exercised over them a soothing influence.

Every morning at an early hour, they went to pay a visit to the château. As they passed in through the gate, they had a view of its entire front, with the five pavilions covered with sharp-pointed roofs, and its staircase of horseshoe-shape opening out to the end of the courtyard, which is hemmed in, to right and left, by two main portions of the building further down. On the paved ground lichens blended their colours here and there with the tawny hue of bricks, and the entire appearance of the palace, rust-coloured like old armour, had about it something of the impassiveness of royalty—a sort of warlike, melancholy grandeur.

At last, a man-servant made his appearance with a bunch of keys in his hand. He first showed them the apartments of the queens, the Pope's oratory, the gallery of Francis I, the mahogany table on which the Emperor signed his abdication, and in one of the rooms cut in two the old Galerie des Cerfs, the place where Christine got Monaldeschi assassinated. Rosanette listened to this narrative attentively, then, turning towards Frederick:

"No doubt it was through jealousy? Mind yourself!" After this they passed through the Council Chamber, the Guards' Room, the Throne Room, and the drawing-room of Louis XIII. The uncurtained windows sent forth a white light. The handles of the window-fastenings and the copper feet of the pier-tables were slightly tarnished with dust. The armchairs were everywhere hidden under coarse linen covers. Above the doors could be seen reliquaries of Louis XIV, and here and there hangings representing the gods of Olympus, Psyche, or the battles of Alexander.

As she was passing in front of the mirrors, Rosanette stopped for a moment to smooth her head-bands.

After passing through the donjon-court and the Saint-Saturnin Chapel, they reached the Festal Hall.

They were dazzled by the magnificence of the ceiling, which was divided into octagonal apartments set off with gold and silver, more finely chiselled than a jewel, and by the vast number of paintings covering the walls, from the immense chimney-piece, where the arms of France were surrounded by crescents and quivers, down to the musicians' gallery, which had been erected at the other end along the entire width of the hall. The ten arched windows were wide open; the sun threw its lustre on the pictures, so that they glowed beneath its rays; the blue sky continued in an endless curve the ultramarine of the arches; and from the depths of the woods, where the lofty summits of the trees filled up the horizon, there seemed to come an echo of flourishes blown by ivory trumpets, and mythological ballets, gathering together under the foliage princesses and nobles disguised as nymphs or fauns—an epoch of ingenuous science, of violent passions, and sumptuous art, when the ideal was to sweep away the world in a vision of the Hesperides, and when the mistresses of kings mingled their glory with the stars. There was a portrait of one of the most beautiful of these celebrated women in the form of Diana the huntress, and even the Infernal Diana, no doubt in order to indicate the power which she possessed even beyond the limits of the tomb. All these symbols confirmed her glory, and there remained about the spot something of her, an indistinct voice, a radiation that stretched out indefinitely. A feeling of mysterious retrospective voluptuousness took possession of Frederick.

In order to divert these passionate longings into another channel, he began to gaze tenderly on Rosanette, and asked her would she not like to have been this woman?

"What woman?"

"Diane de Poitiers!"

He repeated:

"Diane de Poitiers, the mistress of Henry II."

She gave utterance to a little "Ah!" that was all.

Her silence clearly demonstrated that she knew nothing about the matter, and had failed to comprehend his meaning, so that out of complaisance he said to her:

"Perhaps you are getting tired of this?"

"No, no—quite the reverse." And lifting up her chin, and casting around her a glance of the vaguest description, Rosanette let these words escape her lips:

"It recalls some memories to me!"

Meanwhile, it was easy to trace on her countenance a strained expression, a certain sense of awe; and, as this air of gravity made her look all the prettier, Frederick overlooked it.

The carps' pond amused her more. For a quarter of an hour she kept flinging pieces of bread into the water in order to see the fishes skipping about.

Frederick had seated himself by her side under the linden-trees. He saw in imagination all the personages who had haunted these walls—Charles V, the Valois Kings, Henry IV, Peter the Great, Jean Jacques Rousseau, and "the fair mourners of the stage-boxes," Voltaire, Napoleon, Pius VII, and Louis Philippe; and he felt himself environed, elbowed, by these tumultuous dead people. He was stunned by such a confusion of historic figures, even though he found a certain fascination in contemplating them, nevertheless.

At length they descended into the flower-garden.

It is a vast rectangle, which presents to the spectator, at the first glance, its wide yellow walks, its square grass-plots, its ribbons of box-wood, its yew-trees shaped like pyramids, its low-lying green swards, and its narrow borders, in which thinly-sown flowers make spots on the grey soil. At the end of the garden may be seen a park through whose entire length a canal makes its way.

Royal residences have attached to them a peculiar kind of melancholy, due, no doubt, to their dimensions being much too large for the limited number of guests entertained within them, to the silence which one feels astonished to find in them after so many flourishes of trumpets, to the immobility of their luxurious furniture, which attests by the aspect of age and decay it gradually assumes the transitory character of dynasties, the eternal wretchedness of all things; and this exhalation of the centuries, enervating and funereal, like the perfume of a mummy, makes itself felt even in untutored brains. Rosanette yawned immoderately. They went back to the hotel.

After their breakfast an open carriage came round for them. They started from Fontainebleau at a point where several roads diverged, then went up at a walking pace a gravelly road leading towards a little pine-wood. The trees became larger, and, from time to time, the driver would say, "This is the Frères Siamois, the Pharamond, the Bouquet de Roi," not forgetting a single one of these notable sites, sometimes even drawing up to enable them to admire the scene.

They entered the forest of Franchard. The carriage glided over the grass like a sledge; pigeons which they could not see began cooing. Suddenly, the waiter of a café made his appearance, and they alighted before the railing of a garden in which a number of round tables were placed. Then, passing on the left by the walls of a ruined abbey, they made their way over big boulders of stone, and soon reached the lower part of the gorge.

It is covered on one side with sandstones and juniper-trees tangled together, while on the other side the ground, almost quite bare, slopes towards the hollow of the valley, where a foot-track makes a pale line through the brown heather; and far above could be traced a flat cone-shaped summit with a telegraph-tower behind it.

Half-an-hour later they stepped out of the vehicle once more, in order to climb the heights of Aspremont.

The roads form zigzags between the thick-set pine-trees under rocks with angular faces. All this corner of the forest has a sort of choked-up look—a rather wild and solitary aspect. One thinks of hermits in connection with it—companions of huge stags with fiery crosses between their horns, who were wont to welcome with paternal smiles the good kings of France when they knelt before their grottoes. The warm air was filled with a resinous odour, and roots of trees crossed one another like veins close to the soil. Rosanette slipped over them, grew dejected, and felt inclined to shed tears.

But, at the very top, she became joyous once more on finding, under a roof made of branches, a sort of tavern where carved wood was sold. She drank a bottle of lemonade, and bought a holly-stick; and, without one glance towards the landscape which disclosed itself from the plateau, she entered the Brigands' Cave, with a waiter carrying a torch in front of her. Their carriage was awaiting them in the Bas Breau.

A painter in a blue blouse was working at the foot of an oak-tree with his box of colours on his knees. He raised his head and watched them as they passed.   .

In the middle of the hill of Chailly, the sudden breaking of a cloud caused them to turn up the hoods of their cloaks. Almost immediately the rain stopped, and the paving-stones of the street glistened under the sun when they were re-entering the town.

Some travellers, who had recently arrived, informed them that a terrible battle had stained Paris with blood. Rosanette and her lover were not surprised. Then everybody left; the hotel became quiet, the gas was put out, and they were lulled to sleep by the murmur of the fountain in the courtyard.

On the following day they went to see the Wolf's Gorge, the Fairies' Pool, the Long Rock, and the *Marlotte*. Two days later, they began again at random, just as their coachman thought fit to drive them, without asking where they were, and often even neglecting the famous sites.

They felt so comfortable in their old landau, low as a sofa, and covered with a rug made of a striped material which was quite faded. The moats, filled with brushwood, stretched out under their eyes with a gentle, continuous movement. White rays passed like arrows through the tall ferns. Sometimes a road that was no longer used presented itself before them, in a straight line, and here and there might be seen a feeble growth of weeds. In the centre between four cross-roads, a crucifix extended its four arms. In other places, stakes were bending down like dead trees, and little curved paths, which were lost under the leaves, made them feel a longing to pursue them. At the same moment the horse turned round; they entered there; they plunged into the mire. Further down moss had sprouted out at the sides of the deep ruts.

They believed that they were far away from all other people, quite alone. But suddenly a gamekeeper with his gun, or a band of women in rags with big bundles of fagots on their backs, would hurry past them.

When the carriage stopped, there was a universal silence. The only sounds that reached them were the blowing of the horse in the shafts with the faint cry of a bird more than once repeated.

The light at certain points illuminating the outskirts of the wood, left the interior in deep shadow, or else, attenuated in the foreground by a sort of twilight, it exhibited in the background violet vapours, a white radiance. The midday sun, falling directly on wide tracts of greenery, made splashes of light over them, hung gleaming drops of silver from the ends of the branches, streaked the grass with long lines of emeralds, and flung gold spots on the beds of dead leaves. When they let their heads fall back, they could distinguish the sky through the tops of the trees. Some of them, which were enormously high, looked like patriarchs or emperors, or, touching one another at their extremities formed with their long shafts, as it were, triumphal arches; others, sprouting forth obliquely from below, seemed like falling columns. This heap of big vertical lines gaped open. Then, enormous green billows unrolled themselves in unequal embossments as far as the surface of the valleys, towards which advanced the brows of other hills looking down on white plains, which ended by losing themselves in an undefined pale tinge.

Standing side by side, on some rising ground, they felt, as they drank in the air, the pride of a life more free penetrating into the depths of their souls, with a superabundance of energy, a joy which they could not explain.

The variety of trees furnished a spectacle of the most diversified character. The beeches with their smooth white bark twisted their tops together. Ash trees softly curved their bluish branches. In the tufts of the hornbeams rose up holly stiff as bronze. Then came a row of thin birches, bent into elegiac attitudes; and the pine-trees, symmetrical as organ pipes, seemed to be singing a song as they swayed to and fro. There were gigantic oaks with knotted forms, which had been violently shaken, stretched themselves out from the soil and pressed close against each other, and with firm trunks resembling torsos, launched forth to heaven despairing appeals with their bare arms and furious threats, like a group of Titans struck motionless in the midst of their rage. An atmosphere of gloom, a feverish languor, brooded over the pools, whose sheets of water were cut into flakes by the overshadowing thorn-trees. The lichens on their banks, where the wolves come to drink, are of the colour of sulphur, burnt, as it were, by the footprints of witches, and the incessant croaking of the frogs responds to the cawing of the crows as they wheel through the air. After this they passed through the monotonous glades, planted here and there with a staddle. The sound of iron falling with a succession of rapid blows could be heard. On the side of the hill a group of quarrymen were breaking the rocks. These rocks became more and more numerous and finally filled up the entire landscape, cube-shaped like houses, flat like flag-stones, propping up, overhanging, and became intermingled with each other, as if they were the ruins, unrecognisable and monstrous, of some vanished city. But the wild chaos they exhibited made one rather dream of volcanoes, of deluges, of great unknown cataclysms. Frederick said they had been there since the beginning of the world, and would remain so till the end. Rosanette turned aside her head, declaring that this would drive her out of her mind, and went off to collect sweet heather. The little violet blossoms, heaped up near one another, formed unequal plates, and the soil, which was giving way underneath, placed soft dark fringes on the sand spangled with mica.

One day they reached a point half-way up a hill, where the soil was full of sand. Its surface, untrodden till now, was streaked so as to resemble symmetrical waves. Here and there, like promontories on the dry bed of an ocean, rose up rocks with the vague outlines of animals, tortoises thrusting forward their heads, crawling seals, hippopotami, and bears. Not a soul around them. Not a single sound. The shingle glowed under the dazzling rays of the sun, and all at once in this vibration of light the specimens of the brute creation that met their gaze began to move about. They returned home quickly, flying from the dizziness that had seized hold of them, almost dismayed.

The gravity of the forest exercised an influence over them, and hours passed in silence, during which, allowing themselves to yield to the lulling effects of springs, they remained as it were sunk in the torpor of a calm intoxication. With his arm around her waist, he listened to her talking while the birds were warbling, noticed with the same glance the black grapes on her bonnet and the juniper-berries, the draperies of her veil, and the spiral forms assumed by the clouds, and when he bent towards her the freshness of her skin mingled with the strong perfume of the woods. They found amusement in everything. They showed one another, as a curiosity, gossamer threads of the Virgin hanging from bushes, holes full of water in the middle of stones, a squirrel on the branches, the way in which two butterflies kept flying after them; or else, at twenty paces from them, under the trees, a hind strode on peacefully, with an air of nobility and gentleness, its doe walking by its side.

Rosanette would have liked to run after it to embrace it.

She got very much alarmed once, when a man suddenly presenting himself, showed her three vipers in a box. She wildly flung herself on Frederick's breast. He felt happy at the thought that she was weak and that he was strong enough to defend her.

That evening they dined at an inn on the banks of the Seine. The table was near the window, Rosanette sitting opposite him, and he contemplated her little well-shaped white nose, her turned-up lips, her bright eyes, the swelling bands of her nut-brown hair, and her pretty oval face. Her dress of raw silk clung to her somewhat drooping shoulders, and her two hands, emerging from their sleeves, joined close together as if they were one—carved, poured out wine, moved over the table-cloth. The waiters placed before them a chicken with its four limbs stretched out, a stew of eels in a dish of pipe-clay, wine that had got spoiled, bread that was too hard, and knives with notches in them. All these things made the repast more enjoyable and strengthened the illusion. They fancied that they were in the middle of a journey in Italy on their honeymoon. Before starting again they went for a walk along the bank of the river.

The soft blue sky, rounded like a dome, leaned at the horizon on the indentations of the woods. On the opposite side, at the end of the meadow, there was a village steeple; and further away, to the left, the roof of a house made a red spot on the river, which wound its way without any apparent motion. Some rushes bent over it, however, and the water lightly shook some poles fixed at its edge in order to hold nets. An osier bow-net and two or three old fishing-boats might be seen there. Near the inn a girl in a straw hat was drawing buckets out of a well. Every time they came up again, Frederick heard the grating sound of the chain with a feeling of inexpressible delight.

He had no doubt that he would be happy till the end of his days, so natural did his felicity appear to him, so much a part of his life, and so intimately associated with this woman's being. He was irresistibly impelled to address her with words of endearment. She answered with pretty little speeches, light taps on the shoulder, displays of tenderness that charmed him by their unexpectedness. He discovered in her quite a new sort of beauty, in fact, which was perhaps only the reflection of surrounding things, unless it happened to bud forth from their hidden potentialities.

When they were lying down in the middle of the field, he would stretch himself out with his head on her lap, under the shelter of her parasol; or else with their faces turned towards the green sward, in the centre of which they rested, they kept gazing towards one another so that their pupils seemed to intermingle, thirsting for one another and ever satiating their thirst, and then with half-closed eyelids they lay side by side without uttering a single word.

Now and then the distant rolling of a drum reached their ears. It was the signal-drum which was being beaten in the different villages calling on people to go and defend Paris.

"Oh! look here! 'tis the rising!" said Frederick, with a disdainful pity, all this excitement now presenting to his mind a pitiful aspect by the side of their love and of eternal nature.

And they talked about whatever happened to come into their heads, things that were perfectly familiar to them, persons in whom they took no interest, a thousand trifles. She chatted with him about her chambermaid and her hairdresser. One day she was so self-forgetful that she told him her age—twenty-nine years. She was becoming quite an old woman.

Several times, without intending it, she gave him some particulars with reference to her own life. She had been a "shop girl," had taken a trip to England, and had begun studying for the stage; all this she told without any explanation of how these changes had come about; and he found it impossible to reconstruct her entire history.

She related to him more about herself one day when they were seated side by side under a plane-tree at the back of a meadow. At the road-side, further down, a little barefooted girl, standing amid a heap of dust, was making a cow go to pasture. As soon as she caught sight of them she came up to beg, and while with one hand she held up her tattered petticoat, she kept scratching with the other her black hair, which, like a wig of Louis XIV's time, curled round her dark face, lighted by a magnificent pair of eyes.

"She will be very pretty by-and-by," said Frederick.

"How lucky she is, if she has no mother!" remarked Rosanette.

"Eh? How is that?"

"Certainly. I, if it were not for mine—"

She sighed, and began to speak about her childhood. Her parents were weavers in the Croix-Rousse. She acted as an apprentice to her father. In vain did the poor man wear himself out with hard work; his wife was continually abusing him, and sold everything for drink. Rosanette could see, as if it were yesterday, the room they occupied with the looms ranged lengthwise against the windows, the pot boiling on the stove, the bed painted like mahogany, a cupboard facing it, and the obscure loft where she used to sleep up to the time when she was fifteen years old. At length a gentleman made his appearance on the scene—a fat man with a face of the colour of boxwood, the manners of a devotee, and a suit of black clothes. Her mother and this man had a conversation together, with the result that three days afterwards—Rosanette stopped, and with a look in which there was as much bitterness as shamelessness:

"It was done!"

Then, in response to a gesture of Frederick:

"As he was married (he would have been afraid of compromising himself in his own house), I was brought to a private room in a restaurant, and told that I would be happy, that I would get a handsome present.

"At the door, the first thing that struck me was a candelabrum of vermilion on a table, on which there were two covers. A mirror on the ceiling-showed their reflections, and the blue silk hangings on the walls made the entire apartment resemble an alcove; I was seized with astonishment. You understand—a poor creature who had never seen anything before. In spite of my dazed condition of mind, I got frightened. I wanted to go away. However, I remained.

"The only seat in the room was a sofa close beside the table. It was so soft that it gave way under me. The mouth of the hot-air stove in the middle of the carpet sent out towards me a warm breath, and there I sat without taking anything. The waiter, who was standing near me, urged me to eat. He poured out for me immediately a large glass of wine. My head began to swim, I wanted to open the window. He said to me:

" 'No, Mademoiselle! that is forbidden.' "

"And he left me.

"The table was covered with a heap of things that I had no knowledge of. Nothing there seemed to me good. Then I fell back on a pot of jam, and patiently waited. I did not know what prevented him from coming. It was very late—midnight at last—I couldn't bear the fatigue any longer. While pushing aside one of the pillows, in order to hear better, I found under my hand a kind of album—a book of engravings, they were vulgar pictures. I was sleeping on top of it when he entered the room."

She hung down her head and remained pensive.

The leaves rustled around them. Amid the tangled grass a great foxglove was swaying to and fro. The sunlight flowed like a wave over the green expanse, and the silence was interrupted at intervals by the browsing of the cow, which they could no longer see.

Rosanette kept her eyes fixed on a particular spot, three paces away from her, her nostrils heaving, and her mind absorbed in thought. Frederick caught hold of her hand.

"How you suffered, poor darling!"

"Yes," said she, "more than you imagine! So much so that I wanted to make an end of it—they had to fish me up!"

"What?"

"Ah! think no more about it! I love you, I am happy! kiss me!"

And she picked off, one by one, the sprigs of the thistles which clung to the hem of her gown.

Frederick was thinking more than all on what she had not told him. What were the means by which she had gradually emerged from wretchedness? To what lover did she owe her education? What had occurred in her life down to the day when he first came to her house? Her latest avowal was a bar to these questions. All he asked her was how she had made Arnoux's acquaintance.

"Through the Vatnaz."

"Wasn't it you that I once saw with both of them at the Palais-Royal?"

He referred to the exact date. Rosanette made a movement which showed a sense of deep pain.

"Yes, it is true! I was not gay at that time!"

But Arnoux had proved himself a very good fellow. Frederick had no doubt of it. However, their friend was a queer character, full of faults. He took care to re-call them. She quite agreed with him on this point.

"Never mind! One likes him, all the same, this camel!"

"Still—even now?" said Frederick.

She began to redden, half smiling, half angry.

"Oh, no! that's an old story. I don't keep anything hidden from you. Even though it might be so, with him it is different. Besides, I don't think you are nice towards your victim!"

"My victim!"

Rosanette caught hold of his chin.

"No doubt!"

And in the lisping fashion in which nurses talk to babies:

"Have always been so good! Never went a-by-by with his wife?"

"I! never at any time!"

Rosanette smiled. He felt hurt by this smile of hers, which seemed to him a proof of indifference.

But she went on gently, and with one of those looks which seem to appeal for a denial of the truth:

"Are you perfectly certain?"

"Not a doubt of it!"

Frederick solemnly declared on his word of honour that he had never bestowed a thought on Madame Arnoux, as he was too much in love with another woman.

"With whom, pray?"

"Why, with you, my beautiful one!"

"Ah! don't laugh at me! You only annoy me!"

He thought it a prudent course to invent a story—to pretend that he was swayed by a passion. He manufactured some circumstantial details. This woman, however, had rendered him very unhappy.

"Decidedly, you have not been lucky," said Rosanette.

"Oh! oh! I may have been!" wishing to convey in this way that he had been often fortunate in his love-affairs, so that she might have a better opinion of him, just as Rosanette did not avow how many lovers she had had, in order that he might have more respect for her—for there will always be found in the midst of the most intimate confidences restrictions, false shame, delicacy, and pity. You divine either in the other or in yourself precipices or miry paths which prevent you from penetrating any farther; moreover, you feel that you will not be understood. It is hard to express accurately the thing you mean, whatever it may be; and this is the reason why perfect unions are rare.

The poor Maréchale had never known one better than this. Often, when she gazed at Frederick, tears came into her eyes; then she would raise them or cast a glance towards the horizon, as if she saw there some bright dawn, perspectives of boundless felicity. At last, she confessed one day to him that she wished to have a mass said, "so that it might bring a blessing on our love."

How was it, then, that she had resisted him so long? She could not tell herself. He repeated his question a great many times; and she replied, as she clasped him in her arms:

"It was because I was afraid, my darling, of loving you too well!"

On Sunday morning, Frederick read, amongst the list of the wounded given in a newspaper, the name of Dussardier. He uttered a cry, and showing the paper to Rosanette, declared that he was going to start at once for Paris.

"For what purpose?"

"In order to see him, to nurse him!"

"You are not going, I'm sure, to leave me by myself?"

"Come with me!"

"Ha! to poke my nose in a squabble of that sort? Oh, no, thanks!"

"However, I cannot—"

"Ta! ta! ta! as if they had need of nurses in the hospitals! And then, what concern is he of yours any longer? Everyone for himself!"

He was roused to indignation by this egoism on her part, and he reproached himself for not being in the capital with the others. Such indifference to the misfortunes of the nation had in it something shabby, and only worthy of a small shopkeeper. And now, all of a sudden, his intrigue with Rosanette weighed on his mind as if it were a crime. For an hour they were quite cool towards each other.

Then she appealed to him to wait, and not expose himself to danger.

"Suppose you happen to be killed?"

"Well, I should only have done my duty!"

Rosanette gave a jump. His first duty was to love her; but, no doubt, he did not care about her any longer. There was no common sense in what he was going to do. Good heavens! what an idea!

Frederick rang for his bill. But to get back to Paris was not an easy matter. The Leloir stagecoach had just left; the Lecomte berlins would not be starting; the diligence from Bourbonnais would not be passing till a late hour that night, and perhaps it might be full, one could never tell. When he had lost a great deal of time in making enquiries about the various modes of conveyance, the idea occurred to him to travel post. The master of the post-house refused to supply him with horses, as Frederick had no passport. Finally, he hired an open carriage—the same one in which they had driven about the country—and at about five o'clock they arrived in front of the Hotel du Commerce at Melun.

The market-place was covered with piles of arms. The prefect had forbidden the National Guards to proceed towards Paris. Those who did not belong to his department wished to go on. There was a great deal of shouting, and the inn was packed with a noisy crowd.

Rosanette, seized with terror, said she would not go a step further, and once more begged of him to stay. The innkeeper and his wife joined in her entreaties. A decent sort of man who happened to be dining there interposed, and observed that the fighting would be over in a very short time. Besides, one ought to do his duty. Thereupon the Maréchale redoubled her sobs. Frederick got exasperated. He handed her his purse, kissed her quickly, and disappeared.

On reaching Corbeil, he learned at the station that the insurgents had cut the rails at regular distances, and the coachman refused to drive him any farther; he said that his horses were "overspent."

Through his influence, however, Frederick managed to procure an indifferent cabriolet, which, for the sum of sixty francs, without taking into account the price of a drink for the driver, was to convey him as far as the Italian barrier. But at a hundred paces from the barrier his coachman made him descend and turn back. Frederick was walking along the pathway, when suddenly a sentinel thrust out his bayonet. Four men seized him, exclaiming:

"This is one of them! Look out! Search him! Brigand! scoundrel!"

And he was so thoroughly stupefied that he let himself be dragged to the guard-house of the barrier, at the very point where the Boulevards des Gobelins and de l'Hôpital and Rues Godefroy and Mauffetard converge.

Four barricades formed at the ends of four different ways enormous sloping ramparts of paving-stones. Torches were glimmering here and there. In spite of the rising clouds of dust he could distinguish foot-soldiers of the Line and National Guards, all with their faces blackened, their chests uncovered, and an aspect of wild excitement. They had just captured the square, and had shot down a number of men. Their rage had not yet cooled. Frederick said he had come from Fontainebleau to the relief of a wounded comrade who lodged in the Rue Belle-fond. Not one of them would believe him at first. They examined his hands; they even put their noses to his ear to make sure that he did not smell of powder.

However, by dint of repeating the same thing, he finally satisfied a captain, who directed two fusiliers to conduct him to the guard-house of the Jardin des Plantes. They descended the Boulevard de l'Hôpital. A strong breeze was blowing. It restored him to animation.

After this they turned up the Rue du Marché aux Chevaux. The Jardin des Plantes at the right formed a long black mass, whilst at the left the entire front of the Pitié, illuminated at every window, blazed like a conflagration, and shadows passed rapidly over the window-panes.

The two men in charge of Frederick went away. Another accompanied him to the Polytechnic School. The Rue Saint-Victor was quite dark, without a gas-lamp or a light at any window to relieve the gloom. Every ten minutes could be heard the words:

"Sentinels! mind yourselves!"

And this exclamation, cast into the midst of the silence, was prolonged like the repeated striking of a stone against the side of a chasm as it falls through space.

Every now and then the stamp of heavy footsteps could be heard drawing nearer. This was nothing less than a patrol consisting of about a hundred men.

From this confused mass escaped whisperings and the dull clanking of iron; and, moving away with a rhythmic swing, it melted into the darkness.

In the middle of the crossing, where several streets met, a dragoon sat motionless on his horse. From time to time an express rider passed at a rapid gallop; then the silence was renewed. Cannons, which were being drawn along the streets, made, on the pavement, a heavy rolling sound that seemed full of menace—a sound different from every ordinary sound—which oppressed the heart. The sounds thus produced seemed to intensify the silence, which was profound, unlimited—a black silence. Men in white blouses accosted the soldiers, spoke one or two words to them, and then vanished like phantoms.

The guard-house of the Polytechnic School overflowed with people. The threshold was blocked up with women, who had come to see their sons or their husbands. They were sent on to the Panthéon, which had been transformed into a dead-house; and no attention was paid to Frederick. He pressed forward resolutely, solemnly declaring that his friend Dussardier was waiting for him, that he was at death's door. At last they sent a corporal to accompany him to the top of the Rue Saint-Jacques, to the Mayor's office in the twelfth arrondissement.

The Place du Panthéon was filled with soldiers lying asleep on straw. The day was breaking; the bivouac-fires were extinguished.

The insurrection had left terrible traces in this quarter. The soil of the streets, from one end to the other, was covered with risings of various sizes. On the wrecked barricades had been piled up omnibuses, gas-pipes, and cart-wheels. In certain places there were little dark pools, which must have been blood. The houses were riddled with projectiles, and their framework could be seen under the plaster that was peeled off. Window-blinds, each attached only by a single nail, hung like rags. The staircases having fallen in, doors opened on vacancy. The interiors of rooms could be perceived with their papers in strips. In some instances dainty objects had remained in them quite intact. Frederick noticed a timepiece, a parrot-stick, and some engravings.

When he entered the Mayor's office, the National Guards were chattering without a moment's pause about the deaths of Bréa and Négrier, about the deputy Charbonnel, and about the Archbishop of Paris. He heard them saying that the Duc d'Aumale had landed at Boulogne, that Barbès had fled from Vincennes, that the artillery were coming up from Bourges, and that abundant aid was arriving from the provinces. About three o'clock some one brought good news.

Truce-bearers from the insurgents were in conference with the President of the Assembly.

Thereupon they all made merry; and as he had a dozen francs left, Frederick sent for a dozen bottles of wine, hoping by this means to hasten his deliverance.

Suddenly a discharge of musketry was heard. The drinking stopped. They peered with distrustful eyes into the unknown—it might be Henry V.

In order to get rid of responsibility, they took Frederick to the Mayor's office in the eleventh arrondissement, which he was not permitted to leave till nine o'clock in the morning.

He started at a running pace from the Quai Voltaire. At an open window an old man in his shirtsleeves was crying, with his eyes raised. The Seine glided peacefully along. The sky was of a clear blue; and in the trees round the Tuileries birds were singing.

Frederick was just crossing the Place du Carrousel when a litter happened to be passing by. The soldiers at the guard-house immediately presented arms; and the officer, putting his hand to his shako, said: "Honour to unfortunate bravery!" This phrase seemed to have almost become a matter of duty. He who pronounced it appeared to be, on each occasion, filled with profound emotion. A group of people in a state of fierce excitement followed the litter, exclaiming:

"We will avenge you! we will avenge you!"

The vehicles kept moving about on the boulevard, and women were making lint before the doors. Meanwhile, the outbreak had been quelled, or very nearly so. A proclamation from Cavaignac, just posted up, announced the fact. At the top of the Rue Vivienne, a company of the Garde Mobile appeared. Then the citizens uttered cries of enthusiasm. They raised their hats, applauded, danced, wished to embrace them, and to invite them to drink; and flowers, flung by ladies, fell from the balconies.

At last, at ten o'clock, at the moment when the cannon was booming as an attack was being made on the Faubourg Saint-Antoine, Frederick reached the abode of Dussardier. He found the bookkeeper in his garret, lying asleep on his back. From the adjoining apartment a woman came forth with silent tread—Mademoiselle Vatnaz.

She led Frederick aside and explained to him how Dussardier had got wounded.

On Saturday, on the top of a barricade in the Rue Lafayette, a young fellow wrapped in a tricoloured flag cried out to the National Guards: "Are you going to shoot your brothers?" As they advanced, Dussardier threw down his gun, pushed away the others, sprang over the barricade, and, with a blow of an old shoe, knocked down the insurgent, from whom he tore the flag. He had afterwards been found under a heap of rubbish with a slug of copper in his thigh. It was found necessary to make an incision in order to extract the projectile. Mademoiselle Vatnaz arrived the same evening, and since then had not quitted his side.

She intelligently prepared everything that was needed for the dressings, assisted him in taking his medicine or other liquids, attended to his slightest wishes, left and returned again with footsteps more light than those of a fly, and gazed at him with eyes full of tenderness.

Frederick, during the two following weeks, did not fail to come back every morning. One day, while he was speaking about the devotion of the Vatnaz, Dussardier shrugged his shoulders:

"Oh! no! she does this through interested motives."

"Do you think so?"

He replied: "I am sure of it!" without seeming disposed to give any further explanation.

She had loaded him with kindnesses, carrying her attentions so far as to bring him the newspapers in which his gallant action was extolled. He even confessed to Frederick that he felt uneasy in his conscience.

Perhaps he ought to have put himself on the other side with the men in blouses; for, indeed, a heap of promises had been made to them which had not been carried out. Those who had vanquished them hated the Republic; and, in the next place, they had treated them very harshly. No doubt they were in the wrong—not quite, however; and the honest fellow was tormented by the thought that he might have fought against the righteous cause. Sénécal, who was immured in the Tuileries, under the terrace at the water's edge, had none of this mental anguish.

There were nine hundred men in the place, huddled together in the midst of filth, without the slightest order, their faces blackened with powder and clotted blood, shivering with ague and breaking out into cries of rage, and those who were brought there to die were not separated from the rest. Sometimes, on hearing the sound of a detonation, they believed that they were all going to be shot. Then they dashed themselves against the walls, and after that fell back again into their places, so much stupefied by suffering that it seemed to them that they were living in a nightmare, a mournful hallucination. The lamp, which hung from the arched roof, looked like a stain of blood, and little green and yellow flames fluttered about, caused by the emanations from the vault. Through fear of epidemics, a commission was appointed. When he had advanced a few steps, the President recoiled, frightened by the stench from the excrements and from the corpses.

As soon as the prisoners drew near a vent-hole, the National Guards who were on sentry, in order to prevent them from shaking the bars of the grating, prodded them indiscriminately with their bayonets.

As a rule they showed no pity. Those who were not beaten wished to signalise themselves. There was a regular outbreak of fear. They avenged themselves at the same time on newspapers, clubs, mobs, speech-making—everything that had exasperated them during the last three months, and in spite of the victory that had been gained, equality (as if for the punishment of its defenders and the exposure of its enemies to ridicule) manifested itself in a triumphal fashion—an equality of brute beasts, a dead level of sanguinary vileness; for the fanaticism of self-interest balanced the madness of want, aristocracy had the same fits of fury as low debauchery, and the cotton cap did not show itself less hideous than the red cap. The public mind was agitated just as it would be after great convulsions of nature. Sensible men were rendered imbeciles for the rest of their lives on account of it.

Père Roque had become very courageous, almost foolhardy. Having arrived on the 26th at Paris with some of the inhabitants of Nogent, instead of going back at the same time with them, he had gone to give his assistance to the National Guard encamped at the Tuileries; and he was quite satisfied to be placed on sentry in front of the terrace at the water's side. There, at any rate, he had these brigands under his feet! He was delighted to find that they were beaten and humiliated, and he could not refrain from uttering invectives against them.

One of them, a young lad with long fair hair, put his face to the bars, and asked for bread. M. Roque ordered him to hold his tongue. But the young man repeated in a mournful tone:

"Bread!"

"Have I any to give you?"

Other prisoners presented themselves at the vent-hole, with their bristling beards, their burning eyeballs, all pushing forward, and yelling:

"Bread!"

Père Roque was indignant at seeing his authority slighted. In order to frighten them he took aim at them; and, borne onward into the vault by the crush that nearly smothered him, the young man, with his head thrown backward, once more exclaimed:

"Bread!"

"Hold on! here it is!" said Père Roque, firing a shot from his gun. There was a fearful howl—then, silence. At the side of the trough something white could be seen lying.

After this, M. Roque returned to his abode, for he had a house in the Rue Saint-Martin, which he used as a temporary residence; and the injury done to the front of the building during the riots had in no slight degree contributed to excite his rage. It seemed to him, when he next saw it, that he had exaggerated the amount of damage done to it. His recent act had a soothing effect on him, as if it indemnified him for his loss.

It was his daughter herself who opened the door for him. She immediately made the remark that she had felt uneasy at his excessively prolonged absence. She was afraid that he had met with some misfortune—that he had been wounded.

This manifestation of filial love softened Père Roque. He was astonished that she should have set out on a journey without Catherine.

"I sent her out on a message," was Louise's reply.

And she made enquiries about his health, about one thing or another; then, with an air of indifference, she asked him whether he had chanced to come across Frederick:

"No; I didn't see him!"

It was on his account alone that she had come up from the country.

Some one was walking at that moment in the lobby.

"Oh! excuse me—"

And she disappeared.

Catherine had not found Frederick. He had been several days away, and his intimate friend, M. Deslauriers, was now living in the provinces.

Louise once more presented herself, shaking all over, without being able to utter a word. She leaned against the furniture.

"What's the matter with you? Tell me—what's the matter with you?" exclaimed her father.

She indicated by a wave of her hand that it was nothing, and with a great effort of will she regained her composure.

The keeper of the restaurant at the opposite side of the street brought them soup. But Père Roque had passed through too exciting an ordeal to be able to control his emotions. "He is not likely to die;" and at dessert he had a sort of fainting fit. A doctor was at once sent for, and he prescribed a potion. Then, when M. Roque was in bed, he asked to be as well wrapped up as possible in order to bring on perspiration. He gasped; he moaned.

"Thanks, my good Catherine! Kiss your poor father, my chicken! Ah! those revolutions!"

And, when his daughter scolded him for having made himself ill by tormenting his mind on her account, he replied:

"Yes! you are right! But I couldn't help it! I am too sensitive!"

Chapter XV

"How Happy Could I Be With Either"

MADAME DAMBREUSE, IN HER BOUDOIR, BETWEEN HER NIECE AND MISS John, was listening to M. Roque as he described the severe military duties he had been forced to perform.

She was biting her lips, and appeared to be in pain.

"Oh! 'tis nothing! it will pass away!"

And, with a gracious air:

"We are going to have an acquaintance of yours at dinner with us—Monsieur Moreau."

Louise gave a start.

"Oh! we'll only have a few intimate friends there—amongst others, Alfred de Cisy."

And she spoke in terms of high praise about his manners, his personal appearance, and especially his moral character.

Madame Dambreuse was nearer to a correct estimate of the state of affairs than she imagined; the Vicomte was contemplating marriage. He said so to Martinon, adding that Mademoiselle Cécile was certain to like him, and that her parents would accept him.

To warrant him in going so far as to confide to another his intentions on the point, he ought to have satisfactory information with regard to her dowry. Now Martinon had a suspicion that Cécile was M. Dambreuse's natural daughter; and it is probable that it would have been a very strong step on his part to ask for her hand at any risk. Such audacity, of course, was not unaccompanied by danger; and for this reason Martinon had, up to the present, acted in a way that could not compromise him. Besides, he did not see how he could well get rid of the aunt. Cisy's confidence induced him to make up his mind; and he had formally made his proposal to the banker, who, seeing no obstacle to it, had just informed Madame Dambreuse about the matter.

Cisy presently made his appearance. She arose and said:

"You have forgotten us. Cécile, shake hands!"

At the same moment Frederick entered the room.

"Ha! at last we have found you again!" exclaimed Père Roque. "I called with Cécile on you three times this week!"

Frederick had carefully avoided them. He pleaded by way of excuse that he spent all his days beside a wounded comrade.

For a long time, however, a heap of misfortunes had happened to him, and he tried to invent stories to explain his conduct. Luckily the guests arrived in the midst of his explanation. First of all M. Paul de Grémonville, the diplomatist whom he met at the ball; then Fumichon, that manufacturer whose conservative zeal had scandalised him one evening. After them came the old Duchesse de Montreuil Nantua.

But two loud voices in the anteroom reached his ears. They were that of M. de Nonancourt, an old beau with the air of a mummy preserved in cold cream, and that of Madame de Larsillois, the wife of a prefect of Louis Philippe. She was terribly frightened, for she had just heard an organ playing a polka which was a signal amongst the insurgents. Many of the wealthy class of citizens had similar apprehensions; they thought that men in the catacombs were going to blow up the Faubourg Saint-Germain. Some noises escaped from cellars, and things that excited suspicion were passed up to windows.

Everyone in the meantime made an effort to calm Madame de Larsillois. Order was re-established. There was no longer anything to fear.

"Cavaignac has saved us!"

As if the horrors of the insurrection had not been sufficiently numerous, they exaggerated them. There had been twenty-three thousand convicts on the side of the Socialists—no less!

They had no doubt whatever that food had been poisoned, that Gardes Mobiles had been sawn between two planks, and that there had been inscriptions on flags inciting the people to pillage and incendiarism.

"Aye, and something more!" added the ex-prefect.

"Oh, dear!" said Madame Dambreuse, whose modesty was shocked, while she indicated the three young girls with a glance.

M. Dambreuse came forth from his study accompanied by Martinon. She turned her head round and responded to a bow from Pellerin, who was advancing towards her. The artist gazed in a restless fashion towards the walls. The banker took him aside, and conveyed to him that it was desirable for the present to conceal his revolutionary picture.

"No doubt," said Pellerin, the rebuff which he received at the Club of Intellect having modified his opinions.

M. Dambreuse let it slip out very politely that he would give him orders for other works.

"But excuse me. Ah! my dear friend, what a pleasure!"

Arnoux and Madame Arnoux stood before Frederick.

He had a sort of vertigo. Rosanette had been irritating him all the afternoon with her display of admiration for soldiers, and the old passion was reawakened.

The steward came to announce that dinner was on the table. With a look she directed the Vicomte to take Cécile's arm, while she said in a low tone to Martinon, "You wretch!" And then they passed into the dining-room.

Under the green leaves of a pineapple, in the middle of the table-cloth, a dorado stood, with its snout reaching towards a quarter of roebuck and its tail just grazing a bushy dish of crayfish. Figs, huge cherries, pears, and grapes (the first fruits of Parisian cultivation) rose like pyramids in baskets of old Saxe. Here and there a bunch of flowers mingled with the shining silver plate. The white silk blinds, drawn down in front of the windows, filled the apartment with a mellow light. It was cooled by two fountains, in which there were pieces of ice; and tall men-servants, in short breeches, waited on them. All these luxuries seemed more precious after the emotion of the past few days. They felt a fresh delight at possessing things which they had been afraid of losing; and Nonancourt expressed the general sentiment when he said:

"Ah! let us hope that these Republican gentlemen will allow us to dine!"

"In spite of their fraternity!" Père Roque added, with an attempt at wit.

These two personages were placed respectively at the right and at the left of Madame Dambreuse, her husband being exactly opposite her, between Madame Larsillois, at whose side was the diplomatist and the old Duchesse, whom Fumichon elbowed. Then came the painter, the dealer in faïence, and Mademoiselle Louise; and, thanks to Martinon, who had carried her chair to enable her to take a seat near Louise, Frederick found himself beside Madame Arnoux.

She wore a black barège gown, a gold hoop on her wrist, and, as on the first day that he dined at her house, something red in her hair, a branch of fuchsia twisted round her chignon. He could not help saying:

" 'Tis a long time since we saw each other."

"Ah!" she returned coldly.

He went on, in a mild tone, which mitigated the impertinence of his question:

"Have you thought of me now and then?"

"Why should I think of you?"

Frederick was hurt by these words.

"You are right, perhaps, after all."

But very soon, regretting what he had said, he swore that he had not lived a single day without being ravaged by the remembrance of her.

"I don't believe a single word of it, Monsieur."

"However, you know that I love you!"

Madame Arnoux made no reply.

"You know that I love you!"

She still kept silent.

"Well, then, go be hanged!" said Frederick to himself.

And, as he raised his eyes, he perceived Mademoiselle Roque at the other side of Madame Arnoux.

She thought it gave her a coquettish look to dress entirely in green, a colour which contrasted horribly with her red hair. The buckle of her belt was large and her collar cramped her neck. This lack of elegance had, no doubt, contributed to the coldness which Frederick at first displayed towards her. She watched him from where she sat, some distance away from him, with curious glances; and Arnoux, close to her side, in vain lavished his gallantries—he could not get her to utter three words, so that, finally abandoning all hope of making himself agreeable to her, he listened to the conversation. She now began rolling about a slice of Luxembourg pine-apple in her pea-soup.

Louis Blanc, according to Fumichon, owned a large house in the Rue Saint-Dominique, which he refused to let to the workmen.

"For my part, I think it rather a funny thing," said Nonancourt, "to see Ledru-Rollin hunting over the Crown lands."

"He owes twenty thousand francs to a goldsmith!" Cisy interposed, "and 'tis maintained—"

Madame Dambreuse stopped him.

"Ah! how nasty it is to be getting hot about politics! and for such a young man, too! fie, fie! Pay attention rather to your fair neighbour!"

After this, those who were of a grave turn of mind attacked the newspapers. Arnoux took it on himself to defend them. Frederick mixed himself up in the discussion, describing them as commercial establishments just like any other house of business. Those who wrote for them were, as a rule, imbeciles or humbugs; he gave his listeners to understand that he was acquainted with journalists, and combated with sarcasms his friend's generous sentiments.

Madame Arnoux did not notice that this was said through a feeling of spite against her.

Meanwhile, the Vicomte was torturing his brain in the effort to make a conquest of Mademoiselle Cécile. He commenced by finding fault with the shape of the decanters and the graving of the knives, in order to show his artistic tastes. Then he talked about his stable, his tailor and his shirtmaker. Finally, he took up the subject of religion, and seized the opportunity of conveying to her that he fulfilled all his duties.

Martinon set to work in a better fashion. With his eyes fixed on her continually, he praised, in a monotonous fashion, her birdlike profile, her dull fair hair, and her hands, which were unusually short. The plain-looking young girl was delighted at this shower of flatteries.

It was impossible to hear anything, as all present were talking at the tops of their voices. M. Roque wanted "an iron hand" to govern France. Nonancourt even regretted that the political scaffold was abolished. They ought to have all these scoundrels put to death together.

"Now that I think of it, are we speaking of Dussardier?" said M. Dambreuse, turning towards Frederick.

The worthy shopman was now a hero, like Sallesse, the brothers Jeanson, the wife of Pequillet, etc.

Frederick, without waiting to be asked, related his friend's history; it threw around him a kind of halo.

Then they came quite naturally to refer to different traits of courage.

According to the diplomatist, it was not hard to face death, witness the case of men who fight duels.

"We might take the Vicomte's testimony on that point," said Martinon.

The Vicomte's face got very flushed.

The guests stared at him, and Louise, more astonished than the rest, murmured: "What is it, pray?"

"He *sank* before Frederick," returned Arnoux, in a very low tone.

"Do you know anything, Mademoiselle?" said Nonancourt presently, and he repeated her answer to Madame Dambreuse, who, bending forward a little, began to fix her gaze on Frederick.

Martinon did not wait for Cécile's questions. He informed her that this affair had reference to a woman of improper character. The young girl drew back slightly in her chair, as if to escape from contact with such a libertine.

The conversation was renewed. The great wines of Bordeaux were sent round, and the guests became animated. Pellerin had a dislike to the Revolution, because he attributed to it the complete loss of the Spanish Museum.

This is what grieved him most as a painter.

As he made the latter remark, M. Roque asked:

"Are you not yourself the painter of a very notable picture?"

"Perhaps! What is it?"

"It represents a lady in a costume—faith!—a little light, with a purse, and a peacock behind."

Frederick, in his turn, reddened. Pellerin pretended that he had not heard the words.

"Nevertheless, it is certainly by you! For your name is written at the bottom of it, and there is a line on it stating that it is Monsieur Moreau's property."

One day, when Père Roque and his daughter were waiting at his residence to see him, they saw the Maréchale's portrait. The old gentleman had even taken it for "a Gothic painting."

"No," said Pellerin rudely, " 'tis a woman's portrait."

Martinon added:

"And a living woman's, too, and no mistake! Isn't that so, Cisy?"

"Oh! I know nothing about it."

"I thought you were acquainted with her. But, since it causes you pain, I must beg a thousand pardons!"

Cisy lowered his eyes, proving by his embarrassment that he must have played a pitiable part in connection with this portrait. As for Frederick, the model could only be his mistress. It was one of those convictions which are immediately formed, and the faces of the assembly revealed it with the utmost clearness.

"How he lied to me!" said Madame Arnoux to herself.

"It is for her, then, that he left me," thought Louise.

Frederick had an idea that these two stories might compromise him; and when they were in the garden, he uttered reproaches to Martinon on the subject. Mademoiselle Cécile's wooer burst out laughing in his face.

"Oh, not at all! 'twill do you good! Go ahead!"

What did he mean? Besides, what was the cause of this good nature, so contrary to his usual conduct? Without giving any explanation, he proceeded towards the lower end, where the ladies were seated. The men were standing round them, and, in their midst, Pellerin was giving vent to his ideas. The form of government most favourable for the arts was an enlightened monarchy. He was disgusted with modern times, "if it were only on account of the National Guard"—he regretted the Middle Ages and the days of Louis XIV. M. Roque congratulated him on his opinions, confessing that they overcame all his prejudices against artists. But almost without a moment's delay he went off when the voice of Fumichon attracted his attention.

Arnoux tried to prove that there were two Socialisms—a good and a bad. The manufacturer saw no difference whatever between them, his head becoming dizzy with rage at the utterance of the word "property."

" 'Tis a law written on the face of Nature! Children cling to their toys. All peoples, all animals are of my opinion. The lion even, if he were able to speak, would declare himself a proprietor! Thus I myself, messieurs, began with a capital of fifteen thousand francs. Would you be surprised to hear that for thirty years I used to get up at four o'clock every morning? I've had as much pain as five hundred devils in making my fortune! And people will come and tell me I'm not the master, that my money is not my money; in short, that property is theft!"

"But Proudhon—"

"Let me alone with your Proudhon! if he were here I think I'd strangle him!"

He would have strangled him. After the intoxicating drink he had swallowed Fumichon did not know what he was talking about any longer, and his apoplectic face was on the point of bursting like a bombshell.

"Good morrow, Arnoux," said Hussonnet, who was walking briskly over the grass.

He brought M. Dambreuse the first leaf of a pamphlet, bearing the title of "The Hydra," the Bohemian defending the interests of a reactionary club, and in that capacity he was introduced by the banker to his guests.

Hussonnet amused them by relating how the dealers in tallow hired three hundred and ninety-two street boys to bawl out every evening "Lamps," and then turning into ridicule the principles of '89, the emancipation of the negroes, and the orators of the Left; and he even went so far as to do "Prudhonnne on a Barricade," perhaps under the influence of a kind of jealousy of these rich people who had enjoyed a good dinner. The caricature did not please them overmuch. Their faces grew long.

This, however, was not a time for joking, so Nonancourt observed, as he recalled the death of Monseigneur Affre and that of General de Bréa. These events were being constantly alluded to, and arguments were constructed out of them. M. Roque described the archbishop's end as "everything that one could call sublime." Fumichon gave the palm to the military personage, and instead of simply expressing regret for these two murders, they held disputes with a view to determining which ought to excite the greatest indignation. A second comparison was next instituted, namely, between Lamoricière and Cavaignac, M. Dambreuse glorifying Cavaignac, and Nonancourt, Lamoricière.

Not one of the persons present, with the exception of Arnoux, had ever seen either of them engaged in the exercise of his profession. None the less, everyone formulated an irrevocable judgment with reference to their operations.

Frederick, however, declined to give an opinion on the matter, confessing that he had not served as a soldier. The diplomatist and M. Dambreuse gave him an approving nod of the head. In fact, to have fought against the insurrection was to have defended the Republic. The result, although favourable, consolidated it; and now they had got rid of the vanquished, they wanted to be conquerors.

As soon as they had got out into the garden, Madame Dambreuse, taking Cisy aside, chided him for his awkwardness. When she caught sight of Martinon, she sent him away, and then tried to learn from her future nephew the cause of his witticisms at the Vicomte's expense.

"There's nothing of the kind."

"And all this, as it were, for the glory of M. Moreau. What is the object of it?"

"There's no object. Frederick is a charming fellow. I am very fond of him."

"And so am I, too. Let him come here. Go and look for him!"

After two or three commonplace phrases, she began by lightly disparaging her guests, and in this way she placed him on a higher level than the others. He did not fail to run down the rest of the ladies more or less, which was an ingenious way of paying her compliments. But she left his side from time to time, as it was a reception-night, and ladies were every moment arriving; then she returned to her seat, and the entirely accidental arrangement of the chairs enabled them to avoid being overheard.

She showed herself playful and yet grave, melancholy and yet quite rational. Her daily occupations interested her very little—there was an order of sentiments of a less transitory kind. She complained of the poets, who misrepresent the facts of life, then she raised her eyes towards heaven, asking of him what was the name of a star.

Two or three Chinese lanterns had been suspended from the trees; the wind shook them, and lines of coloured light quivered on her white dress. She sat, after her usual fashion, a little back in her armchair, with a footstool in front of her. The tip of a black satin shoe could be seen; and at intervals Madame Dambreuse allowed a louder word than usual, and sometimes even a laugh, to escape her.

These coquetries did not affect Martinon, who was occupied with Cécile; but they were bound to make an impression on M. Roque's daughter, who was chatting with Madame Arnoux. She was the only member of her own sex present whose manners did not appear disdainful. Louise came and sat beside her; then, yielding to the desire to give vent to her emotions:

"Does he not talk well—Frederick Moreau, I mean?"

"Do you know him?"

"Oh! intimately! We are neighbours; and he used to amuse himself with me when I was quite a little girl."

Madame Arnoux cast at her a sidelong glance, which meant:

"I suppose you are not in love with him?"

The young girl's face replied with an untroubled look:

"Yes."

"You see him often, then?"

"Oh, no! only when he comes to his mother's house. 'Tis ten months now since he came. He promised, however, to be more particular."

"The promises of men are not to be too much relied on, my child."

"But he has not deceived me!"

"As he did others!"

Louise shivered: "Can it be by any chance that he promised something to her;" and her features became distracted with distrust and hate.

Madame Arnoux was almost afraid of her; she would have gladly withdrawn what she had said. Then both became silent.

As Frederick was sitting opposite them on a folding-stool, they kept staring at him, the one with propriety out of the corner of her eye, the other boldly, with parted lips, so that Madame Dambreuse said to him:

"Come, now, turn round, and let her have a good look at you!"

"Whom do you mean?"

"Why, Monsieur Roque's daughter!"

And she rallied him on having won the heart of this young girl from the provinces. He denied that this was so, and tried to make a laugh of it.

"Is it credible, I ask you? Such an ugly creature!"

However, he experienced an intense feeling of gratified vanity. He recalled to mind the reunion from which he had returned one night, some time before, his heart filled with bitter humiliation, and he drew a deep breath, for it seemed to him that he was now in the environment that really suited him, as if all these things, including the Dambreuse mansion, belonged to himself. The ladies formed a semicircle around him while they listened to what he was saying, and in order to create an effect, he declared that he was in favor of the re-establishment of divorce, which he maintained should be easily procurable, so as to enable people to quit one another and come back to one another without any limit as often as they liked. They uttered loud protests; a few of them began to talk in whispers. Little exclamations every now and then burst forth from the place where the wall was overshadowed with aristolochia. One would imagine that it was a mirthful cackling of hens; and he developed his theory with that self-complacency which is generated by the consciousness of success. A man-servant brought into the arbour a tray laden with ices. The gentlemen drew close together and began to chat about the recent arrests.

Thereupon Frederick revenged himself on the Vicomte by making him believe that he might be prosecuted as a Legitimist. The other urged by way of reply that he had not stirred outside his own room. His adversary enumerated in a heap the possible mischances. MM. Dambreuse and Grémonville found the discussion very amusing. Then they paid Frederick compliments, while expressing regret at the same time that he did not employ his abilities in the defence of order. They grasped his hand with the utmost warmth; he might for the future count on them. At last, just as everyone was leaving, the Vicomte made a low bow to Cécile:

"Mademoiselle, I have the honour of wishing you a very good evening."

She replied coldly:

"Good evening." But she gave Martinon a parting smile.

Père Roque, in order to continue the conversation between himself and Arnoux, offered to see him home, "as well as Madame"—they were going the same way. Louise and Frederick walked in front of them. She had caught hold of his arm; and, when she was some distance away from the others she said:

"Ah! at last! at last! I've had enough to bear all the evening! How nasty those women were! What haughty airs they had!"

He made an effort to defend them.

"First of all, you might certainly have spoken to me the moment you came in, after being away a whole year!"

"It was not a year," said Frederick, glad to be able to give some sort of rejoinder on this point in order to avoid the other questions.

"Be it so; the time appeared very long to me, that's all. But, during this horrid dinner, one would think you felt ashamed of me. Ah! I understand—I don't possess what is needed in order to please as they do."

"You are mistaken," said Frederick.

"Really! Swear to me that you don't love anyone!"

He did swear.

"You love nobody but me alone?"

"I assure you, I do not."

This assurance filled her with delight. She would have liked to lose her way in the streets, so that they might walk about together the whole night.

"I have been so much tormented down there! Nothing was talked about but barricades. I imagined I saw you falling on your back covered with blood! Your mother was confined to her bed with rheumatism. She knew nothing about what was happening. I had to hold my tongue. I could stand it no longer, so I took Catherine with me."

And she related to him all about her departure, her journey, and the lie she told her father.

"He's bringing me back in two days. Come tomorrow evening, as if you were merely paying a casual visit, and take advantage of the opportunity to ask for my hand in marriage."

Never had Frederick been further from the idea of marriage. Besides, Mademoiselle Roque appeared to him a rather absurd young person. How different she was from a woman like Madame Dambreuse! A very different future was in store for him. He had found reason to-day to feel perfectly certain on that point; and, therefore, this was not the time to involve himself, from mere sentimental motives, in a step of such momentous importance. It was necessary now to be decisive—and then he had seen Madame Arnoux once more. Nevertheless he was rather embarrassed by Louise's candour.

He said in reply to her last words:

"Have you considered this matter?"

"How is that?" she exclaimed, frozen with astonishment and indignation.

He said that to marry at such a time as this would be a piece of folly.

"So you don't want to have me?"

"Nay, you don't understand me!"

And he plunged into a confused mass of verbiage in order to impress upon her that he was kept back by more serious considerations; that he had business on hand which it would take a long time to dispose of; that even his inheritance had been placed in jeopardy (Louise cut all this explanation short with one plain word); that, last of all, the present political situation made the thing undesirable. So, then, the most reasonable course was to wait patiently for some time. Matters would, no doubt, right themselves—at least, he hoped so; and, as he could think of no further grounds to go upon just at that moment, he pretended to have been suddenly reminded that he should have been with Dussardier two hours ago.

Then, bowing to the others, he darted down the Rue Hauteville, took a turn round the Gymnase, returned to the boulevard, and quickly rushed up Rosanette's four flights of stairs.

M. and Madame Arnoux left Père Roque and his daughter at the entrance of the Rue Saint-Denis. Husband and wife returned home without exchanging a word, as he was unable to continue chattering any longer, feeling quite worn out. She even leaned against his shoulder. He was the only man who had displayed any honourable sentiments during the evening. She entertained towards him feelings of the utmost indulgence. Meanwhile, he cherished a certain degree of spite against Frederick.

"Did you notice his face when a question was asked about the portrait? When I told you that he was her lover, you did not wish to believe what I said!"

"Oh! yes, I was wrong!"

Arnoux, gratified with his triumph, pressed the matter even further.

"I'd even make a bet that when he left us, a little while ago, he went to see her again. He's with her at this moment, you may be sure! He's finishing the evening with her!"

Madame Arnoux had pulled down her hat very low.

"Why, you're shaking all over!"

"That's because I feel cold!" was her reply.

As soon as her father was asleep, Louise made her way into Catherine's room, and, catching her by the shoulders, shook her.

"Get up—quick! as quick as ever you can! and go and fetch a cab for me!"

Catherine replied that there was not one to be had at such an hour.

"Will you come with me yourself there, then?"

"Where, might I ask?"

"To Frederick's house!"

"Impossible! What do you want to go there for?"

It was in order to have a talk with him. She could not wait. She must see him immediately.

"Just think of what you're about to do! To present yourself this way at a house in the middle of the night! Besides, he's asleep by this time!"

"I'll wake him up!"

"But this is not a proper thing for a young girl to do!"

"I am not a young girl—I'm his wife! I love him! Come—put on your shawl!"

Catherine, standing at the side of the bed, was trying to make up her mind how to act. She said at last:

"No! I won't go!"

"Well, stay behind then! I'll go there by myself!"

Louise glided like an adder towards the staircase. Catherine rushed after her, and came up with her on the footpath outside the house. Her remonstrances were fruitless; and she followed the girl, fastening her undervest as she hurried along in the rear. The walk appeared to her exceedingly tedious. She complained that her legs were getting weak from age.

"I'll go on after you—faith, I haven't the same, thing to drive me on that you have!"

Then she grew softened.

"Poor soul! You haven't anyone now but your Catau, don't you see?"

From time to time scruples took hold of her mind.

"Ah, this is a nice thing you're making me do! Suppose your father happened to wake and miss you! Lord God, let us hope no misfortune will happen!"

In front of the Théâtre des Variétés, a patrol of National Guards stopped them.

Louise immediately explained that she was going with her servant to look for a doctor in the Rue Rumfort. The patrol allowed them to pass on.

At the corner of the Madeleine they came across a second patrol, and, Louise having given the same explanation, one of the National Guards asked in return:

"Is it for a nine months' ailment, ducky?"

"Oh, damn it!" exclaimed the captain, "no blackguardisms in the ranks! Pass on, ladies!"

In spite of the captain's orders, they still kept cracking jokes.

"I wish you much joy!"

"My respects to the doctor!"

"Mind the wolf!"

"They like laughing," Catherine remarked in a loud tone. "That's the way it is to be young."

At length they reached Frederick's abode.

Louise gave the bell a vigorous pull, which she repeated several times. The door opened a little, and, in answer to her inquiry, the porter said:

"No!"

"But he must be in bed!"

"I tell you he's not. Why, for nearly three months he has not slept at home!"

And the little pane of the lodge fell down sharply, like the blade of a guillotine.

They remained in the darkness under the archway.

An angry voice cried out to them:

"Be off!"

The door was again opened; they went away.

Louise had to sit down on a boundary-stone; and clasping her face with her hands, she wept copious tears welling up from her full heart. The day was breaking, and carts were making their way into the city.

Catherine led her back home, holding her up, kissing her, and offering her every sort of consolation that she could extract from her own experience. She need not give herself so much trouble about a lover. If this one failed her, she could find others.

Chapter XVI

Unpleasant News from Rosanette

WHEN ROSANETTE'S ENTHUSIASM FOR THE GARDES MOBILES HAD calmed down, she became more charming than ever, and Frederick insensibly glided into the habit of living with her.

The best portion of the day was the morning on the terrace. In a light cambric dress, and with her stockingless feet thrust into slippers, she kept moving about him—went and cleaned her canaries' cage, gave her gold-fishes some water, and with a fire-shovel did a little amateur gardening in the box filled with clay, from which arose a trellis of nasturtiums, giving an attractive look to the wall. Then, resting, with their elbows on the balcony, they stood side by side, gazing at the vehicles and the passers-by; and they warmed themselves in the sunlight, and made plans for spending the evening. He absented himself only for two hours at most, and, after that, they would go to some theatre, where they would get seats in front of the stage; and Rosanette, with a large bouquet of flowers in her hand, would listen to the instruments, while Frederick, leaning close to her ear, would tell her comic or amatory stories. At other times they took an open carriage to drive to the Bois de Boulogne. They kept walking about slowly until the middle of the night. At last they made their way home through the Arc de Triomphe and the grand avenue, inhaling the breeze, with the stars above their heads, and with all the gas-lamps ranged in the background of the perspective like a double string of luminous pearls.

Frederick always waited for her when they were going out together. She was a very long time fastening the two ribbons of her bonnet; and she smiled at herself in the mirror set in the wardrobe; then she would draw her arm over his, and, making him look at himself in the glass beside her:

"We produce a good effect in this way, the two of us side by side. Ah! my poor darling, I could eat you!"

He was now her chattel, her property. She wore on her face a continuous radiance, while at the same time she appeared more languishing in manner, more rounded in figure; and, without being able to explain in what way, he found her altered, nevertheless.

One day she informed him, as if it were a very important bit of news, that my lord Arnoux had lately set up a linen-draper's shop for a woman who was formerly employed in his pottery-works. He used to go there every evening—"he spent a great deal on it no later than a week ago; he had even given her a set of rosewood furniture."

"How do you know that?" said Frederick.

"Oh! I'm sure of it."

Delphine, while carrying out some orders for her, had made enquiries about the matter. She must, then, be much attached to Arnoux to take such a deep interest in his movements. He contented himself with saying to her in reply:

"What does this signify to you?"

Rosanette looked surprised at this question.

"Why, the rascal owes me money. Isn't it atrocious to see him keeping beggars?"

Then, with an expression of triumphant hate in her face:

"Besides, she is having a nice laugh at him. She has three others on hand. So much the better; and I'll be glad if she eats him up, even to the last farthing!"

Arnoux had, in fact, let himself be made use of by the girl from Bordeaux with the indulgence which characterises senile attachments. His manufactory was no longer going on. The entire state of his affairs was pitiable; so that, in order to set them afloat again, he was at first projecting the establishment of a *café chantant*, at which only patriotic pieces would be sung. With a grant from the Minister, this establishment would become at the same time a focus for the purpose of propagandism and a source of profit. Now that power had been directed into a different channel, the thing was impossible.

His next idea was a big military hat-making business. He lacked capital, however, to give it a start.

He was not more fortunate in his domestic life. Madame Arnoux was less agreeable in manner towards him, sometimes even a little rude. Berthe always took her father's part. This increased the discord, and the house was becoming intolerable. He often set forth in the morning, passed his day in making long excursions out of the city, in order to divert his thoughts, then dined at a rustic tavern, abandoning himself to his reflections.

The prolonged absence of Frederick disturbed his habits. Then he presented himself one afternoon, begged of him to come and see him as in former days, and obtained from him a promise to do so.

Frederick did not feel sufficient courage within him to go back to Madame Arnoux's house. It seemed to him as if he had betrayed her. But this conduct was very pusillanimous. There was no excuse for it. There was only one way of ending the matter, and so, one evening, he set out on his way.

As the rain was falling, he had just turned up the Passage Jouffroy, when, under the light shed from the shop-windows, a fat little man accosted him. Frederick had no difficulty in recognising Compain, that orator whose motion had excited so much laughter at the club. He was leaning on the arm of an individual whose head was muffled in a zouave's red cap, with a very long upper lip, a complexion as yellow as an orange, a tuft of beard under his jaw, and big staring eyes listening with wonder.

Compain was, no doubt, proud of him, for he said:

"Let me introduce you to this jolly dog! He is a bootmaker whom I include amongst my friends. Come and let us take something!"

Frederick having thanked him, he immediately thundered against Rateau's motion, which he described as a manouevre of the aristocrats. In order to put an end to it, it would be necessary to begin '93 over again! Then he enquired about Regimbart and some others, who were also well known, such as Masselin, Sanson, Lecornu, Maréchal, and a certain Deslauriers, who had been implicated in the case of the carbines lately intercepted at Troyes.

All this was new to Frederick. Compain knew nothing more about the subject. He quitted the young man with these words:

"You'll come soon, will you not? for you belong to it."

"To what?"

"The calf's head!"

"What calf's head?"

"Ha, you rogue!" returned Compain, giving him a tap on the stomach.

And the two terrorists plunged into a café.

Ten minutes later Frederick was no longer thinking of Deslauriers. He was on the footpath of the Rue de Paradis in front of a house; and he was staring at the light which came from a lamp in the second floor behind a curtain.

At length he ascended the stairs.

"Is Arnoux there?"

The chambermaid answered:

"No; but come in all the same."

And, abruptly opening a door:

"Madame, it is Monsieur Moreau!"

She arose, whiter than the collar round her neck.

"To what do I owe the honour—of a visit—so unexpected?"

"Nothing. The pleasure of seeing old friends once more."

And as he took a seat:

"How is the worthy Arnoux going on?"

"Very well. He has gone out."

"Ah, I understand! still following his old nightly practices. A little distraction!"

"And why not? After a day spent in making calculations, the head needs a rest."

She even praised her husband as a hard-working man. Frederick was irritated at hearing this eulogy; and pointing towards a piece of black cloth with a narrow blue braid which lay on her lap:

"What is it you are doing there?"

"A jacket which I am trimming for my daughter."

"Now that you remind me of it, I have not seen her. Where is she, pray?"

"At a boarding-school," was Madame Arnoux's reply.

Tears came into her eyes. She held them back, while she rapidly plied her needle. To keep himself in countenance, he took up a number of *L'Illustration* which had been lying on the table close to where she sat.

"These caricatures of Cham are very funny, are they not?"

"Yes."

Then they relapsed into silence once more.

All of a sudden, a fierce gust of wind shook the window-panes.

"What weather!" said Frederick.

"It was very good of you, indeed, to come here in the midst of this dreadful rain."

"Oh! what do I care about that? I'm not like those whom it prevents, no doubt, from going to keep their appointments."

"What appointments?" she asked with an ingenuous air.

"Don't you remember?"

A shudder ran through her frame and she hung down her head.

He gently laid his hand on her arm.

"I assure you that you have given me great pain."

She replied, with a sort of wail in her voice:

"But I was frightened about my child."

She told him about Eugène's illness, and all the tortures which she had endured on that day.

"Thanks! thanks! I doubt you no longer. I love you as much as ever."

"Ah! no; it is not true!"

"Why so?"

She glanced at him coldly.

"You forget the other! the one you took with you to the races! the woman whose portrait you have—your mistress!"

"Well, yes!" exclaimed Frederick, "I don't deny anything! I am a wretch! Just listen to me!"

If he had done this, it was through despair, as one commits suicide. However, he had made her very unhappy in order to avenge himself on her with his own shame.

"What mental anguish! Do you not realise what it means?"

Madame Arnoux turned away her beautiful face while she held out her hand to him; and they closed their eyes, absorbed in a kind of intoxication that was like a sweet, ceaseless rocking. Then they stood face to face, gazing at one another.

"Could you believe it possible that I no longer loved you?"

She replied in a low voice, full of caressing tenderness:

"No! in spite of everything, I felt at the bottom of my heart that it was impossible, and that one day the obstacle between us two would disappear!"

"So did I; and I was dying to see you again."

"I once passed close to you in the Palais-Royal!"

"Did you really?"

And he spoke to her of the happiness he experienced at coming across her again at the Dambreuses' house.

"But how I hated you that evening as I was leaving the place!"

"Poor boy!"

"My life is so sad!"

"And mine, too! If it were only the vexations, the anxieties, the humiliations, all that I endure as wife and as mother, seeing that one must die, I would not complain; the frightful part of it is my solitude, without anyone."

"But you have me here with you!"

"Oh! yes!"

A sob of deep emotion made her bosom swell. She spread out her arms, and they strained one another, while their lips met in a long kiss.

A creaking sound on the floor not far from them reached their ears. There was a woman standing close to them; it was Rosanette. Madame Arnoux had recognised her. Her eyes, opened to their widest, scanned this woman, full of astonishment and indignation. At length Rosanette said to her:

"I have come to see Monsieur Arnoux about a matter of business."

"You see he is not here."

"Ah! that's true," returned the Maréchal. "Your nurse is right! A thousand apologies!"

And turning towards Frederick:

"So here you are—you?"

The familiar tone in which she addressed him, and in her own presence, too, made Madame Arnoux flush as if she had received a slap right across the face.

"I tell you again, he is not here!"

Then the Maréchale, who was looking this way and that, said quietly:

"Let us go back together! I have a cab waiting below."

He pretended not to hear.

"Come! let us go!"

"Ah! yes! this is a good opportunity! Go! go!" said Madame Arnoux.

They went off together, and she stooped over the head of the stairs in order to see them once more, and a laugh—piercing, heart-rending, reached them from the place where she stood. Frederick pushed Rosanette into the cab, sat down opposite her, and during the entire drive did not utter a word.

The infamy, which it outraged him to see once more flowing back on him, had been brought about by himself alone. He experienced at the same time the dishonour of a crushing humiliation and the regret caused by the loss of his new-found happiness. Just when, at last, he had it in his grasp, it had for ever more become impossible, and that through the fault of this girl of the town, this harlot. He would have liked to strangle her. He was choking with rage. When they had got into the house he flung his hat on a piece of furniture and tore off his cravat.

"Ha! you have just done a nice thing—confess it!"

She planted herself boldly in front of him.

"Ah! well, what of that? Where's the harm?"

"What! You are playing the spy on me?"

"Is that my fault? Why do you go to amuse yourself with virtuous women?"

"Never mind! I don't wish you to insult them."

"How have I insulted them?"

He had no answer to make to this, and in a more spiteful tone:

"But on the other occasion, at the Champ de Mars—"

"Ah! you bore us to death with your old women!"

"Wretch!"

He raised his fist.

"Don't kill me! I'm pregnant!"

Frederick staggered back.

"You are lying!"

"Why, just look at me!"

She seized a candlestick, and pointing at her face:

"Don't you recognise the fact there?"

Little yellow spots dotted her skin, which was strangely swollen. Frederick did not deny the evidence. He went to the window, and opened it, took a few steps up and down the room, and then sank into an armchair.

This event was a calamity which, in the first place, put off their rupture, and, in the next place, upset all his plans. The notion of being a father, moreover, appeared to him grotesque, inadmissible. But why? If, in place of the Maréchale— And his reverie became so deep that he had a kind of hallucination. He saw there, on the carpet, in front of the chimney-piece, a little girl. She resembled Madame

Arnoux and himself a little—dark, and yet fair, with two black eyes, very large eyebrows, and a red ribbon in her curling hair. (Oh, how he would have loved her!) And he seemed to hear her voice saying: "Papa! papa!"

Rosanette, who had just undressed herself, came across to him, and noticing a tear in his eyelids, kissed him gravely on the forehead.

He arose, saying:

"By Jove, we mustn't kill this little one!"

Then she talked a lot of nonsense. To be sure, it would be a boy, and its name would be Frederick. It would be necessary for her to begin making its clothes; and, seeing her so happy, a feeling of pity for her took possession of him. As he no longer cherished any anger against her, he desired to know the explanation of the step she had recently taken. She said it was because Mademoiselle Vatnaz had sent her that day a bill which had been protested for some time past; and so she hastened to Arnoux to get the money from him.

"I'd have given it to you!" said Frederick.

"It is a simpler course for me to get over there what belongs to me, and to pay back to the other one her thousand francs."

"Is this really all you owe her?"

She answered:

"Certainly!"

On the following day, at nine o'clock in the evening (the hour specified by the doorkeeper), Frederick repaired to Mademoiselle Vatnaz's residence.

In the anteroom, he jostled against the furniture, which was heaped together. But the sound of voices and of music guided him. He opened a door, and tumbled into the middle of a rout. Standing up before a piano, which a young lady in spectacles was fingering, Delmar, as serious as a pontiff, was declaiming a humanitarian poem on prostitution; and his hollow voice rolled to the accompaniment of the metallic chords. A row of women sat close to the wall, attired, as a rule, in dark colours without neckbands or sleeves. Five or six men, all people of culture, occupied seats here and there. In an armchair was seated a former writer of fables, a mere wreck now; and the pungent odour of the two lamps was intermingled with the aroma of the chocolate which filled a number of bowls placed on the card-table.

Mademoiselle Vatnaz, with an Oriental shawl thrown over her shoulders, sat at one side of the chimney-piece. Dussardier sat facing her at the other side. He seemed to feel himself in an embarrassing position. Besides, he was rather intimidated by his artistic surroundings. Had the Vatnaz, then, broken off with Delmar? Perhaps not. However, she seemed jealous of the worthy shopman; and Frederick, having asked to let him exchange a word with her, she made a sign to him to go with them into her own apartment. When the thousand francs were paid down before her, she asked, in addition, for interest.

" 'Tisn't worth while," said Dussardier.

"Pray hold your tongue!"

This want of moral courage on the part of so brave a man was agreeable to Frederick as a justification of his own conduct. He took away the bill with him, and never again referred to the scandal at Madame Arnoux's house. But from that time forth he saw clearly all the defects in the Maréchale's character.

She possessed incurable bad taste, incomprehensible laziness, the ignorance of a savage, so much so that she regarded Doctor Derogis as a person of great celebrity, and she felt proud of entertaining himself and his wife, because they were "married people." She lectured with a pedantic air on the affairs of daily life to Mademoiselle Irma, a poor little creature endowed with a little voice, who had as a protector a gentleman "very well off," an ex-clerk in the Custom-house, who had a rare talent for card tricks. Rosanette used to call him "My big Loulou." Frederick could no longer endure the repetition of her stupid words, such as "Some custard," "To Chaillot," "One could never know," etc.; and she persisted in wiping off the dust in the morning from her trinkets with a pair of old white gloves. He was above all disgusted by her treatment of her servant, whose wages were constantly in arrear, and who even lent her money. On the days when they settled their accounts, they used to wrangle like two fish-women; and then, on becoming reconciled, used to embrace each other. It was a relief to him when Madame Dambreuse's evening parties began again.

There, at any rate, he found something to amuse him. She was well versed in the intrigues of society, the changes of ambassadors, the personal character of dressmakers; and, if commonplaces escaped her lips, they did so in such a becoming fashion, that her language might be regarded as the expression of respect for propriety or of polite irony. It was worth while to watch the way in which, in the midst of twenty persons chatting around her, she would, without overlooking any of them, bring about the answers she desired and avoid those that were dangerous. Things of a very simple nature, when related by her, assumed the aspect of confidences. Her slightest smile gave rise to dreams; in short, her charm, like the exquisite scent which she usually carried about with her, was complex and indefinable.

While he was with her, Frederick experienced on each occasion the pleasure of a new discovery, and, nevertheless, he always found her equally serene the next time they met, like the reflection of limpid waters.

But why was there such coldness in her manner towards her niece? At times she even darted strange looks at her.

As soon as the question of marriage was started, she had urged as an objection to it, when discussing the matter with M. Dambreuse, the state of "the dear child's" health, and had at once taken her off to the baths of Balaruc. On her return fresh pretexts were raised by her—that the young man was not in a good position, that this ardent passion did not appear to be a very serious attachment, and that no risk would be run by waiting. Martinon had replied, when the suggestion was made to him, that he would wait. His conduct was sublime. He lectured Frederick. He did more. He enlightened him as to the best means of pleasing Madame Dambreuse, even giving him to understand that he had ascertained from the niece the sentiments of her aunt.

As for M. Dambreuse, far from exhibiting jealousy, he treated his young friend with the utmost attention, consulted him about different things, and even showed anxiety about his future, so that one day, when they were talking about Père Roque, he whispered with a sly air:

"You have done well."

And Cécile, Miss John, the servants and the porter, every one of them exercised a fascination over him in this house. He came there every evening, quitting Rosanette for that purpose. Her approaching maternity rendered her graver in manner, and even a little melancholy, as if she were tortured by anxieties. To every question put to her she replied:

"You are mistaken; I am quite well."

She had, as a matter of fact, signed five notes in her previous transactions, and not having the courage to tell Frederick after the first had been paid, she had gone back to the abode of Arnoux, who had promised her, in writing, the third part of his profits in the lighting of the towns of Languedoc by gas (a marvellous undertaking!), while requesting her not to make use of this letter at the meeting of shareholders. The meeting was put off from week to week.

Meanwhile the Maréchale wanted money. She would have died sooner than ask Frederick for any. She did not wish to get it from him; it would have spoiled their love. He contributed a great deal to the household expenses; but a little carriage, which he hired by the month, and other sacrifices, which were indispensable since he had begun to visit the Dambreuses, prevented him from doing more for his mistress. On two or three occasions, when he came back to the house at a different hour from his usual time, he fancied he could see men's backs disappearing behind the door, and she often went out without wishing to state where she was going. Frederick did not attempt to enquire minutely into these matters. One of these days he would make up his mind as to his future course of action. He dreamed of another life which would be more amusing and more noble. It was the fact that he had such an ideal before his mind that rendered him indulgent towards the Dambreuse mansion.

It was an establishment in the neighbourhood of the Rue de Poitiers. There he met the great M. A., the illustrious B., the profound C., the eloquent Z., the immense Y., the old terrors of the Left Centre, the paladins of the Right, the burgraves of the golden mean; the eternal good old men of the comedy. He was astonished at their abominable style of talking, their meannesses, their rancours, their dishonesty—all these personages, after voting for the Constitution, now striving to destroy it; and they got into a state of great agitation, and launched forth manifestoes, pamphlets, and biographies. Hussonnet's biography of Fumichon was a masterpiece. Nonancourt devoted himself to the work of propagandism in the country districts; M. de Grémonville worked up the clergy; and Martinon brought together the young men of the wealthy class. Each exerted himself according to his resources, including Cisy himself. With his thoughts now all day long absorbed in matters of grave moment, he kept making excursions here and there in a cab in the interests of the party.

M. Dambreuse, like a barometer, constantly gave expression to its latest variation. Lamartine could not be alluded to without eliciting from this gentleman the quotation of a famous phrase of the man of the people: "Enough of poetry!" Cavaignac was, from this time forth, nothing better in his eyes than a traitor. The President, whom he had admired for a period of three months, was beginning to fall off in his esteem (as he did not appear to exhibit the "necessary energy"); and, as he always wanted a savior, his gratitude, since the affair of the Conservatoire, belonged to Changarnier: "Thank God for Changarnier . . . Let us place our reliance on Changarnier . . . Oh, there's nothing to fear as long as Changarnier—"

M. Thiers was praised, above all, for his volume against Socialism, in which he showed that he was quite as much of a thinker as a writer. There was an immense laugh at Pierre Leroux, who had quoted passages from the philosophers in the Chamber. Jokes were made about the phalansterian tail. The "Market of Ideas" came in for a meed of applause, and its authors were compared to Aristophanes. Frederick patronised the work as well as the rest.

Political verbiage and good living had an enervating effect on his morality. Mediocre in capacity as these persons appeared to him, he felt proud of knowing them, and internally longed for the respectability that attached to a wealthy citizen. A mistress like Madame Dambreuse would give him a position.

He set about taking the necessary steps for achieving that object.

He made it his business to cross her path, did not fail to go and greet her with a bow in her box at the theatre, and, being aware of the hours when she went to church, he would plant himself behind a pillar in a melancholy attitude. There was a continual interchange of little notes between them with regard to curiosities to which they drew each other's attention, preparations for a concert, or the borrowing of books or reviews. In addition to his visit each night, he sometimes made a call just as the day was closing; and he experienced a progressive succession of pleasures in passing through the large front entrance, through the courtyard, through the anteroom, and through the two reception-rooms. Finally, he reached her boudoir, which was as quiet as a tomb, as warm as an alcove, and in which one jostled against the upholstered edging of furniture in the midst of objects of every sort placed here and there—chiffoniers, screens, bowls, and trays made of lacquer, or shell, or ivory, or malachite, expensive trifles, to which fresh additions were frequently made. Amongst single specimens of these rarities might be noticed three Etretat rollers which were used as paper-presses, and a Frisian cap hung from a Chinese folding-screen. Nevertheless, there was a harmony between all these things, and one was even impressed by the noble aspect of the entire place, which was, no doubt, due to the loftiness of the ceiling, the richness of the portières, and the long silk fringes that floated over the gold legs of the stools.

She nearly always sat on a little sofa, close to the flower-stand, which garnished the recess of the window. Frederick, seating himself on the edge of a large wheeled ottoman, addressed to her compliments of the most appropriate kind that he could conceive; and she looked at him, with her head a little on one side, and a smile playing round her mouth.

He read for her pieces of poetry, into which he threw his whole soul in order to move her and excite her admiration. She would now and then interrupt him with a disparaging remark or a practical observation; and their conversation relapsed incessantly into the eternal question of Love. They discussed with each other what were the circumstances that produced it, whether women felt it more than men, and what was the difference between them on that point. Frederick tried to express his opinion, and, at the same time, to avoid anything like coarseness or insipidity. This became at length a species of contest between them, sometimes agreeable and at other times tedious.

Whilst at her side, he did not experience that ravishment of his entire being which drew him towards Madame Arnoux, nor the feeling of voluptuous delight with which Rosanette had, at first, inspired him. But he felt a passion for her as a thing that was abnormal and difficult of attainment, because she was of aristocratic rank, because she was wealthy, because she was a devotee—imagining that she had a delicacy of sentiment as rare as the lace she wore, together with amulets on her skin, and modest instincts even in her depravity.

He made a certain use of his old passion for Madame Arnoux, uttering in his new flame's hearing all those amorous sentiments which the other had caused him to feel in downright earnest, and pretending that it was Madame Dambreuse herself who had occasioned them. She received these avowals like one accustomed to such things, and, without giving him a formal repulse, did not yield in the slightest degree; and he came no nearer to seducing her than Martinon did to getting married. In order to bring matters to an end with her niece's suitor, she accused him of having money for his object, and even begged of her husband to put the matter to the test. M. Dambreuse then declared to the young man that Cécile, being the orphan child of poor parents, had neither expectations nor a dowry.

Martinon, not believing that this was true, or feeling that he had gone too far to draw back, or through one of those outbursts of idiotic infatuation which may be described as acts of genius, replied that his patrimony, amounting to fifteen thousand francs a year, would be sufficient for them. The banker was touched by this unexpected display of disinterestedness. He promised the young man a tax-collectorship, undertaking to obtain the post for him; and in the month of May, 1850, Martinon married Mademoiselle Cécile. There was no ball to celebrate the event. The young people started the same evening for Italy. Frederick came next day to pay a visit to Madame Dambreuse. She appeared to him paler than usual. She sharply contradicted him about two or three matters of no importance. However, she went on to observe, all men were egoists.

There were, however, some devoted men, though he might happen himself to be the only one.

"Pooh, pooh! you're just like the rest of them!"

Her eyelids were red; she had been weeping.

Then, forcing a smile:

"Pardon me; I am in the wrong. Sad thoughts have taken possession of my mind."

He could not understand what she meant to convey by the last words.

"No matter! she is not so hard to overcome as I imagined," he thought.

She rang for a glass of water, drank a mouthful of it, sent it away again, and then began to complain of the wretched way in which her servants attended on her. In order to amuse her, he offered to become her servant himself, pretending that he knew how to hand round plates, dust furniture, and announce visitors—in fact, to do the duties of a *valet-de-chambre,* or, rather, of a running-footman, although the latter was now out of fashion. He would have liked to cling on behind her carriage with a hat adorned with cock's feathers.

"And how I would follow you with majestic stride, carrying your pug on my arm!"

"You are facetious," said Madame Dambreuse.

Was it not a piece of folly, he returned, to take everything seriously? There were enough of miseries in the world without creating fresh ones. Nothing was worth the cost of a single pang. Madame Dambreuse raised her eyelids with a sort of vague approval.

This agreement in their views of life impelled Frederick to take a bolder course. His former miscalculations now gave him insight. He went on:

"Our grandsires lived better. Why not obey the impulse that urges us on-ward?" After all, love was not a thing of such importance in itself.

"But what you have just said is immoral!"

She had resumed her seat on the little sofa. He sat down at the side of it, near her feet.

"Don't you see that I am lying! For in order to please women, one must exhibit the thoughtlessness of a buffoon or all the wild passion of tragedy! They only laugh at us when we simply tell them that we love them! For my part, I consider those hyperbolical phrases which tickle their fancy a profanation of true love, so that it is no longer possible to give expression to it, especially when addressing women who possess more than ordinary intelligence."

She gazed at him from under her drooping eyelids. He lowered his voice, while he bent his head closer to her face.

"Yes! you frighten me! Perhaps I am offending you? Forgive me! I did not in-tend to say all that I have said! 'Tis not my fault! You are so beautiful!"

Madame Dambreuse closed her eyes, and he was astonished at his easy victory. The tall trees in the garden stopped their gentle quivering. Motionless clouds streaked the sky with long strips of red, and on every side there seemed to be a sus-pension of vital movements. Then he recalled to mind, in a confused sort of way, evenings just the same as this, filled with the same unbroken silence. Where was it that he had known them?

He sank upon his knees, seized her hand, and swore that he would love her for ever. Then, as he was leaving her, she beckoned to him to come back, and said to him in a low tone:

"Come by-and-by and dine with us! We'll be all alone!"

It seemed to Frederick, as he descended the stairs, that he had become a differ-ent man, that he was surrounded by the balmy temperature of hothouses, and that he was beyond all question entering into the higher sphere of patrician adulteries and lofty intrigues. In order to occupy the first rank there all he required was a woman of this stamp. Greedy, no doubt, of power and of success, and married to a man of inferior calibre, for whom she had done prodigious services, she longed for some one of ability in order to be his guide. Nothing was impossible now. He felt himself capable of riding two hundred leagues on horseback, of travelling for several nights in succession without fatigue. His heart overflowed with pride.

Just in front of him, on the footpath, a man wrapped in a seedy overcoat was walking with downcast eyes, and with such an air of dejection that Frederick, as he passed, turned aside to have a better look at him. The other raised his head. It was Deslauriers. He hesitated. Frederick fell upon his neck.

"Ah! my poor old friend! What! 'tis you!"

And he dragged Deslauriers into his house, at the same time asking his friend a heap of questions.

Ledru-Rollin's ex-commissioner commenced by describing the tortures to which he had been subjected. As he preached fraternity to the Conservatives, and respect for the laws to the Socialists, the former tried to shoot him, and the latter brought cords to hang him with. After June he had been brutally dismissed. He found himself involved in a charge of conspiracy—that which was connected with the seizure of arms at Troyes. He had subsequently been released for want of evidence to sustain the charge. Then the acting committee had sent him to London, where his ears had been boxed in the very middle of a banquet at which he and his colleagues were being entertained. On his return to Paris—

"Why did you not call here, then, to see me?"

"You were always out! Your porter had mysterious airs—I did not know what to think; and, in the next place, I had no desire to reappear before you in the character of a defeated man."

He had knocked at the portals of Democracy, offering to serve it with his pen, with his tongue, with all his energies. He had been everywhere repelled. They had mistrusted him; and he had sold his watch, his bookcase, and even his linen.

"It would be much better to be breaking one's back on the pontoons of Belle Isle with Sénécal!"

Frederick, who had been fastening his cravat, did not appear to be much affected by this news.

"Ha! so he is transported, this good Sénécal?"

Deslauriers replied, while he surveyed the walls with an envious air:

"Not everybody has your luck!"

"Excuse me," said Frederick, without noticing the allusion to his own circumstances, "but I am dining in the city. We must get you something to eat; order whatever you like. Take even my bed!"

This cordial reception dissipated Deslauriers' bitterness.

"Your bed? But that might inconvenience you!"

"Oh, no! I have others!"

"Oh, all right!" returned the advocate, with a laugh. "Pray, where are you dining?"

"At Madame Dambreuse's."

"Can it be that you are—perhaps—?"

"You are too inquisitive," said Frederick, with a smile, which confirmed this hypothesis.

Then, after a glance at the clock, he resumed his seat.

"That's how it is! and we mustn't despair, my ex-defender of the people!"

"Oh, pardon me; let others bother themselves about the people henceforth!"

The advocate detested the working-men, because he had suffered so much on their account in his province, a coal-mining district. Every pit had appointed a provisional government, from which he received orders.

"Besides, their conduct has been everywhere charming—at Lyons, at Lille, at Havre, at Paris! For, in imitation of the manufacturers, who would fain exclude the products of the foreigner, these gentlemen call on us to banish the English, German, Belgian, and Savoyard workmen. As for their intelligence, what was the use of that precious trades' union of theirs which they established under the Restoration? In 1830 they joined the National Guard, without having the common sense to get the upper hand of it. Is it not the fact that, since the morning when 1848 dawned, the various trade-bodies had not reappeared with their banners? They have even demanded popular representatives for themselves, who are not to open their lips except on their own behalf. All this is the same as if the deputies who represent beetroot were to concern themselves about nothing save beetroot. Ah! I've had enough of these dodgers who in turn prostrate themselves before the scaffold of Robespierre, the boots of the Emperor, and the umbrella of Louis Philippe—a rabble who always yield allegiance to the person that flings bread into their mouths. They are always crying out against the venality of Talleyrand and Mirabeau; but the messenger down below there would sell his country for fifty centimes if they'd only promise to fix a tariff of three francs on his walk. Ah! what a wretched state of affairs! We ought to set the four corners of Europe on fire!"

Frederick said in reply:

"The spark is what you lack! You were simply a lot of shopboys, and even the best of you were nothing better than penniless students. As for the workmen, they may well complain; for, if you except a million taken out of the civil list, and of which you made a grant to them with the meanest expressions of flattery, you have done nothing for them, save to talk in stilted phrases! The workman's certificate remains in the hands of the employer, and the person who is paid wages remains (even in the eye of the law), the inferior of his master, because his word is not believed. In short, the Republic seems to me a worn-out institution. Who knows? Perhaps Progress can be realised only through an aristocracy or through a single man? The initiative always comes from the top, and whatever may be the people's pretensions, they are lower than those placed over them!"

"That may be true," said Deslauriers.

According to Frederick, the vast majority of citizens aimed only at a life of peace (he had been improved by his visits to the Dambreuses), and the chances were all on the side of the Conservatives. That party, however, was lacking in new men.

"If you came forward, I am sure—"

He did not finish the sentence. Deslauriers saw what Frederick meant, and passed his two hands over his head; then, all of a sudden:

"But what about yourself? Is there anything to prevent you from doing it? Why would you not be a deputy?"

In consequence of a double election there was in the Aube a vacancy for a candidate. M. Dambreuse, who had been re-elected as a member of the Legislative Assembly, belonged to a different arrondissement.

"Do you wish me to interest myself on your behalf?" He was acquainted with many publicans, schoolmasters, doctors, notaries' clerks and their masters. "Besides, you can make the peasants believe anything you like!"

Frederick felt his ambition rekindling.

Deslauriers added:

"You would find no trouble in getting a situation for me in Paris."

"Oh! it would not be hard to manage it through Monsieur Dambreuse."

"As we happened to have been talking just now about coal-mines," the advocate went on, "what has become of his big company? This is the sort of employment that would suit me, and I could make myself useful to them while preserving my own independence."

Frederick promised that he would introduce him to the banker before three days had passed.

The dinner, which he enjoyed alone with Madame Dambreuse, was a delightful affair. She sat facing him with a smile on her countenance at the opposite side of the table, whereon was placed a basket of flowers, while a lamp suspended above their heads shed its light on the scene; and, as the window was open, they could see the stars. They talked very little, distrusting themselves, no doubt; but, the moment the servants had turned their backs, they sent across a kiss to one another from the tips of their lips. He told her about his idea of becoming a candidate. She approved of the project, promising even to get M. Dambreuse to use every effort on his behalf.

As the evening advanced, some of her friends presented themselves for the purpose of congratulating her, and, at the same time, expressing sympathy with her; she must be so much pained at the loss of her niece. Besides, it was all very well for newly-married people to go on a trip; by-and-by would come incumbrances, children. But really, Italy did not realise one's expectations. They had not as yet passed the age of illusions; and, in the next place, the honeymoon made everything look beautiful. The last two who remained behind were M. de Grémonville and Frederick. The diplomatist was not inclined to leave. At last he departed at midnight. Madame Dambreuse beckoned to Frederick to go with him, and thanked him for this compliance with her wishes by giving him a gentle pressure with her hand more delightful than anything that had gone before.

The Maréchale uttered an exclamation of joy on seeing him again. She had been waiting for him for the last five hours. He gave as an excuse for the delay an indispensable step which he had to lake in the interests of Deslauriers. His face wore a look of triumph, and was surrounded by an aureola which dazzled Rosanette.

" 'Tis perhaps on account of your black coat, which fits you well; but I have never seen you look so handsome! How handsome you are!"

In a transport of tenderness, she made a vow internally never again to belong to any other man, no matter what might be the consequence, even if she were to die of want.

Her pretty eyes sparkled with such intense passion that Frederick took her upon his knees and said to himself:

"What a rascally part I am playing!" while admiring his own perversity.

Chapter XVII

A Strange Betrothal

M. DAMBREUSE, WHEN DESLAURIERS PRESENTED HIMSELF AT HIS HOUSE, WAS THINK-
ing of reviving his great coal-mining speculation. But this fusion of all the companies into one was looked upon unfavourably; there was an outcry against
monopolies, as if immense capital were not needed for carrying out enterprises of
this kind!

Deslauriers, who had read for the purpose the work of Gobet and the articles
of M. Chappe in the *Journal des Mines*, understood the question perfectly. He
demonstrated that the law of 1810 established for the benefit of the grantee a privilege which could not be transferred. Besides, a democratic colour might be given
to the undertaking. To interfere with the formation of coal-mining companies was
against the principle even of association.

M. Dambreuse intrusted to him some notes for the purpose of drawing up a
memorandum. As for the way in which he meant to pay for the work, he was all
the more profuse in his promises from the fact that they were not very definite.

Deslauriers called again at Frederick's house, and gave him an account of the
interview. Moreover, he had caught a glimpse of Madame Dambreuse at the bottom of the stairs, just as he was going out.

"I wish you joy—upon my soul, I do!"

Then they had a chat about the election. There was something to be devised in
order to carry it.

Three days later Deslauriers reappeared with a sheet of paper covered with
handwriting, intended for the newspapers, and which was nothing less than a
friendly letter from M. Dambreuse, expressing approval of their friend's candidature. Supported by a Conservative and praised by a Red, he ought to succeed. How
was it that the capitalist had put his signature to such a lucubration? The advocate
had, of his own motion, and without the least appearance of embarrassment, gone
and shown it to Madame Dambreuse, who, thinking it quite appropriate, had taken
the rest of the business on her own shoulders.

Frederick was astonished at this proceeding. Nevertheless, he approved of it;
then, as Deslauriers was to have an interview with M. Roque, his friend explained
to him how he stood with regard to Louise.

"Tell them anything you like; that my affairs are in an unsettled state, that I am
putting them in order. She is young enough to wait!"

Deslauriers set forth, and Frederick looked upon himself as a very able man. He experienced, moreover, a feeling of gratification, a profound satisfaction. His delight at being the possessor of a rich woman was not spoiled by any contrast. The sentiment harmonised with the surroundings. His life now would be full of joy in every sense.

Perhaps the most delicious sensation of all was to gaze at Madame Dambreuse in the midst of a number of other ladies in her drawing-room. The propriety of her manners made him dream of other attitudes. While she was talking in a tone of coldness, he would recall to mind the loving words which she had murmured in his ear. All the respect which he felt for her virtue gave him a thrill of pleasure, as if it were a homage which was reflected back on himself; and at times he felt a longing to exclaim:

"But I know her better than you! She is mine!"

It was not long ere their relations came to be socially recognised as an established fact. Madame Dambreuse, during the whole winter, brought Frederick with her into fashionable society.

He nearly always arrived before her; and he watched her as she entered the house they were visiting with her arms uncovered, a fan in her hand, and pearls in her hair. She would pause on the threshold (the lintel of the door formed a framework round her head), and she would open and shut her eyes with a certain air of indecision, in order to see whether he was there.

She drove him back in her carriage; the rain lashed the carriage-blinds. The passers-by seemed merely shadows wavering in the mire of the street; and, pressed close to each other, they observed all these things vaguely with a calm disdain. Under various pretexts, he would linger in her room for an entire additional hour.

It was chiefly through a feeling of ennui that Madame Dambreuse had yielded. But this latest experience was not to be wasted. She desired to give herself up to an absorbing passion; and so she began to heap on his head adulations and caresses.

She sent him flowers; she had an upholstered chair made for him. She made presents to him of a cigar-holder, an inkstand, a thousand little things for daily use, so that every act of his life should recall her to his memory. These kind attentions charmed him at first, and in a little while appeared to him very simple.

She would step into a cab, get rid of it at the opening into a by-way, and come out at the other end; and then, gliding along by the walls, with a double veil on her face, she would reach the street where Frederick, who had been keeping watch, would take her arm quickly to lead her towards his house. His two men-servants would have gone out for a walk, and the doorkeeper would have been sent on some errand. She would throw a glance around her—nothing to fear!—and she would breathe forth the sigh of an exile who beholds his country once more. Their good fortune emboldened them. Their appointments became more frequent. One evening, she even presented herself, all of a sudden, in full ball-dress. These surprises might have perilous consequences. He reproached her for her lack of prudence. Nevertheless, he was not taken with her appearance. The low body of her dress exposed her thinness too freely.

It was then that he discovered what had hitherto been hidden from him—the disillusion of his senses. None the less did he make professions of ardent love; but in order to call up such emotions he found it necessary to evoke the images of Rosanette and Madame Arnoux.

This sentimental atrophy left his intellect entirely untrammelled; and he was more ambitious than ever of attaining a high position in society. Inasmuch as he had such a stepping-stone, the very least he could do was to make use of it.

One morning, about the middle of January, Sénécal entered his study, and in response to his exclamation of astonishment, announced that he was Deslauriers' secretary. He even brought Frederick a letter. It contained good news, and yet it took him to task for his negligence; he would have to come down to the scene of action at once. The future deputy said he would set out on his way there in two days' time.

Sénécal gave no opinion on the other's merits as a candidate. He spoke about his own concerns and about the affairs of the country.

Miserable as the state of things happened to be, it gave him pleasure, for they were advancing in the direction of Communism. In the first place, the Administration led towards it of its own accord, since every day a greater number of things were controlled by the Government. As for Property, the Constitution of '48, in spite of its weaknesses, had not spared it. The State might, in the name of public utility, henceforth take whatever it thought would suit it. Sénécal declared himself in favour of authority; and Frederick noticed in his remarks the exaggeration which characterised what he had said himself to Deslauriers. The Republican even inveighed against the masses for their inadequacy.

"Robespierre, by upholding the right of the minority, had brought Louis XVI to acknowledge the National Convention, and saved the people. Things were rendered legitimate by the end towards which they were directed. A dictatorship is sometimes indispensable. Long live tyranny, provided that the tyrant promotes the public welfare!"

Their discussion lasted a long time; and, as he was taking his departure, Sénécal confessed (perhaps it was the real object of his visit) that Deslauriers was getting very impatient at M. Dambreuse's silence.

But M. Dambreuse was ill. Frederick saw him everyday, his character of an intimate friend enabling him to obtain admission to the invalid's bedside.

General Changarnier's recall had powerfully affected the capitalist's mind. He was, on the evening of the occurrence, seized with a burning sensation in his chest, together with an oppression that prevented him from lying down. The application of leeches gave him immediate relief. The dry cough disappeared; the respiration became more easy; and, eight days later, he said, while swallowing some broth:

"Ah! I'm better now—but I was near going on the last long journey!"

"Not without me!" exclaimed Madame Dambreuse, intending by this remark to convey that she would not be able to outlive him.

Instead of replying, he cast upon her and upon her lover a singular smile, in which there was at the same time resignation, indulgence, irony, and even, as it were, a touch of humour, a sort of secret satisfaction almost amounting to actual joy.

Frederick wished to start for Nogent. Madame Dambreuse objected to this; and he unpacked and repacked his luggage by turns according to the changes in the invalid's condition.

Suddenly M. Dambreuse spat forth considerable blood. The "princes of medical science," on being consulted, could not think of any fresh remedy. His legs swelled, and his weakness increased. He had several times evinced a desire to see Cécile, who was at the other end of France with her husband, now a collector of taxes, a position to which he had been appointed a month ago. M. Dambreuse gave express orders to send for her. Madame Dambreuse wrote three letters, which she showed him.

Without trusting him even to the care of the nun, she did not leave him for one second, and no longer went to bed. The ladies who had their names entered at the door-lodge made enquiries about her with feelings of admiration, and the passers-by were filled with respect on seeing the quantity of straw which was placed in the street under the windows.

On the 12th of February, at five o'clock, a frightful hæmoptysis came on. The doctor who had charge of him pointed out that the case had assumed a dangerous aspect. They sent in hot haste for a priest.

While M. Dambreuse was making his confession, Madame kept gazing curiously at him some distance away. After this, the young doctor applied a blister, and awaited the result.

The flame of the lamps, obscured by some of the furniture, lighted up the apartment in an irregular fashion. Frederick and Madame Dambreuse, at the foot of the bed, watched the dying man. In the recess of a window the priest and the doctor chatted in low tones. The good sister on her knees kept mumbling prayers.

At last came a rattling in the throat. The hands grew cold; the face began to turn white. Now and then he drew a deep breath all of a sudden; but gradually this became rarer and rarer. Two or three confused words escaped him. He turned his eyes upward, and at the same moment his respiration became so feeble that it was almost imperceptible. Then his head sank on one side on the pillow.

For a minute, all present remained motionless.

Madame Dambreuse advanced towards the dead body of her husband, and, without an effort—with the unaffectedness of one discharging a duty—she drew down the eyelids. Then she spread out her two arms, her figure writhing as if in a spasm of repressed despair, and quitted the room, supported by the physician and the nun.

A quarter of an hour afterwards, Frederick made his way up to her apartment.

There was in it an indefinable odour, emanating from some delicate substances with which it was filled. In the middle of the bed lay a black dress, which formed a glaring contrast with the pink coverlet.

Madame Dambreuse was standing at the corner of the mantelpiece. Without attributing to her any passionate regret, he thought she looked a little sad; and, in a mournful voice, he said:

"You are enduring pain?"

"I? No—not at all."

As she turned around, her eyes fell on the dress, which she inspected. Then she told him not to stand on ceremony.

"Smoke, if you like! You can make yourself at home with me!"

And, with a great sigh:

"Ah! Blessed Virgin!—what a riddance!"

Frederick was astonished at this exclamation. He replied, as he kissed her hand:

"All the same, you were free!"

This allusion to the facility with which the intrigue between them had been carried on hurt Madame Dambreuse.

"Ah! you don't know the services that I did for him, or the misery in which I lived!"

"What!"

"Why, certainly! Was it a safe thing to have always near him that bastard, a daughter, whom he introduced into the house at the end of five years of married life, and who, were it not for me, might have led him into some act of folly?"

Then she explained how her affairs stood. The arrangement on the occasion of her marriage was that the property of each party should be separate. The amount of her inheritance was three hundred thousand francs. M. Dambreuse had guaranteed by the marriage contract that in the event of her surviving him, she should have an income of fifteen thousand francs a year, together with the ownership of the mansion. But a short time afterwards he had made a will by which he gave her all he possessed, and this she estimated, so far as it was possible to ascertain just at present, at over three millions.

Frederick opened his eyes widely.

"It was worth the trouble, wasn't it? However, I contributed to it! It was my own property I was protecting; Cécile would have unjustly robbed me of it."

"Why did she not come to see her father?"

As he asked her this question Madame Dambreuse eyed him attentively; then, in a dry tone:

"I haven't the least idea! Want of heart, probably! Oh! I know what she is! And for that reason she won't get a farthing from me!"

She had not been very troublesome, he pointed out; at any rate, since her marriage.

"Ha! her marriage!" said Madame Dambreuse, with a sneer. And she grudged having treated only too well this stupid creature, who was jealous, self-interested, and hypocritical. "All the faults of her father! She disparaged him more and more. There was never a person with such profound duplicity, and with such a merciless disposition into the bargain, as hard as a stone—"a bad man, a bad man!"

Even the wisest people fall into errors. Madame Dambreuse had just made a serious one through this overflow of hatred on her part. Frederick, sitting opposite her in an easy chair, was reflecting deeply, scandalised by the language she had used.

She arose and knelt down beside him.

"To be with you is the only real pleasure! You are the only one I love!"

While she gazed at him her heart softened, a nervous reaction brought tears into her eyes, and she murmured:

"Will you marry me?"

At first he thought he had not understood what she meant. He was stunned by his wealth.

She repeated in a louder tone:

"Will you marry me?"

At last he said with a smile:

"Have you any doubt about it?"

Then the thought forced itself on his mind that his conduct was infamous, and in order to make a kind of reparation to the dead man, he offered to watch by his side himself. But, feeling ashamed of this pious sentiment, he added, in a flippant tone:

"It would be perhaps more seemly."

"Perhaps so, indeed," she said, "on account of the servants."

The bed had been drawn completely out of the alcove. The nun was near the foot of it, and at the head of it sat a priest, a different one, a tall, spare man, with the look of a fanatical Spaniard. On the night-table, covered with a white cloth, three wax-tapers were burning.

Frederick took a chair, and gazed at the corpse.

The face was as yellow as straw. At the corners of the mouth there were traces of blood-stained foam. A silk handkerchief was tied around the skull, and on the breast, covered with a knitted waistcoat, lay a silver crucifix between the two crossed hands.

It was over, this life full of anxieties! How many journeys had he not made to various places? How many rows of figures had he not piled together? How many speculations had he not hatched? How many reports had he not heard read? What quackeries, what smiles and curvets! For he had acclaimed Napoleon, the Cossacks, Louis XVIII, 1830, the working-men, every *régime*, loving power so dearly that he would have paid in order to have the opportunity of selling himself.

But he had left behind him the estate of La Fortelle, three factories in Picardy, the woods of Crancé in the Yonne, a farm near Orleans, and a great deal of personal property in the form of bills and papers.

Frederick thus made an estimate of her fortune; and it would soon, nevertheless, belong to him! First of all, he thought of "what people would say"; then he asked himself what present he ought to make to his mother, and he was concerned about his future equipages, and about employing an old coachman belonging to his own family as the doorkeeper. Of course, the livery would not be the same. He would convert the large reception-room into his own study. There was nothing to prevent him by knocking down three walls from setting up a picture-gallery on the second-floor. Perhaps there might be an opportunity for introducing into the lower portion of the house a hall for Turkish baths. As for M. Dambreuse's office, a disagreeable spot, what use could he make of it?

These reflections were from time to time rudely interrupted by the sounds made by the priest in blowing his nose, or by the good sister in settling the fire.

But the actual facts showed that his thoughts rested on a solid foundation. The corpse was there. The eyelids had reopened, and the pupils, although steeped in clammy gloom, had an enigmatic, intolerable expression.

Frederick fancied that he saw there a judgment directed against himself, and he felt almost a sort of remorse, for he had never any complaint to make against this man, who, on the contrary—

"Come, now! an old wretch!" and he looked at the dead man more closely in order to strengthen his mind, mentally addressing him thus:

"Well, what? Have I killed you?"

Meanwhile, the priest read his breviary; the nun, who sat motionless, had fallen asleep. The wicks of the three wax-tapers had grown longer.

For two hours could be heard the heavy rolling of carts making their way to the markets. The window-panes began to admit streaks of white. A cab passed; then a group of donkeys went trotting over the pavement. Then came strokes of hammers, cries of itinerant vendors of wood and blasts of horns. Already every other sound was blended with the great voice of awakening Paris.

Frederick went out to perform the duties assigned to him. He first repaired to the Mayor's office to make the necessary declaration; then, when the medical officer had given him a certificate of death, he called a second time at the municipal buildings in order to name the cemetery which the family had selected, and to make arrangements for the funeral ceremonies.

The clerk in the office showed him a plan which indicated the mode of interment adopted for the various classes, and a programme giving full particulars with regard to the spectacular portion of the funeral. Would he like to have an open funeral-car or a hearse with plumes, plaits on the horses, and aigrettes on the footmen, initials or a coat-of-arms, funeral-lamps, a man to display the family distinctions? and what number of carriages would he require?

Frederick did not economise in the slightest degree. Madame Dambreuse was determined to spare no expense.

After this he made his way to the church.

The curate who had charge of burials found fault with the waste of money on funeral pomps. For instance, the officer for the display of armorial distinctions was really useless. It would be far better to have a goodly display of wax-tapers. A low mass accompanied by music would be appropriate.

Frederick gave written directions to have everything that was agreed upon carried out, with a joint undertaking to defray all the expenses.

He went next to the Hotel de Ville to purchase a piece of ground. A grant of a piece which was two metres in length and one in breadth cost five hundred francs. Did he want a grant for fifty years or forever?

"Oh, forever!" said Frederick.

He took the whole thing seriously and got into a state of intense anxiety about it. In the courtyard of the mansion a marble-cutter was waiting to show him estimates and plans of Greek, Egyptian, and Moorish tombs; but the family architect had already been in consultation with Madame; and on the table in the vestibule there were all sorts of prospectuses with reference to the cleaning of mattresses, the disinfection of rooms, and the various processes of embalming.

After dining, he went back to the tailor's shop to order mourning for the servants; and he had still to discharge another function, for the gloves that he had ordered were of beaver, whereas the right kind for a funeral were floss-silk.

When he arrived next morning, at ten o'clock, the large reception-room was filled with people, and nearly everyone said, on encountering the others, in a melancholy tone:

"It is only a month ago since I saw him! Good heavens! it will be the same way with us all!"

"Yes; but let us try to keep it as far away from us as possible!"

Then there were little smiles of satisfaction; and they even engaged in conversations entirely unsuited to the occasion. At length, the master of the ceremonies, in a black coat in the French fashion and short breeches, with a cloak, cambric mourning-bands, a long sword by his side, and a three-cornered hat under his arm, gave utterance, with a bow, to the customary words:

"Messieurs, when it shall be your pleasure."

The funeral started. It was the market-day for flowers on the Place de la Madeleine. It was a fine day with brilliant sunshine; and the breeze, which shook the canvas tents, a little swelled at the edges the enormous black cloth which was hung over the church-gate. The escutcheon of M. Dambreuse, which covered a square piece of velvet, was repeated there three times. It was: *Sable, with an arm sinister or and a clenched hand with a glove argent;* with the coronet of a count, and this device: *By every path.*

The bearers lifted the heavy coffin to the top of the staircase, and they entered the building. The six chapels, the hemicycles, and the seats were hung with black. The catafalque at the end of the choir formed, with its large wax-tapers, a single focus of yellow lights. At the two corners, over the candelabra, flames of spirits of wine were burning.

The persons of highest rank took up their position in the sanctuary, and the rest in the nave; and then the Office for the Dead began.

With the exception of a few, the religious ignorance of all was so profound that the master of the ceremonies had, from time to time, to make signs to them to rise, to kneel, or to resume their seats. The organ and the two double-basses could be heard alternately with the voices. In the intervals of silence, the only sounds that reached the car were the mumblings of the priest at the altar; then the music and the chanting went on again.

The light of day shone dimly through the three cupolas, but the open door let in, as it were, a stream of white radiance, which, entering in a horizontal direction, fell on every uncovered head; and in the air, half-way towards the ceiling of the church, floated a shadow, which was penetrated by the reflection of the gildings that decorated the ribbing of the pendentives and the foliage of the capitals.

Frederick, in order to distract his attention, listened to the *Dies iroe.* Me gazed at those around him, or tried to catch a glimpse of the pictures hanging too far above his head, wherein the life of the Magdalen was represented. Luckily, Pellerin came to sit down beside him, and immediately plunged into a long dissertation on the subject of frescoes. The bell began to toll. They left the church.

The hearse, adorned with hanging draperies and tall plumes, set out for Père-Lachaise drawn by four black horses, with their manes plaited, their heads decked with tufts of feathers, and with large trappings embroidered with silver flowing down to their shoes. The driver of the vehicle, in Hessian boots, wore a three-cornered hat with a long piece of crape falling down from it. The cords were held by four personages: a questor of the Chamber of Deputies, a member of the General Council of the Aube, a delegate from the coal-mining company, and Fumichon, as a friend. The carriage of the deceased and a dozen mourning-coaches followed. The persons attending at the funeral came in the rear, filling up the middle of the boulevard.

The passers-by stopped to look at the mournful procession. Women, with their brats in their arms, got up on chairs, and people, who had been drinking glasses of beer in the cafés, presented themselves at the windows with billiard-cues in their hands.

The way was long, and, as at formal meals at which people are at first reserved and then expansive, the general deportment speedily relaxed. They talked of nothing but the refusal of an allowance by the Chamber to the President. M. Piscatory had shown himself harsh; Montalembert had been "magnificent, as usual," and MM. Chamballe, Pidoux, Creton, in short, the entire committee would be compelled perhaps to follow the advice of MM. Quentin-Bauchard and Dufour.

This conversation was continued as they passed through the Rue de la Roquette, with shops on each side, in which could be seen only chains of coloured glass and black circular tablets covered with drawings and letters of gold—which made them resemble grottoes full of stalactites and crockery-ware shops. But, when they had reached the cemetery-gate, everyone instantaneously ceased speaking.

The tombs among the trees: broken columns, pyramids, temples, dolmens, obelisks, and Etruscan vaults with doors of bronze. In some of them might be seen funereal boudoirs, so to speak, with rustic armchairs and folding-stools. Spiders' webs hung like rags from the little chains of the urns; and the bouquets of satin ribbons and the crucifixes were covered with dust. Everywhere, between the balusters on the tombstones, may be observed crowns of immortelles and chandeliers, vases, flowers, black discs set off with gold letters, and plaster statuettes—little boys or little girls or little angels sustained in the air by brass wires; several of them have even a roof of zinc overhead. Huge cables made of glass strung together, black, white, or azure, descend from the tops of the monuments to the ends of the flag-stones with long folds, like boas. The rays of the sun, striking on them, made them scintillate in the midst of the black wooden crosses. The hearse advanced along the broad paths, which are paved like the streets of a city. From time to time the axle-trees cracked. Women, kneeling down, with their dresses trailing in the grass, addressed the dead in tones of tenderness. Little white fumes arose from the green leaves of the yew trees. These came from offerings that had been left behind, waste material that had been burnt.

M. Dambreuse's grave was close to the graves of Manuel and Benjamin Constant. The soil in this place slopes with an abrupt decline. One has under his feet there the tops of green trees, further down the chimneys of steam-pumps, then the entire great city.

Frederick found an opportunity of admiring the scene while the various addresses were being delivered.

The first was in the name of the Chamber of Deputies, the second in the name of the General Council of the Aube, the third in the name of the coal-mining company of Saone-et-Loire, the fourth in the name of the Agricultural Society of the Yonne, and there was another in the name of a Philanthropic Society. Finally, just as everyone was going away, a stranger began reading a sixth address, in the name of the Amiens Society of Antiquaries.

And thereupon they all took advantage of the occasion to denounce Socialism, of which M. Dambreuse had died a victim. It was the effect produced on his mind by the exhibitions of anarchic violence, together with his devotion to order, that had shortened his days. They praised his intellectual powers, his integrity, his generosity, and even his silence as a representative of the people, "for, if he was not an orator, he possessed instead those solid qualities a thousand times more useful," etc., with all the requisite phrases—"Premature end; eternal regrets; the better land; farewell, or rather no, *an revoir!*"

The clay, mingled with stones, fell on the coffin, and he would never again be a subject for discussion in society.

However, there were a few allusions to him as the persons who had followed his remains left the cemetery. Hussonnet, who would have to give an account of the interment in the newspapers, took up all the addresses in a chaffing style, for, in truth, the worthy Dambreuse had been one of the most notable *pots-de-vin* of the last reign. Then the citizens were driven in the mourning-coaches to their various places of business; the ceremony had not lasted very long; they congratulated themselves on the circumstance.

Frederick returned to his own abode quite worn out.

When he presented himself next day at Madame Dambreuse's residence, he was informed that she was busy below stairs in the room where M. Dambreuse had kept his papers.

The cardboard receptacles and the different drawers had been opened confusedly, and the account-books had been flung about right and left. A roll of papers on which were endorsed the words "Repayment hopeless" lay on the ground. He was near falling over it, and picked it up. Madame Dambreuse had sunk back in the armchair, so that he did not see her.

"Well? where are you? What is the matter!"

She sprang to her feet with a bound.

"What is the matter? I am ruined, ruined! do you understand?"

M. Adolphe Langlois, the notary, had sent her a message to call at his office, and had informed her about the contents of a will made by her husband before their marriage. He had bequeathed everything to Cécile; and the other will was lost. Frederick turned very pale. No doubt she had not made sufficient search.

"Well, then, look yourself!" said Madame Dambreuse, pointing at the objects contained in the room.

The two strong-boxes were gaping wide, having been broken open with blows of a cleaver, and she had turned up the desk, rummaged in the cupboards, and shaken the straw-mattings, when, all of a sudden, uttering a piercing cry, she dashed into a corner where she had just noticed a little box with a brass lock. She opened it—nothing!

"Ah! the wretch! I, who took such devoted care of him!"

Then she burst into sobs.

"Perhaps it is somewhere else?" said Frederick.

"Oh! no! it was there! in that strong-box. I saw it there lately, 'Tis burned! I'm certain of it!"

One day, in the early stage of his illness, M. Dambreuse had gone down to this room to sign some documents.

" 'Tis then he must have done the trick!"

And she fell back on a chair, crushed. A mother grieving beside an empty cradle was not more woeful than Madame Dambreuse was at the sight of the open strong-boxes. Indeed, her sorrow, in spite of the baseness of the motive which inspired it, appeared so deep that he tried to console her by reminding her that, after all, she was not reduced to sheer want.

"It is want, when I am not in a position to offer you a large fortune!"

She had not more than thirty thousand livres a year, without taking into account the mansion, which was worth from eighteen to twenty thousand, perhaps.

Although to Frederick this would have been opulence, he felt, none the less, a certain amount of disappointment. Farewell to his dreams and to all the splendid existence on which he had intended to enter! Honour compelled him to marry Madame Dambreuse. For a minute he reflected; then, in a tone of tenderness:

"I'll always have yourself!"

She threw herself into his arms, and he clasped her to his breast with an emotion in which there was a slight element of admiration for himself.

Madame Dambreuse, whose tears had ceased to flow, raised her face, beaming all over with happiness, and seizing his hand:

"Ah! I never doubted you! I knew I could count on you!"

The young man did not like this tone of anticipated certainty with regard to what he was pluming himself on as a noble action.

Then she brought him into her own apartment, and they began to arrange their plans for the future. Frederick should now consider the best way of advancing himself in life. She even gave him excellent advice with reference to his candidature.

The first point was to be acquainted with two or three phrases borrowed from political economy. It was necessary to take up a specialty, such as the stud system, for example; to write a number of notes on questions of local interest, to have always at his disposal post-offices or tobacconists' shops, and to do a heap of little services. In this respect M. Dambreuse had shown himself a true model. Thus, on one occasion, in the country, he had drawn up his wagonette, full of friends of his, in front of a cobbler's stall, and had bought a dozen pairs of shoes for his guests, and for himself a dreadful pair of boots, which he had not even the courage to wear for an entire fortnight. This anecdote put them into a good humour. She related others, and that with a renewal of grace, youthfulness, and wit.

She approved of his notion of taking a trip immediately to Nogent. Their parting was an affectionate one; then, on the threshold, she murmured once more:

"You love me—do you not?"

"Eternally," was his reply.

A messenger was waiting for him at his own house with a line written in lead-pencil informing him that Rosanette was about to be confined. He had been so much preoccupied for the past few days that he had not bestowed a thought upon the matter.

She had been placed in a special establishment at Chaillot.

Frederick took a cab and set out for this institution.

At the corner of the Rue de Marbeuf he read on a board in big letters: "Private Lying-in-Hospital, kept by Madame Alessandri, first-class midwife, ex-pupil of the Maternity, author of various works, etc." Then, in the centre of the street, over the door—a little side-door—there was another sign-board: "Private Hospital of Madame Alessandri," with all her titles.

Frederick gave a knock. A chambermaid, with the figure of an Abigail, introduced him into the reception-room, which was adorned with a mahogany table and armchairs of garnet velvet, and with a clock under a globe.

Almost immediately Madame appeared. She was a tall brunette of forty, with a slender waist, fine eyes, and the manners of good society. She apprised Frederick of the mother's happy delivery, and brought him up to her apartment.

Rosanette broke into a smile of unutterable bliss, and, as if drowned in the floods of love that were suffocating her, she said in a low tone:

"A boy—there, there!" pointing towards a cradle close to her bed.

He flung open the curtains, and saw, wrapped up in linen, a yellowish-red object, exceedingly shrivelled-looking, which had a bad smell, and which was bawling lustily.

"Embrace him!"

He replied, in order to hide his repugnance:

"But I am afraid of hurting him."

"No! no!"

Then, with the tips of his lips, he kissed his child.

"How like you he is!"

And with her two weak arms, she clung to his neck with an outburst of feeling which he had never witnessed on her part before.

The remembrance of Madame Dambreuse came back to him. He reproached himself as a monster for having deceived this poor creature, who loved and suffered with all the sincerity of her nature. For several days he remained with her till night.

She felt happy in this quiet place; the window-shutters in front of it remained always closed. Her room, hung with bright chintz, looked out on a large garden. Madame Alessandri, whose only shortcoming was that she liked to talk about her intimate acquaintanceship with eminent physicians, showed her the utmost attention. Her associates, nearly all provincial young ladies, were exceedingly bored, as they had nobody to come to see them. Rosanette saw that they regarded her with envy, and told this to Frederick with pride. It was desirable to speak low, nevertheless. The partitions were thin, and everyone stood listening at hiding-places, in spite of the constant thrumming of the pianos.

At last, he was about to take his departure for Nogent, when he got a letter from Deslauriers. Two fresh candidates had offered themselves, the one a Conservative, the other a Red; a third, whatever he might be, would have no chance. It was all Frederick's fault; he had let the lucky moment pass by; he should have come sooner and stirred himself.

"You have not even been seen at the agricultural assembly!" The advocate blamed him for not having any newspaper connection.

"Ah! if you had followed my advice long ago! If we had only a public print of our own!"

He laid special stress on this point. However, many persons who would have voted for him out of consideration for M. Dambreuse, abandoned him now. Deslauriers was one of the number. Not having anything more to expect from the capitalist, he had thrown over his *protégé*.

Frederick took the letter to show it to Madame Dambreuse.

"You have not been to Nogent, then?" said she.

"Why do you ask?"

"Because I saw Deslauriers three days ago."

Having learned that her husband was dead, the advocate had come to make a report about the coal-mines, and to offer his services to her as a man of business. This seemed strange to Frederick; and what was his friend doing down there?

Madame Dambreuse wanted to know how he had spent his time since they had parted.

"I have been ill," he replied.

"You ought at least to have told me about it."

"Oh! it wasn't worth while;" besides, he had to settle a heap of things, to keep appointments and to pay visits.

From that time forth he led a double life, sleeping religiously at the Maréchale's abode and passing the afternoon with Madame Dambreuse, so that there was scarcely a single hour of freedom left to him in the middle of the day.

The infant was in the country at Andilly. They went to see it once a week.

The wet-nurse's house was on rising ground in the village, at the end of a little yard as dark as a pit, with straw on the ground, hens here and there, and a vegetable-cart under the shed.

Rosanette would begin by frantically kissing her baby, and, seized with a kind of delirium, would keep moving to and fro, trying to milk the she-goat, eating big pieces of bread, and inhaling the odour of manure; she even wanted to put a little of it into her handkerchief.

Then they took long walks, in the course of which she went into the nurseries, tore off branches from the lilac-trees which hung down over the walls, and exclaimed, "Gee ho, donkey!" to the asses that were drawing cars along, and stopped to gaze through the gate into the interior of one of the lovely gardens; or else the wet-nurse would take the child and place it under the shade of a walnut-tree; and for hours the two women would keep talking the most tiresome nonsense.

Frederick, not far away from them, gazed at the beds of vines on the slopes, with here and there a clump of trees; at the dusty paths resembling strips of grey ribbon; at the houses, which showed white and red spots in the midst of the greenery; and sometimes the smoke of a locomotive stretched out horizontally to the bases of the hills, covered with foliage, like a gigantic ostrich's feather, the thin end of which was disappearing from view.

Then his eyes once more rested on his son. He imagined the child grown into a young man; he would make a companion of him; but perhaps he would be a blockhead, a wretched creature, in any event. He was always oppressed by the illegality of the infant's birth; it would have been better if he had never been born! And Frederick would murmur, "Poor child!" his heart swelling with feelings of unutterable sadness.

They often missed the last train. Then Madame Dambreuse would scold him for his want of punctuality. He would invent some falsehood.

It was necessary to invent some explanations, too, to satisfy Rosanette. She could not understand how he spent all his evenings; and when she sent a messenger to his house, he was never there! One day, when he chanced to be at home, the two women made their appearance almost at the same time. He got the Maréchale to go away, and concealed Madame Dambreuse, pretending that his mother was coming up to Paris.

Ere long, he found these lies amusing. He would repeat to one the oath which he had just uttered to the other, send them bouquets of the same sort, write to them at the same time, and then would institute a comparison between them. There was a third always present in his thoughts. The impossibility of possessing her seemed to him a justification of his perfidies, which were intensified by the fact that he had to practise them alternately; and the more he deceived, no matter which of the two, the fonder of him she grew, as if the love of one of them added heat to that of the other, and, as if by a sort of emulation, each of them were seeking to make him forget the other.

"Admire my confidence in you!" said Madame Dambreuse one day to him, opening a sheet of paper, in which she was informed that M. Moreau and a certain Rose Bron were living together as husband and wife.

"Can it be that this is the lady of the races?"

"What an absurdity!" he returned. "Let me have a look at it!"

The letter, written in Roman characters, had no signature. Madame Dambreuse, in the beginning, had tolerated this mistress, who furnished a cloak for their adultery. But, as her passion became stronger, she had insisted on a rupture—a thing which had been effected long since, according to Frederick's account; and when he had ceased to protest, she replied, half closing her eyes, in which shone a look like the point of a stiletto under a muslin robe:

"Well—and the other?"

"What other?"

"The earthenware-dealer's wife!"

He shrugged his shoulders disdainfully. She did not press the matter.

But, a month later, while they were talking about honour and loyalty, and he was boasting about his own (in a casual sort of way, for the sake of precaution), she said to him:

"It is true—you are acting uprightly—you don't go back there any more?"

Frederick, who was at the moment thinking of the Maréchale, stammered:

"Where, pray?"

"To Madame Arnoux's."

He implored her to tell him from whom she got the information. It was through her second dressmaker, Madame Regimbart.

So, she knew all about his life, and he knew nothing about hers!

In the meantime, he had found in her dressing-room the miniature of a gentleman with long moustaches—was this the same person about whose suicide a vague story had been told him at one time? But there was no way of learning any more about it! However, what was the use of it? The hearts of women are like little pieces of furniture wherein things are secreted, full of drawers fitted into each other; one hurts himself, breaks his nails in opening them, and then finds within only some withered flower, a few grains of dust—or emptiness! And then perhaps he felt afraid of learning too much about the matter.

She made him refuse invitations where she was unable to accompany him, stuck to his side, was afraid of losing him; and, in spite of this union which was every day becoming stronger, all of a sudden, abysses disclosed themselves between the pair about the most trifling questions—an estimate of an individual or a work of art.

She had a style of playing on the piano which was correct and hard. Her spiritualism (Madame Dambreuse believed in the transmigration of souls into the stars) did not prevent her from taking the utmost care of her cash-box. She was haughty towards her servants; her eyes remained dry at the sight of the rags of the poor. In the expressions of which she habitually made use a candid egoism manifested itself: "What concern is that of mine? I should be very silly! What need have I?" and a thousand little acts incapable of analysis revealed hateful qualities in her. She would have listened behind doors; she could not help lying to her confessor. Through a spirit of despotism, she insisted on Frederick going to the church with her on Sunday. He obeyed, and carried her prayer-book.

The loss of the property she had expected to inherit had changed her considerably. These marks of grief, which people attributed to the death of M. Dambreuse, rendered her interesting, and, as in former times, she had a great number of visitors. Since Frederick's defeat at the election, she was ambitious of obtaining for both of them an embassy in Germany; therefore, the first thing they should do was to submit to the reigning ideas.

Some persons were in favour of the Empire, others of the Orléans family, and others of the Comte do Chambord; but they were all of one opinion as to the urgency of decentralisation, and several expedients were proposed with that view, such as to cut up Paris into many large streets in order to establish villages there, to transfer the seat of government to Versailles, to have the schools set up at Bourges, to suppress the libraries, and to entrust everything to the generals of division; and they glorified a rustic existence on the assumption that the uneducated man had naturally more sense than other men! Hatreds increased—hatred of primary teachers and wine-merchants, of the classes of philosophy, of the courses of lectures on history, of novels, red waistcoats, long beards, of independence in any shape, or any manifestation of individuality, for it was necessary "to restore the principle of authority"—let it be exercised in the name of no matter whom; let it come from no matter where, as long as it was Force, Authority! The Conservatives now talked in the very same way as Sénécal. Frederick was no longer able to understand their drift, and once more he found at the house of his former mistress the same remarks uttered by the same men.

The salons of the unmarried women (it was from this period that their importance dates) were a sort of neutral ground where reactionaries of different kinds met. Hussonnet, who gave himself up to the depreciation of contemporary glories (a good thing for the restoration of Order), inspired Rosanette with a longing to have evening parties like any other. He undertook to publish accounts of them, and first of all he brought a man of grave deportment, Fumichon; then came Nonancourt, M. de Grémonville, the Sieur de Larsilloix, ex-prefect, and Cisy, who was now an agriculturist in Lower Brittany, and more Christian than ever.

In addition, men who had at one time been the Maréchale's lovers, such as the Baron de Comaing, the Comte de Jumillac, and others, presented themselves; and Frederick was annoyed by their free-and-easy behaviour.

In order that he might assume the attitude of master in the house, he increased the rate of expenditure there. Then he went in for keeping a groom, took a new habitation, and got a fresh supply of furniture. These displays of extravagance were useful for the purpose of making his alliance appear less out of proportion with his pecuniary position. The result was that his means were soon terribly reduced—and Rosanette was entirely ignorant of the fact!

One of the lower middle-class, who had lost caste, she adored a domestic life, a quiet little home. However, it gave her pleasure to have "an at home day." In referring to persons of her own class, she called them "Those women!" She wished to be a society lady, and believed herself to be one. She begged of him not to smoke in the drawing-room any more, and for the sake of good form tried to make herself look thin.

She played her part badly, after all; for she grew serious, and even before going to bed always exhibited a little melancholy, just as there are cypress trees at the door of a tavern.

He found out the cause of it; she was dreaming of marriage—she, too! Frederick was exasperated at this. Besides, he recalled to mind her appearance at Madame Arnoux's house, and then he cherished a certain spite against her for having held out against him so long.

He made enquiries none the less as to who her lovers had been. She denied having had any relations with any of the persons he mentioned. A sort of jealous feeling took possession of him. He irritated her by asking questions about presents that had been made to her, and were still being made to her; and in proportion to the exciting effect which the lower portion of her nature produced upon him, he was drawn towards her by momentary illusions which ended in hate.

Her words, her voice, her smile, all had an unpleasant effect on him, and especially her glances with that woman's eye forever limpid and foolish. Sometimes he felt so tired of her that he would have seen her die without being moved at it. But how could he get into a passion with her? She was so mild that there was no hope of picking a quarrel with her.

Deslauriers reappeared, and explained his sojourn at Nogent by saying that he was making arrangements to buy a lawyer's office. Frederick was glad to see him again. It was somebody! and as a third person in the house, he helped to break the monotony.

The advocate dined with them from time to time, and whenever any little disputes arose, always took Rosanette's part, so that Frederick, on one occasion, said to him:

"Ah! you can have with her, if it amuses you!" so much did he long for some chance of getting rid of her.

About the middle of the month of June, she was served with an order made by the law courts by which Maître Athanase Gautherot, sheriff's officer, called on her to pay him four thousand francs due to Mademoiselle Clémence Vatnaz; if not, he would come to make a seizure on her.

In fact, of the four bills which she had at various times signed, only one had been paid; the money which she happened to get since then having been spent on other things that she required.

She rushed off at once to see Arnoux. He lived now in the Faubourg Saint-Germain, and the porter was unable to tell her the name of the street. She made her way next to the houses of several friends of hers, could not find one of them at home, and came back in a state of utter despair.

She did not wish to tell Frederick anything about it, fearing lest this new occurrence might prejudice the chance of a marriage between them.

On the following morning, M. Athanase Gautherot presented himself with two assistants close behind him, one of them sallow with a mean-looking face and an expression of devouring envy in his glance, the other wearing a collar and straps drawn very tightly, with a sort of thimble of black taffeta on his index-finger—and both ignobly dirty, with greasy necks, and the sleeves of their coats too short.

Their employer, a very good-looking man, on the contrary, began by apologising for the disagreeable duty he had to perform, while at the same time he threw a look round the room, "full of pretty things, upon my word of honour!" He added, "Not to speak of the things that can't be seized." At a gesture the two bailiff's men disappeared.

Then he became twice as polite as before. Could anyone believe that a lady so charming would not have a genuine friend! A sale of her goods under an order of the courts would be a real misfortune. One never gets over a thing like that. He tried to excite her fears; then, seeing that she was very much agitated, suddenly assumed a paternal tone. He knew the world. He had been brought into business relations with all these ladies—and as he mentioned their names, he examined the frames of the pictures on the walls. They were old pictures of the worthy Arnoux, sketches by Sombary, water-colours by Burieu, and three landscapes by Dittmer. It was evident that Rosanette was ignorant of their value. Maître Gautherot turned round to her:

"Look here! to show that I am a decent follow, do one thing: give me up those Dittmers here—and I am ready to pay all. Do you agree?"

At that moment Frederick, who had been informed about the matter by Delphine in the anteroom, and who had just seen the two assistants, came in with his hat on his head, in a rude fashion. Maître Gautherot resumed his dignity; and, as the door had been left open:

"Come on, gentlemen—write down! In the second room, let us say—an oak table with its two leaves, two sideboards—"

Frederick here stopped him, asking whether there was not some way of preventing the seizure.

"Oh! certainly! Who paid for the furniture?"

"I did."

"Well, draw up a claim—you have still time to do it."

Maître Gautherot did not take long in writing out his official report, wherein he directed that Mademoiselle Bron should attend at an enquiry in chambers with reference to the ownership of the furniture, and having done this he withdrew.

Frederick uttered no reproach. He gazed at the traces of mud left on the floor by the bailiff's shoes, and, speaking to himself:

"It will soon be necessary to look about for money!"

"Ah! my God, how stupid I am!" said the Maréchale.

She ransacked a drawer, took out a letter, and made her way rapidly to the Languedoc Gas Lighting Company, in order to get the transfer of her shares.

She came back an hour later. The interest in the shares had been sold to another. The clerk had said, in answer to her demand, while examining the sheet of paper containing Arnoux's written promise to her: "This document in no way constitutes you the proprietor of the shares. The company has no cognisance of the matter." In short, he sent her away unceremoniously, while she choked with rage; and Frederick would have to go to Arnoux's house at once to have the matter cleared up.

But Arnoux would perhaps imagine that he had come to recover in an indirect fashion the fifteen thousand francs due on the mortgage which he had lost; and then this claim from a man who had been his mistress's lover seemed to him a piece of baseness.

Selecting a middle course, he went to the Dambreuse mansion to get Madame Regimbart's address, sent a messenger to her residence, and in this way ascertained the name of the café which the Citizen now haunted.

It was the little café on the Place de la Bastille, in which he sat all day in the corner to the right at the lower end of the establishment, never moving any more than if he were a portion of the building.

After having gone successively through the half-cup of coffee, the glass of grog, the "bishop," the glass of mulled wine, and even the red wine and water, he fell back on beer, and every half hour he let fall this word, "Bock!" having reduced his language to what was actually indispensable. Frederick asked him if he saw Arnoux occasionally.

"No!"

"Look here—why?"

"An imbecile!"

Politics, perhaps, kept them apart, and so Frederick thought it a judicious thing to enquire about Compain.

"What a brute!" said Regimbart.

"How is that?"

"His calf's head!"

"Ha! explain to me what the calf's head is!"

Regimbart's face wore a contemptuous smile.

"Some tomfoolery!"

After a long interval of silence, Frederick went on to ask:

"So, then, he has changed his address?"

"Who?"

"Arnoux!"

"Yes—Rue de Fleurus!"

"What number?"

"Do I associate with the Jesuits?"

"What, Jesuits!"

The Citizen replied angrily:

"With the money of a patriot whom I introduced to him, this pig has set up as a dealer in beads!"

"It isn't possible!"

"Go there, and see for yourself!"

It was perfectly true; Arnoux, enfeebled by a fit of sickness, had turned religious; besides, he had always had a stock of religion in his composition, and (with that mixture of commercialism and ingenuity which was natural to him), in order to gain salvation and fortune both together, he had begun to traffick in religious objects.

Frederick had no difficulty in discovering his establishment, on whose sign-board appeared these words: "*Emporium of Gothic Art*—Restoration of articles used in ecclesiastical ceremonies—Church ornaments—Polychromatic sculpture—Frankincense of the Magi, Kings, etc., etc."

At the two corners of the shop-window rose two wooden statues, streaked with gold, cinnabar, and azure, a Saint John the Baptist with his sheepskin, and a Saint Genevieve with roses in her apron and a distaff under her arm; next, groups in plaster, a good sister teaching a little girl, a mother on her knees beside a little bed, and three collegians before the holy table. The prettiest object there was a kind of châlet representing the interior of a crib with the ass, the ox, and the child Jesus stretched on straw—real straw. From the top to the bottom of the shelves could be seen medals by the dozen, every sort of beads, holy-water basins in the form of shells, and portraits of ecclesiastical dignitaries, amongst whom Monsignor Affre and our Holy Father shone forth with smiles on their faces.

Arnoux sat asleep at his counter with his head down. He had aged terribly. He had even round his temples a wreath of rosebuds, and the reflection of the gold crosses touched by the rays of the sun fell over him.

Frederick was filled with sadness at this spectacle of decay. Through devotion to the Maréchale he, however, submitted to the ordeal, and stepped forward. At the end of the shop Madame Arnoux showed herself; thereupon, he turned on his heel.

"I couldn't see him," he said, when he came back to Rosanette.

And in vain he went on to promise that he would write at once to his notary at Havre for some money—she flew into a rage. She had never seen a man so weak, so flabby. While she was enduring a thousand privations, other people were enjoying themselves.

Frederick was thinking about poor Madame Arnoux, and picturing to himself the heart-rending impoverishment of her surroundings. He had seated himself before the writing-desk; and, as Rosanette's voice still kept up its bitter railing:

"Ah! in the name of Heaven, hold your tongue!"

"Perhaps you are going to defend them?"

"Well, yes!" he exclaimed; "for what's the cause of this display of fury?"

"But why is it that you don't want to make them pay up? 'Tis for fear of vexing your old flame—confess it!"

He felt an inclination to smash her head with the timepiece. Words failed him. He relapsed into silence.

Rosanette, as she walked up and down the room, continued:

"I am going to hurl a writ at this Arnoux of yours. Oh! I don't want your assistance. I'll get legal advice."

Three days later, Delphine rushed abruptly into the room where her mistress sat.

"Madame! madame! there's a man here with a pot of paste who has given me a fright!"

Rosanette made her way down to the kitchen, and saw there a vagabond whose face was pitted with smallpox. Moreover, one of his arms was paralysed, and he was three fourths drunk, and hiccoughed every time he attempted to speak.

This was Maître Gautherot's bill-sticker. The objections raised against the seizure having been overruled, the sale followed as a matter of course.

For his trouble in getting up the stairs he demanded, in the first place, a half-glass of brandy; then he wanted another favour, namely, tickets for the theatre, on the assumption that the lady of the house was an actress. After this he indulged for some minutes in winks, whose import was perfectly incomprehensible. Finally, he declared that for forty sous he would tear off the corners of the poster which he had already affixed to the door below stairs. Rosanette found herself referred to by name in it—a piece of exceptional harshness which showed the spite of the Vatnaz.

She had at one time exhibited sensibility, and had even, while suffering from the effects of a heartache, written to Béranger for his advice. But under the ravages of life's storms, her spirit had become soured, for she had been forced, in turn, to give lessons on the piano, to act as manageress of a *table d'hôte*, to assist others in writing for the fashion journals, to sublet apartments, and to traffic in lace in the world of light women, her relations with whom enabled her to make herself useful to many persons, and amongst others to Arnoux. She had formerly been employed in a commercial establishment.

There it was one of her functions to pay the workwomen; and for each of them there were two livres, one of which always remained in her hands. Dussardier, who, through kindness, kept the amount payable to a girl named Hortense Baslin, presented himself one day at the cash-office at the moment when Mademoiselle Vatnaz was presenting this girl's account, 1,682 francs, which the cashier paid her. Now, on the very day before this, Dussardier had entered down the sum as 1,082 in the girl Baslin's book. He asked to have it given back to him on some pretext; then, anxious to bury out of sight the story of this theft, he stated that he had lost it. The workwoman ingenuously repeated this falsehood to Mademoiselle Vatnaz, and the latter, in order to satisfy her mind about the matter, came with a show of indifference to talk to the shopman on the subject. He contented himself with the answer: "I have burned it!"—that was all. A little while afterwards she quitted the house, without believing that the book had been really destroyed, and filled with the idea that Dussardier had preserved it.

On hearing that he had been wounded, she rushed to his abode, with the object of getting it back. Then, having discovered nothing, in spite of the closest searches, she was seized with respect, and presently with love, for this youth, so loyal, so gentle, so heroic and so strong! At her age such good fortune in an affair of the heart was a thing that one would not expect. She threw herself into it with the appetite of an ogress; and she had given up literature, Socialism, "the consoling doctrines and the generous Utopias," the course of lectures which she had projected on the "Desubalternization of Woman"—everything, even Delmar himself; finally she offered to unite herself to Dussardier in marriage.

Although she was his mistress, he was not at all in love with her. Besides, he had not forgotten her theft. Then she was too wealthy for him. He refused her offer. Thereupon, with tears in her eyes, she told him about what she had dreamed—it was to have for both of them a confectioner's shop. She possessed the capital that was required beforehand for the purpose, and next week this would be increased to the extent of four thousand francs. By way of explanation, she referred to the proceedings she had taken against the Maréchale.

Dussardier was annoyed at this on account of his friend. He recalled to mind the cigar-holder that had been presented to him at the guard-house, the evenings spent in the Quai Napoleon, the many pleasant chats, the books lent to him, the thousand acts of kindness which Frederick had done in his behalf. He begged of the Vatnaz to abandon the proceedings.

She rallied him on his good nature, while exhibiting an antipathy against

Rosanette which he could not understand. She longed only for wealth, in fact, in order to crush her, by-and-by, with her four-wheeled carriage.

Dussardier was terrified by these black abysses of hate, and when he had ascertained what was the exact day fixed for the sale, he hurried out. On the following morning he made his appearance at Frederick's house with an embarrassed countenance.

"I owe you an apology."

"For what, pray?"

"You must take me for an ingrate, I, whom she is the—" He faltered.

"Oh! I'll see no more of her. I am not going to be her accomplice!" And as the other was gazing at him in astonishment:

"Isn't your mistress's furniture to be sold in three days' time?"

"Who told you that?"

"Herself—the Vatnaz! But I am afraid of giving you offence—"

"Impossible, my dear friend!"

"Ah! that is true—you are so good!"

And he held out to him, in a cautious fashion, a hand in which he clasped a little pocket-book made of sheep-leather.

It contained four thousand francs—all his savings.

"What! Oh! no! no!—"

"I knew well I would wound your feelings," returned Dussardier, with a tear in the corner of his eye.

Frederick pressed his hand, and the honest fellow went on in a piteous tone:

"Take the money! Give me that much pleasure! I am in such a state of despair. Can it be, furthermore, that all is over? I thought we should be happy when the Revolution had come. Do you remember what a beautiful thing it was? how freely we breathed! But here we are flung back into a worse condition of things than ever.

"Now, they are killing our Republic, just as they killed the other one—the Roman! ay, and poor Venice! poor Poland! poor Hungary! What abominable deeds! First of all, they knocked down the trees of Liberty, then they restricted the right to vote, shut up the clubs, re-established the censorship and surrendered to the priests the power of teaching, so that we might look out for the Inquisition. Why not? The Conservatives want to give us a taste of the stick. The newspapers are lined merely for pronouncing an opinion in favour of abolishing the death-penalty. Paris is overflowing with bayonets; sixteen departments are in a state of siege; and then the demand for amnesty is again rejected!"

He placed both hands on his forehead, then, spreading out his arms as if his mind were in a distracted state:

"If, however, we only made the effort! if we were only sincere, we might understand each other. But no! The workmen are no better than the capitalists, you see! At Elbœuf recently they refused to help at a fire! There are wretches who profess to regard Barbès as an aristocrat! In order to make the people ridiculous, they want to get nominated for the presidency Nadaud, a mason—just imagine! And there is no way out of it—no remedy! Everybody is against us! For my part, I have never done any harm; and yet this is like a weight pressing down on my stomach. If this state of things continues, I'll go mad. I have a mind to do away with myself. I tell you I want no money for myself! You'll pay it back to me, deuce take it! I am lending it to you."

Frederick, who felt himself constrained by necessity, ended by taking the four thousand francs from him. And so they had no more disquietude so far as the Vatnaz was concerned.

But it was not long ere Rosanette was defeated in her action against Arnoux; and through sheer obstinacy she wished to appeal.

Deslauriers exhausted his energies in trying to make her understand that Arnoux's promise constituted neither a gift nor a regular transfer. She did not even pay the slightest attention to him, her notion being that the law was unjust—it was because she was a woman; men backed up each other amongst themselves. In the end, however, she followed his advice.

He made himself so much at home in the house, that on several occasions he brought Sénécal to dine there. Frederick, who had advanced him money, and even got his own tailor to supply him with clothes, did not like this unceremoniousness; and the advocate gave his old clothes to the Socialist, whose means of existence were now of an exceedingly uncertain character.

He was, however, anxious to be of service to Rosanette. One day, when she showed him a dozen shares in the Kaolin Company (that enterprise which led to Arnoux being cast in damages to the extent of thirty thousand francs), he said to her:

"But this is a shady transaction, and you have now a grand chance!"

She had the right to call on him to pay her debts. In the first place, she could prove that he was jointly bound to pay all the company's liabilities, since he had certified personal debts as collective debts—in short, he had embezzled sums which were payable only to the company.

"All this renders him guilty of fraudulent bankruptcy under articles 586 and 587 of the Commercial Code, and you may be sure, my pet, we'll send him packing."

Rosanette threw herself on his neck. He entrusted her case next day to his former master, not having time to devote attention to it himself, as he had business at Nogent. In case of any urgency, Sénécal could write to him.

His negotiations for the purchase of an office were a mere pretext. He spent his time at M. Roque's house, where he had begun not only by sounding the praises of their friend, but by imitating his manners and language as much as possible; and in this way he had gained Louise's confidence, while he won over that of her father by making an attack on Ledru-Rollin.

If Frederick did not return, it was because he mingled in aristocratic society, and gradually Deslauriers gave them to understand that he was in love with somebody, that he had a child, and that he was keeping a fallen creature.

The despair of Louise was intense. The indignation of Madame Moreau was not less strong. She saw her son whirling towards the bottom of a gulf the depth of which could not be determined, was wounded in her religious ideas as to propriety, and as it were, experienced a sense of personal dishonour; then all of a sudden her physiognomy underwent a change. To the questions which people put to her with regard to Frederick, she replied in a sly fashion:

"He is well, quite well."

She was aware that he was about to be married to Madame Dambreuse.

The date of the event had been fixed, and he was even trying to think of some way of making Rosanette swallow the thing.

About the middle of autumn she won her action with reference to the kaolin shares. Frederick was informed about it by Sénécal, whom he met at his own door, on his way back from the courts.

It had been held that M. Arnoux was privy to all the frauds, and the ex-tutor had such an air of making merry over it that Frederick prevented him from coming further, assuring Sénécal that he would convey the intelligence to Rosanette. He presented himself before her with a look of irritation on his face.

"Well, now you are satisfied!"

But, without minding what he had said:

"Look here!"

And she pointed towards her child, which was lying in a cradle close to the fire. She had found it so sick at the house of the wet-nurse that morning that she had brought it back with her to Paris.

All the infant's limbs were exceedingly thin, and the lips were covered with white specks, which in the interior of the mouth became, so to speak, clots of blood-stained milk.

"What did the doctor say?"

"Oh! the doctor! He pretends that the journey has increased his—I don't know what it is, some name in 'ite'—in short, that he has the thrush. Do you know what that is?"

Frederick replied without hesitation: "Certainly," adding that it was nothing.

But in the evening he was alarmed by the child's debilitated look and by the progress of these whitish spots, resembling mould, as if life, already abandoning this little frame, had left now nothing but matter from which vegetation was sprouting. His hands were cold; he was no longer able to drink anything; and the nurse, another woman, whom the porter had gone and taken on chance at an office, kept repeating:

"It seems to me he's very low, very low!"

Rosanette was up all night with the child.

In the morning she went to look for Frederick.

"Just come and look at him. He doesn't move any longer."

In fact, he was dead. She took him up, shook him, clasped him in her arms, calling him most tender names, covered him with kisses, broke into sobs, turned herself from one side to the other in a state of distraction, tore her hair, uttered a number of shrieks, and then let herself sink on the edge of the divan, where she lay with her mouth open and a flood of tears rushing from her wildly-glaring eyes.

Then a torpor fell upon her, and all became still in the apartment. The furniture was overturned. Two or three napkins were lying on the floor. It struck six. The night-light had gone out.

Frederick, as he gazed at the scene, could almost believe that he was dreaming. His heart was oppressed with anguish. It seemed to him that this death was only a beginning, and that behind it was a worse calamity, which was just about to come on.

Suddenly, Rosanette said in an appealing tone:

"We'll preserve the body—shall we not?"

She wished to have the dead child embalmed. There were many objections to this. The principal one, in Frederick's opinion, was that the thing was impracticable in the case of children so young. A portrait would be better. She adopted this idea. He wrote a line to Pellerin, and Delphine hastened to deliver it.

Pellerin arrived speedily, anxious by this display of zeal to efface all recollection of his former conduct. The first thing he said was:

"Poor little angel! Ah, my God, what a misfortune!"

But gradually (the artist in him getting the upper hand) he declared that nothing could be made out of those yellowish eyes, that livid face, that it was a real case of still-life, and would, therefore, require very great talent to treat it effectively; and so he murmured:

"Oh, 'tisn't easy—'tisn't easy!"

"No matter, as long as it is life-like," urged Rosanette.

"Pooh! what do I care about a thing being life-like? Down with Realism! 'Tis the spirit that must be portrayed by the painter! Let me alone! I am going to try to conjure up what it ought to be!"

He reflected, with his left hand clasping his brow, and with his right hand clutching his elbow; then, all of a sudden:

"Ha, I have an idea! a pastel! With coloured mezzotints, almost spread out flat, a lovely model could be obtained with the outer surface alone!"

He sent the chambermaid to look for his box of colours; then, having a chair under his feet and another by his side, he began to throw out great touches with as much complacency as if he had drawn them in accordance with the bust. He praised the little Saint John of Correggio, the Infanta Rosa of Velasquez, the milk-white flesh-tints of Reynolds, the distinction of Lawrence, and especially the child with long hair that sits in Lady Gower's lap.

"Besides, could you find anything more charming than these little toads? The type of the sublime (Raphael has proved it by his Madonnas) is probably a mother with her child?"

Rosanette, who felt herself stifling, went away; and presently Pellerin said:

"Well, about Arnoux; you know what has happened?"

"No! What?"

"However, it was bound to end that way!"

"What has happened, might I ask?"

"Perhaps by this time he is— Excuse me!"

The artist got up in order to raise the head of the little corpse higher.

"You were saying—" Frederick resumed.

And Pellerin, half-closing his eyes, in order to take his dimensions better:

"I was saying that our friend Arnoux is perhaps by this time locked up!"

Then, in a tone of satisfaction:

"Just give a little glance at it. Is that the thing?"

"Yes, 'tis quite right. But about Arnoux?"

Pellerin laid down his pencil.

"As far as I could understand, he was sued by one Mignot, an intimate friend of Regimbart—a longheaded fellow that, eh? What an idiot! Just imagine! one day—"

"What! it's not Regimbart that's in question, is it?"

"It is, indeed! Well, yesterday evening, Arnoux had to produce twelve thousand francs; if not, he was a ruined man."

"Oh! this perhaps is exaggerated," said Frederick.

"Not a bit. It looked to me a very serious business, very serious!"

At that moment Rosanette reappeared, with red spots under her eyes, which glowed like dabs of paint. She sat down near the drawing and gazed at it. Pellerin made a sign to the other to hold his tongue on account of her. But Frederick, without minding her:

"Nevertheless, I can't believe—"

"I tell you I met him yesterday," said the artist, "at seven o'clock in the evening, in the Rue Jacob. He had even taken the precaution to have his passport with him; and he spoke about embarking from Havre, he and his whole camp."

"What! with his wife?"

"No doubt. He is too much of a family man to live by himself."

"And are you sure of this?"

"Certain, faith! Where do you expect him to find twelve thousand francs?"

Frederick took two or three turns round the room. He panted for breath, bit his lips, and then snatched up his hat.

"Where are you going now?" said Rosanette.

He made no reply, and the next moment he had disappeared.

Chapter XVIII

AN AUCTION

TWELVE THOUSAND FRANCS SHOULD BE PROCURED, OR, IF NOT, HE WOULD see Madame Arnoux no more; and until now there had lingered in his breast an unconquerable hope. Did she not, as it were, constitute the very substance of his heart, the very basis of his life? For some minutes he went staggering along the footpath, his mind tortured with anxiety, and nevertheless gladdened by the thought that he was no longer by the other's side.

Where was he to get the money? Frederick was well aware from his own experience how hard it was to obtain it immediately, no matter at what cost. There was only one person who could help him in the matter—Madame Dambreuse. She always kept a good supply of bank-notes in her escritoire. He called at her house; and in an unblushing fashion:

"Have you twelve thousand francs to lend me?"

"What for?"

That was another person's secret. She wanted to know who this person was. He would not give way on this point. They were equally determined not to yield. Finally, she declared that she would give nothing until she knew for what purpose it was wanted.

Frederick's face became very flushed; and he stated that one of his comrades had committed a theft. It was necessary to replace the sum this very day.

"Let me know his name? His name? Come! what's his name?"

"Dussardier!"

And he threw himself on his knees, imploring of her to say nothing about it.

"What idea have you got into your head about me?" Madame Dambreuse replied. "One would imagine that you were the guilty party yourself. Pray, have done with your tragic airs! Hold on! here's the money! and much good may it do him!"

He hurried off to see Arnoux. That worthy merchant was not in his shop. But he was still residing in the Rue de Paradis, for he had two domiciles.

In the Rue de Paradis, the porter said that M. Arnoux had been away since the evening before. As for Madame, he ventured to say nothing; and Frederick, having rushed like an arrow up the stairs, laid his ear against the keyhole. At length, the door was opened. Madame had gone out with Monsieur. The servant could not say when they would be back; her wages had been paid, and she was leaving herself.

Suddenly he heard the door creaking.

"But is there anyone in the room?"

"Oh, no, Monsieur! it is the wind."

Thereupon he withdrew. There was something inexplicable in such a rapid disappearance.

Regimbart, being Mignot's intimate friend, could perhaps enlighten him? And Frederick got himself driven to that gentleman's house at Montmartre in the Rue l'Empereur.

Attached to the house there was a small garden shut in by a grating which was stopped up with iron plates. Three steps before the hall-door set off the white front; and a person passing along the footpath could see the two rooms on the ground-floor, the first of which was a parlour with ladies' dresses lying on the furniture on every side, and the second the workshop in which Madame Regimbart's female assistants were accustomed to sit.

They were all convinced that Monsieur had important occupations, distinguished connections, that he was a man altogether beyond comparison. When he was passing through the lobby with his hat cocked up at the sides, his long grave face, and his green frock-coat, the girls stopped in the midst of their work. Besides, he never failed to address to them a few words of encouragement, some observation which showed his ceremonious courtesy; and, afterwards, in their own homes they felt unhappy at not having been able to preserve him as their ideal.

No one, however, was so devoted to him as Madame Regimbart, an intelligent little woman, who maintained him by her handicraft.

As soon as M. Moreau had given his name, she came out quickly to meet him, knowing through the servants what his relations were with Madame Dambreuse. Her husband would be back in a moment; and Frederick, while he followed her, admired the appearance of the house and the profusion of oil-cloth that was displayed in it. Then he waited a few minutes in a kind of office, into which the Citizen was in the habit of retiring, in order to be alone with his thoughts.

When they met, Regimbart's manner was less cranky than usual.

He related Arnoux's recent history. The ex-manufacturer of earthenware had excited the vanity of Mignot, a patriot who owned a hundred shares in the *Siècle*, by professing to show that it would be necessary from the democratic standpoint to change the management and the editorship of the newspaper; and under the pretext of making his views prevail in the next meeting of shareholders, he had given the other fifty shares, telling him that he could pass them on to reliable friends who would back up his vote. Mignot would have no personal responsibility, and need not annoy himself about anyone; then, when he had achieved success, he would be able to secure a good place in the administration of at least from live to six thousand francs. The shares had been delivered. But Arnoux had at once sold them, and with the money had entered into partnership with a dealer in religious articles. Thereupon came complaints from Mignot, to which Arnoux sent evasive answers. At last the patriot had threatened to bring against him a charge of cheating if he did not restore his share-certificates or pay an equivalent sum—fifty thousand francs.

Frederick's face wore a look of despondency.

"That is not the whole of it," said the Citizen. "Mignot, who is an honest fellow, has reduced his claim to one fourth. New promises on the part of the other, and, of course, new dodges. In short, on the morning of the day before yesterday Mignot sent him a written application to pay up, within twenty-four hours, twelve thousand francs, without prejudice to the balance."

"But I have the amount!" said Frederick.

The Citizen slowly turned round:

"Humbug!"

"Excuse me! I have the money in my pocket. I brought it with me."

"How you do go at it! By Jove, you do! However, 'tis too late now—the complaint has been lodged, and Arnoux is gone."

"Alone?"

"No! along with his wife. They were seen at the Havre terminus."

Frederick grew exceedingly pale. Madame Regimbart thought he was going to faint. He regained his self-possession with an effort, and had even sufficient presence of mind to ask two or three questions about the occurrence. Regimbart was grieved at the affair, considering that it would injure the cause of Democracy. Arnoux had always been lax in his conduct and disorderly in his life.

"A regular hare-brained fellow! He burned the candle at both ends! The petticoat has ruined him! 'Tis not himself that I pity, but his poor wife!" For the Citizen admired virtuous women, and had a great esteem for Madame Arnoux.

"She must have suffered a nice lot!"

Frederick felt grateful to him for his sympathy; and, as if Regimbart had done him a service, pressed his hand effusively.

"Have you done all that's necessary in the matter?" was Rosanette's greeting to him when she saw him again.

He had not been able to pluck up courage to do it, he answered, and walked about the streets at random to divert his thoughts.

At eight o'clock, they passed into the dining-room; but they remained seated face to face in silence, gave vent each to a deep sigh every now and then, and pushed away their plates.

Frederick drank some brandy. He felt quite shattered, crushed, annihilated, no longer conscious of anything save a sensation of extreme fatigue.

She went to look at the portrait. The red, the yellow, the green, and the indigo made glaring stains that jarred with each other, so that it looked a hideous thing—almost ridiculous.

Besides, the dead child was now unrecognisable. The purple hue of his lips made the whiteness of his skin more remarkable. His nostrils were more drawn than before, his eyes more hollow; and his head rested on a pillow of blue taffeta, surrounded by petals of camelias, autumn roses, and violets. This was an idea suggested by the chambermaid, and both of them had thus with pious care arranged the little corpse. The mantelpiece, covered with a cloth of guipure, supported silver-gilt candlesticks with bunches of consecrated box in the spaces between them. At the corners there were a pair of vases in which pastilles were burning. All these things, taken in conjunction with the cradle, presented the aspect of an altar; and Frederick recalled to mind the night when he had watched beside M. Dambreuse's death-bed.

Nearly every quarter of an hour Rosanette drew aside the curtains in order to take a look at her child. She saw him in imagination, a few months hence, beginning to walk; then at college, in the middle of the recreation-ground, playing a game of base; then at twenty years a full-grown young man; and all these pictures conjured up by her brain created for her, as it were, the son she would have lost, had he only lived, the excess of her grief intensifying in her the maternal instinct.

Frederick, sitting motionless in another armchair, was thinking of Madame Arnoux.

No doubt she was at that moment in a train, with her face leaning against a carriage window, while she watched the country disappearing behind her in the direction of Paris, or else on the deck of a steamboat, as on the occasion when they first met; but this vessel carried her away into distant countries, from which she would never return. He next saw her in a room at an inn, with trunks covering the floor, the wallpaper hanging in shreds, and the door shaking in the wind. And after that—to what would she be compelled to turn? Would she have to become a schoolmistress or a lady's companion, or perhaps a chambermaid? She was exposed to all the vicissitudes of poverty. His utter ignorance as to what her fate might be tortured his mind. He ought either to have opposed her departure or to have followed her. Was he not her real husband? And as the thought impressed itself on his consciousness that he would never meet her again, that it was all over forever, that she was lost to him beyond recall, he felt, so to speak, a rending of his entire being, and the tears that had been gathering since morning in his heart overflowed.

Rosanette noticed the tears in his eyes.

"Ah! you are crying just like me! You are grieving, too?"

"Yes! yes! I am——"

He pressed her to his heart, and they both sobbed, locked in each other's arms.

Madame Dambreuse was weeping too, as she lay, face downwards, on her bed, with her hands clasped over her head.

Olympe Regimbart having come that evening to try on her first coloured gown after mourning, had told her about Frederick's visit, and even about the twelve thousand francs which he had ready to transfer to M. Arnoux.

So, then, this money, the very money which he had got from her, was intended to be used simply for the purpose of preventing the other from leaving Paris—for the purpose, in fact, of preserving a mistress!

At first, she broke into a violent rage, and determined to drive him from her door, as she would have driven a lackey. A copious flow of tears produced a sooth-ing effect upon her. It was better to keep it all to herself, and say nothing about it.

Frederick brought her back the twelve thousand francs on the following day.

She begged of him to keep the money lest he might require it for his friend, and she asked a number of questions about this gentleman. Who, then, had tempted him to such a breach of trust? A woman, no doubt! Women drag you into every kind of crime.

This bantering tone put Frederick out of countenance. He felt deep remorse for the calumny he had invented. He was reassured by the reflection that Madame Dambreuse could not be aware of the facts. All the same, she was very persistent about the subject; for, two days later, she again made enquiries about his young friend, and, after that, about another—Deslauriers.

"Is this young man trustworthy and intelligent?"

Frederick spoke highly of him.

"Ask him to call on me one of these mornings; I want to consult him about a matter of business."

She had found a roll of old papers in which there were some bills of Arnoux, which had been duly protested, and which had been signed by Madame Arnoux. It was about these very bills Frederick had called on M. Dambreuse on one occasion while the latter was at breakfast; and, although the capitalist had not sought to en-force repayment of this outstanding debt, he had not only got judgment on foot of them from the Tribunal of Commerce against Arnoux, but also against his wife, who knew nothing about the matter, as her husband had not thought fit to give her any information on the point.

Here was a weapon placed in Madame Dambreuse's hands—she had no doubt about it. But her notary would advise her to take no step in the affair. She would have preferred to act through some obscure person, and she thought of that big fel-low with such an impudent expression of face, who had offered her his services.

Frederick ingenuously performed this commission for her.

The advocate was enchanted at the idea of having business relations with such an aristocratic lady.

He hurried to Madame Dambreuse's house.

She informed him that the inheritance belonged to her niece, a further reason for liquidating those debts which she should repay, her object being to overwhelm Martinon's wife by a display of greater attention to the deceased's affairs.

Deslauriers guessed that there was some hidden design underlying all this. He reflected while he was examining the bills. Madame Arnoux's name, traced by her own hand, brought once more before his eyes her entire person, and the insult which he had received at her hands. Since vengeance was offered to him, why should he not snatch at it?

He accordingly advised Madame Dambreuse to have the bad debts which went with the inheritance sold by auction. A man of straw, whose name would not be divulged, would buy them up, and would exercise the legal rights thus given him to realise them. He would take it on himself to provide a man to discharge this function.

Towards the end of the month of November, Frederick, happening to pass through the street in which Madame Arnoux had lived, raised his eyes towards the windows of her house, and saw posted on the door a placard on which was printed in large letters:

"Sale of valuable furniture, consisting of kitchen utensils, body and table linen, shirts and chemises, lace, petticoats, trousers, French and Indian cashmeres, an Erard piano, two Renaissance oak chests, Venetian mirrors, Chinese and Japanese pottery."

" 'Tis their furniture!" said Frederick to himself, and his suspicions were confirmed by the door-keeper.

As for the person who had given instructions for the sale, he could get no information on that head. But perhaps the auctioneer, Maître Berthelmot, might be able to throw light on the subject.

The functionary did not at first want to tell what creditor was having the sale carried out. Frederick pressed him on the point. It was a gentleman named Sénécal, an agent; and Maître Berthelmot even carried his politeness so far as to lend his newspaper—the *Petites Affiches*—to Frederick.

The latter, on reaching Rosanette's house, flung down this paper on the table spread wide open.

"Read that!"

"Well, what?" said she with a face so calm that it roused up in him a feeling of revolt.

"Ah! keep up that air of innocence!"

"I don't understand what you mean."

" 'Tis you who are selling out Madame Arnoux yourself!"

She read over the announcement again.

"Where is her name?"

"Oh! 'tis her furniture. You know that as well as I do."

"What does that signify to me?" said Rosanette, shrugging her shoulders.

"What does it signify to you? But you are taking your revenge, that's all. This is the consequence of your persecutions. Haven't you outraged her so far as to call at her house?—you, a worthless creature! and this to the most saintly, the most charming, the best woman that ever lived! Why do you set your heart on ruining her?"

"I assure you, you are mistaken!"

"Come now! As if you had not put Sénécal forward to do this!"

"What nonsense!"

Then he was carried away with rage.

"You lie! you lie! you wretch! You are jealous of her! You have got a judgment against her husband! Sénécal is already mixed up in your affairs. He detests Arnoux; and your two hatreds have entered into a combination with one another. I saw how delighted he was when you won that action of yours about the kaolin shares. Are you going to deny this?"

"I give you my word—"

"Oh, I know what that's worth—your word!"

And Frederick reminded her of her lovers, giving their names and circumstantial details. Rosanette drew back, all the colour fading from her face.

"You are astonished at this. You thought I was blind because I shut my eyes. Now I have had enough of it. We do not die through the treacheries of a woman of your sort. When they become too monstrous we get out of the way. To inflict punishment on account of them would be only to degrade oneself."

She twisted her arms about.

"My God, who can it be that has changed him?"

"Nobody but yourself."

"And all this for Madame Arnoux!" exclaimed Rosanette, weeping.

He replied coldly:

"I have never loved any woman but her!"

At this insult her tears ceased to flow.

"That shows your good taste! A woman of mature years, with a complexion like liquorice, a thick waist, big eyes like the ventholes of a cellar, and just as empty! As you like her so much, go and join her!"

"This is just what I expected. Thank you!"

Rosanette remained motionless, stupefied by this extraordinary behaviour.

She even allowed the door to be shut; then, with a bound, she pulled him back into the anteroom, and flinging her arms around him:

"Why, you are mad! you are mad! this is absurd! I love you!" Then she changed her tone to one of entreaty:

"Good heavens! for the sake of our dead infant!"

"Confess that it was you who did this trick!" said Frederick.

She still protested that she was innocent.

"You will not acknowledge it?"

"No!"

"Well, then, farewell! and forever!"

"Listen to me!"

Frederick turned round:

"If you understood me better, you would know that my decision is irrevocable!"

"Oh! oh! you will come back to me again!"

"Never as long as I live!"

And he slammed the door behind him violently.

Rosanette wrote to Deslauriers saying that she wanted to see him at once.

He called one evening, about five days later; and, when she told him about the rupture:

"That's all! A nice piece of bad luck!"

She thought at first that he would have been able to bring back Frederick; but now all was lost. She ascertained through the doorkeeper that he was about to be married to Madame Dambreuse.

Deslauriers gave her a lecture, and showed himself an exceedingly gay fellow, quite a jolly dog; and, as it was very late, asked permission to pass the night in an armchair.

Then, next morning, he set out again for Nogent, informing her that he was unable to say when they would meet once more. In a little while, there would perhaps be a great change in his life.

Two hours after his return, the town was in a state of revolution. The news went round that M. Frederick was going to marry Madame Dambreuse. At length the three Mesdemoiselles Auger, unable to stand it any longer, made their way to the house of Madame Moreau, who with an air of pride confirmed this intelligence. Père Roque became quite ill when he heard it. Louise locked herself up; it was even rumoured that she had gone mad.

Meanwhile, Frederick was unable to hide his dejection. Madame Dambreuse, in order to divert his mind, no doubt, from gloomy thoughts, redoubled her attentions. Every afternoon they went out for a drive in her carriage; and, on one occasion, as they were passing along the Place de la Bourse, she took the idea into her head to pay a visit to the public auction-rooms for the sake of amusement.

It was the 1st of December, the very day on which the sale of Madame Arnoux's furniture was to take place. He remembered the date, and manifested his repugnance, declaring that this place was intolerable on account of the crush and the noise. She only wanted to get a peep at it. The brougham drew up. He had no alternative but to accompany her.

In the open space could be seen washhand-stands without basins, the wooden portions of armchairs, old hampers, pieces of porcelain, empty bottles, mattresses; and men in blouses or in dirty frock-coats, all grey with dust, and mean-looking faces, some with canvas sacks over their shoulders, were chatting in separate groups or hailing each other in a disorderly fashion.

Frederick urged that it was inconvenient to go on any further.

"Pooh!"

And they ascended the stairs. In the first room, at the right, gentlemen, with catalogues in their hands, were examining pictures; in another, a collection of Chinese weapons were being sold. Madame Dambreuse wanted to go down again. She looked at the numbers over the doors, and she led him to the end of the corridor towards an apartment which was blocked up with people.

He immediately recognised the two whatnots belonging to the office of *L'Art Industriel*, her work-table, all her furniture. Heaped up at the end of the room according to their respective heights, they formed a long slope from the floor to the windows, and at the other sides of the apartment, the carpets and the curtains hung down straight along the walls. There were underneath steps occupied by old men who had fallen asleep. At the left rose a sort of counter at which the auctioneer, in a white cravat, was lightly swinging a little hammer. By his side a young man was writing, and below him stood a sturdy fellow, between a commercial traveller and a vendor of countermarks, crying out: "Furniture for sale." Three attendants placed the articles on a table, at the sides of which sat in a row second-hand dealers and old-clothes' women. The general public at the auction kept walking in a circle behind them.

When Frederick came in, the petticoats, the neckerchiefs, and even the chemises were being passed on from hand to hand, and then given back. Sometimes they were flung some distance, and suddenly strips of whiteness went flying through the air. After that her gowns were sold, and then one of her hats, the broken feather of which was hanging down, then her furs, and then three pairs of boots; and the disposal by sale of these relics, wherein he could trace in a confused sort of way the very outlines of her form, appeared to him an atrocity, as if he had seen carrion crows mangling her corpse. The atmosphere of the room, heavy with so many breaths, made him feel sick. Madame Dambreuse offered him her smelling-bottle. She said that she found all this highly amusing.

The bedroom furniture was now exhibited. Maître Berthelmot named a price. The crier immediately repeated it in a louder voice, and the three auctioneer's assistants quietly waited for the stroke of the hammer, and then carried off the article sold to an adjoining apartment. In this way disappeared, one after the other, the large blue carpet spangled with camellias, which her dainty feet used to touch so lightly as she advanced to meet him, the little upholstered easy-chair, in which he used to sit facing her when they were alone together, the two screens belonging to the mantelpiece, the ivory of which had been rendered smoother by the touch of her hands, and a velvet pincushion, which was still bristling with pins. It was as if portions of his heart had been carried away with these things; and the monotony of the same voices and the same gestures benumbed him with fatigue, and caused within him a mournful torpor, a sensation like that of death itself.

There was a rustle of silk close to his ear. Rosanette touched him.

It was through Frederick himself that she had learned about this auction. When her first feelings of vexation was over, the idea of deriving profit from it occurred to her mind. She had come to see it in a white satin vest with pearl buttons, a furbelowed gown, tight-fitting gloves on her hands, and a look of triumph on her face.

He grew pale with anger. She stared at the woman who was by his side.

Madame Dambreuse had recognised her, and for a minute they examined each other from head to foot minutely, in order to discover the defect, the blemish—the one perhaps envying the other's youth, and the other filled with spite at the extreme good form, the aristocratic simplicity of her rival.

At last Madame Dambreuse turned her head round with a smile of inexpressible insolence.

The crier had opened a piano—her piano! While he remained standing before it he ran the fingers of his right hand over the keys, and put up the instrument at twelve hundred francs; then he brought down the figures to one thousand, then to eight hundred, and finally to seven hundred.

Madame Dambreuse, in a playful tone, laughed at the appearance of some socket that was out of gear.

The next thing placed before the second-hand dealers was a little chest with medallions and silver corners and clasps, the same one which he had seen at the first dinner in the Rue de Choiseul, which had subsequently been in Rosanette's house, and again transferred back to Madame Arnoux's residence. Often during their conversations his eyes wandered towards it. He was bound to it by the dearest memories, and his soul was melting with tender emotions about it, when suddenly Madame Dambreuse said:

"Look here! I am going to buy that!"

"But it is not a very rare article," he returned.

She considered it, on the contrary, very pretty, and the appraiser commended its delicacy.

"A gem of the Renaissance! Eight hundred francs, messieurs! Almost entirely of silver! With a little whiting it can be made to shine brilliantly."

And, as she was pushing forward through the crush of people:

"What an odd idea!" said Frederick.

"You are annoyed at this!"

"No! But what can be done with a fancy article of that sort?"

"Who knows? Love-letters might be kept in it, perhaps!"

She gave him a look which made the allusion very clear.

"A reason the more for not robbing the dead of their secrets."

"I did not imagine she was dead." And then in a loud voice she went on to bid:

"Eight hundred and eighty francs!"

"What you're doing is not right," murmured Frederick.

She began to laugh.

"But this is the first favour, dear, that I am asking from you."

"Come, now! doesn't it strike you that at this rate you won't be a very considerate husband?"

Some one had just at that moment made a higher bid.

"Nine hundred francs!"

"Nine hundred francs!" repeated Maître Berthelmot.

"Nine hundred and ten—fifteen—twenty—thirty!" squeaked the auctioneer's crier, with jerky shakes of his head as he cast a sweeping glance at those assembled around him.

"Show me that I am going to have a wife who is amenable to reason," said Frederick.

And he gently drew her towards the door.

The auctioneer proceeded:

"Come, come, messieurs; nine hundred and thirty. Is there any bidder at nine hundred and thirty?"

Madame Dambreuse, just as she had reached the door, stopped, and raising her voice to a high pitch:

"One thousand francs!"

There was a thrill of astonishment, and then a dead silence.

"A thousand francs, messieurs, a thousand francs! Is nobody advancing on this bid? Is that clear? Very well, then—one thousand francs! going!—gone!"

And down came the ivory hammer. She passed in her card, and the little chest was handed over to her. She thrust it into her muff.

Frederick felt a great chill penetrating his heart.

Madame Dambreuse had not let go her hold of his arm; and she had not the courage to look up at his face in the street, where her carriage was awaiting her.

She flung herself into it, like a thief flying away after a robbery, and then turned towards Frederick. He had his hat in his hand.

"Are you not going to come in?"

"No, Madame!"

And, bowing to her frigidly, he shut the carriage-door, and then made a sign to the coachman to drive away.

The first feeling that he experienced was one of joy at having regained his independence. He was filled with pride at the thought that he had avenged Madame Arnoux by sacrificing a fortune to her; then, he was amazed at his own act, and he felt doubled up with extreme physical exhaustion.

Next morning his man-servant brought him the news.

The city had been declared to be in a state of siege; the Assembly had been dissolved; and a number of the representatives of the people had been imprisoned at Mazas. Public affairs had assumed to his mind an utterly unimportant aspect, so deeply pre-occupied was he by his private troubles.

He wrote to several tradesmen countermanding various orders which he had given for the purchase of articles in connection with his projected marriage, which now appeared to him in the light of a rather mean speculation; and he execrated Madame Dambreuse, because, owing to her, he had been very near perpetrating a vile action. He had forgotten the Maréchale, and did not even bother himself about Madame Arnoux—absorbed only in one thought—lost amid the wreck of his dreams, sick at heart, full of grief and disappointment, and in his hatred of the artificial atmosphere wherein he had suffered so much, he longed for the freshness of green fields, the repose of provincial life, a sleeping existence spent beneath his natal roof in the midst of ingenuous hearts. At last, when Wednesday evening arrived, he made his way out into the open air.

On the boulevard numerous groups had taken up their stand. From time to time a patrol came and dispersed them; they gathered together again in regular order behind it. They talked freely and in loud tones, made chaffing remarks about the soldiers, without anything further happening.

"What! are they not going to fight?" said Frederick to a workman.

"They're not such fools as to get themselves killed for the well-off people! Let them take care of themselves!"

And a gentleman muttered, as he glanced across at the inhabitants of the faubourgs:

"Socialist rascals! If it were only possible, this time, to exterminate them!"

Frederick could not, for the life of him, understand the necessity of so much rancour and vituperative language. His feeling of disgust against Paris was intensified by these occurrences, and two days later he set out for Nogent by the first train.

The houses soon became lost to view; the country stretched out before his gaze. Alone in his carriage, with his feet on the seat in front of him, he pondered over the events of the last few days, and then on his entire past. The recollection of Louise came back to his mind.

"She, indeed, loved me truly! I was wrong not to snatch at this chance of happiness. Pooh! let us not think any more about it!"

Then, five minutes afterwards: "Who knows, after all? Why not, later?"

His reverie, like his eyes, wandered afar towards vague horizons.

"She was artless, a peasant girl, almost a savage; but so good!"

In proportion as he drew nearer to Nogent, her image drew closer to him. As they were passing through the meadows of Sourdun, he saw her once more in imagination under the poplar-trees, as in the old days, cutting rushes on the edges of the pools. And now they had reached their destination; he stepped out of the train.

Then he leaned with his elbows on the bridge, to gaze again at the isle and the garden where they had walked together one sunshiny day, and the dizzy sensation caused by travelling, together with the weakness engendered by his recent emotions, arousing in his breast a sort of exaltation, he said to himself:

"She has gone out, perhaps; suppose I were to go and meet her!"

The bell of Saint-Laurent was ringing, and in the square in front of the church there was a crowd of poor people around an open carriage, the only one in the district—the one which was always hired for weddings. And all of a sudden, under the church-gate, accompanied by a number of well-dressed persons in white cravats, a newly-married couple appeared.

He thought he must be labouring under some hallucination. But no! It was, indeed, Louise! covered with a white veil which flowed from her red hair down to her heels; and with her was no other than Deslauriers, attired in a blue coat embroidered with silver—the costume of a prefect.

How was this?

Frederick concealed himself at the corner of a house to let the procession pass.

Shamefaced, vanquished, crushed, he retraced his steps to the railway-station, and returned to Paris.

The cabman who drove him assured him that the barricades were erected from the Château d'Eau to the Gymnase, and turned down the Faubourg Saint-Martin. At the corner of the Rue de Provence, Frederick stepped out in order to reach the boulevards.

It was five o'clock. A thin shower was falling. A number of citizens blocked up the footpath close to the Opera House. The houses opposite were closed. No one at any of the windows. All along the boulevard, dragoons were galloping behind a row of wagons, leaning with drawn swords over their horses; and the plumes of their helmets, and their large white cloaks, rising up behind them, could be seen under the glare of the gas-lamps, which shook in the wind in the midst of a haze. The crowd gazed at them mute with fear.

In the intervals between the cavalry-charges, squads of policemen arrived on the scene to keep back the people in the streets.

But on the steps of Tortoni, a man—Dussardier—who could be distinguished at a distance by his great height, remained standing as motionless as a caryatide.

One of the police-officers, marching at the head of his men, with his three-cornered hat drawn over his eyes, threatened him with his sword.

The other thereupon took one step forward, and shouted:

"Long live the Republic!"

The next moment he fell on his back with his arms crossed.

A yell of horror arose from the crowd. The police-officer, with a look of command, made a circle around him; and Frederick, gazing at him in open-mouthed astonishment, recognised Sénécal.

Chapter XIX

A BITTER-SWEET REUNION

HE TRAVELLED.

He realised the melancholy associated with packet-boats, the chill one feels on waking up under tents, the dizzy effect of landscapes and ruins, and the bitterness of ruptured sympathies.

He returned home.

He mingled in society, and he conceived attachments to other women. But the constant recollection of his first love made these appear insipid; and besides the vehemence of desire, the bloom of the sensation had vanished. In like manner, his intellectual ambitions had grown weaker. Years passed; and he was forced to support the burthen of a life in which his mind was unoccupied and his heart devoid of energy.

Towards the end of March, 1867, just as it was getting dark, one evening, he was sitting all alone in his study, when a woman suddenly came in.

"Madame Arnoux!"

"Frederick!"

She caught hold of his hands, and drew him gently towards the window, and, as she gazed into his face, she kept repeating:

" 'Tis he! Yes, indeed—'tis he!"

In the growing shadows of the twilight, he could see only her eyes under the black lace veil that hid her face.

When she had laid down on the edge of the mantelpiece a little pocket-book bound in garnet velvet, she seated herself in front of him, and they both remained silent, unable to utter a word, smiling at one another.

At last he asked her a number of questions about herself and her husband.

They had gone to live in a remote part of Brittany for the sake of economy, so as to be able to pay their debts. Arnoux, now almost a chronic invalid, seemed to have become quite an old man. Her daughter had been married and was living at Bordeaux, and her son was in garrison at Mostaganem.

Then she raised her head to look at him again:

"But I see you once more! I am happy!"

He did not fail to let her know that, as soon as he heard of their misfortune, he had hastened to their house.

"I was fully aware of it!"

"How?"

She had seen him in the street outside the house, and had hidden herself.

"Why did you do that?"

Then, in a trembling voice, and with long pauses between her words:

"I was afraid! Yes—afraid of you and of myself!"

This disclosure gave him, as it were, a shock of voluptuous joy. His heart began to throb wildly. She went on:

"Excuse me for not having come sooner." And, pointing towards the little pocket-book covered with golden palm-branches:

"I embroidered it on your account expressly. It contains the amount for which the Belleville property was given as security."

Frederick thanked her for letting him have the money, while chiding her at the same time for having given herself any trouble about it.

"No! 'tis not for this I came! I was determined to pay you this visit—then I would go back there again."

And she spoke about the place where they had taken up their abode.

It was a low-built house of only one story; and there was a garden attached to it full of huge box-trees, and a double avenue of chestnut-trees, reaching up to the top of the hill, from which there was a view of the sea.

"I go there and sit down on a bench, which I have called 'Frederick's bench.' "

Then she proceeded to fix her gaze on the furniture, the objects of virtù, the pictures, with eager intentness, so that she might be able to carry away the impressions of them in her memory. The Maréchale's portrait was half-hidden behind a curtain. But the gilding and the white spaces of the picture, which showed their outlines through the midst of the surrounding darkness, attracted her attention.

"It seems to me I knew that woman?"

"Impossible!" said Frederick. "It is an old Italian painting."

She confessed that she would like to take a walk through the streets on his arm. They went out.

The light from the shop-windows fell, every now and then, on her pale profile; then once more she was wrapped in shadow, and in the midst of the carriages, the crowd, and the din, they walked on without paying any heed to what was happening around them, without hearing anything, like those who make their way across the fields over beds of dead leaves.

They talked about the days which they had formerly spent in each other's society, the dinners at the time when *L'Art Industriel* flourished, Arnoux's fads, his habit of drawing up the ends of his collar and of squeezing cosmetic over his moustache, and other matters of a more intimate and serious character. What delight he experienced on the first occasion when he heard her singing! How lovely she looked on her feast-day at Saint-Cloud! He recalled to her memory the little garden at Auteuil, evenings at the theatre, a chance meeting on the boulevard, and some of her old servants, including the negress.

She was astonished at his vivid recollection of these things.

"Sometimes your words come back to me like a distant echo, like the sound of a bell carried on by the wind, and when I read passages about love in books, it seems to me that it is about you I am reading."

"All that people have found fault with as exaggerated in fiction you have made me feel," said Frederick. "I can understand Werther, who felt no disgust at his Charlotte for eating bread and butter."

"Poor, dear friend!"

She heaved a sigh; and, after a prolonged silence:

"No matter; we shall have loved each other truly!"

"And still without having ever belonged to each other!"

"This perhaps is all the better," she replied.

"No, no! What happiness we might have enjoyed!"

"Oh, I am sure of it with a love like yours!"

And it must have been very strong to endure after such a long separation.

Frederick wished to know from her how she first discovered that he loved her.

"It was when you kissed my wrist one evening between the glove and the cuff. I said to myself, 'Ah! yes, he loves me—he loves me;' nevertheless, I was afraid of being assured of it. So charming was your reserve, that I felt myself the object, as it were, of an involuntary and continuous homage."

He regretted nothing now. He was compensated for all he had suffered in the past.

When they came back to the house, Madame Arnoux took off her bonnet. The lamp, placed on a bracket, threw its light on her white hair. Frederick felt as if some one had given him a blow in the middle of the chest.

In order to conceal from her his sense of disillusion, he flung himself on the floor at her feet, and seizing her hands, began to whisper in her ear words of tenderness:

"Your person, your slightest movements, seemed to me to have a more than human importance in the world. My heart was like dust under your feet. You produced on me the effect of moonlight on a summer's night, when around us we find nothing but perfumes, soft shadows, gleams of whiteness, infinity; and all the delights of the flesh and of the spirit were for me embodied in your name, which I kept repeating to myself while I tried to kiss it with my lips. I thought of nothing further. It was Madame Arnoux such as you were with your two children, tender, grave, dazzlingly beautiful, and yet so good! This image effaced every other. Did

I not think of it alone? for I had always in the very depths of my soul the music of your voice and the brightness of your eyes!"

She accepted with transports of joy these tributes of adoration to the woman whom she could no longer claim to be. Frederick, becoming intoxicated with his own words, came to believe himself in the reality of what he said. Madame Arnoux, with her back turned to the light of the lamp, stooped towards him. He felt the caress of her breath on his forehead, and the undefined touch of her entire body through the garments that kept them apart. Their hands were clasped; the tip of her boot peeped out from beneath her gown, and he said to her, as if ready to faint:

"The sight of your foot makes me lose my self-possession."

An impulse of modesty made her rise. Then, without any further movement, she said, with the strange intonation of a somnambulist:

"At my age!—he—Frederick! Ah! no woman has ever been loved as I have been. No! Where is the use in being young? What do I care about them, indeed? I despise them—all those women who come here!"

"Oh! very few women come to this place," he returned, in a complaisant fashion.

Her face brightened up, and then she asked him whether he meant to be married.

He swore that he never would.

"Are you perfectly sure? Why should you not?"

" 'Tis on your account!" said Frederick, clasping her in his arms.

She remained thus pressed to his heart, with her head thrown back, her lips parted, and her eyes raised. Suddenly she pushed him away from her with a look of despair, and when he implored of her to say something to him in reply, she bent forward and whispered:

"I would have liked to make you happy!"

Frederick had a suspicion that Madame Arnoux had come to offer herself to him, and once more he was seized with a desire to possess her—stronger, fiercer, more desperate than he had ever experienced before. And yet he felt, the next moment, an unaccountable repugnance to the thought of such a thing, and, as it were, a dread of incurring the guilt of incest. Another fear, too, had a different effect on him—lest disgust might afterwards take possession of him. Besides, how embarrassing it would be!—and, abandoning the idea, partly through prudence, and partly through a resolve not to degrade his ideal, he turned on his heel and proceeded to roll a cigarette between his fingers.

She watched him with admiration.

"How dainty you are! There is no one like you! There is no one like you!"

It struck eleven.

"Already!" she exclaimed; "at a quarter-past I must go."

She sat down again, but she kept looking at the clock, and he walked up and down the room, puffing at his cigarette. Neither of them could think of anything further to say to the other. There is a moment at the hour of parting when the person that we love is with us no longer.

At last, when the hands of the clock got past the twenty-five minutes, she slowly took up her bonnet, holding it by the strings.

"Good-bye, my friend—my dear friend! I shall never see you again! This is the closing page in my life as a woman. My soul shall remain with you even when you see me no more. May all the blessings of Heaven be yours!"

And she kissed him on the forehead, like a mother.

But she appeared to be looking for something, and then she asked him for a pair of scissors.

She unfastened her comb, and all her white hair fell down.

With an abrupt movement of the scissors, she cut off a long lock from the roots.

"Keep it! Good-bye!"

When she was gone, Frederick rushed to the window and threw it open. There on the footpath he saw Madame Arnoux beckoning towards a passing cab. She stepped into it. The vehicle disappeared.

And this was all.

Chapter XX

"Wait Till You Come to Forty Year"

ABOUT THE BEGINNING OF THIS WINTER, FREDERICK AND DESLAURIERS were chatting by the fireside, once more reconciled by the fatality of their nature, which made them always reunite and be friends again.

Frederick briefly explained his quarrel with Madame Dambreuse, who had married again, her second husband being an Englishman.

Deslauriers, without telling how he had come to marry Mademoiselle Roque, related to his friend how his wife had one day eloped with a singer. In order to wipe away to some extent the ridicule that this brought upon him, he had compromised himself by an excess of governmental zeal in the exercise of his functions as prefect. He had been dismissed. After that, he had been an agent for colonisation in Algeria, secretary to a pasha, editor of a newspaper, and canvasser for advertisements, his latest employment being the office of settling disputed cases for a manufacturing company.

As for Frederick, having squandered two thirds of his means, he was now living like a citizen of comparatively humble rank.

Then they questioned each other about their friends.

Martinon was now a member of the Senate.

Hussonnet occupied a high position, in which he was fortunate enough to have all the theatres and entire press dependent upon him.

Cisy, given up to religion, and the father of eight children, was living in the château of his ancestors.

Pellerin, after turning his hand to Fourrièrism, homœopathy, table-turning, Gothic art, and humanitarian painting, had become a photographer; and he was to be seen on every dead wall in Paris, where he was represented in a black coat with a very small body and a big head.

"And what about your chum Sénécal?" asked Frederick.

"Disappeared—I can't tell you where! And yourself—what about the woman you were so passionately attached to, Madame Arnoux?"

"She is probably at Rome with her son, a lieutenant of chasseurs."

"And her husband?"

"He died a year ago."

"You don't say so?" exclaimed the advocate. Then, striking his forehead:

"Now that I think of it, the other day in a shop I met that worthy Maréchale, holding by the hand a little boy whom she has adopted. She is the widow of a certain M. Oudry, and is now enormously stout. What a change for the worse!—she who formerly had such a slender waist!"

Deslauriers did not deny that he had taken advantage of the other's despair to assure himself of that fact by personal experience.

"As you gave me permission, however."

This avowal was a compensation for the silence he had maintained with reference to his attempt with Madame Arnoux.

Frederick would have forgiven him, inasmuch as he had not succeeded in the attempt.

Although a little annoyed at the discovery, he pretended to laugh at it; and the allusion to the Maréchale brought back the Vatnaz to his recollection.

Deslauriers had never seen her any more than the others who used to come to the Arnoux's house; but he remembered Regimbart perfectly.

"Is he still living?"

"He is barely alive. Every evening regularly he drags himself from the Rue de Grammont to the Rue Montmartre, to the cafés, enfeebled, bent in two, emaciated, a spectre!"

"Well, and what about Compain?"

Frederick uttered a cry of joy, and begged of the ex-delegate of the provisional government to explain to him the mystery of the calf's head.

" 'Tis an English importation. In order to parody the ceremony which the Royalists celebrated on the thirtieth of January, some Independents founded an annual banquet, at which they have been accustomed to eat calves' heads, and at which they make it their business to drink red wine out of calves' skulls while giving toasts in favour of the extermination of the Stuarts. After Thermidor, the Terrorists organised a brotherhood of a similar description, which proves how prolific folly is."

"You seem to me very dispassionate about politics?"

"Effect of age," said the advocate.

And then they each proceeded to summarise their lives.

They had both failed in their objects—the one who dreamed only of love, and the other of power.

What was the reason of this?

" 'Tis perhaps from not having taken up the proper line," said Frederick.

"In your case that may be so. I, on the contrary, have sinned through excess of rectitude, without taking into account a thousand secondary things more important than any. I had too much logic, and you too much sentiment."

Then they blamed luck, circumstances, the epoch at which they were born.

Frederick went on:

"We have never done what we thought of doing long ago at Sens, when you wished to write a critical history of Philosophy and I a great mediæval romance about Nogent, the subject of which I had found in Froissart: 'How Messire Brokars de Fenestranges and the Archbishop of Troyes attacked Messire Eustache d'Ambrecicourt.' Do you remember?"

And, exhuming their youth with every sentence, they said to each other:

"Do you remember?"

They saw once more the college playground, the chapel, the parlour, the fencing-school at the bottom of the staircase, the faces of the ushers and of the pupils—one named Angelmare, from Versailles, who used to cut off trousers-straps from old boots, M. Mirbal and his red whiskers, the two professors of linear drawing and large drawing, who were always wrangling, and the Pole, the fellow-countryman of Copernicus, with his planetary system on pasteboard, an itinerant astronomer whose lecture had been paid for by a dinner in the refectory, then a terrible debauch while they were out on a walking excursion, the first pipes they had smoked, the distribution of prizes, and the delightful sensation of going home for the holidays.

It was during the vacation of 1837 that they had called at the house of the Turkish woman.

This was the phrase used to designate a woman whose real name was Zoraide Turc; and many persons believed her to be a Mohammedan, a Turk, which added to the poetic character of her establishment, situated at the water's edge behind the rampart. Even in the middle of summer there was a shadow around her house, which could be recognised by a glass bowl of goldfish near a pot of mignonette at a window. Young ladies in white nightdresses, with painted cheeks and long ear-rings, used to tap at the panes as the students passed; and as it grew dark, their custom was to hum softly in their hoarse voices at the doorsteps.

This home of perdition spread its fantastic notoriety over all the arrondisse-ment. Allusions were made to it in a circumlocutory style: "The place you know—a certain street—at the bottom of the Bridges." It made the farmers' wives of the district tremble for their husbands, and the ladies grow apprehensive as to their servants' virtue, inasmuch as the sub-prefect's cook had been caught there; and, to be sure, it exercised a fascination over the minds of all the young lads of the place.

Now, one Sunday, during vesper-time, Frederick and Deslauriers, having previously curled their hair, gathered some flowers in Madame Moreau's garden, then made their way out through the gate leading into the fields, and, after taking a wide sweep round the vineyards, came back through the Fishery, and stole into the Turkish woman's house with their big bouquets still in their hands.

Frederick presented his as a lover does to his betrothed. But the great heat, the fear of the unknown, and even the very pleasure of seeing at one glance so many women placed at his disposal, excited him so strangely that he turned exceedingly pale, and remained there without advancing a single step or uttering a single word. All the girls burst out laughing, amused at his embarrassment. Fancying that they were turning him into ridicule, he ran away; and, as Frederick had the money, Deslauriers was obliged to follow him.

They were seen leaving the house; and the episode furnished material for a bit of local gossip which was not forgotten three years later.

They related the story to each other in a prolix fashion, each supplementing the narrative where the other's memory failed; and, when they had finished the recital:

"That was the best time we ever had!" said Frederick.

"Yes, perhaps so, indeed! It was the best time we ever had," said Deslauriers.

THE TEMPTATION OF SAINT ANTHONY
OR,
A REVELATION OF THE SOUL

CONTENTS

Chapter I

A Holy Saint

IT IS IN THE THEBAÏD, ON THE HEIGHTS OF A MOUNTAIN, WHERE A PLATFORM, shaped like a crescent, is surrounded by huge stones.

The Hermit's cell occupies the background. It is built of mud and reeds, flat-roofed and doorless. Inside are seen a pitcher and a loaf of black bread; in the centre, on a wooden support, a large book; on the ground, here and there, bits of rush-work, a mat or two, a basket and a knife.

Some ten paces or so from the cell a tall cross is planted in the ground; and, at the other end of the platform, a gnarled old palm-tree leans over the abyss, for the side of the mountain is scarped; and at the bottom of the cliff the Nile swells, as it were, into a lake.

To right and left, the view is bounded by the enclosing rocks; but, on the side of the desert, immense undulations of a yellowish ash-colour rise, one above and one beyond the other, like the lines of a sea-coast; while, far off, beyond the sands, the mountains of the Libyan range form a wall of chalk-like whiteness faintly shaded with violet haze. In front, the sun is going down. Towards the north, the sky has a pearl-grey tint; while, at the zenith, purple clouds, like the tufts of a gigantic mane, stretch over the blue vault. These purple streaks grow browner; the patches of blue assume the paleness of mother-of-pearl. The bushes, the pebbles, the earth, now wear the hard colour of bronze, and through space floats a golden dust so fine that it is scarcely distinguishable from the vibrations of light.

Saint Anthony, who has a long beard, unshorn locks, and a tunic of goatskin, is seated, cross-legged, engaged in making mats. No sooner has the sun disappeared than he heaves a deep sigh, and gazing towards the horizon:

"Another day! Another day gone! I was not so miserable in former times as I am now! Before the night was over, I used to begin my prayers; than I would go down to the river to fetch water, and would reascend the rough mountain pathway, singing a hymn, with the water-bottle on my shoulder. After that, I used to amuse myself by arranging everything in my cell. I used to take up my tools, and examine the mats, to see whether they were evenly cut, and the baskets, to see whether they were light; for it seemed to me then that even my most trifling acts were duties which I performed with ease. At regulated hours I left off my work and prayed, with my two arms extended. I felt as if a fountain of mercy were flowing from Heaven above into my heart. But now it is dried up. Why is this? . . ."

He proceeds slowly into the rocky enclosure.

"When I left home, everyone found fault with me. My mother sank into a dying state; my sister, from a distance, made signs to me to come back; and the other one wept, Ammonaria, that child whom I used to meet every evening, beside the cistern, as she was leading away her cattle. She ran after me. The rings on her feet glittered in the dust, and her tunic, open at the hips, fluttered in the wind. The old ascetic who hurried me from the spot addressed her, as we fled, in loud and menacing tones. Then our two camels kept galloping continuously, till at length every familiar object had vanished from my sight.

"At first, I selected for my abode the tomb of one of the Pharaohs. But some enchantment surrounds those subterranean palaces, amid whose gloom the air is stifled with the decayed odour of aromatics. From the depths of the sarcophagi I heard a mournful voice arise, that called me by name—or rather, as it seemed to me, all the fearful pictures on the walls started into hideous life. Then I fled to the borders of the Red Sea into a citadel in ruins. There I had for companions the scorpions that crawled amongst the stones, and, overhead, the eagles who were continually whirling across the azure sky. At night, I was torn by talons, bitten by beaks, or brushed with light wings; and horrible demons, yelling in my ears, hurled me to the earth. At last, the drivers of a caravan, which was journeying towards Alexandria, rescued me, and carried me along with them.

"After this, I became a pupil of the venerable Didymus. Though he was blind, no one equalled him in knowledge of the Scriptures. When our lesson was ended, he used to take my arm, and, with my aid, ascend the Panium, from whose summit could be seen the Pharos and the open sea. Then we would return home, passing along the quays, where we brushed against men of every nation, including the Cimmerians, clad in bearskin, and the Gymnosophists of the Ganges, who smear their bodies with cow-dung. There were continual conflicts in the streets, some of which were caused by the Jews' refusal to pay taxes, and others by the attempts of the seditious to drive out the Romans. Besides, the city is filled with heretics, the followers of Manes, of Valentinus, of Basilides, and of Arius, all of them eagerly striving to discuss with you points of doctrine and to convert you to their views.

"Their discourses sometimes come back to my memory; and, though I try not to dwell upon them, they haunt my thoughts.

"I next took refuge in Colzin, and, when I had undergone a severe penance, I no longer feared the wrath of God. Many persons gathered around me, offering to become anchorites. I imposed on them a rule of life in antagonism to the vagaries of Gnosticism and the sophistries of the philosophers. Communications now reached me from every quarter, and people came a great distance to see me.

"Meanwhile, the populace continued to torture the confessors; and I was led back to Alexandria by an ardent thirst for martyrdom. I found on my arrival that the persecution had ceased three days before. Just as I was returning, my path was blocked by a great crowd in front of the Temple of Serapis. I was told that the Governor was about to make one final example. In the centre of the portico, in the broad light of day, a naked woman was fastened to a pillar, while two soldiers were scourging her. At each stroke her entire frame writhed. Suddenly, she cast a wild look around, her trembling lips parted; and, above the heads of the multitude, her figure wrapped, as it were, in her flowing hair, methought I recognised Ammonaria. . . . Yet this one was taller—and beautiful, exceedingly!"

He draws his hand across his brow.

"No! no! I must not think upon it!

"On another occasion, Athanasius asked me to assist him against the Arians. At that time, they had confined themselves to attacking him with invectives and ridicule. Since then, however, he has been calumniated, deprived of his see, and banished. Where is he now? I know not! People concern themselves so little about bringing me any news! All my disciples have abandoned me, Hilarion like the rest.

"He was, perhaps, fifteen years of age when he came to me, and his mind was so much filled with curiosity that every moment he was asking me questions. Then he would listen with a pensive air; and, without a murmur, he would run to fetch whatever I wanted—more nimble than a kid, and gay enough, moreover, to make even a patriarch laugh. He was a son to me!"

The sky is red; the earth completely dark. Agitated by the wind, clouds of sand rise, like winding-sheets, and then fall again. All at once, in a clear space in the heavens, a flock of birds flits by, forming a kind of triangular battalion, resembling a piece of metal with its edges alone vibrating.

Anthony glances at them.

"Ah! how I should like to follow them! How often, too, have I not wistfully gazed at the long boats with their sails resembling wings, especially when they bore away those who had been my guests! What happy times I used to have with them! What outpourings! None of them interested me more than Ammon. He described to me his journey to Rome, the Catacombs, the Coliseum, the piety of illustrious women, and a thousand other things. And yet I was unwilling to go away with him! How came I to be so obstinate in clinging to this solitary life? It might have been better for me had I stayed with the monks of Nitria when they besought me to do so. They occupy separate cells, and yet communicate with one another. On Sunday the trumpet calls them to the church, where you may see three whips hung up, which are reserved for the punishment of thieves and intruders, for they maintain very severe discipline.

"Nevertheless, they do not stand in need of gifts, for the faithful bring them eggs, fruit, and even instruments for removing thorns from their feet. There are vineyards around Pisperi, and those of Pabenum have a raft, in which they go forth to seek provisions.

"But I should have served my brethren more effectually by being a simple priest. I might succour the poor, administer the sacraments, and guard the purity of domestic life. Besides, all the laity are not lost, and there was nothing to prevent me from being, for example, a grammarian or a philosopher. I should have had in my room a sphere made of reeds, tablets always in my hand, young people around me, and a crown of laurel suspended as an emblem over my door.

"But there is too much pride in such triumphs! Better be a soldier. I was strong and courageous enough to manage engines of war, to traverse gloomy forests, or, with helmet on head, to enter smoking cities. More than this, there would be nothing to hinder me from purchasing with my earnings the office of toll-keeper of some bridge, and travellers would relate to me their histories, pointing out to me heaps of curious objects which they had stowed away in their baggage.

"On festival days the merchants of Alexandria sail along the Canopic branch of the Nile and drink wine from cups of lotus, to the sound of tambourines, which make all the taverns near the river shake. Beyond, trees, cut cone-fashion, protect the peaceful farmsteads against the south wind. The roof of each house rests on slender columns running close to one another, like the framework of a lattice, and, through these spaces, the owner, stretched on a long seat, can gaze out upon his grounds and watch his servants thrashing corn or gathering in the vintage, and the cattle trampling on the straw. His children play along the grass; his wife bends forward to kiss him."

Through the deepening shadows of the night pointed snouts reveal themselves here and there with ears erect and glittering eyes. Anthony advances towards them. Scattering the wind in their wild rush, the animals take flight. It was a troop of jackals.

One of them remains behind, and, resting on two paws, with his body bent and his head on one side, he places himself in an attitude of defiance.

"How pretty he looks! I should like to pass my hand softly over his back."

Anthony whistles to make him come near. The jackal disappears.

"Ah! he is gone to join his fellows. Oh! This solitude! this weariness!"

Laughing bitterly:

"This is such a delightful life—to twist palm branches in the fire to make shepherds' crooks, to turn out baskets and fasten mats together, and then to exchange all this handiwork with the Nomads for bread that breaks your teeth! Ah! wretched me! will there never be an end of this? But, indeed, death would be better! I can bear it no longer! Enough! Enough!"

He stamps his foot, and makes his way through the rocks with rapid step, then stops, out of breath, bursts into sobs, and flings himself upon the ground.

The night is calm; millions of stars are trembling in the sky. No sound is heard save the chattering of the tarantula.

The two arms of the cross cast a shadow on the sand. Anthony, who is weeping, perceives it.

"Am I so weak, my God? Courage! Let us arise!"

He enters his cell, finds there the embers of a fire, lights a torch, and places it on the wooden stand, so as to illumine the big book.

"Suppose I take—the 'Acts of the Apostles'—yes, no matter where!

" *'He saw the sky opened with a great linen sheet which was let down by its four corners, wherein were all kinds of terrestrial animals and wild beasts, reptiles and birds. And a voice said to him: Arise, Peter! Kill and eat!'*

"So, then, the Lord wished that His apostle should eat every kind of food? . . . whilst I . . ."

Anthony lets his chin sink on his breast. The rustling of the pages, which the wind scatters, causes him to lift his head, and he reads:

" *'The Jews slew all their enemies with swords, and made a great carnage of them, so that they disposed at will of those whom they hated.'*

"There follows the enumeration of the people, slain by them—seventy-five thousand. They had endured so much! Besides, their enemies were the enemies of the true God. And how they must have enjoyed their vengeance, completely slaughtering the idolaters! No doubt the city was gorged with the dead! They must have been at the garden gates, on the staircases, and packed so closely together in the various rooms that the doors could not be closed! But here am I plunging into thoughts of murder and bloodshed!"

He opens the book at another passage.

" *'Nebuchadnezzar prostrated himself with his face on the ground and adored Daniel.'*

"Ah! that is good! The Most High exalts His prophets above kings. This monarch spent his life in feasting, always intoxicated with sensuality and pride. But God, to punish him, changed him into a beast, and he walked on four paws!"

Anthony begins to laugh; and, while stretching out his arms, disarranges the leaves of the book with the tips of his fingers. Then his eyes fall on these words:

" *'Ezechias felt great joy in coming to them. He showed them his perfumes, his gold and silver, all his aromatics, his sweet-smelling oils, all his precious vases, and the things that were in his treasures.'*

"I can imagine how they beheld, heaped up to the very ceiling, gems, diamonds, darics. A man who possesses such an accumulation of these things is not the same as others. While handling them, he assumes that he holds the result of innumerable exertions, and that he has absorbed, and can again diffuse, the very life of the people. This is a useful precaution for kings. The wisest of them all was not wanting in it. His fleets brought him ivory—and apes. Where is this? It is—"

He rapidly turns over the leaves.

"Ah! this is the place:

" 'The Queen of Sheba, being aware of the glory of Solomon, came to tempt him, propounding enigmas.'

"How did she hope to tempt him? The Devil was very desirous to tempt Jesus. But Jesus triumphed because He was God, and Solomon owing, perhaps, to his magical science. It is sublime, this science; for—as a philosopher has explained to me—the world forms a whole, all whose parts have an influence on one another, like the different organs of a single body. It is interesting to understand the affinities and antipathies implanted in everything by "Nature, and then to put them into play. In this way one might be able to modify laws that appear to be unchangeable."

At this point the two shadows traced behind him by the arms of the cross project themselves in front of him. They form, as it were, two great horns. Anthony exclaims:

"Help, my God!"

The shadows resume their former position.

"Ah! it was an illusion—nothing more. It is useless for me to torment my soul. I have no need to do so—absolutely no need!"

He sits down and crosses his arms.

"And yet methought I felt the approach . . . But why should *he*, come? Besides, do I not know his artifices? I have repelled the monstrous anchorite who, with a laugh, offered me little hot loaves; the centaur who tried to take me on his back; and that vision of a beautiful dusky maid amid the sands, which revealed itself to me as the spirit of voluptuousness."

Anthony walks up and down rapidly.

"It is by my direction that all these holy retreats have been built, full of monks wearing hair-cloths beneath their goatskins, and numerous enough to furnish forth an army. I have healed diseases at a distance. I have banished demons. I have waded through the river in the midst of crocodiles. The Emperor Constantine has written me three letters; and Balacius, who treated with contempt the letter I sent him, has been torn by his own horses. The people of Alexandria, whenever I reappeared amongst them, fought to get a glimpse of me; and Athanasius was my guide when I took my departure. But what toils, too, I have had to undergo! Here, for more than thirty years, have I been constantly groaning in the desert! I have carried on my loins eighty pounds of bronze, like Eusebius; I have exposed my body to the stings of insects, like Macarius; I have remained fifty-three nights without closing an eye, like Pachomius; and those who are decapitated, torn with pincers, or burnt, possess less virtue, perhaps, inasmuch as my life is a continual martyrdom!"

Anthony slackens his pace.

"Certainly there is no one who undergoes so much mortification. Charitable hearts are growing fewer, and people never give me anything now. My cloak is worn out, and I have no sandals, nor even a porringer; for I gave all my goods and chattels to the poor and my own family, without keeping a single obolus for myself. Should I not need a little money to get the tools that are indispensable for my work? Oh! not much—a little sum! . . . I would husband it.

"The Fathers of Nicæa were ranged in purple robes on thrones along the wall, like the Magi; and they were entertained at a banquet, while honours were heaped upon them, especially on Paphnutius, merely because he has lost an eye and is lame since Dioclesian's persecution! Many a time the Emperor has kissed his injured eye. What folly! Moreover, the Council had such worthless members! Theophilus, a bishop of Scythia; John, another, in Persia; Spiridion, a cattle-drover. Alexander was too old. Athanasius ought to have made himself more agreeable to the Arians in order to get concessions from them!

"How is it they dealt with me? They would not even give me a hearing! He who spoke against me—a tall young man with a curling beard—coolly launched out captious objections; and while I was trying to find words to reply to him, they kept looking at me with malignant glances, barking at me like hyenas. Ah! if I could only get them all sent into exile by the Emperor, or rather smite them, crush them, behold them suffering. I have much to suffer myself!"

He sinks swooning against the wall of his cell.

"This is what it is to have fasted overmuch! My strength is going. If I had eaten, only once, a morsel of meat!"

He half-closes his eyes languidly.

"Ah! for some red flesh . . . a bunch of grapes to nibble, some curds that would quiver on a plate!

"But what ails me now? What ails me now? I feel my heart dilating like the sea when it swells before the storm. An overwhelming weakness bows me down, and the warm atmosphere seems to waft towards me the odour of hair. Still, there is no trace of a woman here."

He turns towards the little pathway amid the rocks.

"This is the way they come, poised in their litters on the black arms of eunuchs. They descend, and, joining together their hands, laden with rings, they kneel down. They tell me their troubles. The need of a superhuman voluptuousness tortures them. They would like to die; in their dreams they have seen gods who called them by name; and the edges of their robes fall round my feet. I repel them. 'Oh! no,' they say to me, 'not yet! What must I do?' Any penance will appear easy to them. They ask me for the most severe: to share in my own, to live with me.

"It is a long time now since I have seen any of them! Perhaps, though, this is what is about to happen? And why not? If suddenly I were to hear the mule-bells ringing in the mountains. It seems to me . . ."

Anthony climbs upon a rock, at the entrance of the path, and bends forward, darting his eyes into the darkness.

"Yes! down there, at the very end, there is a moving mass, like people who are trying to pick their way. Here it is! They are making a mistake."

Calling out:

"On this side! Come! Come!"

The echo repeats:

"Come! Come!"

He lets his arms fall down, quite dazed.

"What a shame! Ah! poor Anthony!"

And immediately he hears a whisper:

"Poor Anthony."

"Is that anyone? Answer!"

It is the wind passing through the spaces between the rocks that causes these intonations, and in their confused sonorities he distinguishes voices, as if the air were speaking. They are low and insinuating, a kind of sibilant utterance:

The first—"Do you wish for women?"

The second—"Nay; rather great piles of money."

The third—"A shining sword."

The others—"All the people admire you."

"Go to sleep."

"You will cut their throats. Yes! you will cut their throats."

At the same time, visible objects undergo a transformation. On the edge of the cliff, the old palm-tree, with its cluster of yellow leaves, becomes the torso of a woman leaning over the abyss, and poised by her mass of hair.

Anthony re-enters his cell, and the stool which sustains the big book, with its pages filled with black letters, seems to him a bush covered with swallows.

"Without doubt, it is the torch that is making this play of light. Let us put it out!"

He puts it out, and finds himself in profound darkness.

And, suddenly, through the midst of the air, passes first, a pool of water, then a prostitute, the corner of a temple, a figure of a soldier, and a chariot with two white horses prancing.

These images make their appearance abruptly, in successive shocks, standing out from the darkness like pictures of scarlet above a background of ebony.

Their motion becomes more rapid; they pass in a dizzy fashion. At other times they stop, and, growing pale by degrees, dissolve—or, rather, they fly away, and instantly others arrive in their stead.

Anthony droops his eyelids.

They multiply, surround, besiege him. An unspeakable terror seizes hold of him, and he no longer has any sensation but that of a burning contraction in the epigastrium. In spite of the confusion of his brain, he is conscious of a tremendous silence which separates him from all the world. He tries to speak; impossible! It is as if the link that bound him to existence was snapped; and, making no further resistance, Anthony falls upon the mat.

Chapter II

THE TEMPTATION OF LOVE AND POWER

THEN, A GREAT SHADOW—MORE SUBTLE THAN AN ORDINARY SHADOW, from whose borders other shadows hang in festoons—traces itself upon the ground.

It is the Devil, resting against the roof of the cell and carrying under his wings—like a gigantic bat that is suckling its young—the Seven Deadly Sins, whose grinning heads disclose themselves confusedly.

Anthony, his eyes still closed, remains languidly passive, and stretches his limbs upon the mat, which seems to him to grow softer every moment, until it swells out and becomes a bed; then the bed becomes a shallop, with water rippling against its sides.

To right and left rise up two necks of black soil that tower above the cultivated plains, with a sycamore here and there. A noise of bells, drums, and singers resounds at a distance. These are caused by people who are going down from Canopus to sleep at the Temple of Serapis. Anthony is aware of this, and he glides, driven by the wind, between the two banks of the canal. The leaves of the papyrus and the red blossoms of the water-lilies, larger than a man, bend over him. He lies extended at the bottom of the vessel. An oar from behind drags through the water. From time to time rises a hot breath of air that shakes the thin reeds. The murmur of the tiny waves grows fainter. A drowsiness takes possession of him. He dreams that he is an Egyptian Solitary.

Then he starts up all of a sudden.

"Have I been dreaming? It was so pleasant that I doubted its reality. My tongue is burning! I am thirsty!"

He enters his cell and searches about everywhere at random.

"The ground is wet! Has it been raining? Stop! Scraps of food! My pitcher broken! But the water-bottle?"

He finds it.

"Empty, completely empty! In order to get down to the river, I should need three hours at least, and the night is so dark I could not see well enough to find my way there. My entrails are writhing. Where is the bread?"

After searching for some time he picks up a crust smaller than an egg.

"How is this? The jackals must have taken it, curse them!"

And he flings the bread furiously upon the ground.

This movement is scarcely completed when a table presents itself to view, covered with all kinds of dainties. The table-cloth of byssus, striated like the fillets of sphinxes, seems to unfold itself in luminous undulations. Upon it there are enormous quarters of flesh-meat, huge fishes, birds with their feathers, quadrupeds with their hair, fruits with an almost natural colouring; and pieces of white ice and flagons of violet crystal shed glowing reflections. In the middle of the table Anthony observes a wild boar smoking from all its pores, its paws beneath its belly, its eyes half-closed—and the idea of being able to eat this formidable animal rejoices his heart exceedingly. Then, there are things he had never seen before—black hashes, jellies of the colour of gold, ragouts, in which mushrooms float like water-lilies on the surface of a pool, whipped creams, so light that they resemble clouds.

And the aroma of all this brings to him the odour of the ocean, the coolness of fountains, the mighty perfume of woods. He dilates his nostrils as much as possible; he drivels, saying to himself that there is enough there to last for a year, for ten years, for his whole life!

In proportion as he fixes his wide-opened eyes upon the dishes, others accumulate, forming a pyramid, whose angles turn downwards. The wines begin to flow, the fishes to palpitate; the blood in the dishes bubbles up; the pulp of the fruits draws nearer, like amorous lips; and the table rises to his breast, to his very chin—with only one seat and one cover, which are exactly in front of him.

He is about to seize the loaf of bread. Other loaves make their appearance.

"For me! . . . all! but—"

Anthony draws back.

"In the place of the one which was there, here are others! It is a miracle, then, exactly like that the Lord performed! . . . With what object? Nay, all the rest of it is not less incomprehensible! Ah! demon, begone! begone!"

He gives a kick to the table. It disappears.

"Nothing more? No!"

He draws a long breath.

"Ah! the temptation was strong. But what an escape I have had!"

He raises up his head, and stumbles against an object which emits a sound.

"What can this be?"

Anthony stoops down.

"Hold! A cup! Someone must have lost it while travelling—nothing extraordinary!—"

He wets his finger and rubs.

"It glitters! Precious metal! However, I cannot distinguish—"

He lights his torch and examines the cup.

"It is made of silver, adorned with ovolos at its rim, with a medal at the bottom."

He makes the medal resound with a touch of his finger-nail.

"It is a piece of money which is worth from seven to eight drachmas—not more. No matter! I can easily with that sum get myself a sheepskin."

The torch's reflection lights up the cup.

"It is not possible! Gold! yes, all gold!"

He finds another piece, larger than the first, at the bottom, and, underneath that many others.

"Why, here's a sum large enough to buy three cows—a little field!"

The cup is now filled with gold pieces.

"Come, then! a hundred slaves, soldiers, a heap wherewith to buy—"

Here the granulations of the cup's rim, detaching themselves, form a pearl necklace.

"With this jewel here, one might even win the Emperor's wife!"

With a shake Anthony makes the necklace slip over his wrist. He holds the cup in his left hand, and with his right arm raises the torch to shed more light upon it. Like water trickling down from a basin, it pours itself out in continuous waves, so as to make a hillock on the sand—diamonds, carbuncles, and sapphires mingled with huge pieces of gold bearing the effigies of kings.

"What? What? Staters, shekels, darics, aryandics! Alexander, Demetrius, the Ptolemies, Cæsar! But each of them had not as much! Nothing impossible in it! More to come! And those rays which dazzle me! Ah! my heart overflows! How good this is! Yes! . . . Yes! . . . more! Never enough! It did not matter even if I kept flinging it into the sea; more would remain. Why lose any of it? I will keep it all, without telling anyone about it. I will dig myself a chamber in the rock, the interior of which will be lined with strips of bronze; and thither will I come to feel the piles of gold sinking under my heels. I will plunge my arms into it as if into sacks of corn. I would like to anoint my face with it—to sleep on top of it!"

He lets go the torch in order to embrace the heap, and falls to the ground on his breast. He gets up again. The place is perfectly empty!

"What have I done? If I died during that brief space of time, the result would have been Hell—irrevocable Hell!"

A shudder runs through his frame.

"So, then, I am accursed? Ah! no, this is all my own fault! I let myself be caught in every trap. There is no one more idiotic or more infamous. I would like to beat myself, or, rather, to tear myself out of my body. I have restrained myself too long. I need to avenge myself, to strike, to kill! It is as if I had a troop of wild beasts in my soul. I would like, with a stroke of a hatchet in the midst of a crowd—Ah! a dagger! . . ."

He flings himself upon his knife, which he has just seen. The knife slips from his hand, and Anthony remains propped against the wall of his cell, his mouth wide open, motionless—like one in a trance.

All the surroundings have disappeared.

He finds himself in Alexandria on the Panium—an artificial mound raised in the centre of the city, with corkscrew stairs on the outside.

In front of it stretches Lake Mareotis, with the sea to the right and the open plain to the left, and, directly under his eyes, an irregular succession of flat roofs, traversed from north to south and from east to west by two streets, which cross each other, and which form, in their entire length, a row of porticoes with Corinthian capitals. The houses overhanging this double colonnade have stained-glass windows. Some have enormous wooden cages outside of them, in which the air from without is swallowed up.

Monuments in various styles of architecture are piled close to one another. Egyptian pylons rise above Greek temples. Obelisks exhibit themselves like spears between battlements of red brick. In the centres of squares there are statues of Hermes with pointed ears, and of Anubis with dogs' heads. Anthony notices the mosaics in the court-yards, and the tapestries hung from the cross-beams of the ceiling.

With a single glance he takes in the two ports (the Grand Port and the Eunostus), both round like two circles, and separated by a mole joining Alexandria to the rocky island, on which stands the tower of the Pharos, quadrangular, five hundred cubits high and in nine storys, with a heap of black charcoal flaming on its summit.

Small ports nearer to the shore intersect the principal ports. The mole is terminated at each end by a bridge built on marble columns fixed in the sea. Vessels pass beneath, and pleasure-boats inlaid with ivory, gondolas covered with awnings, triremes and biremes, all kinds of shipping, move up and down or remain at anchor along the quays.

Around the Grand Port there is an uninterrupted succession of Royal structures: the palace of the Ptolemies, the Museum, the Posideion, the Cæsarium, the Timonium where Mark Anthony took refuge, and the Soma which contains the tomb of Alexander; while at the other extremity of the city, close to the Eunostus, might be seen glass, perfume, and paper factories.

Itinerant vendors, porters, and ass-drivers rush to and fro, jostling against one another. Here and there a priest of Osiris with a panther's skin on his shoulders, a Roman soldier, or a group of negroes, may be observed. Women stop in front of stalls where artisans are at work, and the grinding of chariot-wheels frightens away some birds who are picking up from the ground the sweepings of the shambles and the remnants of fish. Over the uniformity of white houses the plan of the streets casts, as it were, a black network. The markets, filled with herbage, exhibit green bouquets, the drying-sheds of the dyers, plates of colours, and the gold ornaments on the pediments of temples, luminous points—all this contained within the oval enclosure of the greyish walls, under the vault of the blue heavens, hard by the motionless sea.

But the crowd stops and looks towards the eastern side, from which enormous whirlwinds of dust are advancing.

It is the monks of the Thebaïd who are coming, clad in goats' skins, armed with clubs, and howling forth a canticle of war and of religion with this refrain:

"Where are they? Where are they?"

Anthony comprehends that they have come to kill the Arians.

All at once, the streets are deserted, and one sees no longer anything but running feet.

And now the Solitaries are in the city. Their formidable cudgels, studded with nails, whirl around like monstrances of steel. One can hear the crash of things being broken in the houses. Intervals of silence follow, and then the loud cries burst forth again. From one end of the streets to the other there is a continuous eddying of people in a state of terror. Several are armed with pikes. Sometimes two groups meet and form into one; and this multitude, after rushing along the pavements, separates, and those composing it proceed to knock one another down. But the men with long hair always reappear.

Thin wreaths of smoke escape from the corners of buildings. The leaves of the doors burst asunder; the skirts of the walls fall in; the architraves topple over.

Anthony meets all his enemies one after another. He recognises people whom he had forgotten. Before killing them, he outrages them. He rips them open, cuts their throats, knocks them down, drags the old men by their beards, runs over children, and beats those who are wounded. People revenge themselves on luxury. Those who cannot read, tear the books to pieces; others smash and destroy the statues, the paintings, the furniture, the cabinets—a thousand dainty objects whose use they are ignorant of, and which, for that very reason, exasperate them. From time to time they stop, out of breath, and then begin again. The inhabitants, taking refuge in the court-yards, utter lamentations. The women lift their eyes to Heaven, weeping, with their arms bare. In order to move the Solitaries they embrace their knees; but the latter only dash them aside, and the blood gushes up to the ceiling, falls back on the linen clothes that line the walls, streams from the trunks of decapitated corpses, fills the aqueducts, and rolls in great red pools along the ground.

Anthony is steeped in it up to his middle. He steps into it, sucks it up with his lips, and quivers with joy at feeling it on his limbs and under his hair, which is quite wet with it.

The night falls. The terrible clamour abates.

The Solitaries have disappeared.

Suddenly, on the outer galleries lining the nine stages of the Pharos, Anthony perceives thick black lines, as if a flock of crows had alighted there. He hastens thither, and soon finds himself on the summit.

A huge copper mirror turned towards the sea reflects the ships in the offing.

Anthony amuses himself by looking at them; and as he continues looking at them, their number increases.

They are gathered in a gulf formed like a crescent. Behind, upon a promontory, stretches a new city built in the Roman style of architecture, with cupolas of stone, conical roofs, marble work in red and blue, and a profusion of bronze attached to the volutes of capitals, to the tops of houses, and to the angles of cornices. A wood, formed of cypress-trees, overhangs it. The colour of the sea is greener; the air is colder. On the mountains at the horizon there is snow.

Anthony is about to pursue his way when a man accosts him, and says:

"Come! they are waiting for you!"

He traverses a forum, enters a court-yard, stoops under a gate, and he arrives before the front of the palace, adorned with a group in wax representing the Emperor Constantine hurling the dragon to the earth. A porphyry basin supports in its centre a golden conch filled with pistachio-nuts. His guide informs him that he may take some of them. He does so.

Then he loses himself, as it were, in a succession of apartments.

Along the walls may be seen, in mosaic, generals offering conquered cities to the Emperor on the palms of their hands. And on every side are columns of basalt, gratings of silver filigree, seats of ivory, and tapestries embroidered with pearls. The light falls from the vaulted roof, and Anthony proceeds on his way. Tepid exhalations spread around; occasionally he hears the modest patter of a sandal. Posted in the ante-chambers, the custodians—who resemble automatons—bear on their shoulders vermilion-coloured truncheons.

At last, he finds himself in the lower part of a hall with hyacinth curtains at its extreme end. They divide, and reveal the Emperor seated upon a throne, attired in a violet tunic and red buskins with black bands.

A diadem of pearls is wreathed around his hair, which is arranged in symmetrical rolls. He has drooping eyelids, a straight nose, and a heavy and cunning expression of countenance. At the corners of the dais, extended above his head, are placed four golden doves, and, at the foot of the throne, two enamelled lions are squatted. The doves begin to coo, the lions to roar. The Emperor rolls his eyes; Anthony steps forward; and directly, without preamble, they proceed with a narrative of events.

"In the cities of Antioch, Ephesus, and Alexandria, the temples have been pillaged, and the statues of the gods converted into pots and porridge-pans."

The Emperor laughs heartily at this. Anthony reproaches him for his tolerance towards the Novatians. But the Emperor flies into a passion. "Novatians, Arians, Meletians—he is sick of them all!" However, he admires the episcopacy, for the Christians create bishops, who depend on five or six personages, and it is his interest to gain over the latter in order to have the rest on his side. Moreover, he has not failed to furnish them with considerable sums. But he detests the fathers of the Council of Nicæa. "Come, let us have a look at them."

Anthony follows him. And they are found on the same floor under a terrace which commands a view of a hippodrome full of people, and surmounted by porticoes wherein the rest of the crowd are walking to and fro. In the centre of the course there is a narrow platform on which stands a miniature temple of Mercury, a statue of Constantine, and three bronze serpents intertwined with each other; while at one end there are three huge wooden eggs, and at the other seven dolphins with their tails in the air.

Behind the Imperial pavilion, the prefects of the chambers, the lords of the household, and the Patricians are placed at intervals as far as the first story of a church, all whose windows are lined with women. At the right is the gallery of the Blue faction, at the left that of the Green, while below there is a picket of soldiers, and, on a level with the arena, a row of Corinthian pillars, forming the entrance to the stalls.

The races are about to begin; the horses fall into line. Tall plumes fixed between their ears sway in the wind like trees; and in their leaps they shake the chariots in the form of shells, driven by coachmen wearing a kind of many-coloured cuirass with sleeves narrow at the wrists and wide in the arms, with legs uncovered, full beard, and hair shaven above the forehead after the fashion of the Huns.

Anthony is deafened by the murmuring of voices. Above and below he perceives nothing but painted faces, motley garments, and plates of worked gold; and the sand of the arena, perfectly white, shines like a mirror.

The Emperor converses with him, confides to him some important secrets, informs him of the assassination of his own son Crispus, and goes so far as to consult Anthony about his health.

Meanwhile, Anthony perceives slaves at the end of the stalls. They are the fathers of the Council of Nicæa, in rags, abject. The martyr Paphnutius is brushing a horse's mane; Theophilus is scrubbing the legs of another; John is painting the hoofs of a third; while Alexander is picking up their droppings in a basket.

Anthony passes among them. They salaam to him, beg of him to intercede for them, and kiss his hands. The entire crowd hoots at them; and he rejoices in their degradation immeasurably. And now he has become one of the great ones of the Court, the Emperor's confidant, first minister! Constantine places the diadem on his forehead, and Anthony keeps it, as if this honour were quite natural to him.

And presently is disclosed, beneath the darkness, an immense hall, lighted up by candelabra of gold.

Columns, half lost in shadow so tall are they, run in a row behind the tables, which stretch to the horizon, where appear, in a luminous haze, staircases placed one above another, successions of archways, colossi, towers; and, in the background, an unoccupied wing of the palace, which cedars overtop, making blacker masses above the darkness.

The guests, crowned with violets, lean upon their elbows on low-lying couches. Beside each one are placed amphoræ, from which they pour out wine; and, at the very end, by himself, adorned with the tiara and covered with carbuncles, King Nebuchadnezzar is eating and drinking. To right and left of him, two theories of priests, with peaked caps, are swinging censers. Upon the ground are crawling captive kings, without feet or hands, to whom he flings bones to pick. Further down stand his brothers, with shades over their eyes, for they are perfectly blind.

A constant lamentation ascends from the depths of the ergastula. The soft and monotonous sounds of a hydraulic organ alternate with the chorus of voices; and one feels as if all around the hall there was an immense city, an ocean of humanity, whose waves were beating against the walls.

The slaves rush forward carrying plates. Women run about offering drink to the guests. The baskets groan under the load of bread, and a dromedary, laden with leathern bottles, passes to and fro, letting vervain trickle over the floor in order to cool it.

Belluarii lead forth lions; dancing-girls, with their hair in ringlets, turn somersaults, while squirting fire through their nostrils; negro-jugglers perform tricks; naked children fling snowballs, which, in falling, crash against the shining silver plate. The clamour is so dreadful that it might be described as a tempest, and the steam of the viands, as well as the respirations of the guests, spreads, as it were, a cloud over the feast. Now and then, flakes from the huge torches, snatched away by the wind, traverse the night like flying stars.

The King wipes off the perfumes from his visage with his hand. He eats from the sacred vessels, and then breaks them, and he enumerates, mentally, his fleets, his armies, his peoples. Presently, through a whim, he will burn his palace, along with his guests. He calculates on rebuilding the Tower of Babel, and dethroning God.

Anthony reads, at a distance, on his forehead, all his thoughts. They take possession of himself—and he becomes Nebuchadnezzar.

Immediately, he is satiated with conquests and exterminations; and a longing seizes him to plunge into every kind of vileness. Moreover, the degradation wherewith men are terrified is an outrage done to their souls, a means still more of stupefying them; and, as nothing is lower than a brute beast, Anthony falls upon four paws on the table, and bellows like a bull.

He feels a pain in his hand—a pebble, as it happened, has hurt him—and he again finds himself in his cell.

The rocky enclosure is empty. The stars are shining. All is silence.

"Once more I have been deceived. Why these things? They arise from the revolts of the flesh! Ah! miserable man that I am!"

He dashes into his cell, takes out of it a bundle of cords, with iron nails at the ends of them, strips himself to the waist, and raising his eyes towards Heaven:

"Accept my penance, O my God! Do not despise it on account of its insufficiency. Make it sharp, prolonged, excessive. It is time! To work!"

He proceeds to lash himself vigorously.

"Ah! no! no! No pity!"

He begins again.

"Oh! Oh! Oh! Each stroke tears my skin, cuts my limbs. This smarts horribly! Ah! it is not so terrible! One gets used to it. It seems to me even . . ."

Anthony stops.

"Come on, then, coward! Come on, then! Good! good! On the arms, on the back, on the breast, against the belly, everywhere! Hiss, thongs! bite me! tear me! I would like the drops of my blood to gush forth to the stars, to break my back, to strip my nerves bare! Pincers! wooden horses! molten lead! The martyrs bore more than that! Is that not so, Ammonaria?"

The shadows of the Devil's horns reappear.

"I might have been fastened to the pillar next to yours, face to face with you, under your very eyes, responding to your shrieks with my sighs, and our griefs would blend into one, and our souls would commingle."

He flogs himself furiously.

"Hold! hold! for your sake! once more! . . . But this is a mere tickling that passes through my frame. What torture! What delight! Those are like kisses. My marrow is melting! I am dying!"

And in front of him he sees three cavaliers, mounted on wild asses, clad in green garments, holding lilies in their hands, and all resembling one another in figure.

Anthony turns back, and sees three other cavaliers of the same kind, mounted on similar wild asses, in the same attitude.

He draws back. Then the wild asses, all at the same time, step forward a pace or two, and rub their snouts against him, trying to bite his garment. Voices exclaim, "This way! this way! Here is the place!" And banners appear between the clefts of the mountain, with camels' heads in halters of red silk, mules laden with baggage, and women covered with yellow veils, mounted astride on piebald horses.

The panting animals lie down; the slaves fling themselves on the bales of goods, roll out the variegated carpets, and strew the ground with glittering objects.

A white elephant, caparisoned with a fillet of gold, runs along, shaking the bouquet of ostrich feathers attached to his head-band.

On his back, lying on cushions of blue wool, cross-legged, with eyelids half-closed and well-poised head, is a woman so magnificently attired that she emits rays around her. The attendants prostrate themselves, the elephant bends his knees, and the Queen of Sheba, gliding down by his shoulder, steps lightly on the carpet and advances towards Anthony. Her robe of gold brocade, regularly divided by furbelows of pearls, jet and sapphires, is drawn tightly round her waist by a close-fitting corsage, set off with a variety of colours representing the twelve signs of the Zodiac. She wears high-heeled pattens, one of which is black and strewn with silver stars and a crescent, whilst the other is white and is covered with drops of gold, with a sun in their midst.

Her loose sleeves, garnished with emeralds and birds' plumes, exposes to view her little, rounded arms, adorned at the wrists with bracelets of ebony; and her hands, covered with rings, are terminated by nails so pointed that the ends of her fingers are almost like needles.

A chain of plate gold, passing under her chin, runs along her cheeks till it twists itself in spiral fashion around her head, over which blue powder is scattered; then, descending, it slips over her shoulders and is fastened above her bosom by a diamond scorpion, which stretches out its tongue between her breasts. From her ears hang two great white pearls. The edges of her eyelids are painted black. On her left cheek-bone she has a natural brown spot, and when she opens her mouth she breathes with difficulty, as if her bodice distressed her.

As she comes forward, she swings a green parasol with an ivory handle surrounded by vermilion bells; and twelve curly negro boys carry the long train of her robe, the end of which is held by an ape, who raises it every now and then.

She says:

"Ah! handsome hermit! handsome hermit! My heart is faint! By dint of stamping with impatience my heels have grown hard, and I have split one of my toe-nails. I sent out shepherds, who posted themselves on the mountains, with their bands stretched over their eyes, and searchers, who cried out your name in the woods, and scouts, who ran along the different roads, saying to each passer-by: 'Have you seen him?'

"At night I shed tears with my face turned to the wall. My tears, in the long run, made two little holes in the mosaic-work—like pools of water in rocks—for I love you! Oh! yes; very much!"

She catches his beard.

"Smile on me, then, handsome hermit! Smile on me, then! You will find I am very gay! I play on the lyre, I dance like a bee, and I can tell many stories, each one more diverting than the last.

"You cannot imagine what a long journey we have made. Look at the wild asses of the green-clad couriers—dead through fatigue!"

The wild asses are stretched motionless on the ground.

"For three great moons they have journeyed at an even pace, with pebbles in their teeth to cut the wind, their tails always erect, their hams always bent, and always in full gallop. You will not find their equals. They came to me from my maternal grandfather, the Emperor Saharil, son of Jakhschab, son of Jaarab, son of Kastan. Ah! if they were still living, we would put them under a litter in order to get home quickly. But . . . how now? . . . What are you thinking of?"

She inspects him.

"Ah! when you are my husband, I will clothe you, I will fling perfumes over you, I will pick out your hairs."

Anthony remains motionless, stiffer than a stake, pale as a corpse.

"You have a melancholy air: is it at quitting your cell? Why, I have given up everything for your sake—even King Solomon, who has, no doubt, much wisdom, twenty thousand war-chariots, and a lovely beard! I have brought you my wedding presents. Choose."

She walks up and down between the row of slaves and the merchandise.

"Here is balsam of Genesareth, incense from Cape Gardefan, ladanum, cinnamon and silphium, a good thing to put into sauces. There are within Assyrian embroideries, ivories from the Ganges, and the purple cloth of Elissa; and this case of snow contains a bottle of Chalybon, a wine reserved for the Kings of Assyria, which is drunk pure out of the horn of a unicorn. Here are collars, clasps, fillets, parasols, gold dust from Baasa, tin from Tartessus, blue wood from Pandion, white furs from Issidonia, carbuncles from the island of Palæsimundum, and tooth-picks made with the hair of the tachas—an extinct animal found under the earth. These cushions are from Emathia, and these mantle-fringes from Palmyra. Under this Babylonian carpet there are . . . but come, then! Come, then!"

She pulls Saint Anthony along by the beard. He resists. She goes on:

"This light tissue, which crackles under the fingers with the noise of sparks, is the famous yellow linen brought by the merchants from Bactriana. They required no less than forty-three interpreters during their voyage. I will make garments of it for you, which you will put on at home.

"Press the fastenings of that sycamore box, and give me the ivory casket in my elephant's packing-case!"

They draw out of a box some round objects covered with a veil, and bring her a little case covered with carvings.

"Would you like the buckler of Dgian-ben-Dgian, the builder of the Pyramids? Here it is! It is composed of seven dragons' skins placed one above another, joined by diamond screws, and tanned in the bile of a parricide. It represents, on one side, all the wars which have taken place since the invention of arms, and, on the other, all the wars that will take place till the end of the world. Above, the thunderbolt rebounds like a ball of cork. I am going to put it on your arm, and you will carry it to the chase.

"But if you knew what I have in my little case! Try to open it! Nobody has succeeded in doing that. Embrace me, and I will tell you."

She takes Saint Anthony by the two cheeks. He repels her with outstretched arms.

"It was one night when King Solomon had lost his head. At length, we had concluded a bargain. He arose, and, going out with the stride of a wolt..."

She dances a pirouette.

"Ah! ah! handsome hermit! you shall not know it! you shall not know it!"

She shakes her parasol, and all the little bells begin to ring.

"I have many other things besides—there, now! I have treasures shut up in galleries, where they are lost as in a wood. I have summer palaces of lattice-reeds, and winter palaces of black marble. In the midst of great lakes, like seas, I have islands round as pieces of silver all covered with mother-of-pearl, whose shores make music with the beating of the liquid waves that roll over the sand. The slaves of my kitchen catch birds in my aviaries, and angle for fish in my ponds. I have engravers continually sitting to stamp my likeness on hard stones, panting workers in bronze who cast my statues, and perfumers who mix the juice of plants with vinegar and beat up pastes. I have dressmakers who cut out stuffs for me, goldsmiths who make jewels for me, women whose duty it is to select head-dresses for me, and attentive house-painters pouring over my panellings boiling resin, which they cool with fans. I have attendants for my harem, eunuchs enough to make an army. And then I have armies, subjects! I have in my vestibule a guard of dwarfs, carrying on their backs ivory trumpets."

Anthony sighs.

"I have teams of gazelles, quadrigæ of elephants, hundreds of camels, and mares with such long manes that their feet get entangled with them when they are galloping, and flocks with such huge horns that the woods are torn down in front of them when they are pasturing. I have giraffes who walk in my gardens, and who raise their heads over the edge of my roof when I am taking the air after dinner. Seated in a shell, and drawn by dolphins, I go up and down the grottoes, listening to the water flowing from the stalactites. I journey to the diamond country, where my friends the magicians allow me to choose the most beautiful; then I ascend to earth once more, and return home."

She gives a piercing whistle, and a large bird, descending from the sky, alights on the top of her head-dress, from which he scatters the blue powder. His plumage, of orange colour, seems composed of metallic scales. His dainty head, adorned with a silver tuft, exhibits a human visage. He has four wings, a vulture's claws, and an immense peacock's tail, which he displays in a ring behind him. He seizes in his beak the Queen's parasol, staggers a little before he finds his equilibrium, then erects all his feathers, and remains motionless.

"Thanks, fair Simorg-anka! You who have brought me to the place where the lover is concealed! Thanks! thanks! messenger of my heart! He flies like desire. He travels all over the world. In the evening he returns; he lies down at the foot of my couch; he tells me what he has seen, the seas he has flown over, with their fishes and their ships, the great empty deserts which he has looked down upon from his airy height in the skies, all the harvests bending in the fields, and the plants that shoot up on the walls of abandoned cities."

She twists her arms with a languishing air.

"Oh! if you were willing! if you were only willing! . . . I have a pavilion on a promontory, in the midst of an isthmus between two oceans. It is wainscotted with plates of glass, floored with tortoise-shells, and is open to the four winds of Heaven. From above, I watch the return of my fleets and the people who ascend the hill with loads on their shoulders. We should sleep on down softer than clouds; we should drink cool draughts out of the rinds of fruit, and we gaze at the sun through a canopy of emeralds. Come!"

Anthony recoils. She draws close to him, and, in a tone of irritation:

"How so? Rich, coquettish, and in love?—is not that enough for you, eh? But must she be lascivious, gross, with a hoarse voice, a head of hair like fire, and re-bounding flesh? Do you prefer a body cold as a serpent's skin, or, perchance, great black eyes more sombre than mysterious caverns? Look at these eyes of mine, then!"

Anthony gazes at them, in spite of himself.

"All the women you ever have met, from the daughter of the cross-roads singing beneath her lantern to the fair patrician scattering leaves from the top of her litter, all the forms you have caught a glimpse of, all the imaginings of your desire, ask for them! I am not a woman—I am a world. My garments have but to fall, and you shall discover upon my person a succession of mysteries."

Anthony's teeth chattered.

"If you placed your finger on my shoulder, it would be like a stream of fire in your veins. The possession of the least part of my body will fill you with a joy more vehement than the conquest of an empire. Bring your lips near! My kisses have the taste of fruit which would melt in your heart. Ah! how you will lose yourself in my tresses, caress my breasts, marvel at my limbs, and be scorched by my eyes, between my arms, in a whirlwind—"

Anthony makes the sign of the Cross.

"So, then, you disdain me! Farewell!"

She turns away weeping; then she returns.

"Are you quite sure? So lovely a woman?"

She laughs, and the ape who holds the end of her robe lifts it up.

"You will repent, my fine hermit! you will groan; you will be sick of life! but I will mock at you! la! la! la! oh! oh! oh!"

She goes off with her hands on her waist, skipping on one foot.

The slaves file off before Saint Anthony's face, together with the horses, the dromedaries, the elephant, the attendants, the mules, once more covered with their loads, the negro boys, the ape, and the green-clad couriers holding their broken lilies in their hands—and the Queen of Sheba departs, with a spasmodic utterance which might be either a sob or a chuckle.

Chapter III

The Disciple, Hilarion

WHEN SHE HAS DISAPPEARED, ANTHONY PERCEIVES A CHILD ON THE threshold of his cell.

"It is one of the Queen's servants," he thinks.

This child is small, like a dwarf, and yet thickset, like one of the Cabiri, distorted, and with a miserable aspect. White hair covers his prodigiously large head, and he shivers under a sorry tunic, while he grasps in his hand a roll of papyrus. The light of the moon, across which a cloud is passing, falls upon him.

Anthony observes him from a distance, and is afraid of him.

"Who are you?"

The child replies:

"Your former disciple, Hilarion."

Anthony—"You lie! Hilarion has been living for many years in Palestine."

Hilarion—"I have returned from it! It is I, in good sooth!"

Anthony, draws closer and inspects him—"Why, his figure was bright as the dawn, open, joyous. This one is quite sombre, and has an aged look."

Hilarion—"I am worn out with constant toiling."

Anthony—"The voice, too, is different. It has a tone that chills you."

Hilarion—"That is because I nourish myself on bitter fare."

Anthony—"And those white locks?"

Hilarion—"I have had so many griefs."

Anthony, aside—"Can it be possible? . . ."

Hilarion—"I was not so far away as you imagined. The hermit, Paul, paid you a visit this year during the month of Schebar. It is just twenty days since the nomads brought you bread. You told a sailor the day before yesterday to send you three bodkins."

Anthony—"He knows everything!"

Hilarion—"Learn, too, that I have never left you. But you spend long intervals without perceiving me."

Anthony—"How is that? No doubt my head is troubled! To-night especially . . ."

Hilarion—"All the deadly sins have arrived. But their miserable snares are of no avail against a saint like you!"

Anthony—"Oh! no! no! Every minute I give way! Would that I were one of

those whose souls are always intrepid and their minds firm—like the great Athanasius, for example!"

Hilarion—"He was unlawfully ordained by seven bishops!"

Anthony—"What does it matter? If his virtue . . ."

Hilarion—"Come, now! A haughty, cruel man, always mixed up in intrigues,
and finally exiled for being a monopolist."

Anthony—"Calumny!"

Hilarion—"You will not deny that he tried to corrupt Eustatius, the treasurer
of the bounties?"

Anthony—"So it is stated, and I admit it."

Hilarion—"He burned, for revenge, the house of Arsenius."

Anthony—"Alas!"

Hilarion—"At the Council of Nicasa, he said, speaking of Jesus, 'The man of
the Lord.' "

Anthony—"Ah! that is a blasphemy!"

Hilarion—"So limited is he, too, that he acknowledges he knows nothing as to
the nature of the Word."

Anthony, smiling with pleasure—"In fact, he has not a very lofty intellect."

Hilarion—"If they had put you in his place, it would have been a great satisfaction for your brethren, as well as yourself. This life, apart from others, is a bad
thing."

Anthony—"On the contrary! Man, being a spirit, should withdraw himself
from perishable things. All action degrades him. I would like not to cling to the
earth—even with the soles of my feet."

Hilarion—"Hypocrite! who plunges himself into solitude to free himself the
better from the outbreaks of his lusts! You deprive yourself of meat, of wine, of
stoves, of slaves, and of honours; but how you let your imagination offer you banquets, perfumes, naked women, and applauding crowds! Your chastity is but a more
subtle kind of corruption, and your contempt for the world is but the impotence of
your hatred against it! This is the reason that persons like you are so lugubrious, or
perhaps it is because they lack faith. The possession of the truth gives joy. Was Jesus
sad? He used to go about surrounded by friends; He rested under the shade of the
olive, entered the house of the publican, multiplied the cups, pardoned the fallen
woman, healing all sorrows. As for you, you have no pity, save for your own
wretchedness. You are so much swayed by a kind of remorse, and by a ferocious insanity, that you would repel the caress of a dog or the smile of a child."

Anthony, bursts out sobbing—"Enough! Enough! You move my heart too much."

Hilarion—"Shake off the vermin from your rags! Get rid of your filth! Your
God is not a Moloch who requires flesh as a sacrifice!"

Anthony—"Still, suffering is blessed. The cherubim bend down to receive the blood of confessors."

Hilarion—"Then admire the Montanists! They surpass all the rest."

Anthony—"But it is the truth of the doctrine that makes the martyr."

Hilarion—"How can he prove its excellence, seeing that he testifies equally on behalf of error?"

Anthony—"Be silent, viper!"

Hilarion—"It is not perhaps so difficult. The exhortations of friends, the pleasure of outraging popular feeling, the oath they take, a certain giddy excitement—a thousand things, in fact, go to help them."

Anthony draws away from Hilarion. Hilarion follows him—"Besides, this style of dying introduces great disorders. Dionysius, Cyprian, and Gregory avoided it. Peter of Alexandria has disapproved of it; and the Council of Elvira . . ."

Anthony, stops his ears—"I will listen to no more!"

Hilarion, raising his voice—"Here you are again falling into your habitual sin—laziness. Ignorance is the froth of pride. You say, 'My conviction is formed; why discuss the matter?' and you despise the doctors, the philosophers, tradition, and even the text of the law, of which you know nothing. Do you think you hold wisdom in your hand?"

Anthony—"I am always hearing him! His noisy words fill my head."

Hilarion—"The endeavours to comprehend God are better than your mortifications for the purpose of moving him. We have no merit save our thirst for truth. Religion alone does not explain everything; and the solution of the problems which you have ignored might render it more unassailable and more sublime. Therefore, it is essential for each man's salvation that he should hold intercourse with his brethren—otherwise the Church, the assembly of the faithful, would be only a word—and that he should listen to every argument, and not disdain anything, or anyone. Balaam the soothsayer, Æschylus the poet, and the sybil of Cumæ, announced the Saviour. Dionysius the Alexandrian received from Heaven a command to read every book. Saint Clement enjoins us to study Greek literature. Hermas was converted by the illusion of a woman that he loved!"

Anthony—"What an air of authority! It appears to me that you are growing taller . . ."

In fact, Hilarion's height has progressively increased; and, in order not to see him, Anthony closes his eyes.

Hilarion—"Make your mind easy, good hermit. Let us sit down here, on this big stone, as of yore, when, at the break of day, I used to salute you, addressing you as 'Bright morning star'; and you at once began to give me instruction. It is not finished yet. The moon affords us sufficient light. I am all attention."

He has drawn forth a calamus from his girdle, and, cross-legged on the ground, with his roll of papyrus in his hand, he raises his head towards Anthony, who, seated beside him, keeps his forehead bent.

"Is not the word of God confirmed for us by the miracles? And yet the sorcerers of Pharaoh worked miracles. Other impostors could do the same; so here we may be deceived. What, then, is a miracle? An occurrence which seems to us outside the limits of Nature. But do we know all Nature's powers? And, from the mere fact that a thing ordinarily does not astonish us, does it follow that we comprehend it?"

Anthony—"It matters little; we must believe in the Scripture."

Hilarion—"Saint Paul, Origen, and some others did not interpret it literally; but, if we explain it allegorically, it becomes the heritage of a limited number of people, and the evidence of its truth vanishes. What are we to do, then?"

Anthony—"Leave it to the Church."

Hilarion—"Then the Scripture is useless?"

Anthony—"Not at all. Although the Old Testament, I admit, has—well, obscurities . . . But the New shines forth with a pure light."

Hilarion—"And yet the Angel of the Annunciation, in Matthew, appears to Joseph, whilst in Luke it is to Mary. The anointing of Jesus by a woman comes to pass, according to the First Gospel, at the beginning of his public life, but according to the three others, a few days before his death. The drink which they offer him on the Cross is, in Matthew, vinegar and gall, in Mark, wine and myrrh. If we follow Luke and Matthew, the Apostles ought to take neither money nor bag—in fact, not even sandals or a staff; while in Murk, on the contrary, Jesus forbids them to carry with them anything except sandals and a staff. Here is where I get lost. . . ."

Anthony, in amazement—"In fact . . . in fact . . ."

Hilarion—"At the contact of the woman with the issue of blood, Jesus turned round, and said, 'Who has touched me?' So, then, He did not know who touched Him? That is opposed to the omniscience of Jesus. If the tomb was watched by guards, the women had not to worry themselves about an assistant to lift up the stone from the tomb. Therefore, there were no guards there—or rather, the holy women were not there at all. At Emmaus, He eats with His disciples, and makes them feel His wounds. It is a human body, a material object, which can be weighed, and which, nevertheless, passes through stone walls. Is this possible?"

Anthony—"It would take a good deal of time to answer you."

Hilarion—"Why did He receive the Holy Ghost, although He was the Son? What need had He of baptism, if He were the Word? How could the Devil tempt Him—God?

"Have these thoughts never occurred to you?"

Anthony—"Yes! often! Torpid or frantic, they dwell in my conscience. I crush them out; they spring up again, they stifle me; and sometimes I believe that I am accursed."

Hilarion—"Then you have nothing to do but to serve God?"

Anthony—"I have always need to adore Him."

After a prolonged silence, Hilarion resumes:

"But apart from dogma, entire liberty of research is permitted us. Do you wish to become acquainted with the hierarchy of Angels, the virtue of Numbers, the explanation of germs and metamorphoses?"

Anthony—"Yes! yes! My mind is struggling to escape from its prison. It seems to me that, by gathering my forces, I shall be able to effect this. Sometimes—even for an interval brief as a lightning-flash—I feel myself, as it were, suspended in midair; then I fall back again!"

Hilarion—"The secret which you are anxious to possess is guarded by sages. They live in a distant country, sitting under gigantic trees, robed in white, and calm as gods. A warm atmosphere nourishes them. All around leopards stride through the plains. The murmuring of fountains mingles with the neighing of unicorns. You shall hear them; and the face of the Unknown shall be unveiled!"

Anthony, sighing—"The road is long and I am old!"

Hilarion—"Oh! oh! men of learning are not rare! There are some of them even very close to you here! Let us enter!"

Chapter IV

THE FIERY TRIAL

ND ANTHONY SEES IN FRONT OF HIM AN IMMENSE BASILICA. THE LIGHT PROJects itself from the lower end with the magical effect of a many-coloured sun. It lights up the innumerable heads of the multitude which fills the nave and surges between the columns towards the side-aisles, where one can distinguish in the wooden compartments altars, beds, chainlets of little blue stones, and constellations painted on the walls.

In the midst of the crowd groups are stationed here and there; men standing on stools are discoursing with lifted fingers; others are praying with arms crossed, or lying down on the ground, or singing hymns, or drinking wine. Around a table the faithful are carrying on the love-feasts; martyrs are unswathing their limbs to show their wounds; old men, leaning on their staffs, are relating their travels.

Amongst them are people from the country of the Germans, from Thrace, Gaul, Scythia and the Indies—with snow on their beards, feathers in their hair, thorns in the fringes of their garments, sandals covered with lust, and skins burnt by the sun. All costumes are mingled—mantles of purple and robes of linen, embroidered dalmatics, woollen jackets, sailors' caps and bishops' mitres. Their eyes gleam strangely. They have the appearance of executioners or of eunuchs.

Hilarion advances among them. Anthony, pressing against his shoulder, observes them. He notices a great many women. Several of them are dressed like men, with their hair cut short. He is afraid of them.

Hilarion—"These are the Christian women who have converted their husbands. Besides, the women are always for Jesus—even the idolaters—as witness Procula, the wife of Pilate, and Poppæa, the concubine of Nero. Don't tremble any more! Come on!"

There are fresh arrivals every moment.

They multiply; they separate, swift as shadows, all the time making a great uproar, or intermingling yells of rage, exclamations of love, canticles, and upbraidings.

Anthony, in a low tone—"What do they want?"

Hilarion—"The Lord said, 'I may still have to speak to you about many things.' They possess those things."

And he pushes him towards a throne of gold, five paces off, where, surrounded by ninety-five disciples, all anointed with oil, pale and emaciated, sits the prophet

Manes—beautiful as an archangel, motionless as a statue—wearing an Indian robe, with carbuncles in his plaited hair, a book of coloured pictures in his left hand, and a globe under his right. The pictures represent the creatures who are slumbering in chaos. Anthony bends forward to see him. Then Manes makes his globe revolve, and, attuning his words to the music of a lyre, from which bursts forth crystalline sounds, he says:

"The celestial earth is at the upper extremity, the mortal earth at the lower. It is supported by two angels, the Splenditenens and the Omophorus, with six faces.

"At the summit of Heaven, the Impassible Divinity occupies the highest seat; underneath, face to face, are the Son of God and the Prince of Darkness.

"The darkness having made its way into His kingdom, God extracted from His essence a virtue which produced the first man; and He surrounded him with five elements. But the demons of darkness deprived him of one part, and that part is the soul.

"There is but one soul, spread through the universe, like the water of a stream divided into many channels. This it is that sighs in the wind, grinds in the marble which is sawn, howls in the voice of the sea; and it sheds milky tears when the leaves are torn off the fig-tree.

"The souls that leave this world emigrate towards the stars, which are animated beings."

Anthony begins to laugh:

"Ah! ah! what an absurd hallucination!"

A man, beardless, and of austere aspect—"Why?"

Anthony is about to reply. But Hilarion tells him in an undertone, that this man is the mighty Origen; and Manes resumes:

"At first, they stay in the moon, where they are purified. After that, they ascend to the sun."

Anthony, slowly—"I know nothing to prevent us from believing it."

Manes—"The end of every creature is the liberation of the celestial ray shut up in matter. It makes its escape more easily through perfumes, spices, the aroma of old wine, the light substances that resemble thought. But the actions of daily life withhold it. The murderer will be born again in the body of a eunuch; he who slays an animal will become that animal. If you plant a vine-tree, you will be fastened in its branches. Food absorbs those who use it. Therefore, mortify yourselves! fast!"

Hilarion—"They are temperate, as you see!"

Manes—"There is a great deal of it in flesh-meats, less in herbs. Besides, the Pure, by the force of their merits, despoil vegetables of that luminous spark, and it flies towards its source. The animals, by generation, imprison it in the flesh. Therefore, avoid women!"

Hilarion—"Admire their countenance!"

Manes—"Or, rather, act so well that they may not be prolific. It is better for the soul to sink on the earth than to languish in carnal fetters."

Anthony—"Ah! abomination!"

Hilarion—"What matters the hierarchy of iniquities? The Church has done well to make marriage a sacrament!"

Saturninus, in Syrian costume—"He propagates a dismal order of things! The Father, in order to punish the rebel angels, commanded them to create the world. Christ came in order that the God of the Jews, who was one of those angels—"

Anthony—"An angel? He! the Creator?"

Gerdon—"Did He not desire to kill Moses and deceive the prophets? and did He not lead the people astray, spreading lying and idolatry?"

Marcion—"Certainly, the Creator is not the true God!"

Saint Clement of Alexandria—"Matter is eternal!"

Bardesanes, as one of the Babylonian Magi—"It was formed by the seven planetary spirits."

The Hernians—"The angels have made the souls!"

The Priscillianists—"The world was made by the Devil."

Anthony, falls backward—"Horror!"

Hilarion, holding him up—"You drive yourself to despair too quickly! You don't rightly comprehend their doctrine. Here is one who has received his from Theodas, the friend of Saint Paul. Hearken to him!"

And, at a signal from Hilarion, Valentinus, in a tunic of silver cloth, with a hissing voice and a pointed skull, cries:

"The world is the work of a delirious God!"

Anthony, hangs down his head—"The work of a delirious God!"

After a long silence:

"How is that?"

Valentinus—"The most perfect of the Æons, the Abysm, reposed on the bosom of Profundity together with Thought. From their union sprang Intelligence, who had for his consort Truth.

"Intelligence and Truth engendered the Word and Life, which in their turn engendered Man and the Church; and this makes eight Æons."

He reckons on his fingers:

"The Word and Truth produced ten other Æons, that is to say, five couples. Man and the Church produced twelve others, amongst whom were the Paraclete and Faith, Hope and Charity, Perfection and Wisdom, Sophia.

"The entire of those thirty Æons constitutes the Pleroma, or Universality of God. Thus, like the echoes of a voice that is dying away, like the exhalations of a perfume that is evaporating, like the fires of a sun that is setting, the Powers that have emanated from the Highest Powers are always growing feeble.

"But Sophia, desirous of knowing the Father, rushed out of the Pleroma; and the Word then made another pair, Christ and the Holy Ghost, who bound together all the Æons, and all together they formed Jesus, the flower of the Pleroma. Meanwhile, the effort of Sophia to escape had left in the void an image of her, an evil substance, Acharamoth. The Saviour took pity on her, and delivered her from her passions; and from the smile of Acharamoth on being set free Light was born; her tears made the waters, and her sadness engendered gloomy Matter. From Acharamoth sprang the Demiurge, the fabricator of the worlds, the heavens, and the Devil. He dwells much lower down than the Pleroma, without even beholding it, so that he imagines he is the true God, and repeats through the mouths of his prophets: 'Besides me there is no God.' Then he made man, and cast into his soul the immaterial seed, which was the Church, the reflection of the other Church placed in the Pleroma.

"Acharamoth, one day, having reached the highest region, shall unite with the Saviour; the lire hidden in the world shall annihilate all matter, shall then consume itself, and men, having become pure spirits, shall espouse the angels!"

Origen—"Then the Demon shall be conquered, and the reign of God shall begin."

Anthony represses an exclamation, and immediately Basilides, catching him by the elbow:

"The Supreme Being, with his infinite emanations, is called Abraxas, and the Saviour with all his virtues, Kaulakau, otherwise rank-upon-rank, rectitude-upon-rectitude. The power of Kaulakau is obtained by the aid of certain words inscribed on this calcedony to facilitate memory."

And he shows on his neck a little stone on which fantastic lines are engraved.

"Then you shall be transported into the invisible; and, unfettered by law, you shall despise everything, including virtue itself. As for us, the Pure, we must avoid sorrow, after the example of Kaulakau."

Anthony—"What! and the Cross?"

The Elkhesaites, in hyacinthine robes, reply to him:

"The sadness, the vileness, the condemnation, and the oppression of my fathers are effaced, thanks to the new Gospel. We may deny the inferior Christ, the man-Jesus; but we must adore the other Christ generated in his person under the wing of the Dove. Honour marriage! The Holy Spirit is feminine!"

Hilarion has disappeared; and Anthony, pressed forward by the crowd, finds himself facing the Carpocratians, stretched with women upon scarlet cushions:

"Before re-entering the centre of unity, you will have to pass through a series of conditions and actions. In order to free yourself from the Powers of Darkness, do their works for the present! The husband goes to his wife and says, 'Act with charity towards your brother,' and she will kiss you."

The Nicolaites, assembled around a smoking dish:

"This is meat offered to idols; let us take it! Apostacy is permitted when the heart is pure. Glut your flesh with what it asks for. Try to destroy it by means of debaucheries. Prounikos, the mother of Heaven, wallows in iniquity."

The Marcosians, with rings of gold and dripping with balsam:

"Come to us, in order to be united with the Spirit! Come to us, in order to drink immortality!"

And one of them points out to him, behind some tapestry, the body of a man with an ass's head. This represents Sabaoth, the father of the Devil. As a mark of hatred he spits upon it.

Another discloses a very low bed strewn with flowers, saying as he does so:

"The spiritual nuptials are about to be consummated."

A third holds forth a goblet of glass while he utters an invocation. Blood appears in it:

"Ah! there it is! there it is! the blood of Christ!"

Anthony turns aside; but he is splashed by the water, which leaps out of a tub.

The Helvidians cast themselves into it head foremost, muttering:

"Man regenerated by baptism is incapable of sin!"

Then he passes close to a great fire, where the Adamites are warming themselves completely naked to imitate the purity of Paradise; and he jostles up against the Messalians wallowing on the stone door half-asleep, stupid:

"Oh! run over us, if you like; we shall not budge! Work is a sin; all occupation is evil!"

Behind those, the abject Paternians, men, women, and children, pell-mell, on a heap of filth, lift up their hideous faces, besmeared with wine:

"The inferior parts of the body, having been made by the Devil, belong to him. Let us eat, drink, and enjoy!"

Ætius—"Crimes come from the need here below of the love of God!"

But all at once a man, clad in a Carthaginian mantle, jumps among them, with a bundle of thongs in his hand; and striking at random to right and left of him violently:

"Ah! imposters, brigands, simoniacs, heretics, and demons! the vermin of the schools! the dregs of Hell! This fellow here, Marcion, is a sailor from Sinope excommunicated for incest. Carpocras has been banished as a magician; Ætius has stolen his concubine; Nicolas prostituted his own wife; and Manes, who describes himself as the Buddha, and whose name is Cubricus, was flayed with the sharp end of a cane, so that his tanned skin swings at the gates of Ctesiphon."

Anthony has recognised Tertullian, and rushes forward to meet him.

"Help, master! help!"

Tertullian, continuing—"Break the images! Veil the virgins! Pray, fast, weep, mortify yourselves! No philosophy! no books! After Jesus, science is useless!"

All have fled; and Anthony sees, instead of Tertullian, a woman seated on a stone bench. She sobs, her head resting against a pillar, her hair hanging down, and her body wrapped in a long brown simar.

Then they find themselves close to each other far from the crowd; and a silence, an extraordinary peacefulness, ensues, such as one feels in a wood when the wind ceases and the leaves flutter no longer. This woman is very beautiful, though faded and pale as death. They stare at each other, and their eyes mutually exchange a flood of thoughts, as it were, a thousand memories of the past, bewildering and profound. At last Priscilla begins to speak:

"I was in the lowest chamber of the baths, and I was lulled to sleep by the confused murmurs that reached me from the streets. All at once I heard loud exclamations. The people cried, 'It is a magician! it is the Devil!' And the crowd stopped in front of our house opposite to the Temple of Æsculapius. I raised myself with my wrists to the height of the air-hole. On the peristyle of the temple was a man with an iron collar around his neck. He placed lighted coals on a chafing-dish, and with them made large furrows on his breast, calling out, 'Jesus! Jesus!' The people said, 'That is not lawful! let us stone him!' But he did not desist. The things that were occurring were unheard of, astounding. Flowers, large as the sun, turned around before my eyes, and I heard a harp of gold vibrating in mid-air. The day sank to its close. My arms let go the iron bars; my strength was exhausted; and when he bore me away to his house—"

Anthony—"Whom are you talking about?"

Priscilla—"Why, of Montanus!"

Anthony—"But Montanus is dead."

Priscilla—"That is not true."

A voice—"No, Montanus is not dead!"

Anthony comes back; and near him, on the other side upon a bench, a second woman is seated—this one being fair, and paler still, with swellings under her eyelids, as if she had been a long time weeping. Without waiting for him to question her, she says:

Maximilla—"We were returning from Tarsus by the mountains, when, at a turn of the road, we saw a man under a fig-tree. He cried from a distance, 'Stop!' and he sprang forward, pouring out abuse on us. The slaves rushed up to protect us. He burst out laughing. The horses pranced. The mastiffs all began to howl. He was standing up. The perspiration fell down his face. The wind made his cloak flap.

"While addressing us by name, he reproached us for the vanity of our actions, the impurity of our bodies; and he raised his list towards the dromedaries on account of the silver bells which they wore under their jaws. His fury filled my very entrails with terror; nevertheless, it was a voluptuous sensation, which soothed, intoxicated me. At first, the slaves drew near. 'Master,' said they, 'our beasts are fatigued'; then there were the women: 'We are frightened'; and the slaves ran away. After that, the children began to cry, 'We are hungry.' And, as no answer was given to the women, they disappeared. And now he began to speak. I perceived that there was some one close beside me. It was my husband: I listened to the other. The first crawled between the stones, exclaiming, 'Do you abandon me?' and I replied, 'Yes! begone!' in order to accompany Montanus."

Anthony—"A eunuch!"

Priscilla—"Ah! coarse heart, you are astonished at this! Yet Magdalen, Jane, Martha and Susanna did not enter the couch of the Saviour. Souls can be madly embraced more easily than bodies. In order to retain Eustolia with impunity, the Bishop Leontius mutilated himself—cherishing his love more than his virility. And, then, it is not my own fault. A spirit compels me to do it; Eotas cannot cure me. Nevertheless, he is cruel. What does it matter? I am the last of the prophetesses; and, after me, the end of the world will come."

Maximilla—"He has loaded me with his gifts. None of the others loved me so much, nor is any of them better loved."

Priscilla—"You lie! I am the person he loves!"

Maximilla—"No: it is I!"

They fight.

Between their shoulders appears a negro's head.

Montanus, covered with a black cloak, fastened by two dead men's bones:

"Be quiet, my doves! Incapable of terrestrial happiness, we by this union attain to spiritual plenitude. After the age of the Father, the age of the Son; and I inaugurate the third, that of the Paraclete. His light came to me during the forty nights when the heavenly Jerusalem shone in the firmament above my house at Pepuza.

"Ah! how you cry out with anguish when the thongs flagellate you! How your aching limbs offer themselves to my burning caresses! How you languish upon my breast with an inconceivable love! It is so strong that it has revealed new worlds to you, and you can now behold spirits with your mortal eyes."

Anthony makes a gesture of astonishment.

Tertullian, coming up close to Montanus—"No doubt, since the soul has a body, that which has no body exists not."

Montanus—"In order to render it less material I have introduced numerous mortifications—three Lents every year, and, for each night, prayers, in saying which the mouth is kept closed, for fear the breath, in escaping, should sully the mental act. It is necessary to abstain from second marriages—or, rather, from marriage altogether! The angels sinned with women."

The Archontics, in hair-shirts:

"The Saviour said, 'I came to destroy the work of the woman.' "

The Tatianists, in hair-cloths of rushes:

"She is the tree of evil! Our bodies are the garments of skin."

And, ever advancing on the same side, Anthony encounters the Valesians, stretched on the ground, with red plates below their stomachs, beneath their tunics.

They present to him a knife.

"Do like Origen and like us! Is it the pain you fear, coward? Is it the love of your flesh that restrains you, hypocrite?"

And while he watches them struggling, extended on their backs swimming in their own blood, the Cainites, with their hair fastened by vipers, pass close to him, shouting in his ears:

"Glory to Cain! Glory to Sodom! Glory to Judas!

"Cain begot the race of the strong; Sodom terrified the earth with its chastisement, and it is through Judas that God saved the world! Yes, Judas! without him no death and no Redemption!"

They pass out through the band of Circoncellions, clad in wolf-skin, crowned with thorns, and carrying iron clubs.

"Crush the fruit! Attack the fountain-head! Drown the child! Plunder the rich man who is happy, and who eats overmuch! Strike down the poor man who casts an envious glance at the ass's saddle-cloth, the dog's meal, the bird's nest, and who is grieved at not seeing others as miserable as himself.

"As for us—the Saints—in order to hasten the end of the world, we poison, burn, massacre. The only salvation is in martyrdom. We give ourselves up to martyrdom. We take off with pincers the skin of our heads; we spread our limbs under the ploughs; we cast ourselves into the mouths of furnaces. Shame on baptism! Shame on the Eucharist! Shame on marriage! Universal damnation!"

Then, throughout the basilica, there is a fresh accession of frenzy. The Audians draw arrows against the Devil; the Collyridians fling blue veils to the ceiling; the Ascitians prostrate themselves before a wineskin; the Marcionites baptise a corpse with oil. Close beside Appelles, a woman, the better to explain her idea, shows a round loaf of bread in a bottle; another, surrounded by the Sampsians, distributes like a host the dust of her sandals. On the bed of the Marcosians, strewn with roses, two lovers embrace each other. The Circoncellions cut one another's throats; the Velesians make a rattling sound; Bardesanes sings; Carpocras dances; Maximilla and Priscilla utter loud groans; and the false prophetess of Cappadocia, quite naked, resting on a lion and brandishing three torches, yells forth the Terrible Invocation.

The pillars are poised like trunks of trees; the amulets round the necks of the Heresiarchs have lines of flame crossing each other; the constellations in the chapels move to and fro, and the walls recede under the alternate motion of the crowd, in which every head is a wave which leaps and roars.

Meanwhile, from the very depths of the uproar rises a song with bursts of laughter, in which the name of Jesus recurs. These outbursts come from the common people, who all clap their hands in order to keep time with the music. In the midst of them is Arius, in the dress of a deacon:

"The fools who declaim against me pretend to explain the absurd; and, in order to destroy them entirely, I have composed little poems so comical that they are known by heart in the mills, the taverns, and the ports.

"A thousand times no! the Son is not co-eternal with the Father, nor of the same substance. Otherwise He would not have said, 'Father, remove from Me this chalice! Why do ye call Me good? God alone is good! I go to my God, to your God!' and other expressions, proving that He was a created being. It is demonstrated to us besides by all His names: lamb, shepherd, fountain, wisdom, Son of Man, prophet, good way, corner-stone."

Sabellius—"As for me, I maintain that both are identical."

Arius—"The Council of Antioch has decided the other way."

Anthony—"Who, then, is the Word? Who was Jesus?"

The Valentinians—"He was the husband of Acharamoth when she had repented!"

The Sethianians—"He was Sem, son of Noah!"

The Theodotians—"He was Melchisidech!"

The Merinthians—"He was nothing but a man!"

The Apollonarists—"He assumed the appearance of one! He simulated the Passion!"

Marcellus of Ancyra—"He is a development of the Father!"

Pope Calixtus—"Father and Son are the two forms of a single God!"

Methadius—"He was first in Adam, and then in man!"

Cerinthus—"And He will come back to life again!"

Valentinus—"Impossible—His body is celestial."

Paul of Samosta—"He is God only since His baptism."

Hermogenes—"He dwells in the sun."

And all the heresiarchs form a circle around Anthony, who weeps, with his head in his hands.

A Jew, with red beard, and his skin spotted with leprosy, advances close to him, and chuckling horribly:

"His soul was the soul of Esau. He suffered from the disease of Bellerophon; and his mother, the woman who sold perfumes, surrendered herself to Pantherus, a Roman soldier, under the corn-sheaves, one harvest evening."

Anthony eagerly lifts up his head, and gazes at them without uttering a word; then, treading right over them:

"Doctors, magicians, bishops and deacons, men and phantoms, back! back! Ye are all lies!"

The Heresiarchs—"We have martyrs, more martyrs than yours, prayers more difficult, higher outbursts of love, and ecstasies quite as protracted."

Anthony—"But no revelation. No proofs."

Then all brandish in the air rolls of papyrus, tablets of wood, pieces of leather, and strips of cloth; and pushing them one before the other:

The Corinthians—"Here is the Gospel of the Hebrews!"

The Marcionites—"The Gospel of the Lord! The Gospel of Eve!"

The Encratites—"The Gospel of Thomas!"

The Cainites—"The Gospel of Judas!"

Basilides—"The treatise of the spirit that has come!"

Manes—"The prophecy of Barcouf!"

Anthony makes a struggle and escapes them, and he perceives, in a corner filled with shadows, the old Ebionites, dried up like mummies, their glances dull, their eyebrows white.

They speak in a quavering tone:

"We have known, we ourselves have known, the carpenter's son. We were of his own age; we lived in his street. He used to amuse himself by modelling little birds with mud; without being afraid of cutting the benches, he assisted his father in his work, or rolled up, for his mother, balls of dyed wool. Then he made a journey into Egypt, whence he brought back wonderful secrets. We were in Jericho when he discovered the eater of grasshoppers. They talked together in a low tone, without anyone being able to hear them. But it was since that occurrence that he made a noise in Galilee and that many stories have been circulated concerning him."

They repeat, tremulously:

"We have known, we ourselves; we have known him."

Anthony—"One moment! Tell me! pray tell me, what was his face like?"

Tertullian—"Fierce and repulsive in its aspect; for he was laden with all the crimes, all the sorrows, and all the deformities of the world."

Anthony—"Oh! no! no! I imagine, on the contrary, that there was about his entire person a superhuman beauty."

Eusebius of Cæsarea—"There is at Paneadæ, close to an old ruin, in the midst of a rank growth of weeds, a statue of stone, raised, as it is pretended, by the woman with the issue of blood. But time has gnawed away the face, and the rain has obliterated the inscription."

A woman comes forth from the group of Carpocratians.

Marcellina—"I was formerly a deaconess in a little church at Rome, where I used to show the faithful images, in silver, of St. Paul, Homer, Pythagoras and Jesus Christ.

"I have kept only his."

She draws aside the folds of her cloak.

"Do you wish it?"

A voice—"He reappears himself when we invoke him. It is the hour. Come!"

And Anthony feels a brutal hand laid on him, which drags him along.

He ascends a staircase in complete darkness, and, after proceeding for some time, arrives in front of a door. Then his guide (is it Hilarion? he cannot tell) says in the ear of a third person, "The Lord is about to come,"—and they are introduced into an apartment with a low ceiling and no furniture. What strikes him at first is, opposite him, a long chrysalis of the colour of blood, with a man's head, from which rays escape, and the word *Knouphis* written in Greek all around. It rises above a shaft of a column placed in the midst of a pedestal. On the other walls of the apartment, medallions of polished brass represent heads of animals—that of an ox, of a lion, of an eagle, of a dog, and again, an ass's head! The argil lamps, suspended below these images, shed a flickering light. Anthony, through a hole in the wall, perceives the moon, which shines far away on the waves, and he can even distinguish their monotonous ripple, with the dull sound of a ship's keel striking against the stones of a pier.

Men, squatting on the ground, their faces hidden beneath their cloaks, give vent at intervals to a kind of stifled barking. Women are sleeping, with their foreheads clasped by both arms, which are supported by their knees, so completely shrouded by their veils that one would say they were heaps of clothes arranged along the wall. Beside them, children, half-naked, and half devoured with vermin, watch the lamps burning, with an idiotic air;—and they are doing nothing; they are awaiting something.

They speak in low voices about their families, or communicate to one another remedies for their diseases. Many of them are going to embark at the end of the day, the persecution having become too severe. The Pagans, however, are not hard to deceive. "They believe, the fools, that we adore Knouphis!"

But one of the brethren, suddenly inspired, places himself in front of the column, where they have laid a loaf of bread, which is on the top of a basket full of fennel and hartwort.

The others have taken their places, forming, as they stand, three parallel lines.

The inspired one unrolls a paper covered with cylinders joined together, and then begins:

"Upon the darkness the ray of the Word descended, and a violent cry burst forth, which seemed like the voice of light."

All responding, while they sway their bodies to and fro:

"Kyrie eleison!"

The inspired one—"Man, then, was created by the infamous God of Israel, with the assistance of those here,"—pointing towards the medallions—"Aristophaios, Oraios, Sabaoth, Adonai, Eloi and Iaô!

"And he lay on the mud, hideous, feeble, shapeless, without the power of thought."

All, in a plaintive tone:

"Kyrie eleison!"

The inspired one—"But Sophia, taking pity on him, quickened him with a portion of her spirit. Then, seeing man so beautiful, God was seized with anger, and imprisoned him in His kingdom, interdicting him from the tree of knowledge. Still, once more, the other one came to his aid. She sent the serpent, who, with its sinuous advances, prevailed on him to disobey this law of hate. And man, when he had tasted knowledge, understood heavenly matters."

All, with energy:

"Kyrie eleison!"

The inspired one—"But Jaldalaoth, in order to be revenged, plunged man into matter, and the serpent along with him!"

All, in very low tones:

"Kyrie eleison!"

They close their mouths and then become silent.

The odours of the harbour mingle in the warm air with the smoke of the lamps. Their wicks, spluttering, are on the point of being extinguished, and long mosquitoes flutter around them. Anthony gasps with anguish. He has the feeling that some monstrosity is floating around him—the horror of a crime about to be perpetrated.

But the inspired one, stamping with his feet, snapping his fingers, tossing his head, sings a psalm, with a wild refrain, to the sound of cymbals and of a shrill flute:

"Come! come! come! come forth from thy cavern!

"Swift One, that runs without feet, captor that takes without hands! Sinuous as the waves, round as the sun, darkened with spots of gold; like the firmament, strewn with stars! like the twistings of the vine-tree and the windings of entrails!

"Unbegotten! earth-devourer! ever young! perspicacious! honoured at Epidaurus! good for men! who cured King Ptolemy, the soldiers of Moses, and Glaucus, son of Minos!

"Come! come! come! come forth from thy cavern!"

All repeat:

"Come! come! come! come forth from thy cavern!"

However, there is no manifestation.

"Why, what is the matter with him?"

They proceed to deliberate, and to make suggestions. One old man offers a clump of grass. Then there is a rising in the basket. The green herbs are agitated; the flowers fall, and the head of a python appears.

He passes slowly over the edge of the loaf, like a circle turning round a motionless disc; then he develops, lengthens; he becomes of enormous weight. To prevent him from grazing the ground, the men support him with their breasts, the women with their heads, and the children with the tips of their fingers; and his tail, emerging through the hole in the wall, stretches out indefinitely, even to the depths of the sea. His rings unfold themselves, and fill the apartment. They wind themselves round Anthony.

The Faithful, pressing their mouths against his skin, snatch the bread which he has nibbled.

"It is thou! it is thou!

"Raised at first by Moses, crushed by Ezechias, re-established by the Messiah. He drank thee in the waters of baptism; but thou didst quit him in the Garden of Olives, and then he felt all his weakness.

"Writhing on the bar of the Cross, and higher than his head, slavering above the crown of thorns, thou didst behold him dying; for thou art Jesus! yes, thou art the Word! thou art the Christ!"

Anthony swoons in horror, and falls in his cell, upon the splinters of wood, where the torch, which had slipped from his hand, is burning mildly. This commotion causes him to half-open his eyes; and he perceives the Nile, undulating and clear, under the light of the moon, like a great serpent in the midst of the sands—so much so that the hallucination again takes possession of him. He has not quitted the Ophites; they surround him, address him by name, carry off baggages, and descend towards the port. He embarks along with them.

A brief period of time flows by. Then the vault of a prison encircles him. In front of him, iron bars make black lines upon a background of blue; and at its sides, in the shade, are people weeping and praying, surrounded by others who are exhorting and consoling them.

Without, one is attracted by the murmuring of a crowd, as well as by the splendour of a summer's day. Shrill voices are crying out watermelons, water, iced drinks, and cushions of grass to sit down on. From time to time, shouts of applause burst forth. He observes people walking on their heads.

Suddenly, comes a continuous roaring, strong and cavernous, like the noise of water in an aqueduct; and, opposite him, he perceives, behind the bars of another cage, a lion, who is walking up and down; then a row of sandals, of naked legs, and of purple fringes.

Overhead, groups of people, ranged symmetrically, widen out from the lowest circle, which encloses the arena, to the highest, where masts have been raised to support a veil of hyacinth hung in the air on ropes. Staircases, which radiate towards the centre, intersect, at equal distances, those great circles of stone. Their steps disappear from view, owing to the vast audience seated there—knights, senators, soldiers, common people, vestals and courtesans, in woollen hoods, in silk maniples, in tawny tunics with aigrettes of precious stones, tufts of feathers and lictors' rods; and all this assemblage, muttering, exclaiming, tumultuous and frantic, stuns him like an immense tub boiling over. In the midst of the arena, upon an altar, smokes a vessel of incense.

The people who surround him are Christians, delivered up to the wild beasts. The men wear the red cloak of the high-priests of Saturn, the women the fillets of Ceres. Their friends distribute fragments of their garments and rings. In order to gain admittance into the prison, they require, they say, a great deal of money; but what does it matter? They will remain till the end.

Amongst these consolers Anthony observes a bald man in a black tunic, a portion of whose face is plainly visible. He discourses with them on the nothingness of the world, and the happiness of the Elect. Anthony is filled with transports of Divine love. He longs for the opportunity of sacrificing his life for the Saviour, not knowing whether he is himself one of these martyrs. But, save a Phrygian, with long hair, who keeps his arms raised, they all have a melancholy aspect. An old man is sobbing on a bench, and a young man, who is standing, is musing with downcast eyes.

The old man has refused to pay tribute at the angle of a cross-road, before a statue of Minerva; and he regards his companions with a look which signifies:

"You ought to succour me! Communities sometimes make arrangements by which they might be left in peace. Many amongst you have even obtained letters falsely declaring that you have offered sacrifice to idols."

He asks:

"Is it not Peter of Alexandria who has regulated what one ought to do when one is overcome by tortures?"

Then, to himself:

"Ah! this is very hard at my age! my infirmities render me so feeble! Perchance, I might have lived to another winter!"

The recollection of his little garden moves him to tears; and he contemplates the side of the altar.

The young man, who had disturbed by violence a feast of Apollo, murmurs:

"My only chance was to fly to the mountains!"

"The soldiers would have caught you," says one of the brethren.

"Oh! I could have done like Cyprian; I should have come back; and the second time I should have had more strength, you may be sure!"

Then he thinks of the countless days he should have lived, with all the pleasures which he will not have known;—and he, likewise, contemplates the side of the altar.

But the man in the black tunic rushes up to him:

"How scandalous! What? You a victim of election? Think of all those women who are looking al you! And then, God sometimes performs a miracle. Pionius benumbed the hands of his executioners; and the blood of Polycarp extinguished the flames of his funeral-pile."

He turns towards the old man. "Father, father! You ought to edify us by your death. By deferring it, you will, without doubt, commit some bad action which will destroy the fruit of your good deeds. Besides, the power of God is infinite. Perhaps your example will convert the entire people."

And, in the den opposite, the lions stride up and down, without stopping, rapidly, with a continuous movement. The largest of them all at once fixes his eyes on Anthony and emits a roar, and a mass of vapour issues from his jaws.

The women are jammed up against the men.

The consoler goes from one to another:

"What would ye say—what would any of you say—if they burned you with plates of iron; if horses tore you asunder; if your body, coated with honey, was devoured by insects? You will have only the death of a hunter who is surprised in a wood."

Anthony would much prefer all this than the horrible wild beasts; he imagines he feels their teeth and their talons, and that he hears his back cracking under their jaws.

A belluarius enters the dungeon; the martyrs tremble. One alone amongst them is unmoved—the Phrygian, who has gone into a corner to pray. He had burned three temples. He now advances with lifted arms, open mouth, and his head towards Heaven, without seeing anything, like a somnambulist.

The consoler exclaims:

"Keep back! Keep back! The Spirit of Montanus will destroy ye!"

All fall back, vociferating:

"Damnation to the Montanist!"

They insult him, spit upon him, would like to strike him. The lions, prancing, bite one another's manes. The people yell:

"To the beasts! To the beasts!"

The martyrs, bursting into sobs, catch hold of one another. A cup of narcotic wine is offered to them. They quickly pass it from hand to hand.

Near the door of the den another belluarius awaits the signal. It opens; a lion comes out.

He crosses the arena with great irregular strides. Behind him in a row appear the other lions, then a bear, three panthers, and leopards. They scatter like a flock in a prairie.

The cracking of a whip is heard. The Christians stagger, and, in order to make an end of it, their brethren push them forward.

Anthony closes his eyes.

He opens them again. But darkness envelops him. Ere long, it grows bright once more; and he is able to trace the outlines of a plain, arid and covered with knolls, such as may be seen around a deserted quarry. Here and there a clump of shrubs lifts itself in the midst of the slabs, which are on a level with the soil, and above which white forms are bending, more undefined than clouds. Others rapidly make their appearance. Eyes shine through the openings of long veils. By their indolent gait and the perfumes which exhale from them, Anthony knows they are ladies of patrician rank. There are also men, but of inferior condition, for they have visages at the same time simple and coarse.

One of the women, with a long breath:

"Ah! how pleasant is the air of the chilly night in the midst of sepulchres! I am so fatigued with the softness of couches, the noise of day, and the oppressiveness of the sun!"

A woman, panting—"Ah! at last, here I am! But how irksome to have wedded an idolater!"

Another—"The visits to the prisons, the conversations with our brethren, all excite the suspicions of our husbands! And we must even hide ourselves from them when making the sign of the Cross; they would take it for a magical conjuration."

Another—"With mine, there was nothing but quarrelling all day long. I did not like to submit to the abuses to which he subjected my person; and, for revenge, he had me persecuted as a Christian."

Another—"Recall to your memory that young man of such striking beauty who was dragged by the heels behind a chariot, like Hector, from the Esquiline

Gate to the Mountains of Tibur; and his blood stained the bushes on both sides of the road. I collected the drops—here they are!"

She draws from her bosom a sponge perfectly black, covers it with kisses, and then flings herself upon the slab, crying:

"Ah! my friend! my friend!"

A man—"It is just three years to-day since Domitilla's death. She was stoned at the bottom of the Wood of Proserpine. I gathered her bones, which shone like glow-worms in the grass. The earth now covers them."

He flings himself upon a tombstone.

"O my betrothed! my betrothed!"

And all the others, scattered through the plain:

"O my sister!" "O my brother!" "O my daughter!" "O my mother!"

They are on their knees, their foreheads clasped with their hands, or their bodies lying flat with both arms extended; and the sobs which they repress make their bosoms swell almost to bursting. They gaze up at the sky, saying:

"Have pity on her soul, O my God! She is languishing in the abode of shadows. Deign to admit her into the Resurrection, so that she may rejoice in Thy light!"

Or, with eyes fixed on the flagstones, they murmur:

"Be at rest—suffer no more! I have brought thee wine and meat!"

A widow—"Here is pudding, made by me, according to his taste, with many eggs, and a double measure of Hour. We are going to eat together as of yore, is not that so?"

She puts a little of it on her lips, and suddenly begins to laugh in an extravagant fashion, frantically.

The others, like her, nibble a morsel and drink a mouthful; they tell one another the history of their martyrs; their sorrow becomes vehement; their libations increase; their eyes, swimming with tears, are fixed on one another; they stammer with inebriety and desolation. Gradually their hands touch; their lips meet; their veils are torn away, and they embrace one another upon the tombs in the midst of the cups and the torches.

The sky begins to brighten. The mist soaks their garments; and, as if they were strangers to one another, they take their departure by different roads into the country.

The sun shines forth. The grass has grown taller; the plain has become transformed. Across the bamboos, Anthony sees a forest of columns of a bluish-grey colour. Those are trunks of trees springing from a single trunk. From each of its branches descend other branches which penetrate into the soil; and the whole of those horizontal and perpendicular lines, indefinitely multiplied, might be compared to a gigantic framework were it not that here and there appears a little fig-tree with a dark foliage like that of a sycamore. Between the branches he distinguishes bunches of yellow flowers and violets, and ferns as large as birds' feathers. Under the lowest branches may be seen at different points the horns of a buffalo, or the glittering eyes of an antelope. Parrots sit perched, butterflies flutter, lizards crawl upon the ground, flies buzz; and one can hear, as it were, in the midst of the silence, the palpitation of an all-permeating life.

At the entrance of the wood, on a kind of pile, is a strange sight—a man coated over with cows' dung, completely naked, more dried-up than a mummy. His joints form knots at the extremities of his bones, which are like sticks. He has clusters of shells in his ears, his face is very long, and his nose is like a vulture's beak. His left arm is held erect in the air, crooked, and stiff as a stake; and he has remained there so long that birds have made a nest in his hair.

At the four corners of his pile four fires are blazing. The sun is right in his face. He gazes at it with great open eyes, and without looking at Anthony.

"Brahmin of the banks of the Nile, what sayest thou?"

Flames start out on every side through the partings of the beams; and the gymnosophist resumes:

"Like a rhinoceros, I am plunged in solitude. I dwelt in the tree that was behind me."

In fact, the large fig-tree presents in its flutings a natural excavation of the shape of a man.

"And I fed myself on flowers and fruits with such an observance of precepts that not even a dog has seen me eat.

"As existence proceeds from corruption, corruption from desire, desire from sensation, and sensation from contact, I have avoided every kind of action, every kind of contact, and—without stirring any more than the pillar of a tombstone—exhaling my breath through my two nostrils, fixing my glances upon my nose; and, observing the ether in my spirit, the world in my limbs, the moon in my heart, I pondered on the essence of the great soul, whence continually escape, like sparks of fire, the principles of life. I have, at last, grasped the supreme soul in all beings, all beings in the supreme soul; and I have succeeded in making my soul penetrate the place into which my senses used to penetrate.

"I receive knowledge directly from Heaven, like the bird Tchataka, who quenches his thirst only in the droppings of the rain. From the very fact of my having knowledge of things, things no longer exist. For me now there is no hope and no anguish, no goodness, no virtue, neither day nor night, neither thou nor I—absolutely nothing.

"My frightful austerities have made me superior to the Powers. A contraction of my brain can kill a hundred kings' sons, dethrone gods, overrun the world."

He utters all this in a monotonous voice. The leaves all around him are withered. The rats fly over the ground.

He slowly lowers his eyes towards the flames, which are rising, then adds:

"I have become disgusted with form, disgusted with perception, disgusted even with knowledge itself—for thought does not outlive the transitory fact that gives rise to it; and the spirit, like the rest, is but an illusion.

"Everything that is born will perish; everything that is dead will come to life again. The beings that have actually disappeared will sojourn in wombs not yet formed, and will come back to earth to serve with sorrow other creatures. But, as I have resolved through an infinite number of existences, under the guise of gods, men, and animals, I give up travelling, and no longer wish for this fatigue. I abandon the dirty inn of my body, walled in with flesh, reddened with blood, covered with hideous skin, full of uncleanness; and, for my reward, I shall, finally, sleep in the very depths of the absolute, in annihilation."

The flames rise to his breast, then envelop him. His head stretches across as if through the hole of a wall. His eyes are perpetually fixed in a vacant stare.

Anthony gets up again. The torch on the ground has set fire to the splinters of wood, and the flames have singed his beard. Bursting into an exclamation, Anthony tramples on the fire; and, when only a heap of cinders is left:

"Where, then, is Hilarion? He was here just now. I saw him! Ah! no; it is impossible! I am mistaken! How is this? My cell, those stones, the sand, have not, perhaps, any more reality. I must be going mad. Stay! where was I? What was happening here?

"Ah! the gymnosophist! This death is common amongst the Indian sages. Kalanos burned himself before Alexander; another did the same in the time of Augustus. What hatred of life they must have had!—unless, indeed, pride drove them to it. No matter, it is the intrepidity of martyrs! As to the others, I now believe all that has been told me of the excesses they have occasioned.

"And before this? Yes, I recollect! the crowd of heresiarchs . . . What shrieks! what eyes! But why so many outbreaks of the flesh and wanderings of the spirit?

"It is towards God they pretend to direct their thoughts in all these different ways. What right have I to curse them, I who stumble in my own path? When they have disappeared, I shall, perhaps, learn more. This one rushed away too quickly; I had not time to reply to him. Just now it is as if I had in my intellect more space and more light. I am tranquil. I feel myself capable . . . But what is this now? I thought I had extinguished the fire."

A flame flutters between the rocks; and, speedily, a jerky voice makes itself heard from the mountains in the distance.

"Are those the barkings of a hyena, or the lamentations of some lost traveller?"

Anthony listens. The flame draws nearer.

And he sees approaching a woman who is weeping, resting on the shoulder of a man with a white beard. She is covered with a purple garment all in rags. He, like her, is bare-headed, with a tunic of the same colour, and carries a bronze vase, whence arises a small blue flame.

Anthony is filled with fear—and yet he would fain know who this woman is.

The stranger (Simon)—"This is a young girl, a poor child, whom I take everywhere with me."

He raises the bronze vase. Anthony inspects her by the light of this flickering flame. She has on her face marks of bites, and traces of blows along her arms. Her scattered hair is entangled in the rents of her rags; her eyes appear insensible to the light.

Simon—"Sometimes she remains thus a longtime without speaking or eating, and utters marvelous things."

Anthony—"Really?"

Simon—"Eunoia! Eunoia! relate what you have to say!"

She turns around her eyeballs, as if awakening from a dream, passes her fingers slowly across her two lids, and in a mournful voice:

Helena (Eunoia)—"I have a recollection of a distant region, of the colour of emerald. There is only a single tree there."

Anthony gives a start.

"At each step of its huge branches a pair of spirits stand. The branches around them cross each other, like the veins of a body, and they watch the eternal life circulating from the roots, where it is lost in shadow up to the summit, which reaches beyond the sun. I, on the second branch, illumined with my face the summer nights."

Anthony, touching his forehead—"Ah! ah! I understand! the head!"

Simon, with his finger on his lips—"Hush! Hush!"

Helena—"The vessel remained convex: her keel clave the foam. He said to me, 'What does it matter if I disturb my country, if I lose my kingdom! You will be mine, in my own house!'

"How pleasant was the upper chamber of his palace! He would lie down upon the ivory bed, and, smoothing my hair, would sing in an amorous strain. At the end of the day, I could see the two camps and the lanterns which they were lighting; Ulysses at the edge of his tent; Achilles, armed from head to foot, driving a chariot along the seashore."

Anthony—"Why, she is quite mad! Wherefore? . . . ."

Simon—"Hush! Hush!"

Helena—"They rubbed me with unguents, and sold me to the people to amuse them. One evening, standing with the sistrum in my hand, I was coaxing Greek sailors to dance. The rain, like a cataract, fell upon the tavern, and the cups of hot wine were smoking. A man entered without the door having been opened."

Simon—"It was I! I found you. Here she is, Anthony; she who is called Sigeh, Eunoia, Barbelo, Prounikos! The Spirits who govern the world were jealous of her, and they bound her in the body of a woman. She was the Helen of the Trojans, whose memory the poet Stesichorus had rendered infamous. She has been Lucretia, the patrician lady violated by the kings. She was Delilah, who cut off the hair of Samson. She was that daughter of Israel who surrendered herself to he-goats. She has loved adultery, idolatry, lying and folly. She was prostituted by every nation. She has sung in all the cross-ways. She has kissed every face. At Tyre, she, the Syrian, was the mistress of thieves. She drank with them during the nights, and she concealed assassins amid the vermin of her tepid bed."

Anthony—"Ah! what is coming over me?"

Simon, with a furious air—

"I have redeemed her, I tell you, and re-established her in all her splendour, such as Caius Cæsar Agricola became enamoured of when he desired to sleep with the Moon!"

Anthony—"Well! well!"

Simon—"But she really is the Moon! Has not Pope Clement written that she was imprisoned in a tower? Three hundred persons came to surround the tower; and on each of the murderers, at the same time, the moon was seen to appear—though there are not many moons in the world, or many Eunoias!"

Anthony—"Yes! . . . I think I recollect . . ."

And he falls into a reverie.

Simon—"Innocent as Christ, who died for men, she has devoted herself to women. For the powerlessness of Jehovah is demonstrated by the transgression of Adam, and we must shake off the old law, opposed, as it is, to the order of things. I have preached the new Gospel in Ephraim and in Issachar, along the torrent of Bizor, behind the lake of Houleh, in the valley of Mageddo, and beyond the mountains, at Bostra and at Damas. Let those who are covered with wine-dregs, those who are covered with dirt, those who are covered with blood, come to me; and I will wash out their defilement with the Holy Spirit, called by the Greeks, Minerva. She is Minerva! She is the Holy Spirit! I am Jupiter Apollo, the Christ, the Paraclete, the great power of God incarnated in the person of Simon!"

Anthony—"Ah! it is you! . . . it is you! But I know your crimes! You were born at Gittha on the borders of Samaria. Dositheus, your first master, dismissed you! You execrate Saint Paul for having converted one of your women; and, vanquished by Saint Peter, in your rage and terror, you flung into the waves the bag which contained your magical instruments!"

Simon—"Do you desire them?"

Anthony looks at him, and an inner voice murmurs in his breast, "Why not?"

Simon resumes:

"He who understands the powers of Nature and the substance of spirits ought to perform miracles. It is the dream of all sages—and the desire of which gnaws you; confess it!

"Amongst the Romans I flew so high in the circus that they saw me no more. Nero ordered me to be decapitated; but it was a sheep's head that fell to the ground instead of mine. Finally, they buried me alive; but I came back to life on the third day. The proof of it is that I am here!"

He gives him his hands to smell. They have the odour of a corpse. Anthony recoils.

"I can make bronze serpents move, marble statues laugh, and dogs speak. I will show you an immense quantity of gold, I will set up kings, you shall see nations adoring me. I can walk on the clouds and on the waves; pass through mountains; assume the appearance of a young man, or of an old man; of a tiger, or of an ant; take your face, give you mine; and drive the thunderbolt. Do you hear?"

The thunder rolls, followed by flashes of lightning.

"It is the voice of the Most High, 'for the Eternal, thy God, is a fire,' and all creations operate by the emanations of this central fire. You are about to receive the baptism of it—that second baptism, announced by Jesus, which fell on the Apostles one stormy day when the window was open!"

And all the while stirring the flame with his hand, slowly, as if to sprinkle Anthony with it:

"Mother of Mercies, thou who discoverest secrets in order that we may have rest in the eighth house . . ."

Anthony exclaims:

"Ah! if I had holy water!"

The flame goes out, producing much smoke.

Eunoia and Simon have disappeared.

An extremely cold fog, opaque and foetid, fills the atmosphere.

Anthony, extending his arms like a blind man—

"Where am I? . . . I am afraid of falling into the abyss. And the cross, no doubt, is too far away from me. Ah! what a night! what a night!"

A sudden gust of wind cleaves the fog asunder; and he perceives two men covered with long white tunics. The first is of tall stature, with a sweet expression of countenance and grave deportment. His white hair, parted like that of Christ, descends regularly over his shoulders. He has thrown down a wand which he was carrying in his hand, and which his companion has taken up, making a respectful bow after the fashion of Orientals. The other is small, coarse-looking, flat-nosed, with a thick neck, curly hair, and an air of simplicity. Both of them are barefooted, bareheaded, and covered with dust, like people who have come on a long journey.

Anthony, with a start—"What do ye seek? Speak! Go on!"

Damis—He is the little man—

"La, la! . . . worthy hermit! what do you say? I know nothing about it. Here is the Master!"

He sits down; the other remains standing. Silence.

Anthony, resumes—"Ye come in this fashion? . . ."

Damis—"Oh! a great distance—a very great distance!"

Anthony—"And ye are going? . . ."

Damis, pointing at his companion—"Wherever he wishes."

Anthony—"Who, then, is he?"

Damis—"Look at him."

Anthony—"He has the appearance of a saint. If I dared . . ."

The fog by this time is quite gone. The atmosphere has become perfectly clear. The moon shines out.

Damis—"What are you thinking of now that you say nothing more?"

Anthony—"I am thinking of—Oh! nothing."

Damis draws close to Apollonius, makes many turns round him, with his figure bent, and without moving his head.

"Master, this is a Galilean hermit who wishes to know the sources of your wisdom."

Apollonius—"Let him approach."

Anthony hesitates.

Damis—"Approach!"

Apollonius, in a voice of thunder—

"Approach! You would like to know who I am, what I have done, what I am thinking of? Is that not so, child?"

Anthony—". . . If at the same time those things contribute to my salvation."

Apollonius—"Rejoice! I am about to tell them to you!"

Damis, in a low tone to Anthony—

"Is it possible? He must have, at the first glance, recognised your extraordinary inclinations for philosophy! I shall profit by it also myself."

Apollonius—"I will first describe to you the long road I travelled to gain doctrine; and, if you find in all my life one bad action, you will stop me—for he must scandalise by his words who has offended by his actions."

Damis to Anthony:

"What a just man! eh?"

Anthony—"Decidedly, I believe he is sincere."

Apollonius—"The night of my birth, my mother thought she saw herself gathering flowers on the border of a lake. A flash of lightning appeared; and she brought me into the world amid the cries of swans who were singing in her dream. Up to my fifteenth year, they plunged me three times a day into the fountain Asbadeus, whose waters render perjurers dropsical; and they rubbed my body with leaves of cnyza, to make me chaste. A princess from Palmyra sought me out, one evening, and offered me treasures, which she knew were hidden in tombs. A priest of the temple of Diana cut his throat in despair with the sacrificial knife; and the Governor of Cilicia, after repeated promises, declared before my family that he would put me to death; but it was he who died three days after, assassinated by the Romans."

Damis, to Anthony, striking him on the elbow—"Eh? Just as I told you! What a man!"

Apollonius—"I have for four years in succession observed the complete silence of the Pythagoreans. The most unforeseen calamity did not draw one sigh from me; and, at the theatre, when I entered, they turned aside from me as from a phantom."

Damis—"Would you have done that—you?"

Apollonius—"The time of my ordeal ended, I undertook to instruct the priests who had lost the tradition."

Anthony—"What tradition?"

Damis—"Let him continue. Be silent!"

Apollonius—"I have conversed with the Samaneans of the Ganges, with the astrologers of Chaldea, with the magi of Babylon, with the Gaulish druids, with the priests of the negroes. I have climbed the fourteen Olympi; I have sounded the Lakes of Sythia; I have measured the vastness of the desert!"

Damis—"All this is undoubtedly true. I was there myself!"

Apollonius—"At first, I went as far as the Hyrcanian Sea. I have gone all round it, and through the country of the Baraomatæ, where Bucephalus is buried. I have gone down to Nineveh. At the gates of the city a man came up to me."

Damis—"I! I! my good Master! I loved you from the very beginning. You were sweeter than a girl, and more beautiful than a god!"

Apollonius, without listening to him—"He wished to accompany me, in order to act as an interpreter for me."

Damis—"But you replied that you understood every language, and that you divined all thoughts. Then I kissed the end of your mantle, and I walked behind you."

Apollonius—"After Ctesiphon, we entered into the land of Babylon."

Damis—"And the satrap uttered an exclamation on seeing a man so pale."

Anthony, to himself—"Which signifies—?"

Apollonius—"The King received me standing near a throne of silver, in a circular hall studded with stars, and from a cupola hung, from unseen threads, four great golden birds, with both wings extended."

Anthony, musing—"Are there such things on the earth?"

Damis—"That is, indeed, a city—Babylon! Everyone is rich there! The houses, painted blue, have gates of bronze, with staircases that lead down to the river."

Making a sketch with his stick on the ground:

"Like that, do you see? And then there are temples, squares, baths, aqueducts! The palaces are covered with copper! and then the interior, if you only saw it!"

Apollonius—"On the northern wall rises a tower, which supports a second, a third, a fourth, a fifth; and there are three others besides! The eighth is a chapel with a bed in it. Nobody enters there but the woman chosen by the priests for the God Belus. The King of Babylon made me take up my quarters in it."

Damis—"They scarcely paid any heed to me. I was left, too, to walk about the streets by myself. I enquired into the customs of the people; I visited the workshops; I examined the huge machines which bring water into the gardens. But it annoyed me to be separated from the Master."

Apollonius—"At last, we left Babylon; and, by the light of the moon, we suddenly saw a wild mare."

Damis—"Yes, indeed! she sprang forth on her iron hoofs; she neighed like an ass; she galloped amongst the rocks. He burst into angry abuse of her; and she disappeared."

Anthony, aside—"Where can they have come from?"

Apollonius—"At Taxilla, capital of five thousand fortresses, Phraortes, King of the Ganges, showed us his guard of tall black men, five cubits high, and in the gardens of his palace, under a pavilion of green brocade, an enormous elephant, whom the queens used to amuse themselves in perfuming. This was the elephant of Porus, who fled after the death of Alexander."

Damis—"And which was found again in a forest."

Anthony—"They talk a great deal, like drunken people."

Apollonius—"Phraortes made us sit down at his table."

Damis—"What an odd country! The noblemen, while drinking, amuse themselves by flinging arrows under the feet of a child who is dancing. But I do not approve . . ."

Apollonius—"When I was ready to depart, the King gave me a parasol, and said to me: 'I have, on the Indus, a stud of white camels. When you do not want them any longer, blow into their ears, and they will return.' We proceeded along the river, walking in the night by the gleaming of the glowworms, who emitted their radiance through the bamboos. The slave whistled an air to keep off the serpents; and our camels bent the reins while passing under the trees, as if under doors that were too low. One day, a black child, who held in his hand a caduceus of gold, conducted us to the College of Sages. Iarchas, their chief, spoke to me of my ancestors, of all my thoughts, of all my actions, and all my existences. He had been the river Indus, and he recalled to my mind that I had conducted the boats on the Nile in the time of King Sesostris."

Damis—"As for me, they told me nothing, so that I do not know what I was."

Anthony—"They have the unsubstantial air of shadows."

Apollonius—"We met on the seashore the cynocephali, glutted with milk, who were returning from their expedition in the Island of Taprobane. The tepid waves pushed white pearls before us. The amber cracked under our footsteps. Whales' skeletons were bleaching in the crevices of the cliffs. In short, the earth grew more contracted than a sandal;—and, after casting towards the sun drops from the ocean, we turned to the right to go back. We returned through the region of the Aromatæ, through the country of the Gangaridæ, the promontory of Comaria, the land of the Sachalitæ, of the Aramitæ, and the Homeritæ; then across the Cassanian mountains, the Red Sea, and the Island of Topazes, we penetrated into Ethiopia, through the kingdom of the Pygmæi."

Anthony, aside—"How large the earth is!"

Damis—"And when we got home again, all those whom we had known in former days were dead."

Anthony hangs his head. Silence.

Apollonius goes on:

"Then they began talking about me in the world. The plague ravaged Ephesus; I made them stone an old mendicant."

Damis—"And the plague was gone!"

Anthony—"What! He banishes diseases?"

Apollonius—"At Cnidus, I cured the lover of Venus."

Damis—"Yes, a madman, who had even promised to marry her. To love a woman is bad enough; but a statue—what idiocy! The Master placed his hand on this man's heart, and immediately the love was extinguished."

Anthony—"What! He drives out demons?"

Apollonius—"At Tarentum, they brought to the stake a young girl who was dead."

Damis—"The Master touched her lips; and she arose, calling on her mother."

Anthony—"Can it be? He brings the dead back to life?"

Apollonius—"I foretold that Vespasian would be Emperor."

Anthony—"What! He divines the future?"

Damis—"There was at Corinth—"

Apollonius—"While I was supping with him at the waters of Baia—"

Anthony—"Excuse me, strangers; it is late!"

Damis—"—A young man named Menippus."

Anthony—"No! no! go away!"

Apollonius—"—A dog entered, carrying in its mouth a hand that had been cut off."

Damis—"—One evening, in one of the suburbs, he met a woman."

Anthony—"You do not hear me. Take yourselves off!"

Damis—"—He prowled vacantly around the couches."

Anthony—"Enough!"

Apollonius—"—They wanted to drive him away."

Damis—"—Menippus, then, surrendered himself to her; and they became lovers."

Apollonius—"—And, beating the mosaic floor with his tail, he deposited this hand on the knees of Flavius."

Damis—"—But, in the morning, at the school-lectures, Menippus was pale."

Anthony, with a bound—"Still at it! Well, let them go on, since there is not . . ."

Damis—"The Master said to him: 'O beautiful young man, you are caressing a serpent; and a serpent is caressing you. For how long are these nuptials?' Every one of us went to the wedding."

Anthony—"I am doing wrong, surely, in listening to this!"

Damis—"Servants were busily engaged at the vestibule; the doors flew open; nevertheless, one could hear neither the noise of footsteps, nor the sound of opening doors. The Master seated himself beside Menippus. Immediately, the bride was seized with anger against the philosophers. But the vessels of gold, the cup-bearers, the cooks, the attendants, disappeared; the roof flew away; the walls fell in; and Apollonius remained alone, standing with this woman all in tears at his feet. It was a vampire, who satisfied the handsome young men in order to devour their flesh—because nothing is better for phantoms of this kind than the blood of lovers."

Apollonius—"If you wish to know the art—"

Anthony—"I wish to know nothing."

Apollonius—"On the evening of our arrival at the gates of Rome—"

Anthony—"Oh! yes, tell me about the City of the Popes."

Apollonius—"—A drunken man accosted us who sang with a sweet voice. It was an epithalamium of Nero; and he had the power of causing the death of anyone who heard him with indifference. He carried on his back in a box a string taken from the cithara of the Emperor. I shrugged my shoulders. He threw mud in our faces. Then I unfastened my girdle and placed it in his hands."

Damis—"In this instance you were quite wrong!"

Apollonius—"The Emperor, during the night, made me call at his residence. He played at ossicles with Sporus, leaning with his left arm on a table of agate. He turned round, and, knitting his fair brows: 'Why are you not afraid of me?' he asked. 'Because the God who made you terrible has made me intrepid,' I replied."

Anthony, to himself—"Something unaccountable fills me with fear."

Silence.

Damis resumes, in a shrill voice—"All Asia, moreover, could tell you . . ."

Anthony, starting up—"I am sick. Leave me!"

Damis—"Listen now. At Ephesus, he witnessed the death of Domitian, who was at Rome."

Anthony, making an effort to laugh—"Is this possible?"

Damis—"Yes, at the theatre, in broad daylight, on the fourteenth of the Kalends of October, he suddenly exclaimed: 'They are murdering Cæsar!' and he added, every now and then, 'He rolls on the ground! Oh! how he struggles! He gets up again; he attempts to fly; the gates are shut. Ah! it is finished. He is dead!' And that very day, in fact, Titus Flavius Domitianus was assassinated, as you are aware."

Anthony—"Without the aid of the Devil . . . No doubt . . ."

Apollonius—"He wished to put me to death, this Domitian. Damis fled by my direction, and I remained alone in my prison."

Damis—"It was a terrible bit of daring, I must confess!"

Apollonius—"About the fifth hour, the soldiers led me to the tribunal. I had my speech quite ready, which I kept under my cloak."

Damis—"The rest of us were on the bank Puzzoli! We saw you die; we wept; when, towards the sixth hour, all at once, you appeared, and said to us, 'It is I.' "

Anthony, aside—"Just like Him!"

Damis, very loudly—"Absolutely!"

Anthony—"Oh, no! you are lying, are you not? You are lying!"

Apollonius—"He came down from Heaven—I ascend there, thanks to my virtue, which has raised me even to the height of the Most High!"

Damis—"Tyana, his native city, has erected a temple with priests in his honour!"

Apollonius draws close to Anthony, and, bending towards his ear, says:

"The truth is, I know all the gods, all the rites, all the prayers, all the oracles. I have penetrated into the cavern of Trophonius, the son of Apollo. I have moulded for the Syracusans the cakes which they use on the mountains. I have undergone the eighty tests of Mithra. I have pressed against my heart the serpent of Sabacius. I have received the scarf of the Cabiri. I have bathed Cybele in the waves of the Campanian Gulf; and I have passed three moons in the caverns of Samothrace!"

Damis, laughing stupidly—"Ah! ah! ah! at the mysteries of the Bona Dea!"

Apollonius—"And now we are renewing our pilgrimage. We are going to the North, the side of the swans and the snows. On the white plain the blind hippopodes break with the ends of their feet the ultramarine plant."

Damis—"Come! it is morning! The cock has crowed; the horse has neighed; the ship is ready."

Anthony—"The cock has not crowed. I hear the cricket in the sands, and I see the moon, which remains in its place."

Apollonius—"We are going to the South, behind the mountains and the huge waves, to seek in the perfumes for the cause of love. You shall inhale the odour of myrrhodion, which makes the weak die. You shall bathe your body in the lake of pink oil of the Island of Juno. You shall see sleeping under the primroses the lizard who awakens all the centuries when at his maturity the carbuncle falls from his forehead. The stars glitter like eyes, the cascades sing like lyres, an intoxicating fragrance arises from the opening flowers. Your spirit shall expand in this atmosphere, and it will show itself in your heart as well as in your face."

Damis—"Master, it is time! The wind is about to rise; the swallows are awakening; the myrtle-leaf is shed."

Apollonius—"Yes, let us go!"

Anthony—"No—not I! I remain!"

Apollonius—"Do you wish me to show you the plant Balis, which resuscitates the dead?"

Damis—"Ask him rather for the bloodstone, which attracts silver, iron and bronze!"

Anthony—"Oh! how sick I feel! how sick I feel!"

Damis—"You shall understand the voices of all creatures, the roarings, the cooings!"

Apollonius—"I will make you mount the unicorns, the dragons, and the dolphins!"

Anthony, weeps—"Oh! oh! oh!"

Apollonius—"You shall know the demons who dwell in the caverns, those who speak in the woods, those who move about in the waves, those who drive the clouds."

Damis—"Fasten your girdle! tie your sandals!"

Apollonius—"I will explain to you the reasons for the shapes of divinities; why it is that Apollo is upright, Jupiter sitting down, Venus black at Corinth, square at Athens, conical at Paphos."

Anthony, clasping his hands—"I wish they would go away! I wish they would go away!"

Apollonius—"I will snatch off before your eyes the armour of the Gods; we shall force the sanctuaries; I will make you violate the pythoness!"

Anthony—"Help, Lord!"

He flings himself against the cross.

Apollonius—"What is your desire? your dream? There is barely time to think of it . . ."

Anthony—"Jesus, Jesus, come to my aid!"

Apollonius—"Do you wish me to make Jesus appear?"

Anthony—"What? How?"

Apollonius—"It shall be He—and no other! He shall cast off His crown, and we shall speak together face to face!"

Damis, in a low tone—"Say what you wish for most! Say what you wish for most!"

Anthony, at the foot of the cross, murmurs prayers. Damis continues to run around him with wheedling gestures.

"See, worthy hermit, dear Saint Anthony! pure man, illustrious man! man who cannot be sufficiently praised! Do not be alarmed; this is an exaggerated style of speaking, borrowed from the Orientals. It in no way prevents—"

Apollonius—"Let him alone, Damis! He believes, like a brute, in the reality of things. The fear which he has of the gods prevents him from comprehending them; and he eats his own words, just like a jealous king! But you, my son, quit me not!"

He steps back to the verge of the cliffs, passes over it and remains there, hanging in mid-air:

"Above all forms, farther than the earth, beyond the skies, dwells the World of Ideas, entirely filled with the Word. With one bound we leap across Space, and you shall grasp in its infinity the Eternal, the Absolute Being! Come! give me your hand. Let us go!"

The pair, side by side, rise softly into the air.

Anthony, embracing the cross, watches them ascending.

They disappear.

Chapter V

ALL GODS, ALL RELIGIONS

ANTHONY, WALKING SLOWLY—"THAT WAS REALLY HELL!"

"Nebuchadnezzar did not dazzle me so much. The Queen of Sheba did not bewitch me so thoroughly. The way in which he spoke about the gods filled me with a longing to know them.

"I recollect having seen hundreds of them at a time, in the Island of Elephantinum, in the reign of Dioclesian. The Emperor had given up to the nomads a large territory, on condition that they should protect the frontiers; and the treaty was concluded in the name of the invisible Powers. For the gods of every people were ignorant about other people. The Barbarians had brought forward theirs. They occupied the hillocks of sand which line the river. One could see them holding their idols between their arms, like great paralytic children, or else, sailing amid cataracts on trunks of palm-trees, they pointed out from a distance the amulets on their necks and the tattooings on their breasts; and that is not more criminal than the religion of the Greeks, the Asiatics, and the Romans.

"When I dwelt in the Temple of Heliopolis, I used often to contemplate all the objects on the walls: vultures carrying sceptres, crocodiles playing on lyres, men's faces joined to serpents' bodies, women with cows' heads prostrated before the ithyphallic deities; and their supernatural forms carried me away into other worlds. I wished to know what those calm eyes were gazing at. In order that matter should have so much power, it should contain a spirit. The souls of the gods are attached to their images. Those who possess external beauty may fascinate us; but the others, who are abject or terrible . . . how to believe in them? . . ."

And he sees moving past, close to the ground, leaves, stones, shells, branches of trees, vague representations of animals, then a species of dropsical dwarfs. These are gods. He bursts out laughing.

Behind him, he hears another outburst of laughter; and Hilarion presents himself, dressed like a hermit, much bigger than before—in fact, colossal.

Anthony is not surprised at seeing him again.

"What a brute one must be to adore a thing like that!"

Hilarion—"Oh! yes; very much of a brute!"

Then advance before them, one by one, idols of all nations and all ages, in wood, in metal, in granite, in feathers, and in skins sewn together. The oldest of them, anterior to the Deluge, are lost to view beneath the seaweed which hangs from them like hair. Some, too long for their lower portions, crack in their joints and break their loins while walking. Others allow sand to flow out through holes in their bellies.

Anthony and Hilarion are prodigiously amused. They hold their sides from sheer laughter.

After this, idols pass with faces like sheep. They stagger on their bandy legs, open wide their eyelids, and bleat out, like dumb animals: "Ba! ba! ba!"

In proportion as they approach the human type, they irritate Anthony the more. He strikes them with his fist, kicks them, rushes madly upon them. They begin to present a horrible aspect, with high tufts, eyes like bulls, arms terminated with claws, and the jaws of a shark. And, before these gods, men are slaughtered on altars of stone, while others are pounded in vats, crushed under chariot-wheels, or nailed to trees. There is one of them, all in red-hot iron, with the horns of a bull, who devours children.

Anthony—"Horror!"

Hilarion—"But the gods always demand sufferings. Your own, even, has wished—"

Anthony, weeping—"Say no more—hold your tongue!"

The enclosure of rocks changes into a valley. A herd of oxen pastures there on the shorn grass. The shepherd who has charge of them perceives a cloud; and in a sharp voice pierces the air with words of urgent entreaty.

Hilarion—"As he wants rain, he tries, by his strains, to coerce the King of Heaven to open the fruitful cloud."

Anthony, laughing—"This is too silly a form of presumption!"

Hilarion—"Why, then, do you perform exorcisms?"

The valley becomes a sea of milk, motionless and illimitable.

In the midst of it floats a long cradle, formed by the coils of a serpent, all whose heads, bending forward at the same time, overshadow a god who lies there asleep. He is young, beardless, more beautiful than a girl, and covered with diaphanous veils. The pearls of his tiara shine softly, like moons; a chaplet of stars winds itself many times above his breast, and, with one hand under his head and the other arm extended, he reposes with a dreamy and intoxicated air. A woman squatted before his feet awaits his awakening.

Hilarion—"This is the primordial duality of the Brahmans—the absolute not expressing itself by any form."

Upon the navel of the god a stalk of lotus has grown; and in its calyx appears another god with three faces.

Anthony—"Hold! what an invention!"

Hilarion—"Father, Son and Holy Ghost, in the same way make only one person!"

The three heads are turned aside, and three immense gods appear. The first, who is of a rosy hue, bites the end of his toe. The second, who is blue, tosses four arms about. The third, who is green, weaves a necklace of human skulls. Immediately in front of them rise three goddesses, one wrapped in a net, another offering a cup, and the third brandishing a bow.

And these gods, these goddesses multiply, become tenfold. On their shoulders rise arms, and at the ends of their arms are hands holding banners, axes, bucklers, swords, parasols and drums. Fountains spring from their heads, grass hangs from their nostrils.

Riding on birds, cradled on palanquins, throned on seats of gold, standing in niches of ivory, they dream, travel, command, drink wine and inhale flowers. Dancing-girls whirl around; giants pursue monsters; at the entrances to the grottoes, solitaries meditate. Myriads of stars and clouds of streamers mingle in an indistinguishable throng. Peacocks drink from the streams of golden dust. The embroidery of the pavilions blends with the spots of the leopards. Coloured rays cross one another in the blue air, amid the flying of arrows and the swinging of censers. And all this unfolds itself, like a lofty frieze, leaning with its base on the rocks and mounting to the very sky.

Anthony, dazzled—"What a number of them there are! What do they wish?"

Hilarion—"The one who is scratching his abdomen with his elephant's trunk is the solar god, the inspirer of wisdom. That other, whose six heads carry towers and fourteen handles of javelins, is the prince of armies, the fire-devourer. The old man riding on a crocodile is going to bathe the souls of the dead on the seashore. They will be tormented by this black woman with rotten teeth, the governess of hell. The chariot drawn by red mares, which a legless coachman is driving, is carrying about in broad daylight the master of the sun. The moon-god accompanies him in a litter drawn by three gazelles. On her knees, on the back of a parrot, the goddess of beauty is presenting her round breast to Love, her son. Here she is farther on; she leaps with joy in the prairies. Look! look! With a radiant mitre on her head, she runs over the cornfields, over the waves, mounts into the air, and exhibits herself everywhere. Between these gods sit the genii of the winds, of the planets, of the months, of the days, and a hundred thousand others! And their aspects are multiplied, their transformations rapid. Here is one who from a fish has become a tortoise, he assumes the head of a wild boar, the stature of a dwarf!"

Anthony—"For what purpose?"

Hilarion—"To establish equilibrium, to combat evil. Life is exhausted, its forms are used up; and it is necessary to progress by metamorphoses of them."

Suddenly a naked man appears, seated in the middle of the sand with his legs crossed. A large circle vibrates, suspended behind him. The little curls of his

black hair, deepening into an azure tint, twist symmetrically around a protuberance at the top of his head. His arms, of great length, fall straight down his sides.
His two hands, with open palms, rest evenly on his thighs. The lower portions of
his feet present the figures of two suns; and he remains completely motionless in
front of Anthony and Hilarion, with all the gods around him placed at intervals
upon the rocks, as if on the seats of a circus. His lips open, and in a deep voice
he says:

"I am the master of the great charity, the help of creatures, and I expound the
law to believers and to the profane alike. To save the world I wished to be born
amongst men; the gods wept when I went away. At first, I sought a woman suitable
for the purpose—of warlike race, the spouse of a king, exceedingly virtuous and
beautiful, with a deep navel, a body firm as a diamond; and at the time of the full
moon, without the intervention of any male, I entered her womb. I came out
through her right side. Then the stars stopped in their motions."

Hilarion murmurs between his teeth:

" 'And when they saw the stars stop, they conceived a great joy!' "

Anthony looks more attentively at the Buddha, who resumes:

"From the bottom of the Himalaya, a religious centenarian set forth to see
me."

Hilarion—" 'A man called Simeon, who was not to die before he had seen the
Christ!' "

The Buddha—"They brought me to the schools. I knew more than the doctors."

Hilarion—". . . 'In the midst of the doctors; and all those who heard him were
ravished by his wisdom.' "

Anthony makes a sign to Hilarion to keep silent.

The Buddha—"I went continually to meditate in the gardens. The shadows of
the trees used to move; but the shadow of the one that sheltered me did not move.
No one could equal me in the knowledge of the Sacred Writings, the enumeration
of atoms, the management of elephants, waxworks, astronomy, poetry, boxing, all
exercises and all arts. In compliance with custom, I took a wife; and I passed the
days in my royal palace, arrayed in pearls, under a shower of perfumes, fanned by
the fly-flappers of thirty-three thousand women, and gazing at my people from the
tops of my terraces adorned with resounding bells. But the sight of the world's
miseries made me turn aside from pleasures. I lied. I went a-begging on high-ways,
covered with rags collected in the sepulchres; and, as there was a very learned hermit, I offered myself as his servant. I guarded his door; I washed his feet. All sensation, all joy, all languor, were annihilated. Then, concentrating my thoughts on
a larger field of meditation, I came to know the essence of things, the illusion of

forms. I speedily abandoned the science of the Brakhmans. They are eaten up with lusts beneath their austere exterior; they anoint themselves with filth, and sleep upon thorns, believing that they arrive at happiness through the path of death!"

Hilarion—"Pharisees, hypocrites, whited sepulchres, race of vipers!"

The Buddha—"I, too, have done astonishing things—eating for a day only a single grain of rice—and at that time grains of rice were not bigger than they are now—my hair fell off; my body became black; my eyes, sunken in their sockets, seemed like stars seen at the bottom of a well. For six years I never moved, remaining exposed to flies, to lions, and to serpents; and I subjected myself to burning suns, heavy showers, snow, lightning, hail, and tempest, without even shielding myself with my hand. The travellers who passed, assuming that I was dead, flung clods of earth at me from a distance.

"There only remained for me to be tempted by the Devil.

"I invoked him.

"His sons came—hideous, covered with scales, nauseous as charcoal, howling, hissing, bellowing, flinging at each other armour and dead men's bones. Some of them spirted out flames through their nostrils; others spread around darkness with their wings; others carried chaplets of fingers that had been cut off; others drank the venom of serpents out of the hollows of their hands. They have the heads of pigs, rhinoceroses, or toads—all kinds of figures calculated to inspire respect or terror."

Anthony, aside—"I endured that myself in former times."

The Buddha—"Then he sent me his daughters—beautiful, well-attired, with golden girdles, teeth white as the jasmine, and limbs round as an elephant's trunk. Some of them stretched out their arms when they yawned to display the dimples in their elbows; others blinked their eyes; others began to laugh, and others unfastened one another's garments. Amongst them were blushing virgins, matrons full of pride, and queens with great trains of baggage and attendants."

Anthony, aside—"Ah! that also!"

The Buddha—"Having vanquished the demon, I passed twelve years in nourishing myself exclusively on perfumes;—and, as I had acquired the five virtues, the five faculties, the ten forces, the eighteen substances, and penetrated into the four spheres of the invisible world, the Intelligence was mine, and I became the Buddha!"

All the gods bow down, those who have many heads lower them all at the same time. He raises his hand on high in the air, and resumes:

"In view of the deliverance of beings, I have made hundreds of thousands of sacrifices; I have given to the poor robes of silk, beds, chariots, houses, heaps of gold and diamonds. I have given my hands to the one-handed, my legs to the lame, my eyes to the blind; I have cut off my head for the decapitated. At the time when I was king, I distributed the provinces; at the time when I was Brakhman, I despised nobody. When I was a solitary I spoke words of tenderness to the thief who tried to cut my throat. When I was a tiger, I let myself die of hunger. And in this final stage of existence, having preached the law, I have nothing more to do. The great period is accomplished. The men, the animals, the gods, the bamboos, the oceans, the mountains, the grains of sand of the Ganges, with the myriads of myriads of stars, everything, must perish; and, until the new births, a flame will dance on the ruins of a world's overthrow."

Then a vertigo seizes the gods. They stagger, fall into convulsions, and vomit forth their existences. Their crowns break to pieces; their standards fly away. They get rid of their attributes and their sexes, fling over their shoulders the cups from which they drink immortality, strangle themselves with their serpents, and vanish in smoke; and, when they have all disappeared:

Hilarion, slowly—"You have just seen the creed of many hundreds of millions of men!"

Anthony is on the earth, his face in his hands. Standing close to him, and turning his back to the cross, Hilarion watches him.

A rather lengthened period elapses.

Then a singular being appears, with the head of a man and the body of a fish. He advances straight through the air, tossing the sand with his tail; and his patriarchal face and his little arms make Anthony laugh.

Oannes, in a plaintive voice—"Treat me with respect! I am the contemporary of the beginning of things.

"I have dwelt in the shapeless world, where slumbered hermaphrodite animals, under the weight of an opaque, atmosphere, in the depths of gloomy waves—when the fingers, the fins, and the wings were confounded, and eyes without heads floated like molluscs amongst human-faced bulls and dog-footed serpents.

"Over the whole of those beings Omoroca, bent like a hoop, stretched her woman's body. But Belus cut her clean in two halves, made the earth with one, and the heavens with another; and the two worlds alike mutually contemplate each other. I, the first consciousness of chaos, I have arisen from the abyss to harden matter, to regulate forms; and I have taught men fishing, the sowing of seed, the scripture, and the history of the gods. Since then, I live in the ponds that remained after the Deluge. But the desert grows larger around them; the wind flings sand into them; the sun consumes them; and I expire on my bed of lemon while gazing across the water at the stars. Thither am I returning."

He makes a plunge and disappears in the Nile.

Hilarion—"This is an ancient god of the Chaldeans!"

Anthony, ironically—"Who, then, were the gods of Babylon?"

Hilarion—"You can see them!"

And they find themselves upon the platform of a quadrangular tower rising above other towers, which, growing narrower in proportion as they rise, form a monstrous pyramid. You may distinguish below a great, black mass—the city, without doubt—stretching along the plain. The air is cold; the sky is of a sombre blue; the multitudinous stars palpitate.

In the middle of the platform stands a column of white stone. Priests in linen robes pass and return all round, so as to describe in their evolutions a moving circle, and, with heads raised, they contemplate the stars.

Hilarion points out several of them to Saint Anthony:

"There are thirty chief priests. Fifteen gaze upon the region above the earth, and fifteen on the region below it. At regular intervals one of them rushes from the upper regions to the lower, whilst another abandons the lower to mount towards the empyrean.

"Of the seven planets, two are benevolent, two malevolent, and three ambiguous; everything in the world depends on these eternal fires. According to their position and their movements, one may draw prognostications, and you are now treading on the most sacred spot on earth. There Pythagoras and Zoroaster may be met. Two thousand years have these men been observing the sky, the better to comprehend the gods."

Anthony—"The stars are not gods!"

Hilarion—"Yes! say they; for, while things are continually passing around us, the sky, like eternity, remains unchangeable!"

Anthony—"Nevertheless, it has a master."

Hilarion, pointing at the column—"That is Belus, the first ray, the sun, the male!—the other, which is fruitful, is under him!"

Anthony observes a garden lighted up with lamps. He is in the midst of the crowd in an avenue of cypress-trees. To right and left little paths lead towards huts erected in a wood of pomegranate-trees, which protect lattices of reeds. The men, for the most part, have pointed caps with laced robes, like the plumage of peacocks. There are people from the North clad in bearskins; nomads in brown woollen cloaks; pale Gangarides with long ear-rings; and the classes, like the nationalities, appear to be confused, for sailors and stone-cutters jostle against princes wearing tiaras of carbuncles and carrying large walking-sticks with carved heads. All hurry forward with dilated nostrils, filled with the same desire.

From time to time they got out of the way, in order to allow a long, covered chariot, drawn by oxen, to pass, or perhaps it is an ass jolting on his back a woman closely veiled, who also disappears in the direction of the huts.

Anthony is frightened. He desires to turn back. However, an inexpressible curiosity leads him on.

Beneath the cypress-trees women are squatted in rows upon deerskins, each of them having for a diadem a plait of cords. Some of them, magnificently attired, address the passers-by in loud tones. The more timid keep their features hidden between their hands, whilst, from behind, a matron—no doubt, their mother—encourages them. Others, with heads enveloped in black shawls, and the rest of their bodies quite nude, seem, at a distance, like statues of flesh. As soon as a man flings money on their knees, they rise. And one can hear kisses amid the foliage, and sometimes a great, bitter cry.

Hilarion—"Those are the virgins of Babylon who prostitute themselves to the goddess."

Anthony—"What goddess?"

Hilarion—"There she is!"

And he shows Anthony, at the very end of the avenue, on the threshold of an illuminated grotto, a block of stone representing a woman.

Anthony—"Infamy! What an abomination to give a sex to God!"

Hilarion—"You conceive Him, surely, as a living person!"

Once more Anthony finds himself in darkness.

He perceives in the air a luminous circle placed on horizontal wings. This species of ring surrounds, like a girdle that is too loose, the figure of a small man with a mitre on his head and a crown in his hand, the lower part of whose body is shut out from view by the huge feathers exhibited in his kilt.

This is Ormuz, the God of the Persians. He flutters while he exclaims:

"I am terrified! I catch a glimpse of his mouth. I have vanquished thee, Ahriman! But thou art beginning again!

"At first, revolting against me, thou didst destroy the eldest of creatures, Kaiomortz, the man-bull. Then, thou didst seduce the first human pair, Meschia and Meschiana, and didst fill their hearts with darkness, and press forward thy battalions towards Heaven.

"I had my own, the inhabitants of the stars, and I gazed down from my throne on all the planets in their different spheres.

"Mithra, my son, dwelt in an inaccessible spot. There he received souls, and sent them forth, and, each morning he arose to pour out his riches.

"The splendour of the firmament was reflected by the earth. The fire shone on the mountains—image of the other fire with which I have created all beings. To secure it from defilement, they did not burn the dead, who were transported to Heaven on the beaks of birds.

"I have regulated pasturages, labours, the wood of sacrifice, the forms of cups, the words that must be uttered in insomnia; and my priests prayed continually in order that their worship should correspond to the eternity of God. They purified themselves with water; they offered up loaves on the altars; they confessed their sins in loud tones.

"Homa gave himself to men to drink in order to communicate his strength to them.

"While the genii of Heaven were fighting the demons, the children of Iran chased the serpents. The King, whom a countless train of courtiers served on bended knees, was attired so as to resemble me in person, and wore my head-dress. His gardens had the magnificence of a celestial earth; and his tomb represented him slaying a monster—emblem of the good which exterminates evil. For, one day, it came to pass—thanks to the endless course of time—that I triumphed over Ahriman. But the interval that separates us is disappearing; the night is rising! Help, Amschaspands, Irzeds, Ferouers! Come to my assistance, Mithra! take thy sword! Caosyac, who must come back to save the world, defend me! How is this? . . . No one!

"Ah! I am dying! Ahriman, thou art the master!"

Hilarion, behind Anthony, restrains an exclamation of joy, and Ormuz plunges into the darkness.

Then appears the great Diana of Ephesus, black, with enamelled eyes, elbows at her sides, forearms turned out, and hands open.

Lions crouch upon her shoulders; fruits, flowers and stars cross one another upon her chest; further down three rows of breasts exhibit themselves, and from the belly to the feet she is caught in a close sheath, from which sprout forth, in the centre of her body, bulls, stags, griffins and bees. She is seen in the white gleaming caused by a disc of silver, round as the full moon, placed behind her head.

"Where is my temple? Where are my amazons? How is it with me—me, the incorruptible—that I find myself so impotent?"

Her flowers wither; her fruits, over-ripe, hang loose; the lions and the bulls bow down their necks; the stags, exhausted, begin to pant; the bees, with a faint buzzing, fall dying upon the ground. She presses her breasts one after the other. They are empty! But, yielding to a desperate pressure, her sheath bursts open. She clutches the end of it, like the skirt of a dress, flings into it her animals and her flower-wreaths, then goes back into the darkness; and in the distance voices murmur, grumble, roar, cry, or bellow. The density of the night is increased by the winds. A warm shower begins to fall in heavy drops.

Anthony—"How pleasant is this odour of palm-trees, this rustling of green leaves, this transparency of fountains! I would like to lie down flat upon the ground, in order to feel it close to my heart, and my life would be renewed in eternal youth!"

He hears the sound of castanets and cymbals, and, in the midst of a rustic crowd, men clad in white tunics, with red bands, lead out an ass, richly harnessed, his tail adorned with ribands and his hoofs painted. A box, covered with a saddle-cloth of yellow linen, sways to and fro upon his back, between two baskets, one of which receives the offerings deposited there—eggs, grapes, pears, cheeses, poultry, and small coins—while the second is full of roses, which the drivers of the ass scatter before him as they move along. The latter wear pendants in their ears, large cloaks, plaited tresses, and have their cheeks painted. Each of them has an olive crown fastened around his forehead by a figured medallion. They carry daggers in their girdles, and flourish whips with ebony handles, each having three thongs mounted with ossicles. The last in the procession fix in the ground erect, as a chandelier, a huge pine-tree, whose summit is on fire, and the lowest branches of which overshadow a little sheep.

The ass stops. The saddle-cloth is removed; and underneath appears a second covering of black fell. Then one of the men in a white tunic begins to dance, while playing upon castanets; while another, on his knees before the box, beats a tambourine; and the oldest of the band commences:

"Here is the Bona Dea, the divinity of the mountains, the great mother of Syria! Draw hither, honest people! She procures joy, heals the sick, bestows fortunes, and satisfies lovers. It is we who bring her out to walk in the country in fine weather and bad weather. We often sleep in the open air, and we have not a well-served table every day. The thieves dwell in the woods. The beasts rush forth from their dens. Slippery paths line the precipices. Look here! look here!"

They raise the coverlet and disclose a box incrusted with little pebbles.

"Higher than the cedar-trees she hovers in the blue ether. More circumambient than the winds, she surrounds the world. Her respiration is exhaled through the nostrils of tigers; her voice growls beneath the volcanoes; her anger is the storm; and the pallor of her face has made the moon white. She ripens the harvests; she swells out the rinds; she makes the beard grow. Give her something, for she hates the avaricious!"

The box flies open; and beneath an awning of blue silk is seen a little image of Cybele, glittering with spangles, crowned with towers, and seated on a chariot of red stone, drawn by two lions with raised paws.

The crowd presses forward to see.

The archi-gallus continues:

"She loves the sounds of dulcimers, the stamping of feet, the howling of wolves, the echoing mountains and the deep gorges, the flower of the almond-tree, the pomegranate and the green figs, the whirling dance, the high-sounding flute, the sweet sap, the salt tear—blood! Help! help! Mother of mountains!"

They flagellate themselves with their whips, and the strokes resound on their breasts. The skins of the tambourines vibrate till they almost burst. They seize their knives and inflict gashes on their arms:

"She is sad: let us be sad! He who is doomed to suffer must weep! In that way your sins will be remitted. Blood washes out everything: shed drops of it around, then, like flowers. She demands that of another—of one who is pure!"

The archi-gallus raises his knife above the sheep,

Anthony, seized with horror—"Don't slaughter the lamb!"

A purple flood gushes forth. The priests sprinkle the crowd with it; and all—including Anthony and Hilarion—ranged around the burning tree, silently watch the last palpitations of the victim. From the midst of the priests comes a woman, exactly like the image enclosed in the little box. She stops on seeing a young man in a Phrygian cap.

His thighs are covered with tight-fitting breeches opened here and there by lozenges which are fastened with coloured bows. He rests his elbows against one of the branches of the tree, holding a flute in his hand, in a languishing attitude.

Cybele, encircling his figure with her arms—

"To rejoin thee I have travelled through every region—and famine ravaged the fields. Thou hast deceived me! No matter—I love thee! Warm my body! Let us unite!"

Atys—"The spring-time will return no more, O eternal Mother! Despite my love, it is not possible to penetrate thy essence. I should like to cover myself with a coloured robe like thine. I envy thy breasts, swollen with milk, the length of thy tresses, thy mighty sides from which spring living creatures. Would that I were like thee! Would that I were woman! But no! that can never be! My virility fills me with horror!"

With a sharp stone he mutilates himself; then he begins to run madly around.

The priests imitate the god; the faithful, the priests. Men and women exchange their garments and embrace one another; and this whirlwind of blood-stained flesh hurries away, whilst the voices, ever continuing, become more clamorous and shrill, like those one hears at funerals.

A great catafalque hung with purple carries on its summit a bed of ebony, surrounded by torches and baskets of silver filigree, in which are contained green lettuces, mallows, and fennel. Upon the seats, above and below, are seated women, all attired in black, with girdles undone and naked feet, and holding with a melancholy air huge bouquets of flowers.

On the ground, at the corners of the platform, alabaster urns filled with myrrh are sending up light wreaths of smoke. On the bed may be seen the corpse of a man. Blood trickles from his thigh. His arm is hanging down, and a dog, who is howling, licks his nails. The line of torches placed too close to one another prevents his figure from being completely visible. Anthony is seized with anguish. He is afraid of seeing the face of some one he knew.

The women cease their sobbing; and, after an interval of silence, all, at the same time, burst into a psalm:

"Beautiful! beautiful! he is beautiful! Enough of sleep—raise his head! Up! Inhale our bouquets! These are narcissi and anemones gathered in thy gardens to please thee. Return to life! thou fillest us with fear!

"Speak! What dost thou require? Dost thou wish to drink wine? Dost thou wish to sleep in our beds? Dost thou wish to eat the honey-cakes which have the form of little birds?

"Let us press close to his hips! let us kiss his breast! Hold! hold! feel thou our fingers covered with rings which are stealing over thy body, and our lips which are seeking thy mouth, and our hair which is sweeping thy legs, insensible god, deaf to our prayers!"

They burst into shrieks, tearing their faces with their nails, then become silent; and only the howling of the dog is heard.

"Alas! alas! The dark blood rushes over his snowy flesh. See how his knees writhe, how his sides give way! The flowers upon his face have soaked the gore. He is dead! Let us weep! let us lament!"

They come all in a row to fling down between the torches their flowing locks, resembling at a distance black or yellow serpents; and the catafalque is softly lowered to the level of a cave—a gloomy sepulchre, which is yawning in the background.

Then a woman bends over the corpse. Her hair, which never has been cut, covers her from head to foot. She sheds so many tears that her grief does not seem to be like that of others, but superhuman, infinite.

Anthony thinks of the mother of Jesus.

She says:

"Thou didst escape from the East, and thou didst press me in thy arms all quivering with dew, O sun! Doves fluttered above the azure of thy mantle, our kisses caused breezes amid the foliage, and I abandoned myself to thy love, delighting in the exquisite sensation of my own weakness.

"Alas! alas! Why art thou about to rush away over the mountains? At the autumnal equinox a wild boar wounded thee! Thou art dead, and the fountains weep and the trees droop, and the winter wind is whistling through the leafless branches.

"My eyes are about to close, seeing that darkness is covering thee. By this time thou art dwelling on the other side of the world, near my more powerful rival.

"O Persephone, all that is beautiful goes clown to thee and returns no more!"

While she has been speaking, her companions have taken the dead body to lower it into the sepulchre. It remains in their hands. It was only a corpse of wax!

Anthony experiences a kind of relief. The whole scene vanishes, and the cell, the rocks, and the cross reappear! And now he distinguishes on the other side of the Nile a woman standing in the middle of the desert. She holds with her hand the end of a long black veil, which conceals her figure; while she carries on her left arm a little child, which she is suckling. At her side a huge ape is squatted on the sand. She lifts her head towards the sky, and, in spite of the distance, her voice can be heard.

Isis—"O Neith, beginning of things! Ammon, lord of eternity! Ptha, demiurgus! Thoth, his intelligence! Gods of Amenthi! Special Triads of the Nomes! Sparrow-hawks in the azure! Sphinxes on the outsides of temples! Ibises standing between the horns of oxen! Planets! Constellations! River-banks! Murmurs of wind! Reflections of light! Tell me where to find Osiris!

"I have sought for him through all the water-courses and all the lakes, and, farther still, in the Phoenician Byblos. Anubis, with ears erect, jumped round me, barking, and with his nose scenting out the clumps of tamarind. Thanks, good Cynocephalus, thanks!"

She gives the ape two or three friendly little slaps on the head.

"The hideous red-haired Typhon killed him and tore him to pieces. We have found all his members. But I have not got that which made me fruitful!"

She utters bitter lamentations.

Anthony is seized with rage. He casts pebbles at her insultingly:

"Impure one! begone, begone!"

Hilarion—"Respect her! This is the religion of your ancestors! You have worn her amulets in your cradle!"

Isis—"In former times, when the summer returned, the inundation drove to the desert the impure beasts. The dykes flew open; the boats dashed against one another; the panting earth drank the stream till it was glutted. O god! with horns of bull, them didst stretch thyself upon my breast, and the lowing of the eternal cow was heard!

"The new-sown crops, the harvests, the thrashing of corn, and the vintages succeeded each other regularly in unison with the changes of the seasons, in the nights, ever clear, the great stars shed forth their beams. The days were steeped in an unchanging splendour. The sun and the moon were seen like a royal pair on either side of the horizon.

"We were enthroned in a world more sublime—twin monarchs, spouses from the bosom of eternity; he holding a sceptre with the head of a conchoupha, and I a sceptre with a lotus-flower, we stood with hands joined;—and the crash of empires did not change our attitude.

"Egypt lay stretched beneath us, monumental and solemn, long, like the corridor of a temple, with obelisks at the right, pyramids at the left, its labyrinth in the middle; and everywhere avenues of monsters, forests of columns, massive archways flanking gates which have for their summit the earth's sphere between two wings.

"The animals of her zodiac found their counterparts in her plains, and with their forms and colours filled her mysterious writings. Divided into twelve regions, as the year is into twelve months—each month, each day, having its god— she reproduced the immutable order of the heavens; and man, though he died, did not lose his lineaments, but, saturated with perfumes and becoming imperishable, he went to sleep for three thousand years in a silent Egypt.

"The latter, greater than the other, spread out beneath the earth. Thither one descended by means of staircases leading to halls where were reproduced the joys of the good, the tortures of the wicked, everything that takes place in the third invisible world. Ranged along the walls, the dead, in painted coffins, awaited each their turn; and the soul, free from migrations, continued its sleep till it awakened in another life.

"Meanwhile, Osiris sometimes came back to see me. His shade made me the mother of Harpocrates."

She gazes on the child:

"It is he! Those are his eyes; those are his tresses, curling like a ram's horns. Thou shalt begin his works over again. We shall bloom afresh, like the lotus. I am always the great Isis! Nobody has ever yet lifted my veil! My offspring is the sun!

"Sun of spring, let the clouds obscure thy face! The breath of Typhon devours the pyramids. Just now I have seen the Sphinx fly away. He galloped off like a jackal.

"I am seeking for my priests—my priests in their linen robes, with great harps, carrying along a mystic skiff ornamented with pateræ of silver. No more feasts on the lakes! no more illuminations in my Delta! no more cups of milk at Philæ! For a long time Apis has not reappeared.

"Egypt! Egypt! Thy great immovable gods have their shoulders whitened by the dung of birds, and the wind, as it passes along the desert, carries with it the ashes of the dead!—Anubis, protector of shadows, do not leave me!"

The Cynocephalus vanishes.

She gives her child a shaking.

"But what aileth thee? . . . thy hands are cold, thy head fallen back!"

Harpocrates has just died. Then she utters a cry so bitter, mournful, and heartrending, that Anthony replies to it by another cry, while he opens his arms to support her.

She is no longer there. He hangs his head, overwhelmed with shame.

All that he has just seen becomes confused in his mind. It is like the stunning effect of a voyage, the uncomfortable sensation of drunkenness. Fain would he hate; and yet a vague pity softens his heart. He begins to weep abundantly.

Hilarion—"What is it now that makes you sad?"

Anthony, after questioning himself for a long time—"I am thinking of all the souls lost through these false gods!"

Hilarion—"Do you not find that they have—in some respects—resemblances to the true?"

Anthony—"This is a trick of the Devil the better to seduce the faithful. He attacks the strong through the spirit, and the others through the flesh."

Hilarion—"But lust, in its furies, possesses the disinterestedness of penitence. The frantic love of the body accelerates its destruction—and by its weakness proclaims the extent of the impossible."

Anthony—"How is it that this affects me? My heart revolts with disgust against those brutish gods, always occupied with carnage and incest."

Hilarion—"Recall to yourself in the Scriptures all the things that scandalise you because you cannot understand them. In the same way, these gods, under the outward form of criminals, may contain the truth. There are some of them left to see. Turn aside!"

Anthony—"No! no! it is a peril!"

Hilarion—"A moment ago you wished to make their acquaintance. Do falsehoods make your faith totter? What do you fear?"

The rocks in front of Anthony have become a mountain.

A range of clouds intersects it half-way from the top; and overhead appears another mountain, enormous, quite green, which hollows out the valley unevenly, having on its summit, in a wood of laurels, a palace of bronze, with tiles of gold and ivory capitals.

In the midst of the peristyle, upon a throne, Jupiter, colossal, and with a naked torso, holds victory in one hand, and the thunderbolt in the other; and his eagle, between his legs, erects its head.

Juno, close to him, rolls her great eyes, surmounted by a diadem, from which escapes, like a vapour, a veil floating in the wind.

Behind, Minerva, standing on a pedestal, leans upon her spear. The Gorgon's skin covers her breast, and a linen peplum descends in regular folds even to her toenails. Her grey eyes, which shine beneath her vizor, gaze intently into the distance.

At the right of the palace the aged Neptune is riding on a dolphin beating with its fins a vast expanse of azure, which is the sky or the sea, for the perspective of the ocean prolongs the blue ether; the two elements become mingled in one.

On the other side, Pluto, fierce, in a mantle black as night, with a tiara of diamonds and a sceptre of ebony, is in the midst of an isle enclosed by the windings of the Styx;—and this ghostly stream rushes into the darkness, which forms under the cliff a great black gap, a shapeless abyss.

Mars, clad in bronze, brandishes, with an air of fury, his huge sword and shield.

Hercules, standing lower, gazes up at him, leaning on his club.

Apollo, with radiant face, is driving, with his right arm extended, four white horses at a gallop; and Ceres, in a chariot drawn by oxen, is advancing towards him with a sickle in her hand.

Bacchus goes before her on a very low car slowly drawn along by lynxes. Erect, beardless, with vine-branches over his forehead, he passes, holding a goblet from which wine is flowing. Silenus, at his side, is dangling upon an ass. Pan, with pointed ears, is blowing his pipe; the Mimallones beat drums; Monads scatter flowers; the Bacchantes throw back their heads with hair dishevelled.

Diana, with her tunic tucked up, sets out from the wood with her nymphs.

At the bottom of a cavern, Vulcan is hammering the iron between the Cabiri; here and there, the old river-gods, resting upon green stones, water their urns; and the Muses, standing up, are singing in the dales.

The Hours, of equal height, hold each other by the hand; and Mercury is placed in a slanting posture, upon a rainbow, with his magic wand, his winged sandals and his broad-brimmed hat.

But at the top of the staircase of the gods, amid clouds soft as feathers, whose folds as they wind around let fall roses, Venus Anadyomene is gazing at her image in a mirror; her pupils cast languishing glances underneath her rather heavy eyelashes. She has long, fair tresses, which spread out over her shoulders, her dainty breasts, her slender figure, her hips widening like the curves of a lyre, her two rounded thighs, the dimples around her knees, and her delicate feet. Not far from her mouth a butterfly is fluttering. The splendour of her body sheds around her a halo of brilliant mother-of-pearl; and all the rest of Olympus is bathed in a rosy dawn, which, by insensible degrees, reaches the heights of the azure sky.

Anthony—"Ah! my bosom dilates. A joy, which I cannot analyse, descends into the depths of my soul. How beautiful it is! how beautiful it is!"

Hilarion—"They stooped down from the height of the clouds to direct the swords. You might meet them on the roadsides. You kept them in your home; and this familiarity made life divine.

"Her only aim was to be free and beautiful. Her ample robes rendered her movements more graceful. The orator's voice, exercised beside the sea, struck the marble porticoes in unison with the sonorous waves. The stripling, rubbed with oil, wrestled, quite naked, in the full light of day. The most religious action was to expose pure forms.

"Those men, too, respected spouses, the aged and suppliants. Behind the Temple of Hercules, an altar was raised to Pity.

"They used to immolate victims with flowers around their fingers. Memory was not even troubled by the decay of the dead, for there remained of them only a handful of ashes. The soul, mingled with the boundless ether, ascended to the gods!"

Bending towards Anthony's ear:

"And they live for ever! The Emperor Constantine adores Apollo. You will find the Trinity in the mysteries of Samothrace, baptism in the case of Isis, the redemption in that of Mithra, the martyrdom of a god in the feasts of Bacchus. Proserpine is the Virgin; Aristæus, Jesus!"

Anthony keeps his eyes cast down; then all at once he repeats the creed of Jerusalem—as he recollects it—emitting, after each phrase, a long sigh:

" 'I believe in one only God, the Father;—and in one only Lord, Jesus Christ, first-born son of God, who became incarnate and was made man; who was crucified and buried; who ascended into Heaven; who will come to judge the living and the dead; whose kingdom will have no end;—and in one only Holy Ghost;—and in one only baptism of repentance;—and in one holy Catholic Church;—and in the resurrection of the flesh;—and in the life everlasting!' "

Immediately the cross becomes larger, and, piercing the clouds, it casts a shadow over the heaven of the gods.

They all grow dim. Olympus vanishes.

Anthony distinguishes near its base, half lost in the caverns, or supporting the stones on their shoulders, huge bodies chained. These are the Titans, the Giants, the Hecatonchires, and the Cyclops.

A voice rises, indistinct and formidable—like the murmur of the waves, like the sound heard in woods during a storm, like the roaring of the wind down a precipice:

"We knew it, we of all others! The gods were doomed to die. Uranus was mutilated by Saturn, and Saturn by Jupiter. He will be himself annihilated. Each in its turn. It is destiny!"

And, by degrees, they plunge into the mountain, and disappear.

Meanwhile, the roof of the palace of gold flies away.

Jupiter descends from his throne. The thunder at his feet smokes like a brand that is almost extinguished; and the eagle, stretching its neck, gathers with its beak its falling plumes.

"So, then, I am no longer the master of things, all-good, all-powerful, god of the phratriae and of the Greek peoples, ancestor of all the kings, the Agamemnon of Heaven!

"Eagle of the apotheoses, what breath of Erebus has driven thee to me? or, flying from the Campus Martius, dost thou bring to me the soul of the last of the Emperors?

"I no longer desire those of men! Let the earth guard them, and let them be moved on a level with its baseness. They now have hearts of slaves; they forget injuries, ancestors, oaths; and everywhere the folly of mobs, the mediocrity of the individual, and the hideousness of races reign supreme!"

His respiration makes his sides swell even to bursting, and he writhes with his hands. Hebe in tears presents a cup to him. He seizes it:

"No! no! As long as there will be, no matter where, a head enclosing thought which hates disorder and realises the idea of Law, the spirit of Jupiter will live!"

But the cup is empty. He turns it around slowly on his finger-nail.

"Not a drop! When ambrosia fails, there is an end of the Immortals!"

It slips out of his hand, and he leans against a pillar, feeling that he is dying.

Juno—"There was no need of so many loves! Eagle, bull, swan, golden shower, cloud and flame, thou hast assumed every form, scattered thy light in every element, hidden thy head on every couch! This time the divorce is irrevocable—and our sway, our very existence, is dissolved!"

She rushes away into the air!

Minerva no longer has her spear; and the ravens, which nestled in the sculptures of the frieze, whirl round her, and bite at her helmet.

"Let me see whether my vessels, cleaving the shining sea, have returned into my three ports, wherefore the fields are deserted, and what the daughters of Athens are now doing.

"In the month of Hecatombæon, all my people came to me led by their magistrates and priests. Then, in white robes, with chitons of gold, the long files of virgins advanced, holding cups, baskets, and parasols; then, the three hundred oxen for the sacrifice, old men shaking green boughs, soldiers clashing their armour against each other, youths singing hymns, players on the flute and on the lyre, rhapsodists and dancing-girls—and finally, on the mast of a trireme, supported by coils of rope, my great veil embroidered by virgins, who, for the space of a year, had been nourished in a particular fashion; and, when it had been shown in every street, in every square, and before every temple, in the midst of a procession continually chanting, it ascended to the Acropolis, brushed passed the Propylæum, and entered the Parthenon.

"But a difficulty faces me—me, the ingenious one! What! what! not a single idea! Here am I more terrified than a woman."

She perceives behind her a ruin, utters a cry, and, struck on the forehead, falls backward to the ground.

Hercules has cast off his lion's skin, and, resting on his feet, bending his back, and biting his lips, he makes desperate efforts to sustain Olympus, which is toppling down.

"I have vanquished the Cercopes, the Amazons, and the Centaurs. I have slain many kings, I have broken the horn of Achelous, a great river. I have cut through mountains; I have brought oceans together. I have liberated enslaved nations; I have peopled uninhabited countries. I have travelled over Gaul. I have traversed the desert where one feels thirst. I have defended the gods, and I have freed myself from Omphale. But Olympus is too heavy. My arms are growing feeble. I am dying!"

He is crushed beneath the ruins.

Pluto—"It is thine own fault, Amphitrionades! Why didst thou descend into my realms? The vulture who devours the entrails of Tityus has raised its head; Tantalus has had his lips moistened; and Ixion's wheel is stopped.

"Meanwhile, the Keres stretch forth their nails to detain the souls; the Furies in despair twist the serpents in their locks; and Cerberus, fastened by thee with a chain, has a rattling in the throat, while he slavers from his three mouths.

"Thou didst leave the gate ajar. Others have come. The light of human day has penetrated Tartarus!"

He sinks into the darkness.

Neptune—"My trident no longer raises tempests. The monsters who caused terror have rotted at the bottom of the sea.

"Amphitrite, whose white feet rushed over the foam; the green nereids, who could be seen on the horizon; the scaly sirens, who used to stop the ships to tell stories; and the old tritons, who used to blow into shells, all are dead! The gaiety of the sea has vanished!

"I will not survive it! Let the vast ocean cover me."

He disappears into the azure.

Diana, attired in black, among her dogs, who have become wolves—

"The freedom of great woods intoxicated me with its odour of deer and exhalations of swamps. The women, over whose pregnancy I watched, bring dead children into the world. The moon trembles under the incantations of sorcerers. I am filled with violent and boundless desires. I long to drink poisons, to lose myself in vapours or in dreams! . . ."

And a passing cloud bears her away.

Mars, bare-headed and blood-stained—

"At first, I fought single-handed, provoking by insults an entire army, indifferent to countries, and for the pleasure of carnage. Then, I had companions. They marched to the sound of flutes, in good order, with even step, breathing upon their bucklers, with lofty plume and slanting spear. We flung ourselves into the battle with loud cries like those of eagles. War was as joyous as a feast. Three hundred men withstood all Asia.

"But they returned, those barbarians! and in tens of thousands, nay, in millions! Since numbers, war-engines, and strategy are more powerful, it is better to make an end of it, like a brave man!"

He kills himself.

Vulcan, wiping the sweat from his limbs with a sponge—

"The world is getting cold. It is necessary to heat the springs, the volcanoes, and the rivers, which run from metals under the earth!—Strike harder! with vigorous arm! with all your strength!"

The Cabiri hurt themselves with their hammers, blind themselves with the sparks, and, groping their way along, are lost in the shadow.

Ceres, standing in her chariot which is drawn by wheels having wings in their naves—"Stop! Stop!

"They had good reason to exclude the strangers, the atheists, the epicureans, and the Christians! The mystery of the basket is unveiled, the sanctuary profaned—all is lost!"

She descends with a rapid fall—bursting into exclamation of despair, and dragging back the horses.

"Ah! falsehood! Daira is not given up to me. The brazen bell calls me to the dead. It is another kind of Tartarus. There is no returning from it. Horror!"

The abyss swallows her up.

Bacchus, laughing frantically:

"What does it matter! The wife of Archontes is my spouse! Even the law goes down before drunkenness. For me the new song and the multiplied forms!

"The fire which consumed my mother runs in my veins. Let it burn the stronger, even though I perish!

"Male and female, good for both, I deliver myself to ye, Bacchantes! I deliver myself to ye, Bacchantes! and the vine will twist around the trunks of trees! Howl! dance! writhe! Unbind the tiger and the slave! bite the flesh with ferocious teeth!"

And Pan, Silenus, the Satyrs, the Bacchantes, the Mimallones, and the Mænades, with their serpents, their torches, and their black masks, scatter flowers, then shake their dulcimers, strike their thyrsi, pelt each other with shells, crunch grapes, strangle a he-goat, and rend Bacchus.

Apollo, lashing his coursers, whose glistening hairs fly off—

"I have left behind me Delos the stony, so empty that everything there now seems dead; and I am striving to reach the Delphian oracle before its inspiring vapour should be completely lost. The mules browse on its laurel. The pythoness, gone astray, is found there no longer.

"By a stronger concentration, I will have sublime poems, eternal monuments; and all matter will be penetrated with the vibrations of my cithara."

He fingers its chords. They break and snap against his face. He flings down the instrument, and driving his four-horse chariot furiously:

"No! enough of forms! Farther still—to the very summit—to the world of pure thought!"

But the horses, falling back, begin to prance so that the chariot is smashed; and, entangled in the fragments of the pole and the knottings of the horses, he falls head-foremost into the abyss.

The sky is darkened. Venus, blue as a violet from the cold, shivers.

"I covered with my girdle the entire horizon of Hellas. Its fields shone with the roses of my cheeks; its shores were cut according to the form of my lips; and its mountains, whiter than my doves, palpitated under the hands of the sculptors. My spirit showed itself in the order of festivities, the arrangements of head-dresses, the dialogues of philosophers, and the constitution of republics. But I have loved men too much. It is Love that has dishonoured me!"

She falls back in tears.

"The world is abominable. My bosom feels the lack of air.

"O Mercury, inventor of the lyre, and conductor of souls, bear me away!"

She places a finger upon her mouth, and, describing an immense parabola, topples over into the abyss.

And now nothing can be seen. The darkness is complete.

In the meantime two red arrows seem to escape from the pupils of Hilarion.

Anthony at length notices his high stature:

"Many times already, while you were speaking, you appeared to me to be growing tall; and it was not an illusion. How is this? Explain it to me. Your appearance appals me!"

Steps draw nigh.

"What is this now?"

Hilarion stretches forth his arms:

"Look!"

Then, under a pale ray of the moon, Anthony distinguishes an interminable caravan which defiles over the crest of the rocks; and each passenger, one after another, falls from the cliff into the gulf.

First, there are the three great gods of Samothrace—Axieros, Axiokeros, and Axiokersa—joined in a cluster, with purple masks, and their hands raised.

Æsculapius advances with a melancholy air, without even seeing Samos and Telesphorus, who question him with anguish. Sosipolis, the Elean, with the form of a python, rolls out his rings towards the abyss. Doespœna, through vertigo, flings herself in there of her own accord. Britomartis, shrieking with fear, clasps the folds of her fillet. The Centaurs arrive with a great galloping, and dash, pell-mell, into the black hole.

Limping behind them come the sad group of nymphs. Those of the meadows are covered with dust; those of the woods groan and bleed, wounded by the wood-cutters' axes.

The Gelludæ, the Stryges, the Empusæ, all the infernal goddesses intermingling their hooks, their torches, and their snakes, form a pyramid; and at the summit, upon a vulture's skin, Eurynomus, bluish like flesh-flies, devours his own arms.

Then in a whirlwind disappears at the same time, Orthia the sanguinary, Hymnia of Orchomena, the Saphria of the Patræans, Aphia of Ægina, Bendis of Thrace, and Stymphalia with the leg of a bird. Triopas, in place of three eyeballs, has nothing more than three orbits. Erichthonius, with spindle-shanks, crawls like a cripple on his wrists.

Hilarion—"What happiness, is it not, to see all of them in a state of abjectness and agony? Mount with me on this stone, and you will be like Xerxes reviewing his army.

"Yonder, at a great distance, in the midst of fogs, do you perceive that giant with yellow beard who lets fall a sword red with blood? He is the Scythian Zalmoxis between two planets—Artimpasa, Venus; and Orsiloche, the Moon.

"Farther off, emerging out of the pale clouds, are the gods who are adored by the Cimmerians, beyond even Thule!

"Their great halls were warm, and by the light of the naked swords that covered the vault they drank hydromel in horns of ivory. They ate the liver of the whale in copper plates forged by the demons, or else they listened to the captive sorcerers sweeping their hands across the harps of stone. They are weary! they are cold! The snow wears down their bearskins, and their feet are exposed through the rents in their sandals.

"They mourn for the meadows where, upon hillocks of grass, they used to recover breath in the battle, the long ships whose prows cut through the mountains of ice, and the skates they used in order to follow the orbit of the poles while carrying on the extremities of their arms the firmament, which turned around with them."

A shower of hoar-frost pours down upon them. Anthony lowers his glance to the opposite side, and he perceives—outlining themselves in black upon a red background—strange personages with chin-pieces and gauntlets, who throw balls at one another, leap one on top of the other, make grimaces, and dance frantically.

Hilarion—"These are the gods of Etruria, the innumerable Æsars. Here is Tages, the inventor of auguries. He attempts with one hand to increase the divisions of the heavens, while with the other he leans upon the earth. Let him come back to it!

"Nortia is contemplating the wall into which she drove nails to mark the number of the years. Its surface is covered and its last period accomplished. Like two travellers driven about by a tempest, Kastur and Polutuk take shelter under the same mantle."

Anthony, closes his eyes—'Enough! Enough!"

But now through the air with a great noise of wings pass all the Victories of the Capitol, hiding their foreheads in their hands, and losing the trophies suspended from their arms.

Janus, master of the twilight, flies away upon a black ram, and of his two faces one is already putrefied, while the other is benumbed with fatigue.

Summanus—god of the gloomy sky, who no longer has a head—presses against his heart an old cake in the form of a wheel.

Vesta, under a ruined cupola, tries to rekindle her extinguished lamp.

Bellona gashes her cheeks without causing the blood, which used to purify her devotees, to flow out.

Anthony—"Pardon! They weary me!"

Hilarion—"Formerly they used to be entertaining!"

And he points out to Anthony, in a grove of beech-trees a woman perfectly naked—with four paws like a beast—bestridden by a black man holding in each hand a torch.

"This is the goddess Aricia with the demon Virbius. Her priest, the monarch of the woods, happened to be an assassin; and the fugitive slaves, the despoilers of corpses, the brigands of the Salarian road, the cripples of the Sublician bridge, all the vermin of the garrets of the Suburra, had not dearer devotion!

"The patrician ladies of Mark Anthony's time preferred Libitina."

And he shows him under the cypresses and rose-trees another woman clothed in gauze. She smiles, though she is surrounded by pickaxes, litters, black hangings, and all the utensils of funerals. Her diamonds glitter from afar among cobwebs. The Larvæ, like skeletons, display their bones amid the branches, and the Lemures, who are phantoms, spread out their bats' wings.

On the side of a field the god Terma is bent down, torn asunder, and covered with filth.

In the midst of a ridge the huge corpse of Vertumnus is being devoured by red dogs. The rustic gods depart weeping, Sartor, Sarrator, Vervactor, Eollina, Vallona, and Hostilenus—all covered with little hooded cloaks, and each bearing a mattock, a fork, a hurdle, and a boar-spear.

Hilarion—"It was their spirits that made the villa prosper with its dove-cotes, its park for dormice, its poultry-yards protected by snares, and its hot stables embalmed with cedar.

"They protected all the wretched people who dragged the fetters with their legs over the pebbles of the Sabina, those who called the hogs with the sound of the trumpet, those who gathered the grapes on the tops of the elm-trees, those who drove through the byroads the asses laden with dung. The husbandman, while he panted over the handle of his plough, prayed to them to strengthen his arms; and the cow-herds, in the shadow of the lime-trees, beside gourds of milk, chanted their eulogies by turns upon flutes of reeds."

Anthony sighs.

And in the middle of a chamber, upon a platform, a bed of ivory is revealed, surrounded by persons lifting up pine-torches.

"Those are the gods of marriage. They are awaiting the bride.

"Domiduca has to lead her in, Virgo to undo her girdle, Subigo to stretch her upon the bed, and Præma to keep back her arms, whispering sweet words in her ear.

"But she will not come! and they dismiss the others—Nona and Decima, the nurses; the three Nixii, who are to deliver her; the two wet-nurses, Educa and Potina; and Carna, the cradle-rocker, whose bunch of hawthorns drives away bad dreams from the infant. Later, Ossipago will have strengthened its knees, Barbatus will have given the beard, Stimula the first desires, and Volupia the first enjoyment; Fabulinus will have taught it how to speak, Numera how to count, Camœna how to sing, and Consus how to think."

The chamber is empty, and there remains no longer at the side of the bed anyone but Nænia—a hundred years old—muttering to herself the lament which she poured forth on the death of old men.

But soon her voice is lost amid bitter cries, which come from the domestic lares, squatted at the end of the atrium, clad in dogs' skins, with flowers around their bodies, holding their closed hands up to their cheeks, and weeping as much as they can.

"Where is the portion of food which is given to us at each meal, the good attentions of maid-servant, the smile of the matron, and the gaiety of the little boys playing with huckle-bones on the mosaic of the courtyard? Then, when they have grown big, they hang over our breasts their gold or leather bullae.

"What happiness, when, on the evening of a triumph, the master, returning home, turned towards us his humid eyes! He told the story of his contests, and the narrow house was more stately than a palace, and more sacred than a temple.

"How pleasant were the repasts of the family, especially the day after the Feralia! The feeling of tenderness towards the dead dispelled all discords; and people embraced one another, drinking to the glories of the past, and to the hopes of the future.

"But the ancestors in painted wax, shut up behind us, became gradually covered with mouldiness. The new races, to punish us for their own deceptions, have broken our jaws; and under the rats' teeth our bodies of wood have crumbled away."

And the innumerable gods, watching at the doors, in the kitchen, in the cellar, and in the stoves, disperse on all sides, under the appearance of enormous ants running away, or huge butterflies on the wing.

Then a thunderclap.

A voice—"I was the God of armies, the Lord, the Lord God!

"I have unfolded on the hills the tents of Jacob, and nourished in the sands my fugitive people. It was I who burned Sodom! It was I who engulfed the earth beneath the Deluge! It was I who drowned Pharaoh, with the royal princes, the war-chariots, and the charioteers. A jealous God, I execrated the other gods. I crushed the impure; I overthrew the proud; and my desolation rushed to right and left, like a dromedary let loose in a field of maize.

"To set Israel free, I chose the simple. Angels, with wings of flame, spoke to them in the bushes.

"Perfumed with spikenard, cinnamon, and myrrh, with transparent robes and high-heeled shoes, women of intrepid heart went forth to slay the captains. The passing wind bore away the prophets.

"I engraved my law on tablets of stone. It shut in my people as in a citadel. They were my people. I was their God! The earth was mine, and men were mine, with their thoughts, their works, the implements with which they tilled the soil, and their posterity.

"My ark rested in a triple sanctuary, behind purple curtains and flaming lamps. For my ministry I had an entire tribe, who swung the censers, and the high-priest in a robe of hyacinth, and wearing precious stones upon his breast arranged in regular order.

"Woe! woe! The Holy of Holies is flung open; the veil is rent; the odours of the holocaust are scattered to all the winds. The jackals whine in the sepulchres; my temple is destroyed; my people are dispersed!

"They have strangled the priests with the cords of their vestments. The women are captives; the sacred vessels are all melted down!"

The voice, dying away:

"I was the God of armies, the Lord, the Lord God!" Then comes an appalling silence, a profound darkness.

Anthony—"They are all gone!"

"I remain!" says some one.

And, face to face with him stands Hilarion, but transfigured—beautiful as an archangel, luminous as a sun, and so tall that, in order to see him, Anthony lifts up his head—"Who, then, are you?"

Hilarion—"My kingdom is as wide as the universe, and my desire has no limits. I am always going about enfranchising the mind and weighing the worlds, without hate, without fear, without love, and without God. I am called Science."

Anthony, recoiling backwards—"You must be, rather, the Devil!"

Hilarion, fixing his eyes upon him—"Do you wish to see him?"

Anthony no longer avoids his glance. He is seized with curiosity concerning the Devil. His terror increases; his longing becomes measureless.

"If I saw him, however—if I saw him?" . . . Then, in a spasm of rage:

"The horror that I have of him will rid me of him forever. Yes!"

A cloven foot reveals itself. Anthony is filled with regret. But the Devil overshadows him with his horns, and carries him off.

Chapter VI

THE MYSTERY OF SPACE

H E FLIES UNDER ANTHONY'S BODY, EXTENDED LIKE A SWIMMER; HIS TWO great wings, outspread, entirely concealing him, resemble a cloud.

Anthony—"Where am I going? Just now I caught a glimpse of the form of the Accursed One. No! a cloud is carrying me away. Perhaps I am dead, and am mounting up to God? . . .

"Ah! how well I breathe! The untainted air inflates my soul. No more heaviness! no more suffering!

"Beneath me, the thunderbolt darts forth, the horizon widens, rivers cross one another. That light spot is the desert; that pool of water the ocean. And other oceans appear—immense regions of which I had no knowledge. There are black lands that smoke like live embers, a belt of snow ever obscured by the mists. I am trying to discover the mountains where each evening the sun goes to sleep."

The Devil—"The sun never goes to sleep!"

Anthony is not startled by this voice. It appears to him an echo of his thought—a response of his memory.

Meanwhile, the earth takes the form of a ball, and he perceives it in the midst of the azure turning on its poles while it winds around the sun.

The Devil—"So, then, it is not the centre of the world? Pride of man, humble thyself!"

Anthony—"I can scarcely distinguish it now. It is intermingled with the other fires. The firmament is but a tissue of stars."

They continue to ascend.

"No noise! not even the crying of the eagles! Nothing! . . . and I bend down to listen to the music of the spheres."

The Devil—"You cannot hear them! No longer will you see the antichthon of Plato, the focus of Philolaüs, the spheres of Aristotle, or the seven heavens of the Jews with the great waters above the vault of crystal!"

Anthony—"From below it appeared as solid as a wall. But now, on the contrary, I am penetrating it; I am plunging into it!"

And he arrives in front of the moon—which is like a piece of ice, quite round, filled with a motionless light.

The Devil—"This was formerly the abode of souls. The good Pythagoras had even supplied it with birds and magnificent flowers."

Anthony—"I see nothing there save desolate plains, with extinct craters, under a black sky.

"Come towards those stars with a softer radiance, so that we may gaze upon the angels who hold them with the ends of their arms, like torches!"

The Devil carries him into the midst of the stars.

"They attract one another at the same time that they repel one another. The action of each has an effect on the others, and helps to produce their movements—and all this without the medium of an auxiliary, by the force of a law, by the virtue simply of order."

Anthony—"Yes . . . yes! my intelligence grasps it! It is a joy greater than the sweetness of affection! I pant with stupefaction before the immensity of God!"

The Devil—"Like the firmament, which rises in proportion as you ascend, He will become greater according as your imagination mounts higher; and you will feel your joy increase in proportion to the unfolding of the universe, in this enlargement of the Infinite."

Anthony—"Ah! higher! ever higher!"

The stars multiply and shed around their scintillations. The Milky Way at the zenith spreads out like an immense belt, with gaps here and there; in these clefts, amid its brightness, dark tracts reveal themselves. There are showers of stars, trains of golden dust, luminous vapours which float and then dissolve.

Sometimes a comet sweeps by suddenly; then the tranquillity of the countless lights is renewed.

Anthony, with open arms, leans on the Devil's two horns, thus occupying the entire space covered by his wings. He recalls with disdain the ignorance of former days, the limitation of his ideas. Here, then, close beside him, were those luminous globes which he used to gaze at from below. He traces the crossing of their paths, the complexity of their directions. He sees them coming from afar, and, suspended like stones in a sling, describing their orbits and pushing forward their parabolas.

He perceives, with a single glance, the Southern Cross and the Great Bear, the Lynx and the Centaur, the nebulae of the Gold-fish, the six suns in the constellation of Orion, Jupiter with his four satellites, and the triple ring of the monstrous Saturn! all the planets, all the stars which men should, in future days, discover! He fills his eyes with their light; he overloads his mind with a calculation of their distances;—then he lets his head fall once more.

"What is the object of all this?"

The Devil—"There is no object!

"How could God have had an object? What experience could have enlightened Him, what reflection enabled Him to judge? Before the beginning of things, it would not have operated, and now it would be useless."

Anthony—"Nevertheless, He created the world, at one period of time, by His mere word!"

The Devil—"But the beings who inhabit the earth came there successively. In the same way, in the sky, new stars arise—different effects from various causes."

Anthony—"The variety of causes is the will of God!"

The Devil—"But to admit in God several acts of will is to admit several causes, and thus to destroy His unity!

"His will is not separable from His essence. He cannot have a second will, inasmuch as He cannot have a second essence—and, since He exists eternally, He acts eternally.

"Look at the sun! From its borders escape great flames emitting sparks which scatter themselves to become new worlds; and, further than the last, beyond those depths where only night is visible, other suns whirl round, and behind these others again, and others still, to infinity . . ."

Anthony—"Enough! enough! I am terrified! I am about to fall into the abyss."

The Devil stops, and gently balancing himself—

"There is no such thing as nothingness! There is no vacuum! Everywhere there are bodies moving over the unchangeable realms of space—and, as if it had any bounds it would not be space but a body, it consequently has no limits!"

Anthony, open-mouthed—"No limits!"

The Devil—"Ascend into the sky forever and ever, and you will never reach the top! Descend beneath the earth for millions upon millions of centuries, and you will never get to the bottom—inasmuch as there is no bottom, no top, no end, above or below; and space is, in fact, comprised in God, who is not a part of space, of a magnitude that can be measured, but immensity!"

Anthony, slowly—"Matter, in that case, would be part of God?"

The Devil—"Why not? Can you tell where He comes to an end?"

Anthony—"On the contrary, I prostrate myself, I efface myself before His power!"

The Devil—"And you pretend to move Him! You speak to Him, you even adorn Him with virtues—goodness, justice, clemency—in place of recognising the fact that He possesses all perfections!

"To conceive anything beyond is to conceive God outside of God. Being outside of Being. But then He is the only Being, the only Substance.

"If substance could be divided, it would lose its nature—it would not be itself; God would no longer exist. He is, therefore, indivisible as well as infinite, and if He had a body, He would be made up of parts. He would no longer be one; He would no longer be infinite. Therefore, He is not a person!"

Anthony—"What? My prayers, my sobs, the sufferings of my flesh, the transports of my zeal, all these things would be no better than a lie . . . in space . . . uselessly—like a bird's cry, like a whirlwind of dead leaves!"

He weeps.

"Oh! no! There is above everything some One, a Great Spirit, a Lord, a Father, whom my heart adores, and who must love me!"

The Devil—"You desire that God should not be God; for, if He experienced love, anger, or pity, He would pass from His perfection to a greater or less perfection. He cannot descend to a sentiment, or be contained under a form."

Anthony—"One day, however, I shall see Him!"

The Devil—"With the Blessed, is it not? When the finite shall enjoy the Infinite, enclosing the Absolute in a limited space!"

Anthony—"No matter! There must be a Paradise for the good, as well as a Hell for the wicked!"

The Devil—"Does the exigency of your reason constitute the law of things? Without doubt, evil is a matter of indifference to God, seeing that the earth is covered with it!

"Is it from impotence that He endures it, or from cruelty that He preserves it?

"Do you think that He can be continually putting the world in order like an imperfect work, and that He watches over all the movements of all beings, from the flight of the butterfly to the thought of man?

"If He created the universe His providence is superfluous. If Providence exists, creation is defective.

"But good and evil only concern you—like day and night, pleasure and pain, death and birth, which have relationship merely to a corner of space, to a special medium, to a particular interest. Inasmuch as what is infinite alone is permanent, the Infinite exists; and that is all!"

The Devil has gradually extended his huge wings, and now they cover space.

Anthony can no longer see. He is on the point of fainting:

"A horrible chill freezes me to the bottom of my soul. This exceeds the utmost pitch of pain. It is, as it were, a death more profound than death. I wheel through the immensity of darkness. It enters into me. My consciousness is shivered to atoms under this expansion of nothingness."

The Devil—"But things happen only through the medium of your mind. Like a concave mirror, it distorts objects, and you need every resource in order to verify facts.

"Never shall you understand the universe in its full extent; consequently you cannot form an idea as to its cause, so as to have a just notion of God, or even say that the universe is infinite, for you should first comprehend the Infinite!

"Form is perhaps an error of your senses, substance an illusion of your intellect. Unless it be that the world, being a perpetual flux of things, appearances, by a sort of contradiction, would not be a test of truth, and illusion would be the only reality.

"But are you sure that you see? Are you sure that you live? Perhaps nothing at all exists!"

The Devil has seized Anthony, and, holding him by the extremities of his arms, stares at him with open jaws ready to swallow him up.

"Come, adore me! and curse the phantom that you call God!"

Anthony raises his eyes with a last movement of lingering hope.

The Devil quits him.

Chapter VII

THE CHIMERA AND THE SPHINX

ANTHONY FINDS HIMSELF STRETCHED ON HIS BACK AT THE EDGE OF THE CLIFF. The sky is beginning to grow white.

"Is this the brightness of dawn? or is it the reflection of the moon?"

He tries to rise, then sinks back, and with chattering teeth:

"I feel fatigued . . . as if all my bones were broken!

"Why?

"Ah! it is the Devil! I remember; and he even repeated to me all I had learned from old Didymus concerning the opinions of Xenophanes, of Heraclitus, of Melissus, and of Anaxagoras, as well as concerning the Infinite, the creation, and the impossibility of knowing anything!

"And I imagined that I could unite myself to God!"

Laughing bitterly:

"Ah! madness! madness! Is it my fault? Prayer is intolerable to me! My heart is drier than a rock! Formerly it overflowed with love! . . .

"The sand, in the morning, used to send forth exhalations on the horizon, like the fumes of a censer. At the setting of the sun blossoms of fire burst forth from the cross, and, in the middle of the night, it often seemed to me that all creatures and all things, gathered in the same silence, were with me adoring the Lord. Oh! charm of prayer, bliss of ecstasy, gifts of Heaven, what has become of you?

"I remember a journey I made with Ammon in search of a solitude in which we might establish monasteries. It was the last evening, and we quickened our steps, murmuring hymns, side by side, without uttering a word. In proportion as the sun went down, the shadows of our bodies lengthened, like two obelisks, always enlarging and marching on in front of us. With the pieces of our staffs we planted the cross here and there to mark the site of a cell. The night came on slowly, and black waves spread over the earth, while an immense sheet of red still occupied the sky.

"When I was a child, I used to amuse myself in constructing hermitages with pebbles. My mother, close beside me, used to watch what I was doing.

"She was going to curse me for abandoning her, tearing her white locks. And her corpse remained stretched in the middle of the cell, beneath the roof of reeds, between the tottering walls. Through a hole, a hyena, sniffing, thrusts forward his jaws! . . . Horror! horror!"

He sobs.

"No: Ammonaria would not have left her!

"Where is Ammonaria now?

"Perhaps, in a hot bath she is drawing off her garments one by one, first her cloak, then her girdle, then her outer tunic, then her inner one, then the wrappings round her neck; and the vapour of cinnamon envelops her naked limbs. At last she sinks to sleep on the tepid floor. Her hair, falling around her hips, looks like a black fleece—and, almost suffocating in the overheated atmosphere, she draws breath, with her body bent forward and her breasts projecting. Hold! here is my flesh breaking into revolt. In the midst of anguish, I am tortured by voluptuousness. Two punishments at the same time—it is too much! I can no longer endure my own body!"

He stoops down and gazes over the precipice.

"The man who falls over that will be killed. Nothing easier, by simply rolling over on the left side: it is necessary to take only one step! only one!"

Then appears an old woman.

Anthony rises with a start of error. He imagines that he sees his mother risen from the dead.

But this one is much older and excessively emaciated. A winding-sheet, fastened round her head, hangs with her white hair down to the very extremities of her legs, thin as sticks. The brilliancy of her teeth, which are like ivory, makes her clayey skin look darker. The sockets of her eyes are full of gloom, and in their depths flicker two flames, like lamps in a sepulchre.

"Come forward," she says; "what keeps you back?"

Anthony, stammering—"I am afraid of committing a sin!"

She resumes:

"But King Saul was slain! Razias, a just man, was slain! Saint Pelagius of Antioch was slain! Dominius of Aleppo and his two daughters, three more saints, were slain;—and recall to your mind all the confessors who, in their eagerness to die, rushed to meet their executioners. In order to taste death the more speedily, the virgins of Miletus strangled themselves with their cords. The philosopher, Hegesias, at Syracuse preached so well on the subject, that people deserted the brothels to hang themselves in the fields. The Roman patricians sought for death as if it were a debauch."

Anthony—"Yes, it is a powerful passion! Many an anchorite has yielded to it."

The old woman—"To do a thing which makes you equal to God—think of that! He created you; you are about to destroy His work, you, by your courage, freely. The enjoyment of Erostrates was not greater. And then, your body is thus mocked by your soul in order that you may avenge yourself in the end. You will have no pain. It will soon be over. What are you afraid of? A large black hole! It is empty, perhaps!"

Anthony listens without saying anything in reply;—and, on the other side, appears another woman, marvellously young and beautiful. At first, he takes her for Ammonaria. But she is taller, fair as honey, rather plump, with paint on her cheeks, and roses on her head. Her long robe, covered with spangles, is studded with metallic mirrors. Her fleshly lips have a look of blood, and her somewhat heavy eyelashes are so much bathed in languor that one would imagine she was blind. She murmurs:

"Come, then, and enjoy yourself. Solomon recommends pleasure. Go where your heart leads you, and according to the desire of your eyes."

Anthony—"To find what pleasure? My heart is sick; my eyes are dim!"

She replies:

"Hasten to the suburb of Racotis; push open a door painted blue; and, when you are in the atrium, where a jet of water is gurgling, a woman will present herself—in a peplum of white silk edged with gold, her hair dishevelled, and her laugh like sounds made by rattlesnakes. She is clever. In her caress you will taste the pride of an initiation, and the satisfaction of a want. Have you pressed against your bosom a maiden who loved you? Recall to your mind her remorse, which vanished under a flood of sweet tears. You can imagine yourself—can you not?—walking through the woods beneath the light of the moon. At the pressure of your hands joined with hers a shudder runs through both of you; your eyes, brought close together, overflow from one to the other like immaterial waves, and your heart is full; it is bursting; it is a delicious whirlwind, an overpowering intoxication."

The old woman—"You need not experience joys to feel their bitterness! You need only see them from afar, and disgust takes possession of you. You must needs be wearied with the monotony of the same actions, the duration of the days, the ugliness of the world, and the stupidity of the sun!"

Anthony—"Oh! yes; all that it shines upon is displeasing to me."

The young woman—"Hermit! hermit! you shall find diamonds among the pebbles, fountains beneath the sand, a delight in the dangers which you despise; and there are even places on the earth so beautiful that you are filled with a longing to embrace them."

The old woman—"Every evening when you lie down to sleep on the earth, you hope that it may soon cover you."

The young woman—"Nevertheless, you believe in the resurrection of the flesh, which is the transport of life into eternity."

The old woman, while speaking, has been growing more emaciated, and, above her skull, which has no hair upon it, a bat has been making circles in the air.

The young woman has become plumper. Her robe changes colour; her nostrils swell; her eyes roll softly.

The first says, opening her arms:

"Come! I am consolation, rest, oblivion, eternal peace!"

And the second offering her breast:

"I am the soother, the joy, the life, the happiness inexhaustible!"

Anthony turns on his heel to fly. Each of them places a hand upon his shoulder.

The winding-sheet flies open, and reveals the skeleton of Death. The robe bursts open, and presents to view the entire body of Lust, which has a slender figure, with an enormous development behind, and great, undulating masses of hair, disappearing towards the end.

Anthony remains motionless between the pair, contemplating them.

Death says to him—

"This moment, or a little later—what does it matter? You belong to me, like the suns, the nations, the cities, the kings, the snow on the mountains, and the grass in the fields. I fly higher than the sparrow-hawk, I run more quickly than the gazelle; I keep pace even with hope; I have conquered God!"

Lust—"Do not resist; I am omnipotent. The forests echo with my sighs; the waves are stirred by my agitations. Virtue, courage, piety, are dissolved in the perfume of my breath. I accompany man at every step he takes; and on the threshold of the tomb he comes back to me."

Death—"I will reveal to you what you tried to grasp by the light of torches on the features of the dead—or when you rambled beyond the Pyramids in those vast sand-heaps composed of human remains. From time to time, a piece of skull rolled under your sandal. You took it out of the dust; you made it slip between your fingers; and your mind, becoming absorbed in it, was plunged into nothingness."

Lust—"Mine is a deeper gulf! Marble slabs have inspired impure loves. People rush towards meetings that terrify them, and rivet the very chains which they curse. Whence comes the witchery of courtesans, the extravagance of dreams, the immensity of my sadness?"

Death—"My irony surpasses that of all other things. There are convulsions of joy at the funerals of kings and at the extermination of peoples; and they make war with music, plumes, flags, golden harnesses, and a display of ceremony to pay me the greater homage."

Lust—"My anger is as strong as yours. I howl, I bite, I have sweats of agony, and corpse-like appearances."

Death—"It is I who make you serious; let us embrace each other!"

Death chuckles; Lust roars. They seize each other's figures, and sing together:

"I hasten the dissolution of matter."

"I facilitate the scattering of germs!"

"Thou destroyest that I may renew!"

"Thou engenderest that I may destroy!"

"Active my power!"

"Fruitful my decay!"

And their voices, whose echoes, rolling forth, fill the horizon, become so powerful that Anthony falls backward.

A shock, from time to time, causes him to half open his eyes; and he perceives, in the midst of the darkness, a kind of monster before him.

It is a death's-head with a crown of roses. It rises above the torso of a woman white as mother-of-pearl. Beneath, a winding-sheet, starred with points of gold, makes a kind of train;—and the entire body undulates, like a gigantic worm holding itself erect.

The vision grows fainter, and then fades away.

Anthony, rises again—"This time, once more, it was the Devil, and under his two-fold aspect—the spirit of voluptuousness and the spirit of destruction. Neither terrifies me. I thrust happiness aside, and feel that I am eternal.

"Thus, death is only an illusion, a veil, masking at certain points the continuity of life. But substance, being one, why is there a variety of forms? There must be somewhere primordial figures, whose bodies are only images. If one could see, one would know the bond between mind and matter, wherein Being consists!

"There are those figures which were painted at Babylon on the wall of the temple of Belus, and they covered a mosaic in the port of Carthage. I, myself, have sometimes seen in the sky what seemed like forms of spirits. Those who traverse the desert meet animals passing all conception . . ."

And, opposite him, on the other side of the Nile, lo! the Sphinx appears.

It stretches out its feet, shakes the fillets on its forehead, and lies down upon its belly.

Jumping, flying, spirting fire through its nostrils, and striking its wings with its dragon's tail, the Chimera with its green eyes, winds round, and barks. The curls of its head, thrown back on one-side, intermingle with the hair on its haunches; and on the other side they hang over the sand, and move to and fro with the swaying of its entire body.

The Sphinx is motionless, and gazes at the Chimera:

"Here, Chimera; stop!"

The Chimera—"No, never!"

The Sphinx—"Do not run so quickly; do not fly so high; do not bark so loud!"

The Chimera—"Do not address me, do not address me any more, since you remain forever silent!"

The Sphinx—"Cease casting your flames in my face and flinging your yells in my ears; you shall not melt my granite!"

The Chimera—"You will not get hold of me, terrible Sphinx!"

The Sphinx—"You are too foolish to live with me!"

The Chimera—"You are too clumsy to follow me!"

The Sphinx—"And where are you going that you run so quickly?"

The Chimera—"I gallop into the corridors of the labyrinth; I hover over the mountains; I skim along the waves; I yelp at the bottoms of precipices; I hang by my jaws on the skirts of the clouds. With my trailing tail I scratch the coasts, and the hills have taken their curb according to the form of my shoulders. But as for you, I find you perpetually motionless; or, rather, with the end of your claw tracing letters on the sand."

The Sphinx—"That is because I keep my secret! I reflect and I calculate. The sea returns to its bed; the blades of corn balance themselves in the wind; the caravans pass; the dust flies off; the cities crumble;—but my glance, which nothing can turn aside, remains concentrated on the objects which cover an inaccessible horizon."

The Chimera—"As for me, I am light and joyous! I discover in men dazzling perspectives, with Paradises in the clouds and distant felicities. I pour into their souls the eternal insanities, projects of happiness, plans for the future, dreams of glory, and oaths of love, as well as virtuous resolutions. I drive them on perilous voyages and on mighty enterprises. I have carved with my claws the marvels of architecture. It is I that hung the little bells on the tomb of Porsenna, and surrounded with a wall of Corinthian brass the quays of the Atlantides.

"I seek fresh perfumes, larger flowers, pleasures hitherto unknown. If anywhere I find a man whose soul reposes in wisdom, I fall upon him and strangle him."

The Sphinx—"All those whom the desire of God torments, I have devoured.

"The strongest, in order to climb to my royal forehead, mount upon the stripes of my fillets as on the steps of a staircase. Weariness takes possession of them, and they fall back of their own accord."

Anthony begins to tremble. He is not before his cell, but in the desert, having at either side of him those two monstrous animals, whose jaws graze his shoulders.

The Sphinx—"O Fantasy, bear me on thy wings to enliven thy sadness!"

The Chimera—"O Unknown One, I am in love with thine eyes! I turn round thee, soliciting allayment of that which devours me!"

The Sphinx—"My feet cannot raise themselves. The lichen, like a ringworm, has grown over my mouth. By dint of thinking, I have no longer anything to say."

The Chimera—"You lie, hypocritical Sphinx! How is it that you are always addressing me and abjuring me?"

The Sphinx—"It is you, unmanageable caprice, who pass and whirl about."

The Chimera—"Is that my fault? Come, now, just let me be!"

It barks.

The Sphinx—"You move away; you avoid me!"

The Sphinx grumbles.

The Chimera—"Let us make the attempt! You crush me!"

The Sphinx—"No; impossible!"

And sinking, little by little, it disappears in the sand, while the Chimera, crawling, with its tongue out, departs with a winding movement.

The breath issuing from its mouth has produced a fog.

In this fog Anthony traces masses of clouds and imperfect curves. Finally, he distinguishes what appear to be human bodies.

And first advances the group of Astomi, like air-balls passing across the sun.

"Don't puff too strongly! The drops of rain bruise us; the false sounds excoriate us; the darkness blinds us. Composed of breezes and of perfumes, we roll, we float—a little more than dreams, not entirely beings."

The Nisnas have but one eye, one cheek, one hand, one leg, half a body, and half a heart. And they say, in a very loud tone:

"We live quite at our ease in our halves of houses with our halves of wives and our halves of children."

The Blemmyes, absolutely bereft of heads—

"Our shoulders are the largest;—and there is not an ox, a rhinoceros, or an elephant that is capable of carrying what we carry.

"Arrows, and a sort of vague outline are imprinted on our breasts—that is all! We reduce digestion to thought; we subtilise secretions. For us God floats peacefully in the internal chyle.

"We proceed straight on our way, passing through every mire, running along the verge of every abyss; and we are the most industrious, happy, and virtuous people."

The Pygmies—"Little good-fellows, we swarm over the world, like vermin on the hump of a dromedary.

"We are burnt, drowned, or run over; but we always reappear more full of life and more numerous—terrible from the multitude of us that exists!"

The Sciapodes—"Kept on the ground by our flowing locks, long as creeping plants, we vegetate under the shelter of our feet, which are as large as parasols; and the light reaches us through the spaces between our wide heels. No disorder and no toil! To keep the head as low as possible—that is the secret of happiness!"

Their lifted thighs, resembling trunks of trees, increase in number. And now a forest appears in which huge apes rush along on four paws. They are men with dogs' heads.

The Cynocephali—"We leap from branch to branch to suck the eggs, and we pluck the little birds; then we put their nests upon our heads after the fashion of caps.

"We do not fail to snatch away the worst of the cows, and we destroy the lynxes' eyes. Tearing the flowers, crushing the fruits, agitating the springs, we are the masters—by the strength of our arms and the fierceness of our hearts.

"Be bold, comrades, and snap your jaws!"

Blood and milk flow from their lips. The rain streams over their hairy backs.

Anthony inhales the freshness of green leaves which are agitated as the branches of the trees dash against each other. All at once appears a large black stag with a bull's head, carrying between his two ears a mass of white horns.

The Sadhuzag—"My seventy-four antlers are hollow like flutes. When I turn myself towards the south wind, sounds go forth from them that draw around me the ravished beasts. The serpents come winding to my feet; the wasps stick in my nostrils; and the parrots, the doves, and the ibises alight upon my branches. Listen!"

He bends back his horns, from which issues an unutterably sweet music.

Anthony presses both his hands above his heart. It seems to him as if this melody were about to carry off his soul.

The Sadhuzag—"But, when I turn towards the north wind, my horns, more bushy than a battalion of spears, emit a howling noise. The forests thrill; the rivers swell; the husks of the fruit burst, and blades of grass stand erect like a coward's hair. Listen!"

He bows down his branches, from which now come forth discordant cries. Anthony feels as if he were torn asunder, and his horror is increased on seeing the Mantichor, a gigantic red lion with a human figure and three rows of teeth:

"The silky texture of my scarlet hair mingles with the yellowness of the sands. I breathe through my nostrils the terror of solitudes. I spit forth the plague. I devour armies when they venture into the desert. My nails are twisted like gimlets; my teeth are cut like a saw; and my hair, wriggled out of shape, bristles with darts which I scatter, right and left, behind me. Hold! hold!"

The Mantichor casts thorns from his tail, which radiate, like arrows, in all directions. Drops of blood flow, spattering over the foliage.

The Catoblepas appears, a black buffalo, with a pig's head hanging to the earth, and connected with his shoulders by a slender neck, long and flabby as an empty gut. He is wallowing on the ground; and his feet disappear under the enormous mane of hard hairs that descend over his face:

"Fat, melancholy, savage, I remain continually feeling the mire under my stomach. My skull is so heavy that it is impossible for me to carry it. I roll it around slowly; and, opening my jaws, I snatch with my tongue the poisonous herbs that are moistened with my breath. I once devoured my paws without noticing it.

"No one, Anthony, has ever seen my eyes, or those who have seen them are dead. If I but raised my eyelids—my eyelids red and swollen—that instant you would die."

Anthony—"Oh! that thing! . . . Well! well! As if I had any such longing! Its stupidity attracts me. No! no! I will not!" He looks fixedly on the ground. But the grass lights up, and, in the twistings of the flames, stands erect the Basilisk, a huge, violet serpent, with a trilobate crest and two teeth—one above, the other below:

"Take care! You are about to fall into my jaws! I drink fire. I am fire myself; and from every quarter I suck it in—from clouds, from pebbles, from dead trees, from the hair of animals, and from the surface of marshes. My temperature supports the volcanoes. I cause the lustre of precious stones and the colour of metals."

The Griffin, a lion with a vulture's beak, white wings, red paws, and blue neck— "I am the master of the profound splendours. I know the secret of the tombs where the old kings sleep. A chain, which issues from the wall, keeps their heads erect. Near them, in basins of porphyry, women whom they have loved float upon black liquids. Their treasures are ranged in halls, in lozenges, in hillocks, and in pyramids; and, lower, far below the tombs, after long journeys in the midst of suffocating darkness, are rivers of gold with forests of diamonds, meadows of carbuncles, and lakes of quicksilver. With my back against the door of the vault, and my claws in the air, I watch with my flaming eyes those who may think fit to come there. The immense plain, even to the furthest point of the horizon, is quite bare and whitened with travellers' bones. For you the bronze doors will open, and you will inhale the vapour of the mines; you will descend into the caverns. . . . Quick! quick!"

He digs the earth with his claws, crowing like a cock.

A thousand voices reply to him. The forest trembles.

And all sorts of horrible beasts arise: the Tragelaphus, half-stag, half-ox; the Myrmecoleo, a lion in front, an ant behind, whose genitals are turned backwards; the python, Aksar, of sixty cubits, who frightened Moses; the great weasel, Pastinaca, which kills trees by its odour; the Presteros, which renders idiotic those who touch it; the Mirag, a horned hare dwelling in the islands of the sea. The Copard Phalmant bursts his belly by dint of howling; the Senad, a bear with three heads, tears its little ones with its mouth; the dog, Cepus, scatters on the rocks the blue milk of its dugs. Mosquitoes begin to buzz, toads to jump, and serpents to hiss. Lightnings flash; down comes the hail.

Then there are squalls, which reveal anatomical marvels. There are alligators' heads with roebucks' feet, owls with serpents' tails, swine with tigers' muzzles, goats with asses' rumps, frogs covered with hair like bears, chameleons large as hippopotami, calves with two heads, one of which weeps while the other bellows, four fœtuses holding each other by the navel and spinning like tops, and winged bellies which flutter like gnats.

They rain down from the sky; they spring out of the ground; they glide from the rocks. Everywhere eyes flash, mouths roar; the breasts bulge out; the claws lengthen; the teeth gnash; the flesh quivers. Some of them bring forth their young; others with a single bite, devour one another.

Suffocating from their very numbers, multiplying by their contact, they climb on top of one another; and they all keep stirring about Anthony with a regular swaying motion, as if the soil were the deck of a vessel.

He feels close to his calves the trailing of slugs, and on his hands the cold touch of vipers; and spiders spinning their webs enclose him in their network.

But the circle of monsters begins to open; the sky suddenly becomes blue, and the unicorn makes its appearance:

"Off I gallop! Off I gallop!

"I have hoofs of ivory, teeth of steel, a head coloured purple, a body like snow, and the horn on my forehead has the varied hues of the rainbow.

"I travel from Chaldea to the Tartar desert, on the banks of the Ganges, and into Mesopotamia. I outstrip the ostriches. I run so rapidly that I draw the wind along with me. I rub my back against the palm-trees; I roll myself in the bamboos. With one bound I jump across the rivers. Doves fly above my head. Only a virgin can bridle me.

"Off I gallop! Off I gallop!"

Anthony watches him flying away.

And, keeping his eyes still raised, he perceives all the birds that are nourished by the wind: the Gouith, the Ahuti, the Alphalim, the Jukneth from the mountains of Caff, and the Homaï of the Arabs, which are the souls of murdered men. He hears the parrots utter human speech, then the great web-footed Pelasgians, who sob like children or chuckle like old women.

A briny breath of air strikes his nostrils. A seashore is now before him.

At a distance rise waterspouts, lashed up by the whales; and at the extremity of the horizon the beasts of the sea, round, like leather bottles, flat, like strips of metal, or indented, like saws, advance, crawling over the sand:

"You are about to come with us into our unfathomable depths, never penetrated by man before. Different races dwell in the country of the ocean. Some are in the abode of the tempests; others swim openly in the transparency of the cold waves, browse like oxen over the coral plains, sniff in with their nostrils the ebbing tide, or carry on their shoulders the weight of the ocean-springs."

Phosphorescences flash from the hairs of the seals and from the scales of the fishes. Sea-hedgehogs turn around like wheels; Ammon's horns unroll themselves like cables; oysters make sounds with the fastenings of their shells; polypi spread out their tentacles; medusæ quiver like crystal balls; sponges float; anemones squirt out water; and mosses and sea-weed shoot up.

And all kinds of plants spread out into branches, twist themselves into tendrils, lenghten into points, and grow round like fans. Pumpkins present the appearance of bosoms, and creeping plants entwine themselves like serpents.

The Dedaims of Babylon, which are trees, have as their fruits human heads; mandrakes sing; and the root Baaras runs into the grass.

And now the plants can no longer be distinguished from the animals. Polyparies, which have the appearance of sycamores, carry arms on their branches. Anthony fancies he can trace a caterpillar between two leaves; it is a butterfly which flits away. He is on the point of walking over some shingle when up springs a grey grasshopper. Insects, like petals of roses, garnish a bush; the remains of ephemera make a bed of snow upon the soil.

And, next, the plants are indistinguishable from the stones.

Pebbles bear a resemblance to brains, stalactites to udders, and iron-dust to tapestries adorned with figures. In pieces of ice he can trace efflorescences, impressions of bushes and shells—so that one cannot tell whether they are the impressions of those objects or the objects themselves. Diamonds glisten like eyes, and minerals palpitate.

And he is no longer afraid! He lies down flat on his face, resting on his two elbows, and, holding in his breath, he gazes around.

Insects without stomachs keep eating; dried-up ferns begin to bloom afresh; and limbs which were wanting sprout forth again.

Finally, he perceives little globular bodies as large as pins' heads, and garnished all round with eyelashes. A vibration agitates them.

Anthony, in ecstasy—

"O bliss! bliss! I have seen the birth of life; I have seen the beginning of motion. The blood beats so strongly in my veins that it seems about to burst them. I feel a longing to fly, to swim, to bark, to bellow, to howl. I would like to have wings, a tortoise-shell, a rind, to blow out smoke, to wear a trunk, to twist my body, to spread myself everywhere, to be in everything, to emanate with odours, to grow like plants, to flow like water, to vibrate like sound, to shine like light, to be outlined on every form, to penetrate every atom, to descend to the very depths of matter—to be matter!"

The dawn appears at last; and, like the uplifted curtains of a tabernacle, golden clouds, wreathing themselves into large volutes, reveal the sky.

In the very middle of it, and in the disc of the sun itself, shines the face of Jesus Christ.

Anthony makes the sign of the Cross, and resumes his prayers.

BOUVARD AND PÉCUCHET
A TRAGI-COMIC NOVEL OF
BOURGEOIS LIFE

CONTENTS

Chapter I

KINDRED SOULS

A S THERE WERE THIRTY-THREE DEGREES OF HEAT THE BOULEVARD BOUR-
don was absolutely deserted.

Farther down, the Canal St. Martin, confined by two locks, showed in a straight line its water black as ink. In the middle of it was a boat, filled with timber, and on the bank were two rows of casks.

Beyond the canal, between the houses which separated the timber-yards, the great pure sky was cut up into plates of ultramarine; and under the reverberating light of the sun, the white façades, the slate roofs, and the granite wharves glowed dazzlingly. In the distance arose a confused noise in the warm atmosphere; and the idleness of Sunday, as well as the melancholy engendered by the summer heat, seemed to shed around a universal languor.

Two men made their appearance.

One came from the direction of the Bastille; the other from that of the Jardin des Plantes. The taller of the pair, arrayed in linen cloth, walked with his hat back, his waistcoat unbuttoned, and his cravat in his hand. The smaller, whose form was covered with a maroon frock-coat, wore a cap with a pointed peak.

As soon as they reached the middle of the boulevard, they sat down, at the same moment, on the same seat.

In order to wipe their foreheads they took off their headgear, each placing his beside himself; and the little man saw "Bouvard" written in his neighbour's hat, while the latter easily traced "Pécuchet" in the cap of the person who wore the frock-coat.

"Look here!" he said; "we have both had the same idea—to write our names in our head-coverings!"

"Yes, faith, for they might carry off mine from my desk."

" 'Tis the same way with me. I am an employé."

Then they gazed at each other. Bouvard's agreeable visage quite charmed Pécuchet.

His blue eyes, always half-closed, smiled in his fresh-coloured face. His trousers, with big flaps, which creased at the end over beaver shoes, took the shape of his stomach, and made his shirt bulge out at the waist; and his fair hair, which of its own accord grew in tiny curls, gave him a somewhat childish look.

He kept whistling continually with the tips of his lips.

Bouvard was struck by the serious air of Pécuchet. One would have thought that he wore a wig, so flat and black were the locks which adorned his high skull. His face seemed entirely in profile, on account of his nose, which descended very low. His legs, confined in tight wrappings of lasting, were entirely out of proportion with the length of his bust. His voice was loud and hollow.

This exclamation escaped him:

"How pleasant it would be in the country!"

But, according to Bouvard, the suburbs were unendurable on account of the noise of the public-houses outside the city. Pécuchet was of the same opinion. Nevertheless, he was beginning to feel tired of the capital, and so was Bouvard.

And their eyes wandered over heaps of stones for building, over the hideous water in which a truss of straw was floating, over a factory chimney rising towards the horizon. Sewers sent forth their poisonous exhalations. They turned to the opposite side; and they had in front of them the walls of the Public Granary.

Decidedly (and Pécuchet was surprised at the fact), it was still warmer in the street than in his own house. Bouvard persuaded him to put down his overcoat. As for him, he laughed at what people might say about him.

Suddenly, a drunken man staggered along the footpath; and the pair began a political discussion on the subject of working-men. Their opinions were similar, though perhaps Bouvard was rather more liberal in his views.

A noise of wheels sounded on the pavement amid a whirlpool of dust. It turned out to be three hired carriages which were going towards Bercy, carrying a bride with her bouquet, citizens in white cravats, ladies with their petticoats huddled up so as almost to touch their armpits, two or three little girls, and a student.

The sight of this wedding-party led Bouvard and Pécuchet to talk about women, whom they declared to be frivolous, waspish, obstinate. In spite of this, they were often better than men; but at other times they were worse. In short, it was better to live without them. For his part, Pécuchet was a bachelor.

"As for me, I'm a widower," said Bouvard, "and I have no children."

"Perhaps you are lucky there. But, in the long run, solitude is very sad."

Then, on the edge of the wharf, appeared a girl of the town with a soldier—sallow, with black hair, and marked with smallpox. She leaned on the soldier's arm, dragging her feet along, and swaying on her hips.

When she was a short distance from them, Bouvard indulged in a coarse remark. Pécuchet became very red in the face, and, no doubt to avoid answering, gave him a look to indicate the fact that a priest was coming in their direction.

The ecclesiastic slowly descended the avenue, along which lean elm trees were placed as landmarks, and Bouvard, when he no longer saw the priest's three-cornered head-piece, expressed his relief; for he hated Jesuits. Pécuchet, without absolving them from blame, exhibited some respect for religion.

Meanwhile, the twilight was falling, and the window-blinds in front of them were raised. The passers-by became more numerous. Seven o'clock struck.

Their words rushed on in an inexhaustible stream; remarks succeeding to anecdotes, philosophic views to individual considerations. They disparaged the management of the bridges and causeways, the tobacco administration, the theatres, our marine, and the entire human race, like people who had undergone great mortifications. In listening to each other both found again some ideas which had long since slipped out of their minds; and though they had passed the age of simple emotions, they experienced a new pleasure, a kind of expansion, the lender charm associated with their first appearance on life's stage.

Twenty times they had risen and sat down again, and had proceeded along the boulevard from the upper to the lower lock, each time intending to take their departure, but not having the strength to do so, held back by a kind of fascination.

However, they came to parting at last, and they had clasped each other's hands, when Bouvard said all of a sudden:

"Faith! what do you say to our dining together?"

"I had the very same idea in my own head," returned Pécuchet, "but I hadn't the courage to pose it to you."

And he allowed himself to be led towards a restaurant facing the Hotel de Ville, where would be comfortable.

Bouvard called for the *menu*. Pécuchet was afraid of spices, as they might inflame his blood. This led to a medical discussion. Then they glorified the utility of science: how many things could be learned, how many researches one could make, if one had only time! Alas! earning one's bread took up all one's time; and they raised their arms in astonishment, and were near embracing each other over the table on discovering that they were both copyists, Bouvard in a commercial establishment, and Pécuchet in the Admiralty, which did not, however, prevent him from devoting a few spare moments each evening to study. He had noted faults in M. Thiers's work, and he spoke with the utmost respect of a certain professor named Dumouchel.

Bouvard had the advantage of him in other ways. His hair watch-chain, and his manner of whipping-up the mustard-sauce, revealed the greybeard, full of experience; and he ate with the corners of his napkin under his armpits, giving utterance to things which made Pécuchet laugh. It was a peculiar laugh, one very low note, always the same, emitted at long intervals. Bouvard's laugh was explosive, sonorous, uncovering his teeth, shaking his shoulders, and making the customers at the door turn round to stare at him.

When they had dined they went to take coffee in another establishment. Pécuchet, on contemplating the gas-burners, groaned over the spreading torrent of luxury; then, with an imperious movement, he flung aside the newspapers. Bouvard was more indulgent on this point. He liked all authors indiscriminately, having been disposed in his youth to go on the stage.

He had a fancy for trying balancing feats with a billiard-cue and two ivory balls, such as Barberou, one of his friends, had performed. They invariably fell, and, rolling along the floor between people's legs, got lost in some distant corner. The waiter, who had to rise every time to search for them on all-fours under the benches, ended by making complaints. Pécuchet picked a quarrel with him; the coffee-house keeper came on the scene, but Pécuchet would listen to no excuses, and even cavilled over the amount consumed.

He then proposed to finish the evening quietly at his own abode, which was quite near, in the Rue St. Martin. As soon as they had entered he put on a kind of cotton nightgown, and did the honours of his apartment.

A deal desk, placed exactly in the centre of the room caused inconvenience by its sharp corners; and all around, on the boards, on the three chairs, on the old arm-chair, and in the corners, were scattered pell-mell a number of volumes of the *Roret Encyclopædia, The Magnetiser's Manual,* a Fénelon, and other old books, with heaps of waste paper, two cocoa-nuts, various medals, a Turkish cap, and shells brought back from Havre by Dumouchel. A layer of dust velveted the walls, which otherwise had been painted yellow. The shoe-brush was lying at the side of the bed, the coverings of which hung down. On the ceiling could be seen a big black stain, produced by the smoke of the lamp.

Bouvard, on account of the smell no doubt, asked permission to open the window.

"The papers will fly away!" cried Pécuchet, who was more afraid of the currents of air.

However, he panted for breath in this little room, heated since morning by the slates of the roof.

Bouvard said to him: "If I were in your place, I would remove my flannel."

"What!" And Pécuchet cast down his head, frightened at the idea of no longer having his healthful flannel waistcoat.

"Let me take the business in hand," resumed Bouvard; "the air from outside will refresh you."

At last Pécuchet put on his boots again, muttering, "Upon my honour, you are bewitching me." And, notwithstanding the distance, he accompanied Bouvard as far as the latter's house at the corner of the Rue de Béthune, opposite the Pont de la Tournelle.

Bouvard's room, the floor of which was well waxed, and which had curtains of cotton cambric and mahogany furniture, had the advantage of a balcony over-looking the river. The two principal ornaments were a liqueur-frame in the middle of the chest of drawers, and, in a row beside the glass, daguerreotypes represent-ing his friends. An oil painting occupied the alcove.

"My uncle!" said Bouvard. And the taper which he held in his hand shed its light on the portrait of a gentleman.

Red whiskers enlarged his visage, which was surmounted by a forelock curling at its ends. His huge cravat, with the triple collar of his shirt, and his velvet waist-coat and black coat, appeared to cramp him. You would have imagined there were diamonds on his shirt-frill. His eyes seemed fastened to his cheekbones, and he smiled with a cunning little air.

Pécuchet could not keep from saying, "One would rather take him for your father!"

"He is my godfather," replied Bouvard carelessly, adding that his baptismal name was François-Denys-Bartholemée.

Pécuchet's baptismal name was Juste-Romain-Cyrille, and their ages were identical—forty-seven years. This coincidence caused them satisfaction, but sur-prised them, each having thought the other much older. They next vented their ad-miration for Providence, whose combinations are sometimes marvellous.

"For, in fact, if we had not gone out a while ago to take a walk we might have died before knowing each other."

And having given eachother their employers' addresses, they exchanged a cor-dial "good night."

"Don't go to see the women!" cried Bouvard on the stairs.

Pécuchet descended the steps without answering this coarse jest.

Next day, in the space in front of the establishment of MM. Descambos Broth-ers, manufacturers of Alsatian tissues, 92, Rue Hautefeuille, a voice called out:

"Bouvard! Monsieur Bouvard!"

The latter glanced through the window-panes and recognised Pécuchet, who articulated more loudly:

"I am not ill! I have remained away!"

"Why, though?"

"This!" said Pécuchet, pointing at his breast.

All the talk of the day before, together with the temperature of the apartment and the labours of digestion, had prevented him from sleeping, so much so that, unable to stand it any longer, he had flung off his flannel waistcoat. In the morn-ing he recalled his action, which fortunately had no serious consequences, and he came to inform Bouvard about it, showing him in this way that he had placed him very high in his esteem.

He was a small shopkeeper's son, and had no recollection of his mother, who died while he was very young. At fifteen he had been taken away from a boarding-school to be sent into the employment of a process-server. The gendarmes invaded his employer's residence one day, and that worthy was sent off to the galleys—a stern history which still caused him a thrill of terror. Then he had attempted many callings—apothecary's apprentice, usher, book-keeper in a packet-boat on the Upper Seine. At length, a head of a department in the Admiralty, smitten by his handwriting, had employed him as a copying-clerk; but the consciousness of a defective education, with the intellectual needs engendered by it, irritated his temper, and so he lived altogether alone, without relatives, without a mistress. His only distraction was to go out on Sunday to inspect public works.

The earliest recollections of Bouvard carried him back across the banks of the Loire into a farmyard. A man who was his uncle had brought him to Paris to teach him commerce. At his majority, he got a few thousand francs. Then he took a wife, and opened a confectioner's shop. Six months later his wife disappeared, carrying off the cash-box. Friends, good cheer, and above all, idleness, had speedily accomplished his ruin. But he was inspired by the notion of utilising his beautiful chirography, and for the past twelve years he had clung to the same post in the establishment of MM. Descambos Brothers, manufacturers of tissues, 92, Rue Hautefeuille. As for his uncle, who formerly had sent him the celebrated portrait as a memento, Bouvard did not even know his residence, and expected nothing more from him. Fifteen hundred francs a year and his salary as copying-clerk enabled him every evening to take a nap at a coffee-house. Thus their meeting had the importance of an adventure. They were at once drawn together by secret fibres. Besides, how can we explain sympathies? Why does a certain peculiarity, a certain imperfection, indifferent or hateful in one person, prove a fascination in another? That which we call the thunderbolt is true as regards all the passions.

Before the month was over they "thou'd" and "thee'd" eachother.

Frequently they came to see eachother at their respective offices. As soon as one made his appearance, the other shut up his writing-desk, and they went off together into the streets. Bouvard walked with long strides, whilst Pécuchet, taking innumerable steps, with his frock-coat flapping at his heels, seemed to slip along on rollers. In the same way, their peculiar tastes were in harmony. Bouvard smoked his pipe, loved cheese, regularly took his half-glass of brandy. Pécuchet snuffed, at dessert ate only preserves, and soaked a piece of sugar in his coffee. One was self-confident, flighty, generous; the other prudent, thoughtful, and thrifty.

· In order to please him, Bouvard desired to introduce Pécuchet to Barberou. He was an ex-commercial traveller, and now a purse-maker—a good fellow, a patriot, a ladies' man, and one who affected the language of the faubourgs. Pécuchet did not care for him, and he brought Bouvard to the residence of Dumouchel. This author (for he had published a little work on mnemonics) gave lessons in literature at a young ladies' boarding-school, and had orthodox opinions and a grave deportment. He bored Bouvard.

Neither of the two friends concealed his opinion from the other. Each recognised the correctness of the other's view. They altered their habits, they quitting their humdrum lodgings, and ended by dining together every day.

They made observations on the plays at the theatre, on the government, the dearness of living, and the frauds of commerce. From time to time, the history of Collier or the trial of Fualdès turned up in their conversations; and then they sought for the causes of the Revolution.

They lounged along by the old curiosity shops. They visited the School of Arts and Crafts, St. Denis, the Gobelins, the Invalides, and all the public collections.

When they were asked for their passports, they made pretence of having lost them, passing themselves off as two strangers, two Englishmen.

In the galleries of the Museum, they viewed the stuffed quadrupeds with amazement, the butterflies with delight, and the metals with indifference; the fossils made them dream; the conchological specimens bored them. They examined the hot-houses through the glass, and groaned at the thought that all these leaves distilled poisons. What they admired about the cedar was that it had been brought over in a hat.

At the Louvre they tried to get enthusiastic about Raphael. At the great library they desired to know the exact number of volumes.

On one occasion they attended at a lecture on Arabic at the College of France, and the professor was astonished to see these two unknown persons attempting to take notes. Thanks to Barberou, they penetrated into the green-room of a little theatre. Dumouchel got them tickets for a sitting at the Academy. They inquired about discoveries, read the prospectuses, and this curiosity developed their intelligence. At the end of a horizon, growing every day more remote, they perceived things at the same time confused and marvellous.

When they admired an old piece of furniture they regretted that they had not lived at the period when it was used, though they were absolutely ignorant of what period it was. In accordance with certain names, they imagined countries only the more beautiful in proportion to their utter lack of definite information about them. The works of which the titles were to them unintelligible, appeared to their minds to contain some mysterious knowledge.

And the more ideas they had, the more they suffered. When a mail-coach crossed them in the street, they felt the need of going off with it. The Quay of Flowers made them sigh for the country.

One Sunday they started for a walking tour early in the morning, and, passing through Meudon, Bellevue, Suresnes, and Auteuil, they wandered about all day amongst the vineyards, tore up wild poppies by the sides of fields, slept on the grass, drank milk, ate under the acacias in the gardens of country inns, and got home very late—dusty, worn-out, and enchanted.

They often renewed these walks. They felt so sad next day that they ended by depriving themselves of them.

The monotony of the desk became odious to them. Always the eraser and the sandarac, the same inkstand, the same pens, and the same companions. Looking on the latter as stupid fellows, they talked to them less and less. This cost them some annoyances. They came after the regular hour every day, and received reprimands.

Formerly they had been almost happy, but their occupation humiliated them since they had begun to set a higher value on themselves, and their disgust increased while they were mutually glorifying and spoiling each other. Pécuchet contracted Bouvard's bluntness, and Bouvard assumed a little of Pécuchet's moroseness.

"I have a mind to become a mountebank in the streets!" said one to the other.

"As well to be a rag-picker!" exclaimed his friend.

What an abominable situation! And no way out of it. Not even the hope of it!

One afternoon (it was the 20th of January, 1839) Bouvard, while at his desk, received a letter left by the postman.

He lifted up both hands; then his head slowly fell back, and he sank on the floor in a swoon.

The clerks rushed forward; they took off his cravat; they sent for a physician. He re-opened his eyes; then, in answer to the questions they put to him:

"Ah! the fact is—the fact is— A little air will relieve me. No; let me alone. Kindly give me leave to go out."

And, in spite of his corpulence, he rushed, all breathless, to the Admiralty office, and asked for Pécuchet.

Pécuchet appeared.

"My uncle is dead! I am his heir!"

"It isn't possible!"

Bouvard showed him the following lines:

OFFICE OF MAÎTRE TARDIVEL, NOTARY.

Savigny-en-Septaine, 14th January, 1839.

SIR—I beg of you to call at my office in order to take notice there of the will of your natural father, M. François-Denys-Bartholomée Bouvard, ex-merchant in the town of Nantes, who died in this parish on the 10th of the present month. This will contains a very important disposition in your favour.   TARDIVEL, *Notary.*

Pécuchet was obliged to sit down on a boundary-stone in the courtyard outside the office.

Then he returned the paper, saying slowly:

"Provided that this is not—some practical joke."

"You think it is a farce!" replied Bouvard, in a stifled voice like the rattling in the throat of a dying man.

But the postmark, the name of the notary's office in printed characters, the notary's own signature, all proved the genuineness of the news; and they regarded each other with a trembling at the corners of their mouths and tears in their staring eyes.

They wanted space to breathe freely. They went to the Arc de Triomphe, came back by the water's edge, and passed beyond Nôtre Dame. Bouvard was very flushed. He gave Pécuchet blows with his fist in the back, and for five minutes talked utter nonsense.

They chuckled in spite of themselves. This inheritance, surely, ought to mount up—?

"Ah! that would be too much of a good thing. Let's talk no more about it."

They did talk again about it. There was nothing to prevent them from immediately demanding explanations. Bouvard wrote to the notary with that view.

The notary sent a copy of the will, which ended thus:

"Consequently, I give to François-Deny-Bartholemée Bouvard, my recognised natural son, the portion of my property disposable by law."

The old fellow had got this son in his youthful days, but he had carefully kept it dark, making him pass for a nephew; and the "nephew" had always called him "my uncle," though he had his own idea on the matter. When he was about forty, M. Bouvard married; then he was left a widower. His two legitimate sons having gone against his wishes, remorse took possession of him for the desertion of his other child during a long period of years. He would have even sent for the lad but for the influence of his female cook. She left him, thanks to the manouevres of the family, and in his isolation, when death drew nigh, he wished to repair the wrongs he had done by bequeathing to the fruit of his early love all that he could of his fortune. It ran up to half a million francs, thus giving the copying-clerk two hundred and fifty thousand francs. The eldest of the brothers, M. Étienne, had announced that he would respect the will.

Bouvard fell into a kind of stupefied condition. He kept repeating in a low tone, smiling with the peaceful smile of drunkards: "An income of fifteen thousand livres!"—and Pécuchet, whose head, however, was stronger, was not able to get over it.

They were rudely shaken by a letter from Tardivel. The other son, M. Alexandre, declared his intention to have the entire matter decided by law, and even to question the legacy, if he could, requiring, first of all, to have everything sealed, and to have an inventory taken and a sequestrator appointed, etc. Bouvard got a bilious attack in consequence. Scarcely had he recovered when he started for Savigny, from which place he returned without having brought the matter nearer to a settlement, and he could only grumble about having gone to the expense of a journey for nothing. Then followed sleepless nights, alternations of rage and hope, of exaltation and despondency. Finally, after the lapse of six months, his lordship Alexandre was appeased, and Bouvard entered into possession of his inheritance.

His first exclamation was: "We will retire into the country!" And this phrase, which bound up his friend with his good fortune, Pécuchet had found quite natural. For the union of these two men was absolute and profound. But, as he did not wish to live at Bouvard's expense, he would not go before he got his retiring pension. Two years more; no matter! He remained inflexible, and the thing was decided.

In order to know where to settle down, they passed in review all the provinces. The north was fertile, but too cold; the south delightful, so far as the climate was concerned, but inconvenient because of the mosquitoes; and the middle portion of the country, in truth, had nothing about it to excite curiosity. Brittany would have suited them, were it not for the bigoted tendency of its inhabitants. As for the regions of the east, on account of the Germanic *patois* they could not dream of it. But there were other places. For instance, what about Forez, Bugey, and Rumois? The maps said nothing about them. Besides, whether their house happened to be in one place or in another, the important thing was to have one. Already they saw themselves in their shirt-sleeves, at the edge of a plat-band, pruning rose trees, and digging, dressing, settling the ground, growing tulips in pots. They would awaken at the singing of the lark to follow the plough; they would go with baskets to gather apples, would look on at butter-making, the thrashing of corn, sheep-shearing, bee-culture, and would feel delight in the lowing of cows and in the scent of new-mown hay. No more writing! No more heads of departments! No more even quarters' rent to pay! For they had a dwelling-house of their own! And they would eat the hens of their own poultry-yard, the vegetables of their own garden, and would dine without taking off their wooden shoes! "We'll do whatever we like! We'll let our beards grow!"

They would purchase horticultural implements, then a heap of things "that might perhaps be useful," such as a tool-chest (there was always need of one in a house), next, scales, a land-surveyor's chain, a bathing-tub in case they got ill, a thermometer, and even a barometer, "on the Gay-Lussac system," for physical experiences, if they took a fancy that way. It would not be a bad thing either (for a person cannot always be working out of doors), to have some good literary works; and they looked out for them, very embarrassed sometimes to know if such a book was really "a library book."

Bouvard settled the question. "Oh! we shall not want a library. Besides, I have my own."

They prepared their plans beforehand. Bouvard would bring his furniture, Pécuchet his big black table; they would turn the curtains to account; and, with a few kitchen utensils, this would be quite sufficient. They swore to keep silent about all this, but their faces spoke volumes. So their colleagues thought them funny. Bouvard, who wrote spread over his desk, with his elbows out, in order the better to round his letters, gave vent to a kind of whistle while half-closing his heavy eyelids with a waggish air. Pécuchet, squatted on a big straw foot-stool, was always carefully forming the pot-hooks of his large handwriting, but all the while swelling his nostrils and pressing his lips together, as if he were afraid of letting his secret slip.

After eighteen months of inquiries, they had discovered nothing. They made journeys in all the outskirts of Paris, both from Amiens to Evreux, and from Fontainebleau to Havre. They wanted a country place which would be a thorough country place, without exactly insisting on a picturesque site; but a limited horizon saddened them.

They fled from the vicinity of habitations, and only redoubled their solitude.

Sometimes they made up their minds; then, fearing they would repent later, they changed their opinion, the place having appeared unhealthy, or exposed to the sea-breeze, or too close to a factory, or difficult of access.

Barberou came to their rescue. He knew what their dream was, and one fine day he called on them to let them know that he had been told about an estate at Chavignolles, between Caen and Falaise. This comprised a farm of thirty-eight hectares, with a kind of château, and a garden in a very productive state.

They proceeded to Calvados, and were quite enraptured. For the farm, together with the house (one would not be sold without the other), only a hundred and forty-three thousand francs were asked. Bouvard did not want to give more than a hundred and twenty thousand.

Pécuchet combated his obstinacy, begged of him to give way, and finally declared that he would make up the surplus himself. This was his entire fortune, coming from his mother's patrimony and his own savings. Never had he breathed a word, reserving this capital for a great occasion.

The entire amount was paid up about the end of 1840, six months before his retirement.

Bouvard was no longer a copying-clerk. At first he had continued his functions through distrust of the future; but he had resigned once he was certain of his inheritance. However, he willingly went back to MM. Descambos; and the night before his departure he stood drinks to all the clerks.

Pécuchet, on the contrary, was morose towards his colleagues, and went off, on the last day, roughly clapping the door behind him.

He had to look after the packing, to do a heap of commissions, then to make purchases, and to take leave of Dumouchel.

The professor proposed to him an epistolary interchange between them, of which he would make use to keep Pécuchet well up in literature; and, after fresh felicitations, wished him good health.

Barberou exhibited more sensibility in taking leave of Bouvard. He expressly gave up a domino-party, promised to go to see him "over there," ordered two aniseed cordials, and embraced him.

Bouvard, when he got home, inhaled over the balcony a deep breath of air, saying to himself, "At last!" The lights along the quays quivered in the water, the rolling of omnibuses in the distance gradually ceased. He recalled happy days spent in this great city, supper-parties at restaurants, evenings at the theatre, gossips with his portress, all his habitual associations; and he experienced a sinking of the heart, a sadness which he dared not acknowledge even to himself.

Pécuchet was walking in his room up to two o'clock in the morning. He would come back there no more: so much the better! And yet, in order to leave behind something of himself, he printed his name on the plaster over the chimney-piece.

The larger portion of the baggage was gone since the night before. The garden implements, the bedsteads, the mattresses, the tables, the chairs, a cooking apparatus, and three casks of Burgundy would go by the Seine, as far as Havre, and would be despatched thence to Caen, where Bouvard, who would wait for them, would have them brought on to Chavignolles.

But his father's portrait, the armchairs the liqueur-case, the old books, the timepiece, all the precious objects were put into a furniture waggon, which would proceed through Nonancourt, Verneuil, and Falaise. Pécuchet was to accompany it.

He installed himself beside the conductor, upon a seat, and, wrapped up in his oldest frock-coat, with a comforter, mittens, and his office foot-warmer, on Sunday, the 20th of March, at daybreak, he set forth from the capital.

The movement and the novelty of the journey occupied his attention during the first few hours. Then the horses slackened their pace, which led to disputes between the conductor and the driver. They selected execrable inns, and, though they were accountable for everything, Pécuchet, through excess of prudence, slept in the same lodgings.

Next day they started again, at dawn, and the road, always the same, stretched out, uphill, to the verge of the horizon. Yards of stones came after each other; the ditches were full of water; the country showed itself in wide tracts of green, monotonous and cold; clouds scudded through the sky. From time to time there was a fall of rain. On the third day squalls arose. The awning of the waggon, badly fastened on, went clapping with the wind, like the sails of a ship. Pécuchet lowered his face under his cap, and every time he opened his snuff-box it was necessary for him, in order to protect his eyes, to turn round completely.

During the joltings he heard all his baggage swinging behind him, and shouted out a lot of directions. Seeing that they were useless, he changed his tactics. He assumed an air of good-fellowship, and made a display of civilities; in the troublesome ascents he assisted the men in pushing on the wheels: he even went so far as to pay for the coffee and brandy after the meals. From that time they went on more slowly; so much so that, in the neighbourhood of Gauburge, the axletree broke, and the waggon remained tilted over. Pécuchet immediately went to inspect the inside of it: the sets of porcelain lay in bits. He raised his arms, while he gnashed his teeth, and cursed these two idiots; and the following day was lost owing to the waggon-driver getting tipsy: but he had not the energy to complain, the cup of bitterness being full.

Bouvard had quitted Paris only on the third day, as he had to dine once more with Barberou. He arrived in the coach-yard at the last moment; then he woke up before the cathedral of Rouen: he had mistaken the *diligence*.

In the evening, all the places for Caen were booked. Not knowing what to do, he went to the Theatre of Arts, and he smiled at his neighbours, telling them he had retired from business, and had lately purchased an estate in the neighbourhood. When he started on Friday for Caen, his packages were not there. He received them on Sunday, and despatched them in a cart, having given notice to the farmer who was working the land that he would follow in the course of a few hours.

At Falaise, on the ninth day of his journey, Pécuchet took a fresh horse, and even till sunset they kept steadily on. Beyond Bretteville, having left the highroad, he got off into a cross-road, fancying that every moment he could see the gable-ends of Chavignolles. However, the ruts hid them from view; they vanished, and then the party found themselves in the midst of ploughed fields. The night was falling. What was to become of them? At last Pécuchet left the waggon behind, and, splashing in the mire, advanced in front of it to reconnoitre. When he drew near farmhouses, the dogs barked. He called out as loudly as ever he could, asking what was the right road. There was no answer. He was afraid, and got back to the open ground. Suddenly two lanterns flashed. He perceived a cabriolet, and rushed forward to meet it. Bouvard was inside.

But where could the furniture waggon be? For an hour they called out to it through the darkness. At length it was found, and they arrived at Chavignolles.

A great fire of brushwood and pine-apples was blazing in the dining-room. Two covers were placed there. The furniture, which had come by the cart, was piled up near the vestibule. Nothing was wanting. They sat down to table.

Onion soup had been prepared for them, also a chicken, bacon, and hard-boiled eggs. The old woman who cooked came from time to time to inquire about their tastes. They replied, "Oh! very good, very good!" and the big loaf, hard to cut, the cream, the nuts, all delighted them. There were holes in the flooring, and the damp was oozing through the walls. However, they cast around them a glance of satisfaction, while eating on the little table on which a candle was burning. Their faces were reddened by the strong air. They stretched out their stomachs; they leaned on the backs of their chairs, which made a cracking sound in consequence, and they kept repeating: "Here we are in the place, then! What happiness! It seems to me that it is a dream!"

Although it was midnight, Pécuchet conceived the idea of taking a turn round the garden. Bouvard made no objection. They took up the candle, and, screening it with an old newspaper, walked along the paths. They found pleasure in mentioning aloud the names of the vegetables.

"Look here—carrots! Ah!—cabbages!"

Next, they inspected the espaliers. Pécuchet tried to discover the buds. Sometimes a spider would scamper suddenly over the wall, and the two shadows of their bodies appeared magnified, repeating their gestures. The ends of the grass let the dew trickle out. The night was perfectly black, and everything remained motionless in a profound silence, an infinite sweetness. In the distance a cock was crowing.

Their two rooms had between them a little door, which was hidden by the papering of the wall. By knocking a chest of drawers up against it, nails were shaken out; and they found the place gaping open. This was a surprise.

When they had undressed and got into bed, they kept babbling for some time. Then they went asleep—Bouvard on his back, with his mouth open, his head bare; Pécuchet on his right side, his knees in his stomach, his head muffled in a cotton night-cap; and the pair snored under the moonlight which made its way in through the windows.

Chapter II

Experiments in Agriculture

HOW HAPPY THEY FELT WHEN THEY AWOKE NEXT MORNING! BOUVARD smoked a pipe, and Pécuchet took a pinch of snuff, which they declared to be the best they had ever had in their whole lives. Then they went to the window to observe the landscape.

In front of them lay the fields, with a barn and the church-bell at the right and a screen of poplars at the left.

Two principal walks, forming a cross, divided the garden into four parts. The vegetables were contained in wide beds, where, at different spots, arose dwarf cypresses and trees cut in distaff fashion. On one side, an arbour just touched an artificial hillock; while, on the other, the espaliers were supported against a wall; and at the end, a railed opening gave a glimpse of the country outside. Beyond the wall there was an orchard, and, next to a hedge of elm trees, a thicket; and behind the railed opening there was a narrow road.

They were gazing on this spectacle together, when a man, with hair turning grey, and wearing a black overcoat, appeared walking along the pathway, striking with his cane all the bars of the railed fence. The old servant informed them that this was M. Vaucorbeil, a doctor of some reputation in the district. She mentioned that the other people of note were the Comte de Faverges, formerly a deputy, and an extensive owner of land and cattle; M. Foureau, who sold wood, plaster, all sorts of things; M. Marescot, the notary; the Abbé Jeufroy; and the widow Bordin, who lived on her private income. The old woman added that, as for herself, they called her Germaine, on account of the late Germain, her husband. She used to go out as a charwoman, but would be very glad to enter into the gentlemen's service. They accepted her offer, and then went out to take a look at their farm, which was situated over a thousand yards away.

When they entered the farmyard, Maître Gouy, the farmer, was shouting at a servant-boy, while his wife, on a stool, kept pressed between her legs a turkey-hen, which she was stuffing with balls of flour.

The man had a low forehead, a thin nose, a downward look, and broad shoulders. The woman was very fair-haired, with her cheek-bones speckled with bran, and that air of simplicity which may be seen in the faces of peasants on the windows of churches.

In the kitchen, bundles of hemp hung from the ceiling. Three old guns stood in a row over the upper part of the chimneypiece. A dresser loaded with flowered crockery occupied the space in the middle of the wall; and the window-panes with their green bottle-glass threw over the tin and copper utensils a sickly lustre.

The two Parisians wished to inspect the property, which they had seen only once—and that a mere passing glance. Maître Gouy and his wife escorted them, and then began a litany of complaints.

All the appointments, from the carthouse to the boilery, stood in need of repair. It would be necessary to erect an additional store for the cheese, to put fresh iron on the railings, to raise the boundaries, to deepen the ponds, and to plant anew a considerable number of apple trees in the three enclosures.

Then they went to look at the lands under cultivation. Maître Gouy ran them down, saying that they ate up too much manure; cartage was expensive; it was impossible to get rid of stones; and the bad grass poisoned the meadows. This depreciation of his land lessened the pleasure experienced by Bouvard in walking over it.

They came back by the hollow path under an avenue of beech trees. On this side the house revealed its front and its courtyard. It was painted white, with a coating of yellow. The carthouse and the storehouse, the bakehouse and the woodshed, made, by means of a return, two lower wings. The kitchen communicated with a little hall. Next came the vestibule, a second hall larger than the other, and the drawing-room. The four rooms on the first floor opened on the corridor facing the courtyard. Pécuchet selected one of them for his collections. The last was to be the library; and, on opening some of the presses, they found a few ancient volumes, but they had no fancy for reading the titles of them. The most urgent matter was the garden.

Bouvard, while passing close to the row of elm trees, discovered under their branches a plaster figure of a woman. With two fingers she held wide her petticoat, with her knees bent and her head over her shoulder, as if she were afraid of being surprised.

"I beg your pardon! Don't inconvenience yourself!"—and this pleasantry amused them so much that they kept repeating it twenty times a day for three months.

Meanwhile, the people of Chavignolles were desirous to make their acquaintance. Persons came to look at them through the railed fence. They slopped up the openings with boards. This thwarted the inhabitants. To protect himself from the sun Bouvard wore on his head a handkerchief, fastened so as to look like a turban. Pécuchet wore his cap, and he had a big apron with a pocket in front, in which a pair of pruning-shears, his silk handkerchief, and his snuffbox jostled against one another. Bare-armed, side by side, they dug, weeded, and pruned, imposing tasks on eachother, and eating their meals as quickly as ever they could, taking care, however, to drink their coffee on the hillock, in order to enjoy the view.

If they happened to come across a snail, they pounced on it and crushed it, making grimaces with the corners of their mouths, as if they were cracking-nuts. They never went out without their grafting implements, and they used to cut the worms in two with such force that the iron of the implement would sink three inches deep. To get rid of caterpillars, they struck the trees furiously with switches.

Bouvard planted a peony in the middle of the grass plot, and tomatoes so that they would hang down like chandeliers under the arch of the arbour.

Pécuchet had a large pit dug in front of the kitchen, and divided it into three parts, where he could manufacture composts which would grow a heap of things, whose detritus would again bring other crops, providing in this way other manures to a limitless extent; and he fell into reveries on the edge of the pit, seeing in the future mountains of fruits, floods of flowers, and avalanches of vegetables. But the horse-dung, so necessary for the beds, was not to be had, inasmuch as the farmers did not sell it, and the innkeepers refused to supply it. At last, after many searches, in spite of the entreaties of Bouvard, and flinging aside all shamefacedness, he made up his mind to go for the dung himself.

It was in the midst of this occupation that Madame Bordin accosted him one day on the high-road. When she had complimented him, she inquired about his friend. This woman's black eyes, very small and very brilliant, her high complexion, and her assurance (she even had a little moustache) intimidated Pécuchet. He replied curtly, and turned his back on her—an impoliteness of which Bouvard disapproved.

Then the bad weather came on, with frost and snow. They installed themselves in the kitchen, and went in for trellis-work, or else kept going from one room to another, chatted by the chimney corner, or watched the rain coming down.

Since the middle of Lent they had awaited the approach of spring, and each morning repeated: "Everything is starting out!" But the season was late, and they consoled their impatience by saying: "Everything is going to start out!"

At length they were able to gather the green peas. The asparagus gave a good crop; and the vine was promising.

Since they were able to work together at gardening, they must needs succeed at agriculture; and they were seized with an ambition to cultivate the farm. With common sense and study of the subject, they would get through it beyond a doubt.

But they should first see how others carried on operations, and so they drew up a letter in which they begged of M. de Faverges to do them the honour of allowing them to visit the lands which he cultivated.

The count made an appointment immediately to meet them.

After an hour's walking, they reached the side of a hill overlooking the valley of the Orne. The river wound its way to the bottom of the valley. Blocks of red sandstone stood here and there, and in the distance larger masses of stone formed, as it were, a cliff overhanging fields of ripe corn. On the opposite hill the verdure was so abundant that it hid the house from view. Trees divided it into unequal squares, outlining themselves amid the grass by more sombre lines.

Suddenly the entire estate came into view. The tiled roofs showed where the farm stood. To the right rose the château with its white façade, and beyond it was a wood. A lawn descended to the river, into which a row of plane trees cast their shadows.

The two friends entered a field of lucern, which people were spreading. Women wearing straw hats, with cotton handkerchiefs round their heads, and paper shades, were lifting with rakes the hay which lay on the ground, while at the end of the plain, near the stacks, bundles were being rapidly flung into a long cart, yoked to three horses.

The count advanced, followed by his manager. He was dressed in dimity; and his stiff figure and mutton-chop whiskers gave him at the same time the air of a magistrate and a dandy. Even when he was speaking, his features did not appear to move.

As soon as they had exchanged some opening courtesies, he explained his system with regard to fodder: the swathes should be turned without scattering them; the ricks should be conical, and the bundles made immediately on the spot, and then piled together by tens. As for the English rake, the meadow was too uneven for such an implement.

A little girl, with her stockingless feet in old shoes, and showing her skin through the rents in her dress, was supplying the women with cider, which she poured out of a jug supported against her hip. The count asked where this child came from, but nobody could tell. The women who were making the hay had picked her up to wait on them during the harvesting. He shrugged his shoulders, and just as he was moving away from the spot, he gave vent to some complaints as to the immorality of our country districts.

Bouvard eulogised his lucern field.

It was fairly good, in spite of the ravages of the *cuscute*.

The future agriculturists opened their eyes wide at the word "cuscute."

On account of the number of his cattle, he resorted to artificial meadowing; besides, it went well before the other crops—a thing that did not always happen in the case of fodder.

"This at least appears to me incontestable."

"Oh! incontestable," replied Bouvard and Pécuchet in one breath. They were on the borders of a field which had been carefully thinned. A horse, which was being led by hand, was dragging along a large box, mounted on three wheels. Seven plough-shares below were opening in parallel lines small furrows, in which the grain fell through pipes descending to the ground.

"Here," said the count, "I sow turnips. The turnip is the basis of my quadren-nial system of cultivation."

And he was proceeding to deliver a lecture on the drill-plough when a servant came to look for him, and told him that he was wanted at the château.

His manager took his place—a man with a forbidding countenance and obse-quious manners.

He conducted "these gentlemen" to another field, where fourteen harvesters, with bare breasts and legs apart, were cutting down rye. The steels whistled in the chaff, which came pouring straight down. Each of them described in front of him a large semicircle, and, all in a line, they advanced at the same time. The two Parisians admired their arms, and felt smitten with an almost religious veneration for the opulence of the soil. Then they proceeded to inspect some of the ploughed lands. The twilight was falling, and the crows swooped down into the ridges.

As they proceeded they met a flock of sheep pasturing here and there, and they could hear their continual browsing. The shepherd, seated on the stump of a tree, was knitting a woollen stocking, with his dog beside him.

The manager assisted Bouvard and Pécuchet to jump over a wooden fence, and they passed close to two orchards, where cows were ruminating under the apple trees.

All the farm-buildings were contiguous and occupied the three sides of the yard. Work was carried on there mechanically by means of a turbine moved by a stream which had been turned aside for the purpose. Leathern bands stretched from one roof to the other, and in the midst of dung an iron pump performed its operations.

The manager drew their attention to little openings in the sheepfolds nearly on a level with the floor, and ingenious doors in the pigsties which could shut of their own accord.

The barn was vaulted like a cathedral, with brick arches resting on stone walls.

In order to amuse the gentlemen, a servant-girl threw a handful of oats before the hens. The shaft of the press appeared to them enormously big. Next they went up to the pigeon-house. The dairy especially astonished them. By turning cocks in the corners, you could get enough water to flood the flagstones, and, as you en-tered, a sense of grateful coolness came upon you as a surprise. Brown jars, ranged close to the barred opening in the wall, were full to the brim of milk, while the cream was contained in earthen pans of less depth. Then came rolls of butter, like fragments of a column of copper, and froth overflowed from the tin pails which had just been placed on the ground.

But the gem of the farm was the ox-stall. It was divided into two sections by wooden bars standing upright their full length, one portion being reserved for the cattle, and the other for persons who attended on them. You could scarcely see there, as all the loopholes were closed up. The oxen were eating, with little chains attached to them, and their bodies exhaled a heat which was kept down by the low ceiling. But someone let in the light, and suddenly a thin stream of water flowed into the little channel which was beside the racks. Lowings were heard, and the horns of the cattle made a rattling noise like sticks. All the oxen thrust their muzzles between the bars, and proceeded to drink slowly.

The big teams made their way into the farm-yard, and the foals began to neigh. On the ground floor two or three lanterns flashed and then disappeared. The workpeople were passing, dragging their wooden shoes over the pebbles, and the bell was ringing for supper.

The two visitors took their departure.

All they had seen delighted them, and their resolution was taken. After that evening, they took out of their library the four volumes of *La Maison Rustique*, went through Gasperin's course of lectures, and subscribed to an agricultural journal.

In order to be able to attend the fairs more conveniently, they purchased a car, which Bouvard used to drive.

Dressed in blue blouses, with large-brimmed hats, gaiters up to their knees, and horse-dealers' cudgels in their hands, they prowled around cattle, asked questions of labourers, and did not fail to attend at all the agricultural gatherings.

Soon they wearied Maître Gouy with their advice, and especially by their depreciation of his system of fallowing. But the farmer stuck to his routine. He asked to be allowed a quarter, putting forward as a reason the heavy falls of hail. As for the farm-dues, he never furnished any of them. His wife raised an outcry at even the most legitimate claims. At length Bouvard declared his intention not to renew the lease.

Thenceforth Maître Gouy economised the manures, allowed weeds to grow up, ruined the soil; and he took himself off with a fierce air, which showed that he was meditating some scheme of revenge.

Bouvard had calculated that 20,000 francs, that is to say, more than four times the rent of the farm, would be enough to start with. His notary sent the amount from Paris.

The property which they had undertaken to cultivate comprised fifteen hectares of grounds and meadows, twenty-three of arable land, and five of waste land, situated on a hillock covered with stones, and known by the name of La Butte.

They procured all the indispensable requirements for the purpose: four horses, a dozen cows, six hogs, one hundred and sixty sheep, and for the household two carters, two women, a shepherd, and in addition a big dog.

In order to get cash at once, they sold their fodder. The price was paid to them directly, and the gold napoleons counted over a chest of oats appeared to them more glittering than any others, more rare and valuable.

In the month of November they brewed cider. It was Bouvard that whipped the horse, while Pécuchet on the trough shovelled off the strained apples.

They panted while pressing the screw, drew the juice off into the vat, looked after the bung-holes, with heavy wooden shoes on their feet; and in all this they found a huge diversion.

Starting with the principle that you cannot have too much corn, they got rid of about half of their artificial meadows; and, as they had not rich pasturing, they made use of oil-cakes, which they put into the ground without pounding, with the result that the crop was a wretched one.

The following year they sowed the ground very thickly. Storms broke out, and the ears of corn were scattered.

Nevertheless, they set their hearts on the cheese, and undertook to clear away the stones from La Butte. A hamper carried away the stones. The whole year, from morn to eve, in sunshine or in rain, the everlasting hamper was seen, with the same man and the same horse, toiling up the hill, coming down, and going up again. Sometimes Bouvard walked in the rear, making a halt half-way up the hill to dry the sweat off his forehead.

As they had confidence in nobody, they treated the animals themselves, giving them purgatives and clysters.

Serious irregularities occurred in the household. The girl in the poultry-yard became *enceinte*. Then they took married servants; but the place soon swarmed with children, cousins, male and female, uncles, and sisters-in-law. A horde of people lived at their expense; and they resolved to sleep in the farm-house successively.

But when evening came they felt depressed, for the filthiness of the room was offensive to them; and besides, Germaine, who brought in the meals, grumbled at every journey. They were preyed upon in all sorts of ways. The threshers in the barn stuffed corn into the pitchers out of which they drank. Pécuchet caught one of them in the act, and exclaimed, while pushing him out by the shoulders:

"Wretch! You are a disgrace to the village that gave you birth!"

His presence inspired no respect. Moreover, he was plagued with the garden.

All his time would not have sufficed to keep it in order. Bouvard was occupied with the farm. They took counsel and decided on this arrangement.

The first point was to have good hotbeds. Pécuchet got one made of brick. He painted the frames himself; and, being afraid of too much sunlight, he smeared over all the bell-glasses with chalk. He took care to cut off the tops of the leaves for slips. Next he devoted attention to the layers. He attempted many sorts of grafting—flute-graft, crown-graft, shield-graft, herbaceous grafting, and whip-grafting. With what care he adjusted the two libers! how he tightened the ligatures! and what a heap of ointment it took to cover them again!

Twice a day he took his watering-pot and swung it over the plants as if he would have shed incense over them. In proportion as they became green under the water, which fell in a thin shower, it seemed to him as if he were quenching his own thirst and reviving along with them. Then, yielding to a feeling of intoxication, he snatched off the rose of the watering-pot, and poured out the liquid copiously from the open neck.

At the end of the elm hedge, near the female figure in plaster, stood a kind of log hut. Pécuchet locked up his implements there, and spent delightful hours there picking the berries, writing labels, and putting his little pots in order. He sat down to rest himself on a box at the door of the hut, and then planned fresh improvements.

He had put two clumps of geraniums at the end of the front steps. Between the cypresses and the distaff-shaped trees he had planted sunflowers; and as the plots were covered with buttercups, and all the walks with fresh sand, the garden was quite dazzling in its abundance of yellow hues.

But the bed swarmed with larvae. In spite of the dead leaves placed there to heat the plants, under the painted frames and the whitened bell-glasses, only a stunted crop made its appearance. He failed with the broccoli, the mad-apples, the turnips, and the watercress, which he had tried to raise in a tub. After the thaw all the artichokes were ruined. The cabbages gave him some consolation. One of them especially excited his hopes. It expanded and shut up quickly, but ended by becoming prodigious and absolutely uneatable. No matter—Pécuchet was content with being the possessor of a monstrosity!

Then he tried his hand at what he regarded as the *summum* of art—the growing of melons.

He sowed many varieties of seed in plates filled with vegetable mould, which he deposited in the soil of the bed. Then he raised another bed, and when it had put forth its virgin buddings he transplanted the best of them, putting bell-glasses over them. He made all the cuttings in accordance with the precepts of *The Good Gardener*. He treated the flowers tenderly; he let the fruits grow in a tangle, and then

selected one on either arm, removed the others, and, as soon as they were as large
as nuts, he slipped a little board around their rind to prevent them from rotting by
contact with dung. He heated them, gave them air, swept off the mist from the bell-
glasses with his pocket-handkerchief, and, if he saw lowering clouds, he quickly
brought out straw mattings to protect them.

He did not sleep at night on account of them. Many times he even got up out
of bed, and, putting on his boots without stockings, shivering in his shirt, he traversed the entire garden to throw his own counterpane over his hotbed frames.

The melons ripened. Bouvard grinned when he saw the first of them. The second was no better; neither was the third. For each of them Pécuchet found a fresh
excuse, down to the very last, which he threw out of the window, declaring that he
could not understand it at all.

The fact was, he had planted some things beside others of a different species;
and so the sweet melons got mixed up with the kitchen-garden melons, the big Por-
tugal with the Grand Mogul variety; and this anarchy was completed by the prox-
imity of the tomatoes—the result being abominable hybrids that had the taste of
pumpkins.

Then Pécuchet devoted his attention to the flowers. He wrote to Dumouchel
to get shrubs with seeds for him, purchased a stock of heath soil, and set to work
resolutely.

But he planted passion-flowers in the shade and pansies in the sun, covered the
hyacinths with dung, watered the lilies near their blossoms, tried to stimulate the
fuchsias with glue, and actually roasted a pomegranate by exposing it to the heat of
the kitchen fire.

When the weather got cold, he screened the eglantines under domes of strong
paper which had been lubricated with a candle. They looked like sugarloaves held
up by sticks.

The dahlias had enormous props; and between these straight lines could be
seen the winding branches of a Sophora Japonica, which remained motionless,
without either perishing or growing.

However, since even the rarest trees flourish in the gardens of the capital, they
must needs grow successfully at Chavignolles; and Pécuchet provided himself
with the Indian lilac, the Chinese rose, and the eucalyptus, then in the beginning of
its fame. But all his experiments failed; and at each successive failure he was vastly
astonished.

Bouvard, like him, met with obstacles. They held many consultations, opened
a book, then passed on to another, and did not know what to resolve upon when
there was so much divergence of opinion.

Thus, Puvis recommends marl, while the Roret Manual is opposed to it. As for plaster, in spite of the example of Franklin, Riefel and M. Rigaud did not appear to be in raptures about it.

According to Bouvard, fallow lands were a Gothic prejudice. However, Leclerc has noted cases in which they are almost indispensable. Gasparin mentions a native of Lyons who cultivated cereals in the same field for half a century: this upsets the theory as to the variation of crops. Tull extols tillage to the prejudice of rich pasture; and there is Major Beetson, who by means of tillage would abolish pasture altogether.

In order to understand the indications of the weather, they studied the clouds according to the classification of Luke Howard. They contemplated those which spread out like manes, those which resemble islands, and those which might be taken for mountains of snow—trying to distinguish the nimbus from the cirrus and the stratus from the cumulus. The shapes had altered even before they had discovered the names.

The barometer deceived them; the thermometer taught them nothing; and they had recourse to the device invented in the time of Louis XIV by a priest from Touraine. A leech in a glass bottle was to rise up in the event of rain, to stick to the bottom in settled weather, and to move about if a storm were threatening. But nearly always the atmosphere contradicted the leech. Three others were put in along with it. The entire four behaved differently.

After many reflections, Bouvard realised that he had made a mistake. His property required cultivation on a large scale, the concentrated system, and he risked all the disposable capital that he had left—thirty thousand francs.

Stimulated by Pécuchet, he began to rave about pasture. In the pit for composts were heaped up branches of trees, blood, guts, feathers—everything that he could find. He used Belgian cordial, Swiss wash, lye, red herrings, wrack, rags; sent for guano, tried to manufacture it himself; and, pushing his principles to the farthest point, he would not suffer even urine or other refuse to be lost. Into his farmyard were carried carcasses of animals, with which he manured his lands. Their cut-up carrion strewed the fields. Bouvard smiled in the midst of this stench. A pump fixed to a dung-cart spattered the liquid manure over the crops. To those who assumed an air of disgust, he used to say, "But 'tis gold! 'tis gold!" And he was sorry that he had not still more manures. Happy the land where natural grottoes are found lull of the excrements of birds!

The colza was thin; the oats only middling; and the corn sold very badly on account of its smell. A curious circumstance was that La Butte, with the stones cleared away from it at last, yielded less than before.

He deemed it advisable to renew his material. He bought a Guillaume scarifier, a Valcourt weeder, an English drill-machine, and the great swing-plough of Mathieu de Dombasle, but the ploughboy disparaged it.

"Do you learn to use it!"

"Well, do you show me!"

He made an attempt to show, but blundered, and the peasants sneered. He could never make them obey the command of the bell. He was incessantly bawling after them, rushing from one place to another, taking down observations in a notebook, making appointments and forgetting all about them—and his head was boiling over with industrial speculations.

He got the notion into his head of cultivating the poppy for the purpose of getting opium from it, and above all the milk-vetch, which he intended to sell under the name of "family coffee."

Finally, in order to fatten his oxen the more quickly, he blooded them for an entire fortnight.

He killed none of his pigs, and gorged them with salted oats. The pigsty soon became too narrow. The animals obstructed the farmyard, broke down the fences, and went gnawing at everything.

In the hot weather twenty-five sheep began to get spoiled, and shortly afterwards died. The same week three bulls perished owing to Bouvard's bloodlettings.

In order to destroy the maggots, he thought of shutting up the fowls in a hencoop on rollers, which two men had to push along behind the plough—a thing which had only the effect of breaking the claws of the fowls.

He manufactured beer with germander-leaves, and gave it to the harvesters as cider. The children cried, the women moaned, and the men raged. They all threatened to go, and Bouvard gave way to them.

However, to convince them of the harmlessness of his beverage, he swallowed several bottles of it in their presence; then he got cramps, but concealed his pains under a playful exterior. He even got the mixture sent to his own residence. He drank some of it with Pécuchet in the evening, and both of them tried to persuade themselves that it was good. Besides, it was necessary not to let it go to waste. Bouvard's colic having got worse, Germaine went for the doctor.

He was a grave-looking man, with a round forehead, and he began by frightening his patient. He thought the gentleman's attack of cholerine must be connected with the beer which people were talking about in the country. He desired to know what it was composed of, and found fault with it in scientific terms with shruggings of the shoulders. Pécuchet, who had supplied the recipe for it, was mortified.

In spite of pernicious limings, stinted redressings, and unseasonable weedings, Bouvard had in front of him, in the following year, a splendid crop of wheat. He thought of drying it by fermentation, in the Dutch fashion, on the Clap-Meyer system: that is to say, he got it thrown down all of a heap and piled up in stacks, which would be overturned as soon as the damp escaped from them, and then exposed to the open air—after which Bouvard went off without the least uneasiness.

Next day, while they were at dinner, they heard under the beech trees the beating of a drum. Germaine ran out to know what was the matter, but the man was by this time some distance away. Almost at the same moment the church-bell rang violently.

Bouvard and Pécuchet felt alarmed, and, impatient to learn what had happened, they rushed bareheaded along the Chavignolles road.

An old woman passed them. She knew nothing about it. They stopped a little boy, who replied:

"I believe it's a fire!"

And the drum continued beating and the bell ringing more loudly than before. At length they reached the nearest houses in the village. The grocer, some yards away, exclaimed:

"The fire is at your place!"

Pécuchet stepped out in double-quick time; and he said to Bouvard, who trotted by his side with equal speed:

"One, two! one, two!"—counting his steps regularly, like the chasseurs of Vincennes.

The road which they took was a continuously uphill one; the sloping ground hid the horizon from their view. They reached a height close to La Butte, and at a single glance the disaster was revealed to them.

All the stacks, here and there, were flaming like volcanoes in the midst of the plain, stripped bare in the evening stillness. Around the biggest of them there were about three hundred persons, perhaps; and under the command of M. Foureau, the mayor, in a tricoloured scarf, youngsters, with poles and crooks, were dragging down the straw from the top in order to save the rest of it.

Bouvard, in his eagerness, was near knocking down Madame Bordin, who happened to be there. Then, seeing one of his servant-boys, he loaded him with insults for not having given him warning. The servant-boy, on the contrary, through excess of zeal, had at first rushed to the house, then to the church, next to where Monsieur himself was staying, and had returned by the other road.

Bouvard lost his head. His entire household gathered round him, all talking together, and he forbade them to knock down the stacks, begged of them to give him some help, called for water, and asked where were the firemen.

"We've got to get them first!" exclaimed the mayor.

"That's your fault!" replied Bouvard.

He flew into a passion, and made use of improper language, and everyone wondered at the patience of M. Foureau, who, all the same, was a surly individual, as might be seen from his big lips and bulldog jaw.

The heat of the stacks became so great that nobody could come close to them any longer. Under the devouring flames the straw writhed with a crackling sound, and the grains of corn lashed one's face as if they were buckshot. Then the stack fell in a huge burning pile to the ground, and a shower of sparks flew out of it, while fiery waves floated above the red mass, which presented in its alternations of colour parts rosy as vermilion and others like clotted blood. The night had come, the wind was swelling; from time to time, a flake of fire passed across the black sky.

Bouvard viewed the conflagration with tears in his eyes, which were veiled by his moist lids, and his whole face was swollen with grief. Madame Bordin, while playing with the fringes of her green shawl, called him "Poor Monsieur!" and tried to console him. Since nothing could be done, he ought to do himself justice.

Pécuchet did not weep. Very pale, or rather livid, with open mouth, and hair stuck together with cold sweat, he stood apart, brooding. But the curé who had suddenly arrived on the scene, murmured, in a wheedling tone:

"Ah! really, what a misfortune! It is very annoying. Be sure that I enter into your feelings."

The others did not affect any regret. They chatted and smiled, with hands spread out before the flame. An old man picked out burning straws to light his pipe with; and one blackguard cried out that it was very funny.

"Yes, 'tis nice fun!" retorted Bouvard, who had just overheard him.

The fire abated, the burning piles subsided, and an hour later only ashes remained, making round, black marks on the plain. Then all withdrew.

Madame Bordin and the Abbé Jeufroy led MM. Bouvard and Pécuchet back to their abode.

On the way the widow addressed very polite reproaches to her neighbour on his unsociableness, and the ecclesiastic expressed his great surprise at not having up to the present known such a distinguished parishioner of his.

When they were alone together, they inquired into the cause of the conflagration, and, in place of recognising, like the rest of the world, that the moist straw had taken fire of its own accord, they suspected that it was a case of revenge. It proceeded, no doubt, from Maître Gouy, or perhaps from the mole-catcher. Six months before Bouvard had refused to accept his services, and even maintained, before a circle of listeners, that his trade was a baneful one, and that the government ought to prohibit it. Since that time the man prowled about the locality. He wore his beard full-grown, and appeared to them frightful-looking, especially in the evening, when he presented himself outside the farmyard, shaking his long pole garnished with hanging moles.

The damage done was considerable, and in order to know their exact position, Pécuchet for eight days worked at Bouvard's books, which he pronounced to be "a veritable labyrinth." After he had compared the day-book, the correspondence, and the ledger covered with pencil-notes and discharges, he realised the truth: no goods to sell, no funds to get in, and in the cash-box zero. The capital showed a deficit of thirty-three thousand francs.

Bouvard would not believe it, and more than twenty times they went over the accounts. They always arrived at the same conclusion. Two years more of such farming, and their fortune would be spent on it! The only remedy was to sell out.

To do that, it was necessary to consult a notary. The step was a disagreeable one: Pécuchet took it on himself.

In M. Marescot's opinion, it was better not to put up any posters. He would speak about the farm to respectable clients, and would let them make proposals.

"Very well," said Bouvard, "we have time before us." He intended to get a tenant; then they would see. "We shall not be more unlucky than before; only now we are forced to practise economy!"

Pécuchet was disgusted with gardening, and a few days later he remarked:

"We ought to give ourselves up exclusively to tree culture—not for pleasure, but as a speculation. A pear which is the product of three soils is sometimes sold in the capital for five or six francs. Gardeners make out of apricots twenty-five thousand livres in the year! At St. Petersburg, during the winter, grapes are sold at a napoleon per grape. It is a beautiful industry, you must admit! And what does it cost? Attention, manuring, and a fresh touch of the pruning-knife."

It excited Bouvard's imagination so much that they sought immediately in their books for a nomenclature for purchasable plants, and, having selected names which appeared to them wonderful, they applied to a nurseryman from Falaise, who busied himself in supplying them with three hundred stalks for which he had not found a sale. They got a locksmith for the props, an iron-worker for the fasteners, and a carpenter for the rests. The forms of the trees were designed beforehand. Pieces of lath on the wall represented candelabra. Two posts at the ends of the plat-bands supported steel threads in a horizontal position; and in the orchard, hoops indicated the structure of vases, cone-shaped switches that of pyramids, so well that, in arriving in the midst of them, you imagined you saw pieces of some unknown machinery or the framework of a pyrotechnic apparatus.

The holes having been dug, they cut the ends of all the roots, good or bad, and buried them in a compost. Six months later the plants were dead. Fresh orders to the nurseryman, and fresh plantings in still deeper holes. But the rain softening the soil, the grafts buried themselves in the ground of their own accord, and the trees sprouted out.

When spring had come, Pécuchet set about the pruning of pear trees. He did not cut down the shoots, spared the superfluous side branches, and, persisting in trying to lay the "duchesses" out in a square when they ought to go in a string on one side, he broke them or tore them down invariably. As for the peach trees, he got mixed up with over-mother branches, under-mother branches, and second-under-mother branches. The empty and the full always presented themselves when they were not wanted, and it was impossible to obtain on an espalier a perfect rectangle, with six branches to the right and six to the left, not including the two principal ones, the whole forming a fine bit of herringbone work.

Bouvard tried to manage the apricot trees, but they rebelled. He lowered their stems nearly to a level with the ground; none of them shot up again. The cherry trees, in which he had made notches, produced gum.

At first, they cut very long, which destroyed the principal buds, and then very short, which led to excessive branching; and they often hesitated, not knowing how to distinguish between buds of trees and buds of flowers. They were delighted to have flowers, but when they recognised their mistake, they tore off three fourths of them to strengthen the remainder.

Incessantly they kept talking about "sap" and "cambium," "paling up," "breaking down," and "blinding of an eye." In the middle of their dining-room they had in a frame the list of their young growths, as if they were pupils, with a number which was repeated in the garden on a little piece of wood, at the foot of the tree. Out of bed at dawn, they kept working till nightfall with their twigs carried in their belts. In the cold mornings of spring. Bouvard wore his knitted vest under his blouse, and Pécuchet his old frock-coat under his packcloth wrapper; and the people passing by the open fence heard them coughing in the damp atmosphere.

Sometimes Pécuchet drew forth his manual from his pocket, and he studied a paragraph of it standing up with his grafting-tool near him in the attitude of the gardener who decorated the frontispiece of the book: This resemblance flattered him exceedingly, and made him entertain more esteem for the author.

Bouvard was continually perched on a high ladder before the pyramids. One day he was seized with dizziness, and, not daring to come down farther, he called on Pécuchet to come to his aid.

At length pears made their appearance, and there were plums in the orchard. Then they made use of all the devices which had been recommended to them against the birds. But the bits of glass made dazzling reflections, the clapper of the wind-mill woke them during the night, and the sparrows perched on the lay figure. They made a second, and even a third, varying the dress, but without any useful result.

However, they could hope for some fruit. Pécuchet had just given an intimation of the fact to Bouvard, when suddenly the thunder resounded and the rain fell—a heavy and violent downpour. The wind at intervals shook the entire surface of the espalier. The props gave way one after the other, and the unfortunate distaff-shaped trees, while swaying under the storm, dashed their pears against one another.

Pécuchet, surprised by the shower, had taken refuge in the hut. Bouvard stuck to the kitchen. They saw splinters of wood, branches, and slates whirling in front of them; and the sailors' wives who, on the sea-shore ten leagues away, were gazing out at the sea, had not eyes more wistful or hearts more anxious. Then, suddenly, the supports and wooden bars of espaliers facing one another, together with the rail-work, toppled down into the garden beds.

What a picture when they went to inspect the scene! The cherries and plums covered the grass, amid the dissolving hailstones. The Passe Colmars were destroyed, as well as the Besi des Vétérans and the Triomphes de Jordoigne. There was barely left amongst the apples even a few Bon Papas; and a dozen Tetons de Venus, the entire crop of peaches, rolled into the pools of water by the side of the box trees, which had been torn up by the roots.

After dinner, at which they ate very little, Pécuchet said softly:

"We should do well to see after the farm, lest anything has happened to it."

"Bah! only to find fresh causes of sadness."

"Perhaps so; for we are not exactly lucky."

And they made complaints against Providence and against nature.

Bouvard, with his elbows on the table, spoke in little whispers; and as all their troubles began to subside, their former agricultural projects came back to their recollection, especially the starch manufacture and the invention of a new sort of cheese.

Pécuchet drew a loud breath; and while he crammed several pinches of snuff into his nostrils, he reflected that, if fate had so willed it, he might now be a member of an agricultural society, might be delivering brilliant lectures, and might be referred to as an authority in the newspapers.

Bouvard cast a gloomy look around him.

"Faith! I'm anxious to get rid of all this, in order that we may settle down somewhere else!"

"Just as you like," said Pécuchet; and the next moment: "The authors recommend us to suppress every direct passage. In this way the sap is counteracted, and

the tree necessarily suffers thereby. In order to be in good health, it would be necessary for it to have no fruit! However, those which we prune and which we never
manure produce them not so big, it is true, but more luscious. I require them to
give me a reason for this! And not only each kind demands its particular attentions,
but still more each individual tree, according to climate, temperature, and a heap
of things! Where, then, is the rule? and what hope have we of any success or
profit?"

Bouvard replied to him, "You will see in Gasparin that the profit cannot exceed
the tenth of the capital. Therefore, we should be doing better by investing this capital in a banking-house. At the end of fifteen years, by the accumulation of interest, we'd have it doubled, without having our constitutions ground down."

Pécuchet hung down his head.

"Arboriculture may be a humbug!"

"Like agriculture!" replied Bouvard.

Then they blamed themselves for having been too ambitious, and they resolved to husband thenceforth their labour and their money. An occasional pruning would suffice for the orchard. The counter-espaliers were forbidden, and dead
or fallen trees should not be replaced; but he was going to do a nasty job—nothing
less than to destroy all the others which remained standing. How was he to set
about the work?

Pécuchet made several diagrams, while using his mathematical case. Bouvard
gave him advice. They arrived at no satisfactory result. Fortunately, they discovered amongst their collection of books Boitard's work entitled *L'Architecte des
Jardins.*

The author divides them into a great number of styles. First there is the melancholy and romantic style, which is distinguished by immortelles, ruins, tombs, and
"a votive offering to the Virgin, indicating the place where a lord has fallen under
the blade of an assassin." The terrible style is composed of overhanging rocks,
shattered trees, burning huts; the exotic style, by planting Peruvian torch-thistles,
"in order to arouse memories in a colonist or a traveller." The grave style should,
like Ermenonville, offer a temple to philosophy. The majestic style is characterised
by obelisks and triumphal arches; the mysterious style by moss and by grottoes;
while a lake is appropriate to the dreamy style. There is even the fantastic style, of
which the most beautiful specimen might have been lately seen in a garden at
Würtemberg—for there might have been met successively a wild boar, a hermit,
several sepulchres, and a barque detaching itself from the shore of its own accord,
in order to lead you into a boudoir where water-spouts lave you when you are settling yourself down upon a sofa.

Before this horizon of marvels, Bouvard and Pécuchet experienced a kind of bedazzlement. The fantastic style appeared to them reserved for princes. The temple to philosophy would be cumbersome. The votive offering of the Madonna would have no signification, having regard to the lack of assassins, and—so much the worse for the colonists and the travellers—the American plants would cost too much. But the rocks were possible, as well as the shattered trees, the immortelles, and the moss; and in their enthusiasm for new ideas, after many experiments, with the assistance of a single man-servant, and for a trifling sum, they made for themselves a residence which had no analogy to it in the entire department.

The elm hedge, open here and there, allowed the light of day to fall on the thicket, which was full of winding paths in the fashion of a labyrinth. They had conceived the idea of making in the espalier wall an archway, through which the prospect could be seen. As the arch could not remain suspended, the result was an enormous breach and a fall of wreckage to the ground.

They had sacrificed the asparagus in order to build on the spot an Etruscan tomb, that is to say, a quadrilateral figure in dark plaster, six feet in height, and looking like a dog-hole. Four little pine trees at the corners flanked the monument, which was to be surmounted by an urn and enriched by an inscription.

In the other part of the kitchen garden, a kind of Rialto projected over a basin, presenting on its margin encrusted shells of mussels. The soil drank up the water—no matter! they would contrive a glass bottom which would keep it back.

The hut had been transformed into a rustic summer-house with the aid of coloured glass.

At the top of the hillock, six trees, cut square, supported a tin headpiece with the edges turned up, and the whole was meant to signify a Chinese pagoda.

They had gone to the banks of the Orne to select granite, and had broken it, marked the pieces with numbers, and carried them back themselves in a cart, then had joined the fragments together with cement, placing them one above the other in a mass; and in the middle of the grass arose a rock resembling a gigantic potato.

Something further was needed to complete the harmony. They pulled down the largest linden tree they had (however, it was three quarters dead), and laid it down the entire length of the garden, in such a way that one would imagine it had been carried thither by a torrent or levelled to the ground by a thunderstorm.

The task finished, Bouvard, who was on the steps, cried from a distance:

"Here! you can see best!"—"See best!" was repeated in the air.

Pécuchet answered:

"I am going there!"—"Going there!"

"Hold on! 'Tis an echo!"—"Echo!"

The linden tree had hitherto prevented it from being produced, and it was assisted by the pagoda, as it faced the barn, whose gables rose above the row of trees.

In order to try the effect of the echo, they amused themselves by giving vent to comical phrases: Bouvard yelled out language of a blackguard description.

He had been several times at Falaise, under the pretence of going there to receive money, and he always came back with little parcels, which he locked up in the chest of drawers. Pécuchet started one morning to repair to Bretteville, and returned very late with a basket, which he hid under his bed. Next day, when he awoke, Bouvard was surprised. The first two yew trees of the principal walk, which the day before were still spherical, had the appearance of peacocks, and a horn with two porcelain knobs represented the beak and the eyes. Pécuchet had risen at dawn, and trembling lest he should be discovered, he had cut the two trees according to the measurement given in the written instructions sent him by Dumouchel.

For six months the others behind the two above mentioned assumed the forms of pyramids, cubes, cylinders, stags, or armchairs; but there was nothing equal to the peacocks. Bouvard acknowledged it with many eulogies.

Under pretext of having forgotten his spade, he drew his comrade into the labyrinth, for he had profited by Pécuchet's absence to do, himself too, something sublime.

The gate leading into the fields was covered over with a coating of plaster, under which were ranged in beautiful order five or six bowls of pipes, representing Abd-el-Kader, negroes, naked women, horses' feet, and death's-heads.

"Do you understand my impatience?"

"I rather think so!"

And in their emotion they embraced eachother.

Like all artists, they felt the need of being applauded, and Bouvard thought of giving a great dinner.

"Take care!" said Pécuchet, "you are going to plunge into entertainments. It is a whirlpool!"

The matter, however, was decided. Since they had come to live in the country, they had kept themselves isolated. Everybody, through eagerness to make their acquaintance, accepted their invitation, except the Count de Faverges, who had been summoned to the capital by business. They fell back on M. Hurel, his factotum.

Beljambe, the innkeeper, formerly a *chef* at Lisieux, was to cook certain dishes; Germaine had engaged the services of the poultry-wench; and Marianne, Madame Bordin's servant-girl, would also come. Since four o'clock the range was wide open; and the two proprietors, full of impatience, awaited their guests.

Hurel stopped under the beech row to adjust his frock-coat. Then the curé stepped forward, arrayed in a new cassock, and, a second later, M. Foureau, in a velvet waistcoat. The doctor gave his arm to his wife, who walked with some difficulty, assisting herself with her parasol. A stream of red ribbons fluttered behind them—it was the cap of Madame Bordin, who was dressed in a lovely robe of shot silk. The gold chain of her watch dangled over her breast, and rings glittered on both her hands, which were partly covered with black mittens. Finally appeared the notary, with a Panama hat on his head, and an eyeglass—for the professional practitioner had not stifled in him the man of the world. The drawing-room floor was waxed so that one could not stand upright there. The eight Utrecht armchairs had their backs to the wall; a round table in the centre supported the liqueur case; and above the mantelpiece could be seen the portrait of Père Bouvard. The shades, reappearing in the imperfect light, made the mouth grin and the eyes squint, and a slight mouldiness on the cheek-bones seemed to produce the illusion of real whiskers. The guests traced a resemblance between him and his son, and Madame Bordin added, glancing at Bouvard, that he must have been a very fine man.

After an hour's waiting, Pécuchet announced that they might pass into the dining-room.

The white calico curtains with red borders were, like those of the drawing-room, completely drawn before the windows, and the sun's rays passing across them, flung a brilliant light on the wainscotings, the only ornament of which was a barometer.

Bouvard placed the two ladies beside him, while Pécuchet had the mayor on his left and the curé on his right.

They began with the oysters. They had the taste of mud. Bouvard was annoyed, and was prodigal of excuses, and Pécuchet got up in order to go into the kitchen and make a scene with Beljambe.

During the whole of the first course, which consisted of a brill with a vol-au-vent and stewed pigeons, the conversation turned on the mode of manufacturing cider; after which they discussed what meats were digestible or indigestible. Naturally, the doctor was consulted. He looked at matters sceptically, like a man who had dived into the depths of science, and yet did not brook the slightest contradiction.

At the same time, with the sirloin of beef, Burgundy was supplied. It was muddy. Bouvard, attributing this accident to the rinsing of the bottles, got them to try three others without more success; then he poured out some St. Julien, manifestly not long enough in bottle, and all the guests were mute. Hurel smiled without discontinuing; the heavy steps of the waiters resounded over the flooring.

Madame Vaucorbeil, who was dumpy and waddling in her gait (she was near her confinement), had maintained absolute silence. Bouvard, not knowing what to talk to her about, spoke of the theatre at Caen.

"My wife never goes to the play," interposed the doctor.

M. Marescot observed that, when he lived in Paris, he used to go only to the Italian operas.

"For my part," said Bouvard, "I used to pay for a seat in the pit sometimes at the Vaudeville to hear farces."

Foureau asked Madame Bordin whether she liked farces.

"That depends on what kind they are," she said.

The mayor rallied her. She made sharp rejoinders to his pleasantries. Then she mentioned a recipe for preparing gherkins. However, her talents for housekeeping were well known, and she had a little farm, which was admirably looked after.

Foureau asked Bouvard, "Is it your intention to sell yours?"

"Upon my word, up to this I don't know what to do exactly."

"What! not even the Escalles piece?" interposed the notary. "That would suit you, Madame Bordin."

The widow replied in an affected manner:

"The demands of M. Bouvard would be too high."

"Perhaps someone could soften him."

"I will not try."

"Bah! if you embraced him?"

"Let us try, all the same," said Bouvard.

And he kissed her on both cheeks, amid the plaudits of the guests.

Almost immediately after this incident, they uncorked the champagne, whose detonations caused an additional sense of enjoyment. Pécuchet made a sign; the curtains opened, and the garden showed itself.

In the twilight it looked dreadful. The rockery, like a mountain, covered the entire grass plot; the tomb formed a cube in the midst of spinaches, the Venetian bridge a circumflex accent over the kidney-beans, and the summer-house beyond a big black spot, for they had burned its straw roof to make it more poetic. The yew trees, shaped like stags or armchairs, succeeded to the tree that seemed thunder-stricken, extending transversely from the elm row to the arbour, where tomatoes hung like stalactites. Here and there a sunflower showed its yellow disk. The Chinese pagoda, painted red, seemed a lighthouse on the hillock. The peacocks' beaks, struck by the sun, reflected back the rays, and behind the railed gate, now freed from its boards, a perfectly flat landscape bounded the horizon.

In the face of their guests' astonishment Bouvard and Pécuchet experienced a veritable delight.

Madame Bordin admired the peacocks above all; but the tomb was not appreciated, nor the cot in flames, nor the wall in ruins. Then each in turn passed over the bridge. In order to fill the basin, Bouvard and Pécuchet had been carrying water in carts all the morning. It had escaped between the foundation stones, which were imperfectly joined together, and covered them over again with lime.

While they were walking about, the guests indulged in criticism.

"In your place that's what I'd have done."—"The green peas are late."—"Candidly, this corner is not all right."—"With such pruning you'll never get fruit."

Bouvard was obliged to answer that he did not care a jot for fruit.

As they walked past the hedge of trees, he said with a sly air:

"Ah! here's a lady that puts us out of countenance: a thousand excuses!"

It was a well-seasoned joke; everyone knew "the lady in plaster."

Finally, after many turns in the labyrinth, they arrived in front of the gate with the pipes. Looks of amazement were exchanged. Bouvard observed the faces of his guests, and, impatient to learn what was their opinion, asked:

"What do you say to it?"

Madame Bordin burst out laughing. All the others followed her example, after their respective ways—the curé giving a sort of cluck like a hen, Hurel coughing, the doctor mourning over it, while his wife had a nervous spasm, and Foureau. an unceremonious type of man, breaking an Abd-el-Kader and putting it into his pocket as a souvenir.

When they had left the tree-hedge, Bouvard, to astonish the company with the echo, exclaimed with all his strength:

"Servant, ladies!"

Nothing! No echo. This was owing to the repairs made in the barn, the gable and the roof having been demolished.

The coffee was served on the hillock; and the gentlemen were about to begin a game of ball, when they saw in front of them, behind the railed fence, a man staring at them.

He was lean and sunburnt, with a pair of red trousers in rags, a blue waistcoat, no shirt, his black beard cut like a brush. He articulated, in a hoarse voice:

"Give me a glass of wine!"

The mayor and the Abbé Jeufroy bad at once recognised him. He had formerly been a joiner at Chavignolles.

"Come, Gorju! take yourself off," said M. Foureau. "You ought not to be asking for alms."

"I! Alms!" cried the exasperated man. "I served seven years in the wars in Africa. I've only just got up out of a hospital. Good God! must I turn cutthroat?"

His anger subsided of its own accord, and, with his two fists on his hips, he surveyed the assembled guests with a melancholy and defiant air. The fatigue of bivouacs, absinthe, and fever, an entire existence of wretchedness and debauchery, stood revealed in his dull eyes. His white lips quivered, exposing the gums. The vast sky, empurpled, enveloped him in a blood-red light; and his obstinacy in remaining there caused a species of terror.

Bouvard, to have done with him, went to look for the remnants of a bottle. The vagabond swallowed the wine greedily, then disappeared amongst the oats, gesticulating as he went.

After this, blame was attached by those present to Bouvard. Such kindnesses encouraged disorder. But Bouvard, irritated at the ill-success of his garden, took up the defence of the people. They all began talking at the same time.

Foureau extolled the government. Hurel saw nothing in the world but landed property. The Abbé Jeufroy complained of the fact that it did not protect religion. Pécuchet attacked the taxes. Madame Bordin exclaimed at intervals, "As for me, I detest the Republic." And the doctor declared himself in favour of progress: "For, indeed, gentlemen, we have need of reforms."

"Possibly," said Foureau; "but all these ideas are injurious to business."

"I laugh at business!" cried Pécuchet.

Vaucorbeil went on: "At least let us make allowance for abilities."

Bouvard would not go so far.

"That is your opinion," replied the doctor; "there's an end of you, then! Good evening. And I wish you a deluge in order to sail in your basin!"

"And I, too, am going," said M. Foureau the next moment; and, pointing to the pocket where the Abd-el-Kader was, "If I feel the want of another, I'll come back."

The curé, before departing, timidly confided to Pécuchet that he did not think this imitation of a tomb in the midst of vegetables quite decorous. Hurel, as he withdrew, made a low bow to the company. M. Marescot had disappeared after dessert. Madame Bordin again went over her recipe for gherkins, promised a second for plums with brandy, and made three turns in the large walk; but, passing close to the linden tree, the end of her dress got caught, and they heard her murmuring:

"My God! what a piece of idiocy this tree is!"

At midnight the two hosts, beneath the arbour, gave vent to their resentment.

No doubt one might find fault with two or three, little details here and there in the dinner; and yet the guests had gorged themselves like ogres, showing that it was not so bad. But, as for the garden, so much depreciation sprang from the blackest jealousy. And both of them, lashing themselves into a rage, went on:

"Ha! water is needed in the basin, is it? Patience! they may see even a swan and fishes in it!"

"They scarcely noticed the pagoda."

"To pretend that the ruins are not proper is an imbecile's view."

"And the tomb objectionable! Why objectionable? Hasn't a man the right to erect one in his own demesne? I even intend to be buried in it!"

"Don't talk like that!" said Pécuchet.

Then they passed the guests in review.

"The doctor seems to me a nice snob!"

"Did you notice the sneer of M. Marescot before the portrait?"

"What a low fellow the mayor is! When you dine in a house, hang it! you should show some respect towards the curios."

"Madame Bordin!" said Bouvard.

"Ah! that one's a schemer. Don't annoy me by talking about her."

Disgusted with society, they resolved to see nobody any more, but live exclusively by themselves and for themselves.

And they spent days in the wine-cellar, picking the tartar off the bottles, revarnished all the furniture, enamelled the rooms; and each evening, as they watched the wood burning, they discussed the best system of fuel.

Through economy they tried to smoke hams, and attempted to do the washing themselves. Germaine, whom they inconvenienced, used to shrug her shoulders. When the time came for making preserves she got angry, and they took up their station in the bakehouse. It was a disused wash-house, where there was, under the faggots, a big, old-fashioned tub, excellently fitted for their projects, the ambition having seized them to manufacture preserves.

Fourteen glass bottles were filled with tomatoes and green peas. They coated the stoppers with quicklime and cheese, attached to the rims silk cords, and then plunged them into boiling water. It evaporated; they poured in cold water; the difference of temperature caused the bowls to burst. Only three of them were saved. Then they procured old sardine boxes, put veal cutlets into them, and plunged them into a vessel of boiling water. They came out as round as balloons. The cold flattened them out afterwards. To continue their experiments, they shut up in other boxes eggs, chiccory, lobsters, a hotchpotch of fish, and a soup!—and they applauded themselves like M. Appert, "on having fixed the seasons." Such discoveries, according to Pécuchet, carried him beyond the exploits of conquerors.

They improved upon Madame Bordin's pickles by spicing the vinegar with pepper; and their brandy plums were very much superior. By the process of steeping ratafia, they obtained raspberry and absinthe. With honey and angelica in a cask of Bagnolles, they tried to make Malaga wine; and they likewise undertook the manufacture of champagne! The bottles of Châblis diluted with water must burst of themselves. Then he no longer was doubtful of success.

Their studies widening, they came to suspect frauds in all articles of food.

They cavilled with the baker on the colour of his bread; they made the grocer their enemy by maintaining that he adulterated his chocolate. They went to Falaise for a jujube, and, even under the apothecary's own eyes, they submitted his paste to the test of water. It assumed the appearance of a piece of bacon, which indicated gelatine.

After this triumph, their pride rose to a high pitch. They bought up the stock of a bankrupt distiller, and soon there arrived in the house sieves, barrels, funnels, skimmers, filters, and scales, without counting a bowl of wood with a ball attached and a Moreshead still, which required a reflecting-furnace with a basket funnel. They learned how sugar is clarified, and the different kinds of boilings, the large and the small system of boiling twice over, the blowing system, the methods of making up in balls, the reduction of sugar to a viscous state, and the making of burnt sugar. But they longed to use the still; and they broached the fine liqueurs, beginning with the aniseed cordial. The liquid nearly always drew away the materials with it, or rather they stuck together at the bottom; at other times they were mistaken as to the amount of the ingredients. Around them shone great copper pans; egg-shaped vessels projected their narrow openings; saucepans hung from the walls. Frequently one of them culled herbs on the table, while the other made the ball swing in the suspended bowl. They stirred the ladles; they tasted the mashes.

Bouvard, always in a perspiration, had no garment on save his shirt and his trousers, drawn up to the pit of his stomach by his short braces; but, giddy as a bird, he would forget the opening in the centre of the cucurbit, or would make the fire too strong.

Pécuchet kept muttering calculations, motionless in his long blouse, a kind of child's smock-frock with sleeves; and they looked upon themselves as very serious people engaged in very useful occupations.

At length they dreamed of a cream which would surpass all others. They would put into it coriander as in Kummel, kirsch as in Maraschino, hyssop as in Chartreuse, amber-seed as in Vespetro cordial, and sweet calamus as in Krambambuly; and it would be coloured red with sandalwood. But under what name should they introduce it for commercial purposes?—for they would want a name easy to retain and yet fanciful. Having turned the matter over a long time, they determined that it should be called "Bouvarine."

About the end of autumn stains appeared in the three glass bowls containing the preserves. The tomatoes and green peas were rotten. That must have been due to the way they had stopped up the vessels. Then the problem of stoppage tormented them. In order to try the new methods, they required money; and the farm had eaten up their resources.

Many times tenants had offered themselves; but Bouvard would not have them. His principal farm-servant carried on the cultivation according to his directions, with a risky economy, to such an extent that the crops diminished and everything was imperilled; and they were talking about their embarrassments when Maître Gouy entered the laboratory, escorted by his wife, who remained timidly in the background.

Thanks to all the dressings they had got, the lands were improved, and he had come to take up the farm again. He ran it down. In spite of all their toils, the profits were uncertain; in short, if he wanted it, that was because of his love for the country, and his regret for such good masters.

They dismissed him coldly. He came back the same evening.

Pécuchet had preached at Bouvard; they were on the point of giving way. Gouy asked for a reduction of rent; and when the others protested, he began to bellow rather than speak, invoking the name of God, enumerating his labours, and extolling his merits. When they called on him to state his terms, he hung down his head instead of answering. Then his wife, seated near the door, with a big basket on her knees, made similar protestations, screeching in a sharp voice, like a hen that has been hurt.

At last the lease was agreed on, the rent being fixed at three thousand francs a year—a third less than it had been formerly.

Before they had separated, Maître Gouy offered to buy up the stock, and the bargaining was renewed.

The valuation of the chattels occupied fifteen days. Bouvard was dying of fatigue. He let everything go for a sum so contemptible that Gouy at first opened his eyes wide, and exclaiming, "Agreed!" slapped his palm.

After which the proprietors, following the old custom, proposed that they should take a "nip" at the house, and Pécuchet opened a bottle of his Malaga, less through generosity than in the hope of eliciting eulogies on the wine.

But the husbandman said, with a sour look, "It's like liquorice syrup." And his wife, "in order to get rid of the taste," asked for a glass of brandy.

A graver matter engaged their attention. All the ingredients of the "Bouvarine" were now collected. They heaped them together in the cucurbit, with the alcohol, lighted the fire, and waited. However, Pécuchet, annoyed by the misadventure about the Malaga, took the tin boxes out of the cupboard and pulled the lid off the first, then off the second, and then off the third. He angrily flung them down, and called out to Bouvard. The latter had fastened the cock of the worm in order to try the effect on the preserves.

The disillusion was complete. The slices of veal were like boiled boot-soles; a muddy fluid had taken the place of the lobster; the fish-stew was unrecognisable;

mushroom growths had sprouted over the soup, and an intolerable smell tainted the laboratory.

Suddenly, with the noise of a bombshell, the still burst into twenty pieces, which jumped up to the ceiling, smashing the pots, flattening out the skimmers, and shattering the glasses. The coal was scattered about, the furnace was demolished, and next day Germaine found a spatula in the yard.

The force of the steam had broken the instrument to such an extent that the cucurbit was pinned to the head of the still.

Pécuchet immediately found himself squatted behind the vat, and Bouvard lay like one who had fallen over a stool. For ten minutes they remained in this posture, not daring to venture on a single movement, pale with terror, in the midst of broken glass. When they were able to recover the power of speech, they asked themselves what was the cause of so many misfortunes, and of the last above all? And they could understand nothing about the matter except that they were near being killed. Pécuchet finished with these words:

"It is, perhaps, because we do not know chemistry!"

Chapter III

AMATEUR CHEMISTS

IN ORDER TO UNDERSTAND CHEMISTRY THEY PROCURED REGNAULT'S COURSE of lectures, and were, in the first place, informed that "simple bodies are perhaps compound." They are divided into metalloids and metals—a difference in which, the author observes, there is "nothing absolute." So with acids and bases, "a body being able to behave in the manner of acids or of bases, according to circumstances."

The notation appeared to them irregular. The multiple proportions perplexed Pécuchet.

"Since one molecule of *a*, I suppose, is combined with several particles of *b*, it seems to me that this molecule ought to be divided into as many particles; but, if it is divided, it ceases to be unity, the primordial molecule. In short, I do not understand."

"No more do I," said Bouvard.

And they had recourse to a work less difficult, that of Girardin, from which they acquired the certainty that ten litres of air weigh a hundred grammes, that lead does not go into pencils, and that the diamond is only carbon.

What amazed them above all is that the earth, as an element, does not exist.

They grasped the working of straw, gold, silver, the lye-washing of linen, the tinning of saucepans; then, without the least scruple, Bouvard and Pécuchet launched into organic chemistry.

What a marvel to find again in living beings the same substances of which the minerals are composed! Nevertheless they experienced a sort of humiliation at the idea that their own personality contained phosphorus, like matches; albumen, like the whites of eggs; and hydrogen gas, like street-lamps.

After colours and oily substances came the turn of fermentation. This brought them to acids—and the law of equivalents once more confused them. They tried to elucidate it by means of the atomic theory, which fairly swamped them.

In Bouvard's opinion instruments would have been necessary to understand all this. The expense was very great, and they had incurred too much already. But, no doubt, Dr. Vaucorbeil could enlighten them.

They presented themselves during his consultation hours.

"I hear you, gentlemen. What is your ailment?"

Pécuchet replied that they were not patients, and, having stated the object of their visit:

"We want to understand, in the first place, the higher atomicity."

The physician got very red, then blamed them for being desirous to learn chemistry.

"I am not denying its importance, you may be sure; but really they are shoving it in everywhere! It exercises a deplorable influence on medicine."

And the authority of his language was strengthened by the appearance of his surroundings. Over the chimney-piece trailed some diachylum and strips for binding. In the middle of the desk stood the surgical case. A basin in a corner was full of probes, and close to the wall there was a representation of a human figure deprived of the skin.

Pécuchet complimented the doctor on it.

"It must be a lovely study, anatomy."

M. Vaucorbeil expatiated on the fascination he had formerly found in dissections; and Bouvard inquired what were the analogies between the interior of a woman and that of a man.

In order to satisfy him, the doctor fetched from his library a collection of anatomical plates.

"Take them with you! You can look at them more at your ease in your own house."

The skeleton astonished them by the prominence of the jawbone, the holes for the eyes, and the frightful length of the hands.

They stood in need of an explanatory work. They returned to M. Vaucorbeil's residence, and, thanks to the manual of Alexander Lauth, they learned the divisions of the frame, wondering at the backbone, sixteen times stronger, it is said, than if the Creator had made it straight (why sixteen times exactly?). The metacarpals drove Bouvard crazy; and Pécuchet, who was in a desperate state over the cranium, lost courage before the sphenoid, although it resembles a Turkish or "Turkesque" saddle.

As for the articulations, they were hidden under too many ligaments; so they attacked the muscles. But the insertions were not easily discovered; and when they came to the vertebral grooves they gave it up completely.

Then Pécuchet said:

"If we took up chemistry again, would not this be only utilising the laboratory?"

Bouvard protested, and he thought he had a recollection of artificial corpses being manufactured according to the custom of hot countries.

Barberou, with whom he communicated, gave him some information about the matter. For ten francs a month they could have one of the manikins of M. Auzoux; and the following week the carrier from Falaise deposited before their gate an oblong box.

Full of emotion, they carried it into the bake-house. When the boards were unfastened, the straw fell down, the silver paper slipped off, and the anatomical fig-ure made its appearance.

It was brick-coloured, without hair or skin, and variegated with innumerable strings, red, blue, and white. It did not look like a corpse, but rather like a kind of plaything, very ugly, very clean, and smelling of varnish.

They next took off the thorax; and they perceived the two lungs, like a pair of sponges, the heart like a big egg, slightly sidewise behind the diaphragm, the kid-neys, the entire bundle of entrails.

"To work!" said Pécuchet. The day and the evening were spent at it. They had put blouses on, just as medical students do in the dissecting-rooms; and, by the light of three candles, they were working at their pieces of pasteboard, when a list knocked at the door.

"Open!"

It was M. Foureau, followed by the keeper.

Germaine's masters were pleased to show him the manikin. She had rushed im-mediately to the grocer's shop to tell the thing, and the whole village now imagined that they had a real corpse concealed in their house. Foureau, yielding to the pub-lic clamour, had come to make sure about the fact. A number of persons, anxious for information, stood outside the porch.

When he entered, the manikin was lying on its side, and the muscles of the face, having been loosened, caused a monstrous protrusion, and looked frightful.

"What brings you here?" said Pécuchet.

Foureau stammered: "Nothing, nothing at all." And, taking up one of the pieces from the table, "What is this?"

"The buccinator," replied Bouvard.

Foureau said nothing, but smiled in a sly fashion, jealous of their having an amusement which he could not afford.

The two anatomists pretended to be pursuing their investigations. The people outside, getting bored with waiting, made their way into the bake-house, and, as they began pushing one another a little, the table shook.

"Ah! this is too annoying," exclaimed Pécuchet. "Let us be rid of the public!"

The keeper made the busybodies take themselves off.

"Very well," said Bouvard; "we don't want anyone."

Foureau understood the allusion, and put it to them whether, not being med-ical men, they had the right to keep such an object in their possession. However, he was going to write to the prefect.

What a country district it was! There could be nothing more foolish, bar-barous, and retrograde. The comparison which they instituted between themselves and the others consoled them—they felt a longing to suffer in the cause of science.

The doctor, too, came to see them. He disparaged the model as too far removed from nature, but took advantage of the occasion to give them a lecture.

Bouvard and Pécuchet were delighted; and at their request M. Vaucorbeil lent them several volumes out of his library, declaring at the same time that they would not reach the end of them. They took note of the cases of childbirth, longevity, obesity, and extraordinary constipation given in the *Dictionary of Medical Sciences*. Would that they had known the famous Canadian, De Beaumont, the polyphagi, Tarare and Bijou, the dropsical woman from the department of Eure, the Piedmontese who went every twenty days to the water-closet, Simon de Mirepoix, who was ossified at the time of his death, and that ancient mayor of Angoulême whose nose weighed three pounds!

The brain inspired them with philosophic reflections. They easily distinguished in the interior of it the *septum lucidum*, composed of two lamellæ, and the pineal gland, which is like a litlle red pea. But there were peduncles and ventricles, arches, columns, strata, ganglions, and fibres of all kinds, and the foramen of Pacchioni and the "body" of Paccini; in short, an inextricable mass of details, enough to wear their lives out.

Sometimes, in a fit of dizziness, they would take the figure completely to pieces, then would get perplexed about putting back each part in its proper place. This was troublesome work, especially after breakfast, and it was not long before they were both asleep, Bouvard with drooping chin and protruding stomach, and Pécuchet with his hands over his head and both elbows on the table.

Often at that moment M. Vaucorbeil, having finished his morning rounds, would open the door.

"Well, comrades, how goes anatomy?"

"Splendidly," they would answer.

Then he would put questions to them, for the pleasure of confusing them.

When they were tired of one organ they went on to another, in this way taking up and then throwing aside the heart, the stomach, the ear, the intestines; for the pasteboard manikin bored them to death, despite their efforts to become interested in him. At last the doctor came on them suddenly, just as they were nailing him up again in his box.

"Bravo! I expected that."

At their age they could not undertake such studies; and the smile that accompanied these words wounded them deeply.

What right had he to consider them incapable? Did science belong to this gentleman, as if he were himself a very superior personage? Then, accepting his challenge, they went all the way to Bayeux to purchase books there. What they required was physiology, and a second-hand bookseller procured for them the treatises of Richerand and Adelon, celebrated at the period.

All the commonplaces as to ages, sexes, and temperaments appeared to them of the highest importance. They were much pleased to learn that there are in the tartar of the teeth three kinds of animalcules, that the seat of taste is in the tongue, and the sensation of hunger in the stomach.

In order to grasp its functions better, they regretted that they had not the faculty of ruminating, as Montègre, M. Gosse, and the brother of Gerard had; and they masticated slowly, reduced the food to pulp, and insalivated it, accompanying in thought the alimentary mass passing into their intestines, and following it with methodical scrupulosity and an almost religious attention to its final consequences.

In order to produce digestion artificially, they piled up meat in a bottle, in which was the gastric juice of a duck, and they carried it under their armpits for a fortnight, without any other result, save making their persons smell unpleasantly. You might have seen them running along the high-road in wet clothes under a burning sun. This was for the purpose of determining whether thirst is quenched by the application of water to the epidermis. They came back out of breath, both of them having caught cold.

Experiments in hearing, speech, and vision were then made in a lively fashion; but Bouvard made a show-off on the subject of generation.

Pécuchet's reserve with regard to this question had always surprised him. His friend's ignorance appeared to him so complete that Bouvard pressed him for an explanation, and Pécuchet, colouring, ended by making an avowal.

Some rascals had on one occasion dragged him into a house of ill-fame, from which he made his escape, preserving himself for the woman whom he might fall in love with some day. A fortunate opportunity had never come to him, so that, what with bashfulness, limited means, obstinacy, the force of custom, at fifty-two years, and in spite of his residence in the capital, he still possessed his virginity.

Bouvard found difficulty in believing it; then he laughed hugely, but stopped on perceiving tears in Pécuchet's eyes—for he had not been without attachments, having by turns been smitten by a rope-dancer, the sister-in-law of an architect, a bar-maid, and a young washerwoman; and the marriage had even been arranged when he had discovered that she was *enceinte* by another man.

Bouvard said to him:

"There is always a way to make up for lost time. Come—no sadness! I will take it on myself, if you like."

Pécuchet answered, with a sigh, that he need not think any more about it; and they went on with their physiology.

Is it true that the surfaces of our bodies are always letting out a subtle vapour? The proof of it is that the weight of a man is decreasing every minute. If each day what is wanting is added and what is excessive subtracted, the health would be kept in perfect equilibrium. Sanctorius, the discoverer of this law, spent half a century weighing his food every day together with its excretions, and took the weights himself, giving himself no rest, save for the purpose of writing down his computations.

They tried to imitate Sanctorius; but, as their scales could not bear the weight of both of them, it was Pécuchet who began.

He took his clothes off, in order not to impede the perspiration, and he stood on the platform of the scales perfectly naked, exposing to view, in spite of his modesty, his unusually long torso, resembling a cylinder, together with his short legs and his brown skin. Beside him, on his chair, his friend read for him:

" 'Learned men maintain that animal heat is developed by the contractions of the muscles, and that it is possible by moving the thorax and the pelvic regions to raise the temperature of a warm bath.' "

Bouvard went to look for their bathing-tub, and, when everything was ready, plunged into it, provided with a thermometer. The wreckage of the distillery, swept towards the end of the room, presented in the shadow the indistinct outlines of a hillock. Every now and then they could hear the mice nibbling; there was a stale odour of aromatic plants, and finding it rather agreeable, they chatted serenely.

However, Bouvard felt a little cool.

"Move your members about!" said Pécuchet.

He moved them, without at all changing with the thermometer. " 'Tis decidedly cold."

"I am not hot either," returned Pécuchet, himself seized with a fit of shivering. "But move about your pelvic regions—move them about!"

Bouvard spread open his thighs, wriggled his sides, balanced his stomach, pulled like a whale, then looked at the thermometer, which was always falling.

"I don't understand this at all! Anyhow, I am stirring myself!"

"Not enough!"

And he continued his gymnastics.

This had gone on for three hours when once more he grasped the tube.

"What! twelve degrees! Oh, good-night! I'm off to bed!"

A dog came in, half mastiff, half hound, mangy, with yellowish hair and lolling tongue.

What were they to do? There was no bell, and their housekeeper was deaf. They were quaking, but did not venture to budge, for fear of being bitten.

Pécuchet thought it a good idea to hurl threats at him, and at the same time to roll his eyes about.

Then the dog began to bark; and he jumped about the scales, in which Pécuchet, by clinging on to the cords and bending his knees, tried to raise himself up as high as ever he could.

"You're getting your death of cold up there!" said Bouvard; and he began making smiling faces at the dog, while pretending to give him things.

The dog, no doubt, understood these advances. Bouvard went so far as to caress him, stuck the animal's paws on his shoulders, and rubbed them with his finger-nails.

"Hollo! look here! there, he's off with my breeches!"

The clog cuddled himself upon them, and lay quiet.

At last, with the utmost precautions, they ventured the one to come down from the platform of the scales, and the other to get out of the bathing-tub; and when Pécuchet had got his clothes on again, he gave vent to this exclamation:

"You, my good fellow, will be of use for our experiments."

What experiments? They might inject phosphorus into him, and then shut him up in a cellar, in order to see whether he would emit fire through the nostrils.

But how were they to inject it? and furthermore, they could not get anyone to sell them phosphorus.

They thought of putting him under a pneumatic bell, of making him inhale gas, and of giving him poison to drink. All this, perhaps, would not be funny! Eventually, they thought the best thing they could do was to apply a steel magnet to his spinal marrow.

Bouvard, repressing his emotion, handed some needles on a plate to Pécuchet, who fixed them against the vertebra. They broke, slipped, and fell on the ground. He took others, and quickly applied them at random. The dog burst his bonds, passed like a cannon-ball through the window, ran across the yard to the vestibule, and presented himself in the kitchen.

Germaine screamed when she saw him soaked with blood, and with twine round his paws.

Her masters, who had followed him, came in at the same moment. He made one spring and disappeared.

The old servant turned on them.

"This is another of your tomfooleries, I'm sure! And my kitchen, too! It's nice! This perhaps will drive him mad! People are in jail who are not as bad as you!"

They got back to the laboratory in order to examine the magnetic needles.

Not one of them had the least particle of the filings drawn off.

Then Germaine's assumption made them uneasy. He might get rabies, come back unawares, and make a dash at them.

Next day they went making inquiries everywhere, and for many years they turned up a by-path whenever they saw in the open country a dog at all resembling this one.

Their other experiments were unsuccessful. Contrary to the statements in the text-books, the pigeons which they bled, whether their stomachs were full or empty, died in the same space of time. Kittens sunk under water perished at the end of five minutes; and a goose, which they had stuffed with madder, presented periostea that were perfectly white.

The question of nutrition puzzled them.

How did it happen that the same juice is produced by bones, blood, lymph, and excrementitious materials? But one cannot follow the metamorphoses of an article of food. The man who uses only one of them is chemically equal to him who absorbs several. Vauquelin, having made a calculation of all the lime contained in the oats given as food to a hen, found a greater quantity of it in the shells of her eggs. So, then, a creation of substance takes place. In what way? Nothing is known about it.

It is not even known what is the strength of the heart. Borelli says it is what is necesssary for lifting a weight of one hundred and eighty thousand pounds, while Kiell estimates it at about eight ounces; and from this they drew the conclusion that physiology is—as a well-worn phrase expresses it—the romance of medicine. As they were unable to understand it, they did not believe in it.

A month slipped away in doing nothing. Then they thought of their garden. The dead tree, displayed in the middle of it, was annoying, and accordingly they squared it. This exercise fatigued them. Bouvard very often found it necessary to get the blacksmith to put his tools in order.

One day, as he was making his way to the forge, he was accosted by a man carrying a canvas bag on his back, who offered to sell him almanacs, pious books, holy medals, and lastly, the *Health Manual* of François Raspail.

This little book pleased him so much that he wrote to Barberou to send him the large work. Barberou sent it on, and in his letter mentioned an apothecary's shop for the prescriptions given in the work.

The simplicity of the doctrine charmed them. All diseases proceed from worms. They spoil the teeth, make the lungs hollow, enlarge the liver, ravage the intestines, and cause noises therein. The best thing for getting rid of them is camphor. Bouvard and Pécuchet adopted it. They took it in snuff, they chewed it and distributed it in cigarettes, in bottles of sedative water and pills of aloes. They even undertook the care of a hunchback. It was a child whom they had come across one fair-day. His mother, a beggar woman, brought him to them every morning. They rubbed his hump with camphorated grease, placed there for twenty minutes a mustard poultice, then covered it over with diachylum, and, in order to make sure of his coming back, gave him his breakfast.

As his mind was fixed on intestinal worms, Pécuchet noticed a singular spot on Madame Bordin's cheek. The doctor had for a long time been treating it with bitters. Round at first as a twenty-sou piece, this spot had enlarged and formed a red circle. They offered to cure it for her. She consented, but made it a condition that the ointment should be applied by Bouvard. She took a seat before the window, un-fastened the upper portion of her corset, and remained with her cheek turned up, looking at him with a glance of her eye which would have been dangerous were it not for Pécuchet's presence. In the prescribed doses, and in spite of the horror felt with regard to mercury, they administered calomel. One month afterwards Madame Bordin was cured. She became a propagandist in their behalf, and the tax-collector, the mayor's secretary, the mayor himself, and everybody in Chavignolles sucked camphor by the aid of quills.

However, the hunchback did not get straight; the collector gave up his ciga-rette; it stopped up his chest twice as much. Foureau made complaints that the pills of aloes gave him hemorrhoids. Bouvard got a stomachache, and Pécuchet fearful headaches. They lost confidence in Raspail, but took care to say nothing about it, fearing that they might lessen their own importance.

They now exhibited great zeal about vaccine, learned how to bleed people over cabbage leaves, and even purchased a pair of lancets.

They accompanied the doctor to the houses of the poor, and then consulted their books. The symptoms noticed by the writers were not those which they had just observed. As for the names of diseases, they were Latin, Greek, French—a medley of every language. They are to be counted by thousands; and Linnæus's system of classification, with its genera and its species, is exceedingly convenient; but how was the species to be fixed? Then they got lost in the philosophy of med-icine. They raved about the life-principle of Van Helmont, vitalism, Brownism, or-ganicism, inquired of the doctor whence comes the germ of scrofula, towards what point the infectious miasma inclines, and the means in all cases of disease to distin-guish the cause from its effects.

"The cause and the effect are entangled in one another," replied Vaucorbeil.

His want of logic disgusted them—and they went by themselves to visit the sick, making their way into the houses on the pretext of philanthropy. At the fur-ther end of rooms, on dirty mattresses, lay persons with faces hanging on one side, others who had them swollen or scarlet, or lemon-coloured, or very violet-hued, with pinched nostrils, trembling mouths, rattlings in the throat, hiccoughs, perspi-rations, and emissions like leather or stale cheese.

They read the prescriptions of their physicians, and were surprised at the fact that anodynes are sometimes excitants, and emetics purgatives, that the same rem-edy suits different ailments, and that a malady may disappear under opposite sys-tems of treatment.

Nevertheless, they gave advice, got on the moral hobby again, and had the assurance to auscultate. Their imagination began to ferment. They wrote to the king, in order that there might be established in Calvados an institute of nurses for the sick, of which they would be the professors.

They would go to the apothecary at Bayeux (the one at Falaise had always a grudge against them on account of the jujube affair), and they gave him directions to manufacture, like the ancients, *pila purgatoria,* that is to say, medicaments in the shape of pellets, which, by dint of handling, become absorbed in the individual.

In accordance with the theory that by diminishing the heat we impede the watery humours, they suspended in her armchair to the beams of the ceiling a woman suffering from meningitis, and they were swinging her with all their force when the husband, coming on the scene, kicked them out. Finally, they scandalised the curé thoroughly by introducing the new fashion of thermometers in the rectum.

Typhoid fever broke out in the neighbourhood. Bouvard declared that he would not have anything to do with it. But the wife of Gouy, their farmer, came groaning to them. Her man was a fortnight sick, and M. Vaucorbeil was neglecting him. Pécuchet devoted himself to the case.

Lenticular spots on the chest, pains in the joints, stomach distended, tongue red, these were all symptoms of dothienenteritis. Recalling the statement of Raspail that by taking away the regulation of diet the fever may be suppressed, he ordered broth and a little meat.

The doctor suddenly made his appearance. His patient was on the point of eating, with two pillows behind his back, between his wife and Pécuchet, who were sustaining him. He drew near the bed, and flung the plate out through the window, exclaiming:

"This is a veritable murder!"

"Why?"

"You perforate the intestine, since typhoid fever is an alteration of its follicular membrane."

"Not always!"

And a dispute ensued as to the nature of fevers. Pécuchet believed that they were essential in themselves; Vaucorbeil made them dependent, on our bodily organs.

"Therefore, I remove everything that might excite them excessively."

"But regimen weakens the vital principle."

"What twaddle are you talking with your vital principle? What is it? Who has seen it?"

Pécuchet got confused.

"Besides," said the physician, "Gouy does not want food."

The patient made a gesture of assent under his cotton nightcap.

"No matter, he requires it!"

"Not a bit! his pulse is at ninety-eight!"

"What matters about his pulse?" And Pécuchet proceeded to give authorities.

"Let systems alone!" said the doctor.

Pécuchet folded his arms. "So then, you are an empiric?"

"By no means; but by observing——"

"But if one observes badly?"

Vaucorbeil took this phrase for an allusion to Madame Bordin's skin eruption—a story about which the widow had made a great outcry, and the recollection of which irritated him.

"To start with, it is necessary to have practised."

"Those who revolutionised the science did not practise—Van Helmont, Boerhaave, Broussais himself."

Without replying, Vaucorbeil stooped towards Gouy, and raising his voice:

"Which of us two do you select as your doctor?"

The patient, who was falling asleep, perceived angry faces, and began to blubber. His wife did not know either what answer to make, for the one was clever, but the other had perhaps a secret.

"Very well," said Vaucorbeil, "since you hesitate between a man furnished with a diploma——"

Pécuchet sneered.

"Why do you laugh?"

"Because a diploma is not always an argument."

The doctor saw himself attacked in his means of livelihood, in his prerogative, in his social importance. His wrath gave itself full vent.

"We shall see that when you are brought up before the courts for illegally practising medicine!" Then, turning round to the farmer's wife, "Get him killed by this gentleman at your ease, and I'm hanged if ever I come back to your house!"

And he dashed past the beech trees, shaking his walking-stick as he went.

When Pécuchet returned, Bouvard was himself in a very excited state. He had just had a visit from Foureau, who was exasperated about his hemorrhoids. Vainly had he contended that they were a safeguard against every disease. Foureau, who would listen to nothing, had threatened him with an action for damages. He lost his head over it.

Pécuchet told him the other story, which he considered more serious, and was a little shocked at Bouvard's indifference.

Gouy, next day, had a pain in his abdomen. This might be due to the ingestion of the food. Perhaps Vaucorbeil was not mistaken. A physician, after all, ought to have some knowledge of this! And a feeling of remorse took possession of Pécuchet! He was afraid lest he might turn out a homicide.

For prudence' sake they sent the hunchback away. But his mother cried a great deal at his losing the breakfast, not to speak of the infliction of having made them come every day from Barneval to Chavignolles.

Foureau calmed down, and Gouy recovered his strength. At the present moment the cure was certain. A success like this emboldened Pécuchet.

"If we studied obstetrics with the aid of one of these manikins—"

"Enough of manikins!"

"There are half-bodies made with skin invented for the use of students of midwifery. It seems to me that I could turn over the foetus!"

But Bouvard was tired of medicine.

"The springs of life are hidden from us, the ailments too numerous, the remedies problematical. No reasonable definitions are to be found in the authors of health, disease, diathesis, or even pus."

However, all this reading had disturbed their brains.

Bouvard, whenever he caught a cold, imagined he was getting inflammation of the lungs. When leeches did not abate a stitch in the side, he had recourse to a blister, whose action affected the kidneys. Then he fancied he had an attack of stone.

Pécuchet caught lumbago while lopping the elm trees, and vomited after his dinner—a circumstance which frightened him very much. Then, noticing that his colour was rather yellow, suspected a liver complaint, and asked himself, "Have I pains?" and ended by having them.

Mutually becoming afflicted, they looked at their tongues, felt each other's pulses, made a change as to the use of mineral waters, purged themselves—and dreaded cold, heat, wind, rain, flies, and principally currents of air.

Pécuchet imagined that taking snuff was fatal. Besides, sneezing sometimes causes the rupture of an aneurism; and so he gave up the snuff-box altogether. From force of habit he would thrust his fingers into it, then suddenly become conscious of his imprudence.

As black coffee shakes the nerves, Bouvard wished to give up his half cup; but he used to fall asleep after his meals, and was afraid when he woke up, for prolonged sleep is a foreboding of apoplexy.

Their ideal was Cornaro, that Venetian gentleman who by the regulation of his diet attained to an extreme old age. Without actually imitating him, they might take the same precautions; and Pécuchet took down from his bookshelves a *Manual of Hygiene* by Doctor Morin.

"How had they managed to live till now?"

Their favourite dishes were there prohibited. Germaine, in a state of perplexity, did not know any longer what to serve up to them.

Every kind of meat had its inconveniences. Puddings and sausages, red herrings, lobsters, and game are "refractory." The bigger a fish is, the more gelatine it contains, and consequently the heavier it is. Vegetables cause acidity, macaroni makes people dream; cheeses, "considered generally, are difficult of digestion." A glass of water in the morning is "dangerous." Everything you eat or drink being accompanied by a similar warning, or rather by these words: "Bad!" "Beware of the abuse of it!" "Does not suit everyone!" Why bad? Wherein is the abuse of it? How are you to know whether a thing like this suits you?

What a problem was that of breakfast! They gave up coffee and milk on account of its detestable reputation, and, after that, chocolate, for it is "a mass of indigestible substances." There remained, then, tea. But "nervous persons ought to forbid themselves the use of it completely." Yet Decker, in the seventeenth century, prescribed twenty decalitres of it a day, in order to cleanse the spongy parts of the pancreas.

This direction shook Morin in their estimation, the more so as he condemns every kind of headdress, hats, women's caps, and men's caps—a requirement which was revolting to Pécuchet.

Then they purchased Becquerel's treatise, in which they saw that pork is in itself "a good aliment," tobacco "perfectly harmless in its character," and coffee "indispensable to military men."

Up to that time they had believed in the un-healthiness of damp places. Not at all! Casper declares them less deadly than others. One does not bathe in the sea without refreshing one's skin. Bégin advises people to cast themselves into it while they are perspiring freely. Wine taken neat after soup is considered excellent for the stomach; Levy lays the blame on it of impairing the teeth. Lastly, the flannel waistcoat—that safeguard, that preserver of health, that palladium cherished by Bouvard and inherent to Pécuchet, without any evasions or fear of the opinions of others—is considered unsuitable by some authors for men of a plethoric and sanguine temperament!

What, then, is hygiene? "Truth on this side of the Pyrenees, error on the other side," M. Levy asserts; and Becquerel adds that it is not a science.

So then they ordered for their dinner oysters, a duck, pork and cabbage, cream, a Pont l'Evêque cheese, and a bottle of Burgundy. It was an enfranchisement, almost a revenge; and they laughed at Cornaro! It was only an imbecile that could be tyrannised over as he had been! What vileness to be always thinking about prolonging one's existence! Life is good only on the condition that it is enjoyed.

"Another piece?"

"Yes, I will."

"So will I."

"Your health."

"Yours."

"And let us laugh at the rest of the world."

They became elated. Bouvard announced that he wanted three cups of coffee, though he was not a military man. Pécuchet, with his cap over his ears, took pinch after pinch, and sneezed without fear; and. feeling the need of a little champagne, they ordered Germaine to go at once to the wine-shop to buy a bottle of it. The village was too far away; she refused. Pécuchet got indignant:

"I command you—understand!—I command you to hurry off there."

She obeyed, but, grumbling, resolved soon to have done with her masters; they were so incomprehensible and fantastic.

Then, as in former days, they went to drink their coffee and brandy on the hillock.

The harvest was just over, and the stacks in the middle of the fields rose in dark heaps against the tender blue of a calm night. Nothing was astir about the farms. Even the crickets were no longer heard. The fields were all wrapped in sleep.

The pair digested while they inhaled the breeze which blew refreshingly against their cheeks.

Above, the sky was covered with stars; some shone in clusters, others in a row, or rather alone, at certain distances from each other. A zone of luminous dust, extending from north to south, bifurcated above their heads. Amid these splendours there were vast empty spaces, and the firmament seemed a sea of azure with archipelagoes and islets.

"What a quantity!" exclaimed Bouvard.

"We do not see all," replied Pécuchet. "Behind the Milky Way are the nebulæ, and behind the nebulæ,. stars still; the most distant is separated from us by three millions of myriamètres."

He had often looked into the telescope of the Place Vendôme, and he recalled the figures.

"The sun is a million times bigger than the earth; Sirius is twelve times the size of the sun; comets measure thirty-four millions of leagues."

" 'Tis enough to make one crazy!" said Bouvard.

He lamented his ignorance, and even regretted that he had not been in his youth at the Polytechnic School.

Then Pécuchet, turning him in the direction of the Great Bear, showed him the polar star; then Cassiopeia, whose constellation forms a Y; Vega, of the Lyra constellation—all scintillating; and at the lower part of the horizon, the red Aldebaran.

Bouvard, with his head thrown back, followed with difficulty the angles, quadrilaterals, and pentagons, which it is necessary to imagine in order to make yourself at home in the sky.

Pécuchet went on:

"The swiftness of light is eighty thousand leagues a second; one ray of the Milky Way takes six centuries to reach us; so that a star at the moment we observe it may have disappeared. Several are intermittent; others never come back; and they change positions. Every one of them is in motion; every one of them is passing on."

"However, the sun is motionless."

"It was believed to be so formerly. But to-day men of science declare that it rushes towards the constellation of Hercules!"

This put Bouvard's ideas out of order—and, after a minute's reflection:

"Science is constructed according to the data furnished by a corner of space. Perhaps it does not agree with all the rest that we are ignorant of, which is much vaster, and which we cannot discover."

So they talked, standing on the hillock, in the light of the stars; and their conversation was interrupted by long intervals of silence.

At last they asked one another whether there were men in the stars. Why not? And as creation is harmonious, the inhabitants of Sirius ought to be gigantic, those of Mars of middle stature, those of Venus very small. Unless it should be everywhere the same thing. There are merchants up there, and gendarmes; they trade there; they fight there; they dethrone kings there.

Some shooting stars slipped suddenly, describing on the sky, as it were, the parabola of an enormous rocket.

"Stop!" said Bouvard; "here are vanishing worlds."

Pécuchet replied:

"If ours, in its turn, kicks the bucket, the citizens of the stars will not be more moved than we are now. Ideas like this may pull down your pride."

"What is the object of all this?"

"Perhaps it has no object."

"However—" And Pécuchet repeated two or three times "however," without finding anything more to say.

"No matter. I should very much like to know how the universe is made."

"That should be in Buffon," returned Bouvard, whose eyes were closing.

"I am not equal to any more of it. I am going to bed."

The *Epoques de la Nature* informed them that a comet by knocking against the sun had detached one portion of it, which became the earth. First, the poles had cooled; all the waters had enveloped the globe; they subsided into the caverns; then the continents separated from each other, and the beasts and man appeared.

The majesty of creation engendered in them an amazement infinite as itself. Their heads got enlarged. They were proud of reflecting on such lofty themes.

The minerals ere long proved wearisome to them, and for distraction they sought refuge in the *Harmonies* of Bernardin de Saint-Pierre.

Vegetable and terrestrial harmonies, aërial, aquatic, human, fraternal, and even conjugal—every one of them is here dealt with, not omitting the invocations to Venus, to the Zephyrs, and to the Loves. They exhibited astonishment at fishes having fins, birds wings, seeds an envelope; full of that philosophy which discovers virtuous intentions in Nature, and regards her as a kind of St. Vincent de Paul, always occupied in performing acts of benevolence.

Then they wondered at her prodigies, the waterspouts, the volcanoes, the virgin forests; and they bought M. Depping's work on the *Marvels and Beauties of Nature in France*. Cantal possesses three of them, Hérault five, Burgundy two—no more, while Dauphiné reckons for itself alone up to fifteen marvels. But soon we shall find no more of them. The grottoes with stalactites are stopped up; the burning mountains are extinguished; the natural icehouses have become heated; and the old trees in which they said mass are falling under the leveller's axe, or are on the point of dying.

Their curiosity next turned towards the beasts.

They reopened their Buffon, and got into ecstasies over the strange tastes of certain animals.

But all the books are not worth one personal observation. They hurried out into the farmyard, and asked the labourers whether they had seen bulls consorting with mares, hogs seeking after cows, and the males of partridges doing strange things among themselves.

"Never in their lives." They thought such questions even a little queer for gentlemen of their age.

They took a fancy to try abnormal unions. The least difficult is that of the he-goat and the ewe. Their farmer had not a he-goat in his possession; a neighbour lent his, and, as it was the period of rutting, they shut the two beasts up in the press, concealing themselves behind the casks in order that the event might be quietly accomplished.

Each first ate a little heap of hay; then they ruminated; the ewe lay down, and she bleated continuously, while the he-goat, standing erect on his crooked legs, with his big beard and his drooping ears, fixed on her his eyes, which glittered in the shade.

At length, on the evening of the third day, they deemed it advisable to assist nature, but the goat, turning round on Pécuchet, hit him in the lower part of the stomach with his horns. The ewe, seized with fear, began turning about in the press as if in a riding-school. Bouvard ran after her, threw himself on top of her to hold her, and fell on the ground with both hands full of wool.

They renewed their experiments on hens and a drake, on a mastiff and a sow, in the hope that monsters might be the result, not understanding anything about the question of species.

This word denotes a group of individuals whose descendants reproduce themselves, but animals classed as of different species may possess the power of reproduction, while others comprised in the same species have lost the capacity. They flattered themselves that they would obtain clear ideas on this subject by studying the development of germs; and Pécuchet wrote to Dumouchel in order to get a microscope.

By turns they put on the glass surface hairs, tobacco, finger-nails, and a fly's claw, but they forgot the drop of water which is indispensable; at other times it was the little lamel, and they pushed each other forward, and put the instrument out of order; then, when they saw only a haze, they blamed the optician. They went so far as to have doubts about the microscope. Perhaps the discoveries that have been attributed to it are not so certain?

Dumouchel, in sending on the invoice to them, begged of them to collect on his account some serpent-stones and sea-urchins, of which he had always been an admirer, and which were commonly found in country districts. In order to interest them in geology he sent them the *Lettres* of Bertrand with the *Discours* of Cuvier on the revolutions of the globe.

After the perusal of these two works they imagined the following state of things:

First, an immense sheet of water, from which emerged promontories speckled with lichens, and not one human being, not one sound. It was a world silent, motionless, and bare; there long plants swayed to and fro in a fog that resembled the vapour of a sweating-room. A red sun overheated the humid atmosphere. Then volcanoes burst forth; the igneous rocks sent up mountains of liquid flame, and the paste of the streaming porphyry and basalt began to congeal. Third picture: in shallow seas have sprung up isles of madrepore; a cluster of palm trees overhangs them here and there. There are shells like carriage wheels, tortoises three metres in length, lizards of sixty feet; amphibians stretch out amid the reeds their ostrich necks and crocodile jaws; winged serpents fly about. Finally, on the large continents, huge mammifers make their appearance, their limbs misshapen, like pieces of wood badly squared, their hides thicker than plates of bronze, or else shaggy, thick-lipped, with manes and crooked fangs. Flocks of mammoths browsed on the plains where, since, the Atlantic has been; the paleotherium, half horse, half tapir, overturned with his tumbling the ant-hills of Montmartre; and the *cervus giganteus* trembled under the chestnut trees at the growls of the bears of the caverns, who made the dog of Beaugency, three times as big as a wolf, yelp in his den.

All these periods had been separated from one another by cataclysms, of which the latest is our Deluge. It was like a drama of fairyland in several acts, with man for apotheosis.

They were astounded when they learned that there existed on stones imprints of dragon-flies and birds' claws; and, having run through one of the Roret manuals, they looked out for fossils.

One afternoon, as they were turning over some flints in the middle of the high-road, the curé passed, and, accosting them in a wheedling tone:

"These gentlemen are busying themselves with geology. Very good."

For he held this science in esteem. It confirmed the authority of the Scriptures by proving the fact of the Deluge.

Bouvard talked about coproliles, which are animals' excrements in a petrified state.

The Abbé Jeufroy appeared surprised at the matter. After all, if it were so, it was a reason the more for wondering at Providence.

Pécuchet confessed that, up to the present, their inquiries had not been fruitful; and yet the environs of Falaise, like all Jurassic soils, should abound in remains of animals.

"I have been told," replied the Abbé Jeufroy, "that the jawbone of an elephant was at one time found at Villers."

However, one of his friends, M. Larsoneur, advocate, member of the bar at Lisieux, and archaeologist, would probably supply them with information about it. He had written a history of Port-en-Bessin, in which the discovery of an alligator was noticed.

Bouvard and Pécuchet exchanged glances: the same hope took possession of both; and, in spite of the heat, they remained standing a long time questioning the ecclesiastic, who sheltered himself from the sun under a blue cotton umbrella. The lower part of his face was rather heavy, and his nose was pointed. He was perpetually smiling, or bent his head while he closed his eyelids.

The church-bell rang the Angelus.

"A very good evening, gentlemen! You will allow me, will you not?"

At his suggestion they waited three weeks for Larsoneur's reply. At length it arrived.

The name of the man who had dug up the tooth of the mastodon was Louis Bloche. Details were wanting. As to his history, it was comprised in one of the volumes of the Lisieux Academy, and he could not lend his own copy, as he was afraid of spoiling the collection. With regard to the alligator, it had been discovered in the month of November, 1825, under the cliff of the Hachettes of Sainte-Honorine, near Port-en-Bessin, in the arrondissement of Bayeux. His compliments followed.

The obscurity that enshrouded the mastodon provoked in Pécuchet's mind a longing to search for it. He would fain have gone to Villers forthwith.

Bouvard objected that, to save themselves a possibly useless and certainly expensive journey, it would be desirable to make inquiries. So they wrote a letter to the mayor of the district, in which they asked him what had become of one Louis Bloche. On the assumption of his death, his descendants or collateral relations might be able to enlighten them as to his precious discovery, when he made it, and in what public place in the township this testimony of primitive times was deposited? Were there any prospects of finding similar ones? What was the cost of a man and a car for a day?

And vainly did they make application to the deputy-mayor, and then to the first municipal councillor. They received no news from Villers. No doubt the inhabitants were jealous about their fossils—unless they had sold them to the English. The journey to the Hachettes was determined upon.

Bouvard and Pécuchet took the public conveyance from Falaise to Caen. Then a covered car brought them from Caen to Bayeux; from Bayeux, they walked to Port-en-Bessin.

They had not been deceived. There were curious stones alongside the Hachettes; and, assisted by the directions of the innkeeper, they succeeded in reaching the strand.

The tide was low. It exposed to view all its shingles, with a prairie of sea-wrack as far as the edge of the waves. Grassy slopes cut the cliff, which was composed of soft brown earth that had hardened and become in its lower strata a rampart, of greyish stone. Tiny streams of water kept flowing down incessantly, while in the distance the sea rumbled. It seemed sometimes to suspend its throbbing, and then the only sound heard was the murmur of the little springs.

They staggered over the sticky soil, or rather they had to jump over holes.

Bouvard sat down on a mound overlooking the sea and contemplated the waves, thinking of nothing, fascinated, inert. Pécuchet brought him over to the side of the cliff to show him a serpent-stone incrusted in the rock, like a diamond in its gangue. It broke their nails; they would require instruments; besides, night was coming on. The sky was empurpled towards the west, and the entire sea-shore was wrapped in shadow. In the midst of the blackish wrack the pools of water were growing wider. The sea was coming towards them. It was time to go back.

Next day, at dawn, with a mattock and a pick, they made an attack on their fossil, whose covering cracked. It was an ammonite nodosus, corroded at the ends but weighing quite six pounds; and in his enthusiasm Pécuchet exclaimed:

"We cannot do less than present it to Dumouchel!"

They next chanced upon sponges, lampshells, orks—but no alligator. In default of it, they were hoping to get the backbone of a hippopotamus or an ichthyosaurus, the bones of any animals whatever that were contemporaneous with the Deluge, when they discovered against the cliff, at a man's height, outlines which assumed the form of a gigantic fish.

They deliberated as to the means by which they could get possession of it. Bouvard would extricate it at the top, while Pécuchet beneath would demolish the rock in order to make it descend gently without spoiling it.

Just as they were taking breath they saw above their heads a custom-house officer in a cloak, who was gesticulating with a commanding air.

"Well! What! Let us alone!" And they went on with their work, Bouvard on the tips of his toes, trapping with his mattock, Pécuchet, with his back bent, digging with his pick.

But the custom-house officer reappeared farther down, in an open space between the rocks, making repeated signals. They treated him with contempt. An oval body bulged out under the thinned soil, and sloped down, was on the point of slipping.

Suddenly another individual, with a sabre, presented himself.

"Your passports?"

It was the field-guard on his rounds, and, at the same instant, the man from the custom-house came up, having hastened through a ravine.

"Take them into custody for me, Père Morin, or the cliff will fall in!"

"It is for a scientific object," replied Pécuchet.

Then a mass of stone fell, grazing them all four so closely that a little more and they were dead men.

When the dust was scattered, they recognised the mast of a ship, which crumbled under the custom-house officer's boot.

Bouvard said with a sigh, "We did no great harm!"

"One should not do anything within the fortification limits," returned the guard.

"In the first place, who are you, in order that I may take out a summons against you?"

Pécuchet refused to give his name, cried out against such injustice.

"Don't argue! follow me!"

As soon as they reached the port a crowd of ragamuffins ran after them. Bouvard, red as a poppy, put on an air of dignity; Pécuchet, exceedingly pale, darted furious looks around; and these two strangers, carrying stones in their pocket-handkerchiefs, did not present a good appearance. Provisionally, they put them up at the inn, whose master on the threshold guarded the entrance. Then the mason came to demand back his tools. They were paying him for them, and still there were incidental expenses!—and the field-guard did not come back! Wherefore? At last, a gentleman, who wore the cross of the Legion of Honour, set them free, and they went away, after giving their Christian names, surnames, and their domicile, with an undertaking on their part to be more circumspect in future.

Besides a passport, they were in need of many things, and before undertaking fresh explorations they consulted the *Geological Traveller's Guide*, by Boné. It was necessary to have, in the first place, a good soldier's knapsack, then a surveyor's chain, a file, a pair of nippers, a compass, and three hammers, passed into a belt, which is hidden under the frock-coat, and "thus preserves you from that original appearance which one ought to avoid on a journey." As for the stick, Pécuchet freely adopted the tourist's stick, six feet high, with a long iron point. Bouvard preferred the walking-stick umbrella, or many-branched umbrella, the knob of which is removed in order to clasp on the silk, which is kept separately in a little bag. They did not forget strong shoes with gaiters, "two pairs of braces" each "on account of perspiration," and, although one cannot present himself everywhere in a cap, they shrank from the expense of "one of those folding hats, which bear the name of 'Gibus,' their inventor."

The same work gives precepts for conduct: "To know the language of the part of the country you visit": they knew it. "To preserve a modest deportment": this was their custom. "Not to have too much money about you": nothing simpler. Finally, in order to spare yourself embarrassments of all descriptions, it is a good thing to adopt the "description of engineer."

"Well, we will adopt it."

Thus prepared, they began their excursions; were sometimes eight days away, and passed their lives in the open air.

Sometimes they saw, on the banks of the Orne, in a rent, pieces of rock raising their slanting surfaces between some poplar trees and heather; or else they were grieved by meeting, for the entire length of the road, nothing but layers of clay. In the presence of a landscape they admired neither the series of perspectives nor the depth of the backgrounds, nor the undulations of the green surfaces; but that which was not visible to them, the underpart, the earth: and for them every hill was only a fresh proof of the Deluge.

To the Deluge mania succeeded that of erratic blocks. The big stones alone in the fields must come from vanished glaciers, and they searched for moraines and faluns.

They were several times taken for pedlars on account of their equipage; and when they had answered that they were "engineers," a dread seized them—the usurpation of such a title might entail unpleasant consequences.

At the end of each day they panted beneath the weight of their specimens; but they dauntlessly carried them off home with them. They were deposited on the doorsteps, on the stairs, in the bedrooms, in the dining-room, and in the kitchen; and Germaine used to make a hubbub about the quantity of dust. It was no slight task, before pasting on the labels, to know the names of the rocks; the variety of colours and of grain made them confuse argil and marl, granite and gneiss, quartz and limestone.

And the nomenclature plagued them. Why Devonian, Cambrian, Jurassic—as if the portions of the earth designated by these names were not in other places as well as in Devonshire, near Cambridge, and in the Jura? It was impossible to know where you are there. That which is a system for one is for another a stratum, for a third a mere layer. The plates of the layers get intermingled and entangled in one another; but Omalius d'Halloy warns you not to believe in geological divisions.

This statement was a relief to them; and when they had seen coral limestones in the plain of Caen, phillades at Balleroy, kaolin at St. Blaise, and oolite everywhere, and searched for coal at Cartigny and for mercury at Chapelle-en-Juger, near St. Lô, they decided on a longer excursion: a journey to Havre, to study the fire-resisting quartz and the clay of Kimmeridge.

As soon as they had stepped out of the packet-boat they asked what road led under the lighthouses.

Landslips blocked up the way; it was dangerous to venture along it.

A man who let out vehicles accosted them, and offered them drives around the neighbourhood—Ingouville, Octeville, Fécamp, Lillebonne, "Rome, if it was necessary."

His charges were preposterous, but the name of Falaise had struck them. By turning off the main road a little, they could see Etretat, and they took the coach that started from Fécamp to go to the farthest point first.

In the vehicle Bouvard and Pécuchet had a conversation with three peasants, two old women, and a seminarist, and did not hesitate to style themselves engineers.

They stopped in front of the bay. They gained the cliff, and five minutes after, rubbed up against it to avoid a big pool of water which was advancing like a gulf stream in the middle of the sea-shore. Then they saw an archway which opened above a deep grotto; it was sonorous and very blight, like a church, with descending columns and a carpet of sea-wrack all along its stone flooring.

This work of nature astonished them, and as they went on their way collecting shells, they started considerations as to the origin of the world.

Bouvard inclined towards Neptunism; Pécuchet, on the contrary, was a Plutonist.

"The central fire had broken the crust of the globe, heaved up the masses of earth, and made fissures. It is, as it were, an interior sea, which has its flow and ebb, its tempests; a thin film separates us from it. We could not sleep if we thought of all that is under our heels. However, the central fire diminishes, and the sun grows more feeble, so much so that one day the earth will perish of refrigeration. It will become sterile; all the wood and all the coal will be converted into carbonic acid, and no life can subsist there."

"We haven't come to that yet," said Bouvard.

"Let us expect it," returned Pécuchet.

No matter, this end of the world, far away as it might be, made them gloomy; and, side by side, they walked in silence over the shingles.

The cliff, perpendicular, a mass of white, striped with black here and there by lines of flint, stretched towards the horizon like the curve of a rampart five leagues wide. An east wind, bitter and cold, was blowing; the sky was grey; the sea greenish and, as it were, swollen. From the highest points of rocks birds took wing, wheeled round, and speedily re-entered their hiding places. Sometimes a stone, getting loosened, would rebound from one place to another before reaching them.

Pécuchet continued his reflections aloud:

"Unless the earth should be destroyed by a cataclysm! We do not know the length of our period. The central fire has only to overflow."

"However, it is diminishing."

"That does not prevent its explosions from having produced the Julia Island, Monte Nuovo, and many others."

Bouvard remembered having read these details in Bertrand.

"But such catastrophes do not happen in Europe."

"A thousand pardons! Witness that of Lisbon. As for our own countries, the coal-mines and the firestone useful for war are numerous, and may very well, when decomposing, form the mouths of volcanoes. Moreover, the volcanoes always burst near the sea."

Bouvard cast his eyes over the waves, and fancied he could distinguish in the distance a volume of smoke ascending to the sky.

"Since the Julia Island," returned Pécuchet, "has disappeared, the fragments of the earth formed by the same cause will perhaps have the same fate. An islet in the Archipelago is as important as Normandy and even as Europe."

Bouvard imagined Europe swallowed up in an abyss.

"Admit," said Pécuchet, "that an earthquake takes place under the British Channel: the waters rush into the Atlantic; the coasts of France and England, tottering on their bases, bend forward and reunite—and there you are! The entire space between is wiped out."

Instead of answering, Bouvard began walking so quickly that he was soon a hundred paces away from Pécuchet. Being alone, the idea of a cataclysm disturbed him. He had eaten nothing since morning; his temples were throbbing. All at once the soil appeared to him to be shaking, and the cliff over his head to be bending forward at its summit. At that moment a shower of gravel rolled down from the top of it. Pécuchet observed him scampering off wildly, understood his fright, and cried from a distance:

"Stop! stop! The period is not completed!"

And in order to overtake him he made enormous bounds with the aid of his tourist's stick, all the while shouting out:

"The period is not completed! The period is not completed!"

Bouvard, in a mad state, kept running without stopping. The many-branched umbrella fell down, the skirts of his coat were flying, the knapsack was tossing on his back. He was like a tortoise with wings about to gallop amongst the rocks. One bigger than the rest concealed him from view.

Pécuchet reached the spot out of breath, saw nobody, then returned in order to gain the fields through a defile, which Bouvard, no doubt, had taken.

This narrow ascent was cut by four great steps in the cliff, as lofty as the heights of two men, and glittering like polished alabaster.

At an elevation of fifty feet Pécuchet wished to descend; but as the sea was dashing against him in front, he set about clambering up further. At the second turning, when he beheld the empty space, terror froze him. As he approached the third, his legs were becoming weak. Volumes of air vibrated around him, a cramp gripped his epigastrium; he sat down on the ground, with eyes closed, no longer having consciousness of aught save the beatings of his own heart, which were suffocating him; then he flung his tourist's stick on the ground, and on his hands and knees resumed his ascent. But the three hammers attached to his belt began to press against his stomach; the stones with which he had crammed his pockets knocked against his sides; the peak of his cap blinded him; the wind increased in violence. At length he reached the upper ground, and there found Bouvard, who had ascended higher through a less difficult defile. A cart picked them up. They forgot all about Étretat.

The next evening, at Havre, while waiting for the packet-boat, they saw at the tail-end of a newspaper, a short scientific essay headed, "On the Teaching of Geology." This article, full of facts, explained the subject as it was understood at the period.

There has never been a complete cataclysm of the globe, but the same space has not always the same duration, and is exhausted more quickly in one place than in another. Lands of the same age contain different fossils, just as depositaries very far distant from each other enclose similar ones. The ferns of former times are identical with the ferns of to-day. Many contemporary zoophytes are found again in the most ancient layers. To sum up, actual modifications explain former convulsions. The same causes are always in operation; Nature does not proceed by leaps; and the periods, Brogniart asserts, are, after all, only abstractions.

Cuvier's work up to this time had appeared to them surrounded with the glory of an aureola at the summit of an incontestable science. It was sapped. Creation had no longer the same discipline, and their respect for this great man diminished.

From biographies and extracts they learned something of the doctrines of Lamarck and Geoffroy Saint-Hilaire.

All that was contrary to accepted ideas, the authority of the Church.

Bouvard experienced relief as if from a broken yoke. "I should like to see now what answer Citizen Jeufroy would make to me about the Deluge!"

They found him in his little garden, where he was awaiting the members of the vestry, who were to meet presently with a view to the purchase of a chasuble.

"These gentlemen wish for——?"

"An explanation, if you please."

And Bouvard began, "What means, in Genesis, 'The abyss which was broken up,' and 'The cataracts of heaven?' For an abyss does not get broken up, and heaven has no cataracts."

The abbé closed his eyelids, then replied that it was always necessary to distinguish between the sense and the letter. Things which shock you at first, turn out right when they are sifted.

"Very well, but how do you explain the rain which passed over the highest mountains—those that are two leagues in height. Just think of it! Two leagues!—a depth of water that makes two leagues!"

And the mayor, coming up, added:

"Bless my soul! What a bath!"

"Admit," said Bouvard, "that Moses exaggerates like the devil."

The curé had read Bonald, and answered:

"I am ignorant of his motives; it was, no doubt, to inspire a salutary fear in the people of whom he was the leader."

"Finally, this mass of water—where did it come from?"

"How do I know? The air was changed into water, just as happens every day."

Through the garden gate they saw M. Girbal, superintendent of taxes, making his way in, together with Captain Heurteaux, a landowner; and Beljambe, the innkeeper, appeared, assisting with his arm Langlois, the grocer, who walked with difficulty on account of his catarrh.

Pécuchet, without bestowing a thought on them, took up the argument:

"Excuse me, M. Jeufroy. The weight of the atmosphere, science demonstrates to us, is equal to that of a mass of water which would make a covering of ten metres around the globe. Consequently, if all the air that had been condensed fell down in a liquid state, it would augment very little the mass of existing waters."

The vestrymen opened their eyes wide, and listened.

The curé lost patience. "Will you deny that shells have been found on the mountains? What put them there, if not the Deluge? They are not accustomed, I believe, to grow out of the ground of themselves alone, like carrots!" And this joke having made the assembly laugh, he added, pressing his lips together: "Unless this be another discovery of science!"

Bouvard was pleased to reply by referring to the rising of mountains, the theory of Elie de Beaumont.

"Don't know him," returned the abbé.

Foureau hastened to explain: "He is from Caen. I have seen him at the Prefecture."

"But if your Deluge," Bouvard broke in "had sent shells drifting, they would be broken on the surface, and not at depths of three hundred metres sometimes."

The priest fell back on the truth of the Scriptures, the tradition of the human race, and the animals discovered in the ice in Siberia.

"That does not prove that man existed at the time they did."

The earth, in Pécuchet's view, was much older. "The delta of the Mississippi goes back to tens of thousands of years. The actual epoch is a hundred thousand, at least. The lists of Manetho—"

The Count de Faverges appeared on the scene. They were all silent at his approach.

"Go on, pray. What were you talking about?"

"These gentlemen are wrangling with me," replied the abbé.

"About what?"

"About Holy Writ, M. le Comte."

Bouvard immediately pleaded that they had a right, as geologists, to discuss religion.

"Take care," said the count; "you know the phrase, my dear sir, 'A little science takes us away from it, a great deal leads us back to it'?" And in a tone at the same time haughty and paternal: "Believe me, you will come back to it! you will come back to it!"

"Perhaps so. But what were we to think of a book in which it is pretended that the light was created before the sun? as if the sun were not the sole cause of light!"

"You forget the light which we call boreal," said the ecclesiastic.

Bouvard, without answering this point, strongly denied that light could be on one side and darkness on the other, that evening and morning could have existed when there were no stars, or that the animals made their appearance suddenly, instead of being formed by crystallisation.

As the walks were too narrow, while gesticulating, they trod on the flower-borders. Langlois took a fit of coughing.

The captain exclaimed: "You are revolutionaries!"

Girbal: "Peace! peace!"

The priest: "What materialism!"

Foureau: "Let us rather occupy ourselves with our chasuble!"

"No! let me speak!" And Bouvard, growing more heated, went on to say that man was descended from the ape!

All the vestrymen looked at each other, much amazed, and as if to assure themselves that they were not apes.

Bouvard went on: "By comparing the foetus of a woman, of a bitch, of a bird, of a frog—"

"Enough!"

"For my part, I go farther!" cried Pécuchet. "Man is descended from the fishes!"

There was a burst of laughter. But without being disturbed:

"The *Telliamed*—an Arab book—"

"Come, gentlemen, let us hold our meeting."

And they entered the sacristy.

The two comrades had not given the Abbé Jeufroy such a fall as they expected; therefore, Pécuchet found in him "the stamp of Jesuitism." His "boreal light," however, caused them uneasiness. They searched for it in Orbigny's manual.

"This is a hypothesis to explain why the vegetable fossils of Baffin's Bay resemble the Equatorial plants. We suppose, in place of the sun, a great luminous source of heat which has now disappeared, and of which the Aurora Borealis is but perhaps a vestige."

Then a doubt came to them as to what proceeds from man, and, in their perplexity, they thought of Vaucorbeil.

He had not followed up his threats. As of yore, he passed every morning before their grating, striking all the bars with his walking-stick one after the other.

Bouvard watched him, and, having stopped him, said he wanted to submit to him a curious point in anthropology.

"Do you believe that the human race is descended from fishes?"

"What nonsense!"

"From apes rather—isn't that so?"

"Directly, that is impossible!"

On whom could they depend? For, in fact, the doctor was not a Catholic!

They continued their studies, but without enthusiasm, being weary of eocene and miocene, of Mount Jurillo, of the Julia Island, of the mammoths of Siberia and of the fossils, invariably compared in all the authors to "medals which are authentic testimonies," so much so that one day Bouvard threw his knapsack on the ground, declaring that he would not go any farther.

"Geology is too defective. Some parts of Europe are hardly known. As for the rest, together with the foundation of the oceans, we shall always be in a state of ignorance on the subject."

Finally, Pécuchet having pronounced the word "mineral kingdom":

"I don't believe in it, this mineral kingdom, since organic substances have taken part in the formation of flint, of chalk, and perhaps of gold. Hasn't the diamond been charcoal; coal a collection of vegetables? and by heating it to I know not how many degrees, we get the sawdust of wood, so that everything passes, everything goes to ruin, and everything is transformed. Creation is carried out in an undulating and fugitive fashion. Much better to occupy ourselves with something else."

He stretched himself on his back and went to sleep, while Pécuchet, with his head down and one knee between his hands, gave himself up to his own reflections.

A border of moss stood on the edge of a hollow path overhung by ash trees, whose slender tops quivered; angelica, mint, and lavender exhaled warm, pungent odours. The atmosphere was drowsy, and Pécuchet, in a kind of stupor, dreamed of the innumerable existences scattered around him—of the insects that buzzed, the springs hidden beneath the grass, the sap of plants, the birds in their nests, the wind, the clouds—of all Nature, without seeking to unveil her mysteries, enchanted by her power, lost in her grandeur.

"I'm thirsty!" said Bouvard, waking up.

"So am I. I should be glad to drink something."

"That's easy," answered a man who was passing by in his shirt-sleeves with a plank on his shoulder. And they recognised that vagabond to whom, on a former occasion, Bouvard had given a glass of wine. He seemed ten years younger, wore his hair foppishly curled, his moustache well waxed, and twisted his figure about in quite a Parisian fashion. After walking about a hundred paces, he opened the gateway of a farmyard, threw down his plank against the wall, and led them into a large kitchen.

"Mélie! are you there, Mélie?"

A young girl appeared. At a word from him she drew some liquor and came back to the table to serve the gentlemen.

Her wheat-coloured head-bands fell over a cap of grey linen. Her worn dress of poor material fell down her entire body without a crease, and, with her straight nose and blue eyes, she had about her something dainty, rustic, and ingenuous.

"She's nice, eh?" said the joiner, while she was bringing them the glasses. "You might take her for a lady dressed up as a peasant-girl, and yet able to do rough work! Poor little heart, come! When I'm rich I'll marry you!"

"You are always talking nonsense, *Monsieur* Gorju," she replied, in a soft voice, with a slightly drawling accent.

A stable boy came in to get some oats out of an old chest, and let the lid fall down so awkwardly that it made splinters of wood fly upwards.

Gorju declaimed against the clumsiness of all "these country fellows," then, on his knees in front of the article of furniture, he tried to put the piece in its place. Pécuchet, while offering to assist him, traced beneath the dust faces of notable characters.

It was a chest of the Renaissance period, with a twisted fringe below, vine branches in the corner, and little columns dividing its front into five portions. In the centre might be seen Venus-Anadyomene standing on a shell, then Hercules and Omphale, Samson and Delilah, Circe and her swine, the daughters of Lot making their father drunk; and all this in a state of complete decay, the chest being worm-eaten, and even its right panel wanting.

Gorju took a candle, in order to give Pécuchet a better view of the left one, which exhibited Adam and Eve under a tree in Paradise in an affectionate attitude.

Bouvard equally admired the chest.

"If you keep it they'll give it to you cheap."

They hesitated, thinking of the necessary repairs.

Gorju might do them, cabinet-making being a branch of his trade.

"Let us go. Come on."

And he dragged Pécuchet towards the fruit-garden, where Madame Castillon, the mistress, was spreading linen.

Mélie, when she had washed her hands, took from where it lay beside the window her lace-frame, sat down in the broad daylight and worked.

The lintel of the door enclosed her like a picture-frame. The bobbins disentangled themselves under her fingers with a sound like the clicking of castanets. Her profile remained bent.

Bouvard asked her questions as to her family, the part of the country she came from, and the wages she got.

She was from Ouistreham, had no relations alive, and earned seventeen shillings a month; in short, she, pleased him so much that he wished to take her into his service to assist old Germaine.

Pécuchet reappeared with the mistress of the farmhouse, and, while they went on with their bargaining, Bouvard asked Gorju in a very low tone whether the girl would consent to become their servant.

"Lord, yes."

"However," said Bouvard, "I must consult my friend."

The bargain had just been concluded, the price fixed for the chest being thirty-five francs. They were to come to an understanding about the repairs.

They had scarcely got out into the yard when Bouvard spoke of his intentions with regard to Mélie.

Pécuchet stopped (in order the better to reflect), opened his snuff-box, took a pinch, and, wiping the snuff off his nose:

"Indeed, it is a good idea. Good heavens! yes! why not? Besides, you are the master."

Ten minutes afterwards, Gorju showed himself on the top of a ditch, and questioning them: "When do you want me to bring you the chest?"

"To-morrow."

"And about the other question, have you both made up your minds?"

"It's all right," replied Pécuchet.

Chapter IV

RESEARCHES IN ARCHAEOLOGY

SIX MONTHS LATER THEY HAD BECOME ARCHAEOLOGISTS, AND THEIR HOUSE was like a museum.

In the vestibule stood an old wooden beam. The staircase was encumbered with the geological specimens, and an enormous chain was stretched on the ground all along the corridor. They had taken off its hinges the door between the two rooms in which they did not sleep, and had condemned the outer door of the second in order to convert both into a single apartment.

As soon as you crossed the threshold, you came in contact with a stone trough (a Gallo-Roman sarcophagus); the ironwork next attracted your attention. Fixed to the opposite wall, a warming-pan looked down on two andirons and a hearthplate representing a monk caressing a shepherdess. On the boards all around, you saw torches, locks, bolts, and nuts of screws. The floor was rendered invisible beneath fragments of red tiles. A table in the centre exhibited curiosities of the rarest description: the shell of a Cauchoise cap, two argil urns, medals, and a phial of opaline glass. An upholstered armchair had at its back a triangle worked with guipure. A piece of a coat of mail adorned the partition to the right, and on the other side sharp spikes sustained in a horizontal position a unique specimen of a halberd.

The second room, into which two steps led down, contained the old books which they had brought with them from Paris, and those which, on their arrival, they had found in a press. The leaves of the folding-doors had been removed hither. They called it the library.

The back of the door was entirely covered by the genealogical tree of the Croixmare family. In the panelling on the return side, a pastel of a lady in the dress of the period of Louis XV made a companion picture to the portrait of Père Bouvard. The casing of the glass was decorated with a sombrero of black felt, and a monstrous galoche filled with leaves, the remains of a nest.

Two cocoanuts (which had belonged to Pécuchet since his younger days) flanked on the chimney-piece an earthenware cask on which a peasant sat astride. Close by, in a straw basket, was a little coin brought up by a duck.

In front of the bookcase stood a shell chest of drawers trimmed with plush. The cover of it supported a cat with a mouse in its mouth—a petrifaction from St. Allyre; a work-box, also of shell work, and on this box a decanter of brandy contained a Bon Chrétien pear.

But the finest thing was a statue of St. Peter in the embrasure of the window. His right hand, covered with a glove of apple-green colour, was pressing the key of Paradise. His chasuble, ornamented with fleurs-de-luce, was azure blue, and his tiara very yellow, pointed like a pagoda. He had flabby cheeks, big round eyes, a gaping mouth, and a crooked nose shaped like a trumpet. Above him hung a canopy made of an old carpet in which you could distinguish two Cupids in a circle of roses, and at his feet, like a pillar, rose a butter-pot bearing these words in white letters on a chocolate ground: "Executed in the presence of H.R.H. the Duke of Angoulême at Noron, 3rd of October, 1847."

Pécuchet, from his bed, saw all these things in a row, and sometimes he went as far as Bouvard's room to lengthen the perspective.

One spot remained empty, exactly opposite to the coat of arms, that intended for the Renaissance chest. It was not finished; Gorju was still working at it, jointing the panels in the bakehouse, squaring them or undoing them.

At eleven o'clock he took his breakfast, chatted after that with Mélie, and often did not make his appearance again for the rest of the day.

In order to have pieces of furniture in good style, Bouvard and Pécuchet went scouring the country. What they brought back was not suitable; but they had come across a heap of curious things. Their first passion was a taste for articles of *virtù;* then came the love of the Middle Ages.

To begin with, they visited cathedrals; and the lofty naves mirroring themselves in the holy-water fonts, the glass ornaments dazzling as hangings of precious stones, the tombs in the recesses of the chapels, the uncertain light of crypts—everything, even to the coolness of the walls, thrilled them with a shudder of joy, a religious emotion.

They were soon able to distinguish the epochs, and, disdainful of sacristans, they would say: "Ha! a Romanesque apsis!" "That's of the twelfth century!" "Here we are falling back again into the flamboyant!"

They strove to interpret the sculptured symbols on the capitals, such as the two griffins of Marigny pecking at a tree in blossom; Pécuchet read a satire in the singers with grotesque jaws which terminate the mouldings at Feugerolles; and as for the exuberance of the man that covers one of the mullions at Hérouville, that was a proof, according to Bouvard, of our ancestors' love of broad jokes.

They ended by not tolerating the least symptom of decadence. All was decadence, and they deplored vandalism, and thundered against badigeon.

But the style of a monument does not always agree with its supposed date. The semicircular arch of the thirteenth century still holds sway in Provence. The ogive is, perhaps, very ancient; and authors dispute as to the anteriority of the Romanesque to the Gothic. This want of certainty disappointed them.

After the churches they studied fortresses—those of Domfront and Falaise. They admired under the gate the grooves of the portcullis, and, having reached the top, they first saw all the country around them, then the roofs of the houses in the town, the streets intersecting one another, the carts on the square, the women at the washhouse. The wall descended perpendicularly as far as the palisade; and they grew pale as they thought that men had mounted there, hanging to ladders. They would have ventured into the subterranean passages but that Bouvard found an obstacle in his stomach and Pécuchet in his horror of vipers.

They desired to make the acquaintance of the old manor-houses—Curcy, Bully, Fontenay, Lemarmion, Argonge. Sometimes a Carlovingian tower would show itself at the corner of some farm-buildings behind a heap of manure. The kitchen, garnished with stone benches, made them dream of feudal junketings. Others had a forbiddingly fierce aspect with their three enceintes still visible, their loopholes under the staircase, and their high turrets with pointed sides. Then they came to an apartment in which a window of the Valois period, chased so as to resemble ivory, let in the sun, which heated the grains of colza that strewed the floor. Abbeys were used as barns. The inscriptions on tombstones were effaced. In the midst of fields a gable-end remained standing, clad from top to bottom in ivy which trembled in the wind.

A number of things excited in their breasts a longing to possess them—a tin pot, a paste buckle, printed calicoes with large flowerings. The shortness of money restrained them.

By a happy chance, they unearthed at Balleroy in a tinman's house a Gothic church window, and it was big enough to cover, near the armchair, the right side of the casement up to the second pane. The steeple of Chavignolles displayed itself in the distance, producing a magnificent effect. With the lower part of a cupboard Gorju manufactured a prie-dieu to put under the Gothic window, for he humoured their hobby. So pronounced was it that they regretted monuments about which nothing at all is known—such as the villa residence of the bishops of Séez.

"Bayeux," says M. de Caumont, "must have possessed a theatre." They searched for the site of it without success.

The village of Montrecy contained a meadow celebrated for the number of medals which chanced formerly to have been found there. They calculated on making a fine harvest in this place. The caretaker refused to admit them.

They were not more fortunate as to the connection which existed between a cistern at Falaise and the faubourg of Caen. Ducks which had been put in there reappeared at Vaucelles, quacking, "Can, can, can"—whence is derived the name of the town!

No step, no sacrifice, was too great for them.

At the inn of Mesnil-Villement, in 1816, M. Galeron got a breakfast for the sum of four sous. They took the same meal there, and ascertained with surprise that things were altered!

Who was the founder of the abbey of St. Anne? Is there any relationship between Marin Onfroy, who, in the twelfth century, imported a new kind of potato, and Onfroy, governor of Hastings at the period of the Conquest? How were they to procure *L'Astucieuse Pythonisse*, a comedy in verse by one Dutrezor, produced at Bayeux, and just now exceedingly rare? Under Louis XIV, Hérambert Dupaty, or Dupastis Hérambert, composed a work which has never appeared, full of anecdotes about Argentan: the question was how to recover these anecdotes. What have become of the autograph memoirs of Madame Dubois de la Pierre, consulted for the unpublished history of L'Aigle by Louis Dasprès, curate of St. Martin? So many problems, so many curious points, to clear up.

But a slight mark often puts one on the track of an invaluable discovery.

Accordingly, they put on their blouses, in order not to put people on their guard, and, in the guise of hawkers, they presented themselves at houses, where they expressed a desire to buy up old papers. They obtained heaps of them. These included school copybooks, invoices, newspapers that were out of date—nothing of any value.

At last Bouvard and Pécuchet addressed themselves to Larsoneur.

He was absorbed in Celtic studies, and while summarily replying to their questions put others to them.

Had they observed in their rounds any traces of dog-worship, such as are seen at Montargis, or any special circumstances with regard to the fires on St. John's night, marriages, popular sayings, etc.? He even begged of them to collect for him some of those flint axes, then called *celtæ*, which the Druids used in their criminal holocausts.

They procured a dozen of them through Gorju, sent him the smallest of them, and with the others enriched the museum. There they walked with delight, swept the place themselves, and talked about it to all their acquaintances.

One afternoon Madame Bordin and M. Marescot came to see it.

Bouvard welcomed them, and began the demonstration in the porch.

The beam was nothing less than the old gibbet of Falaise, according to the joiner who had sold it, and who had got this information from his grandfather.

The big chain in the corridor came from the subterranean cells of the keep of Torteval. In the notary's opinion it resembled the boundary chains in front of the entrance-courts of manor-houses. Bouvard was convinced that it had been used in former times to bind the captives. He opened the door of the first chamber.

"What are all these tiles for?" exclaimed Madame Bordin.

"To heat the stoves. But let us be a little regular, if you please. This is a tomb discovered in an inn where they made use of it as a horse-trough."

After this, Bouvard took up the two urns filled with a substance which consisted of human dust, and he drew the phials up to his eyes, for the purpose of showing the way the Romans used to shed tears in it.

"But one sees only dismal things at your house!"

Indeed it was a rather grave subject for a lady. So he next drew out of a case several copper coins, together with a silver denarius.

Madame Bordin asked the notary what sum this would be worth at the present day.

The coat of mail which he was examining slipped out of his fingers; some of the links snapped.

Bouvard stifled his annoyance. He had even the politeness to unfasten the halberd, and, bending forward, raising his arms and stamping with his heels, he made a show of hamstringing a horse, stabbing as if with a bayonet and overpowering an enemy.

The widow inwardly voted him a rough person.

She went into raptures over the shell chest of drawers.

The cat of St. Allyre much astonished her, the pear in the decanter not quite so much; then, when she came to the chimney-piece: "Ha! here's a hat that would need mending!"

Three holes, marks of bullets, pierced its brims.

It was the head-piece of a robber chief under the Directory, David de la Bazoque, caught in the act of treason, and immediately put to death.

"So much the better! They did right," said Madame Bordin.

Marescot smiled disdainfully as he gazed at the different objects. He did not understand this galoche having been the sign of a hosier, nor the purport of the earthenware cask—a common cider-keg—and, to be candid, the St. Peter was lamentable with his drunkard's physiognomy.

Madame Bordin made this observation:

"All the same, it must have cost you a good deal?"

"Oh! not too much, not too much."

A slater had given it to him for fifteen francs.

After this, she found fault on the score of propriety with the low dress of the lady in the powdered wig.

"Where is the harm," replied Bouvard, "when one possesses something beautiful?" And he added in a lower tone: "Just as you are yourself, I'm sure."

(The notary turned his back on them, and studied the branches of the Croixmare family.)

She made no response but began to play with her long gold chain. Her bosom swelled out the black taffeta of her corsage, and, with her eyelashes slightly drawn together, she lowered her chin like a turtledove bridling up; then, with an ingenuous air:

"What is this lady's name?"

"It is unknown; she was one of the Regent's mistresses, you know; he who played so many pranks."

"I believe you; the memoirs of the time—"

And the notary, without giving her time to finish the sentence, deplored this example of a prince carried away by his passions.

"But you are all like that!"

The two gentlemen protested, and then followed a dialogue on women and on love. Marescot declared that there were many happy unions; sometimes even, without suspecting it, we have close beside us what we require for our happiness.

The allusion was direct. The widow's cheeks flushed scarlet; but, recovering her composure almost the next moment:

"We are past the age for folly, are we not, M. Bouvard?"

"Ha! ha! For my part, I don't admit that."

And he offered his arm to lead her towards the adjoining room.

"Be careful about the steps. All right? Now observe the church window."

They traced on its surface a scarlet cloak and two angels' wings. All the rest was lost under the leads which held in equilibrium the numerous breakages in the glass. The day was declining; the shadows were lengthening; Madame Bordin had become grave.

Bouvard withdrew, and presently reappeared muffled up in a woollen wrapper, then knelt down at the prie-dieu with his elbows out, his face in his hands, the light of the sun falling on his bald patch; and he was conscious of this effect, for he said:

"Don't I look like a monk of the Middle Ages?"

Then he raised his forehead on one side, with swimming eyes, and trying to give a mystical expression to his face. The solemn voice of Pécuchet was heard in the corridor:

"Don't be afraid. It is I." And he entered, his head covered with a helmet—an iron pot with pointed ear-pieces.

Bouvard did not quit the prie-dieu. The two others remained standing. A minute slipped away in glances of amazement.

Madame Bordin appeared rather cold to Pécuchet. However he wished to know whether everything had been shown to them.

"It seems to me so." And pointing towards the wall: "Ah! pray excuse us; there is an object which we may restore in a moment."

The widow and Marescot thereupon took their leave. The two friends conceived the idea of counterfeiting a competition. They set out on a race after each other; one giving the other the start. Pécuchet won the helmet.

Bouvard congratulated him upon it, and received praises from his friend on the subject of the wrapper.

Mélie arranged it with cords, in the fashion of a gown. They took turns about in receiving visits.

They had visits from Girbal, Foureau, and Captain Heurteaux, and then from inferior persons—Langlois, Beljambe, their husbandmen, and even the servant-girls of their neighbours; and, on each occasion, they went over the same explanations, showed the place where the chest would be, affected a tone of modesty, and claimed indulgence for the obstruction.

Pécuchet on these days wore the Zouave's cap which he had formerly in Paris, considering it more in harmony with an artistic environment. At a particular moment, he would put the helmet on his head, and incline it over the back of his neck, in order to have his face free. Bouvard did not forget the movement with the halberd; finally, with one glance, they would ask each other whether the visitor was worthy of having "the monk of the Middle Ages" represented.

What a thrill they felt when M. de Faverges' carriage drew up before the garden gate! He had only a word to say to them. This was the occasion of his visit:

Hurel, his man of business, had informed him that, while searching everywhere for documents, they had bought up old papers at the farm of Aubrye.

That was perfectly true.

Had they not discovered some letters of Baron de Gonneval, a former aide-de-camp of the Duke of Angoulême, who had stayed at Aubrye? He wished to have this correspondence for family reasons.

They had not got it in the house, but they had in their possession something that would interest him if he would be good enough to follow them into their library.

Never before had such well-polished boots creaked in the corridor. They knocked against the sarcophagus. He even went near smashing several tiles, moved an armchair about, descended two steps; and, when they reached the second chamber, they showed him under the canopy, in front of the St. Peter, the butter-pot made at Noron.

Bouvard and Pécuchet thought that the date might some time be of use. Through politeness, the nobleman inspected their museum. He kept repeating, "Charming! very nice!" all the time giving his mouth little taps with the handle of his switch; and said that, for his part, he thanked them for having rescued those remains of the Middle Ages, an epoch of religious faith and chivalrous devotion. He loved progress, and would have given himself up like them to these interesting studies, but that politics, the General Council, agriculture, a veritable whirlwind, drove him away from them.

"After you, however, one would have merely gleanings, for soon you will have captured all the curiosities of the department."

"Without vanity, we think so," said Pécuchet.

However, one might still discover some at Chavignolles; for example, there was, close to the cemetery wall in the lane, a holy-water basin buried under the grass from time immemorial.

They were pleased with the information, then exchanged a significant glance—"Is it worth the trouble?"—but already the Count was opening the door.

Mélie, who was behind it, fled abruptly.

As he passed out of the house into the grounds, he observed Gorju smoking his pipe with folded arms.

"You employ this fellow? I would not put much confidence in him in a time of disturbance."

And M. de Faverges sprang lightly into his tilbury.

Why did their servant-maid seem to be afraid of him?

They questioned her, and she told them she had been employed on his farm. She was that little girl who poured out drink for the harvesters when they came there two years before. They had taken her on as a help at the château, and dismissed her in consequence of false reports.

As for Gorju, how could they find fault with him? He was very handy, and showed the utmost consideration for them.

Next day, at dawn, they repaired to the cemetery. Bouvard felt with his walking-stick at the spot indicated. They heard the sound of a hard substance. They pulled up some nettles, and discovered a stone basin, a baptismal font, out of which plants were sprouting. It is not usual, however, to bury baptismal fonts outside churches.

Pécuchet made a sketch of it; Bouvard wrote out a description of it; and they sent both to Larsoneur. His reply came immediately.

"Victory, my dear associates! Unquestionably, it is a druidical bowl!"

However, let them be careful about the matter. The axe was doubtful; and as much for his sake as for their own, he pointed out a series of works to be consulted.

In a postscript, Larsoneur confessed his longing to have a look at this bowl, which opportunity would be afforded him in a few days, when he would be starting on a trip from Brittany.

Then Bouvard and Pécuchet plunged into Celtic archaeology.

According to this science, the ancient Gauls, our ancestors, adored Kirk and

Kron, Taranis Esus, Nelalemnia, Heaven and Earth, the Wind, the Waters, and, above all, the great Teutates, who is the Saturn of the Pagans; for Saturn, when he reigned in Phœnicia, wedded a nymph named Anobret, by whom he had a child called Jeüd. And Anobret presents the same traits as Sara; Jeüd was sacrificed (or near being so), like Isaac; therefore, Saturn is Abraham; whence the conclusion must be drawn that the religion of the Gauls had the same principles as that of the Jews.

Their society was very well organised. The first class of persons amongst them included the people, the nobility, and the king; the second, the jurisconsults; and in the third, the highest, were ranged, according to Taillepied, "the various kinds of philosophers," that is to say, the Druids or Saronides, themselves divided into Eubages, Bards, and Vates.

One section of them prophesied, another sang, while a third gave instruction in botany, medicine, history, and literature, in short, all the arts of their time.

Pythagoras and Plato were their pupils. They taught metaphysics to the Greeks, sorcery to the Persians, aruspicy to the Etruscans, and to the Romans the plating of copper and the traffic in hams.

But of this people, who ruled the ancient world, there remain only stones either isolated or in groups of three, or placed together so as to resemble a rude chamber, or forming enclosures.

Bouvard and Pécuchet, filled with enthusiasm, studied in succession the stone on the Post-farm at Ussy, the Coupled Stone at Quest, the Standing Stone near L'Aigle, and others besides.

All these blocks, of equal insignificance, speedily bored them; and one day, when they had just seen the menhir at Passais, they were about to return from it when their guide led them into a beech wood, which was blocked up with masses of granite, like pedestals or monstrous tortoises. The most remarkable of them is hollowed like a basin. One of its sides rises, and at the further end two channels run down to the ground; this must have been for the flowing of blood—impossible to doubt it! Chance does not make these things.

The roots of the trees were intertwined with these rugged pedestals. In the distance rose columns of fog like huge phantoms. It was easy to imagine under the leaves the priests in golden tiaras and white robes, and their human victims with arms bound behind their backs, and at the side of the bowl the Druidess watching the red stream, whilst around her the multitude yelled, to the accompaniment of cymbals and of trumpets made from the horns of the wild bull.

Immediately they decided on their plan. And one night, by the light of the moon, they took the road to the cemetery, stealing in like thieves, in the shadows of the houses. The shutters were fastened, and quiet reigned around every dwelling-place; not a dog barked.

Gorju accompanied them. They set to work. All that could be heard was the noise of stones knocking against the spade as it dug through the soil.

The vicinity of the dead was disagreeable to them. The church clock struck with a rattling sound, and the rosework on its tympanum looked like an eye espying a sacrilege. At last they carried off the bowl.

They came next morning to the cemetery to see the traces of the operation.

The abbé, who was taking the air at his door, begged of them to do him the honour of a visit, and, having introduced them into his breakfast-parlour, he gazed at them in a singular fashion.

In the middle of the sideboard, between the plates, was a soup-tureen decorated with yellow bouquets.

Pécuchet praised it, at a loss for something to say.

"It is old Rouen," returned the curé; "an heirloom. Amateurs set a high value on it—M. Marescot especially." As for him, thank God, he had no love of curiosities; and, as they appeared not to understand, he declared that he had seen them himself stealing the baptismal font.

The two archaeologists were quite abashed. The article in question was not in actual use.

No matter! they should give it back.

No doubt! But, at least, let them be permitted to get a painter to make a drawing of it.

"Be it so, gentlemen."

"Between ourselves, is it not?" said Bouvard, "under the seal of confession."

The ecclesiastic, smiling, reassured them with a gesture.

It was not he whom they feared, but rather Larsoneur. When he would he passing through Chavignolles, he would feel a hankering after the bowl; and his chatterings might reach the ears of the Government. Out of prudence they kept it hidden in the bakehouse, then in the arbour, in the trunk, in a cupboard. Gorju was tired of dragging it about.

The possession of such a rare piece of furniture bound them the closer to the Celticism of Normandy.

Its sources were Egyptian. Séez, in the department of the Orne, is sometimes written Saïs, like the city of the Delta. The Gauls swore by the bull, an idea derived from the bull Apis. The Latin name of Bellocastes, which was that of the people of Bayeux, comes from Beli Casa, dwelling, sanctuary of Belus—Belus and Osiris, the same divinity!

"There is nothing," says Mangou de la Londe, "opposed to the idea that druidical monuments existed near Bayeux." "This country," adds M. Roussel, "is like the country in which the Egyptians built the temple of Jupiter Ammon."

So then there was a temple in which riches were shut up. All the Celtic monuments contain them.

"In 1715," relates Dom Martin, "one Sieur Heribel exhumed in the vicinity of Bayeux, several argil vases full of bones, and concluded (in accordance with tradition and authorities which had disappeared) that this place, a necropolis, was the Mount Faunus in which the Golden Calf is buried."

In the first place, where is Mount Faunus? The authors do not point it out. The natives know nothing about it. It would be necessary to devote themselves to excavations, and with that view they forwarded a petition to the prefect, to which they got no response.

Perhaps Mount Faunus had disappeared, and was not a hill but a barrow?

Several of them contain skeletons that have the position of the foetus in the mother's womb. This meant that for them the tomb was, as it were, a second gestation, preparing them for another life. Therefore the barrow symbolises the female organ, just as the raised stone is the male organ.

In fact, where menhirs are found, an obscene creed has persisted. Witness what took place at Guerande, at Chichebouche, at Croissic, at Livarot. In former times the towers, the pyramids, the wax tapers, the boundaries of roads, and even the trees had a phallic meaning. Bouvard and Pécuchet collected whipple-trees of carriages, legs of armchairs, bolts of cellars, apothecaries' pestles. When people came to see them they would ask, "What do you think that is like?" and then they would confide the secret. And, if anyone uttered an exclamation, they would shrug their shoulders in pity.

One evening as they were dreaming about the dogmas of the Druids, the abbé cautiously stole in.

Immediately they showed the museum, beginning with the church window; but they longed to reach the new compartment—that of the phallus. The ecclesiastic stopped them, considering the exhibition indecent. He came to demand back his baptismal font.

Bouvard and Pécuchet begged for another fortnight, the time necessary for taking a moulding of it.

"The sooner the better," said the abbé.

Then he chatted on general topics.

Pécuchet, who had left the room a minute, on coming back slipped a napoleon into his hand.

The priest made a backward movement.

"Oh! for your poor!"

And, colouring, M. Jeufroy crammed the gold piece into his cassock.

To give back the bowl, the bowl for sacrifices! Never, while they lived! They were even anxious to learn Hebrew, which is the mother-tongue of Celtic, unless indeed the former language be derived from it! And they had planned a journey into Brittany, commencing with Rennes, where they had an appointment with Larsoneur, with a view of studying that urn mentioned in the Memorials of the Celtic Academy, which appeared to have contained the ashes of Queen Artimesia, when the mayor entered unceremoniously with his hat on, like the boorish individual he was.

"All this won't do, my fine fellows! You must give it up!"

"What, pray?"

"Rogues! I know well you are concealing it!"

Someone had betrayed them.

They replied that they had the curé's permission to keep it.

"We'll soon see that!"

Foureau went away. An hour later he came back.

They were obstinate.

In the first place, this holy-water basin was not wanted, as it really was not a holy-water basin at all. They would prove this by a vast number of scientific reasons. Next, they offered to acknowledge in their will that it belonged to the parish. They even proposed to buy it.

"And, besides, it is my property," Pécuchet asseverated.

The twenty francs accepted by M. Jeufroy furnished a proof of the contract, and if he compelled them to go before a justice of the peace, so much the worse: he would be taking a false oath!

During these disputes he had again seen the soup-tureen many times, and in his soul had sprung up the desire, the thirst for possession of this piece of earthenware. If the curé was willing to give it to him, he would restore the bowl, otherwise not.

Through weariness or fear of scandal, M. Jeufroy yielded it up. It was placed amongst their collection near the Cauchoise cap. The bowl decorated the church porch; and they consoled themselves for the loss of it with the reflection that the people of Chavignolles were ignorant of its value.

But the soup-tureen inspired them with a taste for earthenware—a new subject for study and for explorations through the country.

It was the period when persons of good position were looking out for old Rouen dishes. The notary possessed a few of them, and derived from the lad, as it were, an artistic reputation which was prejudicial to his profession, but for which he made up by the serious side of his character.

When he learned that Bouvard and Pécuchet had got the soup-tureen, he came to propose to them an exchange.

Pécuchet would not consent to this.

"Let us say no more about it!" and Marescot proceeded to examine their ceramic collection.

All the specimens hung up along the wall were blue on a background of dirty white, and some showed their horn of plenty in green or reddish tones. There were shaving-dishes, plates and saucers, objects long sought for, and brought back in the recesses of one's frock-coat close to one's heart.

Marescot praised them, and then talked about other kinds of faïence, the Hispano-Arabian, the Dutch, the English, and the Italian, and having dazzled them with his erudition:

"Might I see your soup-tureen again?"

He made it ring by rapping on it with his fingers, then he contemplated the two S's painted on the lid.

"The mark of Rouen!" said Pécuchet.

"Ho! ho! Rouen, properly speaking, would not have any mark. When Moutiers was unknown, all the French faïence came from Nevers. So with Rouen to-day. Besides, they imitate it to perfection at Elbœuf."

"It isn't possible!"

"Majolica is cleverly imitated. Your specimen is of no value; and as for me, I was about to do a downright foolish thing."

When the notary had gone, Pécuchet sank into an armchair in a state of nervous prostration.

"We shouldn't have given back the bowl," said Bouvard; "but you get excited, and always lose your head."

"Yes, I do lose my head"; and Pécuchet, snatching up the soup-tureen, flung it some distance away from him against the sarcophagus.

Bouvard, more self-possessed, picked up the broken pieces one by one; and some time afterwards this idea occurred to him: "Marescot, through jealousy, might have been making fools of us!"

"How?"

"There's nothing to show me that the soup-tureen was not genuine! Whereas the other specimens which he pretended to admire are perhaps counterfeit."

And so the day closed with uncertainties and regrets.

This was no reason for abandoning their tour into Brittany.

They even purposed to take Gorju along with them to assist them in their excavations.

For some time past, he had slept at the house, in order to finish the more quickly the repairing of the chest.

The prospect of a change of place annoyed him, and when they talked about menhirs and barrows which they calculated on seeing: "I know better ones," said he to them; "in Algeria, in the South, near the sources of Bou-Mursoug, you meet quantities of them." He then gave a description of a tomb which chanced to be open right in front of him, and which contained a skeleton squalling like an ape with its two arms around its legs.

Larsoneur, when they informed him of the circumstance, would not believe a word of it.

Bouvard sifted the matter, and started the question again.

How does it happen that the monuments of the Gauls are shapeless, whereas these same Gauls were civilised in the time of Julius Cæsar? No doubt they were traceable to a more ancient people.

Such a hypothesis, in Larsoneur's opinion, betrayed a lack of patriotism.

No matter; there is nothing to show that these monuments are the work of Gauls. "Show us a text!"

The Academician was displeased, and made no reply; and they were very glad of it, so much had the Druids bored them.

If they did not know what conclusion to arrive at as to earthenware and as to Celticism, it was because they were ignorant of history, especially the history of France.

The work of Anquetil was in their library; but the series of "do-nothing kings" amused them very little. The villainy of the mayors of the Palace did not excite their indignation, and they gave Anquetil up, repelled by the ineptitude of his reflections.

Then they asked Dumouchel, "What is the best history of France?"

Dumouchel subscribed, in their names, to a circulating library, and forwarded to them the work of Augustin Thierry, together with two volumes of M. de Genoude.

According to Genoude, royalty, religion, and the national assemblies—here are "the principles" of the French nation, which go back to the Merovingians. The Carlovingians fell away from them. The Capetians, being in accord with the people, made an effort to maintain them. Absolute power was established under Louis XIII, in order to conquer Protestantism, the final effort of feudalism; and '89 is a return to the constitution of our ancestors.

Pécuchet admired his ideas. They excited Bouvard's pity, as he had read Augustin Thierry first: "What trash you talk with your French nation, seeing that France did not exist! nor the national assemblies! and the Carlovingians usurped nothing at all! and the kings did not set free the communes! Read for yourself."

Pécuchet gave way before the evidence, and surpassed him in scientific strictness. He would have considered himself dishonoured if he had said "Charlemagne" and not "Karl the Great," "Clovis" in place of "Clodowig."

Nevertheless he was beguiled by Genoude, deeming it a clever thing to join together both ends of French history, so that the middle period becomes rubbish; and, in order to ease their minds about it, they took up the collection of Buchez and Roux.

But the fustian of the preface, that medley of Socialism and Catholicism, disgusted them; and the excessive accumulation of details prevented them from grasping the whole.

They had recourse to M. Thiers.

It was during the summer of 1845, in the garden beneath the arbour. Pécuchet, his feet resting on a small chair, read aloud in his cavernous voice, without feeling tired, stopping to plunge his fingers into his snuff-box. Bouvard listened, his pipe in his mouth, his legs wide apart, and the upper part of his trousers unbuttoned.

Old men had spoken to them of '93, and recollections that were almost personal gave life to the prosy descriptions of the author. At that time the highroads were covered with soldiers singing the "Marseillaise." At the thresholds of doors women sat sewing canvas to make tents. Sometimes came a wave of men in red caps, bending forward a pike, at the end of which could be seen a discoloured head with the hair hanging down. The lofty tribune of the Convention looked down upon a cloud of dust, amid which wild faces were yelling cries "Death!" Anyone who passed, at midday, close to the basin of the Tuileries could hear each blow of the guillotine, as if they were cutting up sheep.

And the breeze moved the vine-leaves of the arbour; the ripe barley swayed at intervals; a blackbird was singing. And, casting glances around them, they relished this tranquil scene.

What a pity that from the beginning they had failed to understand one another! For if the royalists had reflected like the patriots, if the court had exhibited more candour, and its adversaries less violence, many of the calamities would not have happened.

By force of chattering in this way they roused themselves into a state of excitement. Bouvard, being liberal-minded and of a sensitive nature, was a Constitutionalist, a Girondist, a Thermidorian; Pécuchet, being of a bilious temperament and a lover of authority, declared himself a *sans-culotte,* and even a Robespierrist. He expressed approval of the condemnation of the King, the most violent decrees, the worship of the Supreme Being. Bouvard preferred that of Nature. He would have saluted with pleasure the image of a big woman pouring out from her breasts to her adorers not water but Chambertin.

In order to have more facts for the support of their arguments they procured other works: Montgaillard, Prudhomme, Gallois, Lacretelle, etc.; and the contradictions of these books in no way embarrassed them. Each took from them what might vindicate the cause that he espoused.

Thus Bouvard had no doubt that Danton accepted a hundred thousand crowns to bring forward motions that would destroy the Republic; while in Pécuchet's opinion Vergniaud would have asked for six thousand francs a month.

"Never! Explain to me, rather, why Robespierre's sister had a pension from Louis XVIII."

"Not at all! It was from Bonaparte. And, since you take it that way, who is the person that a few months before Égalité's death had a secret conference with him? I wish they would reinsert in the *Memoirs of La Campan* the suppressed paragraphs. The death of the Dauphin appears to me equivocal. The powder magazine at Grenelle by exploding killed two thousand persons. The cause was unknown, they tell us: what nonsense!" For Pécuchet was not far from understanding it, and threw the blame for every crime on the manouevres of the aristocrats, gold, and the foreigner.

In the mind of Bouvard there could be no dispute as to the use of the words, "Ascend to heaven, son of St. Louis," as to the incident about the virgins of Verdun, or as to the *culottes* clothed in human skin. He accepted Prudhomme's lists, a million of victims, exactly.

But the Loire, red with gore from Saumur to Nantes, in a line of eighteen leagues, made him wonder. Pécuchet in the same degree entertained doubts, and they began to distrust the historians.

For some the Revolution is a Satanic event; others declare it to be a sublime exception. The vanquished on each side naturally play the part of martyrs.

Thierry demonstrates, with reference to the Barbarians, that it is foolish to institute an inquiry as to whether such a prince was good or was bad. Why not follow this method in the examination of more recent epochs? But history must needs avenge morality: we feel grateful to Tacitus for having lacerated Tiberius. After all, whether the Queen had lovers; whether Dumouriez, since Valmy, intended to betray her; whether in Prairial it was the Mountain or the Girondist party that began, and in Thermidor the Jacobins or the Plain; what matters it to the development of the Revolution, of which the causes were far to seek and the results incalculable?

Therefore it was bound to accomplish itself, to be what it was; but, suppose the flight of the King without impediment, Robespierre escaping or Bonaparte assassinated—chances which depended upon an innkeeper proving less scrupulous, a door being left open, or a sentinel falling asleep—and the progress of the world would have taken a different direction.

They had no longer on the men and the events of that period a single well-balanced idea. In order to form an impartial judgment upon it, it would have been necessary to have read all the histories, all the memoirs, all the newspapers, and all the manuscript productions, for through the least omission might arise an error, which might lead to others without limit.

They abandoned the subject. But the taste for history had come to them, the need of truth for its own sake.

Perhaps it is easier to find it in more ancient epochs? The authors, being far removed from the events, ought to speak of them without passion. And they began the good Rollin.

"What a heap of rubbish!" exclaimed Bouvard, after the first chapter.

"Wait a bit," said Pécuchet, rummaging at the end of their library, where lay heaped up the books of the last proprietor, an old lawyer, an accomplished man with a mania for literature; and, having put out of their places a number of novels and plays, together with an edition of Montesquieu and translations of Horace, he obtained what he was looking for—Beaufort's work on Roman History.

Titus Livius attributes the foundation of Rome to Romulus; Sallust gives the credit of it to the Trojans under Æneas. Coriolanus died in exile, according to Fabius Pictor; through the stratagems of Attius Tullius, if we may believe Dionysius. Seneca states that Horatius Cocles came back victorious; and Dionysius that he was wounded in the leg. And La Mothe le Vayer gives expression to similar doubts with reference to other nations.

There is no agreement as to the antiquity of the Chaldeans, the age of Homer, the existence of Zoroaster, the two empires of Assyria. Quintus Curtius has manufactured fables. Plutarch gives the lie to Herodotus. We should have a different idea of Cæsar if Vercingetorix had written his Commentaries.

Ancient history is obscure through want of documents. There is an abundance of them in modern history; and Bouvard and Pécuchet came back to France, and began Sismondi.

The succession of so many men filled them with a desire to understand them more thoroughly, to enter into their lives. They wanted to read the originals— Gregory of Tours, Monstrelet, Commines, all those whose names were odd or agreeable. But the events got confused through want of knowledge of the dates.

Fortunately they possessed Dumouchel's work on mnemonics, a duodecimo in boards with this epigraph: "To instruct while amusing."

It combined the three systems of Allevy, of Pâris, and of Fenaigle.

Allevy transforms numbers into external objects, the number 1 being expressed by a tower, 2 by a bird, 3 by a camel, and so on. Pâris strikes the imagination by means of rebuses: an armchair garnished with clincher-nails will give "Clou, vis—Clovis"; and, as the sound of frying makes "ric, ric," whitings in a stove will recall "Chilperic." Fenaigle divides the universe into houses, which contain rooms, each having four walls with nine panels, and each panel bearing an emblem. A pharos on a mountain will tell the name of "Phar-a-mond" in Pâris's system; and, according to Allevy's directions, by placing above a mirror, which signifies 4, a bird 2, and a hoop o, we shall obtain 420, the date of that prince's accession.

For greater clearness, they took as their mnemotechnic basis their own house, their domicile, associating a distinct fact with each part of it; and the courtyard, the garden, the outskirts, the entire country, had for them no meaning any longer except as objects for facilitating memory. The boundaries in the fields defined certain epochs; the apple trees were genealogical stems, the bushes battles; everything became symbolic. They sought for quantities of absent things on their walls, ended by seeing them, but lost the recollection of what dates they represented.

Besides the dates are not always authentic. They learned out of a manual for colleges that the birth of Jesus ought to be carried back five years earlier than the date usually assigned for it; that there were amongst the Greeks three ways of counting the Olympiads, and eight amongst the Latin of making the year begin. So many opportunities for mistakes outside of those which result from the zodiacs, from the epochs, and from the different calendars!

And from carelessness as to dates they passed to contempt for facts.

What is important is the philosophy of history!

Bouvard could not finish the celebrated discourse of Bossuet.

"The eagle of Meaux is a farce-actor! He forgets China, the Indies, and America; but is careful to let us know that Theodosius was 'the joy of the universe,' that Abraham 'treated kings as his equals,' and that the philosophy of the Greeks has come down from the Hebrews. His preoccupation with the Hebrews provokes me."

Pécuchet shared this opinion, and wished to make him read Vico.

"Why admit," objected Bouvard, "that fables are more true than the truths of historians?"

Pécuchet tried to explain myths, and got lost in the *Scienza Nuova*.

"Will you deny the design of Providence?"

"I don't know it!" said Bouvard. And they decided to refer to Dumouchel.

The professor confessed that he was now at sea on the subject of history.

"It is changing everyday. There is a controversy as to the kings of Rome and the journeys of Pythagoras. Doubts have been thrown on Belisarius, William Tell, and even on the Cid, who has become, thanks to the latest discoveries, a common robber. It is desirable that no more discoveries should be made, and the Institute ought even to lay down a kind of canon prescribing what it is necessary to believe!"

In a postscript he sent them some rules of criticism taken from Daunou's course of lectures:

"To cite by way of proof the testimony of multitudes is a bad method of proof; they are not there to reply.

"To reject impossible things. Pausanias was shown the stone swallowed by Saturn.

"Architecture may lie: instance, the arch of the Forum, in which Titus is called the first conqueror of Jerusalem, which had been conquered before him by Pompey.

"Medals sometimes deceive. Under Charles IX money was minted from the coinage of Henry II.

"Take into account the skill of forgers and the interestedness of apologists and calumniators."

Few historians have worked in accordance with these rules, but all in view of one special cause, of one religion, of one nation, of one party, of one system, in order to curb kings, to advise the people, or to offer moral examples.

The others, who pretend merely to narrate, are no better; for everything cannot be told—some selection must be made. But in the selection of documents some special predilection will have the upper hand, and, as this varies according to the conditions under which the writer views the matter, history will never be fixed.

"It is sad," was their reflection. However, one might take a subject, exhaust the sources of information concerning it, make a good analysis of them, then condense it into a narrative, which would be, as it were, an epitome of the facts reflecting the entire truth.

"Do you wish that we should attempt to compose a history?"

"I ask for nothing better. But of what?"

"Suppose we write the life of the Duke of Angoulême?"

"But he was an idiot!" returned Bouvard.

"What matter? Personages of an inferior mould have sometimes an enormous influence, and he may have controlled the machinery of public affairs."

The books would furnish them with information; and M. de Faverges, no doubt, would have them himself, or could procure them from some elderly gentleman of his acquaintance.

They thought over this project, discussed it, and finally determined to spend a fortnight at the municipal library at Caen in making researches there.

The librarian placed at their disposal some general histories and some pamphlets with a coloured lithograph portrait representing at three-quarters' length Monseigneur the Duke of Angoulême.

The blue cloth of his uniform disappeared under the epaulets, the stars, and the large red ribbon of the Legion of Honour; a very high collar surrounded his long neck; his pear-shaped head was framed by the curls of his hair and by his scanty whiskers and heavy eyelashes; and a very big nose and thick lips gave his face an expression of commonplace good-nature.

When they had taken notes, they drew up a programme:

"Birth and childhood but slightly interesting. One of his tutors is the Abbé Guénée, Voltaire's enemy. At Turin he is made to cast a cannon; and he studies the campaigns of Charles VIII. Also he is nominated, despite his youth, colonel of a regiment of noble guards.

"1797.—His marriage.

"1814.—The English take possession of Bordeaux. He runs up behind them and shows his person to the inhabitants. Description of the prince's person.

"1815.—Bonaparte surprises him. Immediately he appeals to the King of Spain; and Toulon, were it not for Masséna, would have been surrendered to England.

"Operations in the South. He is beaten, but released under the promise to restore the crown diamonds carried off at full gallop by the King, his uncle.

"After the Hundred Days he returns with his parents and lives in peace. Several years glide away.

"War with Spain. Once he has crossed the Pyrenees, victories everywhere follow the grandson of Henry IV He takes the Trocadéro, reaches the pillars of Hercules, crushes the factions, embraces Ferdinand, and returns.

"Triumphal arches; flowers presented by young girls; dinners at the Prefecture; 'Te Deum' in the cathedrals. The Parisians are at the height of intoxication. The city offers him a banquet. Songs containing allusions to the hero are sung at the theatre.

"The enthusiasm diminishes; for in 1827 a ball organised by subscription proves a failure.

"As he is High Admiral of France, he inspects the fleet, which is going to start for Algiers.

"July 1830.—Marmont informs him of the state of affairs. Then he gets into such a rage that he wounds himself in the hand with the general's sword. The King entrusts him with the command of all the forces.

"He meets detachments of the line in the Bois de Boulogne, and has not a word to say to them.

"From St. Cloud he flies to the bridge of Sèvres. Coldness of the troops. That does not shake him. The Royal family leave Trianon. He sits down at the foot of an oak, unrolls a map, meditates, remounts his horse, passes in front of St. Cyr, and sends to the students words of hope.

"At Rambouillet the bodyguards bid him goodbye. He embarks, and during the entire passage is ill. End of his career.

"The importance possessed by the bridges ought here to be noticed. First, he exposes himself needlessly on the bridge of the Inn; he carries the bridge St. Esprit and the bridge of Lauriol; at Lyons the two bridges are fatal to him, and his fortune dies before the bridge of Sèvres.

"List of his virtues. Needless to praise his courage, to which he joined a far-seeing policy. For he offered every soldier sixty francs to desert the Emperor, and in Spain he tried to corrupt the Constitutionalists with ready money.

"His reserve was so profound that he consented to the marriage arranged between his father and the Queen of Etruria, to the formation of a new cabinet after the Ordinances, to the abdication in favour of Chambord—to everything that they asked him.

"Firmness, however, was not wanting in him. At Angers, he cashiered the infantry of the National Guard, who, jealous of the cavalry, had succeeded by means of a stratagem in forming his escort, so that his Highness found himself jammed into the ranks at the cost of having his knees squeezed. But he censured the cavalry, the cause of the disorder, and pardoned the infantry—a veritable judgment of Solomon.

"His piety manifested itself by numerous devotions, and his clemency by obtaining the pardon of General Debelle, who had borne arms against him.

"Intimate details; characteristics of the Prince:

"At the château of Beauregard, in his childhood, he took pleasure in deepening, along with his brother, a sheet of water, which may still be seen. On one occasion, he visited the barracks of the chasseurs, called for a glass of wine, and drank the King's health.

"While walking, in order to mark the step, he used to keep repeating to himself: 'One, two—one, two—one, two!'

"Some of his sayings have been preserved—

"To a deputation from Bordeaux:

" 'What consoles me for not being at Bordeaux is to find myself amidst you.'

"To the Protestants of Nismes:

" 'I am a good Catholic, but I shall never forget that my distinguished ancestor was a Protestant.'

"To the pupils of St. Cyr, when all was lost:

" 'Right, my friends! The news is good! This is right—all right!'

"After Charles X's abdication:

" 'Since they don't want me, let them settle it themselves.'

"And in 1814, at every turn, in the smallest village:

" 'No more war; no more conscription; no more united rights.'

"His style was as good as his utterance. His proclamations surpassed everything.

"The first, of the Count of Artois, began thus:

" 'Frenchmen, your King's brother has arrived!'

"That of the prince:

" 'I come. I am the son of your kings. You are Frenchmen!'

"Order of the day, dated from Bayonne:

" 'Soldiers, I come!'

"Another, in the midst of disaffection:

" 'Continue to sustain with the vigour which befits the French soldier the struggle which you have begun. France expects it of you.'

"Lastly, at Rambouillet:

" 'The King has entered into an arrangement with the government established at Paris, and everything brings us to believe that this arrangement is on the point of being concluded.'

" 'Everything brings us to believe' was sublime."

"One thing vexed me," said Bouvard, "that there is no mention of his love affairs!" And they made a marginal note: "To search for the prince's amours."

At the moment when they were taking their leave, the librarian, bethinking himself of it, showed them another portrait of the Duke of Angoulême.

In this one he appeared as a colonel of cuirassiers, on a vaulting-horse, his eyes still smaller, his mouth open, and his hair straight.

How were they to reconcile the two portraits? Had he straight hair, or rather crisped—unless he carried affectation so far as to get it curled?

A grave question, from Pécuchet's point of view, for the mode of wearing the hair indicates the temperament, and the temperament the individual.

Bouvard considered that we know nothing of a man as long as we are ignorant of his passions; and in order to clear up these two points, they presented themselves at the château of Faverges. The count was not there; this retarded their work. They returned home annoyed.

The door of the house was wide open; there was nobody in the kitchen. They went upstairs, and who should they see in the middle of Bouvard's room but Madame Bordin, looking about her right and left!

"Excuse me," she said, with a forced laugh, "I have for the last hour been searching for your cook, whom I wanted for my preserves."

They found her in the wood-house on a chair fast asleep. They shook her. She opened her eyes.

"What is it now? You are always prodding at me with your questions!"

It was clear that Madame Bordin had been putting some to her in their absence.

Germaine got out of her torpor, and complained of indigestion.

"I am remaining to take care of you," said the widow.

Then they perceived in the courtyard a big cap, the lappets of which were fluttering. It was Madame Castillon, proprietress of a neighbouring farm. She was calling out: "Gorju! Gorju!"

And from the corn-loft the voice of their little servant-maid answered loudly: "He is not there!"

At the end of five minutes she came down, with her cheeks flushed and looking excited. Bouvard and Pécuchet reprimanded her for having been so slow. She unfastened their gaiters without a murmur.

Then they went to look at the chest. The bake-house was covered with its scattered fragments; the carvings were damaged, the leaves broken.

At this sight, in the face of this fresh disaster, Bouvard had to keep back his tears, and Pécuchet got a fit of nervous shivering.

Gorju, making his appearance almost immediately, explained the matter. He had just put the chest outside in order to varnish it, when a wandering cow knocked it down on the ground.

"Whose cow?" said Pécuchet.

"I don't know."

"Ah! you left the door open, as you did some time ago. It is your fault."

At any rate, they would have nothing more to do with him. He had been trifling with them too long, and they wanted no more of him or his work.

"These gentlemen were wrong. The damage was not so great. It would be all settled before three weeks." And Gorju accompanied them into the kitchen, where Germaine was seen dragging herself along to see after the dinner.

They noticed on the table a bottle of Calvados, three quarters emptied.

"By you, no doubt," said Pécuchet to Gorju.

"By me! never!"

Bouvard met his protest by observing:

"You are the only man in the house."

"Well, and what about the women?" rejoined the workman, with a side wink.

Germaine caught him up:

"You'd better say 'twas I!"

"Certainly it was you."

"And perhaps 'twas I smashed the press?"

Gorju danced about.

"Don't you see that she's drunk?"

Then they squabbled violently with eachother, he with a pale face and a biting manner, she purple with rage, tearing tufts of grey hair from under her cotton cap. Madame Bordin took Germaine's part, while Mélie took Gorju's.

The old woman burst out:

"Isn't it an abomination that you two should be spending days together in the grove, not to speak of the nights?—a sort of Parisian, eating up honest women, who comes to our master's house to play tricks on them!"

Bouvard opened his eyes wide.

"What tricks?"

"I tell you he's making fools of you!"

"Nobody can make a fool of me!" exclaimed Pécuchet, and, indignant at her insolence, exasperated by the mortification inflicted on him, he dismissed her, telling her to go and pack. Bouvard did not oppose this decision, and they went out, leaving Germaine in sobs over her misfortune, while Madame Bordin was trying to console her.

In the course of the evening, as they grew calmer, they went over these occurrences, asked themselves who had drunk the Calvados, how the chest got broken, what Madame Castillon wanted when she was calling Gorju, and whether he had dishonoured Mélie.

"We are not able to tell," said Bouvard, "what is happening in our own household, and we lay claim to discover all about the hair and the love affairs of the Duke of Angoulême."

Pécuchet added: "How many questions there are in other respects important and still more difficult!"

Whence they concluded that external facts are not everything. It is necessary to complete them by means of psychology. Without imagination, history is defective.

"Let us send for some historical romances!"

Chapter V

ROMANCE AND THE DRAMA

THEY FIRST READ WALTER SCOTT.

It was like the surprise of a new world.

The men of the past who had for them been only phantoms or names, became living beings, kings, princes, wizards, footmen, gamekeepers, monks, gipsies, merchants, and soldiers, who deliberate, fight, travel, trade, eat and drink, sing and pray, in the armouries of castles, on the blackened benches of inns, in the winding streets of cities, under the sloping roofs of booths, in the cloisters of monasteries. Landscapes artistically arranged formed backgrounds for the narratives, like the scenery of a theatre. You follow with your eyes a horseman galloping along the strand; you breathe amid the heather the freshness of the wind; the moon shines on the lake, over which a boat is skimming; the sun glitters on the breast-plates; the rain falls over leafy huts. Without having any knowledge of the models, they thought these pictures lifelike and the illusion was complete.

And so the winter was spent.

When they had breakfasted, they would instal themselves in the little room, one at each side of the chimneypiece, and, facing each other, book in hand, they would begin to read in silence. When the day wore apace, they would go out for a walk along the road, then, having snatched a hurried dinner, they would resume their reading far into the night. In order to protect himself from the lamp, Bouvard wore blue spectacles, while Pécuchet kept the peak of his cap drawn over his forehead.

Germaine had not gone, and Gorju now and again came to dig in the garden; for they had yielded through indifference, forgetful of material things.

After Walter Scott, Alexandre Dumas diverted them after the fashion of a magic-lantern. His personages, active as apes, strong as bulls, gay as chaffinches, enter on the scene and talk abruptly, jump off roofs to the pavement, receive frightful wounds from which they recover, are believed to be dead, and yet reappear. There are trap-doors under the boards, antidotes, disguises; and all things get entangled, hurry along, and are finally unravelled without a minute for reflection. Love observes the proprieties, fanaticism is cheerful, and massacres excite a smile.

Rendered hard to please by these two masters, they could not tolerate the balderdash of the *Belisaraire*, the foolery of the *Numa Pompilius*, of Marchangy, and Vicomte d'Arlincourt. The colouring of Frédéric Soulié (like that of the book-lover Jacob) appeared to them insufficient; and M. Villemain scandalised them by showing at page 85 of his *Lascaris*, a Spaniard smoking a pipe—a long Arab pipe— in the middle of the fifteenth century.

Pécuchet consulted the *Biographie Universelle,* and undertook to revise Dumas from the point of view of science.

The author in *Les Deux Dianes* makes a mistake with regard to dates. The marriage of the Dauphin, Francis, took place on the 15th of October, 1548, and not on the 20th of May, 1549. How does he know (see *Le Page du Duc de Savoie*) that Catherine de Medicis, after her husband's death, wished to resume the war? It is not very probable that the Duke of Anjou was crowned at night in a church, an episode which adorns *La Dame de Montsoreau. La Reine Margot* especially swarms with errors. The Duke of Nevers was not absent. He gave his opinion at the council before the feast of St. Bartholomew, and Henry of Navarre did not follow the procession four days after. Henry III did not come back from Poland so quickly. Besides, how many flimsy devices! The miracle of the hawthorn, the balcony of Charles IX, the poisoned glass of Jeanne d'Albret—Pécuchet no longer had any confidence in Dumas.

He even lost all respect for Walter Scott on account of the oversights in his *Quentin Durward*. The murder of the Archbishop of Liège is anticipated by fifteen years. The wife of Robert de Lamarck was Jeanne d'Arschel and not Hameline de Croy. Far from being killed by a soldier, he was put to death by Maximilian; and the face of Temeraire, when his corpse was found, did not express any menace, inasmuch as the wolves had half devoured it.

None the less, Bouvard went on with Walter Scott, but ended by getting weary of the repetition of the same effects. The heroine usually lives in the country with her father, and the lover, a plundered heir, is re-established in his rights and triumphs over his rivals. There are always a mendicant philosopher, a morose nobleman, pure young girls, facetious retainers, and interminable dialogues, stupid prudishness, and an utter absence of depth.

In his dislike to bric-à-brac, Bouvard took up George Sand.

He went into raptures over the beautiful adulteresses and noble lovers, would have liked to be Jacques, Simon, Lélio, and to have lived in Venice. He uttered sighs, did not know what was the matter with him, and felt himself changed.

Pécuchet, who was working up historical literature studied plays. He swallowed two *Pharamonds*, three *Clovises*, four *Charlemagnes*, several *Philip Augustuses*, a crowd of *Joan of Arcs*, many *Marquises de Pompadours*, and some *Conspiracies of Cellamare*.

Nearly all of them appeared still more stupid than the romances. For there exists for the stage a conventional history which nothing can destroy. Louis XI will not fail to kneel before the little images in his hat; Henry IV will be constantly jovial, Mary Stuart tearful, Richelieu cruel; in short, all the characters seem taken from a single block, from love of simplicity and regard for ignorance, so that the playwright, far from elevating, lowers, and, instead of instructing, stupefies.

As Bouvard had spoken eulogistically to him about George Sand, Pécuchet proceeded to read *Consuelo, Horace,* and *Mauprat* was beguiled by the author's vindication of the oppressed, the socialistic and republican aspect of her works, and the discussions contained in them.

According to Bouvard, however, these elements spoiled the story, and he asked for love-tales at the circulating library.

They read aloud, one after the other, *La Nouvelle Héloïse, Delphine, Adolphe,* and *Ourika.* But the listener's yawns proved contagious, for the book slipped out of the reader's hand to the floor.

They found fault with the last-mentioned works for making no reference to the environment, the period, the costume of the various personages. The heart alone is the theme—nothing but sentiment! as if there were nothing else in the world.

They next went in for novels of the humorous order, such as the *Voyage autour de ma Chambre,* by Xavier de Maistre, and *Sous les Tilleuls,* by Alphonse Karr. In books of this description the author must interrupt the narrative in order to talk about his dog, his slippers, or his mistress.

A style so free from formality charmed them at first, then appeared stupid to them, for the author effaces his work while displaying in it his personal surroundings.

Through need of the dramatic element, they plunged into romances of adventure. The more entangled, extraordinary, and impossible the plot was, the more it interested them. They did their best to foresee the *dénouement,* became very excited over it, and tired themselves out with a piece of child's play unworthy of serious minds.

The work of Balzac amazed them like a Babylon, and at the same time like grains of dust under the microscope.

In the most commonplace things arise new aspects. They never suspected that there were such depths in modern life.

"What an observer!" exclaimed Bouvard.

"For my part I consider him chimerical," Pécuchet ended by declaring. "He believes in the occult sciences, in monarchy, in rank; is dazzled by rascals; turns up millions for you like centimes; and middle-class people are not with him middle-class people at all, but giants. Why inflate what is unimportant, and waste description on silly things? He wrote one novel on chemistry, another on banking, another on printing-machines, just as one Ricard produced *The Cabman, The Water-Carrier* and *The Cocoa-Nut Seller.* We should soon have books on every trade and on every province; then on every town and on the different stories of every house, and on every individual—which would be no longer literature but statistics or ethnography."

The process was of little consequence in Bouvard's estimation. He wanted to get information—to acquire a deeper knowledge of human nature. He read Paul de Kock again, and ran through the *Old Hermits of the Chaussée d' Antin.*

"Why lose one's time with such absurdities?" said Pécuchet.

"But they might be very interesting as a series of documents."

"Go away with your documents! I want something to lift me up, and take me away from the miseries of this world."

And Pécuchet, craving for the ideal, led Bouvard unconsciously towards tragedy.

The far-off times in which the action takes place, the interests with which it is concerned, and the high station of its leading personages impressed them with a certain sense of grandeur.

One day Bouvard took up *Athalie,* and recited the dream so well that Pécuchet wished to attempt it in his turn. From the opening sentence his voice got lost in a sort of humming sound. It was monotonous and, though strong, indistinct.

Bouvard, full of experience, advised him, in order to render it well-modulated, to roll it out from the lowest tone to the highest, and to draw it back by making use of an ascending and descending scale; and he himself went through this exercise every morning in bed, according to the precept of the Greeks. Pécuchet, at the time mentioned, worked in the same fashion: each had his door closed, and they went on bawling separately.

The features that pleased them in tragedy were the emphasis, the political declamations, and the maxims on the perversity of things.

They learned by heart the most celebrated dialogues of Racine and Voltaire, and they used to declaim them in the corridor. Bouvard, as if he were at the Théâtre Français, strutted, with his hand on Pécuchet's shoulder, stopping at intervals; and, with rolling eyes, he would open wide his arms, and accuse the Fates. He would give forth fine bursts of grief from the *Philoctète* of La Harpe, a nice death-rattle from *Gabrielle de Vergy,* and, when he played Dionysius, tyrant of Syracuse, the way in which he represented that personage gazing at his son while exclaiming, "Monster, worthy of me!" was indeed terrible. Pécuchet forgot his part in it. The ability, and not the will, was what he lacked.

On one occasion, in the *Cléopâtre* of Marmontel, he fancied that he could reproduce the hissing of the asp, just as the automaton invented for the purpose by Vaucanson might have done it. The abortive effort made them laugh all the evening. The tragedy sank in their estimation.

Bouvard was the first to grow tired of it, and, dealing frankly with the subject, demonstrated how artificial and limping it was, the silliness of its incidents, and the absurdity of the disclosures made to confidants.

They then went in for comedy, which is the school for fine shading. Every sentence must be dislocated, every word must be underlined, and every syllable must be weighed. Pécuchet could not manage it, and got quite stranded in *Celimène*. Moreover, he thought the lovers very cold, the disputes a bore, and the valets intolerable—Clitandre and Sganarelle as unreal as Ægistheus and Agamemnon.

There remained the serious comedy or tragedy of everyday life, where we see fathers of families afflicted, servants saving their masters, rich men offering others their fortunes, innocent seamstresses and villainous corrupters, a species which extends from Diderot to Pixérécourt. All these plays preaching about virtue disgusted them by their triviality.

The drama of 1830 fascinated them by its movement, its colouring, its youthfulness. They made scarcely any distinction between Victor Hugo, Dumas, or Bouchardy, and the diction was no longer to be pompous or fine, but lyrical, extravagant.

One day, as Bouvard was trying to make Pécuchet understand Frédéric Lemaître's acting, Madame Bordin suddenly presented herself in a green shawl, carrying with her a volume of Pigault-Lebrun, the two gentlemen being so polite as to lend her novels now and then.

"But go on!" for she had been a minute there already, and had listened to them with pleasure.

They hoped she would excuse them. She insisted.

"Faith!" said Bouvard, "there's nothing to prevent—"

Pécuchet, through bashfulness, remarked that he could not act unprepared and without costume.

"To do it effectively, we should need to disguise ourselves!"

And Bouvard looked about for something to put on, but found only the Greek cap, which he snatched up.

As the corridor was not big enough, they went down to the drawing-room. Spiders crawled along the walls, and the geological specimens that encumbered the floor had whitened with their dust the velvet of the armchairs. On the chair which had least dirt on it they spread a cover, so that Madame Bordin might sit down.

It was necessary to give her something good.

Bouvard was in favour of the *Tour de Nesle*. But Pécuchet was afraid of parts which called for too much action.

"She would prefer some classical piece! *Phèdre*, for instance."

"Be it so."

Bouvard set forth the theme: "It is about a queen whose husband has a son by another wife. She has fallen madly in love with the young man. Are we there? Start!

> *"Yes, prince! for Theseus I grow faint, I burn—*
> *I love him!"*

And, addressing Pécuchet's side-face, he gushed out admiration of his port, his visage, "that charming head"; grieved at not having met him with the Greek fleet; would have gladly been lost with him in the labyrinth.

The border of the red cap bent forward amorously, and his trembling voice and his appealing face begged of the cruel one to take pity on a hopeless flame.

Pécuchet, turning aside, breathed hard to emphasise his emotion.

Madame Bordin, without moving, kept her eyes wide open, as if gazing at people whirling round; Mélie was listening behind the door; Gorju, in his shirt-sleeves, was staring at them through the window. Bouvard made a dash into the second part. His acting gave expression to the delirium of the senses, remorse, despair; and he flung himself on the imaginary sword of Pécuchet with such violence that, slipping over some of the stone specimens, he was near tumbling on the ground.

"Pay no attention! Then Theseus arrives, and she poisons herself."

"Poor woman!" said Madame Bordin.

After this they begged of her to choose a piece for them.

She felt perplexed about making a selection. She had seen only three pieces: *Robert le Diable* in the capital, *Le Jeune Mari* at Rouen, and another at Falaise which was very funny, and which was called *La Brouette du Vinaigrier.*

Finally, Bouvard suggested to her the great scene of Tartuffe in the second act.

Pécuchet thought an explanation was desirable:

"You must know that Tartuffe—"

Madame Bordin interrupted him: "We know what a Tartuffe is."

Bouvard had wished for a robe for a certain passage.

"I see only the monk's habit," said Pécuchet.

"No matter; bring it here."

He reappeared with it and a copy of Molière.

The opening was tame, but at the place where Tartuffe caresses Elmire's knees, Pécuchet assumed the tone of a gendarme:

"What is your hand doing there?"

Bouvard instantly replied in a sugary voice:

"I am feeling your dress; the stuff of it is marrowy."

And he shot forth glances from his eyes, bent forward his mouth, sniffed with an exceedingly lecherous air, and ended by even addressing himself to Madame Bordin.

His impassioned gaze embarrassed her, and when he stopped, humble and palpitating, she almost sought for something to say in reply.

Pécuchet took refuge in the book: *"The declaration is quite gallant."*

"Ha! yes," cried she; "he is a bold wheedler."

"Is it not so?" returned Bouvard confidently. "But here's another with a more modern touch about it." And, having opened his coat, he squatted over a piece of ashlar, and, with his head thrown back, burst forth:

> *"Your eyes' bright flame my vision floods with joy.*
> *Sing me some song like those, in bygone years,*
> *You sang at eve, your dark eye filled with tears."*

"That is like me," she thought.

> *"Drink and be merry! let the wine-cup flow:*
> *Give me this hour, and all the rest may go!"*

"How droll you are!" And she laughed with a little laugh, which made her throat rise up, and exposed her teeth.

> *"Ah! say, is it not sweet*
> *To love and see your lover at your feet?"*

He knelt down.

"Finish, then."

> *" 'Oh! let me sleep and dream upon thy breast,*
> *My beauty, Doña Sol, my love!'*

Here the bells are heard, and they are disturbed by a mountaineer."

"Fortunately; for, but for that—" And Madame Bordin smiled, in place of finishing the sentence.

It was getting dark. She arose.

It had been raining a short time before, and the path through the beech grove not being dry enough, it was more convenient to return across the fields. Bouvard accompanied her into the garden, in order to open the gate for her.

At first they walked past the trees cut like distaffs, without a word being spo-

ken on either side. He was still moved by his declamation, and she, at the bottom
of her heart, felt a certain kind of fascination, a charm which was generated by the
influence of literature. There are occasions when art excites commonplace natures;
and worlds may be unveiled by the clumsiest interpreters.

The sun had reappeared, making the leaves glisten, and casting luminous spots
here and there amongst the brakes. Three sparrows with little chirpings hopped on
the trunk of an old linden tree which had fallen to the ground. A hawthorn in blossom exhibited its pink sheath; lilacs drooped, borne down by their foliage.

"Ah! that does one good!" said Bouvard, inhaling the air till it filled his lungs.

"You are so painstaking."

"It is not that I have talent; but as for fire, I possess some of that."

"One can see," she returned, pausing between the words, "that you—were in
love—in your early days."

"Only in my early days, you believe?"

She stopped. "I know nothing about it."

"What does she mean?" And Bouvard felt his heart beating.

A little pool in the middle of the gravel obliging them to step aside, they got
up on the hedgerow.

Then they chatted about the recital.

"What is the name of your last piece?"

"It is taken from *Hernani,* a drama."

"Ha!" then slowly and as if in soliloquy, "it must be nice to have a gentleman
say such things to you—in downright earnest."

"I am at your service," replied Bouvard.

"You?"

"Yes, I."

"What a joke!"

"Not the least in the world!"

And, having cast a look about him, he caught her from behind round the waist
and kissed the nape of her neck vigorously.

She became very pale as if she were going to faint, and leaned one hand against
a tree, then opened her eyes and shook her head.

"It is past."

He looked at her in amazement.

The grating being open, she got up on the threshold of the little gateway.

There was a water-channel at the opposite side. She gathered up all the folds
of her petticoat and stood on the brink hesitatingly.

"Do you want my assistance?"

"Unnecessary."

"Why not?"

"Ha! you are too dangerous!" And as she jumped down, he could see her white stocking.

Bouvard blamed himself for having wasted an opportunity. Bah! he should have one again—and then not all women are alike. With some of them you must be blunt, while audacity destroys you with others. In short, he was satisfied with himself—and he did not confide his hope to Pécuchet; this was through fear of the remarks that would be passed, and not at all through delicacy.

From that time forth they used to recite in the presence of Mélie and Gorju, all the time regretting that they had not a private theatre.

The little servant-girl was amused without understanding a bit of it, wondering at the language, charmed at the roll of the verses. Gorju applauded the philosophic passages in the tragedies, and everything in the people's favour in the melodramas, so that, delighted at his good taste, they thought of giving him lessons, with a view to making an actor of him subsequently. This prospect dazzled the workman.

Their performances by this time became the subject of general gossip. Vaucorbeil spoke to them about the matter in a sly fashion. Most people regarded their acting with contempt.

They only prided themselves the more upon it. They crowned themselves artists. Pécuchet wore moustaches, and Bouvard thought he could not do anything better, with his round face and his bald patch, than to give himself a head à la Béranger. Finally, they determined to write a play.

The subject was the difficulty. They searched for it while they were at breakfast, and drank coffee, a stimulant indispensable for the brain, then two or three little glasses. They would next take a nap on their beds, after which they would make their way down to the fruit garden and take a turn there; and at length they would leave the house to find inspiration outside, and, after walking side by side, they would come back quite worn out.

Or else they would shut themselves up together. Bouvard would sweep the table, lay down paper in front of him, dip his pen, and remain with his eyes on the ceiling; whilst Pécuchet, in the armchair, would be plunged in meditation, with his legs stretched out and his head down.

Sometimes they felt a shivering sensation, and, as it were, the passing breath of an idea, but at the very moment when they were seizing it, it had vanished.

But methods exist for discovering subjects. You take a title at random, and a fact trickles out of it. You develop a proverb; you combine a number of adventures so as to form only one. None of these devices came to anything. In vain they ran through collections of anecdotes, several volumes of celebrated trials, and a heap of historical works.

And they dreamed of being acted at the Odéon, had their thoughts fixed on theatrical performances, and sighed for Paris.

"I was born to be an author instead of being buried in the country!" said Bouvard.

"And I likewise," chimed in Pécuchet.

Then came an illumination to their minds. If they had so much trouble about it, the reason was their ignorance of the rules.

They studied them in the *Pratique du Théâtre*, by D'Aubignac, and in some works not quite so old-fashioned.

Important questions are discussed in them: Whether comedy can be written in verse; whether tragedy does not go outside its limits by taking its subject from modern history; whether the homes ought to be virtuous; what kinds of villains it allows; up to what point horrors are permissible in it; that the details should verge towards a single end; that the interest should increase; that the conclusion should harmonise with the opening—these were unquestionable propositions.

> *"Invent resorts that can take hold of me."*

says Boileau. By what means were they to "invent resorts?"

> *"So that in all your speeches passion's dart*
> *May penetrate, and warm, and move the heart."*

How were they to "warm the heart?"

Rules, therefore, were not sufficient; there was need, in addition, for genius. And genius is not sufficient either. Corneille, according to the French Academy, understands nothing about the stage; Geoffroy disparaged Voltaire; Souligny scoffed at Racine; La Harpe blushed at Shakespeare's name.

Becoming disgusted with the old criticism, they wished to make acquaintance with the new, and sent for the notices of plays in the newspapers.

What assurance! What obstinacy! What dishonesty! Outrages on masterpieces; respect shown for platitudes; the gross ignorance of those who pass for scholars, and the stupidity of others whom they describe as witty.

Perhaps it is to the public that one must appeal.

But works that have been applauded sometimes displeased them, and amongst plays that were hissed there were some that they admired.

Thus the opinions of persons of taste are unreliable, while the judgment of the multitude is incomprehensible.

Bouvard submitted the problem to Barberou. Pécuchet, on his side, wrote to Dumouchel.

The ex-commercial traveller was astonished at the effeminacy engendered by provincial life. His old Bouvard was turning into a blockhead; in short, "he was no longer in it at all."

"The theatre is an article of consumption like any other. It is advertised in the newspapers. We go to the theatre to be amused. The good thing is the thing that amuses."

"But, idiot," exclaimed Pécuchet, "what amuses you is not what amuses me; and the others, as well as yourself, will be weary of it by and by. If plays are written expressly to be acted, how is it that the best of them can be always read?"

And he awaited Dumouchel's reply. According to the professor, the immediate fate of a play proved nothing. The *Misanthrope* and *Athalie* are dying out. *Zaïre* is no longer understood. Who speaks to-day of Ducange or of Picard? And he recalled all the great contemporary successes from *Fanchon la Vielleuse* to *Gaspardo le Pêcheur,* and deplored the decline of our stage. The cause of it is the contempt for literature, or rather for style; and, with the aid of certain authors mentioned by Dumouchel, they learned the secret of the various styles; how we get the majestic, the temperate, the ingenuous, the touches that are noble and the expressions that are low. "Dogs" may be heightened by "devouring"; "to vomit" is to be used only figuratively; "fever" is applied to the passions; "valiance" is beautiful in verse.

"Suppose we made verses?" said Pécuchet.

"Yes, later. Let us occupy ourselves with prose first."

A strict recommendation is given to choose a classic in order to mould yourself upon it; but all of them have their dangers, and not only have they sinned in point of style, but still more in point of phraseology.

This assertion disconcerted Bouvard and Pécuchet, and they set about studying grammar.

Has the French language, in its idiomatic structure definite articles and indefinite, as in Latin? Some think that it has, others that it has not. They did not venture to decide.

The subject is always in agreement with the verb, save on the occasions when the subject is not in agreement with it.

There was formerly no distinction between the verbal adjective and the present participle; but the Academy lays down one not very easy to grasp.

They were much pleased to learn that the pronoun *leur* is used for persons, but also for things, while *où* and *en* are used for things and sometimes for persons.

Ought we to say *Cette femme a l'air bon* or *l'air bonne?*—*une bûche de bois sec,* or *de bois sèche?*—*ne pas laisser de,* or *que de?*—*une troupe de voleurs survint,* or *survinrent?*

Other difficulties: *Autour* and *á l'entour* of which Racine and Boileau did not see the difference; *imposer,* or *en imposer,* synonyms with Massillon and Voltaire; *croasser* and *coasser,* confounded by La Fontaine, who knew, however, how to distinguish a crow from a frog.

The grammarians, it is true, are at variance. Some see a beauty where others discover a fault. They admit principles of which they reject the consequences, announce consequences of which they repudiate the principles, lean on tradition, throw over the masters, and adopt whimsical refinements.

Ménage, instead of *lentilles* and *cassonade,* approves of *nentilles* and *castonade;* Bonhours, *jérarchie* and not *hiérarchie* and M. Chapsal speaks of *les oeils de la soupe.*

Pécuchet was amazed above all at Jénin. What! *ʒ'annetons* would be better than *hannetons, ʒ'aricots* than *haricots!* and, under Louis XIV, the pronunciation was *Roume* and *Monsieur de Lioune,* instead of *Rome* and *Monsieur de Lionne!*

Littré gave them the finishing stroke by declaring that there never had been, and never could be positive orthography. They concluded that syntax is a whim and grammar an illusion.

At this period, moreover, a new school of rhetoric declared that we should write as we speak, and that all would be well so long as we felt and observed.

As they had felt and believed that they had observed, they considered themselves qualified to write. A play is troublesome on account of the narrowness of its framework, but the novel has more freedom. In order to write one they searched among their personal recollections.

Pécuchet recalled to mind one of the head-clerks in his own office, a very nasty customer, and he felt a longing to take revenge on him by means of a book.

Bouvard had, at the smoking saloon, made the acquaintance of an old writing-master, who was a miserable drunkard. Nothing could be so ludicrous as this character.

At the end of the week, they imagined that they could fuse these two subjects into one. They left off there, and passed on to the following: a woman who causes the unhappiness of a family; a wife, her husband, and her lover; a woman who would be virtuous through a defect in her conformation; an ambitious man; a bad priest. They tried to bind together with these vague conceptions things supplied by their memory, and then made abridgments or additions.

Pécuchet was for sentiment and ideality, Bouvard for imagery and colouring; and they began to understand each other no longer, each wondering that the other should be so shallow.

The science which is known as æsthetics would perhaps settle their differences. A friend of Dumouchel, a professor of philosophy, sent them a list of works on the subject. They worked separately and communicated their ideas to one another.

In the first place, what is the Beautiful?

For Schelling, it is the infinite expressing itself through the finite; for Reid, an occult quality; for Jouffroy, an indecomposable fact; for De Maistre, that which is pleasing to virtue; for P. André, that which agrees with reason.

And there are many kinds of beauty: a beauty in the sciences—geometry is beautiful; a beauty in morals—it cannot be denied that the death of Socrates was beautiful; a beauty in the animal kingdom—the beauty of the dog consists in his sense of smell. A pig could not be beautiful, having regard to his dirty habits; no more could a serpent, for it awakens in us ideas of vileness. The flowers, the butterflies, the birds may be beautiful. Finally, the first condition of beauty is unity in variety: there is the principle.

"Yet," said Bouvard, "two squint eyes are more varied than two straight eyes, and produce an effect which is not so good—as a rule."

They entered upon the question of the Sublime.

Certain objects are sublime in themselves: the noise of a torrent, profound darkness, a tree flung down by the storm. A character is beautiful when it triumphs, and sublime when it struggles.

"I understand," said Bouvard; "the Beautiful is the beautiful, and the Sublime the very beautiful."

But how were they to be distinguished?

"By means of tact," answered Pécuchet.

"And tact—where does that come from?"

"From taste."

"What is taste?"

It is defined as a special discernment, a rapid judgment, the power of distinguishing certain relationships.

"In short, taste is taste; but all that does not tell the way to have it."

It is necessary to observe the proprieties. But the proprieties vary; and, let a work be ever so beautiful, it will not be always irreproachable. There is, however, a beauty which is indestructible, and of whose laws we are ignorant, for its genesis is mysterious.

Since an idea cannot be interpreted in every form, we ought to recognise limits amongst the arts, and in each of the arts many forms; but combinations arise in which the style of one will enter into another without the ill result of deviating from the end—of not being true.

The too rigid application of truth is hurtful to beauty, and preoccupation with beauty impedes truth. However, without an ideal there is no truth; this is why types are of a more continuous reality than portraits. Art, besides, only aims at verisimilitude; but verisimilitude depends on the observer, and is a relative and transitory thing.

So they got lost in discussions. Bouvard believed less and less in æsthetics.

"If it is not a humbug, its correctness will be demonstrated by examples. Now listen."

And he read a note which had called for much research on his part:

" 'Bouhours accuses Tacitus of not having the simplicity which history demands. M. Droz, a professor, blames Shakespeare for his mixture of the serious and the comic. Nisard, another professor, thinks that André Chénier is, as a poet, beneath the seventeenth century. Blair, an Englishman, finds fault with the picture of the harpies in Virgil. Marmontel groans over the liberties taken by Homer. Lamotte does not admit the immortality of his heroes. Vida is indignant at his similes. In short, all the makers of rhetorics, poetics, and æsthetics, appear to me idiots."

"You are exaggerating," said Pécuchet.

He was disturbed by doubts; for, if (as Longinus observes) ordinary minds are incapable of faults, the faults must be associated with the masters, and we are bound to admire them. This is going too far. However, the masters are the masters. He would have liked to make the doctrines harmonise with the works, the critics with the poets, to grasp the essence of the Beautiful; and these questions exercised him so much that his bile was stirred up. He got a jaundice from it.

It was at its crisis when Marianne, Madame Bordin's cook, came with a request from her mistress for an interview with Bouvard.

The widow had not made her appearance since the dramatic performance. Was this an advance? But why should she employ Marianne as an intermediary? And all night Bouvard's imagination wandered.

Next day, about two o'clock, he was walking in the corridor, and glancing out through the window from time to time. The door-bell rang. It was the notary.

He crossed the threshold, ascended the staircase, and seated himself in the armchair, and, after a preliminary exchange of courtesies, said that, tired of waiting for Madame Bordin, he had started before her. She wished to buy the Ecalles from him.

Bouvard experienced a kind of chilling sensation, and he hurried towards Pécuchet's room.

Pécuchet did not know what reply to make. He was in an anxious frame of mind, as M. Vaucorbeil was to be there presently.

At length Madame Bordin arrived. The delay was explained by the manifest attention she had given to her toilette, which consisted of a cashmere frock, a hat, and fine kid gloves—a costume befitting a serious occasion.

After much frivolous preliminary talk, she asked whether a thousand crown-pieces would not be sufficient.

"One acre! A thousand crown-pieces! Never!"

She half closed her eyes. "Oh! for me!"

And all three remained silent.

M. de Faverges entered. He had a morocco case under his arm, like a solicitor; and, depositing it on the table, said:

"These are pamphlets! They deal with reform—a burning question; but here is a thing which no doubt belongs to you."

And he handed Bouvard the second volume of the *Mémoires du Diable*.

Mélie, just now, had been reading it in the kitchen; and, as one ought to watch over the morals of persons of that class, he thought he was doing the right thing in confiscating the book.

Bouvard had lent it to his servant-maid. They chatted about novels. Madame Bordin liked them when they were not dismal.

"Writers," said M. de Faverges, "paint life in colours that are too flattering."

"It is necessary to paint," urged Bouvard.

"Then nothing can be done save to follow the example."

"It is not a question of example."

"At least, you will admit that they might fall into the hands of a young daughter. I have one."

"And a charming one!" said the notary, with the expression of countenance he wore on the days of marriage contracts.

"Well, for her sake, or rather for that of the persons that surround her, I prohibit them in my house, for the people, my dear sir—"

"What have the people done?" said Vaucorbeil, appearing suddenly at the door.

Pécuchet, who had recognised his voice, came to mingle with the company.

"I maintain," returned the count, "that it is necessary to prevent them from reading certain books."

Vaucorbeil observed: "Then you are not in favour of education?"

"Yes, certainly. Allow me—"

"When every day," said Marescot, "an attack is made on the government."

"Where's the harm?"

And the nobleman and the physician proceeded to disparage Louis Philippe, recalling the Pritchard case, and the September laws against the liberty of the press.

"And that of the stage," added Pécuchet.

Marescot could stand this no longer.

"It goes too far, this stage of yours!"

"That I grant you," said the count—"plays that glorify suicide."

"Suicide is a fine thing! Witness Cato," protested Pécuchet.

Without replying to the argument, M. de Faverges stigmatised those works in which the holiest things are scoffed at: the family, property, marriage.

"Well, and Molière?" said Bouvard.

Marescot, a man of literary taste, retorted that Molière would not pass muster any longer, and was, furthermore, a little overrated.

"Finally," said the count, "Victor Hugo has been pitiless—yes, pitiless—towards Marie Antoinette, by dragging over the hurdle the type of the Queen in the character of Mary Tudor."

"What!" exclaimed Bouvard, "I, an author, I have no right—"

"No, sir, you have no right to show us crime without putting beside it a corrective—without presenting to us a lesson."

Vaucorbeil thought also that art ought to have an object—to aim at the improvement of the masses. "Let us chant science, our discoveries, patriotism," and he broke into admiration of Casimir Delavigne.

Madame Bordin praised the Marquis de Foudras.

The notary replied: "But the language—are you thinking of that?"

"The language? How?"

"He refers to the style," said Pécuchet. "Do you consider his works well written?"

"No doubt, exceedingly interesting."

He shrugged his shoulders, and she blushed at the impertinence.

Madame Bordin had several times attempted to come back to her own business transaction. It was too late to conclude it. She went off on Marescot's arm.

The count distributed his pamphlets, requesting them to hand them round to other people.

Vaucorbeil was leaving, when Pécuchet stopped him.

"You are forgetting me, doctor."

His yellow physiognomy was pitiable, with his moustaches and his black hair, which was hanging down under a silk handkerchief badly fastened.

"Purge yourself," said the doctor. And, giving him two little slaps as if to a child: "Too much nerves, too much artist!"

"No, surely!"

They summed up what they had just heard. The morality of art is contained for every person in that which flatters that person's interests. No one has any love for literature.

After this they turned over the count's pamphlets.

They found in all of a demand for universal suffrage.

"It seems to me," said Pécuchet, "that we shall soon have some squabbling."

For he saw everything in dark colours, perhaps on account of his jaundice.

Chapter VI

REVOLT OF THE PEOPLE

ON THE MORNING OF THE 25TH OF FEBRUARY, 1848, THE NEWS WAS BROUGHT to chavignolles, by a person who had come from Falaise, that Paris was covered with barricades, and the next day the proclamation of the Republic was posted up outside the mayor's office.

This great event astonished the inhabitants.

But when they learned that the Court of Cassation, the Court of Appeal, the Court of Exchequer, the Chamber of Notaries, the order of advocates, the Council of State, the University, the generals, and M. de la Roche-Jacquelein himself had given promise of their adherence to the provisional government, their breasts began to expand; and, as trees of liberty were planted at Paris, the municipal council decided that they ought to have them at Chavignolles.

Bouvard made an offer of one, his patriotism exulting in the triumph of the people; as for Pécuchet, the fall of royalty confirmed his anticipations so exactly that he must needs be satisfied.

Gorju, obeying them with zeal, removed one of the poplar trees that skirted the meadow above La Butte, and transported it to "the Cows' Pass," at the entrance of the village, the place appointed for the purpose.

Before the hour for the ceremony, all three awaited the procession. They heard a drum beating, and then beheld a silver cross. After this appeared two torches borne by the chanters, then the curé, with stole, surplice, cope, and biretta. Four altar-boys escorted him, a fifth carried the holy-water basin, and in the rear came the sacristan. He got up on the raised edge of the hole in which stood the poplar tree, adorned with tri-coloured ribbons. On the opposite side could be seen the mayor and his two deputies, Beljambe and Marescot; then the principal personages of the district, M. de Faverges, Vaucorbeil, Coulon, the justice of the peace, an old fogy with a sleepy face. Heurtaux wore a foraging-cap, and Alexandre Petit, the new schoolmaster, had put on his frock-coat, a threadbare green garment—his Sunday coat. The firemen, whom Girbal commanded, sword in hand, stood in single file. On the other side shone the white plates of some old shakos of the time of Lafayette—five or six, no more—the National Guard having fallen into desuetude at Chavignolles. Peasants and their wives, workmen from neighbouring factories, and village brats, crowded together in the background; and Placquevent, the keeper, five feet eight inches in height, kept them in check with a look as he walked to and fro with folded arms.

The curé's speech was like that of other priests in similar circumstances. After thundering against kings, he glorified the Republic. "Do we not say 'the republic of letters,' 'the Christian republic'? What more innocent than the one, more beautiful than the other? Jesus Christ formulated our sublime device: the tree of the people was the tree of the Cross. In order that religion may give her fruits, she has need of charity." And, in the name of charity, the ecclesiastic implored his brethren not to commit any disorder; to return home peaceably.

Then he sprinkled the tree while he invoked the blessing of God. "May it grow, and may it recall to us our enfranchisement from all servitude, and that fraternity more bountiful than the shade of its branches. Amen."

Some voices repeated "Amen"; and, after an interval of drum-beating, the clergy, chanting a *Te Deum*, returned along the road to the church.

Their intervention had produced an excellent effect. The simple saw in it a promise of happiness, the patriotic a mark of deference, a sort of homage rendered to their principles.

Bouvard and Pécuchet thought they should have been thanked for their present, or at least that an allusion should have been made to it; and they unbosomed themselves on the subject to Faverges and the doctor.

What mattered wretched considerations of that sort? Vaucorbeil was delighted with the Revolution; so was the count. He execrated the Orléans family. They would never see them any more! Good-bye to them! All for the people henceforth! And followed by Hurel, his factotum, he went to meet the curé.

Foureau was walking with his head down, between the notary and the innkeeper, irritated by the ceremony, as he was apprehensive of a riot; and instinctively he turned round towards Placquevent, who, together with the captain, gave vent to loud regrets at Girbal's unsatisfactoriness and the sorry appearance of his men.

Some workmen passed along the road singing the "Marseillaise," with Gorju among them brandishing a stick; Petit was escorting them, with fire in his eyes.

"I don't like that!" said Marescot. "They are making a great outcry, and getting too excited."

"Oh, bless my soul!" replied Coulon; "young people must amuse themselves."

Foureau heaved a sigh. "Queer amusement! and then the guillotine at the end of it!" He had visions of the scaffold, and was anticipating horrors.

Chavignolles felt the rebound of the agitation in Paris. The villagers subscribed to the newspapers. Every morning people crowded to the post-office, and the postmistress would not have been able to get herself free from them had it not been for the captain, who sometimes assisted her. Then would follow a chat on the green.

The first violent discussion was on the subject of Poland.

Heurtaux and Bouvard called for its liberation.

M. de Faverges took a different view.

"What right have we to go there? That would be to let loose Europe against us. No imprudence!"

And everybody approving of this, the two Poles held their tongues.

On another occasion, Vaucorbeil spoke in favour of Ledru-Rollin's circulars.

Foureau retorted with a reference to the forty-five centimes.

"But the government," said Pécuchet, "has suppressed slavery."

"What does slavery matter to me?"

"Well, what about the abolition of the death-penalty in political cases?"

"Faith," replied Foureau, "they would like to abolish everything. However, who knows? the tenants are already showing themselves very exacting."

"So much the better! The proprietors," according to Pécuchet, "had been too much favoured. He that owns an estate—"

Foureau and Marescot interrupted him, exclaiming that he was a communist.

"I—a communist!"

And all kept talking at the same time. When Pécuchet proposed to establish a club, Foureau had the hardihood to reply that they would never see such a thing at Chavignolles.

After this, Gorju demanded guns for the National Guard, the general opinion having fixed on him as instructor. The only guns in the place were those of the firemen. Girbal had possession of them. Foureau did not care to deliver them up.

Gorju looked at him.

"You will find, however, that I know how to use them."

For he added to his other occupations that of poaching, and the innkeeper often bought from him a hare or a rabbit.

"Faith! take them!" said Foureau.

The same evening they began drilling. It was under the lawn, in front of the church. Gorju, in a blue smock-frock, with a neckcloth around his loins, went through the movements in an automatic fashion. When he gave the orders, his voice was gruff.

"Draw in your bellies!"

And immediately, Bouvard, keeping back his breath, drew in his stomach, and stretched out his buttocks.

"Good God! you're not told to make an arch."

Pécuchet confused the ranks and the files, half-turns to the right and half-turns to the left; but the most pitiable sight was the schoolmaster: weak and of a slim figure, with a ring of fair beard around his neck, he staggered under the weight of his gun, the bayonet of which incommoded his neighbours.

They wore trousers of every colour, dirty shoulder-belts, old regimentals that were too short, leaving their shirts visible over their flanks; and each of them pretended that he had not the means of doing otherwise. A subscription was started to clothe the poorest of them. Foureau was niggardly, while women made themselves conspicuous. Madame Bordin gave five francs, in spite of her hatred of the Republic. M. de Faverges equipped a dozen men, and was not missing at the drill. Then he took up his quarters at the grocer's, and gave those who came in first a drink.

The powerful then began fawning on the lower class. Everyone went after the working-men. People intrigued for the favour of being associated with them. They became nobles.

Those of the canton were, for the most part, weavers; others worked in the cotton mills or at a paper factory lately established.

Gorju fascinated them by his bluster, taught them the shoe trick, and brought those whom he treated as chums to Madame Castillon's house for a drink.

But the peasants were more numerous, and on market days M. de Faverges would walk about the green, make inquiries as to their wants, and try to convert them to his own ideas. They listened without answering, like Père Gouy, ready to accept any government so long as it reduced the taxes.

By dint of babbling, Gorju was making a name for himself. Perhaps they might send him into the Assembly!

M. de Faverges also was thinking of it, while seeking not to compromise himself.

The Conservatives oscillated between Foureau and Marescot, but, as the notary stuck to his office, Foureau was chosen—a boor, an idiot. The doctor waxed indignant. Rejected in the competition, he regretted Paris, and the consciousness of his wasted life gave him a morose air. A more distinguished career was about to open for him—what a revenge! He drew up a profession of faith, and went to read it to MM. Bouvard and Pécuchet.

They congratulated him upon it. Their opinions were identical with his. However, they wrote better, had a knowledge of history, and could cut as good a figure as he in the Chamber. Why not? But which of them ought to offer himself? And they entered upon a contest of delicacy.

Pécuchet preferred that it should be his friend rather than himself.

"No, it suits you better! you have a better deportment!"

"Perhaps so," returned Bouvard, "but you have a better tuft of hair!" And, without solving the difficulty, they arranged their plans of conduct.

This vertigo of deputyship had seized on others. The captain dreamed of it under his foraging-cap while puffing at his pipe, and the schoolmaster too in his school, and the curé also between two prayers, so that he sometimes surprised himself with his eyes towards heaven, in the act of saying, "Grant, O my God, that I may be a deputy!"

The doctor having received some encouragement, repaired to the house of Heurtaux, and explained to him what his chances were. The captain did not stand on ceremony about it. Vaucorbeil was known, undoubtedly, but little liked by his professional brethren, especially in the case of chemists. Everyone would bark at him; the people did not want a gentleman; his best patients would leave him. And, when he weighed these arguments, the physician regretted his weakness.

As soon as he had gone, Heurtaux went to see Placquevent. Between old soldiers there should be mutual courtesy, but the rural guard, devoted though he was to Foureau, flatly refused to help him.

The curé demonstrated to M. de Faverges that the hour had not come. It was necessary to give the Republic time to get used up.

Bouvard and Pécuchet represented to Gorju that he would never be strong enough to overcome the coalition of the peasants and the village shop-keepers, filled him with uncertainty, and deprived him of all confidence.

Petit, through pride, had allowed his ambition to be seen. Beljambe warned him that, if he failed, his dismissal was certain.

Finally, the curé got orders from the bishop to keep quiet.

Then, only Foureau remained.

Bouvard and Pécuchet opposed him, bringing up against him his unfriendly attitude about the guns, his opposition to the club, his reactionary views, his avarice; and even persuaded Gouy that he wished to bring back the old *régime.* Vague as was the meaning of this word to the peasant's mind, he execrated it with a hatred that had accumulated in the souls of his forefathers throughout ten centuries; and he turned all his relatives, and those of his wife, brothers-in-law, cousins, grand-nephews (a horde of them), against Foureau.

Gorju, Vaucorbeil, and Petit kept working for the overthrow of the mayor; and, the ground being thus cleared, Bouvard and Pécuchet, without any doubt, were likely to succeed.

They drew lots to know which would present himself. The drawing decided nothing, and they went to consult the doctor on the subject.

He had news for them: Flacardoux, editor of *Le Calvados,* had announced his candidature. The two friends had a keen sense of having been deceived. Each felt the other's disappointment more than his own. But politics had an exciting influence on them. When the election-day arrived they went to inspect the urns. Flacardoux had carried it!

M. de Faverges had fallen back on the National Guard, without obtaining the epaulet of commander. The people of Chavignolles contrived to get Beljambe nominated.

This favouritism on the part of the public, so whimsical and unforeseen, dismayed Heurtaux. He had neglected his duties, confining himself to inspecting the military operations now and then, and giving utterance to a few remarks. No matter! He considered it a monstrous thing that an innkeeper should be preferred to one who had been formerly a captain in the Imperial service, and he said, after the invasion of the Chamber on the 15th of May: "If the military grades give themselves away like that in the capital, I shall be no longer astonished at what may happen."

The reaction began.

People believed in Louis Blanc's pineapple soup, in Flocon's bed of gold, and Ledru-Rollin's royal orgies; and as the province pretends to know everything that happens in Paris, the inhabitants of Chavignolles had no doubt about these inventions, and gave credence to the most absurd reports.

M. de Faverges one evening came to look for the curé, in order to tell him that the Count de Chambord had arrived in Normandy.

Joinville, according to Foureau, had made preparations with his sailors to put down "these socialists of yours." Heurtaux declared that Louis Napoleon would shortly be consul.

The factories had stopped. Poor people wandered in large groups about the country.

One Sunday (it was in the early days of June) a gendarme suddenly started in the direction of Falaise. The workmen of Acqueville, Liffard, Pierre-Pont, and Saint-Rémy were marching on Chavignolles. The sheds were shut up. The municipal council assembled and passed a resolution, to prevent catastrophes, that no resistance should be offered. The gendarmes were kept in, and orders were given to them not to show themselves. Soon was heard, as it were, the rumbling of a storm. Then the song of the Girondists shook the windows, and men, arm in arm, passed along the road from Caen, dusty, sweating, in rags. They filled up the entire space in front of the council chamber, and a great hurly-burly arose.

Gorju and two of his comrades entered the chamber. One of them was lean and wretched-looking, with a knitted waistcoat, the ribbons of which were hanging down; the other, black as coal—a machinist, no doubt—with hair like a brush, thick eyebrows, and old list shoes. Gorju, like a hussar, wore his waistcoat slung over his shoulder.

All three remained standing, and the councillors, seated round the table, which was covered with a blue cloth, gazed at their faces, pale from privation.

"Citizens!" said Gorju, "we want work."

The mayor trembled. He could not find his voice.

Marescot replied from the place where he sat that the council would consider the matter directly; and when the comrades had gone out they discussed several suggestions.

The first was to have stones drawn.

In order to utilise the stones, Girbal proposed a road from Angleville to Tournebu.

That from Bayeux had positively rendered the same service.

They could clear out the pond! This was not sufficient as a public work. Or rather, dig a second pond! But in what place?

Langlois' advice was to construct an embankment along the Mortins as a protection against an inundation. It would be better, Beljambe thought, to clear away the heather.

It was impossible to arrive at any conclusion. To appease the crowd, Coulon went down over the peristyle and announced that they were preparing charity workshops.

"Chanty! Thanks!" cried Gorju. "Down with the aristocrats! We want the right to work!"

It was the question of the time. He made use of it as a source of popularity. He was applauded.

In turning round he elbowed Bouvard, whom Pécuchet had dragged to the spot, and they entered into conversation. Nothing could keep them back; the municipal building was surrounded; the council could not escape.

"Where shall you get money?" said Bouvard.

"In the rich people's houses. Besides, the government will give orders for public works."

"And if works are not wanted?"

"They will have them made in advance."

"But wages will fall," urged Pécuchet. "When work happens to be lacking, it is because there are too many products; and you demand to have them increased!"

Gorju bit his moustache. "However, with the organisation of labour—"

"Then the government will be the master!"

Some of those around murmured:

"No, no! no more masters!"

Gorju got angry. "No matter! Workers should be supplied with capital, or rather credit should be established."

"In what way?"

"Ah! I don't know; but credit ought to be established."

"We've had enough of that," said the machinist. "They are only plaguing us, these farce-actors!"

And he climbed up the steps, declaring that he would break open the door.

There he was met by Placquevent, with his right knee bent and his fists clenched:

"Advance one inch further!"

The machinist recoiled. The shouting of the mob reached the chamber. All arose with the desire to run away. The help from Falaise had not arrived. They bewailed the count's absence. Marescot kept twisting a pen; Père Coulon groaned; Heurtaux lashed himself into a fury to make them send for the gendarmes.

"Command them to come!" said Foureau.

"I have no authority."

The noise, however, redoubled. The whole green was covered with people, and they were all staring at the first story of the building when, at the window in the middle, under the clock, Pécuchet made his appearance.

He had ingeniously gone up by the back-stairs, and, wishing to be like Lamartine, he began a harangue to the populace:

"Citizens!—"

But his cap, his nose, his frock-coat, his entire personality lacked distinction.

The man in the knitted waistcoat asked him:

"Are you a workman?"

"No."

"A master, then?"

"Nor that either."

"Well, take yourself off, then."

"Why?" returned Pécuchet, haughtily.

And the next moment he disappeared, in the machinist's clutch, into the recess of the window.

Gorju came to his assistance. "Let him alone! He's a decent fellow." They clenched.

The door flew open, and Marescot, on the threshold, announced the decision of the council. Hurel had suggested his doing so.

The road from Tournebu would have a branch road in the direction of Angleville and leading towards the château of Faverges.

It was a sacrifice which the commune took upon itself in the interest of the working-men.

They dispersed.

When Bouvard and Pécuchet re-entered their house, women's voices fell upon their ears. The servants and Madame Bordin were breaking into exclamations, the widow's screams being the loudest; and at sight of them she cried:

"Ha! this is very fortunate! I have been waiting for you for the last three hours!

My poor garden has not a single tulip left! Filth everywhere on the grass! No way of getting rid of him!"

"Who is it?"

"Père Gouy."

He had come with a cartload of manure, and had scattered it pell-mell over the grass.

"He is now digging it up. Hurry on and make him stop."

"I am going with you," said Bouvard.

At the bottom of the steps outside, a horse in the shafts of a dung-cart was gnawing at a bunch of oleanders. The wheels, in grazing the flower borders, had bruised the box trees, broken a rhododendron, knocked down the dahlias; and clods of black muck, like molehills, embossed the green sward. Gouy was vigorously digging it up.

One day Madame Bordin had carelessly said to him that she would like to have it turned up. He set about the job, and, in spite of her orders to desist, went on with it. This was the way that he interpreted the right to work, Gorju's talk having turned his brain.

He went away only after violent threats from Bouvard.

Madame Bordin, by way of compensation, did not pay for the manual labour, and kept the manure. She was wise: the doctor's wife, and even the notary's, though of higher social position, respected her for it.

The charity workshops lasted a week. No trouble occurred. Gorju left the neighbourhood.

Meanwhile, the National Guard was always on foot: on Sunday, a review; military promenades, occasionally; and, every night, patrols. They disturbed the village. They rang the bells of houses for fun; they made their way into the bedrooms where married couples were snoring on the same bolster; then they uttered broad jokes, and the husband, rising, would go and get them a glass each. Afterwards, they would return to the guard-house to play a hundred of dominoes, would consume a quantity of cider there, and eat cheese, while the sentinel, worn out, would keep opening the door every other minute. There was a prevailing absence of discipline, owing to Beljambe's laxity.

When the days of June came, everyone was in favour of "flying to the relief of Paris"; but Foureau could not leave the mayoral premises, Marescot his office, the doctor his patients, or Girbal his firemen. M. de Faverges was at Cherbourg. Beljambe kept his bed. The captain grumbled: "They did not want me; so much the worse!"—and Bouvard had the wisdom to put restraint on Pécuchet.

The patrols throughout the country were extended farther. They were panic-stricken by the shadow of a haystack, or by the forms of branches. On one occasion the entire National Guard turned and ran. In the moonlight they had observed, under an apple tree, a man with a gun, taking aim at them. At another time, on a dark night, the patrol halting under the beech trees, heard someone close at hand.

"Who is there?"

No answer.

They allowed the person to pursue his course, following him at a distance, for he might have a pistol or a tomahawk; but when they were in the village, within reach of help, the dozen men of the company rushed together upon him, exclaiming:

"Your papers!" They pulled him about and overwhelmed him with insults. The men at the guardhouse had gone out. They dragged him there; and by the light of the candle that was burning on top of the stove they at last recognised Gorju.

A wretched greatcoat of lasting was flapping over his shoulders. His toes could be seen through the holes in his boots. Scratches and bruises stained his face with blood. He was fearfully emaciated, and rolled his eyes about like a wolf.

Foureau, coming up speedily, questioned him as to how he chanced to be under the beech trees, what his object was in coming back to Chavignolles, and also as to the employment of his time for the past six weeks.

"That is no business of yours. I have my liberty."

Placquevent searched him to find out whether he had cartridges about him.

They were about to imprison him provisionally.

Bouvard interposed.

"No use," replied the mayor; "we know your opinions."

"Nevertheless—"

"Ha! be careful; I give you warning. Be careful."

Bouvard persisted no further.

Gorju then turned towards Pécuchet: "And you, master, have you not a word to say for me?"

Pécuchet hung down his head, as if he had a suspicion against his innocence.

The poor wretch smiled bitterly.

"I protected you, all the same."

At daybreak, two gendarmes took him to Falaise.

He was not tried before a court-martial, but was sentenced by the civil tribunal to three months' imprisonment for the misdemeanour of language tending towards the destruction of society. From Falaise he wrote to his former employers to send him soon a certificate of good life and morals, and as their signature required to be legalised by the mayor or the deputy, they preferred to ask Marescot to do this little service for them.

They were introduced into a dining-room, decorated with dishes of fine old earthenware; a Boule clock occupied the narrowest shelf. On the mahogany table, without a cloth, were two napkins, a teapot and finger-glasses. Madame Marescot crossed the room in a dressing-gown of blue cashmere. She was a Parisian who was bored with the country. Then the notary came in, with his cap in one hand, a newspaper in the other; and at once, in the most polite fashion, he affixed his seal, although their *protégé* was a dangerous man.

"Really," said Bouvard, "for a few words—"

"But words lead to crimes, my dear sir, give me leave to say."

"And yet," said Pécuchet, "what line of demarcation can you lay down between innocent and guilty phrases? The thing that just now is prohibited may be subsequently applauded." And he censured the harshness with which the insurgents had been treated.

Marescot naturally rested his case on the necessity of protecting society, the public safety—the supreme law.

"Pardon me!" said Pécuchet, "the right of a single individual is as much entitled to respect as those of all, and you have nothing to oppose to him but force if he turns your axiom upon yourself."

Instead of replying, Marescot lifted his brows disdainfully. Provided that he continued to draw up legal documents, and to live among his plates, in his comfortable little home, injustices of every kind might present themselves without affecting him. Business called him away. He excused himself.

His theory of public safety excited their indignation. The Conservatives now talked like Robespierre.

Another matter for astonishment: Cavaignac was flagging; the Garde Mobile was exposing itself to suspicion. Ledru-Rollin had ruined himself even in Vaucorbeil's estimation. The debates on the Constitution interested nobody, and on the 10th of December all the inhabitants of Chavignolles voted for Bonaparte. The six millions of votes made Pécuchet grow cold with regard to the people, and Bouvard and he proceeded to study the question of universal suffrage.

As it belongs to everybody, it cannot possess intelligence. One ambitious man will always be the leader; the others will follow him like a flock of sheep, the electors not being compelled even to know how to read. This was the reason, in Bouvard's opinion, that there were so many frauds at presidential elections.

"None," replied Bouvard; "I believe rather in the gullibility of the people. Think of all who buy the patent health-restorer, the Dupuytren pomatum, the Châtelaine's water, etc. Those boobies constitute the majority of the electorate, and we submit to their will. Why cannot an income of three thousand francs be made out of rabbits? Because the overcrowding of them is a cause of death. In the same way, through the mere fact of its being a multitude, the germs of stupidity contained in it are developed, and thence result consequences that are incalculable."

"Your scepticism frightens me," said Pécuchet.

At a later period, in the spring, they met M. de Faverges, who apprised them of the expedition to Rome. We should not attack the Italians, but we should require guaranties. Otherwise our influence would be destroyed. Nothing would be more legitimate than this intervention.

Bouvard opened his eyes wide. "On the subject of Poland, you expressed a contrary opinion."

"It is no longer the same thing." It was now a question of the Pope.

And M. de Faverges, when he said, "We wish," "We shall do," "We calculate clearly," represented a group.

Bouvard and Pécuchet were disgusted with the minority quite as much as with the majority. The common people, in short, were just the same as the aristocracy.

The right of intervention appeared dubious to them. They sought for its principles in Calvo, Martens, Vattel; and Bouvard's conclusion was this:

"There may be intervention to restore a prince to the throne, to emancipate a people, or, for the sake of precaution, in view of a public danger. In other cases it is an outrage on the rights of others, an abuse of force, a piece of hypocritical violence."

"And yet," said Pécuchet, "peoples have a solidarity as well as men."

"Perhaps so." And Bouvard sank into a reverie.

The expedition to Rome soon began.

At home, through hatred of revolutionary ideas, the leaders of the Parisian middle class got two printing-offices sacked. The great party of order was formed.

It had for its chiefs in the arrondissement the count, Foureau, Marescot, and the curé. Everyday, about four o'clock, they walked from one end of the green to the other, and talked over the events of the day. The principal business was the distribution of pamphlets. The titles did not lack attractiveness: "God will be pleased with it"; "The sharing"; "Let us get out of the mess"; "Where are we going?" The finest things among them were the dialogues in the style of villagers, with oaths and bad French, to elevate the mental faculties of the peasants. By a new law, the hawking of pamphlets would be in the hands of the prefects; and they had just crammed Proudhon into St. Pélagie—gigantic triumph!

The trees of liberty were generally torn down. Chavignolles obeyed orders. Bouvard saw with his own eyes the fragments of his poplar on a wheelbarrow. They helped to warm the gendarmes, and the stump was offered to the curé, who had blessed it. What a mockery!

The schoolmaster did not hide his way of thinking.

Bouvard and Pécuchet congratulated him on it one day as they were passing in front of his door. Next day he presented himself at their residence.

At the end of the week they returned his visit.

The day was declining. The brats had just gone home, and the schoolmaster, in half-sleeves, was sweeping the yard. His wife, with a neckerchief tied round her head, was suckling a baby. A little girl was hiding herself behind her petticoat; a hideous-looking child was playing on the ground at her feet. The water from the washing she had been doing in the kitchen was flowing to the lower end of the house.

"You see," said the schoolmaster, "how the government treats us."

And forthwith he began finding fault with capital as an infamous thing. It was necessary to democratise it, to enfranchise matter.

"I ask for nothing better," said Pécuchet.

At least, they ought to have recognised the right to assistance.

"One more right!" said Bouvard.

No matter! The provisional government had acted in a flabby fashion by not ordaining fraternity.

"Then try to establish it."

As there was no longer daylight, Petit rudely ordered his wife to carry a candle to his study.

The lithograph portraits of the orators of the Left were fastened with pins to the plaster walls. A bookshelf stood above a deal writing-desk. There were a chair, stool, and an old soap-box for persons to sit down upon. He made a show of laughing. But want had laid its traces on his cheeks, and his narrow temples indicated the stubbornness of a ram, an intractable pride. He never would yield.

"Besides, see what sustains me!"

It was a pile of newspapers on a shelf, and in feverish phrases he explained the articles of his faith: disarmament of troops, abolition of the magistracy, equality of salaries, a levelling process by which the golden age was to be brought about under the form of the Republic, with a dictator at its head—a fellow that would carry this out for us briskly!

Then he reached for a bottle of aniseed cordial and three glasses, in order to propose the toast of the hero, the immortal victim, the great Maximilian.

On the threshold appeared the black cassock of the priest. Having saluted those present in an animated fashion, he addressed the schoolmaster, speaking almost in a whisper:

"Our business about St. Joseph, what stage is it at?"

"They have given nothing," replied the schoolmaster.

"That is your fault!"

"I have done what I could."

"Ha! really?"

Bouvard and Pécuchet discreetly rose. Petit made them sit down again, and addressing the curé:

"Is that all?"

The Abbé Jeufroy hesitated. Then, with a smile which tempered his reprimand:

"It is supposed that you are rather negligent about sacred history."

"Oh, sacred history!" interrupted Bouvard.

"What fault have you to find with it, sir?"

"I—none. Only there are perhaps more useful things to be learned than the anecdote of Jonas and the story of the kings of Israel."

"You are free to do as you please," replied the priest drily.

And without regard for the strangers, or on account of their presence:

"The catechism hour is too short."

Petit shrugged his shoulders.

"Mind! You will lose your boarders!"

The ten francs a month for these pupils formed the best part of his remuneration. But the cassock exasperated him.

"So much the worse; take your revenge!"

"A man of my character does not revenge himself," said the priest, without being moved. "Only I would remind you that the law of the fifteenth of March assigns us to the superintendence of primary education."

"Ah! I know that well," cried the schoolmaster. "It is given even to colonels of gendarmes. Why not to the rural guard? That would complete the thing!"

And he sank upon the stool, biting his fingers, repressing his rage, stifled by the feeling of his own powerlessness.

The priest touched him lightly on the shoulder.

"I did not intend to annoy you, my friend. Keep yourself quiet. Be a little reasonable. Here is Easter close at hand; I hope you will show an example by going to communion along with the others."

"That is too much! I—I submit to such absurdities!"

At this blasphemy the curé turned pale, his eyeballs gleamed, his jaw quivered.

"Silence, unhappy man! silence! And it is his wife who looks after the church linen!"

"Well, what then? What has she done to you?"

"She always stays away from mass. Like yourself, for that matter!"

"Oh! a schoolmaster is not sent away for a thing of that kind!"

"He can be removed."

The priest said no more.

He was at the end of the room, in the shadow.

Petit was thinking, with his head resting on his chest.

They would arrive at the other end of France, their last sou eaten up by the journey, and they would again find down there, under different names, the same curé, the same superintendent, the same prefect—all, even to the minister, were like links in a chain dragging him down. He had already had one warning—others would follow. After that?—and in a kind of hallucination he saw himself walking along a high-road, a bag on his back, those whom he loved by his side, and his hand held out towards a post-chaise.

At that moment his wife was seized with a fit of coughing in the kitchen, the new-born infant began to squeal, and the boy was crying.

"Poor children!" said the priest in a softened voice.

The father thereupon broke into sobs:

"Yes, yes! whatever you require!"

"I count upon it," replied the curé.

And, having made the customary bow:

"Well, good evening to you, gentlemen."

The schoolmaster remained with his face in his hands.

He pushed away Bouvard. "No! let me alone. I feel as if I'd like to die. I am an unfortunate man."

The two friends, when they reached their own house, congratulated themselves on their independence. The power of the clergy terrified them.

It was now employed for the purpose of strengthening public order. The Republic was about to disappear.

Three millions of electors found themselves excluded from universal suffrage. The security required from newspapers was raised; the press censorship was re-established. It was even suggested that it should be put in force against the fiction columns. Classical philosophy was considered dangerous. The commercial classes preached the dogma of material interests; and the populace seemed satisfied.

The country-people came back to their old masters.

M. de Faverges, who had estates in Eure, was declared a member of the Legislative Assembly, and his re-election for the general council of Calvados was certain beforehand.

He thought proper to invite the leading personages in the district to a luncheon.

The vestibule in which three servants were waiting to take their overcoats, the billiard-room and the pair of drawing-rooms, the plants in china vases, the bronzes on the mantel-shelves, the gold wands on the panelled walls, the heavy curtains, the wide armchairs—this display of luxury struck them at once as a mark of courtesy towards them; and, when they entered the dining-room, at the sight of the table laden with meats in silver dishes, together with the row of glasses before each plate, the side-dishes here and there, and a salmon in the middle, every face brightened up.

The party numbered seventeen, including two sturdy agriculturists, the sub-prefect of Bayeux and one person from Cherbourg. M. de Faverges begged his guests to excuse the countess, who was absent owing to a headache; and, after some commendations of the pears and grapes, which filled four baskets at the corners, he asked about the great news—the project of a descent on England by Changarnier.

Heurtaux desired it as a soldier, the curé through hatred of the Protestants, and Foureau in the interests of commerce.

"You are giving expression," said Pécuchet, "to the sentiments of the Middle Ages."

"The Middle Ages had their good side," returned Marescot. "For instance, our cathedrals."

"However, sir, the abuses—"

"No matter—the Revolution would not have come."

"Ha! the Revolution—there's the misfortune," said the ecclesiastic with a sigh.

"But everyone contributed towards it, and (excuse me, Monsieur le Comte) the nobles themselves by their alliance with the philosophers."

"What is it you want? Louis XVIII legalised spoliation. Since that time the parlimentary system is sapping the foundations."

A joint of roast beef made its appearance, and for some minutes nothing was heard save the sounds made by forks and moving jaws, and by the servants crossing the floor with the two words on their lips, which they repeated continually:

"Madeira! Sauterne!"

The conversation was resumed by the gentleman from Cherbourg:

"How were they to stop on the slope of an abyss?"

"Amongst the Athenians," said Marescot—"amongst the Athenians, towards whom we bear certain resemblances, Solon checkmated the democrats by raising the electoral census."

"It would be better," said Hurel, "to suppress the Chamber: every disorder comes from Paris."

"Let us decentralise," said the notary.

"On a large scale," added the count.

In Foureau's opinion, the communal authorities should have absolute control, even to the extent of prohibiting travellers from using their roads, if they thought fit.

And whilst the dishes followed one another—fowl with gravy, lobsters, mushrooms, salads, roast larks—many topics were handled: the best system of taxation, the advantages of the large system of land cultivation, the abolition of the death penalty. The sub-prefect did not forget to cite that charming witticism of a clever man: "Let Messieurs the Assassins begin!"

Bouvard was astonished at the contrast between the surroundings and the remarks that reached his ears; for one would think that the language used should always harmonise with the environment, and that lofty ceilings should be made for great thoughts. Nevertheless, he was flushed at dessert, and saw the fruit-dishes as if through a fog. Bordeaux, Burgundy, and Malaga were amongst the wines sent round. M. de Faverges, who knew the people he had to deal with, made the champagne flow. The guests, touching glasses, drank to his success at the election; and more than three hours elapsed before they passed out into the smoking-room, where coffee was served.

A caricature from *Charivari* was trailing on the floor between some copies of the *Univers*. It represented a citizen the skirts of whose frock-coat allowed a tail to be seen with an eye at the end of it. Marescot explained it amid much laughter.

They swallowed their liqueurs, and the ashes of their cigars fell on the paddings of the furniture.

The abbê, desirous to convince Girbal, began an attack on Voltaire. Coulon fell asleep. M. de Faverges avowed his devotion to Chambord.

"The bees furnish an argument for monarchy."

"But the ants for the Republic." However, the doctor adhered to it no longer.

"You are right," said the sub-prefect; "the form of government matters little."

"With liberty," suggested Pécuchet.

"An honest man has no need of it," replied Foureau. "I make no speeches, for my part. I am not a journalist. And I tell you that France requires to be governed with a rod of iron."

All called for a deliverer. As they were going out, Bouvard and Pécuchet heard M. de Faverges saying to the Abbé Jeufroy:

"We must re-establish obedience. Authority perishes if it be made the subject of discussion. The Divine Right—there is nothing but that!"

"Exactly, Monsieur le Comte."

The pale rays of an October sun were lengthening out behind the woods. A moist wind was blowing, and as they walked over the dead leaves they breathed like men who had just been set free.

All that they had not found the opportunity of saying escaped from them in exclamations:

"What idiots!"

"What baseness!"

"How is it possible to imagine such obstinacy!"

"In the first place, what is the meaning of the Divine Right?"

Dumouchel's friend, that professor who had supplied them with instruction on the subject of aesthetics, replied to their inquiries in a learned letter.

"The theory of Divine Right was formulated in the reign of Charles II by the Englishman Filmer. Here it is:

" 'The Creator gave the first man dominion over the world. It was transmitted to his descendants, and the power of the king emanates from God.'

" 'He is His image,' writes Bossuet. 'The paternal empire accustoms us to the domination of one alone. Kings have been made after the model of parents.'

"Locke refuted this doctrine: 'The paternal power is distinguished from the monarchic, every subject having the same right over his children that the monarch has over his own. Royalty exists only through the popular choice; and even the election was recalled at the ceremony of coronation, in which two bishops, pointing towards the king, asked both nobles and peasants whether they accepted him as such.'

"Therefore, authority comes from the people.

" 'They have the right to do what they like,' says Helvetius; to 'change their constitution,' says Vattel; to 'revolt against injustice,' according to the contention of Glafey, Hotman, Mably, and others; and St. Thomas Aquinas authorises them to 'deliver themselves from a tyrant.' 'They are even,' says Jurieu, 'dispensed from being right.' "

Astonished at the axiom, they took up Rousseau's *Contrat Social.* Pécuchet went through to the end. Then closing his eyes, and throwing back his head, he made an analysis of it.

"A convention is assumed whereby the individual gives up his liberty.

"The people at the same time undertook to protect him against the inequalities of nature, and made him owner of the things he had in his possession."

"Where is the proof of the contract?"

"Nowhere! And the community does not offer any guaranty. The citizens occupy themselves exclusively with politics. But as callings are necessary, Rousseau is in favour of slavery. 'The sciences have destroyed the human race. The theatre is corrupting, money fatal, and the state ought to impose a religion under the penalty of death.' "

"What!" said they, "here is the pontiff of democracy."

All the champions of reform had copied him; and they procured the *Examen du Socialisme,* by Morant.

The first chapter explained the doctrine of Saint-Simon.

At the top the Father, at the same time Pope and Emperor. Abolition of inheritance; all property movable and immovable forming a social fund, which should be worked on a hierarchical basis. The manufacturers are to govern the public fortune. But there is nothing to be afraid of; they will have as a leader the "one who loves the most."

One thing is lacking: woman. On the advent of woman depends the salvation of the world.

"I do not understand."

"Nor I."

And they turned to Fourierism:

" 'All misfortunes come from constraint. Let the attraction be free, and harmony will be established.

" 'In our souls are shut up a dozen leading passions: five egoistical, four animistic, and three distributive. The first class have reference to individuals, the second to groups, the last to groups of groups, or series, of which the whole forms a phalanx, a society of eighteen hundred persons dwelling in a palace. Every morning carriages convey the workers into the country, and bring them back in the evening. Standards are carried, festivities are held, cakes are eaten. Every woman, if she desires it, can have three men—the husband, the lover, and the pro-creator. For celibates, the Bayadère system is established—' "

"That fits me!" said Bouvard. And he lost himself in dreams of the harmonious world.

" 'By the restoration of climatures, the earth will become more beautiful; by the crossing of races, human life will become longer. The clouds will be guided as the thunderbolt is now: it will rain at night in the cities so that they will be clean. Ships will cross the polar seas, thawed beneath the Aurora Borealis. For everything is produced by the conjunction of two fluids, male and female, gushing out from the poles, and the northern lights are a symptom of the blending of the planets— a prolific emission.' "

"This is beyond me!" said Pécuchet.

After Saint-Simon and Fourier the problem resolves itself into questions of wages.

Louis Blanc, in the interests of the working class, wishes to abolish external commerce; Lafarelle to tax machinery; another to take off the drink duties, to restore trade wardenships, or to distribute soups.

Proudhon conceives the idea of a uniform tariff, and claims for the state the monopoly of sugar.

"These socialists," said Bouvard, "always call for tyranny."

"Oh, no!"

"Yes, indeed!"

"You are absurd!"

"Well, I am shocked at you!"

They sent for the works of which they had only summaries. Bouvard noted a number of passages, and, pointing them out, said:

"Read for yourself. They offer as examples to us the Essenes, the Moravian Brethren, the Jesuits of Paraguay, and even the government of prisons."

" 'Amongst the Icarians breakfast was over in twenty minutes; women were delivered at the hospitals. As for books, it was forbidden to print them without the authorisation of the Republic.' "

"But Cabet is an idiot."

"Here, now, we have from Saint-Simon: 'The publicists should submit their works to a committee of manufacturers.'

"And from Pierre Leroux: 'The law will compel the citizens to listen to an orator.'

"And from Auguste Comte: 'The priests will educate the youth, will exercise supervision over literary works, and will reserve to themselves the power of regulating procreation.' "

These quotations troubled Pécuchet. In the evening, at dinner, he replied:

"I admit that there are absurdities in the works of the inventors of Utopias; nevertheless they deserve our sympathy. The hideousness of the world tormented them, and, in order to make it beautiful, they endured everything. Recall to mind More decapitated, Campanella put seven times to the torture, Buonarotti with a chain round his neck, Saint-Simon dying of want; many others. They might have lived in peace; but no! they marched on their way with their heads towards the sky, like heroes."

"Do you believe," said Bouvard, "that the world will change, thanks to the theories of some particular gentleman?"

"What does it matter?" said Pécuchet; "it is time to cease stagnating in selfishness. Let us look out for the best system."

"Then you expect to find it?"

"Certainly."

"You?"

And, in the fit of laughter with which Bouvard was seized, his shoulders and stomach kept shaking in harmony. Redder than the jams before them, with his napkin under his armpits, he kept repeating, "Ha! ha! ha!" in an irritating fashion.

Pécuchet left the room, slamming the door after him.

Germaine went all over the house to call him, and he was found at the end of his own apartment in an easy chair, without fire or candle, his cap drawn over his eyes. He was not unwell, but had given himself up to his own broodings.

When the quarrel was over they recognised that a foundation was needed for their studies—political economy.

They inquired into supply and demand, capital and rent, importation and prohibition.

One night Pécuchet was awakened by the creaking of a boot in the corridor. The evening before, according to custom, he had himself drawn all the bolts; and he called out to Bouvard, who was fast asleep.

They remained motionless under the coverlets. The noise was not repeated.

The servants, on being questioned, said they had heard nothing.

But, while walking through the garden, they remarked in the middle of a flower-bed, near the gateway, the imprint of a boot-sole, and two of the sticks used as supports for the trees were broken. Evidently some one had climbed over.

It was necessary to give notice of it to the rural guard.

As he was not at the municipal building, Pécuchet thought of going to the grocer's shop.

Who should they see in the back shop, beside Placquevent, in the midst of the topers, but Gorju—Gorju, rigged out like a well-to-do citizen, entertaining the company!

This meeting was taken as a matter of course.

So on they lapsed into a discussion about progress.

Bouvard had no doubt it existed in the domain of science. But in that of literature it was not so manifest; and if comfort increases, the poetic side of life disappears.

Pécuchet, in order to bring home conviction on the point, took a piece of paper: "I trace across here an undulating line. Those who happen to travel over it, whenever it sinks, can no longer see the horizon. It rises again nevertheless, and, in spite of its windings, they reach the top. This is an image of progress."

Madame Bordin entered at this point.

It was the 3rd of December, 1851. She had the newspaper in her hand.

They read very quickly, side by side, the news of the appeal to the people, the dissolution of the Chamber, and the imprisonment of the deputies.

Pécuchet turned pale. Bouvard gazed at the widow.

"What! have you nothing to say?"

"What do you wish me to do here?" (They had forgotten to offer her a seat.) "I came here simply out of courtesy towards you, and you are scarcely civil to-day."

And out she went, disgusted at their want of politeness.

The astonishing news had struck them dumb. Then they went about the village venting their indignation.

Marescot, whom they found surrounded by a pile of deeds, took a different view. The babbling of the Chamber was at an end, thank Heaven! Henceforth they would have a business policy.

Beljambe knew nothing about the occurrences, and, furthermore, he laughed at them.

In the market-place they stopped Vaucorbeil.

The physician had got over all that. "You are very foolish to bother yourselves."

Foureau passed them by, remarking with a sly air, "The democrats are swamped."

And the captain, with Girbal's arm in his, exclaimed from a distance, "Long live the Emperor!"

But Petit would be sure to understand them, and Bouvard having tapped at a window-pane, the schoolmaster quitted his class.

He thought it a good joke to have Thiers in prison. This would avenge the people.

"Ha! ha! my gentlemen deputies, your turn now!"

The volley of musketry on the boulevards met with the approval of the people of Chavignolles. No mercy for the vanquished, no pity for the victims! Once you revolt, you are a scoundrel!

"Let us be grateful to Providence," said the curé, "and under Providence to Louis Bonaparte. He gathers around him the most distinguished men. The Count de Faverges will be made a senator."

Next day they had a visit from Placquevent.

"These gentlemen" had talked a great deal. He required a promise from them to hold their tongues.

"Do you wish to know my opinion?" said Pécuchet. "Since the middle class is ferocious and the working-men jealous-minded, whilst the people, after all, accept every tyrant, so long as they are allowed to keep their snouts in the mess, Napoleon has done right. Let him gag them, the rabble, and exterminate them—this will never be too much for their hatred of right, their cowardice, their incapacity, and their blindness."

Bouvard mused: "Hey! progress! what humbug!" He added: "And politics, a nice heap of dirt!"

"It is not a science," returned Pécuchet. "The military art is better: you can tell what will happen—we ought to turn our hands to it."

"Oh, thanks," was Bouvard's answer. "I am disgusted with everything. Better for us to sell our barrack, and go in the name of God's thunder amongst the savages."

"Just as you like."

Mélie was drawing water out in the yard.

The wooden pump had a long lever. In order to make it work, she bent her back, so that her blue stockings could be seen as high as the calf of her legs. Then, with a rapid movement, she raised her right arm, while she turned her head a little to one side; and Pécuchet, as he gazed at her, felt quite a new sensation, a charm, a thrill of intense delight.

Chapter VII

"Unlucky in Love"

AND NOW THE DAYS BEGAN TO BE SAD. THEY STUDIED NO LONGER, FEARING lest they might be disillusioned. The inhabitants of Chavignolles avoided them. The newspapers they tolerated gave them no information; and so their solitude was unbroken, their time completely unoccupied.

Sometimes they would open a book, and then shut it again—what was the use of it? On other days they would be seized with the idea of cleaning up the garden: at the end of a quarter of an hour they would be fatigued; or they would set out to have a look at the farm, and come back disenchanted; or they tried to interest themselves in household affairs, with the result of making Germaine break out into lamentations. They gave it up.

Bouvard wanted to draw up a catalogue for the museum, and declared their curios stupid.

Pécuchet borrowed Langlois' duck-gun to shoot larks with; the weapon burst at the first shot, and was near killing him.

Then they lived in the midst of that rural solitude so depressing when the grey sky covers in its monotony a heart without hope. The step of a man in wooden shoes is heard as he steals along by the wall, or perchance it is the rain dripping from the roof to the ground. From time to time a dead leaf just grazes one of the windows, then whirls about and flies away. The indistinct echoes of some funeral bell are borne to the ear by the wind. From a corner of the stable comes the lowing of a cow. They yawned in eachother's faces, consulted the almanac, looked at the deck, waited for meal-time; and the horizon was ever the same—fields in front, the church to the right, a screen of poplars to the left, their tops swaying incessantly in the hazy atmosphere with a melancholy air.

Habits which they formerly tolerated now gave them annoyance. Pécuchet became quite a bore from his mania for putting his handkerchief on the tablecloth. Bouvard never gave up his pipe, and would keep twisting himself about while he was talking. They started disputes about the dishes, or about the quality of the butter; and while they were chatting face to face each was thinking of different things.

A certain occurrence had upset Pécuchet's mind.

Two days after the riot at Chavignolles, while he was airing his political grievance, he had reached a road covered with tufted elms, and heard behind his back a voice exclaiming, "Stop!"

It was Madame Castillon. She was rushing across from the opposite side without perceiving him.

A man who was walking along in front of her turned round. It was Gorju; and they met some six feet away from Pécuchet, the row of trees separating them from him.

"Is it true," said she, "you are going to fight?"

Pécuchet slipped behind the ditch to listen.

"Well, yes," replied Gorju; "I am going to fight. What has that to do with you?"

"He asks *me* such a question!" cried she, flinging her arms about him. "But, if you are killed, my love! Oh! remain!"

And her blue eyes appealed to him, still more than her words.

"Let me alone. I have to go."

There was an angry sneer on her face.

"The other has permitted it, eh?"

"Don't speak of her."

He raised his fist.

"No, dear; no. I don't say anything." And big tears trickled down her cheeks as far as the frilling of her collarette.

It was midday. The sun shone down upon the fields covered with yellow grain. Far in the distance carriage-wheels softly slipped along the road. There was a torpor in the air—not a bird's cry, not an insect's hum. Gorju cut himself a switch and scraped off the bark.

Madame Castillon did not raise her head again. She, poor woman, was thinking of her vain sacrifices for him, the debts she had paid for him, her future liabilities, and her lost reputation. Instead of complaining, she recalled for him the first days of their love, when she used to go every night to meet him in the barn, so that her husband on one occasion, fancying it was a thief, fired a pistol-shot through the window. The bullet was in the wall still. "From the moment I first knew you, you seemed to me as handsome as a prince. I love your eyes, your voice, your walk, your smell," and in a lower tone she added: "and as for your person, I am fairly crazy about it."

He listened with a smile of gratified vanity.

She clasped him with both hands round the waist, her head bent as if in adoration.

"My dear heart! my dear love! my soul! my life! Come! speak! What is it you want? Is it money? We'll get it. I was in the wrong. I annoyed you. Forgive me; and order clothes from the tailor, drink champagne—enjoy yourself. I will allow everything—everything."

She murmured with a supreme effort, "Even her—as long as you come back to me."

He just touched her lips with his, drawing one arm around her to prevent her from falling; and she kept murmuring, "Dear heart! dear love! how handsome you are! My God! how handsome you are!"

Pécuchet, without moving an inch, his chin just touching the top of the ditch, stared at them in breathless astonishment.

"Come, no swooning," said Gorju. "You'll only have me missing the coach. A glorious bit of devilment is getting ready, and I'm in the swim; so just give me ten sous to stand the conductor a drink."

She took five francs out of her purse. "You will soon give them back to me. Have a little patience. He has been a good while paralysed. Think of that! And, if you liked, we could go to the chapel of Croix-Janval, and there, my love, I would swear before the Blessed Virgin to marry you as soon as he is dead."

"Ah! he'll never die—that husband of yours."

Gorju had turned on his heel. She caught hold of him again, and clinging to his shoulders:

"Let me go with you. I will be your servant. You want someone. But don't go away! don't leave me! Death rather! Kill me!"

She crawled towards him on her knees, trying to seize his hands in order to kiss them. Her cap fell off, then her comb, and her hair got dishevelled. It was turning white around her ears, and, as she looked up at him, sobbing bitterly, with red eyes and swollen lips, he got quite exasperated, and pushed her back.

"Be off, old woman! Good evening."

When she had got up, she tore off the gold cross that hung round her neck, and flinging it at him, cried:

"There, you ruffian!"

Gorju went off, lashing the leaves of the trees with his switch.

Madame Castillon ceased weeping. With fallen jaw and tear-dimmed eyes she stood motionless, petrified with despair; no longer a being, but a thing in ruins.

What he had just chanced upon was for Pécuchet like the discovery of a new world—a world in which there were dazzling splendours, wild blossomings, oceans, tempests, treasures, and abysses of infinite depth. There was something about it that excited terror; but what of that? He dreamed of love, desired to feel it as she felt it, to inspire it as he inspired it.

However, he execrated Gorju, and could hardly keep from giving information about him at the guardhouse.

Pécuchet was mortified by the slim waist, the regular curls, and the smooth beard of Madame Castillon's lover, as well as by the air of a conquering hero which the fellow assumed, while his own hair was pasted to his skull like a soaked wig, his torso wrapped in a greatcoat resembled a bolster, two of his front teeth were out, and his physiognomy had a harsh expression. He thought that Heaven had dealt unkindly with him, and felt that he was one of the disinherited; moreover, his friend no longer cared for him.

Bouvard deserted him every evening. Since his wife was dead, there was nothing to prevent him from taking another, who, by this time, might be coddling him up and looking after his house. And now he was getting too old to think of it.

But Bouvard examined himself in the glass. His cheeks had kept their colour; his hair curled just the same as of yore; not a tooth was loose; and, at the idea that he had still the power to please, he felt a return of youthfulness. Madame Bordin rose in his memory. She had made advances to him, first on the occasion of the burning of the stacks, next at the dinner which they gave, then in the museum at the recital, and lastly, without resenting any want of attention on his part, she had called three Sundays in succession. He paid her a return visit, and repeated it, making up his mind to woo and win her.

Since the day when Pécuchet had watched the little servant-maid drawing water, he had frequently talked to her, and whether she was sweeping the corridor or spreading out the linen, or taking up the saucepans, he could never grow tired of looking at her—surprised himself at his emotions, as in the days of adolescence. He had fevers and languors on account of her, and he was stung by the picture left in his memory of Madame Castillon straining Gorju to her breast.

He questioned Bouvard as to the way libertines set about seducing women.

"They make them presents; they bring them to restaurants for supper."

"Very good. But after that?"

"Some of them pretend to faint, in order that you may carry them over to a sofa; others let their handkerchiefs fall on the ground. The best of them plainly make an appointment with you." And Bouvard launched forth into descriptions which inflamed Pécuchet's imagination, like engravings of voluptuous scenes.

"The first rule is not to believe what they say. I have known those who, under the appearance of saints, were regular Messalinas. Above all, you must be bold."

But boldness cannot be had to order.

From day to day Pécuchet put off his determination, and besides he was intimidated by the presence of Germaine.

Hoping that she would ask to have her wages paid, he exacted additional work from her, took notice every time she got tipsy, referred in a loud voice to her want of cleanliness, her quarrelsomeness, and did it all so effectively that she had to go.

Then Pécuchet was free! With what impatience he waited for Bouvard to go out! What a throbbing of the heart he felt as soon as the door closed!

Mélie was working at a round table near the window by the light of a candle; from time to time she broke the threads with her teeth, then she half-closed her eyes while adjusting it in the slit of the needle.

At first he asked her what kind of men she liked. Was it, for instance, Bouvard's style?

"Oh, no." She preferred thin men.

He ventured to ask her if she ever had had any lovers.

"Never."

Then, drawing closer to her, he surveyed her piquant nose, her small mouth, her charmingly-rounded figure. He paid her some compliments, and exhorted her to prudence.

In bending over her he got a glimpse, under her corsage, of her white skin, from which emanated a warm odour that made his cheeks tingle. One evening he touched with his lips the wanton hairs at the back of her neck, and he felt shaken even to the marrow of his bones. Another time he kissed her on the chin, and had to restrain himself from pulling his teeth in her flesh, so savoury was it. She returned his kiss. The apartment whirled round; he no longer saw anything.

He made her a present of a pair of lady's boots, and often treated her to a glass of aniseed cordial.

To save her trouble he rose early, chopped up the wood, lighted the fire, and was so attentive as to clean Bouvard's shoes.

Mélie did not faint or let her handkerchief fall, and Pécuchet did not know what to do, his passion increasing through the fear of satisfying it.

Bouvard was assiduously paying his addresses to Madame Bordin. She used to receive him rather cramped in her gown of shot silk, which creaked like a horse's harness, all the while fingering her long gold chain to keep herself in countenance.

Their conversations turned on the people of Chavignolles or on "the dear departed," who had been an usher at Livarot.

Then she inquired about Bouvard's past, curious to know something of his "youthful freaks," the way in which he had fallen heir to his fortune, and the interests by which he was bound to Pécuchet.

He admired the appearance of her house, and when he came to dinner there was struck by the neatness with which it was served and the excellent fare placed on the table. A succession of dishes of the most savoury description, which intermingled at regular intervals with a bottle of old Pomard, brought them to the dessert, at which they remained a long time sipping their coffee; and, with dilating nostrils, Madame Bordin dipped into her saucer her thick lip, lightly shaded with a black down.

One day she appeared in a low dress. Her shoulders fascinated Bouvard. As he sat in a little chair before her, he began to pass his hands along her arms. The widow seemed offended. He did not repeat this attention, but he pictured to himself those ample curves, so marvellously smooth and fine.

Any evening when he felt dissatisfied with Mélie's cooking, it gave him pleasure to enter Madame Bordin's drawing-room. It was there he should have lived.

The globe of the lamp, covered with a red shade, shed a tranquil light. She was seated close to the fire, and his foot touched the hem of her skirt.

After a few opening words the conversation flagged.

However, she kept gazing at him, with half-closed lids, in a languid fashion, but unbending withal.

Bouvard could not stand it any longer, and, sinking on his knees to the floor, he stammered:

"I love you! Marry me!"

Madame Bordin drew a strong breath; then, with an ingenuous air, said he was jesting; no doubt he was trying to have a laugh at her expense—it was not fair. This declaration stunned her.

Bouvard returned that she did not require anyone's consent. "What's to hinder you? Is it the trousseau? Our linen has the same mark, a B—we'll unite our capital letters!"

The idea caught her fancy. But a more important matter prevented her from arriving at a decision before the end of the month. And Bouvard groaned.

She had the politeness to accompany him to the gate, escorted by Marianne, who carried a lantern.

The two friends kept their love affairs hidden from each other.

Pécuchet counted on always cloaking his intrigue with the servant-maid. If Bouvard made any opposition to it, he could carry her off to other places, even though it were to Algeria, where living is not so dear. But he rarely indulged in such speculations, full as he was of his passion, without thinking of the consequences.

Bouvard conceived the idea of converting the museum into the bridal chamber, unless Pécuchet objected, in which case he might take up his residence at his wife's house.

One afternoon in the following week—it was in her garden; the buds were just opening, and between the clouds there were great blue spaces—she stopped to gather some violets, and said as she offered them to him:

"Salute Madame Bouvard!"

"What! Is it true?"

"Perfectly true."

He was about to clasp her in his arms. She kept him back. "What a man!"

Then, growing serious, she warned him that she would shortly be asking him for a favour.

" 'Tis granted."

They fixed the following Thursday for the formality of signing the marriage contract.

Nobody should know anything about it up to the last moment.

"Agreed."

And off he went, looking up towards the sky, nimble as a roebuck.

Pécuchet on the morning of the same day said in his own mind that he would die if he did not obtain the favours of his little maid, and he followed her into the cellar, hoping the darkness would give him courage.

She tried to go away several times, but he detained her in order to count the bottles, to choose laths, or to look into the bottoms of casks—and this occupied a considerable time.

She stood facing him under the light that penetrated through an air-hole, with her eyes cast down, and the corner of her mouth slightly raised.

"Do you love me?" said Pécuchet abruptly.

"Yes, I do love you."

"Well, then prove it to me."

And throwing his left arm around her, he embraced her with ardour.

"You're going to do me some harm."

"No, my little angel. Don't be afraid."

"If Monsieur Bouvard—"

"I'll tell him nothing. Make your mind easy."

There was a heap of faggots behind them. She sank upon them, and hid her face under one arm—and another man would have understood that she was no novice.

Bouvard arrived soon for dinner.

The meal passed in silence, each of them being afraid of betraying himself, while Mélie attended them with her usual impassiveness.

Pécuchet turned away his eyes to avoid hers; and Bouvard, his gaze resting on the walls, pondered meanwhile on his projected improvements.

Eight days after he came back in a towering rage.

"The damned traitress!"

"Who, pray?"

"Madame Bordin."

And he related how he had been so infatuated as to offer to make her his wife, but all had come to an end a quarter of an hour since at Marescot's office. She wished to have for her marriage portion the Ecalles meadow, which he could not dispose of, having partly retained it, like the farm, with the money of another person.

"Exactly," said Pécuchet.

"I had had the folly to promise her any favour she asked—and this was what she was after! I attribute her obstinacy to this; for if she loved me she would have given way to me."

The widow, on the contrary, had attacked him in insulting language, and referred disparagingly to his physique, his big paunch.

"My paunch! Just imagine for a moment!"

Meanwhile Pécuchet had risen several times, and seemed to be in pain.

Bouvard asked him what was the matter, and thereupon Pécuchet, having first taken the precaution to shut the door, explained in a hesitating manner that he was affected with a certain disease.

"What! You?"

"I—myself."

"Oh, my poor fellow! And who is the cause of this?"

Pécuchet became redder than before, and said in a still lower tone:

"It can be only Mélie."

Bouvard remained stupefied.

The first thing to do was to send the young woman away.

She protested with an air of candour.

Pécuchet's case was, however, serious; but he was ashamed to consult a physician.

Bouvard thought of applying to Barberou.

They gave him particulars about the matter, in order that he might communicate with a doctor who would deal with the case by correspondence.

Barberou set to work with zeal, believing it was Bouvard's own case, and calling him an old dotard, even though he congratulated him about it.

"At my age!" said Pécuchet. "Is it not a melancholy thing? But why did she do this?"

"You pleased her."

"She ought to have given me warning."

"Does passion reason?" And Bouvard renewed his complaints about Madame Bordin.

Often had he surprised her before the Ecalles, in Marescot's company, having a gossip with Germaine. So many manouevres for a little bit of land!

"She is avaricious! That's the explanation."

So they ruminated over their disappointments by the fireside in the breakfast parlour, Pécuchet swallowing his medicines and Bouvard puffing at his pipe; and they began a discussion about women.

"Strange want!—or is it a want?" "They drive men to crime—to heroism as well as to brutishness." "Hell under a petticoat," "paradise in a kiss," "the turtle's warbling," "the serpent's windings," "the cat's claws," "the sea's treachery," "the moon's changeableness." They repeated all the commonplaces that have been uttered about the sex.

It was the desire for women that had suspended their friendship. A feeling of remorse took possession of them. "No more women. Is not that so? Let us live without them!" And they embraced each other tenderly.

There should be a reaction; and Bouvard, when Pécuchet was better, considered that a course of hydropathic treatment would be beneficial.

Germaine, who had come back since the other servant's departure, carried the bathing-tub each morning into the corridor.

The two worthies, naked as savages, poured over themselves big buckets of water; they then rushed back to their rooms. They were seen through the garden fence, and people were scandalised.

Chapter VIII

NEW DIVERSIONS

SATISFIED WITH THEIR REGIMEN, THEY DESIRED TO IMPROVE THEIR CONSTITU-
tions by gymnastics; and taking up the *Manual of Amoros*, they went
through its atlas. All those young lads squatting, lying back, standing, bending their legs, lifting weights, riding on beams, climbing ladders, cutting capers on
trapezes—such a display of strength and agility excited their envy.

However, they were saddened by the splendour of the gymnasium described
in the preface; for they would never be able to get a vestibule for the equipages, a
hippodrome for the races, a sweep of water for the swimming, or a "mountain of
glory"—an artificial hillock over one hundred feet in height.

A wooden vaulting-horse with the stuffing would have been expensive: they abandoned the idea. The linden tree, thrown down in the garden, might have been used as
a horizontal pole; and, when they were skilful enough to go over it from one end to the
other, in order to have a vertical one, they set up a beam of counter-espaliers. Pécuchet
clambered to the top; Bouvard slipped off, always fell back, finally gave it up.

The "orthosomatic sticks" pleased him better; that is to say, two broomsticks
bound by two cords, the first of which passes under the armpits, and the second
over the wrists; and for hours he would remain in this apparatus, with his chin
raised, his chest extended, and his elbows close to his sides.

For want of dumbbells, the wheelwright turned out four pieces of ash resembling sugar-loaves with necks of bottles at the ends. These should be carried to the
right and to the left, to the front and to the back; but being too heavy they fell out
of their hands, at the risk of bruising their legs. No matter! They set their hearts
on Persian clubs, and even fearing lest they might break, they rubbed them every
evening with wax and a piece of cloth.

Then they looked out for ditches. When they found one suitable for their purpose, they rested a long pole in the centre, sprang forward on the left foot, reached
the opposite side, and then repeated the performance. The country being flat, they
could be seen at a distance; and the villagers asked one another what were these extraordinary things skipping towards the horizon.

When autumn arrived they went in for chamber gymnastics, which completely
bored them. Why had they not the indoor apparatus or post-armchair invented in
Louis XIV's time by the Abbé of St. Pierre? How was it made? Where could they
get the information?

Dumouchel did not deign to answer their letter on the subject.

Then they erected in the bakehouse a brachial weighing-machine. Over two pulleys attached to the ceiling a rope was passed, holding a crossbeam at each end. As soon as they had caught hold of it one pushed against the ground with his toes, while the other lowered his arms to a level with the floor; the first by his weight would draw towards him the second, who, slackening his rope a little, would ascend in his turn. In less than five minutes their limbs were dripping with perspiration.

In order to follow the prescriptions of the Manual, they tried to make themselves ambidextrous, even to the extent of depriving themselves for a time of the use of their right hands. They did more: Amoros points out certain snatches of verse which ought to be sung during the manouevres, and Bouvard and Pécuchet, as they proceeded, kept repeating the hymn No. 9: "A king, a just king is a blessing on earth."

When they beat their breast-bones: "Friends, the crown and the glory," etc.

At the various steps of the race:

> *"Let us catch the beast that cowers!*
> *Soon tile swift stag shall be ours!*
> *Yes! the race shall soon be won,*
> *Come, run! come, run! come, run!"*

And, panting more than hounds, they cheered each other on with the sounds of their voices.

One side of gymnastics excited their enthusiasm—its employment as a means of saving life. But they would have required children in order to learn how to carry them in sacks, and they begged the schoolmaster to furnish them with some. Petit objected that their families would be annoyed at it. They fell back on the succour of the wounded. One pretended to have swooned: the other rolled him away in a wheelbarrow with the utmost precaution.

As for military escalades, the author extols the ladder of Bois-Rosé, so called from the captain who surprised Fécamp in former days by climbing up the cliff.

In accordance with the engraving in the book, they trimmed a rope with little sticks and fixed it under the cart-shed. As soon as the first stick is bestridden and the third grasped, the limbs are thrown out in order that the second, which a moment before was against the chest, might be directly under the thighs. The climber then springs up and grasps the fourth, and so goes on.

In spite of prodigious strainings of the hips, they found it impossible to reach the second step. Perhaps there is less trouble in hanging on to stones with your hands, just as Bonaparte's soldiers did at the attack of Fort Chambray? and to make one capable of such an action, Amoros has a tower in his establishment.

The wall in ruins might do as a substitute for it. They attempted the assault with it. But Bouvard, having withdrawn his foot too quickly from a hole, got frightened, and was seized with dizziness.

Pécuchet blamed their method for it. They had neglected that which relates to the phalanxes, so that they should go back to first principles.

His exhortations were fruitless; and then, in his pride and presumption, he went in for stilts.

Nature seemed to have destined him for them, for he immediately made use of the great model with flat boards four feet from the ground, and, balanced thereon, he stalked over the garden like a gigantic stork taking exercise.

Bouvard, at the window, saw him stagger and then flop down all of a heap over the kidney-beans, whose props, giving way as he descended, broke his fall.

He was picked up covered with mould, his nostrils bleeding—livid; and he fancied that he had strained himself.

Decidedly, gymnastics did not agree with men of their age. They abandoned them, did not venture to move about any longer for fear of accidents, and they remained the whole day sitting in the museum dreaming of other occupations.

This change of habits had an influence on Bouvard's health. He became very heavy, puffed like a whale after his meals, tried to make himself thin, ate less, and began to grow weak.

Pécuchet, in like manner, felt himself "undermined," had itchings in his skin and lumps in his throat.

"This won't do," said they; "this won't do."

Bouvard thought of going to select at the inn some bottles of Spanish wine in order to put his bodily machinery in order.

As he was going out, Marescot's clerk and three men brought from Beljambe a large walnut table. "Monsieur" was much obliged to him for it. It had been conveyed in perfect order.

Bouvard in this way learned about the new fashion of table-turning. He joked about it with the clerk.

However, all over Europe, America, Australia and the Indies, millions of mortals passed their lives in making tables turn; and they discovered the way to make prophets of canaries, to give conceits without instruments, and to correspond by means of snails. The press, seriously offering these impostures to the public, increased its credulity.

The spirit-rappers had alighted at the château of Faverges, and thence had spread through the village; and the notary questioned them particularly.

Shocked at Bouvard's scepticism, he invited the two friends to an evening party at table-turning.

Was this a trap? Madame Bordin was to be there. Pécuchet went alone.

There were present as spectators the mayor, the tax-collector, the captain, other residents and their wives, Madame Vaucorbeil, Madame Bordin, of course, besides Mademoiselle Laverrière, Madame Marescot's former schoolmistress, a rather squint-eyed lady with her hair falling over her shoulders in the corkscrew fashion of 1830. In an armchair sat a cousin from Paris, attired in a blue coat and wearing an air of insolence.

The two bronze lamps, the whatnot containing a number of curiosities, ballads embellished with vignettes on the piano, and small water-colours in huge frames, had always excited astonishment in Chavignolles. But this evening all eyes were directed towards the mahogany table. They would test it by and by, and it had the importance of things which contain a mystery. A dozen guests took their places around it with outstretched hands and their little fingers touching one another. Only the ticking of the clock could be heard. The faces indicated profound attention. At the end of ten minutes several complained of tinglings in the arms.

Pécuchet was incommoded.

"You are pushing!" said the captain to Foureau.

"Not at all."

"Yes, you are!"

"Ah! sir."

The notary made them keep quiet.

By dint of straining their ears they thought they could distinguish cracklings of wood.

An illusion! Nothing had budged.

The other day when the Aubert and Lorraine families had come from Lisieux and they had expressly borrowed Beljambe's table for the occasion, everything had gone on so well. But this to-day exhibited a certain obstinacy. Why?

The carpet undoubtedly counteracted it, and they changed to the dining-room.

The round table, which was on rollers, glided towards the right-hand side. The operators, without displacing their fingers, followed its movements, and of its own accord it made two turns. They were astounded.

Then M. Alfred articulated in a loud voice:

"Spirit, how do you find my cousin?"

The table, slowly oscillating, struck nine raps. According to a slip of paper, in which the number of raps were translated by letters, this meant "Charming."

A number of voices exclaimed "Bravo!"

Then Marescot, to tease Madame Bordin, called on the spirit to declare her exact age.

The foot of the table came down with five taps.

"What? five years!" cried Girbal.

"The tens don't count," replied Foureau.

The widow smiled, though she was inwardly annoyed.

The replies to the other questions were missing, so complicated was the alphabet.

Much better was the plane table—an expeditious medium of which Mademoiselle Laverrière had made use for the purpose of noting down in an album the direct communications of Louis XII, Clémence Isaure, Franklin, Jean-Jacques Rousseau, and others. These mechanical contrivances are sold in the Rue d'Aumale. M. Alfred promised one of them; then addressing the schoolmistress: "But for a quarter of an hour we should have a little music; don't you think so? A mazurka!"

Two metal chords vibrated. He took his cousin by the waist, disappeared with her, and came back again.

The sweep of her dress, which just brushed the doors as they passed, cooled their faces. She flung back her head; he curved his arms. The gracefulness of the one, the playful air of the other, excited general admiration; and, without waiting for the rout cakes, Pécuchet took himself off, amazed at the evening's exhibition.

In vain did he repeat: "But I have seen it! I have seen it!".

Bouvard denied the facts, but nevertheless consented to make an experiment himself.

For a fortnight they spent every afternoon facing each other, with their hands over a table, then over a hat, over a basket, and over plates. All these remained motionless.

The phenomenon of table-turning is none the less certain. The common herd attribute it to spirits; Faraday to prolonged nervous action; Chevreuil to unconscious efforts; or perhaps, as Segouin admits, there is evolved from the assembly of persons an impulse, a magnetic current.

This hypothesis made Pécuchet reflect. He took into his library the *Magnetiser's Guide,* by Montacabère, read it over attentively, and initiated Bouvard in the theory: All animated bodies receive and communicate the influence of the stars—a property analogous to the virtue of the loadstone. By directing this force we may cure the sick; there is the principle. Science has developed since Mesmer; but it is always an important thing to pour out the fluid and to make passes, which, in the first place, must have the effect of inducing sleep.

"Well! send me to sleep," said Bouvard.

"Impossible!" replied Pécuchet: "in order to be subject to the magnetic action, and to transmit it, faith is indispensable."

Then, gazing at Bouvard: "Ah! what a pity!"

"How?"

"Yes, if you wished, with a little practice, there would not be a magnetiser anywhere like you."

For he possessed everything that was needed: easiness of access, a robust constitution, and a solid mind.

The discovery just made of such a faculty in himself was flattering to Bouvard. He took a plunge into Montacabère's book on the sly.

Then, as Germaine used to feel buzzings in her ears that deafened her, he said to her one evening in a careless tone:

"Suppose we try magnetism?"

She did not make any objection to it. He sat down in front of her, took her two thumbs in his hands, and looked fixedly at her, as if he had not done anything else all his life.

The old dame, with her feet on a footwarmer, began by bending her neck; her eyes closed, and quite gently she began to snore. At the end of an hour, during which they had been staring at her, Pécuchet said in a low tone:

"What do you feel?"

She awoke.

Later, no doubt, would come lucidity.

This success emboldened them, and, resuming with self-confidence, the practice of medicine, they nursed Chamberlan, the beadle, for pains in his ribs; Migraine the mason, who had a nervous affection of the stomach; Mère Varin, whose encephaloid under the collar-bone required, in order to nourish her, plasters of meat; a gouty patient, Père Lemoine, who used to crawl by the side of taverns; a consumptive; a person afflicted with hemiplegia, and many others. They also treated corns and chilblains.

After an investigation into the disease, they cast questioning glances at each other to determine what passes to use, whether the currents should be1 large or small, ascending or descending, longitudinal, transversal, bidigital, tridigital, or even quindigital.

When the one had had too much of it, the other replaced him. Then, when they had come back to their own house, they noted down their observation in their diary of treatment.

Their suave manners captivated everyone. However, Bouvard was liked better, and his reputation spread as far as Falaise, where he had cured La Barbée, the daughter of Père Barbée, a retired captain of long standing.

She had felt something like a nail in the back of her head, spoke in a hoarse voice, often remained several days without eating, and then would devour plaster or coal. Her nervous crises, beginning with sobs, ended in floods of tears; and every kind of remedy, from diet-drinks to moxas, had been employed, so that, through sheer weariness, she accepted Bouvard's offer to cure her.

When he had dismissed the servant-maid and bolted the door, he began rubbing her abdomen, while leaning over the seat of the ovaries. A sense of relief manifested itself by sighs and yawns. He placed his finger between her eyebrows and the top of her nose: all at once she became inert. If one lifted her arms, they fell down again. Her head remained in whatever attitude he wished, and her lids, half closed, vibrating with a spasmodic movement, allowed her eyeballs to be seen rolling slowly about; they riveted themselves on the corners convulsively.

Bouvard asked her if she were in pain. She replied that she was not. Then he inquired what she felt now. She indicated the inside of her body.

"What do you see there?"

"A worm."

"What is necessary in order to kill it?"

She wrinkled her brow. "I am looking for—I am not able! I am not able!"

At the second sitting she prescribed for herself nettle-broth; at the third, cat-nip. The crises became mitigated, then disappeared. It was truly a miracle. The nasal addigitation did not succeed with the others, and, in order to bring on somnambulism, they projected the construction of a mesmeric tub. Pécuchet already had even collected the filings and cleaned a score of bottles, when a scruple made him hesitate.

Amongst the patients there would be persons of the other sex.

"And what are we to do if this should give rise to an outburst of erotic mania?"

This would not have proved any impediment to Bouvard; but for fear of impostures and attempts to extort hush-money, it was better to put aside the project. They contented themselves with a collection of musical glasses, which they carried about with them to the different houses, so as to delight the children.

One day, when Migraine was worse, they had recourse to the musical glasses. The crystalline sounds exasperated him; but Deleuze enjoins that one should not be frightened by complaints; and so they went on with the music.

"Enough! enough!" he cried.

"A little patience!" Bouvard kept repeating.

Pécuchet tapped more quickly on the glass plates, and the instrument was vibrating in the midst of the poor man's cries when the doctor appeared, attracted by the hubbub.

"What! you again?" he exclaimed, enraged at finding them always with his patients.

They explained their magnetic method of curing. Then he declaimed against magnetism—"a heap of juggleries, whose effects came only from the imagination."

However, animals are magnetised. Montacabère so states, and M. Fontaine succeeded in magnetising a lion. They had not a lion, but chance had offered them another animal.

For on the following day a ploughboy came to inform them that they were wanted up at the farm for a cow in a hopeless condition.

They hurried thither. The apple trees were in bloom, and the herbage in the farmyard was steaming under the rays of the rising sun.

At the side of a pond, half covered with a cloth, a cow was lowing, while she shivered under the pails of water that were being emptied over her body, and, enormously swollen, she looked like a hippopotamus.

Without doubt she had got "venom" while grazing amid the clover. Père Gouy and his wife were afflicted because the veterinary surgeon was not able to come, and the wheelwright who had a charm against swelling did not choose to put himself out of his way; but "these gentlemen, whose library was famous, must know the secret."

Having tucked up their sleeves, they placed themselves one in front of the horns, the other at the rump, and, with great internal efforts and frantic gesticulations, they spread wide their fingers in order to scatter streams of fluid over the animal, while the farmer, his wife, their son, and the neighbours regarded them almost with terror.

The rumblings which were heard in the cow's belly caused borborygms in the interior of her bowels. She emitted wind.

Pécuchet thereupon said: "This is an opening door for hope—an outlet, perhaps."

The outlet produced its effect: the hope gushed forth in a bundle of yellow stuff, bursting with the force of a shell. The hide got loose; the cow got rid of her swelling. An hour later there was no longer any sign of it.

This was certainly not the result of imagination. Therefore the fluid contained some special virtue. It lets itself be shut up in the objects to whom it is given without being impaired. Such an expedient saves displacements. They adopted it; and they sent their clients magnetised tokens, magnetised handkerchiefs, magnetised water, and magnetised bread.

Then, continuing their studies, they abandoned the passes for the system of Puységur, which replaces the magnetiser by means of an old tree, about the trunk of which a cord is rolled.

A pear tree in their fruit garden seemed made expressly for the purpose. They prepared it by vigorously encircling it with many pressures. A bench was placed underneath. Their clients sat in a row, and the results obtained there were so marvellous that, in order to get the better of Vaucorbeil, they invited him to a *séance* along with the leading personages of the locality.

Not one failed to attend. Germaine received them in the breakfast-room, making excuses on behalf of her masters, who would join them presently.

From time to time they heard the bell ringing. It was the patients whom she was bringing in by another way. The guests nudged one another, drawing attention to the windows covered with dust, the stains on the panels, the frayed pictures; and the garden, too, was in a wretched state. Dead wood everywhere! The orchard was barricaded with two sticks thrust into a gap in the wall.

Pécuchet made his appearance. "At your service, gentlemen."

And they saw at the end of the garden, under the Edouïn pear tree, a number of persons seated.

Chamberlan, clean-shaven like a priest, in a short cassock of lasting, with a leathern cap, gave himself up to the shivering sensations engendered by the pains in his ribs. Migraine, whose stomach was always tormenting him, made wry faces close beside him. Mère Varin, to hide her tumour, wore a shawl with many folds. Père Lemoine, his feet stockingless in his old shoes, had his crutches under his knees; and La Barbée, who wore her Sunday clothes, looked exceedingly pale.

At the opposite side of the tree were other persons. A woman with an albino type of countenance was sponging the suppurating glands of her neck; a little girl's face half disappeared under her blue glasses; an old man, whose spine was deformed by a contraction, with his involuntary movements knocked against Marcel, a sort of idiot clad in a tattered blouse and a patched pair of trousers. His hare-lip, badly stitched, allowed his incisors to be seen, and his jaw, which was swollen by an enormous inflammation, was muffled up in linen.

They were all holding in their hands pieces of twine that hung down from the tree. The birds were singing, and the air was impregnated with the refreshing smell of grass. The sun played with the branches, and the ground was smooth as moss.

Meanwhile, instead of going to sleep, the subjects of the experiment were straining their eyes.

"Up to the present," said Foureau, "it is not funny. Begin. I am going away for a minute."

And he came back smoking an Abd-el-Kader, the last that was left from the gate with the pipes.

Pécuchet recalled to mind an admirable method of magnetising. He put into his mouth the noses of all the patients in succession, and inhaled their breath, in order to attract the electricity to himself; and at the same time Bouvard clasped the tree, with the object of augmenting the fluid.

The mason interrupted his hiccoughs; the beadle was agitated; the man with the contraction moved no more. It was possible now to approach them, and make them submit to all the tests.

The doctor, with his lancet, pricked Chamberlan's ear, which trembled a little. Sensibility in the case of the others was manifest. The gouty man uttered a cry. As for La Barbée, she smiled, as if in a dream, and a stream of blood trickled under her jaw.

Foureau, in order to make the experiment himself, would fain have seized the lancet, but the doctor having refused, he vigorously pinched the invalid.

The captain tickled her nostrils with a feather; the tax-collector plunged a pin under her skin.

"Let her alone now," said Vaucorbeil; "it is nothing astonishing, after all. Simply a hysterical female! The devil will have his pains for nothing."

"That one there," said Pécuchet, pointing towards Victoire, the scrofulous woman, "is a physician. She recognises diseases, and indicates the remedies."

Langlois burned to consult her about his catarrh; but Coulon, more courageous, asked her for something for his rheumatism.

Pécuchet placed his right hand in Victoire's left, and, with her lids closed uninterruptedly, her cheeks a little red, her lips quivering, the somnambulist, after some rambling utterances, ordered *valum becum.*

She had assisted in an apothecary's shop at Bayeux. Vaucorbeil drew the inference that what she wanted to say was *album Groecum* a term which is to be found in pharmacy.

Then they accosted Père Lemoine, who, according to Bouvard, could see objects through opaque bodies. He was an ex-schoolmaster, who had sunk into debauchery. White hairs were scattered about his face, and, with his back against the tree and his palms open, he was sleeping in the broad sunlight in a majestic fashion.

The physician drew over his eyes a double neckcloth; and Bouvard, extending a newspaper towards him, said imperiously:

"Read!"

He lowered his brow, moved the muscles of his face, then threw back his head, and ended by spelling out:

"Cons-ti-tu-tion-al."

But with skill the muffler could be slipped off!

These denials by the physician roused Pécuchet's indignation. He even ventured to pretend that La Barbée could describe what was actually taking place in his own house.

"May be so," returned the doctor.

Then, taking out his watch:

"What is my wife occupying herself with?"

For a long time La Barbée hesitated; then with a sullen air:

"Hey! what? I am there! She is sewing ribbons on a straw hat."

Vaucorbeil snatched a leaf from his note-book and wrote a few lines on it, which Marescot's clerk hastened to deliver.

The *séance* was over. The patients went away. Bouvard and Pécuchet, on the whole, had not succeeded. Was this due to the temperature, or to the smell of tobacco, or to the Abbé Jeufroy's umbrella, which had a lining of copper, a metal unfavourable to the emission of the fluid?

Vaucorbeil shrugged his shoulders. However, he could not deny the honesty of MM. Deleuze, Bertrand, Morin, Jules Cloquet. Now these masters lay down that somnambulists have predicted events, and submitted without pain to cruel operations.

The abbé related stories more astonishing. A missionary had seen Brahmins rushing, heads down, through a street; the Grand Lama of Thibet rips open his bowels in order to deliver oracles.

"Are you joking?" said the physician.

"By no means."

"Come, now, what tomfoolery that is!"

And the question being dropped, each of them furnished an anecdote.

"As for me," said the grocer, "I had a dog who was always sick when the month began on a Friday."

"We were fourteen children," observed the justice of the peace. "I was born on the 14th, my marriage took place on the 14th, and my saint's-day falls on the 14th. Explain this to me."

Beljambe had often reckoned in a dream the number of travellers he would have next day at his inn; and Petit told about the supper of Cazotte.

The curé then made this reflection:

"Why do we not see into it quite easily?"

"The demons—is that what you say?" asked Vaucorbeil.

Instead of again opening his lips, the abbé nodded his head.

Marescot spoke of the Pythia of Delphi.

"Beyond all question, miasmas."

"Oh! miasmas now!"

"As for me, I admit the existence of a fluid," remarked Bouvard.

"Nervoso-siderial," added Pécuchet.

"But prove it, show it, this fluid of yours! Besides, fluids are out of fashion. Listen to me."

Vaucorbeil moved further up to get into the shade. The others followed him.

"If you say to a child, 'I am a wolf; I am going to eat you,' he imagines that you are a wolf, and he is frightened. Therefore, this is a vision conjured up by words. In the same way the somnambulist accepts any fancies that you desire him to accept. He recollects instead of imagining, and has merely sensations when he believes that he is thinking. In this manner it is possible for crimes to be suggested, and virtuous people may see themselves ferocious beasts, and involuntarily become cannibals."

Glances were cast towards Bouvard and Pécuchet. Their scientific pursuits were fraught with dangers to society.

Marescot's clerk reappeared in the garden flourishing a letter from Madame Vaucorbeil.

The doctor tore it open, turned pale, and finally read these words:

"I am sewing ribbons on a straw hat."

Amazement prevented them from bursting into a laugh.

"A mere coincidence, deuce take it! It proves nothing."

And as the two magnetisers wore looks of triumph, he turned round at the door to say to them:

"Don't go further. These are risky amusements."

The curé, while leading away his beadle, reproved them sternly:

"Are you mad? Without my permission! Practices forbidden by the Church!"

They had all just taken their leave; Bouvard and Pécuchet were talking to the schoolmaster on the hillock, when Marcel rushed from the orchard, the bandage of his chin undone, and stuttered:

"Cured! cured! good gentlemen."

"All right! enough! Let us alone."

Petit, a man of advanced ideas, thought the doctor's explanation commonplace and unenlightened. Science is a monopoly in the hands of the rich. She excludes the people. To the old-fashioned analysis of the Middle Ages it is time that a large and ready-witted synthesis should succeed. Truth should be arrived at through the heart. And, declaring himself a spiritualist, he pointed out several works, no doubt imperfect, but the heralds of a new dawn.

They sent for them.

Spiritualism lays down as a dogma the fated amelioration of our species. Earth will one day become Heaven. And this is the reason why the doctrine fascinated the schoolmaster. Without being Catholic, it was known to St. Augustine and St. Louis. Allan Kardec even has published some fragments dictated by them which are in accordance with contemporary opinions. It is practical as well as benevolent, and reveals to us, like the telescope, the supernal worlds. Spirits, after death and in a state of ecstasy, are transported thither. But sometimes they descend upon our globe, where they make furniture creak, mingle in our amusements, taste the beauties of Nature, and the pleasures of the arts.

Nevertheless, there are amongst us many who possess an astral trunk—that is to say, behind the ear a long tube which ascends from the hair to the planets, and permits us to converse with the spirits of Saturn. Intangible things are not less real, and from the earth to the stars, from the stars to the earth, a see-saw motion takes place, a transmission, a continual change of place.

Then Pécuchet's heart swelled with extravagant aspirations, and when night had come Bouvard surprised him at the window contemplating those luminous spaces which are peopled with spirits.

Swedenborg made rapid journeys to them. For in less than a year he explored Venus, Mars, Saturn, and, twenty-three times, Jupiter. Moreover, he saw Jesus Christ in London; he saw St. Paul; he saw St. John; he saw Moses; and in 1736 he saw the Last Judgment.

He has also given us descriptions of Heaven.

Flowers, palaces, market-places, and churches are found there, just as with us. The angels, who were formerly human beings, lay their thoughts upon leaves, chat about domestic affairs or else on spiritual matters; and the ecclesiastical posts are assigned to those who, in their earthly career, cultivated the Holy Scripture.

As for Hell, it is filled with a nauseous smell, with hovels, heaps of filth, quagmires, and ill-clad persons.

And Pécuchet racked his brain in order to comprehend what was beautiful in these revelations. To Bouvard they seemed the delirium of an imbecile. All such matters transcend the bounds of Nature. Who, however, can know anything about them? And they surrendered themselves to the following reflections:

Jugglers can cause illusions amongst a crowd; a man with violent passions can excite other people by them; but how can the will alone act upon inert matter? A Bavarian, it is said, was able to ripen grapes; M. Gervais revived a heliotrope; one with greater power scattered the clouds at Toulouse.

It is necessary to admit an intermediary substance between the universe and ourselves? The od, a new imponderable, a sort of electricity, is perhaps nothing else. Its emissions explain the light that those who have been magnetised believe they see: the wandering flames in cemeteries, the forms of phantoms.

These images would not, therefore, be illusions, and the extraordinary gifts of persons who are possessed, like those of clairvoyants, would have a physical cause.

Whatever be their origin, there is an essence, a secret and universal agent. If we could take possession of it, there would be no need of force, of duration. That which requires ages would develop in a minute; every miracle would be practicable, and the universe would be at our disposal.

Magic springs from this eternal yearning of the human mind. Its value has no doubt been exaggerated, but it is not a falsehood. Some Orientals who are skilled in it perform prodigies. All travellers have vouched for its existence, and at the Palais Royal M. Dupotet moves with his finger the magnetic needle.

How to become magicians? This idea appeared to them foolish at first, but it returned, tormented them, and they yielded to it, even while affecting to laugh.

A course of preparation is indispensable.

In order to excite themselves the better, they kept awake at night, fasted, and, wishing to convert Germaine into a more delicate medium, they limited her diet. She indemnified herself by drinking, and consumed so much brandy that she speedily ended in becoming intoxicated. Their promenades in the corridor awakened her. She confused the noise of their footsteps with the hummings in her ears and the voices which she imagined she heard coming from the walls. One day, when she had put a plaice into the pantry, she was frightened on seeing it covered with flame; she became worse than ever after that, and ended by believing that they had cast a spell over her.

Hoping to behold visions, they pressed the napes of each other's necks; they made themselves little bags of belladonna; finally they adopted the magic box, out of which rises a mushroom bristling with nails, to be worn over the heart by means of a ribbon attached to the breast. Everything proved unsuccessful. But they might make use of the sphere of Dupotet!

Pécuchet, with a piece of charcoal, traced on the ground a black shield, in order to enclose within its compass the animal spirits whose duty it is to assist the ambient spirits, and rejoicing at having the mastery over Bouvard, he said to him, with a pontifical air:

"I defy you to cross it!"

Bouvard viewed this circular space. Soon his heart began throbbing, his eyes became clouded.

"Ha! let us make an end of it!" And he jumped over it, to get rid of an inexpressible sense of unpleasantness.

Pécuchet, whose exultation was increasing, desired to make a corpse appear.

Under the Directory a man in the Rue de l'Échiquier exhibited the victims of the Terror. There are innumerable examples of persons coming back from the other world. Though it may be a mere appearance, what matter? The thing was to produce the effect.

The nearer to us we feel the phantom, the more promptly it responds to our appeal. But he had no relic of his family—ring, miniature, or lock of hair—while

Bouvard was in a position to conjure up his father; but, as he testified a certain repugnance on the subject, Pécuchet asked him:

"What are you afraid of?"

"I? Oh! nothing at all! Do what you like."

They kept Chamberlan in their pay, and he supplied them by stealth with an old death's-head. A seamster cut out for them two long black robes with hoods attached, like monks' habits. The Falaise coach brought them a large parcel in a wrapper. Then they set about the work, the one interested in executing it, the other afraid to believe in it.

The museum was spread out like a catafalque. Three wax tapers burned at the side of the table pushed against the wall beneath the portrait of Père Bouvard, above which rose the death's-head. They had even stuffed a candle into the interior of the skull, and rays of light shot out through the two eyeholes.

In the centre, on a chafing-dish, incense was smoking. Bouvard kept in the background, and Pécuchet, turning his back to him, cast handfuls of sulphur into the fireplace.

Before invoking a corpse the consent of the demons is required. Now, this day being a Friday—a day which is assigned to Béchet—they should occupy themselves with Béchet first of all.

Bouvard, having bowed to the right and to the left, bent his chin, and raised his arms, began:

"In the names of Ethaniel, Anazin, Ischyros——"

He forgot the rest.

Pécuchet rapidly breathed forth the words, which had been jotted down on a piece of pasteboard:

"Ischyros, Athanatos, Adonaï, Sadaï, Eloy, Messiasös" (the litany was a long one), "I implore thee, I look to thee, I command thee, O Béchet!"

Then, lowering his voice:

"Where art thou, Béchet? Béchet! Béchet! Béchet!"

Bouvard sank into the armchair, and he was very pleased at not seeing Béchet, a certain instinct reproaching him with making an experiment which was a kind of sacrilege.

Where was his father's soul? Could it hear him? What if, all at once, it were about to appear?

The curtains slowly moved under the wind, which made its way in through a cracked pane of glass, and the wax-tapers caused shadows to oscillate above the corpse's skull and also above the painted face. An earthy colour made them equally brown. The cheek-bones were consumed by mouldiness, the eyes no longer possessed any lustre; but a flame shone above them in the eyeholes of the empty skull.

It seemed sometimes to take the other's place, to rest on the collar of the frock-coat, to have a beard on it; and the canvas, half unfastened, swayed and palpitated.

Little by little they felt, as it were, the sensation of being touched by a breath, the approach of an impalpable being. Drops of sweat moistened Pécuchet's forehead, and Bouvard began to gnash his teeth: a cramp gripped his epigastrium; the floor, like a wave, seemed to flow under his heels; the sulphur burning in the chimney fell down in spirals. At the same moment bats flitted about. A cry arose. Who was it?

And their faces under their hoods presented such a distorted aspect that, gazing at each other, they were becoming more frightened than before, not venturing either to move or to speak, when behind the door they heard groans like those of a soul in torture.

At length they ran the risk. It was their old housekeeper, who, espying them through a slit in the partition, imagined she saw the devil, and, falling on her knees in the corridor, kept repeatedly making the sign of the Cross.

All reasoning was futile. She left them the same evening, having no desire to be employed by such people.

Germaine babbled. Chambelan lost his place, and he formed against them a secret coalition, supported by the Abbé Jeufroy, Madame Bordin, and Foureau.

Their way of living, so unlike that of other people, gave offence. They became objects of suspicion, and even inspired a vague terror.

What destroyed them above all in public opinion was their choice of a servant. For want of another, they had taken Marcel.

His hare-lip, his hideousness, and the gibberish he talked made people avoid him. A deserted child, he had grown up, the sport of chance, in the fields, and from his long-continued privations he became possessed by an insatiable appetite. Animals that had died of disease, putrid bacon, a crushed dog—everything agreed with him so long as the piece was thick; and he was as gentle as a sheep, but utterly stupid.

Gratitude had driven him to offer himself as a servant to MM. Bouvard and Pécuchet; and then, believing that they were wizards, he hoped for extraordinary gains.

Soon after the first days of his employment with them, he confided to them a secret. On the heath of Poligny a man had formerly found an ingot of gold. The anecdote is related by the historians of Falaise; they were ignorant of its sequel: Twelve brothers, before setting out on a voyage, had concealed twelve similar ingots along the road from Chavignolles to Bretteville, and Marcel begged of his masters to begin a search for them over again. These ingots, said they to eachother, had perhaps been buried just before emigration.

This was a case for the use of the divining-rod. Its virtues are doubtful. They studied the question, however, and learned that a certain Pierre Garnier gives scientific reasons to vindicate its claims: springs and metals throw out corpuscles which have an affinity with the wood.

"This is scarcely probable. Who knows, however? Let us make the attempt."

They cut themselves a forked branch from a hazel tree, and one morning set forth to discover the treasure.

"It must be given up," said Bouvard.

"Oh, no! bless your soul!"

After they had been three hours travelling, a thought made them draw up: "The road from Chavignolles to Bretteville!—was it the old or the new road? It must be the old!"

They went back, and rushed through the neighbourhood at random, the direction of the old road not being easy to discover.

Marcel went jumping from right to left, like a spaniel running at field-sports. Bouvard was compelled to call him back every five minutes. Pécuchet advanced step by step, holding the rod by the two branches, with the point upwards. Often it seemed to him that a force and, as it were, a cramp-iron drew it towards the ground; and Marcel very rapidly made a notch in the neighbouring trees, in order to find the place later.

Pécuchet, however, slackened his pace. His mouth was open; the pupils of his eyes were contracted. Bouvard questioned him, caught hold of his shoulders, and shook him. He did not stir, and remained inert, exactly like La Barbée. Then he said he felt around his heart a kind of compression, a singular experience, arising from the rod, no doubt, and he no longer wished to touch it.

They returned next day to the place where the marks had been made on the trees. Marcel dug holes with a spade; nothing, however, came of it, and each time they felt exceedingly sheepish. Pécuchet sat down by the side of a ditch, and while he mused, with his head raised, striving to hear the voices of the spirits through his astral body, asking himself whether he even had one, he fixed his eyes on the peak of his cap; the ecstasy of the previous day once more took possession of him. It lasted a long time, and became dreadful.

Above some oats in a by-path appeared a felt hat: it was that of M. Vaucorbeil on his mare.

Bouvard and Marcel called out to him.

The crisis was drawing to an end when the physician arrived. In order to examine Pécuchet he lifted his cap, and perceiving a forehead covered with coppery marks:

"Ha! ha! *Fructus belli!* Those are love-spots, my fine fellow! Take care of yourself. The deuce! let us not trifle with love."

Pécuchet, ashamed, again put on his cap, a sort of head-piece that swelled over a peak shaped like a half-moon, the model of which he had taken from the Atlas of Amoros.

The doctor's words astounded him. He kept thinking of them with his eyes staring before him, and suddenly had another seizure.

Vaucorbeil watched him, then, with a fillip, knocked off his cap.

Pécuchet recovered his faculties.

"I suspected as much," said the physician; "the glazed peak hypnotises you like a mirror; and this phenomenon is not rare with persons who look at a shining substance too attentively."

He pointed out how the experiment might be made on hens, then mounted his nag, and slowly disappeared from their view.

Half a league further on they noticed, in a farmyard, a pyramidal object stretched out towards the horizon. It might have been compared to an enormous bunch of black grapes marked here and there with red dots. It was, in fact, a long pole, garnished, according to the Norman custom, with cross-bars, on which were perched turkeys bridling in the sunshine.

"Let us go in." And Pécuchet accosted the farmer, who yielded to their request.

They traced a line with whiting in the middle of the press, tied down the claws of a turkey-cock, then stretched him flat on his belly, with his beak placed on the line. The fowl shut his eyes, and soon presented the appearance of being dead. The same process was gone through with the others. Bouvard passed them quickly across to Pécuchet, who ranged them on the side on which they had become torpid.

The people about the farm-house exhibited uneasiness. The mistress screamed, and a little girl began to cry.

Bouvard loosened all the turkeys. They gradually revived; but one could not tell what might be the consequences.

At a rather tart remark of Pécuchet, the farmer grasped his pitchfork tightly.

"Clear out, in God's name, or I'll smash your head!"

They scampered off.

No matter! the problem was solved: ecstasy is dependent on material causes.

What, then, is matter? What is spirit? Whence comes the influence of the one on the other, and the reciprocal exchange of influence?

In order to inform themselves on the subject, they made researches in the works of Voltaire, Bossuet, Fénelon; and they renewed their subscription to a circulating library.

The ancient teachers were inaccessible owing to the length of their works, or the difficulty of the language; but Jouffroy and Damiron initiated them into modern philosophy, and they had authors who dealt with that of the last century.

Bouvard derived his arguments from Lamettrie, Locke, and Helvetius; Pécuchet from M. Cousin, Thomas Reid, and Gérando. The former adhered to experience; for the latter, the ideal was everything. The one belonged to the school of Aristotle, the other to that of Plato; and they proceeded to discuss the subject.

"The soul is immaterial," said Pécuchet.

"By no means," said his friend. "Lunacy, chloroform, a bleeding will overthrow it; and, inasmuch as it is not always thinking, it is not a substance which does nothing but think."

"Nevertheless," rejoined Pécuchet, "I have in myself something superior to my body, which sometimes confutes it."

"A being in a being—*homo duplex!* Look here, now! Different tendencies disclose opposite motives. That's all!"

"But this something, this soul, remains identical amid all changes from without. Therefore, it is simple, indivisible, and thus spiritual."

"If the soul were simple," replied Bouvard, "the newly-born would recollect, would imagine, like the adult. Thought, on the contrary, follows the development of the brain. As to its being indivisible, neither the perfume of a rose nor the appetite of a wolf, any more than a volition or an affirmation, is cut in two."

"That makes no difference," said Pécuchet. "The soul is exempt from the qualities of matter."

"Do you admit weight?" returned Bouvard. "Now, if matter can fall, it can in the same way think. Having had a beginning, the soul must come to an end, and as it is dependent on certain organs, it must disappear with them."

"For my part, I maintain that it is immortal. God could not intend—"

"But if God does not exist?"

"What?" And Pécuchet gave utterance to the three Cartesian proofs: " '*Primo:* God is comprehended in the idea that we have of Him; *secundo:* Existence is possible to Him; *tertio:* How can I, a finite being, have an idea of the Infinite? And, since we have this idea, it comes to us from God; therefore, God exists.' "

He passed on to the testimony of conscience, the traditions of different races, and the need of a Creator.

"When I see a clock—"

"Yes! yes! That's a well-known argument. But where is the clockmaker's father?"

"However, a cause is necessary."

Bouvard was doubtful about causes. "From the fact that one phenomenon succeeds another phenomenon, the conclusion is drawn that it is caused by the first. Prove it."

"But the spectacle of the universe indicates an intention and a plan."

"Why? Evil is as perfectly organised as good. The worm that works its way into a sheep's head and causes it to die, is as valuable from an anatomical point of view as the sheep itself. Abnormalities surpass the normal functions. The human body could be better constructed. Three fourths of the globe are sterile. That celestial lamp-post, the moon, does not always show itself! Do you think the ocean was destined for ships, and the wood of trees for fuel for our houses?"

Pécuchet answered: "Yet the stomach is made to digest, the leg to walk, the eye to see, although there are dyspepsias, fractures, and cataracts. No arrangements without an end. The effects came on at the exact time or at a later period. Everything depends on laws; therefore, there are final causes."

Bouvard imagined that perhaps Spinoza would furnish him with some arguments, and he wrote to Dumouchel to get him Saisset's translation.

Dumouchel sent him a copy belonging to his friend Professor Varelot, exiled on the 2nd of December.

Ethics terrified them with its axioms, its corollaries. They read only the pages marked with pencil, and understood this:

" 'The substance is that which is of itself, by itself, without cause, without origin. This substance is God. He alone is extension, and extension is without bounds.' "

"What can it be bound with?"

" 'But, though it be infinite, it is not the absolute infinite, for it contains only one kind of perfection, and the Absolute contains all.' "

They frequently stopped to think it out the better. Pécuchet took pinches of snuff, and Bouvard's face glowed with concentrated attention.

"Does this amuse you?"

"Yes, undoubtedly. Go on forever."

" 'God displays Himself in an infinite number of attributes which express, each in its own way, the infinite character of His being. We know only two of them—extension and thought.

" 'From thought and extension flow innumerable modes, which contain others. He who would at the same time embrace all extension and all thought would see there no contingency, nothing accidental, but a geometrical succession of terms, bound amongst themselves by necessary laws.' "

"Ah! that would be beautiful!" exclaimed Bouvard.

" 'If God had a will, an end, if He acted for a cause, that would mean that He would have some want, that He would lack some one perfection. He would not be God.

" 'Thus our world is but one point in the whole of things, and the universe, impenetrable by our knowledge, is a portion of an infinite number of universes emitting close to ours infinite modifications. Extension envelops our universe, but is enveloped by God, who contains in His thought all possible universes, and His thought itself is enveloped in His substance.' "

It appeared to them that this substance was filled at night with an icy coldness, carried away in an endless course towards a bottomless abyss, leaving nothing around them but the Unseizable, the Immovable, the Eternal.

This was too much for them, and they renounced it. And wishing for something less harsh, they bought the course of philosophy, by M. Guesnier, for the use of classes.

The author asks himself what would be the proper method, the ontological or the psychological.

The first suited the infancy of societies, when man directed his attention towards the external world. But at present, when he turns it in upon himself, "we believe the second to be more scientific."

The object of psychology is to study the acts which take place in our own breasts. We discover them by observation.

"Let us observe." And for a fortnight, after breakfast, they regularly searched their consciousness at random, hoping to make great discoveries there—and made none, which considerably astonished them.

" 'One phenomenon occupies the ego, viz., the idea. What is its nature? It has been supposed that the objects are put into the brain, and that the brain transmits these images to our souls, which gives us the knowledge of them.' "

But if the idea is spiritual, how are we to represent matter? Thence comes scepticism as to external perceptions. If it is material, spiritual objects could not be represented. Thence scepticism as to the reality of internal notions.

"For another reason let us here be careful. This hypothesis will lead us to atheism."

For an image, being a finite thing, cannot possibly represent the Infinite.

"Yet" argued Bouvard, "when I think of a forest, of a person, of a dog, I see this forest, this person, this dog. Therefore the ideas do represent them."

And they proceeded to deal with the origin of ideas.

According to Locke, there are two originating causes—sensation and reflection; and Condillac reduces everything to sensation.

But then reflection will lack a basis. It has need of a subject, of a sentient being; and it is powerless to furnish us with the great fundamental truths: God, merit and demerit, the Just, the Beautiful—ideas which are all *innate*, that is to say, anterior to facts, and to experience, and universal.

"If they were universal we should have them from our birth."

"By this word is meant dispositions to have them; and Descartes—"

"Your Descartes is muddled, for he maintains that the foetus possesses them, and he confesses in another place that this is in an implied fashion."

Pécuchet was astonished. "Where is this found?"

"In Gérando." And Bouvard tapped him lightly on the stomach.

"Make an end of it, then," said Pécuchet.

Then, coming to Condillac:

" 'Our thoughts are not metamorphoses of sensation. It causes them, puts them in play. In order to put them in play a motive power is necessary, for matter of itself cannot produce movement.' And I found that in your Voltaire," Pécuchet added, making a low bow to him.

Thus they repeated again and again the same arguments, each treating the other's opinion with contempt, without persuading his companion that his own was right.

But philosophy elevated them in their own estimation. They recalled with disdain their agricultural and political preoccupations.

At present they were disgusted with the museum. They would have asked nothing better than to sell the articles of *virtù* contained in it. So they passed on to the second chapter: "Faculties of the Soul."

" 'They are three in number, no more: that of feeling, that of knowing, and that of willing.

" 'In the faculty of feeling we should distinguish physical sensibility from moral sensibility. Physical sensations are naturally classified into five species, being transmitted through the medium of the senses. The facts of moral sensibility, on the contrary, owe nothing to the body. What is there in common between the pleasure of Archimedes in discovering the laws of weight and the filthy gratification of Apicius in devouring a wild-boar's head?

" 'This moral sensibility has five *genera,* and its second genus, moral desires, is divided into five species, and the phenomena of the fourth genus, affection, are subdivided into two other species, amongst which is the love of oneself—a legitimate propensity, no doubt, but one which, when it becomes exaggerated, takes the name of egoism.

" 'In the faculty of knowing we find rational perception, in which there are two principal movements and four degrees.

" 'Abstraction may present perils to whimsical minds.

" 'Memory brings us into contact with the past, as foresight does with the future.

" 'Imagination is rather a special faculty, *sui generis.*' "

So many intricacies in order to demonstrate platitudes, the pedantic tone of the author, and the monotony of his forms of expression—"We are prepared to acknowledge it," "Far from us be the thought," "Let us interrogate our consciousness"—the sempiternal eulogy on Dugald Stewart; in short, all this verbiage, disgusted them so much that, jumping over the faculty of willing, they went into logic.

It taught them the nature of analysis, synthesis, induction, deduction, and the principal causes of our errors.

Nearly all come from the misuse of words.

"The sun is going to bed." "The weather is becoming brown," "The winter is drawing near"—vicious modes of speech which would make us believe in personal entities, when it is only a question of very simple occurrences. "I remember such an object," "such an axiom," "such a truth"—illusion! These are ideas and not at all things which remain in me; and the rigour of language requires, "I remember such an act of my mind by which I perceived that object," "whereby I have deduced that axiom," "whereby I have admitted this truth."

As the term that describes an incident does not embrace it in all its aspects, they try to employ only abstract words, so that in place of saying, "Let us make a tour," "It is time to dine," "I have the colic," they give utterance to the following phrases: "A promenade would be salutary," "This is the hour for absorbing aliments," "I experience a necessity for disburdenment."

Once masters of logic, they passed in review the different criterions; first, that of common sense.

If the individual can know nothing, why should all individuals know more? An error, were it a hundred thousand years old, does not by the mere fact of its being old constitute truth. The multitude invariably pursues the path of routine. It is, on the contrary, the few who are guided by progress.

Is it better to trust to the evidence of the senses? They sometimes deceive, and never give information save as to externals. The innermost core escapes them.

Reason offers more safeguards, being immovable and impersonal; but in order that it may be manifested it is necessary that it should incarnate itself. Then, reason becomes my reason; a rule is of little value if it is false. Nothing can show such a rule to be right.

We are recommended to control it with the senses; but they may make the darkness thicker. From a confused sensation a defective law will be inferred, which, later, will obstruct the clear view of things.

Morality remains.

This would make God descend to the level of the useful, as if our wants were the measure of the Absolute.

As for the evidence—denied by the one, affirmed by the other—it is its own criterion. M. Cousin has demonstrated it.

"I see no longer anything but revelation," said Bouvard. "But, to believe it, it is necessary to admit two preliminary cognitions—that of the body which has felt, and that of the intelligence which has perceived; to admit sensation and reason. Human testimonies! and consequently open to suspicion."

Pécuchet reflected—folded his arms. "But we are about to fall into the frightful abyss of scepticism."

In Bouvard's opinion it frightened only weak brains.

"Thank you for the compliment," returned Pécuchet. "However, there are indisputable facts. We can arrive at truth within a certain limit."

"Which? Do two and two always make four? Is that which is contained in some degree less than that which contains it? What is the meaning of nearly true, a fraction of God, the part of an indivisible thing?"

"Oh, you are a mere sophist!" And Pécuchet, annoyed, remained for three days in a sulk.

They employed themselves in running through the contents of several volumes. Bouvard smiled from time to time, and renewing the conversation, said:

"The fact is, it is hard to avoid doubt; thus, for the existence of God, Descartes', Kant's, and Leibnitz's proofs are not the same, and mutually destroy one another. The creation of the world by atoms, or by a spirit, remains inconceivable. I feel myself, at the same time, matter and thought, while all the time I am ignorant of what one or the other really is. Impenetrability, solidity, weight, seem to me to be mysteries just as much as my soul, and, with much stronger reason, the union of the soul and the body. In order to explain it, Leibnitz invented his harmony, Malebranche premotion, Cudworth a mediator, and Bossuet sees in it a perpetual miracle."

"Exactly," said Pécuchet. And they both confessed that they were tired of philosophy. Such a number of systems confused them. Metaphysics is of no use: one can live without it. Besides, their pecuniary embarrassments were increasing. They owed one bill to Beljambe for three hogsheads of wine, another to Langlois for two stone of sugar, a sum of one hundred francs to the tailor, and sixty to the shoemaker.

Their expenditures were continuous, of course, and meantime Maître Gouy did not pay up.

They went to Marescot to ask him to raise money for them, either by the sale of the Ecalles meadow, or by a mortgage on their farm, or by giving up their house on the condition of getting a life annuity and keeping the usufruct.

In Marescot's opinion this would be an impracticable course; but a better means might be devised, and they should be informed about it.

After this they thought of their poor garden. Bouvard undertook the pruning of the row of elms and Pécuchet the trimming of the espalier. Marcel would have to dig the borders.

At the end of a quarter of an hour they stopped. The one closed his pruning-knife, the other laid down his scissors, and they began to walk to and fro quietly, Bouvard in the shade of the linden trees, with his waistcoat off, his chest held out and his arms bare; Pécuchet close to the wall, with his head hanging down, his arms behind his back, the peak of his cap turned over his neck for precaution; and thus they proceeded in parallel lines without even seeing Marcel, who was resting at the side of the hut eating a scrap of bread.

In this reflective mood thoughts arose in their minds. They grasped at them, fearing to lose them; and metaphysics came back again—came back with respect to the rain and the sun, the gravel in their shoes, the flowers on the grass—with respect to everything. When they looked at the candle burning, they asked themselves whether the light is in the object or in our eyes. Since stars may have disappeared by the time their radiance has reached us, we admire, perhaps, things that have no existence.

Having found a Raspail cigarette in the depths of a waistcoat, they crumbled it over some water, and the camphor moved about. Here, then, is movement in matter. One degree more of movement might bring on life!

But if matter in movement were sufficient to create beings, they would not be so varied. For in the beginning lands, water, men, and plants had no existence. What, then, is this primordial matter, which we have never seen, which is no portion of created things, and which yet has produced them all?

Sometimes they wanted a book. Dumouchel, tired of assisting them, no longer answered their letters. They enthusiastically took up the new question, especially Pécuchet. His need of truth became a burning thirst.

Moved by Bouvard's preachings, he gave up spiritualism, but soon resumed it again only to abandon it once more, and, clasping his head with his hands, he would exclaim:

"Oh, doubt! doubt! I would much prefer nothingness."

Bouvard perceived the insufficiency of materialism, and tried to stop at that, declaring, however, that he had lost his head over it.

They began with arguments on a solid basis, but the basis gave way; and suddenly they had no longer a single idea—just as a bird takes wing the moment we wish to catch it.

During the winter evenings they chatted in the museum at the corner of the fire, staring at the coals. The wind, whistling in the corridor, shook the window-panes; the black masses of trees swayed to and fro, and the dreariness of the night intensified the seriousness of their thoughts.

Bouvard from time to time walked towards the further end of the apartment and then came back. The torches and the pans on the walls threw slanting shadows on the ground; and the St. Peter, seen in profile, showed on the ceiling the silhouette of his nose, resembling a monstrous hunting-horn.

They found it hard to move about amongst the various articles, and Bouvard, by not taking precautions, often knocked against the statue. With its big eyes, its drooping lip, and its air of a drunkard, it also annoyed Pécuchet. For a long time he had wished to get rid of it, but through carelessness put it off from day to day.

One evening, in the middle of a dispute on the monad, Bouvard hit his big toe against St. Peter's thumb, and turning on him in a rage, exclaimed:

"He plagues me, this jackanapes! Let us toss him out!"

It was difficult to do this over the staircase. They flung open the window, and gently tried to tip St. Peter over the edge. Pécuchet, on his knees, attempted to raise his heels, while Bouvard pressed against his shoulders. The old codger in stone did not budge. After this they had recourse to the halberd as a lever, and finally succeeded in stretching him out quite straight. Then, after a see-saw motion, he dashed into the open space, his tiara going before him. A heavy crash reached their ears, and next day they found him broken into a dozen pieces in the old pit for composts.

An hour afterwards the notary came in, bringing good news to them. A lady in the neighbourhood was willing to advance a thousand crown-pieces on the security of a mortgage of their farm, and, as they were expressing their satisfaction at the proposal:

"Pardon me. She adds, as a condition, that you should sell her the Ecalles meadow for fifteen hundred francs. The loan will be advanced this very day. The money is in my office."

They were both disposed to give way.

Bouvard ended by saying: "Good God! be it so, then."

"Agreed," said Marescot. And then he mentioned the lender's name: it was Madame Bordin.

"I suspected 'twas she!" exclaimed Pécuchet.

Bouvard, who felt humiliated, had not a word to say.

She or someone else—what did it matter? The principal thing was to get out of their difficulties.

When they received the money (they were to get the sum for the Ecalles later) they immediately paid all their bills; and they were returning to their abode when, at the corner of the market-place, they were stopped by Farmer Gouy.

He had been on his way to their house to apprise them of a misfortune. The wind, the night before, had blown down twenty apple trees into the farmyard, overturned the boilery, and carried away the roof of the barn.

They spent the remainder of the afternoon in estimating the amount of the damage, and they continued the inquiry on the following day with the assistance of the carpenter, the mason, and the slater. The repairs would cost at least about eighteen hundred francs.

Then, in the evening, Gouy presented himself. Marianne herself had, a short time before, told him all about the sale of the Ecalles meadow—a piece of land with a splendid yield, suitable in every way, and scarcely requiring any cultivation at all, the best bit in the whole farm!—and he asked for a reduction.

The two gentlemen refused it. The matter was submitted to the justice of the peace, who decided in favour of the farmer. The loss of the Ecalles, which was valued at two thousand francs per acre, caused him an annual depreciation of seventy, and he was sure to win in the courts.

Their fortune was diminished. What were they to do? And soon the question would be, How were they to live?

They both sat down to table full of discouragement. Marcel knew nothing about it in the kitchen. His dinner this time was better than theirs.

The soup was like dish-water, the rabbit had a bad smell, the kidney-beans were underdone, the plates were dirty, and at dessert Bouvard burst into a passion and threatened to break everything on Marcel's head.

"Let us be philosophers," said Pécuchet. "A little less money, the intrigues of a woman, the clumsiness of a servant—what is it but this? You are too much immersed in matter."

"But when it annoys me?" said Bouvard.

"For my part, I don't admit it," rejoined Pécuchet.

He had recently been reading an analysis of Berkeley, and added:

"I deny extension, time, space, even substance! for the true substance is the mind-perceiving qualities."

"Quite so," said Bouvard; "but get rid of the world, and you'll have no proof left of God's existence."

Pécuchet uttered a cry, and a long one too, although he had a cold in his head, caused by the iodine of potassium, and a continual feverishness increased his excitement. Bouvard, being uneasy about him, sent for the doctor.

Vaucorbeil ordered orange-syrup with the iodine, and for a later stage cinnabar baths.

"What's, the use?" replied Pécuchet. "One day or another the form will die out. The essence does not perish."

"No doubt," said the physician, "matter is indestructible. However—"

"Ah, no!—ah, no! The indestructible thing is being. This body which is there before me—yours, doctor—prevents me from knowing your real self, and is, so to speak, only a garment, or rather a mask."

Vaucorbeil believed he was mad.

"Good evening. Take care of your mask."

Pécuchet did not stop. He procured an introduction to the Hegelian philosophy, and wished to explain it to Bouvard.

"All that is rational is real. There is not even any reality save the idea. The laws of the mind are laws of the universe; the reason of man is identical with that of God."

Bouvard pretended to understand.

"Therefore the absolute is, at the same time, the subject and the object, the unity whereby all differences come to be settled. Thus, things that are contradictory are reconciled. The shadow permits the light; heat and cold intermingled produce temperature. Organism maintains itself only by the destruction of organism; everywhere there is a principle that disunites, a principle that connects."

They were on the hillock, and the curé was walking past the gateway with his breviary in his hand.

Pécuchet asked him to come in, as he desired to finish the explanation of Hegel, and to get some notion of what the curé would say about it.

The man of the cassock sat down beside them, and Pécuchet broached the question of Christianity.

"No religion has established this truth so well: 'Nature is but a moment of the idea.' "

"A moment of the idea!" murmured the priest in astonishment.

"Why, yes. God in taking a visible envelope showed his consubstantial union with it."

"With nature—oh! oh!"

"By His decease He bore testimony to the essence of death; therefore, death was in Him, made and makes part of God."

The ecclesiastic frowned.

"No blasphemies! it was for the salvation of the human race that He endured sufferings."

"Error! We look at death in the case of the individual, where, no doubt, it is a calamity; but with relation to things it is different. Do not separate mind from matter."

"However, sir, before the Creation—"

"There was no Creation. It has always existed. Otherwise this would be a new being adding itself to the Divine idea, which is absurd."

The priest arose; business matters called him elsewhere.

"I flatter myself I've floored him!" said Pécuchet. "One word more. Since the existence of the world is but a continual passage from life to death, and from death to life, so far from everything existing, nothing is. But everything is becoming— do you understand?"

"Yes; I do understand—or rather I don't."

Idealism in the end exasperated Bouvard.

"I don't want anymore of it. The famous *cogito* stupefies me. Ideas of things are taken for the things themselves. What we understand very slightly is explained by means of words which we don't understand at all—substance, extension, force, matter, and soul. So much abstraction, imagination. As for God, it is impossible to know in what way He is, if He is at all. Formerly, He used to cause the wind, the thunderstorms, revolutions. At present, He is diminishing. Besides, I don't see the utility of Him."

"And morality—in this state of affairs."

"Ah! so much the worse."

"It lacks a foundation in fact," said Pécuchet.

And he remained silent, driven into a corner by premises which he had himself laid down. It was a surprise—a crushing bit of logic.

Bouvard no longer even believed in matter.

The certainty that nothing exists (deplorable though it may be) is none the less a certainty. Few persons are capable of possessing it. This transcendency on their part inspired them with pride, and they would have liked to make a display of it. An opportunity presented itself.

One morning, while they were going to buy tobacco, they saw a crowd in front of Langlois' door. The public conveyance from Falaise was surrounded, and there was much excitement about a convict named Touache, who was wandering about the country. The conductor had met him at Croix-Verte between two gendarmes, and the people of Chavignolles breathed a sigh of relief.

Girbal and the captain remained on the green; then the justice of the peace made his appearance, curious to obtain information, and after him came M. Marescot in a velvet cap and sheepskin slippers.

Langlois invited them to honour his shop with their presence; they would be more at their ease; and in spite of the customers and the loud ringing of the bell, the gentlemen continued their discussion as to Touache's offences.

"Goodness gracious!" said Bouvard, "he had bad instincts. That was the whole of it!"

"They are conquered by virtue," replied the notary.

"But if a person has not virtue?"

And Bouvard positively denied free-will.

"Yet," said the captain, "I can do what I like. I am free, for instance, to move my leg."

"No, sir, for you have a motive for moving it."

The captain looked out for something to say in reply, and found nothing. But Girbal discharged this shaft:

"A Republican speaking against liberty. That is funny."

"A droll story," chimed in Langlois.

Bouvard turned on him with this question:

"Why don't you give all you possess to the poor?"

The grocer cast an uneasy glance over his entire shop.

"Look here, now, I'm not such an idiot! I keep it for myself."

"If you were St. Vincent de Paul, you would act differently, since you would have his character. You obey your own. Therefore, you are not free."

"That's a quibble!" replied the company in chorus.

Bouvard did not flinch, and said, pointing towards the scales on the counter:

"It will remain motionless so long as each scale is empty. So with the will; and the oscillation of the scales between two weights which seem equal represents the strain on our mind when it is hesitating between different motives, till the moment when the more powerful motive gets the better of it and leads it to a determination."

"All that," said Girbal, "makes no difference for Touache, and does not prevent him from being a downright vicious rogue."

Pécuchet addressed the company:

"Vices are properties of Nature, like floods, tempests."

The notary stopped, and raising himself on tiptoe at every word:

"I consider your system one of complete immorality. It gives scope to every kind of excess, excuses crimes, and declares the guilty innocent."

"Exactly," replied Bouvard; "the wretch who follows his appetites is right from his own point of view just as much as the honest man who listens to reason."

"Do not defend monsters!"

"Wherefore monsters? When a person is born blind, an idiot, a homicide, this appears to us to be opposed to order, as if order were known to us, as if Nature were striving towards an end."

"You then raise a question about Providence?"

"I do raise a question about it."

"Look rather to history," exclaimed Pécuchet. "Recall to mind the assassina-

tions of kings, the massacres amongst peoples, the dissensions in families, the affliction of individuals."

"And at the same time," added Bouvard, for they mutually excited eachother,
"this Providence takes care of little birds, and makes the claws of crayfishes grow
again. Oh! if by Providence you mean a law which rules everything, I am of the
same opinion, and even more so."

"However, sir," said the notary, "there are principles."

"What stuff is that you're talking? A science, according to Condillac, is so
much the better the less need it has of them. They do nothing but summarise acquired knowledge, and they bring us back to those conceptions which are exactly
the disputable ones."

"Have you, like us," went on Pécuchet, "scrutinised and explored the arcana of
metaphysics?"

"It is true, gentlemen—it is true!"

Then the company broke up.

But Coulon, drawing them aside, told them in a paternal tone that he was no
devotee certainly, and that he even hated the Jesuits. However, he did not go as far
as they did. Oh, no! certainly not. And at the corner of the green they passed in
front of the captain, who, as he lighted his pipe, growled:

"All the same, I do what I like, by God!"

Bouvard and Pécuchet gave utterance on other occasions to their scandalous
paradoxes. They threw doubt on the honesty of men, the chastity of women, the
intelligence of government, the good sense of the people—in short, they sapped
the foundations of everything.

Foureau was provoked by their behaviour, and threatened them with imprisonment if they went on with such discourses.

The evidence of their own superiority caused them pain. As they maintained
immoral propositions, they must needs be immoral: calumnies were invented about
them. Then a pitiable faculty developed itself in their minds, that of observing stupidity and no longer tolerating it. Trifling things made them feel sad: the advertisements in the newspapers, the profile of a shopkeeper, an idiotic remark
overheard by chance. Thinking over what was said in their own village, and on the
fact that there were even as far as the Antipodes other Coulons, other Marescots,
other Foureaus, they felt, as it were, the heaviness of all the earth weighing down
upon them.

They no longer went out of doors, and received no visitors.

One afternoon a dialogue arose, outside the front entrance, between Marcel
and a gentleman who wore dark spectacles and a hat with a large brim. It was the
academician Larsoneur. He observed a curtain half-opening and doors being shut.

This step on his part was an attempt at reconciliation; and he went away in a rage, directing the man-servant to tell his masters that he regarded them as a pair of common fellows.

Bouvard and Pécuchet did not care about this. The world was diminishing in importance, and they saw it as if through a cloud that had descended from their brains over their eyes.

Is it not, moreover, an illusion, a bad dream? Perhaps, on the whole, prosperity and misfortune are equally balanced. But the welfare of the species does not console the individual.

"And what do others matter to me?" said Pécuchet.

His despair afflicted Bouvard. It was he who had brought his friend to this pass, and the ruinous condition of their house kept their grief fresh by daily irritations.

In order to revive their spirits they tried discussions, and prescribed tasks for themselves, but speedily fell back into greater sluggishness, into more profound discouragement.

At the end of each meal they would remain with their elbows on the table groaning with a lugubrious air.

Marcel would give them a scared look, and then go back to his kitchen, where he stuffed himself in solitude.

About the middle of midsummer they received a circular announcing the marriage of Dumouchel with Madame Olympe-Zulma Poulet, a widow.

"God bless him!"

And they recalled the time when they were happy.

Why were they no longer following the harvesters? Where were the days when they went through the different farm-houses looking everywhere for antiquities? Nothing now gave them such hours of delight as those which were occupied with the distillery and with literature. A gulf lay between them and that time. It was irrevocable.

They thought of taking a walk as of yore through the fields, wandered too far, and got lost. The sky was dotted with little fleecy clouds, the wind was shaking the tiny bells of the oats; a stream was purling along through a meadow—and then, all at once, an infectious odour made them halt, and they saw on the pebbles between the thorn trees the putrid carcass of a dog.

The four limbs were dried up. The grinning jaws disclosed teeth of ivory under the bluish lips; in place of the stomach there was a mass of earth-coloured flesh which seemed to be palpitating with the vermin that swarmed all over it. It writhed, with the sun's rays falling on it, under the gnawing of so many mouths, in this intolerable stench—a stench which was fierce and, as it were, devouring.

Yet wrinkles gathered on Bouvard's forehead, and his eyes filled with tears.

Pécuchet said in a stoical fashion, "One day we shall be like that."

The idea of death had taken hold of them. They talked about it on their way back.

After all, it has no existence. We pass away into the dew, into the breeze, into the stars. We become part of the sap of trees, the brilliance of precious stones, the plumage of birds. We give back to Nature what she lent to each of us, and the nothingness before us is not a bit more frightful than the nothingness behind us.

They tried to picture it to themselves under the form of an intense night, a bottomless pit, a continual swoon. Anything would be better than such an existence—monotonous, absurd, and hopeless.

They enumerated their unsatisfied wants. Bouvard had always wished for horses, equipages, a big supply of Burgundy, and lovely women ready to accommodate him in a splendid habitation. Pécuchet's ambition was philosophical knowledge. Now, the vastest of problems, that which contains all others, can be solved in one minute. When would it come, then? "As well to make an end of it at once."

"Just as you like," said Bouvard.

And they investigated the question of suicide.

Where is the evil of casting aside a burden which is crushing you? and of doing an act harmful to nobody? If it offended God, should we have this power? It is not cowardice, though people say so, and to scoff at human pride is a fine thing, even at the price of injury to oneself—the thing that men regard most highly.

They deliberated as to the different kinds of death. Poison makes you suffer. In order to cut your throat you require too much courage. In the case of asphyxia, people often fail to effect their object.

Finally, Pécuchet carried up to the garret two ropes belonging to their gymnastic apparatus. Then, having fastened them to the same cross-beam of the roof, he let a slip-knot hang down from the end of each, and drew two chairs underneath to reach the ropes.

This method was the one they selected.

They asked themselves what impression it would cause in the district, what would become of their library, their papers, their collections. The thought of death made them feel tenderly about themselves. However, they did not abandon their project, and by dint of talking about it they grew accustomed to the idea.

On the evening of the 24th of December, between ten and eleven o'clock, they sat thinking in the museum, both differently attired. Bouvard wore a blouse over his knitted waistcoat, and Pécuchet, through economy, had not left off his monk's habit for the past three months.

As they were very hungry (for Marcel, having gone out at daybreak, had not reappeared), Bouvard thought it would be a healthful thing for him to drink a quart bottle of brandy, and for Pécuchet to take some tea.

While he was lifting up the kettle he spilled some water on the floor.

"Awkward!" exclaimed Bouvard.

Then, thinking the infusion too small, he wanted to strengthen it with two additional spoonfuls.

"This will be execrable," said Pécuchet.

"Not at all."

And while each of them was trying to draw the work-box closer to himself, the tray upset and fell down. One of the cups was smashed—the last of their fine porcelain tea-service.

Bouvard turned pale.

"Go on! Confusion! Don't put yourself about!"

"Truly, a great misfortune! I attribute it to my father."

"Your natural father," corrected Pécuchet, with a sneer.

"Ha! you insult me!"

"No; but I am tiring you out! I see it plainly! Confess it!"

And Pécuchet was seized with anger, or rather with madness. So was Bouvard. The pair began shrieking, the one excited by hunger, the other by alcohol. Pécuchet's throat at length emitted no sound save a rattling.

"It is infernal, a life like this. I much prefer death. Adieu!"

He snatched up the candlestick and rushed out, slamming the door behind him.

Bouvard, plunged in darkness, found some difficulty in opening it. He ran after Pécuchet, and followed him up to the garret.

The candle was on the floor, and Pécuchet was standing on one of the chairs, with a rope in his hand. The spirit of imitation got the better of Bouvard.

"Wait for me!"

And he had just got up on the other chair when, suddenly stopping:

"Why, we have not made our wills!"

"Hold on! That's quite true!"

Their breasts swelled with sobs. They leaned against the skylight to take breath.

The air was chilly and a multitude of stars glittered in a sky of inky blackness.

The whiteness of the snow that covered the earth was lost in the haze of the horizon.

They perceived, close to the ground, little lights, which, as they drew near, looked larger, all reaching up to the side of the church.

Curiosity drove them to the spot. It was the midnight mass. These lights came from shepherds' lanterns. Some of them were shaking their cloaks under the porch.

The serpent snorted; the incense smoked. Glasses suspended along the nave represented three crowns of many-coloured flames; and, at the end of the perspective at the two sides of the tabernacle, immense wax tapers were pointed with red flames. Above the heads of the crowd and the broad-brimmed hats of the women, beyond the chanters, the priest could be distinguished in his chasuble of gold. To his sharp voice responded the strong voices of the men who filled up the gallery, and the wooden vault quivered above its stone arches. The walls were decorated with the stations of the Cross. In the midst of the choir, before the altar, a lamb was lying down, with its feet under its belly and its ears erect.

The warm temperature imparted to them both a strange feeling of comfort, and their thoughts, which had been so tempestuous only a short time before, became peaceful, like waves when they are calmed.

They listened to the Gospel and the *Credo*, and watched the movements of the priest. Meanwhile, the old, the young, the beggar women in rags, the mothers in high caps, the strong young fellows with tufts of fair down on their faces, were all praying, absorbed in the same deep joy, and saw the body of the Infant Christ shining, like a sun, upon the straw of a stable. This faith on the part of others touched Bouvard in spite of his reason, and Pécuchet in spite of the hardness of his heart.

There was a silence; every back was bent, and, at the tinkling of a bell, the little lamb bleated.

The host was displayed by the priest, as high as possible between his two hands. Then burst forth a strain of gladness inviting the whole world to the feet of the King of Angels. Bouvard and Pécuchet involuntarily joined in it, and they felt, as it were, a new dawn rising in their souls.

Chapter IX

SONS OF THE CHURCH

MARCEL REAPPEARED NEXT DAY AT THREE O'CLOCK, HIS FACE GREEN, HIS eyes bloodshot, a lump on his forehead, his breeches torn, his breath tainted with a strong smell of brandy, and his person covered with dirt.

He had been, according to an annual custom of his, six leagues away at Iqueville to enjoy a midnight repast with a friend; and, stuttering more than ever, crying, wishing to beat himself, he begged of them for pardon, as if he had committed a crime. His masters granted it to him. A singular feeling of serenity rendered them indulgent.

The snow had suddenly melted, and they walked about the garden, inhaling the genial air, delighted merely with living.

Was it only chance that had kept them from death? Bouvard felt deeply affected. Pécuchet recalled his first commission, and, full of gratitude to the Force, the Cause, on which they depended, the idea took possession of them to read pious works.

The Gospel dilated their souls, dazzled them like a sun. They perceived Jesus standing on a mountain, with one arm raised, while below the multitude listened to Him; or else on the margin of a lake in the midst of the apostles, while they drew in their nets; next on the ass, in the clamour of the "alleluias," His hair fanned by the quivering palms; finally, lifted high upon the Cross, bending down His head, from which eternally falls a dew of blood upon the world. What won them, what ravished them, was His tenderness for the humble, His defence of the poor, His exaltation of the oppressed; and they found in that Book, wherein Heaven unfolds itself, nothing theological in the midst of so many precepts, no dogma, no requirement, save purity of heart.

As for the miracles, their reason was not astonished by them. They had been acquainted with them from their childhood. The loftiness of St. John enchanted Pécuchet, and better disposed him to appreciate the *Imitation*.

Here were no more parables, flowers, birds, but lamentations—a compression of the soul into itself.

Bouvard grew sad as he turned over these pages, which seemed to have been written in foggy weather, in the depths of a cloister, between a belfry and a tomb. Our mortal life appeared there so wretched that one must needs forget it and return to God. And the two poor men, after all their disappointments, experienced that need of simple natures—to love something, to find rest for their souls.

They studied *Ecclesiastes, Isaiah, Jeremiah.*

But the Bible dismayed them with its lion-voiced prophets, the crashing of thunder in the skies, all the sobbings of Gehenna, and its God scattering empires as the wind scatters clouds.

They read it on Sunday at the hour of vespers, while the bell was ringing.

One day they went to mass, and then came back. It was a kind of recreation at the end of the week. The Count and Countess de Faverges bowed to them from the distance, a circumstance which was remarked. The justice of the peace said to them with blinking eyes:

"Excellent! You have my approval."

All the village dames now sent them consecrated bread. The Abbé Jeufroy paid them a visit; they returned it; friendly intercourse followed; and the priest avoided talking about religion.

They were astonished at this reserve, so much so that Pécuchet, with an assumption of indifference, asked him what was the way to set about obtaining faith.

"Practise first of all."

They began to practise, the one with hope, the other with defiance, Bouvard being convinced that he would never be a devotee. For a month he regularly followed all the services; but, unlike Pécuchet, he did not wish to subject himself to Lenten fare.

Was this a hygienic measure? We know what hygiene is worth. A matter of the proprieties? Down with the proprieties! A mark of submission towards the Church? He laughed at it just as much; in short, he declared the rule absurd, pharisaical, and contrary to the spirit of the Gospel.

On Good Friday in other years they used to eat whatever Germaine served up to them. But on this occasion Bouvard ordered a beefsteak. He sat down and cut up the meat, and Marcel, scandalised, kept staring at him, while Pécuchet gravely took the skin off his slice of codfish.

Bouvard remained with his fork in one hand, his knife in the other. At length, making up his mind, he raised a mouthful to his lips. All at once his hand began to tremble, his heavy countenance grew pale, his head fell back.

"Are you ill?"

"No. But—" And he made an avowal. In consequence of his education (it was stronger than himself), he could not eat meat on this day for fear of dying.

Pécuchet, without misusing his victory, took advantage of it to live in his own fashion. One evening he returned home with a look of sober joy imprinted on his face, and, letting the word escape, said that he had just been at confession.

Thereupon they argued about the importance of confession.

Bouvard acknowledged that of the early Christians, which was made publicly:

the modern is too easy. However, he did not deny that this examination concerning ourselves might be an element of progress, a leaven of morality.

Pécuchet, desirous of perfection, searched for his vices: for some time past the puffings of pride were gone. His taste for work freed him from idleness; as for gluttony, nobody was more moderate. Sometimes he was carried away by anger.

He made a vow that he would be so no more.

In the next place, it would be necessary to acquire the virtues: first of all, humility, that is to say, to believe yourself incapable of any merit, unworthy of the least recompense, to immolate your spirit, and to place yourself so low that people may trample you under their feet like the mud of the roads. He was far as yet from these dispositions.

Another virtue was wanting in him—chastity. For inwardly he regretted Mélie, and the pastel of the lady in the Louis XV dress disturbed him by her ample display of bosom. He shut it up in a cupboard, and redoubled his modesty, so much so that he feared to cast glances at his own person.

In order to mortify himself, Pécuchet gave up his little glass after meals, confined himself to four pinches of snuff in the day, and even in the coldest weather he did not any longer put on his cap.

One day, Bouvard, who was fastening up the vine, placed a ladder against the wall of the terrace near the house, and, without intending it, found himself landed in Pécuchet's room.

His friend, naked up to the middle, first gently smacked his shoulders with the cat-o'-nine-tails without quite undressing; then, getting animated, pulled off his shirt, lashed his back, and sank breathless on a chair.

Bouvard was troubled, as if at the unveiling of a mystery on which he should not have gazed.

For some time he had noticed a greater cleanliness about the floor, fewer holes in the napkins, and an improvement in the diet—changes which were due to the intervention of Reine, the curé's housekeeper. Mixing up the affairs of the Church with those of her kitchen, strong as a ploughman, and devoted though disrespectful, she gained admittance into households, gave advice, and became mistress in them. Pécuchet placed implicit confidence in her experience.

On one occasion she brought to him a corpulent man with narrow eyes like a Chinaman, and a nose like a vulture's beak. This was M. Gouttman, a dealer in pious articles. He unpacked some of them shut up in boxes under the cart-shed: a cross, medals, and beads of all sizes; candelabra for oratories, portable altars, tinsel bouquets, and sacred hearts of blue pasteboard, St. Josephs with red beards, and porcelain crucifixes. The price alone stood in his way.

Gouttman did not ask for money. He preferred barterings; and, having gone up to the museum, he offered a number of his wares for their collection of old iron and lead.

They appeared hideous to Bouvard. But Pécuchet's glance, the persistency of Reine, and the bluster of the dealer were effectual in making him yield.

Gouttman, seeing him so accommodating, wanted the halberd in addition; Bouvard, tired of having exhibited its working, surrendered it. The entire valuation was made. "These gentlemen still owed a hundred francs." It was settled by three bills payable at three months; and they congratulated themselves on a good bargain.

Their acquisitions were distributed through the various rooms. A crib filled with hay and a cork cathedral decorated the museum.

On Pécuchet's chimney-piece there was a St. John the Baptist in wax; along the corridor were ranged the portraits of episcopal dignitaries; and at the bottom of the staircase, under a chained lamp, stood a Blessed Virgin in an azure mantle and a crown of stars. Marcel cleaned up those splendours, unable to imagine anything more beautiful in Paradise.

What a pity that the St. Peter was broken, and how nicely it would have done in the vestibule!

Pécuchet stopped sometimes before the old pit for composts, where he discovered the tiara, one sandal, and the tip of an ear; allowed sighs to escape him, then went on gardening, for now he combined manual labour with religious exercises, and dug the soil attired in the monk's habit, comparing himself to Bruno. This disguise might be a sacrilege. He gave it up.

But he assumed the ecclesiastical style, no doubt owing to his intimacy with the curé. He had the same smile, the same tone of voice, and, like the priest too, he slipped both hands with a chilly air into his sleeves up to the wrists. A day came when he was pestered by the crowing of the cock and disgusted with the roses; he no longer went out, or only cast sullen glances over the fields.

Bouvard suffered himself to be led to the May devotions. The children singing hymns, the gorgeous display of lilacs, the festoons of verdure, had imparted to him, so to speak, a feeling of imperishable youth. God manifested Himself to his heart through the fashioning of nests, the transparency of fountains, the bounty of the sun; and his friend's devotion appeared to him extravagant, fastidious.

"Why do you groan during mealtime?"

"We ought to eat with groans," returned Pécuchet, "for it was in that way that man lost his innocence"—a phrase which he had read in the *Seminarist's Manual*, two duodecimo volumes he had borrowed from M. Jeufroy: and he drank some of the water of La Salette, gave himself up with closed doors to ejaculatory prayers, and aspired to join the confraternity of St. Francis.

In order to obtain the gift of perseverance, he resolved to make a pilgrimage in honour of the Blessed Virgin. He was perplexed as to the choice of a locality. Should it be Nôtre Dame de Fourviers, de Chartres, d'Embrun, de Marseille, or d'Auray? Nôtre Dame de la Délivrande was nearer, and it suited just as well.

"You will accompany me?"

"I should look like a greenhorn," said Bouvard.

After all, he might come back a believer; he did not object to being one; and so he yielded through complaisance.

Pilgrimages ought to be made on foot. But forty-three kilometers would be trying; and the public conveyances not being adapted for meditation, they hired an old cabriolet, which, after a twelve hours' journey, set them down before the inn.

They got an apartment with two beds and two chests of drawers, supporting two water-jugs in little oval basins; and "mine host" informed them that this was "the chamber of the Capuchins" under the Terror. There La Dame de la Délivrande had been concealed with so much precaution that the good fathers said mass there clandestinely.

This gave Pécuchet pleasure, and he read aloud a sketch of the history of the chapel, which had been taken downstairs into the kitchen.

It had been founded in the beginning of the second century by St. Régnobert, first bishop of Lisieux, or by St. Ragnebert, who lived in the seventh, or by Robert the Magnificent in the middle of the eleventh.

The Danes, the Normans, and, above all, the Protestants, had burnt and ravaged it at various epochs. About 1112, the original statue was discovered by a sheep, which indicated the place where it was by tapping with its foot in a field of grass; and on this spot Count Baudouin erected a sanctury.

" 'Her miracles are innumerable. A merchant of Bayeux, taken captive by the Saracens, invoked her: his fetters fell off, and he escaped. A miser found a nest of rats in his corn loft, appealed to her aid, and the rats went away. The touch of a medal, which had been rubbed over her effigy, caused an old materialist from Versailles to repent on his death-bed. She gave back speech to Sieur Adeline, who lost it for having blasphemed; and by her protection, M. and Madame de Becqueville had sufficient strength to live chastely in the married state.

" 'Amongst those whom she cured of irremediable diseases are mentioned Mademoiselle de Palfresne, Anne Lirieux, Marie Duchemin, François Dufai, and Madame de Jumillac née d'Osseville.

" 'Persons of high rank have visited her: Louis XI, Louis XIII, two daughters of Gaston of Orléans, Cardinal Wiseman, Samirrhi, patriarch of Antioch, Monseigneur Véroles, vicar apostolic of Manchuria; and the Archbishop of Quelen came to return thanks to her for the conversion of Prince Talleyrand.' "

"She might," said Pécuchet, "convert you also!"

Bouvard, already in bed, gave vent to a species of grunt, and presently was fast asleep.

Next morning at six o'clock they entered the chapel.

Another was in course of construction. Canvas and boards blocked up the nave; and the monument, in a rococo style, displeased Bouvard, above all, the altar of red marble with its Corinthian pilasters.

The miraculous statue, in a niche at the left of the choir, was enveloped in a spangled robe. The beadle came up with a wax taper for each of them. He fixed it in a kind of candlestick overlooking the balustrade, asked for three francs, made a bow, and disappeared.

Then they surveyed the votive offerings. Inscriptions on slabs bore testimony to the gratitude of the faithful. They admired two swords in the form of a cross presented by a pupil of the Polytechnic School, brides' bouquets, military medals, silver hearts, and in the corner, along the floor, a forest of crutches.

A priest passed out of the sacristy carrying the holy pyx.

When he had remained for a few minutes at the bottom of the altar, he ascended the three steps, said the *Oremus,* the *Introit,* and the *Kyrie,* which the boy who served mass recited all in one breath on bended knees.

The number present was small—a dozen or fifteen old women. The rattling of their beads could be heard accompanying the noise of a hammer driving in stones. Pécuchet bent over his prie-dieu and responded to the "Amens." During the elevation, he implored Our Lady to send him a constant and indestructible faith. Bouvard, in a chair beside him, took up his Euchology, and stopped at the litany of the Blessed Virgin.

"Most pure, most chaste, most venerable, most amiable, most powerful— Tower of ivory—House of gold—Gate of the morning."

These words of adoration, these hyperboles drew him towards the being who has been the object of so much reverence. He dreamed of her as she is represented in church paintings, above a mass of clouds, cherubims at her feet, the Infant Jesus on her breast—Mother of tendernesses, upon whom all the sorrows of the earth have a claim—ideal of woman carried up to heaven; for man exalts that love arising out of the depths of the soul, and his highest aspiration is to rest upon her heart.

The mass was finished. They passed along by the dealers' sheds which lined the walls in front of the church. They saw there images, holy-water basins, urns with fillets of gold, Jesus Christs made of cocoa-nuts, and ivory chaplets; and the sun brought into prominence the rudeness of the paintings, the hideousness of the drawings. Bouvard, who had some abominable specimens at his own residence, was indulgent towards these. He bought a little Virgin of blue paste. Pécuchet contented himself with a rosary as a memento.

The dealers called out: "Come on! come on! For five francs, for three francs, for sixty centimes, for two sous, don't refuse Our Lady!"

The two pilgrims sauntered about without making any selections from the proffered wares. Uncomplimentary remarks were made about them.

"What is it they want, these creatures?"

"Perhaps they are Turks."

"Protestants, rather."

A big girl dragged Pécuchet by the frock-coat; an old man in spectacles placed a hand on his shoulder; all were bawling at the same time; and a number of them left their sheds, and, surrounding the pair, redoubled their solicitations and effronteries.

Bouvard could not stand this any longer.

"Let us alone, for God's sake!" The crowd dispersed. But one fat woman followed them for some distance, and exclaimed that they would repent of it.

When they got back to the inn they found Gouttman in the café. His business called him to these quarters, and he was talking to a man who was examining accounts at a table.

This person had a leather cap, a very wide pair of trousers, a red complexion, and a good figure in spite of his white hair: he had the appearance at the same time of a retired officer and an old strolling player.

From time to time he rapped out an oath; then, when Gouttman replied in a mild tone, he calmed down at once and passed to another part of the accounts.

Bouvard who had been closely watching him, at the end of a quarter of an hour came up to his side.

"Barberou, I believe?"

"Bouvard!" exclaimed the man in the cap, and they embraced each other.

Barberou had in the course of twenty years experienced many changes of fortune. He had been editor of a newspaper, an insurance agent, and manager of an oyster-bed.

"I will tell you all about it," he said.

At last, having returned to his original calling, he was travelling for a Bordeaux house, and Gouttman, who took care of the diocese, disposed of wines for him to the ecclesiastics. "But," he hurriedly added, "you must pardon me one minute; then I shall be at your service."

He was proceeding with the examination of the accounts, and all of a sudden he jumped up excitedly.

"What! two thousand?"

"Certainly."

"Ha! it's wrong, that's what it is!"

"What do you say?"

"I say that I've seen Hérambert myself," replied Barberou in a passion. "The invoice makes it four thousand. No humbug!"

The dealer was not put out of countenance.

"Well, it discharges you—what next?"

Barberou, as he stood there with his face at first pale and then purple, impressed Bouvard and Pécuchet with the apprehension that he was about to strangle Gouttman.

He sat down, folded his arms, and said:

"You are a vile rascal, you must admit."

"No insults, Monsieur Barberou. There are witnesses. Be careful!"

"I'll bring an action against you!"

"Ta! ta! ta!" Then having fastened together his books, Gouttman lifted the brim of his hat: "I wish you luck on't!" With these words he went off.

Barberou explained the facts: For a credit of a thousand francs doubled by a succession of renewals with interest, he had delivered to Gouttman three thousand francs' worth of wines. This would pay his debt with a profit of a thousand francs; but, on the contrary, he owed three thousand on the transaction! His employers might dismiss him; they might even prosecute him!

"Blackguard! robber! dirty Jew! And this fellow dines at priests' houses! Besides, everything that touches the clerical headpiece—"

And he went on railing against the priests, and he struck the table with such violence that the little statue was near falling.

"Gently!" said Bouvard.

"Hold on! What's this here?" And Barberou having removed the covering of the little Virgin: "A pilgrimage bauble! Yours?"

" 'Tis mine," said Pécuchet.

"You grieve me," returned Barberou; "but I'll give you a wrinkle on that point. Don't be afraid." And as one must be a philosopher, and as there is no use in fretting, he invited them to come and lunch with him.

The three sat down together at table.

Barberou was agreeable, recalled old times, took hold of the maid-servant's waist, and wished to measure the breadth of Bouvard's stomach. He would soon see them again, and would bring them a droll book.

The idea of his visit was rather pleasant to them. They chatted about it in the omnibus for an hour, while the horse was trotting. Then Pécuchet shut his eyes. Bouvard also relapsed into silence. Internally he felt an inclination towards religion.

"M. Marescot had the day before called to make an important communication"— Marcel knew no more about it.

They did not see the notary till three days after; and at once he explained the matter.

Madame Bordin offered to buy the farm from M. Bouvard, and to pay him seven thousand five hundred francs a year.

She had been casting sheep's eyes on it since her youth, knew the boundaries and lands all around it, its defects and its advantages; and this desire consumed her like a cancer.

For the good lady, like a true Norman, cherished above everything landed estate, less for the security of the capital than for the happiness of treading on soil that belonged to herself. In that hope she had devoted herself to inquiries and inspections from day to day, and had practised prolonged economies; and she waited with impatience for Bouvard's answer.

He was perplexed, not desiring that Pécuchet one day should be fortuneless; but it was necessary to seize the opportunity—which was the result of the pilgrimage, for the second time Providence had shown itself favourable to them. They proposed the following conditions: An annual payment, not of seven thousand five hundred francs, but of six thousand francs, provided it should pass to the survivor.

Marescot made the point that one of them was in delicate health. The constitution of the other gave him an apoplectic tendency. Madame Bordin, carried away by her ruling passion, signed the contract.

Bouvard got into a melancholy frame of mind about it. Somebody might desire his death; and this reflection inspired him with serious thoughts, ideas about God and eternity.

Three days after, M. Jeufroy invited them to the annual dinner which it was his custom to give to his colleagues. The dinner began at two o'clock in the afternoon, and was to finish at eleven at night.

Perry was used at it as a beverage, and puns were circulated. The Abbé Pruneau, before they broke up, composed an acrostic; M. Bougon performed card-tricks; and Cerpet, a young curate, sang a little ballad which bordered on gallantry.

The curé frequently came to see them. He presented religion under graceful colours. And, after all, what risk would they run? So Bouvard expressed his willingness to approach the holy table shortly, and Pécuchet was to participate in the sacrament on the same occasion.

The great day arrived. The church, on account of the first communions, was thronged with worshippers. The village shopkeepers and their womenfolk were crowded close together in their seats, and the common people either remained standing up behind or occupied the gallery over the church door.

What was about to take place was inexplicable—so Bouvard reflected; but reason does not suffice for the comprehension of certain things. Great men have admitted that. Let him do as much as they had done; and so, in a kind of torpor, he contemplated the altar, the censer, the tapers, with his head a little light, for he had eaten nothing, and experienced a singular weakness.

Pécuchet, by meditating on the Passion of Jesus Christ, excited himself to outbursts of love. He would have liked to offer his soul up to Him as well as the souls of others—and the ecstasies, the transports, the illumination of the saints, all beings, the entire universe. Though he prayed with fervour, the different parts of the mass seemed to him a little long.

At length the little boys knelt down on the first step of the altar, forming with their coats a black band, above which rose light or dark heads of hair at unequal elevations. Then the little girls took their places, with their veils falling from beneath their wreaths. From a distance they resembled a row of white clouds at the end of the choir.

Then it was the turn of the great personages.

The first on the gospel-side was Pécuchet; but, too much moved, no doubt, he kept swaying his head right and left. The curé found difficulty in putting the host into his mouth, and as he received it he turned up the whites of his eyes.

Bouvard, on the contrary, opened his jaws so widely, that his tongue hung over his lip like a streamer. On rising he jostled against Madame Bordin. Their eyes met. She smiled; without knowing the reason why, he reddened.

After Madame Bordin, Mademoiselle de Faverges, the countess, their lady companion, and a gentleman who was not known at Chavignolles approached the altar in a body.

The last two were Placquevent and Petit, the schoolmaster, and then, all of a sudden, Gorju made his appearance. He had got rid of the tuft on his chin; and, as he went back to his place, he had his arms crossed over his breast in a very edifying fashion.

The curé harangued the little boys. Let them take care later on in life not to act like Judas, who betrayed his God, but to preserve always their robe of innocence.

Pécuchet was regretting his when there was a sudden moving of the seats: the mothers were impatient to embrace their children.

The parishioners, on their way out, exchanged felicitations. Some shed tears. Madame de Faverges, while waiting for her carriage, turned round towards Bouvard and Pécuchet, and presented her future son-in-law: "Baron de Mahurot, engineer." The count was sorry not to have the pleasure of their company. He would return the following week. "Pray bear it in mind."

The carriage having now come up, the ladies of the château departed, and the throng dispersed.

They found a parcel inside their own grounds in the middle of the grass. The postman, as the house had been shut up, had thrown it over the wall. It was the work which Barberou had promised to send, *Examination of Christianity,* by Louis Hervieu, a former pupil of the Normal School. Pécuchet would have nothing to say to it, and Bouvard had no desire to make himself acquainted with it.

He had been repeatedly told that the sacrament would transform him. For several days he awaited its blossomings in his conscience. He remained the same as ever, and a painful astonishment took possession of him.

What! The Flesh of God mingles with our flesh, and it produces no effect there! The Thought which governs the world does not illuminate our spirits! The Supreme Power abandons us to impotence!

M. Jeufroy, while reassuring him, prescribed for him the catechism of the Abbé Gaume.

On the other hand, Pécuchet's devotion had become developed. He would have liked to communicate under two species, kept singing psalms as he walked along the corridor, and stopped the people of Chavignolles to argue with, and to convert them. Vaucorbeil laughed in his face; Girbal shrugged his shoulders; and the captain called him "Tartuffe."

It was now thought that they were going too far.

It is an excellent custom to consider things as so many symbols. If the thunder rumbles, imagine to yourself the Last Judgment; at sight of a cloudless sky, think of the abode of the blessed; say to yourself in your walks that every step brings you nearer to death. Pécuchet observed this method. When he took hold of his clothes, he thought of the carnal envelope in which the Second Person of the Trinity was clad; the ticking of the clock recalled to him the beatings of His heart, and the prick of a pin the nails of the Cross. But in vain did he remain on his knees for hours and multiply his fasts and strain his imagination. He did not succeed in getting detached from self; it was impossible to attain to perfect contemplation.

He had recourse to mystic authors: St. Theresa, John of the Cross, Louis of Granada, Simpoli, and, of the more modern, Monseigneur Chaillot. Instead of the sublimities which he expected, he encountered only platitudes, a very disjointed style, frigid imagery, and many comparisons drawn from lapidaries' shops.

He learned, however, that there is an active purgation and a passive purgation, an internal vision and an external vision, four kinds of prayers, nine excellencies in love, six degrees in humility, and that the wounding of the soul is not very different from spiritual theft.

Some points embarrassed him.

"Since the flesh is accursed, how is it that we are bound to thank God for the boon of existence?" "What proportion must be observed between the fear indispensable to the salvation and the hope which is no less so?" "Where is the sign of grace?" etc.

M. Jeufroy's answers were simple.

"Don't worry yourself. By desiring to sift everything we rush along a perilous slope."

The *Catechism of Perseverance*, by Gaume, had disgusted Pécuchet so much that he took up Louis Hervieu's book. It was a summary of modern exegesis, prohibited by the government. Barberou, as a republican, had bought the book.

It awakened doubts in Bouvard's mind, and, first of all, on original sin. "If God had created man peccable, He ought not to punish him; and evil is anterior to the Fall, since there were already volcanoes and wild beasts. In short, this dogma upsets my notions of justice."

"What would you have?" said the curé. "It is one of those truths about which everybody is agreed, without being able to furnish proofs of it; and we ourselves make the crimes of their fathers rebound on the children. Thus morality and law justify this decree of Providence, since we find it in nature."

Bouvard shook his head. He had also doubts about hell.

"For every punishment should look to the amelioration of the guilty person, which is impossible where the penalty is eternal; and how many are enduring it? Just think! All the ancients, the Jews, the Mussulmans, the idolaters, the heretics, and the children who have died without baptism—those children created by God, and for what end?—for the purpose of being punished for a sin which they did not commit!"

"Such is St. Augustine's opinion," added the curé; "and St. Fulgentius involves even the unborn child in damnation. The Church, it is true, has come to no decision on this matter. One remark, however. It is not God, but the sinner who damns himself; and the offence being infinite, since God is infinite, the punishment must be infinite. Is that all, sir?"

"Explain the Trinity to me." said Bouvard.

"With pleasure. Let us take a comparison: the three sides of a triangle, or rather our soul, which contains being, knowing, and willing; what we call faculty in the case of man is person in God. There is the mystery."

"But the three sides of the triangle are not each the triangle; these three faculties of the soul do not make three souls, and your persons of the Trinity are three Gods."

"Blasphemy!"

"So then there is only one person, one God, one substance affected in three ways!"

"Let us adore without understanding," said the curé.

"Be it so," said Bouvard. He was afraid of being taken for an atheist, and getting into bad odour at the château.

They now visited there three times a week, about five o'clock in winter, and the cup of tea warmed them. The count's manners recalled the ease of the ancient court; the countess, placid and plump, exhibited much discernment about everything. Mademoiselle Yolande, their daughter, was the type of the young person, the angel of "keepsakes"; and Madame de Noares, their lady companion, resembled Pécuchet in having a pointed nose like him.

The first time they entered the drawing-room she was defending somebody.

"I assure you he is changed. His gift is a proof of it."

This somebody was Gorju. He had made the betrothed couple an offer of a Gothic prie-dieu. It was brought. The arms of the two houses appeared on it in coloured relief. M. de Mahurot seemed satisfied with it, and Madame de Noares said to him:

"You will remember my *protégés?*"

Then she brought in two children, a boy of a dozen years and his sister, who was perhaps ten. Through the holes in their rags could be seen their limbs, reddened with cold. The one was shod in old slippers, the other wore only one wooden shoe. Their foreheads disappeared under their hair, and they stared around them with burning eyeballs like famished wolves.

Madame de Noares told how she had met them that morning on the high-road. Placquevent could not give any information about them.

They were asked their names.

"Victor—Victorine."

"Where was their father?"

"In jail."

"And what was he doing before that?"

"Nothing."

"Their country?"

"St. Pierre."

"But which St. Pierre?"

The two little ones for sole response, said, snivelling:

"Don't know—don't know."

Their mother was dead, and they were begging.

Madame de Noares explained how dangerous it would be to abandon them; she moved the countess, piqued the count's sense of honour, was backed up by mademoiselle, pressed the matter—succeeded.

The gamekeeper's wife would take charge of them. Later, work would be found for them, and, as they did not know how to read or write, Madame de Noares gave them lessons herself, with a view to preparing them for catechism.

When M. Jeufroy used to come to the château, the two youngsters would be sent for; he would question them, and then deliver a lecture, into which he would import a certain amount of display on account of his audience.

On one occasion, when the abbé had discoursed about the patriarchs, Bouvard, on the way home with him and Pécuchet, disparaged them very much.

"Jacob is notorious for his thieveries, David for his murders, Solomon for his debaucheries."

The abbé replied that we should look further into the matter. Abraham's sacrifice is a prefigurement of the Passion; Jacob is another type of the Messiah, just like Joseph, like the Brazen Serpent, like Moses.

"Do you believe," said Bouvard, "that he composed the 'Pentateuch'?"

"Yes, no doubt."

"And yet his death is recorded in it; the same observation applies to Joshua; and, as for the Judges, the author informs us that, at the period whose history he was writing, Israel had not yet kings. The work was, therefore, written under the Kings. The Prophets, too, astonish me."

"He's going to deny the Prophets now!"

"Not at all! but their overheated imagination saw Jehovah under different forms—that of a fire, of a bush, of an old man, of a dove; and they were not certain of revelation since they are always asking for a sign."

"Ha! and where have you found out these nice things?"

"In Spinoza."

At this word, the curé jumped.

"Have you read him?"

"God forbid!"

"Nevertheless, sir, science—"

"Sir, no one can be a scholar without being a Christian."

Science furnished a subject for sarcasms on his part:

"Will it make an ear of corn sprout, this science of yours? What do we know?" he said.

But he did know that the world was created for us; he did know that archangels are above the angels; he did know that the human body will rise again such as it was about the age of thirty.

His ecclesiastical self-complacency provoked Bouvard, who, through want of confidence in Louis Hervieu, had written to Varlot; and Pécuchet, better informed, asked M. Jeufroy for explanations of Scripture.

The six days of Genesis mean six great epochs. The pillage of the precious vessels made by the Jews from the Egyptians must be interpreted to mean intellectual riches, the arts of which they had stolen the secret. Isaiah did not strip himself completely, *nudus* in Latin signifying "up to the hips": thus Virgil advises people to go naked in order to plough, and that writer would not have given a precept opposed to decency. Ezekiel devouring a book has nothing extraordinary in it; do we not speak of devouring a pamphlet, a newspaper?

"But if we see metaphors everywhere, what will become of the facts?"

The abbé maintained, nevertheless, that they were realities.

This way of understanding them appeared disloyal to Pécuchet. He pushed his investigations further, and brought a note on the contradictions of the Bible.

"Exodus teaches us that for forty years they offered up sacrifices in the desert; according to Amos and Jeremiah they offered up none. Paralipomenon and the book of Esdras are not in agreement as to the enumeration of the people. In Deuteronomy, Moses saw the Lord face to face; according to Exodus, he could not see Him. Where, then, is the inspiration?"

"An additional ground for admitting it," replied M. Jeufroy smiling. "Impostors have need of connivance; the sincere take no such precautions. In perplexity, have recourse to the Church. She is always infallible."

"On whom does her infallibility depend?"

"The Councils of Basle and of Constance attribute it to the councils. But often the councils are at variance—witness that which decided in favour of Athanasius and of Arius; those of Florence and Lateran award it to the Pope."

"But Adrian VI declares that the Pope may be mistaken, like any other person."

"Quibbles! All that does not affect the permanence of dogma."

"Louis Hervieu's work points out the variations: baptism was formerly reserved for adults, extreme unction was not a sacrament till the ninth century, the Real Presence was decreed in the eighth, purgatory recognised in the fifteenth, the Immaculate Conception is a thing of yesterday."

And so it came to pass that Pécuchet did not know what to think of Jesus. Three Evangelists make him out to be a man. In one passage of St. John he appears to be equal to God; in another, all the same, to acknowledge himself His inferior.

The abbé rejoined by citing the letter of King Abgar, the acts of Pilate, and the testimony of the sibyls, "the foundation of which is genuine." He found the Virgin again amongst the Gauls, the announcement of a Redeemer in China, the Trinity everywhere, the Cross on the cap of the Grand Lama, and in Egypt in the closed hands of the gods; and he even exhibited an engraving representing a nilometer, which, according to Pécuchet, was a phallus.

M. Jeufroy secretly consulted his friend Pruneau, who searched for proofs for him in the authors. A conflict of erudition was waged, and, lashed by conceit, Pécuchet became abstruse, mythological. He compared the Virgin to Isis, the Eucharist to the Homa of the Persians, Bacchus to Moses, Noah's ark to the ship of Xithurus. These analogies demonstrated to his satisfaction the identity of religions.

But there cannot be several religions, since there is only one God. And when he was at the end of his arguments, the man in the cassock exclaimed: "It is a mystery!"

"What is the meaning of that word? Want of knowledge: very good. But if it denotes a thing the mere statement of which involves contradiction, it is a piece of stupidity."

And now Pécuchet would never let M. Jeufroy alone. He would surprise him in the garden, wait for him in the confessional, and take up the argument again in the sacristy.

The priest had to invent plans in order to escape from him.

One day, after he had started for Sassetot on a sick call, Pécuchet proceeded along the road in front of him in such a way as to render conversation inevitable.

It was an evening about the end of August. The red sky began to darken, and a large cloud lowered above them, regular at the base and forming volutes at the top.

Pécuchet at first talked about indifferent subjects, then, having slipped out the word "martyr":

"How many do you think there were of them?"

"A score of millions at least."

"Their number is not so great, according to Origen."

"Origen, you know, is open to suspicion."

A big gust of wind swept past, violently shaking the grass beside the ditches and the two rows of young elm trees that stretched towards the end of the horizon.

Pécuchet went on:

"Amongst the martyrs we include many Gaulish bishops killed while resisting the barbarians, which is no longer the question at issue."

"Do you wish to defend the emperors?"

According to Pécuchet, they had been calumniated.

"The history of the Theban legion is a fable. I also question Symphorosa and her seven sons, Felicitas and her seven daughters, and the seven virgins of Ancyra condemned to violation, though septuagenarians, and the eleven thousand virgins of St. Ursula, of whom one companion was called *Undecemilla*, a name taken for a figure; still more, the ten martyrs of Alexandria!"

"And yet—and yet they are found in authors worthy of credit."

Raindrops fell, and the curé unrolled his umbrella; and Pécuchet, when he was under it, went so far as to maintain that the Catholics had made more martyrs than the Jews, the Mussulmans, the Protestants, and the Freethinkers—than all those of Rome in former days.

The priest exclaimed:

"But we find ten persecutions from the reign of Nero to that of Cæsar Galba!"

"Well! and the massacres of the Albigenses? and St. Bartholomew? and the revocation of the Edict of Nantes?"

"Deplorable excesses, no doubt; but you do not mean to compare these people to St. Étienne, St. Lawrence, Cyprian, Polycarp, a crowd of missionaries?"

"Excuse me! I will remind you of Hypatia, Jerome of Prague, John Huss, Bruno, Vanini, Anne Dubourg!"

The rain increased, and its drops dashed down with such force that they rebounded from the ground like little white rockets.

Pécuchet and M. Jeufroy walked on slowly, pressed close to one another, and the curé said:

"After abominable tortures they were flung into vessels of boiling water."

"The Inquisition made use of the same kind of torture, and it burned very well for you."

"Illustrious ladies were exhibited to the public gaze in the *lupanars*."

"Do you believe Louis XIV's dragoons regarded decency?"

"And mark well that the Christians had done nothing against the State."

"No more had the Huguenots."

The wind swept the rain into the air. It clattered on the leaves, trickled at the side of the road; and the mud-coloured sky intermingled with the fields, which lay bare after the close of harvest. Not a root was to be seen. Only, in the distance, a shepherd's hut.

Pécuchet's thin overcoat had no longer a dry thread in it. The water ran along his spine, got into his boots, into his ears, into his eyes, in spite of the Amoros headpiece. The curé, while lifting up with one hand the tail of his cassock, uncovered his legs; and the points of his three-cornered hat sputtered the water over his shoulders, like the gargoyles of a cathedral.

They had to stop, and, turning their backs to the storm, they remained face to face, belly to belly, holding with their four hands the swaying umbrella.

M. Jeufroy had not interrupted his vindication of the Catholics.

"Did they crucify your Protestants, as was done to St. Simeon; or get a man devoured by two tigers, as happened to St. Ignatius?"

"But make some allowance for the number of women separated from their husbands, children snatched from their mothers, and the exile of the poor across the snow, in the midst of precipices. They huddled them together in prisons; just when they were at the point of death they were dragged along on the hurdle."

The abbé sneered. "You will allow me not to believe a word of it. And our martyrs are less doubtful. St. Blandina was delivered over naked in a net to a furious cow. St. Julia was beaten to death. St. Taracus, St. Probus, and St. Andronicus had their teeth broken with a hammer, their sides torn with iron combs, their hands pierced with reddened nails, and their scalps carried off."

"You are exaggerating," said Pécuchet. "The death of the martyrs was at that time an amplification of rhetoric."

"What! of rhetoric?"

"Why, yes; whilst what I relate to you, sir, is history. The Catholics in Ireland disembowelled pregnant women in order to take their children—"

"Never!"

"—and give them to the pigs."

"Come now!"

"In Belgium they buried women alive."

"What nonsense!"

"We have their names."

"And even so," objected the priest, angrily shaking his umbrella, "they cannot be called martyrs. There are no martyrs outside the Church."

"One word. If the value of a martyr depends on the doctrine, how could he serve to demonstrate its existence?"

The rain ceased; they did not speak again till they reached the village. But, on the threshold of the presbytery, the curé said:

"I pity you! really, I pity you!"

Pécuchet immediately told Bouvard about the wrangle. It had filled him with an antipathy to religion, and, an hour later, seated before a brushwood fire, they both read the *Curé Meslier*. These dull negations disgusted Pécuchet; then, reproaching himself for perhaps having misunderstood heroes, he ran through the history of the most illustrious martyrs in the Biography.

What a clamour from the populace when they entered the arena! and, if the lions and the jaguars were too quiet, the people urged them to come forward by their gestures and their cries. The victims could be seen covered with gore, smiling where they stood, with their gaze towards heaven. St. Perpetua bound up her hair in order that she might not look dejected.

Pécuchet began to reflect. The window was open, the night tranquil; many stars were shining. There must have passed through these martyrs' souls things of which we have no idea—a joy, a divine spasm! And Pécuchet, by dwelling on the subject, believed that he understood this emotion, and that he would have done the same himself.

"You?"

"Certainly."

"No fudge! Do you believe—yes or no?"

"I don't know."

He lighted a candle; then, his eyes falling on the crucifix in the alcove:

"How many wretches have sought help from that!"

And, after a brief silence:

"They have denaturalised Him. It is the fault of Rome—the policy of the Vatican."

But Bouvard admired the Church for her magnificence, and would have brought back the Middle Ages provided he might be a cardinal.

"You must admit I should have looked well in the purple."

Pécuchet's headpiece, placed in front of the fire, was not yet dry. While stretching it out he felt something in the lining, and out tumbled a medal of St. Joseph.

Madame de Noares wished to ascertain from Pécuchet whether he had not experienced some kind of change, bringing him happiness, and betrayed herself by her questions. On one occasion, whilst he was playing billiards, she had sewn the medal in his cap.

Evidently she was in love with him: they might marry; she was a widow, and he had had no suspicion of this attachment, which might have brought about his life's happiness.

Though he exhibited a more religious tendency than M. Bouvard, she had dedicated him to St. Joseph, whose succour is favourable to conversions.

No one knew so well as she all the beads and the indulgences which they procure, the effect of relics, the privileges of blessed waters. Her watch was attached to a chain that had touched the bonds of St. Peter. Amongst her trinkets glittered a pearl of gold, in imitation of the one in the church of Allouagne containing a tear of Our Lord; a ring on her little finger enclosed some of the hair of the curé of Ars, and, as she was in the habit of collecting simples for the sick, her apartment was like a sacristy combined with an apothecary's laboratory.

Her time was passed in writing letters, in visiting the poor, in dissolving irregular connections, and in distributing photographs of the Sacred Heart. A gentleman had promised to send her some "martyr's paste," a mixture of paschal wax and human dust taken from the Catacombs, and used in desperate cases in the shape of fly-blisters and pills. She promised some of it to Pécuchet.

He appeared shocked at such materialism.

In the evening a footman from the château brought him a basketful of little books relating pious phrases of the great Napoleon, witticisms of clergymen at inns, frightful deaths that had happened to atheists. All those things Madame de

Noares knew by heart, along with an infinite number of miracles. She related several stupid ones—miracles without an object, as if God had performed them to excite the wonder of the world. Her own grandmother had locked up in a cupboard some prunes covered with a piece of linen, and when the cupboard was opened a year later they saw thirteen of them on the cloth forming a cross.

"Explain this to me."

This was the phrase she used after her marvellous tales, which she declared to be true, with the obstinacy of a mule. Apart from this she was a harmless woman of lively disposition.

On one occasion, however, she deviated from her character.

Bouvard was disputing with her about the miracle of Pezilla: this was a fruit-dish in which wafers had been hidden during the Revolution and which had become gilded of itself.

"Perhaps there was at the bottom a little yellow colour caused by humidity?"

"Not at all! I repeat it, there was not! The cause of the gilding was the contact with the Eucharist."

By way of proof she relied on the attestations of bishops.

"It is, they say, like a buckler, a—a palladium over the diocese of Perpignan. Ask Monsieur Jeufroy, then!"

Bouvard could not stand this kind of talk any longer; and, after he had looked over his Louis Hervieu, he took Pécuchet off with them.

The clergyman was finishing his dinner. Reine offered them chairs, and, at a gesture from her master, she went to fetch two little glasses, which she filled with Rosolio.

After this Bouvard explained what had brought him there.

The abbé did not reply candidly.

"Everything is possible to God, and the miracles are a proof of religion."

"However, there are laws of nature—"

"That makes no difference to Him. He sets them aside in order to instruct, to correct."

"How do you know whether He sets them aside?" returned Bouvard. "So long as Nature follows her routine we never bestow a thought on it, but in an extraordinary phenomenon we believe we see the hand of God."

"It may be there," replied the ecclesiastic; "and when an occurrence has been certified by witnesses—"

"The witnesses swallow everything, for there are spurious miracles."

The priest grew red.

"Undoubtedly; sometimes."

"How can we distinguish them from the genuine ones? If the genuine ones, given as proofs, have themselves need of proofs, why perform them?"

Reine interposed, and, preaching like her master, said it was necessary to obey.

"Life is a passage, but death is eternal."

"In short," suggested Bouvard, guzzling the Rosolio, "the miracles of former times are not better demonstrated than the miracles of to-day; analogous reasonings uphold those of Christians and Pagans."

The curé flung down his fork on the table.

"Again I tell you those miracles were spurious! There are no miracles outside of the Church."

"Stop!" said Pécuchet, "that is the same argument you used regarding the martyrs: the doctrine rests on the facts and the facts on the doctrine."

M. Jeufroy, having swallowed a glass of water, replied:

"Even while denying them you believe in them. The world which twelve fishermen converted—look at that! it seems to me a fine miracle."

"Not at all!"

Pécuchet gave a different account of the matter: "Monotheism comes from the Hebrews; the Trinity from the Indians; the Logos belongs to Plato, and the Virgin Mother to Asia."

No matter! M. Jeufroy clung to the supernatural and did not desire that Christianity should have humanly the least reason for its existence, though he saw amongst all peoples foreshadowings or deformations of it. The scoffing impiety of the eighteenth century he would have tolerated, but modern criticism, with its politeness, exasperated him.

"I prefer the atheist who blasphemes to the sceptic who cavils."

Then he looked at them with an air of bravado, as if to dismiss them.

Pécuchet returned home in a melancholy frame of mind. He had hoped for a reconciliation between faith and reason.

Bouvard made him read this passage from Louis Hervieu:

"In order to know the abyss which separates them, oppose their axioms.

"Reason says to you: 'The whole comprehends the part,' and faith replies to you: 'By substantiation, Jesus, while communicating with the apostles, had His body in His hand and His head in His mouth.'

"Reason says to you: 'No one is responsible for the crime of another,' and faith replies to you: 'By original sin.'

"Reason says to you: 'Three make three,' and faith declares that 'Three make one.' "

They no longer associated with the abbé.

It was the period of the war with Italy. The respectable people were trembling for the Pope. They were thundering against Victor Emmanuel. Madame de Noares went so far as to wish for his death. Bouvard and Pécuchet alone protested timidly.

When the door of the drawing-room flew open in front of them and they looked at themselves in the lofty mirrors, as they passed, whilst through the windows they caught a glimpse of the walks where glared above the grass the red waistcoat of a manservant, they felt a sensation of delight; and the luxuriousness of their surroundings rendered them indulgent to the words that were uttered there.

The count lent them all the works of M. de Maistre. He expounded the principles contained in them before a circle of intimate friends—Hurel, the curé, the justice of the peace, the notary, and the baron, his future son-in-law, who used to come from time to time for twenty-four hours to the château.

"What is abominable," said the count, "is the spirit of 'eighty-nine. First of all they question the existence of God; then they dispute about government; then comes liberty—liberty for insults, for revolt, for enjoyments, or rather for plunder, so that religion and authority ought to proscribe the independents, the heretics. No doubt they will protest against what they call persecution, as if the executioners persecuted the criminals. Let me resume: No State without God! the law being unable to command respect unless it comes from on high, and, in fact, it is not a question of the Italians, but of determining which shall have the best of it, the Revolution or the Pope, Satan or Jesus Christ."

M. Jeufroy expressed his approval by monosyllables, Hurel by means of a smile, and the justice of the peace by nodding his head. Bouvard and Pécuchet kept their eyes fixed on the ceiling; Madame de Noares, the countess, and Yolande were making clothes for the poor, and M. de Mahurot, beside his betrothed, was turning over the leaves of a book.

Then came intervals of silence, during which everyone seemed to be absorbed in the investigation of a problem. Napoleon III was no longer a saviour, and he had even given a deplorable example by allowing the masons at the Tuileries to work on Sunday.

"It ought not to be permitted," was the ordinary phrase of the count.

Social economy, fine arts, literature, history, scientific doctrines—on all he decided in his quality of Christian and father of a family; and would to God that the government, in this respect, exercised the same severity that he exhibited in his household! Authority alone is the judge of the dangers of science: spread too extensively, it inspires fatal ambitions in the breasts of the people. They were happier, these poor people, when the nobles and the bishops tempered the absolutism of the king. The manufacturers now make use of them. They are on the point of sinking into slavery.

And all looked back with regret to the old *régime*, Hurel through meanness, Coulon through ignorance, Marescot as a man of artistic tastes.

Bouvard, when he found himself at home once more, fortified his mind with a course of Lamettrie, Holbach, and others; whilst Pécuchet forsook a religion which had become a medium of government.

M. de Mahurot had communicated in order the better to charm the ladies, and, if he adopted it as a practice, it was in the interests of the servants.

A mathematician and *dilettante,* who played waltzes on the piano and admired Topffer, he was distinguished by a tasteful scepticism. What was said about feudal abuses, the Inquisition, and the Jesuits, was the result of prejudice. He extolled progress, though he despised everyone who was not a gentleman, or who had not come from the Polytechnic School!

M. Jeufroy likewise displeased the two friends. He believed in sorcery, made jokes about idolatry, declared that all idioms are derived from the Hebrew. His rhetoric lacked the element of novelty: it was invariably the stag at bay, honey and absinthe, gold and lead, perfumes, urns, and the comparison of the Christian soul to the soldier who ought to say in the face of sin: "Thou shall not pass!"

In order to avoid his discourses they used to come to the château at as late an hour as possible.

One day, however, they encountered him there. He had been an hour awaiting his two pupils. Suddenly Madame de Noares entered.

"The little girl has disappeared. I am bringing Victor in. Ah! the wretch!"

She had found in his pocket a silver thimble which she had lost three days ago. Then, stifled with sobs:

"That is not all! While I was giving him a scolding, he turned his back on me!"

And, ere the count and countess could have said a word:

"However, it is my own fault: pardon me!"

She had concealed from them the fact that the two orphans were the children of Touache, who was now in prison.

What was to be done?

If the count sent them away they would be lost, and his act of charity would be taken for a caprice.

M. Jeufroy was not surprised. Since man is corrupt, our natural duty is to punish him in order to improve him.

Bouvard protested. Leniency was better. But the count once more expatiated on the iron hand indispensable for children as well as for the people. These two children were full of vices—the little girl was untruthful, the boy brutish. This theft, after all, might have been excused, the impertinence never. Education should be the school of respect.

Therefore Sorel, the gamekeeper, would immediately administer to the youngster a good flogging.

M. de Mahurot, who had something to say to him, undertook the commission. He went to the anteroom for a gun, and called Victor, who had remained in the centre of the courtyard with downcast head.

"Follow me," said the baron. As the way to the gamekeeper's lodge turned off a little from Chavignolles, M. Jeufroy, Bouvard, and Pécuchet accompanied him.

At a hundred paces from the château, he begged them not to speak any more while he was walking along the wood.

The ground sloped down to the river's edge, where rose great blocks of stone. At sunset they looked like slabs of gold. On the opposite side the green hillocks were wrapped in shadow. A keen wind was blowing. Rabbits came out of their burrows, and began browsing on the grass.

A shot went off; a second; a third: and the rabbits jumped up, then rolled over. Victor flung himself on them to seize hold of them, and panted, soaking with perspiration.

"You have your clothes in nice condition!" said the baron.

There was blood on his ragged blouse.

Bouvard shrank from the sight of blood. He would not admit that it ever should be shed.

M. Jeufroy returned:

"Circumstances sometimes make it necessary. If the guilty person does not give his own, there is need of another's—a truth which the Redemption teaches us."

According to Bouvard, it had been of hardly any use, since nearly all mankind would be damned, in spite of the sacrifice of Our Lord.

"But everyday He renews it in the Eucharist."

"And whatever be the unworthiness of the priest," said Pécuchet, "the miracle takes place at the words."

"There is the mystery, sir."

Meanwhile Victor had riveted his eyes on the gun, and he even tried to touch it.

"Down with your paws!" And M. de Mahurot took a long path through the wood.

The clergyman had placed Pécuchet on one side of him and Bouvard at the other, and said to the latter:

"Attention, you know. *Debetur pueris.*"

Bouvard assured him that he humbled himself in the presence of the Creator, but was indignant at their having made Him a man. We fear His vengeance; we work for His glory. He has every virtue: an arm, an eye, a policy, a habitation.

" 'Our Father, who art in heaven,' what does that mean?"

And Pécuchet added: "The universe has become enlarged; the earth is no longer its central point. It revolves amongst an infinite multitude of other worlds.

Many of them surpass it in grandeur, and this belittlement of our globe shows a more sublime ideal of God.

"So, then, religion must change. Paradise is something infantile, with its blessed always in a state of contemplation, always chanting hymns, and looking from on high at the tortures of the damned. When one reflects that Christianity had for its basis an apple!"

The curé was annoyed. "Deny revelation; that would be simpler."

"How do you make, out that God spoke?" said Bouvard.

"Prove that he did not speak!" said M. Jeufroy.

"Once again, who affirms it?"

"The Church."

"Nice testimony!"

This discussion bored M. de Mahurot, and, as he walked along: "Pray listen to the curé. He knows more than you."

Bouvard and Pécuchet made signs to indicate that they were taking another road; then, at Croix-Verte:

"A very good evening."

"Your servant," said the baron.

All this would be told to M. de Faverges, and perhaps a rupture would result. So much the worse. They felt that they were despised by those people of rank. They were never asked to dinner, and they were tired of Madame de Noares, with her continual remonstrances.

They could not, however, keep the De Maistre; and a fortnight after they returned to the château, not expecting to be welcomed, but they were. All the family were in the boudoir, and amongst those present were Hurel and, strangely enough, Foureau.

Correction had failed to correct Victor. He refused to learn his catechism; and Victorine gave utterance to vulgar words. In short, the boy should go to a reformatory, and the girl to a nunnery. Foureau was charged with carrying out the measure, and he was about to go when the countess called him back.

They were waiting for M. Jeufroy to fix the date of the marriage, which was to take place at the mayor's office before being celebrated in the church, in order to show that they looked on civil marriage with contempt.

Foureau tried to defend it. The count and Hurel attacked it. What was a municipal function beside a priesthood?—and the baron would not have believed himself to be really wedded if he had been married only in the presence of a tri-coloured scarf.

"Bravo!" said M. Jeufroy, who had just come in. "Marriage having been established by Jesus Christ—"

Pécuchet stopped him: "In which Gospel? In the Apostolic times they respected it so little that Tertullian compares it to adultery."

"Oh! upon my word!"

"Yes, certainly! and it is not a sacrament. A sign is necessary for a sacrament. Show me the sign in marriage."

In vain did the curé reply that it represented the union of God with the Church.

"You do not understand Christianity either! And the law—"

"The law preserves the stamp of Christianity," said M. de Faverges. "Without that, it would permit polygamy."

A voice rejoined: "Where would be the harm?"

It was Bouvard, half hidden by a curtain.

"You might have many wives, like the Patriarchs, the Mormons, the Mussulmans, and nevertheless be an honest man."

"Never!" exclaimed the priest; "honesty consists in rendering what is due. We owe homage to God. So he who is not a Christian is not honest."

"Just as much as others," said Bouvard.

The count, believing that he saw in this rejoinder an attack on religion, extolled it. It had set free the slaves.

Bouvard referred to authorities to prove the contrary:

"St. Paul recommends them to obey their masters as they would obey Jesus. St. Ambrose calls servitude a gift of God. Leviticus, Exodus, and the Councils have sanctioned it. Bossuet treats it as a part of the law of nations. And Monseigneur Bouvier approves of it."

The count objected that, none the less, Christianity had developed civilisation.

"Ay, and idleness, by making a virtue of poverty."

"However, sir, the morality of the Gospel?"

"Ha! ha! not so moral! Those who labour only during the last hour are paid as much as those who labour from the first hour. To him who hath is given, and from him who hath not is taken away. As for the precept of receiving blows without returning them and of letting yourself be robbed, it encourages the audacious, the cowardly, and the dissolute."

They were doubly scandalised when Pécuchet declared that he liked Buddhism as well.

The priest burst out laughing.

"Ha! ha! ha! Buddhism!"

Madame de Noares lifted up her hands: "Buddhism!"

"What! Buddhism!" repeated the count.

"Do you understand it?" said Pécuchet to M. Jeufroy, who had become confused. "Well, then, learn something about it. Better than Christianity, and before it, it has recognised the nothingness of earthly things. Its practices are austere, its faithful more numerous than the entire body of Christians; and, as for incarnation, Vishnu had not merely one, but nine of them. So judge."

"Travellers' lies!" said Madame de Noares.

"Backed up by the Freemasons!" added the curé.

And all talking at the same time:

"Come, then, go on!"

"Very pretty!"

"For my part, I think it funny!"

"Not possible!"

Finally, Pécuchet, exasperated, declared that he would become a Buddhist!

"You are insulting Christian ladies," said the baron.

Madame de Noares sank into an armchair. The countess and Yolande remained silent. The count kept rolling his eyes; Hurel was waiting for his orders. The abbé, to contain himself, read his breviary.

This sight calmed M. de Faverges; and, looking at the two worthies:

"Before you find fault with the Gospel, and that when there may be stains on your own lives, there is some reparation—"

"Reparation?"

"For stains?"

"Enough! gentlemen. You don't understand me." Then, addressing Foureau: "Sorel is informed about it. Go to him."

Bouvard and Pécuchet withdrew without bowing.

At the end of the avenue they all three gave vent to their indignation.

"They treated me as if I were a servant," grumbled Foureau; and, as his companions agreed with him, in spite of their recollection of the affair of the hemorrhoids, he exhibited towards them a kind of sympathy.

Road-menders were working in the neighbourhood. The man who was over them drew near: it was Gorju. They began to chat.

He was overseeing the macadamisation of the road, voted in 1848, and he owed this post to M. de Mahurot, the engineer. "The one that's going to marry Mademoiselle de Faverges. I suppose 'tis from the house below you were just coming?"

"For the last time," said Pécuchet gruffly.

Gorju assumed an innocent air. "A quarrel! Come, come!"

And if they could have seen his countenance when they had turned on their heels, they might have observed that he had scented the cause of it.

A little further on, they stopped before a trellised enclosure, inside which there were kennels, and also a red-tiled cottage.

Victorine was on the threshold. They heard dogs barking. The gamekeeper's wife came out. Knowing the object of the mayor's visit, she called to Victor. Everything was ready beforehand, and their outfit was contained in two pocket-handkerchiefs fastened together with pins.

"A pleasant journey," said the woman to the children, too glad to have no more to do with such vermin.

Was it their fault if they owed their birth to a convict father? On the contrary, they seemed very quiet, and did not even betray any alarm as to the place to which they were being conveyed.

Bouvard and Pécuchet watched them as they walked in front of them.

Victorine muttered some unintelligible words, with her little bundle over her arm, like a milliner carrying a bandbox.

Every now and then she would turn round, and Pécuchet, at the sight of her fair curls and her pretty figure, regretted that he had not such a child. Brought up under different conditions, she would be charming later. What happiness only to see her growing tall, to hear day after day her bird-like warbling, to kiss her when the fancy seized him!—and a feeling of tenderness, rising from his heart to his lips, made his eyes grow moist and somewhat oppressed his spirit.

Victor, like a soldier, had slung his baggage over his shoulder. He whistled, threw stones at the crows in the furrows, and went to cut switches off the trees.

Foureau called him back; and Bouvard, holding him by the hand, was delighted at feeling within his own those fingers of a robust and vigorous lad. The poor little wretch asked for nothing but to grow freely, like a flower in the open air! and he would rot between closed walls with tasks, punishment, a heap of tomfooleries! Bouvard was seized with pity, springing from a sense of revolt, a feeling of indignation against Fate, one of those fits of rage in which one longs to destroy government altogether.

"Jump about!" he said, "amuse yourself! Have a bit of fun as long as you can!"

The youngster scampered off.

His sister and he were to sleep at the inn, and at daybreak the messenger from Falaise would take Victor and set him down at the reformatory of Beaubourg; while a nun belonging to the orphanage of Grand-Camp would come to fetch Victorine.

Foureau having gone into these details, was once more lost in his own thoughts. But Bouvard wished to know how much the maintenance of the youngsters would cost.

"Bah! a matter perhaps of three hundred francs. The count has given me twenty-five for the first disbursements. What a stingy fellow!"

And, stung to the heart by the contempt shown towards his scarf, Foureau quickened his pace in silence.

Bouvard murmured: "They make me feel sad. I will take the charge of them."

"And so will I," said Pécuchet, the same idea having occurred to both of them.

No doubt there were impediments?

"None," returned Foureau. Besides, he had the right as mayor to entrust deserted children to whomsoever he thought fit. And, after a prolonged hesitation:

"Well, yes; take them! That will annoy *him*."

Bouvard and Pécuchet carried them off.

When they returned to their abode they found at the end of the staircase, under the Madonna, Marcel upon his knees praying with fervour. With his head thrown back, his eyes half closed, and his hare-lip gaping, he had the appearance of a fakir in ecstasy.

"What a brute!" said Bouvard.

"Why? He is perhaps attending to things that would make you envy him if you could only see them. Are there not two worlds entirely distinct? The aim of a process of reasoning is of less consequence than the manner of reasoning. What does the form of belief matter? The great thing is to believe."

Such were the objections of Pécuchet to Bouvard's observation.

Chapter X

LESSONS IN ART AND SCIENCE

THEY PROCURED A NUMBER OF WORKS RELATING TO EDUCATION, AND RE-solved to adopt a system of their own. It was necessary to banish every metaphysical idea, and, in accordance with the experimental method, to follow in the lines of natural development. There was no haste, for the two pupils might forget what they had learned.

Though they had strong constitutions, Pécuchet wished, like a Spartan, to make them more hardy, to accustom them to hunger, thirst, and severe weather, and even insisted on having their feet badly shod in order that they might be prepared for colds. Bouvard was opposed to this.

The dark closet at the end of the corridor was used as their sleeping apartment. Its furniture consisted of two folding beds, two couches, and a jug. Above their heads the top window was open, and spiders crawled along the plaster. Often the children recalled to mind the interior of a cabin where they used to wrangle. One night their father came home with blood on his hands. Some time afterwards the gendarmes arrived. After that they lived in a wood. Men who made wooden shoes used to kiss their mother. She died, and was carried off in a cart. They used to get severe beatings; they got lost. Then they could see once more Madame de Noares and Sorel; and, without asking themselves the reason why they were in this house, they felt happy, there. But they were disagreeably surprised when at the end of eight months the lessons began again. Bouvard took charge of the little girl, and Pécuchet of the boy.

Victor was able to distinguish letters, but did not succeed in forming syllables. He stammered over them, then stopped suddenly, and looked like an idiot. Victorine put questions. How was it that "ch" in "orchestra" had the sound of a "q," and that of a "k" in "archaeology." We must sometimes join two vowels and at other times separate them. All this did not seem to her right. She grew indignant at it.

The teachers gave instruction at the same hour in their respective apartments, and, as the partition was thin, these four voices, one soft, one deep, and two sharp, made a hideous concert. To finish the business and to stimulate the youngsters by means of emulation, they conceived the idea of making them work together in the museum; and they proceeded to teach them writing. The two pupils, one at each end of the table, copied written words that were set for them; but the position of their bodies was awkward. It was necessary to straighten them; their copybooks fell down; their pens broke, and their ink bottles were turned upside down.

Victorine, on certain days, went on capitally for about three minutes, then she would begin to scrawl, and, seized with discouragement, she would sit with her eyes fixed on the ceiling. Victor was not long before he fell asleep, lying over his desk.

Perhaps they were distressed by it? Too great a strain was bad for young heads. "Let us stop," said Bouvard.

There is nothing so stupid as to make children learn by heart; yet, if the memory is not exercised, it will go to waste, and so they taught the youngsters to recite like parrots the first fables of La Fontaine. The children expressed their approval of the ant that heaped up treasure, of the wolf that devoured the lamb, and of the lion that took everyone's share.

When they had become more audacious, they spoiled the garden. But what amusement could be provided for them?

Jean Jacques Rousseau in *Emile* advises the teacher to get the pupil to make his own playthings. Bouvard could not contrive to make a hoop or Pécuchet to sew up a ball. They passed on to toys that were instructive, such as cut-paper work. Pécuchet showed them his microscope. When the candle was lighted, Bouvard would sketch with the shadow of his finger on the wall the profile of a hare or a pig. But the pupils grew tired of it.

Writers have gone into raptures about the delightfulness of an open-air luncheon or a boating excursion. Was it possible for them really to have such recreations? Fénelon recommends from time to time "an innocent conversation." They could not invent one. So they had to come back to the lessons—the multiplying bowls, the erasures of their scrawlings, and the process of teaching them how to read by copying printed characters. All had proved failures, when suddenly a bright idea struck them.

As Victor was prone to gluttony, they showed him the name of a dish: he soon ran through *Le Cuisinier Français* with ease. Victorine, being a coquette, was promised a new dress if she wrote to the dressmaker for it: in less than three weeks she accomplished this feat. This was playing on their vices—a pernicious method, no doubt; but it had succeeded.

Now that they had learned to read and write, what should they be taught? Another puzzle.

Girls have no need of learning, as in the case of boys. All the same, they are usually brought up like mere animals, their sole intellectual baggage being confined to mystical follies.

Is it expedient to teach them languages? "Spanish and Italian," the Swan of

Cambray lays down, "scarcely serve any purpose save to enable people to read dangerous books."

Such a motive appeared silly to them. However, Victorine would have to do only with these languages; whereas English is more widely used. Pécuchet proceeded to study the rules of the language. He seriously demonstrated the mode of expressing the "th"—"like this, now, *the, the, the.*"

But before instructing a child we must be acquainted with its aptitudes. They may be divined by phrenology. They plunged into it, then sought to verify its assertions by experiments on their own persons. Bouvard exhibited the bumps of benevolence, imagination, veneration, and amorous energy—*vulgo*, eroticism. On Pécuchet's temples were found philosophy and enthusiasm allied with a crafty disposition. Such, in fact, were their characters. What surprised them more was to recognise in the one as well as in the other a propensity towards friendship, and, charmed with the discovery, they embraced each other with emotion.

They next made an examination of Marcel. His greatest fault, of which they were not ignorant, was an excessive appetite. Nevertheless Bouvard and Pécuchet were dismayed to find above the top of the ear, on a level with the eye, the organ of alimentivity. With advancing years their servant would perhaps become like the woman in the Salpêtrière, who everyday ate eight pounds of bread, swallowed at one time fourteen different soups, and at another sixty bowls of coffee. They might not have enough to keep him.

The heads of their pupils presented no curious characteristics. No doubt they had gone the wrong way to work with them. A very simple expedient enabled them to develop their experience.

On market days they insinuated themselves among groups of country people on the green, amid the sacks of oats, the baskets of cheese, the calves and the horses, indifferent to the jostlings; and whenever they found a young fellow with his father, they asked leave to feel his skull for a scientific purpose. The majority vouchsafed no reply; others, fancying it was pomatum for ringworm of the scalp, refused testily. A few, through indifference, allowed themselves to be led towards the porch of the church, where they would be undisturbed.

One morning, just as Bouvard and Pécuchet were beginning operations, the curé suddenly presented himself, and seeing what they were about, denounced phrenology as leading to materialism and to fatalism. The thief, the assassin, the adulterer, have henceforth only to cast the blame of their crimes on their bumps.

Bouvard retorted that the organ predisposes towards the act without forcing one to do it. From the fact that a man has in him the germ of a vice, there is nothing to show that he will be vicious.

"However, I wonder at the orthodox, for, while upholding innate ideas, they reject propensities. What a contradiction!"

But phrenology, according to M. Jeufroy, denied Divine Omnipotence, and it was unseemly to practise under the shadow of the holy place, in the very face of the altar.

"Take yourselves off! No!—take yourselves off!"

They established themselves in the shop of Ganot, the hairdresser. Bouvard and Pécuchet went so far as to treat their subjects' relations to a shave or a clip. One afternoon the doctor came to get his hair cut. While seating himself in the armchair he saw in the glass the reflection of the two phrenologists passing their fingers over a child's pate.

"So you are at these fooleries?" he said.

"Why foolery?"

Vaucorbeil smiled contemptuously, then declared that there were not several organs in the brain. Thus one man can digest food which another cannot digest. Are we to assume that there are as many stomachs in the stomach as there are varieties of taste?

They pointed out that one kind of work is a relaxation after another; an intellectual effort does not strain all the faculties at the same time; each has its distinct seat.

"The anatomists have not discovered it," said Vaucorbeil.

"That's because they have dissected badly," replied Pécuchet.

"What?"

"Oh, yes! they cut off slices without regard to the connection of the parts"— a phrase out of a book which recurred to his mind.

"What a piece of nonsense!" exclaimed the physician. "The cranium is not moulded over the brain, the exterior over the interior. Gall is mistaken, and I defy you to justify his doctrine by taking at random three persons in the shop."

The first was a country woman, with big blue eyes.

Pécuchet, looking at her, said:

"She has a good memory."

Her husband attested the fact, and offered himself for examination.

"Oh! you, my worthy fellow, it is hard to lead you."

According to the others, there was not in the world such a headstrong fellow.

The third experiment was made on a boy who was accompanied by his grandmother.

Pécuchet observed that he must be fond of music.

"I assure you it is so," said the good woman. "Show these gentlemen, that they may see for themselves."

He drew a Jew's-harp from under his blouse and began blowing into it.

There was a crashing sound—it was the violent slamming of the door by the doctor as he went out.

They were no longer in doubt about themselves, and summoning their two pupils, they resumed the analysis of their skull-bones.

That of Victorine was even all around, a sign of ponderation; but her brother had an unfortunate cranium—a very large protuberance in the mastoid angle of the parietal bones indicated the organ of destructiveness, of murder; and a swelling farther down was the sign of covetousness, of theft. Bouvard and Pécuchet remained dejected for eight days.

But it was necessary to comprehend the exact sense of words: what we call combativeness implies contempt for death. If it causes homicides, it may, likewise bring about the saving of lives. Acquisitiveness includes the tact of pickpockets and the ardour of merchants. Irreverence has its parallel in the spirit of criticism, craft in circumspection. An instinct always resolves itself into two parts, a bad one and a good one. The one may be destroyed by cultivating the other, and by this system a daring child, far from being a vagabond, may become a general. The sluggish man will have only prudence; the penurious, economy; the extravagant, generosity.

A magnificent dream filled their minds. If they carried to a successful end the education of their pupils, they would later found an establishment having for its object to correct the intellect, to subdue tempers, and to ennoble the heart. Already they talked about subscriptions and about the building.

Their triumph in Ganot's shop had made them famous, and people came to consult them in order that they might tell them their chances of good luck.

All sorts of skulls were examined for this purpose—bowl-shaped, pear-shaped, those rising like sugar loaves, square heads, high heads, contracted skulls and flat skulls, with bulls' jaws, birds' faces, and eyes like pigs'; but such a crowd of people disturbed the hairdresser in his work. Their elbows rubbed against the glass cupboard that contained the perfumery, they put the combs out of order, the wash-hand stand was broken; so he turned out all the idlers, begging of Bouvard and Pécuchet to follow them, an ultimatum which they unmurmuringly accepted, being a little worn out with cranioscopy.

Next day, as they were passing before the little garden of the captain, they saw, chatting with him, Girbal, Coulon, the keeper, and his younger son, Zephyrin, dressed as an altar-boy. His robe was quite new, and he was walking below before returning to the sacristy, and they were complimenting him.

Curious to know what they thought of him, Placquevent asked "these gentlemen" to feel his young man's head.

The skin of his forehead looked tightly drawn; his nose, thin and very gristly at the tip, drooped slantwise over his pinched lips; his chin was pointed, his expression evasive, and his right shoulder was too high.

"Take off your cap," said his father to him.

Bouvard slipped his hands through his straw-coloured hair; then it was Pécuchet's turn, and they communicated to each other their observations in low tones:

"Evident *love of books!* Ha! ha! *approbativeness! Conscientiousness* wanting! No *amativeness!*

"Well?" said the keeper.

Pécuchet opened his snuff-box, and took a pinch.

"Faith!" replied Bouvard, "this is scarcely a genius."

Placquevent reddened with humiliation.

"All the same, he will do my bidding."

"Oho! Oho!"

"But I am his father, by God! and I have certainly the right—"

"Within certain limits," observed Pécuchet.

Girbal interposed. "The paternal authority is indispensable."

"But if the father is an idiot?"

"No matter," said the captain; "his power is none the less absolute."

"In the interests of the children," added Coulon.

According to Bouvard and Pécuchet, they owed nothing to the authors of their being; and the parents, on the other hand, owed them food, education, forethought—in fact, everything.

Their good neighbours protested against this opinion as immoral. Placquevent was hurt by it as if it were an insult.

"For all that, they are a nice lot that you collect on the high-roads. They will go far. Take care!"

"Care of what?" said Pécuchet sourly.

"Oh! I am not afraid of you."

"Nor I of you either."

Coulon here used his influence to restrain the keeper and induce him to go away quietly.

For some minutes there was silence. Then there was some talk about the dahlias of the captain, who would not let his friends depart till he had exhibited every one of them.

Bouvard and Pécuchet were returning homeward when, a hundred paces in front of them, they noticed Placquevent; and close beside him Zephyrin was lifting up his elbow, like a shield, to save his ear from being boxed.

What they had just heard expressed, in another form, were the opinions of the count; but the example of their pupils proved how much liberty had the advantage over coercion. However, a little discipline was desirable.

Pécuchet nailed up a blackboard in the museum for the purpose of demonstrations. They each resolved to keep a journal wherein the things done by the pupil, noted down every evening, could be read next morning, and, to regulate the work by ringing the bell when it should be finished. Like Dupont de Nemours, they would, at first, make use of the paternal injunction, then of the military injunction, and familiarity in addressing them would be forbidden.

Bouvard tried to teach Victorine ciphering. Sometimes he would make mistakes, and both of them would laugh. Then she would kiss him on the part of his neck which was smoothest and ask leave to go, and he would give his permission.

Pécuchet at the hour for lessons in vain rang the bell and shouted out the military injunction through the window. The brat did not come. His socks were always hanging over his ankles; even at table he thrust his fingers into his nostrils, and did not even keep in his wind. Broussais objects to reprimands on this point on the ground that "it is necessary to obey the promptings of a conservative instinct."

Victorine and he made use of frightful language, saying, *mé itou* instead of *moi aussi*, *bère* instead of *boire*, *al* instead of *elle*, and *deventiau* with the *iau;* but, as grammar cannot be understood by children, and as they would learn the use of language by hearing others speak correctly, the two worthy men watched their own words till they found it quite distressing.

They held different views about the way to teach geography. Bouvard thought it more logical to begin with the commune, Pécuchet with the entire world.

With a watering-pot and some sand he sought to demonstrate what was meant by a river, an island, a gulf, and even sacrificed three flower-beds to explain three continents; but the cardinal points could not be got into Victor's head.

On a night in January Pécuchet carried him off in the open country. While they walked along he held forth on astronomy: mariners find it useful on their voyages; without it Christopher Columbus would not have made his discovery. We owe a debt of gratitude to Copernicus, to Galileo, and to Newton.

It was freezing hard, and in the dark blue sky countless stars were scintillating. Pécuchet raised his eyes.

"What! No Ursa Major!"

The last time he had seen it, it was turned to the other side. At length he recognised it, then pointed out the polar star, which is always turned towards the north, and by means of which travellers can find out their exact situation.

Next day he placed an armchair in the middle of the room and began to waltz round it.

"Imagine that this armchair is the sun and that I am the earth; it moves like this."

Victor stared at him, filled with astonishment.

After this he took an orange, passed through it a piece of stick to indicate the poles, then drew a circle across it with charcoal to mark the equator. He next moved the orange round a wax candle, drawing attention to the fact that the various points on the surface were not illuminated at the same time—which causes the difference of climates; and for that of the seasons he sloped the orange, inasmuch as the earth does not stand up straight—which brings about the equinoxes and the solstices.

Victor did not understand a bit of it. He believed that the earth turns around in a long needle, and that the equator is a ring pressing its circumference.

By means of an atlas Pécuchet exhibited Europe to him; but, dazzled by so many lines and colours, he could no longer distinguish the names of different places. The bays and the mountains did not harmonise with the respective nations; the political order confused the physical order. All this, perhaps, might be cleared up by studying history.

It would have been more practical to begin with the village, and go on next to the arrondissement, the department, and the province; but, as Chavignolles had no annals, it was absolutely necessary to stick to universal history. It was rendered embarrassing by such a variety of details that one ought only to select its beautiful features. For Greek history there are: "We shall fight in the shade," the banishment of Aristides by the envious, and the confidence of Alexander in his physician. For Roman, the geese of the Capitol, the tripod of Scævola, the barrel of Regulus. The bed of roses of Guatimozin is noteworthy for America. As for France, it supplies the vase of Soissons, the oak of St. Louis, the death of Joan of Arc, the boiled hen of Bearnais—you have only too extensive a field to select from, not to speak of *À moi d'Auvergne!* and the shipwreck of the *Vengeur*.

Victor confused the men, the centuries, and the countries. Pécuchet, however, was not going to plunge him into subtle considerations, and the mass of facts is a veritable labyrinth. He confined himself to the names of the kings of France. Victor forgot them through not knowing the dates. But, if Dumouchel's system of mnemonics had been insufficient for themselves, what would it be for him! Conclusion: history can be learned only by reading a great deal. He would do this.

Drawing is useful where there are numerous details; and Pécuchet was courageous enough to try to learn it himself from Nature by working at the landscape forthwith. A bookseller at Bayeux sent him paper, india-rubber, pasteboard, pencils, and fixtures, with a view to the works, which, framed and glazed, would adorn the museum.

Out of bed at dawn, they started each with a piece of bread in his pocket, and much time was lost in finding a suitable scene. Pécuchet wished to reproduce what he found under his feet, the extreme horizon, and the clouds, all at the same time; but the backgrounds always got the better of the foregrounds; the river tumbled down from the sky; the shepherd walked over his flock; and a dog asleep looked as if he were hunting. For his part, he gave it up, remembering that he had read this definition:

"Drawing is composed of three things: line, grain, and fine graining, and, furthermore, the powerful touch. But it is only the master who can give the powerful touch."

He rectified the line, assisted in the graining process, watched over the fine graining, and waited for the opportunity of giving the powerful touch. It never arrived, so incomprehensible was the pupil's landscape.

Victorine, who was very lazy, used to yawn over the multiplication table. Mademoiselle Reine showed her how to stitch, and when she was marking linen she lifted her fingers so nicely that Bouvard afterwards had not the heart to torment her with his lesson in ciphering. One of these days they would resume it. No doubt arithmetic and sewing are necessary in a household; but it is cruel, Pécuchet urged, to bring up girls merely with an eye to the husbands they might marry. Not all of them are destined for wedlock; if we wish them later to do without men, we ought to teach them many things.

The sciences can be taught in connection with the commonest objects; for instance, by telling what wine is made of; and when the explanation was given, Victor and Victorine had to repeat it. It was the same with groceries, furniture, illumination; but for them light meant the lamp, and it had nothing in common with the spark of a flint, the flame of a candle, the radiance of the moon.

One day Victorine asked, "How is it that wood burns?" Her masters looked at each other in confusion. The theory of combustion was beyond them.

Another time Bouvard, from the soup to the cheese, kept talking of nutritious elements, and dazed the two youngsters with fibrine, caseine, fat and gluten.

After this, Pécuchet desired to explain to them how the blood is renewed, and he became puzzled over the explanation of circulation.

The dilemma is not an easy one; if you start with facts, the simplest require proofs that are too involved, and by laying down principles first, you begin with the absolute—faith.

How is it to be solved? By combining the two methods of teaching, the rational and the empirical; but a double means towards a single end is the reverse of method. Ah! so much the worse, then.

To initiate them in natural history, they tried some scientific excursions.

"You see," said they, pointing towards an ass, a horse, an ox, "beasts with four feet—they are called quadrupeds. As a rule, birds have feathers, reptiles scales, and butterflies belong to the insect class."

They had a net to catch them with, and Pécuchet, holding the insect up daintily, made them take notice of the four wings, the six claws, the two feelers, and of its bony proboscis, which drinks in the nectar of flowers.

He gathered herbs behind the ditches, mentioned their names, and, when he did not know them, invented them, in order to keep up his prestige. Besides, nomenclature is the least important thing in botany.

He wrote this axiom on the blackboard: "Every plant has leaves, a calyx, and a corolla enclosing an ovary or pericarp, which contains the seed." Then he ordered his pupils to go looking for plants through the fields, and to collect the first that came to hand.

Victor brought him buttercups; Victorine a bunch of strawberries. He searched vainly for the pericarp.

Bouvard, who distrusted his own knowledge, rummaged in the library, and discovered in *Le Redouté des Dames* a sketch of an iris in which the ovaries were not situated in the corolla, but beneath the petals in the stem. In their garden were some scratchweeds and lilies-of-the-valley in flower. These rubiaceae had no calyx; therefore the principle laid down on the blackboard was false.

"It is an exception," said Pécuchet.

But chance led to the discovery of a field-madder in the grass, and it had a calyx.

"Goodness gracious! If the exceptions themselves are not true, what are we to put any reliance on?"

One day, in one of these excursions, they heard the cries of peacocks, glanced over the wall, and at first did not recognise their own farm. The barn had a slate roof; the railings were new; the pathways had been metalled.

Père Gouy made his appearance.

" 'Tisn't possible! Is it you?"

How many sad stories he had to tell of the past three years, amongst others the death of his wife! As for himself, he had always been as strong as an oak.

"Come in a minute."

It was early in April, and in the three fruit-gardens rows of apple trees in full blossom showed their white and red clusters; the sky, which was like blue satin, was perfectly cloudless. Table-cloths, sheets, and napkins hung down, vertically attached to tightly-drawn ropes by wooden pins. Père Gouy lifted them as they passed; and suddenly they came face to face with Madame Bordin, bareheaded, in a dressing-gown, and Marianne offering her armfuls of linen.

"Your servant, gentlemen. Make yourselves at home. As for me, I shall sit down; I am worn out."

The farmer offered to get some refreshment for the entire party.

"Not now," said she; "I am too hot."

Pécuchet consented, and disappeared into the cellar with Père Gouy, Marianne and Victor.

Bouvard sat down on the grass beside Madame Bordin.

He received the annual payment punctually; he had nothing to complain of; and he wished for nothing more.

The bright sunshine lighted up her profile. One of her black head-bands had come loose, and the little curls behind her neck clung to her brown skin, moistened with perspiration. With each breath her bosom heaved. The smell of the grass mingled with the odour of her solid flesh, and Bouvard felt a revival of his attachment, which filled him with joy. Then he complimented her about her property.

She was greatly charmed with it; and she told him about her plans. In order to enlarge the farmyard, she intended to take down the upper bank.

Victorine was at that moment climbing up the slopes, and gathering primroses, hyacinths, and violets, without being afraid of an old horse that was browsing on the grass at her feet.

"Isn't she pretty?" said Bouvard.

"Yes, she is pretty, for a little girl."

And the widow heaved a sigh, which seemed charged with life-long regret.

"You might have had one yourself."

She hung down her head.

"That depended on you."

"How?"

He gave her such a look that she grew purple, as if at the sensation of a rough caress; but, immediately fanning herself with her pocket-handkerchief:

"You have let the opportunity slip, my dear."

"I don't quite understand." And without rising he drew closer to her.

She remained looking down at him for some time; then smiling, with moist eyes:

"It is your fault."

The sheets, hanging around them, hemmed them in, like the curtains of a bed.

He leaned forward on his elbow, so that his face touched her knees.

"Why?—eh?—why?"

And as she remained silent, while he was in a condition in which words cost nothing, he tried to justify himself; accused himself of folly, of pride.

"Forgive me! Let everything be as it was before. Do you wish it?" And he caught her hand, which she allowed to remain in his.

A sudden gust of wind blew up the sheets, and they saw two peacocks, a male and a female. The female stood motionless, with her tail in the air. The male marched around her, erected his tail into a fan and bridled up, making a clucking noise.

Bouvard was clasping the hand of Madame Bordin. She very quickly loosed herself. Before them, open-mouthed and, as it were, petrified, was young Victor staring at them; a short distance away Victorine, stretched on her back, in the full light of day, was inhaling all the flowers which she had gathered.

The old horse, frightened by the peacocks, broke one of the lines with a kick, got his legs entangled in it, and, galloping through the farmyard, dragged the washed linen after him.

At Madame Bordin's wild screams Marianne rushed up. Père Gouy abused his horse: "Fool of a beast! Old bag of bones! Infernal thief of a horse!"—kicked him in the belly, and lashed his ears with the handle of a whip.

Bouvard was shocked at seeing the animal maltreated.

The countryman, in answer to his protest, said:

"I've a right to do it; he's my own."

This was no justification. And Pécuchet, coming on the scene, added that animals too have their rights, for they have souls like ourselves—if indeed ours have any existence.

"You are an impious man!" exclaimed Madame Bordin.

Three things excited her anger: the necessity for beginning the washing over again, the outrage on her faith, and the fear of having been seen just now in a compromising attitude.

"I thought you were more liberal," said Bouvard.

She replied, in a magisterial manner, "I don't like scamps."

And Gouy laid the blame on them for having injured his horse, whose nostrils were bleeding. He growled in a smothered voice:

"Damned unlucky people! I was going to put him away when they turned up."

The two worthies took themselves off, shrugging their shoulders.

Victor asked them why they had been vexed with Gouy.

"He abuses his strength, which is wrong."

"Why is it wrong?"

Could it be that the children had no idea of justice? Perhaps so.

And the same evening, Pécuchet, with Bouvard sitting at his right, and facing the two pupils with some notes in his hand, began a course of lectures on morality.

"This science teaches us to exercise control over our actions.

"They have two motives—pleasure and interest, and a third, more imperious—duty.

"Duties are divided into two classes: first, duties towards ourselves, which consist in taking care of our bodies, protecting ourselves against all injury." (They understood this perfectly.) "Secondly, duties towards others; that is to say, to be always loyal, good-natured, and even fraternal, the human race being only one single family. A thing often pleases us which is injurious to our fellows; interest is a different thing from good, for good is in itself irreducible." (The children did not comprehend.) He put off the sanction of duties until the next occasion.

In the entire lecture, according to Bouvard, he had not defined "good."

"Why do you wish to define it? We feel it."

So, then, the lessons of morality would suit only moral people—and Pécuchet's course did not go further.

They made their pupils read little tales tending to inspire them with the love of virtue. They plagued Victor to death.

In order to strike his imagination, Pécuchet suspended from the walls of his apartment representations of the lives of the good person and the bad person respectively. The first, Adolphe, embraced his mother, studied German, assisted a blind man, and was admitted into the Polytechnic School. The bad person, Eugène, began by disobeying his father, had a quarrel in a café, beat his wife, fell down dead drunk, smashed a cupboard—and a final picture represented him in jail, where a gentleman, accompanied by a young lad, pointed him out, saying, "You see, my son, the dangers of misconduct."

But for the children, the future had no existence. In vain were their minds saturated with the maxim that "work is honourable," and that "the rich are sometimes unhappy." They had known workmen in no way honoured, and had recollections of the château, where life seemed good. The pangs of remorse were depicted for them with so much exaggeration that they smelled humbug, and after that became distrustful. Attempts were then made to govern their conduct by a sense of honour, the idea of public opinion, and the sentiment of glory, by holding up to their admiration great men; above all, men who made themselves useful, like Belzunce, Franklin, and Jacquard. Victor displayed no longing to resemble them.

One day, when he had done a sum in addition without a mistake, Bouvard sewed to his jacket a ribbon to symbolise the Cross. He strutted about with it; but, when he forgot about the death of Henry IV, Pécuchet put an ass's cap on his head. Victor began to bray with so much violence and for so long a time, that it was found necessary to take off his pasteboard ears.

Like him, his sister showed herself vain of praise, and indifferent to blame.

In order to make them more sensitive, a black cat was given to them, that they might take care of it; and two or three coppers were presented to them, so that they might bestow alms. They thought the requirement unjust; this money belonged to them.

In compliance with the wish of the pedagogues, they called Bouvard "my uncle," and Pécuchet "good friend;" but they "thee'd" and "thou'd" them, and half the lessons were usually lost in disputes.

Victorine ill-treated Marcel, mounted on his back, dragged him by the hair. In order to make game of his hare-lip, she spoke through her nose like him; and the poor fellow did not venture to complain, so fond was he of the little girl. One evening his hoarse voice was unusually raised. Bouvard and Pécuchet went down to the kitchen. The two pupils were staring at the chimneypiece, and Marcel, with clasped hands, was crying out:

"Take him away! It's too much—it's too much!"

The lid of the pot flew off like the bursting of a shell. A greyish mass bounded towards the ceiling, then wriggled about frantically, emitting fearful howls.

They recognised the cat, quite emaciated, with its hair gone, its tail like a piece of string, and its dilated eyes starting out of its head. They were as white as milk, vacant, so to speak, and yet glaring.

The hideous animal continued its howling till it flung itself into the fireplace, disappeared, then rolled back in the middle of the cinders lifeless.

It was Victor who had perpetrated this atrocity; and the two worthy men recoiled, pale with stupefaction and horror. To the reproaches which they addressed to him, he replied, as the keeper had done with reference to his son and the farmer with reference to his horse: "Well! since it's my own," without ceremony and with an air of innocence, in the placidity of a satiated instinct.

The boiling water from the pot was scattered over the floor, and saucepans, tongs, and candlesticks lay everywhere thrown about.

Marcel was some time cleaning up the kitchen, and his masters and he buried the poor cat in the garden under the pagoda.

After this Bouvard and Pécuchet had a long chat about Victor. The paternal blood was showing itself. What were they to do? To give him back to M. de Faverges or to entrust him to others would be an admission of impotence. Perhaps he would reform.

No matter! It was a doubtful hope; and they no longer felt any tenderness towards him. What a pleasure it would have been, however, to have near them a youth interested in their ideas, whose progress they could watch, who would by and by have become a brother to them! But Victor lacked intellect, and heart still more. And Pécuchet sighed, with his hands clasped over his bent knee.

"The sister is not much better," said Bouvard.

He pictured to himself a girl of nearly fifteen years, with a refined nature, a playful humour, adorning the house with the elegant tastes of a young lady; and, as if he had been her father and she had just died, the poor man began to weep.

Then, seeking an excuse for Victor, he quoted Rousseau's opinion: "The child has no responsibility, and cannot be moral or immoral."

Pécuchet's view was that these children had reached the age of discretion, and that they should study some method whereby they could be corrected. Bentham lays down that a punishment, in order to be effectual, should be in proportion to the offence—its natural consequence. The child has broken a pane of glass—a new one will not be put in: let him suffer from cold. If, not being hungry any longer, he asks to be served again, give way to him: a fit of indigestion will quickly make him repent. Suppose he is lazy—let him remain without work: boredom of itself will make him go back to it.

But Victor would not endure cold; his constitution could stand excesses; and doing nothing would agree with him.

They adopted the reverse system: medicinal punishment. Impositions were given to him; he only became more idle. They deprived him of sweet things; his greediness for them redoubled. Perhaps irony might have success with him? On one occasion, when he came to breakfast with dirty hands, Bouvard jeered at him, calling him a "gay cavalier," a "dandy," "yellow gloves." Victor listened with lowering brow, suddenly turned pale, and flung his plate at Bouvard's head; then, wild at having missed him, made a rush at him. It took three men to hold him. He rolled himself on the floor, trying to bite. Pécuchet, at some distance, sprinkled water over him out of a carafe: he immediately calmed down; but for two days he was hoarse. The method had not proved of any use.

They adopted another. At the least symptom of anger, treating him as if he were ill, they put him to bed. Victor was quite contented there, and showed it by singing.

One day he took out of its place in the library an old cocoanut, and was beginning to split it open, when Pécuchet came up:

"My cocoanut!"

It was a memento of Dumouchel! He had brought it from Paris to Chavignolles. He raised his arms in indignation. Victor burst out laughing. "Good friend" could not stand it any longer, and with one good box sent him rolling to the end of the room, then, quivering with emotion, went to complain to Bouvard.

Bouvard rebuked him.

"Are you crazy with your cocoanut? Blows only brutalise; terror enervates. You are disgracing yourself!"

Pécuchet returned that corporal chastisements were sometimes indispensable. Pestalozzi made use of them; and the celebrated Melancthon confesses that without them he would have learned nothing.

His friend observed that cruel punishments, on the other hand, had driven children to suicide. He had in his reading found examples of it.

Victor had barricaded himself in his room.

Bouvard parleyed with him outside the door, and, to make him open it, promised him a plum tart.

From that time he grew worse.

There remained a method extolled by Monseigneur Dupanloup: "the severe look." They tried to impress on their countenances a dreadful expression, and they produced no effect.

"We have no longer any resource but to try religion."

Pécuchet protested. They had banished it from their programme.

But reasoning does not satisfy every want. The heart and the imagination desire something else. The supernatural is for many souls indispensable. So they resolved to send the children to catechism.

Reine offered to conduct them there. She again came to the house, and knew how to make herself liked by her caressing ways.

Victorine suddenly changed, became shy, honey-tongued, knelt down before the Madonna, admired the sacrifice of Abraham, and sneered disdainfully at the name of Protestant.

She said that fasting had been enjoined upon her. They made inquiries: it was not true. On the feast of Corpus Christi some damask violets disappeared from one of the flower-beds to decorate the processional altar: she impudently denied having cut them. At another time she took from Bouvard twenty sous, which she placed at vesper-time in the sacristan's collecting-plate.

They drew from this the conclusion that morality is distinguishable from religion; when it has not another basis, its importance is secondary.

One evening, while they were dining, M. Marescot entered. Victor fled immediately.

The notary, having declined to sit down, told what had brought him there.

Young Touache had beaten—all but killed—his son. As Victor's origin was known, and as he was unpopular, the other brats called him "Convict," and not long since he had given Master Arnold Marescot a drubbing, which was an insult. "Dear Arnold" bore the marks of it on his body.

"His mother is in despair, his clothes are in rags, his health is imperilled. What are we coming to?"

The notary insisted on severe chastisement, and, amongst other things, on Victor being henceforth kept away from catechism, to prevent fresh collisions.

Bouvard and Pécuchet, although wounded by his haughty tone, promised everything he wished—yielded.

Had Victor obeyed a sentiment of honour or of revenge? In any case, he was no coward.

But his brutality frightened them. Music softens manners. Pécuchet conceived the notion of teaching him the solfeggio.

Victor had much difficulty in reading the notes readily and not confounding the terms *adagio, presto,* and *sforzando.* His master strove to explain to him the gamut, perfect harmony, the diatonic, the chromatic, and the two kinds of intervals called major and minor.

He made him stand up straight, with his chest advanced, his shoulders thrown back, his mouth wide open, and, in order to teach by example, gave out intonations in a voice that was out of tune. Victor's voice came forth painfully from his larynx, so contracted was it. When the bar began with a crotchet rest, he started either too soon or too late.

Nevertheless Pécuchet took up an air in two parts. He used a rod as a substitute for a fiddlestick, and moved his arm like a conductor, as if he had an orchestra behind him; but, engaged as he was in two tasks, he sometimes made a mistake; his blunder led to others on the part of the pupil; and, knitting their brows, straining the muscles of their necks, they went on at random down to the end of the page.

At length Pécuchet said to Victor:

"You're not likely to shine in a choral society."

And he abandoned the teaching of music.

Besides, perhaps Locke is right: "Music is associated with so much profligate company that it is better to occupy oneself with something else."

Without desiring to make an author of him, it would be convenient for Victor to know how to despatch a letter. A reflection stopped them: the epistolary style cannot be acquired, for it belongs exclusively to women.

They next thought of cramming his memory with literary fragments, and, perplexed about making selections, consulted Madame Campan's work. She recommends the scene of Eliakim, the choruses in *Esther,* and the entire works of Jean Baptiste Rousseau.

These are a little old-fashioned. As for romances, she prohibits them, as depicting the world under too favourable colours. However, she permits *Clarissa Harlowe* and *The Father of a Family,* by Mrs. Opie. Who is this Mrs. Opie?

They did not find her name in the Biographie of Michaud.

There remained fairy tales. "They would be expecting palaces of diamonds," said Pécuchet. Literature develops the intellect, but excites the passions.

Victorine was sent away from catechism on account of her conduct. She had been caught kissing the notary's son, and Reine made no joke of it: her face looked grave under her cap with its big frills.

After such a scandal, why keep a young girl so corrupted?

Bouvard and Pécuchet called the curé an old fool. His housekeeper defended him, muttering:

"We know you!—we know you!"

They made a sharp rejoinder, and she went off rolling her eyes in a fearful manner.

Victorine was, in fact, smitten with a fancy for Arnold, so nice did she think him, with his embroidered collar, his velvet jacket, and his well-scented hair; and she had been bringing bouquets to him up to the time when Zephyrin told about her.

What foolishness was exhibited regarding this adventure, the two children being perfectly innocent!

The two guardians thought Victor required a stirring amusement like hunting; this would lead to the expense of a gun, of a dog. They thought it better to fatigue him, in order to tame the exuberance of his animal spirits, and went in for coursing in the fields.

The young fellow escaped from them, although they relieved eachother. They could do nothing more; and in the evening they had not the strength to hold up the newspaper.

Whilst they were waiting for Victor they talked to the passers-by, and through the sheer necessity of playing the pedagogue, they tried to teach them hygiene, deplored the injuries from floods and the waste of manures, thundered against such superstitions as leaving the skeleton of a blackbird in a barn, putting consecrated wood at the end of a stable and a bag of worms on the big toes of people suffering from fever.

They next took to inspecting wet nurses, and were incensed at their management of babies: some soaked them in gruel, causing them to die of exhaustion; others stuffed them with meat before they were six months old, and so they fell victims to indigestion; several cleaned them with their own spittle; all managed them barbarously.

When they saw over a door an owl that had been crucified, they went into the farmhouse and said:

"You are wrong; these animals live on rats and field-mice. There has been found in a screech-owl's stomach a quantity of caterpillars' larvae."

The country-folk knew them from having seen them, in the first place, as physicians, then searching for old furniture, and afterwards looking for stones; and they replied:

"Come, now, you pair of play-actors! don't try to teach us."

Their conviction was shaken, for the sparrows cleanse the kitchen-gardens, but eat up the cherries. The owls devour insects, and at the same time bats, which are useful; and, if the moles eat the slugs, they upset the soil. There was one thing of which they were certain: that all game should be destroyed as fatal to agriculture.

One evening, as they were passing along by the wood of Faverges, they found themselves in front of Sorel's house, at the side of the road. Sorel was gesticulating in the presence of three persons. The first was a certain Dauphin, a cobbler, small, thin, and with a sly expression of countenance; the second, Père Aubain, a village porter, wore an old yellow frock-coat, with a pair of coarse blue linen trousers; the third, Eugéne, a man-servant employed by M. Marescot, was distinguished by his beard cut like that of a magistrate.

Sorel was showing them a noose in copper wire attached to a silk thread, which was held by a clamp—what is called a snare—and he had discovered the cobbler in the act of setting it.

"You are witnesses, are you not?"

Eugène lowered his chin by way of assent, and Père Aubain replied:

"Once you say so."

What enraged Sorel was that anyone should have the audacity to set up a snare at the entrance of his lodge, the rascal imagining that one would have no idea of suspecting it in such a place.

Dauphin adopted the blubbering system:

"I was walking over it; I even tried to break it." They were always accusing him. They had a grudge against him; he was most unlucky.

Sorel, without answering him, had drawn out of his pocket a note-book and a pen and ink, in order to make out an official report.

"Oh, no!" said Pécuchet.

Bouvard added: "Let him go. He is a decent fellow."

"He—a poacher!"

"Well, such things will happen."

And they proceeded to defend poaching: "We know, to start with, that the rabbits nibble at the young sprouts, and that the hares destroy the corn crops—except, perhaps, the woodcock—"

"Let me alone, now." And the gamekeeper went on writing with clenched teeth.

"What obstinacy!" murmured Bouvard.

"Another word, and I shall send for the gendarmes!"

"You are an ill-mannered fellow!" said Pécuchet.

"You are no great things!" retorted Sorel.

Bouvard, forgetting himself, referred to him as a blockhead, a bully; and Eugène kept repeating, "Peace! peace! let us respect the law"; while Père Aubain was groaning three paces away from them on a heap of pebbles.

Disturbed by these voices, all the dogs of the pack rushed out of their kennels.

Through the railings their black snouts could be seen, and, rushing hither and thither they kept barking loudly.

"Don't plague me further," cried their master, "or I'll make them go for your breeches!"

The two friends departed, satisfied, however, with having upheld progress and civilisation.

Next day a summons was served on them to appear at the police court for offering insults to the gamekeeper, and to pay a hundred francs' compensation, "reserving an appeal to the public administration, having regard to the contraventions committed by them. Costs: 6 francs 75 centimes.—TIERCELIN, Summoner."

Wherefore a public administration? Their heads became giddy; then, becoming calm, they set about preparing their defence.

On the day named, Bouvard and Pécuchet repaired to the court-house an hour too early. No one was there; chairs and three cushioned seats surrounded an oval table covered with a cloth; a niche had been made in the wall for the purpose of placing a stove there; and the Emperor's bust, which was on a pedestal, overlooked the scene.

They strolled up to the top room of the building, where there was a fire-engine, a number of flags, and in a corner, on the floor, other plaster busts—the great Napoleon without a diadem; Louis XVIII with epaulets on a dress-coat; Charles X, recognisable by his hanging lip; Louis Philippe, with arched eyebrows and hair dressed in pyramid fashion, the slope of the roof grazing the nape of his neck; and all these objects were befouled by flies and dust. This spectacle had a demoralising effect on Bouvard and Pécuchet. Governing powers excited their pity as they made their way back to the main hall.

There they found Sorel and the field-keeper, the one wearing his badge on his arm, and the other his military cap.

A dozen persons were talking, having been summoned for not having swept in front of their houses, or for having let their dogs go at large, or neglecting to attach lanterns to their carts, or for keeping a public-house open during mass-time.

At length Coulon presented himself, wrapped in a robe of black serge and wearing a round cap with velvet edgings. His clerk sat down at his left, the mayor, scarfed, at his right; and shortly afterwards the case of Sorel against Bouvard and Pécuchet was called.

Louis-Martial-Eugène Lenepveur, valet at Chavignolles (Calvados), availed himself of his character as a witness to unburden himself of all he knew about a great many things that were foreign to the issue.

Nicolas-Juste Aubain, day-labourer, was afraid both of displeasing Sorel and of injuring "these gentlemen." He had heard abusive words, and yet he had his doubts about it. He pleaded that he was deaf.

The justice of the peace made him sit down; then, addressing himself to the gamekeeper: "Do you persist in your declarations?"

"Certainly."

Coulon then asked the two defendants what they had to say.

Bouvard maintained that he had not insulted Sorel, but that in taking the poacher's part he had vindicated the rights of the peasantry. He recalled the abuses of feudal times and the ruinous huntings of the nobles.

"No matter! The contravention—"

"Allow me to stop you," exclaimed Pécuchet.

The words "contravention," "crime," and "delict" were of no value. To seek in this way to class punishable acts was to take an arbitrary basis. As much as to say to citizens: "Don't bother yourself as to the value of your actions; that is determined by the punishment inflicted by authority." However, the penal code appeared to him an absurd production devoid of principles.

"That may be," replied Coulon; and he proceeded to pronounce his judgment.

But here Foureau, who represented the public administration, arose. They had outraged the gamekeeper in the exercise of his functions. If no regard were shown for propriety, everything would be destroyed.

"In short, may it please Monsieur the Justice of the Peace to apply the maximum penalty."

This was ten francs, in the form of damages to Sorel.

"Bravo!" exclaimed Bouvard.

Coulon had not finished.

"Impose on them, in addition, a fine of five francs for having been guilty of the contravention mentioned by the public administration."

Pécuchet turned around to the audience:

"The fine is a trifle to the rich man, but a disaster to the poor man. As for myself, it matters nothing to me."

And he presented the appearance of defying the court.

"Really," said Coulon, "I am astonished that people of intelligence—"

"The law dispenses you from the possession of it," retorted Pécuchet. "The justice of the peace occupies his post indefinitely, while the judge of the supreme court is reputed capable up to seventy-five years, and the judge of first instance is no longer so at seventy."

But, at a gesture from Foureau, Placquevent advanced.

They protested.

"Ah! if you were appointed by competition!"

"Or by the General Council!"

"Or a committee of experts, and according to a proper list!"

Placquevent moved them on, and they went out while the other defendants' names were being called, believing that they had made a good show in the course of these vile proceedings.

To give vent to their indignation they went that evening to Beljambe's hostelry. His café was empty, the principal customers being in the habit of leaving about ten o'clock. The lamp had been lowered; the walls and the counter seemed shrouded in a fog. A female attendant came on the scene. It was Mélie. She did not appear agitated, and, smiling, she poured them out two bocks. Pécuchet, ill at ease, quickly left the establishment.

Bouvard came back there alone, entertained some of the villagers with sarcasms at the mayor's expense, and after that went into the smoking-room.

Six months later Dauphin was acquitted for want of evidence. What a shame! These very witnesses who had been believed when testifying against them were now regarded with suspicion. And their anger knew no bounds when the registrar gave them notice to pay the fine. Bouvard attacked the registry as injurious to property.

"You are mistaken," said the collector. "Why, it bears a third of the public expenditure!"

"I would have proceedings with regard to taxes less vexatious, a better system of land registration, alterations in the law as to mortgages, and would abolish the Bank of France, which has the privilege of usury."

Girbal, not being strong on the subject, let the argument fall to the ground, and departed. However, Bouvard made himself agreeable to the innkeeper; he would attract a crowd around him; and, while he was waiting for the guests, he chatted familiarly with the barmaid.

He gave utterance to odd ideas on primary education. On leaving school, pupils ought to be capable of nursing the sick, understanding scientific discoveries, and taking an interest in the arts. The requirements of his programme made him fall out with Petit; and he offended the captain by maintaining that soldiers, instead of losing their time with drilling, would be better occupied in growing vegetables.

When the question of free trade turned up he brought Pécuchet along with him, and the whole winter there were in the café angry looks, contemptuous attitudes, insults and vociferations, with blows of fists on the table that made the beer-glasses jump.

Langlois and the other merchants defended national commerce; Oudot, owner of a spinning factory, and Mathieu, a goldsmith, national industry; the landowners and the farmers, national agriculture: everyone claiming privileges for himself to the detriment of the public at large.

The observations of Bouvard and Pécuchet had an alarming effect.

As they were accused of ignoring the practical side of life, of having a tendency towards levelling, and of immorality, they developed these three ideas: to replace the family name by a registered number; to arrange the French people in a hierarchy, and in such a way that, in order to preserve his grade, it would be necessary for one to submit from time to time to an examination; no more punishments, no more rewards, but in every village an individual chronicle of all persons living there, which would pass on to posterity.

Their system was treated with disdain. They wrote an article about it for the Bayeux daily paper, drew up a note to the prefect, a petition to the Chambers, and a memorial to the Emperor.

The newspaper did not publish their article.

The prefect did not condescend to reply.

The Chambers were silent; and they waited along time for a communication from the Tuileries.

What, then, was the Emperor occupying his time with?

With women, no doubt.

Foureau, on the part of the sub-prefect, suggested the desirability of more reserve.

They laughed at the sub-prefect, the prefect, the councillors of the prefecture, even the council of state. Administrative justice was a monstrosity, for the administration by means of favours and threats unjustly controls its functionaries. In short, they came to be regarded as a nuisance, and the leading men of the place gave injunctions to Beljambe not to entertain two such fellows.

At this period, Bouvard and Pécuchet were burning to signalise themselves by a work which would dazzle their neighbours; and they saw nothing better than plans for the embellishment of Chavignolles.

Three fourths of the houses should be demolished. They would construct in the centre of the village a monumental square, on the way to Falaise a hospital, slaughter-houses on the way to Caen, and at the "Cows' Pass" a Roman church of many colours.

Pécuchet manufactured a colouring mixture with Indian ink, and did not forget in preparing his plans to give a yellow tint to the woods, a red to the buildings, and a green to the meadows, for the pictures of an ideal Chavignolles pursued him in his daydreams, and he came back to them as he lay on his mattress.

Bouvard was awakened by him one night.

"Are you unwell?"

Pécuchet stammered, "Haussmann prevents me from going to sleep."

About this time he received a letter from Dumouchel to know the cost of sea-baths on the Norman coast.

"Let him go about his business with his baths! Have we any time to write?"

And, when they had procured a land-surveyor's chain, a semicircle, a water-level, and a compass, they began at other studies.

They encroached on private properties. The inhabitants were frequently surprised to see the pair fixing stakes in the ground for surveying purposes. Bouvard and Pécuchet announced their plans, and what would be the outcome of them, with the utmost self-complacency. The people became uneasy, for, perchance, authority might at length fall in with these men's views! Sometimes they rudely drove them away.

Victor scaled the walls and crept up to the roof to hang up signals there; he exhibited good-will, and even a degree of enthusiasm.

They were also better satisfied with Victorine.

When she was ironing the linen she hummed in a sweet voice as she moved her smoothing-iron over the board, interested herself in looking after the household, and made a cap for Bouvard, with a well-pointed peak that won compliments for her from Romiche.

This man was one of those tailors who go about mending clothes in farm-houses. He was taken into the house for a fortnight.

Hunchbacked, with bloodshot eyes, he made up for his bodily defects by a facetious disposition. While the masters were out, he used to amuse Marcel and Victorine by telling them funny stories. He would put out his tongue as far as his chin, imitate the cuckoo, or give exhibitions of ventriloquism; and at night, saving the cost of an inn, he went to sleep in the bakehouse.

Now, one morning, at a very early hour, Bouvard, being cold, happened to go there to get chips to light his fire.

What he saw petrified him. Behind the remains of the chest, upon a straw mattress, Romiche and Victorine lay asleep together.

He had passed his arm around her waist, and his other hand, long as that of an ape, clutched one of her knees. She was smiling, stretched on her back. Her fair hair hung loose, and the whiteness of the dawn threw its pale light upon the pair.

Bouvard for a moment felt as if he had received a blow in the chest; then a sense of shame prevented him from making a single movement. He was oppressed by painful reflections.

"So young! Lost! lost!" He then went to awaken Pécuchet, and briefly told him everything.

"Ah! the wretch!"

"We cannot help it. Be calm!" And for some time they remained sighing, one after the other—Bouvard, with his coat off and his arms folded; Pécuchet, at the side of his bed, sitting barefooted in a cotton nightcap.

Romiche should leave that very day, when his work was finished. They would pay him in a haughty fashion, and in silence.

But Providence had some spite against them.

Marcel, a short time afterwards, led them to Victor's room and showed them at the bottom of his chest of drawers a twenty-franc piece. The youngster had asked him to get the change of it.

Where did it come from? No doubt it was got by a theft committed while they were going about as engineers. But in order to restore it they would require to know the person; and if some one came to claim it they would look like accomplices.

At length, having sent for Victor, they ordered him to open his drawer: the napoleon was no longer there. He pretended not to understand. A short time before, however, they had seen it, this very coin, and Marcel was incapable of lying. This affair had revolutionised Pécuchet so much that he had, since morning, kept in his pocket a letter for Bouvard:

"Sir—Fearing lest M. Pécuchet may be ill, I have recourse to your kindness—"

"Whose is the signature, then?"

"Olympe Dumouchel, *née* Charpeau."

She and her husband were anxious to know in which bathing-place—Courseulles, Langrune, or Lucques—the best society was to be found, which was least noisy, and as to the means of transport, the cost of washing, etc.

This importunity made them angry with Dumouchel; then weariness plunged them into deeper despondency.

They went over all the pains that they had taken—so many lessons, precautions, torments!

"And to think that we intended at one time to make Victorine a teacher, and Victor an overseer of works!"

"Ah! how deceived we were in her!"

"If she is vicious, it is not the fault of the lessons she got."

"For my part, to make her virtuous, I would have learned Cartouche's biography."

"Perhaps they needed family life—the care of a mother?"

"I was like one to them," protested Bouvard.

"Alas!" replied Pécuchet. "But there are natures bereft of moral sense; and education in that case can do nothing."

"Ah! yes, 'tis a fine thing, education!"

As the orphans had not learned any trade, they would seek two situations for them as servants; and then, with the help of God, they would have nothing more to do with them.

And henceforth "My uncle" and "Good friend" made them take their meals in the kitchen.

But soon they grew restless, their minds feeling the need of work, their existence of an aim.

Besides, what does one failure prove? What had proved abortive in the case of children might be more successful with men. And they conceived the idea of preparing a course of lectures for adults.

In order to explain their views, a conference would be necessary. The great hall of the inn would be perfectly suitable for this purpose.

Beljambe, as deputy mayor, was afraid to compromise himself, refused at first, then, thinking that he might make something out of it, changed his mind, and sent word to that effect by his servant-maid.

Bouvard, in the excess of his joy, kissed her on both cheeks.

The mayor was absent. The other deputy, M. Marescot, entirely taken up with his office, would pay little attention to the conference. So it was to take place; and, to the beating of the drum, the hour was announced as three o'clock on the following Sunday.

It was only on the day before that they thought about their costumes. Pécuchet, thank Heaven, had preserved an old ceremonial coat with a velvet collar, two white cravats, and black gloves. Bouvard put on his blue frock-coat, a nankeen waistcoat and beaver shoes; and they were strongly moved when they had passed through the village and arrived at the hostelry of the Golden Cross.

ABOUT THE AUTHOR

G USTAVE FLAUBERT (1821–1880) WAS BORN INTO A MIDDLE-CLASS FAMILY AND grew up in comfortable surroundings in Rouen, France, the town where he would spend most of his life. He enrolled in law school in 1841 but was unable to complete his studies owing to illness. For much of the next decade, Flaubert traveled but showed little inclination to take up a profession. He had written narratives and dramas while in school, but did not become a published author until *Madame Bovary*, which he began writing in 1851, appeared in 1857. Experimental and controversial, the novel initially was prosecuted by censors on charges of immorality and its notoriety catapulted Flaubert to the front ranks of the French literary scene, where he was warmly received by Charles Baudelaire, Theophile Gautier, and other distinguished contemporaries. In time it was recognized as a groundbreaking work of fiction and Flaubert was lionized as a master of literary realism. Over the next twenty years he published the novels *Salammbô* (1862), *Sentimental Education* (1869), and *The Temptation of Saint Anthony* (1874), as well as the collection *Three Tales* (1877). He also wrote several plays, none of them successfully produced. Although highly respected by colleagues and friends, Flaubert suffered straitened financial circumstances and poor health for much of his later life. His last novel, *Bouvard and Pécuchet*, was published posthumously in 1881. Flaubert's letters, which contain reflections on the art of literature and writing, are considered landmarks of literary criticism.

LIBRARY OF ESSENTIAL WRITERS

2007

LEWIS CARROLL *Complete Works*

✦

JOSEPH CONRAD *Complete Short Stories*

✦

JAMES FENIMORE COOPER *Five Novels*

✦

DANIEL DEFOE *Five Novels*

✦

GUSTAVE FLAUBERT *Five Novels*

✦

E. M. FORSTER *Four Novels*

✦

ERNEST HEMINGWAY *Four Novels*

✦

LEO TOLSTOY *Three Novels*

2006

JANE AUSTEN *Seven Novels*

✦

CHARLOTTE BRONTË *Four Novels*

✦

CHARLES DICKENS *Five Novels*

✦

ALEXANDRE DUMAS *Three Novels*

✦

GEORGE ELIOT *Four Novels*

✦

THOMAS HARDY *Five Novels*

✦

NATHANIEL HAWTHORNE *Five Novels*

✦

O. HENRY *The Fiction*

✦

HENRY JAMES *Five Novels*

✦

JACK LONDON *Six Novels*

✦

W. SOMERSET MAUGHAM *Five Novels*

✦

EDGAR ALLAN POE *Fiction and Poetry*

✦

SAKI *The Fiction*

✦

ROBERT LOUIS STEVENSON *Seven Novels*

✦

BRAM STOKER *Five Novels*

✦

MARK TWAIN *Five Novels*

✦

JULES VERNE *Seven Novels*

✦

H. G. WELLS *Seven Novels*

✦

EDITH WHARTON *Five Novels*

✦

OSCAR WILDE *Collected Works*